THE
KEEPER
CHRONICLES

THE COMPLETE TRILOGY

Cover Illustration: Billy Christian.
Cover Design: STK Kreations.
Art Director: Bryce O'Connor
Illustrations © 2018, 2019 by Wojtek Depczynski
Map © 2018 by Ren

J.A. ANDREWS

THE KEEPER CHRONICLES

THE COMPLETE TRILOGY

Map of

TALLUS

HOARFROST RANGE

THE SCALE MOUNTAINS

ENCLAVE MOUNTAIN

KOLLMAN PASS

Morrow Clan

ROVEN SWEEP

Bermea
BOAN CLAN

Muun
PANOS CLAN

Tun
SUNN CLAN

Sendel
ODO CLAN

Ratun
TEMUR CLAN

Porreen
MORROW CLAN

N

SOUTHERN
SEA

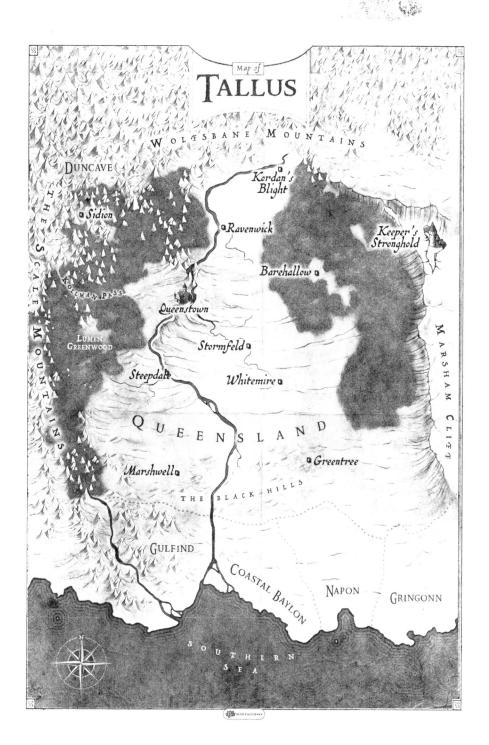

Map of

TALLUS

WOLFSBANE MOUNTAINS

DUNCAVE

Kordan's
Blight

Sidion

Ravenwick

Keeper's
Stronghold

Barehallow

KOLLMAN PASS

Queenstown

LUMEN
GREENWOOD

Stormfeld

Steepdale

Whitemire

QUEENSLAND

Greentree

Marshwell

THE BLACK HILLS

Gulfind

COASTAL BAYLON

NAPON

GRINGONN

SOUTHERN
SEA

N

A THREAT OF SHADOWS

The Keeper Chronicles Book 1

ONE

The deeper Alaric rode into the woods, the more something felt... off. This forest had always fit like a well-worn cloak. But tonight, the way the forest wrapped around felt familiar, but not quite comfortable, as though it remembered wrapping around a slightly different shape.

"This path used to be easier to follow," Alaric said to his horse, Beast, as they paused between patches of late spring moonlight. Alaric peered ahead, looking for the trail leading to the Stronghold. He found it running like a scratch through the low brush to the right. "If the Keepers weren't too meek to hold grudges, I'd think the old men were hiding it from me."

All the usual smells of pine and moss and dirt wove through the air, the usual sounds of little animals going about their lives, but Alaric kept catching a hint of something different. Something more complicated than he wanted to deal with.

Around the next turn, the trail ran straight into a wide tree trunk. Alaric leaned as far to the side as he could, but he couldn't see around it. "I could be wrong about the Keepers holding grudges."

Well, if they didn't want him at the Stronghold, that was too bad. He didn't need a warm welcome. He just needed to find one book with one antidote. With a little luck, the book would be easy to find and he could leave quickly. With a lot of luck, he'd get in and out without having to answer anyone's questions about what he'd been doing for the past year.

Beast circled the tree and found the path again, snaking out the other side. As his hooves thudded down on it, a howl echoed through the woods.

The horse froze, and Alaric grabbed the pouch hanging around his neck, protecting it against his chest. He closed his eyes, casting out past the nearest trees and through the woods, searching for the blazing energy of the wolf. He sensed nothing beyond the tranquil glow of the trees and the dashing flashes of frightened rabbits.

"That's new." Alaric opened his eyes and peered into the darkness.

A louder howl broke through the night. Beast shuddered.

"It's all right." Alaric patted Beast's neck as he cast farther out. The life energy of an animal as large as a wolf would be like a bonfire among the trees, but there was nothing near them. "It's not wolves. Just disembodied howls." He kept his voice soothing, hoping to calm the animal.

"That didn't sound as reassuring as I meant it to. But a real wolf pack wouldn't keep howling as they got closer. If we were being tracked by wolves, we wouldn't know it."

Beast's ears flicked back and forth, alert for another howl.

"Okay, that wasn't reassuring, either." Alaric nudged him forward. "C'mon we're almost to the Wall."

A third howl tore out of the darkness right beside them.

Beast reared back, whinnying in terror. Alaric grabbed for the saddle and swore. He pressed his hand to Beast's neck.

"*Paxa*," he said, focusing energy through his hand and into Beast. A shock of pain raced across Alaric's palm where it touched the horse, as the energy rushed through.

Mid-snort, Beast settled and stood still.

Alaric shook out his hand and looked thoughtfully into the woods. This wasn't about a grudge, or at least the howls weren't directed at him. Any Keeper would know there were no wolves. Even one as inadequate as he would know there was no energy, no *vitalle*, behind the sounds. So what was the purpose of it? The path had never been like this before.

With Beast calm, Alaric set him back into a steady walk. Two more howls rang out from the woods, but Beast ambled along, unruffled. Alaric rubbed his still-tingling palm.

Beast paused again as the trail ran into another wide tree.

Alaric growled in frustration. The path to the Keepers' Stronghold shouldn't be this troublesome for a Keeper.

Unless it no longer recognized him as one. That was a sobering thought.

As they skirted around the tree, a white face thrust itself out of the trunk. Alaric jerked away as the hazy form of a man leaned out toward him. When the figure didn't move, Alaric reined in Beast and forced himself to study it. It held no life energy, it was just an illusion—like the wolves.

The figure was a young man. He had faded yellow hair and milky white skin. Once the initial shock wore off, the man was not particularly frightening.

"What are you supposed be? A friendly ghost?" Alaric asked.

It hung silent on the tree. Alaric leaned forward and backward, but the ghost remained still, staring off into the woods.

"The howls were more frightening than you." Alaric set Beast to walking again.

"You are lost," the ghost whispered as he passed.

Alaric gave a short laugh. "I've been lost many times in my life, but this isn't one of them. And if it's your job to scare people off, you should consider saying something more chilling and less… depressing."

Beast kept walking, and Alaric turned to watch the ghost fade into the darkness behind them.

A rasp pulled his attention forward. Another white form slid out of the tree they were approaching. This one was a young woman. She was rather pretty, for a ghost.

"Hello." Alaric gave her a polite nod.

"You have failed," she whispered. "You have failed everyone."

Alaric scowled. The words rang uncomfortably true.

Alaric stopped Beast in front of the ghost. Behind the woman's face, Alaric saw thin, silver runes carved on the bark. He couldn't read them through the ghost, but he didn't need to. Narrowing his focus, he cast out ahead of them along the trail, brushing against the trunks with his senses. Now that he knew what he was looking for, he felt the subtle humming runes dotting the trees ahead.

Alaric sat back in the saddle. This wasn't what he expected from the Keepers. The old men protected their privacy like paranoid hermits, but they'd never tried to scare people away before. Of course, these ghosts weren't frightening. If the Keepers were going to make ghosts, these are the kind they would make.

Years ago, during his "Defeat by Demoralization" lesson, Keeper Gerone had declared, "Control the emotions, control the man!" Gerone was probably responsible for the depressing ghosts.

The ghost runes were on almost every tree now, faces appearing every few steps.

"Your powers are worthless," the next whispered and Alaric flinched.

"It's your fault," another rasped. "All your fault."

Alaric clenched his jaw and stared ahead as the whispers surrounded him.

When he passed close to one large tree, a ghost thrust out close to him. Alaric turned toward it and saw his own face looking back at him. A pale, wasted version of himself. His black hair was faded to a lifeless grey, and his skin, far from being tanned from traveling, was bleached a wrinkly bone white. Only his eyes had stayed dark, sinking from a healthy brown to deep, black pits.

Alaric stared, repulsed, at the withered apparition of himself—it was decades older than his forty years. The ghost looked tired, a deep crease furrowed between its brows. Alaric reached up and rubbed his own forehead.

The ghost leaned closer.

"She's dead," it whispered.

Guilt stabbed into him, deep and familiar. He shuddered, grabbing the pouch at his neck, his mind flooded with the image of Evangeline's sunken face.

Alaric slammed his palm against the rune on the trunk.

"*Uro!*" Pain raced through his hand again. He poured energy into the tree, willing it to burn. The bark smoked as he seared the rune off.

Out of the corner of his eye, pulses of white light appeared along the path ahead of them. He glanced at them, but the distraction had consequences, and the pain flared, arcing up each finger. He gasped and narrowed his focus back to the energy flowing through his palm. The pain receded slightly. The ghost stared a moment longer, then faded away. Alaric dropped his arm, leaving a hand-shaped scorch mark on the trunk where the rune had been.

"She's dead."

Alaric's head snapped forward.

The trees ahead of him were full of ghosts, each a washed-out version of himself.

"Dead… She's dead… Dead." The words filled the air.

Alaric clutched the pouch at his neck until he felt the rough stone inside.

A ghost reached toward him. "She's dead…" Its voice rattled in a long sigh.

Alaric spurred Beast into a gallop, trusting the horse to follow the trail. The whispers clung to them as they ran. Alaric shrank down, hunching his shoulders, wresting his mind away from the memory of his wife's tired eyes, her pale skin.

The trees ended, and they raced out into a silent swath of grass, running up to the base of an immense cliff. Alaric pulled Beast to a stop, both of them breathing hard. Gripping the saddle, Alaric looked back into the trees. The forest was dark and quiet.

"I take it back," he said, catching his breath, "the ghosts were worse than the wolves." He sat in the saddle, pushing back the dread that was enveloping him. She wasn't dead. The ghosts were just illusions. He'd get the antidote tonight. She'd be fine.

When his heart finally slowed, he gave Beast an exhausted pat on the neck.

"This path used to be a *lot* easier to follow."

TWO

laric turned away from the forest. Before him stood a short section of stone wall twice his height. The unusual thing about the Wall was that, instead of enclosing anything, it sat flush against the base of the Marsham Cliffs.

Ignoring the looming presence of the forest behind him, Alaric cast out toward the Wall until he sensed the stone with the vibrating runes. His left hand ached from the last two spells, but there was no point in having both hands sore. This time, he gathered some *vitalle* from the grass around him. With a grim smile, he pulled some from the nearest ghost-trees as well and lifted his hand toward the Wall.

"*Aperi.*" Pain burst through his hand like fire. He let out a groan as the stones shifted. An arch opened, revealing a dark tunnel boring deep into the cliff.

Alaric walked Beast inside and turned to look back at the trees. He caught sight of a milky white face, and his stomach clenched.

Alaric thrust his hand toward the entrance. "*Cluda.*"

This time, the shock raced all the way up to his elbow. Alaric gasped and clutched his arm to his chest as the opening of the tunnel sealed itself off, leaving them in blackness. He clenched his jaw until the pain faded. He should have used the other hand for that last one.

Alaric started Beast toward the bright moonlight at the far end of the tunnel, wishing he could use the *paxa* spell to calm himself.

In the calmness of the tunnel, the memory of Evangeline's hollowed face flooded his mind again, followed by the familiar anguish.

He pushed that image away and drew out the memory of the night they had walked together along the edge of the Greenwood. She had peered into the woods hoping to catch a glimpse of an elf. He had explained that no one caught sight of an elf by chance, but she had ignored him, jumping at every flash of a bird or a squirrel.

He held that idea for a long moment. The way she had looked. The way she had been. The way she would be again.

He tucked the memory away and refocused on tonight. All he needed was to slip into the library and find one book. It should be easy.

Of course, the path should have been easy, too. The wolves and ghosts made no sense. Alaric had lived at the Stronghold for two decades and had traveled that path countless times. It had never given him trouble. It had never needed to. The Wall was more than enough defense for the Stronghold.

To anyone but a Keeper, the Wall would appear to be just an odd bit of wall sitting right against a cliff face. None but a Keeper knew how to open the tunnel, and the tunnel was the only entrance to the valley holding the Keepers' Stronghold.

The obvious question was whether the Keepers had changed the path in the year since Alaric had stormed out, or whether Alaric had changed, and this was how the path had always treated strangers.

Beast nickered as the tunnel spilled out into a grassy field in a narrow valley. Ahead of them a tower rose, its white stones shining in the moonlight. The smells of the day lingered in the valley, bread and smoke and drying herbs, but this late at night, everything was quiet.

A glitter of light from the very top of the tower beckoned him. The Wellstone.

It tempted him to go up, to dive into the pool of Keeper memories that it held. It was the other option besides the book, the quicker option. He needed knowledge from Kordan, and Kordan had been a Keeper. He would have stored his memories in the Wellstone, just like every other Keeper for the last two hundred years. Certainly, the information Alaric needed would be there.

But the price to use the Wellstone was too high. Evangeline was safe for now. The reference Alaric had found about Kordan had mentioned a book, so he was here for a book. *Please let the antidote be in the book.*

Alaric crossed the grass to the wooden front doors of the tower, bleached to grey in the moonlight and flung wide open as always. Alaric stepped through them into the heavy stillness of the entry hall. He ignored the lanterns sitting on the shelf next to the door, reluctant to disturb the darkness. Hopefully, he could find the book and leave without having to explain himself, or his long absence, to anyone.

On his left, the wall was dark with cloaks. Reaching out, he brushed his hand along the soft fabric. True Keepers' robes, managing to be both substantial and light, might be the thing he missed the most.

Before he left, he would take one. He'd leave this thin, worn cloak behind, the one that wasn't quite black and wasn't quite right, and take a real Keeper's robe with him.

He walked out the end of the hall, through the open center of the tower to the entrance of the library.

He paused near the door, hanging back in the shadows. The library was lit by glowing golden orbs tucked into nooks between the bookshelves. He could hear the scratching of a pen as a Keeper wrote somewhere deep in the library, but there was no one to be seen. He stepped up to the wooden railing in front of him and looked out into an immense circular room. Four stories below him lay a tiled floor with patterns swirling like eddies in a stream. Three stories above him, a glass ceiling showed the starry sky. A narrow walkway stretched around the room alongside age-darkened bookshelves.

If the Keepers could be relied on for anything, it was to record things. And then cross-reference that knowledge. Repeatedly. Alaric wasn't sure where Kordan's book would be shelved, but all of his works should be recorded in the Keeper's Registry.

Alaric walked to the winding ramp spiraling along the inside of the railing, connecting each floor to the next, grateful for the thick rugs that muffled his steps. He climbed up two floors, still seeing no one, and made his way to the thick black tome that recorded the life's work of each Keeper.

A puff of air breezed past him as he opened the Registry, as though the book was crammed with more knowledge than it could hold. It had always felt strange to hold this book, knowing that one day, there would be an entry in it under his own name.

Alaric flipped to the index. No listing for Kordan. He tried alternate spellings, but found nothing. He growled in frustration.

"That has got to be the most boring book in the library," a voice said from behind him.

Alaric's heart skipped a beat at the sound of the Shield's voice. Silently cursing the thick step-muffling rugs, he turned to face the leader of the Keepers.

"You've been gone over a year, Alaric. Please tell me you didn't come back just to browse the Registry."

The tiny form of the Shield stood behind him smiling, his bald head barely above Alaric's elbow. His clear eyes peered up at Alaric from below wooly white eyebrows. Alaric braced for questions, but the Shield just smiled benignly, displaying none of the accusation that Alaric expected.

"How did you know I was here?"

The Shield shrugged. "I'm so old that at this point, I'm bordering on omniscient."

Alaric let out a short laugh, his tension releasing with it.

The Shield glanced down at the book in Alaric's hand. "As any omniscient would ask, what are you looking for? And can I help you find it?"

Alaric almost said no, but though the Shield was not omniscient, the amount of knowledge contained behind those fluffy brows was astounding. He could save Alaric hours of research.

Alaric offered the book to him. "I'm looking for information on a Keeper named Kordan. He lived about a hundred years ago."

The Shield weighed the words for a moment, and Alaric knew he was making connections and filling in blanks until he understood far more than Alaric had said. The old man waved away the Registry and turned toward the shelves. "You're looking in the wrong book. Kordan was a Keeper, but after dabbling in some darker magic, he left the Stronghold and requested to be removed from the ranks of Keepers. He'll be recorded over here." He pulled another book off the shelf, *Histories and Works of the Gifted*. "Specifically, he'll be under the *Magic-Capable, Affiliation-Unknown* section since he never aligned himself with any other group. He's under Kordan the Harvester."

Magic-Capable, Affiliation-Unknown. Alaric sighed. *I'm right there with you, Kordan.*

"He has a town named after him," the Shield continued. "Kordan's Blight. It's up near the foot of the Wolfsbane Mountains."

"Kordan's Blight? That sounds... ominous." Alaric slid the Registry back into place on the shelf.

"Mmm," the Shield agreed, flipping pages. "There wasn't much of a town when he lived there, just a few homesteads. Kordan lived there for some time doing experiments. I'm sure you can guess that his time there didn't end well. You know how local legends are. The memory of him stuck, and when a town did grow there, it inherited the name. Ahh, here it is." The Shield set his finger on a paragraph then looked up at Alaric with a searching look.

"So... you came back looking for information on a Keeper, and you decided to come down here. To the library..."

Alaric didn't answer the unspoken question.

"...when we have a Wellstone upstairs which holds all of Kordan's memories."

"I'm not using it," Alaric said flatly. He wouldn't pay the Wellstone's fee. He wouldn't share with it all his memories since the last time he used it. The memories of meeting Evangeline, of when she was poisoned, of the things he had done to save her and the dark days since. "My memories are my own. I'm not interested in sharing them with the Wellstone so they can be studied and analyzed." His voice came out sharper than he had intended.

The Shield considered him for a long moment. "Then it is safe to assume you don't intend to stay."

Alaric let his eyes run over the books in front of him. Shelves and shelves of annals, a running history of Queensland kept by the Keepers for hundreds of years.

"But I need you back at court," the Shield said when Alaric didn't answer. "The queen needs you back."

"I can't."

"Queen Saren needs a Keeper to advise her."

"Send someone else."

"Who?" The calmness in the Shield's voice cracked. "Who here has the strength to travel two days to the palace, then keep up with the pressure of life at court?"

The answer to that was obvious. There was only one other Keeper young enough to travel. "Send Will."

"Will never came back from the Greenwood. It's been over a year, and we've received no word."

Alaric looked sharply at the Shield. Will should have only been gone a couple of months. He was in his thirties, barely younger than Alaric. He'd been like a brother to Alaric since they had joined the Keepers twenty years ago.

"Well, let someone else read some books and take over," Alaric snapped.

"If all Saren needed was books, I'd send her books. But I don't even have another Keeper who can piece together history and politics and answers the way you can. No one else who can draw out the important parts of history and make it useful."

Alaric shook his head. He couldn't go back to court. Not right now.

The Shield's voice grew quieter. "How is Evangeline?"

Alaric felt the familiar stab of guilt. He took a deep breath. The library air smelled of paper and ink and knowledge. He'd missed that smell. He took another breath. That was all he seemed to do these days, take deep breaths.

The Shield let the question drop. "What are you looking for from Kordan?"

Another hard question. It wasn't that he didn't want to tell the Shield, exactly, but it was hard to say out loud. The hope was too fragile, like the new skin of ice over a pond. Just the effort of shaping it into words could shatter it.

But that fear was irrational. He looked down into the Shield's face. "I'm looking for the antidote to rock snake venom."

The old man's eyebrows shot up in surprise. "I wouldn't have thought to look in Kordan's work."

Under other circumstances, Alaric would be pleased that he'd told the Shield something he didn't already know.

The Shield turned back to the book, and his surprise turned into a scowl. "This lists one reference in the library from Kordan, a scroll. But it's not in the medicinal section." He glanced up at Alaric. "It's on the restricted shelves."

The restricted shelves? Alaric felt the hope he'd been carrying so carefully crack.

The Shield gave Alaric a long, measured look. "I hope you find the answers you need, Alaric." He turned to go.

"There were ghosts outside the Wall," Alaric said quietly.

The Shield paused and turned back. "There are always ghosts on the path back home. They must have never had anything to say to you before."

Alaric looked at the old man in surprise. "You see them?"

The Shield gave a short, bitter laugh. "Every time. The sentinels may be the reason that so few of the older Keepers ever leave. They're too afraid to take the path back. You live long enough, Alaric, and you build up quite a few ghosts." The smile he gave Alaric now was tinged with sadness. "I meant what I told you before you left. No one is defined by a single choice. All of us have ghosts. And regrets. If you ever see a road back to us, I will be glad of it."

Alaric felt a momentary swell of gratitude. But the Shield didn't know what Alaric had done, the places he'd gone, the things he'd been a part of. He didn't know how many lines Alaric had crossed trying to save Evangeline, only to fail again and again. He tried to return the old man's parting smile, but he couldn't quite force one out before the Shield was too far away to see it.

THREE

Alaric watched the Shield leave the library before he moved. Then he went to the ramp and headed to the lowest floor. Two levels down, he almost ran into another Keeper walking with his nose in a book.

The man looked up with an apologetic smile. When he saw Alaric's face, his smile withered. Alaric held in a sigh.

"Mikal," Alaric said, nodding his head slightly. Of course it had to be Mikal.

Mikal narrowed his eyes. "Back so soon?"

Alaric felt a pang of regret at the Keeper's reaction. But here, at least, was the welcome Alaric had expected. "I'm not really back at all."

Mikal gave a little snort, his eyes running down Alaric's worn cloak. "Never thought you would be." He stepped around Alaric and disappeared up the ramp.

Alaric stood still for a moment. It was surprisingly depressing to realize he was living up to Mikal's expectations, not the Shield's.

Alaric descended quickly all the way to the deepest floor of the library where the oldest books were stored. Their spines, even with the meticulous preservation of the Keepers, were flaking off, leaving a fine dust along the front of the shelves. There were books on this level written in runes so ancient that none but a Keeper could read them.

He crossed the floor to a bookshelf covered by a wooden gate. When Alaric touched the wood, red words flared into existence.

Herein lie words of darkness and death.

A year ago when he'd touched this gate, he'd been looking for a way to save Evangeline's life among these restricted books. A way that was different from all the ways a Keeper would try. A way that might work. Most of these writings were from Sidion, works the Shade Seekers had written. They spoke of dark magic that the Keepers would not consider using. When the red warning had sprung up that time, Alaric had almost walked away.

Almost. He hadn't heeded the words. He thought he had found new paths of life. He had been wrong.

"Darkness and death," he agreed quietly.

He opened the gate and began to look carefully through the first shelf that held scrolls. At one end of it, he found one ruined, crumpled red scroll. Alaric winced in guilt and skipped down to the lower shelves. On the very bottom sat the unassuming brown scroll labeled, *Death and Life of a Seed* by Kordan the Harvester.

He pulled the parchment from its place and moved to a nearby desk positioned between the shelves. The cheerful glow of the golden orb above it felt out of place.

He unrolled the thin, crinkling paper.

Herein, I write the final record of my work. I cannot bear to write any more. I will store all of my memories in the Wellstone, and bury my treasure beneath a young oak. Then I am finished with it all.

It is only now that I see the darkness in what I have been studying.

I realized, as every farmer does, it is only in dying that a seed creates a new plant. I remembered that the Shade Seekers have a way of manipulating the energy of a creature at the moment of its death. If I could use that power with a seed, I might grow a plant greater than expected. I failed many times before I finally succeeded. I was elated when a sunflower sprouted and grew to an enormous height overnight.

I was coming to understand the exact nature of the seeds, the exact way in which they died, the exact moment in which to impart my magic. I began to see that I could control death, even stop it and replace it with life. Far from frightening me, I was thrilled by this new power.

Everything went perfectly for a quarter of a year.

Then came the day when Peros, the farmer's son, was bitten by a rock snake. Roused by the commotion, I ran outside and saw his parents holding him in despair. A man had killed the snake, but too late. Blackness was seeping up the boy's leg. There was nothing to do. No way to stop it.

Sometimes, I try to justify myself by remembering that I had been cooped up for months, focused exclusively on my seeds. But I know that does not excuse me.

When I saw the boy dying, it was as though he were a seed. I could see the life in him and knew how it would leave. I knew the moment of action. The despair of his parents drove any thought from my head, and I raced to the boy, cradling his head in my hands, whispering the words of death and life. Through his pain, he looked up at me, and I know that at the last moment, he understood what I did. Oh, worthless man! To have that moment back and watch the life fade from his eyes!

The boy did not die. A seed, when it is 'reborn', splits open and a new life springs from within it. But a boy is not a seed—Peros had nothing inside him to grow. There was nothing but the snake's venom and death.

The fear that he would split open paralyzed me for a moment, but he did not. He writhed and screamed in agony, an agony far worse than the bite. His parents tried to calm him, but everyone else drew back in terror. What came out of him was his energy, the essence of him. I can still hear the scream he let out as a green glow radiated from every part of his body. This glow swirled and pulled away from him, causing him terrible pain. It coalesced into a green focus of light as the last tendrils were torn from him.

The screaming stopped, and he collapsed to the ground. His eyes were glazed and empty, but he breathed. An enormous rough emerald dropped onto his chest, the solid form of the green light, the solid form of the boy's vitalle. His father cast the gem off the boy and clung to him. He spoke his son's name, but there was no response. The boy's eyes stared vacantly. He was alive, but hollow.

Eventually, they stood him up and led him away. He followed their every command, but lifelessly. They had never trusted my powers, but now they looked at me in horror as they left.

I picked up the emerald. It was warm and pulsed with a swirling green light. The Shade Seekers call it a Reservoir Stone. I almost took it to his family, but I did not. I do not know what I hoped to learn from it. Maybe it was a sort of punishment to keep it with me and remember what I had done.

I did nothing with the gem but look at it and weep.

Although the boy felt no more pain, the venom continued to eat away at him.

The light in the emerald dimmed through the night. When the boy died near dawn, the gem grew dark and cold.

It wasn't until days later that I realized that I have an antidote to the snakebite. It had never occurred to me. Perhaps this is the danger the Keepers warned me of. Not that my experiments were evil, but that they focused on death to the extent that I stopped looking for life.

Tonight, I end the record of my experiments. I have not the heart to work even with the seeds again. I will return to the Stronghold one last time. I know they will accept this scroll, even if they no longer can accept me. After what I have done, I can no longer call myself a Keeper. There are decisions that can't be unmade, paths that cannot be unchosen, choices that change us too much for us to ever change back.

The emerald sits next to me now, dark and empty.

I will leave here and give the villagers their peace.

Tomorrow, I deliver this scroll to the Stronghold. May it serve as a warning.

Alaric stared at the page in horror. His hand reached for the pouch around his neck. Trembling, he yanked it open, dropping its contents into his hand.

Out fell a huge, rough, uncut ruby filled with swirls of blood-red light.

Alaric rested his forehead against the warm gem, shutting his eyes against the red light. The same red light that had glowed while Evangeline had screamed in agony as he'd slowly drained her of her life energy to form the Reservoir Stone.

He opened his eyes and watched the eddies move through the ruby, the light scattering between the irregular faces of the gem. The energy was still there, still moving, just as it had for the last year. The crystal he had placed around her body to preserve it was working. She lived, and would until he removed the crystal. But that wouldn't matter, not if he couldn't find the antidote.

Alaric set the ruby off to the side and picked up Kordan's scroll and scanned it again, desperation rising. Kordan must have written something more. He had an antidote to rock snake venom. He must have recorded it somewhere.

With a growl of frustration, he flung the scroll away.

I will store all of my memories in the Wellstone.

Alaric dropped his head onto the table with a thud. How hard would it have been to write out one antidote?

He turned his head to look at the ruby again, letting the swirls of light calm him.

A sliver of darkness spun past the surface.

Alaric grabbed the ruby. He watched it closely. The currents flowed around each other until the black line appeared again, no wider than a blade of grass, wrapped around and through one of the streams of light.

Alaric's hand clenched the stone.

When the boy died near dawn, the gem grew dark and cold.

Alaric held the ruby with shaking hands. The bit of blackness continued to swirl in with the red. When had the darkness appeared? He studied it for a long time, but the black line didn't change. How long did he have before the ruby went dark?

He needed the antidote. Soon. If Kordan had put it in the Wellstone, then Alaric would use the Wellstone.

Alaric put the ruby back into the pouch at his neck. A tight ball of anger began to grow in his gut at the thought of sharing with the Keepers the things he had done during the last year. Once they knew, Alaric would never be welcomed back here. They wouldn't be able to look past it.

But he needed the antidote, so he would use the Wellstone, and then he would leave before they had to ask him to. He would get the antidote and go back to Evangeline.

Alaric stood up and placed Kordan's scroll back where it belonged. The warning gate closed on the bookshelf with a click.

He left the library quickly. The center of the Stronghold tower was open to the ceiling, its white walls rising up a half-dozen stories, drawing closer together as the diameter of the tower shrank. Along the wall, a ramp led upward. Dotted with arched doorways, it spiraled up until it passed through the ceiling. Through that opening, he could see flashes of light from the Wellstone.

Alaric began to climb the ramp. He passed his favorite study, the one with the deep fireplace and deep chair that always smelled like bread from the kitchen below.

Up near the top of the tower, Alaric passed his old room. It was thickly rugged, the walls blanketed by shelves of books, scrolls, and jars. All the things he used to value sat patiently, waiting for him to come back.

He moved on, climbing upward until the ramp led up through the opening in the ceiling and out into the night. The room at the top of the tower was walled almost entirely with open windows. The warm breeze swirled through, tucking dried leaves and dirt deeper into the corners.

The Wellstone, more valuable than everything else the Keepers owned, sat on a small silver pedestal in the center of a table.

It was a round, multifaceted crystal the size of a small melon. Colors flashed erratically through each of its facets, a few of them shining brilliantly.

The Wellstone served as a vessel, storing both energy and memories. The Keepers had been sharing their memories with it for centuries, helping to keep the things they recorded as close to fact as possible.

A chair sat next to the table, and Alaric sank into it. He touched the Wellstone, the edges cold and sharp beneath his fingers.

It would be here, all the knowledge Kordan had shared with the Wellstone when he had come to the Stronghold to deliver his book.

I might have an antidote to the snakebite.

Alaric took a deep breath and steeled himself for what was about to happen. Forcing himself not to consider it any longer, he reached out and cupped his hands around the Wellstone.

Connecting his mind to the crystal was like stepping into a raging storm. Images and sounds battered against him, not because it was trying to push him out, but because Alaric was too insignificant for the Wellstone to notice. He fought for a place in the chaos, fought to be stronger, louder.

When the Wellstone finally noticed him, it drew him in hungrily, the chaos shifting to swirl around him. He stayed still in the center of it all, still reluctant to release his memories. It tugged on his mind. With a groan, Alaric let go.

FOUR

T he chaos faded, and the Wellstone swept him along through his own memories. The first images were from court, flashes of the queen, the beginning of his trip to investigate troubling rumors from countries to the south.

Then two eyes, somewhere between green and brown, caught his attention. Alaric grabbed at the stream of memories, slowing them, watching them unfold.

The eyes peered out of a window at him, curious and amused.

Alaric froze, tottering on an upturned bucket, reaching his arm up as high as he could toward one specific apple high on the tree. He laughed self-consciously. With the break in his concentration, his spell faltered and the apple hanging far above him stopped quivering.

"Hello," the woman said politely.

"Hello," he answered, smoothing out his black robe and stepping off the bucket.

The woman raised her eyebrows and looked up at the tree laden with apples.

"Would you like a boost up?"

"No, thank you," Alaric said. "There's something undignified about a grown man climbing to the top of an apple tree for an apple when there are perfectly good ones within arm's reach."

"Was dignified the look you were going for?"

Alaric laughed again. He looked back up at the apple high on the tree and sighed in resignation. "I'd love a boost up."

The woman came outside and looked up at the tree. She was almost as tall as Alaric, with golden hair that was trying valiantly to escape from a long braid. Her face, while not striking, was open and happy.

"That particular apple is worth this much work?" She gestured to his robe with a grin. "Not to mention the destruction of your reputation as a respectable Keeper?"

Alaric considered the apple for a moment, knowing it seemed odd. "It's worth at least that much."

She offered her hands as a step, and between the two of them, Alaric was able to scramble up onto the first branch of the apple tree. Several minutes later, Alaric dropped back down out of the tree, holding his apple victoriously.

"I hate to tell you this," the woman said, "but your prize apple has been nibbled on."

Alaric turned the apple around to look at the bites taken from the side of the fruit.

"I know," he said. "That's why I wanted it."

"You're a very strange man," she said.

"This apple was bitten by a green-breasted robin," Alaric explained. "The saliva of a green-breasted robin is very rare and has some unusual qualities. It's very exciting to find this apple."

"Thrilling."

Alaric grinned and gave the woman a bow. "I'm Alaric. You have the thanks of the Keepers for your assistance in my quest. If there is any way the Keepers or I can repay you, we are in your debt."

She laughed and curtsied. "Well, Keeper Alaric, I am Evangeline, and this is my inn. If you would honor me with your patronage and some Keeper-storytelling for my customers, I would feel overpaid."

Alaric agreed to the storytelling and followed Evangeline into the inn. The walls were rough grey stone. The wooden planks of the floor were worn smooth by years of traffic. The hearth held a cheery fire, and smells of dinner and comfort wafted out of the kitchen. It was everything an inn should be. Alaric found himself relaxing, wanting nothing more than to prop his feet up on the hearth and enjoy a meal.

The common room was full for mid-afternoon. Workers wandered in and out for quick drinks, and a gaggle of old women played a noisy game of cards at a corner table. Three equally old men sat nearby, heckling the card players. Evangeline walked Alaric to a table near the fire.

"I bring you all a treat today," Evangeline announced to the room, handing Alaric a mug of cider. "A storyteller!"

A cheer went up from the room, and there was a scuffle of chairs as people rearranged themselves to take advantage of the new entertainment.

Alaric rubbed his hands together. "Are there any requests?"

Several suggestions were shouted from different parts of the room.

"Tomkin and the Dragon," Evangeline said.

A round of hollers agreed with the choice and Alaric nodded. It was a good choice. He took a deep drink of cider, pulled his hood up over his head, and looked down at the floor, letting the room fall into silence. From beneath his hood, he glanced at Evangeline and saw her leaning on the bar, her face set in a look of anticipation. Pleased by her interest, he began.

Images flashed by, of him and Evangeline traveling south. How nervous she had been to meet with the king of Napon.

His memories reached the evening on the sea cliffs.

Did the Wellstone know that some of these memories were more worn than others? Pulled out more often and clung to?

The moon sat low over the ocean, embodying every bit of poetry ever written about such a moment. Evangeline held his hands while the local holy man spoke the wedding pledges.

The image shifted.

The two of them pulled the unwieldy rowboat up onto the lakeshore and collapsed on the sand, half laughing, half groaning. Alaric could barely move his arms, and his back ached. The wind that had risen, making the water so choppy, blew across the beach, cooling him off so quickly he began to shiver.

"That is the worst rowboat ever made," she said, panting.

"With the world's smallest oars," he added. So much for a relaxing afternoon of fishing.

"If we find that obnoxious woman who was yelling, 'Row! Row!' from the shore, can you turn her into a rock?"

Alaric laughed. "I'm not good at messing with the boundary between the living and the *non-living."*

"A frog, then?"

"A frog is a possibility."

Alaric loosened his grip, letting images flow past faster, like water through his fingers. Images of walking a forested road with Evangeline, talking about everything and nothing. Sitting around a bonfire, watching village children dance. Scenes of easy happiness.

But then he caught a glimpse of the Lumen Greenwood in the distance, and a small village. The village that had been terrorized by an enormous fire lizard, which had been preying on their flocks and killed a child.

Alaric's heart faltered, and he grabbed at the flow of memories to stop them, but the Wellstone pulled him on.

Alaric set out with the three villagers to find and kill the fire lizard. Evangeline hadn't wanted to stay behind, but he'd gotten her to agree at last.

The dull orange lizard attacked them when they were barely out of the village.

Alaric drew vitalle out from it, slowing the lizard, but it was still so fast. The men shot arrows at it, most of them missing wildly as the creature darted around them, spitting burning liquid, raking the men with its claws.

The beast was finally brought down, its body prickling with black-fletched arrows. Alaric stumbled over to the men strewn on the ground. Not one had survived.

There was a noise behind him, and he spun around. Evangeline staggered toward him, a black-fletched arrow lodged in her thigh. His heart faltered.

"No," he cried, catching her as she fell. "I thought you were in the village."

She clutched at him, her face white with pain.

Alaric set her down gently. The arrow wasn't deep. A simple, clean wound like this would heal relatively quickly.

He gave her a moment to brace for the pain before he pulled it out.

She screamed.

Alaric clawed at the memories, frantically trying to stop them, to change them, to block the arrow, to change the story.

The wound had been simple, but it had not been clean. Of course the villagers had poisoned the arrows. But in their terror, they had poisoned them with things they didn't even have an antidote for.

Alaric climbed the stone steps of the small mountain keep, carrying her in his arms. Her breath came in shallow gasps. Her face was gaunt and pale.

The blanket he had wrapped her in slid off her black, swollen leg. Lines of dark red snaked up her thigh, tracing the poison's path. He tried to carry her gently, but she shuddered in pain with each step.

Alaric reeled away from the memory, but the Wellstone dragged him relentlessly on.

Alaric stood in the Stronghold council chamber trying not to crush the red scroll in his fist. Sixteen Keepers in black robes were seated at the long, map-strewn table, looking at him with troubled faces.

The Shield smiled warmly. "Brother Alaric, you have a request for the council?"

Alaric held the red scroll from Sidion securely in his hand, feeling the rich thrum of power it held. A power with more fire than the Keepers' books held. "I would like to travel to Sidion."

Most of the faces remained impassive. Keeper Gerone sighed, and Keeper Mikal huffed in disapproval.

"For what purpose?" the Shield asked.

They already knew the answer, but Alaric forced the words out, anyway.

"All my attempts have failed. Evangeline is at rest in a holding trance, but I cannot completely stop the progression of the rock snake venom. Our skills cannot save her. I need a way to extract it from her body without killing her."

Several men murmured in disapproval.

"And you think this is wise?"

"I think my wife is too young to die," Alaric snapped. "It's arrogant to think we have all the answers. There are references"—he waved the red scroll at them, causing little bits to crumble off—"of magic beyond what we practice. The Shade Seekers can sever the vitalle from the body—"

"Sever!" cried out Keeper Mikal above the muttering that filled the room. "The body is nothing without vitalle. The life energy and the body are intertwined—"

"Peace, brother," the Shield broke in. The room fell silent. "Alaric knows all these things. His learning has never been deficient."

"Any man can become a fool," muttered Mikal.

"Yes, and any man can stop being a fool and become something better," the Shield answered. "I, myself, have done both—more than once." He turned to Alaric. "You knew that we wouldn't approve this, and you knew why."

Alaric thought of Evangeline, the blackness of the venom twisting through her body. "Your reasons aren't as compelling as they used to be."

The Shield sighed. "No, I don't suppose they are."

"This is why Keepers don't waste time marrying," Mikal said. "It divides loyalties."

Alaric's anger flared, but he refused to look at Mikal, refused to have this fight again. "Will you give me leave to go?"

"No." The Shield's answer was simple. More sad than angry.

"Then you sentence my wife to death." Alaric flung the word across the table.

The Shield did not flinch. "I would save her, and you, from something worse."

"You sit here in your tower," Alaric said, biting off each word, "isolated from the world, judging and recording only part of it. You disregard and forbid things you are ignorant of."

"It is not from ignorance that we have banned the practices of Sidion."

"You've been there? You've studied their arts?" Alaric shot at the Shield.

"Yes."

Several heads turned sharply toward their leader.

"One of those choices that made me more of a fool."

Alaric paused at that. But then her face came back to him. Her desperate eyes, her hollowed cheeks.

"I must go."

"Then you will no longer be a Keeper." Mikal shoved his chair back as he stood.

"No one is discussing casting Alaric out," the Shield said firmly.

Mikal glared at Alaric before slamming back down into his chair.

The Shield looked around the room. "We do not cast men out for a single choice because no man is defined by a single choice. With each day, we decide anew who we are, what we will grow toward. Alaric has chosen to be a Keeper a thousand times in a thousand ways. No one is discussing his place here, only his request to travel to Sidion." He turned back to Alaric. "We cannot give you leave to go. It is forbidden."

Alaric stood, looking down the table at the frail old man. "I asked as a courtesy. I don't need your permission."

"We will not stop you, of course, and you will be welcomed back when you return." The Shield met Alaric's gaze. "But I beg you to reconsider. This is not what you want. Shade Seekers do not value the things we do. Please do not go. For her sake."

Alaric stared hard at the man. "I will not sit by and watch her die," Alaric said, crushing the scroll in his hand. Keeper Gerone's face grew white, and he stretched his hand toward the ruined red parchment.

Alaric would not be swayed.

He would not lose her.

The Wellstone continued to pull him on. Alaric was at Sidion, reading dark, heartless books. Then he was standing over Evangeline, drawing the red light out from her, apologizing over and over while she screamed in pain. Finally, the ruby solidified, swirling with red light.

Alaric let the memories flow, letting the Wellstone pull them out as quickly as it wanted. When Alaric reached the Death Caves of the southern blood doctors in Napon, the memories slowed. Alaric tried to push them faster, but the Stone recognized that here was a place no Keeper had ever been before. It spent too long absorbing the horrors of that place. Watching healthy people, even women and young children, poisoned. Their symptoms, responses to antidotes, and deaths recorded meticulously. There was so much blood and sickness in those caves you could taste it in the air.

The Wellstone sifted through every memory as Alaric stood by, watching the doctors perform experiment after experiment with the rock snake venom he had brought. They didn't have rock snakes this far south. He hadn't known what they would do when he brought it to them. He hadn't known how many people they would kill trying to develop an antidote. How many people Alaric would have to watch die, unable to stop them.

And even the blood doctors found no antidote.

The Wellstone's pull on him lessened as the pool of unshared memories shrank. It settled finally on an image of the small keep where Evangeline lay, pale and still. Moonlight fell through the balcony doors onto her thin face, her limp hair. It glinted off the crystal surrounding her, keeping her body alive.

With a moan, Alaric pulled his hands off the Wellstone.

FIVE

Alaric leaned his head on the table and closed his eyes, clasping his hands together to stop their shaking. He wanted to run, to run and forget the fact that those memories were shared now, held permanently in the Wellstone to be studied by Keepers whenever they wished.

Alaric shook out his hands. He shoved the thoughts of what he had just done away. It was done, and with it, his time as a Keeper. He would find Kordan's antidote, and then he would leave. He thought of the swirl of darkness in the ruby and felt a wave of anguish. How long did he have before that darkness spread? How long did Evangeline have left?

But the Wellstone demanded focus, and it was a long time before he was calm enough to try. Finally, he set his hands on it and concentrated on the entry he had read in Kordan's journal. The boy, the snake, the emerald.

It was a process, looking for information in the seemingly bottomless pool of memories in the Wellstone. Slowly, painstakingly, he nudged the chaos toward the memories Kordan had left. When he finally found them, he found the boy, writhing in pain while a green glow radiated from his body.

The emerald formed, and the boy was led away by his parents. If Alaric could see where Kordan kept his notes, he could sift back through memories until he found the Keeper writing the antidote. But Kordan's home was bare. There was only one book, the small brown journal Alaric had already read. Where did Kordan record his work?

Kordan pulled the emerald out of his pocket, watching the light swirl. He picked up a box from the mantle, a sprawling oak tree carved into the lid. Gently, he wrapped the emerald in a red hand-kerchief and placed it in the box.

Then he dropped into a chair. On the table next to him, sitting on a silver, three-pronged stand, was a small crystal with irregular surfaces, but each facet flashed with color.

Kordan had a Wellstone.

Alaric tried to see more, tried to draw out more memories from Kordan. But all he could see was Kordan looking into his own Wellstone.

Alaric's stomach dropped. Wellstones must not record memories recorded in other Wellstones. No matter what he tried, he found no more of Kordan's life.

He let his hands fall off the crystal.

He was looking in the wrong place. Kordan had kept all of his knowledge in his own Wellstone. This one was useless.

He sank back into the chair, dropping his face into his hands. His dismay was so great that he could hardly breathe. He had just used the wrong Wellstone. There was no antidote here.

Alaric had just shared all his memories with the Keepers for nothing.

I will store all of my memories in the Wellstone, and bury my treasure here beneath a young oak, Kordan had written.

Alaric thought of Kordan's sparse home. The Keeper had had no treasure besides the Wellstone. One even as small and irregular as his would be worth a fortune.

Somewhere in Kordan's Blight, under what must now be a hundred-year-old oak, the antidote Alaric needed was buried.

He stood up, refusing to look at the useless Wellstone, refusing to think about the memories he'd just shared. The Shield would come see them soon enough and realize that Alaric wasn't really a Keeper any longer. Kordan was right. There were choices that changed a person too much.

Alaric strode back down the ramp into the dark tower. When he reached the council chamber, he stopped to check a map, slipping in and closing the door behind him before lighting a lantern.

The council table was spread with woefully incomplete maps of the Lumen Greenwood, the forest of the elves.

For eight years, the Keepers had been trying to find out what had happened the day Mallon, a ruthless Shade Seeker with seemingly limitless power, had disappeared. He had bent the country to his will, leading an army of nomadic warriors right to the walls of the capital. Neither Queen Saren nor the Keepers had had any real hope of stopping Mallon. But then he had turned his attention toward the elves and disappeared into their woods.

That day, half of the Greenwood had burned and Mallon had disappeared along with every trace of his power. The thousands under his control had been released, and his nomadic army had drained back through the Scale Mountains.

But the elves had disappeared as well. It was challenging to find the elves in the best of times, but since Mallon, it had been impossible.

Alaric pulled maps off a shelf, tossing aside assorted maps of Queensland, the Dwarves' capital of Duncave, and other miscellaneous maps until he found one showing Kordan's Blight. It was far north, the last village before the Wolfsbane Mountains began.

He took a moment to memorize the map, then blew out the lantern and went quickly downstairs.

When he reached the ground floor, he could hear the thwump-thwumping of Keeper Gerone kneading the morning bread. It must be close to dawn. Alaric walked over to the kitchen door and saw the Keeper's bent back as he steadily worked the dough. Alaric breathed in the smell of home and belonging.

He opened his mouth to greet Gerone, eyeing a kitchen chair he could drop into and spill his troubles out to the old man. In the quiet, while it was still dark, had always been a good time to talk to the brilliant man, looking for new perspectives or connections or answers.

But Alaric couldn't bring himself to tell Gerone what he had done. He'd see the memories in the Wellstone soon enough.

Gerone began to turn around and Alaric ducked quickly past the door.

He paused for just a moment at the Keepers' robes on the way out. He let his fingers run across the fabric again. He could leave the worn-out one he was wearing and put on a proper robe. The robes were made to look common, giving Keepers a measure of anonymity when they traveled. But they weren't common. They were perfect. The perfect weight, the perfect warmth, the perfect black. The first time he had worn one was the first time he had really believed he was a Keeper.

Alaric let his hand drop. Leaving the robes on their hooks, he left.

The woods allowed Alaric to leave without being visited by ghosts or wolves, and by the time the sun had fully risen, he was on the King's Highway heading north. When dusk came, he stopped for the night at a small tavern in a small town. It had been before lunchtime when he had passed the last thing that could be called a city. From here north, it was just scattered homesteads and the occasional village.

In the tavern, even though he was exhausted from not sleeping the night before, he settled into the commotion and camaraderie of the dining room. He was reluctant to call himself a Keeper tonight, so he introduced himself as a royal historian tasked with recording local histories. Several men joined him at a table and talked over each other to tell a legend of a crazy miller woman who haunted Dead Man's Hollow.

When the sun set, Alaric continued recording stories by candlelight. The room was alive with laughter and folktales. For the first time in a long time, his enjoyment of the world around him drowned out his own worry and guilt.

The tavern brightened slightly as the front door opened. A hush fell over the room. Alaric glanced up to see where the extra light was coming from.

It took a moment to understand what he was seeing.

Standing in the doorway was a group of travelers. A young man, an old man, a stocky dwarf, and glittering like her own candle flame, was an elf.

SIX

The people around Alaric sat perfectly still, staring unabashedly at what was surely the only elf they had ever seen. Alaric stared along with them. He had forgotten how luminous they were.

"Good evening," she said, gracing them with a smile that spread through the room like a wave of warm water. Alaric smiled back at her. She was so very elfish—like a sparkle of sunlight. Her simple white dress reached down to her knees and was belted by a ring of purple flowers. The waves of her hair, and maybe even her skin, shimmered with specks of gold.

The sounds of the rest of the room faded—she lit up like a beacon of light in a dull world. Like a beacon of pure, stunning, mesmerizing brilliance.

Alaric realized he was gazing oafishly at her and blinked. He shook off the unfocused feeling creeping across his mind and studied her. She was pretty, but not nearly as lovely as he had thought. Or maybe she was. She was mesmerizing.

Alaric tore his gaze away from her. Scowling, he braced his mind against her, willfully choosing to focus on his own hands, the bread on the table, the smell of onions and roasting meat. He took control of his own thoughts, leaving no room for any outside influence. His mind cleared, and the room settled back into perspective.

That was disconcerting.

Elves could sense more about living creatures than humans could. They could see emotions and the general state of well-being that a person had just by looking at them. But this elf was doing more than that. Alaric glanced around the enthralled tavern. It sure looked like this elf wasn't just reading emotions. She was controlling them.

"Are you done?" the dwarf asked the elf as he jostled past her. "I'm hungry."

She let out a tinkle of laughter, and everyone blinked and moved again, leaning toward their neighbors and whispering.

The man next to Alaric tore his gaze away from the elf and continued his story. Alaric gave enough attention to him to write it down, but like everyone else, he mostly watched this new group. Now that his mind was clearer, he realized the full impact of what he was seeing.

The elf by herself would be astonishing enough, but she had settled into a chair right next to the dwarf. Alaric had never heard of an elf and a dwarf interacting. As far as he knew, there had never even been a meeting between the two peoples. If a dwarf happened to be in the capital during the short time an elf had visited, the two avoided each other.

But these two seemed perfectly at ease with each other.

When the barmaid took drinks to the table, the dwarf lifted his glass. "To the richest family in Kordan's Blight."

Alaric's quill stuttered. Kordan's Blight?

He wrapped up the story with the man, crossed the room to where the group was sitting, and introduced himself.

"A royal historian?" the dwarf asked, glancing down at Alaric's worn cloak. "So you're a cheaper version of those Keepers you humans like so much?"

Alaric forced a smile at the dwarf. "Precisely."

"You'll have to excuse Douglon," the young man said, shooting the dwarf a disapproving look. He had an open face topped by a tousle of indistinct brown hair. "He's hungry. Please, have a seat. I'm Brandson."

Alaric took the seat. "I must say, you are the most interesting group that I have ever come across in my travels."

"You have no idea," the elf said, smiling at him. Then she peered at him as though working out a puzzle. "Is this place calming your soul?" she asked curiously.

"It is," Alaric admitted.

"Wonderful," she said, bathing him with a radiant smile. "A soul with burdens such as yours needs some calming."

Her smile sank into him, sending tendrils of comfort deep into his chest.

Alaric liked elves. They kept you on your toes. He firmed up the focus of his mind so that she couldn't influence his thoughts. It was stimulating to be around a people who had such casual intuition. She wouldn't care enough about a human to wonder what his burdens were, but she'd see that he carried them as easily as she'd see his brown hair.

The dwarf rolled his eyes. "Good evening," he grunted. "I don't care about your soul."

Alaric laughed. "And I don't care about yours, master dwarf." Douglon was exactly what Alaric expected from a dwarf, with the darkened leather armor and his long copper beard, beaded and tucked into his belt alongside his scarred battle-axe.

Douglon flicked his hand toward the elf. "The annoyingly cheerful elf is Ayda."

"And I," the old man proclaimed in a nasal voice, "am Wizendorenfurderfur the Wondrous." He wiggled his fingers through the air. "Holder of Secrets, Caster of Spells, and Spinner of Dreams!" He wore a long, dark blue robe, embroidered with stars, moons, and swirls of lighter blue thread. Matched, of course, by his pointy hat.

Brandson bit his lip to keep from smiling, and Douglon snorted in annoyance.

It was rare to run across someone with a talent for magic. Not as rare as elves, but if the man was telling the truth, this group just kept getting more interesting. "Wizendorenfurderfur," Alaric repeated.

"Close enough," the old man replied with a dismissive wave of his hand. "I don't expect common folk to be able to pronounce my name. I allow these people to call me Gustav."

"Naturally," answered Alaric, keeping his face serious while he gave the wizard a slight bow.

Alaric looked back at Douglon and Ayda. "I've never heard of an elf and a dwarf traveling together."

"You still haven't," Douglon said, grumbling but not moving away from her. "I travel with Brandson. Ayda just shows up sometimes, and Brandson is too kind to send her away. No one would choose to travel with an elf."

Ayda smiled sweetly at the dwarf.

Alaric glanced around the table as the tavern keeper brought them all some dinner. Taken together, they were an odd collection, but when he looked at them individually, they each embodied their own people perfectly. The elf was flighty, the dwarf was gruff, the young man was friendly, and the wizard wore a pointy hat. Alaric smiled at them all. He couldn't have put together a more entertaining group if he had tried.

"I heard you mention Kordan's Blight," Alaric said. "That is one of the towns I'm planning on visiting."

Brandson nodded. "That's where we live. We're headed home from the market at Queenstown."

"Brandson is the town blacksmith," Douglon said.

"A town with the name Kordan's Blight promises some interesting local legends," Alaric said.

"I can tell you how the town was named!" said Gustav. He took a dramatic pause, then shot an impatient look at Alaric. "Aren't you going to write this down, historian?"

"Um, of course," Alaric said. He pulled out his book and quill, receiving an approving nod from the old man.

Gustav narrowed his eyes and began in a hushed voice. "Long ago, the evil wizard Kordan dwelt in the town. He tyrannized the people, stealing their crops and murdering their cattle. Then one day, he took an innocent boy and turned him into a demon! The people were terrified until my great-great-grandfather, Meisterfoltergast, cast the wizard out and killed the demon. Meisterfoltergast spent days cleansing the town of Kordan's evil. He restored their crops and blessed their cattle but renamed the town Kordan's Blight as a warning to the people to remember what evil is."

Gustav fixed Alaric with a glare and whispered, "People always forget that there is evil nearby. Always."

The old man picked up a piece of chicken and tore off a bite.

Silence reigned for a moment while everyone stared at the wizard.

"I'd bet my beard there's not a lick of truth to that," Douglon said to Ayda.

Gustav huffed and glared at the dwarf.

Brandson shrugged. "I've lived there most of my life, and that's essentially the tale I've always heard. Although until I met Gustav, I hadn't known the part about Meisterfoltergast." He gave Gustav a small smile.

Alaric looked back at his paper and kept writing. The tale of Kordan these people knew was warped, but he was definitely the same Keeper that Alaric was interested in.

"Is there anything left of Kordan? A monument? Signs of destruction? His home?" Alaric kept his eyes on his work. "Any of his valuables the town kept?"

When no one answered, Alaric glanced up. Brandson, Douglon, and Gustav were focusing intently on their food. Ayda was smirking at them.

"It was a very long time ago," Gustav pointed out.

"Of course," Alaric said, letting the question drop. "It would be strange to keep mementos of an evil wizard."

Alaric didn't glance up at the group, but the tension in the men was palpable. Alaric blotted the page he had written and turned to Gustav.

"You seem quite knowledgeable. I'd be honored if you shared some of your stories with me."

"I suppose I could do that." Gustav sniffed. "I'll have to select the best. We don't have time tonight for all of them."

"You could come along with us tomorrow if you are going to Kordan's Blight," Brandson said, causing Douglon and Gustav to scowl.

Alaric gave the blacksmith a warm smile. "I would love to."

Ayda cocked her head and looked at Alaric. "What are you looking for there?" She sparkled captivatingly.

Alaric pulled his eyes away, focusing on the concrete things around him, the feel of his quill, the sounds of the tavern. "Just looking for old stories, wives tales, histories."

She narrowed her eyes.

"Any local knowledge I can find, really. Recipes for local dishes, remedies for sicknesses, anything people can tell me." The remedies part was true, and it seemed best to throw in a little truth when talking to an elf.

She nodded slowly. "And the queen cares about all of this?"

"The queen cares about all of her subjects." That, at least, was completely true. "I'd love to hear some stories from you as well. The world has been asking a lot of questions about the elves since Mallon disappeared."

Ayda's smile froze, and her eyes flashed with an anger so deep that Alaric drew back. "The elves are fine." She bit off each word.

Her gaze pinned him to his seat. He forced himself not to shift in discomfort.

Brandson, Douglon, and Gustav looked anywhere but at Ayda.

"Good," Alaric answered, forcing a smile. "The queen will be glad to hear it."

Ayda nodded curtly.

"So, Alaric," Brandson broke in, "have you come across many interesting stories?"

Alaric turned toward the smith and grabbed for the change of subject. With more enthusiasm than was probably necessary, he launched into a legend from a southern town about their haunted chicken coop.

The next time he glanced at Ayda, she had relaxed back into her chair, smiling and laughing with the others. He braced his mind against her again, but he couldn't quite shake the fuzziness that had been on him since she walked through the door. It was going to be a long trip with her if the elf made him feel like this the whole way.

Alaric set aside the question of the elves. Maybe once he got to know her better she would give him at least some hints. Whatever had happened with the elves, they obviously weren't fine.

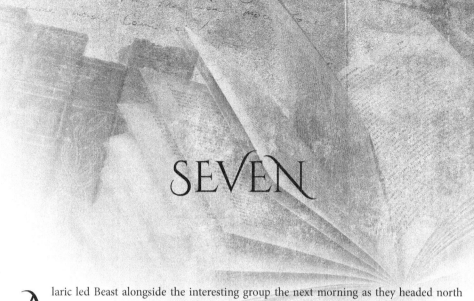

SEVEN

Alaric led Beast alongside the interesting group the next morning as they headed north along the King's Highway. Brandson drove a slow horse cart loaded down with assorted blades, horseshoes, and wagon parts from his smithy. Gustav and Douglon walked while Ayda traveled through the edge of the woods along the road, placing her hand on trunks as she passed in the elfish way of listening to the trees.

It had been a year since Alaric had traveled with anyone, a year since he'd wanted to. But there was such an easy camaraderie about this group that he found himself enjoying it.

"Oh, look at that oak tree!" Ayda cried out.

Alaric glanced at the oak. It was one of a dozen he could see around them. Hopefully, there weren't this many oaks in Kordan's Blight, or it was going to be hard to figure out which one Kordan had used as a marker for his buried treasure.

"Which tree?" Douglon asked. "The boring one right there?"

Alaric tried not to laugh. It wasn't exactly boring, but there was nothing unusual about it.

Ignoring the dwarf, Ayda stepped over to the oak, slipping in under the heavy branches.

"I think it's a nice tree," Brandson said.

"It's a tree," Douglon said. "Like that one and that one and that one."

Ayda came back weaving a chain of leaves together. Alaric watched her hands closely. It almost looked like she was creating new leaves as she walked, but that was impossible.

"Here you are, noble dwarf," Ayda said, holding out the chain. "A gift from Harwood."

"Harwood?" asked Alaric.

"Probably the stupid tree's name," explained Douglon, backing away as Ayda tried to put the chain around his neck.

"It is his name," Ayda said. "And stand still, dwarf, or I'll enchant this so that you can never remove it."

Douglon paused, and Ayda took the opportunity to fling the necklace of leaves around his neck. They fell over his shoulders, the bright green leaves lying across the front of his red beard. Douglon stopped and glared at her.

"Come now," she said, patting his bearded cheek.

Alaric was caught between admiration for her bravery and concern for her safety. He certainly wouldn't have patted a dwarf wearing that expression.

"Wear it a bit for old Harwood," Ayda said. "At least until he's out of sight. It makes you look ferocious."

The dwarf growled and leaned toward her menacingly. Ayda laughed. "See?"

Douglon's hand went to the chain of leaves, but he didn't pull it off.

"You can write this down, historian," Gustav said in a nasal voice from beside the cart where he had been walking. "In ancient times, the leaves of the oak tree were used to form crowns for the victors of war. I myself have formed weapons out of oak leaves, using spells to harden them and hurl them at my enemies!"

Alaric forced an interested look onto his face. "I'll add that to my notes tonight." The part about the crowns was true, but hardening leaves into projectiles seemed like a waste of energy. If you needed to hurl something hard, just pick up a rock.

"Not the dreaded leaf attack," Douglon muttered. He began to peel the green blade off each leaf, leaving only a wiry chain of stems around his neck.

"That sounds impressive," said Brandson to Gustav, giving the old man a smile. "I hope we'll never be in a position to need that useful trick."

"Surely we will, my boy," Gustav said. "Surely we will. Danger is always close at hand." With those ominous words, the wizard moved ahead of them down the road, peering into the underbrush.

Brandson glanced at Alaric and shrugged.

Alaric still couldn't completely shake the unfocused feeling that he'd had since the group walked in the door of the tavern last night. He couldn't sense Ayda actually trying to influence his mind, but he also couldn't quite shake the feeling that his mind wasn't completely his own.

But in spite of that fuzziness, part of his mind felt more alert. It required a vigilance that he hadn't needed in a very long time to make sure Ayda wasn't influencing him. Nothing about her was particularly threatening, but he wasn't going to be able to relax until they reached Kordan's Blight and he could put some distance between himself and the elf.

Alaric let the wizard, the dwarf, and the elf pull ahead of Brandson and his slow cart. The young smith would be the easiest person to start a conversation with about Kordan's Blight.

Brandson hadn't been any more forthcoming than the others last night when Alaric had asked them if anything of Kordan's was left in Kordan's Blight. Would the young man need encouragement to talk? The Keepers wouldn't approve, because they didn't use magic to manipulate people. But the spell wouldn't really change Brandson, just make him a little more…whatever he already was. Brandson was already a trusting sort, so it would encourage that a little. Still, it was a morally hazy area.

Last night, when Alaric had pulled the ruby out of its pouch, the inky line had seemed darker. It had still been the only dark line in a sea of red, but each time it had swirled across one of the faces of the Reservoir Stone, it had felt more ominous. The thought pushed away any remaining guilt about using his magic. A little information up front could save Alaric a lot of time searching for Kordan's Wellstone. Alaric wrapped his hand around the reins to hide any tremor and made sure the rest of the group was far enough away to not be affected by the magic.

"*Augmenta*," he whispered. He fisted his hand against the pain as the energy was released.

"You have a unique family," Alaric said to Brandson.

"Yes," Brandson agreed. He continued in a confiding whisper, "You may be surprised to learn that we are not blood relatives."

Alaric laughed. "Astonishing."

"We are all orphans of one sort or another and have thrown our lots in together. I am an orphan of the sort that is actually an orphan. My parents died from one of the outbreaks of the yellow plague during the Riving of the north."

Alaric made a sympathetic noise. The people of the north were spread out into such small villages and towns that Mallon, when he had come here, hadn't bothered bringing an army. Instead, he had sent a sickness. The yellow plague had been especially deadly to healthy men. In many parts of the north, not a single man between fifteen and fifty survived. Most of Brandson's generation were fatherless.

"When I was fifteen, the blacksmith in Kordan's Blight took me in and taught me his trade. He died five years ago and I have been the town blacksmith ever since."

Ahead of them, Gustav stalked along the road by himself, muttering.

Brandson smiled after the wizard. "Wizendorenfurderfur appeared half dead on my doorstep during a blizzard late last winter. I dragged him in and thawed him out. The story of his life before that is so... complex... that I can't follow it. But I don't think he has any family. He's hung around ever since. We haven't seen much of his dazzling magical powers, but he's a good cook, and my stomach is glad of his company."

"Is he really a wizard?" Alaric asked, his voice pitched low so Gustav couldn't hear.

"I think so." Brandson wrinkled his brow. "At least he tells an awful lot of stories about his magical skills. I have seen him start a fire with just a word."

Manipulating energy to light a fire wasn't difficult. The old man might have some minimal talent. Maybe a touch more than the average street magician who could often sense energy without being able to manipulate it.

"And those two?" Alaric asked, looking at the dwarf and the elf who were haggling over the color of a blackberry.

"Black," Douglon said, "it's a blackberry."

"The berry is purple. And there is a hint of gold," Ayda said.

"Gold? Let me see."

Smiling triumphantly, she handed it to him.

Douglon popped the berry in his mouth. "Tastes black."

Ayda glared at his mouth for a moment as though she might reach in and get the berry back. Then she shrugged. "I'll find more. I wonder if they will all have gold in them?"

Brandson let out a laugh. "I found Ayda when I was hunting not long after the snow melted. She was wandering through the forest chatting with trees. I had never seen an elf before, so I invited her to my home for a meal. She agreed, which surprised me. I didn't think elves bothered with humans."

Alaric watched Ayda scampering along the bushes next to the road. "They usually don't. I'm not only surprised she came to your home, I'm surprised that she would travel with you on a trip as long as this. She isn't anxious to get home?"

Brandson shook his head. "No. And it's not just this trip. Ayda's been staying at my smithy for almost three months. She does leave every once in a while, but then she shows back up again."

Three months? Elves that had come to the capital to meet with Saren were unhappy if they were out of the Greenwood for three days.

Brandson watched Ayda for a moment. "I think she left her family, but I don't know why. As far as I know, that is unusual for an elf."

It wasn't unusual. It was unheard of. The elves shared a communal life force. If something were urgent enough, an elf would leave the Greenwood, but they always hurried back. Some Keepers went as far as to believe that isolating an elf would lead to its death.

"She's been with you that long? Elves never form attachments to anyone but other elves."

Brandson shrugged. "She's become friends with us."

Alaric looked closely at the elf, wondering if Brandson was bestowing her feelings with a name they didn't deserve.

"I met Douglon that same day. Ayda and I discovered him in the woods on our way back home. He was standing in a clearing, poring over a map. He hid it as soon as he noticed me. I approached him first, in case he was hostile, but he was nice enough. Especially when he saw my hunting knife."

Alaric glanced down at the knife on Brandson's belt. He looked closer. "Is that dwarf-made?"

"No, I made it, but I modeled it after the dwarfish blades. Douglon was intrigued. I invited him to my forge to see my work, and he accepted. But when Ayda stepped out of the trees, he almost left. Said his beard would fall out if he had to listen to the prattling of an elf for an entire meal.

"It was the most serious I'd seen Ayda all day. She told him he was in need of a bath. It turns out Douglon is proud of his hygiene. Her words almost sent him into a frenzy.

"I managed to calm the two and remind them that as my guests they would do well to respect my friends. They agreed, but it was a tense walk back. Part way through dinner, though, we had a breakthrough. Douglon, who'd had several pints of ale, confided to us that he possessed a treasure map. But he'd gotten himself stuck since he was unable to interpret the runes on the map."

Alaric was part fascinated, part alarmed. His *augmenta* spell might have worked too well. He had only wanted the blacksmith to feel comfortable, but if Brandson started spilling secrets, he might grow suspicious as to why. Alaric cast about for a moment, but could think of no way to end the spell.

"Gustav, as you will soon learn," Brandson continued, "has enormous amounts of knowledge of all things, including runes, and offered to interpret them. After some haggling, we decided that between Gustav's knowledge, my familiarity with the region, Ayda's ability to talk to the trees, and Douglon's map, we might be able to find this treasure. Gustav, when he had interpreted the map, claimed he had heard of it. His great-great-grand uncle or some such person had passed down information about it."

Brandson sighed. "But that was months ago, and we still have found nothing. Not for lack of trying. We've dug in dozens of places, but we haven't found—"

He stopped and looked at Alaric in dismay. "I shouldn't be telling you this. We swore an oath of secrecy to each other."

Alaric worked hard to keep his face bland. "That's the way of the road, isn't it? Talking to strangers. I've had no one but Beast to talk to for a long time. By now, he knows all my history." He patted Beast's neck. "He's probably thrilled to hear someone else's for once."

Brandson paused and Alaric waited, trying to look unconcerned. Finally, he sighed. "It's actually something you might be interested in writing about. The treasure supposedly belonged to the wizard Kordan. It's some sort of enormous gem that might have magical powers. Kordan buried it before he was driven from town."

Alaric's hand clenched on the reins, and he whipped his head around toward Brandson so quickly that the blacksmith drew back.

Ayda stepped into view around the carthorse, her hands overflowing with blackberries.

Alaric focused on her quickly, an inept cover up for showing the surprise he had to Brandson. But that was another mistake. As soon as he focused on Ayda, he realized the fuzziness had crept across his mind again. Pulling his eyes away from her, he fixed his eyes resolutely on the berries while she laid them out on the seat next to Brandson. Being with these people was like being caught in a mental whirlwind. He took a deep breath, trying to calm his mind and to school his features into a more reasonable level of surprise.

Ayda beamed at Alaric and offered him a berry. "You look like you've seen a ghost."

He managed a weak smile. "Not since yesterday."

She cocked her head at him, her expression bemused. "Well, there's nothing like a juicy berry to remind you you're still among the living." With a grin, she walked off ahead of them.

Alaric stuck the berry into his mouth to give himself an extra moment to recover. It burst with juices, the tartness clearing his head. He grabbed another one before even trying to think straight.

These people were searching for Kordan's Wellstone? The same Wellstone that he had learned existed only yesterday? He shoved against that fuzzy feeling in his mind again. What was he missing here?

"That's quite a treasure," Alaric said finally. "And it is exactly the sort of thing I would love to write about."

Brandson nodded slowly.

"It does seem strange that Gustav happened to have information about a treasure Douglon was looking for," Alaric said, attempting to move the focus of the conversation off himself.

"That's what Douglon thinks, too," Brandson said. "He doesn't believe Gustav knows anything. Thinks he's just along to steal the treasure. It doesn't help that Gustav's clue is too cryptic to make sense of. '*The stone lies beneath the oatry,*' whatever that means."

Alaric reached for some more berries and forced his face to stay neutral even though his mind spun.

The stone lies beneath the oak tree.

How exactly had the dimwitted wizard discovered that piece of information?

EIGHT

"You told him what?" Douglon hurled a stick into the fire that evening and glared from Brandson to Alaric.

Alaric toyed with the idea of using *augmenta* again to bring Brandson more firmly onto his side. But with everyone this close, it would influence everyone. Gustav and Douglon would become angrier. It probably wouldn't affect an elf, but it wouldn't stop Ayda from watching him with that odd look, either.

"You told him all that without him influencing you in any way?" she asked Brandson, eyeing Alaric.

"Of course," Brandson said. "I told him because I trust him."

"I'm honored that Brandson entrusted me with your secret," Alaric said, stepping back from her. "And to prove my goodwill, I will help you find your treasure."

"We don't need help," Douglon said. "Or anyone else to split it with."

"What help could you offer?" Brandson asked, talking over Douglon.

Alaric was tempted for a moment to tell them he was a Keeper. For Brandson and Gustav, that would put him in a position of authority. But it wouldn't convince Douglon. All Douglon would see was that he was still a human, and dwarves were unimpressed with humans. Mostly, though, he was reluctant to claim the title.

"I have found a decent amount of treasure myself," Alaric said instead. "And I have a good sense of an object's worth."

"We can figure out how much it's worth," the dwarf said.

"Probably," agreed Alaric, "but I do bring one more thing. A buyer."

Brandson looked curious, but Douglon scowled.

"If the gem is as large as you think it is, the queen would be interested in it. I'd imagine she would pay you generously for it." It wasn't exactly a lie. "If this stone is even a quarter as grand as you say it is, I will talk to Saren about buying it." The Keepers would pay any price for a Wellstone. And Saren would help.

The group exchanged wary glances.

"And *Saren* will just do as you say?" Gustav asked.

"*Queen Saren*," Alaric corrected, berating himself for being so careless, "likes gemstones. She buys them at a generous price from miners. I'm sure she would do the same for yours."

Douglon and Gustav were watching Alaric with distrust. This wasn't going all that well.

"If you decide you don't want to sell it, the queen will have to be satisfied with that, of course," Alaric said. "But a gem doesn't split four ways. A pile of gold does."

"That's a good point," Ayda said. She sat a little off to the side, thoroughly entertained by the discussion.

"If you tell your queen about it, she's likely to take it from us by force," Douglon said.

Alaric let out a laugh. "You don't know much about Queen Saren, do you?"

"Queen Saren is known for her fairness and generosity," Brandson said. "She wouldn't take it by force."

"That doesn't mean a lot coming from you." Douglon shot a glare at Brandson and gestured toward Alaric. "You trust people a little too easily, don't you think?"

Brandson scowled.

"It seems to me that you've benefitted from that trust a bit," Ayda pointed out to the dwarf.

Douglon included her in his general glare, then turned to Gustav. "Is it true what they say about the queen?"

"You could probably convince her to pay you more than it's worth," Gustav said. "She's never been particularly strong."

Alaric bristled, but clamped his mouth shut.

"How generous would she be?" Douglon asked, his expression calculating.

"Very generous," Alaric said. "I've seen her pay almost twice what a gem was worth if she thought it was beautiful." Not to mention powerful and magical.

Douglon stroked his beard absently.

Brandson cleared his throat. "I vote to let Alaric join us."

"Me, too!" Ayda burst out, as though she'd been waiting for the chance.

Alaric didn't meet her eyes. It would be nice to keep his wits clear right now.

He looked at Gustav and was surprised to be greeted by a shrewd look. When Alaric met his eyes, though, the old man's gaze faltered and dropped to the fire. "Fine with me," he muttered.

Douglon stood and approached Alaric. The dwarf extended his hand. "Your word that the treasure is ours unless we agree to sell it?"

Alaric didn't need to own the Wellstone, just get his hands on it for a few minutes. He stood and shook the dwarf's hand.

Hours later, the talk of treasure dwindled and all parties settled down to sleep. Alaric leaned against a tree at the edge of the firelight, surrounded by the lingering warmth of the day. The only sounds were the chirps of the forest bugs and the crackle of the fire.

It was odd that he had run into this group. More than odd. To find people searching for Kordan's buried treasure? It was impossible to think that was coincidence. If it was something else, though, Alaric didn't have any idea what it was.

"Are you going to try to influence me?" Ayda's voice slipped out of the darkness next to Alaric's ear, causing him to start.

"Of course not," he answered. It wasn't worth pretending he hadn't used *augmenta* on Brandson. Ayda probably knew he had. "You seem to be an expert at influencing people. Even for an elf."

Ayda laughed, stepping out of the darkness and settling herself beside him on the grass.

"Influencing is such a vague idea, isn't it? It comes in all different forms. Am I still influencing people if they just like me?" She cocked her head to the side, looking at Alaric. "But I don't know that I could affect you, at least not without some actual effort. That is unusual, you know."

Alaric snorted. "You don't actually believe that."

He couldn't quite pull his eyes away from her. There was something fascinating about Ayda. Something shimmery around the edges, something warm radiating out, something troubling tucked in the background. Elves had a sort of intensity about them that humans and dwarves lacked, but Alaric had never met one whose intensity was so… visible. So glittery.

"Why are you such a challenge, I wonder?" She rose up and walked to the fire.

He focused on the skin of her arm, trying to catch what sparkled.

She knelt and stretched her hand straight into the fire. Alaric gasped and started forward, but she pulled her hand back out, pinching off one small flickering flame between her unharmed fingers. There was no kindling or fuel, just a single flame. She gazed at it with a pleased expression while Alaric stared at her open-mouthed. Lifting it close to her mouth, she blew on it. Starting from the bottom, the flame grew still and hardened, forming a smooth crystal.

She walked back to Alaric, pulling up a piece of long grass on her way. Stretching it between her fingers, she set the end of it against the side of the crystal and pushed. The blade of grass pierced it, leaving the orange flame dangling like a gem on a chain.

"There you are," she said. She knelt down next to him and tied the necklace around his neck.

Alaric sat, too stunned to move.

"You are better suited to fire than leaves," she added, motioning to Douglon who still wore his chain of oak leaf stems.

Alaric reached up to touch the necklace. It felt like a piece of glass slightly warmed from the sun. The gem was the exact likeness of the flame.

It would have taken Alaric weeks to theorize a way to do that, and even then, he probably would have only ended up with burnt fingers. Elves' magic was elemental, but this was different. They talked to trees and helped flowers grow, but he had never heard of an elf manipulating fire like that. Fire couldn't be changed to stone. The two things were too different. What she had done should be impossible.

He raised his eyes to hers warily. She showed no sign of pain. It was as though she paid no price for the magic.

"Why are you such a challenge?" she repeated. Even though her smile remained pleasant, her gaze pierced into his mind.

He tried to wrench his gaze away, but he was pinned.

He couldn't even blink.

She stepped into his thoughts and began to look around. He shoved against her presence, but it was like shoving a mountain. Disregarding him completely, she stood still in his mind and peered around as though she were in an interesting room.

Alaric focused his entire mind on her face, filling his consciousness with her eyes and smile, dragging all of his thoughts and emotions together. He felt his other thoughts strangled out by this single image.

After a moment, she blinked and was once again merely sitting in front of him, looking at him with eyes that were the soul of innocence.

"That was more interesting than I expected," she said.

Alaric stared at her, his mind staggering, furious.

"I saw the woman in the crystal box."

Alaric grabbed the pouch at his neck, the image of Evangeline lying still beneath the crystal flooding his mind.

"She's the answer, you know."

"What?" His mind was grasping about, trying to understand what had just happened.

"The answer to why you're such a challenge. What is her name? Evangeline?"

Alaric's gut clenched.

"A man who loves a woman that fiercely isn't easily influenced by another." She smirked at him. "Even by an expert influencer like me."

Again, Alaric tensed.

"Don't worry," she said, her eyes still bright. "I'll keep your secret. Interesting, though. Very interesting. I'm glad to meet you… Keeper."

Alaric darted glances at the others, but they were asleep.

Ayda looked at him questioningly. "Do all Keepers have minds as distracted and fuzzy as yours?"

Alaric stared at her, incredulous. "What is wrong with you?"

She let out a peal of laughter. "I feel fuzzy sometimes, too. It's so hard to keep our minds to ourselves, isn't it? Evangeline looks kind. I like her."

She faded into the darkness, leaving Alaric breathing fast, his fist clenched around the ruby at his neck.

NINE

Alaric sat up for a long time, his eyes and ears straining for any sign of Ayda. He couldn't remember the last time he had felt this vulnerable.

Even though they knew how, Keepers did not invade each other's minds and few others had the ability to do so. Alaric hadn't practiced protecting his mind since eight years ago when Mallon had spread terror across Queensland, stepping into men's minds and ripping out their wills. It was clearly time to brush up on that skill again.

Regardless, it shouldn't have been hard to push Ayda out. He knew his Keeper skills were rusty, but this was more than that. Entering someone else's mind wasn't like walking into a library and opening a book. Each mind was a layered labyrinth, the darkest secrets hidden so deeply they were impossible to find. The only thing evident when entering another's mind was what they were most focused on. But Ayda had stepped in and seen Alaric's most protected thoughts with ease. And despite his efforts, he was certain she had left only because she wanted to.

And he still couldn't completely shake the haziness she caused in his mind.

The stars had traveled a good distance across the sky before the vulnerable feeling faded and he could assess the situation he was in.

He had found a group looking for the exact same gem he was. Even though they didn't know who Alaric was or that the gem was a Wellstone, it was still too much of a coincidence to ignore.

Far from being troubling, the thought was invigorating. It had been a long time since he had anything to focus on besides looking for the antidote. And here, right in the direction he needed to go, sat the tantalizing prickle of a new, unsolved mystery.

Besides, this group, whoever they were, had a map—an actual map—to where Kordan had buried his Wellstone. They could be a group of Mallon's personal Shade Seekers whose entire purpose was to lure Alaric to his death, and he would still go along with them.

It was almost fun.

* * *

"We should be home by dinner," Brandson told Alaric after several hours of walking the next morning. Alaric led Beast alongside Brandson's cart like he had the day before. The smith called ahead, "With any luck, Douglon, by tomorrow night, I'll have that axe head finished for you."

The dwarf turned and waited for them to catch up.

"Brandson is pretty handy in the smithy," Douglon said to Alaric. "He makes blades that look dwarfish, and they're strong, but they're also light."

"When he says 'light' he doesn't really mean light," Brandson said. "I'd have a hard time swinging it. But it is lighter than the axe he carries now."

Douglon rubbed his hands together in anticipation. "It's light. And the blade holds an edge. My cousin will finally be jealous of my axe."

"Are you usually jealous of his?" Alaric asked.

"Hardly," Douglon said, "but he thinks everyone is. You should see him strutting around with that purple-shafted axe on his hip."

"Purple?"

"Exactly. Patlon is a good warrior and has proved it often enough, but he drives us all crazy with his stupid axe. He insisted on wearing it in the presence of the High Dwarf so he would be able to describe it to the royal blacksmith when he wants a replica." Douglon threw his arms into the air. "It's purple!"

"Why?"

"Some rubbish about it being blessed by an elf maiden with purple hair. There's no way Patlon has ever seen an elf. Even if he had, who wants the blessings of an elf for their weapon? It would probably just make the axe giggle." He cast an annoyed look at Ayda. "Or refuse to cut down trees."

Alaric laughed. "Is Patlon a close cousin?" Dwarf families were vast and complex, with every relative outside immediate family, no matter how distant, called cousins.

"As close as they come. He's my uncle's son. We've been like brothers since birth." He paused. "Or we used to be."

Alaric let a moment pass. He considered using *augmenta* on the dwarf, but these people were growing on him. He'd rather have Douglon actually trust him. "Did your break with him happen to involve a treasure map?"

Douglon stiffened. "How'd you know?"

Alaric shrugged. "You have a treasure map, but no cousin-like-a-brother here searching with you."

Douglon studied Alaric for a long moment. "If you're going to tag along with us, I suppose you should hear the story. It has some interesting parts, anyway, you might want to include it in your notes.

"Patlon and I were digging in the Scale Mountains looking for a diamond deposit that he had heard of when we found a strange piece of wall. It didn't enclose anything, just leaned up against the base of a cliff."

Alaric looked at the dwarf in surprise. That sounded an awful lot like the Wall at the Stronghold. But Douglon was talking about a place in the Scale Mountains, two days' ride to the west.

"There had been a rockslide on the mountain behind the wall, and part of the slope had collapsed, exposing a tunnel. It wasn't dwarf-made. It was too straight and smooth." He shook his head in disapproval. "Didn't take into account the natural flow of the mountain. Looked like something a human would dig. Anyway, the tunnel started at the wall—even though the wall had no door in it—and continued straight under the mountain." Here Douglon paused to gauge Alaric's response to this fact.

Douglon was describing a wall and tunnel exactly like that of the Stronghold.

"This sounds like a story worth writing down," Alaric said. "Do you mind?" At Douglon's nod,

Alaric pulled out his book and a coal pencil. He quickly took down what the dwarf had already said.

"The tunnel led straight ahead several hundred feet under the mountain," Douglon continued, warming up to his story and his audience, "until it came out into a valley we hadn't seen before. It was just an oversized crack in the mountains, really, left behind when the slopes beside it were thrust up. But it was inaccessible except from this tunnel.

"In the valley were the beginnings of a tower. A circle of iron-laced sandstone. It rose about twenty feet before it stopped, as though the builder had been interrupted. Only one room on the ground floor had been completed. A dusty bedroom." Douglon leaned closer. "It had belonged to a wizard."

Alaric's mind was racing. Douglon had found a Wall, a tunnel, and a valley complete with the beginnings of a new Stronghold? In the Scale Mountains? More questions than he could voice swirled in his head.

"A wizard?" he asked finally.

Douglon nodded. "It was full of wizardy things. There were shelves of scrolls and pouches and boxes. The scrolls were written in runes we couldn't read. But the pouches and boxes, every one held some marvel. The boxes held things like a spinning top that bounced off the sides, a pile of ancient gold coins, three dried mushrooms that hummed. One pouch held bright blue beetles that smelled of rosemary, all dead. Another was filled with pure silver sand."

Douglon's voice grew quieter. "All these things were fascinating, but we found the real treasure on a shelf near the bed. Next to a book, written in runes we couldn't read, lay this." Reaching into his cloak, Douglon pulled out a worn roll of leather.

Alaric unrolled it, reading a short, scrawled paragraph.

It feels wrong to bury something of such value. Perhaps I should give the stone to them, but I can't bear to look at it. The memories haunt me. I will bury it in a place of honor and leave it behind. I pray this map remains useless, and I am never in need of finding it again.

The handwriting was the same as the scroll at the Stronghold. The page had been written by Kordan.

Alaric read and reread the paragraph, his heart pounding. The map really was to Kordan's Wellstone. The new Stronghold the dwarves had found must have been built by the old Keeper as well. What had he done? Left the real Stronghold and tried to continue as a Keeper by himself?

Alaric flipped the leather over. Time had faded the ink, and there were blotches where the leather had been soiled, but most of the map was decipherable. Several sets of runes, meticulously drawn dotted the page.

Alaric let his eyes wander over the runes. There was no doubt that this was written by a Keeper. The precision and clarity of the writing made him surprisingly nostalgic. Whatever their other faults, the Keepers could write.

The map showed a valley at the base of the Wolfsbane Mountains containing some buildings. Two rock formations were labeled. In the center of the map was a tree with a gem drawn beneath it.

"And the town is Kordan's Blight?" asked Alaric.

"Judging from the rock formations, yes," answered the dwarf. "But whenever this map was drawn, the town was much smaller than it is today. And Kordan's Blight is full of trees. How on earth do we know which one the map refers to?"

"These are the runes that Gustav translated?"

"If you can call it translation. Either Gustav is an idiot, or whoever wrote this was a lunatic. Everything is gibberish." Douglon's finger stabbed at a point on the map where a cluster of runes stood. "This says: *The falling stars cool the turtle's back*." Douglon glared at the wizard walking ahead of them on the road. "I'm willing to believe he's an idiot."

Alaric took the moment to study the runes. He could see what Gustav had translated, but the writing was off slightly. An extra tail here, an odd dot there.

These weren't modern runes at all. They were ancient.

The Keepers had some books old enough to use them, and each Keeper was schooled in how to read them, but they were too nuanced and open to interpretation to be of use for most things today. The fascinating thing about the runes on the map was that even though they were ancient, each was similar to a modern rune with a different meaning. Sometimes radically different.

"Falling stars" was a decent modern translation, but in the ancient language, it read: damned soul. "Turtle's back" should roughly translate to: a place of sanctuary. The word "cool" was a complicated rune that indicated vengeance and justice. That rune also had the sense of turning the entire phrase into a question. The amount of nuance that was drawn into the runes was impressive. After piecing it together, Alaric decided that what the cluster really said was, *Shall the soul that has been damned seek vengeance or discover a place of sanctuary?*

Alaric tried hard to hide the smile that kept creeping onto his face. First of all, the writing wasn't part of the map. It was just Kordan's musings. Secondly, almost no one besides a Keeper would be able to read the ancient runes. Barely anyone in Queensland read even modern runes. Gustav must be well educated to be able to translate the modern runes he had, but he would have them chasing after nonsense. Alaric marveled at the complexity of the writing.

Douglon reached over for the map, and Alaric forced himself to hand it back. He'd been so focused on that one set of runes, he'd barely looked at the map itself.

"So you ended up with the map," Alaric said, watching Douglon roll it up and tuck it into his pocket. "Did you give Patlon the rest of the treasure?"

Douglon looked uncomfortable. "Patlon thought we should take all the wizardy things home before following the map. But since the stone sounded more valuable than everything else we'd found, I wanted to go get the treasure."

Douglon's voice trailed off. He shook his head and continued in an offhanded way. "In the end, we split up. He took all the stuff we had found, and I took the map."

Alaric looked at the dwarf in disbelief. "He agreed to that?"

Douglon shifted. "'Agreed' might be the wrong word for it."

"Smoke!" Gustav shouted from a turn in the road ahead.

A dark plume of smoke was visible over the hill to their left, roiling up into the blue sky.

Ayda and Douglon began to run. Ayda outpaced him quickly, racing down the road.

"Kordan's Blight?" asked Alaric. The look on Brandson's face as he urged the slow carthorse forward was his answer.

"Take Beast," Alaric said tossing Brandson the reins. The blacksmith leapt into the saddle and galloped toward the smoke. Alaric climbed onto the lumbering cart and followed.

Once the carthorse plodded around the turn, the entire town was visible. A crowd was gathered before the nearest building, milling around under the sign with an anvil standing untouched at the road. The acrid smell of smoke cut through the air, and as Alaric drew the carthorse closer, he could feel the lingering heat from the fire. Nothing was still burning. What had been the smithy was now a smoldering pile of charred wood.

TEN

Brandson sat on Beast, staring at what was left of his home. There was nothing to be done.

Ayda walked up to Brandson and put her arm around his shoulder. Gustav ran through the crowd, grabbing leftover buckets and throwing water toward the already doused building.

"It's a little late for him to decide to do something useful," Douglon said to Ayda.

Gustav tossed a large bucket full of water that splashed into a puddle near the front of the structure, not remotely close to any of the parts that were still smoking.

"Well, not useful exactly," Douglon said.

Gustav glared at the two of them. Throwing the bucket down, he stalked away.

"I'm sorry, son," a man said to Brandson. "'Twas burning good by the time anyone saw it. 'Twas naught to do but keep th' other buildings safe."

Brandson slid down from Beast and stood staring at the husk of his home. The roof was gone, and the walls were sagging. Behind the smithy, the remains of Brandson's living quarters let out swirls of smoke. The smith began to walk toward them, his arm raised against the heat, but he couldn't even reach what was left of the walls. Even from back where Alaric stood, waves of heat rolled off the building.

Alaric doubted there was anything salvageable, but something white caught his eye. He stepped up next to Brandson and found a light-colored rock leaning against the base of a burned wall. Chiseled into the stone was a symbol, or two symbols, one over the other.

"What's that?" he asked Brandson.

The blacksmith looked at the rock blankly.

"That wasn't there when we left," Ayda said, squinting down at it. "The top symbol looks like an axe. I can't tell what the bottom part is."

Alaric crept toward the rock, the heat burning against the exposed skin of his face. He knelt and wiped wet ashes off of it, using the bunched corner of his robe. Then he stepped back quickly, and the three of them peered at the rock, trying to decipher the shape.

"What did you find?" Gustav demanded. "Move over. Let me see."

"It's a dwarf," Douglon said from behind them.

"It doesn't look like a dwarf," said Ayda. "It looks like a lizard."

"It is a dwarf, lying dead, smited by the axe," Douglon said dully.

"How do you know?" Alaric asked. Ayda's description was more accurate.

Douglon stepped up beside them, glowering at the white rock. "Because it's Patlon's symbol."

———•—•———

Brandson stared into the bottom of his empty ale tankard. He hadn't moved since collapsing into a chair in the tavern. His expression had gone from depressed to bleary. Alaric, returning from making sure that Beast and the carthorse were stabled behind the tavern, joined the rest of them at a table in the corner of the empty dining hall. The entire building was stuffy and smelled of onions.

"Are you sure that was Patlon's symbol?" Alaric asked Douglon.

The dwarf nodded. "We invented it as children. He claimed that he needed a warning to scare his enemies. I never thought that would mean me."

"It might not," Ayda said. "Patlon didn't hurt anything of yours. But he did destroy every single thing Brandson owned. Even though Brandson is guilty of nothing but generosity and goodness."

Douglon looked stricken. "I'll rebuild the entire smithy," he said to Brandson. "Twice as big. With diamonds for windows."

Brandson grunted and everyone fell into an uncomfortable silence.

"So..."Alaric said to Douglon, "Patlon just let you have the map?"

"I told him I was taking it, and he said nothing." The dwarf shifted in his chair. "Course he was passed out at the time."

Brandson dropped his tankard to the table with a thunk and turned to the dwarf. "You didn't think to tell us that you'd stolen the map and a fire-wielding dwarf was going to come burn down my home?"

"I didn't think he'd find me! It took me months to figure out that the mountains and rock formations the map was talking about were here. I have no idea how he found me."

"He has a point," Ayda said, and Douglon looked at her gratefully. "Who would have expected a dwarf to be that clever?"

Douglon's smile turned to a glare.

She brightened. "I know! His purple elf helped him!"

Alaric let out a laugh at that, and even Brandson allowed a small smile before dropping his face into his hands. Ayda wrapped her arm around his shoulders.

"If Patlon found the smithy, why isn't he still here?" asked Alaric.

"I'm sure he is, somewhere," said Douglon. "He prides himself on his hunting ability. Claims he can wait for a week without food or water or sleep if he's tracking his prey."

"I doubt he can go that long," Alaric said, "but if that fire was just set this morning, I'm sure he saw us come into town."

Brandson groaned. "What are we going to do?"

"There are five of us and only one of him. He's not much of a threat if we stick together," Alaric answered. "We need to find a way to talk to him."

"Brandson might need to sleep off all the ale before we plan anything," Ayda said.

"Where are we going to sleep? If we stay here, he'll probably just burn the tavern down on us," Brandson said, raising his head enough to glare at Douglon with one eye.

The tavern door swung open letting in a swirl of fresh air. They all tensed. Douglon stood, his hand going to his axe. Gustav hunched over, glaring at the door and raising his hands as though he meant to shoot lightning at whoever entered. Alaric turned as well, but it was only a milkmaid carrying an enormous jug.

She stopped when she saw everyone looking at her.

Ayda gave her a friendly wave. Douglon nodded to her, dropping back into his chair.

The milkmaid gave a self-conscious smile and carried her jug into the kitchen. She returned a minute later. Catching sight of Brandson, she paused. Her gaze flicked uncertainly to Ayda's arm draped over the smith's shoulder, but she pushed one of her long, brown braids behind her shoulder, smoothed the front of her dress, and approached the table.

"Brandson, I'm so sorry," she said.

Brandson squinted at her. A foolish smile crept across his face. "Milly?" He tried to sit up a little straighter, but kept listing to the side. Douglon gave the smith a small shove to push him back up.

"I saw the smithy," Milly said. "That's terrible. Truly terrible." Her voice trailed off, and she stood uncomfortably next to their table.

Douglon pushed an empty chair out toward her, and she dropped into it. When Ayda introduced Alaric, Milly nodded politely.

"You can all come out to the farm," she said. "There's more than enough room. You can stay as long as you need to."

"We can pay you, Milly," Brandson said.

"Pay me? For taking in my homeless neighbor? You had better not say that again, blacksmith." Brandson shrank back in his chair a bit.

Ayda clapped. "We'd love to! Can I milk another cow?"

"That's not a good idea," Gustav interrupted.

"Why not?" Milly asked.

"I did a good job last time," Ayda said.

Gustav ignored the elf and leaned toward Milly, his dramatic whisper barely lower than a shout. "The fire wasn't an accident."

Milly's eyes widened. "Someone tried to hurt Brandson?"

"Someone tried to hurt *someone*," Gustav said, looking at Douglon.

The dwarf shifted uncomfortably.

"Do they know you're here?" Milly asked.

"Probably," Ayda said. "It's the dwarf's cousin. He dragged his family feud all the way here, and now Brandson's life is ruined."

Douglon grimaced, and Brandson let out a groan and dropped his head back into his hands.

"Well if he knows you're here, you're stuck. There's no way out of the tavern without being seen."

"We'll wait until dark," Douglon said.

"Or you could come with me," Milly said. "My wagon is parked against the stable. You could hide in the back, and I can drive you out of town."

"We're not going to endanger you, Milly," Brandson said.

"Then you're stuck here until nightfall," she said. "And with the full moon tonight, good luck sneaking anywhere."

The table was quiet for a long moment. Douglon glanced at Brandson, but the smith's expression was vacant. The dwarf turned to Alaric with a questioning look.

Milly seemed like a competent sort of girl. She was right about being stuck here. There wasn't another easy way out of the tavern that he could see.

"I don't know," Alaric began.

"Oh, stop dallying and go," Milly said. "You can each take turns guarding my house tonight if it makes you feel better. There's a window in the stable, and the wagon's just outside of it. There should be plenty of room."

Brandson looked worried, but Milly shooed him toward the back door.

"Thank you so much, Milly," Ayda said.

"Go on. I'll wait a couple of minutes before I come out."

The rest of the group went quickly into the kitchen. Alaric glanced after them for a moment. It wasn't really necessary for him to hide from Patlon, but he was unwilling to let Douglon and his map out of his sight. Alaric paid the tavern keeper for a loaf of bread and a generous cut of ham. Then he set an extra gold coin on the counter.

"If a dwarf comes in looking for us, it would be helpful if you couldn't remember where we've gone," he said.

The woman picked up the gold coin and tucked it into her apron. "Where who's gone?"

Alaric smiled at her and followed the others out the back door of the tavern. When he slipped into the back of Milly's wagon, it smelled reliable, like hay and hard work. Like the stables at the Stronghold.

He pulled his legs up close, trying not to bump into the others. This was hardly the most dignified way he'd ever traveled. But he'd cram into a wagon half this size if it meant he got to see Douglon's map.

"Which tree?" Douglon asked. "The boring one right there?"

ELEVEN

"We can't leave Kordan's Blight," roared Douglon. "Not without my treasure!"

"Your treasure?" Gustav demanded.

"We can't stay here waiting for your cousin to murder us," Brandson tossed over his shoulder from where he sat adjusting the door on Milly's wood stove.

They'd arrived at her farm a couple of hours earlier. Milly, who already knew about the group's treasure hunting, had demanded that they explain about the smithy. She had taken it all in with surprising level-headedness. Once everyone had eaten and Brandson's ale had worn off, the conversation deteriorated into an argument.

The kitchen was dotted with cups and pitchers of fresh wild flowers, making the room smell and feel like a serene mountain glen. Except for the smell of half-eaten ham. And all the yelling.

Alaric sat at one end of the table, letting the group holler at each other. Douglon's map was spread out on the other end, too far away to read.

"If only we could understand the runes," Brandson said, gesturing at the map. "Then we could find the treasure and be done with it."

"Maybe we need to find someone who can translate them," muttered Douglon.

"Translate them!" huffed Gustav in outrage. "I have translated them. It is not my fault that you're too stupid to understand them."

"You don't understand them, either," Ayda said. "Which might make people wonder if you're a fraud."

"I don't have to wonder," Douglon said.

"There'll be no talk like that around my table," Milly said. "Gustav is as much my guest as you two are, and I'm sure he's doing his best."

"Sorry," Douglon muttered, crossing his arms and settling back in his seat.

Gustav snorted and rose from the table, turning his back to them and staring into the fire.

"May I?" asked Alaric, pointing to the map. He tried to keep his voice level.

Gustav shot him a suspicious look.

"Sure," said Douglon, handing it to him. "Maybe you can see something we've missed."

"I doubt that," Alaric said, "but I've had a pretty thorough education."

"Of course," Brandson said, peering over the stove door. "I can't believe we haven't asked you yet."

"I'm sure I won't find anything the worthy wizard didn't." Alaric took the map and ran his fingers over the runes.

There wasn't much written on the map and none of it involved directions, but the structure was mesmerizing. Each cluster of runes, its own sentence, ran into others complementing and subtly altering their meanings. There in the center of the map was the gem sitting beneath a tree.

"Do you see anything?" Brandson asked, his voice polite.

"There is something here," Alaric said pointing to large runes at the top of the map. "What do you make of this, Gustav?"

The wizard glanced where Alaric was pointing and snorted. "*The valley of Kordan.* That's one we understand."

"Yes," Alaric answered, "but this here, what you translated 'of' could have another meaning."

Everyone was looking at him.

"Literally it means: *which is the same as*," Alaric continued. "So instead of: *the valley of Kordan*, it would be: *that which is the same as the valley of Kordan.*" He met five blank stares.

"Meaning," he said, "that there are two valleys. The valley of Kordan, which is what we're in, and the valley that is similar to it."

"We're looking in the wrong place?" asked Brandson, his face stunned.

"It's possible."

"Let me see that," snapped Gustav, snatching the map from Alaric's hands. He pored over the runes, holding the map inches from his nose. "I suppose that could be one interpretation," he said, "but it's hardly the most straightforward reading."

Douglon took the map back across the table and set it squarely in front of himself. "Another valley with these two rocks?" The dwarf pointed to two notations on the map. "There's the Rocks of the Bear at the top of the map, and Mother's Rock halfway down the left side."

"Mother's Rock?" asked Alaric.

Brandson nodded. "It's on the ridge west of town. It looks like a mother holding a child."

Gustav cleared his throat. "The legend says that a woman, Kessera, was so beautiful that an elf lord fell in love with her. They married, some say against her will, and a year later, she bore him a son. The elf was so jealous of Kessera's love for her child that he cursed them," he dropped his voice to a dramatic whisper, "and turned them to stone!"

"That's a charming story," Alaric said, glancing at Ayda. "What's the moral? Never marry an elf?"

"Never anger an elf," she corrected him.

"Probably good advice," Alaric said.

"Seems like an elf would turn someone into a tree rather than a stone," Douglon said.

"Elves turn themselves into trees," Ayda corrected him. "And it isn't a punishment. It's lovely."

"Anyway," Brandson said, coming up beside Alaric, "those two rocks put Kordan's Blight right in the middle of the map. The valley we are in is wider than the one on the map, but besides that—" Brandson cocked his head to the side, peering at the upside down map. "It's Bone Valley!"

Milly, standing next to Douglon, shook her head. "The rocks are in the wrong place."

"Not from where I'm standing," Brandson answered. He grabbed the map. "Bone Valley is over the ridge to the west of us—the ridge that has Mother's Rock. If we flip the map over, like this, so that Mother's Rock is on the east side of the map, instead of the west, then the map fits Bone Valley, complete with a set of ruins at its southern end named Bear Stronghold." Brandson grinned at everyone.

"You people need to stop naming things after bears around here," Douglon said, but he was grinning, too.

"Bear Stronghold wasn't named after the animal," Milly said. "It was a small fortress where the chieftain of a mountain clan defended his people from an attack. It is said he fought as fiercely as a bear."

Gustav grabbed the map. "Yes! That could be what it says. It is an old-fashioned word that today would translate to rock, but it has the idea of solidness and strength. I would say that 'stronghold' would be a fine translation."

Alaric had come to the same conclusion, but he was impressed Gustav had picked up on the nuance. Alaric felt his pulse quicken. Kordan's Wellstone was in the next valley. The antidote was almost within his reach. He rubbed the ruby at his neck through the pouch, picturing the darkness swirling around with the red light.

Douglon rubbed his hands together. "Well, at first light, we should stop wasting time and find our treasure. Brandson, please tell me there's just one lone tree in the center of the valley."

Brandson and Milly exchanged glances. "I'm not sure."

"It's right over the hill. Haven't you ever hunted there?"

"No one hunts in Bone Valley," Brandson said. "There aren't any animals. The lake there has no outlet, so the water's gone bitter. Besides…"

Everyone looked at him expectantly.

"It's supposed to be haunted," Milly finished.

"By what?" Douglon asked. "People who bury treasure?"

"By the ghosts of people who were killed by a dragon," Brandson said.

Gustav looked sharply at Brandson, his eyes eager. "A dragon?"

"A local legend about a dragon?" Alaric said, reaching for paper to write it down.

"It was a long time ago," Brandson said, "I don't know any more of the story than that a dragon came and ate people. But no one goes into Bone Valley today. I went over the top of the ridge on a dare when I was a kid, but I didn't go all the way down the other side. It was eerie. Part of the valley is forested, but it was unnaturally quiet."

"Well, ghosts don't scare me, and you'd know if there was still a dragon in that valley," Douglon said. "If no one goes there, then there's a good chance our treasure has been left alone. I say tomorrow morning, we go see what it's like over there."

"Yes," said Ayda. "Bone Valley sounds lovely."

TWELVE

The sky had barely begun to lighten when they left the next morning. A mist skulked along the ground, and Alaric crept behind the others, beads of moisture clinging to him and dampening his clothes before they even reached the forest at the edge of Milly's farm.

Alaric's eyes were gritty from lack of sleep. After the others had finally gone to bed, he had lain awake, longing to steal Douglon's map and set out immediately, but it would be faster to stay with the others. Brandson could get them into Bone Valley more quickly than Alaric could wandering around in the dark. That fact didn't alleviate his anxiety to get moving. He had finally fallen asleep only to be woken up for his turn watching for Patlon.

The night had passed peacefully, though, and this morning, he carried one of the small packs Brandson had cobbled together for their trip. According to the smith, they'd reach the valley by dinnertime.

Douglon glared at Milly as she walked next to Brandson. "One more person wanting a share of the treasure."

"Maybe she'll turn out to be useful," Gustav whispered to the dwarf so loudly that everyone heard. "You never know who will. That's why I like to embrace the people around me."

Alaric tried to keep an incredulous look off his face, but Douglon didn't.

"You embrace me, and I'll break your scrawny neck," Douglon said.

"I don't want any of your treasure, master dwarf," Milly said over her shoulder. "I just don't want to be home alone when your cousin shows up."

"It's your fault that she's here," Ayda said, pointing to the dwarf. "Which means she should share your part of the treasure."

Douglon growled at her and trudged up the hill.

"How are you going to split up one gem?" Milly asked.

Alaric glanced around the group. Ayda didn't appear to be listening, but Douglon's face turned stony. They didn't really expect Douglon to share with them, did they?

"We're all friends," Brandson told her. "It will work out."

Gustav, on the other side of Alaric, gave a small snort, muttering to himself and shooting glances at Douglon.

As the ground rose, they entered a sparse forest smelling of pine and moss. Ayda picked small purple flowers, occasionally poking them into Douglon's beard. Holding a handful of flowers, she waited for Alaric to catch up to her.

"Are you going to put those on me?" he asked.

Ayda considered him for a moment, then she tossed the flowers aside and gestured to the flame that still hung around his neck. "You're better suited to fire than flowers."

Alaric had thought about removing the little flame, but it was so lifelike, he'd decided, cautiously, he liked it. "That's the second time you've said that. I don't feel well suited to fire."

"Of course you are. You have that tight burning core of anger. Or pain. Or guilt?" She waved the question away. "Whatever it is, it's deep, but it's bright."

That deep core was anger, and it flared at her attention. "Stay out of my mind."

Ayda laughed, "I'm not in your mind. I'm just looking at you. Can't you see someone's color?"

See someone's color? He didn't even know what that meant. "Let me guess, my color is red?"

"Fiery orange. But not all of you. Just that blazing center. Most of you is a tenacious green."

"Tenacious."

"Yes. Like a mossy stone under scuffling water. It's soothing, really. Except the fire part. You think the fire part is all there is, but that's not true. The anger is only there because of how much you love."

Right, that tenacious green love. "Does everyone have colors?"

Ayda nodded.

"What color is Milly?"

"A dauntless pitch purple. That first color the sky turns before the dawn."

"The color of the sunrise isn't usually called dauntless. Delicate or fresh, but not dauntless."

"Of course it is. The world is flooded with blackness every night before that purple glides over the horizon and presses it back to make room for the sun. No other color braves the darkness like that every morning, or holds it off as long every night."

Milly was walking next to Brandson, talking quietly with him. She looked more like a farm girl than a dauntless sunrise.

"What color is Douglon?" Alaric asked.

"Molten coppery red. Like his beard. Molten enough to be dangerous, but still easily shaped."

Alaric laughed. "Easily shaped?"

"Yes. He's quite tender hearted."

"And Brandson?"

"Cozy brown."

"Gustav?"

"Oh, who cares about the wizard?" Ayda said, shrugging. "People are colors. If you can't see them, I'm not going to explain everyone to you." With that, she turned and headed up the hill toward Douglon.

Alaric shook his head at her. He was either getting used to the influence she exerted over him, or it was fading. The walk through the cool morning air left his mind feeling clearer than it had in days. He needed to consider what he would do once they found the Wellstone. He couldn't let Douglon, or Gustav, take it. Then Alaric would have to chase them, and he was tired of chasing things.

Alaric would explain who he was and what the Wellstone was. When Douglon heard how much Saren and the Keepers would pay him for it, he would sell it. And hopefully, Gustav wasn't a good enough wizard to even know how to use it.

They trudged up the steep ridge that separated Kordan's Blight from Bone Valley. It would have been impassible if Brandson had not known a game trail that wound up toward Mother's Rock. Even with the trail, Alaric was winded and hot before they were even halfway up.

Just before midday, they reached the highest trees, which were stunted and twisted by the mountain winds. Alaric's back was sweaty underneath the pack Brandson had put together. The game trail turned back down the slope, leaving nothing above them but a steep slope of loose rock. Ayda had been lagging behind as they climbed, looking bored at the scrawny trees around them. At Brandson's suggestion, they all dropped their packs in the shade of the last trees, deciding to eat lunch before trying to scramble over the rocks. The sky, which had started out clear, was beginning to cloud over. With any luck, by the end of their meal, the ridge would be encased in cloud, hiding them from any watching eyes.

If nothing else, it would block the sun.

Milly and Brandson began to lay out some food.

Gustav stood at the edge of the trees, arms spread wide and eyes closed.

Alaric's skin tingled as though a warm wind had blown past him. He looked at the wizard in surprise. Gustav had just cast out, looking for the energy of living things around them.

"I sense no danger," Gustav proclaimed. "Neither ahead nor behind. I think our presence has gone undetected by the evil dwarf."

"He's not evil!" Douglon broke in, but at Brandson's annoyed look, he shut his mouth.

Alaric, who had been planning on doing what Gustav claimed to have done, considered the wizard. Casting out was different from manipulating energy. It was just a seeking, sending out a wave of awareness and feeling for the reflections sent back by living things. Alaric couldn't feel the reflections from someone else's wave with any accuracy, but he could feel impressions. Keeper Gerone had called it a sympathetic resonance. Alaric always thought it was more like eavesdropping on a whispered conversation. You couldn't hear the exact words, but you got a notion of how many people were talking.

Gustav had produced a wave, but it was clunky. Alaric doubted it had traveled past the first few trees.

So the wizard did have some familiarity with magic.

Alaric weighed his options for a moment. He did want to know whether Patlon was following them, but if he sent out his own wave and Gustav picked up on it, the wizard would know Alaric wasn't just a historian. Announcing that he was a Keeper right now, out of the blue, felt awkward. Unfortunately, the whole secret was beginning to feel awkward.

There was an art to casting out. Nuances of strength and speed and direction. Alaric kept his eye on Gustav and sent out the most subtle wave he could, sending it mostly downhill. Alaric felt the reflection of Gustav's energy, so some ripples had made it that way. But Gustav made no indication that he noticed Alaric's wave.

Alaric's wave made it a good way down the slope and all the way to the top. He came to the same conclusion Gustav had. There was nothing on the ridge larger than a squirrel.

The clouds had rolled down over the ridge by the time they finished eating.

After they had packed up, Ayda dusted her hands off on her dress and turned to the group. "Well, it's been lovely searching about with you people. You've all been entertaining, but I can't see any point in continuing this climb when I just have to climb back out tomorrow." She looked distastefully at the bare, rocky slope rising steeply above them. "I'm going to go find a nice forest with interesting trees."

Alaric turned to Ayda in surprise.

"You're leaving again?" Douglon asked, bored.

"You can't leave now!" Brandson said. "We're so close!"

"You know I don't care about your little stone," Ayda looked at the thin, wind-stunted pine trees around them. "These trees make me miss my home."

"You're not even slightly interested in whether we find the gem?" Douglon asked.

"Not really. I'm vaguely interested in seeing if the tree it was buried under is still alive, but not enough to keep climbing this endless slope."

It made sense, of course, Alaric thought. It was more surprising that Ayda was still with them than that she'd want to leave. Any normal elf would have run home months ago.

Alaric stood a bit back from the group and was the only one who saw Gustav, his brow drawn, step away from the others. The wizard focused his gaze on Ayda and his lips started to move. A moment later, his hand clenched in pain and his face reddened with effort.

Alaric looked back and forth between Ayda and Gustav. Was the wizard really trying to influence an elf? She would know it instantly.

But Ayda continued chatting with the others, unconcerned.

"But you're part of the treasure hunt," Milly said. "You can't leave the group."

Ayda gave her a skeptical look.

"She's right," Brandson said. "Right, Douglon?"

Douglon, whose scowl had deepened as the conversation continued, shrugged. "Doesn't matter to me. I'm here for a sparkling gemstone, not a sparkling elf."

Brandson shot Douglon a glare before turning back to Ayda. "Please stay just a little longer. I wouldn't feel right if you weren't there."

Gustav stopped muttering and hid his shaking fist behind his back. He slumped, exhausted, against a tree.

Alaric could still see no sign that Ayda had noticed the wizard's attempts, nor was there any change in her attitude. Had the wizard even cast a spell?

"That makes no sense, blacksmith. You all will find your treasure, and I will find a forest with better trees than these. How could that feel wrong?"

Brandson looked around at the others for support, then turned back to Ayda and said, "We might need you. What if we need to talk to the trees? They might know where to look. They might remember a treasure... or someone digging... a really long time ago... or something," he finished lamely.

A small smile crept across Ayda's face. "I need to teach you a little bit about trees." But she nodded. "All right, I'll go over the hill with you."

She met Alaric's gaze and beamed. Alaric grinned back before he realized that the fog had returned. His grin turned to a scowl.

Maybe he should have encouraged her to leave.

They continued up, slipping on wet rocks in a dull grey mist. All around him, the endless grey was punctuated with thumps and curses and the skittering of rocks down behind them.

Reaching the top of the ridge in clouds so thick the group could barely see ahead of them, they hurried over, glad that no one in Kordan's Blight could have seen them leave and glad that the other side, although steep, was more grass and low brush than rocks. Brandson, after a short nervous glance toward the greyness filling Bone Valley and an encouraging nod from Milly, led them down the slope.

Alaric brought up the rear of their group, focused on each step, concentrating on the slope before him.

With a shriek, Gustav tripped and tumbled down the hill, a blur of skinny limbs and a pointy hat. He fell a good way before his foot caught, yanking him to a stop with a yelp. He lay there stunned, his head lower on the hill than the white legs sticking out from beneath his robe. Gustav didn't move and Alaric peered down past the rest of them at the old man.

"Are you all right, Gustav?" Brandson asked.

"If he's dead, I get his share of the treasure," Douglon called out.

"Shut up," Gustav groaned, and Ayda let out a peal of laughter that echoed through the fog.

Gustav cursed and floundered, trying to right himself. As Alaric made his way down toward the old man, his own foot slipped, and he barely caught himself.

It was Milly who got to the wizard first, slipping and sliding down to reach him.

Gustav waved her away, scolding and complaining. Patiently, she ignored his protests and helped him untangle his foot, then retrieved his pointy, star-swirled hat, which had tumbled a bit farther down the hill.

He smoothed out his muddy robe.

"Thank you," he muttered to Milly as he crammed on his bent hat. "I'm fine," and he marched down the hill.

Milly waited while the others made their way down to her.

"You're too good, Milly," Ayda said. "Your kindness is wasted on that old man."

"Kindness can't be wasted," Milly replied. "If it needs gratitude, it isn't really kindness."

"It might not be wasted, but it's certainly unappreciated." Ayda glanced at Brandson who was watching Milly with bright eyes. "Or at least unappreciated by the wizard."

When the rain started, it came with huge drops that plopped onto Alaric's head and shoulders with irritating force. He pulled his cloak tight against his neck, but drop after drop found their way through, dribbling down his back. It took close to an hour before the ground leveled off and they reached the edge of a pine forest. Sunset was still hours away, but between the rain and the trees, they walked through a deep gloom.

With the pattering of rain sounding distant on the branches high above them, Alaric noticed the unnatural silence for the first time. There were no birds, no squirrels, not even many bugs. The forest smelled stale and forgotten.

Brandson caught his eye. "Creepy, isn't it?"

Alaric cast out a thin, subtle wave, unnoticed by Gustav, but found no animal larger than a bug. The trees held a deep, ponderous hum of energy, like a rumble of thunder.

Ayda walked by them, brushing her fingertips against their trunks and peering up into the canopy. "The trees are old. They've almost forgotten how to talk."

"How will we ever bear the loss?" Douglon muttered.

The rain fell on the canopy of the trees above them. The water cascaded down from above, here and there making the ground a patchwork of dry dirt and mud. They walked, their eyes mostly up, watching for the water and winding from dry patch to dry patch.

A dry crack from under Douglon's boot echoed through the forest. Everyone stopped.

The ground ahead of them was littered with pale sticks.

"These didn't come from the pines," Brandson said looking up at the dark trees around them. "They're not dark enough." He dropped down to one knee and picked up a stick. It crumbled in his hand. "Bones! They're all bones!"

A slight chill ran down Alaric's spine. As far as he could see, bones of different sizes poked up out of the ground like misshapen fingers trying to claw free of their graves.

The party stared in silence until Ayda spoke.

"What did you expect to find in Bone Valley?"

THIRTEEN

Alaric knelt down. These weren't complete skeletons, just scattered bones. A lot of scattered bones.

Douglon crept backward, cringing at every crunch under his feet. "Where did they all come from?" he asked, an edge of panic in his voice.

"Quite a few of these came from chickens," answered Milly, moving some of the bones around with her feet.

"Chickens?" said Brandson.

"Some of them. But these over here are bigger. From a pig, maybe," she said, reaching down to pick up one of the bones.

"Don't touch it!" Douglon said.

Milly looked at him in surprise. "Why not? It's very old. Look how smooth the edges are."

Douglon didn't move any closer. Milly looked at him puzzled.

"They're just bones," she said.

"I know that," he said scowling, "but there are so many of them."

"This one's big. Horse, do you think?" Milly asked.

Alaric stepped in among the bones. Milly was right. They were all old. Broken edges were smoothed over from years of exposure to weather, and since little weather made it down beneath these trees, the bones must have been here a very long time.

A roundish lump lay half buried in the ground. "This one isn't a horse."

It was a human skull.

The sound of the rain above them lessened and the forest lightened. Alaric scanned the ground and saw a number of skulls.

"What happened here?" Milly asked.

Alaric caught sight of Gustav standing at the edge of the bones, squinting into the gloom. His befuddled expression slowly turned sly.

"There's only one thing that leaves carnage like this." Gustav's voice rang out so loudly that the others jumped. They all turned to look at him. All except Alaric. He knew what the wizard was going to say.

"A dragon!" the old man proclaimed, throwing his arms out and searching the treetops.

Milly took a step closer to Brandson, and everyone looked up toward the tops of the trees.

"A dragon big enough to eat a horse wouldn't fit in between these trees," Alaric pointed out. "And one shot of dragon fire would have burned up this entire forest. If these bones were left by a dragon, they were left here a long time ago, as Milly has already pointed out. Before this forest grew."

They considered his logic for a moment and nodded. All except Gustav, who glared at Alaric.

"It does look like the legend of Bone Valley's dragon has some truth behind it, though," Alaric said to Brandson.

"Can we please get out of here?" Douglon asked through clenched teeth.

Ahead of them, in the direction of all the bones, the forest lightened.

Brandson straightened. "I'm afraid there's no way out but through the bones." He stepped forward, cringing when his foot crunched down onto the eerie bed of bones.

Ayda and Milly picked their way through carefully, discussing the bones they came across. Brandson stepped through, gingerly testing each step before moving on. Douglon followed right behind Brandson, cringing and shuddering with each step.

"It was a dragon," Gustav said petulantly to Alaric.

"That's the most obvious answer," Alaric said. "And it fits with the legend of Bone Valley. But we certainly don't need to be frightened of a dragon from a hundred years ago."

Gustav scowled at him and continued ahead. Alaric shook his head. That old man certainly had a love for the dramatic.

The bones ended with the trees. The sun had broken through the clouds, and they stood at the edge of a meadow stretching across Bone Valley, dotted with stands of pine trees. Above them, the clouds were chasing each other on the wind. Snow-covered mountains soared above the western side of the valley.

"We'd better find a place to camp," Brandson said glancing at the sun, which sat low above the mountains. "Twilight is going to come earlier here."

"How about away from the bones?" said Douglon.

They struck out along the edge of the trees searching for some other shelter. The sun had dropped behind the mountains by the time they reached a little grove of pines set out in the middle of the meadow. After Douglon inspected the ground for any bones, they set up camp between the trunks.

Brandson carried an armful of wood for the fire. "I don't suppose you could do that thing again where you see if Patlon followed us?" he asked Gustav.

"Of course, my boy," the wizard answered. "I was just about to." Standing up tall and spreading his arms wide apart, the wizard closed his eyes and began to mutter, spinning in a circle.

Alaric watched him, keeping his face bland. He felt Gustav's wave limp past again.

"We are still alone," Gustav announced. "That monster did not follow us."

"He's not a—" Douglon started, but at Gustav's glare he stopped. "We'll set a watch tonight," he grumbled.

Alaric cast out his own wave without any movement or sound, but his findings agreed with the old man's.

Gustav ambled over to where Milly and Brandson were setting wood for a small fire. The wizard shooed them away. As he did, Alaric saw a glimmer of silver drop onto the wood. With a flourish, Gustav shouted, "*Incende!*" and stabbed his staff into the wood. There was a tiny spark and then an explosion as the wood burst into flames. Milly scrambled back and stifled a scream. Smiling in satisfaction, Gustav strode away from the flames, waving them back to the fire.

Alaric knelt to rummage in his pack, trying to hide his smile. Fire powder! The old man had used fire powder and passed it off as magic. Alaric thought for the hundredth time that he should give up everything else and bring fire powder to Queensland. It was prohibitively expensive, but the wealthy in countries far to the south sprinkled the silvery powder in ovens and over wood. A quick rap would ignite the powder and result in what had occurred in their own fire. How had Gustav managed to get ahold of some?

"Amazing, Gustav!" exclaimed Milly.

"Wondrous," Alaric agreed.

The evening stretched out, perfectly quiet, as the group settled down around the small fire. It was a little eerie that there were so few noises, and Alaric found himself constantly straining to hear something. Anything.

Brandson volunteered to take first watch and ambled to the edge of their small pine grove. Milly watched him for a moment. Seeing Ayda's encouraging nod, she prepared a plate of food and took it over to him.

"Thanks, Milly," Alaric could just hear Brandson say to her.

"She's a nice girl," Ayda said, following Alaric's gaze.

Alaric nodded.

"I think Brandson should marry her. I've been trying forever to get the two of them together."

"Marry her?"

"Yes. Brandson is lonely. He has been since his parents died," Ayda said, her face thoughtful. "I think he needs a more satisfying family than a bunch of misfits."

"Who are you calling a misfit?" Douglon asked.

"You," she laughed, stepping over to him and poking another flower into his beard.

Alaric glanced around at the ground but didn't see any flowers. Where did she find these things?

"Alaric is a handsome man with good prospects," Ayda said, "and I'm— Well… me. So the misfits are you and the crazy wizard."

Gustav harrumphed and stood up from the fire, stalking away to sit on the opposite side of the camp from Brandson.

"I'm glad you're here, Milly." Brandson's voice drifted through the darkening trees.

"Me, too," she answered. "Those trees over there are lovely."

"The oaks?" Brandson said. "They are. Strange to see a stand of oaks when the rest of the valley is full of pines."

Alaric looked up and caught Gustav whipping his head around toward Milly.

Alaric waited for a grand announcement from Gustav claiming to have solved the riddle, but the wizard hunched back around and studied his fingernails.

So Gustav didn't plan on sharing his knowledge with the rest of the group. That was interesting. Alaric settled himself back against the tree. What was the old man's plan?

For a long time, Alaric rested against his tree, watching Gustav who was busy looking bored. The Wellstone was close. It was past time to let this group know that he knew what the 'oatry' clue meant. With that, there'd be nothing to stop them from finding the treasure. Tomorrow morning, Alaric decided, he would tell everyone he was a Keeper. It might not be precisely true, but it was as good of a title for him as anything else. The nagging guilt of lying to this group had become too strong to ignore. It would be a relief to tell them.

One by one, the others fell asleep. When Gustav hadn't stopped snoring for at least an hour,

Alaric allowed himself to close his eyes as well.

It was still dark when Alaric awoke to a shriek. From across the campsite, Gustav ran screeching toward the fire. He reached the group and bunched up his robe, catapulting himself over the fire, white bony legs still pumping in mid-air.

"Dragon!" he yelled as he barely cleared the small fire and landed, legs still pumping as he raced through their grove of trees and toward the grass separating them from the main forest.

Alaric leapt up and searched the clear, moonlit sky with his eyes and mind. The night was quiet and empty.

Then an enormous power burst into the valley. A dragon shot through the night sky. Dark red flashes glittered off its scales in the moonlight. It flew in front of the moon, and for a moment, its thin wings glowed scarlet. It was massive, its wings blocking out ragged sections of the stars as it soared across the sky. It turned and dove, making straight for them.

Gustav, still shrieking, had reached the grassy meadow and ran toward the main woods.

Alaric's blood thrummed with the energy of the dragon. *A dragon!*

Milly screamed and cowered behind a tree. Brandson threw his arm around her.

"Gustav!" yelled Brandson, "Get back here!"

But the old man ran heedlessly on.

"Idiot!" Douglon swore.

Alaric snapped into motion, running to the edge of the grove, searching for a spell to protect Gustav.

But the dragon reached the wizard first. The dragon's roar shook the ground, and the blast of energy created as it produced its fire knocked Alaric off his feet.

Its massive body hurtled through the air, spraying out a jet of flame, which enveloped the old man. The huge jaw opened, and the teeth snapped shut around Gustav. The dragon spun around, shooting high into the air and leaving behind empty, charred grass.

FOURTEEN

A dragon—a real dragon! And Gustav...

But there hadn't been a dragon in Queensland for a hundred years.

Silence reigned in the valley. The clouds had cleared, and the wet grass glinted silver in the moonlight. Alaric stood with everyone else, frozen, staring at the scorched ground where Gustav had been.

High above them, the dragon roared. The sky lit up with red flames, startling them all into action.

Alaric scrambled to his feet and moved to the edge of the trees, searching the sky. He caught sight of the dark shape spiraling impossibly high before turning back toward them. What were they going to do against a dragon?

Alaric glanced around at the group. Brandson held his knife uncertainly. It was a knife for skinning animals, not fighting a dragon. Douglon hefted his axe, which was a *little* better. But the two looked small and insignificant. Milly ran to the fire and smothered it with dirt. Alaric gave her an approving nod. Looking around for a weapon, she grabbed a frying pan.

Alaric noticed in passing how clear his mind felt, and he glanced at Ayda. She was focused on the sky.

Don't fight a dragon, Keeper Gerone would say. *Leave that sort of business to warriors. Distract it and flee.*

Distract it with what? They were in an empty valley. But they certainly weren't equipped to fight it. Not this group. Douglon was the only one even close to a warrior. There was no archer. No one even had a sword. Alaric could protect them somewhat, but only from the fire. He had no defense against dragon teeth.

"Any ideas?" he asked Ayda.

"Befriend it?" she offered.

Useless elf.

"If he lands," Douglon said, "we might have a chance to injure it and drive it off." His voice didn't hold any real hope, though. "Stay in the trees until he does."

"What if he sets the forest on fire first?" Milly asked.

Alaric gathered some energy. He began to weave an invisible shield over the nearby trees, enclosing the group in it. It wouldn't stop the fire completely, dragon's breath was too hot, but it would protect the trees from enough heat that they shouldn't burst immediately into flames. And hopefully, it would stop the flames from reaching them down on the ground. His hands began to burn as he stretched the shield farther. He had guarded Douglon, Brandson, and Milly from the heat and was turning toward Ayda when she flashed him an irritated look.

"I don't need your help," she said. "Take care of the others."

"Sorry," he said, pulling the shield away from her and anchoring it above the rest of them.

"Here it comes!" Douglon warned.

A rushing sound began high above them, then plummeted down.

Douglon was right. Any chance they had of even injuring the creature depended on it being on the ground.

Maybe a strong wind could ground it. Alaric began to gather energy again, pulling it in as fast as he dared, feeling the pressure of it building inside of him. He wove a web across the space between their grove of trees and the main forest, containing a portion of air. When the web was complete, he drew energy out of the air above it, pulling out the heat, making it colder and colder. The cool air pressed down on his web, getting heavier the colder he made it. He drew out more and more heat until the air was frigid. An erratic wind began to move at the edges of his web, and the trees on either side where he had anchored it bent down toward the ground.

The dragon pelted toward them. An ear-splitting roar cracked the night.

Alaric's hands were in agony, and his arms burned as he forced more and more energy into the net. He stretched clawed hands forward one more time. The grass at his feet withered as he pulled energy from it to replenish his own. The leaves of the nearest tree shriveled. Alaric reached farther, searching for more strength to put toward his task.

The dragon sped down along the grass. With a surge, Alaric tore his net off the trees and let the cold air plummet down. The dragon, caught in the draft, crashed to the ground. But in a moment, it bunched its legs and launched itself back into the air.

He caught a glimpse of Brandson's knife as he threw it. It tinked harmlessly off the red scales of the dragon's belly and tumbled into the grass.

Alaric sank back on his heels, his stomach dropping. His arms were like rocks in his lap, and he had barely affected the dragon. The trees Alaric had protected were smoking, but one more pass would light them like torches.

The dragon roared high above them.

Ayda came over to Alaric. It took most of his strength to lift his head and look up at her.

"I thought you'd do better than that," she said, looking a little disappointed. "You didn't do much better than the wizard."

Alaric stared after her, unable to move as she stalked toward the grass where Gustav had disappeared.

"You stupid elf!" Douglon shouted, watching Ayda walk toward her destruction. "It's a *dragon!* Get back here!"

Ayda ignored him and kept walking. With one last look at the sky, the dwarf rushed after Ayda spewing curses.

Ayda shot him a furious glance and flicked her hand at him.

The dwarf jerked to a stop. Thin roots had snaked up out of the ground and wrapped around his feet, growing and hardening over his boots. He shouted at Ayda, waving his axe wildly and tugging with all his might at his stationary feet. He took his axe and chopped at the edges of the roots. For every root he cut through, another slithered out of the ground.

Ayda continued walking into the open grass. Brandson began to run after her, but at another dangerous look from the elf, he stopped and backed up next to Milly.

The dragon's roar came closer, and the sky lit again. On Alaric's chest, a flash of light reflected off the flame that Ayda had frozen for him.

Maybe the elf standing in the center of the charred circle of grass wasn't so vulnerable.

But then the dragon appeared, impossibly huge and fast. The rush of wings grew louder, and the world glowed red. Milly screamed and hid her face in Brandson's shoulder as the dragon hurtled toward Ayda.

Alaric couldn't pull his gaze away. With the dragon bearing down on her, Ayda was nothing more than a golden wisp in the moonlight.

Ayda waited, looking up at the descending monster, watching until it was so close that the flames were inches from her face. With a wave of her hand, she cast the flames away, solidifying them and sending them splintering into countless pieces. They landed on the ground near Alaric's feet with the ringing of a thousand tiny bells. The grass was covered with glinting shards of deep red.

Enormous jaws crushed the end of the flame, which had solidified while still in the dragon's mouth, and the creature shot back into the sky.

Ayda looked pleased at the pile of hardened flames. "That was pretty." She crinkled her brow. "I think I'll make the next set blue. There's much too much red over there now, don't you think, Milly?"

Milly, staring with her mouth wide open, said nothing.

"Yes, blue." Ayda turned to see the dragon approaching again.

This time, the beast dove near to the ground farther up the valley and raced toward her. With its blood-red belly skimming the grass, it waited until it was right on her before spewing out flames. Another wave of her hand diverted the flame, this time, turning it a brilliant blue as it hardened.

Milly screamed as the dragon bore down on Ayda. But the elf, with an exasperated flip of her hand, sent the dragon tumbling over her as though it had caught a clawed toe on a rock. The dragon plunged to the ground behind her, crashing down on its back. The valley shook, and Alaric ducked, shielding his head from the branches and pinecones that rained down on him.

In a breath, the dragon twisted back to its feet. Crouched with its chin brushing the ground, the beast let out a low, vicious hiss.

Ayda cocked her head to one side.

"You're not going to try the fire again, are you?" she asked.

The dragon flared its nostrils but did nothing. It seemed to be contemplating the same question. Alaric slowly let out his breath, but drew it in again when Ayda walked toward the beast as though he were an angry house cat who needed soothing.

"Sir Dragon," she began, "if I may call you that since I don't know your proper name. I'm afraid that you have attacked a group that would have been better left alone."

The dragon stared at her with a mixture of hatred and confusion.

"We realize that you are a truly terrifying beast and that there are few who would dare to stand against a beast such as you, but we are among those few." She had reached the dragon now. Although the dragon's chin was on the ground, the top of its nose was shoulder height to the elf.

"It's not just me," she continued. "There's a fearsome dwarf warrior in those trees." The dragon flicked its eyes toward the trees. Douglon, who had been slouched in shock, his feet still frozen, straightened himself up and gripped his axe.

"There's a young blacksmith who is quite strong and equally determined." Brandson stood taller. "And there's a milkmaid with a frying pan. Between you and me, I don't think she was planning to cook over dragon fire." Milly hid the pan behind her back.

"And, if you had gotten by all of us, there is still a magic worker in those trees who I had *assumed* was fairly adept." She cast a critical look at Alaric.

Alaric felt Douglon, Brandson, and Milly look at him as well. The dragon turned intelligent eyes toward Alaric for a long moment.

Ayda stretched her hand out to touch the dragon's snout, but its eyes whipped back toward her and narrowed. A loud, threatening growl rumbled deep in its chest.

Ayda paused. Douglon made a strangled noise.

Alaric's heart was in his throat, waiting for the jaws to open and Ayda to disappear.

She dropped her hand back down, and the dragon's nose inched forward. Its head lashed forward, and it snapped its teeth. Ayda jerked back, crying out and grabbing her arm. Blood seeped through her fingers.

"A little help?" Ayda said, bracing herself as the dragon's snout drew closer again.

"What am I supposed to do?" Alaric hissed at her.

The dragon growled again, vibrating the ground. The breath from its nostrils swirled Ayda's hair. The dragon's eyes lit for a moment, watching the golden sparkles from her hair.

Distract it. Right. Dragons liked sparkly things.

Alaric pulled some energy in from the trees near him again and, ignoring the fact that his hands were still throbbing, began to pour energy into the air behind Ayda's feet. The air warmed and rose, lifting strands of her hair with it. More and more locks lifted and swirled around her head. In the middle of the moonlit grass, she looked like she was surrounded by sparks.

The dragon's eyes glazed slightly.

Alaric crept forward, feeding energy slowly into the air and gathering more at the same time until he thought he would burst with the pressure of it. When he was right next to the dragon's neck, he stopped feeding the air near Ayda and braced himself.

This was going to hurt.

The dragon blinked as Ayda's hair stilled. Alaric pushed both hands onto the dragon's scales at the base of its neck.

The dragon twisted and lashed out at Alaric, his claw tearing through Alaric's shoulder. Pain ripped across Alaric's arm. He dove to the side while Ayda yelled, drawing the dragon's attention back to her. Alaric scrambled back close to it and slammed his palms against the dragon's neck.

"*Paxa!*" Energy surged out through his palms, searing his skin as it poured into the dragon. The dragon's entire body relaxed.

Alaric dropped to his knees and fell forward. Blisters formed on his palms, and his arms ached too much to move. Blood was running down his left arm from his shoulder. His head swam, and it took him a moment to realize he was leaning on the dragon's neck.

He used his elbows to push himself off the monster. Brandson, Milly, and Douglon were staring at him in amazement.

Ayda let out a whoosh of air. "That's better," she said, her voice quavering slightly. She reached out to touch the dragon's snout, but wrinkled her nose when she saw the blood on her hand. She wiped it off on her dress, leaving a dark stain, then set her hand on the dragon's nose.

Its eyes softened, and it made a sound less like a growl than a purr.

"Yes, I like you, too," she said kindly. "But it's time you were going. I'm afraid that we can't all share this valley and since we have some business here…"

Brandson cleared his throat.

"Oh, right," Ayda said. "We would appreciate it if you would leave the next valley alone also. It is our home, of sorts." With a final pat of the dragon's nose, she turned away.

The dragon blinked at her.

"By the way, what is your name?" she asked, turning back to it. She paused, her head cocked. "Anguine? Well it was lovely to meet you, Anguine. You are a very fierce dragon. I did think the old man you ate would have caused you a bit more trouble," she said with a crinkled brow. "I guess he wasn't too calm under pressure." The dragon shifted, and Ayda fixed it with a piercing gaze. "I see," she said. "Well, off with you."

Turning her back to the dragon, she walked back to the others. The dragon shook its head once. The clawed foot near Alaric flexed, and he scrambled back away from it. With one final confused look at the departing elf, it vaulted itself into the sky and disappeared northward toward the mountains.

FIFTEEN

Alaric sank back against the nearest tree trunk and watched the red glint of the dragon disappear over the mountains. At least it had flown west toward the Roven Sweep and not south into the heart of Queensland. Although the nomads on the Sweep were going to have a tough time dealing with it.

The gash in his shoulder burned, and his arms hung down on his lap, aching. He gingerly turned over his palms and saw a circle of blisters on each, shiny and taut in the moonlight. He rested his head back on the tree trunk and closed his eyes.

His mind churned up questions he was too exhausted to consider. A dragon? Here? Where had it come from? *Paxa* had worked on it—had anyone ever tried that before? Had a Keeper ever touched a dragon before? And survived? He'd have to send the Shield a letter. Alaric closed his fingers slightly, but the blisters shot searing pains across his palms. Writing a letter might have to wait.

"Ayda?" Milly's voice sounded far away and weak. "Is it gone?"

Alaric heard someone rekindle the fire and realized he was shivering. Part of the pain in his fingers, he realized, was because they were ice cold. The active part of his brain pointed out that was to be expected after pushing so much energy out of them. The exhausted part told it to shut up. He heaved himself forward and using his elbows, managed to get to his knees. The fire flickered through the trees, an impossible distance away.

Then Brandson was there, tugging Alaric to his feet and half leading, half dragging him to the fire. Alaric sank down close to it.

Milly stepped over to him and, with a wary look, handed him a piece of bread. He smiled gratefully at her. The smile she gave back was strained. He tore off a piece of bread that seemed to weigh as much as a boulder. One bite at a time, he ate, waiting for his strength to return.

Alaric could feel blood dripping down his arm. In his pack was tucked a salve that would help. It would help with the burns, too. He eyed his bag all the way across the campsite, another impossible distance.

Ayda would need some, too. He glanced at her, but her arm looked clean and whole. Her dress was spotless and white.

"That was amazing," Milly said in a hushed voice, glancing from Ayda to Alaric.

Ayda beamed at her. "Thank you. It's been some time since I've seen a dragon, but they are all the same. Always attacking with fire and teeth."

"They really should attack with something dangerous," Douglon said.

Ayda laughed a silvery laugh. "Exactly. And I am sorry about the whole tied to the ground thing," she said, motioning to the tree that Douglon had been stuck under. "But I'm afraid you would have been less handsome if that dragon had singed off your beard."

Douglon muttered something and stroked his beard, running his hand over the flowers Ayda had stuck in earlier. He brushed them out in disgust. "I guess we owe you our lives," he said grudgingly.

"You're welcome," she beamed at him.

Milly studied Ayda for a moment. "I've never heard of anyone who could do what you just did with the fire."

"Everybody has the same magic," Ayda said. She gestured at Alaric. "He could have done the same thing."

All eyes turned to Alaric, and a heavy silence filled the trees.

"So you're just a royal historian?" Douglon said.

Alaric started to shrug, but the shooting pain in his shoulder stopped him with a gasp. "That's part of my job."

Douglon scowled and the others waited.

Alaric sighed. "I'm a Keeper." The title didn't feel completely false.

Brandson and Milly gasped.

Douglon's scowl deepened. "Didn't it occur to you to mention that?"

"It's not something we announce," Alaric said.

"You're after the gem, aren't you?" demanded Douglon. "You were going to steal it."

"Douglon!" Brandson said. "Alaric's a Keeper! He wouldn't do such a thing!"

The title didn't feel completely true, either.

"Yes, he seems very noble," Douglon said.

Alaric sighed. Turned out having his secret revealed wasn't much of a relief after all.

"You, of all people, can't be upset at someone keeping his personal history to himself," Ayda said to the dwarf.

"It's all right," Alaric said. "He has a right to be angry. I should have told you sooner."

"Is Ayda telling the truth?" asked Milly. "Could you have done that with the dragon fire?"

Maybe. If he had a thousand years. And a thousand Keepers.

"I don't know," Alaric said after a short hesitation. "Certainly not with as much style."

"Why did you join up with us in the first place?" Douglon demanded.

"I was interested in your group because you lived in Kordan's Blight, and I was looking for information about Kordan. He was a Keeper."

"He was?" Milly asked. "The stories of him aren't very... Keeper-like."

"Maybe you people don't know what Keepers are like," Douglon pointed out.

"Neither Kordan nor I are model Keepers," Alaric admitted. "But Kordan started out as one. He did leave the Keepers after he lived here, though."

"How did you know we were looking for Kordan's gem?" Douglon asked.

"I didn't."

"You expect us to believe you just happened to come across a group looking for a treasure you're also looking for?"

Alaric shook his head. "I know. The chances of that are... nonexistent. But I had no idea who any of you were or what you were looking for. I have no explanation."

Douglon gave him an incredulous look.

Alaric's hands were throbbing, but the bread was starting to help. "I will offer you what I promised for the gem."

"Why so generous?" asked Douglon.

Alaric hesitated, but there was nothing to be gained from secrecy. "Because the gem we are looking for is that valuable to me. To all the Keepers. I believe what we are going to find is called a Wellstone. To you, it is a treasure, and a treasure is worth money. To me, it is an artifact to be studied."

Douglon harrumphed and turned his scowl toward the elf. "What did you do to the dragon?"

"I befriended it," Ayda answered.

There was silence for a long moment.

Ayda shrugged and gave a small, self-conscious smile. "Everyone likes me, if they just get close enough."

Douglon snorted, but the words had the ring of truth in them. Everyone *did* like Ayda. Even Alaric liked Ayda, despite, well, despite everything.

"Do you think the dragon will return tonight?" Milly asked Ayda.

"Oh, no. He agreed to stay away as long as we are in the valley." The elf scrunched up her nose. "I suppose I didn't tell him to leave us alone after we left, but I don't think he'd try again."

Alaric reached for a skin of water, but the tear in his shoulder sent a lance of pain down his arm and he groaned.

"Alaric," Milly said, rushing over, "I forgot you were hurt."

She worked the ripped fabric away from his shoulder and cringed. The cut was deep and ragged.

Ayda stepped over and glanced at it. "That's not too bad."

"It feels bad," Alaric said.

Ayda reached past Milly and pushed her hand against the wound. Pain knifed through his shoulder and he gasped. But a warmth flowed out of Ayda's hand along with a tightening sensation, and the wound knit itself back together. In a moment, the pain was gone, and Ayda stepped back, smiling. There was nothing on his shoulder but a white scar and a lot of leftover blood.

Alaric rotated his arm gingerly. There was no pain at all. He looked up into Ayda's face, stunned. How had she done that? It took the body days, weeks to heal a wound like that. The amount of energy expended was enormous. Yet Ayda had done it effortlessly.

"We do not have the same magic," he said.

Her face darkened, and an odd look crept into her eyes.

"Yes, we do. Just in different amounts." She caught sight of Alaric's palms and frowned, "Those I can't do much with. A cut just needs to be cleaned out and pulled back together. But a burn is different. I could heal them, but it will leave terrible scars. Scars you might not want on your hands."

Alaric had met a man once with a burned hand. The scarred skin didn't stretch right, he couldn't grip anything well. Alaric thought of not being able to hold a pen. "I'll just wait for them to heal."

"I can do something about the pain, though," Ayda said. She set her hands on Alaric's palms. Her fingers felt cool against his flaming skin. A numbness spread across his hands, and the pain receded. He let out a sigh of relief.

Milly brought over some strips of fabric and began to bandage Alaric's hand. At his questioning look, she gave an apologetic shrug. "One of Gustav's shirts."

"I can't believe he's gone," Brandson said, poking a stick into the coals.

It had all happened so quickly. So finally.

"If the dragon had to eat anyone," Ayda said, "I'm glad it was the wizard."

"Ayda!" Brandson said, aghast.

"It's true," she said. "I'll take the next watch in case that dwarf did follow us and decides to attack us tonight as well." She wandered over to the edge of the trees. "Although, after the dragon, a dwarf will be boring."

Brandson stared after her.

"You can't expect too much from her," Alaric told him. "Elves don't attach to anyone who's not an elf. It's astonishing that she stays with you at all, but she won't feel the same sort of bond to the group that you do. No matter how long she spends with you."

"I'm not sure that makes me feel any better," Brandson said, watching Ayda disappear between the trees.

Alaric managed to stand and get to his blanket. He sank down and rested his head on his pack.

Douglon crashed and clattered around on the other side of the fire, moving Gustav's belongings out of the way so he could move his own sleeping roll closer to the fire. He dropped Gustav's shovel on his foot and swore before throwing it into some nearby bushes. "I thought wizards were powerful, but Gustav obviously wasn't. That Mallon turned out to be a fraud, too. Wasn't he killed by a forest fire?"

"Mallon was *not* a fraud," Brandson snapped. "He controlled whole cities, killed thousands with his armies and sent diseases that—" Brandson's voice broke. He took a deep breath. "Diseases that murdered thousands more. Among them, my parents."

The clearing went quiet. Douglon cleared his throat. "Mallon never came near the dwarves. We knew he had an army and was attacking your cities, but I didn't know…"

"There are few families in Queensland who didn't lose someone," Milly said. "Mallon seemed unstoppable."

Alaric nodded. "There are some wizards with power, but not many."

"Aren't Keepers wizards?" asked Douglon.

"Not primarily. We know how to manipulate energy, but it's not our first priority. Actually, historian is closer to the mark. The official term used by the crown is 'Advisor and Protector of the Realm.' We see magic as a tool, one of many, that can be used to keep Queensland safe." Alaric was surprised that he had said 'we.' And that he had meant it. It had been a long time since he had thought of Keepers' ideals in a positive light.

"Most minor wizards, like Gustav, are independent. Some are Shade Seekers, a group who use what the Keepers, and probably most everyone else, would call darker magic. The magic is more important to them than anything, and they are not against killing for it. Mallon was a Shade Seeker, but no one had ever heard of one as powerful as he was. We had no defense. He controlled or destroyed at will." He looked into the woods after Ayda. "Ayda must know what happened, but I don't know what the elves did. We didn't know of anything that could stop him. I assure you whatever killed Mallon the Rivor, it wasn't a forest fire."

"Maybe Ayda killed him," Milly whispered.

Alaric felt a chill.

"Maybe Ayda ate him and stole his power," Douglon whispered.

Milly stifled a giggle.

"Why do you call him the Rivor?" Douglon asked.

"The first town that Mallon took over was along the edge of the Scale Mountains," Alaric said. "It was home to the gem cutters' guild. Mallon entered the town alone, found the town leaders and… turned them into his instruments.

"The people reported to the king, and the word they used for it was riving. It's the word for when a gem cutter cracks or damages a stone so deeply that it's worthless. It was an accurate description for what he was doing to people's minds. The name stuck."

Douglon looked troubled. "Seems the dwarves underestimated him."

Silence fell over the group. Alaric's eyes closed. He felt like he was falling, falling through the earth, falling into sweet, inescapable sleep.

But his mind still spun. Ayda, dragons, Gustav, Mallon. Thoughts chased themselves pell-mell around his mind.

His perfectly clear mind.

Alaric's eyes snapped open. He was tired, unbelievably tired, but his mind was alert. Not the least bit of fuzziness remained. He looked again in the direction Ayda had gone and took a deep breath, reveling in the new lightness. Was she done trying to influence him? He should have fought a dragon with her days ago.

His eyes sank closed.

———•—•——

Despite the events of the night before, Alaric stirred with the others at dawn.

"This is the day!" Douglon said. "We'll find the gem by lunch. Let's take another look at that map."

"After we bury Gustav," Milly said firmly.

Everyone paused.

"What would you have us bury?" asked Douglon, eyeing the charred bit of grass where the wizard had met his end.

"Well, fine, not bury then," said Milly, "but he deserves some sort of funeral."

"Yes, he does," Brandson agreed.

"Can't we pretend the dragon was a grand funeral pyre?" asked Douglon.

Milly gave him a withering look.

"Brandson," she said, "please go find something we could use as a tombstone. And go help him, Douglon. We're going to do something for the poor old man."

Brandson nodded and headed into the trees.

"We'll need something to write with," Milly said.

Ayda pulled a charred stick from the fire and offered it to Milly with an amused smile.

"What's she gonna write?" Douglon asked Brandson as they walked away. "'Here doesn't lie the body of a wizard who didn't beat a dragon'?"

Milly scowled after the dwarf. She turned to Alaric. "Can you think of anything else we should do?"

He was taken aback for a moment at being asked, but she looked so earnest that he shook his head. "I think the tombstone is perfect."

A few minutes later, the five of them gathered on the scorched grass and watched as Brandson shoved a large flat stone into place. Milly knelt before it and raised her stick to write.

She paused. "How do you spell Wizendorenfurderfur?"

Douglon shrugged. "Just put Gustav."

"Right," Milly agreed. "Gustav the Wondrous."

Ayda tried to hide her smile until Douglon whispered, "He wasn't a wondrous runner."

Milly ignored them both and finished. Standing back with the others, she cleared her throat.

"Gustav is gone and we'll miss him," she began. "We'll miss his... um, knowledge and... um... that way he could start fires. He was a noble wizard... At least, I think he was." She paused, looking at the others. At Douglon's grin, she flung the stick to the ground and glared at them all. "Oh, for pity's sake, I barely knew the man! You stone-hearted scoundrels say something!"

Ayda laughed and stepped forward. "Well, old man, none of us believed you were much of a wizard. I guess you proved us right."

"I, for one, will miss you," Brandson said. "My house was too quiet before you came. And you were an excellent cook."

Milly slipped her hand into Brandson's.

"Um," Douglon began, searching for something to say. "Even though it makes no sense, thanks for the tip about the 'oatry.'"

"What about an oak tree?" asked Milly. "Didn't we see oak trees last night?"

Brandson and Douglon stared at her.

"Oak tree!" they both yelled and rushed off toward the campsite.

Milly gave the tombstone one last apologetic look then followed them, leaving Alaric and Ayda at the makeshift grave.

Ayda cocked her head and looked at Alaric. "Do you think the wizard knew the treasure was so close by?" She looked at Gustav's tombstone and gave a thoughtful, "Huh," before she turned and walked back toward the camp.

Alaric followed her and reached the campsite as the others were gathering shovels.

"Does anyone see Gustav's shovel?" Douglon asked, rummaging in the bushes where he'd thrown it.

"You don't need another shovel," Brandson said. "C'mon!"

The excitement was contagious and Alaric hurried after them. He set his bandaged palm against the pouch at his neck. Kordan's Wellstone was buried nearby. The antidote. Alaric's heartbeat raced ahead as well. He cast out, feeling the stand of trees ahead of him and one old, ponderous oak.

All thoughts of wizards and dragons and strange elves disappeared in a breath. Once he had the antidote and reached Kordan's Blight, it would take three days to reach Evangeline. Two if he pushed Beast hard. He could wake her. Heal her.

He rushed to catch up to the others.

Only Ayda trailed behind.

It was a large group of trees with one, near the center, reaching above the rest.

"It must be there!" Brandson said. "Under the oldest one."

Ahead of him, Douglon, Brandson, and Milly threaded their way through the oaks. The largest tree was massive, its trunk wider across than Alaric's reach, thick roots snaking across the ground. Branches spread out, sheltering an area as large as a house.

"Ayda is going to explode with excitement when she sees this tree," Alaric heard Brandson say as he walked around the trunk.

"Where should we dig?" asked Milly.

No one answered her for a moment.

From the other side of the tree, Douglon started swearing loudly.

Alaric finally caught up, stepping carefully over the jutting roots as he rounded the trunk, only to see Brandson and Douglon leaning on their clean shovels next to a freshly dug hole. Alaric joined them and peered in. His stomach dropped.

The hole was rough as though it had been dug in a hurry. It was about three feet deep and was completely empty. Even the small indentation at the bottom, which clearly used to hold a box.

It was gone. Kordan's Wellstone was gone.

Alaric felt fury rising inside of him, looking for a target. He raised his gaze and found one.

Leaning against the trunk above the hole was a pointy, star-covered hat and Gustav's shovel, now covered in dirt.

SIXTEEN

Gustav wasn't dead.

He had survived the dragon.

He had dug up the Wellstone.

Alaric's mind crashed up against a single thought. The Wellstone was gone.

Ayda rounded the tree and took in scene before her… and the pointy hat. "Stupid wizard." She kicked the hat, sending it tumbling down into the hole.

"He's alive." Brandson's voice was a combination of shock and hope.

"I'm going to kill him." Douglon swung his axe, glaring through the trees.

"The wizard's long gone," Ayda said. "He has no more use for you or your map, dwarf."

Douglon growled and slammed his axe into a nearby tree. Ayda shot him a disapproving look. She flicked her hand, sending the axe spinning out of the tree. Douglon snatched it back up off the ground.

"He has no use for any of us now," Ayda said, giving Brandson a small smile. "Our milkmaid's not the only one who wasted kindness on that old man."

Milly walked up to Brandson and slipped her arm into his.

"I can't decide if I'm glad or furious," Brandson said.

Douglon stomped past them. "…lying, cheating, backstabbing, two-faced…"

Alaric stared into the empty hole. Gustav had duped him, had duped all of them.

"Gustav must be a powerful wizard if he escaped from the dragon," Milly said.

"He escaped," Brandson said, "and let us think he was dead." Anger began to simmer behind Brandson's eyes.

"He didn't escape the dragon," Ayda said. "He used it to fool us. I think it's his pet."

"Gustav has a pet dragon?" Brandson asked, the anger now moving beyond simmering.

Ayda shrugged. "What would you call it if you had a dragon that did what you wanted?"

"Dangerous," Alaric said.

"When I was talking to the dragon, I got the feeling that it knew the wizard."

Douglon fixed Ayda with a venomous glare. "You knew Gustav was alive?"

"No," Ayda said. "Just that the dragon knew him. I didn't ask if the wizard was still alive."

Douglon opened his mouth and sputtered. "You didn't *ask?*" His voice rose louder. "You didn't think to tell us? You didn't think—"

"Dragons eat people," Ayda interrupted, casting a bored look into the hole. "And I never cared for the old man." With that, she turned and walked back toward the campsite.

"I hate that elf," Douglon said, slamming his axe back into the tree. "I *hate* her."

Brandson was staring after Ayda, his mouth wide open in shock. He looked at Alaric. "Would she care that little about any of us dying?"

Alaric watched Ayda disappear through the stand of oaks. "Most likely. Elves don't usually care about anyone but other elves."

Brandson rubbed his hands on his face and growled in frustration. "Gustav betrays us. Ayda doesn't care about us. Why couldn't normal people have fallen into my life?"

"Look!" Milly slid down into the hole. "Something glinted down here."

"The gem?" Douglon asked, pushing past Brandson to get to the hole.

Brandson pulled Douglon back with a dangerous light in his eye. "If it's the gem and you decide to steal it because none of us matters to you either, I will track you down and chop off your beard."

Douglon looked at Brandson with raised eyebrows. He shook his head. "Anything we find, Brandson, we share." He held out his hand to the blacksmith.

Brandson let out a long breath. "Sorry." He shook the dwarf's hand.

"It's not the gem," Milly gave them an apologetic smile. "Just this."

She held up a small medallion of some sort. Brandson took it and helped Milly back out of the hole. It was bronze, hammered flat into an oval and inscribed with runes. Two off-centered lines, one vertical and one horizontal, split the oval into four sections.

Alaric leaned forward to study the piece. What appeared to be incomprehensible runes grew sinister the longer he looked at them. A letter placed oddly, the way the shape of the runes seemed to suggest images. The symbols tugged at his mind, drawing him in.

He tore his eyes away from the mesmerizing symbols. The oval called to him. "That thing's dangerous."

The others looked up at him in surprise.

"It would be best if you threw it back into the hole and covered it up," Alaric said. "Or better yet dig a new hole for it then forget where you bury it."

"It was buried with the treasure. It could be valuable," said Douglon. "Gustav must not have noticed it in the dark."

"That was not buried with the Wellstone." Alaric's voice was harsher than he intended. He took a deep breath. He glanced again at it. It hummed with malevolence. "Those markings are corrupt. I don't know exactly what it says, but it is evil. Very evil."

"It still might have been buried with the gem," Douglon pointed out. "The stories of Kordan aren't pleasant. Maybe your Keeper went bad."

Alaric felt as though he had a rock in his gut. This medallion couldn't have been Kordan's. He had done some questionable things, but certainly nothing this evil. Alaric reached up to feel the pouch at his neck, feeling the echoes of Kordan's actions in his own life.

"Wherever it came from," he said, again pulling his eyes away from the medallion, "it is evil. You should get rid of it. Destroy it. If it will let you." He turned away from them and walked back to the camp.

At their campsite, Ayda was building up a cook fire. He stood aimlessly for a moment at the edge of the clearing. Gustav had the Wellstone. The knowledge felt like lead in his stomach. On the far side of the clearing, Gustav's pack leaned against a tree. Alaric knelt down by it and dumped out the contents. He wasn't sure what he was looking for, except answers.

There was nothing to find until a small, clay bottle rolled out of one of the many unmatched, poorly darned socks. Alaric worked the cork out, and a sharp metallic smell cut through the air.

Fire powder. It's a good thing Gustav hadn't had this with him during his dragon stunt. A bottle, even this small, ignited by dragon fire would have caused an explosion big enough to kill Gustav, the dragon, and the rest of them, too. Alaric put the bottle in his pocket and pushed the rest of Gustav's things back into his pack. Footsteps approached behind him.

"If you think this thing is dangerous," Milly said, "we would like you to destroy it. It does seem a little… dark." Douglon and Brandson nodded behind her.

Ayda glanced over at them. "What are you doing with the wizard's medallion?"

"This is Gustav's?" asked Brandson. "What is it?"

The medallion really wasn't Kordan's. A wave of relief washed over Alaric.

"I don't know, but he was very protective of it. I saw it one night when he was rummaging through his bag. I asked if I could see it and he hid it." Ayda hunched her shoulders and scrunched her face into an imitation of Gustav. "*No one can touch it! NO ONE! GET AWAY!*"

Douglon laughed, reached over and set one finger on the medallion. "I'm touching it."

Ayda let out a peal of laughter and took the oval from Milly.

"If Gustav cared about it so much," Milly said, "isn't it odd that he left it behind?"

Douglon shook his head. "He's an idiot. It's not surprising that he screws up anything. The only not-surprising thing is that he succeeded in stealing our treasure from us."

Ayda sat down, turning the medallion over in her hands. "I think these are part of the design," she said to Alaric, pointing to the thick lines cut across the oval.

Alaric reluctantly sat down next to her. Ayda held it out to him, but he shook his head. "I don't want to touch it."

"It keeps trying to pull me in, too." She held the medallion so Alaric could look at it. "See these small tails on the lines? They connect the different strings of runes to each other. Like the ugliest flower chain I've ever seen."

Alaric looked at the lines and felt himself pulled into the medallion. It was a gentle sinking, like falling asleep, but at its core, it felt malevolent. He braced his mind against the pull and studied the runes. Ayda was right. The entire design drew his eye in a serpentine path around the oval. There was no specific starting point, just a twisted loop.

The longer he looked at it, the stronger the pull.

Alaric blinked and looked away. "You're right. The lines are important. It's some sort of instructions. I can't read all of it, but it talks about sacrifice, death, and"—he cast a troubled look at the medallion—"bleeding the life out of someone."

Ayda crinkled her nose and tossed the oval to the ground near the fire. She wiped her hands off on her dress and stood.

Alaric's eyes were drawn back to it. It looked like bronze, but it was missing something. Warmth, maybe. It was too muted to be bronze, as though it sucked in the light that hit it instead of reflecting it. It sat there, a blemish in the dirt, too dark to fit into the sunny day.

"So Gustav really is… evil?" Brandson sank down beside him. He looked hard at the medallion. "When we found out he was alive, I hoped… I don't know what."

"I haven't seen anything this dark since Mallon was alive," Alaric said.

"Did you know Gustav was really a wizard?"

"Yes, but I thought his powers were minimal," Alaric said.

"I thought he was an idiot," Douglon said dropping to the ground beside them.

"Maybe he's a genius," Milly said. "If he played a role that well for so long."

"Impossible," the dwarf said. "He's too much of an idiot."

Alaric looked back down at the medallion. It sat dull and slightly too dark. The dirt around it looked wholesome by comparison. Disconnected thoughts swirled in Alaric's mind. This dark thing was Gustav's. He *hadn't* seen anything that dark since Mallon. The dragon couldn't have been Gustav's pet. Dragons weren't pets. Gustav must have been controlling it. Gustav was good enough at manipulating things to control a dragon.

Thoughts of the oval, the dragon, and Gustav flitted through Alaric's mind. His perfectly clear mind. His mind that had been fuzzy since the moment he had laid eyes on Ayda. Which was the exact moment he had laid eyes on Gustav. And his mind had been clear since Gustav had disappeared with the dragon.

The truth snapped into place.

How had he not seen it?

"Gustav is a Shade Seeker," he said.

Across the clearing, Ayda froze. Slowly, she turned toward him, her face dark and frightening. Something terrifying glinted in her eyes. "My, my. We did underestimate the old man, didn't we?"

SEVENTEEN

Gustav was a Shade Seeker. If there had been any doubt in Alaric's mind before about whether he was still a Keeper, the fact that he had traveled for four days with a Shade Seeker and never noticed settled it.

To have pulled that off, Gustav must be far more powerful than Alaric had thought. And the wizard had even fooled Ayda. She had figured out Alaric was a Keeper the first night he traveled with them, but she had lived at Brandson's with Gustav for a quarter of a year. The thoughts swirled, dragging him farther into doubt. How was he going to find the Wellstone?

Douglon had tried to destroy Gustav's medallion. He'd stomped on it, hit it with his axe, thrown it into the fire, but nothing had any effect on it. While the group numbly gathered their belongings, Alaric wrapped it in a cloth and buried it in the bottom of his pack. The oval didn't exert any pull on him unless he looked at it, but the knowledge that it was there weighed down his pack in an unsettling way.

"Patlon might find us if we go back to Kordan's Blight," Brandson pointed out.

"Doesn't matter anymore," Douglon said. "We don't have what he's looking for. Whenever he shows up, I'll talk to him. The sooner, the better, as far as I'm concerned."

The group trudged back toward the village. Brandson tossed out idea after idea as to Gustav's whereabouts, each as unlikely as the next. Douglon kept up a perpetual rumble under his breath, cursing the old wizard in every conceivable way and kicking rocks as he walked. Milly and Ayda, less gloomy than the others, pulled ahead a little and chatted.

"Not all trees are worth talking to," Ayda explained to Milly. The elf was like a glitter of sunlight passing among the trees. "Whisperwillows are silly, and oaks think too highly of themselves, but a lot of trees are interesting."

Douglon rolled his eyes and kicked the next rock at a tree.

"Can elves really change into trees?" Milly asked. "Does it feel… strange?"

"No, it's lovely. You can drink in the sunshine, and rain on your leaves is the most beautiful feeling in the world."

"I doubt it," Douglon muttered.

Brandson walked up next to Alaric. "Are you going to follow Gustav?"

Alaric nodded. "I need the Wellstone. It holds information that I desperately need."

"What kind of information can a stone hold?"

"An antidote."

Brandson glanced at him, but didn't press further. "How will you find him?"

"I don't know. Shade Seekers have a keep at Sidion. If I can't find Gustav there, maybe I can find some information about him."

They had walked into a small clearing when Ayda spun toward the north and froze, her eyes boring through the trees. Alaric turned almost as fast, catching a snippet of a tune on the breeze. The others halted as well. The next gust of wind carried the sound of a whistled, jaunty tune.

"That's not Patlon," Douglon said. "Dwarves don't whistle stupid songs. Sounds more like an elf if you ask me."

Ayda ignored him, and Alaric motioned him to be quiet.

Another breeze brought the whistling back to their ears. This time, a throbbing hum could be heard as well. A low purr moving on the air like a warm blanket, wrapping around the things it passed.

"That's lovely," said Milly, pushing past Alaric and taking a step toward the trees.

Alaric grabbed her arm, making the blisters on his palm scream.

"Get her out of here!" Alaric commanded Brandson. "Caves! Are there caves nearby?"

Milly pulled her arm away from Alaric in irritation.

"Bear Stronghold's not far," Brandson said.

The humming and whistling grew closer. Milly smiled and took another step.

Alaric stepped in front of her and grabbed her by both arms, trying to hold on to her without hurting her, or his own hands, any more than he needed to. She shoved against him, glaring at Alaric, but he didn't let go. "Take her," he told Brandson.

"Knock it off!" Brandson said stepping between the Keeper and Milly.

"That is a borrey," Alaric said. "Milly's in grave danger."

"Just mischievous little sprites. No danger," scoffed Douglon.

"Borreys are all male," Alaric said. "That humming you hear is a mating call. It will draw Milly in, she won't be able to resist. They use women to reproduce." Milly was trying to get past Brandson, her eyes fixed on the woods. "The woman does not survive the process."

Milly attempted one more step toward the noise, but Brandson grabbed her.

"Get her to a protected place in the Stronghold," Alaric instructed. "She won't want to go. Get her there and keep her there however you can. And do it fast. Build a fire across the opening. A big one. Borreys hate fire."

Brandson nodded and began to pull Milly across the clearing.

"Help him," Alaric told Douglon. "You may need to carry her."

Douglon hesitated, glancing at Ayda.

"I'm in no danger," she said.

"Go," Alaric urged the dwarf. "Brandson will need your help. We'll come find you. Take this." Alaric pressed Gustav's small bottle into Douglon's hand. "It's Gustav's fire powder. Sprinkle a little on something then strike it with a stick or a stone. It will ignite."

Douglon took the bag and snorted. "This was how he started his 'magical' fires?"

"A little bit goes a long way," warned Alaric.

Douglon flashed a wicked smile. "Will it kill the borrey?"

"Probably not, they're hard to kill. But it should hold it at bay. We'll try to give you some time."

Douglon nodded and ran toward the edge of the clearing where Brandson stood tugging on Milly's arm and pleading with her to follow him. The dwarf ran up, tossed Milly up onto his shoulder and darted off through the trees while she shrieked and pounded on his back. Brandson stared after them in shock.

"Show me the way!" the dwarf bellowed as he ran. Brandson ran after them.

Alaric nodded in approval, then turned back to Ayda.

"And you are still here because…?"

She was watching the woods in the direction of the whistling. "I don't think I'm in any danger. I can help."

Alaric didn't know if borreys took elves for mates. He stood beside her, facing the coming creature. The humming grew louder, and Ayda's eyes glazed. She shifted toward the trees.

"Ayda!" Alaric's voice cracked like a whip. She blinked and looked at him. "You can't be here. Run!"

"Too late," Ayda said, seeing a flicker of movement deep in the trees. She stepped back, her eyes wide.

"I can't protect you," Alaric said, desperate. "If it takes control of you. You'll fight me, too."

"I know," she said, clenching her jaw against the hum. She turned and focused on Alaric. "I can change. Can you help me change back?"

"I can help," Alaric said. The whistling was getting louder. "But you don't have time."

"Of course I do. You've restored an elf before?"

When would he have had the chance to restore an elf from a tree back to their elfin form? "No. But I understand the process."

"Understand the process?"

"You'd be doing the hard part, right? I just have to anchor you with an image to help you snap back to…"—he waved his hand at her—"…this. But you're out of time. I saw Prince Elryn change into a tree, and it took almost five minutes. The elves thought that was fast. I can't hold the borrey off that long."

Ayda looked at Alaric sharply. "You were at the Tree of Hope when Elryn changed?" The humming grew still louder, and Ayda slapped her hands over her ears. Then she squeezed her eyes shut and hummed loudly, drowning out the sound of the borrey. She reached her arms up and took a deep breath in. Closing her eyes, she breathed out. Her feet and toes lengthened, followed by her arms and fingers. Her toes wriggled down into the earth, splitting into roots digging into the dirt. Her legs and torso thickened into a trunk. Her hair flowed along her branches and burst into bright green leaves. By the end of the breath, she had transformed into a slender, silvery tree. Only her face, an oddly tree-like face, remained. It had taken mere seconds. Alaric stared at her dumbfounded.

"An elf, Keeper," she said to him, her voice barely audible. "Help me change back to an elf."

He looked blankly at her for a heartbeat. "Can elves change into anything else?"

"No," she answered, and the tree mouth twitched into a small smile as her face hardened and faded into the trunk.

There was a rustling at the edge of the clearing, and a short young man with wide-set green eyes stepped out of the trees. The creature might have been mistaken for a human except that its sandy hair did not cover the top of its ears, each of which split into two sharp points. The throbbing hum was louder now, emanating from inside the creature. The thing stopped whistling and took a deep breath, smelling the air. A wide smile spread across its face, revealing pointed teeth. Its eyes lit on Alaric, then scanned the rest of the clearing.

"Good morning," the borrey greeted him.

"Good morning," Alaric responded, leaning against the Ayda tree. In his pocket, his fingers began tracing protective runes, concentrating on the magic and trying not to be distracted by the borrey.

"Beautiful day." The creature continued speaking pleasantly even as a small crease of annoyance appeared between its eyebrows. It began walking around the clearing peering into the surrounding trees. "I thought I heard you speaking with a woman as I approached. Have you no companion?"

Alaric looked around the empty clearing. "Just me and the trees."

The borrey turned toward Alaric, its face hungry. Its eyes fell on the Ayda tree. It looked at the silver trunk with its bright green leaves, and its brow furrowed. The creature walked closer. "Do you often talk to trees?"

"Well, not all trees. Whisperwillows are silly, and oaks think too highly of themselves, but some trees are interesting."

The borrey moved within inches of the Ayda tree. Alaric continued to lean against the tree, but his fingers quickened their tracing of protective runes. The energy burned his fingertips and flowed across his blisters like scalding water. The borrey breathed in, its nose brushing the bark of the tree. Then its eyes flashed open and it drew back. Alaric pushed away from the tree quickly as the borrey shot him a look of fury from eyes that were now seething red.

"I wonder what happens to the elf if you kill the tree?" The borrey flexed its hands, and sharp claws flashed out. With a snarl, it stabbed toward the base of the trunk.

Alaric made no move, but an inch from the trunk, the claws deflected as though they'd hit an invisible wall.

"I'm afraid I can't let you do that," Alaric said. "I'm fond of this tree."

The borrey stepped back, eyeing the Keeper. "Not bad," it said, moving forward again and breathing the scent of the tree. This time, the claws flicked out, not at Ayda but straight at Alaric's gut. When they reached his shirt, they twisted to the side again.

"You cannot stop me." The borrey fixed him with a chilling look. "You cannot hurt me. I will wear you down, destroy you, and then deal with the elf."

The creature closed its eyes and took a deep breath, drawing itself up. Alaric braced himself for an attack, but the creature's eyes snapped open.

"Ahhhh," the borrey sighed, relaxing. "You are protecting more than the elf." It lifted its head and smelled again. "A human woman… young…. close."

Alaric tensed, and the borrey's lips curled into a grin.

"How will you protect the human when you are here?" Light glinted off pointed teeth as the borrey flashed a smile. Then it turned, dropping to all fours, and raced off after Milly.

EIGHTEEN

Alaric sprinted through the woods after the borrey already out of sight ahead of him. The ground kept rising and his lungs burned. He was never going to catch the creature.

Even if the others had managed to find a safe place to put Milly, what were they going to do against the borrey? Its skin looked human, but was tough as boiled leather. Douglon's axe *might* hurt it, if he could hit it. But the borrey's reflexes would outmatch the dwarf.

The other problem was that if they ran the borrey off from Milly, it could still return to Ayda. It didn't take much imagination to figure out that damaging the tree would damage Ayda.

No, the borrey would have to be chased off for good. When a borrey found itself in life-threatening danger, it transported itself back to the place of its birth, ice caves in the far north.

Unfortunately, there was a good chance that he, Brandson, and Douglon would not be able to produce that level of threat. By the time Alaric reached Bear Stronghold, he was going to be exhausted. Even if he could think of a spell to use, it was going to be hard to find the strength. He couldn't just trap the creature. They were too close to Kordan's Blight. The borrey would ultimately get free and just pick a new victim in the village. Somehow, he was going to have to generate a legitimate threat.

Early in Alaric's years at the Keepers' Stronghold, they had covered the topic of borreys. Alaric remembered how dissatisfied Keeper Gerone had been.

"Is the transport willful or instinctual?" he had asked. "We do not know. There is too much we do not know! We need to send someone to study them. But borreys never make it high enough on the list of dangers to warrant any attention.

"They are not dangerous to the public at large, but I'm afraid that for the unfortunate woman whom the borrey captures, it is always fatal.

"Borreys are rare and only mate every twelve years, but still… If you find yourself defending such a woman, my only advice for you is fire. Lots of fire."

First a dragon. Now a borrey. What was it about this group that drew exceptionally dangerous trouble?

If Douglon had managed to get a fire lit and Alaric was close enough, he could make it burn brighter. The flame Ayda had solidified into a necklace hung from his neck and glinted in the sun. This was a bad time for her to be unavailable.

Alaric swore for the hundredth time and pushed farther up the hill. He finally reached the edge of the trees. Above him, stretching out in both directions was a rocky cliff face. Sitting part-way up the cliff was a stout wall enclosing two towers. There was a narrow arch cut into the wall, and the borrey crouched in front of it. Douglon stood before the doorway, swinging his axe with Brandson off to the side.

There was no fire anywhere. Alaric ran toward the path that wound up to the Stronghold. He rounded the first turn as an enormous explosion rocked the ground, shaking the Stronghold and knocking him to his knees. Alaric's palms slammed against the ground, and his blisters burst. He gasped in pain.

An inhuman shriek of rage echoed off the rocks, and Alaric saw the silhouette of the borrey cringing back from an enormous wall of flames. Behind Brandson, a section of the Stronghold wall cracked and crashed down in a cloud of dust and rock. Alaric shoved himself back up and ran closer. The borrey was on a small ledge in front of the entrance. On either side of the ledge, the ground dropped off steeply. Douglon and Brandson had chosen a good place. The borrey howled at the wall of flame in front of him.

"What troubles you?" bellowed Douglon over the fire. "Afraid you'll burn your pretty hair?"

The borrey snarled and dropped to all fours as it paced.

That fire wouldn't last long on the rocky ledge. Once the fire powder burned up, there would be no fuel to keep it going. Already, the flames were shrinking. If Alaric could get closer, he could add more energy to the fire, make it bigger.

"Come, pretty boy," Douglon called, "come meet my axe. Do you fear a little fire? Like a common dog?"

The borrey hissed, its long claws reflecting the firelight. The flames between Douglon and the creature sank lower.

The borrey crept closer.

From the edge of the wall of fire, Brandson started throwing stones. The borrey paused to glare at him, but every stone flew wide of the creature. Douglon shouted at it again, drawing its attention back to him. The flames were shrinking quickly. In a matter of moments, the borrey would leap across them.

Brandson was still throwing rocks. The blacksmith had never looked so incompetent. The stones would not have done the borrey any real harm, but Brandson had thrown a half dozen already, and each had sailed over the creature's head, landing an arm span behind him.

"Where's your aim, boy?" Douglon shouted, taking a step back toward the wall.

Brandson swore and scrambled about for another rock.

Alaric reached the ledge behind the borrey. He started to gather some energy to add to the fire. He could see nothing living around him, though, and he himself was exhausted. He was too far from the borrey to steal any of his. He began drawing from his own energy when Brandson threw a rock in a high arc toward the Keeper.

"Alaric! Get back! The powder!" Brandson pointed to Alaric's feet.

Alaric looked down an instant before the stone landed and saw the sparkle of fire powder. He dove behind the nearest boulder.

There was a deafening explosion when Brandson's stone hit the fire powder. Alaric lay there stunned, the world strangely muffled and a dizzying pressure in his ears. He shook his head to clear it and scrambled to his knees. Leaning around the boulder, he saw an arc of flames behind the borrey trapping it in a cage of fire. Alaric's hearing began to return, and he heard the borrey scream in rage as it spun around, finding itself encircled in flame. It stepped forward, hissing and spitting at Brandson.

Tucked in behind the boulder with Alaric was a stand of brown scrub brush. It was alive, barely, but that was something. Alaric drew the *vitalle* from the scrub brush and pushed it toward the fire. His hands seared as though they were in the flames themselves, but Alaric forced himself to focus on the fire, pulling every last bit of energy from the scrub brush. The flames rose higher and brighter. Douglon and Brandson stepped back and shielded their faces.

The next moment, lines of fire powder leading in toward the borrey ignited and streams of flame shot toward it. Alaric poured all the energy he could find into the fire, his outstretched hands clenched as the pain seared through them.

The borrey turned, cringing away from the fire. It raised its head and let out a piercing shriek. One last pile of fire powder ignited right next to the borrey and it screamed again. Looking around frantically, it raised its hands to the sky and let out a howl. The flame flickered brightly for a second, then a thunderous clap reverberated through the air. Alaric felt the boom deep in his chest.

The borrey was gone.

Alaric cut off the flow of energy, and the ring of fire weakened. Through the flames, Brandson peered at him. Alaric lifted his hand slightly in a wave.

Brandson threw his arms into the air and let out a shout. Douglon bellowed something and pounded Brandson on the back.

When the flames died out, Brandson crossed over the blackened lines on the ground to clap Alaric on the shoulder.

"Don't know where the rotten beast went," Douglon said with a wicked grin, "but we sure pissed it off."

Brandson looked around. "Where did it go? Where's the rest of the powder?"

Alaric shook his head, "No need for that. You two have managed to pull off the only solution to a Borrey attack. You sent it scurrying back home, far, far away."

Brandson grinned.

"In that case, well done us." Douglon glanced at the black scorch marks then at Alaric. "Thanks for the help with the flames."

Alaric nodded. A line of pus and blood ran out from under one of his bandages. "It's a good thing the flames didn't need any more help."

Douglon looked down the slope, "Where's the elf?"

"She's… waiting down in the valley. Where's Milly?"

Brandson cleared his throat and his eyes flicked toward the tower. "Uh, she wouldn't stay inside, so…"

"We had to tie her to a post." Douglon shook his head. "For a little thing, she put up a good fight."

"She was pretty mad." Brandson pulled up his sleeve, showing long, red scratches running up to his elbow. "I guess we should go untie her," he said, not moving.

Douglon grunted and looked through the arch in the wall, not moving, either.

Alaric heaved himself up. "She'll be fine now that the borrey's gone."

Alaric followed the others into the Stronghold. The air inside the wall was thick with dust, and their feet crunched on loose rock spilled across the courtyard from the collapsed wall. A shriek and sounds of a scuffle came from inside the leftmost tower.

"Milly!" Brandson shouted as he rushed inside followed by Douglon.

Alaric dragged his feet forward after the others, trying to hurry.

A loud clang rang out. "Stay back, you... you... you..." Milly yelled.

Alaric made it to the doorway of the tower. The inside was dark and stale. Brandson and Douglon stepped inside and Alaric followed, slumping back against the wall next to the doorway. As his eyes adjusted to the gloom, he saw Milly brandishing a frying pan.

"Milly," Brandson pleaded, "we had no choice. It was for your own good."

"Tying me to a rock?" she shrieked. "In a room with a monster?"

"We saved your life," Douglon pointed out. "Where'd you find a pan?"

"The monster was outside the walls," Brandson said, his arms spread out in a placating sort of way as he inched closer to Milly. "Put down the pan. Please. It's okay. We fought it off." A little bit of pride crept into his voice.

"Outside?" she asked. Her voice rose an octave. "Outside?"

She took a long, shuddering breath, then, as though talking to children, she said, "While you two *heroes* left me tied up in here, this monster"—she waved the frying pan at a lump on the floor—"crept out of the dark and tried to kill me! If you hadn't tied such pathetic knots, I'd be dead!"

The form on the floor shifted and groaned. A hand rose and grabbed its head. Alaric could make out a beard and deep-set eyes.

There was a creak of leather as Douglon approached, holding his axe. "Get up slowly."

"Drop your axe, you meathead," the figure grumbled. "You're so slow with it, I could sit up, eat a meal, and saunter out of the tower before your blow ever fell."

Douglon's eyes narrowed. "On your feet! Now!"

The figure raised its head, wincing. It was a dwarf. With a moan, his head fell back to the floor.

"I'm afraid you'll have to kill me here, cousin. It seems I'm not quite ready to rise."

Alaric slid down the wall to sit on the floor. If he weren't so exhausted, he would laugh.

Douglon gestured to the dwarf on the floor. "Everyone, meet my cousin, Patlon."

NINETEEN

Alaric sat against the wall of the tower, exhausted. The split blisters on his palms throbbed. The more his eyes grew accustomed to the dim room, the more he could tell that Patlon must have been staying here. There was a large fireplace along the far wall with a scattering of cooking supplies near it. Milly stomped over to it and dropped the pan with a clatter, while Douglon hoisted Patlon up against one of the thick posts supporting the ceiling.

Milly took the rope out of Douglon's hands. "If you tie him up, he'll be out in no time. You can't just tangle ropes together and call it a knot."

Patlon let out a low chuckle as Milly tugged and tied the rope. "He's always been terrible at knots."

"You'd best shut your mouth, cousin," Douglon said. "You're not well thought of here."

Brandson rummaged through Patlon's cooking wares and brought a piece of thick-crusted bread to Alaric. "You look a bit worn out."

When Alaric lifted his hand to take it, Brandson's eyes widened at the bloody bandage. "Here." He tore off a piece of the loaf.

Alaric took it gratefully and sank his teeth into the bread. It was dry and coarse and possibly the most delicious thing he had ever eaten.

Brandson and Milly unwrapped Alaric's hands one at a time before rewrapping them in clean bandages. Alaric ate the last bite of bread and flexed his hands. It was going to be days before his hands were useful.

Leaving Brandson, Milly, and Douglon to watch Patlon, Alaric began the long walk back to the clearing with the Ayda tree.

When Alaric reached the tree, one thin branch brushed across the top of his head.

"It's nice to see you, too," he answered. "I didn't realize you could control your branches. I suppose it makes sense, though. The branches are sort of your fingers, aren't they?" Where sunlight trickled through the pale green leaves, her bark was glimmering silver. "What kind of tree are you?"

The tree quivered a little.

"You invented it, didn't you?"

It quivered again.

"Well, don't drop any seeds. I don't think the world is ready for a forest of Ayda-trees.

"We scared off the borrey. But then we found Patlon hiding where they stashed Milly. I don't know if I can trust the dwarves not to kill each other, so let's change you back."

Alaric reached out his hand toward the trunk but paused at the thought of putting his blistered palm on her trunk. As far as he knew, he wasn't going to contribute any energy to this process, just provide Ayda with an image of herself, something she could focus on. Still, it took some effort of will to put his aching palm on the trunk.

"All right," he said, "I've got you fixed in my mind."

He stood still for several moments, eyes closed, mind focused on an image of Ayda. When nothing happened, he glanced up. She was still a tree. A tree reaching toward the sun and swaying in the breeze with more exuberance than the others.

"Ayda! Pay attention."

The tree settled down a bit. Alaric focused on Ayda as an elf again.

No energy flowed out of his hand, but where his skin touched the trunk, the warmth of his hand leeched out, leaving his fingers ice cold. He gasped and tried to pull his hand away, but it was fixed on the tree. His fingers grew white until they were as pale as the trunk.

The coldness moved up his arm, the warmth being leeched out from deep within muscle and bone. It crept higher, and Alaric tugged on his arm with his other hand.

A branch snapped down and swatted the Keeper across the cheek. Alaric looked up at the tree, realizing that he had lost his focus.

He froze. The tree was not turning back into Ayda. Instead of resolving down into her body, the branches were stretching out farther, solidifying into a disjointed tangle of limbs, eyes, and gaping mouths. Directly above his head, a tortured face emerged out of the wood, its mouth open in a silent scream. Branches stretched out into clawed hands and twisted legs. Eyes bulged out, wide and sightless.

Alaric stared in horror until another branch stung him across the arm. Squeezing his eyes shut, he dragged his focus back onto the idea of Ayda, desperately holding an image of her as an elf in his mind. The cold seeped into his chest. He clung to the image of Ayda as his knees buckled and he dropped to the ground.

The darkness stirred sluggishly and warm hands pulled at him. He dragged his eyes open to see Ayda, once again an elf, standing over him.

"Now I know why we use elves instead of humans as our anchors," she said, her voice far away. "I almost sucked the life right out of you." She knelt down next to him.

He couldn't breathe, his body was heavy and dull, and blackness flowed into the edges of his vision. Ayda took his numb, white hand and held it close to her mouth. She breathed across his fingertips. Warmth surged up his arm like a wave. It flowed into his chest, and Alaric's lungs drew in a rush of air.

Alaric sat up as though he'd just woken up from a long sleep. His vision was clear, and every trace of exhaustion was gone. Only the burns on his hands still hurt, and even that pain was deadened. He looked up at Ayda. She was fair and glittery and normal. Or as normal as Ayda could be. "What happened?"

"I drew too much out of you," Ayda said as she sat down beside him.

"I didn't know I was contributing to the process."

"You weren't supposed to," Ayda said. "I just needed an image to grab on to."

Alaric rubbed his fingers, which were now back to their proper color. "Well, the grabbing hurt more than I thought it would."

"It shouldn't have. Sorry. I wasn't paying quite as much attention as I should have been. You see, there was a lovely sunbeam that I had caught in my upper branch, and…" She paused and smiled at Alaric's glare. "I didn't notice how hard I grabbed."

"Do you know of any other time when a human was used for an anchor? What if I hadn't been able to bring you back?" Alaric asked. "Were you just willing to live out the rest of your centuries as a tree?"

"You aren't just a human, you're a Keeper. That makes you slightly more useful. And you make it sound like it would be bad not to change back. I like being a tree." She looked exactly as she always had, with no trace of disjointed limbs or eyes.

"You were terrifying," he told her. "I thought the anchor was just a focus because trees are distractible. What were all the arms and legs and faces? I didn't know you could change into anything other than…you."

"I suppose in a way that is me, too."

She was a monster with dozens of limbs and heads? Alaric opened his mouth to ask more, but at the dark expression on Ayda's face, he paused.

"Now," she said briskly, "it is easy to get distracted as a tree, but did you mention Patlon?"

Alaric groaned and stood. "Oh, I almost forgot. He was making camp inside the Stronghold. I'll be amazed if they haven't killed each other yet."

They started across the clearing.

"You seemed surprised that I was at Prince Elryn's changing," Alaric said. "It was during my years at court, so I attended with Queen Saren. I don't remember meeting you there, but there were a lot of elves."

Ayda continued walking for a moment before answering. "I wasn't there."

"Really? Were there many absent?"

She shook her head. "Only one."

"Where were you?"

She ignored the question. "You understand what the ceremony meant?"

"It named Elryn heir to the elven throne. Sometime you need to sit down with me and explain the elven royal family tree. The Keepers are always annoyed that we can't pin down exactly how you are all related, and no elves ever explain it. But Elryn is King Andolin's eldest son, right? Isn't it your custom for the eldest child to be the next ruler?"

Ayda laughed, "The custom is not mine, but it is what my people do. We aren't as bound by the idea of inheriting the throne as you humans are, but more often than not, the crown is accepted by the eldest child." She shrugged. "I had a role to play in the ceremony that I wasn't interested in. So I left and let someone else do it."

Alaric snorted. Elves didn't shirk responsibilities. Whether it was because of a sense of communal consciousness or just a cultural trait, they accepted their roles in elven society without complaint. True, there was little structure to the elven culture, but Alaric had never heard of one refusing to do what was asked of them.

"Ayda, sometimes when you talk, you sound more human than elf."

"That's what my father said. He blamed it on my mother."

Alaric looked at her in surprise. "Was she human?"

Ayda's peal of laughter rang through the trees. "Do I look like my mother was a human? You're a Keeper, so you must have heard of Ayala."

Alaric stopped. "Queen Ayala was your mother?"

Ayda nodded and stopped as well. She turned toward him and smiled a patient little smile.

"If she's your… then you…"

Ayda nodded encouragingly.

"Princess Aydalya?" he asked in amazement.

"At your service," she curtsied. "I am Aydalya, daughter of Queen Ayala. First born of King Andolin, elder half-sister to the crowned Prince Elryn."

"Elder!" He stared at her for a long moment. "You should have been named heir!"

"That was the role I didn't want."

TWENTY

rincess Aydalya? Not only had he found an elf, he'd found the only living elf princess. What was Princess Aydalya doing wandering around the northern edges of the kingdom with a bunch of treasure hunters?

"My brother was the better choice for heir," she continued. "His mind was built for ruling and planning and listening." Ayda reached up and touched a leaf. "Mine is… less steadfast."

"More human?"

Ayda laughed again, "That's what my father would say."

"So, your mother was captured by goblins and rescued by the human, Boman. She then lived with him for the rest of his life."

"For forty years, yes," Ayda said. "When she returned to the forest, she had developed some human-like tendencies. When she married my father, he said she proved that humanness was contagious. When I was born, he decided it was also hereditary." She looked ahead to where the forest still blocked their view of the caves. "May we continue now, Keeper?"

Alaric fell into step beside her again. She was Princess Aydalya. Even traveling with Queen Saren to the elves, he had barely received more than a nod from King Andolin. Elves just weren't interested in humans. A few elves had been assigned the job of making the human visitors comfortable, and they had been polite but distant. His mind swirled with questions for her.

"So was that when you left your people? The day of the ceremony?" It was hardly the most important question, but he needed somewhere to start.

"No. I went to the southern edge of the Greenwood for that day only. Once the ceremony was finished, I returned." She was silent a long moment. "I thought I had ended any plans my father had for me."

"He had another?"

Ayda's face shadowed again. "He didn't plan it, but he still forced me into a terrible fate."

"More terrible than becoming queen?" Alaric asked wryly.

Ayda took a deep breath, and the trees around them stilled. Alaric glanced around uneasily.

"More terrible than you can imagine," she answered.

The moment passed, and the forest breathed again.

They walked in silence for several minutes. Alaric kept a watch on her from the corner of his eye. It was unnerving that she walked so somberly beside him. His mind still shot out question after question. She was an elven princess who had first refused the throne, then left her people. Each of those facts alone demanded a long explanation, but she was walking so pensively, he couldn't bring himself to ask.

"The elves thought that Elryn had changed into a tree very quickly," he said, looking for a new subject, "but it took him several minutes."

A smile cracked her somberness.

When she didn't comment, he continued, "They said Elryn was faster than any elf they had ever seen."

"It drove him mad!" she said, bursting into laughter. "He had praise heaped upon him for how fast he could change, and the whole time, he knew what I could do. When we were children, we used to race. If you can call it a race."

"He never told anyone?"

She shook her head. "It wasn't his secret to tell. Until today, no one else has seen me change."

"How do you do it? Are you some sort of... elf prodigy?"

Ayda's laughter rang off the nearby trees. "Hardly. I've always been mediocre at everything. Except changing. And I don't know why I'm so fast at that. Elryn says he has to coax his body into changing shape. For me, it's like stretching. At any given moment, I think my body would rather be a tree."

"You're good at that freeze-the-fire trick," Alaric motioned to the flame that still hung around his neck.

Ayda's smile faded from her face. "That's a more recent skill."

"I've never seen anything like it."

She sighed. "Neither had I."

"What is it?" Alaric raised the flame toward her. "Is it flame or stone?"

"It's a flame still. Well, it has the potential to be a flame still. Or maybe the longing to be a flame."

"Can you turn it back into a flame?"

Ayda's eyes widened. "Oh, you don't want that. The potential it has keeps building up in it. I changed one back, once. It had only been still for a few minutes, but when I changed it back, it quickly grew to several times bigger than it had been. The one you have has been still for so long, it would be huge if I changed it back."

Alaric held the flame as far away from him as the necklace would allow. "Is it going to happen on its own?"

Ayda laughed. "No, it takes some very specific manipulating to coax it back into a flame. It couldn't do it on its own."

She turned away from him and continued walking. Alaric cast out toward the flame to see if he could detect any energy, but it was completely dormant. He let the flame fall back down onto his chest, hoping he wasn't carrying around some sort of bomb.

"What do you want Kordan's treasure for?" Ayda motioned to the pouch hanging beneath Alaric's robe. "It has to do with Evangeline, doesn't it? Can it raise the dead?"

Alaric grabbed the pouch, protecting it against his chest. "Evangeline's not dead!"

Ayda raised an eyebrow. "She's not really alive, though, is she?"

Alaric pulled the pouch out of his shirt and loosened it. He dropped the warm, swirling ruby out into his hand. "Still alive," he answered, "but still sick."

Ayda's eyes widened. She leaned toward the Reservoir Stone but made no move to touch it.

The light filled his palm, casting red light over his hand and Ayda's face. There was a pulse to the swirling, like a heartbeat. Alaric let his eyes follow the currents diving and dancing from one irregular surface to another for a moment. It was several breaths before the dark line surfaced. It stretched out longer than before. Alaric clenched the ruby in his hand before returning it to his pouch.

"Kordan's treasure is a Wellstone that holds the antidote I need to heal her."

"What will you do with the ruby?" Ayda asked.

"Wake her up." He shook his head.

"Do you know how?"

"I understand the process."

Ayda let out a short laugh. "That worked out well for you last time. Maybe I should be there in case you almost die again."

Alaric scowled and walked faster.

"The real question is," Ayda continued, "why did the wizard steal the Wellstone? I doubt he has a wife in a crystal box."

"Stay out of my head!" Alaric snapped.

She skipped a little to keep up. "You think about Evangeline constantly."

Alaric stopped.

Ayda stopped, too. "I don't try to listen, you know, but sometimes you shout your thoughts at me. And your thoughts of Evangeline are usually so sad. Although sometimes they're sweet. Like this." Ayda reached out and touched Alaric's arm.

Alaric stood in the Napon market. The southern sun poured down on the awnings slung between booths, lighting the stalls in hues of reds and yellows. It was still too deep in summer, too stiflingly hot, for there to be many shoppers. The few vendors that bothered to open booths today called out lazily in deep, southern accents.

Alaric set down another bottle of ink. Just a dark bluish black, like the others. The vendor called after him, dropping the price as he walked away, but Alaric gave him a smile and moved on. In the corner of the next booth sat a mismatched collection of little glass bottles filled with inks. Alaric held several up to the light to see their color. Behind him, he heard Evangeline ask a question.

"Six coppers," the vendor said. "Six coppers for the pretty flower bowl."

"Six?" Evangeline laughed. "Two coppers for the pretty flower bowl."

She was holding a small, clay bowl. The red clay formed an almost round bowl with a blue and yellow flower painted on the inside. It was a happy bowl, if not a high quality one. Two coppers was generous.

The vendor shook his head. "Six coppers. Flower bowls are six coppers."

Alaric turned back to the inks, hoping to find a red.

"Four coppers?" Evangeline's voice was less certain now.

"Six." The vendor's voice was firm.

The last bottle Alaric held up to the light was dark blue. Red ink was too rare to find in a naponese tourist market, but it never hurt to check.

He turned to find Evangeline behind him, smiling and holding the bowl. The pottery vendor flashed him a big smile, and Alaric put his arm around Evangeline's shoulder as they walked away. Her shoulders quivered with little laughs.

"You bought it?" The bowl was not even close to being round.

She looked up at him ruefully. "He wouldn't change his price."

Alaric laughed. "He didn't need to."

"I know," she laughed, "but shouldn't he have at least pretended to bargain with me?"

"He bargained very well." Alaric held his hand out for the bowl. "I think you're the one who didn't really bargain."

She laughed and gave it to him. "It didn't quite go as I had planned."

"Why didn't you walk away?"

"Because I like the bowl," she said, considering the colors painted on it. "The flower reminds me of the sky and sunshine."

Alaric held the bowl out in front of them and squinted at it. "Well, I do see blue and yellow. What exactly does the brownish red clay remind you of?"

"Someday," she said, taking it back and admiring it, "it will remind me of a naponese market I visited with you. It will remind me how great Keepers are always rummaging through the things around them, looking for what they need—whether it's knowledge or red ink. And it will remind me that maybe sometimes, it is better to stop rummaging and just ask someone." With a flourish, she produced a small glass bottle.

Alaric reached for it in astonishment. He held it up toward a ray of sunlight trickling through the fabric above them. The ink inside glowed like dark red wine. "This is perfect!"

"You can repay me at dinner tonight. When they request a story from you, tell Tomkin and the Dragon. I love that one."

"I will." Alaric kissed the top of her head. "I have the best wife."

"Yes, you do."

He glanced at her out of the corner of his eye. "Do I want to know how much you paid for this?" She grinned. "No, you do not."

"I like that memory," Ayda said. "You two are so happy."

Alaric yanked his hand away from Ayda. "Stay out of my head!"

Ayda resumed walking. "Keep your thoughts to yourself."

Alaric followed her, off guard. It was his own memory she had shown him. He was partly furious that she knew it, partly heartbroken because he and Evangeline had been happy. He watched Ayda walk ahead of him, settling on an emotion somewhere near irritation. "Can you read everyone's mind as easily as you read mine?"

Ayda crinkled her brow. "No, yours is the clearest. Maybe because it's more… open? You could read my mind if you wanted, couldn't you?"

"I could try."

"Maybe that's why, then. You've trained your mind to reach outside of itself, so to me, it's open."

"Wasn't Gustav's mind open?"

Ayda cringed. "No." She paused. "Maybe that's why I never thought he was a wizard. Even Brandson and Douglon occasionally shout their thoughts when they're excited, but Gustav was always shut tight. I assumed he was just incredibly boring."

Alaric wished he knew how Gustav had done that. Add that to the list of questions he had for the wizard.

"Maybe he wants the Wellstone for a different reason than you do." Ayda said. "What else is in it?"

"Records of Kordan's work. He worked with seeds and…" Alaric reached for the ruby again, "he created a stone like this one. An emerald."

"Maybe the wizard is after that knowledge. Maybe he needs to bring someone back from the brink of death, like you do."

"Who would a Shade Seeker want to wake?"

Ayda stopped walking and spun toward Alaric.

Her eyes burned and her hair darkened until it was the deep red of a glowing coal. Waves of heat radiated from her, pushing Alaric back a step.

Her hair lifted, blown by a wind Alaric couldn't feel, and sparks whipped out from the ends. She clenched her fists, and Alaric took another step back.

When she spoke, it was in a deadly whisper that shook the ground beneath his feet.

"He's going to wake Mallon."

Her hair lifted, blown by a wind Alaric couldn't feel and sparks whipped out from the ends. She clenched her fists and Alaric took another step back.

TWENTY-ONE

Alaric stared at Ayda and took yet another step back. She seethed with fury, her eyes glinting with cold light.

Wake Mallon?

Mallon was dead.

Ayda reached down, picked up a stick, and stared hard at it. She muttered angrily and began stalking up the hill.

Alaric followed behind her, a fear stealing over him that he hadn't felt in years. Was it possible that Mallon was still alive? He had disappeared and all signs of his power had ended. What could cause that aside from death?

He opened his mouth twice to ask her a question, any of the questions he had, but each time, she shot him such a glare that he shut his mouth again.

The stick in her hand shifted until it was a perfect likeness of Gustav's face and pointy hat, with a distinctly idiotic expression.

She hissed a vicious-sounding word and crushed the visage into her palm sending an explosion of splinters out from her tiny white hand.

Alaric hung back a moment, letting her move up the hill away from him. He stared at the settling shards of wood then watched the elf warily as she continued toward the Stronghold.

Ayda stopped and turned to wait for Alaric. He approached her with every sense alert, waiting for something terrifying to happen, but her hair was golden again and the fury had settled to the back of her eyes.

"I'm going to kill him."

"Oh." Gustav or Mallon?

Ayda looked straight into Alaric's eyes, and he braced himself for… something. But she just smiled a humorless smile.

"I like you, Alaric." She gave an elfish lilt to his name that caught his attention. It was the first time she had ever spoken his name. With that word, something changed. The glow that surrounded Ayda faded slightly, and she looked more concrete, more solid.

"I'm going to kill that idiot wizard before he can wake Mallon. You can come with me, if you'd like." Ayda turned and headed toward the Stronghold. "Bring whomever you'd like along," she tossed over her shoulder.

When they reached the others, the smell of roasting meat drifted out of the Stronghold along with echoes of laughter.

"So much for killing each other," Alaric said as they walked in.

"She dragged King Horgoth out," Patlon was saying, sitting next to the others by the fire, "by his beard!"

Douglon howled with laughter and pounded on the floor. Brandson was doubled over, and Milly wiped her eyes.

"Did he marry her?" Milly asked.

Patlon nodded. "That evening."

Alaric cleared his throat, and Douglon waved him over.

"Patlon, this is Keeper Alaric. He's been traveling with us."

Patlon nodded his head in greeting.

"And the elf is Ayda."

Patlon smiled at her. "My axe was blessed by an elf," Patlon said, lifting up his purple-shafted axe for Ayda to see. "Do you know any purple-haired elves?"

"Pella's hair was purple once," Ayda said, walking over to run her fingers along the purple wood. "It changed with the seasons."

"Her blessing did something to the wood, and it's near unbreakable. Do you—" Patlon paused. "Do you think she'd remember me? It was many years ago."

Ayda looked at the axe for a long moment. "She remembers you. Elves don't forget."

Patlon sat up straighter, throwing a smug look at Douglon.

Ayda turned back to Douglon. "Speaking of not forgetting, aren't we very angry with Patlon? I vividly remember a burned smithy."

"He's offered to rebuild it," Brandson said. "Twice as big and closer to the river." The blacksmith grinned. "And he's going to give me enough dwarfish rock steel to make five knives."

"One of which I get back," Patlon added. "I didn't mean to burn it down. I've been here for several weeks, hunting about near these rocks, but I just recently learned that Douglon was here. I went to confront him at the smithy, but I upended a bucket of ashes, and before I knew it, the whole place was ablaze."

"And so you stopped to carve a threatening symbol on a rock for us to find?" Alaric said.

"I had made it already," Patlon hedged, "and the damage was done. I figured I could at least make Douglon mad."

Douglon waved off the apologetic look from his cousin. "The rockslide has settled, cousin. No worries."

"You haven't told me if you've had any luck with the treasure, though," Patlon said.

Douglon leaned forward. "We found it."

Patlon looked eagerly at the others for confirmation.

"We almost found it," Brandson said. "But it was stolen by someone we were searching with."

"You found the treasure, then someone you trusted stole it?" Patlon asked Douglon, deadpan. "How dreadful for you."

Douglon glared at him. "It was stolen by a powerful wizard."

Alaric raised his eyebrow. That was more credit than Douglon had ever given Gustav.

"Then let's go find him!" Patlon rose and hefted his purple axe. "Where would he go to sell it around here?"

"We are not going to find him by wandering aimlessly," Alaric broke in. "He's a Shade Seeker."

Patlon looked around quickly. "You forgot to mention that."

"Well," Douglon said, "If you knew him, you'd forget, too. He's sort of bumbly."

"I think it's safe to say that the bumbling was an act," Alaric said.

"I don't know," Brandson said. "He lived with us for months. It was very convincing."

"The only non-bumbly thing he did was steal the gem out from under us." Douglon said.

"And sic his dragon on us," Ayda said.

"He has a dragon?" Patlon asked, dropping back down onto the floor.

"And he's not going to sell the gem," Alaric said. "He took it for a specific reason."

Everyone turned toward him except Ayda. She turned her back on them and looked out the door.

"Ayda thinks he took it to raise Mallon," Alaric said.

The room went perfectly still.

"Mallon?" said Milly faintly.

"He stole a gem to raise the Rivor from the dead?" Douglon looked at Alaric as though he was joking. "Is he going to buy him back from the underworld?"

Patlon chuckled. "I didn't realize the dead were for sale."

"He's not dead," Ayda said, still facing the door, her back stiff.

"Of course he's dead," scoffed Patlon. "Even the dwarves know the story of how he strode into the Greenwood to conquer you but your people destroyed him."

Ayda turned slowly from the wall and passed her gaze over each of them, ending with Patlon. Each one of them drew back at her expression. When she looked at Patlon, he wilted.

"I was there when he was bound," she continued, walking to Patlon and towering over him. Her face grew dark, and she seemed to stretch taller. "He is not dead," she ended with a whisper.

No one breathed for a moment.

"Bound?" Alaric asked, finally.

Ayda turned away from Patlon. "For lack of a better word. The Rivor can't be killed or trapped like a mortal. He's only connected loosely to his physical body. Not enough of him inhabits his body for hurting it to cause him any real harm."

The others exchanged puzzled looks.

"How did your people bind him?" Alaric asked.

"We made a net to catch him and drew it close around his body. Then we froze him there."

"In ice?" Patlon asked.

Ayda gave a short laugh. "No, it's not like he's stuck in a crystal box."

Alaric scowled at her.

"It's almost impossible to stop a will that strong, but we set his mind on a path that leads back to itself. He is fighting to get out, but the route he is taking is circular. The hope is that he cannot escape."

"So that is why all of his spells ended?" Alaric said. "Because his will is confined to himself now?"

Ayda nodded. "He could spread his will far from himself. He could attach it to a person and leave part of it there. It took my people a long time to figure out what he was doing. It was Prince

Elryn who first detached one of Mallon's spells from someone.

"The spell needed somewhere to go, though, so it attached itself to Elryn. He was able to destroy it by transforming into a tree. This is where we got the idea of how to defeat him. We realized that if we could collect all of the spells and destroy them at once, there would be nothing left of Mallon outside of his own body. He would be mortal.

"That is when I began to travel," Ayda continued. "I visited every town I could find and marked any cursed people I found."

"Marked?" asked Douglon.

"In a way another elf could find, yes. I was returning from the far south, but not yet home when the elves began. It was earlier than planned, but there was no doubt. I could feel elves, hundreds of them, stretching out toward the marked ones." She looked far away and fell silent.

"Did it work?" Milly asked timidly.

Ayda blinked and looked around.

"Yes, but the Rivor arrived too soon, and the battle began before they had destroyed all the spells. Mallon was gravely wounded… but at a terrible price." Ayda turned back toward the wall. "All of my people were lost."

"No!" Milly said.

Alaric listened, stunned. All of the elves were dead?

The room was silent.

Ayda sighed. "I was too late. When I got to my people, they had taken Mallon's power onto themselves, but it was too much. My people were dead, and Mallon was senseless, but alive. I tried to kill him, but nothing I could do harmed his body. He was trapped, but not defeated."

She took a deep breath and looked around. "I carried his body to the Elder Grove, an ancient place. It is surrounded by the oldest trees in the forest, which will let none but elves enter. It took a bit of convincing for the trees to let me take him there." Ayda smiled sadly. "I left him there, secure in their deep magic, in the hopes of discovering a way to kill him."

Alaric realized he had been holding his breath and let it out. This was why no elves had been found in eight years. It wasn't that they were being secretive. Ayda was the only one left to be found.

TWENTY-TWO

A great loss swept through Alaric. He knew there had never been many elves in the Greenwood, but he couldn't believe all but Ayda were gone.

Patlon frowned. "You know, I had discounted them as rumors, but we've heard news that nomadic tribes have been gathering in the Scales."

Alaric turned sharply. "Do nomads usually come into the Scale Mountains?"

"The last time was eight years ago when they joined with Mallon. I think those rumors need some investigating." Patlon slapped Douglon on the shoulder. "Cousin, you'll have to chase the single, solitary, old man by yourself. I need to go face hordes of vicious nomads."

Alaric nodded. "Tell King Horgoth to tell Queen Saren what the dwarves know."

Patlon raised an eyebrow. "I can't tell the High Dwarf what to do."

"Well, tell him I told you to," Douglon grumbled. "Tell him to get off that ugly throne and start doing something useful."

Alaric raised an eyebrow at Douglon's brashness.

Patlon winced. "It won't be any better coming from you. In fact, it would be a lot worse. It's going to take me a little time to smooth things over between you and Horgoth."

"Smooth what over?"

"Your banishment," Patlon said apologetically.

"My *what*?"

"Well, I might have mentioned to Horgoth that you stole the map from me."

"How does that get me banished?"

"He thought that we had intended to bring him the treasure. He decided that you had stolen the map so you could keep the gem from him, and I couldn't correct him without saying that neither of us had ever considered giving it to him."

"Why would we?"

"Exactly! Since when do we drop all the treasure we find off with him? Did we give him the gold from that crown?"

"Or the barrels of whiskey from the monastery?" Douglon added.

"Don't worry, cousin," Patlon said. "I'll smooth things over with him. It will be taken care of long before you get back there."

"What will happen to you if it's not smoothed over?" Brandson asked Douglon.

"Jail," Douglon said.

"Well," Patlon tugged nervously at his beard. "Actually, he would be executed."

"You said banished," Douglon said in a low voice.

"Did I?"

"But execution isn't the penalty for breaking a banishment. It's the penalty for treason."

"I didn't mean for him to leap to treason," Patlon said, holding his hands out to keep Douglon back. "But somehow, Horgoth convinced himself that you were collecting wealth so that you could set yourself up as High Dwarf."

"What?" Douglon shouted. "You got me banished by convincing Horgoth that I wanted to be king? And he *believed* you?"

"I didn't do anything! You know how he is," Patlon said, inching backward. "He's always been a little insecure about your claim to the throne."

"Douglon has a claim to the throne?" Brandson asked.

"It's nothing," Douglon tossed the words at Brandson and turned back to Patlon.

"Sort of," Patlon said, leaning around his fuming cousin to look at Brandson. "Douglon's grandfather was the twin brother of King Horgoth's grandfather. There's this interesting story that draws into question which twin was actually born first. Douglon's grandfather had six toes on one foot, and one midwife claims—"

"Enough!" roared Douglon. "I do not want to be king. Neither did my grandfather. I hope Horgoth has a litter of sons so that their family line is indestructible. I would chop off my beard and live with an elf before I would submit to sitting day in and day out on that ugly throne. I cannot believe Horgoth believed you!" Douglon looked plaintively at his cousin. "He really charged me with treason?"

Patlon winced. "In front of a full court."

Douglon dropped his head into his hands. Then he looked back at his cousin. "And how exactly are you going to smooth this over?"

Patlon began tugging at his beard again. "I'm going to have to tell him it turns out you were just waylaid and you're on your way to bring it to him now."

"I'm not giving that treasure to my addle-headed cousin! Even if it were mine to give."

"If you can think of another idea," Patlon said, "let me know."

"King Horgoth dislikes wizards, doesn't he?" Alaric asked.

"Hates 'em," Patlon said.

"Tell him the treasure belonged to a wizard and Douglon was bewitched."

"Ooh! That's good! Then you're innocent, Douglon!"

"And Horgoth will never want the treasure," Douglon said, nodding at Alaric.

"Good, because he can't have it," Alaric said. "I need it."

"You?" Patlon asked.

"It's a Keeper's Wellstone, and I'm a Keeper." The claim rolled off his tongue almost easily.

"I keep forgetting that Kordan was a Keeper," Douglon said. "He seemed so evil."

"Did you hear that from anyone besides Gustav?" Alaric asked.

Douglon narrowed his eyes.

"No," Ayda answered for him.

"Kordan was a Keeper," Alaric said. "I have read the records of his work. He wasn't evil. There was an accident while Kordan was performing some magic, and a boy died, despite Kordan's efforts to save him."

Ayda leaned toward Douglon and whispered loudly, "Kordan sounds diabolical."

"Shut up," the dwarf said. He turned to Alaric. "What do you need the Wellstone for?"

Alaric almost gave a generic answer about Keepers loving knowledge. But as he reached for the pouch at his neck, he realized that he *wanted* to tell them about Evangeline.

As the silence dragged on, the faces of his companions grew concerned. Looking from face to face, something loosened inside of him and he began to talk. He told them of meeting Evangeline, marrying her, of the stupid accident when she had been poisoned, about how he had searched and searched for an antidote and finally had real hope that it was held in Kordan's Wellstone.

There was silence for a long moment.

"Oh, Alaric," Milly said quietly.

"I didn't realize Keepers married," Brandson said.

Milly smacked him in the arm. "What Brandson *means* is that is terrible and we will do everything we can to get the stone back."

"Not many Keepers marry," Alaric said. "Most spend too much time stuck in the Stronghold or libraries to meet anyone. But it happens occasionally."

"Do you think Gustav knew Kordan was a Keeper?" Brandson asked.

"I'm sure of it, if he knew about the Wellstone," Alaric said. "Although I don't know where he heard about it."

Patlon looked at them all curiously. "What story did Gustav tell you about Kordan to get you all to look for the treasure?"

"Douglon was the one looking for the gem," Brandson explained. "Gustav was already at my house when Douglon showed up."

Patlon tilted his head in confusion. "But Gustav's been looking for it since last summer." He stopped and snapped his mouth shut.

"You're getting old, cousin," Douglon said dangerously. "Brandson didn't meet Gustav until last winter. How do you know that Gustav was looking for the treasure before that?"

"You knew Gustav," Alaric said.

"'*Knew him*' is a little strong," Patlon began.

Douglon growled.

"I met Gustav last summer while I was hunting," Patlon said quickly. "He was sneaking along a game trail, and I almost shot him. We got to talking, and he told me he had found a cave the night before with veins of silver in the walls. He'd scraped some off for his potions but had no need of the rest of it. He gave me directions to it and said he was seeking a different sort of treasure. He had heard rumors of a valley with no beginning and no end. It was said to hold both treasure and magical objects."

"He told you about the valley where we found the map?" Douglon asked. "And you never told me?"

"I was going to, but when I followed the old man's directions to his cave with 'huge veins of silver', all I found was one streak so thin it was barely visible. I had spent my whole hunting day on a wild goose chase." Patlon's scowl turned a little sheepish as he looked at Douglon. "I didn't feel like telling you I'd been duped. Then when we really did find the valley, it seemed too late..."

"You never saw Gustav again?" Alaric broke in before Douglon could answer.

Patlon shook his head again, then paused. "Now that you ask... maybe." He tugged absently on his beard. "After you ran off with the map, Douglon, I stopped by the tavern at the river crossing and had a drink. Partway through the evening, an old man came in and sat near me. Hulgrat and Swenrich were there, and"—he glanced at Douglon—"I may have been telling them about what you did."

Douglon growled again.

"You stole from me!" Patlon exclaimed.

"The old man?" Alaric reminded him.

"Yes, well there was something familiar about him, but I couldn't seem to look at him clearly enough to figure out what. He just sat nearby, and I had the impression he was listening. Then at one point, I looked over and he was gone. I honestly haven't thought about him again until right now. But now that I think about it, he did remind me of Gustav."

"It was him," Alaric said. "Shade Seekers have a way of affecting what people focus on. They call it influence. Gustav could have manipulated you until you didn't care enough about him to pay attention."

"Then he knew I had the map," Douglon said, "months before I ever met him."

Alaric nodded absently, struck by an idea. Influence. Gustav used influence. The questions that had been fluttering through his mind since he met this group settled. Answer after answer burst into light.

"If Gustav is skilled at influence, that explains everything." Every single thing. "It's easy to make people not notice someone they weren't looking for in the first place, like an old man in a tavern, but I think Gustav's influence may range far past that.

"I think Gustav is the reason you are all together," Alaric said. "If he had tracked Douglon near Kordan's Blight, Gustav could have used influence to draw Douglon to him."

"No one drew me," Douglon objected.

"If Gustav was good at it, you would have thought it was your own choices that guided you," Alaric said. He gestured to Milly, "It's similar to the magic the borrey used."

"That doesn't explain why Ayda is here," Brandson pointed out.

"They both came to you at about the same time, right?" Alaric asked. "Then it makes sense. An influence spell to draw someone isn't one that Keepers use, but I understand the concept." He ignored Ayda's snort. "You can draw a specific person if you know a great deal about them. The better you know them, the more specific to an individual the spell will be, but it will work over a smaller distance.

"Gustav knew little about Douglon. Just that he was a dwarf, really, but since Douglon's probably the only dwarf within two days' walk, Gustav could afford to be vague. Since he didn't know how close Douglon was, he would have wanted to make the spell as general as possible. I'm guessing he drew any intelligent, non-human. That would bring Ayda as well."

"You might be right," Ayda said. "I hadn't planned on going to Kordan's Blight, but I never thought much about it. I have a hard time paying attention to things sometimes."

Douglon rolled his eyes. "Sometimes?"

"And it explains why I just couldn't focus on him. Ever," Ayda said. "I thought he was just boring, but I could barely look at him."

"I'm sure he knew you would notice too much about him if you did," Alaric said.

An irritated line creased her brow. "That's why I don't know what color he is, why I didn't ask how the dragon knew him, why I never wondered about the wizard at all."

"So Gustav kept drawing Ayda back whenever she left?" Brandson asked.

Alaric groaned. How had he not seen any of this? That's what Gustav had been doing in the woods when Ayda had wanted to leave. It wasn't Brandson that had convinced her to stay at all.

Gustav had used his influence. "I thought elves were hard to influence," he said to Ayda.

She winced. "That's another thing my father said was human about me. I'm easy to fool."

Milly looked at Ayda, her brows drawn together. "Why would he keep drawing Ayda back? He needed Douglon's map, but what did he need Ayda for?"

Alaric looked at Ayda. Why did Gustav want her there?

Ayda shrugged. "Maybe he just liked me."

"That can't be it." Douglon shook his head. "He must have had some other crazy reason."

Ayda ignored him and looked to Alaric for an answer.

"I'm not sure," he said. "Maybe it was because you have such unusual powers." Alaric certainly felt better knowing where Ayda was. Maybe Gustav had noticed the same sort of thing; the idea that Ayda had the potential for something extraordinary. Or devastating.

"So if Gustav was just after the treasure," Brandson said, "why not just steal Douglon's map?"

"He couldn't read it," Alaric said. "The runes on that map are complicated. To anyone other than a Keeper, they would say the gibberish Gustav read. Shade Seekers study runes, but not to the extent Keepers do. I'm not sure anyone studies ancient runes the way Keepers do."

"Which means," Ayda said, "not only did Gustav draw the map to him, but he also drew one of the only people on earth who can read it." She smiled sweetly. "I think it's reasonable to think that Gustav drew you as well."

Alaric snorted. That old wizard hadn't drawn him. He had already been seeking information about Kordan. His own journey had brought him here.

Except here was finally an explanation for the ridiculous coincidence of finding this exact group. Gustav had drawn them together. And it explained the slight fuzziness Alaric had felt the whole time they were together. It was Gustav, subtly controlling everyone's decisions for his own gain. Alaric had never heard of anyone using influence so subtly.

"A troubling idea," he said. "Gustav seems to use influence as a kind of net, sending out ideas of what he wants and then drawing in whatever it catches. What's even more troubling is that it still might be working. Borreys are ridiculously rare. What are the chances that we would stumble across one right when we decide to follow Gustav?"

"Do you think Gustav's still around then?" Milly asked.

"I don't know why he would be," Alaric said, "but he could have set things in motion before he left. It's still a big coincidence, but every other coincidence so far has been Gustav's doing."

"Well," Brandson said, "there's one thing Gustav didn't plan. In attempting to collect a team to find his treasure, he's also brought together the perfect group to stop him—dwarves who know what the nomads are doing, a Keeper who knows about the Wellstone, and an elf who knows where Mallon's body is."

Alaric looked around the group as they all nodded.

"So where do we find Gustav?" Brandson asked.

Alaric felt the pressure as one gaze after another turned toward him. It would have been nice if he had an answer.

TWENTY-THREE

Alaric looked around the group. "We're not on a treasure hunt in the safety of these hills any longer," he began.

"Yeah, nothing dangerous here…" Douglon muttered to Ayda.

Alaric ignored him. "Since Gustav is a Shade Seeker, he is most likely headed to Sidion."

At this, Milly paled and Brandson shifted.

"Do you know where it is?" Brandson asked.

Alaric nodded. "I haven't been to the Shade Seekers' Keep itself, but I've been close enough to know where it is. Douglon probably does too."

The dwarf nodded.

"It's not an easy place to get into." Alaric looked at Milly. "We need to go through Kordan's Blight and get horses. We'll drop you off at your home. Now that things are settled with Patlon, you'll be in no danger."

"Home?" Milly asked, one eyebrow rising. "You're not sending me home."

"I suppose I can't convince you to stay home, either, Brandson?" Alaric asked.

Brandson leveled a steely gaze at the Keeper. "Mallon killed my parents. I'm not going to just sit by and let Gustav bring him back."

"We may not be great wizards or powerful warriors," Milly said, "but we aren't just going to go sit at home while you all go off to stop Gustav. A lot of regular people like us are going to suffer if Mallon is raised. It's only fair that we should get to help stop him. You don't have to be some great hero to contribute something good, you know."

Brandson and Milly were sitting, chins raised, daring the others to disagree. Alaric nodded to them. "All right then. Does anyone have any ingenious ideas on how to stop him besides chasing him across the country? I think we have to assume he has the cooperation of his dragon, so he'll be moving a lot faster than we will on horses."

"Could you draw Gustav back here the way he drew everyone?" Milly asked.

Alaric shook his head. "An influence spell can prod someone in the direction that you want them to go, but once they realize it's happening, it's worthless. I don't think I could fool Gustav into thinking he wanted to come back and find us."

"Can you do something else magical?" Brandson asked. "Grab him and bring him here or make some sort of glowing trail to find him?"

"It doesn't work that way. Magic is pretty limited. Everything living has energy. Magic involves redirecting that energy. To do that, it has to travel through me. But it's like heat—a little is okay, too much burns." He held up his bandaged palms.

"But Keepers in the past have done amazing things," Milly said. "What about when Chesavia fought the water demon?"

"Chesavia was killed by the water demon," Brandson pointed out.

"Actually, she wasn't," Alaric said. "Keeper Chesavia died because she used too much magic. The demon was strong, too strong to be destroyed without Chesavia using more energy than she could manage. She knew it. She chose to continue past what her body could handle. She defeated the demon, but it cost her her life.

"Keepers aren't great wizards or powerful warriors, either. Chesavia was one of the few who single-handedly saved the day."

"Then what good are they?" Douglon asked.

"We work more with knowledge than magic. We spend a lot of time watching for trouble, searching out the truth if we find the rumor of any. Then we try to assemble the people that could do something about it and provide them with the knowledge they need."

"Well, that is perfect," Brandson said, rubbing his hands together. "We've definitely found trouble, and the group's assembled. Provide us with knowledge."

Alaric laughed and Douglon spread a map of Queensland out on the floor. At the top, in tiny detail, rose the Wolfsbane Mountains. The great river snaked south from them until it flowed off the southern end of the map. The Scale Mountains ran down the western edge, and the Marsham Cliffs lined the eastern side.

Patlon pointed out the location where the nomads were rumored to be gathering to Douglon.

"That's a huge valley," Douglon told Alaric. "It's well supplied with water. A large force could gather there."

"How many are there?" Alaric asked.

"No idea," Patlon said. "It's all just rumors."

"Isn't that near the entrance of Duncave? Haven't the dwarves bothered to see what's going on right above their heads?" Alaric asked.

Patlon shrugged. "Humans are always wandering around on the surface. It's hard to keep track of them."

"You need to convince King Horgoth that he needs to," Alaric said. "Queen Saren needs to know if there's an army on her border. Douglon, where did you and Patlon find that valley with Kordan's tower and the treasure map?" He marked the area Douglon showed him on the map, west and a little south of Queenstown along the edge of the Scale Mountains. "I don't know why Gustav would go there, but he was looking for it when you met him, Patlon." Alaric turned to Ayda. "Gustav will need to get Mallon's body. Is it well hidden?"

"It's safe in the Elder Grove, but not hidden. I didn't know anyone would look for him. It might take the wizard some time, but he'll find it."

"I think we need to fix that," Alaric said. "I doubt we can hide him so well that Gustav will never find him, but we can buy some time. How long would it take us to reach the Grove?"

"Three or four days," Ayda answered. "But I don't know a way to hide him that a Shade Seeker won't figure out."

"I think I can come up with some tricks that should slow Gustav down." None of which would be pleasant. "I can at least guess how he'll go about looking. Can you show me where the Elder

Grove is?" Alaric asked Ayda.

Ayda glanced at the map. "It wouldn't help you for me to mark it on the map. I'll need to take you there. It's near the northern end of the Greenwood."

Alaric looked over the map. "I think we should go there first. Gustav will have to spend time searching while we can go directly there. It might help us catch up."

"Then we'd better get moving," Douglon said.

"Is it safe to assume that Gustav has left Kordan's Blight?" Milly asked.

"He has no reason to stay," Alaric answered.

"Then, if we head out now, we can have one good night sleep in my house before setting out tomorrow."

The mood of the group was lighter as they headed to Milly's. Alaric could hear the dwarves' laughter ringing off the trees. Ayda walked along merrily near Milly, the two of them giggling and whispering to each other. In reality, they were in a far worse predicament than they had imagined when they trudged out of their camp that morning, but now they had a goal.

Brandson fell in beside Alaric. "Do you think we have a chance of stopping Gustav?"

If the wizard wasn't on a dragon, it would be a lot easier. "We have a chance."

Brandson was quiet for a moment.

"I was only twelve when the yellow plague broke out. My father got sick. My mother wouldn't leave him, but she sent me off to the hills with my uncle." He paused again. "No one who stayed in the village survived. My uncle went back with a group of men a couple of weeks later and burned it to the ground. Then he brought me to Kordan's Blight where the blacksmith took me in. My uncle left to join the King's army before the battle of Turning Creek."

Turning Creek. King Kendren's army had made their stand there against Mallon. The Rivor had brought legions of nomads and monsters no one could name. He had annihilated Kendren's army. The king himself had been wounded with a poisoned blade. Alaric had tried to save him, tried to find some way to stop the poison, to draw it out. The king had only lived for two days.

"I never saw my uncle again," Brandson said.

Alaric put his hand on the smith's shoulder. "We'll stop Gustav. And maybe in the process, find the way to kill Mallon."

Brandson nodded. "Good, because Mallon keeps taking people from me. My parents, my uncle, and now Gustav, too."

That night, the group sat around Milly's table. The room was warm and noisy, full of smells of roast chicken and hot cider. Douglon and Patlon spun tales of ancient treasures lost and found.

The fire in the hearth had burned low and the conversation lulled when Ayda turned to Alaric. "Tell us a story, Keeper."

There was enthusiastic agreement, and Alaric nodded. "Do you have one in mind?"

"Tomkin and the Dragon," Ayda said.

Evangeline's face, waiting expectantly the day he met her sprang up before his mind. Alaric looked sharply at the elf, but there was no mischief in her look.

"It's a night to remember better times," Ayda said.

Alaric looked into the fire for a long moment. He let his mind linger on the memory of Evangeline's face, the eagerness in her eyes. Outside, the night deepened, drawing the edges of the world down into the small, fire-lit room. Ayda was right. It was that sort of night.

He pulled his hood up over his head and looked down at the floor, remembering an inn and letting the room fall into silence before he began.

TWENTY-FOUR

Patlon parted from them early the next morning, choosing to head southwest, cross-country toward Duncave instead of following the King's Highway south.

Alaric retrieved Beast from the tavern's stables while Brandson borrowed several horses from his neighbors, leaving the slow carthorse behind. They headed south through a cool morning, following the road over sun-steeped hills and down into pockets of mist.

As they dropped into a long, low valley thick with mist, Alaric pulled out the ruby. In the dim morning, the core was the red of old embers, pulsing and breathing beneath the brighter streams of light. Droplets of mist clung to the surface, twinkling like blood-red stars. Alaric waited, watching the interplay of the currents of light through one of the faces of the rough gem. There was no break in the light and his hand tightened on the ruby. The energy spun beneath the surface in darker and lighter hues of red, but no black swirl appeared. His heart beat faster. The darkness had disappeared.

But then a wide band of light shifted. Deep in the core of the ruby, he glimpsed a knot of blackness before the light swirled back in front of it. Alaric felt his heart falter, and he clutched the ruby to his chest. The darkness was growing—slowly, but it was growing. And Gustav was so far ahead of them. How long did he have before the ruby went dark? How long could Evangeline wait for the antidote?

The road before them gamboled over hills and in and out of forests. At the top of each rise, Alaric scanned the sky as though he would find Gustav on his red dragon, just a short distance ahead of them.

They rose early and rode late each day trying to reach Queenstown by lunch the third day. Alaric had no doubt that Queen Saren would have her people keeping an eye out for him, but as long as Alaric didn't run into anyone he knew, they should be through in a couple of hours.

Alaric had a letter penned and ready to post to Saren in the city. She was going to be furious that he wasn't stopping. The fact that Mallon wasn't dead and might be a threat again soon wasn't really the sort of message to put in a letter, but he didn't want to take the time to go to the palace. Gustav was already too far ahead of them. The palace would mean councils and waiting and discussions and more waiting.

And explaining to Saren why her closest advisor had deserted her for two years without an explanation. He felt a pang of guilt at the idea of Saren, never quite sure of herself, carrying on for so long without a Keeper there for support. Probably, she had been fine, but the Court Keeper played a pivotal role in the politics of the palace. Without someone there who was obligated to work only for the good of the country, it was possible for things to become unbalanced quickly. Of course, he had thought that the Stronghold would send someone else to take his place when it became obvious he wasn't coming back. He'd always expected Keeper Will to be here.

The morning they approached the capital, a dark bank of clouds piled up against the western horizon. By the time they could see the city, sprawled out on both sides of the great river, the wind was sharp with the smell of the storm. They joined the slow plodding pace of wagons walking through clusters of houses and an increasing number of shops, toward the thick city walls.

When they rode through the city gates, the darkness of the approaching storm devoured the early afternoon sun, dropping the city into twilight. The winds rose, whipping dust and refuse down the streets in mad dashes. The flow of travelers continued doggedly into the city, funneling into busy avenues. All of the main thoroughfares in the city ran into the central market like spokes of a wheel. The quickest way through the city was straight through that market and out the avenue on the other side. There was no use fighting against the current of humanity moving in that direction.

It had been two years since Alaric was in the capital. The city hadn't changed. It had the same tumult of biting smells and jostling motion. Alaric had spent eight years at court, advising first King Kendren and then Queen Saren. Today, he felt like he was visiting a foreign city, wide-eyed and nervous. He searched the faces of the crowd, pulling back into his hood if he saw anyone who might be familiar.

When they turned into the open market square, the full force of the wind hit him, pelting his face with bits of rock and dust, and jostling Beast into the other horses.

The gale thrashed through a sea of booths and humanity. Vendors struggled to finish tying down their tents and their wares while thunder rolled over the rooftops. Alaric slid off Beast and pressed against him for protection. The others did the same, and he led them against the wind, pressing along the southern edge of the square until they huddled in the relative shelter of the buildings on the western side.

"We need to get moving," Alaric shouted above the wind. "Once we leave the city, we'll be back in the forest and the wind shouldn't be as bad."

The door of the smithy next to them crashed open, caught by the wind. A black-bearded dwarf exited, swinging an axe and watching it arc through the air with a pleased expression. Three palace guards fell into place behind him.

Alaric stepped back, letting Beast's head come between himself and the guards.

"Another dwarf!" Ayda said cheerfully.

Alaric could just see the dwarf glance at her, his brow knitting together in disgust when he saw the elf.

Next to Alaric, Douglon caught sight of the dwarf and let out a small growl. "Menwoth." His voice was steely.

Menwoth's mouth dropped open in surprise before fury filled his face. "Traitor!" he rushed at Douglon, axe raised. "Seize him! This dwarf is wanted by High King Horgoth!"

"Ambassador! Please restrain yourself, sir!" The lead guard's voice cut through the wind as he stepped forward, his own sword drawn.

Menwoth lowered his axe, but stood glowering at Douglon. "Arrest this dwarf." When the guards hesitated, he snapped at them, "I demand it. High King Horgoth has declared him a traitor.

His execution awaits him in Duncave."

The guard, his uniform showing him to be a lieutenant, stepped up to Douglon. "You'll need to come with us."

Douglon's face darkened, and he reached for his axe.

Alaric set a hand on Douglon's shoulder and pushed back his hood. He stepped forward. "This man is not a traitor."

The guard looked at him dismissively. "If Ambassador Menwoth requests that we detain this dwarf, he will be brought to the palace."

Clearly, Alaric hadn't needed to worry about being recognized. "I don't know you, Lieutenant, but my name is Alaric. I'm the Keeper serving at Her Majesty's court." Well, serving might not be the exact word for it, but 'avoiding Her Majesty's court' didn't have as good a ring to it.

The guard looked at him sharply, taking in Alaric's not-quite-as-black-as-a-Keeper's robe. Alaric tried to look impressive, but judging from the guard's face, he wasn't succeeding.

"Keeper Alaric has not been at court for two years."

"Yes, well, I'm here now. And this dwarf is not a traitor. You can't arrest him."

The lieutenant's eyebrows rose and Menwoth sputtered, "That is for King Horgoth to decide, not some man claiming to be Queen Saren's historian."

"Keepers are well regarded here." There was mild disapproval in the lieutenant's voice. "Keeper Alaric is among the most respected men in our land."

"That means nothing to a dwarf," Menwoth said.

The guard narrowed his eyes at Alaric for a long moment. "I'm afraid, sir, that you'll need to bring your complaints about the detainment of this dwarf to Her Majesty herself."

Alaric clenched his jaw. Of course the guard shouldn't just believe him. Alaric looked like a dirty traveler who happened to be wearing black. But still.

Douglon bristled. "I'm not a traitor, and you're not arresting me. If Horgoth wants me, he can get his fat head out of that throne room and come get me."

Alaric looked at the guards surrounding them. "Douglon, I'll talk to the queen. We'll sort this out."

Douglon growled.

Menwoth looked wildly at the guard. "You can't trust him! He wants Horgoth's throne! He's plotting to kill him!"

Douglon rolled his eyes. "The only dwarf here who wishes he had the throne is you."

Menwoth began to shake with fury. "I serve Horgoth faithfully. And I always have, which is why he trusted me with this position at Saren's court."

Douglon snorted. "He just wanted you far away from Duncave."

"Douglon," Alaric broke in, "just go with them so we can get this over with."

Douglon ground his teeth then nodded. At the lieutenant's pointed look, Douglon handed his axe to Brandson. The guards drew up around him and led the way through the wind-blown market toward the palace.

So much for getting through Queenstown quickly. Alaric took the reins of Douglon's horse and followed the others into the beginnings of the storm.

TWENTY-FIVE

The air was heavy with the coming rain, and the wind smelled of the damp hills to the west. They were not quite halfway to the palace, leading their horses to keep pace with the guards, when the rain came. When it did, it was torrential. Alaric hunched down under his hood, pulling his cloak close. Within seconds, it was soaked through. Relentless fingers of wind wound around his neck, dribbling cold rain down his back, down his legs, and into his already sloshing boots. The crackle of lightning and constant rumble of thunder followed them as they hurried along the deserted streets.

They turned onto a wide avenue leading to the palace gates. Through the rain, the building was a grey, hulking shape behind grey, hulking walls. As they drew closer, the grey lightened into pale rock. They entered the palace grounds through an enormous portico and ducked into the nearest building, soaked to the bone.

Alaric stood impatiently, letting water drip off of him to puddle on the floor while the lieutenant ducked into a nearby room and returned with Captain Rold, captain of the queen's guard. Alaric felt an odd combination of relief at being recognized and guilt at being gone for so long that all this was necessary, when the captain snapped off a quick bow to him. "My apologies, Keeper Alaric. You understand that my lieutenant needed confirmation of who you were. Since Her Majesty will be most anxious to see you, if you could all hang your wet cloaks in here, I will take you to her immediately."

"This dwarf is a traitor," Menwoth said, pointing at Douglon. "I demand that he be thrown into the dungeon until he can be transferred to Duncave."

"Douglon is not a traitor," Alaric said. "It is just a misunderstanding."

"Yes, I understand there is some disagreement about a dwarf." Captain Rold turned to Douglon. "If you will come with me willingly to the queen right now, you will not be bound until Her Majesty has made a decision regarding you." He turned to Menwoth who was livid. "Your excellency, I will inform Her Majesty that you are anxious to discuss this situation."

With a curt nod at the other guards to fall in around them, Captain Rold started off through the palace. Alaric fell into step behind him, his boots squelching with each step. The others followed, leaving Menwoth dripping and swearing behind them in the hall.

Alaric followed the captain through the familiar halls of the palace, the sounds of the storm now muffled by the stone walls. When they reached a set of enormous doors, two guards snapped off salutes and heaved the doors open.

Entering the room was like walking into a map. Painted on the walls was a detailed map of Queensland. To the right of the door, the Wolfsbane Mountains dwindled into rolling hills at the northern end of the country. The great river wrapped around the room, meandering south until it passed into the southern kingdoms just to the left of the door. The large square table that filled the center of the room was inlaid with lighter wood showing streets and major buildings of Queenstown. This map, Alaric remembered rather than saw, since the clutter on the table obscured it.

"Your Majesty," the captain said, "Keeper Alaric."

A stout woman looked up from the sea of papers, which were drowning the city on the table. The queen glanced at Alaric for a moment before her eyes lit up and her mouth split into a broad smile. Alaric dropped into a low bow.

"Alaric!" She crossed the room to embrace him.

He had forgotten how short Saren was. Her head barely came up to his shoulders. She had aged more than two years since he had seen her. Her thick braid held much more grey than it had, and deep creases were carved between her brows. More than just a greeting, there was a deep relief in her words.

"It's been so long," she said.

Alaric opened his mouth, but couldn't settle on one answer to that.

Saren looked around at his companions, her eyes widening when she saw Ayda.

"Your Majesty," Alaric said, "may I present Aydalya, princess of the western elves."

Ayda curtsied gracefully, and Saren's eyes widened even further.

"My dear, you are most welcome! I was a child last time one of your people visited us. We are honored to have you as our guest."

Alaric introduced Douglon as well, and Queen Saren nodded her head at the dwarf. "We see far too few of your good people as well, master dwarf. Please consider yourself our honored guest." Saren looked at Milly and Brandson, who were hanging back behind the others. She gave them a warm, welcoming smile. "Are you going to tell me that these two young people are also royalty? A young king and his queen from the Winter Island, perhaps?"

Milly and Brandson both smiled stiffly.

"This is Brandson and Milly, blacksmith and milkmaid from the village of Kordan's Blight."

Queen Saren nodded to them. "Companions of Alaric are always welcome. My house is at your disposal."

At that moment, the door behind them flung open, and a tall, angular man strode into the room. The queen's eyes went flat, and the man, taking in the group before her, drew up short. A flicker of irritation crossed his face before he tossed off a bow so shallow it was barely a bob of his head.

Saren's smile grew icy.

"My apologies, Your Majesty," he said, striding forward to stand a step ahead of Alaric without glancing at him. "I didn't realize there would be guests at our discussion."

The man's fingers were weighted down with gold rings. A thick gold chain hung around his neck holding a ponderous disc printed with the seal of the Black Hills. He was a hand taller than Alaric, and he used his height to tower over the queen. He must be the son of the Black Hills duke who had governed when Alaric had been at court. Although no older than thirty, this man's face was already carved with arrogance.

The smile fell off her face completely as Saren lifted her chin to look the man in the eye.

"Duke Thornton," she began, "we've been honored this afternoon with important guests. We'll have to postpone our discussion until a later date."

Thornton kept his eyes on the queen, "Your Majesty, I'm afraid I have other obligations at a later date."

A surge of anger rolled through Alaric at the duke's arrogance. He stepped forward, positioning himself alongside Saren, facing the man.

The duke flicked an unconcerned glance at Alaric, then returned it to Saren.

"You're too new to court to recognize our guest, Thornton, so I'm sure he'll excuse your rudeness." Saren set her hand on Alaric's arm. "Allow me to introduce Keeper Alaric to you."

Alaric put on a courteous smile.

The duke stiffened and turned toward Alaric. He took in the Keeper's worn travel clothes with a slight raise of his brow. His expression remained haughty, and he gave the slightest nod in acknowledgment. "I didn't realize a Keeper was needed at court any longer."

Alaric didn't have to look down to know what he looked like. He wasn't even wearing his blackish robe any longer. His smile soured.

Saren's face took on a decidedly dangerous look. "There are many people at court who aren't needed, but a Keeper is not one of them. We'll find another time to have that discussion you were looking for. A time when Alaric is available as well." She turned away from Thornton and back toward the others.

The duke gave her a stony glare. He turned it on Alaric for a long moment before striding out of the room.

Saren watched the duke leave with a troubled expression settling on her face. "Alaric, there are a few problems I could use your assistance with."

"Speaking of problems," Alaric said, glancing at Douglon, "we brought one with us."

The queen gave a tired sigh. "Of course you did."

TWENTY-SIX

"Not just a problem, then." Saren frowned after Alaric explained the issue. "A problem with the dwarves, who are notoriously stubborn."

Douglon's brow creased.

"Don't scowl," Ayda whispered loudly to him. "It makes you look stubborn."

Saren gave Ayda a weak smile. "I'll talk to Menwoth."

"It might take more than that," Alaric said. "If Douglon isn't arrested, Menwoth has threatened to tell Horgoth that you shelter those bent on his overthrow."

"Menwoth did all this? He's usually so reserved."

"He has a special place in his heart for me, Your Highness," Douglon said. "I am closer to the throne than he is, and he feels that he deserves my place. In truth, he does. Menwoth has been working to make himself useful to the crown his entire life. I avoid the throne room like quicksand for fear it'll suck me in and force me to do something royal."

Saren narrowed her eyes. "Are you the dwarf who lined Horgoth's crown with lead before his coronation?"

Douglon laughed. "His head kept tipping to the side. He'd never worn the crown before, so he didn't know anything was wrong."

Saren allowed a small smile but shook her head. "This will definitely take more than a word from me to fix."

"Douglon is innocent, Your Majesty," Alaric said. "He can't be arrested."

Saren turned to the captain who still stood by the door. "Why *hasn't* he been arrested?"

"With Keeper Alaric and Ambassador Menwoth disagreeing, my lieutenant thought it best that you make the decision regarding his arrest."

The queen scowled at Douglon. "Menwoth will feel insulted. It might have made things easier if you'd just let him arrest you."

"I'm not keen on entering a dungeon, Your Majesty," Douglon said. "More people go into them than come out."

Saren shook her head. "The whole reason Menwoth is here is so we can reach some trade agreements with King Horgoth. It won't help anything if I harbor a dwarf they think is a traitor. Douglon is Horgoth's subject. I'm not willing to strain relations with Duncave over this. "

Douglon let out a low growl, and Alaric laid a hand on his shoulder.

Alaric said, "I assure you, Your Majesty, Douglon is not a traitor. A misunderstanding between him and his cousin Patlon was… misconstrued by King Horgoth. The matter is being cleared up as we speak."

"It will be your word against a royal decree from Horgoth. Your word won't be enough for Menwoth," Saren said. "The dwarves have no regard for Keepers. You are just another human to him. I would have to offer the ambassador something very valuable to get him to forget about this whole affair. Now that I realize who you are, Douglon, even that might not be enough. The hatred between you and Menwoth is almost legendary."

"I'm beginning to see that," Alaric said. "Douglon's problems often have a root in his personal relationships."

The dwarf had the decency to drop his eyes.

Saren rubbed the end of her braid while she contemplated Douglon. It was such a familiar motion that Alaric smiled. When she had first married Kendren, it had been her nervous habit, running her thumb down to the end of her braid while she tried to answer questions posed by the people who had intimidated her. But now, the motion was slow and calculating as she contemplated the problem before her.

Her eyes flicked to Alaric, and irritation flashed across her face. "What are you smiling about?"

Alaric smiled more broadly. "It's nice to see you again."

"It would be nicer if you hadn't brought problems with you." A small smile crept into her eyes, despite her sharp voice.

Alaric's smile faded. "This thing with Menwoth is nothing. We have a great deal to talk about. Urgently."

Saren's shoulders drooped, and she gave Alaric a tired look. "One problem at a time, please. Let's take care of this, and then I will clear my afternoon." She turned back to Douglon. "What if we took the question out of Menwoth's hands? Nurthrum arrives from Duncave sometime today for an annual discussion of our relationship with King Horgoth. He outranks Menwoth, doesn't he?"

Douglon considered for a moment. "Not officially, but Nurthrum is older than the mountains. Menwoth would feel compelled to respect his decision."

"And would Nurthrum consider you a traitor?"

"He's got a clear head and can be reasoned with. I could convince him it's all a mistake."

Saren nodded. "Then until we can talk to him, you are officially my guest. I will hear grievances between you and Menwoth, and we'll make sure Nurthrum is present as well." She looked at the dwarf sternly. "Until then, do not leave the palace. Unless you want all of my resources, as well as Horgoth's, tracking you down."

Douglon grumbled something into his beard, but gave her a reluctant nod.

Saren let out a long breath. "Good. Alaric, there is a small council meeting tonight. Since you're finally back, I think I'll make it a full council. It will be a good way to get you up to speed."

"Your Majesty," Alaric said, "we're leaving at dawn."

Saren's eyebrows shot up. "Leaving? You just arrived."

"We were just passing through Queenstown. This thing with Douglon is the only reason we stopped."

Saren studied Alaric, her eyes hard. "Well, it's good to know that military force will bring you back."

"You will understand my need for haste once I explain to you what's going on."

"I expect an explanation of many things," she said curtly. "First, there are things that require my attention this afternoon. Let me take care of those, and I will send for you afterward."

She rang a bell on the table, and a smartly dressed steward entered the room.

"Send word to my full council that we meet tonight. And see our guests to their rooms so they can change. Alaric, I'll send for you shortly."

The steward bowed and turned to lead them from the room.

Alaric bowed, frustration gnawing at him. Outside, he could still hear the thrumming of the rain. Even if he could get everyone out of the palace, this storm would make any progress slow. He resigned himself to an afternoon and evening of plodding through the cumbersome workings of palace life.

Alaric's feet could have found his room by themselves. At the end of a long hall of apartments and separated from them by a wide-open room with chairs and a large fireplace, a black door greeted him. This apartment had been his home for the eight years he had lived in Queenstown, advising first King Kendren, then his widowed queen.

Alaric stepped in to find it unchanged. Bookshelves dotted the room, shelves of scrolled maps filled one corner, and there were at least a half-dozen small tables and desks scattered around the large room. The doorway to the bedroom opened in the wall to his right.

He walked along in front of the bookshelf, running his hands over the spines of the books like greeting old friends. At the door to the balcony, he watched the rain pour down into the garden. Everything outside was too large, as altered as any garden would be after an absence of a couple of years. Alaric felt the time wash over him. The man who had lived here before had been so sure of everything, so confident in his place, his beliefs. Now, he felt more like one of the leaves careening by, tossed by the wind and battered down by the rain.

He washed and changed into clothes waiting in the room for him before he returned to the window. Across the courtyard, a student of the apothecary hurried out of Ewan's quarters, ducking through the rain. Alaric's hand went absently to the pouch hanging at his chest. His fingers rubbed the stone through the worn leather bag.

He thought about going over there now, but knowing Saren would call him soon, he turned his back on the window and began to pace the room. A polite knock sounded, and he opened the door to the queen's grey-haired steward.

"Is the room acceptable, Keeper Alaric? If it doesn't suit you, we can find you another."

"No, Matthew," Alaric said, smiling at the man, "the room is perfect, just as it was when I left. If anything has changed, it has been myself."

"Her Majesty is pleased that you are back."

Alaric shook his head. "I'm not sure she's entirely pleased." Alaric looked around the room. It was *exactly* how he had left it. "I thought they would send another Keeper."

"As did Her Majesty."

Alaric sank down into the nearest chair. Of course the queen's last years had been hard. She had relied on Alaric heavily. And he had still left.

"Everyone has felt the absence of a Keeper. Having one here gives us all hope." Matthew bowed and left.

Alaric stared at the closed door for a long time.

TWENTY-SEVEN

An hour later, Alaric followed a messenger all the way through the palace to the royal apartments where he found the queen reading at an immense wooden desk. The room smelled of blackberry tart and fresh bread.

"Alaric," she greeted him with an apologetic smile. She motioned him toward a table set with bread, fruit, and two enormous servings of tart. "Come eat, old friend. Let's start over, shall we?"

Alaric made her a bow, but she waved it away as she sat and began to serve herself. Alaric joined her, realizing how hungry he was.

"I see you have been well, Your Majesty."

The smile she gave had a hint of steel behind it. "I know you didn't plan it, but your return to the palace is timely. Some members of the council at tonight's meeting may find the presence of a Keeper at court to be detrimental to their plans."

So much for easing into the role of Keeper again. Alaric tore off a piece of bread. "I doubt my presence will make much difference. I am too out of touch with what is going on."

"Of course it will make a difference. By now, rumors of your presence have spread throughout the palace." Saren took a slow, savoring bite of tart. "The winds are changing already."

Her face was different than Alaric remembered. There was less youth and gentleness. Saren hadn't been ready for the throne when Kendren died. She had been raised the daughter of a noble family, one that spent little time at court. King Kendren had married her because she was kind and good and honest—too much of all these things to naturally take to the political games played around her.

"I'm sorry I left for so long," Alaric said.

Saren let his worlds hang in the air for a moment.

"Come now, Alaric," she said, an edge to her voice. "It's been two years. Where have you been?"

"When I left you to see if the nomads were allying themselves with the southern kingdoms, I had every intention of returning here when I was done. It took almost a year, but I found the rumors to be groundless.

"I didn't come back because on my way south, I met a woman."

The queen's eyebrow shot up. "A woman worth keeping you from returning to your queen?"

Alaric let the obvious answer speak for itself.

"Send for her."

Alaric flinched at the note of command. It was going to be hard to get used to being ordered about again. He took a deep breath to push down the irritation. "She's not here."

There was a long pause. Saren's eyes narrowed as she waited for him to continue.

"Her name is Evangeline. She was an innkeeper before she traveled with me." Alaric's throat tightened. "She's not here because she's dying. She was poisoned. She is... asleep while I search for the antidote."

Alaric looked at the bread in his hands. Across the table, Saren did not move.

"I have slowed the spread of the poison, but it is not stopped. It will take a long time, but it will kill her." Alaric met the queen's gaze, seeing the sympathy there. "That's where I've been. Searching through every corner of the world for an antidote, crawling through the darkest pits of humanity in search of anything that would help me."

The queen spun her wedding ring around her finger. "I often wondered, while Kendren was dying, if all the waiting and hoping and dreading was worse than the death would ever be." She didn't look at Alaric. "It turns out neither is better than the other. Mourning is just a continuation of the same dreadful waiting. Except now, I'm waiting for something that will never come."

Alaric looked at her, remembering when her hair was still brown, her eyes still young. "I think of your husband often. While searching for an antidote for Evangeline, I often found myself searching for an antidote that might have helped him, too, wondering if there was something else we could have done to save him."

She shook her head. "Such questions lead to madness. Kendren's wounds were not the kind that could be healed." She took a deep breath. "It is so good to see you, Alaric. The last time I saw a Keeper was when Will was here. That was not long after you left.

"His visit was over my birthday feast. Will treated us to stories three nights in a row." She shook her head and smiled. "I can still see the tales in my mind. Three old tales: Tomkin and the Dragon, The Fall of kin Elenned, and Mylen the Destroyer. That man can tell stories better than anyone I've ever heard."

Alaric smiled. "He could leave me breathless just telling me what was for dinner."

"He delayed his departure in the hope you would return."

Alaric felt a jab of guilt. Another person he'd let down. He picked up a small blueberry and rolled it between his fingers. "The last I knew, Will had gone to look for the elves. Evangeline and I were close to the Greenwood on the way back here when I decided to go look for him.

"We had been catching glimpses of the Lumen Greenwood whenever we crested a hill, and she had been giddy at the sight. We reached a village that had been plagued by a fire lizard." Alaric let the story spill out, telling her of the fire lizard and the arrow.

"I didn't know the villagers had poisoned their arrows." He raised his eyes to Saren. "They were all killed by the fire lizard. They hadn't told me."

Alaric looked at the table, the grain in the wood echoing the red lines that had wound their way up Evangeline's leg. "It took more than a day for any sign of the poison to appear. By that time..."

"I took her west, into the Scale Mountains to one of the deserted small keeps. I created a chamber around her, but even that does not stop the poison."

"I doubt there's anything in our own records that you don't already know about, but now that you're back, the entire library is at your disposal, of course. And anything else I can offer. Anything at all."

Alaric shook his head. "As I mentioned earlier, I'm not really back. I need to leave. The sooner the better."

Saren's brow contracted. "To go to Evangeline?"

"No, where I am going now affects the whole country." Alaric pushed his plate away. "Mallon was not killed by the elves."

Saren sat, pale-faced, while Alaric told her of Gustav and Mallon and the elves. When he told her of the gathering nomads, her eyes hardened and she rang a bell that sat on the table. The door opened and a guard appeared.

"Summon General Viso and the map keeper. Have the quartermaster begin preparations for a full army supply and deployment."

The guard bowed and left.

The queen smiled tightly at Alaric. "There's not much I can do against Mallon, but I will not be unprepared with a nomad army on my border."

The queen shoved papers off her table and began to unroll another large map.

"This news needs to be acted on. I'm moving the full council meeting to this afternoon. We'll convene in two hours." She glanced at him. "If—When you stop Gustav and heal Evangeline, you will come back to court."

He bit back irritation at the imperiousness of her demand. She waited for his agreement, but he couldn't bring himself to nod. He'd been too long on his own to have a knee-jerk agreement with the crown.

Saren turned her full gaze on him. "You were my closest advisor, Alaric. You were the one with the most influence over the nobles, the other council members, the people. And you left. The void you left in the court was swarmed by every power-hungry parasite that could reach it." The queen's voice shook slightly. "You have no idea the mess you left me in. There has always been a Keeper at court, Alaric. And with Will gone, there are no other Keepers the Shield can send to me."

Alaric shook his head. "You don't know the things I've done. I'm not sure I can be the court Keeper anymore."

"The world is falling apart, Alaric," Saren snapped. "We don't have the luxury of you falling apart as well. If you're not a Keeper anymore, you are the closest thing I have to one. And I need a Keeper. So whatever doubts you have, deal with them."

He opened his mouth, but she raised a hand to silence him.

Her eyes glittered with anger. "There is a full council meeting in two hours. I don't care if you feel like a Keeper, Alaric. Act like one."

TWENTY-EIGHT

laric left the queen's room and strode toward the apothecary.

There was a grim satisfaction in finding out that his return to court was as frustrating as he had expected. He'd spent too long making his own decisions and choosing his own path. He chafed against the commands of the queen.

Alaric took a calming breath. None of this mattered right now, anyway. He just needed to deal with Gustav. And he needed this blasted storm to end.

The rain had settled into a drenching downpour. Alaric pulled up his hood and dashed across the courtyard to reach the apothecary.

Ewan's door stood open, as always, and Alaric paused on the threshold, letting the water drip off of his cloak. The mossy smell of drying plants wafted out past him. Ewan, his white hair rumpled and his long beard braided to keep it out of his work, was hunched down on a spindly stool. Candlelight glinted off a honey-colored liquid as Ewan meticulously dripped it into a small clay bowl.

Alaric held himself still, not wanting to interrupt. He glanced around at the familiar chaos of the room. The table was littered with pages covered in tightly packed writing and peppered with diagrams. A fire burning in the large fireplace reflected off hundreds of glass vials and bottles.

Ewan set down his dropper and peered into the bowl. For a long moment, the only sound was the rain hammering on the roof, then a thin wisp of reddish smoke rose from the bowl. Ewan let out a whoop and grabbed for a nearby pile of papers.

Alaric laughed, and Ewan spun about to face the door.

"Alaric!" Ewan sprang to his feet and reached the Keeper in two long strides.

Alaric hugged his friend fiercely. The old apothecary's shoulders were nothing but bones.

"Everyone who's stepped through my door this afternoon has been giddy with the rumor of a Keeper in the palace."

"I didn't know it'd cause such a fuss."

"Yes, well, you always did underestimate yourself." Ewan motioned toward the corner of the room. "I hear you travel with an interesting group."

Alaric stepped around a silver apparatus and piles of papers on the floor to drop into the same smooth wooden chair that he always sat in. He leaned back in the chair and felt himself relax. How long had it been since he'd sat somewhere comfortable? Settling back, he told Ewan about his traveling companions.

Ewan's gaze searched Alaric's face. Whatever he saw there, the apothecary's face showed only warmth. "It is good to see you, Alaric."

"It's good to see you, too," Alaric answered. The apothecary had aged as Saren had. Not physically, it was something in his eyes. Something weary. "I know I've been gone too long."

Ewan's mouth twitched into a half smile, and he shook his head. "You were gone as long as you needed to be. There's no changing it now."

Alaric looked up at his friend, but he could find no reproach. Ewan wasn't the queen, wanting to bend him to her will. He saw only friendship. Something deep inside him loosened. A thread that had been twisted around his failures and doubts unwound, and the snarled mass relaxed the slightest bit.

"You don't look like a man who found what he was looking for," Ewan said. "What brought you back?"

"The most immediate reason I'm here is this blasted storm. But the reason I'm passing through Queenstown at all is rather troubling." Alaric told him of Gustav and Mallon and the elves. The apothecary's frown deepened as the story continued. "And so now I am here, trapped because of the storm and at the beck and call of the queen."

Ewan let the words hang in the air for a moment before he said, "Your absence has been hard on the queen. I'm afraid you'll have some more bitterness to wade through before she's done." There was no judgment in the words, just truth. "In the months after you left, a handful of nobles, led by Lord Leuthro, staged a coup."

"Leuthro? He's always supported the queen."

Ewan nodded. "That's one of the many things that made the situation even worse. Leuthro had positioned himself as Saren's closest advisor." Ewan shook his head. "When the truth came out about the planned coup, Saren had to charge him with treason."

Alaric sank back into the chair. "She had to execute him?"

Ewan nodded. "It changed something in her."

Alaric groaned. "And if I had been here, Leuthro wouldn't have been so bold. My entire absence has been a series of failures, each greater than the last."

Ewan shrugged. "I have no idea what your presence would have accomplished. But I know the queen felt very alone and very unsure of herself. It shook the foundation of her rule. Even today, there are pockets of trouble in the kingdom."

Alaric looked up at him sharply. "Who?"

"Currently, the most troublesome are a pack of southern dukes led by Duke Thornton of the Black Hills. No matter what Saren does, Thornton is in the middle of it, stirring up dissent and maneuvering to gain more power for the southern duchies."

"I met Thornton already." Alaric ran his hand through his hair. "He doesn't have the power to cause Saren much trouble."

"Maybe not on his own, but he's gained the loyalty of the southern duchies. He claims there are problems with bandits, but Saren suspects that he's just creating a stranglehold on the gold trade between Queensland and the south. He keeps demanding money for training more troops. Unless Saren complies, the trade routes stagnate. Gold prices are astronomically high and merchants and nobles are up in arms."

"Still, Thornton is in no position to make demands like that of the queen."

"Saren thinks he is. And he's blackmailed or bribed enough of the court to have gained himself an unreasonable amount of power."

Alaric shook his head and smiled. Here was something he could fix. "That's one problem I can easily solve for Saren. How long has this been going on with Thornton?"

"Since early last winter."

Alaric closed his eyes. "I should have come back sooner. There is so much Saren doesn't know. There's a treaty with the Black Hills duchy, but she probably doesn't know about it."

Anyone could have found the treaty with some research, if they had known to look for it. The problem was, no one but King Bowman and Gerone, who had been the court Keeper at the time, had witnessed the treaty. It would be stored in the royal library, but such an insignificant document would have been easily overlooked.

Ewan shook his head. "You have a ridiculous amount of knowledge stuffed into that head of yours. The Keepers were right to send you here to court."

"I wish I'd come back sooner..." Alaric looked at Ewan and felt desperation rise, "but I couldn't."

Ewan waited patiently. Alaric let the words spill out for the second time that day, telling of Evangeline and the poisoning.

Ewan listened as Alaric listed Evangeline's symptoms and the progression of the sickness. "There was no antidote." It was a statement, not a question.

"For each individual poison, yes there was. But not for the rock snake venom." Alaric pulled a small vial from inside his robe, a slip of paper that listed the poisons the villagers had used wrapped tightly around it. He handed both to his friend.

Ewan unrolled the paper and read the list. "May I use a bit of it?"

Alaric nodded.

Ewan held the small glass vial up before a candle and peered at it through bushy eyebrows. The liquid inside was a murky grey.

Perching on the stool by his workbench, he placed six separate drops on a large tray. Then with a clatter of glass and much muttering and clucking, he dripped, scooped, and mixed things into the poison. He soaked a small cloth with a white liquid then touched the corner to the poison. Black, rancid smoke rose from the point of contact.

"Remarkable," Ewan said, waving the smoke away. "These woodsmen created a masterpiece of a poison." He glanced at Alaric. "Her leg? The poisoned one?"

"Black and cold." Alaric squeezed his eyes shut against the image. "She has no feeling left in her foot. The blackness seeps up into her side."

"Lungs?"

"Full. It pains her to breathe."

"The blackroot would infect her spine."

Alaric nodded. "Her left side is weaker. Or it was back when she had the strength to move."

Ewan looked down at the tray before him. "The symptoms didn't appear until a day had passed because the blackroot weakened the rock snake venom. Neither would affect her until the looseweed had exhausted her body. She didn't seem poisoned at first because she wasn't. Just lethargic. But the looseweed would have weakened her body enough to let all the other poisons begin to work.

"The exhaustion could be treated with lionsroot, but once the symptoms of the other poisons appeared..." Ewan leaned back and peered at a dark, empty corner of the ceiling. He scratched absently at his beard. He shook his head and looked back at Alaric. "I can treat everything but the venom. For that I know of no cure."

"I'm on the trail of one," Alaric said, telling Ewan of Kordan.

When he finished, Ewan picked up the vial again. "Do the villagers make this often?"

Alaric shook his head. "They made it just for the fire lizard. They mixed every poison they could find. They had trouble even reproducing a list of the ingredients."

"Good. The thought of this poison being around is unsettling. Whenever you are done with it, it should be destroyed."

Alaric looked at the grey liquid. He was tired of carrying it. There was nothing left to learn from it. "I have no more need of it."

Ewan nodded briskly. He picked up a large glass vial full of a milky white fluid. Uncorking the poison again, he poured it in. The mixture fizzed, and Ewan held it at arms' length, turning his face away from the smoke. In a moment, the bubbles subsided, and he was left holding a vial of dark brown sludge.

Ewan walked to the fire, stoked it, then tossed the vial into the back of the fire place. The mixture spluttered and hissed before it caught fire. In moments, it was gone.

Silence filled the room like a heavy blanket.

Ewan sat back down across from Alaric. "With such a sickness, how is it that she still lives?" he asked quietly.

Alaric thought of the darkness that had spread up her leg, the way her skin had burned with fever.

He whispered, "She lives because I have done terrible things."

TWENTY-NINE

Alaric stared into the fireplace, watching the flames sweep across the surface of the wood, curling and burning the edges slowly and inexorably. He didn't want to remember it all, didn't want to voice the words, didn't want to taint this room. Those things were better locked deep inside.

Ewan sat silent and still.

Alaric let his gaze flick to the face of his old friend. There was still no judgment, just an invitation to unburden himself.

The words swelled, pushing their way up his throat, telling Ewan how he had traveled south looking for the antidote.

"I sent word to you here," he said to Ewan, "but heard you were in a small village at the southeast edge of the realm. After King Kendren's poisoning, I knew every book the library here had on the subject, so it wouldn't have been worthwhile to come back if you weren't here.

"I spent months traveling all over the south in increasingly desperate searches for anything that would help, but I found nothing. I was about to set out in search of you when I discovered that the mayor of Bortaine had an unusual interest in Shade Seekers. He had a small library of histories and writings of some of the lesser Shade Seekers. In several of the scrolls, there were mentions of revivals of those almost dead. I had exhausted every other place I could think of, so I went back to the Stronghold to see if they had any insight into the Shade Seekers' work. They were… unwilling to help with what I needed." Alaric paused. "So I left."

Ewan sank back in his seat, a slight nod the only sign that he understood the permanence of that sentence.

"I went to the library at Sidion."

Ewan's eyes widened. "The Shade Seekers let you in?"

Alaric shook his head. "There weren't any there. I don't know if there usually are, but I found it empty. Their library is in a tower at the southern end of a valley. They have a keep somewhere beyond it, but I didn't go that far."

It had taken all morning to direct a vine in between the library door and the wall, then swell it until the wood cracked. "I could only get into the ground floor. I didn't even see a way to go higher, although I'm sure there were more rooms above me.

"But the books I was looking for were all on the first floor. Their records of poisons were extensive and well organized, with antidotes listed and cross-referenced, but still I didn't find an antidote to the venom. But it didn't matter because what I was looking for didn't have anything to do with poison."

In that tower, he had pulled the dark blue book down from the shelf where it sat alone. The cover was lined with iron, and the volume felt heavier than it should have. The pages smelled of decay and unwholesome things. He had drawn back from the book for a moment. In the Stronghold, this would be locked behind the warning gate. Maybe locked up more than that. When he flipped open the book, he had found thick paper pages with ink that had sunk into the paper, as though it had corroded it.

Alaric glanced up at Ewan. "Keeper magic involves transferring energy between living things. Shade Seekers have no problem transferring energy across the boundary between living and inanimate things.

"But the balance between life and… not life always favors the dead. When the boundary is crossed, the living thing is always depleted, but the dead thing cannot be made alive. Keepers are leery of moving energy over that boundary because they value the living over the dead. Shade Seekers value power over both.

"I found a book explaining how Shade Seekers pull the energy out of a living thing. When they do, a stone is formed to hold the energy. Not quite a living thing, but not quite dead.

"They call it a Reservoir Stone and use it as storage for *vitalle*. They create these… monsters that guard their valley. The creatures are a crossbreed of human and animal. They store the *vitalle* of a human in one of these Reservoir Stones until they press it into a living animal." He grimaced at the memory of a bear he had seen from the library. It was lurching through the woods on misshapen legs, while it chewed on the hind leg of a small deer. The deer was still alive.

"Their use for it was repulsive, but the idea itself was fascinating. It was similar, in a way, to what Keepers do with runes. We infuse them with energy and store it there until the rune needs to work. Except instead of forcing the energy into something, the Shade Seekers allowed the energy to create a vessel for itself.

"I spent a week in Sidion and never saw another soul. When I returned to Evangeline, I found that, despite the trance I had put her in, the poison had progressed." Her face had been so pale he had thought her dead. The desperation of that day caught in his breath. There had been no hesitation, no debate as to the rightness of it.

Alaric pulled the ruby from the pouch at his neck. It filled his palm with a rich, red light. He fisted his hand and squeezed, letting its warmth seep into his fingers, then opened his hand and held it out toward his friend.

Ewan drew in a breath and leaned forward. He stared at the swirling light, his face a mix of horror and amazement. "Where is her body?" The apothecary's voice was barely above a whisper.

"The body lives when the *vitalle* is removed, but it lacks a will. It will neither eat nor sleep. And if I had left her body alone, the poison would have just continued to spread.

"The knowledge from the Shade Seekers opened up new ways of using *vitalle* that I had never considered. I created a crystal to encase her body, to merge with her, keeping her alive while it kept her from changing."

Ewan's eyes were wide and his face was very still. "You stopped her from… aging?"

"Not stopped, but slowed down. It will take years for her to age a month." Alaric dropped his eyes to the ruby. "But the poison needs much less than a month."

Ewan's eyes were locked on the ruby again. "How long ago...?"

"A little over a year."

His eyes lifted to Alaric's face. "You've carried that this whole time?"

Alaric nodded. "I needed to know how to stop the poison, so I traveled south. I tracked down the blood doctors in Napon, any that were competent."

Ewan's eyes went flat.

Alaric forced himself to meet his friend's gaze. "I studied with them for a time, learning about the poisons they used and the antidotes. Their methods are as brutal as we had heard. They perform all their experiments on prisoners, and if they run out of those, they round up the poor off the street.

"The elderly, women, children. There are death caves beneath the city where the fires that burn the bodies never go out. Even there, I found no antidote to the rock snake. So I left."

Ewan's face mirrored the repulsion Alaric felt. "I destroyed some things on my way out." He squeezed his eyes shut, banishing the memory of the cave, the stench of decay and blood, the constant background hum of moaning cut through with shrieks. "What I should have done was burn it down.

"After that, I went to Coastal Baylon and spent time at their library and at the university." The shelves of books there had been endless. "They have so much knowledge there. Books on every topic imaginable bursting off the shelves. And they research new things constantly. Building after building with labs and experiments and research. It's no wonder they have no regard for us. We're barbarians in comparison." He shook his head.

"The experiments they do with poisons, though, are gruesome." He pictured the long line of cells, the stench, the screams of the dying. "They use prisoners for study also."

Alaric shook off the memory. "They even have a small number of books on Keepers. In one, I found a reference to Kordan the Harvester. He was credited with having an antidote to the bite of a rock snake.

"So a few weeks ago, I came back to Queensland to see what the Keepers knew of Kordan. And you know the rest."

"Can you reverse this?" Ewan gestured to the gem that Alaric was still rubbing between his fingers.

"I think so." Alaric stared at the ruby. "I know how they take this energy and put it into another creature. I will put it back into Evangeline instead.

"None of it matters, though, unless Kordan really recorded an antidote and I can get to it. If I can't, my choice lies in leaving her asleep to die a lingering death, or wake her to a quick one. Painful, but quick. And I'm running out of time. The light in the ruby is beginning to fade."

Alaric tucked the ruby back into its pouch.

"I've been thinking of what Gustav wants the Wellstone for. Once he has learned the knowledge it holds, I think he will use it as a well of energy. If he fills it with *vitalle*, it will hold a great deal of power. Whatever his plan is to raise Mallon, it is going to take a lot of energy. And when Gustav fills the Wellstone with energy, if he really takes advantage of every bit of power it will hold, I am certain when he pours it out into Mallon, the memories in the Wellstone will be destroyed."

Alaric raised his gaze to his friend again, looking for hope that he knew he wouldn't find. "Gustav is so far ahead of us that I can't believe we are going to catch him. There is nothing to stop him from finding Mallon's body and waking him."

Alaric gripped the ruby through the pouch. He wasn't going to get the Wellstone. After everything, the antidote was going to slip through his fingers. All the pain he had caused Evangeline, all the pain he had endured, all the people he had let down, it was for nothing.

Alaric dropped his head into his hands. "I should have let her die."

THIRTY

The truth filled the room.

It was useless to believe anything else. It was time to stop looking away from it. He faced it squarely.

"I should have let her die," he repeated. The words, even though just a whisper, opened something inside of him. Some dark corner that he had kept closed cracked open. He saw himself, withered and pale, coiled around the hope of an antidote. Wrapped so tightly that the beauty of that hope was gone. What should have been bright was crushed and deformed into something else, something unrecognizable.

"Maybe," Ewan said quietly, "but letting those we love die is no easy thing. Nor should it be."

Alaric did not move, but the coiled creature inside him unwound the slightest bit more at the apothecary's words. There was permission to stop. An invitation to stop turning away. To face what was done and release it. His actions could not be undone anymore than the poisoning. But he could let go of the mess he had made of it.

He met Ewan's sympathetic gaze. For the first time, the words came out not as a desperate cry, but as a statement. "I should have let her die."

Ewan's eyes were wet, but he did not argue. "What will you do?"

Alaric took a deep breath and stared into the fire, watching the flame devouring the wood, leaving nothing but a small pile of ash.

"I will try to stop Gustav. But if I can't, then there is nothing left to be done," Alaric said, "beyond begging her forgiveness and letting her go."

Ewan motioned around the room. "Alaric, you know that everything I have is yours. If there is anything that I have that would help you in any way…"

Alaric gave a slight smile. "I've collected a fairly impressive store of medicinal plants for myself. You should come see it."

"Maybe you could bring it back here." At Alaric's silence, Ewan continued. "Whatever you decide to do, when it is done, please consider coming back and continuing in your role of Keeper."

"Continuing?" Alaric gave a bitter laugh. "I haven't played a Keeper role in… a lifetime."

"You're orchestrating a group of mismatched, powerful people to, what was it? Take care of some 'significant trouble brewing to the west?' That sounds very much like something a Keeper might do."

After a long moment, Alaric sighed. "It does, doesn't it?"

"You're rather good at it, you know."

Alaric stared into the fire. Yes, he was acting like a Keeper, but that is all it was. Just acting. What he wanted to do was go to Evangeline. "When I think of what will happen if we fail to stop Gustav, my first thought is that it won't be safe for Evangeline to be cured in such a world. Saving the world is lower on the list than saving her."

Ewan shrugged. "Heaped together, the world doesn't look like anything worth saving. It only looks valuable when we think of it in terms of those we love."

"Still. It's not a very Keeperish sentiment."

"It would be if more Keepers left their tower and loved someone in the world."

The apothecary rose and went to the fire. He puttered around for several minutes before producing two cups of tea.

Alaric sat with an empty mind. He let the familiar sounds and smells seep into him, filling an emptiness he hadn't realized was there.

"Reece died last year," Ewan said, still facing the fire.

Alaric's gaze snapped up to his friend.

"No! Ewan, I'm so sorry. I've been talking and talking, and I never even asked..."

"It was an infection in her lungs that wouldn't heal." Ewan looked out the window at the pouring rain. "I knew I couldn't fix it, but I still tried everything I could. I even tried things I knew wouldn't work. The darkest day was the one when I admitted there was nothing I could do."

Silence stretched out between them. Reece and Ewan had been married for years before Alaric had met them. Their marriage, with its easy camaraderie, was the first one Alaric had ever envied.

"She lived four more days. Four days." Ewan sighed deeply. "I wish I had some great wisdom for you."

Alaric could think of nothing to say. How had he not recognized the grief that rolled off his friend? Maybe because it was different from his own. There was no taint of hope in Ewan's. It was worn in, draping familiarly over him, bowing his shoulders. Is this what Alaric would look like in a year? Would this frantic, clawing grief that threatened him turn into something so quiet?

"May I pay my respects to her?" Alaric asked.

Ewan led Alaric outside and around the house, hugging the walls to stay out of the rain. Behind the apothecary, an enormous oak tree grew, dozens of huge branches twisting out in different directions. "I'm glad they buried her on the royal grounds," Alaric said.

Ewan nodded. "The queen herself ordered it and set the stone workers to make the headstone."

Alaric raised one eyebrow.

"Don't worry," Ewan said. "I talked her down from an eight-foot-tall angel to a stone marker."

Alaric laughed. "She's probably saving those angel plans for you."

Ewan winced. "I should design something for myself. Plans she'll feel obligated to follow after my death."

Beneath the oak, nestled between two enormous roots was a grey stone marker. It read, "Reece ~ Beloved wife and friend."

Sitting on top was a delicate, pale pink flower.

"Lambsbreath always was her favorite," Ewan said. "That's one of the last blooms of the season."

"When I first arrived at the palace," Alaric said, "it had been years since I had lived in a city. I told Reece I missed sprawling pine forests, that the city smelled stale. A week later, she appeared with a tray of dirt and moss formed into a little hill. She had planted a handful of pine tree shoots.

She said it was my own forest, and anytime I needed to smell it, it would be on my desk."

Ewan smiled. "She was proud of that little forest. You should have seen how excited she was when she thought of it."

"It worked. My desk smelled like pine trees every day."

Alaric leaned forward over the flower. He cast out to feel the *vitalle* from the grass around him, from the enormous oak and from the surrounding gardens. He laid his finger on the lambsbreath and found what was left of its own life. The edges of its petals were beginning to curl and wilt, the stem was dry. A trickle of energy swirled deep inside the flower, a combination of the white *vitalle* that made up its essence, giving it shape and scent, and the little veins of purple *vitalle* winding through it, letting the cut flower cling to life.

His finger began to tingle as he drew out the purple, separating strand after strand and gathering it just above the flower. A violet haze appeared and brightened.

The fog of purple flickered, and Alaric pulled small amounts of the *vitalle* from the grass beneath his knees, infusing the mist, giving it strength. The glow brightened again, tingeing the delicate pink petals with purple.

He set his other hand on the gravestone and felt the deep, slow essence of the stone. No energy swirled through it, no light, no color. But the stone was infused with its own dense sense of being.

It was this Alaric gathered, like collecting dewdrops. He felt down into the stone and stripped tiny beads of its essence out, pressing them into the glowing purple light above the flower.

His hand on the gravestone burned, but Alaric pressed it to the surface of the rock. He was almost done.

The bits of the stone he had added to the prick of purple light began to weigh it down. Alaric guided it back into the flower, spreading it along the surface of each petal and down the stem. The light diffused easily, flowing out into a lavender gauze covering the lambsbreath.

The flower pulled energy from him now, drawing what it needed. Alaric opened the channel wider from the grass through to his finger. He felt a blister begin to form on his fingertip where it touched the flower and moved more of his fingers to touch it, spreading out the pain.

The energy slowed, then stopped. He took his finger off the flower and pulled his other hand away from the gravestone. His palm where the skin was still new from the blisters in Bone Valley was a dark, angry red, and his finger had a long line of shiny new blisters stretching from the tip to the first knuckle.

Ewan was standing perfectly still next to him. Alaric gave him a small smile and nodded. Ewan hesitated, then reached out his hand to touch the lambsbreath which looked unchanged. When he turned back to Alaric, there were tears on his cheeks. "It's stone," he whispered.

"She deserves to have flowers year round." Alaric looked at the stone flower, its thin petals still a delicate pink against the tombstone. "Maybe not everything I learned from the Shade Seekers was useless, it's just a different way of thinking of the connection between things. Of course, there aren't many wholesome applications for turning living things to stone."

"You've found one."

The flower sat atop the grave, part of the stone. It would be there long past the time when he or Ewan would visit.

"Using the tools of a Shade Seeker doesn't make you one, Alaric. And the one choice of walking out of the Stronghold doesn't negate the thousands of times you chose to be a Keeper. It is only one choice of many. We aren't defined only by our darkest choices. There is much more to us than those."

"Our pasts are complicated, what we've done, what has happened to us, but the beauty of life is that each day, we choose again which parts of that past we will allow to shape our actions. Most of the worst decisions in history have been motivated by love of some kind or another. The decisions you are haunted by certainly were. The path we take away from those choices is dependent on whether we let the choices compel us, or refocus on the love that motivated us in the first place.

"If you don't want to be a Keeper today, then don't be one. But if the only thing holding you back is choices you made in the past, well, those choices are done. Let the past inform your choices today, but don't let it rule them."

THIRTY-ONE

laric stood before the mirror in a formal Keeper's robe. He had found the robe hanging in the closet of his room. It was just a black robe, hooded and reaching down to the floor. Even formal robes had no decorations, only a slightly thicker material.

Still, the robe gave Alaric pause.

The Keeper's robe he had worn when he left the palace had fallen apart almost a year ago. He had replaced it with the first black robe he could find, but it was the black of a storm cloud or a shadow. This robe was the warm black of the night, weighted with the night's stillness.

And there were pockets. Eight pockets just on one side. Eight pockets and nothing to put in them.

His mind slid back over the past year: the library at Sidion, the caves of the southern blood doctors, the dark searches for dark things, Evangeline's withered face always driving him on, a relentless, hollow fire.

The map hanging on the wall above the mantle was shaded in grey over the areas Mallon had controlled eight years ago. It was a looming cloud seeping in from the edges of the country toward Queenstown. If Mallon were raised, that would all begin again, the death, the fear. Something deep inside Alaric rebelled against that cloud. There could be no more ruined villages, no more plagues, no more riving of the people. It didn't matter how far Gustav was ahead of them. Alaric would reach him and stop him.

Alaric turned back to the mirror. A Keeper blazed back at him, cloaked in black, eyes burning. He stepped back in surprise, and the fire died. A knock at his door pulled his attention away.

"The scrolls you requested from the archives, sir," a servant at the door said, bowing.

Alaric took the two small scrolls and glanced at them. At least there was something good he could do. It was satisfying to tuck them into one of his pockets. Over the servant's shoulder, he saw Ayda and Milly seated in some chairs outside his room.

"Did you ever meet Will?" Alaric asked, walking over to Ayda. "Saren said he had visited the elves last time she saw him."

Ayda cocked her head to the side. "Another Keeper?" She nodded. "Two springs ago."

"And in all of the vast Greenwood, he managed to find the one remaining elf?"

"I found him."

"Why?"

"Because he asked the trees to find me. He was very polite to the trees." She smiled. "He stayed with me for several weeks. The first night, he told me a tale of one of your ancient heroes. I'd never heard a human tell a story so well. We traded stories each night, besting each other. He said that the bards should sing songs of our battle."

"Did he tell you where he was going when he left?"

"To the queen, then the Keepers."

Why hadn't Will gone back to the Keepers after coming to the palace? And why hadn't he sent them a message explaining where he had gone?

Douglon and Brandson appeared, complaining about the rain. Alaric led them all through the palace to the council chamber. A long rectangular table filled the center of the room with enough chairs to accommodate a dozen people, but the chamber was empty.

At the head of the table stood Saren's throne-like chair. To the left of it, in the position reserved for the court Keeper, sat a chair shorter than Saren's but decidedly larger than the rest. Alaric raised an eyebrow. He'd never had a special chair before. This wasn't set up just for a council. Saren didn't want anyone to miss the fact that there was a Keeper back at court.

A door at the far end of the room was open, and raised voices came through it. He led the group through the door and into a smaller chamber reserved for the queen and her small council. Saren sat in a large chair, her husband's old chair. It was too big for her, but Alaric had never been able to convince her to get a different one. It made her look like a child pretending to rule. She hadn't taken it well when he'd told her that, though. Now Queen Saren was sitting in her too-large chair and looking troubled as Menwoth stomped back and forth in front of her, shouting.

"He's been charged with treason against King Horgoth! He stole from the crown and is storing up wealth for the purpose of stealing the throne!"

Saren gave a little sigh of relief when Alaric and the others walked into the room.

Menwoth whirled around. "Why is that dwarf not bound?"

Douglon rolled his eyes. "Stuff it Menwoth," he muttered.

Saren held up her hand for silence. "I'm not sure how King Horgoth runs his court, but in mine, things are run in an orderly fashion."

Menwoth glared at Douglon but shut his mouth.

Another dwarf entered the room. His beard was streaked with grey, but his eyes were bright and he carried himself with the ease of a young man. Alaric had met few dwarves with grey beards. Nurthrum must be quite old, a fact that didn't seem to be slowing him down.

"Nurthrum," Saren greeted him. "Thank you for coming."

Douglon nodded respectfully to Nurthrum.

Menwoth looked sharply at the older dwarf and shot Douglon a smug smile. "I didn't know you had arrived, Master Nurthrum. I am so glad you are here."

Nurthrum bowed to Saren. "Just this hour. I received a message from Her Majesty that there was an issue between some dwarves and she would appreciate as many opinions in the matter as possible."

"We have much to do this afternoon, gentlemen," Saren said, motioning for everyone to sit. "If someone could close the door, we can get this sorted out. Menwoth, if you could, in a clear and calm manner, explain your grievance against Douglon?"

Menwoth, with a quick glance at Nurthrum, stated his accusations again, this time, in a more subdued tone. Saren listened patiently, and Douglon, with a few snorts and shakes of his head, listened as well.

"Do you have anything to say, Douglon?" Saren asked when Menwoth had finished.

With surprising restraint, Douglon stated his own case.

"Nurthrum," Saren said, "do you have an opinion on this matter?"

The older dwarf bowed. "Your Majesty, I have known both of these fine dwarves since they were knee high. I do not doubt either of their stories. Anyone who knows Douglon knows that he has no interest in the crown at all. It has been a trial to King Horgoth on many occasions that Douglon is unwilling to do anything related to the throne."

Douglon straightened up proudly at this dubious support.

"I know that Menwoth also speaks the truth, that King Horgoth has indeed accused Douglon of treason before a full court."

"Then what are we to do?" Saren asked.

Nurthrum turned to Douglon. "I have your word that the accusations are false?"

"Good Grayven's Beard! Of course they're false!"

Nurthrum nodded and turned back to Saren. "I will inform King Horgoth that the charges are disputed. If Douglon will agree to come to Duncave as soon as he can to present his case to Horgoth, I will vouch for him until then."

Saren blinked in surprise at the easy solution. "Menwoth, are you willing to stand by Nurthrum's decision?"

Menwoth glowered at Douglon, his mouth clamped shut. He gave a quick nod.

"Excellent," Saren said with a relieved air. "Then we have a great many other things to discuss with the council. Thank you each for coming—"

"Excuse me, Your Majesty," Nurthrum said, "We may have a slight problem convincing King Horgoth that this is the right decision."

Saren leveled a gaze at the dwarf.

"Perhaps a gesture of good will to go along with the news?"

"What do you want, Nurthrum," Saren asked tiredly.

"Kollman Pass."

Menwoth looked quickly at Nurthrum, then a little too eagerly back at Saren.

The queen's eyebrows rose. "Kollman Pass? You want the only western pass out of my lands? In response to this situation? The High Dwarf has been trying to get Kollman Pass since before my husband died. I'm not about to hand it over to keep one dwarf out of trouble."

Nurthrum glanced around the room and his gaze stopped on Alaric.

"Rumors are flying about the palace, Your Majesty. They say a Keeper has returned and that he travels with elves and dwarves and that his presence here means there is great trouble on the horizon."

Alaric watched the dwarf closely. Whatever game Nurthrum was playing, it was working. Saren's eyes shifted apprehensively between the Nurthrum and Alaric.

"I was under the impression that it was important to you, Your Majesty, that Douglon retain his freedom in order to help the Keeper with whatever it is that is so urgent." Nurthrum shrugged. "If it is not, then let us drop this discussion all together and arrest Douglon. King Horgoth can have the headache of sorting all this out, and we can continue about our day."

Saren's eyes narrowed as she considered the dwarf for a long moment. A sense of foreboding began to gnaw at Alaric. Saren hadn't gotten any better at negotiating in the past two years. Nurthrum had cornered her. Saren couldn't give the Pass to the dwarves. It was the only pass through the Scale Mountains. No one in Queensland ever used it, but the army had an outpost there. It was the easiest way for nomads to enter Queensland. The dwarves wouldn't protect the pass. An army of nomads could be at Saren's doorstep before she had any clue.

And the small castle Alaric shared with Evangeline was on Kollman Pass.

Saren gripped her hands together in her lap. "Perhaps it is time for an era of cooperation between our people to begin. There are two watchtowers along Kollman Pass. I want one company of my soldiers for each tower and guaranteed safe passage to and from them. They will be limited in their activities to the immediate area of the towers."

Menwoth's eyebrows rose and Nurthrum smiled widely.

Alaric opened his mouth to object. That was a terrible idea. In practical terms, if the dwarves owned the pass, there were limitless ways they could trouble and harry the soldiers. This would end with Saren losing the Pass completely. She had backed herself into a corner.

Before Alaric could speak, Saren turned to him. "There is one more condition. When you are finished with your current work, Alaric, you will return to court and remain here until I dismiss you."

Alaric stared at her for a moment, then closed his mouth.

Nurthrum glanced at him in surprise, realizing at the same moment as Alaric that the negotiation had never been between the dwarves and Saren.

THIRTY-TWO

I t had never been Saren who was cornered.

Alaric couldn't let Douglon be arrested for treason just because Alaric was reluctant to come back to court. He clenched his jaw and gave Saren a short nod. "When I am done with what I need to do."

Saren let out a breath. "Nurthrum, draft up a treaty for the Pass. We will sign it, and you can take it to Horgoth with the news that Douglon will present himself and his case in Duncave as soon as he is finished helping Alaric."

Alaric watched Saren closely, realizing that the lines on her face looked less like exhaustion and more like experience.

"Now," Saren said, rising and heading toward the formal council chamber, "we have a council meeting to attend."

The dwarves filed out of the room, and Alaric set his hand on Saren's arm to stop her as she walked past. "You gave up Kollman Pass? Just to have me back here?"

Saren's brow snapped together. "Kollman Pass is just one of the pieces in a complicated agreement I am working on with the dwarves. I've been planning to trade the Pass to them for a very long time. Frankly, I never thought I would get the promise of something so valuable in return." She stepped past Alaric, the corner of her mouth curling up in a triumphant smile. "Once you're finally back, I'll take the time to explain it all."

Alaric stared after her for a long moment, holding down the irritation forming in his chest. She had trapped him. She had played into what everyone thought of her and she had trapped him. Worse, she had played into what Alaric thought of her, complete with sitting in the too-big chair. His irritation broke apart and came out as a huff that was very close to a laugh. His mouth twisted into a rueful smile. Reluctantly, he admitted she had won.

The council table was now full of soldiers in military uniforms, a small man rummaging through a pile of maps, and several others from the nobility. A woman with a large book opened on the table before her was glancing around the room and making notes. Brandson and Milly took seats at the foot of the table near the door. Douglon leaned against the back wall behind them. Ayda looked curiously at the people at the table and sat cross-legged on top of a huge chest that sat near a column close to the queen. Saren gave her a courteous smile as she took her seat, and Ayda beamed back at her.

Alaric walked over to his seat at the table and stood behind it. His black robe felt more conspicuous than before. General Marton, the stalwart leader of Saren's forces, gave him a friendly nod. It was nice to see a familiar face. There were empty seats at the end of the table next to Milly. The woman with the book opened, who must be the current court scribe, looked at Saren questioningly.

"Duke Thornton and the southern dukes were invited to the council," Saren said. She pursed her lips and tapped her fingers on the table. Then she glanced at Alaric. "Let's begin, anyway."

The woman with the book raised her eyebrow almost imperceptibly before raising her pen.

Saren cleared her throat and the room quieted. "Today, we welcome Keeper Alaric back to court after far too long without him."

Alaric nodded to the queen.

"We also welcome his companions Brandson, Milly, Douglon, and Princess Aydalya of the Greenwood. Ayda brings us the news we have long feared. She is all that remains of the elven kingdom. The rest of her people were destroyed by Mallon."

There was a collective gasp as the room looked quickly at Ayda and murmured to each other.

"Alaric brings us some more dire news," Saren continued, bringing the room to order. She turned toward him.

Alaric decided to begin with the most straightforward. "The nomads are gathering to the west."

The mapmaker started rummaging through scrolls, and the scribe began scribbling fiercely. "Where?"

Douglon walked up to the table. "They are rumored to be gathering in the valley below Mt. Dorten." He pulled a map closer to himself. "This map is terrible. The valley is here. You don't have it marked." He pointed at a blank space on the map. "It's large and flat with good supply of water and plenty of game. There are several ravines that lead to it from the Roven Sweep. A large force could gather there and be supported by the valley for the entire summer."

The mapmaker began to sketch the valley onto the map.

"Rumored?" General Marton asked.

Douglon nodded. "The dwarves have been finding evidence of them since early spring."

"And they have sent no one to check it out?" Saren asked.

"No, Your Majesty," Douglon answered, looking apologetic. "The dwarves don't think that the actions of humans are particularly important. I've sent my cousin to convince the king to look into it."

Saren considered the map for a moment, then looked at the court scribe. "Didn't Lord Horwen arrive at court yesterday?" At the woman's nod, Saren turned to the guard standing near the door.

"Go find Lord Horwen," Saren told him. She turned back to the room. "Horwen is Lord of Penchen. His lands lie here along the feet of the Scale Mountains. If anyone would have knowledge of that part of the mountains it would be he."

General Marton leaned over the map, asking Douglon questions while the mapmaker scribbled notes furiously. The general called for and then sent a half-dozen messengers out of the room on assorted errands.

A few minutes later, the door opened and the guard escorted an elderly nobleman into the room, his cane tapping on the floor as he tottered off a bow toward Queen Saren. His doublet was black velvet, emblazoned with a white hawk. She motioned him to the empty chair next to Milly. He tussled with his cane for a moment, thumping it against the chair and table, before sitting. Queen Saren introduced the lord to Alaric.

Horwen blinked. "A Keeper! How wonderful!"

Alaric bowed his head slightly toward the man.

Queen Saren addressed Horwen. "These good dwarves bring news of nomads gathering here in the Scale Mountains."

"Nomads? Impossible," Horwen declared. "I've heard no such thing."

"How many scouts do you have in the mountains?" Saren asked.

"None. Nothing ever happens there."

Saren's lips tightened. "If you don't patrol, how do you know there are no nomads there?"

"My people tell me everything," Horwen said expansively. "And I've heard no news of any nomads."

Queen Saren's lips grew even thinner.

"Nevertheless, Your Majesty," Alaric said, "the dwarves are certain there are some nomads there." Alaric glanced around the room again. He took a deep breath and continued, "The reason the nomads are especially troubling is that we believe a Shade Seeker is attempting to raise the Rivor."

There was shocked silence for a moment in the room, then a rumble of conversation.

"What did he say about the Rivor?" Horwen demanded. "Speak up, young man! The Rivor died years ago."

"Maybe not," Saren said.

"Oh," Lord Horwen said. "Oh dear."

As briefly as he could, Alaric told the council about the sacrifice of the elves. Ayda sat close-lipped on the chest.

"How do you know this about the Shade Seeker?" General Marton asked.

"The Shade Seeker's name is Gustav, and he traveled with us for a while."

The general raised his eyebrow.

"No," Alaric answered the obvious question, "we didn't know he was a Shade Seeker."

"We thought he was an idiot," Ayda said.

"How did you figure it out?" Marton asked.

Alaric opened his mouth, but Ayda beat him to it.

"We had been looking for a treasure," Ayda began.

"Ooh!" Horwen said. "A treasure hunt!"

"We figured out that he really was a wizard when he stole it right out from under us," Ayda continued. "Alaric hadn't told us it was a magical treasure created by a Keeper long ago. It turns out the Shade Seeker had been controlling each of us, including Alaric, in order to find it." She shrugged. "Then the Shade Seeker flew off on his dragon."

The queen turned back to Alaric. "That's a lot of things that didn't go well, Alaric. Do you know where Gustav is now?"

Alaric paused. "Ahead of us."

"Do you know where he is going?"

Another pause. "I have some theories."

Queen Saren sighed and sank back in her chair.

"I thought that man was a Keeper," Horwen said loudly to Milly.

Alaric scowled.

"As did I," said the queen tiredly.

THIRTY-THREE

Alaric refused to drop his gaze from the queen's.

"I didn't begin this"—he waved his hand at the group—"treasure hunt as a Keeper. I fell in with a group searching for something I was interested in." He paused. "And I had nowhere else to go."

"Not even back to court where you belong?" she asked.

Alaric clenched his jaw, fighting to keep his voice calm. "I'm not done with what I need to do."

"There's more going on in the world than your problems," she snapped.

Alaric closed his mouth, fuming. The rest of the room was perfectly still. The court scribe's pen, scratching down the words, was the only sound.

"Stop being mean to Alaric," Ayda said peevishly.

The queen's eyes blazed as she turned to the impertinent elf.

"Yes, he did all those things," Ayda said. "He even helped the Shade Seeker translate some troublesome runes on the map so he could find the treasure."

Alaric glared at her, and she shot him a cheerful smile back.

"And, no, Alaric doesn't really want to be a Keeper. Well, most days he doesn't. At this point, he wishes he could pass this off to someone else or at least get some useful advice instead of having to explain himself to people who didn't even know there was a threat, much less know how to neutralize it."

The queen stood to face Ayda, and Alaric rose, too. Douglon pushed himself away from the wall where he had been leaning.

Ayda slid off the chest and stepped forward into the light of a large torch. The room flashed with coppery reflections from her hair. "But there are no other Keepers to rescue you," Ayda said in a quiet voice that filled the room. "And there are no other elves to sacrifice themselves to save your miserable race that did nothing but fall under Mallon's power."

Alaric glanced around the room. Every single face was staring at the elf. The scribe's pen hovered frozen over the paper. Even Lord Horwen's eyes were alert.

"So I'd suggest you stop posturing and ask Alaric what it is that he needs you to do in order to save your weak little kingdom from a threat that has destroyed far more powerful races than your own." Ayda held the queen's eyes a moment longer. Then giving the queen a cold smile, the elf sat back down on the chest.

Alaric let out a breath.

"Uppity little thing," Horwen whispered loudly to Milly.

The look Ayda shot Alaric was fierce and, dare he say, loyal? He bowed his head to her and she grinned.

Alaric looked back at Saren, making his voice as calm as possible. "The nomads are gathering no matter what Lord Horwen's people tell him." Alaric nodded toward Horwen who was sitting back in his chair, looking confused. "And if Gustav succeeds in raising Mallon, you should be ready for an invasion."

The council door swung open, and Duke Thornton strode in, followed by two other smug young noblemen. Thornton tossed off the slightest nod to Queen Saren before dropping into one of the chairs. He looked around the table, his eyes falling on the scribe's book. Noticing that she had already begun taking notes, he scowled at the queen.

Alaric could almost feel the pressure of her fury pull away from him and refocus on the duke. Saren, her hands gripped tightly in her lap below the table, pierced Thornton with her gaze. "How nice of you to join us."

Thornton's eyes flicked to Alaric then back to the queen. He opened his mouth to speak, but the queen continued. "These dwarves bring news that nomads are gathering in the Scale Mountains because a Shade Seeker is attempting to raise Mallon."

Duke Thornton snorted. "The dwarves wouldn't know an army was gathering above them if the troops were stomping and shouting down every muddy hole they could find. And you expect us to believe that Mallon's been what? Sleeping for eight years?"

The two dukes next to him smirked.

"Duke Thornton," Alaric said, keeping his voice level as he targeted the duke with all of his own frustrations. He stood, reaching into his pocket for the scrolls he had requested from the library. "I knew your father."

Thornton gave him a bored look.

"I met your grandfather, Morlan, once as well," Alaric said. "I hear that, unlike your father and grandfather, you're having a hard time keeping the southern passes safe."

Thornton raised an eyebrow. "The passes are crawling with brigands who worm their way up from the south to harass the gold merchants. My soldiers keep the passes open."

"Well, that is your job," Alaric said.

The table had gone quiet. The mapmaker was looking between Alaric and Thornton. The scribe was scribbling away madly, recording each word.

"Yes it is," Thornton answered. "And what exactly is your job, Keeper? Did you notice that while you've been away, the court has continued running just the same? Makes many of us wonder what it is you did when you were here. And it makes us wonder why you came back? Out of a deep loyalty to the queen, was it?"

The anger that had been growing since the meeting with Menwoth surged to the surface. Alaric forced his jaw to relax. Out of the corner of his eye, he could see Saren sitting perfectly still in her chair, her back stiff.

Alaric let his gaze travel around the room. The rest of the council sat waiting, barely breathing. It was impressive how much weight the young duke carried. Not a single person spoke up against him.

"As far as I've heard," Thornton continued, "wherever you've been and whatever you've been doing, Her Majesty was displeased with it. So if you haven't been serving the queen, what have you been doing?"

Alaric let out his breath in a laugh. Whatever this duke deserved, it wasn't an explanation of Alaric's actions. He opened his mouth to answer, but Saren spoke first.

"What Keeper Alaric has been doing is not the concern of a lesser southern duke."

The scribe smirked and wrote the queen's words with obvious pleasure. Thornton turned furious eyes on the queen.

"My apologies, Your Majesty," he said in a scathing voice. "This man is the first Keeper I've ever met, and I find him less impressive than I had expected."

"I, on the other hand," Alaric said, "am impressed by the power you've amassed in such a short time at court. The Black Hills are such an insignificant duchy that the nobles from there are rarely even noticed at court."

Duke Thornton's eyes went flat, but Alaric ignored him, unrolling one of his scrolls and spreading it out on the table. "But it doesn't seem to me that court is running quite as well as it did before I left and before you showed up. It seems to me that there is a bit of dishonesty and exploitation going on." He set his finger on a passage of the scroll and looked back at Thornton. "One of my jobs here is to make sure the truth of things doesn't get lost."

Thornton's eyes narrowed.

"For instance, I have a bit of truth here that deserves to be found." Alaric cleared his throat and read. *"I, Morlan, Duke of the Black Hills, do hereby bind myself as protector of the southern passes. My family is responsible, financially and militarily, for the safety of the three passes leading south from the Black Hills. All financial and military needs will be seen to by myself and my posterity, up to the exhaustion of our resources, before requesting assistance from the crown. In return, King Bowman graciously pardons my treason."*

Alaric raised his eyes to meet Thornton's stare.

"Do you know what this treason is he's speaking of?" Alaric asked conversationally. Alaric spread out the other scroll and scanned down it. "King Bowman kept the matter fairly quiet. Here it is. *During the twelfth year of King Bowman's reign, Duke Morlan of the Black Hills was caught pilfering gold from the merchants along the southern trade routes. His men, disguised as highwaymen, robbed and murdered southern merchants, keeping the gold for the Black Hills family and using it to bribe members of the king's court. When caught, King Bowman generously forgave Morlan the charge of treason in exchange for repayment of the gold stolen, with interest, and Morlan's agreement to protect the southern trade routes with his own resources. From Midsummer's Day, year twelve of King Bowman's reign, the Black Hills duchy is responsible exclusively for the safety of merchants traveling the southern passes. Any losses experienced by the merchants will be repaid by the Black Hills treasury. This treaty is binding to Duke Morlan and his posterity for the duration of the duchy."*

Alaric glanced at Thornton. The duke's face was white with fury.

"That is an interesting bit of truth," Queen Saren said.

Thornton opened his mouth to speak, then shut it.

"If you had knowledge of this," Alaric said, walking around the table toward the duke. "Your recent actions would be treason."

Thornton's hands were at his side, clenched into fists.

"These copies are for you," Alaric said dropping them on the table before the duke. "If I were you, I'd work on how to convince the queen that you didn't know any of this, that somehow, your father neglected to teach you your family's duty. I'm sure Her Majesty will be requiring an explanation. Soon. The royal treasury is calculating how much money you have mistakenly accepted from Her Majesty to protect the passes you are responsible for. I suggest you contact your own treasury to begin collecting the funds."

Thornton shoved his chair back and stood up, glaring at Alaric. His two friends rose, too, backing up toward the door.

"And I also suggest you get that brigand problem under control quickly. Her Majesty will be checking with the gold merchants who enter Queenstown to make sure they've received safe passage."

Thornton turned blazing eyes to the queen.

She looked back at him calmly. "I'll send for you when I have time. Do not leave the palace."

Duke Thornton grabbed the scrolls, spun on his heels, and stormed from the room, followed quickly by the other two.

Saren sank back in her chair, a genuine smile spreading across her face.

Alaric bowed to her. It didn't make up for everything, but it was a start.

THIRTY-FOUR

With the exit of Duke Thornton, the tension in the room dissolved. Alaric walked back to his seat amidst a sea of murmuring.

Saren cocked her head to the side. "Alaric, how did you find out about Gustav and what he was doing?"

"I was searching for some information from an old Keeper named Kordan when I met this group. Douglon had discovered the remains of Kordan's home in a valley in the Scales."

"The Keeper didn't live at the Stronghold?" Saren asked.

"Not at the end of his life. He left the Keepers and built his own home, west of here at the edge of the Scales. Douglon had found a map there to where Kordan had buried a Wellstone."

The queen and Lord Horwen looked impressed by this. Most of the other faces in the room were blank.

"What's a Wellstone?" asked General Marton.

"A gem that holds memories or energy. They are extremely rare, and it is what I had been searching for. Unfortunately, it's what Gustav was looking for as well. To raise Mallon, Gustav is going to have to find a lot of energy and store it somewhere. The Wellstone would be the perfect tool for that."

"What are you planning next, Alaric?" Saren asked.

"We're going to the Greenwood to move the Rivor's body to a more protected place. It won't stop Gustav forever, but it will slow him down and give us more time to find him."

General Marton cleared his throat. "This Shade Seeker is in Queensland preparing to raise Mallon. So who is organizing the nomads?"

Alaric shrugged. "I have no idea. But I can't believe the two things are unrelated."

"It was Gustav!" Milly said suddenly. The entire room turned toward her and she shrank back into her chair. "I mean, it could have been."

Alaric shook his head. "He's been in Kordan's Blight for months."

"I know," Milly said. "But he told me once that before he came to Kordan's Blight, he traveled the Roven Sweep among the nomads. He said they loved him."

Lord Horwen was looking in amazement at Milly, "This is the queen's council, young woman! Not a tavern where peasants shout out rumors. Hold your tongue!"

"Lord Horwen," the queen said sharply, "she is welcome to speak. If I didn't allow rumors in my council meetings, we would have very little to discuss. Milly, do you think Gustav was telling the truth?"

She paused. "Well, I didn't. He also told me once that he could move the moon." She looked at Alaric. "That's impossible, right?"

Alaric nodded at her. "Definitely."

"So I thought he was just making more things up," she continued. "He doesn't seem like a man anyone would follow, but…"

"But what?" the queen said impatiently.

Milly looked at Alaric again. "He always gets what he wants. None of you really liked him, but you all did exactly what he wanted."

"He managed to influence us," Douglon said. "But he could hardly do that to an entire army."

"He wouldn't have to control the entire army," General Marton said, "just the leaders."

Alaric shook his head again. Gustav couldn't have done that, too. Could he? The idea had the unsettling feeling of being… probable. And if the dwarves were right, the nomads had been slowly gathering for months. Theoretically, Gustav could have set things in motion before going to Kordan's Blight.

"This wizard fellow doesn't sound as foolish as you all made him sound," Horwen said with a chuckle. "Sounds like an evil mastermind!"

General Marton nodded.

Saren nodded as well. "Whether Gustav is the mastermind behind this or not, it is clear that we face a threat. One we didn't even dream possible." She looked at the maps and then turned toward Alaric. "What do you need us to do?"

"Ready the army and send some scouts to figure out what the nomads are doing. If we can stop Gustav, I think the nomads will disperse. But if he is successful…" Alaric looked around the room, knowing he didn't need to finish. "We might as well put up a fight."

The queen nodded. "There are things to plan," she said to the council. "You all know your jobs." The council members rose, talking among themselves and moving out of the room.

"You live in the Scale Mountains," Horwen was saying loudly to Menwoth. "You should come to the library with me. I've been studying maps of the mountains near my lands, but they are woefully incomplete. Your expertise would help."

Menwoth nodded. "I have spent a great deal of time with High Dwarf Horgoth's maps, sir. It is possible that I could fill in some gaps."

"He's never actually spent any time in the mountains, though," Douglon muttered to Brandson. Menwoth shot him a glare.

"Excellent!" the old man boomed, his cane tapping quickly on the floor as he walked toward the door with Menwoth. "It's nice to talk to someone of sense. I'm stuck with commoners so often. My steward sent me a message today claiming they've seen a red dragon over the Greenwood." He waved his arms around. "*Help, Lord Horwen! A blood-red dragon rides the sky at night!*" He shook his head. "Peasants! There hasn't been a dragon in Queensland since before I was born."

Menwoth snorted and the two disappeared out the door, his voice fading away.

Alaric's stomach dropped. Gustav was already west of here, searching for Mallon's body. Through the council chamber ceiling, the rain drummed loudly. Alaric growled in frustration. It was going to take them the better part of a day to reach the Greenwood, and Gustav was already there.

It was people like Lord Horwen and his nervous peasants who would suffer if Mallon was raised. People who didn't completely understand what was going on and who didn't have the power to do anything about it. The same people who Alaric had once spent a great deal of energy to protect. How had they fallen so far out of his view? Alaric looked in annoyance at the table spread with maps and papers. He needed to leave, to chase down that stupid wizard and stop him before he managed to pull off another thing he shouldn't be able to.

General Marton looked after the departing lord with a troubled face. "That's strange," he said. "We received a report of a red dragon seen in the area yesterday."

Alaric looked sharply at the general. "What area?"

"This area. Near the city. The report came this morning from a farmer whose land lies a half day's journey north of here." Marton looked thoughtful. "I sent a soldier back with him to check it out, but I admit I didn't believe him. If there's a dragon in the area, it's not acting very dragon-like."

"Gustav flies on a red dragon," Alaric told the general. "I'm sure Horwen's people are telling the truth. I expect him to be over the Greenwood looking for Mallon. But I can't imagine that he would come back east to Queenstown. There's nothing here for him. If your soldier finds anything, let me know."

THIRTY-FIVE

Hours later, Alaric closed the door of his room behind him. He had offered Saren the help he could. The army would be assembled and some general plans were underway.

As the day had gone on, Alaric had felt more and more overwhelmed. Something about the seemingly unattainable expectations everyone had of him, and the constant reminders that if he hadn't been gone for so long, a good many problems could have been avoided. It all combined to leave him feeling like he was fighting against a cloud of guilt and judgment. Saren had ordered food brought to the council chamber, and they had feasted and talked and planned, but Alaric had spent much of the time wishing he could just return to his room for peace and quiet.

Night had fallen, and his room was filled with the comforting red light of a fire someone had lit in the hearth. On the desk, a single candle was lit for him, and Alaric didn't bother to light any more of them. When he dropped into the chair in front of the fireplace, he saw that his bag and cloak had been tidied up over in the corner. He let out a groan that he knew expressed more frustration than some cleaning deserved, but couldn't even the cleaning staff leave him alone for a single day? He had forgotten how diligent the servants were in the palace. After one incident, years ago, of a servant sweeping up and burning the tatters of an ancient scroll he had been trying to reconstruct, he had greatly curtailed their duties. It was going to be hard to come back here.

Having someone prepare a warm fire was nice, though.

A book on the mantle caught his eye, and he leaned forward to get a better view of it. It was one of several decorating the shelf along with candles and a vase of flowers. The rest of the books he was familiar with, but not that one. The title read, *True Light*. He heaved himself out of the chair, grabbed the book, and sank back down. He flipped open the book. The pages were blank.

He turned back to the cover. *True Light*.

Alaric picked up the unlit candle that was sitting on the side table. Touching the wick gently, he said, "*Verus lumen.*" A rush of energy barreled through his finger, and a tiny dot of bluish-white light appeared. Alaric forced his finger to stay steady while the energy burned through it, far more energy than a normal flame required. The light grew brighter, casting a stark white light. Alaric pulled away, clenching his finger for a few breaths until the pain faded.

He set the candle next to him on the table and opened the book to the first page. Silver words leapt into existence.

Brother,

I have a troubling matter and no one to turn to.

If it is you, speak your name.

Alaric stared at the words for a moment. "Alaric."

The writing shimmered slightly, but remained unchanged. Who had left this? No Keeper had stayed here since he left.

No, Will had been here. If this was from Will, what did he want Alaric to say?

Of course. "Alaric the Feckless."

The words shimmered, faded, and reappeared.

Speak your full name.

Alaric grinned. "Alaric the Feckless, Keeper of Trivia, Pawn of Queens."

The words shimmered brightly and then faded. In a breath, the entire page sparkled with silver writing.

Yes you are.

Brother,

I leave this message because I do not trust it to a raven. I have no time to return to the Stronghold myself. I have lingered as long as I dare. I hope you return soon.

I have been to the elves and met an elf named Ayda. She appears to be the last living elf. She said the elven people fought the Rivor and imprisoned him.

I have seen Mallon's body. He is not dead. In fact, he is still strong. The elves have his mind trapped, however, and he is not conscious of anything around him. I could find no way to wound the body.

Something must be done. Although Ayda was complacent, I believe the Rivor will find a way to escape. Without the elves to help, I fear his return would be unstoppable. Tell the Shield. We need to destroy Mallon now while he is weakened. Although how we are to do that, I have no idea.

The other thing that troubles me concerns the elf, Ayda. I spent three weeks in the Greenwood as her guest. I probably shouldn't have stayed so long, but you know how I love the elves. She didn't act as I expected—polite, but really just waiting for me to leave. Instead, she seemed genuinely pleased to have me around.

We spent the time in a contest of storytelling. The first time I realized she was unusual was when I was taking my time getting to the end of Isond and Gondrey's tragic tale. Ayda had been leaning forward, eager as a child, listening when suddenly she stepped… no, crashed into my mind.

I was powerless. She entered my mind as if it were her personal library, picked up the end of the story and stepped back out. It wasn't that she had done anything harmful to me, but the ease with which she'd done it and my utter lack of power to stop her were terrifying.

Several other times, always in a similarly negligent way, she displayed extraordinary power. But mostly she was pleasant. Pleasant and lovely. I know I found her lovelier than I should have, and I often wondered if she had a hand in that.

It was the day before I left when I saw what was truly troubling.

She had found a stone along the river and tossed it to me. The sunlight had caught in the stone, and when I held it in my palm, it started to collect my memories. Milky scenes chased each other through it. My hand on my old knife, writing that report about elves in the library of the Stronghold, throwing stones into a creek during my childhood. Each scene, although mundane, seemed to speak a sort of truth to me. Or perhaps a truth about me. As though the stone were sifting through my memories to find out who I was.

It was a Wellstone. I tried to direct it, but could get nothing coherent out of it. It was too wild. I realized that by studying it, we could gain insight into how our Wellstone thought—or whatever thinking is called when it's done by a rock. Perhaps that knowledge could help us decipher the visions from our own cut stone. Or teach us to ask better questions.

Thrilled with the possibilities, I lifted it up to Ayda, intending to ask if I could keep it. But as I lifted it toward her, I was practically blinded by the light that shone through it.

Through the Wellstone, I caught a glimpse of her standing alone in the center of a glen, power radiating out from her until the very trees bent away.

Then the real Ayda, who had been watching me curiously, shifted slightly. In that moment, the light in her was swallowed up by a darkness so deep and so complete that I was terrified. The stone pulled me into blackness—a very old, very angry blackness.

I knew that all was lost.

Then the Wellstone was knocked from my hand, and Ayda stood before me as lovely and real as ever.

"Those stones don't like me," she said, kicking it into the river. Then she looked at me, a look of piercing loneliness and sadness. "They expect the worst from me. As though one small thing that I carry could destroy everything else."

Please travel to the Stronghold and tell the Shield that the Rivor is not dead, but he may be weaker than he has ever been. Now is the time to act.

And tell him that Ayda—she should be watched. You may not understand this until you meet her, but there is something about her. When I am with her, I am incredibly fond of her. Still, I am afraid. Afraid of the darkness she carries. And not only her darkness, I am afraid even of her light.

I do not trust her. Find her, if you can, but do not trust her.

I will try to return to the Stronghold by year's end.

I wish you were here. I am out of my depth and crave your insight.

Your brother,

Will

Alaric sat back, his nerves thrumming with apprehension. He lifted the flame Ayda had frozen that still hung around his neck, watching it glint in the light.

Did he trust her? If he was honest, he had started to. And if he was honest, he had no reason to. She was hiding something about when the elves fought Mallon. She wouldn't explain to him why her magic was so powerful. Until the meeting with Saren earlier today, she had never even shown any loyalty to him.

Will feared that Ayda was manipulating him, and it was easy to see that she did manipulate almost everyone she met. But it had always felt relatively harmless, a childish desire to be liked. Was it more than that? Brandson and Milly obviously cared about her. Douglon, a dwarf, had overcome his dislike of elves to such an extent that Alaric wondered if there was anything the dwarf wouldn't do for Ayda. Even Gustav had seemed to like her.

The logical conclusion was that Alaric trusted her because she wanted him to.

And the darkness Will saw, what was that? Will was fun to the point of being reckless—at least the Keepers' idea of reckless. Yet there had been real gravity in his warning. The fact that Will had gone to such lengths to keep the message secret was astonishing.

Alaric was a little surprised he hadn't found a crumpled, stained letter stuck to his door with tree sap labeled, "Secret information for Keeper Alaric."

Alaric sat back and rubbed his eyes. He shouldn't be mocking Will's Keeper skills. At least Will had noticed something off about Ayda. Alaric had been completely taken in by her. If this little side trip to the palace had done nothing else, at least it had shown Alaric all of the ways that he had missed things a Keeper should have seen.

A bell somewhere in the city tolled midnight. The rain had lightened to a pattering outside his window.

He looked again at the frozen flame necklace he had. Who was Ayda? He started to pull it over his head, but paused. There was something about the necklace that felt like it should be kept close. Maybe he shouldn't be trusting his own judgment any longer, but he let it drop back down next to the ruby.

This collecting of troubling stone necklaces was getting to be a habit.

THIRTY-SIX

laric turned back to the book. Will's warning had filled the page, and Alaric, flipping idly to the next, was surprised to see a postscript spring into view, filling the page completely. One more thing.

I go west directly. Beyond the Scale Mountains are rumors of a gathering war. A holy man walks among the nomadic tribes recalling them to the Rivor's banner.

A village that I visited near the Greenwood told me tales of a Shade Seeker who had served Mallon. An elderly man who still comes through their village, demanding food and money. Mallon had left him in their village the day he had gone into the Greenwood. They said the Shade Seeker had never harmed any of them and that he wasn't even particularly threatening, but they were still afraid. The fear Mallon spread still lingers, even after all this time. When the Shade Seeker left, some young men from the village followed him on a dare. He went to the Roven Sweep. I think this Shade Seeker is the one gathering the Nomads. Could he know the Rivor is not dead?

Was Will talking about Gustav? If Brandson was right and Gustav had spent time among the nomads, then it could be. There were not many Shade Seekers, and it was highly unlikely there would be two of them interacting with the nomads.

But that would mean the wizard had been close to Mallon, trusted by him. Which meant Gustav wasn't an idiot at all. If Mallon found him useful, Gustav must be powerful.

The Rivor cared for nothing but power.

A cold knot sat in Alaric's stomach. He had underestimated Gustav to a dangerous extent.

Duke Thornton's estimation of Alaric's worth as a Keeper was feeling more and more accurate.

Alaric turned back to the book and flipped the page one more time, just to be sure he was at the end. He found one last line of writing.

Last I heard, the Shade Seeker was masquerading as some elderly western lord.

Lord Horwen.

The exhausted fog in his mind stirred. Lord Horwen was Gustav. The truth of it blew through his mind like a breeze, clearing away the cloud that had hung over him all afternoon.

Alaric dropped the book and swore. The wizard had done it again. He wasn't exhausted. He was being manipulated by Gustav's influence. Again.

Alaric dropped the book and raced into the hall, calling out for the nearest guard to take him to Lord Horwen's rooms. The guard ran ahead of Alaric leading him to Lord Horwen's apartment in a different part of the palace.

Alaric turned the doorknob, expecting it to be locked, but the door swung open. He ran into the lavish quarters. They were empty.

A servant girl stood inside, looking wide-eyed at the guard and Alaric.

"Where is he?" Alaric demanded.

"Lord Horwen left hours ago," she answered, shrinking away from his scowl.

The room was messy, trunks rummaged through, and drawers left open, as though it had been hastily vacated. Gustav was gone.

"Close the gates," Alaric commanded the guard. "Inform Queen Saren that Lord Horwen is an imposter. Search the premises for him." At the man's hesitation, Alaric snapped, "Now!"

If Gustav had left hours ago, it wouldn't matter, but Alaric had to do something. The guard raced off, and Alaric stepped into the room, letting his eyes roam across the mess. The room smelled earthy, like mud. Alaric looked around for the source and saw a grungy canvas bag tossed on a table by the window.

He walked over to it and saw smudges of dirt all over the table and chairs. He picked up the bag and under it found a wide-open box holding a grimy red handkerchief. Alaric stared at the box, his stomach sinking. He reached forward slowly and flipped the box lid closed, revealing the cover, carved with a sprawling oak tree.

He had seen this box before in the memories of the Keepers' Wellstone. It was the box Kordan had used to store the emerald he had created when he had tried to save that young boy's life. The emerald he had wrapped in a red handkerchief.

Alaric sank into a chair. This box, covered in dirt, was what Gustav had dug up in Bone Valley. A box containing an emerald. Not a Wellstone.

Kordan hadn't even buried the Wellstone in Bone Valley.

The book Alaric had found in the Stronghold had read: *I will store all of my memories in the Wellstone, and bury my treasure here beneath a young oak.* Alaric had assumed the treasure was the Wellstone, never thinking that Kordan would have valued the emerald after the boy had died.

Alaric's head thumped down on the table. It made perfect sense. Kordan had buried the emerald under the oak tree for the exact same reason Ewan had buried his wife under one, to give the boy a burial place of honor.

Alaric had been chasing the wrong treasure this entire time.

Alaric fell into bed in his own room. His body felt like it was made of stone, like it would be a simple thing to just lie on this bed forever.

The guards weren't going to find Gustav. He had left the palace hours ago. He was probably back with his dragon, a half day's journey north of here. But why had Gustav come to the palace? What did he want?

Alaric groaned and threw his arm over his face.

And where was Kordan's Wellstone? Alaric had thought back over everything, but he could think of nothing that had specifically said that the treasure buried in Bone Valley was the Wellstone. Alaric had supplied that idea all on his own. Of course Kordan would have buried the emerald. It had gone dark after the boy had died. Why would Kordan have kept a Reservoir Stone that didn't hold any energy?

Which meant that Kordan's Wellstone was probably in the place where he went after he left Kordan's Blight, after he left the Keepers. Kordan's Wellstone was sitting in the very tower where Douglon had found the map.

There was a polite knock at the door, and Alaric heaved himself into a sitting position before calling for them to enter. Matthew, the queen's steward opened the door.

"I'm sorry, sir. No trace has been found of Lord Horwen."

Alaric nodded.

"Her Majesty also wants you to know that your horses will be saddled and ready for you at first light."

"Thank you."

"If you need anything before then, anything cleaned or brought to you, please let us know."

"I think I will be fine, Matthew," Alaric said. "Besides, your conscientious cleaning crew already came by this afternoon."

Matthew's eyes narrowed as he looked around the room. Following his gaze, Alaric saw muddy stains on the tile by the door from when he had first arrived, drapes still pushed back unevenly from when he had first looked out the window, and a candle knocked over on his desk lying in a hardened puddle of wax.

"I sent no one to clean your room today," Matthew said. "And if any of my people had done this shoddy a job, they would be unemployed by now."

Alaric's heart stuttered. It was only his pack and his cloak that had been tidied.

He pushed himself off the bed and sank down next to his pack, dumping it upside down on the floor. He searched through the contents before swearing. It wasn't here.

Gustav had taken back his ominous medallion.

THIRTY-SEVEN

By the time the sky began to lighten the next morning, Alaric wasn't sure he had slept at all. His mind churned with the same thoughts that had plagued him all night. Ayda, Gustav, the Wellstone. The theme of Alaric's failure to see the truth of things wound through his thoughts. It was like a snake, hissing accusations and constricting tighter and tighter.

After taking leave of the queen who was already awake and in her study, Alaric went to the stables. In the east, the sun rose behind the remnants of the storm clouds, turning them a molten orange-red. The vibrancy of the morning felt like a personal affront to the despondency settled deep in Alaric's bones.

Their horses had been readied, and the others were preparing to leave when Alaric joined them. Alaric studied Ayda for a moment. She was chatting easily with Milly, her hair glittering with flashes of copper. Alaric readied Beast mechanically, realizing he had absolutely no idea what to do about Ayda.

He gathered the others together and told them about Gustav.

"I hate that wizard," Ayda said. "It's even harder to pay attention to him than it is to the rest of you. I couldn't even work up the interest to look at that lord."

Alaric had spent a good portion of the restless night wondering how he had missed noticing Gustav again. Alaric couldn't even reconstruct a good picture of Horwen's face. He mostly remembered his doublet with the white hawk. That and the fact that he was old and slightly daft. Horwen had seemed unimportant, a nuisance to be suffered. And the day had been full of so many distractions. Ewan, Saren, Duke Thornton. Gustav had taken advantage of all those things to distract him.

The nuance of the wizard's influence spell was staggering. A normal influence spell would distract someone by suggesting something particular to them. This is how you could recognize an influence spell. If someone suddenly had an overwhelming interest in mushrooms, or staring at a blank wall, it was a sign. But Gustav's was different. Somehow, he managed to cause each person to be distracted by the things they would most naturally be distracted by.

"I have never heard of anyone using influence in such a far-reaching, subtle way as Gustav does," Alaric said. "I'm not even positive he knows what his spells will draw. I don't think he expected to see us at the palace. I think he just casts out nets for things he needs and sees what is drawn in. Maybe a web is a better analogy. And he's the spider waiting to see what is caught. It's entirely possible that the fact we ran into Menwoth was Gustav's doing."

"Why was Gustav even at the palace?" Brandson asked.

"His official reason was studying maps in the library," Alaric said. "I'm guessing he was looking for some clue as to where Mallon might be in the Greenwood. The Keepers are on good terms with the elves, and we know barely anything about their woods. I can't imagine the Shade Seekers know anything at all."

They saddled up, all subdued, and headed out of the palace in silence.

"This isn't all bad," Milly said as they passed out of the western city gates. She ignored all the eyebrows that statement raised. "We missed our chance to stop Gustav at the palace, but we now know that he's not as far ahead of us as we thought."

"True," Alaric said. "And I think he may not be heading straight to the Greenwood. The stone Gustav dug up in Bone Valley was Kordan's emerald, not his Wellstone. The emerald was probably what Gustav was after all along, but after yesterday's council meeting, he knows that Kordan also had a Wellstone.

"I believe the Wellstone is at Kordan's tower where you found the map, Douglon. Gustav would have come to the same conclusion. A Wellstone would help Gustav hold all the energy he's going to need when he tries to wake Mallon. Since the valley with Kordan's tower is between here and the Greenwood, I think he'll go look for that first."

"That's the Wellstone you need, isn't it?" Brandson asked. "The one with the antidote for Evangeline?"

Alaric nodded. The thought of Gustav having the Wellstone rankled deep inside of him.

"It won't take long to stop there," Douglon said. "To get to the northern edge of the Greenwood, we'll pass right by the valley. It'll just take a couple hours to get to it and back."

As the day went on, Alaric kept Beast near Ayda. She was riding quietly, not bothering Douglon or paying attention to the trees. Something was different about her this morning. Ever since she had defended Alaric in the council meeting, she was more open and honest. More present than she normally was. This morning, it felt less like he was keeping tabs on an unpredictable elf and more like he was riding alongside a friend.

Alaric tried to come up with ways of broaching the subject of the darkness Will had seen in her. But there really wasn't a good way to ask someone to share their deepest, darkest secret while you rode with them on a sunny morning. Not a way that seemed likely to work, anyway. It was Ayda who finally spoke first.

"Will you return to the palace when this is over?"

That agreement hung over him like a cloud. "I told Saren I would. After we stop Gustav and after I…"

"Let Evangeline go to sleep?" Ayda asked, not unkindly.

Alaric felt a knife blade of anguish in his gut. To 'go to sleep' was the elven term for death. "No, if we find the Wellstone, I'll wake her and stop the poison."

Ayda looked at him steadily, but said nothing.

Alaric refused to answer the unspoken doubt in her eyes. Unless the Wellstone was absolutely destroyed, he would not give up this hope. "Where will you go after this is over?"

Ayda's eyes swept southwest as though she could see the Greenwood past the miles of hills between them. "Perhaps it will be time to sleep," she answered, a dreamy, hopeful expression on her face.

Alaric turned sharply toward her. "Your kind of sleep? Or mine?"

"Your kind of sleep," she answered with a wistful smile, "will not cure the sort of weariness I have."

Alaric stared at her in amazement. "But you are the last of your people," he said. "If you die, everything of your people dies with you. Think of how much the world could learn, could benefit, from your knowledge!"

"That is my only regret," she said softly, "that the lore of my people will end. But not for the world's sake, for the fact that there will never be another elf who will learn it. We have never felt compelled to share our knowledge with the world. Why should I begin now?"

"But there can't be no more elves. The world needs elves."

Ayda snorted. "There haven't been any elves for eight years, and the world has barely noticed."

Alaric looked ahead without answering, and the two rode together in silence for several minutes.

"I can't continue like this." Her voice was full of exhaustion.

He glanced at her and saw her face drawn with pain. "Because all your people are dead?" He cringed as soon as the words were out at how insensitive they were. But she'd never expressed anything about this before.

She shook her head. "Because my people are not dead."

Not dead? He turned to face her completely, and she looked back at him. The rage was back, deep in her eyes. A small crease appeared between her eyebrows while she studied him.

Alaric braced himself. For what, he didn't know.

But she only gave a slow nod. "You are a Keeper, and my people's story should be kept." Her brow smoothed, and her face opened up somehow. The guarded look in her eyes dropped away. What he had taken to be rage was something worse. She was brimming with a deep, shattering pain. "Will you take the story of the elves?"

Alaric drew back from her, from her eyes. The depth of the pain and hopelessness there threatened to swallow him. She sat patiently, waiting, knowing the weight of what she asked.

He wanted the story, wanted it very much. But the suffering in her eyes was so cavernous, he was afraid to go near it. "I'm not a very good Keeper," he whispered.

"Then do it because you are my friend, Alaric," she said.

Ayda held out her hand to him.

Alaric's was shaking slightly as he reached out and took it.

THIRTY-EIGHT

He raced through the trees, their branches reaching for him, their murmurs of fear and confusion clinging to him. The ground below him was covered with life, tendrils of energy reached down into the dirt, the fragrance of moss and grass filled the air.

He looked down to see Ayda's feet leap over the slow, pulsing energy of a gnarled tree root.

He was in her mind, in her memory.

Ayda raced toward the last bend in the path before the clearing, the fear from the trees urging her on. When she turned, instead of being greeted with warm sunlight, she stumbled to a halt at the edge of a snarled forest.

Directly in front of her was an elf partially transformed into a tall birch. His torso melted into the trunk of the tree, his arms, past the elbow, were covered in bark. His eyes stared unblinking past her as he bent his will toward his goal.

She stepped back a moment, frightened.

"Just a changing," she said quietly to herself. A changing was smooth and graceful. Like stretching. There was nothing frightening about it.

And yet she drew away.

A groan farther ahead drew her attention.

Another elf, partway through changing stared out of an aspen, his face stretched in pain. Why pain? Changing wasn't painful.

There was something terribly wrong. She stood before the tree, trying to understand. The deep pulse of energy that should have flowed through his roots was sluggish. She reached forward and touched the side of the tree, looking into the elf's tortured face. The life energy didn't flow; it swirled and dribbled and pressed in all the wrong places. And there was a darkness, a growing mass of blackness sending tendrils out, wrapping around what was left of the elf and smothering it.

She yanked her hand off the tree and looked around her. Every tree was the same. She could see it now, the blackness sitting inside each one of them.

She walked past one after another, each a tangle of elf and tree segments spliced together. There were so many.

Her gaze scanned the glen as she took faltering steps forward. Her eyes finally fell on the basin sitting at the foot of the steps to her father's house. The surface still bubbled slightly with the power of the links to the cursed ones, links to the people controlled by fragments of Mallon's will.

Ayda looked around at all of the half-changed elves. They should have used those links to pull Mallon's curses off the people he controlled and onto themselves. Once they finished changing into trees, the curses would be released, the dark energy returning to Mallon. Then, with all his power back inside of his own body, he would be mortal. Then, they had a chance to destroy him.

They just needed to finish changing.

Ayda ran toward the basin, ready to take one of the curses upon herself.

"Ayda, stop!" Prince Elryn called from the steps. He rushed to embrace her.

She clung to him, burying her face in her brother's chest, feeling his energy flow smoothly through his body. She hid against him for a moment, blocking out the other elves.

"I can help," she said finally, pulling away toward the basin.

He held her firmly. His face was pale, his eyes tense. Cornered. "I didn't think you'd make it."

"What's happening?"

Elryn shook his head and turned away, leading her up the stairs winding around the trunk of the greenwood tree to her father's house. As they climbed, Ayda could see that the glen was full of elves in different stages of changing. She paused in her climb. The elves stood or kneeled on the ground, looking ill or exhausted. Some looked dead.

"Elryn, what's happening?"

He stepped down toward her, gently took her hand, and began leading her up the stairs again.

"We don't know, exactly," he began. "We've collected the curses, but somehow, they are keeping our people from changing." He looked down toward the glen, dismayed. "There may be too much of the Rivor in one place."

Ayda stopped again, staring at Elryn. "They can't change as fast as you, so the spells have time to stop them."

Elryn looked stricken. "I didn't know it would make a difference."

Ayda began to run up the stairs, now pulling her brother after her. They ran to the top and into her father's house. Rushing through rooms created out of the tree itself, she ran into King Andolin's council chamber where she slid to a halt.

The king stood with his head bowed before a large window. Off to the east, smoke rose lazily above the trees.

"He has crossed the eastern border of the Greenwood," the king said. "He spreads fire and darkness. We have very little time."

Ayda looked at her father. His shoulders were bowed and his skin was white as moonlight.

"Who?" Ayda demanded. "Mallon? Is he coming here?"

Her father did not move. Elryn closed his eyes.

Ayda stared at the two of them just standing there. Mallon was coming to the glen. A seething rage grew deep within her. The darkness in the elves was his doing. He would not bring more of that darkness here.

"We have to fight him!"

"There will be no fight," the king said quietly. "There will only be death."

Ayda looked angrily at her brother and father. "Of course we will fight," she said. "Every elf alive is here. Why would we not fight?"

"Every elf alive is trapped," Elryn said. "Trapped in themselves having willingly taken on the power of the Rivor."

She stared at him, then looked out the window at the elves below. Those changing were still caught, others sat senseless on the ground or stumbled about as though in darkness.

"How many are free?"

Elryn looked at her. "Three."

King Andolin dropped his head into his hands.

"Father," Elryn said matter-of-factly, "it is time."

The king sighed deeply then straightened his shoulders and looked at Ayda. His eyes drew her in and surrounded her.

"I have always loved you, my daughter," he said, pulling her into an embrace. Then he stepped back and held her firmly by the shoulders. "Will you help me?" His voice was pleading. His eyes burned with the question.

"Of course," she answered. "Anything you need."

He opened his mouth for a moment, then closed it again. Turning abruptly away, he strode from the room followed by Elryn.

Ayda looked again at the eastern sky. The smoke spread across the blue sky like a stain.

She ran after them back down to the glen.

Elryn was standing at the eastern entrance of the clearing. He faced down the avenue that wound away under the tree, holding a longbow in his hand.

"What are you doing?" she asked, running up to him. She looked down at the handful of arrows stuck into the ground by his feet, waiting to be shot. "What are we going to do against him with a few arrows?" Still, she turned and stood next to him, facing down the quiet forest path.

"Not we," he said. "Me. Our father has need of you."

"I'm not leaving you," Ayda said. "You can't defeat him alone."

"Our father has need of you," he repeated. Then he pulled his eyes from the path and looked at her, smiling reassuringly. "I can if everything goes right. Now, go."

She hesitated a moment. Elryn's face was filled with... something. Fury? Determination? Agony? He leaned forward and kissed Ayda on the forehead. "I love you."

His kiss burned slightly, as though she had been touched with a coal. Or maybe some ice. "And I love you." Her brother nodded and turned to face the avenue again.

Ayda ran to the king who was shepherding the elves into one large group. She began helping, guiding the ones that could walk to sit among the half-transformed trees. The ones that couldn't walk, they carried. Some rocked, curled on the ground like infants, some shrieked, some were bent and deformed, some had boils and sores.

As gently as she could, with tears spilling down her cheeks, Ayda herded them together.

"Someday," her father had told her the day she had refused to be named his heir. "Someday, you will realize how much you love your people."

And here, with the fire and darkness approaching from the east, she knew. She worked tirelessly, her heart breaking over and over.

When they were as collected as was possible with only a few of the half-formed trees sitting outside of a tight circle, Ayda sank down onto her knees.

Her father was pale.

"How do we protect them?" she asked.

He looked at her with desperate eyes. "I wanted you to be queen because there is a strength in you that is different," he said, coming to her and grasping her hands. Then he closed his eyes. "May that strength sustain you."

"Father?" she said uncertainly.

He dropped her hands and turned back to the circle of elves. Without looking, he waved in her direction. Ayda felt the air stir around her. She looked down and saw that her clothes had changed into a white robe covered in clear crystals.

The queen's gown.

"Father," she said with more steel in her voice. "This belongs to the queen."

King Andolin looked sadly at the closest tree. There, her face frozen in pain and confusion, stood Queen Alaine, not fully a tree but far from an elf.

"She's not dead!" Ayda cried. "And even if she were, you are still here and so is Elryn." She gestured across the clearing to where the crown prince still stood firmly before the eastern entrance. The smoke and darkness were almost upon him.

Suddenly, flames blazed out from between the trees, and a thin, black figure strode into the clearing. The air around him rippled slightly, and even from across the glen, Ayda could feel that the trees near him were filled with loathing.

"This will be your end, Rivor," Elryn said calmly.

Mallon laughed and looked across the clearing. "You don't have many to fight with you."

"We have what matters."

"Yes, I see you've collected my curses. You do realize that just means that now I control all of you as I once controlled others. I could take all your brethren and use them as my own personal army, if I needed an army. Or just set them to killing each other." Mallon smiled. "Or I could just leave them here to rot, haunted by my spirit for the rest of their long lives."

"That's what we were counting on," Elryn said with a smile.

Before Ayda could understand what he was doing, Elryn nocked an arrow and sent it deep into the Rivor's heart.

Mallon stumbled back a step, then stood straight and looked quizzically at Elryn. "Do you think you can kill me with an arrow?"

"Not yet," Elryn answered.

Ayda was distracted by the movement of her father as he reached his arms out over the elves. He closed his eyes, and Ayda felt the spirits of the elves fight to give him their attention. Each elf pushed aside the power of their curse for just a moment to answer the call of their king. She felt their agreement, but her attention was too divided between them and Elryn for her to understand what was happening.

"Aydalya," the king said gently.

She turned back to him just as he opened his eyes.

"It was our only choice."

She wasn't sure if it was an explanation or an apology.

At that moment, each elf gave a long sigh and toppled lifelessly to the ground. Thin wisps of light rose from their bodies, slowly curling toward the sky.

Ayda's breath caught in her throat in horror. "No!"

Her mind spun as a darkness tore out of each figure and rushed across the clearing toward the Rivor.

This was how they would defeat him. As each elf died, each curse was set loose and flew back to its master. Almost all of his power would be held again in his body, and that body would be mortal.

Mallon cried out and grabbed at his chest where the arrow sat.

Elryn smoothly drew another and sent it sinking in next to the first. The Rivor hissed and threw a burst of flame at Elryn. He screamed as flames engulfed him. Ayda took a step toward her brother.

Her father stepped between her and Elryn, stopping her. The flames grew and a growing darkness spread out behind him.

A terrible blackness, solid and living, shot out of Mallon toward the prince. The Rivor dropped to his knees as Elryn raised one hand and the darkness shattered. Pieces shot off him and flew throughout the glen. Elryn faltered then collapsed. Ayda screamed his name. A sliver of darkness shot toward her father's back. She shoved him out of the way.

The shard spun deep into her chest. It stabbed into her, shooting out tendrils, wrapping and crushing her.

"Ayda" her father's voice was strangled as he reached for her.

Inside of her, the darkness spread, consuming her. She dropped to her knees, gasping for breath while everything inside her burned with darkness.

The king reached his arm out toward the wisps of light floating up from the elves. He breathed out a command, and the tendrils streamed over to Ayda, as though carried by a wind.

A flood rushed into her. Voices clamored and wept and commanded. An enormous weight settled on her and she fell to her knees. She clamped her hands over her ears to block out the roar, but it was within her, stretching her, deafening her.

There was a roar of fury, and the elves inside of her tore into the darkness, ripping the fingers of darkness out of her and shoving them into a small ball. Then they wrapped themselves around it, smothering it inside of her. With the darkness contained, the voices stilled and drew back to the edges of her mind, but they did not leave.

Fire spread across the glen. The trees burned, their cries of anger filling Ayda's mind.

Her father moved in front of her again, sheltering her from the backdrop of flames and darkness. Tears streamed down his cheeks.

"I will stay to finish this. You must leave, Ayda. You are all that is left."

She pushed at him, trying to get to Elryn. Past the king's shoulder burned a wall of fire. Mallon stumbled out of the flames, but the prince was gone.

"Ayda," her father's voice snapped her attention back to him. "Run!"

THIRTY-NINE

laric blinked. He was staring at Ayda, their horses walking calmly along the road still damp from last night's deluge. Ayda dropped his hand. She looked down, letting her hair fall forward in front of her face.

"My people are not dead," she said softly. "But they are not alive, either."

Alaric couldn't find any words. The elves, all of the elves who had sacrificed themselves were inside of her. No wonder energy flowed out of her. She was like a dam holding back a flood.

"My people are bound to me. They exist in a half-life, a shadow world contained inside of me. They give me their power, but it bleeds them dry of their own... essence... their own souls. Yet they cannot die. They cannot change or heal or free themselves. They just continue, tattered remnants of a once formidable people.

"They crowd my mind. They fill everything. They infest..." Her voice trailed off. She picked a twig from her horse's mane.

Alaric's attention was caught by a movement of the stick in her hand. What had been nothing more than a sliver of wood swelled to the size of a nut. Ayda's hands still rolled it unconsciously between her fingers as it lengthened into a thin stick. The stick sprouted branches with tiny green buds.

"They saved me from being consumed by Mallon's darkness. I should be grateful." Ayda's features hardened. She squeezed the small tree, now clearly a maple, in her fist. "But they left me alone, and yet I'm never actually alone. I carry the weight of them always, every day, no matter where I am." Her voice rose. "I can't speak to them, but I also can't get away from their presence."

The little maple tree burst into flames.

She looked back at Alaric. Her eyes were dark with anguish. "So yes, when this is done, I will sleep. What was my life ended eight years ago."

Alaric pulled Beast away a step, looking at her warily. Catching sight of the burning tree, Ayda snorted in irritation and tossed it aside. As it fell, the flames solidified, just like the flame on Alaric's necklace, and a perfect model of a burning tree fell to the ground. She didn't even look back as the spot of orange disappeared behind them on the road.

"There is too much power..." she said. "Too much for one body. It flows out too quickly. It trickles out when I don't know it. This... person, this... thing that I have become is not a good thing. No one should be able to flatten hills or level a city on a whim."

"Like Mallon?" Alaric asked.

Ayda nodded. "And so I am still with you, and not sleeping yet." Her face grew pensive again. "I wasn't there when they began to fight him."

Alaric nodded, remembering her racing to the glen. "Would you have made a difference?"

"No. I was no stronger than the others. Weaker than many. I would have died like the rest. But my people sacrificed our whole race to try to destroy his power. I cannot stop before I have tried to do the same."

Ayda fell back into silence. Everything about her made sense now. The effortless way she performed magic, the tortured limbs and faces when she was changing back from a tree. And the fact that she was now part of this group, truly part of it, because she wanted to defeat Mallon. At least that was a goal that Alaric could trust. As long as he was trying to destroy Mallon, Ayda would be with him.

They rode on next to each other in silence. Alaric mulled over her memory for a long time. Will was right. Ayda did have darkness within her. Whatever blackness Mallon had attacked the glen with, a piece of it was inside her. If it weren't for the power of the elves, she surely would have been destroyed.

The only question now was what that darkness had been doing for the last eight years.

The Scale Mountains drew closer as the day went on, their barren slopes rising like jagged teeth. The lower foothills were carpeted with dark green pines, but the taller slopes were bare rock.

The western road ran up against the foothills of the Scales before intersecting a narrow dirt track that ran north and south along the edge of the range. They turned south and Douglon took the lead, walking off the road along the base of the slope, looking closely at every nick in the mountains. He stopped them several times while he explored small paths they came across, but came back each time shaking his head.

"Faster, dwarf," Ayda chided him. "I thought you'd been here before."

"I came from the mountains north of here last time, not from the east like this," Douglon said, glowering at her. "I only passed this way on the way out, and it was quite dark. But these hills are wrong. These were carved by a glacier. Kordan's valley was behind a mountain that jutted up from the west."

Alaric looked down the range of foothills that ran along the road. They looked like mountains, not carved mountains or jutted mountains, just mountains. But it wasn't much later when the dwarf gave a satisfied grunt and pulled over next to a barely visible path that ran through the trees toward the roots of the mountains.

Brandson gave a hoot and clapped Douglon on the shoulder as he rode into it.

The ground from the lowlands next to them ran smoothly up the front of the next hill. Down the ravine Douglon pointed at, Alaric could see the rocky backside did look like it had been thrust up out of the ground. Jutted fit after all.

Brandson called out that the trail had disappeared.

"How sure are you?" Alaric asked.

"As sure as I am that I'm a better woodsman than the blacksmith," Douglon said, grinning.

The trees grew close together, and the path wound into a narrow gap between two hills. The floor of the valley was dotted with large rocks and the thin path wandered slowly through them.

A small knot of anxiety formed in Alaric's chest as they drew closer to Kordan's valley. Kordan had walked down paths similar to Alaric's and had left the Keepers to begin a life here. What sorts of things had he created? Had Kordan built something better than the Stronghold?

A shout rang out from beside the path, and a man lunged at Brandson. Milly screamed as the smith was knocked off his horse, with his attacker landing on top of him.

Two more men attacked Douglon, one leaping off a large boulder to knock him from his horse.

Douglon shoved him off, then slid to the ground, loosing his axe. The men before him crouched down, spreading out and leveling swords at the dwarf. Their clothes were worn, and they had the wild look of brigands. Douglon swung his axe smoothly before him, keeping the men at bay.

Alaric reached toward the man who was straddling Brandson, choking the smith.

"*Dormio,*" Alaric directed the burst of energy toward him. The man fell limp and collapsed on Brandson.

Swearing, the blacksmith shoved the body off him. He stood up, pointing his knife at the man.

"He's asleep," Alaric called out, sliding down off of Beast.

Brandson ran back toward Douglon. The dwarf had knocked the sword out of one man's hand and was facing the other. The weaponless man grabbed at Douglon from behind until Brandson ran up and pulled him off. The smith pinned the man's arms behind him, easily overpowering the thin brigand. Brandson pulled out his knife and thumped the man on the head, knocking him out.

Ayda had stopped up ahead on the path, watching a campsite. More men were tumbling out of the camp and rushing toward them. Alaric ran up next to her, lifting his hand to help. Ayda ignored him, smiling slightly and flicking her fingers at the bandits.

One man yanked to a stop when tiny roots shot out of the ground and wrapped around his feet. Another stumbled to his knees, blinked foolishly at them, then stood and wandered off into the trees. A third stopped, spun around, and started to grab at his companions, calling for them to stop fighting.

Ayda giggled, and Alaric let his arms fall as he watched her take care of them, one after another.

There was a howl and a thud, and they turned to find that Douglon had knocked out the last man who had attacked him and was turning, axe raised, to survey the area. The area had quieted, the bandits escaping off into the forest. Brandson went to help Milly dismount from her horse. Douglon glanced around, then walked back toward Alaric and Ayda, surveying the trees.

Brandson joined them, looking into the clearing and giving them all a grin. "Here's a group of bandits who won't be bothering anyone for a wh—"

Douglon shouted and lunged forward, shoving Alaric out of the way and back against a boulder. The dwarf dove in front of Ayda.

Brandson pointed up a tree, shouted a warning, and threw his knife up into the branches.

There was a soft umphing noise, and Douglon staggered. He spun slowly around, and Alaric felt his stomach drop as he saw the fletching of an arrow sticking through the dwarf's beard.

There was a series of crashes, and a body dropped lifelessly out of a nearby tree, Brandson's knife in his chest. The bandit's bow fell after him.

Ayda stood and stared at Douglon. The dwarf stumbled a step toward her then sank to his knees.

"Douglon!" Brandson yelled, rushing to grab the dwarf's shoulders and lay him gingerly on the ground.

Alaric knelt closer to look. The arrow was sitting in the center of the dwarf's chest. It quivered with each beat of the dwarf's heart.

Milly squeezed her lips together and held Douglon's hand. Brandson knelt next to her, alternately reaching a hand forward, then pulling it back.

Alaric's mind raced. He had to stop the bleeding, had to do something. He reached out, gathering energy from the forest around him. He felt it build in him, pressing against him like a flood.

Douglon's breath came in gasps, his skin was frighteningly white. With every breath, the arrow shuddered. Milly began to cry.

There was so much blood. Too much blood. Douglon was losing more life than Alaric could replace. If he tried, if he began, the dwarf would pull too much energy through him. More than Alaric could handle. And once the magic burned Alaric out, once the energy drained all the life out of himself and into the dwarf, Douglon would probably still die.

Alaric's mind spun helplessly. There was nothing to be done.

Douglon looked down at the arrow and let out a ragged breath. It ended in a gurgle.

FORTY

A laric sank back on his heels.

Douglon looked at him, and his head jerked forward in a quick nod. The dwarf knew it was pointless. Milly held Douglon's hand with tears streaming down her face.

Ayda shoved Alaric out of the way. "Why did you do that?" she demanded of Douglon.

"Ayda!" Milly said aghast.

Douglon tried to scowl, but coughed, and his face crumpled in pain.

Ayda glared at him. "I didn't ask you to do that."

The pool of dark blood seeped into the ground beneath Douglon. The arrow moved less with each breath.

"Ayda, there isn't much time," Milly whispered.

Ayda waved away Milly's words impatiently. "Why?" she demanded again.

"Why?" Douglon's voice came out in a gasp. "Because you weren't paying attention." A spasm of coughing wracked his body. "You are never paying attention," he whispered.

Ayda stared at him uncomprehendingly. "But why did you do it?"

Douglon groaned. "Any of us would have."

She glared at the rest of them. "That's not true."

"Of course we would, Ayda," Brandson said.

"I would want to," Milly said. "I'm not sure I would be brave enough."

Ayda spun to look at Alaric.

"But *you* wouldn't," she said to Alaric. "You have… a lot of things to do."

Ayda was genuinely confused. The anger was back in her eyes, and she was leaning toward Alaric with the look that said if he didn't answer her soon, she was going to step into his mind and rip out the answer.

"I think any of us would try to save each other, Ayda," Alaric said, stepping back.

"Ayda," Milly said, watching Douglon's face grow pale, "I think the time is almost up."

Ayda dropped to her knees and leaned close to Douglon. She was so slight next to him. A sliver of bright copper next to the stocky dwarf. She reached out and turned his face toward her, her hand small and pale against his red beard. "But why?"

Douglon looked at her directly. "I would die for you a hundred times without regret."

She drew back slightly and her eyes widened. Milly and Brandson froze. Alaric felt suddenly intrusive, but he couldn't bear to move back, couldn't look away. Douglon lifted a hand toward her, but it fell back to the earth.

"But I didn't ask you to," she said helplessly.

Douglon rolled his eyes. "Never mind, I regret even doing it once."

"It might be time to thank him," Milly said softly as Douglon's eyes began to close.

Ayda shot Milly an annoyed look. "Stop it, Milly," she snapped. "He's not going to die." With that she reached forward and yanked the arrow from Douglon's chest.

Douglon's body lurched up off the ground, and a cry ripped out of him.

Alaric's whole body clenched. Brandson cried out and Milly fell back. Ayda ignored them all and pushed her hand against the dwarf's chest. She looked off into the distance for a moment, then lifted her hand. Looking distastefully at the blood on her palm, she wiped it on Douglon's shirt, then stood and stalked away.

From the ground, Alaric heard a cough. Milly scrambled back to Douglon's side.

Douglon coughed again, then struggled to sit up. He pushed his beard over and pulled apart the hole in his shirt from the arrow. The shirt was soaked with blood, but the skin beneath it was whole. A jagged scar sat in the center of his chest.

"What is *wrong* with that elf?" Douglon demanded.

"Douglon?" Milly asked, reaching timidly for his shoulder. "Are you… okay?"

Douglon took a deep breath. It sounded clear. The color had returned to his face. "I'm fine," he said, staring after Ayda.

Alaric shook his head. The ground where Douglon had lain was saturated with blood. There was no way the dwarf should be alive. What had Ayda done?

Douglon was glaring after the elf. He began to swear colorfully, then added in a few dwarfish terms, some of which Alaric didn't understand.

Milly still had her hand on Douglon's shoulder. "She saved your life," she pointed out.

"She let me lie on the ground bleeding and then tore an arrow out of my chest!" Douglon shuddered. "Do you have any idea what that *felt* like?"

"Well, n-no," Milly said. "But she did save your life."

Douglon let out a growl and continued to glare after Ayda.

The bandit Alaric had put to sleep began to stir.

Douglon turned his scowl toward the bandits' camp. "Why are there bandits this low in the mountains? They never come this low."

Alaric knelt down next to the bandit "What's your name. What are you doing here?"

The man blinked up at Alaric and grabbed for his sword lying nearby. Brandson kicked it away and stood beside Alaric, glaring down at the man.

"Name's Elrich, sir," the bandit said, shrinking away from them. "And we're here because we ain't got no other choice. We had a village of sorts farther up th' hills. But the nomads have been creepin' closer and closer. Simmon went scoutin', and he says there was thousands of them. They were filling all the valleys below the Pass, with more arriving every day. 'Twasn't a safe place for us to stay, you understand."

"And you're very concerned with safety," Douglon growled.

"Oh yes. We always tries to eat healthy and keep a double watch on the camp at night," he said earnestly to Douglon. "You never know what dangers are out there." Elrich's gaze flicked to the sky.

Douglon just stared at the man.

Alaric glanced up to the sky, too. "Elrich, are there dangers in the sky?"

Elrich chewed on his lip, then said quietly. "We saw a dragon."

"When?"

Elrich looked surprised at being believed. "Couple hours ago. Well, I see'd it, but no one else did, and they din't believe me."

"What time?"

"A bit after lunch. I was tendin' to the horses and glad I din't have the job of hunting because the forest had grown quiet—unnat'rally quiet. The horses was all spooky-like, too. While I was brushing down my own dear brown mare, she got so skittish she almost kicked me! Been together three years, and almost kicked me while gettin' her brushin'!

"That's when I sawed a flash of somethin' in the sky." He leaned forward conspiratorially. "Somethin' red."

Alaric nodded. "A dragon."

"'Twas, indeed, sir. I ain't never seen a dragon before, but that's what this was. Sure as my mama loves me, 'twas a dragon."

"Did you see it again?"

"No, sir, just for that moment, flying deeper into the mountains. But I reckon that's why the woods was so quiet. Ain't no creature done want to be near a dragon."

Alaric nodded. "Thank you, Elrich. You can sleep again," and he raised his hand toward the man.

"And Elrich," Brandson said, looking down at the man. "When you wake up, it's time to stop being a bandit. The next group you try to rob might not just put you to sleep." Elrich shifted uncomfortably. "Go do something useful with your life."

Milly had walked up next to Brandson.

"Like what?" Elrich asked. "I dunno anything but stealing."

Milly gave the man a disapproving look. "Then it's long past time you learned something else."

Douglon heaved himself to his feet and rolled his shoulders, stretching out his chest. He stepped over to the top of Elrich's head and scowled down at him. "Did you know dwarves patrol these hills? I'm going to let them know that you attacked me. Your group here is going to wake up one night just in time to see the axes fall."

Elrich paled and shrank away from the dwarf.

"I think that's enough," Alaric said. He set his hand on Elrich's forehead. "*Dormio.*"

The bandit sank back asleep.

"Let's keep moving," Alaric said. He looked at Douglon. "Are you okay to ride?"

Douglon nodded, stretching again. "I feel fine. Better than fine, really. Whatever Ayda did, it worked," he said, rubbing his chest.

"Does anyone know where she is?" Milly asked.

Alaric looked around but saw no sign of her.

"She's over there." Douglon retrieved his axe from the ground and motioned to the trees. "She's up in that big, strong oak."

Alaric's eyebrow rose. "The big, strong one?"

"I don't see her," Milly said.

"Well, she's there," Douglon said. "The oak is all excited about it."

Milly and Brandson turned to Douglon, too.

"It is?" Brandson asked.

Douglon turned slowly to look at them, the color draining from his face. "Good Grayven's

Beard! What did that elf do to me?" He looked around at the forest, his eyes growing wilder. "I can feel them!" he whispered. "I can feel the trees!"

FORTY-ONE

"Of course you can," Ayda's voice rang out. "I couldn't put as much of myself into you as was required to save your bearded neck without giving you some perks."

"You put yourself…" Douglon looked at her, growing paler still.

"You were almost dead. There wasn't enough blood in you to animate a rabbit. And you're large. Well, you're dwarf-sized. But you had managed to dump most of your own life out onto the ground. I had to replace it with something."

Douglon was holding his chest protectively, cowering slightly as his eyes flitted around the trees.

"You're fine now, Douglon," Ayda said.

Douglon jumped slightly at his name, which she spoke with that strange elfish lilt she used with Alaric's. Had she ever said Douglon's name before?

Douglon looked at her sharply. "What?"

"You're fine now, Douglon." She was watching him impatiently. "So let's go."

When she said his name again, he relaxed a little but stood very still, watching her.

She let out a sigh. "You're the one who knows where we are going. We're waiting to follow you."

Douglon rubbed his chest and, giving the trees one last suspicious look, went to his horse.

He led them up the path, hunkered down slightly in his saddle. Any time a tree was right next to the path, he skirted along the other side, but it wasn't long before the trees dropped away and what had been the trace of a trail became nothing more than a narrow dry stream bed in a barren valley. As the trees disappeared, Douglon sat straighter in his saddle.

"We're almost there." He pointed to the layer of red-stained rocks that ran through the valley walls a little more than halfway up. "The iron layer is almost thick enough." He doggedly led them on while the way twisted left and wandered through another stone-dotted ravine. The layer of rust-colored rock grew a bit thicker just before the streambed turned right around an enormous boulder.

"Here we are," Douglon said.

Alaric turned the corner and stopped short. Ahead of him, set directly against the base of a steep slope, was a stone wall. It was not large, maybe a bit taller than he was, running thirty steps in either direction.

Unlike the grey Wall of the real Stronghold, this wall was made up of the dusty sandstone from the ravine. The stones were small and pieced together well, but not perfectly, leaving the top of the wall tilted and rippled.

Douglon turned left and headed along the wall to a twisted tree trunk growing against it. The dwarf approached the tree cautiously as though it were a wild animal. Gingerly, he reached out and set his hand on the trunk. His eyes widened, and he snatched his hand back. He shot Ayda a murderous look. She smiled proudly at him. He quickly tethered his horse to a low branch, avoiding actually touching it. Then taking a deep breath, he grabbed the lowest branch and clambered up, heaving himself over the top of the wall and away from the tree.

Alaric dismounted and brushed his hand along the wall. Though more crudely made, there was no mistaking the way the stones fit together, as though they had cooperated with each other. He ran his finger along the tiny space between two stones that held no mortar. This wall was made by a Keeper.

The others followed Douglon's lead, climbing the tree and jumping over the top of the wall. When the last of them was gone, Alaric stepped back from the wall.

"*Aperi.*" The familiar burst of pain in his hand was slightly stronger than the Stronghold Wall needed, taking more energy, lacking a little of its sophistication.

Off to his right, the stones shifted and the opening to a tunnel appeared. Not too far in it was choked with stone.

So much effort. So much energy had gone into making this. It wasn't a perfect replica of the Wall, but it would have been exhausting to make. Alaric glanced around at the barren slopes around him. There was nothing to pull energy from, either. Kordan would have had to find it all inside himself. It must have taken him ages.

The small voice in him that still spoke like a Keeper gave a disapproving grunt at all this energy spent and yet the job not done completely right. The other part marveled that it had been done at all.

The voices of the others floated over the wall, and Alaric stepped away from the tunnel.

"*Cluda.*" He said, clenching his hand and watching the stone shift back to a solid wall.

Alaric scrambled up the tree and stood on the top of the wall. The slope behind it met the wall just a couple of feet from the top. A thin game trail meandered away from it around the base of the mountain. He hurried to catch up with Douglon who was leading the others down a wash in the slope. They crunched through the loose rock that filled the wash until they reached the gash of a rockslide in the mountain. At the base of the slide was a heap of stones and a dark hole where the ground had caved in.

Alaric joined the group peering down into the hole. Though stones littered the floor, Alaric realized it was the tunnel that had begun at the door in the wall and continued under the mountain.

Exactly like the one at the real Stronghold, the tunnel they climbed down into ran straight and dry underneath the mountain, ending at the edge of a valley. The tunnel wasn't as large as the real Stronghold's, but again, Kordan must have put an incredible amount of work into creating it.

Alaric followed the others slowly, running his hand along the rippled wall of the tunnel.

Something about this bothered him, but it took several minutes to figure out what. He had started to feel a sense of kindred with Kordan. A sense of someone else understanding his need to leave the Keepers. Someone else who knew he'd be cast out for the decisions he had made. Someone else who had left.

But Alaric wouldn't have done this. He wouldn't have tried to be a Keeper, anyway. He didn't want to recreate a shadow of that life. He just wanted to live on his own.

He didn't want to be sent on missions and do research. He had loved those things before Evangeline. After her, it had all felt so pointless. How could he care about the intricacies of politics in southern countries when he needed to think about her? Countries were going to war with each other. It had always been so and would always be. The futility of trying to help a world bent on destroying itself had been too much.

By the time Alaric reached the end of the tunnel, he knew Kordan hadn't felt the same way. The beginnings of a pale tower rose a couple of stories into the air and stopped, as though it had been chopped off. Again, the main difference from the real Stronghold was the scale and the quality of the work.

But none of that mattered, because the Wellstone was here. He would have the antidote in his hands. His heart was racing and his palms began to sweat at the thought of it. He tried to hold the hope at bay, but it surged forward like a wave.

The group stopped at the mouth of the tunnel and everyone stood quietly, peering out into Kordan's valley.

"Gustav's dragon's not here, is it?" Milly asked.

Alaric stepped to the very edge of the tunnel and cast out for any *vitalle*. "There's no one here," he said.

"Do you think Gustav has been here yet?" Milly asked.

"I don't know," Alaric answered, walking out.

Like the Stronghold, this valley was enclosed by mountains, so none of the afternoon sunlight reached the floor of the valley. Unlike the real Stronghold, Kordan's unfinished tower did not rise high enough to reflect light into the rest of the valley, leaving it in a dim twilight.

Douglon started toward the tower, and Alaric followed right behind him. The others lingered near the tunnel. Even though the valley was empty, everyone spoke in hushed tones and kept looking toward the sky. Alaric glanced up at the clear afternoon sky, too.

Alaric followed Douglon to the empty arch at the front entrance of the tower. It was a poor reproduction of the Keepers' Stronghold. The very air was wrong. There was no sense of solidity to the place, no sense of peace, no sense of permanence. It was a child's attempt at a man's creation.

Something crashed against the wall inside the tower ahead of him. Douglon started swearing.

Alaric followed the short hallway to the center of the tower which was open to the sky. The beginnings of a ramp wound up against the wall starting on his left and ending at nothing. Douglon was staring at the back of the tower.

"Yes," the dwarf said. "Gustav has been here already."

Ahead of them, the entire back of the tower was destroyed, stones torn down and shoved away. Deep dragon-sized claw marks stretched like scars across the floor, through the rubble, and into the grass outside.

"That was the room we found everything in," Douglon said.

Alaric stared at the destruction, defeat flowing over him. He climbed over the fallen stones to stand in the center of the room. Following one claw mark, his gaze fell on a small trunk open in the middle of the floor, a long scuff mark in the dirt showing that it had been pulled from the rubble into the middle of the floor. Alaric stepped around it to see if any of the shelves on the far wall were intact. Behind him, Douglon grunted as he walked right into the trunk. Alaric turned to consider it. The brown trunk was unremarkable in every way.

With a little effort, Alaric forced himself to walk back to the squat, rustic trunk. He nudged the lid with his foot, flipping it shut, displaying a set of runes carved into the top. Influence runes.

"Have you ever seen this trunk before?" Alaric asked Douglon.

The dwarf squinted at the trunk. "It seems vaguely familiar."

Alaric pointed at the runes. "These were placed here to make the trunk seem unremarkable. I bet it was right here in the room when you and Patlon were exploring."

Douglon flipped the trunk back open, and Alaric knelt down next to it. Shoved into the back corner was a three-pronged silver stand, darkened with age.

Alaric sank down, his stomach dropping through the clawed floor. It was the stand he had seen in the Keepers' Wellstone. The stand that had held Kordan's own Wellstone. This trunk was where it had been stored. And now Gustav had it.

FORTY-TWO

A knot of desperation formed in his chest. Alaric looked around the room wildly, looking for the flash of the Wellstone. He stood up and scrambled over loose rock to reach the shelves that lined the wall.

The shelves were damaged, some hanging precariously, some lying on the floor. Scrolls and books had slid off onto the floor, but Alaric shoved them aside, searching for the glitter of the Wellstone.

It wasn't here. He sank down onto Kordan's bed, crunching the pebbles scattered across it. His eyes kept roaming the room, but it was hopeless.

Next to the head of Kordan's bed, a shelf was affixed to the wall. It held a small book covered with thick dust, but Alaric could see by the edges that it had been well used. He reached out and picked it up. After wiping it with the edge of Kordan's blanket he gently opened the cover.

A small cloud of dust puffed out. The smell of it stretched gentle fingers into his mind, drawing out memories of the Stronghold. The first books he had ever cracked open as a Keeper had the same scent. Knowledge and magic and power. And hope.

The queen's library wasn't the same, somehow. Her books smelled like dust and paper. It was a nice smell, but not like this. This book, he knew, had more than just words poured into it. Before he read a word, he knew he had found Kordan's journal.

He flipped toward the back of the book and caught a fragment of another smell. One that gave him pause. Sharper fingers scraped across his mind.

It smelled like the books of the Shade Seekers. Those had more power, more whispering secrets, more lurking shadows.

When he had first read books in Sidion, the difference had struck him, and although a part of him had been wary, the larger part reached for it. He had been tired of the dryness of the Keepers' books, had needed the power and life he could feel in the Shade Seekers' writing.

Life. Alaric shook his head. No, it hadn't been life that he had found there.

Alaric turned back to the first page. Kordan's handwriting covered the page.

This valley is perfect. It is not as large as the Stronghold's, but it will hold what I need. I didn't stay to ask the Shield what he thought. I knew what they would think once they read the work. I have no place among them. But I will do what I can to redeem myself. Here, in this valley, I will create a new Stronghold. A place of learning and peace and—

Alaric closed the book and dropped it into his pocket. He looked around the rest of the room, feeling the echoes of Kordan's attempted new life. Now that he was here, now that he could see the tower and stand inside it, the place was a disappointment. Just a poorly made building dressed in the trappings of a Keeper.

And the Wellstone wasn't here. With a final look at all of Kordan's scrolls, Alaric climbed back over the broken wall and out of the room. He joined the others, who were waiting for him by the tunnel. Not waiting for them and not returning any of their sympathetic glances, he walked out of the valley.

Alaric climbed back over the wall and set out back down the ravine on Beast, urging the horse on as quickly as he could. He was pushed forward by the image of Gustav emptying the Wellstone of Kordan's memories. The others followed him quickly until they reached the road and turned south toward the Greenwood.

Alaric didn't feel hopeful that they'd reach Mallon's body before Gustav. The wizard was ahead of them at every turn. But maybe the Elder Grove would keep him out somehow. Maybe it wouldn't let Gustav take the body away.

It grew dark quickly. After Alaric had cast out to make sure there was no one in the area, the group made camp off the side of the road.

The campsite was subdued. Ayda was unusually quiet, while Douglon kept catching himself talking about the trees around them, then clamping his mouth shut and glaring at Ayda. Sitting near the fire, Alaric pulled out Kordan's journal and flipped through the first few entries.

Kordan had begun to build his tower, but had soon been distracted by other things. He had become increasingly obsessed with the idea of stopping death. He found wounded animals in the forest and brought them back to his valley to try to save them.

The more Alaric read, the more of Sidion he could smell in the words. Kordan had healed the foot of a small mouse, but the effort had almost exhausted him. He had poured out some of his own blood to do it and leached the power from that. The mouse had run off, but Kordan had been in bed for days.

Alaric's heart quickened. Was this the answer to Evangeline? Could Alaric sacrifice some of his own life for hers?

Alaric read of Kordan's elation after this success. He had stumbled onto the knowledge that, besides the spark of life that his magic could give, to really heal something, it required pulling that life from something else. He began with plants and tried to draw life from them to reanimate small bugs, but the plants provided barely any power. Alaric could believe that. The energy from the largest tree didn't compare to that of even a small animal.

Then one day, Kordan had found two wounded beetles. He sacrificed the one to save the other. It almost worked. Almost, but not quite. The bug was partially healed, but it died the next morning.

He found another beetle and caught a large, healthy spider. The beetle wasn't injured, so Kordan, unhappily, injured it, then killed the spider to save it.

Alaric reread the paragraph. Kordan's reluctance to hurt the beetle was plain, but he showed no qualms at all about killing the spider.

It succeeded and the subsequent experiments grew. Soon, Kordan was healing larger animals.

The lamb has walked away! It seems fine, and yesterday, when I found it, it was almost dead. A leg had been broken and there was a terrible wound in its neck.

As I watched it prance away this morning, I felt so much joy. That tiny creature, which would have died if left alone, will now grow and live.

But then I returned to the room and saw the body of the pig.

It was old, so I don't know why it gave me pause, but it did. When I entered the room, its vacant eyes were facing me, and for a moment, they looked reproachful.

I think I must need company if I'm feeling judgment from a dead pig. A dead pig that I would have barely thought about if I were killing it to fill my table.

I have thought about using its meat. Since I drained the blood for the magic, there's really no reason not to, but I find that I can't. He wasn't sacrificed for that.

I know that doesn't make sense. I even went to get the cleaver, but when I got back, there were the eyes again. I swear they were blaming me. Blaming me for counting the lamb's life as more important than his.

But that is what we do all the time, right? We kill animals to feed ourselves. We judge which animals are worth money and which are pests. We rank the value of lives all the time.

I'm just doing the same.

Alaric flipped ahead in the book until an underlined phrase stopped him.

The magic bleeds away some of the life.

During the spell, the magic itself bleeds away some of the power from the life that is being sacrificed. I can feel it. It's as though there is another force in the room. A force directing it all and taking its share of the power.

I have tried everything I can think of to stop the bleed. I have created runes to hold the power before using it. I have put the most protective spells I know around the two creatures to keep the energy between only them. But nothing works. No matter what I do, some of the power is lost.

And the greater the sacrifice, the greater the loss.

For the lamb, a larger animal worked. But for the horse last week, the large cow was not enough. He lived, but in great pain. In the end, it took an entire second cow.

I find that the Shade Seekers know this. I have visited with them and seen the creatures they have made. To make their monsters, they take a man, almost kill him, then revive him through the death of some creature. Every time they try to impart life, the source they use is… diluted before it creates the new thing. If you take a person and save him with a bear, you don't get a full human. You get a half-breed that is not as strong as a bear but still bear-like, with some remnant of human intelligence. But it is not the sum of the two. It is much less. This, of course, makes them easier to control.

This concept is essential to their work: The sacrifice exceeds the reward.

Kordan had studied with the Shade Seekers? Alaric felt his discomfort growing. Kordan was more like him than he had thought. The matter-of-fact way he had spoken of the Shade Seekers mirrored Alaric's own thoughts when he had first encountered their writings. Mirrored some of his thoughts still today. Yet reading Kordan's words made him shudder. Why exactly was that? Why was it harder to justify for Kordan than for himself?

Which makes me wonder, what would it take to heal a human? If a human body were close to death, what would need to be sacrificed to save it?

Alaric's breath caught.

What is greater than a person? It's not so much size as…vitality. Some undefined quantity of life. A large animal wouldn't work. I don't even have to try it. The vitality of the animal just isn't enough. But what would be?

I've thought long about this, and I think there are only two answers. The first is some sort of powerful, magical beast. Somehow, I think it would need to be intelligent also.

If one could catch a dragon, well, there's a chance that would work.

Alaric looked up from his book.

Gustav had a dragon. Gustav could raise Mallon by sacrificing the dragon.

The other answer is more difficult to accept. I believe the sacrifice of more than one person would do it. For instance, the death of two adults, I believe, could save a child from the brink of death.

Alaric drew back as he continued to read Kordan's detached calculations on exactly how many humans would need to be killed to save another.

A Keeper, however, being more than human and having magical qualities, would certainly be worth more than a normal human. Perhaps even enough to save one. But I don't think killing off Keepers in order to save common folk is the answer.

The sacrifice exceeds the reward. But by how much? Perhaps the Shade Seekers know.

Alaric closed the book and let it fall to the ground. Kordan didn't hold answers to his problem with Evangeline. Kordan played with death and life like a child, with no care for the value of either.

Alaric closed his eyes and remembered Kordan's tower. He thought of the smaller stones, the unfinished walls, the attempt to imitate the Stronghold, and the lack of goodness that had been there. When he walked into the valley of the real Stronghold, there was goodness and hope and a desire to battle the darkness, even though it would never stop coming.

But here, in Kordan's work, he found a man who was fiddling with the edges of that darkness. Trying to pull tendrils out into the light and failing to notice how much darkness came with it.

FORTY-THREE

"**C**ould Gustav really use the dragon to wake Mallon?" Brandson asked Alaric the next morning. "I mean, having a dragon obey you is one thing. Maybe you can get the dragon to like you or something. But how do you get a dragon to sacrifice itself for you? Or stay still long enough to sacrifice it yourself?"

"I don't know," Alaric agreed. "The instances I've read of in which someone was paired with a dragon, it was more of an agreement between the two, not the person controlling the dragon. And those situations rarely end well for the person."

"I keep hoping that Gustav will annoy the dragon as much as he annoys everyone else, and that Anguine will take care of our problem for us," Douglon said.

"But it's possible to control it," Milly pointed out. When everyone looked at her she went on. "Ayda did it. Ayda got it to do exactly what she wanted."

Ayda shook her head. "When I touched its nose, I encouraged it to like me. We became friends. I asked it not to hurt us and to leave the valley, it agreed. But not hurting each other is the sort of thing friends do. I didn't ask it to kill itself."

"Would it have?" Milly asked.

Ayda looked off into the sky for a long moment. "I don't know. I can't imagine asking it to."

"Do you think Gustav could?"

Ayda looked at Alaric.

Alaric shrugged. "I'd say Gustav's using a form of influence on the dragon to get it to follow him. But I can't imagine the extent of influence you would need to use to have a creature like a dragon submit to being killed."

"Maybe he'll poison it or something," Milly offered.

"Dragons eat rocks and dead things," Brandson pointed out. "It's got to be hard to find something that's bad for their health."

"And he'd need the dragon healthy before sacrificing it," Alaric said. "The whole point would be to sacrifice a strong, powerful life to provide power for the Rivor."

Milly sighed. "Doesn't it seem like Gustav should be easier to figure out than all this?"

Everyone nodded.

"He probably doesn't know himself how he's going to kill that dragon." Douglon smiled wickedly. "I hope he's terrified about it."

Ayda grinned. "And he and the dragon will be communicating by thought, which means that if the wizard tries to think about the problem, Anguine will know it."

"Still," Alaric pointed out, "Gustav has everything he needs but the body, and he's moving much faster than we are." He glanced at Ayda. "Do you think it will take him long to find the Elder Grove on Anguine?"

Ayda's smile disappeared and her eyes turned instantly to steel. "I can get us to the Elder Grove by this evening."

She climbed on her horse and, neglecting the path, headed straight into the woods.

They followed Ayda through the trees at a brisk rate. Even though there was never a proper trail, the forest itself seemed to be obliging her as she drove a straight line toward the Elder Grove. There were never obstacles, there were convenient streams whenever they needed water, and the trees themselves seemed to lean a bit to clear a path through the woods.

Around lunchtime, Milly came down the line handing out pieces of bread and cheese.

"I didn't ask her if she wanted to stop for lunch," Milly said apologetically to Alaric.

The Keeper shook his head. "Don't blame you."

Ayda had sat straight in her saddle all morning. It was probably good that he couldn't see the expression on her face.

They reached a wide, slow-moving river by mid-afternoon. Alaric realized it must be the Sang River, the northern boundary of the Greenwood. They had come farther than he had thought.

Ayda didn't slow, just walked her horse directly into the river. The water never even rose to her horse's stomach, so the others followed her in.

When Alaric reached the other side, Ayda was frozen in her saddle, her head cocked slightly. The others huddled silently a short distance away from her. Ayda's hair blew slightly in a breeze that Alaric couldn't feel. She reached out slowly, hesitantly, and touched the nearest tree.

She began to breathe heavily. Then, terrifyingly, she darkened. Her hair, her skin against the tree trunk, the very air around her darkened. Beast and the other horses shied nervously. Alaric leaned forward to catch a glimpse of her face. It was drawn in fury. She closed her eyes for a moment, then her eyes flashed open. They burned a fiery red.

A cry ripped from the elf, and she spurred her horse forward, tearing into the woods.

Alaric tried to chase her, but drew up, having no idea where she had gone. The others piled up around him and looked around the woods.

"Where did she—" Milly began before she was cut off by a scream of rage.

The trees around them shuddered. The horses and riders all froze and looked in the direction of the sound. Alaric swallowed hard and pointed Beast toward it. He had to prod the animal twice before he would move.

Before long, he came to the edge of a clearing. Ayda was standing in a circle of destruction, her hands at her side and her head hanging forward. Her hair fell down around her face, covering it.

The ground was scarred with deep gashes of dragon claws between tufts of grass. A few flowers bravely stood amidst the destruction. Around Ayda, a ring of seven colossal trees lay torn down and flung outward. Their roots twisted up into the air like gnarled fingers grabbing at the sky.

The Elder Grove had been destroyed.

And there was no Mallon. Gustav had taken him already and was probably on his way back to Sidion by now.

Beast had taken a step into the clearing before drawing back under the trees. Alaric pulled him back a step farther. He dismounted, but kept a firm rein on Beast, who was nickering nervously.

"Oh no," Milly breathed.

Ayda looked up at them, her eyes burning red. They all drew back an extra step.

Ayda walked slowly to each huge trunk and put her hand on it for a long moment.

"The dragon destroyed them," Douglon said quietly, his eyes wide. "It ripped them up by the roots." He looked warily at the trees around him. "They're so angry." He closed his eyes as though concentrating. "It was beautiful here." He opened his eyes again and they glinted with wrath. "Gustav made the dragon rip them up by the roots."

Ayda walked by each tree again, splintering off a piece of each. Stalking in a wide circle, she stabbed them into the ground, like an upright circle of miniature spears.

Stepping into the middle, she held her arms out and closed her eyes again. The ground began to rumble and the sticks swelled. Before Alaric understood that they were growing, the sticks were up to Ayda's knees. Then her shoulders, then she was hidden from view by the hedge of trees that surrounded her.

But these trees weren't like the fallen ones. The trees that lay on the ground were green and gentle. The new trees, which were now nearing the height of the rest of the forest, had a vicious look to them. Their leaves, a malevolent dark green, had serrated edges and between them shot out thick crimson thorns.

The trees expanded, digging up the earth with roots stretching out toward the edges of the grove. The horses tucked themselves farther back into the forest. When the trees reached a height well over that of the rest of the forest, they stopped.

"I've never been afraid of trees before," Douglon said quietly.

Alaric craned to see between the trunks, hoping Ayda would come out. He certainly didn't want to go in after her.

A moment later, the thorns nearest them parted and Ayda strode out. She walked toward Alaric, and he fought to keep Beast from bolting.

Everything about her was dark. Too dark for an elf.

Her eyes still burned red and her face was terrifying. Alaric stood his ground, but everything in him wanted to run. She walked right up to him until her face was inches from his chest. It was like looking down at a fire demon.

"Yes, it is too dark for an elf," she said. "But I think it's time you stopped expecting me to be an elf."

She reached up and lifted the pouch at his neck gently with her fingers. Alaric's gut clenched as she tapped it, causing the ruby to bounce against her fingers.

"After all, I've stopped expecting you to be a Keeper." She let the pouch drop. And looked into his face again. "Take me to the wizard," she hissed.

FORTY-FOUR

ake her to the wizard. Douglon led the way through the forests heading north. No one spoke much and Alaric found his mind wandering.

Gustav had a dragon. He would reach the Shade Seekers' valley in a matter of hours. Crossing the hills and valleys like they would have to do was going to take more than a day. By the time they reached him, it would be too late. And even with Ayda, Alaric didn't think they stood much of a chance against Mallon once he was raised.

All of them were drooping in their saddles when Alaric finally called a halt. Ayda looked at him stonily and dismounted.

As the camp lay quiet, Alaric stared at the sky. The stars above him twinkled peacefully. The stars always seemed more unattainable when he was unsettled. He took a deep breath trying to draw in their serenity. He waited for the soothing sense he got from the night sky to settle in, but it refused.

There was no way they were going to reach Sidion before Gustav revived Mallon. No way. He was probably preparing right now. Tonight might be the last night of peace that Queensland would know.

He let his gaze wander through the sky. If only he could look at the stars long enough, his mind would calm. Their light was so constant, so emotionless. No, not emotionless, serene. They burned with a serene hope because they burned so purely. And if there could be that much purity in the universe, maybe it outweighed all the mess down here.

Alaric's eyes scanned west and his chest tightened. The starred sky outlined a deep V in the mountains to their west. Kollman Pass.

Through that pass, a half-day's journey would take him to her. She was lying there, only hours away from him.

He wanted to go, to gather his things and slip off to the west. To stop this futile hunt for a wizard who kept beating him.

His eyes lingered on Kollman Pass.

He could go to her. He could see her again. If he followed Gustav, if he found the Rivor awake, there was no way they would survive it. Not even with Ayda.

Not even if Ayda would go back to being Ayda and stop growing darker and darker. He didn't need the Wellstone to see the darkness in her, and the thought of bringing her closer to

Mallon was terrifying.

They were on a hopeless journey. Five eclectic travelers stood no chance against Mallon. This journey would be their death.

But he could be with Evangeline by dawn. He could hold her again.

The familiar ache flared up inside of him. That could not last, either. She had been in so much pain, how could he wake her again without the antidote? Could he sit with her and let her die?

Not that it mattered any longer. Even if he could cure her, he would bring her back to a world enslaved to Mallon.

Alaric sighed and closed his eyes against the Pass. No, he would see this to its inevitable finish. Perhaps between himself and Ayda, they could… wound Mallon. Slow him down. Give the world time for…

What?

Still he would go. He would try.

A humorless smile twisted his face. How Keeperish of him. Perhaps there was more Keeper left in him than he thought. Reading Kordan's journal had reminded Alaric of what true Keepers valued. Their ideas had regained that ring of truth.

Alaric rolled onto his side, turning his back on Kollman Pass. He was going to need some sleep. This journey to his death was bound to be exhausting.

Before dawn, Ayda was up again, commanding the others into their saddles.

Alaric called for everyone's attention. "This evening, we'll be nearing Sidion, and we're going to meet some trouble." They were all looking at him: Brandson and Milly attentively, Douglon nodding, and Ayda looking scornful. "The Shade Seekers have a particular way of dealing with their enemies. They capture them, almost kill them, then revive them by putting them into an animal. It creates something new. Something monstrous."

Milly's eyes were wide.

"I've encountered some of them," Alaric said, "and they are dangerous. Some of them look human, some of them look like animals, but most are some sort of combination. The Shade Seekers use them to protect their valley. I'm not positive that there will be any other Shade Seekers there, but Gustav will be, and I think it's safe to say that whatever creatures are there will be doing what he wants. We may encounter them as early as this afternoon, so we should be cautious."

"We're not going to catch up with Gustav, are we?" Brandson asked.

Alaric shook his head. "I don't think so. It wouldn't take very long to get to Sidion on a dragon."

"Then we'll be too late?" Milly asked.

"Possibly."

She looked uncertainly around the group. "But… if we're too late, won't he have raised the Rivor by the time we get there?"

Douglon looked grim. Ayda glared toward the north.

"That's possible, too." Alaric looked around the group. "We're not far from the road back to the capital. Anyone who's not interested in going to what's most likely a death trap is free to leave." He looked at Milly closely. "In fact, we should let the queen know what's going on. You and Brandson could get there by tomorrow morning and—"

"Are you ever going to stop trying to send me home?" Milly demanded.

"I've only tried it once before. And it's an even better idea now than it was then."

"Don't make her get a frying pan," Douglon said with a grin. Then he prodded his horse forward, and the others followed.

Alaric held Beast back. His eyes found Kollman Pass again. It stood clear against the pale morning sky. In the dawn light, it looked close enough to touch.

He cast out, trying to feel her life. But it was too far. He felt vibrant sparks of birds and creatures, but even if he could reach all the way to her, he wouldn't find that. He would find only the dimmest flicker, barely surviving.

"I'm sorry," he whispered.

For what? For not being able to save her? For putting her near the poison in the first place? For the fact that he was about to follow the others into the trees instead of going back to her?

He closed his eyes and sighed and released Beast to follow the group, bringing them back into view.

It was only hours after lunch when the first creature attacked. Douglon, who had been riding in the lead, was bowled off his horse by a shaggy creature approximately the size of a wolf. Brandson was there in a moment, his knife out and through the creature almost before they were on the ground.

Brandson heaved it off the dwarf revealing a vaguely wolf-like face over a misshapen body. Ayda came up and knelt down beside the creature. She set her hand on its head and closed her eyes for a moment.

"This was a man once. Long ago. So long ago, the memory of it has almost left him."

She looked at the rest of them. "We can't kill any more of these."

"Can't kill them?" Douglon said. "Wait until one jumps on you."

"No," she said firmly. "These aren't evil. We can't kill any more unless they are too far gone to save."

"If we can't kill them, what exactly would you like us to do?" Douglon demanded.

"I'll take care of them," Ayda said. "You just make sure you don't kill them. But keep Milly and the others safe."

"Sure," Douglon grunted. "We'll just play with them 'til you take care of it."

She ignored him and remounted her horse.

It was several hours before they encountered the next monster. They turned a corner, and there in the path was a lion. A lion with wickedly intelligent eyes. It hunched before them, growling slightly. The group froze, the horses shifting in fear. Ayda walked forward. As she got close, the lion crouched lower.

"It's going to attack," Douglon warned, his voice low. He slid to the ground and pulled out his axe as he moved over as far to the side as the trail would allow.

"It's fine," Ayda said.

She took one more step, and the lion lunged toward her. She flicked her hand, and a shimmery blue net appeared in front of the lion. It roared once and the net flickered out. Then the lion hit Ayda and drove her to the ground. Douglon cried out and rushed forward.

Milly screamed from the back of the group. Alaric whipped around to see a huge ape hanging down out of the tree, pulling Milly up out of her saddle. Brandson was racing toward her, his knife out.

Alaric dropped to the ground and grabbed a moss-covered rock. He thrust some energy into it, igniting the moss, and threw it at the ape. The rock hit the creature in the shoulder, and it dropped Milly back into her saddle. She spurred her horse away as the ape dropped to the ground to face Brandson. Alaric gathered energy, looking from Brandson to Ayda, who was pinned beneath the lion, holding it back with one hand.

"Don't kill it!" Ayda yelled at Brandson.

Douglon rushed forward, but a swipe of the lion's paw threw him against a tree.

"Sleep," Ayda commanded, setting her hand on the lion's forehead. The beast stumbled slightly then toppled to the side.

Ayda shoved its legs off of her and raced back to Brandson.

Alaric lit another rock and hurled it at the ape.

The ape bellowed at Brandson and swung an arm out at him. Brandson fell back, letting out a cry as the ape's nails dragged across his calf.

Ayda rushed past him to stand in front of the beast. It bellowed at her as she reached out and placed her hand between its eyes.

"Sleep," she commanded quietly.

The ape leaned closer, his mouth open, breathing fury into her face. She stood calmly before him for a moment before he blinked then sank to the ground.

Brandson was leaning heavily against a tree with blood dripping down his leg.

Ayda walked up to him and touched his leg gently. Then she stood and walked over to where Douglon still lay stunned.

Brandson's eyes widened, and he stood, gingerly putting weight on his leg. Then he pulled his tattered pants to the side and looked at his leg, which held only a dark red scar.

"A scar?" he said dumbly.

"I can heal it," Ayda answered tartly. "I can't make it so that it never happened."

"No, I didn't mean—" Brandson protested. "It's wonderful!"

Ayda smiled slightly.

Douglon stood slowly, shaking his head to clear it. "How long are these things going to sleep?"

Ayda looked at them sadly. "The rest of the day. They're terribly sad, aren't they?"

Milly looked at her as though she were crazy. "That thing was going to carry me off into the trees!"

"That ape used to be a farmer. I could see it in his mind. He refused to give a Shade Seeker his only pig. They took him and did this." She paused. "He had a wife and a tiny baby."

Milly's brow crinkled. "Can you… put him back to normal?"

"No," Ayda answered. "There's not enough of him left in there."

Milly looked at the ape sadly, then tentatively reached out her hand to stroke his head.

"Is there nothing you can do?" she asked, looking at Ayda, then Alaric.

Alaric looked at the two creatures and shook his head. What was there to be done? They couldn't be restored to what they once were. They were too changed.

Ayda cocked her head to the side and crouched down before the ape. Placing both hands on the sides of his head, she closed her eyes for a long moment. Finally, she opened them and shook her head.

"I thought that maybe I could cut the Shade Seeker's hold on him. But he's too much monster now for it to make a difference. He can do nothing but hunt and kill. What was a man has been long forgotten."

"Of course it has," Milly said softly. She reached out to take the ape's enormous hand in her own, avoiding its long, red nails. "How could it not be? We become what we act like, don't we. And after so much time, what would be the point of remembering?"

There was a pulse to the swirling, like a heartbeat. Alaric le
his eyes follow the currents diving and dancing for a
moment. It was several breaths before the dark line surfaced

FORTY-FIVE

laric watched Milly, her words echoing through his mind. *We become what we act like.* Kordan shouldn't have made his own Stronghold. He should have come here, to the Shade Seekers. It was a Shade Seeker Kordan had ended up acting like, not a Keeper.

Alaric reached up and rubbed the ruby at his neck. And where, he thought, should he go himself?

Light from the setting sun stretched out across the path.

"We need to keep moving," he said.

Quietly, the group remounted and, skirting the sleeping lion, continued into the valley of the monsters.

The sun sank lower as they went. Ayda rode in the center of the group with Milly so the elf could get to the front or back of the line easily. Alaric and Brandson led, and Douglon took the rear. Every few minutes, Alaric cast out, looking for monsters, but found the forest near them empty. But far off in the woods, he caught glimpses of large creatures.

"We might want to find a place to camp before it gets dark," Brandson said, looking warily around him. "Somewhere that might be defensible."

A few minutes later, the trail went by a cluster of large boulders with a small clearing inside of it. There was only one way into the rocks making it the most protected place they'd seen all day. The group set up camp in the fading light.

"How much farther?" Ayda demanded.

"Only an hour or two," Alaric said. "But we can't do it at night with all the creatures here. We need to stay someplace we can defend. Tomorrow, at first light, we'll go to the keep."

Ayda glared at him. "We're wasting time," she hissed as she walked away.

They set a fire at the entrance to the clearing to light their camp as well as hold off any but the bravest beasts.

"I'm sure the animals know we're here already," Alaric told them. "But we can try to dissuade them from bothering us."

They took shifts on watch, two at a time, while the others attempted to sleep. Milly and Brandson took first watch, and Alaric lay wide-awake. He was exhausted, but he couldn't sleep. Every few minutes, he could hear rustling outside the ring of boulders. There were creatures out there. Whether the fire would hold them off or not, he didn't know. There were enough people here and the fire, so they might be held at bay, but Gustav certainly wouldn't want to be disturbed, and since things seemed to work out the way Gustav wanted…

Alaric must have dozed off eventually, because he woke to a scream by Milly. He sat up and saw her pointing into the darkness, but he could see nothing. Then the shadow on the top of the largest boulder slithered, and a head lifted off the rock. Its eyes glinted back firelight, but its body was all shadows.

Brandson stepped in front of Milly and drew his knife. Douglon leapt up and held his axe, but backed slowly away from the boulder. Alaric stood, too, and stepped back as a black lizard slithered down the rock to the ground. Ayda stepped forward. The beast snapped its head toward her and dropped low. It hissed deep in its throat, causing lines of molten red to glow beneath the dark scales of its neck.

A fire lizard. Alaric's breath caught and his palms began to sweat. This one was larger than the one he'd fought when Evangeline was poisoned. That one had been sleek and fast. This one was thick with strength. Its head, slithering smoothly on a thick neck, was almost as high as Alaric's waist. Alaric began to gather energy from the trees and grass around him.

Ayda stepped forward purposefully and held out her hand toward the beast.

The lizard crouched down, ready to spring.

"Ayda," Alaric whispered, "please be careful. That's a fire lizard."

"You're not a lizard," she said softly. "Do you remember who you are?"

The beast paused and cocked its head. Then it crept closer. The lizard's snout was inches from Ayda's hand. Ayda knelt down and leaned forward, reaching out her hand slowly. Its eyes slimmed to slits and it drew in a breath.

"Ayda—" Alaric whispered in warning.

But the elf pushed her hand forward and closed her eyes. She set her hand on its snout.

The lizard's eyes snapped open wide and a deep growl began in its chest.

"Can you remember?" Her voice melted through the air.

The growl stopped. The creature blinked. It sniffed Ayda's hand several times, then sank back onto its haunches.

I remember, elf, a voice rang out in Alaric's mind.

Milly, Brandson, and Douglon started and looked at the lizard in amazement. He must be speaking into all of their minds.

Ayda smiled warmly. "I'm Ayda. May I?" she asked, reaching for its head.

The lizard, which had drawn back, gave a stuttered nod and closed its eyes.

Ayda placed her hands on either side of its enormous head. She closed her eyes as well, and the two stayed like that for several breaths. When the creature finally opened its eyes, they were clearer.

Ayda stepped back and gestured around the circle. "This is Keeper Alaric, Douglon, Brandson, and Milly."

No one relaxed, but Milly peeked around Brandson. "What is your name?" she asked, her voice a little higher than normal.

The lizard shook its head.

"It has been too long," Ayda said quietly. "He has been changed for so long that he can't remember who he was before." She looked at the others. "It's been a very long time. Maybe a hundred years."

The creature's eyes were wary. A hundred years. A hundred years trapped in the body of an animal. Most of the Shade Seekers' monsters were crossbreeds of humans and common animals. They had normal sorts of lifespans. But to cross someone with a fire lizard? Fire lizards were a relative of dragons. They lived for centuries.

The creature lifted its head and looked directly at Alaric.

A Keeper, his voice rang out slowly in Alaric's mind again. *It has been a long time since I saw a Keeper.*

Alaric stepped forward. He could find nothing to say.

Do you know my name?

Ayda and the others were watching expectantly. The creature looked at him desperately.

"Ayda would know more than I would," Alaric answered. "She can enter your mind easily. I don't know if I can."

You're a Keeper.

Alaric opened his mouth to object, but Ayda cut in. "Don't tell me, Keeper, that you don't understand the concept of how to do this."

Alaric shot her a glare. "I've done it before," he snapped. "Just not the way you do. My way involves permission. And I can only see what he wants me to."

"Well, this man wants you to see his name. There was too much in there for me to look through. But maybe your way will work."

Taking a deep breath, Alaric stepped forward and reached out toward the lizard's head. The creature reached forward as well. Alaric's hand touched the small, black scales on the side of his face. The lizard flinched away, then moved his head back against Alaric's hand. The scales were smooth and warm, like river stone lying in the sun.

Alaric took another deep breath. Closing his eyes, he reached out tentatively toward the man's mind.

What he found was the mind of an animal. There was hunger and watchfulness and the feel of the earth beneath his feet, the rock beneath his tail, the smell of the people in front of him. He was a beast, but he was intelligent. His mind held caution and planning, and through it all wove bright strands of anger.

Alaric moved carefully, following the anger deeper into the creature's mind until he found a place that was full of fury. There were snippets of memories there. Memories of mountains and trees, of people.

But that was all he could find. Impressions of life and sadness. Regret. The rest of the mind was closed firmly.

Alaric pulled himself out and let his hand fall off the scales. "I'm sorry."

The lizard shook his head slightly. *It was long ago.*

Milly, who had been peering intently at the lizard walked closer to him. "I think you are quite lovely."

The creature snorted softly but bowed to her.

"If you don't remember your old name, do you have a new one? Is there something we can call you?"

The lizard considered her for a long moment. *You may pick one for me.*

Milly gave him an uncertain smile. "You're so very black, like the color of night. Alaric, is there a word that mean darkness, but in a good way?"

"Nox?" he offered.

"Yes," Milly said. "Nox. Will that do?"

That will do very well. Nox sounded pleased.

"How did you end up like this?" Ayda asked.

This fire lizard. The Shade Seekers were going to hurt it. I tried to stop them. They weren't pleased.

"Were you a Shade Seeker?" Alaric asked.

I don't think so. Nox paused, then shook his head. *I don't know. The Shade Seekers talk to me. Many of the other beasts have forgotten how to speak. They use me to control the others. We stay in the valley and attack anyone who comes here without the Shade Seekers' permission.*

"Then why aren't you attacking us?" Milly asked.

"I could tell the Shade Seekers' control over him had weakened," Ayda answered. "It wasn't hard to break."

The lizard bowed his head to her. *I owe you a great debt.*

"Why has their control weakened?" Alaric said.

Maybe because they are all gone from here. Except the one who is here now. He has appeared once before, but did not stay long.

"The Shade Seeker who is here now," Ayda said. "Where is he?"

At the keep, Nox answered. *He passed through the woods late this afternoon.*

"He came through the woods?" Alaric asked in surprise. "Not on his dragon?"

Dragon? There has been no dragon near here.

"Are you sure?"

He looked levelly at Alaric. *I am sure.*

"Of course you are. Sorry." Alaric exchanged glances with Ayda. "We thought he was on a dragon."

"Then he's not far ahead of us!" Milly said. "We're not too late."

Too late for what?

"The wizard is trying to revive the Rivor," Ayda said, her eyes glinting.

Nox growled again, deep in his chest, and his eyes went flat. *That should not happen. The Rivor lived in this valley for years. During that time, the other Shade Seekers disappeared one by one, and the Rivor's power grew. He killed many creatures, too.*

"Mallon killed the other Shade Seekers?" Alaric asked.

Nox nodded. *Many of them.*

"Can you take us to the keep?" Ayda asked.

Nox nodded. *The Shade Seeker will do nothing until morning, though. Raising a creature is a long process, usually requiring hours of preparation and more than one Shade Seeker. Alone, this wizard could not do all of the preparations he needs in the dark.*

Alaric agreed. "The runes he needs to write are extensive. But there's another reason. If his dragon isn't here, then Gustav has nothing to sacrifice."

He had only a donkey and a wagon. In the wagon was a large object wrapped in cloth.

"Mallon's body," Milly said. "What will Gustav sacrifice that is powerful enough?"

He has summoned all the creatures in the valley to meet at the keep tomorrow at midday.

"All of them?" Milly gasped. "He's going to sacrifice all of you?"

Nox's eyes glared into the darkness. *He could not do that. A single Shade Seeker would not be strong enough to control all of us at once.*

"We keep assuming he can't do things," Brandson said.

The Shade Seekers all together could command us to kill ourselves, perhaps. But not one alone. And not one like this.

"Gustav is particularly good at influence," Alaric said. "Maybe he plans to have you kill each other."

"Take us to him tonight," Ayda demanded.

Alaric shook his head. "The other creatures will be out in the dark."

This valley is dangerous at night. Even were I to be with you, we might encounter more monsters than I could fight.

"I'm not afraid of monsters," Ayda said quietly.

"There's very little chance that we are going to make it safely through the valley tomorrow during daylight," Alaric said. "We can't risk it at night. Especially knowing that Gustav isn't going to do anything immediately. He won't start until close to midday tomorrow when the creatures come. He needs something to sacrifice."

Ayda glared at him, her eyes burning into him. Alaric swallowed hard and braced himself for... something.

She finally let out a long breath. "Fine," she hissed. "I'll take watch." And she stalked off past the fire and into the darkness.

The rest of the group looked at one another uneasily.

"She's a little angry at Gustav," Milly said to Nox, smiling apologetically.

Indeed. The elf is powerful and lonely. And angry. Do you think you can stop the Shade Seeker?

"We're not here to stop him," Ayda called back over her shoulder. "We're here to kill him."

FORTY-SIX

"No we're not!" Brandson protested. "We're not here to kill him." He looked around the group. "Are we?"

"No," Milly said. "We aren't. We're here to stop him from raising Mallon."

Douglon let out a short laugh. "We're here to kill him."

"Alaric," Milly appealed to him.

Alaric took a deep breath. "I would rather not kill the old man."

"You won't need to," Ayda said.

"It should be easy enough to stop him," Alaric said, ignoring her.

Ayda snorted again. "Because it's been so easy to stop him all the other times?"

"This is different," Alaric said. "We know where he is, and we know what he is planning. Even if he gets everything set up before we get there, he will be relying heavily on the runes he draws before he begins. He won't be able to begin until the monsters arrive for him to sacrifice. That should give us plenty of time. And we will stop him this time."

"Oh," Ayda said, her eyebrow arched, "so we finally have a Keeper in charge. It's nice that you've decided to break away from wallowing in your past long enough to commit to something. Tell me, Keeper, how do you plan on stopping him from doing this exact same thing again sometime when we aren't following him?"

"We're going to take the Rivor's body and destroy it."

"Don't you think I've tried? What do you think I've been doing since my people fought him? I don't know if he can be destroyed."

Alaric nodded slowly. "Maybe not. But we can try again. Together."

"It is the Shade Seeker who wants to raise him," Ayda pointed out. "There's a simple answer to how to keep him from trying again. He wants the power that the Rivor can bring to him. He is not nice, nor does he care for any of us. He used us, manipulated us, destroyed my home." Ayda's eyes glowed with fury. "And he will pay for it."

"We'll stop him, Ayda," Alaric said.

"Stopping him isn't enough."

Alaric turned to Nox. "Is there a way for us to enter the keep unnoticed?"

There's an entrance in the back. It will not take long to reach it tomorrow morning. The Shade Seeker shouldn't be able to see us approach.

"Then we should get some sleep," Alaric says.

Ayda glared at Alaric, then turned and stalked over to the fire.

One more day and this would be done.

Morning couldn't come soon enough.

Unfortunately, dawn's early light came a little too late.

The sky had turned a dauntless pitch purple when Douglon shook Alaric awake.

"She's gone," Douglon hissed.

Alaric sat up and tried to focus on the dwarf. "Who's gone?"

"The stupid elf. She's gone. She left sometime during the night. She never woke anyone for the next watch." Douglon scowled into the forest.

Alaric looked around. Ayda was nowhere to be seen. Alaric swore, jumping to his feet. "He's still doing it," he said, slamming his pack together.

The others stared at him blankly.

"Gustav doesn't have his dragon," Alaric said, "so he drew something more powerful to himself. He drew Ayda."

Everyone had slept soundly, even Nox, who had curled up in front of one of the gaps in the boulders. That must have been Ayda's doing as well. Alaric felt like he hadn't slept that deeply in years.

"How long ago do you think she left?" Milly asked.

"As soon as we fell asleep… Or more accurately, as soon as she put us to sleep," Alaric answered.

Brandson tried to stand, but cried out and fell against the boulder next to him. Milly ran over to him as he slid back down to the ground. She pulled up the leg of his pants and drew in a quick breath. The skin around the scar where the ape had gashed him had turned dark red.

Alaric went over to look at Brandson's leg and swore again. Not just an infection. The ape's nails must have been poisonous. He hadn't thought of looking at it last night. He couldn't leave Brandson like this.

"We need to drain this. It should be quick."

Alaric sent Douglon off in search of a couple of plants while Milly began boiling water.

I can follow the elf's trail, Nox offered.

Alaric nodded.

With a rustle, Nox slithered over the nearest boulder and into the forest.

Alaric took his knife and held it in the fire. He turned to Brandson. "I'm sorry. This is going to hurt."

He washed Brandson's leg thoroughly, then took his knife and slid it carefully through the center of the scar. Greenish pus seeped out while Brandson bit back cries of pain. Douglon returned, and he and Milly began making a paste while Alaric directed them. Once Alaric had drained out as much pus as he could, he rinsed the wound with water and pressed the paste onto it. Then he ripped up a shirt for some bandages and wrapped the leg.

It felt like ages before Brandson was ready to be helped to his feet. Milly slipped under his arm to stabilize him.

Nox wasn't back yet, but they hurried, packing up their things as quickly as they could. Ayda must have reached the keep hours ago. Alaric slammed his things together. Ayda *should* be more than a match for Gustav, but she had been so angry. Dread anchored deep into Alaric's gut.

Milly let out a loud gasp. Alaric looked at her in alarm, wondering what had happened. She was staring wide-eyed at something behind him.

"Good morning," a nasal voice said from outside the rocks.

Alaric spun around.

Gustav was standing just beyond the coals from last night's fire. He still wore his blue robe with the swirling stars, but it was rumpled and dirty.

Douglon growled and pulled out his axe.

"You came back?" Brandson said.

"That was unwise," Douglon said, stepping toward the old man.

"*Alligo!*" Gustav shouted, waving his arms dramatically toward them.

Alaric started to laugh at the ridiculous motion until he felt his legs freeze to the ground. The paralysis moved quickly up his torso. He grabbed for the pouch at his neck just as his arms went rigid. Only his head was free to move.

Behind him, he heard Douglon grunting against the spell as well.

Alaric felt the humming of the magic focused on the ground around his feet. He began to gather energy to attack Gustav.

"*Liquo!*" Gustav shrieked, this time waving his hand frantically at Alaric.

Alaric felt the energy drain from him, sinking down into the ground. As fast as he could gather it, it ran out of him.

Gustav shook his hands out and looked at Alaric warily for a moment. Then he grinned.

"Don't try to fight me," Gustav said, motioning to the top of the boulders surrounding them.

There was a slither and a scraping of claws as monstrous creatures crawled up onto the tops of the rocks. On the boulder closest to Alaric, an enormous badger appeared. It scraped long, black claws against the rock as it leaned toward them. Instead of the black eyes of a badger, it had human eyes, light brown and shrewd. On other boulders sat a long, mottled snake, a small bear, and a golden-haired lion, all looking at them with unnerving intelligence.

"Gustav?" Brandson asked. "What are you doing?"

Gustav didn't look at Brandson.

Alaric strained against the magic holding him in place. He pulled in energy again and again, only to have it drain out just as quickly into the ground beneath his feet.

"What do you want?" Alaric demanded through a clenched jaw.

"I want peace and quiet to finish my work. And you weren't going to give me that. So I'm afraid you'll need to stay here. I'm leaving my creatures here to keep you under control."

"You mean to kill us," Douglon growled.

"Not yet. I'm not sure you all won't still be useful to me for something. So for now, I've commanded them to leave you alone as long as you remain inside the boulders. If you try to leave, I'm afraid they will kill you." Gustav studied them all. "And after everything, I find that I'm a little fond of all of you."

"Well, we hate you," Douglon said. "Where's Ayda?"

Gustav smiled. "Ayda has agreed to help me in my work."

"She wouldn't," Milly said.

Gustav flashed her an irritated look. "Ayda is helping me. And with her energy, there is nothing to stop me."

"She's not working with you," Alaric said. "Even your influence couldn't convince her to help you. You're using her."

Gustav smirked.

"I'd be careful," Alaric warned. "Ayda isn't someone to trifle with."

"Ayda will be no trouble," Gustav said, waving off Alaric's words. "And neither will you. Now if you'll excuse me, I need to take your weapons."

Gustav walked slowly up to Douglon, reaching tentatively toward his axe. When Douglon didn't do anything more than snarl at him, Gustav took the axe from his hand.

Brandson stared at the wizard, a mixture of anger and hurt in his eyes. Gustav walked past him quickly, not meeting his eye and took Brandson's knife from his saddle and two more knives out of Douglon's. The wizard held them pell-mell across his chest and walked out of the ring of boulders.

"I'm afraid it's time for me to go," Gustav said, hoisting the weapons up higher in his arms with a clatter. He looked at each of them for a long moment. "Um, goodbye."

As Gustav stepped out of the ring of boulders, Alaric threw his entire will against the spell holding him still. His hand holding the pouch jerked forward, breaking the cord that it hung from and leaving the pouch hanging from his clenched hand. Nothing else moved. He was filled with fury.

"Let me see the Wellstone." Alaric's voice broke with desperation. "Before you do it. Please let me see the Wellstone."

Gustav paused and turned back. "What do you need the Wellstone for?" He tilted his head as he looked at Alaric's hand. "What do you keep in that pouch?" Dropping the weapons to the ground, Gustav walked back between the boulders and stepped up to Alaric.

Alaric reached for energy, but again, felt it drain away. He strained against the immobilizing spell, but could do nothing beyond grind his teeth furiously at the old wizard.

Gustav ignored him and pulled the pouch out from Alaric's stiff fingers. He pulled open the strings and dropped the rough ruby into his hand.

FORTY-SEVEN

Gustav's mouth fell open. He slowly raised his eyes to Alaric in disbelief. "A Reservoir Stone? I thought you had been drawn to me because I needed you to read the map. But you were drawn to me because I needed a Reservoir Stone."

Gustav looked at the ruby in wonder.

"Now, I don't need Kordan's emerald. I'm not particularly good at creating Reservoir Stones, you understand. And since I haven't been able to find any other Shade Seekers since I came back from the Roven Sweep a year ago, I started looking for Reservoirs that already existed. When I heard that Keeper Kordan had buried an empty one, I knew I could use it. Just fill it with someone else's energy.

"But this Reservoir Stone still swirls with the flame of a sacrifice. It will be so much easier to add energy to this one than to Kordan's dead emerald." Gustav flashed a wickedly gleeful smile toward Alaric.

"It will be messy and leaky, but enough energy should get to Lord Mallon to wake him up. When he's awake, he can find other sacrifices himself."

"Hm," Douglon grunted, "I wonder where he'll find one of those."

Gustav's brow creased. "He won't sacrifice me. I'm the only servant loyal enough to help him return."

"I'm sure he'll be very grateful," Alaric said, glaring at Gustav with more fury than he had ever felt.

"Oh, you've made it so easy! It's already holding a sacrifice!"

"It's not a sacrifice!"

Gustav looked at the Keeper in surprise. "You don't even know what you have, do you? You don't know the power this holds."

The old man's fingers were wrapped around the ruby like a parasite.

Gustav's smile spread. "A Reservoir Stone is a vessel, a vessel to hold the power of a life which has been sacrificed until it is poured into someone else. They are Mallon's specialty. He has used dozens of them. Absorbing the power of other strong men, including any Shade Seekers who weren't useful to him, made him almost invincible. He strengthened himself by the sacrifice of others."

Alaric's stomach clenched. "She is not a sacrifice."

Gustav's eyes widened, then he burst out laughing. "You sacrificed someone you know? You proved in Queenstown that you weren't much of a Keeper, but that is even darker than I expected. Thank you, by the way, for bringing my medallion to Queenstown. I had thought it lost. My task is much easier with those instructions."

Alaric strained against the magic, his breath coming in gasps.

"Why did you do it?" Gustav asked curiously, looking at the ruby.

The words rose unbidden. "I had no choice. I needed time. I needed time to save her."

"Save her?" Gustav's brow creased. "You didn't save her. You sacrificed her. Shade Seekers don't pull the life out of someone to save them. They pull it out to sacrifice them. Then they use the energy for themselves." Gustav raised his gaze back up to Alaric's face. Sudden understanding filled his face, turning to a look that almost held compassion. "You didn't mean to sacrifice her, did you?"

"She will not be a sacrifice!"

Gustav looked at Alaric hesitantly, then he began to speak almost kindly. "She already is. Whatever she was before this—whoever she was—she isn't here any longer. At least not all of her."

Alaric stopped struggling. He looked from Gustav to the ruby. The old man couldn't know that. He didn't know what he was talking about.

"Too much of her has been lost," Gustav explained. "Too much energy is lost when the vessel is created. The Reservoir holds the life energy of a person, but not enough of it to make a whole person again. *The sacrifice exceeds the reward.* I thought even the Keepers knew that much."

Gustav looked at the Reservoir Stone closely, then closed his eyes. Alaric felt him cast out toward the energy in the ruby. A wave of fury rose at the thought of Gustav's mind brushing against her.

Gustav looked up at Alaric puzzled. "There's not much life here at all. Whatever you planned on doing, this does not hold enough life to do it."

Alaric glared at the old man's wrinkled hand grasping the red stone.

"It's certainly not enough for what I need." Gustav shrugged. "But I can add more. Every little bit helps, I suppose." He tossed Alaric's leather pouch on the ground and dropped the ruby into his pocket. With one final look at each of them, Gustav stepped out of the circle of rocks and disappeared.

The ruby. Gustav had his ruby. He had Evangeline.

Alaric's gut felt like ice.

His wife was going to be sacrificed to Mallon.

Fury built up in him. He strained against the spell holding him in place. It was as though he had been turned to stone.

Douglon was swearing and grunting behind him.

Gustav was getting farther away and Alaric couldn't move.

His rage boiled over into a roar as he reached out gathering energy as quickly as he could, only to have it drained out into the ground once again. Alaric ground his teeth and gathered more, faster. He drew from the ground, from the trees, from the embers of last night's fire. He reached into the boulders and pulled the slow, dark solid *vitalle* of the rock itself.

The energy from the boulders held. Before it could drain out, Alaric focused his energy on the ground around him.

"*Lacero!*"

The energy stabbed down into the ground, slicing Gustav's spell, tearing out of Alaric's palm like a knife. He fell to his knees.

Gustav's spell to drain his energy must have been focused at his feet, because Alaric felt a rush of *vitalle* flow into him. He turned to the others. Quickly, not noticing the pain, he cut through the spells, setting the others free.

Douglon ran through the opening where Gustav had stood, lunging for their weapons. A shriek rang out above them, and an enormous vulture swooped down out of the treetops in front of them, diving for Douglon. The dwarf raised his arm to defend against the attack. Talons ripped across it.

From the woods behind the boulders, Nox lunged for the vulture, his jaw closing on one of the bird's legs. The vulture gave a scream, but Nox yanked the bird out of the air and the two tumbled into the trees. The forest beyond the rocks swayed with the crashes of their fight.

Douglon scrambled back into the circle of boulders, holding his arm to his chest. He swore loudly, glaring at the beasts poised at the tops of the boulders.

The group backed up to the center of the clearing, standing with their backs together. Alaric glanced around the clearing. Their weapons were still outside the ring of boulders. The only weapons within reach were long, thick sticks by their feet. Those wouldn't hurt anything.

Atop the boulders, four monsters shifted, watching them with glittering eyes, content to stay there for now. There had to be a way to get them to leave, to break Gustav's control over them. He reached down slowly, picking up the four closest sticks.

"Those aren't very good weapons, Keeper," Douglon growled.

Alaric held them together and reached up to touch their ends.

"*Incende.*"

The sticks burst into flame. He handed them out to the others before shaking out his hand. Then Alaric cast out his mind toward the badger, its mind full of stealth and power. It knew the people below it were of little consequence.

Alaric felt the tether on its mind, the thin leash of control of what was left of the Shade Seeker's control. With a quick burst of energy, Alaric snapped the tether.

The badger twitched, then lifted its head and sniffed the air. Alaric took a step toward it, raising the fire closer. The badger shied back, then dropped off the back of the boulder.

The other animals crept forward. The snake slithered toward them and dropped to the ground, coiling itself into a loose pile. Milly held her torch out toward it, pushing it back against the rock as it hissed.

"Keep the bear back," Alaric called to Douglon and Brandson.

The two of them stepped toward the boulder with the bear, holding their torches out ahead of them. The bear swung its head back and forth, watching them but shying back from the fire. Alaric held his own torch up toward the lynx. Before the cat could spring, Alaric broke the Shade Seeker's hold on its mind. He shoved the torch toward it until the cat turned and jumped down the other side of the boulder.

He turned to the other two creatures, doing the same thing until they disappeared into the woods as well.

Alaric's hands were burning. He picked up the leather pouch Gustav had dropped and followed Douglon to the gap between the rocks where Gustav had left. Warily, Douglon stepped out. Nothing moved in the woods. The others followed him out, gathering their horses and weapons.

There was a loud rustling in the trees, and Alaric spun toward the sound. Nox's head pushed out from the undergrowth. He shook his head, shaking a vulture feather off onto the ground. *I followed the elf's scent to the keep. She is there.*

"Let's go," Douglon said.

Nox led the way up the valley through the forest. Alaric moved up next to Douglon to check his arm. The cuts were deep and the dwarf grimaced in pain.

"Where's the stupid elf when you need her to heal something?" Douglon asked.

FORTY-EIGHT

Alaric pulled out some of the cloth strips he had leftover from when he'd bandaged Brandson. He looked ahead, searching for any sign of the keep. The way things were going, no one in the group was going to make it there unharmed.

Several times, Alaric caught the sound of creatures skirting the forest near them, but it seemed that Nox's presence deterred them. Whether they were intimidated by the fire lizard or whether they thought Nox was escorting them to the keep, he didn't know.

The keep is just ahead of us.

Almost immediately, the path turned sharply and they found themselves at a large tower at the corner of the keep, crumbled off above the first floor. Nox stood quietly by the door while Alaric opened it.

Good luck, Keeper, Nox said, hanging back.

"Will you come with us?" Alaric asked.

The lizard shook his head. *I don't think I can help beyond this. I want to leave the valley before he calls us all to the sacrifice. I have spent too many years being the Shade Seekers' slave.*

"You weren't their slave this morning," Alaric said.

For that, I thank you all. I am free, but I have forgotten who I am, and I'm not sure I want to remember. I do not think I was good even before the Shade Seekers enslaved me. And by now, I have done too many dark things for them to forget. I just want to leave before the Shade Seeker has the chance to enslave me again.

Alaric nodded. "Thank you for your help."

"Yes," Douglon said, motioning to his arm. "Thank you."

"A friend of mine told me that we're not defined by the darkest parts of our past," Alaric said, remembering Ewan's words. "We can leave them behind as easily as we leave our best moments. We're not confined to be what we have been."

Some things are too much to come back from, he answered. *That's a very pretty idea. I'm not sure it works that way, but it's a pretty idea. Good luck to you all. And Keeper, I'm glad you are here. Your presence here brings hope.*

"Don't get too excited," Alaric said. "I'm a terrible Keeper."

Well, we're not confined to being what we have been, you know. The lizard's laughter echoed in Alaric's mind. *Good luck to you.*

Nox turned and disappeared into the trees, and Alaric entered the tower. It consisted of a large circular room with several old chairs. Stairs reached up toward the broken roof. Across the tower, another door opened into the keep. The tower was so large that they brought the horses in and closed the door behind them.

Brandson sagged down against a wall and slid slowly to the floor. Milly rushed over to him and lifted his pants again. Dark streaks of red radiated up his leg.

Douglon fell heavily into a chair of his own, his arm held protectively to his chest.

Alaric looked at the two of them. "You can stay here with the animals," he began.

"Shut up." Douglon shoved himself back up and walked over to Brandson, offering his good arm. Brandson took it and tried to stand.

Alaric sighed at their stubbornness.

"We're not staying behind," Brandson said.

Alaric nodded. "Then let's go find Gustav. And Ayda."

With no way of knowing where they were headed, Alaric randomly picked the corridor to their left. The walls around them were crumbling, and water ran in little rivulets along the floor of the damp hall. They crept stealthily down hall after hall, but the keep remained silent.

After several more turns, a large archway appeared ahead of them. Alaric paused a little back from it and cast out into the large room beyond it. The room was empty. They walked into the silent room and looked around. It was a great hall. It was deserted and, like the rest of the keep, in the process of crumbling to dust.

Alaric looked around, comparing it to the Stronghold, which would probably last for centuries. He couldn't imagine this keep lasting more than a few rainy seasons.

Sunlight fell on the floor from open doors at the end of the hall.

As they approached, they could see a large courtyard.

Outside, someone was grunting and swearing.

They crept forward until they reached the door. Alaric peered out.

The center of the enormous courtyard had been hastily cleared of leaves and twigs so that the area around a white altar was clear. At this distance, the sides of the altar looked lumpy, but Alaric couldn't quite make out why. There was a circle of runes on the ground, drawn in black winding around the altar. The noises were coming from the other side of it. Gustav had to be over there, although Alaric couldn't see him.

On top of the altar, set far to one corner, were Gustav's medallion and the Wellstone, which was glowing and humming gently. Sparks sputtered between the two. Alaric studied the Wellstone. It didn't seem bright enough yet for Gustav to have filled it. The flashes of light were normal. Gustav must be planning to fill it once the spell was begun. Alaric blew out a quick breath in relief. The cure was still there.

A loud grunt came from the other side of the altar. Gustav's head came over the top as he strained to lift something. The top of another head came briefly into view before Gustav swore and the head fell out of view with a thunk.

Gustav stood, breathing heavily, and gave the body a kick. A foot flipped into sight around the end of the altar. Gustav stomped off past the altar, leaving the body where it had fallen against the altar.

"Is that...*Mallon*?" Brandson asked quietly.

Alaric bit his lip to keep from laughing.

"He is a little bit of an idiot," Douglon whispered.

"Those markings on the ground are runes," Alaric told them. "They form a circle around him. Gustav will use them to store the energy of the spell while he creates it. He'll be relying heavily on them. If we erase a couple, he might not be able to complete the spell."

The others nodded.

"Once he begins the spell, the circle of runes will glow blue. From that point on, they'll have a life of their own. We won't be able to damage them any longer, nor will we be able to take away any of the things he's using. It will all be tied together. So we need to stop him before he begins." Alaric peered as far around the door as he could without stepping out. "Anyone see Ayda?"

Douglon's brow contracted. "I think she's past the altar."

"How do you know that?"

Douglon cringed. "What did she do to me? I can *feel* her." He shook his head. "Sort of."

"I haven't heard any noise from her," Milly said.

"Wouldn't blame him if he gagged her," Douglon said.

"There's no way Gustav got a gag on Ayda," Brandson whispered.

Gustav returned to Mallon's body. He unrolled a bundle of fabric spilling out a flash of green and something bright red. Kordan's emerald and Alaric's ruby.

The fury Alaric had been feeling since Gustav took the ruby rose again.

Gustav bent down, out of sight behind the altar. When he stood back up, the stones were gone.

Alaric imagined the ruby sitting on Mallon's chest, swirling slowly. He took a deep breath, forcing the emotions back and watching Gustav closely.

"Let's go," Alaric said.

Gustav dusted off his robes and looked around critically at his runes. He stepped over Mallon to look closely at the medallion on the altar. Gustav took a deep breath, shook out his arms dramatically, raised his voice, and began to chant.

Alaric stepped out into the courtyard.

In that moment, he saw two things.

The first, with the circle of runes stretched out awkwardly to include her, was Ayda.

Sort of.

Anchored firmly in the rocky ground of the courtyard stood a tree with pale green leaves and glimmering silver bark.

The second was the dull bluish glow of the runes as Gustav began the spell.

FORTY-NINE

Alaric's stomach dropped as the circle of runes glowed blue.

The runes stretched around the Ayda-tree, standing still and bright in the courtyard. How had Gustav managed to get her to change?

Alaric strode out toward the wizard.

Gustav's head snapped up. His mouth froze open in the middle of a word. Shutting his mouth and swallowing hard, he looked down, finished saying the word, then carefully set his foot next to one of the runes on the ground to mark his place. Finally, he looked back up at Alaric, glaring.

"Good morning," Alaric said. He walked along the circle of runes, studying them. They were redundant to the point of being ridiculous. "I see you've decided to be overly cautious. Most of these runes are unnecessary, but"—the smile he flashed at Gustav felt vicious—"every little bit helps, I always say."

Douglon stomped out into the courtyard, his face set like stone, and Gustav's gaze flicked to the dwarf. Douglon looked at Ayda. "Stupid elf. No wonder I can feel her." Douglon cocked his head to the side. "She is *really* angry."

Gustav darted a nervous glance at Ayda.

Douglon made a little strangled noise, and Alaric looked at him quickly. The dwarf's face was twisted in revulsion, and he was looking at the altar. Alaric followed his gaze, realizing that the sides of the altar looked lumpy because they were composed entirely of bones. Skulls of different shapes and sizes leered out in all directions across the courtyard.

"That is unnecessarily creepy," the dwarf muttered.

Milly came up beside him, letting Brandson lean on her shoulder. Brandson stared hard at the wizard. Gustav met his gaze for only a moment before dropping his eyes back down to the string of runes.

"Nice to have the group back together." Douglon pulled his axe out.

"How exactly did you get Ayda to change into a tree?" Alaric asked conversationally, knowing Gustav couldn't stop the spell to tell him. Alaric kept walking slowly around the circle of runes, deciphering each one.

Saying that Gustav had been overly cautious was an understatement. Any other time, it would have been funny. Runes were double and triple written to make sure there could be absolutely no doubt as to their meaning, yet each individual mark was sloppy.

"You really aren't very good at runes, are you?" Alaric asked. "You weren't pretending with Douglon's map. These are awful."

Gustav glared harder, then turned and looked intently at the runes directly before him and began to mutter again.

"Afraid to talk to us, Shade Seeker?" Douglon asked.

"He can't," Alaric said, smiling. "He's begun the spell. If he does anything besides read these excellent runes he's worked so very hard on, the spell will unravel. Or worse, mutate."

Douglon sniggered. "Maybe I should throw my axe at him. Think he can read and dodge at the same time?"

Gustav's head whipped up again, and he pointed frantically to some runes set off from the others.

"Ahh," Alaric said, glancing toward the runes. "He has put some protection in place. You probably can't actually touch him. Even with your axe. Were you nervous someone would disapprove of what you're doing here, old man?"

"Gustav, what are you doing?" Brandson asked quietly. "Mallon killed my parents."

Gustav looked up at the smith and a flicker of doubt crossed his face. But he brushed the doubt away with a scowl and turned back to reciting his spell.

Douglon growled and threw his axe straight at Gustav. The blade hit an invisible wall and rang out, bouncing away from the wizard and landing near Douglon's feet.

Gustav jumped back, glaring at Douglon.

"Yup," Douglon said, picking up his axe. "He's protected."

"Why *are* you doing this?" Alaric asked Gustav. "Everyone was perfectly happy thinking Mallon was dead and gone. What possible reason would you have for raising him?"

Gustav narrowed his eyes, then went back to work.

"I'm actually interested," Alaric said. "Power? Prestige? Did Mallon promise you a dukedom?"

"You had better things than that when you had these people's friendship," Milly said. "Somehow, I doubt you'll get that from Mallon. You picked the wrong side."

"Mallon just needs a puppet," Douglon scoffed. "Most people would have been smart enough to cut the strings when Mallon disappeared."

Gustav's face was red. He clamped his mouth shut and shook his head vehemently.

"Do you hate the entire world so much you just want to see it die?" Brandson asked. "Even those who thought of you as a friend?"

Gustav opened his mouth to Brandson, then snapped it shut in frustration. He turned toward Alaric and stared at him intently. He pointed to his own head, then to Alaric's. The old man was pointing and staring so frantically that Alaric almost laughed.

"You want me to read your mind?"

Gustav nodded vehemently.

"Okay," Alaric said, "I can't say I don't have a morbid interest in what I'll find."

He closed his eyes and reached his mind out toward Gustav. The wizard stood perfectly still, his mind still focused primarily on the rune at his feet, but there was one image sitting prominently in Gustav's mind. A tall, angular man stood on a hill, the Greenwood spread out before him. It was Mallon, his glittering black eyes looking impressed and pleased. The Rivor's face showing clearly that he saw Gustav as useful—valuable even.

Alaric pulled back out of Gustav's mind and opened his eyes. The wizard stood before him, chin raised, eyes blazing defiantly. He looked old, and Alaric was struck by the great loneliness that Gustav carried within himself.

"There are better things to crave than being useful to a man who sees everyone as a tool," Alaric said.

Gustav looked at him for a long moment, his face indecipherable. Taking a deep breath, he continued to read the runes.

"I need some time to read all these runes," Alaric told the others. "Distract him. Do anything you can think of that will slow him down. But don't get too close. I don't know what other sorts of protection he's set up."

Douglon grunted and moved directly across the runes from Gustav, training his gaze at the wizard and pacing him step for step. Gustav attempted a sneer, but it looked rather sickly.

Milly and Brandson whispered together for a minute before Brandson sat down with a groan and Milly ran toward Douglon and Gustav, tossing something shimmery on the ground near the runes before grabbing Douglon's arm and scooting them both back. Brandson tossed a small rock to the same place. Flames burst from the ground, shooting higher than Gustav's head. The wizard jumped back.

"This fire powder is great," Douglon said. "You could have saved Brandson a lot of work, though, by lighting his forge with it every morning."

"What's the word he used when he pretended it was magic?" Milly asked.

"*Incende!*" Brandson shouted as he tossed another stone into some powder.

Gustav leaned forward, trying to concentrate on the runes amidst their distractions.

"Can you read through fire?" Milly said. She walked close to the next rune past Gustav and threw some fire powder directly on in. Brandson grinned and threw a rock, sparking a flame that obscured the rune for several seconds before beginning to die down. Gustav snarled at Milly and had to wait until the flames were low enough for him to stomp out so he could see the rune again. Meanwhile, Milly moved to the next rune and sprinkled on some powder.

Alaric continued to decipher runes until he reached those that stretched out around the Ayda-tree. The more runes he read, the more his sympathy for the wizard disappeared. "So this is how you chose to name Ayda?" he asked, joining the efforts to distract Gustav. "'*The enclosed creature*'? That's vague. Really, all you needed to do was assign an energy rune to Ayda near the beginning, then refer to it here. You should rely more on your mental focus and less on descriptive runes. Let's erase these and start over. We could probably use a third of the runes you've scribbled here.

"And watch this one. It looks a bit like 'pig' instead of 'blood.' That could make things interesting."

Gustav slapped his hands over his ears as he leaned down closer to the runes and kept muttering.

"Will it work?" Milly asked from across the circle.

Alaric sighed. "Surprisingly, it will." He pointed to the rune about Ayda. "He must have originally meant the dragon when he wrote 'creature.'" Alaric turned to Gustav. "Where is your dragon, by the way?"

Gustav kept his eyes on the ground, muttering quickly as he crept around the circle.

"Did he find out what you intended to do with him?"

Gustav ignored him. Douglon had taken to pacing near Gustav, growling. Gustav was trying his best to look only at the runes, but with each growl, he flinched.

Alaric had reached the rune that would draw energy from Ayda to reanimate Mallon. He was close to the Rivor's crumpled body. Mallon's long legs were akimbo and his gaunt cheek was shoved against the altar so that a skull leered out over his black hair. Sitting on his chest was Kordan's dark emerald. And next to it, its red currents swirling unperturbed, sat Evangeline's ruby.

Alaric stepped closer to read a particularly messy rune, the rune he had been looking for. There it was, drawn out on the ground, a rune set to draw the latent energy out of Evangeline's Reservoir Stone. The energy that swirled in the ruby, the little life Evangeline had left, was now bound to Mallon. Alaric stepped forward again to pick up the ruby, but paused. Even if he removed it from the circle, the rune was linked to the ruby. It would still claim the energy. In a matter of minutes, the Reservoir Stone was going to darken, the red light seeping out of the ruby and into the still body below it.

Alaric glared at the rune as though he could burn it off with sheer force of will.

The spell was going to work.

He was too late.

The rune circle was complete. It was ridiculously overcomplicated and messy, and not even remotely close to being a circle, but it was going to work.

The Wellstone sat on the altar just waiting for Gustav to call it out and fill it.

The Ayda-tree was firmly rooted in the flagstones of the courtyard. She was unmovable. And as long as she stood inside the rune circle, it would be her life's energy that Gustav would sacrifice to wake Mallon.

The runes called out Mallon's name, so removing his body from the circle would do no good. Gustav had protected himself from weapons and interference.

Alaric was going to have to sit here and watch that wizard do exactly what he wanted to do, destroying what was left of Evangeline in the process.

And once the Rivor was raised? There was no way Alaric was going to be able to fight him alone.

Alaric sank down to his knees.

After all this, he was going to fail.

A rustling behind him caused him to turn. Nox had slithered up behind him, looking grave. Gustav's eyes lit up for a moment seeing the lizard approach, but when Nox settled down next to Alaric, Gustav scowled again and went back to his runes.

Alaric almost asked what had brought Nox back, but he realized that, in the end, it didn't matter. "You should leave. There's nothing we can do to stop him."

I heard what you said, and I have an idea.

Alaric looked at him, the vaguest stirrings of curiosity rising in his heart.

The rune that speaks of Ayda, Nox began, scooting up alongside Alaric. The lizard's voice was quiet in Alaric's mind. *We could…*

Nox paused thoughtfully, then let his head sink down to the ground. *Never mind, it won't work. You would think that after all these years, I would stop trying to fight the Shade Seekers.*

Alaric looked at the enormous lizard head settled next to him and thought about the long years that Nox had been enslaved here. Years with no hope. And just when Alaric had offered him some, it was pulled away.

Alaric glanced up at Gustav to check his progress, knowing the wizard was moving inexorably closer to finishing the spell.

Inside the circle of runes, the wizard let slip a sly smile.

FIFTY

laric glared at Gustav who went back to muttering and moving with terrific slowness around the circle.

The ruby still swirled on Mallon's chest. Alaric's hands itched to go pick it up. But it wouldn't matter. The Reservoir Stone was called out by the runes. If he picked it up and ran as fast as he could, maybe he could get it far enough away that the spell wouldn't drain it. But what would be the point of that? With Mallon raised, everyone would die sooner or later.

It made no difference. He might as well let her go this way.

His mind recoiled from the idea. Let her be absorbed into the power of a man who murdered and destroyed? There was a big difference between living in a dangerous world and being devoured by evil.

Alaric looked back at Nox, something tugging at his mind. The lizard was so despondent. Not that Alaric could blame him. Still…

Nox was just lying there. He had decided to come back to help, but now, he was just lying there. And Alaric was considering letting Gustav use Evangeline to raise Mallon.

Gustav was going to get exactly what he wanted. Again.

Alaric's head snapped up.

They were doing exactly what the wizard wanted them to do. Again.

Some of the haze in his mind stirred sluggishly.

Alaric looked at the ground behind where he knelt. Not that he was going to find anything. There was no point.

"No," he said out loud and shook his head to clear it. He focused again on the ground.

There behind him was a thin line scraped carefully through the dirt. It crossed right behind Alaric, went under Nox's neck, and wiggled off around the circle.

Taking a deep breath, Alaric tensed all his muscles and lunged backward. It felt like he was pushing through mud or quicksand. With a final heave, he toppled past the line.

Fresh air hit his face and he took a deep breath. The haze in his mind scattered.

An influence ring. That stupid wizard had tricked him again. Alaric grabbed at Nox's neck and yanked at him. The lizard glared toward him and left his head still, lying on the ground inside the ring.

Alaric tugged again but there was no way he was going to move the creature.

"Nox," he urged, but the lizard turned away.

Alaric stepped back. "Sorry about this." He swung his foot as hard as he could, kicking the lizard in the most vulnerable place he could find, the area covered in smaller, thinner scales right behind his front leg.

The fire lizard let out a roar and whipped around faster than Alaric had thought possible.

The Keeper threw himself backward and scrambled away from the enormous head lunging toward him. He heard Milly scream.

The jaws, wide open, froze inches from Alaric's face.

"Nox?" Alaric asked nervously.

The lizard closed his mouth slowly and pulled back, blinking.

"There's an influence ring there," he pointed at the thin line drawn on the ground running around the outside of the rune circle, trying to explain. "Gustav was using it to make us feel hopeless. We needed to get out of it."

Nox turned to look at the wizard and growled. Gustav was staring at them, the color draining from his face.

"At least now I know how he planned to keep his dragon still while he sacrificed it," Alaric said.

The rune that is applied to Ayda just calls out a creature, so if we could get her out, we could replace her with a different creature, right? Nox asked. *Can you get Ayda out of the rune circle?*

Alaric looked at Ayda. One of Ayda's branches hung a few inches outside of Gustav's influence ring. He couldn't move her as a tree, but he could certainly help her change back to an elf. How had he not thought of this sooner? Alaric shot a venomous look at Gustav. It was impossible to think clearly around that stupid wizard. The wizard opened his mouth to shout at him, but then snapped it shut again.

Alaric stretched out a hand to touch the Ayda-tree, but froze, remembering the last time he had helped her change. He reached out with his mind to find other sources of energy. He reached for the dense forest just outside the walls of the keep. He took a moment and felt all the life and energy sitting in those trees. Past Gustav's protective wall, he caught a glimpse of the energy that was the wizard. Alaric grabbed onto that as well. Keeping ahold of that energy, he fixed a firm image of Ayda in his mind then touched a leaf on the nearest branch.

His hand clenched the leaf as a rush of power surged through his body so fast that his knees buckled. The trees along the wall of the keep withered, and Gustav fell to his knees with a yell. In a rush of fury, the tree transformed almost instantly into Ayda. Alaric fell to the ground.

He could feel fury rolling off Ayda in waves as he tried to catch his breath. She caught sight of Gustav and began to stalk toward him.

Gustav had frozen kneeling next to the altar and was looking at Ayda open-mouthed, white as the bones next to him.

"Ayda!" Alaric called. "Get out of the rune circle! He's going to sacrifice you!"

Ayda's step faltered. She dropped her eyes to the runes and to Mallon's body propped awkwardly against the altar. Gustav turned away from her and stared desperately at the runes, chanting again.

Ayda stopped and stood still. Then her shoulders sank in despair as all of the fury drained out of her.

"Ayda!" Alaric yelled. "Gustav is doing this to you! There's an influence ring making you feel like that! Come out!"

But Ayda didn't move. She stood motionless.

Gustav cast one final glance at her then bent over and began muttering faster. He was approaching the runes that had surrounded the Ayda-tree and still enclosed the elf. Once the wizard read them, it would be too late to get her out.

There was one answer.

Alaric looked once more at the ruby swirling on Mallon's chest. He knew, deep inside of him, that Gustav was right. There was not enough life in the Reservoir Stone to bring back Evangeline. He wanted to grab the ruby and run. Run all the way back to Evangeline and save her, fix everything, undo all the pain and suffering and death. But the reality of it all sat heavy on his chest, crushing him with the weight of all the dark things he had done—all in vain. There was no way to save her. There never had been.

Alaric gave the ruby one last, long look before turning away. He had spent a year trying to save her, not caring if the rest of the world burned. And all this time, there wasn't enough of her left to bring back.

He couldn't save the ruby, but maybe he could keep the world from burning. If Ayda were sacrificed, Mallon would gain all the power of the elves. The solution here, the only solution, was to give Mallon a weaker sacrifice. A sacrifice that Ayda could easily best.

Milly and Brandson were still busy trying to slow Gustav using the fire powder, so Alaric called Douglon over to where he stood. "Stand near the edge, but don't cross the influence ring. I'm going to shove Ayda out. You may need to grab her and pull." The dwarf nodded and positioned himself as close to her as he could. Alaric walked back around next to Nox.

And how will you get out, Keeper?

Alaric gave Nox a tight smile. "Ayda's sacrifice would be so big that Gustav would be able to raise Mallon easily. My sacrifice will be much smaller. The sacrifice exceeds the reward."

Nox's eyes flashed. The lizard twisted his head to look at Mallon. A low growl started deep in the lizard's chest.

Gustav continued reading.

There was no time left. Alaric cast a lingering look at the ruby swirling on Mallon's chest. Then he took a deep breath and filled his mind with the desire to get Ayda out of the rune circle no matter what. He focused on that idea until there was nothing else in his mind. With a shout, he threw himself across the influence ring.

Alaric's legs slowed, as though he were running though water, but his momentum crashed him into Ayda. The two of them faltered, but she didn't fall.

Alaric felt his heart slow. The futility of his actions crashed in against him, and no matter how much he clung to the idea of getting out of the circle, the edge was too far away. He would never make it.

He stood there next to Ayda, both of them encircled by the runes. Douglon, Brandson, and Milly were shouting and waving, but Alaric could barely hear them. It didn't matter. It would all be over soon.

Gustav bent over and began reading faster.

Alaric fixed his gaze on the swirling ruby. He had never imagined that he and Evangeline would both die at the same time.

A roar shattered the haze, and a huge force slammed into Alaric's side, shoving him sideways into Ayda. The two of them tumbled away, to the other side of the circle.

Douglon grabbed for them, pulling them clear.

Nox sat inside the circle. He looked pleased, but as Alaric watched, the lizard's eyes faded and his head drooped down to the ground.

Ayda sat up and started back toward the creature, but Alaric grabbed her arm.

"We'll never get him out. If we cross the influence ring, Gustav will control us again and all three of us will be trapped."

"But… Nox…" Ayda said, looking at the runes around him.

You were right, Alaric. This is the answer, Nox said, his thoughts coming sluggishly to them. *The wizard has his creature, a much weaker being than either of you.*

Alaric shook his head. "Nox, focus on us. Come out."

Nox looked at Alaric through his dark, reptilian eyes. *I remember.* His thoughts staggered out to Alaric, desperate and reaching. *The sacrifice exceeds the reward. I remember that emerald. I remember my name. I remember why I chose to forget it.*

Nox opened his mind and Alaric saw a boy, writhing in pain. A man held a snake and the boy's mother wept. He dropped down next to the boy and cradled his head, pouring energy into him. A green light pulled out of the boy's body, the child screamed. Then the light condensed into an emerald that dropped heavily onto the boy's chest.

Alaric pulled his mind away. "Kordan?"

FIFTY-ONE

"Kordan," Alaric repeated, his mind spinning.

You were right, Kordan said, *I have made many choices I regret, but those choices do not control today. Today, I choose to be a Keeper again. I choose to stand up against something evil instead of toying with the edges of it.*

Alaric shook his head again. "This isn't the answer. The spell will kill you."

It is the only answer. The spell will claim a creature, but he needs a creature at least as great as a human to revive Mallon. I am the only one here who is not. Even if I have enough energy to revive him, the Rivor will not rise powerful. He will be a shadow of himself.

"It will kill you," Alaric said again weakly.

Kordan nodded. *I thought I had died a useless death many years ago. If my death will stop this, it will be more than I ever imagined.* He looked at Alaric intensely. *Give me this chance.*

Alaric looked at the lizard again, then nodded. "I've been searching for your Wellstone, searching for anything I could find of yours. My wife…" His voice dropped to a whisper. "You have the antidote for rock snake venom."

Kordan fixed Alaric with a long stare. *Acadanthus leaves,* the words slipped weakly into Alaric's mind. *Acadanthus leaves boiled to a strong tea.*

Alaric stared at the lizard. "Does it work?" he whispered.

Kordan nodded. He bowed his head briefly to his newfound companions before turning his head and glaring at Gustav. Gustav was looking at Kordan frantically. Every time Kordan's eyes began to sink closed, he would shake his head vigorously and growl, re-fixing his glare on the wizard.

"This still hasn't stopped him," Douglon pointed out.

"No, but Kordan is right. If Gustav can raise Mallon with just the energy that Kordan has, Mallon will be terribly weak." He glanced at Ayda.

Ayda was looking at Kordan with tears in her eyes. She looked up at Alaric, fury building again.

Alaric nodded. "Yes, get angry."

Ayda stalked around the influence ring until she stood as close as she dared to Gustav. She glared at him, her fingers flexing. The courtyard darkened and a breeze swirled through it.

The wind didn't ruffle Gustav at all.

"Your spells protect you for now, wizard," Ayda said. "But when you are done, you will no longer be safe."

Milly helped Brandson over to where Douglon stood.

"Be ready," Alaric said. "When Mallon wakes up, we need to attack. I have no idea what he'll be capable of. Gustav should be exhausted. I doubt he'll be able to do much. But focus on Mallon. There will be time to deal with Gustav afterward."

They moved closer to the edge of the influence ring, closer to Mallon's body.

"Your ruby," Milly said, looking toward where it rested on Mallon's chest.

Alaric's heart clenched. "Even if I pull it out of the spell, it won't matter. This rune links the spell to 'the stone with latent energy,' meaning the Reservoir Stone."

"Can you replace it with something else?" Milly asked.

"Yes," Alaric said with a short laugh. "If you have another stone with latent energy."

Milly's shoulders slumped. "You can't just leave it there."

Alaric looked at the swirling red light. A matching flash of red reflected off his chest. He looked down at the flame Ayda had frozen. The stone with the potential to be a flame. Alaric grabbed the necklace and yanked it off his neck. "I'd say the potential to explode into flame qualifies as latent energy."

He just needed to overcome the influence ring and reach Mallon's body. He began to fill his mind with Evangeline, with how desperately he wanted to see her again. Bracing himself, he stepped over the line and strode toward Mallon's body.

The ruby swirled weakly. Too weakly to do anything. Would he ever see her again? Despair crashed over Alaric. He couldn't bring himself to pick it up.

A flash of fiery red from Ayda's flame dangling in his hand caught his eye.

You are better suited to fire than flowers, Ayda had said. *You have that tight burning core of anger, or pain. Or guilt. It's deep, but it's bright.*

He reached inside himself, looking for the anger. He found it, a burning core of fury. Clinging to it, he tried to shake the haze of Gustav's influence, but the anger just kept leading him to despair.

He had to let go of the anger. What else had Ayda said? That the anger wasn't all of him. That the anger was only there because of the love he had. Ewan had said the same.

They were right. He was angry because Evangeline was dying. And he *loved* her. He was angry because the role of Keeper didn't feel right, but that role sat inside the deep well of knowledge that he *loved.*

There was more there than the anger. There was more there than the decision to save Evangeline, to create a ruby, and to turn his back on the Keepers.

No one is defined by a single choice, the Shield had said. *With each day, we decided anew who we are, what we will grow toward. Alaric has chosen to be a Keeper a thousand times in a thousand ways.*

A thousand times in a thousand ways. Alaric pushed away the despair. It was time to choose to be a Keeper one more time. Right now.

This time, when Alaric looked for strength to fight the influence ring, he didn't reach for his anger. He reached for the things he loved. The things that made him who he was: Evangeline, his life as a Keeper, the queen, Ewan, Ayda, Douglon, Brandson, and Milly. He found them, a solid, indestructible foundation beneath the rushing despair of Gustav's influence ring and beneath the fire of his own anger.

He anchored himself to that foundation. This moment was his to choose, and he would choose to follow his own mind, not Gustav's.

The despair receded.

Alaric reached down and picked up the ruby. He almost dropped the flame in its place, but paused. He didn't want the flame touching Mallon, either. Instead, he set it on the altar. Then, clinging to the truth that this moment was for him to choose, he stepped back out of the influence ring.

Alaric clenched the ruby to his chest until the rough edges dug into his hand. He could still feel its warmth. Her warmth. But it was so faint compared to what it had been.

Gustav was sweating and panting. He stared at the ruby in Alaric's hand.

"Gustav," Brandson pleaded. "Don't do this."

The wizard shuddered.

Alaric walked along the outer edge of the influence ring until he stood next to Ayda, close to the wizard. "Not going how you had planned? Well, you can't stop now."

With a shaking voice, Gustav picked up reading where he had stopped and walked the last short distance until he had gone all the way around the circle of runes.

The runes suddenly glowed a vivid blue. The Wellstone burst into light and sent a rush of scalding white energy at Mallon's body. The flame from Alaric's necklace remained unchanged. There was no life inside it for the spell to take. The runes on the ground grew brighter and brighter until both Ayda and Alaric stepped farther away. Gustav sank to the ground, exhausted.

"No," Brandson said, a broken whisper.

With a sigh, Kordan's head settled to the ground. His eyes stared lifelessly across the court-yard. Alaric felt a pang of regret, and Ayda let out a small groan.

A moment later, there was a rustle from the side of the altar, and Mallon's legs stirred.

Ayda began to breathe furiously, and Alaric, after a glance at Gustav, who was lying senselessly on the ground, reached forward and rubbed his foot across the influence ring. The line rubbed off and the influence ring was broken.

"He's too exhausted to keep it up," Alaric said. Grinning, he strode across it with Ayda on his heels.

Their motion roused Gustav who cast a frightened glance at them then rushed to Mallon. The wizard shook him and started yelling for the Rivor to awaken.

With a groan, Mallon opened his black eyes and slowly turned his gaze on each of them in turn.

Douglon let out a war cry and rushed toward the Rivor, his axe raised. Mallon's eyes narrowed, and he hissed at the dwarf. Douglon went flying backward, crashing into a heap against the keep wall.

Brandson hobbled forward a step and threw his knife at Mallon. The Rivor swatted it away and with a look, knocked Brandson flat on his back.

Ayda and Alaric paused.

Mallon focused his eyes on Gustav, then flexed his hands. A smile spread across his face. He pulled himself up, leaning on the side of the bone altar.

"Well done, servant," he said, his voice cutting through the courtyard.

Gustav dropped into a fawning bow.

Ayda, who had begun to shake with fury, stepped forward. The Rivor's eyes fell on her. He studied her for a moment before his grin widened even farther.

"Very well done," Mallon murmured. "You have even brought one who holds some of my soul."

Gustav looked in surprise at Ayda. "She what? I didn't... um... I thought..."

"Shut up, wizard," Ayda said, never taking her eyes off Mallon.

"Come to me, my child," Mallon commanded. His body still leaned heavily on the altar, but his voice burned with power.

Ayda lurched forward as though on a chain. Her hands clenched into fists at her sides, but her body was dragged slowly forward.

The Rivor looked at her hungrily. "Come closer. I am still weak, but the darkness you hold will change that. The darkness you have kept for me all of these years."

Alaric looked at Ayda in fear. This was the darkness Will had warned him of. The darkness he could almost see sometimes.

"Come to me," Mallon called to her. "I will give you power even an elf cannot imagine."

Ayda cast a frightened look at Alaric. Her feet stepped forward again.

In desperation, Alaric held her eyes and opened his mind up to hers. He felt her presence in his mind as her gaze clung desperately to him. He saw her, standing in the Greenwood while the elves died around her. She was tiny and dim and alone.

Her eyes glazed over.

Alaric threw images at her. The image of her standing in Queen Saren's council, defending Alaric. The moment when Douglon had told her he would die for her, lying on the ground with an arrow in his chest. The time she had held out her hand to Alaric, willing to share the story of how her people died. Ayda chatting with Milly as they walked along a road. Any image he could think of to show her she was not alone.

Ayda's eyes refocused on Alaric, and he could see her thoughts clear. She smiled, then turned back to Mallon.

"Come!" he commanded, his voice growing harsher.

"You want your darkness back?" she asked him sweetly. "It would be my pleasure. I am *tired* of carrying it."

A flicker of uncertainty crossed the Rivor's face.

Ayda held out her hand and took a deep breath. Breathing slowly out, she formed her hand into a claw. Inside the claw, a swirl of darkness appeared surrounded by wisps of light. Tendrils of black kept slipping out, reaching between her fingers, but then the light pulled them back in. The light slowly tightened, spinning the dark into a ball of utter blackness.

Alaric could feel it pulling at him. He leaned back, pulling away from the void she was holding. A single tendril of black snaked out toward him, but just as fast, a finger of light snatched it back and trapped it in the ball.

The lights were the elves—what was left of the elves that had been trapped in Ayda.

Mallon shifted backward, his eyes widening.

Finally, Ayda looked up and smiled. "A gift from my people."

With that, she gave the ball, engulfed by light, a nonchalant toss.

It tumbled through the air and landed next to Mallon on the altar. The Rivor drew back. He reached out to touch it, but a spark from the light whipped out at his hand, and he drew it back sharply.

"Keep him near it," Ayda whispered.

Alaric gathered as much energy as he could in the space of a breath. Before Mallon could step back, Alaric reached his hand toward the Rivor. "*Alligo!*" He hissed the same spell Gustav had used to keep them rooted to the ground this morning.

Mallon froze, everything below his head locked into place. Gustav, at the very edge of the spell's range, bent over and tugged on his feet, struggling to move them. Both of them cursed and struggled against the spell.

"That won't last long," Alaric said. He could already feel fractures in the spell holding Gustav's feet.

Ayda was staring at the white lights wrapping the ball of darkness. "They need more power, more energy."

Alaric looked desperately around for something, anything. There was nothing to draw from. The courtyard was stone. There wasn't even a fire to pull energy out of. His eyes fell on the frozen flame sitting on the altar.

"Would the potential for a big fire help?" he asked, nodding toward the frozen flame sitting on the altar.

Her eyes widened and a wild grin spread across her face. She took the flame and turned back to Mallon. He was still looking uncertainly at the dark ball spinning on the altar completely enclosed in a web of light.

Ayda walked up to him and looked him squarely in the eye. She pointed to the bundle of light encasing the dark ball. "You did not destroy my people. I just want to make sure you understand that it was the elves that defeated you." She glanced over her shoulder toward Alaric and the others. "With a little help."

Then Ayda held the tiny crystal flame in her palm. She blew on it, setting it to quivering. It burst into a living flame.

Mallon's eyes widened and she smiled at him.

"Everyone knows that darkness is only dark until you throw in a little light," she said and tossed the flame at the altar. It landed on the little ball of darkness and light, spreading out and dancing over the surface.

Ayda turned and walked over to Kordan's still body. She kissed his scaled head gently then turned toward Alaric.

Alaric stared at her for a moment. Her face was bright and easy. Nothing about her sparkled or flashed, yet she looked more alive and real than he had ever seen her.

"We should go," she said, glancing at the flame that was spreading across the ball of darkness. "Quickly."

FIFTY-TWO

laric called to Douglon, who was stirring against the wall. The dwarf staggered over and helped Alaric drag Brandson to his feet. The three of them stumbled back toward the keep, following Ayda and Milly.

At the door of the keep, Alaric paused and looked back. The others crowded behind him, watching breathlessly.

The blackness was spreading, now covered in orange flame. The white lights that had held it in a ball were stretching out, reaching for each other and creating a web that stretched over the darkness. Mallon strained back against Alaric's spell. He shot spell after spell at the ball, trying to destroy it, but each one was merely absorbed, swelling the size of the darkness trapped there. Gustav snapped his feet free and raced to Mallon, clutching at his arms and tugging at him, but the Rivor didn't move.

"Gustav!" Brandson yelled, "Get away from there!"

Gustav looked toward Brandson for a moment, then went back to pulling on the Rivor.

With a rush of noise like a great wind, or a blazing fire, the ball shot out into an enormous size, enveloping Mallon, Gustav, the altar, and half of the courtyard.

The orange flame, which had been stretched almost to invisibility, flared up. The web of white lights joined with it, creating a shell of brilliant white fire. Alaric shielded his eyes from the searing brightness as a wave of heat rolled over him.

There was a low trembling in the ground. The circle of darkness and flame collapsed down with a concussion like thunder. The ground shook and debris shot out from it, pelting Alaric with pebbles and spreading a thick cloud of dust.

The earth shuddered, and the nearest wall of the courtyard trembled and collapsed. Alaric and the others lurched away from the keep, shielding their heads from the stone and rubble raining down.

The ground rumbled for several more seconds, stones continuing to fall from the keep, then slowly, everything fell silent.

No one moved for a long moment, then Alaric stepped quietly through the haze toward the place where Mallon had been. A breeze stirred the cloud of dust and revealed a gaping hole in the ground where the altar had stood. It spread halfway across the courtyard and was deeper than Alaric was tall.

There was nothing inside it but rubble. No altar, no Gustav, no Kordan, no Mallon.

Ayda stepped up next to him and beamed. She drew a deep breath and flung her arms out. "It's gone!" she sang.

"What was that dark thing?" Milly asked.

"A piece of Mallon," Ayda said, "He infested me with it the day my people sacrificed themselves." She smiled impishly. "I just gave it back to him."

"Gave it back?" Douglon asked.

Ayda smirked. "Well, I gave it back surrounded by a web of my people."

"Your people?" Milly asked faintly.

"What was left of them," Ayda answered. "They were very angry. And then we added some fire." Her smile widened to a grin. "Turns out that's a destructive combination."

"Turns out?" Alaric asked. "You didn't know?"

"I didn't know for sure, but I had a suspicion. You could say that I understood the concept of what would happen."

"However you did it, it was well done." Douglon motioned to the crater. Then he grimaced and pulled his arm back protectively to his chest.

Ayda looked at him in exasperation. "I only left you alone for one night." She walked up to the dwarf and grabbed his arm.

Douglon grunted but didn't pull his arm away. "I don't need you to fix it," he grumbled. "It'll be fine."

Ayda touched the wound gently. Douglon let out a sigh of relief and Ayda patted his cheek sweetly. "Now stop getting hurt."

"The lights around the darkness," Milly said, still looking puzzled at the great hole in the ground, "were they...?"

Ayda sobered. "The elves have held the darkness in check for eight years. They continued to hold it until the flames destroyed the darkness."

"And destroyed them?" Alaric asked.

"And them."

Alaric looked at the pit, a surge of loss rolling through him. So many elves destroyed. Not that they had exactly been alive before, but the price of killing Mallon had been a heavy one. Next to him, he caught sight of Ayda's face, blazing with pride.

"It's all they wanted," she said. "To destroy him. They've waited for too long."

She breathed deeply again and laughed. Seeing Alaric's sober face, she leaned over and kissed him on the cheek. "Don't be so serious, Alaric. This is a good day. The best day in a very long time. We've won. And the only losses on our side today were those who went willingly."

Alaric looked cautiously at Ayda. "So are all the elves... gone?"

Ayda wrinkled her nose. "No, not all of them. Just some." Then she cocked her head slightly. "The ones that are left do seem a little more withdrawn than usual, though."

"Perhaps they can be, now that they don't have to hold the darkness back."

Ayda nodded. "Perhaps. They are small and tired now." She sighed. "And I suppose they will be bored for the rest of my life."

Alaric smiled. "Maybe we can find some other great force of evil to fight."

Brandson groaned quietly, and Ayda looked at him, noticing for the first time that he was slumped against the wall.

She walked quickly to Brandson and knelt down next to him.

"Can you fix it?" Milly asked, her voice breaking a little.

Ayda sat back on her heels and looked helplessly at Milly. "I'm sorry. It's animal poison. I can heal wounds. That's just putting things back together. But poison—poison spreads and… and things aren't broken, they're changed. I don't know how to change them back."

Brandson groaned.

Alaric walked up to Brandson and knelt across from Ayda. He gently lifted the pants Milly had cut open out of the way so that he could see the wound more clearly. There were streaks of dark red climbing up his leg and the flesh was hot.

"We need to get him some medicine," Alaric said. "Let's get him to his horse."

"What are we going to do?" Douglon demanded. "Find some sort of poison doctor out here in the middle of nowhere?"

Alaric grimaced. "You already have."

They all looked at him blankly.

"Evangeline was poisoned. What do you think I've been studying this whole time?"

"And you have antidotes stashed nearby?" Douglon asked.

Alaric sighed. "Let's get Brandson to his horse. It should take less than a day to get to my castle."

"You have a castle?" Milly asked.

Alaric smiled weakly. "Well, no one else has claimed it for over a hundred years, so yes. I have a castle."

They just kept looking at him.

"And Evangeline is there. And all of my research on poisons."

Then Brandson moaned and the group jumped into action. Alaric and Milly each ducked under one of Brandson's arms, helping him walk. Douglon led the way back through the keep, shoving any large debris out of their way. They reached the room with the horses and Brandson sank into a chair.

Alaric led Beast to the doorway and cast out to see if any monsters were nearby. The explosion must have scared them off, because there were no large life forms down in the valley. Everything he felt was far off on the hills.

"The valley is relatively safe, for now. We should hurry."

Alaric and Douglon helped Brandson claw his way up onto his horse. Douglon mounted his horse next to him and tugged and pushed the smith into a better position on his saddle.

"Sorry," Douglon muttered gruffly, his eyes showing far more concern than his voice.

"Here," Alaric said, moving next to Brandson. "Someone will need to ride next to him to make sure he doesn't fall, but I think I can help him a little."

Closing his eyes, Alaric took a deep breath and recalled spells he hadn't tried in a year.

He found the one that he'd first tried on Evangeline. The one meant to slow the spread of the poison. It sat in his mind discarded where he had thrown it when he was furious that it couldn't work well enough.

Taking a deep breath, he set his hand on Brandson's leg and whispered the words he couldn't quite bring himself to say out loud.

When he opened his eyes, everyone was looking expectantly at him. Brandson moaned again.

"I don't think it worked," Douglon said.

Alaric ignored him and closed his eyes again. It had worked. He could feel it. He could feel the energy stopping the spread of the poison, blocking it at the edges. He felt the smallest bit of poison slip through his net and knew that Brandson's time was still limited. But now, he might have the time he needed.

Then Alaric reached up and held his hand toward Brandson's face. "*Dormio,*" he told the blacksmith, and Brandson's head slowly slumped down on his chest, his brow relaxing and his breath calming.

Milly, eyes wide in alarm, rushed up to him.

"He's fine," Alaric assured her.

"He's not fine," Ayda pointed out.

Alaric glared at her again. "He can't feel the poison. And I slowed the spread of it, too. We should have several days before…"

Milly nodded tersely.

"Then what are we waiting for?" Douglon demanded.

The group headed out of the valley with Milly riding behind Brandson, helping to keep him seated. Douglon rode alongside, ready to help if needed.

Alaric led them south, back out of the valley and along the same trail they had taken to get there. That night, when they set up camp, the exhaustion of the last few days settled heavily on him. He could sense Kollman Pass getting closer. For Brandson's sake, he wanted to rush, but his own desire to get back there was steeped in reluctance.

The ruby hung around his neck again, its weight familiar but no longer comforting against his chest. He now had the antidote for the rock snake venom, but it didn't matter. If the energy in her ruby wasn't enough to bring her back, what good was an antidote? The swirls of red light felt fragile and delicate.

He was never going to be with her. This would be the end. He would heal Brandson and send them all on their way. And then? Then the only question was whether he would wake her to say goodbye or just let her slip painlessly away.

FIFTY-THREE

They rose early the next morning, trying to reach the castle by evening. As they saddled the horses, Alaric looked at Ayda. "You never told us how Gustav managed to trap you as a tree."

"I was stupid," she answered. She glanced at Douglon with a rueful smile. "I wasn't paying attention."

"That's surprising," the dwarf answered.

"I had reached the courtyard and could see that the wizard was planning something, because there were some runes scratched into the ground, but I couldn't see him anywhere. It was still dark and as I wondered what to do, four creatures came slinking toward me from all directions."

"And let me guess," Douglon said, "you didn't want to kill them, so you turned yourself into a tree."

Ayda looked guiltily at him for a moment, then giggled. "That's exactly what happened." Her face sobered. "They were so sad. They were so lonely and twisted, and they were only attacking because they were commanded to. I didn't know where the wizard was, but they hated him. They hated the keep, and they hated themselves. The only thing they didn't hate was me." She paused. "But they couldn't stop."

She took a deep breath. "So I couldn't kill them. And I couldn't free them fast enough. I would have needed to touch each one, and I didn't have that much time. But they all were supposed to attack an elf. So I figured that if I were a tree, maybe they would be able to give up. And they did." She shrugged. "It seemed like a good idea until the wizard stepped out of the shadows."

"She just loses the big picture," Douglon explained to the rest of them. "It's not that she makes bad decisions, she's just never paying attention to the big picture."

"And how were you expecting to get back to your own shape?" Alaric asked her.

"I didn't see another choice," she answered. "But I did know you all were close by. You wouldn't have left me as a tree, Alaric."

They pressed on, hoping to reach Kollman Pass in the early afternoon. Alaric spent the day focused on Brandson, contemplating which herbs he would use to fight the poison. He concentrated on the fact that he would need to notify the queen of what had happened. And that he'd need to send Douglon to the dwarves as soon as he would consent to leave, which wouldn't happen until Brandson was healed. Which led him back to his consideration of the antidotes.

What his mind refused to land on was her. The image of Evangeline lying in the crystal filled his mind, but he refused to look at it. Every other time he had envisioned her, he had been driven by hope, driven by ideas of how to heal her. But now…

The sun was lowering toward the horizon when they finally reached the road that led to his castle. They turned a corner in the broken old path and there it sat.

It was small and grey. It had three turrets that rose to different heights and was surrounded by a storybook wall. There was even a drawbridge and a moat. Milly gasped and Ayda clapped in delight at the old castle glowing in the afternoon light.

When they entered, Alaric led them to the tower that held the bedrooms. He told them to choose whichever they liked. They lay Brandson on a luxurious bed in one of the higher rooms.

Alaric saw Brandson safely to the bed and renewed his spell to help him sleep. Then he asked Milly to get some water from the kitchen and headed toward his workroom.

He walked up the stairs, his steps getting heavier as he approached the carved door on his left. He paused beside it for a moment, raising his hand to touch it. But instead, he let his hand drop and continued up the stairs at a brisker pace.

He pushed open the next door on the right and entered his workroom. When the smell hit him, he took a deep breath. It smelled like herbs and dust and medicine. And even though everything in there was meant to stop poison, to restore life, he couldn't hold back the thought that the room smelled like death.

It was lined with tables and bookshelves. He lit a lantern that hung from the center of the ceiling and banished the dark thoughts from his mind. Moving from shelf to table to shelf, he collected things quickly, setting them onto a small tray. When he slipped one round nut into his pocket to keep it from rolling around the tray, it dropped to the floor. Alaric looked down at his robe. It was torn and filthy, the pocket ripped straight across the bottom. He shrugged out of it and tossed it into a corner. The cold of the castle stones seeped into him.

Next to the door hung a black Keeper's robe. It was clean and it was warm. Alaric reached out tentatively and lifted it off the hook. He slid his arms in, and the robe draped over his shoulders like a blanket, wrapping around him and welcoming him home.

He picked up the nut, put it in one of the many pockets of this robe and headed back to Brandson's room, closing the door of the workroom firmly behind him. He passed the carved door again without pausing.

In Brandson's room, Alaric sat quietly at a table, measuring and mixing while the others stood awkwardly around Brandson's bed, sometimes looking at their sick friend, sometimes letting their eyes roam around the room.

There wasn't much in it, but the furniture that was there was carved of rich wood. The bed was covered in thick blankets and fluffy pillows. There were dark red drapes that hung at the balcony. Someone had started a fire in the fireplace and set a kettle above it.

Ayda walked over to the balcony and looked out.

"This place is beautiful," she said.

Alaric grunted, measuring out exactly fourteen simbo seeds.

She opened her mouth as though to say something else, but after glancing at Alaric, fell silent.

When he was finished mixing, Alaric used Milly's water to make a thick paste, then brought it over to Brandson. Gently, he cleaned the wound out again. He smoothed the paste over the wound and bound it with a fresh bandage. Then he gave Milly some leaves and asked her to brew Brandson some strong tea from them.

With all those tasks done, Alaric sank back onto the chair at the table and watched Milly coax the tea down Brandson's throat.

"That's all I can do," he said quietly. "I think the antidote will help, but we won't know until at least tomorrow morning. Every four hours, he should drink another cup of tea."

"How do you know what antidote to use?" Milly asked from her seat next to Brandson, holding his hand again. "Don't you need to know what he was poisoned with?"

"Sometimes, that matters," Alaric said, "but there are combinations of herbs that are good at fighting a broad range of poisons. I gave him the strongest blend I know of for animal poison." Alaric sighed and looked down at his hands as he cleaned the paste off of them. "I spent many months researching antidotes for animal poisons, specifically against the rock snake. So I am now quite familiar with the antidotes to most of them. There are very few that don't have a known antidote, and most of those are reptiles."

Ayda turned and looked directly at Alaric.

"May I see her?" she asked.

Alaric's heart clenched. When he didn't answer, Ayda took a step toward him, her eyes kind.

"She is your wife, Alaric. May we meet her?"

At the word wife, Alaric flinched. He looked around the room at the others. They stood looking hopeful and uncomfortable. Their faces were so familiar that suddenly, he wanted them to meet her.

He stood slowly and walked out into the hallway, turning up the stairs. He heard the others following after him. This time, when he reached the carved door he raised his hand and pushed.

A wave of fresh air hit him. The doors to the balcony were open and the room was flooded with evening light. There were pots of flowers in the corner with blooms growing cheerfully, Alaric's painstakingly created spells keeping them in a state of perpetual summer. Two small trees grew in blue pots on the balcony, just outside the doors. The drapes on the balcony rustled free of dust. The floor was smooth, clean stone.

And in the middle of the room, up on an intricately carved table, lay Evangeline, encased in a thin layer of crystal. Alaric walked up to her, his gaze still heavily on the floor. He walked up to her side, only able to focus on her hand.

It looked smooth and soft as it lay perfectly still. He set his hand against the crystal and his heart almost stopped.

By contrast to his own, her fingertips, halfway up each finger, were blue.

The group behind him filed in. Douglon held back by the wall while Ayda and Milly approached the crystal.

"She's beautiful," Milly said.

Alaric stared at her fingertips.

Ayda set a hand on the top of the crystal, above Evangeline's face. She closed her eyes and stood perfectly still.

"Nice to meet you, Evangeline," she said softly.

Alaric lifted his eyes to Evangeline's face, serene, free of worry.

"Is the crystal what's keeping her alive?" Milly asked quietly.

Alaric nodded. "Partially. The crystal is keeping her body from aging, or at least making it age very slowly." His gaze dropped to thin, small runes that were marked with ink on her neck. "And there are spells that are protecting her body, giving it strength."

The room fell silent. Alaric sank into a chair next to Evangeline and dropped his head into his hands. With quiet rustling, he heard the others leave.

The room was silent for a long time. There was a noise by the door, and Alaric looked up to see Douglon still standing in the back of the room. He had lowered his axe to the ground before him and bowed his head in the dwarfs' posture of mourning.

At Alaric's movement, Douglon looked up. Then he nodded to Alaric, picked up his axe, and left the Keeper in peace.

Alaric was a little surprised to realize that he was glad they were all here. They brought a warmth and life to the castle that had been missing for too long. Alaric sighed and leaned his forehead on the crystal.

His eyes caught on her blue fingers again and his heart lurched. He pulled a small pouch out of one of his pockets. Acadanthus leaves. He'd had them in his workroom all along. Acadanthus vines grew on holly trees, wound so tightly into the tree that it was all but impossible to pick holly leaves or berries without also getting acadanthus leaves. So he had sorted them into their own bag and tossed them on a shelf. He'd never heard of them having any sort of medicinal use. He took out some leaves and dropped them into a kettle hung over the fire.

It doesn't matter, his brain told him. *Providing the antidote to the poison does nothing but heal this husk of a body. You still won't be able to get her back.*

He pulled the boiling kettle off the fire to let the leaves sit until he could smell the acadanthus tea. He stood before his wife, running his hand over the thin layer of clear crystal that encased her.

It won't work, his mind whispered. But he had to know. Somehow, he had to know if it could have worked. All of the other poisons were taken care of. It was just the venom left.

Was it wrong to keep trying things when nothing would truly heal her?

The smell of the acadanthus leaves filled the room.

He had to know.

Alaric took a deep, shuddering breath. He closed his eyes and laid his hands on the crystal right above her heart. He reached out to feel the energy there, the ponderous essence of the crystal that he had placed around her, through her.

Alaric focused on the structure of the crystal where it touched her body. "*Amoveo.*"

The crystal vanished.

FIFTY-FOUR

vangeline lay still, but her chest began to rise with shallow breaths and a weak, slow pulse was visible in her neck.

Alaric poured the acadanthus tea into a cup. Using a small medicine dropper, he dripped the tea into her mouth, watching her neck for signs that she was swallowing. After he'd fed her half the cup, he dredged the leaves from the kettle and mashed them into a paste. He lifted her dress up to just above her knee where the swollen, black wound gaped. Purplish red streaks wound up her leg. He began to gently clean and drain the wound, focusing his mind completely on the task, working at it until it was as clean as he could get it. He packed the wound with the paste of acadanthus leaves and wrapped her leg with clean bandages. Then he resumed his seat next to her and filled the dropper again with tea.

The next morning, Alaric awoke stiff. He had fallen asleep in a cot near Evangeline. It was his bed whenever he was at the castle. The morning sunlight was behind the mountains, and Evangeline's room was still dim. He lit a candle and brought it close to her.

She still slept. He set his hand on her forehead and drew in a sharp breath. It was cooler. Not completely back to normal, but her fever was definitely lower. He set the candle down and unwrapped her leg. Underneath, the lines reaching up her leg had faded to a dull red and the swelling was almost gone.

It was working.

He put some more acadanthus leaves in the kettle, his stomach in knots. It was working.

He pulled the ruby out of the pouch at his neck and laid it on the pillow near her head. The Reservoir Stone did not hold enough life to wake her up. Seeing her here, seeing how little of her was left, he knew Gustav had been right.

He dropped his forehead down on the edge of Evangeline's pillow. Healing her would take the sacrifice of something healthy, something strong. But maybe that price could be paid, somehow. Maybe…

He lay there for hours until Milly came to let him know there was lunch in Brandson's room. He stood and stretched, dragging his mind back to the present.

Alaric was pleased to see the smith sitting up and talking with the others. His leg looked better and his fever was gone. Brandson smiled gratefully at Alaric and thanked him. The group chatted with each other while they ate the cold sausage from last night's dinner. Alaric found himself staring out the window.

Finally, he excused himself and went back to Evangeline's room.

He pulled his chair close to the table and sank into it, taking her hand.

It was time. With the crystal gone, he imagined that the blue had moved infinitesimally farther up her fingers. He cast out to feel the *vitalle* in her body. It was so weak and thin that he could barely sense it. Next to her head, the *vitalle* in the ruby was similarly thin. There was no way that energy would be enough to fill her whole body.

There was no point to this waiting, this lingering. There were only two choices. One was to let her die, the other to sacrifice someone else to save her…

She'd hate him for it, but it might give her a chance.

"Forget what you are planning, Keeper," Ayda said softly.

Alaric whipped his head toward her. She stood just inside the door, watching him with large, troubled eyes.

Alaric looked at the elf with narrow eyes. "I told you to stay out of my head," he said flatly.

Ayda gave a short laugh. "I don't need to read your mind to know what you are thinking." Then she walked over to the other side of Evangeline. "Your sacrifice would be more than useless. It would be cruel."

Alaric glared at Ayda, saying nothing.

Ayda held his gaze. "There is too much death in her, Alaric," she said gently. "All of the life inside of you will not wipe it out. Your death would bring her back barely, but only to be trapped in a broken body. She would revive to find herself in pain and you dead beside her. Then she would still die herself."

Alaric dropped his head into his hands, his fingers digging into his skull.

"There are worse things than death," Ayda whispered.

Alaric looked up at her. Ayda's face was strangely taut. She looked at him sadly.

"Alaric, there is only one thing left for you to do."

"I can't even say goodbye." His voice sounded like someone else's, as though the words tore themselves out of him. "If I wake her, she'll be in so much pain."

The room was silent for a long time.

Ayda moved first. She went to one of the pots of flowers and snapped off a few blossoms, then she stepped out onto the balcony, walked to the potted trees and set the flowers near the base of each trunk. With a whisper, the blooms began sending out tendrils, winding their way up the trunks with thin green vines, sprouting out tiny buds every few inches until the trees looked like they were about to burst into bloom.

She touched a few buds on each tree, and the breeze brought in a soft smell of spring. Ayda stood looking out, with her back to the room. Finally, she nodded and turned to Alaric.

"I can help," Ayda said. "We can help," she gestured to herself. "I can make it so she doesn't feel much pain." Then she looked at him intently, clarifying. "I can't take all the pain away, but whatever she feels should be mild, compared to…"

Alaric looked at her, a faint flicker of hope igniting.

"You could remove the healing spells and wake her," Ayda continued. "All these spells have served their purpose. They gave you the time you needed to look for the antidote. But they serve no purpose now."

No purpose. The words rang dully in Alaric's head. But there was a way. Gustav had done it, Kordan had. The flicker of hope turned to fury. Why did he not have enough life? Where could he find more?

You cannot find more. What would you do? Sacrifice us all? Ayda asked, her voice speaking quietly in his mind.

Alaric's head whipped up and he glared at her. He shoved at her presence in his mind, pushing her away, but she stood firm. Standing just on the edge of his mind. Not invading him, but not leaving, either.

This is not what you want.

The words rang in his mind, echoing the Shield's words. *This is not what you want.*

But he did. He wanted it more than anything.

"No," Ayda spoke firmly out loud. "You do not…. and neither does she."

Alaric's eyes tightened. "How would you know what she wants?" he growled.

Ayda looked down at Evangeline, warring emotions crossing her face. Then she looked back up at Alaric her expression wretched. Reluctantly, she spoke.

"Because she's not really asleep."

FIFTY-FIVE

Alaric's blood froze. Evangeline wasn't asleep?

Ayda continued softly. "I can feel her mind. She's not really awake, and she can't move, but she's not sleeping, either. She knows she's been alone and she knows that now you are back."

Alaric shrank back in his chair. He looked at Evangeline's face, smooth and peaceful. She knew she'd been alone? His hands began to shake. He had left her alone for so very, very long. "Is she in pain?" he whispered.

Ayda was silent for a long moment. "Not in terrible pain."

The breath rushed out of Alaric as guilt clenched inside of him. He had left her here alone and in pain.

"She's happy you are here and she wants to see you," Ayda said. "And then she wants to rest."

Alaric slipped forward out of the chair and reached for her with trembling hands. "I'm so sorry." He leaned his head against her forehead and felt the decision click into place. He couldn't sacrifice himself for her. She would still die. He couldn't sacrifice others for her. No matter what Kordan or Gustav thought, that wasn't something you could calculate, the worth of one person versus another.

The Keepers had been right. This power to pull the life out of someone was not used for a reason. Not because of some antiquated rule, just because the shifting about of people's lives couldn't be done with a clear conscience. It couldn't be done well.

Alaric was tired of not doing things well.

He was tired of feeling angry toward the world, toward the Keepers. Tired of distancing himself from a way of life that he had loved and respected. Tired of living in a desperate world of questionable actions. Tired of fighting against the truth that there were some sicknesses that couldn't be healed.

He wanted the truth back.

And the truth was she was awake and she was dying.

This had gone on far too long.

He nodded at Ayda. "How long can you keep her from feeling the pain?"

Ayda looked at him for a long moment. "For as long as she needs it."

Alaric felt tears start to fill his eyes and he nodded. "Thank you." His gaze dropped back down to Evangeline's fingertips. "It won't be long."

Ayda nodded and picked up Evangeline's hand.

Alaric looked at the ruby. The red light swirled slowly through the stone and it pulsed, slightly warm in his hand. Every breath or two, a swirl of darkness touched one of the irregular surfaces.

He leaned and focused on the thin lines that he could just see on her neck. He began to read them quietly. The runes at her neck glowed a dim blue.

The first words were rough, but as he continued, focusing all of his attention on the thin runes, his voice strengthened and the glow on the tiny lines began to fade.

He narrowed his focus, just concentrating on each line in her skin. He spoke until it faded, releasing the power held there, then he moved on to the next. One by one, moving slowly along the faint path, releasing branches that snaked off, releasing the ones that protected her heart, releasing the ones protecting her mind, releasing the lines that protected her life.

Energy trickled out of his hand, so little needed to end what had cost him so much energy to build.

When the last line faded, he stopped. Nothing had changed. The ruby still swirled slowly. Evangeline lay still, but now he could feel her body living.

Alaric set the ruby on her stomach. Reaching toward the ruby, feeling the energy that spun through it, he began the process of pulling it out and letting it fall back into Evangeline's body.

It happened more quickly than he expected, the amount of *vitalle* in the ruby was so much less than it had originally been. In the span of a few breaths, the ruby sat dark and cold. He moved it off to the side, then set his hand on Evangeline's forehead.

"*Excita,*" he said gently, feeling the rush of energy flow out of his palm.

Evangeline gasped a weak, shallow breath. Her body twitched and her brow drew down in pain.

Alaric heard a strangled noise and realized it was his own breath. He grabbed for her hand and leaned over her. Her fingers were ice cold. Evangeline's body began to thrash, her head tossing from side to side, her back arching.

Alaric remembered. He remembered the pain she had endured. He remembered how inadequate his skills had been to give her comfort. He remembered knowing she was going to die. And he remembered the terror of that idea.

Then Evangeline's body relaxed. She breathed heavily, for a few breaths, but even that began to calm. Alaric looked at Ayda. She was using both hands to hold onto Evangeline's. The elf's eyes were shut, her brow drawn slightly.

A small sigh escaped Evangeline's mouth, and Alaric whipped his attention back to her.

Her eyes were open and looking at him.

He felt his breath catch in his throat and he leaned close to her.

"I've missed you," she whispered.

Alaric reached out and brushed her hair back from her face, bringing his forehead down on hers. She closed her eyes and smiled.

Alaric pulled back, unable to take his eyes off her, but unable to speak. He wanted to apologize, to tell her how much he loved her, but he could barely breathe. He just gripped her hand and stared at her face. She looked so peaceful, so normal. Her cheeks had regained some color and her eyes were bright.

Evangeline looked at Ayda, and Alaric opened his mouth, but no words came out.

Ayda, whose face was pale and drawn, gave a little snort. "I'm Ayda," she said. "I've been traveling with your husband for a bit. Fighting dragons, saving the world, things like that."

Evangeline gave a weak smile. "That's the sort of thing he does." She looked down at her hand encased in the elf's small hands. "You're pulling the pain back, aren't you?"

Ayda gave her a tight, tired smile.

"Thank you," Evangeline whispered.

Alaric stared at her for a moment. She looked so healthy. He hadn't seen her look so healthy in… so very long. He barely remembered that her skin was always a little golden. It had been pale and waxy for so long.

"Evangeline," Alaric said, his voice barely audible, "we don't have much time." His hands gripped her so hard that he had begun to drive away some of the coldness. "I'm so very, very sorry. I couldn't…" He found himself floundering. "I found the antidote. But it's not enough. I'm so sorry." He reached for her face. "I've missed you every second."

"And I you," she said, her voice growing a little stronger. She looked at him with those clear eyes and smiled. "It wasn't your job to stop death, Alaric. Even great Keepers can't do that."

"They should be able to," he whispered.

"I'm glad I met you, Alaric," she said softly. "And I'm glad you will soon be free of"—she looked down at herself—"of this burden. You should have more of a life than this."

"He saved the world just yesterday," Ayda said. "Fought a great wizard and defeated Mallon."

Evangeline raised one eyebrow. "Not to take away from your victory, but wasn't Mallon already dead?"

"Mostly," Alaric said, smiling slightly.

"Well," Evangeline said, "it's been a long time since you've done Keeper things. You should ease back into it. Maybe you can work your way up to fighting someone who is fully alive."

Evangeline's eyebrows drew down suddenly, and she looked over at the hand Ayda was holding. "Whatever you're doing," she said to the elf, "it's working. I feel… wonderful."

Ayda smiled again, but her face was pale.

A noise near the door caught Alaric's attention. Brandson and Douglon were standing against the wall, looking as though they would like to sink into it. Milly had tears in her eyes.

Evangeline glanced at Alaric. "I think I could sit up."

Alaric looked at her in surprise and noticed a strong pulse in her neck. He pulled up her hand and saw fingertips pink and healthy. Evangeline lifted her head, and Alaric quickly reached an arm behind her to help her sit.

Suddenly, there was a strangled yell and Douglon threw himself across the room.

The dwarf reached Ayda just as she toppled to the floor.

FIFTY-SIX

E vangeline took a deep breath and stretched her hands. They looked healthy and strong. Alaric reached down quickly to see where the arrow had pierced her. Instead of the scabbed, swollen, black thigh he had seen for the past year, he saw smooth, clean skin with a small scar sitting right above the knee.

"Ayda!" he breathed, turning toward the elf. "How?"

Ayda lay in Douglon's arms, her face white, barely breathing.

"What have you done?" Alaric demanded.

Ayda smiled weakly.

Douglon's arms gripped her tighter. "You stupid elf," he whispered. "You stupid, stupid, stupid elf."

Evangeline was sitting steadily so Alaric pulled his arm away from her and knelt next to Ayda.

"It turns out," Ayda said, "that there is someone who had enough life in her to heal your wife."

He reached out and took Ayda's hand, which was ice cold. Her fingers were snowy white.

"Oh, Ayda," he says quietly, "you didn't."

She smiled weakly at him. "You were willing to sacrifice yourself. Is it so strange that I should do the same? You know, sometimes people break away from wallowing in their pasts long enough to commit to something."

"But… you're the last elf."

"What better reason is there?"

"You sacrificed all your people, too?"

"My people agreed to die eight years ago. Their lives have not been their own since. I have needed them for many things. I needed them to hold back the darkness. I needed them to take that darkness and destroy Mallon. And now I needed them to heal Evangeline."

"But…"

"I told you I wanted to sleep," she said quietly.

A sob tore out of Douglon, and Ayda looked up at him. She reached up and lifted his chin a bit so that she could see his face. There were tears streaming down his cheeks. His eyes bored into the elf, and now it was Alaric who felt suddenly intrusive. But he didn't want to move and break the moment.

"You stupid elf," Douglon said.

"You can stop looking at me like that, Douglon. It's just a charm," Ayda said. "Just a charm to burn off some of this power."

She looked around the room again, her brow puckered slightly with guilt. "I had too much power. It kept leaking out." A short giggle escaped her, sounding bitter. "I kept dropping little flames without knowing it. I was afraid I was going to burn down the world."

She looked back at Douglon and continued, an edge of self-loathing in her voice, "So I created a charm that worked constantly. A small, steady stream of power that would trickle out in the hopes that the destructive things would stop. Now animals like me, trees talk to me constantly, and even dwarves can set aside their disgust for us a bit.

"So you can stop looking like that Douglon. What you're feeling is just the charm. When I'm gone, the feelings will be, too."

Douglon had looked at her steadily the whole time she had been speaking, not moving. Alaric searched his face for some sign of his thoughts, but the dwarf just stared at Ayda with that burning intensity that made Alaric feel intrusive again.

"It's not a charm," Douglon said finally. His words were so quiet that Alaric found himself leaning forward. "I know about the charm. Everyone knows about the charm."

Ayda turned her head quickly around the room. Brandson nodded slightly. Milly shrugged and looked apologetic. When Ayda turned toward Alaric, he smiled slightly.

"Well," she said petulantly, "just knowing about it doesn't keep it from working."

"It's not working now." Douglon had not looked away from her face.

Ayda's eyes snapped back to him.

"It hasn't worked since you destroyed Mallon."

Alaric shifted slightly. That could be true. Ayda had been much less sparkly since then.

"The charm wanted me to think your eyes were darker and your hair glittered more than it does." He ran one dark hand across the golden curl that spilled over her shoulder. "And that you were taller than you really are."

She let out a small laugh. "I'm short, you know. For an elf."

Douglon let a small smile curl up the corner of his mouth. "Dwarves aren't particularly attracted to height," he pointed out. "It only works when you are around. I never think of you as tall when you are too far away."

"See?" she said, reaching her hand up tentatively to touch his beard.

Douglon stared at her a long moment. "The charm would make me want you to stay because I would think the room a gloomier place once you leave. But what do you think it is that makes me know now that the room really will be gloomy with you gone?"

Douglon reached up and pressed her hand against his cheek. Ayda's eyes widened slightly.

"What do you think it is that helps me to know that I love the real color of your hair, not that awful glittery nonsense you try to make me *think* you have?"

Alaric barely dared to breath for fear of interrupting. Out of the corner of his eye, he saw Milly reach over and hold Brandson's hand.

"What makes me wonder whether I'll ever return home again? Whether it wouldn't be better just to travel with you?"

Ayda was looking up at him, her eyes wide, her hand still pressed against his cheek. Alaric could almost see her slip into Douglon's mind. The dwarf sat perfectly still.

After a long moment, Ayda drew in a long breath. "I'm sorry," she whispered. "I didn't know."

Douglon shrugged, but his eyes burned into her. "That's because you are never paying attention."

Ayda reached up behind him, reaching for his axe blade. "It was selfish of Patlon's elf to choose purple. She thought only of herself. You, Douglon, should have red," she said to him, reaching her hand out to touch the handle of his axe. From the tip of her finger, tendrils of red fire spread along the axe handle, freezing to look like real flames.

"There you are," she said sweetly, sinking a little lower against him. "Now it's an unbreakable axe."

Douglon looked back at his axe handle, then cupped Ayda's face gently in his hand. She met his gaze and something passed between them.

She looked around the room, finding Brandson, Milly, and even Evangeline's eyes.

Finally, Ayda turned to Alaric and he felt her mind. He drew back slightly when he felt how weak it was. It was just an elven mind, a plain, weakened, elven mind.

Alaric sat very still, his mind probing hers slightly. Her mind was so very small, its power almost depleted. He found himself casting around for something to do, some way to give her more power, some strength.

Stop it, her voice snapped through his mind. *I have made my choice. My people are finally gone. It took them all, in the end, to replace all of the death that was in Evangeline. They were so much weaker than they had once been. Stop feeling sorry for them. There was never going to be a different ending.*

Alaric shook his head, but she continued.

Thank you. All I wanted, all we wanted, was to destroy Mallon. And I would have failed without you. Healing Evangeline is my thank you.

Alaric felt her mind waver, then it slipped back out of his mind, leaving him feeling empty.

Ayda smiled weakly at him, then sank back into Douglon's arms. Her head drooped forward, and a curtain of golden hair fell across it.

Douglon let out a shuddering sob and pulled her close, but she did not move again.

FIFTY-SEVEN

The sun sat low over the mountains, the sky stretched out overhead in a clear blue that felt serene, but empty. Alaric stood with his arm around Evangeline on the balcony of the room he had always intended to share with her, near the top of the tower. He listened to her speak, but her words were interrupted by the thrumming of her heart and the sound of her breathing. He cast out wave after wave just to sense the blazing core of energy inside of her. Beneath his arm, she leaned against him, warm and secure, not quite strong enough to stand on her own. But she was alive. Her face was bright and animated and so very alive.

"You're doing it again," she said, her smile teasing.

Alaric blinked and laughed. "Sorry. I have no idea what you just said." He pulled her around and kissed her. She wrapped her arms around his neck, kissing him back. "It's just that your alive-ness is so distracting."

"Alive-ness? Is that a technical Keeper term?"

"Yes. Don't be intimidated by my sophistication."

She looked at him curiously. "Are you still a Keeper?"

Alaric dropped his forehead down to hers. It had taken some getting used to, learning that she hadn't really been asleep all that time. He had been terrified that she'd be angry, but when they'd had their first moments alone, she had just stretched her hands out, flexing her fingers and then touching his face. "I'm too happy to be mad," she'd said. "I know what you did and why. Besides, it wouldn't be entirely fair if I'd just gotten to sleep while you were spending all that time tortured." But she had smiled when she said it, and just like that, the issue was dismissed, dropped back into the realm of things in the past that are over now.

She knew all the things he had spoken to her during her long sickness. All the confessions of failure, all the fury at the Keepers for not helping him, all the anger, all the desperation. All the times he had sworn he was done being a Keeper.

"I'm not sure I'm the same Keeper I used to be, but… yes, I still am one. I have some ideas about how things need to change at the Stronghold, but I think there's a chance it can all work out reasonably well. How do you feel about spending some time at court?"

Her eyebrows rose. "Well, I'm fancy enough for it." She gave a little curtsey in her old traveling dress and bare feet, holding onto his arm to steady herself.

He smiled. "It's busy there and there are some horrific people, but I think you'll like Saren.

And Ewan is there.

"At some point, I need to go see if I can figure out what happened to Will. When he left the palace, he was headed to the Roven Sweep to look into something with the nomads. But he should have been back a long time ago."

"As long as we don't volunteer for any fire lizard hunts on the way," she said, "I'm willing."

Alaric rested his chin on her head. There were too many emotions swirling inside him to pick just one. Evangeline was right here, standing, talking, breathing. But in a room below them, Ayda lay still and cold.

He let his mind stop spinning. He breathed in the scent of Evangeline's skin. He felt the cool breeze and the cooler stones of the balcony. He listened to the quiet rustling of the world.

In the midst of all the emotions, he felt a small green shoot of peace begin to grow. It was a peace tinged with sorrow and loss, but it was rooted in a profound rightness.

———————◆———————

Ayda was laid out peacefully on Evangeline's table.

Alaric and Douglon had moved it to the balcony, and placed one tree on each side of her, their blooms just waiting to burst open.

Douglon stood stationed at her feet.

Alaric stepped up to Ayda's side, his arm still around Evangeline.

Milly straightened Ayda's dress and touched the ring of purple flowers that encircled her waist.

"These flowers are still alive!" she said, looking closely at one tiny daisy-like bloom. "How long has she worn this?"

Brandson stepped forward, his eyes red. His brow drew a bit and he said, "I think always."

"She was wearing it the day we met her," Douglon said.

"They're beginning to fade a bit at the edges," Milly said.

The very edge of each petal was curling. Alaric looked at Douglon, and the dwarf nodded.

Alaric traced some runes in the air above Ayda's body, letting the slow energy pour out of his hands. A shimmer appeared. It stretched until it encompassed all of her, then hardened, perfectly clear.

Alaric set his hand lightly on the crystal. Beneath it, Ayda's body lay perfectly still.

"Will it keep her like this forever?" Milly asked quietly.

"Not forever," Alaric said. "But for a long time. It should take years for even the flowers to wilt." He studied the flowers for a moment. "I don't even know what sort of flowers those are. I wonder if they have any healing properties?" The question came out more out of habit than curiosity.

Evangeline peered down at the little purple flowers. "Those are Lumen Daisies. They grow everywhere in the Greenwood."

Alaric raised his eyebrow. "You've never been in the Greenwood."

Evangeline's brow creased and she looked up at Alaric. "I know. But I also know that these flowers have no medicinal value and are a favorite gift among the elves. They symbolize... home."

Alaric stared at her, an idea taking hold of him. "Why was the Elder Grove so powerful?" He tried to keep his eagerness under control.

"Because it was the burial ground for the first elven king and queen. They sacrificed themselves to the woods to create a place of power."

Alaric took both of her hands. "How much do you know? How much did Ayda tell you?"

Evangeline shook her head. "I don't know. I didn't know I knew any of that until you asked."

Alaric grinned at her. "That's okay. I have a lot of questions."

THE END

PURSUIT OF SHADOWS

The Keeper Chronicles Book 2

THE FLAMES

The air in the normally drab village square shivered with magic.

Will felt as though he'd stepped into a different world. More people than he'd ever seen were gathered together, the high-spirited crowd causing the weathered buildings around them to fade into the background. The nutty smell of roasted sorren seeds wafted out from the wayfarer's wagon, and Will's mother had bought him not one, but two sweet rolls.

Vahe of the Flames stood far back on the stage, surrounded by dark walls and an arched roof, his voice low as he told of three children trapped deep in the lair of a mountain troll. His fingers toyed slowly with a handful of fire, flickering just above his palm, seemingly burning nothing but air. Will couldn't pull his eyes away.

The wayfarer's black hair and pointed beard mixed with the shadows on the stage. His voice rolled out with dark menace as the trolls crept closer to the children. Will's fist clamped into the sticky dough of his sweet roll, and he leaned closer to his mother. When his arm brushed hers, a jab of disapproval flashed into his chest, off-center and too muted to be his own. His mother watched Vahe with the same sternness she turned on Will whenever he played too roughly with baby Ilsa.

Pulling his arm away from her, the feeling faded. He rubbed his skin as though he could erase the memory of it. It happened more and more often lately, these echoes of what other people were feeling when he touched them.

Vahe continued, his voice still low and foreboding but the spell had been broken. Will remembered that the stage was a wagon. Not a normal wagon—a wayfarer's wagon. Like a house with wheels. Except houses didn't come in dazzling colors, or have fronts that could lay open like a ramp, leading down to the village dirt. Vibrant ribbons fluttered from the edges of the roof, quivering brightly in the evening breeze, but inside, Vahe's dark orange flame lent a brooding feel to the shadows. It caught on unknown things, flashing back glints of burnished copper.

The tale ended with a quick escape by the children and Will's mother put her arm around his shoulder.

"Let's get home." Her disapproval rushed into him again, filling the left side of his chest and leaving a mildly sour taste in his mouth.

"But wayfarers never come here. And he might tell more stories."

"I've heard enough." Her tone made it clear the decision had been made. "Tussy needs milking. And that man takes entirely too much pleasure in frightening children."

Milking a goat was a terrible reason to leave. If only Tussy would run away one of the times she broke out of her pen. With a sigh he felt down to his toes, Will followed her, weaving through the crowd of villagers in the dusty square, hoping Vahe would start a story his mother would be interested in hearing.

Instead Vahe began to do tricks with the strange orange flame in his hand, making it appear and disappear, tossing it through the air, even dropping it onto a pile of dry grass without setting it aflame. He tossed it toward the crowd. It disappeared for a moment when it reached the sunlight, then Will caught a glimmer of it hovering over someone's head. It slid over another, and another, people's hands reaching up and passing through it unharmed. It came close and Will held his breath. When it shifted above Will, the top of his head tingled for a heartbeat. A jolt like lightning shot through him. Every bit of his skin stung like the prickles of a hundred tiny thorns, and the air around him shimmered with yellow light. The flame winked out and the sparkles disappeared.

"The fire likes you, boy!" Vahe cried.

Will rubbed his hands across his arms, trying to brush away the last of the prickly feeling. The crowd oohed appreciatively, and Vahe started another trick. But Will's mother waited at the edge of the crowd, her mouth pressed into that thin line and her brow creased with worry.

The sun beat down on the dirt road leading out of the dingy village, and the whole way home through the low, winding hills, Will couldn't shake the tingly feeling that crawled across his skin.

At the edge of their yard the creak of the goat pen caught his attention. Tussy was shoving her little horns under the bar, pushing open the gate—again. The brand new shoots in the garden almost within her reach.

Will ran forward, stretching his hand out as though he could reach across the entire yard. Too far away to reach her, he could do nothing but hurl fury at the stupid goat for interrupting the storytelling, and for endlessly escaping her pen.

Except the fury *did* hurl out of his hand with a ripping pain and the gate slammed shut.

Agony stabbed up his arms and he dropped to his knees, his own cry of pain drowning out Tussy's insulted bleat. A new circle of winter-brown grass around him marred the summer yard, brittle and dry, like the old, worn out grass of fall.

Shiny blisters swelled on his palms and he curled forward, gasping and choking on the pain. Worry and pity washed over him like cool water even before his mother's arms wrapped around him.

"A Keeper," she whispered, looking from his hands to the withered grass. A fierce pride blazed up in Will and he sank against her, letting her emotions drown out his own fear and pain.

———————◆————————

Hours later, he lay in the cool quiet of the cottage and the roiling turmoil in his chest was thankfully all his own. His parents and Ilsa slept in their curtained alcove, the barrage of emotions from them finally quiet. Since he'd closed the gate that had changed. He could feel everything they felt. No one had to touch him now, they only needed to be close.

He rubbed his thumb over the frayed edge of the cloth his mother had wrapped around his blistered hands, his mind spinning.

Magic. He'd done magic. He'd somehow sucked life out of the grass and used it to shut the gate.

The idea hung in the silent cottage both alien and obvious. Part of him was still shocked, but if he was honest, he knew something magical had been happening for months and months. Not with searing, hand-burning pain, but with mumbled, nudging hints. That empty, endless hollowness he'd felt when he shook hands with the butcher at his wife's funeral. Or the day they cheered as Ilsa took her first, wobbling steps—when Will's mother had grasped his shoulder, he thought his heart might burst into a million pieces.

But he couldn't really be a Keeper, could he?

He'd closed a gate from across the yard, and everyone knew the sign of new Keeper magic was burned hands. He stretched his fingers until shots of pain lanced across his palms. If he'd done magic, would the Keepers have to take him? His heart quickened. He'd get to go to the hidden Stronghold. He'd see the queen in her palace. He'd never have to weed the garden or milk Tussy. He'd be rich. He could buy his father a mule, and Ilsa a real doll instead of that ugly rag she carried everywhere.

Will pulled the thin blanket up to his chin, trying not to get too excited. He wasn't the sort of boy who became a Keeper. He was the sort of boy who could never get the goat pen to stay closed.

A foreign terror crashed into him, stronger and darker than anything he'd ever felt and he shrank down into his bed. He strained to hear any sound, but his father's snoring continued, low and steady, and nothing else stirred in the cottage.

He squeezed his eyes shut. *Please don't let me feel their dreams.*

The sensation swelled until he couldn't stay still any longer. He rolled out of bed and tiptoed toward the curtain. The sensation grew stronger. His breath grew shallow and his heart thrummed in his ears as though he stood atop a cliff—or was being chased by something monstrous.

Will pulled the curtain back, desperate to wake them from such a nightmare.

Bright moonlight poured in the window, landing on the bed where his parents lay sleeping. Ilsa and her rag doll curled between them and the wall in a tangle of dark curls. All three were still.

But in the window above them perched a man with a black pointed beard.

Vahe.

Will froze, his hand clutching the curtain. Vahe's gaze snapped up, and Will's gut clenched, whether from his own fear or the wayfarer's, it was impossible to tell. A silver knife appeared in the man's hand, glinting in the moonlight. Slowly, the man raised a finger to his lips.

Will's breath caught in his throat. He needed to yell, scream, something. But his body refused to move.

Vahe shifted his grip on the knife until it pointed down at Will's father's chest.

"Come with me, boy," he whispered, the words barely more than a rustle of wind.

The muscles of Vahe's arm rippled as he shifted the knife over the thin form of Will's parents. Even if Will woke them, they were no match for this man.

A fierce anger stirred in his gut, an anger all his own at this man for threatening them, for daring to come into their house. For being stronger than his parents.

Will stepped forward and let the curtain fall behind him. He flexed his hands slightly. It had worked on the gate. He just needed to push Vahe out the window. Then he could lock the shutters and yell until the neighbors woke.

The desire to push the wayfarer grew stronger and stronger until it filled him, shoving out Vahe's storm of emotions. Every bit of Will wanted that wicked face, that silver knife, and that dreadful excitement out of his home. And out of himself. Will lifted one hand and pointed it toward the wayfarer. Pain shot across his palm as he focused all his fury at the man.

Vahe's eyes widened and he grabbed at the window, bracing himself. "Come," he ordered between clenched teeth. "No one needs to get hurt."

Will pushed harder until his palm burned and the wayfarer threw all his weight against the force of it. Vahe's black hair and beard blended into the night. Will could see only pale cheeks and glittering eyes.

A stray thought wandered across Will's mind, a memory of the withered grass this afternoon. Was the garden outside withering now, fueling whatever he was doing?

He didn't care.

Slowly, a finger's breadth at a time, Vahe slipped backwards.

A small gasp yanked Will's attention down. His mother lay on the bed in front of him, white as moonlight, gasping for breath, her fingers scrabbling against Will's other hand where he clutched her arm. Will snatched his hand back, and the fire racing through him stopped. His fury turned to horror.

It wasn't from the garden. He'd been pulling all that power out of her body.

Everything moved at once.

His mother took a deep, shuddering breath.

His father stirred.

Released from Will's fury, the wayfarer toppled forward, falling into the room, the knife slamming into Will's father's chest. His mother screamed and Ilsa woke, adding her small cries to the chaos. Terror and fury filled Will and he didn't know if it was his or theirs. Pain and panic and desire rushed in, threatening to tear him apart.

Vahe looked up from the knife, his face shocked. He reached toward Will again. "Come here, boy!" he hissed.

Will backed away from Vahe's anger, his mother's terror, and his father's too-still form.

A shout and pounding on the cottage door behind Will made the wayfarer's anger flare hotter. Vahe's eyes bored into Will, his fury thrumming in Will's chest.

Will's mother screamed for help. Vahe hurled a last glare at Will, then snatched up Ilsa. She cried, reaching out toward her mother, her dark curls pressed against Vahe's neck.

"Stop," Will pleaded, taking a step closer.

The door to the cottage splintered and flew open. Neighbors rushed into the small cottage, bringing in a frenzy of emotion.

The wayfarer yanked his bloody knife from Will's father's chest with a snarl. Still clutching Ilsa, Vahe plunged out the window, his anger tearing out of Will, leaving him hollow of everything but his mother's screams.

ONE

Will rode up the interminable slope at a trudging pace, running his fingers through his beard and wondering for the thousandth time why everything on the Sweep was so deceptive. The ceaseless grassland made it impossible to tell distances, and every rise turned out to be twice as long as it looked. On top of that, the seaside road had become mostly sand, and with each step his horse's hooves sank in and backwards, making the climb feel like a continual progression of small defeats.

Endless, faded, tiresome grass rolled down from the far reaches of the northern Sweep to dwindle here, choked out by the sandy beach. In Queensland, or any other wholesome place, the world would be bursting with the greenness and flowers and warmth of spring. But here the grass left over from last year was brown and brittle, the sea was grey, even the sky was barely blue. The emptiness of the Sweep slithered inside him, deepening its roots, tinging everything with hopelessness.

Over the top of the hill, the tip of a jagged peak appeared, and an ache of homesickness squeezed his chest. It was long past time to go home. He'd accomplished nothing here. For his foreignness, he'd been ignored or scorned everywhere he'd gone. All he had to show for the past year were a lingering loneliness and two books crammed full of overheard Roven stories. Granted the books he'd written held more information about the Roven Sweep than the entire Keeper's library, but even that might not cancel out his failure to find the things he'd actually been looking for.

When he finally crested the hill, the Scale Mountains spread out along the horizon like the barren, rocky spine of some ancient monster, guarding the eastern edge of the Sweep. From here the road would take him past the southern tip of the mountains in a day and he'd be in Gulfind. A respectable land with something besides grass. He'd see bushes and trees. He'd be within two easy days of Queensland where he'd have no reason to hide. If people found out he was a Keeper, they'd treat him like an honored guest, instead of calling for his execution.

Something moved in the distance on the road ahead and a mild curiosity stirred his listlessness. He hadn't seen another traveler all day. The Roven clans had already headed north to graze their herds on the well-watered plains near the Hoarfrost Mountains, and there was nothing but grass left here on the southern edge of the Sweep.

A flicker of color caught his eye, and his hand tightened on the reins.

A gaudy wagon with tall sides and a rounded roof stuttered its way over the next long hill. Its garish paint and gleefully clashing ribbons fluttered against the backdrop of the mountains before cresting the hill and disappearing.

A wayfarer's wagon.

A surge of fury and hope blazed up in him. He spurred Shadow forward.

It had been months since he'd found one. The wayfarers were impossible to track. They wandered aimlessly in isolated wagons, spread out across the known world, peddling magical trinkets and cheap performances. Even the Keepers didn't know whether the solitary groups were connected with each other, or whether they hailed from any particular country. The only thing Will had learned in the twenty years since his sister had been taken was that anything he learned from one set of wayfarers was always contradicted by the next.

Will blew out a long breath and relaxed his hands on the reins.

It wouldn't be *the* wagon. It was never *the* wagon. In twenty years he'd found almost two dozen of them, but none of them carried Vahe. None of them even admitted to knowing the man.

Still, Will urged Shadow a little faster down the far side of the hill.

Far to the north, a speck winged through the sky before diving down to disappear into the grass. In the space of a few heartbeats it climbed into the air again and flew closer, growing into the shape of an undersized hawk, thin leather jesses dangling from its legs. Talen flapped down, settling on the blue bedroll tucked against Will's saddle horn. The hawk dropped a dead mouse onto the blanket and fixed Will with unblinking eyes.

"That is just as disgusting as the others." Will leaned back from the gift. "You are the worst payment I've ever received. It would almost be worth backtracking a day and losing sight of the wayfarers just to give you back."

Will couldn't flick the thing into the grass until Talen flew away or the bird would think they were playing some grotesque game of fetch and bring it back.

He'd fully expected the sad excuse for payment to have flown off at the first opportunity. But it had been a full day since a herdsman had offered the miniature hawk as payment for scribe work, and he was still here. He'd wing away to hunt, out of sight across the grass, and just when Will thought he'd left forever, the hawk would come back, dangling a dead mouse in his beak.

"Would you like to come with me to Queensland?" Will considered the hawk who merely stared back. "I can see you don't plan on talking back to me. Shadow never does either, and he's been with me for several weeks now." Will patted the mottled neck of the pinto. "But until we reach a place where *people* will talk to me, you two are all I have.

"Can you do anything useful?" He reached out a finger slowly toward the bird. Talen twitched his gaze to Will's hand, but didn't move. Will ran the back of his finger lightly down the bird's chest, brushing over white feathers speckled with veins of brown. "If I drew you a picture of the man I'm looking for, could you fly up to that wagon and give me some sort of signal if you see him? Because he's someone I've been hunting for much longer than a year. And as soon as I've confirmed he's not there, I'm going home." Talen's back and head were darker with ripples of black and auburn. The feathers were so soft they felt almost liquid.

Talon fixed Will with a round, golden eye.

"I'll take your lack of response as a no.

"While you were off hunting mice, I realized I know four different stories where an animal allowed itself to be linked to its master, giving them unique powers. Two of those stories were about Keepers."

Will cast out toward the bird. He found the bright bundle of *vitalle* wound up in its body, strands of energy humming with the potential to burst into flight or dive after yet another mouse. The bird's *vitalle* sat compacted above the broader, slower energy of the horse. Beyond them both, the grass spread out in countless pinpoints of energy, until it ended at the sea.

"Of course, they were a different sort of Keeper than me. Both of them were adept at magic. If you and I are going to communicate, we'll need to keep it more…simple."

Will focused on Talen. "There is one thing I can do, though." *Dispend*, Keeper Gerone would say, *Reach out*. But Gerone had never quite understood Will's unusual talent. It wasn't really the casting out that all Keepers could do to locate energy, this was more of an unlocking or an opening.

Something in his chest loosened, and a nebulous feeling of expectation, or waiting, poured in from the little bird. Not a fully formed emotion, just a…prodding sort of sensation. That was always the way with animals, broad sensations and hungers. They were recognizable. Loyalty, hunger, satisfaction. But only a single emotion at a time. None of the chaotic tangles of emotions that humans had.

"There are no records of Keepers feeling others' emotions." He stroked Talen's head. A warm, contented feeling surfaced on the left side of Will's chest from the bird, in contrast to his own worn-in frustration with himself, which sat more centered and more comfortably inside him. "But it's not a terribly useful substitute for being proficient at magic. Knowing someone wants something isn't the same as knowing what they want."

Thundering hoofbeats sounded ahead of him and two red-haired Roven rangers crested the hill, bearing down on him at a gallop. He had time to wrap one arm protectively around Talen and grab hold of his jesses to keep the small hawk from flying into one of the Roven before they raced past on either side him. Two distinct sensations of scorn blossomed in his chest.

"Off the road, fetter bait," one barked in the harsh Roven accent.

The other ranger kicked out his foot, catching Will's saddle bag, sending it bouncing and clanging, causing Shadow to prance to the side. "Move, fett!"

The Roven tore away down the road, their emotions fading from his chest, leaving only Talen's fear, Shadow's startled wariness, and Will's own irritation.

"I hate this country." Will spoke softly and ran his finger down the back of Talen's head. "You know one of the main problems with the Roven? They think people are fetter bait." When the hawk quieted, Will loosened his grip on Talen's jesses. "Setting aside the fact that you're sort of fettered, I think we can both agree that humans shouldn't be."

Will glanced over his shoulder. The two Roven were heading the wrong way. All the clans that way had gone north for the summer already. With the bird calm, Will closed himself off and the bird's emotions faded from his chest.

They were almost to the top of the rise when Talon let out a piercing screech. Like a needle to the ear. The bird tilted its head and pinned Will with a hard stare.

"A signal like that is exactly what I'm talking about. Although maybe we could pick a more pleasant sound. You could use it to warn me before I'm charged by rangers—"

A jangle of far-off music caught his attention just as the smell of roasting fish tumbled through the air. Will reached the top of the hill and stopped. A wide, low plain stretched ahead of him all the way to the feet of the Scales. Nestled against the ocean sat the small city of Porreen, the winter home of the Morrow Clan.

And around the wall, tents and people crowded together, proclaiming that here, at the very eastern edge of the Sweep, the spring festival was still going on.

"—or ambushed by festivals."

Talen gave another screech.

"Don't try to take credit for warning me." Will nudged Shadow down the hill. "A screech is not a warning."

Like all Roven cities, Porreen consisted of a roundish jumble of lumpy buildings that looked like cattle corralled by a thick earthen wall. With no trees on the Sweep for wood, everything was made exclusively of cob, a mixture of earth and dried grass, shaped by hand without any attempt to make straight walls or sharp angles. The city sat close enough to the sea that the lumpy cob buildings looked like a city built by children on the beach.

The wayfarer's wagon moved along the edge of the festival, heading out of sight around the city wall. Crowds of red-headed, red-bearded, blue-eyed Roven mingled around the tents. Any head that wasn't red was either a foreign merchant braving the unfriendliness of the Sweep, or a foreign slave in a grey tunic.

With a screech that sounded disapproving, Talen launched off the bedroll and soared away over the empty grassland. Will couldn't blame him. The Roven would probably capture the hawk and cage him. It's what they did to foreign things.

Will scratched at his black beard. It hadn't helped, really, to grow the beard. Every man on the Sweep had one and so he'd let his grow to blend in. But theirs were all hues of red, from bright or-angey-flame to dark coppery russet. Will's was black. Not a tint of red to be seen. Between that, the rest of his black hair, and his dark brown eyes, his head felt like a signal fire made of shadows, her-alding his foreignness. The Morrow Clan's spring festival was bound to be like the others, a mad scramble to buy supplies before the clan moved north for the summer. The hostile stares he was about to encounter dragged at him. He could almost hear muttered "fett" and "fetter bait" already.

The Scale Mountains were so close, and the idea of leaving the Sweep rushed over him like a fresh breeze. He'd glance at the wayfarers, then go. He could be half-way to the mountains by dark. Will flicked the dead mouse off his blanket.

Dismounting, he led his pinto horse off the road, cutting through the grass toward the nearest tents. The tufts at the top of the winter-dried stalks tugged at his pants like greedy little fairies. After a year trying to move unobtrusively through the Roven Sweep, he'd mastered one bit of vaguely sophisticated magic. He cast out, reaching past the dead grass and finding the bits of new growth, just starting to peek out of the ground.

Slowly he extended his fingers toward the ground and began pulling the *vitalle* out of them, drawing it through his hand and into himself as he altered the tiny snips of life-energy into some-thing more elusive. He let the *vitalle* slide out from his other hand, stinging his fingertips as he spread a cloak of disinterest around himself. A suggestion that there was nothing about him worth noticing.

It was done before his fingertips were even singed, accompanied by the usual twinge of guilt at the fact that the other Keepers wouldn't approve.

The influence spell had become unsettlingly easy. Like every other bit of magic Will had ever tried, it had been challenging to cast at first, and even more challenging to sustain.

When he'd first come to the Sweep, he'd only used the influence spell occasionally. But the farther he traveled among the Roven, the more he realized that the Sweep was always unsafe. They distrusted all foreigners, but had a special hatred for Queensland. Parents frightened their children with stories of evil Keepers who didn't use stones to hold their magic, but pulled it out of living things. It became easier not to be noticed, and now putting on the influence spell was like part of getting dressed. He'd renewed it so often it felt as though it never completely wore off.

The other Keepers definitely would not approve of that. Gerone's eyebrows would dive down into a hairy scowl and he'd say there was something dishonest in it, something slightly dangerous. Which was true, but there was something definitely dangerous about having the people of the Roven Sweep find out Will came from Queensland. Or worse, was a Keeper. So Gerone and his eyebrows could say what they pleased.

Will drew close to the crowd, his hand tight on the reins. But the first person's gaze slipped past him without notice, and he let himself relax. He skirted the edge of the festival. Runes of protection and good luck decorated each tent. The leather vests of the Roven were marked around the armholes and the neck with runes. More were painted onto their bowls and tables, and woven into their rugs. Small gems glittered everywhere. They flashed in rings, hung around necks and wrists, many of them glowing with trace amounts of *vitalle*. The Roven called them burning stones if they held any energy, and Will sighed at how much money he could have made on the Sweep if he'd had any idea how to put the energy of living things into a lifeless rock. The Roven filled the festival covered in runes and gems in an effort to be safe, or lucky, or shrewd.

The wayfarers, with their trinkets that looked magical, whether they were or not, were going to make a fortune in this city. They were probably the only foreign people who walked freely through the Sweep.

Will caught a glimpse of long, brown hair coming toward him, and his fist clenched on Shadow's lead. Opening up without meaning to, the emotions of the crowd rushed into his chest with a cacophony of feelings, shoving aside his own blaze of hope.

The crowd slithered past and the slave woman shuffled into view carrying a pile of fabric. An ordinary clutter of emotions from her blossomed in him. Worry, exhaustion, mild curiosity.

Will searched her face, looking so hard for the resemblance to Ilsa that it took a moment to actually see her and recognize it was all wrong. More than that, she was too old, much older than twenty. She paid no more attention to him than anyone else, and didn't raise her eyes from the ground as she passed. When her emotions faded, Will shoved the chaos of the rest of the crowd out of his chest.

Butter-yellow fruit caught his eye. When he offered the Roven vendor his copper half-talen for three avak, the woman looked surprised to see him for just a breath. Her eyes took in his not-red hair and the fact that he didn't wear a grey slave's tunic, and her lips curled in disgust. She snatched the copper out of his hand with a "fett" and went back to her Roven customers.

Will turned away, blending back into the crowd. To chase away the bitter taste of the slur, he took a bite of the fruit, and the tangy juice burst into his mouth like a splash of brightness in the dusty Sweep. Avak was one of those glorious things that was always better than expected. Like the smell of the air after rain. Or the vividness of a lightning strike. One of those things that breaks into life with the truth that there is far more…*something* in the world than people usually notice.

Will took another bite.

Avak didn't fit here on the Sweep.

The sharp tanginess perked up his mind, as it always did. The afternoon sunlight danced over the orange fabric of the tent next to him. It glinted off a set of metal spoons and shimmered down the red-gold braid of the Roven woman considering them. To the south, the ocean rose in small swells glittering like scales on a sea monster.

A bit ahead of him the flutter of the wayfarer's wagon caught his eye.

The last bite of avak flesh pulled cleanly off the smooth pit and Will tucked it in his pocket. The Keepers' Stronghold needed an avak bush. Gerone would be thrilled. He could plant an orchard of them.

The freshness clarified the reality of Will's situation too. This was just another random, solitary wayfarer wagon. The search for his sister was nothing more than a far-fetched dream, and being on the Sweep was a waste of time.

Will led Shadow around a large red tent filled with blankets and stopped.

At the edge of the festival, flashing with gaudy colors and snapping ribbons, sat over a dozen wayfarer wagons lined up one after the other, in an arc.

Rooted to the ground, Will stared at the cacophony of color ahead of him.

He'd had never seen so many wayfarers in one place. Never even heard of a gathering like this.

Wagons with rounded, stout roofs parked next to ones with tall, pointed roofs. One blood-red wagon even had a flat roof, crenelated like a castle. Wildly colored shutters were thrown open and a few of the crooked chimneys dribbled out smoke. A raised stage nestled up against one painted the spiky yellow of a bumblebee, creating the impression that Will stood in a theater.

The stage sat empty, but handfuls of people sat along a row of benches stretching across the back of the makeshift theater, and he sank down on the end, dazed. He let Shadow graze, and watched wayfarers dressed in garish colors unload even more garish costumes and props for the evening's show. A young girl holding a pot passed, trailing the earthy smell of sorren seeds. Tiny shells edging her amber shawl jostled each other with a quiet clatter.

The wagon Will had been following settled at the other end of the arc, calling greetings to the other wayfarers. Will cast out toward the people around him and the energy teeming in their bodies and the bright pinpoints of *vitalle* humming from the burning stones they wore echoed back to him. Countless colored gems, set in rings or pendants, swirled with light and tiny snippets of power.

Will took a bite of the second avak, his surprise fading. He'd found a band of wayfarers doing what wayfarers always did, entertaining crowds and selling marginally magical trifles. The familiar frustration gnawed at him.

A woman stepped up onto the stage wrapped in flowing layers of ocean blues and greens. "Come! Listen to old Estinn!" she called out to the milling crowd with a lilt that made her accent impossible to trace. Bits of grey hair snuck out from under her emerald scarf and her voice rang out loudly from her thin, hunched body. The crowd paused. "When the sun drops over the edge of the world, come witness a battle! Storytellers from near and far will gather, pitting their skills against the skills of Borto Mildiani, in a contest of..." She stopped, then smiled a toothy smile. "*Skills!*

"Are your stories duller than last year's grass? Then keep them to yourself. But if your tales ensnare the ear, come test your mettle against the legendary Borto!" Estinn flung her hand toward the yellow wagon behind the stage.

A black-bearded man in a loose rust-red shirt stepped out, bowing to the crowd with a flourish.

Will's heart froze for a beat.

Vahe.

TWO

Will surged to his feet before he caught himself. Rage and disbelief crashed into each other like wild, frothing waves in a storm.

Will stared at that face, opening up toward the man, as though he could reach past the crowd and feel only Vahe's emotions. There were so many people between them a torrent of indecipherable feelings rushed into him.

Old Estinn stepped off the stage and several other wayfarers joined Vahe. The man greeted them warmly, leading them behind the wagons and out of sight. Will's emotions were so taut he felt almost numb.

A bright dart of curiosity burst into his chest and Will's attention snapped back to the bench. A little slave girl peered at him through strands of long, pale hair from the corner of the nearest wagon. Her emotions were a blazing fire of interest, full of wonder and enthusiasm so strong they shoved everything else inside him to the periphery. She stared at him with large green eyes, as light as spring grass. Her face was so gaunt it was angular.

At her attention he sank back down onto the bench, pushing the deluge of her emotions out of his chest. What he was left with felt almost as foreign. Seeing Vahe's face, after wondering and searching for twenty years, loosed something inside him. Anger and relief strained against each other, but above it all rose a hope, so wild and fierce that it felt almost like terror.

It prodded him to jump up and follow the man. But throttling Vahe and demanding to know where Ilsa was, while he stood among a crowd of his own wayfarers, probably wasn't going to get positive results.

"Are you alright?" The little girl asked, still watching him.

"I…" Why *was* she watching him? He glanced around to see if his influence spell had worn off, but no one else paid him any attention. "I don't know."

She was maybe eight years old, her blond hair as out of place on the Sweep as his black. He took a calming breath, trying to get control of his emotions. Influence spells were always less effective on children. They spent too much time fascinated by new things to be convinced to overlook a stranger.

The little girl inched around the edge of the wagon. Everything about her was dusty in a permanent way, as though she had never been clean. The bones of her shoulder pressed up against her shift like jagged stones and skeletal fingers pushed her hair back. Sitting here among the lurid colors of the wayfarers, her slave's tunic was almost too drab to be called grey.

The Roven bought their slaves from Coastal Baylon and Napon in the east. Criminals in those countries could find themselves as easily on the slave block as in a prison. Debtors were treated the same. A debt large enough would enslave their entire family. But the Roven felt that young slaves were more trouble than they were worth. Until an age where they could be useful, they were kept in a shabby little commune, only fed when they could prove they'd found work. The smallest slaves scurried through the cities with menial jobs, gaunt faces, and tattered clothes.

Will grabbed his last avak.

"Would you like some fruit?" He held it out.

She looked at it suspiciously.

He set the avak as close to the end of the bench as he could. Slowly, she reached forward, then snatched the fruit off the bench. It looked heavy in her hand, like the weight of it might snap her thin wrist.

"It's avak," Will said. "They're my favorite." He glanced around the theater, but Vahe was still out of sight.

She took a nibble of the fruit and cocked her head to the side. "If it's your favorite, why'd you give it to me?"

Will paused. "Would you believe it's my way of countering great evil?"

One of her little eyebrows rose skeptically.

"And," he added, "because you look like me. And I haven't talked to many people lately that do."

She glanced at his black beard and scrunched her nose.

"Well, not exactly like me." He motioned to the Scales. "But where I come from, across those mountains, there are a lot of people who look like you and me. Not everyone has red hair."

She studied the Scales with narrowed eyes. "I don't like those mountains. They don't have any grass at all."

The stony range rose up in a dull brown, jagged and unwelcoming. "True. The mountains are barren, but on the other side the world turns green again and there's grass. Not like here. Over there it's greener and shorter and out of it grows bushes and trees taller than a house." Motion of several people between two of the wagons caught his eye.

She took another bite of the fruit. "There's nothing more wonderful than grass."

Despite everything, the declaration was so unexpected that Will let out a laugh.

She fixed him with a severe look. "Don't you like it?"

"I'm not sure." Will studied the faces between the gaps of the wagons, trying to catch a glimpse of Vahe. "It's a little…empty."

She let out a huff of indignation. "Empty? You could walk for days and not find a bare spot. And all the roots tangle together so the whole world is an endless living thing."

Will dragged his attention back to the strange little girl. He had to press his mouth shut to keep from smiling at the intensity of her enthusiasm. "I've never thought of the grass as being a thing in itself."

"It's the biggest, most powerful thing in the world! It's where everything comes from, and where everything goes when it's too old to move. And"—she glared at him, setting her tiny fists on her hips—"it's beautiful!"

Will sat back. "I stand corrected. I've obviously not been giving the Sweep the respect it deserves." He set his fist on his chest and bowed his head. "I promise not to make the same mistake again."

She pursed her lips in consideration. "And you'll see how beautiful it is?"

Beautiful? Grass too tall to feel like grass, but too grassy to feel like anything else, spread out over the land like the worn, sparse pelt of some massive creature? She waited expectantly.

"I'll try."

"It'll be easy." She leaned forward, her face fairly bursting with excitement. "Summer is coming."

He found himself smiling at her with a smile that felt rusty from disuse. She took another bite of the avak. Vahe still hadn't returned. Will was just about to follow him when the man stepped into view and stood on the stage, calling instructions to a handful of wayfarers, and the surge of hatred that Will felt toward the man almost overwhelmed him.

But Vahe clearly wasn't going anywhere soon. Will settled back and took a deep breath. He couldn't ruin this by rushing into it.

He settled back on the bench. The slave girl still watched him curiously.

"I'm Will."

She considered him seriously for a moment. "I'm…" She let her eyes wander over to the Sweep. "Rass."

Will raised an eyebrow. "Rass sounds a lot like grass."

She grinned at him. "That's why I picked it."

"You're the most interesting girl I've met in a long time." Will paused. He glanced at Vahe. Did Rass know anything about him? He searched for a way to word his next question. *Who owns you?* felt insensitive. He glanced to where she'd been hiding. "Do you live with the wayfarers?"

She let out a giggle. "No."

"You live in Porreen?"

"In the stinky city?" She shuddered. "I live on the grass."

The grass?

"I just came because the colored wagons tell good stories. I love stories."

"So do I," Will said. "I like stories more than maybe anything else in the world."

She cocked her head to the side. "You look like someone out of a story. Sitting here and hiding in plain sight." Her face turned wistful. "I wish I could do that."

Will felt a squeeze of fear in his chest. She could sense his influence spell? Children were unsettling, sometimes. Like they weren't exactly human yet. They were something wilder, brighter. Of course, now that he thought about it that way, maybe it was the adults who'd stopped being human.

Will grasped for a different topic. "I've never seen so many wayfarers together."

Rass sat down on the far edge of the bench. "They come every spring."

"Did…" Will hesitated, but couldn't come up with a better way to ask it. "Did the wayfarers bring you here?"

Rass looked up at him in surprise, then let out a long, rippling laugh. "No one brought me." She licked the last of the avak juice off the pit and held it out to Will. "Thank you."

Will hesitated before holding out his hand and letting her drop the wet pit in his palm. He tucked it quickly into his pocket with the other pit, and wiped his hand on his pants.

"I just come to hear the stories." She pointed at Vahe. "My favorite is Borto."

"Borto?" The name was wrong. Will studied the wayfarer's face. That wasn't exactly right either. The man had too much chin. Or not enough forehead.

"He's the best storyteller on the Sweep."

"The best?" Vahe had told stories, but even as a child Will wouldn't have ranked him any better than the men who told stories in his own village. "Does he do tricks with fire?"

Rass shook her head. "You're looking for Borto's brother, Vahe of the Flames."

Will flinched at the name.

"He comes sometimes, but not as often as Borto."

"Is he here now?" The words came out strained.

"I haven't seen him."

Will's fingers went mindlessly to the gold ring on his finger. The ring had a wide central band that spun with a satisfying smoothness between two thin edges. Will watched Borto closely, a hundred thoughts warring with each other in his head.

"How does your ring spin like that?" Rass asked.

Will held out his hand, showing her. "A friend gave this to me a long time ago."

The Shield, the leader of the Keepers, had gifted it to him over ten years ago, the first time he'd left the Stronghold on his own. *Most rings are a single entity,* he'd told Will. *I've always thought it was interesting that part of this is free to move and spin, affected by the world, while the core of it remains true to the wearer.* The Shield had considered Will for a long moment before nodding approvingly and grinning. *It fits you. And it's extremely satisfying to spin while you think.*

Borto let out a loud laugh and shouted at some approaching wayfarers.

"It's nice to meet you, Rass." Will stood. "I think I'll join the story contest tonight."

Rass's eyebrows shot up. "You tell stories?"

Will leaned toward her and whispered. "Maybe better than Borto."

She clapped her hands and grinned.

Will gave her a slight bow and walked around the edge of the closest wagon.

The influence spell shouldn't have worn off yet, regardless of Rass's attention. And it was awkward trying to have a conversation with someone while the spell tried to distract them. He drew a little energy from the grass at his feet and sent the *vitalle* out through his other hand cutting through the influence spell, letting it dissolve around him. He almost never ended the spell before it wore off, and unlike the ease of putting it on, the unfamiliar act of banishing it burned the ends of his fingers.

Now that it was done, he itched to put it back on. Even back here, away from the crowds of the festival, he felt exposed. The haggling and hawking from the festival seemed louder than before and the smell of smoked fish and roasting sorren seeds was distractingly strong. This might not have been a good idea.

Will started along the wagons toward the place Borto had gone, forcing himself to walk calmly. He caught sight of the man's red sleeve as he sat on a low stool, leaning on his elbows and tinkering with a small box. Will's heart pounded so loudly it was astonishing the wayfarer couldn't hear it.

Borto caught sight of him and rose. His fingers were loaded down with rings that glinted with gems, and at least three larger stones hung around his neck on leather thongs. "Looking for something?"

"You," Will answered, trying to keep his voice pleasant. The resemblance to Vahe made his heart shove up into his throat. He pressed his fist to his chest and bowed, giving himself a moment to calm down. "Do you have room in your contest this evening for one more storyteller?"

Borto took in Will's dirty, drab clothes and worn boots, looking unimpressed.

"I may not best a wayfarer in storytelling," Will said, "but in my own small corner of the world, I once spun a tale so sad it brought a troll to tears."

Borto fixed Will with a probing look. "And what small corner of the world is that? Your accent says southwestern Queensland. Near Marshwell, perhaps?"

Will hid his discomfort at the extremely accurate guess with a smile. "Marshwell is not far at all from where I was raised." Which was true. "But I'm from just over the border in Gulfind." Which was not true. Much smaller than Queensland, Gulfind was surrounded by mountains full of gold mines, making the small population excessively wealthy. It was on excellent terms with Queensland however, and the people along the border from both countries were almost impossible to tell apart. Also, merchants from Gulfind traveled widely and were known for being a bit eccentric. A traveling storyteller from there was unusual, but not unheard of. The lie had served him for the last year on the Sweep.

"I think we can fit in one more storyman." Borto ushered Will back into the stage area. "But I'll warn you, this isn't your homeland. There's no gold for the winner."

"I'm just thrilled to be a part of it." Will wished his pulse would slow. The more he looked at the man, the more differences he saw from his memory of Vahe. "I'm fascinated by wayfarers, and I've never seen so many in one place. There's no better way to learn about people than to hear them tell stories."

"But we won't be telling wayfarer stories. Here on the Sweep, the stories we'll tell are mostly Roven tales."

"It doesn't matter," Will answered, trying to keep the man talking. Borto's voice was different from Vahe's too.

"It doesn't?" Borto looked at Will appraisingly. "If a man tells you of his home and his family, you'll learn something about him. But if he tells you foreign tales, you only learn about foreign places."

"You learn that too," Will agreed. The voice was definitely not Vahe's. "But if everyone knew the same story, we'd still tell it differently from each other." He shrugged. "I think the way a man tells a story reveals more about the man than it does about the story."

Borto studied him. Then a grin spread across the wayfarer's face. "A storyman and a philosopher!" Borto clapped Will on the shoulder and gestured at the old woman standing by the stage. "Welcome to the contest. Give Estinn your name. I want to hear a tale that'd make a troll cry."

Will gave the man another bow and turned toward Estinn. His heart raced like he'd just sprinted across the Sweep, and he took a couple deep breaths trying to calm it. Now he needed to find a place to spend the night and choose a tale. Apparently a sad one. And something that would impress the greatest storyteller on the Sweep.

He could tell The Black Horn. Technically it was from Queensland, and included a Keeper, and it didn't positively end as a tragedy. But it was obscure enough that no one would know if he switched the country. The Keeper would be easy to change to a wise woman and the emotional parts amplified until it would feel like a tragedy. And the only magic in the story was firmly anchored in the horn, leaving it the sort of magic that the stonesteeps on the Sweep used. It never mentioned Keeper magic, drawn from living things.

Will nodded pleasantly at the wayfarers who greeted him as he walked through their area. Leaving off the influence spell felt surprisingly free. It felt like a chain had fallen off, or a window had opened.

Borto knew Vahe. All Will needed to do was befriend him. Here, finally, after twenty years, he had a lead to finding the man who'd taken Ilsa. And following it only depended on telling a good story. There weren't many things Will did well, but storytelling—that was easy.

Will introduced himself to old Estinn and she noted his name.

After getting directions to an inn that served foreigners where he could stable Shadow and stow his bag for the evening, he turned, looking for Rass with a half-formed idea of getting the little girl a real dinner. Instead of Rass, a Roven woman dressed in hunting leathers leaned against the wagon next to his horse. Her hair draped over one shoulder in a long, thick copper braid.

She stood with her arms crossed, watching Will.

Her eyes were narrow, gauging, and her mouth pressed into a thin, flinty line. A hint of unease rolled across the back of Will's neck, but he forced himself to smile at her.

She did not smile back.

THREE

When he reached the woman, he paused and bowed his head slightly in her direction.

"Lovely evening, m'lady." His smile felt wooden.

She said nothing.

The "m'lady" had been too much. Judging from her leather vest, plain boots, and brown cotton pants, all of which were more functional than fashionable, she was a ranger who spent her life hunting on the Sweep. This wasn't a woman who wanted m'ladying.

Above them a seabird squawked indignantly and Will could still hear the noises from the festival, but an awkward silence filled the small void of space around them.

"I guess it's not a lovely evening if you don't like festivals."

Her foot rested on the bench, pinning down the reins of his horse.

"In which case we could hope for something that will end the festivities, like…" He paused. "A pestilence. Or a plague."

She stayed straight-faced, studying him coldly.

He opened up out toward her to read her emotions and felt…nothing.

Her emptiness seeped into him. She had no anger, no suspicion, no dislike. Just nothing. He'd met people with all different intensities of emotions, but never one with none.

A chill wormed its way through his newfound freedom and he backed up a step before stopping himself.

This woman was dreadful.

"One hour until the epic battle of storytellers commences!" Estinn called out to the crowd.

"That's me." Will took a step closer to Lady Dreadful. He put his hand on the reins, and slowly she moved her boot. He gave her a stiff nod, and led Shadow toward the nearest tents.

It took an age to get to them, feeling awkward the entire time, like his legs had forgotten the rhythm of a smooth gait. Her eyes were probably staring into his back, watching empty and cold. When he'd passed two tents, he glanced back, but saw no sign of her. Climbing into the saddle, he shook off her strangeness and turned Shadow toward the city gate.

Away from the woman, the thrum of excitement at finding Borto resurfaced. What was the best way to befriend the man? Telling a story better than anyone else in the competition tonight was obviously the first step.

He ran over the story of the Black Horn in his mind, as he passed through the gate and into the city. He barely noticed the sharp eyes of the city guards or the way Roven purposefully did not move when he approached, but let him move around them. His gaze ran past the lumpy cob buildings, barely seeing them.

His inn slouched against the shop next to it. Around the door, a stonesteep recarved fading protective runes into the cob, muttering to himself while a faint orange glow hovered around his tools. Will cast out toward the man and felt barely a wisp of *vitalle*. Just enough to make his tools glow. No actual magic was being pressed into the runes. It wasn't surprising. Most of the Roven stonesteeps he'd seen put only enough magic into their work to make it look real. In fact *steep* was such an exaggeration Will had often thought they should be called stonedribbles. But Roven were so used to relying on protective runes and burning stones, they paid the stonesteeps without question. These particular runes were so rough and blocky as to be almost illegible. Protection against weather most likely, a simple spell meant to keep the house safe over the summer while the Roven were in the grasses to the north grazing their herds.

The topmost one could be rain. Or sea, maybe. Definitely something watery.

For the thousandth time, Will wished he'd brought Alaric with him to the Sweep. Alaric was the sort of Keeper who would know immediately what the runes said, what they were intended to do, and why they looked different from the ones the Keepers used. He'd also know how to press magic into them, strong enough to last the summer. Any Keeper besides Will would, for that matter.

He left the stonesteep to his ineffective work and settled his horse in a dingy stable, leaving him with a pile of the cleanest hay he could find. The inn's common room smelled stale, a mixture of old food and neglect, and it took more money than it should have to rent a room. But the innkeeper took his coin without any disparaging comment or look, which was worth something.

The room was as filthy and irregular as the outside of the inn promised. It bent in an elongated triangle shape, one side following the curving outer wall. A low bed smelling of moldy, dried grass filled one side, and the other curved around into a point of empty gloom. A thin rug, still clinging to the memory of bright colors, covered the floor. When Will got back to civilized lands, he was going to stay in the nicest inn he could find. He'd pay ridiculously high prices just to be somewhere clean and bright and friendly.

He spread his bedroll over the windowsill to air. Dropping his bag down on the bed and ignoring the puff of dust that ballooned out of the mattress, he pulled out a bundle and unwrapped two small books. He sat and thumbed through the pages, the soft corners familiar under his fingers, checking for dampness or paper mites. His own handwriting covered the pages from edge to edge, with small drawings and diagrams crammed wherever they fit.

There was a flutter at the window and Talen landed on the bedroll, the usual mouse dangling from his beak.

Will grinned at the little hawk and dug into his bag, pulling out an old bit of dried meat. He set it next to the candle on the little table. Talen dropped the mouse and hopped down, snatching up the meat and giving Will an emotionless stare.

"You're welcome." Will went back to checking his book. Talen moved to the bed with a little hop and fixed his eyes on the flipping pages.

"Shall I teach you to read?" Will flipped back to the beginning. "That would make you a more interesting bird. These are my notes from the past year." He tilted the book toward the hawk, and Talen backed up slightly. "Originally I went to see the elves. Which was the most exciting thing I've ever been asked to do. I only ever found one, though."

A sketch of Ayda filled the next page. "This doesn't do her justice. She's…" She was vibrant and fanciful and her golden hair had almost sparkled. "Mesmerizing. I don't know why she spent so much time with me, but it was weeks. And she never introduced me to any other elves.

"She did show me Mallon the Rivor's body, though. Here on the Sweep you'd know him as Mallon the Undying. Which is a bit dramatic, even if it might be true. He attacked Queensland eight years ago, and was on the verge of conquering us. Until the elves stopped him. We thought they'd killed him, but it turns out they'd just trapped him inside his own mind." He glanced at Talen. "I'd imagine it's like he's a man stuck in a small, drab, little room only talking to himself. And a bird.

"I was headed back to tell Alaric, one of the other Keepers, that Mallon wasn't actually dead, when I heard of an old man named Wizendor who was supposedly coming to the Sweep to raise an army for Mallon. That was troubling enough that a Keeper needed to come to this wretched land." He smoothed the page flat. "At least I assume the other Keepers would have agreed that someone needed to come here. I didn't ask. I wasn't doing anything useful in Queensland. I'd been traveling the country looking for children with the ability to be Keepers for years and hadn't found any. At least Wizendor was someone I might actually find."

With the pages lying still, Talen twitched and looked around the room.

"Maybe I should have stayed, but if there's any Keeper *not* cut out for fighting an enemy with inexplicably strong powers, it's me.

Talen cocked his head at Will, looking at him out of one eye.

"Don't look at me like that. I left a note. Alaric is the Keeper who needed to know, anyway, and he was off in the south running errands for the Queen. I left that note at the palace for him nearly a year ago. By now he's probably been back there for ages, doing important Court Keeper sorts of things like straightening out the world and killing Mallon." He paused. "I wish I could have talked to him before coming here, though. I have no idea what was taking him so long to get back."

"Anyway, all this"—he flipped again and Talen snapped his focus back to the pages—"records me *not* finding Wizendor. Which is dull." He stopped at a page where the writing oozed disappointment. "When I did finally hear him speak to a crowd of Roven, it was still dull. Because the man was not worth the chase I'd just been on. If that old fool succeeded in raising a Roven army, then I'm the best Keeper that ever lived."

Past that, the entries in the book grew shorter and less related.

"By then I was deep in the Sweep, so I decided to learn what I could of the Roven on my way back out. Because, honestly, it feels a little embarrassing to have come all the way here and learned essentially nothing." He flipped past maps of the Sweep, notes on Roven culture, and overheard Roven stories. Records of searches that had begun as fascinating questions, but ended fruitlessly.

Like his attempt to find Kachig the Bloodless, a stonesteep so powerful that he was only mentioned in hushed voices. People were so frightened of the man, it had taken a whole month to discover he'd been dead for ten years.

It was unreasonably irritating that he couldn't even find out the reason for the "Bloodless." A title like that had a story behind it, but whatever it was, no one on the Sweep would talk about it.

The final entries all documented rumors of wayfarers on the Sweep, and any hints at where Ilsa might be.

Talen hopped forward to shove his beak into Will's bag.

"There's no more food in there." Will flipped through the last few pages of failure after failure, but closed the book without his usual sense of crushing despair. Because tonight, none of that mattered. Even though his hope of finding Ilsa hung by the slightest thread—he finally had a thread.

The scent of paper and ink wafted past. It smelled like comfort and home and rooms full of books. He held it close to his face for another breath.

What he wouldn't give to be in a library. Besides these two books, in the entire last year on the Sweep he had only seen five others. Two had been genealogies of the Sunn Clan kept in the wealthy district of Tun, and the other three had been carried by a severe looking stonesteep in a parade at Bermea. Almost no one on the Sweep read or cared to learn how. Limited documents were held in each clan recording births and deaths of the wealthy, business men kept minimal ledgers, and very occasionally a contract was drawn up. Will had earned a small amount, including one miniature hawk, by offering to record genealogies for families on the Sweep. The spelling of names was more of an art than a set of rules, but seeing as none of his customers could read, it didn't really matter.

Will shook out the scarf and Talen hopped back away from it. With a tweeting sort of whistle that sounded annoyed, he took off out the window.

Will wrapped his books back up. There was nothing alive in his room to draw energy from, so Will set his hand on the books and pulled a tiny bit of energy out of himself.

It took so little effort. His palm barely tingled against the books as the energy went into them, wrapping an influence spell around the bundle. It said something that the only magic he was good at involved hiding things. Or himself. He tucked the books in the darkest corner under the bed. Between the shadows and the spell, even if someone came into his room, they wouldn't notice them.

He pulled a red wool shirt from his bag. It wasn't exactly like the traditional scarlet tunics storymen from Gulfind wore, but it was close enough that it would fool anyone but an actual storyman from Gulfind. Hopefully Borto would be convinced. He changed into it and straightened his shoulders. The role of storyteller settled over him like a cloud, and he let himself settle into the safety of it. It would be nicer to get to put on the full role of a Keeper. To keep the storytelling but add in the freedom to do magic and keep records and sit in the library and read books for days at a time. To have the camaraderie of the Keepers, to visit court.

He sighed and tucked a small coin purse inside his shirt and left his bag on the bed. The things left in it weren't worth anything.

The story contest wouldn't begin for a while, but this room was depressing and at the festival he could work on a way to talk to Borto again. He had nothing to draw energy from for an influence spell. Bracing himself against the hostility he was about to encounter from the Roven, he left the inn and hurried back toward the festival.

When the wayfarers came into view he paused to look for Lady Dreadful. Seeing no sign of her or Rass, he sat down on a bench, watching for Borto. As the sky darkened, the area swelled with people. Parents spread out brightly colored rugs on the ground while their children scampered and squealed around them. A sweetbread vendor walked by with a sugary smell of cinnamon. The benches along the back were filling and Will sat along the very edge, avoiding contact with them as much as he could.

A quarter of an hour passed before Will caught a glimpse of Borto passing behind the arc of wagons. With a surge of emotions too tangled to name, Will slipped around behind the nearest wagon to follow him.

There was little commotion back here and Will opened himself up. When he caught sight of Borto, a writhing mass of the man's eagerness and anxiety rushed into Will's chest. He drew back against a red wagon wall and glanced around. There was nothing here to cause so much anxiety.

Borto leaned back against his wagon, his arms crossed, one finger tapping quickly against his arm. A young man with a heavy limp came from the other side, and Borto's emotions flared. Will pressed himself against the red wall until he could just see the two of them.

"Lukas!" The wayfarer greeted him with a wide smile that belied his anxiety.

Lukas answered with a curt nod. He wasn't Roven. Even though his hair and beard were styled like one, they were light brown instead of red. His clothes were the undyed grey of a slave, but they were fitted and clean. He wore half a dozen rings and three necklaces. Even in the sunlight several of the burning stones held enough energy to be visibly bright. Over his slave's tunic he wore a grey leather vest stamped with lines and swirls of runes. One of his legs twisted at an odd angle, and he shifted his weight away from it.

He stood farther from Will, so his emotions were faint, but Will caught a hint of greed, and the twists of fear that always wrapped around it. And behind it all sat a deep, ugly hatred.

The emotions of the two men jumbled together and Will closed himself off to them.

If Lukas was a slave, he was better dressed and he wore more burning stones than any Will had seen. He stood next to Borto like a young lord addressing a servant.

Borto held out a bundle wrapped in a worn, brown cloth. Lukas kept his face impassive as he took it, but his movements were too quick to hide his eagerness. He unwrapped the cloth and Will's breath caught.

A book.

Will took a half step forward before he caught himself.

Not just any book. This was thick, covered with a blue leather binding dark as the night sky with a silver medallion on the front. Even from here, Will could see it promised stories and knowledge. And secrets.

A hungry smile twisted across Lukas's face, and he tossed the wayfarer a bulging bag of coins.

"No trouble getting it?" The words were more of a threatening statement than a question.

"Nothing this doesn't make up for." Borto dropped the bag inside his wagon. It let out a substantial thunk.

What book was worth that much money?

Lukas rubbed his hand across the cover.

"Always glad to help out our favorite clan." Borto leaned back. "And visit our favorite festival. Is the Torch coming to the contest tonight?"

The Torch? If Lukas served the clan chief of the Morrow, that would explain the way he was dressed.

"When he has this to read?" Lukas gave a derisive snort and flipped open the book and thumbed through a few pages. "And he says you're to leave at dawn."

Will stifled a laugh. The Roven Torch was trying to control a band of wayfarers?

"Before the festival is over?" Borto asked sharply. "You'll cost my people thousands of talens."

"Not all of you." Lukas's face turned malicious. "Just you. Says the information he sent you is…" His voice cut through the air as sharp as a shard of glass. "Promising, and you shouldn't dally on the Sweep." Carefully wrapping the book back up in the cloth and without looking at Borto for a response, Lukas turned and limped away.

Borto glared in Lukas's direction for a long moment before turning and ducking back between the wagons, slamming his fist into the side of one.

FOUR

Will took a few steps toward the empty space they'd left.

That had been intriguing on so many levels.

The Torch of a Roven clan just ordered a wayfarer to go do...something. And it certainly looked like Borto planned to obey, despite his obvious frustration.

Will stepped along the wagons until he could see Lukas's grey form limping quickly toward the city gate. His leg twisting painfully with each step.

Will took a step after him, his longing to see the book outweighing the obvious fact that he wasn't going to be able to get near it. There was no way a Roven Clan chief would let a foreigner into his house, never mind let him read the expensive book he'd just bought in a secret deal from the wayfarers.

Still...

How could he not follow a book like that?

He took another step forward.

"Take your seats!" Estinn's voice called as a jangle of music started. "Come hear stories that will boil your blood, mesmerize your mind, and seize your soul!"

Will lingered for another moment until Lukas disappeared into the crowd near the gate, before retracing his steps back to the wayfarers' theater.

As fascinating as the book was, if Borto planned to leave the Sweep in the morning, Will had only tonight to impress him. Maybe a good enough tale would convince Borto to let Will travel with them for a few days. If not, he'd follow him anyway.

The sun hung low behind the city, casting the festival into shadows. Smells of roasted barley crackers and smoked fish trickled behind the stage to where Will stood with the other performers, a mix of colorfully dressed wayfarers and leather clad Roven. The wayfarers greeted him cheerfully, questioning him about himself and his story. The Roven stood to the side, coldly.

Estinn settled down the crowd and Will shifted until he could see most of the stage and a slice of the audience between the hanging fabric.

"Our first tale of the night is Yervant, come to share the story of when he followed Mallon to Queensland," Estinn called out, "and killed the Keeper!"

The crowd erupted into cheers and Will's gaze snapped over to the people beside him.

Mallon? No Keepers had been killed when Mallon had invaded. He'd passed through

Queensland like some kind of plague, gaining control over people's minds in town after town, holding sway over them even after he'd left. And when he'd controlled enough, he'd brought his armies of Roven to destroy the rest.

One of the Roven, a thick, disheveled man carrying a mug of ale and smelling unwashed, pushed past Will and stepped up onto the stage. Voices called out to him from the crowd, taunting but friendly, and he held up his hand for silence. With a few final jeers, the audience stilled.

"When Mallon the Undying"—Yervant raised his mug reverently at the name—"led our great people 'cross the Scales to crush the farmers o' Queensland, I traveled with him. Our company had men o' the Morrow Clan—" Cheers rang from the crowd. "—and from the Panos Clan." He looked around slowly and the audience quieted.

Will glanced at the faces in the crowd that he could see. Mallon had attacked Queensland only eight years ago. How many of these men were there?

"And we had a giant, with feet so large he crushed three houses with each step!"

The people were nodding along, muttering approvingly and Will held in a snort. Maybe none of these people had fought. Giants' feet were barely large enough to crush a bush, never mind three houses.

Yervant told how the troops had slunk through the woods, approaching a small town right on the northern edge of the Scales. How the giant had gone out first, destroying building after building, then the Roven warriors had swept in. Until Queensland's soldiers had appeared.

"And behind 'em, black like a shadow, a Keeper snuck through the mornin'." Yervant's voice was low and angry. "He had no amulets, no stones, no books. All his magic he sucked from the world around him." The crowd rumbled. "And he didn't help Queensland's soldiers. Not a single soldier had an amulet or a charmed sword. The enemy fell before our blades like grass, and the Keeper didn't even look at the bodies."

Will clenched his jaw in an effort to keep his face impassive. The only Keeper who'd been along the northern Scales was Mikal. And he had done everything he could to protect those men. He'd knocked aside arrows, softened the enemy's steel, thrown illusions onto the field to confuse the Roven.

"Just when we thought we had 'em beat," Yervant said, bitterness creeping into his voice, "the black Keeper stepped up to a burning house and took the fire *in his hands*." A ripple of revulsion swept across the crowd.

Mikal had never spoken of how the battle ended, and Will had never pressed him. He'd been tempted to look into the Wellstone where Mikal had recorded his memories of it, but it had felt invasive. And so he'd only known there'd been a fire. Mikal had always been good at moving flames. He used to light his candles by walking near the hearth. He'd just pull out a bit of flame, dancing on nothing but air, and bring it to his wick.

"The Keeper took the fire in his hands," Yervant continued, "and threw it at us, sending streams o' fire across our men. Burnin' Roven where they stood, poor Andro and Adaom among 'em."

A swell of anger grumbled through the crowd.

Mikal had wept for those men as well. Even all these years later, the Keeper carried those deaths with him like a shadow.

"The black demon burned our men alive!" Yervant shouted. "He drove off the giant with his dark arts. But at the last moment, I drew my bow, and with Andro and Adaom's bodies at my feet, I shot arrow after arrow at the monster."

"And you killed him!" Someone cried out from the crowd.

Yervant nodded. "My last arrow struck home, sinking into his black heart. I saw him fall t' the ground. Dead."

A wildly inappropriate smile threatened to spread across Will's face. Mikal hadn't been shot in the chest. He'd been shot in the shoulder. The arrow had knocked him down, and when he'd gotten to his feet, the Roven were fleeing. Will had changed the bandages on that wound, and it had healed cleanly. The arrow had been nothing. It was the rest of the battle that had left scars.

Yervant finished his tale and bowed to cheers, sloshing his ale across the front of the stage before climbing down and disappearing into the audience.

Estinn stepped back up on the stage. "Thank you, Yervant. Even though you only have one tale to tell"—she paused for some jeers from the crowd—"it's one we don't mind hearing. Year after year after year."

She raised her hand for silence. "Our next storyman is sure to tell something we haven't heard before. A foreigner has offered to entertain us with tales from distant lands." She turned and held a hand out toward Will. "Good people of the Morrow Clan, I present storyman Will of Gulfind!"

A spattering of applause came from the crowd, mixed with murmurs. Will stepped onto the torchlit stage and found himself alone. The sun had set while Yervant talked. The light from the stage torches made the faces of the crowd indistinct, and he imagined they were an audience from back home. Maybe a gathering from a large village. It felt better than a crowd of Roven, but neither really mattered. Tonight the only audience that mattered was Borto.

Will brought a stool from near the back of the stage forward, and settled on to it. He glanced around to make sure the wayfarer was watching, and catching a quick glimpse of the man standing off to the side, he began.

"Good evening. Tonight I bring you the tale of the Black Horn. A tale of old magic worn thin and new magic just born. Of love and sacrifice. Of a vast army and a single soul."

Will opened himself up to the crowd finding skepticism mixed with curiosity. He breathed in the earthy smell of the torch oil spiced with sorren seeds, and looked down at the stage for a long moment, waiting until the crowd settled into silence, their emotions swinging toward curiosity.

"The bag with the Black Horn bounced against Eliese's back like the prodding of a little sprite, cheering her on to adventure and victory..."

As he told of Eliese's early adventures, it began to happen. The two children directly in front of him were drawn in, and their amusement seeped out, mixing with that of their family, with the Roven warrior behind them.

By the time he reached the heart of the story, the emotions of the crowd had risen, each individual's anticipation merging with their neighbors' until it filled the small theater. Instead of feeling it in his chest, it became something more—almost a visible cloud, almost a living thing.

"...on the mantle," Will continued, "the ram's horn sat like a curl of blackness, darker than the shadows. Eliese reached up, her hand hesitating only a moment before picking it up."

Will gauged the audience. Only at the very edges did the mist begin to tatter with distracted people out on the fringes. A dead spot farther along the side circled around someone keeping themselves isolated from the story. But around Borto, the crowd hung together, utterly focused.

The Black Horn moved along simple and well-made, needing little help on his part. An obscure story he'd found tucked away in the queen's library, he'd stitched it together with a similar account at the Stronghold. They'd been easy to merge and the story had become one of his favorites.

Even exchanging the Keeper for a wise woman and leaving out any mentions of Queensland took minimal thought. He just needed to pick up the spool of the story and follow the thread. The words lined up, one after the other. They stretched ahead of him as easy to follow as a wide path through the grass.

Keeping tabs on the emotions of the audience, he slowed down or sped up the tale. And like all audiences, they let themselves be pulled into it, delighting in the feel of the story.

A bright spot of fascination off to his left in the mist of emotions caught his attention. He glanced over to see Rass perched on a wagon wheel in her little grey slave's shift, beaming at him.

At the darkest moment he paused, letting the tragedy seep through the air. The audience sat silent, somber while the darkness of the tragedy felt complete. Speaking just loud enough to carry over the quiet crowd, he drew them back toward the light, with the slightest hope of finding what was lost.

When the final words had been spoken and allowed to fade away, the crowd erupted into cheers and Borto applauded enthusiastically. The emotions of the crowd splintered into individual people feeling individual things, and Will pressed his fist to his chest and bowed his head to the crowd.

He moved to a seat just off the stage to watch the next storyteller. A Roven woman sang next, a long ballad that warbled on the high notes. She finished and the audience talked and laughed and argued with each other while waiting for the next performer. Will sat half-listening to the conversations around him, half-watching Borto. Two men were arguing about whether or not the ubiquitous rumors of frost goblins on the Sweep were true.

The Sweep was obsessed with the idea of frost goblins this spring.

A story about frost goblins would be fascinating to hear. Until recently, he'd always heard the little creatures mentioned as only a nuisance. But this year, the stories sounded more threatening.

"Another report came today," the first man said. "Eight rangers dead."

The second man shook his head. "Just more rumors."

"Magar says they're not," the first insisted.

"Your cousin will say anything to scare you…"

Will opened up toward them, feeling an acidic fear blossom in his chest, even from the protestor.

Will stretched out farther through the crowd, catching more uncertainty than usual. Every town he'd passed through for the last several weeks had an undercurrent of uneasiness. Will had attributed it to the clans readying themselves for the long migration north to their summer valleys, but maybe it was more.

Past everyone, Will felt that dead spot again. A place where emotions were being held tight. He shifted to see past the torches.

Lady Dreadful leaned against a wagon, partially shadowed from the torchlight studying him. His own uneasiness filled his chest.

At least a dozen Roven sat between him and her, but he closed himself off to all but the frost goblin men, then stretched out past people one by one. A young woman with loose, fiery hair spoke to the man beside her, her emotions swirling bright, just under the surface, edged with jealousy. A man whose beard had streaks of grey chatted with the woman beside him, comfort and contentedness running deep. An older man sat alone, humming with a worn, hollow fear. When he reached Lady Dreadful, he found nothing but emptiness.

Night had truly fallen and a boy scurried across the stage adding more torches. Excitement and pride broke Will's concentration on the woman and her blank hollowness faded from his chest. The extra torches drenched the stage with light, obscuring anything past it. Will shifted on the blanket, trying to shrink back into the shadows, wishing he could see Lady Dreadful. But he might as well be on stage, perfectly lit up and unable to see anything.

He turned his attention to the next wayfarer woman who'd taken the stage, trying to push Lady Dreadful out of his mind. Tomorrow morning he'd leave with Borto, or following right behind him. The cold woman could stay here in Porreen and rot.

Borto Mildiani took the stage and Will turned all his attention to the man. It wasn't difficult. From his first words, the man had the audience enthralled.

Even more than his face or his name, this set him apart from Vahe.

Will had forgotten little about the wayfarer's visit to his childhood home. Vahe had told three tales that morning, tales of danger and suspense. As a child, Will hadn't been able to pinpoint what he hadn't liked about them, but he'd told enough stories by now to know. The way Vahe lingered on frightening ideas, the turns of phrase—he enjoyed his audience's fear.

Borto, on the other hand, made the festival laugh. The crowd threw themselves into his hands and he rewarded them with excitement and intrigue. He told the tale of a young Roven girl lost on the Sweep who'd called out to the Serpent Queen for help and Will listened closely, absorbing the story to write down tonight. Most stories were easy to remember, this one was so well crafted and told, it would be effortless. The thread of the story ran perfectly true from the lost girl calling for help, to the sinuous, black shape of the Serpent Queen descending from the night sky, and instead of leading the girl back home, changing her into a shadow and bringing her up to live among the stars.

Will found the Roven myth of the Serpent Queen fascinating. In Queensland, the black cloud-like darkness that wound through the sky was a shadow trail left by the ogre whose constellation sat at one end. Just a lack of stars, a nothing.

But the Roven viewed the darkness as a serpent, slowly devouring every other star. She was the part of the night sky they claimed as their own, different from the rest and bent on destroying it.

Borto finished to thunderous applause and Will rose with the rest of the crowd.

Estinn took the stage long enough to declare Borto the winner of the contest. Will stepped forward to talk to him, but everyone else in the crowd had the same idea and the stage swarmed with people.

Several wayfarers and even a handful of Roven congratulated Will on his excellent story, but the crowd inexorably pushed him back and shut him out. Borto thundered something enthusiastically to the crowd around him. It would be hours before they left the man alone, but Will didn't need to talk to him tonight. He'd be back at dawn, just happening to be leaving at the same time as Borto. Only one route led off the Sweep this far south, and they'd have days on the lonely Sea Road to talk before they'd have a chance to go separate ways.

The obscurity of Will's room called to him. He looked around for Lady Dreadful, but saw no sign of her. Instead of relief, a wave of vulnerability swept over him, like he'd been tossed into murky water where anything might be slithering past.

He slipped into the throng moving toward the city gate and with the darkness and the mood of the crowd, reached the unsavory alley leading to the inn with a minimal number of distrustful glances and no sign of a thick copper braid. The moon wouldn't rise for hours, and the alley sat in heavy shadows. Will paused at the beginning of it. That woman had him rattled.

Still he hesitated. He let out a huff of annoyance at his own fear, even as he cast out down the dark alley, checking for the *vitalle* of anyone hiding in the shadows. He found nothing.

Walking quickly to his room, he slid the insubstantial latch into place, and leaned against the door. Across the dark room on the windowsill he could just make out a lump. It only took a couple steps closer to make it out. A dead mouse. With a small laugh, Will leaned out the window, half expecting an undersized hawk to wing through the sky, but it was empty of everything but distant, cold stars. With a flick, he shot the mouse out the window to land in the alley.

A candle sat on a tiny table beneath the window. Will set his finger against the wick. "*Incende*," he breathed. His fingertip tingled as energy passed through it and a small flame burst into life.

He sank down onto the bed, dropping his head into his hands and staring at the floor, letting the silence and emptiness wrap around him like a breath of fresh air.

"Who are you?"

The woman's voice cut through the room and Will's head snapped up.

Leaning against the wall, tucked back in the narrowest corner of his room, the candlelight showing barely more than her face, stood Lady Dreadful.

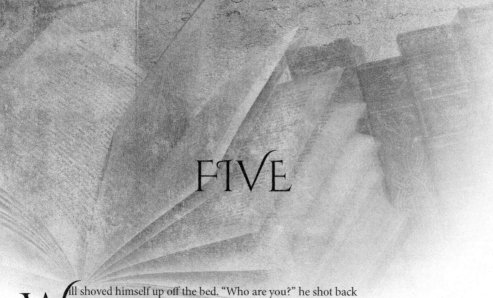

FIVE

Will shoved himself up off the bed. "Who are you?" he shot back

She ignored the question. "You shouldn't be here." Her Roven accent bit the words off harshly.

Will stared at her for a moment. "This is my room."

Trying to gauge her emotions, he opened up toward her. The same emptiness blossomed in his chest. He focused more, searching until he felt an undercurrent of anger, deep and...old. Foundational. The sort of emotion that had been there her entire life. Anger surrounded by coldness and emptiness.

He could see her face, but her dark ranger leathers blurred into the shadows. Making her somehow part of the darkness except a glint of silver from a knife hilt at her belt.

She stepped forward and he forced himself to hold his ground.

"I'm usually better at reading people." The shock of her presence quickly wore off and was replaced with anger at her audacity. "I had the impression you didn't like me. Not that you were headed to my room for a midnight visit."

He still felt nothing. This woman exuded less emotion than anyone he'd ever met. His own body, on the other hand, thrummed with wariness and alarm. The door stood between them and Will had the urge to run, but outside this room he would still be just as trapped. A foreigner running down the streets chased by a Roven? That story did not end well.

"Who are you?" she repeated.

Will gestured to his bright red shirt. "I thought the shirt made it obvious. And the story I told tonight."

She said nothing.

"I'm a storyteller." *...from Gulfind,* he almost added. But the lie felt too blatant.

Her eyes glittered out of the dimness, giving Will the wild impression that she could see through shadows and somehow into him.

"You sound like you're from Queensland."

Will's chest tightened but he kept his voice light. "The people from Queensland and Gulfind sound remarkably alike." Which was one of the main reasons he'd picked Gulfind as his pretend home. "The countries are on such good terms that the family trees along the border are muddled with folk from both countries."

He waited for her to do or say anything. "There's a whole history behind that, but since I make my living as a storyteller, you'll have to pay me if you want to hear it."

"Leave the Sweep."

Her imperious tone was irritating. He sat on the bed and kicked his feet out with a hundred times more nonchalance than he felt.

"I was just considering staying." That lie was blatant, but it was worth it to see the scowl deepen on her face. Will shifted farther onto the bed so he could lean against the wall.

She took a step forward and Will tensed.

He cast out through the room again, looking for a source of energy. The candle flame held too little *vitalle* to do anything. If she attacked, he'd have to pull energy out of her. Which was distasteful. And then he'd—do what? The only spells he worked well were subtle and slow.

His mind offered up outlandish suggestions from old stories: he could split open the ground like Keeper Chesavia had done. Except even when he told that tale he had no idea how she'd done that. He could call fire from the candle and build it into a wall, pressing her back like Keeper Terrane had done against the trolls.

Of course when Will had tried to manipulate flames, even with a bonfire to draw from, all he'd managed was a little tumbleweed of fire that had scuttled erratically across the ground before fizzling out.

He smiled at her, not bothering to make it look sincere. "Now, I think it's time you tell me who you are, and why you're lurking in my room. It's obviously not to hear me tell a story."

She shrugged. "Maybe I am. There's no better way to learn about people than to hear them tell stories, isn't that right?"

Will's stomach clenched at the echo of his words to Borto. "Have you been following me all day?"

She ignored his question again. "When you tell stories, all I hear are lies," she said, her voice cold. "Go back to…wherever you are from, Will." Her lip curled as she said his name, as though she doubted even that. "You are not what you seem."

Will flinched, and tried to cover it up by running his hand through his beard. "What exactly do you think I am?"

She narrowed her eyes and Will opened up toward her one more time. But her emotions were still clamped down out of his reach. She took two more steps, moving within arm's reach, glaring down at him. The clay wall pressed unyieldingly against his back.

"Go home. Things will not go well for you if you stay."

Irritation flickered at the threat and he took some grim pleasure in letting it show on his face. A bit of breeze slipped into the room swirling the scent of grass with the woman's worn leather and causing the candle to stutter. She glanced toward it and Will's heart stuttered with the flame.

She leaned closer and the uneven clay wall pressed harder into Will's back. "I see you." Her accent dragged the smallest bit along the s, almost like a hiss.

The words cut through him. It took everything he had to not shove away from her.

"Leave." She held his gaze for a long moment before turning and striding the few steps to the door. She glanced back at him with her hand on the latch. "There is much to fear on the Roven Sweep…" Her eyes flickered toward the candle. "For a man like you."

The door closed, leaving Will in the darkness of the empty room. He strained to hear her in the hall. The flickering candle and the wobbling shadows it cast were the only movement.

How long had she been here waiting for him? His gaze searched the room as though it would give him a clue.

His books—

With a rush of fear that splintered like shards of glass, he dropped to his knees and his fingers scrambled back under the bed. For a heart-stopping breath he felt nothing. Then he brushed against the bundle and dragged it out. He clutched the books for a moment, the scarf around them undisturbed, before shoving them into his bag.

He could leave tonight. He could head down the sea road, find a place far from Porreen to wait out the night and wait for Borto to catch up.

He glanced into his mostly empty bag. He needed supplies. Dawn would have to be good enough.

There was no way the woman could prove he had used magic to light the candle, but justice on the Sweep rarely worried about things as trivial as proof. The Roven weren't against magic, but if they found out he could do it, they'd know he wasn't just a storyman. And if they knew anything about Gulfind, they'd know that almost no one there used magic. The questioning from there could only go downhill.

He blew out the candle, dropping the room into darkness.

A raised voice echoed down the alley. Will crawled quietly to the window, and lifted his head just high enough to look out.

Two men stumbled drunkenly down the street. No clan warriors coming to arrest him, no empty woman with narrow eyes.

Will looked for something to push in front of the door, but the only furniture in the room was the light table and the bed. And if Roven warriors came for him tonight, it wouldn't be furniture or weapons he'd have to use against them. If they came, he'd just have to hope he woke up quickly enough to work some magic.

He let his head fall back against the wall. Except he didn't exactly have an arsenal of magic at the ready.

Blackness bloomed around him, managing to be both smothering and empty. Normally manageable fears grew and shifted, looming like living things. Tentacles of anxiety pried him open.

Even assuming he could befriend Borto, would he find out where Vahe had taken Ilsa? Would Borto even know? It had been twenty years, even if he found Vahe, would the man remember?

Dawn couldn't come soon enough. The hope he'd been feeling faded, strangled out by questions. The fear of failing surrounded him like a wall. No, a wall was too thin. It surrounded him like the grassland outside, vast and empty. He rolled back onto his bed. Fears that felt too real swirled around him. He pushed them back over and over, waiting for sleep that didn't come.

Life felt like one long search after another. He'd spent a year on the Sweep searching for an army that didn't exist, and for Kachig the Bloodless who was dead.

And it hadn't started here. How many years had he spent looking for children born with the skills to be Keepers?

For the past two centuries, Keepers had appeared about every seven to ten years with barely a gap.

Until Will.

After Will had joined the Keepers twenty years ago, not a single new Keeper had surfaced. There should have been at least two more, maybe three. Instead, the existing Keepers grew older and weaker until only Alaric and Will ever left the Stronghold. When fifteen years had passed, Will had begun searching in earnest, traveling Queensland as often as possible, visiting even the smallest towns while the Keepers worried that no more would ever come.

And he'd searched for twenty years for Ilsa. Twenty years of rumors and dead ends. Would this time be any different?

Sometime in the interminable hours of darkness, sleep must have crept into his room, because early morning sounds from the street and a gust of chilly air woke him. The sky had lightened to pale slate, anticipating the dawn.

With as little movement as he could, Will glanced around the room, finding it empty.

Of course it was empty. He rolled his eyes at himself. It was time to get out of the Sweep. He was going to turn into a paranoid mess if he stayed any longer.

The sky was clear. He searched it for a moment, looking for Talen, before rolling up his bedroll and grabbing his bag. Half uneasy, half annoyed with himself for the uneasiness, he cracked the door open just enough to peer into the empty hallway.

It was obviously too late to stop himself from turning into a paranoid mess.

The smell of warm bread floated upstairs from the common room. He let the homey, daytime scent fill up the hollowness that lingered from last night's fear and followed the smell down to where the squinty-eyed innkeeper puttered in the kitchen. Will bought several small loaves and some smoked fish.

Near the door, something rustled. A shadow shifted and the morning light caught on a coppery-red braid.

SIX

Will's hand clenched his bag. The woman gestured out the door.

"Didn't guess Sora was here for you." The innkeeper leaned his elbows on the counter. "Careful, storyman. That's not a woman t' be taken lightly."

"I'd noticed," Will said. She stood between him and the door. Not that running was an option. Everyone who saw him would vividly remember the black-haired foreigner who'd run through the street. Like a coward.

Even as Will opened up, he knew it would be useless. The innkeeper's curiosity darted into him with an eager brightness, but Sora was nothing but emptiness. In the grey-blue morning light, she looked less like a vicious sliver of darkness and more like a woman. A hostile, unreadable woman, but still a woman.

Behind her the alley lightened. Borto's wagon could be trundling down the road already, the distance between them stretching like a cord. Frustration surged up, battling against his fear. He loosened his hand on his bag.

"Good morning…Sora." He tried to cram as much of his irritation into her name as possible. "Coming to my room wasn't enough last night? You needed to come back this morning?"

A spike of shock and amusement came from the innkeeper.

"Come with me," she ordered.

Will looked around for any other option, but she stood at the only exit. He leaned against the bar, focusing only on her, blocking out the emotions coming from the innkeeper. "No."

She raised an eyebrow, but he felt nothing from her. "Your services are required."

"That's flattering, I suppose. But I'm going to have to decline." He felt the slightest irritation from her.

"Last night," he pressed, looking for more, "you snuck into my room like a gutless thief"—her lips pressed into a thin line—"and ordered me to leave the Sweep. Setting aside the fact that I don't take orders from you, I've decided it's time for me to go home."

He pushed himself off the bar and walked toward the door, but she didn't move out of his way.

"So," he continued, "if your plans for me have changed, and I'd like to point out that it's strange that you have plans for me, I'm afraid you're going to be disappointed."

She crossed her arms. "It's not my plans that have changed. This morning the Torch requires your services."

A cold fear stabbed into his gut. The clan chief?

"You'd be wise to come with me. I'm your polite invitation."

"Yes, you're like a beam of sunshine."

The edge of her mouth quirked up the slightest bit. "If you refuse to come with me, the next people Killien sends won't be as pleasant. And if you try to leave the city…it won't go well."

The walls of the dingy inn pushed in a bit closer. He'd never heard of any foreigner taken to a Torch for a pleasant reason.

"It's not wise to keep a Torch waiting," she said.

"That's true," agreed the innkeeper.

Sora stepped out into the alley and he followed her, his mind racing. He saddled Shadow while she stood in the stable door, blocking his exit. When they reached the end of the alley, the city gate would be within view. He led Shadow out of the stable, his mind scrambling to find a way away from this woman.

But when they reached the street, four guards stood in front of the barred gate.

"You don't want to try that." Sora walked the other way.

Because she'd stop him? Or because the gate was closed for him? Will tightened his hold on Shadow's reins. It was barely dawn, the gate was probably just not open yet. The knot in his stomach didn't go away with the thought, and he followed Sora numbly.

A spattering of Roven moved in the streets, casting unfriendly looks at Will's black hair and beard. Sora turned down one street, then another. Each curved and doubled back intersecting others at odd angles. He felt like he'd shrunk and been trapped in the winding tunnels bookgrubs bored through books. He felt a sudden envy for the grubs. It'd be easier to get out of Porreen if he could burrow himself a new path.

I'm a storyteller from Gulfind, he told himself, attempting to reignite some small hope. *It's worked for months. Everyone has believed me. It'll work a little longer.*

Sora turned onto yet another road.

Everyone had believed him but Sora. The little flick of hope disappeared.

"What's wrong?" A hint of amusement crept into her voice. "Afraid?"

"Yes." He shot her a glare he hoped she could feel. "The Boan Torch is rumored to occasionally arrest any non-Roven he finds in Bermea and sell them on the slave block. I personally saw the Sunn Torch marching a chain of blond-haired slaves to be fed to their *dragon*. No one but Roven live on the Sweep, the only outsiders I've met were passing through. Quickly." He didn't bother to add that the Roven were so uneducated and barbaric that no one wanted to come to the Sweep. "Every foreigner with any sense is afraid to meet a Roven Torch."

Which was why no Keeper had ever met one. The thought caught his attention. Was he about to be the first?

"Ours has nothing against storymen from Gulfind. He's thrilled to meet you."

She didn't sound sarcastic. Maybe this wasn't as dire as it felt. He wasn't under arrest. The Torch had sent a single woman to bring him. And being the first Keeper to meet a Torch did feel significant. Granted the Morrow Clan was the smallest clan on the Sweep, so this was the least significant Torch. But if he had to meet a vicious warlord, it seemed best to meet the smallest one. And offered the opportunity to meet a clan chief, he could hardly run away scared.

Will breathed in a deep breath of the cool morning air. He would meet the Torch and get a sense of the man.

Then he'd run away.

If he could find his way out of this mess of a city.

Borto was getting farther east by the moment, but he pushed the thought away. An hour's head start shouldn't be a problem. Shadow could catch up to the slow wagon.

"You didn't answer my question before," he said. "Why are we going to the Torch?"

She ignored him and he opened up to her again, trying to eek any information out of her that he could. Why couldn't he feel any emotions in her? It was irritating and fascinating. But mostly irritating. He'd never met anyone who could control their feelings this well. Maybe she needed some prodding.

"You do realize I'm a storyteller? If you don't answer me, I'll make something up."

That earned him a response that could almost be called an eye roll, but no emotion.

"The obvious reason," he said loudly enough for the few other people in the street to hear, "is that you've fallen in love with me and we're headed to the Torch to be wed."

She shot him a glare so venomous that he shifted away. But at the same time a jab of indignation shot into the side of his chest from her.

It was thoroughly satisfying.

"Not love then." Maybe more prodding would draw out more emotions. "You must be after money. Has the Torch offered a reward for finding the greatest storyteller in the world?"

She tamped down her emotions again. "If there was a reward, this would be less irritating."

Will stopped. "You're dragging me through town with you at the break of dawn because your Torch wants to hear a story? What are you? His Master of Entertainment?"

She glanced over her shoulder. "Hurry."

He started moving again. The sun crept above the mountains, and in the morning light something about Sora's leathers nagged at him. It took a moment to realize they were plain. Not a single rune marked the dark leather around the armholes or the neck or anywhere. None were sewn into her grey-blue sleeves. The only thing she wore that could be called decorative was a brown cloth wrapped around her upper arm. Leather strips wound around it, fastening on a vicious white claw.

When he didn't look away, she shot him a glare from eyes that were bright green. Green. Roven eyes were always blue. Weren't they? This woman was an enigma. She should be in a story.

The streets widened and the buildings ordered themselves into less primitive shapes. Soon the ends of actual beams of wood, a rich brown against the dull mud, protruded out of the walls holding second floors above them.

Sora made one final turn onto a broad street. It ran past two sprawling houses on each side before ending at one that could only be described as massive.

The entire first level was stone. He hadn't seen a building with this much stone in months. The rock rose out of the ground, unyielding and severe next to all the clay buildings. Wide stone steps spilled into the street like a stack of petrified puddles. Sora motioned to a blond-haired slave who took Shadow. Will spun his ring as he followed Sora past a line of empty wagons and up the steps. He was fiercely envious of her calmness.

An intricate carving of a snake surrounded by stars flowed across the thick wood door. The tiny scales of the Serpent Queen were coated in something faintly green that caught the morning light and shimmered, one lidless eye flashed red from an inset gem. Light rippled along the snake, making it appear to slither across the door. Knife-thin fangs tipped in a shimmer of red stretched wide around the star-shaped doorknob.

Sora reached for the knob, putting her hand in between the fangs, and Will straightened his shoulders. He needed to keep this quick. Get in, meet the warlord, get out. Easy.

For such an easy thing, it took an inordinate amount of effort to step through the door and follow Sora into the large room. A slave worked along shelves, packing things into reed baskets. The warmth of the room smothered him after the chill outside. A fire burned along the side and torches flickered with the opening of the door, sending a flurry of shadows darting over walls and Roven faces.

The room quieted a little as Sora strode in, and more as Will stepped in behind her. He heard murmurs of "fetter bait" and "storyman" trickle through the room. Sora crossed to a small table where two men sat. One of them was enormous, with a bright red beard and hair so wild and wiry it lay like a lion's mane around his face. Two braids as thick as Will's thumb hung from the bottom of the beard, the ends cinched with thick silver bands. His leather vest was decorated with plenty of runes, tooled in and dyed a deep red. Will paused in the center of the room, feeling awkward.

"Killien, Torch of the Morrow Clan," Sora introduced flatly, "meet Will, storyman from Gulfind."

Will pressed his fist to his chest and bowed low, knowing that when he straightened the enormous man would be towering over him.

But it was the other man who rose with a wide smile.

"Thank the black queen!" He extended his hand. "Someone who can spin me a tale!"

Will reached out grasped the Torch's wrist, the man's hand locking around his own like a shackle. Killien wore three wide silver rings encircled with runes and inset with small gems on that hand, two more on his other.

The Torch was an average-sized man, dressed in warrior leathers that were not purely functional like Sora's. Intricate protective markings ringed the shoulders and neck, some inset with a coppery dye that caught the firelight. His auburn hair was cut short. His beard was trimmed to a shape only slightly too wild to be called neat, and decorated with thin, subtle braids, bound off with silver beads. He couldn't be much older than Will. At least a handful of years from forty.

"A storyman...from Gulfind." The Torch looked pointedly at Will's fingers spinning his ring. "And with gold to prove it. I've always thought it takes a certain kind of bravery for your people to wear gold out into the world."

"Or stupidity," Sora said.

"Probably a bit of both." Will held up his hand so Killien could see the ring. "I wear this more because it was a gift and because it spins than because it's gold." He turned the band so Killien could see it spin. "That and because I can't get it off anymore. But I don't carry any other gold with me. I'd rather pay for my lodging and meals with stories. Not many brigands want to steal them, and if they do, they have to keep me alive to do it."

The Torch grinned. "Stories work as payment here, too. It's been ages since a storyman came to the Morrow." His accent cut cleanly against the words, refining the Roven harshness a bit.

Will let out some of the tension that had been building in him. Sora had been serious about the Torch. He really did want a story. Maybe this wouldn't be as terrifying of a meeting as he'd expected. A half-dozen short but entertaining stories popped into Will's mind. "I heard a wayfarer, Borto, tell an excellent story last night."

"Yes, Borto's entertaining," Killien agreed, "but I've heard him a hundred times. No one new ever comes to the Morrow. The good ones never manage to get this far away from Bermea and Tun."

"I didn't say he was good," Sora objected.

"Ignore Sora," Killien said. "She told me you had the festival enthralled. That she hadn't seen a storyteller beguile a crowd like that since her childhood."

"Really?" Will turned toward Sora. "I hadn't realized you'd enjoyed it that much."

Sora's gaze turned flinty. "I said, 'manipulate' not 'beguile.'"

"I'm sure she didn't enjoy it at all." Killien waved away her words. "But if we based our decisions on what Sora liked, we'd never do anything fun. We'd just hunt. Alone." Unperturbed by Sora's expression, the Torch turned back to Will.

"Tell me about yourself, Will." His voice stayed light, but his eyes turned stony. "What brings you all the way to the Morrow?"

"I've been to Bermea and Tun already, and they were…" Will paused, thinking of how to describe the two largest Roven cities without being insulting.

"Festering slums whose resources are squandered by Torches too stupid to know how to lead?" Killien offered.

Grunts of agreement echoed in the room.

"Well"—Will spun his ring slowly—"I was going to say crowded…but 'festering slums' works too. Everything in Bermea was gray with smoke from that army camp outside the city. And Tun smelled like fish." The smell had lingered on his clothing for days. "They need to move that fish market. I got tired of trying to tell stories while gagging through every breath."

Killien grinned. "I hate those cities." He considered Will for a moment. "But I like you."

Sora made an exasperated sound.

"The Morrow Clan heads north to the summer rifts tomorrow," Killien continued. "You can entertain us tonight in the square and stay here as my personal guest. There's a room upstairs that's been vacant since a piggish stonesteep from Tun was here, charging me too much to renew the wards on our herds."

Will's hand stilled on his ring. Stay here? For the whole day?

"He's leaving the Sweep today," Sora informed the Torch. "I caught him on his way out."

Will could have hugged her. "I am."

But Killien's expression tightened. "A day's delay is nothing."

A day's delay would put him far behind Borto. He might catch up to the wayfarer again, but there was too big of a risk of losing him. Will opened his mouth, desperately searching for a way out.

The enormous man with the wild beard stood up from the table and stepped up next to Killien amused. "Surely an invitation from a Roven Torch is enough of a reason to stay."

No. The only reason he'd had to stay in barbaric, uneducated Porreen was at this moment riding away in a wayfarer's wagon. Will searched for the words to tell a Roven Torch that he wasn't interested in being his guest. He glanced around the room. He was completely surrounded by Roven. His gaze caught on the wall by the door and he stopped, stunned.

Shelves filled the entire end of the room. They were mostly empty, but one shelf held at least fifty—

"Books." His words came out barely above a whisper. "You have books."

SEVEN

H e took a step toward them, trying to make out titles. Along the floor in front of the shelves, packed neatly into large baskets, were more books.

Hundreds of them.

"I have a lot of books." Killien led the way over to the shelves. "Most have been packed for the trip north, but you're welcome to read the ones that are left."

Will walked along the shelf reading the titles.

The Clans and the Clashes of the Sweep, History of War in Coastal Baylon, The Gods of Gulfind.

His opinion of the Torch was quickly reforming. Not only were there books, there were a decent number of books about people other than the Roven.

"Do all storymen get this excited about books?" Sora asked. "Or just ones from Gulfind?"

Will's finger froze on the shelf and he glanced up. Sora eyed him with a raised eyebrow, but Killien looked thoroughly pleased to see his books getting so much attention.

Will turned back to the books and tried to keep his voice light. "I don't think you have to be from anywhere in particular to love books."

He slid out a thin book covered in yellow leather and tilted it toward the fire to read the silvery title. *Neighbors Should Be Friends*, by Flibbet the Peddler. Will's eyes tripped over the words and he read it again to be sure. He looked up at Killien. "You have a book by Flibbet?"

"I have three." Killien grinned. "The other two are packed."

A book by Flibbet the Peddler.

Here on the Sweep.

Had anyone found books from the crazy old peddler this far from Queensland? He flipped it open. Flibbet's quirky, multicolored scrawl spread across the page. This book was mentioned twice in other works by Flibbet. The Shield had wanted a copy in the Keeper's library for…for longer than Will had been alive.

"I've never met anyone who knew who he was." Killien crossed his arms and considered Will. "My father met Flibbet just before I was born. The peddler sold him the books and a sword."

Will stared at the Torch speechless for a moment. "*Met* Flibbet?"

Killien nodded. "Said he was the oddest old man he'd ever met. Which, after reading his books, I believe."

"That's impossible."

Killien raised an eyebrow and Sora let out a snort.

"I assure you it happened," the Torch said mildly.

Will bit back his protest. "I just meant that I can't believe the man was still alive. No one's seen him in ages."

"Who hasn't seen him?" Killien looked at him narrowly.

The Keepers. None of the Keepers had seen Flibbet for at least eighty years.

"He's famous in Queensland and in parts of Coastal Baylon. But everyone thinks he's dead. At least everyone I've ever met. The earliest stories of him are a hundred and fifty years old."

"My father said he was old, but one hundred and fifty seems a bit much. Maybe he was an imposter."

Will nodded, then a thought snagged in his mind. "He sold your father a sword?"

"Gave it to him actually." Killien motioned to a short sword hanging on pegs on the wall. It had a wooden grip, a roughly smithed guard, and weathered leather sheath. "Or gave it to me, I suppose. It's a seax, a short sword. Flibbet told my father its name was Svard Naj and it was a gift for his new son 'to help mend the torn'. Seeing as I wasn't even born yet so no one knew if I was a boy, my father assumed the old man was a bit cracked."

Will had never heard of Flibbet giving anyone a weapon. So much of his writing centered around ideas of peace, it felt out of character. But it was more than that.

"He just *gave* it to your father? I've never heard of Flibbet giving away anything. I've heard him make stupid trades, like offering a silver goblet in trade for a handful of chicken feathers, but never just a gift. Is it a good sword?"

"It seems to be. I only use it for ceremonial sorts of things. It's shorter than the one I learned to fight with. And it has a feel to it. Like it's somehow…too serious for a mere fight." Killien laughed and ran one of his hands through his hair. "That sounds a bit ridiculous now that I've said it out loud."

"Not if Flibbet the Peddler really gave it to you."

"Especially if he was already dead," Sora added.

Killien grinned at her.

"I'm glad Sora found you, Will." Killien pointed to the book in Will's hand. "It goes without saying that guests in my house are free to read my books."

Will wanted to read this book. Very much. Whether or not it had really been given to the Morrow by Flibbet, it looked genuine. If he could just read it through once, maybe twice, he'd be able to remember it. Memorizing books was almost as easy as storytelling. He could rewrite it for the Shield later.

But Borto was getting farther away by the moment.

Sora tilted her head and studied Will. "I don't believe he ever agreed to stay."

Killien looked at Will appraisingly. "He doesn't look stupid enough to decline an offer of hospitality."

Sora leaned against the bookshelf and sized Will up. "I don't know…"

Will thought for just a moment about the wayfarer's wagon, trundling east toward the Scales, slipping farther away, the cord between them growing thread-thin.

But he was still surrounded by a room of Roven in the middle of a city of more Roven.

He'd just have to hope that Borto was slow and his yellow wagon was memorable enough that it would be easy to track.

With a nod, he let the idea of Borto go. "What sort of story would you like to hear tonight?"

"Something we haven't heard before. I'm sick of Roven tales with clans massacring each other. Tell me something from a foreign land. Something brave and dangerous and clever."

"The tales from Gulfind are generally clever, if you like tales that revolve around gold. I also have some from Coastal Baylon. Those people are a bit strange and their gods are so…mystifying they end up with curious stories."

"Do you know anything from Queensland?"

The room stilled and Will felt eyes on him. He turned back to the Torch, trying to keep his face nonchalant.

"A few."

"What are they like?" Killien's face stayed friendly, but his eyes were sharp.

"Queensland stories have a certain feel to them. A sort of brightness."

The Torch's eyes narrowed so slightly Will thought he might have imagined it. He did not imagine how much Sora's narrowed.

"Or maybe naivety," Will added. "They really love their heroes."

The Torch looked at Will calculatingly. "I'd like to hear some tales from our enemies. I'd imagine in Queensland the Roven always play the villain."

Out of the hundreds of tales Will knew, he couldn't think of a single story that didn't portray the Roven as the enemy. "The stories I know well"—Or the stories he'd decided he officially knew while he was on the Sweep—"don't mention the Roven at all. But others there are no more flattering to you than your stories are to them."

Killien grinned. "Everyone from Queensland is a villain."

Will forced a smile at that. "As for stories I know best, one is about a young man who is captured by a dragon, and the other is about one of their Keepers."

"Which one?" Killien's voice was sharp and something tightened in Will's gut.

"Chesavia," Will answered. He should have picked something less Queenslandish. Some general adventure story instead of something about magic and Keepers.

"Didn't she die fighting some sort of demon?"

"A water demon." Will's estimation of the Torch rose again. "I'm impressed. I haven't met anyone on the Sweep who knows tales from Queensland."

"I don't know many, but I do know who the Keepers are." Killien's smile held nothing pleasant. He nodded toward the baskets. "I have several books that mention them."

He studied Will. "Tonight, tell us a story from Queensland. It will be fascinating to learn what my enemy thinks is entertaining."

Will nodded. It would be.

EIGHT

"Sora," Killien said, "show Will to his room."

Sora's gaze never faltered from Will's face. "The storyman has managed to travel all the way from—where was it? Gulfind? I think he can find his way upstairs." Without a glance at the Torch, she strode out the door.

Will watched it close before letting his gaze flick back to Killien, expecting anger at Sora's defiance. Instead, Killien looked at the door with a rueful expression.

"I think Sora likes you, storyman." The huge man who'd been sitting with Killien rose.

Laughter rippled through the room and Will glanced around. These people weren't like any Roven he'd ever met. His fear had almost completely dissolved, replaced by a reluctant curiosity. "I'd hate to see how she treats someone she didn't like."

"Don't mind Sora," Killien said. "She doesn't like anyone. But the woman can stalk a white fox in a snowstorm, so we tolerate her attitude."

"I'm Hal." The huge man stepped closer, rising to a full head taller than Will. Everything from his vest to his linen pants to the thick beads in his beard spoke of wealth, but his expression was good-humored. "Do you know any stories about dwarves?"

A spattering of groans greeted his question.

Hal extended his hand and Will grasped it, his fingers barely reaching around the huge man's wrist. "Because you're part dwarf?"

Hal grinned widely. He was dressed much like Killien, runes lining the edges of a wide leather vest, several silver rings spread out across his fingers.

"I know a few dwarf tales," Will said.

"Hal is obsessed with dwarves," Killien said. "No one understands why."

"I do," Will said. "They're strong, they're vicious warriors, they're funny, and did you know they can"—he paused trying to think of the word— "sense rocks? When I was in Duncave, a dwarf gave me a tour of an unused tunnel system and he followed a thin vein of quartz along three different tunnels without ever shining his light on the wall. They say that when there's a different sort of rock, they can taste the difference in the air."

Hal's mouth hung open. "You've been to Duncave?"

"Had an audience with the High Dwarf." Which sounded more formal than whatever had happened. "But it turns out King Horgoth isn't fond of foreigners. He offered me an armed escort on my way out."

"Thank the black queen," Hal breathed, "a real storyman!"

"But he doesn't have to tell the entire story right now," Killien broke in, looking around the room. "Because you all have work to do. It's light enough to get these baskets packed."

Unlike Sora, all of the other Roven obeyed Killien without hesitation.

"I want to hear about Duncave," Hal said.

"After the herds are sorted," Killien said, irritated.

Hal paused on his way to the door. "I'm glad you're here, storyman."

"As am I," Killien said. "I didn't expect someone as…well-traveled as you."

Will shrugged. "You don't learn new stories by sitting at home."

"You do if a storyman comes to visit. Come, I'll show you your room." Killien led Will out of the back of the room.

"You're not exactly what I was expecting in a Torch, either." Will followed Killien to the dark wood stairs. The amount of wood in the house was astonishing. Will slid his hand up the smooth banister as they walked. It was refreshingly solid and unclaylike.

"What did you expect?" Killien asked without turning.

A *bloodthirsty villain* didn't seem like the best answer.

"I've visited three other clans," Will said. "Admittedly I never met their Torches in person, but the Odo Torch had a decidedly unwelcoming way about him, the Sunn Torch only came out to lead slaves to the dragon's cave, rarely gracing anyone with his attention. And the Boan Torch…" Will paused.

"Was a pompous lump of dead weight?" Killien offered over his shoulder.

Will laughed. "I only saw him from a distance during a parade, but…that is a good description. The Boan with their huge army, and the Sunn Clan with their dragon and their stonesteeps—don't they see the benefit of working together?"

"They see nothing but their own grab for power." Killien turned into a short hallway with two doors on each side—actual wooden doors. "Those two are responsible for spilling more Roven blood than any war." Killien stepped into the last room on the left.

It was more Roven than the downstairs level of the house. Killien walked into the clay room and over to a window where orange drapes sighed in the breeze.

Someone outside shouted out commands and there was a bustle of activity. Killien parted the curtains, his shoulders sagging. "We'll be poor hosts today. At this point I see little hope that we'll be ready to leave tomorrow." He rubbed his hands over his face and gave a tired sigh. "You don't by chance know some foreign magic spell that would pack an entire city, do you?"

Will gave a small laugh that had a tinge of panic. "I'm not really good at magic spells."

Killien turned away from the window and shook his head. "Neither am I." He walked to the door. "Breakfast will be served out back shortly. There are things I need to take care of before then."

Will pressed his fist to his chest and gave the Torch a bow as the man left.

When he straightened, he stared at the empty doorway.

That had been…unexpected. Who knew a Roven Torch could be so…unRoven.

Will put his bag into a corner and dropped down onto the bed. Instead of crunching with dried grass, the mattress cushioned him like…like a mattress. Will lay back with a sigh and closed his eyes. This had to be full of wool. He grabbed the pillow. Feathers. After the restless night, his body sank down into the softness.

Borto must be gone by now, trundling east. At least wayfarer wagons were slow. He'd be four days on the Sea Road before any other large roads branched off. If Will pushed hard tomorrow, he could catch up.

Frustration at being here bubbled at the surface, but underneath, there was a layer of guilt. He had a chance to find Ilsa, and that chance was dwindling. He should have…his mind spun through ways he could have escaped this morning, but none of them would have worked. He probably would have had trouble fighting past Sora, never mind armed guards at the gate. Whatever chance he'd had to leave had disappeared during the night.

The fact that Killien's house was fascinating fed the guilt. How could a stack of books have distracted him from his sister?

Had it? Had he given up a chance to leave just to read some books? Will scrubbed his hands across his face. No. Will had never had a choice. Killien had brought him for entertainment. From the moment Sora had appeared this morning, Will's fate had been sealed.

Will heaved himself up off the bed and walked over to the window. He splashed some water over his face from a small red bowl. The sun had risen and the wide avenue was filling with people. The smell of roasting saltfish filled the street mixing with the ever-present smells of the grass and the ocean. To his left, over the low clay buildings of Porreen, the Southern Sea spread out like a blue carpet speckled with fishing boats.

He pushed aside the guilt. The delay was inevitable and moping about it would make it harder to redeem the day into something valuable. Will picked up the yellow book and sank back into the bed.

In all of Queensland, the Keepers had only found a handful of Flibbet's books, outside the ones in the Keeper's library. The curious little peddler, who used to show up every few years, brought the Keepers new books. He had first appeared one hundred fifty years ago at the top of the tall cliffs above the Keeper's Stronghold. Before that, the Keepers didn't know anyone had ever looked down on their valley from the inhospitable desert above. And yet he had appeared, over and over again, disappearing for two years or five years, then dropping bundles of books filled with strange stories, foreign tales, lost histories down from high above. At least he had until about fifty years ago.

Despite the exotic nature of his books, for some reason Will had never imagined that Flibbet went anywhere outside of Queensland. Yet here was a book the Keepers had been looking for. The Shield would be ecstatic to learn what it said. The leader of the Keepers had a fascination with Flibbet that went beyond normal curiosity.

Will opened the cover slowly. The faint smell of paper and old ink wafted past. He flipped to the first page with a mixture of excitement and hesitation. It had been a long time since he'd committed an entire book to memory. When he'd first arrived at the Stronghold and read all the works Keeper Gerone had assigned him, he'd been faster than he was now. Gerone hadn't expected him to memorize them, but how could he not? He'd read them, and once a book was read, if it was well-written, the words laid out a path in his mind. He could recall them whenever he wanted. The only hard part was remembering the beginning. Once it started, you just had to travel down the path.

Here, at last, was a job he was good at. Probably better than any other Keeper. Alaric wouldn't be able to memorize Flibbet in a morning.

His eyes felt gritty from the long night, but he focused on the beginning and picked up the thread of the swirly blue writing. Flibbet began this book with theories on where the people of the

Sweep, Queensland, and the southern countries had come from, positing that they were descended from a common ancestor who had once lived far west over the endless desert.

True to form, Flibbet's words wandered off on tangents and nonsensical tales, peppered by complex diagrams, unexplained symbols, and things that looked like pointless doodles. But somehow the thread ran true through the entire book. There was a special sort of …joy in reading Flibbet. A sort of whimsy and lightness, all anchored to truths that felt as deeply rooted as the mountains.

The original thread of the story thickened into roots, then the thick trunk of a tree, then split off into branches both individual yet similar. The small scattered warlords of Coastal Baylon, the strong central throne of Queensland, the disparate, isolated clans of the Roven. All branches, all related, all somehow the same at their core.

The book was short and the world was still muffled in the quiet of early morning by the time Will finished.

He let the book close, his mind drifting around the ideas, toying with concepts of brotherhood and ancestry and the interrelatedness of everything. The different accents of their shared language feeling suddenly closer than they ever had before.

A spattering of rough Roven voices called to each other outside his window, and Will pushed aside the drapes to watch a half-dozen people organizing baskets of books into a wide, wooden wagon.

Two children squealed and raced in circles, keeping just out of reach of an older man who kept grabbing for their baskets, while a young woman laughed and herded them forward. It was the right kind of laughter, effortless and free, and he had the sudden urge to join them. He leaned against the windowsill, setting his hands on the cool cob that was familiar, if not comfortable. A little girl ran close to the house and glanced up. Her laughter stuttered and she pointed up at him.

"Dirty fett," the man muttered, loud enough to reach the window. He pulled her away and the game ended.

Will dropped down on the bed.

Flibbet's words were just words.

If Queensland and the Sweep had ever shared a common ancestor, they'd grown too distant by now for it to matter.

NINE

S mells of fish and bread wafted through the window.

He took Flibbet, went back down to the main room, and set *Neighbors Should be Friends* back on the shelf. A clatter of activity came from the back of the house.

He walked down a short hall and out into a wide, walled yard scattered with Roven sitting on colorful rugs, eating in a hurried sort of way. A long ledge ran along the back of the house surrounded by people piling plates with prairie hen eggs, red fish wrapped in salted barley flatbread, or butter-yellow avak fruit. Will filled a plate. At the end of the table was a covered clay jar. He opened the lid and smelled saso, Roven coffee. This wasn't the watered-down saso he'd been drinking at out-of-the-way inns. This was rich, full coffee that smelled of roasted nuts and caramel so thick he could almost feel it. He poured himself a cup and breathed in the warm steam.

Will glanced around for a rug on the fringes where he could sit out of the way.

"Come sit, storyman," the enormous Hal called, waving Will over to a large blue blanket. "It's like this every year." Hal looked annoyed as a woman pushed past Will. "Chaotic and rushed. We go to the rifts every year, but no one ever seems ready."

Killien's voice barked something from inside the house.

Hal shook his head. "Every year."

The Torch strode out of the house and toward a blanket with two men and a woman sitting on it nearby. They each straightened and gave the Torch their attention.

"We leave as soon as the horses are prepared, Torch," one man said.

"Take a distress raven with you."

The man's eyes snapped up to the Torch's face. The rest of the group exchanged glances. Even Hal glanced up in surprise.

"We have three messenger ravens already," the woman said.

"Take a distress raven also. And as soon as you reach the rifts, send back a report." The Torch looked around the group, his eyes guarded. "Watch each other."

The back door opened and a burst of *vitalle* rushed into the yard so strong that Will clenched a piece of fish in his hand. Heart pounding, he began to gather *vitalle*, drawing it out of the grass beneath him, his mind racing to think of a protective spell. He hadn't felt that much power since…since he'd been in the Keeper's Stronghold. Not a single stonesteep he'd met on the Sweep had been remotely this powerful.

Lukas, the young man who'd bought the book from Borto, limped out of the house, his thin arms wrapped around a large lumpy leather bag. The rings on his hands glittered in the morning light.

Killien crossed over to him. "Is that the first set?"

The Torch reached into the bag, pulling out a palm-sized yellow crystal swirling with energy. Nodding approvingly, he dropped it back into the bag with a clink, and Will caught a glimpse of more yellow gems.

Will blinked and let the energy he'd gathered drain out of him. All that *vitalle* was from the gems, not the man. These weren't the usual worthless magical talismans found on the Sweep. Whatever those stones held, it was powerful.

"Forty here, and a hundred more promised by tonight." Lukas smirked at the Torch. "He tried to convince me eighty would be enough."

Killien let out a derisive snort. "Lazy dog. A hundred and forty is already less than half of what he claimed he could make."

The yellow light of the stones lit Lukas's face like he stood over a fire. "After this we shouldn't need him."

Killien nodded and clapped Lukas on the shoulder. "Well done. Divide them into three bags. Make one light enough for Sini, and give Rett the other."

Lukas gave the Torch a quick bow and left, taking the *vitalle* with him. The energy of the stones faded away.

Will turned back to his food, letting his heart slow. The amount of power held in that bag was astonishing.

"What were those?" he asked Hal quietly.

"Heatstones," Hal answered. "For our trip north. I didn't think the stonesteep would deliver."

"I've never met a stonesteep." Will paused, wondering how much Hal would talk about. "I've heard some stories, though. I know a bit about Mallon since he invaded Queensland. He's called Mallon the Rivor there, instead of Mallon the Undying."

"He didn't earn the Undying until after the war."

Will turned in surprise. "But the war ended because of his death."

"No one knows if he's dead. They never found his body."

Hal was unconcerned, but a chill passed through Will at the sentiment. Mallon wasn't dead. At least he hadn't been dead a year ago when the elf Ayda, had showed him Mallon, still alive, but trapped inside his own body, held prisoner by the elves.

Of course it'd been ages since he left the message for Alaric at the palace. The Keepers must have found a way to kill him by now.

"The other stonesteep that comes up often," Will continued, "is Kachig the Bloodless."

Hal raised an eyebrow.

"He's a stonesteep right? I can't get anyone to actually tell me about him."

Hal let out a short laugh. "He's the one who trained Mallon. No one knows which was more powerful, but Kachig was more vicious. He's been dead for ten years, and we still don't speak his name if we can help it."

"Why not?"

"Because we're not stupid."

"Hal," Killien interrupted, heading into the house, his voice sharp. "Get to work."

Hal finished his saso in one long drink. "Every year." He pushed himself up and left.

Will watched him go, torn between curiosity and irritation. Why would people not talk about a dead man?

He finished his fish quickly and headed back inside to Killien's bookshelf.

Children ran in the front door, jostling past Will, grabbing baskets of books and lugging them out to the wagon.

"I've got *Sightings of Dragons*," one called out.

Another peered into his basket and grimaced. "All I've got is barley recipes."

Will stared after them as Killien walked up.

"The children can read?" Will watched them haul the baskets outside. "I've barely met any adults on the Sweep who can."

"Most of the Morrow can read. I like my people to be free. But we're the smallest clan on the Sweep, so we're always in danger. The more we learn, the more we understand the past, the easier it is to decipher the present. And the easier it is to remain free."

Will took these words and let them sink in. "I couldn't agree more."

The Torch raised an eyebrow. "I didn't realize the people of Gulfind valued reading so highly."

Will paused, thinking of the massive amounts of ignorance among the people of Gulfind. The hills of Gulfind were full of gold, all of life was spent on entertainment and paying for guards to protect their wealth.

"I wish the people of Gulfind would value things like history," Will answered. "But it's not entertaining enough for most of them."

Killien straightened the books on the shelf. "How long have you been away from home?"

Will dropped into his usual story. "Almost a year. I spent last summer traveling among some of the northern cities. Last winter I came south to Bermea, Tun and any other cities I could find. Then all the Roven headed north, and I was on my way home. I had reached Porreen yesterday and since you were still here, I stayed the night."

"And why did a storyman from Gulfind come to the Sweep in the first place?"

"I like to travel." Will shrugged. "I didn't intend to get as far as I did, honestly. I started traveling, ended up on the edge of the Sweep, and just kept going."

Killien gave him a slight smile. "That's what the grasses do, they call to you, pulling you on over the next rise, through the next valley."

It hadn't been the grasses pulling him, but Will nodded anyway.

"Have you learned many Roven stories while you've been here?"

"A good number."

"Which is your favorite?"

None. The Roven stories all felt...foreign. Like they had the wrong pacing. Or the wrong ending. There were endless tales of battles between clans, most of which were only told in the victors' clans. He hadn't heard a single one that named the Morrow Clan as the winner. In fact, the Morrow Clan was so small and insignificant, it barely made it into any tales at all.

"Roven tales have a strong sense of...location." Will tried to think of a diplomatic answer. "For instance I heard a tale in Bermea about besting the Tun in a battle. Then I heard the same story in Tun, except with the Tun winning." Will paused. "So I guess I don't know about a favorite story. Every time I find one I like, I discover that it's told differently in the next town."

Killien grinned. "That's the rule of the grassland. The truth changes between hilltops."

"It does seem to." Will paused and glanced around the room. "Lately I've heard a lot of stories about frost goblins."

Killien's smile faded.

"I wasn't sure they were real," Will said, "or that if they were, that they ever came out of the northern mountains, but the Roven I've met in the past weeks seem to believe that the frost goblins could be responsible for raids in the north."

"They haven't come out of the northern ice since my father was a child. That year they came in the fall, killed entire hunting parties and decimated herds. They're more like a hive than like individual creatures. They're not big, no taller than your waist, but they swarm over whatever they're attacking. Often they don't have weapons. They overrun with teeth and claws."

The Torch's voice had a dreadfulness to it that chilled Will, despite the bright morning around him. "That's…unsettling."

"It is," Killien agreed. "They burrow in the ground. They can dig tunnels into deep snow or under the grass almost as fast as you can walk. If they've come onto the prairies this spring…" He glanced around at the people in the room. "So far it's just rumors from clans farther to the west. But the rumors have the ring of truth to them."

"How long will it take the clan to reach the rifts?"

"A fortnight. Maybe a couple days faster, if there's perfect weather. If we encounter any rain storms or, stars help us, a heavy spring snow, it'll slow us down."

Killien caught sight of Flibbet's book on the shelf and turned to Will with an impressed look. "Finished with the book already?"

Will nodded slowly. "Flibbet always manages to both ramble and be concise at the same time."

"I've always thought the same." Killien stepped up next to Will and ran his fingers along the spine of Flibbet's book. "I can't decide if he's brilliant, or a little touched in the head."

"Or just old." Will laughed. "*Old enough to know that most things are a waste of time. And that wasting time can be a beautiful thing.*"

Killien raised an eyebrow.

"He wrote that about himself." Will could still picture the small library in Marshwell where he'd found the skinny volume. "In a book titled *Flibbet's Rules for Life.*"

"That is something I would like to read."

"I can write it out for you." The book had been thin, but the pages had been crammed with numbered rules written in a chaos of colors, the words sideways or upside down or spiraling into tiny print.

Killien's other eyebrow rose. "You memorized it?"

Will paused. "I don't memorize it exactly." He was oddly reluctant to explain. "Once I read a book, if I can remember the beginning, the rest of the book just sort of…follows."

Killien studied him. "A useful skill for a storyman."

Will bowed his head slightly in acknowledgment.

"No wonder you're good at your job. Could you tell me everything you read this morning?"

Will glanced back at Flibbet. "Flibbet's always been easy for me. The better written a book is, the easier it is for me to remember. The peddler, even though his books seem disjointed and capricious, somehow has this…thread that winds through his words. They lead to each other. And that makes them easy to remember."

Killien looked at Will for a long, searching moment. "I would very much like a copy of

Flibbet's Rules."

    Something in Killien's eyes made Will feel exposed. He pulled the edges of his mouth up into what hopefully looked like a smile. "If you have some paper, I'll work on it this morning."

    Killien's gaze pinned Will where he stood. "A day may not be long enough to enjoy your company, Will."

TEN

Settled with a stack of paper and a new reed pen, Will began writing out Flibbet's rules.

There were simple rules: *Be more generous than you feel.*

There were practical rules: *Never poke a mountain bear.* Or *Never eat blue tunnel beetles.* This one was followed by an adamant, *Never.*

There were ridiculous rules: *Don't dip your cuffs in the washing water.* Or *Keep an eye on the moon. She'll cause no end of trouble if you don't.*

And tucked amid all these were the ones that Will had read the book for.

Everyone is clear-minded in their own mind.

Too much time alone traps a man in his own mind. Not enough time alone traps him in other's.

It is a terrifying thing to be truly seen—but it is infinitely worse not to be.

There were 213 rules altogether.

When he finished, he had four blank pages left, so he wrote out a short, funny tale from Napon about a serving girl who'd run off to be a pirate.

Then, leaving the papers on the bookshelf, he picked out several history books about the Sweep and sat down to read.

He skimmed dull accounts of obscure Roven battles until the bustle made him feel useless. He offered to help a passing Roven. Everyone in Killien's house seemed to know who he was. Whatever Killien had told them, if he wasn't greeted with friendliness, they were at least polite, which was refreshing.

It occurred to him that he'd never spent so much time with Roven and not been called fetter bait. He spent the next several hours loading wagons with rugs, food, weapons, and leathers, which turned out to be far more educational than the books had been.

He learned that the furniture was left here to wait for their return in the fall. He learned that the wooden wagons had come mostly from merchants who'd brought their wares to the Sweep. Wood was in such high demand, it was more profitable to sell their wagon and buy a new one when they got home. There were enough in Porreen for every four or five families to share one. Unless they were wealthy like Killien, whose household filled three. And he learned that even helping someone with something like packing didn't really earn you trust. Just mild goodwill.

He thought of Borto often, moving ever farther away with whatever knowledge he had of Ilsa, but, as Killien continued to shout at everyone, the clan was leaving at dawn tomorrow. Will would be on his way by then too. He checked on Shadow and found him well cared for and fed, and repeated to himself often that Borto would be easy to catch on the long, lonesome Sea Road.

Killien's slaves and the Roven worked side by side. Will caught sight of Lukas several times, limping along with a pile of books in his arms or patiently directing some children on how to pack them into baskets.

In the end, he found Hal. The enormous man was in charge of the herds of the clan and his afternoon was spent directing people and animals in preparation for the journey north. For the first time in a year, Will began to feel at ease. Hal laughed and joked and complained with utter disregard to Will's foreignness, his voice rumbling over the Roven accent like a wagon crunching along over hard clay.

Hours later Will leaned against the railing at the end of a long porch stretching across the largest building on the main square. He spun his ring, watching the crowd gather.

High, thin clouds reached across the sky like flame-colored fingers. He searched the sky, wondering where Talen had gone. Maybe the little hawk had finally flown off to another part of the Sweep. Feeling surprisingly disappointed at the idea, Will let his eyes follow the trails of light from the setting sun, wishing it was sunrise instead. It would be good to be on his way out of Porreen and off the Sweep, following Borto.

Killien's words from this morning haunted him. *A day may not be long enough.* But this day had been more than enough. Tonight Will needed to tell a story that wouldn't disappoint the Torch, but also wouldn't be good enough for Killien to want him to stay.

He dropped his gaze back down to the square, mentally trimming out parts of the story, making it weaker.

Lukas limped up onto the far corner of the porch, followed by two more slaves. Their grey tunics were as well-made and clean as Lukas's. The first was a large man who towered over Lukas and most of the Roven nearby. He was probably almost forty, with a receding hairline but a full unruly beard of dusty brown hair didn't quite cover his pleasantly distant expression.

The other was maybe fifteen years old, still more of a willowy girl than a woman. The top of her blond head didn't even come up to the larger slave's shoulder. She stood against the railing, talking quietly, but animatedly while both men listened to her with a sort of brotherly patience.

The orange of the sky had tinged the square with a flamelike glow. The clay houses were a dull amber, the packed ground of the square was the color of trampled honey, and the head of every single person was flaming red. An enormous fire of dung patties flared to life in front of the balcony with a smoky, grassy smell, casting a flickering red light into any existing shadows.

Hal leaned against the wall of the house beside Will, peppering him with questions about dwarves.

"Is it true they have a treasure room filled with jewels?"

"I didn't see any, but I imagine they do." Will looked out over the crowd, hoping this would get started soon. "Probably more than one. Any jewels in Duncave belong to all the dwarves and are taken to the High Dwarf. But every dwarf I've seen has jewels on their weapons, on their tools, on thick rings. One had twelve rubies set in the handle of her favorite pitcher. She told me it was a family heirloom. These, for some reason, don't need to be given to the High Dwarf, so you can imagine how many family heirlooms there are."

"Are the walls decorated with gold and gems that sparkle in the torchlight?"

"You're not fascinated with dwarves, Hal." Sora came up onto the porch. "You're fascinated with treasure."

Hal ignored her.

"Actually," Will answered him, "the tunnel walls are mostly earth and stone. And the dwarves don't carry torches. Which makes sense when you think what it would be like to live in caves filled with smoke. They have a moss that puts off an orange glow. It gets brighter if they put water on it, so they carry lanterns made from shallow bowls with moss and water in them. They don't make as much light as a torch, but maybe as much as a candle. And once you've been in the tunnels for several minutes, it's more than enough."

Hal shook his head. "I've never been so envious of any man. You should come north with us and entertain us on the long, boring journey."

Will's fingers tensed on his ring.

Sora raised an eyebrow. "I bet he would love that."

Even without the need to hurry after Borto, the idea of spending weeks traveling with the Roven sounded tortuous. He was spared the pressure of a polite answer by Killien striding up onto the porch. Will hadn't seen the Torch for hours and he gave the man a slight bow. Behind Killien a small Roven woman climbed the steps. She was in the end stages of pregnancy and a slave woman held her elbow cautiously. Will's eyes caught on the slave's dark curls. She bent over, arranging some cushions on a chair for the Roven woman and helped her sit. Then she sat on the porch behind the woman's chair.

She sat forward and something painful clamped down on Will's heart.

The slave was the spitting image of Will's mother. It was his mother's face from years ago. Before Will had left to join the Keepers. Before his father had been killed. Before Ilsa had been taken.

The Roven woman leaned forward, blocking Will's view of the slave and fixed Will with a look that pierced through him. "Fett," she hissed.

Will tore his eyes away from them, his heart pounding so loud he almost didn't hear Hal.

"Pick someone else to stare at." Hal's voice was pitched low but urgent. "That's Lilit, Killien's wife. She doesn't share his…interest in foreigners."

Killien's wife? Will shot a quick glance over. Lilit had turned away dismissively. She was younger than Killien, in her mid-twenties to his thirties. An intricate weave of braids held back mahogany hair that seemed to glow red under the ruddy sky. She wore a dress dyed a vibrant green and stitched with yellow runes along every seam.

Beside her the slave woman, dressed in a simple grey dress, brushed her own loose hair back with a motion that was achingly like Will's mother's.

It couldn't be Ilsa, could it? He tried to match up this face to the last time he'd seen her, terrified, disappearing into the night, his mind grabbing for similarities.

The slave woman smiled at something Lilit said and the image of Ilsa's terrified face blew away like a puff of mist. A different memory surfaced. One he hadn't thought of for so long it had turned brittle, like old paper. His baby sister, smiling and chasing that stupid goat through the grass. That was the face he was looking at. That was the smile.

He wanted to take a step forward, but his legs wouldn't cooperate. His entire body thrummed with a sort of terror. He was desperate for her to look at him, but terrified that she would.

Killien stepped between them to the front of the balcony. Will pulled his gaze away from the slave woman. The world spun and Will put his hand on the railing to steady himself. Killien raised his hand for silence, and within moments the square obeyed.

"Tomorrow the main caravan will leave at dawn," Killien announced. "By nightfall we'll be out of view of Porreen and surrounded by the grasses."

The audience broke out into a loud cheer.

"What about the frost goblins?" A voice called out and the cheers died off.

"We don't know if the stories are true or not," Killien answered. "But it is time to move north. The hay is gone, the herds need the grasses." He paused. "And we need the grasses around us again. The dusting grass has come and the green of the Sweep is waking up. These city walls are starting to feel like a cage."

They roared in approval.

Will risked a glance toward the slave, but Killien's wife blocked his view.

"We have heatstones," Killien continued. Lukas stepped forward, his limp barely noticeable and handed Killien one of the swirling stones. "If there are frost goblins, we will fight them off as our ancestors did, with these burning stones and our swords." There were rumblings of agreement. "But let us hope the tales of goblins prove only to be rumors.

"Speaking of tales, tonight I bring you something different. A storyman from Gulfind has found our clan."

The response to this was more curious chatter than applause. Will bowed toward the crowd. The urge to look at the woman who might be Ilsa was almost overpowering, but he could feel every eye in the square fixed on him.

"Will knows stories from many lands," Killien said. "Tonight he's offered to tell us a tale from Queensland. I know it's easy to think of Queensland as the enemy, as the people who hundreds of years ago took the good land, with rich soil and mild seasons, and left us to the harsher world of the Sweep."

The words cut through the turmoil in Will's mind and caught his attention. Stern faces nodded in the crowd. The Roven thought they'd been forced out of the Queensland? He'd never heard that. Although it would explain the animosity.

"But it is always important to remember," Killien said, "that those we consider enemies are more like us than we think. They have homes and families and worries."

Will held his face neutral as he listened. That was the most humanizing thing he'd heard said about Queensland since he'd come to the Sweep. Was this man actually Roven?

"We must remember our enemies are human," Killien continued, "if we ever hope to defeat them."

Yes. He was Roven.

Thousands of eyes were fixed on the porch. A cool breeze brushed past Will and he breathed it in, gathering the chaos of thoughts and emotions swirling inside him, and breathing them out. The need to follow Borto blew away. That might not be Ilsa, but everything about her was right. The idea of being left in Porreen tomorrow while the clan and this woman went north made his stomach drop.

He threw away all his ideas of how to make his story weaker. What he needed tonight was the best telling of Tomkin and the Dragon that anyone had ever heard. Something so good that Killien couldn't bear to let Will leave.

He resisted the urge to look back, and focused on the tale. It had been a long time since he'd told it. He pulled the beginning of Tomkin to his mind gingerly, hoping it was still intact. This was the right story to tell. Everyone loved Tomkin.

Would the Roven? A little dagger of ice shot into his stomach. How could they not?

"Much can be learned about a people from their stories." Killien's voice rolled over the whole square. "Tonight, he has agreed to tell us one of Queensland's most beloved tales. A story about a young man and a dragon."

Killien turned and motioned Will to the front of the porch. Something scraped behind him and Will turned too quickly to pretend it hadn't startled him.

Sora dragged a thin stool over. "Nervous?" she said softly enough that only he and Killien heard. "No one is stupid enough to tell stories from Queensland on the Sweep."

Killien studied Sora for a moment, then turned to Will with an unreadable expression.

"Maybe they don't know the good ones," Will answered quietly, taking the stool. "Get comfortable, Sora. Even you might like this."

Killien let out a little laugh and sat down next to a disapproving Lilit. Will caught a glimpse of the slave's shoulder, but turned away. A distracted storyteller was poor entertainment.

Facing the crowd, he pushed everything but the story out of his head. Will did a poor job of many things, but telling stories wasn't one of them. And though there was probably no way to get Sora to like him, by the end of the evening, the crowd would. And hopefully the Torch.

But the faces in the audience were unenthused. This was not a crowd ready for a story.

"I have spent all winter in the Roven cities along the sea." Will stepped to the railing, speaking loud enough that the entire square could hear him, searching for common ground. "But now, when I look north, the land isn't white with snow. I see hints of new green grass growing out of last year's brown."

A few heads nodded.

"Across the Scale Mountains, the seasons change gradually. The snows melt slowly, it takes from one full moon to the next for green to return to the land. But only days ago the grasses here were pale with snow. And then yesterday I saw a hint of green."

The mood of the square rose. "And this afternoon, it wasn't a hint." Will paused. "It was…a flood of it." At the edge of the square, movement caught his eye. Sitting on a porch railing with her skinny legs dangling down, sat Rass, beaming at him. Will bowed his head slightly in her direction. "And I was reminded that the Sweep is enormous and powerful. That everything is born there and everything goes there when it is too old to move." Rass's face split into an even wider grin. "There was a thrumming of life on the hills."

Will let his eyes pass over the crowd, feeling their approval.

Hoping he remembered it right, he took a breath. "Life has returned!"

"We will return!" thundered the crowd in the traditional response, erupting into cheers.

When that faded, Will sat on the stool. "In Queensland, there are men called Keepers who protect stories of the past. I have heard one tell a tale in the hall of the Queen herself." The crowd muttered and Will let the complicatedness of the response grow. "This is one of their favorite stories. It is an old tale, not a sweeping epic. Only a small story meant to entertain." He could feel the crowd's skepticism. He gave them a shrug. "Let's see if it's as entertaining as the people of Queensland seem to think." When the spattering of laughter died, he looked down, not moving or speaking while he waited for the square to quiet.

Once it was still, he began.

"Along the southern border, a company of soldiers surged forward, like the waters of the Great River, battling a deadly foe and performing acts of heroism.

"At his desk, Tomkin Thornhewn sat still, like the waters of a small puddle, shuffling through a pile of paper and only dreaming of such renown."

Thousands of eyes fixed on Will, and he opened himself up to them. The words continued on, building a scene, a question, a dragon. The power of the story drew out the minds of the listeners and unified them into something more.

But this wasn't Queensland. The crowd felt too negative toward Tomkin. It had been a mistake to tell them this was a foreign tale, it separated them too much from it. Will shifted his descriptions of Tomkin slightly, less insecurity, more misplaced determinedness. Less fanciful daydreaming, more shock and indignation at his insultingly poor marriage arrangement. The moment when Tomkin picked duty and adventure over complacency, the crowd stopped feeling foreign. That was the point when they stopped comparing themselves to the story, stopped even being aware of themselves. They fell together into a single entity, amused, leery, fatalistic, or hopeful in turn as Tomkin dug himself deeper into trouble.

The wide, empty, open feeling of the Sweep receded. Will felt only the ruins as Tomkin explored the castle, saw only the orange-red scales of the dragon, imagined himself huddled bruised and cold in the rain.

Stars glittered in a black sky by the time the story drew to its close.

Almost reluctantly, Will spoke the final words, feeling the crowd before him settle into a satisfied pleasure. "I cannot say that Tomkin and the Dragon lived happily to the end of their days, because happiness is trickier than that. They had plenty of hard days, and plenty of sad days, but they did try to be kind to each other. And kindness takes you a long way on the path to happiness. So I think it is safe to say that Tomkin and the Dragon lived, on the balance, happy-ish to the end of their days."

Shouts of approval accompanied the slapping of thighs, the Roven's lower, more rumbling form of clapping. Will stood, set his hand on his chest and bowed his head to the crowd. Thrumming with the triumph and satisfaction filling the square.

"Thank the black queen!" Killien stepped up next to him and pounded him on the back. Will staggered a bit under the force. "That was the best story I've heard in years."

Will bowed, darting a look toward Ilsa. The slave woman helped Lilit stand. With every movement and every expression, Will became more convinced this was his sister. He'd never imagined she could be this much like their mother.

"Killien!" Hal called out. "I like Will. Invite him north with us. We'd have stories for the entire, endless walk."

Will pressed his fist to his chest, desperately hoping the story had been good enough. When he looked up, Killien's eyebrows were raised.

"Would you like to come north with us, Will?" Killien held out his hand.

"He doesn't want—" Sora began.

"I'd love to," Will interrupted her. He grasped Killien's wrist, feeling the Torch's hand wrap around his own like a vise.

Sora's eyes sharpened.

Killien's other hand clamped down on Will's shoulder and the Torch leaned in close to him, a wide smile spread across his face.

"Welcome to the Morrow Clan, Will."

ELEVEN

A bite of cold morning air slid down Will's neck, feeling more like the lingering end of winter than the beginning of summer. The sun had been over the Scales for an hour before the wagons had rolled out into the grasslands. He breathed in the cool, placid air, trying to calm the tangle of fury and hope and desperation that had kept him awake much of the night.

Ilsa was here.

He'd wanted to follow Lilit and Ilsa when they disappeared down a wide hallway in the Torch's enormous house. But acting as though he was stalking Killien's wife, even if he was actually trailing her slave, didn't seem like the best way to ingratiate himself with the Torch.

In Will's own room, he'd spent most of the night imagining what he would say to Ilsa, what she would think of his words. And him. The rest of the night had been spent wondering how exactly one went about rescuing a sister from the midst of a Roven clan. Beyond extricating her from the side of the Torch's wife, sneaking past all of the Roven, and somehow escaping across flat, featureless grassland, how would he possibly convince her he was her brother? Every conversation he imagined left him sounding like a desperate lunatic.

If only he knew a story about a man, unskilled in any sort of fighting, who rescued a woman who didn't trust him, from the midst of a traveling clan of Roven. Unfortunately, none of the Roven stories he knew were that interesting.

He'd been left to his own devices all morning and ended up riding near the front of the enormous caravan where he'd tried to stay within sight of Killien and the rangers who surrounded him. Several covered wagons stayed near the front and he watched for Lilit, but he couldn't see her past the Roven that rode between them. More importantly, he couldn't see Ilsa.

Behind him, the Morrow stretched in a long, ragged line that still rolled out of the city of Porreen. Ox-drawn wagons, horses laden down with burdens or pulling carts, herds of sheep and goats. The Roven walked with a sort of contentment. Children ran along the sides of the column, flurries of races or chases sending them skirting out onto the closest hills. Will opened up toward them, feeling a wild freedom.

The Roven were happy to be on the Sweep.

Will let his eyes run over the grass, spinning his ring and trying to match the pale green emptiness he saw with their happiness. But the Sweep was just faded grass and empty sky. The Scale Mountains to the east were dry and rocky, the sea falling behind them to the south was flat and smudgy blue.

Ahead wound the scar left by the Morrow's last migration, stretching north as far as he could see, wide enough for twenty men to walk side-by-side. The serpent's wake, they called it, as though the Serpent Queen herself had descended out of the night sky to lay them a path leading north to their summer homes. He didn't like the imagery. Following a snake that large could lead to nothing good.

He entertained himself by thinking of every rescue story he knew. Out of the countless stories in his head, there must be something helpful to his situation. His favorite rescue story was Pelonia's rescue of her cousins from the marauders. But Will didn't have a sleeping draught to knock out the entire Roven clan. Or a freezing lake. And he doubted he would look fetching enough in a dress to distract his enemy at the crucial moment.

There was also the story of when Petar rescued Taramin from the bandits. But Will did not have Petar's skill with a bow. He rubbed the inside of his forearm where the string had skidded off his skin the one time he'd shot one. That arrow had landed so far from the target, he'd never found it. No, it was safe to rule out any stories that depended on archery skills.

With a sea of Roven around him and Ilsa while they traveled north, escaping would be nearly impossible even if he had Petar himself here. It was best to focus on first steps: getting to know Ilsa and ingratiating himself to both Killien and Lilit.

Above him, a flicker of darkness in the clear sky caught his eye. With a dip of its wings, a hawk plummeted toward him and settled on Will's bedroll, dangling a mouse from its beak.

"I can't believe you found me." Will pulled a piece of dried fish from his bag and Talen dropped the mouse to snatch it up. Will ran the back of his finger down the hawk's impossibly soft chest, feeling Talen's heart patter so quickly it almost vibrated. "And I can't believe how happy I am to see someone familiar." He leaned closer to the bird. "I saw her," he whispered. "She's here."

Talen peered intensely at Will's hand.

"That was the end of the fish." Will spread out his palms.

Talen let out two quick screeches and took off into the sky.

"I'll take that as a display of great excitement on your part." Will flung the mouse into the grass.

A nearby ranger watched Talen leave with a derisive expression. He said something and the rangers around him laughed. They watched him for a few heartbeats, and Will tensed for something more, but they turned away with only a few mutters among themselves.

The absence of the little hawk made the air around him feel empty. The rangers continued to treat him with a cold distance, and the feeling of isolation spread slowly until it surrounded him.

"Do you see the grass?" Rass chirped near midday, running up alongside Will, her dirty face lit up with joy. "It's growing so fast!" She grabbed his foot and tugged him to a stop. "Look look at this blade coming through the dirt. It's brand new!"

Will climbed down out of the saddle and squatted to look at the tiny bit of grass. It was an unearthly green, almost glowing against the dark earth and the pale old grass around it.

"And there are ones just like it *everywhere*!" Rass exclaimed, throwing her arms out.

Will cast out over the nearest hill, almost expecting to feel Rass's enthusiasm echoed back in wild, growing energy from a million newborn blades of grass. But he felt nothing other than the bright energy of Rass herself. Because regardless of the girl's enthusiasm, it was still just grass.

Dirt clung to Rass's little grey shift, and he was appalled again at how poorly the Roven cared for slave children. What was the point of keeping them as slaves if they were going to starve before they were old enough to work? Her body was so gaunt she looked like her own happiness might break her.

An idea struck him. "Rass, do you know many of the slave women?"

She wrinkled her nose. "Do you want your own?"

"What?" The idea was repulsive he drew back. "No! I don't—" She cocked her head to the side like a little bird and Will pressed his mouth shut against all the things he wanted to say about slavery. "I was just wondering if you knew many of the adult slaves in Porreen."

"I don't know any of them." She turned toward the grass again. "So much new grass," she murmured, taking a few steps into it.

"You're welcome to ride with me."

She glanced at the Roven near him. "Not until I'm stronger."

Will bit back a laugh. "When will that be?"

She looked thoughtfully across the Sweep. "Soon, I think."

Will offered the odd little slave girl a hard roll from his bag. "Well, if you need anything at all, come find me."

She considered the roll for a moment, then took it and laughed. "You're funny." She gave Will a little wave and scampered away from the caravan, out onto the Sweep. Her skinny legs flashed as she ran, her head bobbed into the thick, old grass, then disappeared down the nearest gully.

Will mounted Shadow, feeling impotent to help her. The front of the caravan had moved on with Killien's rangers, and the Roven here looked at him distastefully. He trotted Shadow back toward the front. When he drew alongside a handful of slaves, he paused, weighing the risk of asking them about Ilsa.

He opened up to them and a mixture of envy and loathing filled his chest.

"Come to tell us a story, did you?" one of the old men asked quietly. His hair was white and his back bowed beneath his grey tunic.

"He came to offer us that fine horse," another said, "because he doesn't want his elders to walk for a fortnight while he rides up and down the line, whenever he pleases."

"I…" Will stopped, searching for a response.

"Move past, fetter bait," a sharp voice called from past them. A small Roven woman moved through the crowd toward them, her face furious. "The Torch may want your company, but the rest of us do not."

Will bowed his head slightly to the Roven woman, and again to the slaves. He turned Shadow toward the front of the caravan, an odd mix of insult and embarrassment washing over him.

He finally caught a glimpse of Hal and trotted towards him, relieved until Sora rode up as well. Hal greeted him enthusiastically. Sora gave him her usual scowl.

"The Torch ordered you to walk with him," she told Will.

"Ordered me?"

"His exact word was *invite*, but I thought I'd translate it for you. Because you don't seem very bright."

Hal laughed. "He seems bright enough to me."

"He comes to a Roven clan as a foreigner"—Sora's gaze dug into Will—"and then spins stories and lies."

"Sora doesn't like stories," Hal explained.

"You don't like *stories*? Everyone likes stories of some kind or another."

She just looked at him, her face set.

"Did you like the story I told last night? About Tomkin and the dragon?" He hadn't bothered to read Sora after the story ended. Killien had been entertained, Hal and the crowd had loved it.

"You stretched the tale and molded it to manipulate the crowd," she said. "Every word was chosen to do something. Every word was a lie."

A thin claw of fear squeezed Will's chest. The lie part was wrong, but not the rest. He had judged every word, every line, weighing it against the audience, drawing out the parts that pleased the Roven, softening the parts that would feel foreign to them.

He opened his mouth to answer her, to find some sort of defense for it, but Hal spoke first.

"That's the point of a storyman, Sora. If we wanted to hear something boring, we'd ask about your last hunt."

She turned and trotted ahead. "It's not bright to keep the Torch waiting."

Will nudged Shadow to follow her. "This is the second morning you've come to find me. Should I start expecting it? I could have a cup of saso ready for you."

She shot him another glare, the hundredth he'd received that morning. "Unless you don't drink saso." His voice sounded snippier than he'd intended. "Then we could have tea. I know of a red tea from Baylon that would be perfect for you. It's bitter and disagrees with almost everyone."

That earned him the slightest uptick of the very edge of her mouth. She turned into the caravan and led him past dozens of rangers.

The Torch came into view, walking alongside his small fiery-haired wife. Will straightened, looking for any sign of Ilsa. Lilit caught sight of Sora and Will, and her expression sharpened.

"I've brought you your liar," Sora announced.

Killien turned with a raised eyebrow.

Will flung a glare at her. "They're stories. Not lies."

Sora didn't bother to look away from the Torch. "I ride west today." Without waiting for acknowledgement, she rode into the grass.

Lilit whispered something to the Torch that ended with a harsh "fett". Sending a cutting glare toward Will, she walked away.

Killien mounted his horse and glanced back toward her. "I didn't introduce you last night, but that is Lilit, my wife. Flame of the Morrow Clan." He worried his thumb across his lips, watching her walk away, and the burning stones in the rings on his fingers glinted in the morning light. "Carrying our first child. The healers assure me that the child will not come until we reach the rifts."

Lilit walked back to a wagon covered with a tall canopy of undyed wool, colored silks draping the front and back to make fluttering doorways. A hand reached through the silks to help her climb in and Will's breath caught at a glimpse of brown hair. Both disappeared into the wagon.

"Flame?"

"A Torch is not much use without a Flame." Killien squinted back towards her. "She's not happy that I invited you along. I'm expecting you to be so entertaining she changes her mind."

"I could ride with her," Will offered, a little quicker than he'd intended, "tell stories to pass the time."

"That's a terrible idea. Last night she called you a danger to the clan. Thought I should kill you in your sleep. I pointed out that you were a protected guest, she said you weren't her guest, and if she killed me in my sleep, she'd be free to kill you." Killien smiled, but it was a bit strained. "The best thing you can do is stay away from her. Your new goal here is not to entertain the clan, it's to convince my wife to like you. So she stops being mad at me."

The curtains shifted at the front of Lilit's wagon and Will caught a glimpse of movement inside. "I'll do my very best."

"Lilit will come around," Killien said, pulling Will's attention away from the slaves. He did not sound entirely hopeful, "But Sora was right, it's your familiarity with lies I'm interested in."

Will threw up his hands. "A story is very different from a lie."

"Is a rumor? My rangers have found rumors of frost goblins as far west as they've traveled. But since you have been quite a bit farther, I was wondering how far west the rumors went."

"Rumors of frost goblins was the only thing I heard agreed on in every city along the entire coast. They're talking about them in Bermea just as much as here."

Killien blew out a long breath. "That's not the answer I was hoping for."

They topped a small rise and the emptiness of the Sweep felt like a facade. The serpent's wake slithered over the hills ahead of them, dipping into countless unseen valleys. There could be hidden ravines everywhere, full of frost goblins. The earth beneath them could be riddled with warrens.

"Frost goblins aren't a threat to a caravan of this size, are they?"

Killien didn't answer right away. "It's been generations since anyone's seen hives large enough to attack a clan."

"What do they want?"

"Meat and metal. They are especially drawn to silver and gold, but they also gouge out nails, hinges, any metal they find. And they eat raw meat. They'll rip chunks of meat off an animal and leave the rest to rot."

"Do they—" Will hesitated. "—eat people?"

"They seem to prefer animals."

The empty expanse of the sky settled down heavily over the grass, the wind rippled across one hill and spread onto the next, jostling against them constantly.

"They dislike heat. Usually the spring weather drives them into the mountains, which is why we have heatstones. If you bring a stone near a fire, it'll give off tremendous heat for an hour or two."

Killien turned and gave instructions to a nearby ranger, who rode off down the line.

Pairs of riders cantered out from the main caravan, taking up positions on a perimeter around the main group. Killien gave the riders a brief glance before turning back to Will. "Yesterday you mentioned you'd been to three other clans. How does a storyman from Gulfind end up so well-traveled through the Roven Sweep?"

"I didn't intend to be." When he'd first stepped foot on the Sweep, following rumors of a gathering war, he'd thought it would be easy to confirm or refute. How hard could it be to find a single holy man proclaiming that Mallon the Rivor still lived and calling warriors to his banner? He thought he'd find the old man, figure out whether the Roven were amassing an army, and get back to Queensland within a fortnight. "I was chasing a story, actually. Following rumors of an elderly fellow who claimed a dead man had sent him on a mission." Which was true, from a certain point of view.

"Did you find him?"

"It took a while." A long while. Weeks and weeks of following rumors about the man. "And when I found him, he was a complete disappointment." The old man had been so ridiculous. Will had finally caught up to him in the summer valleys of the Boan Clan and instantly dismissed any rumors he'd heard of the man actually gathering an army. "He was just a doddering old man giving foolish speeches that no one listened to.

"But by then it was late in the fall, and the clans were heading south, so I followed and got caught up learning Roven stories." Especially Roven rumors about wayfarers and whether or not they sold foreign slaves on the Sweep. "It's taken months to work my way east again. I planned to go back to Gulfind before I met you." He kept himself from glancing back at Lilit's wagon. "And your offer was too interesting to refuse."

Killien studied him before nodding slowly. "All my books are in crates, sealed against the weather. But the ones you saw in my house are in a red oilcloth sack at the back corner of the book wagon. I've left them available for you."

Will sat straighter in surprise. "Thank you." The long trip north suddenly felt a bit less grim.

"There is also paper," Killien continued. "Write stories for me that I don't know and we can discuss them as we ride."

Will gave him a bow of acknowledgement.

"Everything you know about Queensland."

Will's bow stuttered before he recovered.

"And don't wander far from the front of the caravan. These are my rangers and won't trouble you. Everyone else in the clan knows the storyman from Gulfind is my guest, but accidents happen to foreigners on the Sweep." He glanced at Will's shirt. "Stay dressed like a storyman. And stay close to me."

Behind them, the line of the Morrow stretched back over the next rise filled with thousands of Roven. "I won't wander."

"Wise choice. The book wagon is that one with the orange oilcloth covering the back."

Will bowed at the obvious dismissal and turned Shadow toward the books.

He hadn't gone far when he reached Lukas riding toward Killien, his face bleak. The slave rode directly into Will's path. "Enjoy wearing the red shirt while you can," he said quietly. "It'll be grey soon enough."

Will reined in Shadow and opened up toward Lukas. A coiled, venomous hatred slithered into his chest.

"The only difference between you and me"—Lukas continued, his voice pitched low—"is that Killien's wayfarer dogs dragged me here, fighting the entire way. You just walked right in."

Will drew back, both from the man's fury and his words. "*Killien's* wayfarers?"

With a last hateful look, Lukas turned his horse away. "The wayfarers may not have brought you," he said over his shoulder, "but Killien owns you all the same."

TWELVE

The rest of the day passed in a vaguely unsettled way, Will's mind gnawing on the problem of how to reach Ilsa. He rode Shadow along the eastern edge of the caravan, keeping Lilit's wagon and Killien in view. Lukas's warning left a knot in his gut and there was something reassuring about being closer to the Scale Mountains than the Roven. Even if only by a handful of paces.

The path of the serpent's wake stretched ahead of them, slithering over the hills, the trail of years of migrations etched into the Sweep. It was strange how a place as vastly open as this could feel so confining.

He kept busy thinking of rescue stories, hoping he'd land on some idea of how to get Ilsa away from the Roven. Keeper Terre had rescued six children from a pack of direwolves, but even if Will had mastered the skill of making trees topple strategically, there were no trees on the Sweep. Knocking over blades of grass was bound to have a less terrifying effect.

It was a much needed distraction when Rass appeared. He dismounted and walked with her for a few hours. She ate the food he offered and chattered at him about the grass or the sky or whatever struck her fancy. It had been such a long time since anyone had talked with him so comfortably, it felt both delightful and overwhelming.

Around midday she ran out into the Sweep and Will found Killien's book wagon, wide with low side walls, open in the back. A burnt-orange oilcloth spread across the bed. The last arm's length of the wagon was open and he climbed onto it, lifting the edge of the oilcloth. Beneath it he found crates of books wrapped tightly in more oilcloth. In the nearest corner sat a red bag holding the books from Killien's shelf, a thick stack of paper, four pens, and a bottle of ink. Sitting on the back of the wagon, he set to writing some innocuous stories from Queensland.

As the sun set, riders came by ordering the wagons to a central location. A haphazard city grew along the top of one wide hill with wagons spilling down into the shallow valleys around it. The entire perimeter of the clan was dotted with fires as well, each with a mound of dried grass and dung next to it, ready to be thrown on if larger flames were needed.

Around him the Roven gathered into small knots talking and laughing and eating together and he sat feeling awkward, wondering where he was supposed to find his dinner. The night cooled quickly and a cold breeze blew across Will's back.

He cast out toward the nearest fire, feeling the *vitalle* blazing up in it. It was too bad Alaric wasn't here. He could pull a blanket of warmth from a fire all the way across a room. *Don't move the heat itself, create a…sort of a net around it. Then pull the net, not the heat,* he'd say.

A net. Will stretched his fingers toward the fire. He gathered its *vitalle,* imagining it forming a close woven net, capturing the heat and pulling it toward him. His fingertips stung, but he felt a wave of warmish air. He sat up straighter.

A net had too many holes. He began again, imagining a cloth wrapping around the heat. Slowly, his fingers starting to ache in earnest, he drew the cloth closer.

The enormous form of Hal stepped between him and the fire, and Will's concentration broke. The cloth dissolved and the heat escaped into the night.

"What are you doing over here?" Hal said. "Come get dinner. Unless all this wagon gathering is your fault, in which case I hate you."

"I may have had a part in it," Will admitted. "Killien and I talked about goblins this morning. The entire Sweep is worried about them."

Hal glared at the sprawling mass of Roven. "This will cost an hour of travel each night. It'll add at least a day to the trip." Hal motioned for Will to follow him. "You can pay for it by entertaining us with a story. Something about dwarves."

They wound through wagons, Hal keeping up a continual grumble until they reached a small fire near the edge of the clan where he dropped down next to Sora. She offered Will her usual scowl and Will gave her an especially wide smile back.

Hal passed a basket of thin bread and smoked fish before a young girl arrived, asking him a question about a herd. Will ate his piece of salty, dried fish half listening to Hal's herd management, half watching Roven children carrying baskets of food.

Killien walked up talking to some rangers. Neither Lilit nor Ilsa was with him, but he was followed by Lukas and the two other slaves from the porch in Porreen. Lukas and the younger girl swung bags of heatstones off their shoulders and sat a little ways back from the fire. When the big man sat next to them, he clutched his own bag to his chest.

Lukas spread a book on his lap and flipped through the pages before finding a place to read. The girl leaned over and ran her finger along the page. Will stared at the two of them. Did all of Killien's slaves know how to read? They were obviously well cared for. Maybe slavery in Killien's household wasn't as bad as other places. Was it possible that Ilsa's life had been better than he'd feared?

The big slave stared disinterestedly at the fire, relaxing until his bag slouched and two heatstones rolled out, unnoticed.

"Keep them in the sack, Rett," the girl said kindly, tucking the yellow stones back into the bag and cinching the top closed.

"I'm sorry, Sini," he said absently. "I forgot."

"It's alright." She patted his large hand reassuringly with her own small one.

Rett pulled the bag onto his lap, wrapping one hand firmly around the drawstring and his other arm around the bag. With it secure, he lifted his head and looked around with an aimless curiosity. There was a familial type of ease among the three of them.

Sini watched him for a moment, a little crease of worry in her brow. Lukas reached into a pocket and pulled out a small, glowing green stone.

"Don't," Sini pleaded.

But Lukas held the stone out toward Rett.

The large man's eyes locked on the stone and a wide smile crossed his face. "You found one!"

He reached out gingerly to take it, then cupped it in his hands, curling his body over it.

"Don't watch it too long." The gentleness in Lukas's voice caught Will off guard. "It'll hurt your head."

Rett nodded and kept his eyes fixed on the green glow, a look of utter contentment on his face.

"I wish you'd stop giving him those," Sini said.

"I've said no for weeks. If he begged you all the time, you'd give in too." Lukas watched the man. "Sometimes I think he needs them."

The little bit of green glow was almost hidden in Rett's hands. He watched it with a desperate sort of fascination, as though if he blinked, it might disappear.

Sini looked down at her hands. "I can't bear how sad it makes him."

"But it makes him happy first." Lukas turned back to his book.

She pinched her mouth into a thin, disapproving line and sat silent for a moment before glancing at Lukas's book. "Did you figure it out? Does it work?"

Lukas shrugged. "Killien won't try it." He shot a glare at the Torch. "He's so fixated that he's missing opportunities."

Sini shushed him and Lukas answered her too quietly for Will to catch.

Two Roven children stepped up to him, delivering more piles of flatbread and fish. During the day, all the children of the clan had romped along the side of the caravan doing as they pleased, but now that the camp was settling, those old enough were busy hurrying about just like the slaves, helping the clan settle down.

"What was it like," Will asked Sora, "growing up with the Morrow?"

She looked away and took a bite of fish.

"You won't get any information from Sora," Killien said, sitting across the fire and reaching for the basket of fish. "She's angry tonight."

Sora didn't acknowledge the Torch.

"Are there some nights she's not?" Will asked.

That she acknowledged with a glare.

"She's especially angry tonight because I didn't send her out with the latest scouting party."

"What's the point of sending out a scouting party when none of them can scout?" Sora asked.

"They're all rangers," Killien said mildly.

"They all wear ranger leathers," she corrected him. "Not one of them could track a black sheep in a field of snow."

"See?" Killien said. "She's angry."

Sora went back to scowling at her fish.

"I didn't know there was an alternative," Will said, feeling a grim, if childish, satisfaction at her annoyance. "This is how she talks to me all the time."

Hal reached for the basket of food. "She can't answer your question anyway. Sora didn't grow up in the Morrow. She's from a mountain tribe."

"Really?" Will turned back to her, several things clicking into place. "Of course, your eyes are green."

Sora looked at him with a stony face. "Your beard is stupid."

Will's hand went to his beard. "What?"

"I thought we were stating obvious things."

Will waved away her comments. "I've never met anyone from the mountain tribes. You live in the Hoarfrost Range year round, don't you? How? In the winter the mountains are so…"

"Cold?" offered Hal.

"Yes, cold. How do you stay warm?"

She gave him an exasperated look but didn't answer.

"Alright, we'll play the 'I make up your answer' game again," Will said. "You live in huge communal buildings and keep fires burning all the time?"

"Yes." She graced him with a flat look. "Because everyone knows the Hoarfrost Range is full of huge communal buildings."

"Good point." Will's mind skipped to other ideas. "Do you build houses out of snow?"

"Good guess, storyman," Hal broke in with a wide grin. "That's how we met Sora. Killien and I were in the Hoarfrost hunting when a blizzard rolled in. We thought we were going to freeze to death." He gestured at Sora. "Until, thank the black queen, an angel appeared."

Sora raised an eyebrow.

"She bossed us into helping her make a snow hut, then crawled inside."

Killien smiled and even the corner of Sora's lips rose slightly.

"We didn't know what else to do, so we followed her. When she learned that we were hunting a snow cat, she looked at us." He nodded to Will. "With that angry, scary look."

"I'm familiar with that one," Will said.

"Then she left."

Will laughed. "She left?"

Hal nodded. "Wasn't even gone long enough for us to decide whether she'd deserted us, when she came back, dragging...a dead snow cat."

Will turned to Sora. "You hunted it that fast?"

Sora started to shake her head, but Hal nodded. "That's when we knew she had creepy magic."

"You do?" Will asked.

Sora let out a long suffering sigh. "I didn't use magic. I hunted it with a bow and a knife. It was dead before I found these idiots."

"So she claims," Hal finished.

Will cast out toward Sora, but there was nothing unusual about her *vitalle*. If she could do magic, she wasn't doing anything right now. Not that she'd have a reason to. He opened up to her as well, assuming he'd still feel nothing. But here, sitting with people she was comfortable around, she had relaxed slightly. Her emotions were still muted, but he found hints of both amusement and irritation. He closed himself off to her, wondering if she ever relaxed enough to let her emotions be fully felt. "So the mountain clans live in ice houses?"

"Caves!" Sora said in exasperation, "Caves large enough to house a village. Wide and clean with crystal clear streams. Rooms. Chimneys. Walls that glitter with silver and gems."

Will stared at her in amazement. "Really?" He glanced at Killien who grinned openly, then turned back to Sora. The mountain tribes lived in caves? Like dwarves? "How big are they?" His mind toyed with the idea, turning it slowly around. "Will you take me there?" The Keepers knew next to nothing about the mountain clans. "You can tell me the tales of your people. Has anyone ever written them down? I'll make you a book of them!"

"Sora's the one you'd want to write stories about," Killien said.

Sora dropped her bread, her eyes thin slits of green, and stood up. "I'm not your personal guide, storyman. I have no desire to travel anywhere with you, and I wouldn't subject my people to your..." Her eyes searched his face for a long moment before she gestured at him.

"My what?" Will demanded.

"Your everything."

Will hadn't even realized he'd opened up toward her until he felt her deep, pulsing anger bloom in his chest. Jaw clenched, she turned and walked off into the darkness. Will took a breath, clearing her anger away until all he felt was the now familiar knot of worry that was all his own. He glanced at the Torch and saw nothing but amusement.

Hal's eyes glinted in the firelight and his teeth shone white through his beard. "She's definitely starting to like you, storyman."

Will let out a laugh that sounded weak even to his own ears. "It seems that way." He glanced at Hal. "Can she really do magic?"

Hal shook his head. "It's just uncanny how good she is at tracking. And it's fun to say because it makes her so mad."

"Never mind Sora," Killien said. "It's time for you to earn your keep, storyman. Tell us a tale."

"Something about dwarves," Hal added.

"Shut up, Hal." Killien glanced toward where Sora had disappeared. "Do you know any about angry women?"

Will ran through the tales he knew from Gulfind and Coastal Baylon. No angry women jumped out at him.

"What about Keeper Chesavia from Queensland?" Killien's eyes were bright. "I haven't heard the entire tale, but from what I know, she was angry."

Will shifted, giving himself a moment. Chesavia was very angry. But it was going to be tricky to tell that story without showing how well he knew the Keepers.

"Have you visited Queensland a lot?" Hal asked.

Will nodded. "I'd venture to say I've visited every country you've ever heard of."

Killien raised an eyebrow. "Have you crossed the Roven Sweep west to the land of the white rocks?"

"No." Past the westernmost Roven cities the grassland turned to desert and continued for days, lifeless and barren. "Have you ever met anyone who has?" Will asked.

"Legend says once a wizard crossed the desert on a dragon."

"Well, if I ever have access to a dragon," Will said, "I'd consider it."

"If I had a dragon," Hal said, "I'd make it hunt for me. And cook."

"If I had a dragon," Killien said, "I would destroy my enemies quickly and utterly. I'd destroy all those who keep the Roven weak and divided. Then I would kill all the Keepers in Queensland so the Roven could take back that land with barely a fight."

Will kept his face mild like a disinterested storyman from Gulfind. "Give me a little warning first. I'd love to learn more of their stories before you wipe them out."

A bleak smile twisted the edge of Killien's mouth. "Agreed."

"One of the times I was in Queensland, I visited the queen's court."

Both Hal and Killien looked impressed.

"The night I was there, a Keeper told the story of Chesavia." This was also true. The first time he'd gone to court, Will had arrived just in time for a feast and Alaric's storytelling. "She lived years ago and had battled a water demon. By the end of the tale, Chesavia's angry. I'll warn you, though, it's not a happy story."

"Most tales with angry women aren't." Killien laughed.

"You can remember the story, after hearing it only once?" Hal asked.

"I don't have many skills in life," Will said. "I can't fight, I can't make anything." *I'm fairly weak at magic and I'm not great at translating old runes,* he added silently. "But I can remember every story I've ever heard, or ever read."

Hal raised his eyebrow. "Every one?"

"If I've only heard it once, or if it was poorly told, I have to work a bit to remember it. This story was told by a Keeper. You may not be fond of them, but they are excellent storytellers."

The small fire in front of them flickered, tossed about by the wind. Will looked into it, considering how well he should tell the story. "The tale becomes interesting the day her childhood friend arrived at the palace, wounded and begging to see her."

Will fell into the story, minimizing the way he spoke of Keeper magic. Killien watched him closely, seemingly hungry for more of the tale, and at the end, he thanked Will and looked into the fire for a long time.

"Do you know more tales about Keepers?" Killien asked.

Will glanced at him, then looked into the fire too. He knew every story of every Keeper recorded in the Stronghold. Dozens of which he had rewritten himself, combining different tellings into complete tales. "A few."

"I want to hear them," Killien said. "As many as you can remember."

"Do you see the grass?" Rass chirped near midday, running up alongside Will, her dirty face lit up with joy. "It's growing so fast!"

THIRTEEN

The sun disappeared over the horizon, and the sky pulled the last lingering light up into itself, turning the Sweep into a puddle of darkness. Will tried twice to walk among the wagons where Lilit and Ilsa were, but both times rangers efficiently directed him away. The second time was barely civil. Whatever orders Killien had given them regarding the foreign storyman, Will doubted it would keep him safe if they decided he was paying too much attention to the Torch's wife.

Killien offered Will a place to sleep in one of his wagons along with a pile of blankets. Between a bundle of fabric for a pillow, and wool blankets from the Torch, he had a reasonably comfortable place to sleep.

At least at first. The ever-present wind sent swirls of cold night air jostling around him. His emotions were just as blustery.

First there was Ilsa. All day he'd strained to see her near Lilit's wagon, but in vain.

Then there was Killien. On the one hand, he was more civilized than Will had ever expected. Even his slaves could read. But he *had* slaves, ripped from their homes and brought here. The truth of that was so stark he felt furious and sick at the same time. And just in case Will ever started feeling too comfortable, there was Killien's hatred of Keepers to keep things interesting.

Finally there was Lukas's warning. Was Will fooling himself thinking he'd be free to leave?

Just above the Scales, the sinuous trail of black emptiness rose. A cold darkness crept into Will's chest at the sight of the snake. The Serpent Queen kept drawing his eye back to her utter blackness. As though she were drawing in the whole world. She'd moved halfway across the sky before he fell asleep.

The caravan rumbled to a start as soon as the grasslands were visible. Will walked, trying to work the aches out of his muscles. He stayed close to Shadow, using the horse to block the relentless wind. It wasn't terribly strong this morning, but the constant pushing of it was tiresome. He kept his eye on the covered wagons trailing behind Killien, wondering which one held Ilsa.

He'd remembered a story of a woman who'd rescued her sister from the Naponese blood doctors. She'd disguised herself as one of the servants who disposed of the dead bodies and carted her sister out with the corpses. But unless he and Ilsa could camouflage themselves as a hill of grass, it was unlikely any disguise was going to help them.

Not long after dawn, a noise behind him made Will turn sharply. There was Sora, walking behind him, leading her own horse.

"Is there a reason you're sneaking up on me?" he demanded, his heart racing.

Her eyes took him in, narrowed, and she drew her lips into her usual tight line. "You seem nervous."

He ignored that and took a calming breath. He really shouldn't try to irritate this woman. She was too close to Killien. And now that she was here, he felt the slightest sense of relief. Like he'd been waiting for her without realizing it.

"Does Killien want me?" he asked, hoping he'd be saved from the boredom of walking.

She shook her head. "He's busy."

She came up next to him anyway, wearing the same hunting leathers she had since he'd met her, well-used and plain. Where her arms had been bare yesterday, she now wore a blue wool shirt under her leathers, her shoulders shielded by a flap of chainmail, her wrists covered in thick leather bracers. Her braid lay heavy on her back, catching the sunlight in strands of bright copper. The entire Morrow Clan stretched out around them, but as he walked with her, the two horses blocking out the world around them, it felt almost like they were alone. She didn't seem as annoyed today, so he risked some conversation.

"How long have you been with the Morrow?"

She gave him a long, searching look, as though weighing whether the question was safe to answer. "Almost three years."

A twinge of sympathy caught him off guard. He was exhausted after only one year in the Sweep. "That's a long time."

She turned her gaze back forward. "Not to the Morrow."

"Do they…" He paused, trying to find words for his questions. "Are you still a foreigner to them? Or do they see you for who you actually are?"

Her face tightened a little but she didn't answer him.

"They don't see me either," he said.

Silence stretched out between them. It felt like camaraderie at first. Until the chill of her silence crept in and turned it into just a new form of isolation. Will spun his ring on his finger.

"Why are you here, Sora?"

"I don't trust you." She sounded more thoughtful than hostile.

"The Torch trusts me."

"He doesn't trust anyone."

That was unsettling. "Hal likes me."

She fixed him with her inscrutable look. "I don't trust you, storyman. And I intend to keep an eye on you."

"Well, anytime you feel the need to walk with me, please do. You're far from the most pleasant person I've ever met, but you are opinionated. And that's entertaining."

Sora stopped and put her hand on his shoulder, stopping him and turning him toward her with one motion. Will's heart lurched as she stepped right up to him. She stood almost as tall as him, her eyes sharp and cold.

"I'm watching you all the time." Her hand weighed like stone on his shoulder. She was so close to him he could see the stark green of her eyes, the dark copper lashes. Will was sure she could feel his heart pounding.

"Are you waiting for a goodbye kiss?" Will whispered.

Her eyes went flat and she dropped her hand. With a withering look she mounted her horse and disappeared into the crowd. Will stood for a moment, letting out his breath, still feeling the weight of her hand on his shoulder.

———◆———

Will sat on the back of the book wagon and stared dully across the grass. It was the third morning and he already felt like he'd done nothing in his life but trundle slowly northward across the Sweep. He'd wanted to ride among the wagons that held Lilit and Ilsa, but between Killien commanding him to keep his distance and the number of Roven rangers that surrounded Lilit, he couldn't figure out a way to do so. When he wasn't talking with Killien, riding among the other rangers who merely tolerated him for Killien's sake felt awkward and lonely. He'd ended up spending most of the day yesterday and all of this morning near the books. He'd written out four stories for Killien and read a good portion of one of the Torch's books.

His mind continued its useless search through stories for a rescue plan, but he'd thrown out three more ideas. He had neither floating firebrands nor a broken dam, and it would be hard to time his escape during the distraction provided by an attacking gryffon. If any gryffons still existed.

Last night, Will had given in to Rass's pestering and let her put three thin braids in his beard, each sporting a silver bead. She'd pronounced it "much better."

Talen had come and landed next to him on the wagon until he'd eaten all of Will's dried fish, then launched into the sky again and Will found himself wishing the little bird would stay.

The Clans and Clashes of the Sweep lay open on his lap to a page that mentioned the Morrow Clan. "Insignificant… weak… probably the only reason they survived is that they remain relegated to the easternmost margin of the Sweep, and have nothing worth plundering."

He toyed with his braids. The slight weight of the beads felt odd—empowering almost. As though adding those small beads gave him an unexpected measure of strength, or courage.

Sora rode up to the back of the wagon. "Killien wants you."

"Good." He tucked the book into the bag. "I'm terribly bored."

She had a knife strapped to each ankle and a bow slung across her back.

"Expecting me to put up a fight this morning?" Will mounted Shadow.

"Yes. The entire clan is preparing for an attack from *you*."

He let out a short laugh, until a thought struck him. "That's all for frost goblins?"

She leveled a pointed gaze at him. "Do you know of any other enemies nearby?"

"You feel a bit like an enemy sometimes."

This earned him a small smile. She motioned to his beard. "Getting more Roven by the day."

He felt the beads. "Do you like it?"

She raised one eyebrow.

"I mean—" He shifted. "—does it look right?"

She leaned toward him and he pulled back.

"You're a very nervous man."

"I'm not nervous." Even he could hear the petulance in his voice. "You're just scary."

She let out a short laugh. "If goblins attack, I wouldn't have that silver anywhere so easily grabbed."

Will rubbed one of the beads between his fingers. He imagined a bony goblin hand reaching for his face, and shuddered. Sora trotted ahead and he followed.

When he caught up, her armband caught his eye. The wide, dark fabric wrapped around her upper arm, and the claw tied to it with thin leather strips was viciously sharp. Under the band, a white, puckered scar ran down to her elbow.

"What sort of claw is that?"

Sora glanced down at her arm. "Snow cat." Turning away she added, "Killien's just ahead of the wagons," and rode away.

A handful of tall covered wagons, including the one with Lilit and Ilsa, rolled along in a clump. There were fewer rangers around today, and none near Lilit's wagon. Making sure Sora had disappeared, Will turned so he would ride through them to reach Killien. From the back of Lilit's wagon he caught a glimpse of long brown hair and his heart squeezed out several painfully strong beats. Will angled Shadow closer, feeling his pulse all the way down to where his palms gripped the reins.

A horse laden with a tall load of blankets was hitched to the back of the wagon, plodding along after it. Colored silks hung over the back, fluttering in the breeze.

Ilsa stepped out from between them.

She climbed down, grabbed a bundle of blankets, pushed them into the fluttering silks and disappeared after them. Will slid off Shadow and walked toward her, too many emotions churning inside of him to name. He picked up the next bundle, intending to offer his help, but when the silks opened and she saw him, she froze. The sight of her made everything in his chest claw its way up into his throat, and his offer was strangled out into the single word, "—help?"

Her face grew alarmed. "You need help?"

The idea was so wrong he let out a laugh that sounded a bit unhinged, and she drew back. "No." He stepped closer, desperately trying to speak normally. "I was wondering if you would like some help."

She eyed him a little warily, but when he held out the blankets, she took them and went back into the wagon. He wiped his sweaty palms and picked up the next bundle. This wasn't going well.

When she appeared again, he managed a reasonably normal smile. She pulled the silks shut behind her and climbed down, glancing around with a worried expression.

"You shouldn't be here," she whispered. "If the Flame saw you…" Her voice reminded him so much of their mother, but her accent—the rough Roven-ness of it cut at him.

"I'll just help for a minute." He felt as though he were trying to absorb everything about her. Now that he was closer, there was something of their father around her eyes. She looked healthy, and her grey slave's dress was well-made. She reached for the blankets. A line of thin scars from a switch ran across the back of her hands.

"Thank you." She glanced around again before continuing in a whisper, "I liked the story you told about Tomkin and the dragon." Tomkin's name sounded sharper the way she said it. Like the Roven accent could even make bookish Tomkin more savage.

"I'm Will," he whispered, something inside him breaking at the need to introduce himself.

She glanced back at the wagon. "You should go."

A jab of disappointment shot through him at her answer, but he tried not to let it show. There really wasn't any other way this relationship could begin. In her eyes he was nothing but a stranger. A dangerous stranger as far as Lilit was concerned.

"It's just…" He fumbled around for something to say. "It's just nice talking to someone who's like me."

She pulled the blankets out of his hands. "There's not much the same between you and me."

With a flick of silk, she disappeared into the wagon.

Will stared numbly at the back of the wagon until Lilit's voice floated out, jolting him back into motion. He mounted Shadow and wove his way out from between the wagons toward Killien.

Unnecessarily close behind the Torch rode Lukas, with a book spread open in front of him, making small notes in the margins and eating a roll. Nearby, Sini balanced on her toes on the wide saddle, her knees tucked up against her chest and her arms outstretched. She was such a little thing that even balled up she didn't fill the saddle. Her blond hair was busy falling out of a ponytail, her bag of heatstones hung from the saddle, and she chattered at Rett who rode silent beside her. He held one hand fisted on his saddle horn, and when he opened it to peer inside, Will caught a dim glow of green. The stone Lukas had given him last night was fading. Rett looked at it, then clenched his hand closed, his face worried.

Sini glanced over at the big man, a little crease of worry forming in her brow too. "Look, Rett, I'm a bird."

The big man considered her solemnly. "If you fly away, can I come with you?"

"Of course."

"You don't look like a bird, you look like a shrew." Lukas's face was serious, but his voice was light.

Sini dropped her arms. "With wings?"

"Her nose isn't pointy enough for a shrew," Rett disagreed, looking back at his stone with a troubled expression.

"He's teasing, Rett. Lukas is just envious because I have two good legs." Sini wiggled her knees from side to side. "One leg—" Sini balanced on one foot and stretched the other leg to the side. "—two legs." She switched feet and stuck the other out. "One leg, two legs…"

Lukas laughed and threw the end of the roll at her. It bounced off her grinning cheek, and even Rett managed a smile. Lukas glanced forward, catching Will's eye, and his expression soured.

Killien spared a quick glance at Sini and Lukas as he greeted Will. Between the unusual slaves and the nearness of Ilsa, Killien was hard to pay attention to. But the Torch had read the histories Will had written, and the rest of the morning passed discussing them.

It was irritating to talk to the man. Killien had thought-provoking questions and sharp insights into the minds of other leaders. His thoughts about a historically weak king of Coastal Baylon made Will see the story in a whole new light. Will kept finding himself enjoying the conversation no matter how often he reminded himself not to.

The sun was high in the sky when Lukas closed his book with a snap. Out of the corner of his eye, Will saw him take a bracing breath, set his face into a mask of determination, and ride away.

Not long after, several rangers rode up to Killien, and Will excused himself. There were too many people around Lilit's wagon to even consider trying to see Ilsa, so he set off for the books. To the northwest, clouds were piling up in the blue sky like glowing swells of whiteness, while underneath a dark line sat heavy on the horizon.

When the wagon came into view, Lukas knelt on the back of it, looking into a dark grey sack. Will wove through the crowd until he trailed a little way behind. Lukas pulled out a book, pushed the bag into a crate, and tucked the oilcloth back around the books.

Lukas's brow was drawn, his jaw set. His eyes burned with something jagged. He took a breath and shifted his legs off the back of the wagon. A snarl of pain crossed his face and he pushed himself off, dropping into the grass, one leg twisting underneath him. With obvious effort, he limped to his horse and pulled himself into the saddle.

Will waited until Lukas had disappeared before spurring Shadow closer. He climbed down near the corner where his own red bag was, while the rangers driving the wagon watched him. Will reached into his own bag of books and pulled out a few titles. When the ranger turned back, Will pushed the orange cloth to the side and saw the crate with Lukas's bag. He reached in and pulled out the first book he found.

Methods of Transference.

Will stared at the brown leather cover, his mind tangled up in the odd words. He flipped the book open and his hand froze on the page.

Methods of Transference
based on the stonesteep practices of
Mallon the Undying.

FOURTEEN

Will stared at the name.

Mallon the Undying.

The title Undying was chilling. He was Mallon the Rivor in Queensland. When he'd invaded eight years ago with an army of Roven, the first people to bring a report to the queen were gem cutters, and they called what Mallon did *riving*—cutting a gem so deeply that it became worthless. It was a good description of what he did to people's minds. He cut something so profound inside them that they lost their will to refuse him.

What was unsettling about the Undying title was how true it felt. Everyone in Queensland had thought Mallon had been killed by the elves eight years ago. Until Ayda the elf showed his body to Will, not dead, just trapped.

Will lifted his gaze up to the Scales, as though he could see through the mountains to Alaric and see if the other Keepers had found a way to deal with Mallon.

Will set the book on the back of the wagon and flipped to the first page. Diagrams of stones and energy and animals filled the pages, detailing how to suck the energy out of a living creature and store it in burning stones.

This is what Killien had Lukas reading?

It discussed the sacrifice of the animal coldly, mathematically, as though it was of no importance. The focus was on how the energy, forced into lifeless gems, created the burning stones. Distaste and fascination warred with each other as he skimmed the pages. It was unnatural to put living energy into something not made to hold life. The entire process was ugly. And terribly inefficient. More time was spent on how to keep the energy from fading out of the burning stone than on how to put it there in the first place. Energy did not like to be contained.

A quarter of the way through the book he found pages heavily notated with small, wiry script.

Compulsion Stones

The transference of thought is relatively simple. A gem can be filled to hold an idea with relatively little sacrifice, a cat or other small animal, will provide more than enough.

But the idea in the compulsion stone is only a suggestion. The closer it matches the target's natural inclinations, the more effective the process. While it is occasionally successful with animals, results are not positive in humans. The foreign nature of the idea is recognized too quickly.

Will scanned the rest of the page. This was essentially a cumbersome way to do an influence spell, with similar limitations. An idea that was too foreign wouldn't work. Convincing someone to not notice a single person among a crowd was easy. Convincing them to not notice a single person walking into their room at night was almost impossible.

The rest described how to infuse a burning stone (aquamarine worked best) with a single thought. The process was messy and complicated, with a dozen reasons it could fail. It ended with a comment that Mallon was one of the few who could create compulsion stones reliably, but his methods were unknown.

The scribbled notes on the page were far more interesting.

Not thoughts—Emotions.

Mallon used natural resonance of emotions. Humans inherently susceptible to foreign emotions.

Will ran his finger over the note.

The natural resonance of emotions.

The phrase caught his attention like a glint of light out of the grimness of the book and something profound shifted in his mind. He spun his ring, turning the idea over in his mind.

He'd always thought of reading people as an extension of his other abilities. Emotions weren't exactly like *vitalle*, but he'd always thought of them as a form of energy other Keepers couldn't draw into themselves. But he didn't draw emotions in, he opened himself up and let his own body resound with them.

Resonance fit it perfectly. Because everyone was affected by other's emotions to some extent. A happy friend could lift one's spirits, anger could spread from person to person like a flame. Emotions were contagious.

He spun his ring slowly. Maybe Will's particular gift was that he could isolate others' emotions from his own so he could feel them clearly. The idea sat inside him like a lamp, shining onto other ideas, linking things together that he'd never connected.

Along the very bottom of the page, was scrawled:

Emotions resonate—they do not move. Once the stone is created, transference of emotions, unlike thoughts, requires NO ENERGY.

The lines under the final words were dark and thick and victoriously emphatic.

Will nodded slowly in agreement. It took no effort for him to feel the emotions of others.

He traced the wiry script. Was it Lukas's?

Whoever's it was, this much enthusiasm for controlling people was unsettling. The fact that it reminded Will of the influence spells he'd been using throughout the Sweep made it even worse.

A distant rumble rolled across the grasses. The clouds were closer, climbing high against the blue sky. Their tops so bright white they were almost blinding, and the dark line beneath them as dark as a sliver of night.

"Stow those books, fett," the ranger barked at Will.

Will shot him a scowl and tucked Lukas's book back into its grey sack. He was about to close the bag when he remembered the book Lukas had bought from Borto—the blue one with the silver medallion.

He peered inside, but none of the books were blue.

Grabbing *Clans of the Eastern Sweep* from the bag he was supposed to use, he tucked the oilcloth snugly around everything. Back on Shadow, he took his place along the eastern side of the clan, his mind still toying with the ideas of resonance, and that Lukas was reading books about magic.

Killien didn't have any stonesteeps. He'd paid an outsider to create the heatstones, another to bless the herds. What was Killien planning to do with knowledge he couldn't use? When he didn't come up with an answer, he turned his attention to his own book.

Clans of the Eastern Sweep was short and boring. There were only two tribes besides the Morrow this close to the Scales, the Temur and the Panos. The end of the book was dedicated to the Morrow's history. It was uninspiring.

Always the smallest clan, they were conscripted by whatever nearby clan needed them when infighting broke out in the Sweep. The book ended with Tevien, 17th Torch of the Morrow Clan. It was noted that he had one son named Killien.

A new hand began beneath it.

Tevien, Torch of the Morrow, led his people for 23 years. His goal was to unite the Roven clans. He brought Torches together who had never met in peace.

On Midsummer's Day, in his twenty-third year as Torch, Tevien was summoned to mediate a skirmish between the Temur and the Panos. He was struck by a stray arrow and returned to the grass, giving his life and his strength back to the Sweep.

Killien, 18th Torch of the Morrow, took his father's place at age 18, uncontested.

Will looked toward the front of the caravan where Killien rode.

Eighteen was so young.

At eighteen, Will had been seven years into his training at the Keeper Stronghold and just starting to travel Queensland in what would end up being fruitless searching for new Keeper children, traveling through a safe land, and telling stories to small towns. Not exactly the same as becoming the Torch of a small, vulnerable Roven clan.

A raindrop slapped against his neck and Will snapped the book shut and tucked it into his saddlebag just as the real rain hit. Around him, the caravan moved on unperturbed. Hoods were up and heads were down, but every horse, wagon, and person plodded forward, as if nothing was happening.

The storm was fierce and blustery and short-lived. Killien didn't send for him when the wagons stopped, and he jotted stories for the Torch until it was late enough to try and sleep. The boards of the wagon were hard against his back, the chill of the night seeped through his blankets, and the black Serpent Queen snaked through the stars like a stain.

The pale light of morning came too soon. Will rolled himself out of the wagon, toying with the idea of walking until his body loosened up, but weariness won out and he mounted Shadow, riding along the eastern side of the caravan.

They'd barely started when Sora appeared. A fresh wave of exhaustion rolled over him at the thought of talking to her.

"Good morning," he said, without enthusiasm.

She raised an eyebrow. "No unwarranted cheerfulness this morning?"

He didn't bother to answer, and they rode in silence until Talen's tiny form dove down and landed on Will's bedroll.

"Good morning," Will said, ignoring the mouse he dropped.

"I was wondering if I'd get to meet your hawk." Sora looked at the bird with keen interest and ran a finger down its feathers. The hawk fixed her with its expressionless gaze.

"Sora," Will introduced her, trying to sound polite, "meet Talen."

Sora took in the bird's drab, tiny feet. "Talon? Did you name your horse Hoof?"

"My horse is Shadow," Will said, patting the pinto's mottled neck with affection, "because I've always wanted a black horse named Shadow. The Roven wouldn't sell me a black one, so I bought this one instead. And named him Shadow."

Sora fixed him with an unreadable expression. "It's fitting that you would take something as beautiful as a brown and white pinto and, just by changing the words you say about it, think you can change it into what you really want."

Will stared at her. "Do you ever have any fun? Shadow's name makes me happy. And Talen's name isn't 'Talon' like the claw, its 'Talen' like the coin because he was payment for a job. Although whether he was a good payment or not, I haven't decided."

"He's a grass hawk. And he's beautiful."

"A grass hawk? Is anything in this land *not* named after grass?"

Sora shrugged. "The grass is everything here."

"He's not full grown, is he? Because he's too small to hunt anything but mice."

"Just a yearling." She reached out again and ran her finger along Talen's brown and white chest. "But he won't grow much bigger. A female would be half again as big and a better hunter." The edges of her lips lifted slightly. "And faster and smarter and all around more capable."

Talen fluttered his wings and hopped onto Sora's fist—and she smiled a wide, genuine smile at the bird.

It was utterly transformative, like the time Will had seen a brown lizard skitter onto a leaf, and its rough skin had shifted to a vibrant, shimmery green. He was torn between shock and a sudden possessiveness toward Talen.

"Stop seducing my hawk." Will pulled out a bit of meat. Talen hopped back onto Will's saddle horn and snatched it up. "He's small and not particularly useful, but he and I are a good fit."

She sat back, the smile lingering. "Grass hawks are difficult to catch."

He almost opened up toward her. It'd be unusual to feel any pleasant emotions from her. But it felt refreshing to take the smile as enough. He did soften his voice a little. "Don't try to convince me he's valuable. I'm very comfortable with the long-suffering caretaker role I've developed with him."

"He's not valuable, just intriguing."

Talen peered at Will's saddlebag.

Will spread his hands out. "You're going to have to be hawk-like and hunt for yourself if you're still hungry."

Talen let out a whistling call and sped off into the sky.

Will watched him go until he was only a small black speck. He flung the dead mouse past Sora into the grass.

A small crinkle of disgust wrinkled Sora's nose, but it was accompanied by another smile. She kept her eyes trained on the disappearing hawk. "Killien wants you."

Will looked at her sharply. "Why didn't you say so before?"

She shrugged. "He's up near the front." She seemed to have no intention of coming with him. So, spurring Shadow forward, he left her looking thoughtfully after Talen.

As he rode up to Lilit's wagon, the silk scarves hanging across the back fluttered and he caught a glimpse of the Torch's wife lying on a thick bed of blankets. Her eyes were closed, her face set in an expression of exhaustion and irritation. She pressed painfully swollen hands against her belly. The wagon lurched. Her eyes flew open and she hissed something at the driver.

A grey sleeve came into view and laid a wet cloth across the front of her neck.

Lilit's eyes closed again. "I'd sell everything I own for more wet cloths."

"I'll be right back with more water, Flame."

"Thank you," Lilit said.

Will urged Shadow alongside the back corner of the wagon and came face to face with Ilsa. She cast an alarmed glance toward Lilit, who still lay with her eyes closed, and waved him away.

He motioned for her to be quiet, and offered his water skin. She paused, then gave him a begrudging smile which still looked vaguely disapproving. He poured water onto the cloths in her hand until they were soaked.

Thank you, she mouthed, before turning back into the wagon

"I found some," she said to Lilit, spreading another cloth across the Flame's forehead. The Flame let out a long sigh of relief.

Will rode up toward Killien, feeling almost euphoric but trying to school his expression into something less intense.

Lukas rode next to the Torch, bent over a book Killien held. The Torch watched Will, disapproving. With a quick word to Lukas, he shut the book and handed it to the slave. Lukas gave him a nod and glanced back at Will. Whatever he muttered as he rode away made Killien laugh.

When Will reached the Torch, the man glanced back at Lilit's wagon. "Lilit does *not* like foreigners, and she will *not* be pleased if she finds you loitering around her wagon. You don't want to cross that woman, Will. Stay away from her."

Will's buoyant mood deflated. At least Lilit's hostility of foreigners didn't extend to her slaves. "Is she alright? She seems...uncomfortable."

"The healers assure me everything is as expected." The wagon hit a bump and Lilit snapped at the driver. Killien grimaced. "She wanted to stay in Porreen until the child was born."

Will couldn't blame her for that. "Does no one stay behind?"

"Not this year. With the reports of the frost goblins. I couldn't let her come north with only a small guard. She was...not pleased with that decision." Lilit's voice rang out behind them again, scathing. Killien winced. "She's usually not so..."

Lukas had fallen in close behind them, the book spread across his saddle again. A bit behind him Sini talked to Rett, enthusiastically waving her hands while Rett still looked anxiously at the green stone he held.

"Have you been enjoying my books?" Killien changed the subject.

Will nodded. "I read the account of your father yesterday. He sounded like a fascinating man."

"My father led the Morrow with honesty and strength. He said that fear could punish and rule, but never lead."

Will felt a reluctant approval of the sentiment.

Killien didn't continue right away, but his hands tightened on the reins. "What you read is the official version of his death. The Torch of the Panos had refused my father's help several times. But other nearby clans had begun to mend their differences. My father had a way of making people... see each other. Clans who had been enemies for generations were trying a tentative peace.

"Suddenly the Panos wanted help, said they wanted peace. But I think the truth is that my father was uniting their enemies." Killien stared ahead, unseeing, at the serpent's wake that wound ahead of them on the Sweep. "Two reliable witnesses say there was no fighting the night my father died. There would have been no stray arrows. And when he died, all the old feuds were revived."

Killien rode with an unnatural stillness.

Cautiously, Will opened himself up to Killien. A hollow, worn out grief laced with a savage need for vengeance filled his chest. The anguish and anger at his own father's death rose up.

Yes, emotions had resonance.

A tightening in Will's chest shoved the words out without him meaning to. "My father was killed when I was eleven."

Killien turned toward him and Will felt a glimmer of sympathy from the man. He shoved the emotions out of his chest.

"He was murdered." *By one of your wayfarers.* "A man broke into our house…" Will rubbed his scarred palms together. "I could do nothing."

Killien's eyes focused on some unseen point. "You seem like a man of peace, Will. But if you could find the man responsible, what would you do?"

The pressure in Will's chest climbed up into his throat, threatening to spill out. Killien shifted to watch him closely. "I ask myself that often lately…and I never have an answer."

Killien's face was stony. "I do."

They rode for a long stretch in silence while Will battled the anger that filled his chest. Had Killien sent Vahe twenty years ago?

He glanced at Killien. "How long have you been Torch?"

"Seventeen years."

Not Killien then. His father.

Not that it mattered. Killien would have, if he'd been Torch then. Lukas's grey presence behind him felt like a dagger cutting into the afternoon. Spread out behind them, slaves peppered the caravan. So many lives stolen and broken.

"I would like to continue my father's work to unite the clans. But I've become convinced the only thing that will work is a common enemy. I need an attacking army to destroy." He turned to Will, his eyes brighter than they should be.

Will shook his head slowly. "I don't know of any disposable ones."

The Torch turned back toward the grasses with a fierce smile. "A disposable army. That's exactly what I need. With that I could unify the Sweep. I could solve the world's problems."

"Or you could raze it to the ground."

Killien let out a boyish laugh. "No Will, for that, I'd need a dragon."

"I hope you're not offended," Will said, forcing a lightness into his words that he didn't feel, "that I don't share your enthusiasm for the disposable army or the dragon."

Killien grinned at him. "I never expected you to, storyman." The smile slid off his face. "But the Roven need a way to see that they have more in common than they think. And there's nothing more effective than fear to make people see the truth."

Will hesitated before asking, "What happened to your father's words that fear could punish and rule, but never lead?"

"You have to rule them before you can lead, Will."

FIFTEEN

It was days before he spoke to Ilsa again.

Over the next three days Killien summoned him only twice for short discussions about things Will had written. Both times he'd been surprised to find he left thinking better of the Torch than when he'd arrived. Almost worse was how much Will enjoyed the conversations himself. A large part of him hated Killien more each time he saw a grey slave's tunic. But a newer, smaller part of him had formed a firm respect for the man who seemed so unlike the other Roven. He was endlessly interested in other lands and their people, he treated Will with simple friendship, and as far as Will could tell, treated his slaves better than many men treated their own families.

But both times he'd been near Killien, Lilit's wagon had been surrounded by people and he'd had no chance to even see Ilsa.

The days fell into a blur of pale green grasslands. The wind blew constantly out of the northwest. Sometimes a mild breeze, sometimes so fierce it tore away anything not tied down. On warm afternoons, the clouds piled up and rolled across the Sweep with sheets of rain, plunging it into darkness and thunder. And with every day his frustration at not making progress with Ilsa grew. The Morrow would reach their rifts in a week, and if Killien decided he had no more use of a storyman, any chance to talk to Ilsa might be at an end.

To pass the time, Will continued working his way through the books in the red bag and writing out stories for Killien. Whenever he could, he snuck a glance into Lukas's grey bag, but only one book was interesting. Will had enough chances to read *Methods of Transference* to fully understand compulsion stones.

Killien and Lukas were very focused on the idea of transferring emotions or thoughts into someone. Which was troubling.

Most days he spent a portion of the time with Killien, talking about history or stories. Will often found the Torch discussing some book or another with Lukas, but Will's appearance always prompted the slave to close the book and fall back. Although Will was always answering Killien's summons, Lukas didn't bother to hide his feelings about the interruptions.

Most nights Will ate with the Torch. The man continued to request stories from Queensland, and Will felt that each night was spent downplaying his knowledge of Queensland while still satisfying Killien's curiosity. Hal was always there, a constantly friendly face who worked in questions about dwarves whenever he could. Sora joined them if she wasn't out scouting. Lilit too, a scowling, hateful addition to the group no matter how much Will tried to entertain her. But, shadowing Lilit, came Ilsa, who never made eye contact, but seemed to listen with rapt attention. Will found himself tailoring each story to his sister, pleasing Killien falling into a secondary goal.

Killien's other slaves were always close by, but never actually with the group. Lukas, Sini, and Rett sat together a little removed, but usually listening to any story Will told. Lukas watched him with an unrelenting coldness, but Sini and Rett watched curiously.

The nights Will didn't eat with Killien, he sat with Rass in the back of a wagon and let her prattle on about the little creatures she'd seen that day. Each night it got easier to fall asleep on the hard wagon, each morning he rose less sore and less enthusiastic about the walk that was about to begin. Every other day they reached a large cistern dug deep into the ground and covered with a thick metal lid. Will stood on the edge of the first one, looking down into the dark, still water, feeling cool air seep out from it. The well looked endless and the water poured into his canteen tasted stale.

It was the evening of the sixth day before Will caught sight of Ilsa in the crowd near the cistern. He wove his way through the crowd until he reached her.

She met his eye for only a moment before looking away. "I can't talk to you."

"I won't move my lips," he said through a stiff jaw, falling in beside her and looking forward stoically.

She let out a little laugh, then pressed her lips into a straight line again. "You don't have anything to hold water," she pointed out.

Which was true. He searched for some reason he could give her for being there. He wanted to ask her how her life had been. If she remembered her home or their parents. If she remembered him.

He wanted a way to pour all his memories into her mind and show her the childhood she'd lost. A way to figure out how she'd survived here, how hard it had been, who she'd turned into. But those were hardly conversation starters.

Tossing out the first hundred things he thought of to say, he managed, "I just need your help."

Ilsa shook her head, keeping her eyes forward. "If Lilit hears of me talking to you," she whispered, "she'll be furious. She hates you."

True. Will glanced around. "That's what I need help with. Is there any sort of story she would like? Anything that might make her think better of me? Killien keeps asking for things from foreign lands, and with each one, I swear the Flame hates me more."

"She does."

Ilsa was shorter than him by a hand, and she glanced up at him. Being close to her was such a strange combination of familiarity and awkwardness. Such familiar features set in a face he didn't quite recognize. What sort of stories would *she* like to hear?

"Pick something with a powerful woman," Ilsa said. "One who is the driving force of the story."

Will smiled. "That I can do."

"Now go away before you get us both in trouble."

He paused, trying to think of some reason to stay. An idea occurred to him. "Can Lilit read?"

She nodded. "Now leave. Please, Will."

At the sound of his name, his breath caught. For the briefest moment he thought maybe it signified that she knew him. But there was nothing in her face beyond a worry they'd be noticed.

His mother had always teased him that he couldn't resist his baby sister. He'd retrieve anything for her that she couldn't reach, carry her on his back whenever she asked, act out ridiculous stories just to make her laugh. It didn't matter that Ilsa had no idea who he was today. For him, nothing had changed.

He gave her a slight nod and pulled himself away. At least now he had an idea of how to ingratiate himself to Lilit.

When he got back to the book wagon, he pulled out some fresh paper and set to writing out a story with the most powerful woman he could think of. Sable's story was epic enough in proportions to need a whole book, but certain episodes of her life were excellent tales themselves.

He wrote until darkness hid the page, then rose with the sun to finish. By the time the caravan began moving, he had left Shadow hitched to the wagon and woven toward Lilit's wagon.

He reached the side of it and heard a thunk from the back. Moving quickly before any of the nearby rangers noticed him, he ducked around the corner.

"Ilsa," he whispered, walking along with the wagon.

But it wasn't Ilsa sitting there, shifting her weight uncomfortably.

Lilit's eyes flashed in recognition and her lips curled into a sneer. "What do you want with my girl, fett?"

"I don't…" Will almost stumbled. He tried to give her a disarming smile, but it probably looked panicked. He glanced into the wagon, but Ilsa wasn't there. "I have something for you, actually. I thought you might be bored so I wrote down a story for you about a woman named Sable who began with nothing and ended up essentially ruling the world."

Lilit's expression didn't soften and Will held the papers out to her. She glared for a moment before pulling them out of his hand and flicking them to the ground. They fanned out in front of the next wagon, smashed into the grass by the horses' hooves.

Will stared at the trampled pages disappearing under the wagon.

"My husband may see you as some exotic pet," she said, her voice cold, "but I know you're nothing but a field roach slinking in through a crack, spreading disease and filth."

Will opened his mouth to object, but she leaned forward and fixed him with a look of utter hatred. "If you come near my wagon again, Killien will lose his pet."

Will pulled back. So much for ingratiating himself to her. Will gave her a quick bow and turned away. He cast one last glance around, looking for Ilsa, but all he saw was a page of his story fluttering further behind them under the feet of the caravan. Before Lilit could call for any of the rangers, he hurried around the next wagon and headed back toward the books.

———————•—•———————

The next few days were torturously uneventful. Ilsa stayed at Lilit's side, which was now firmly off limits. Will had failed to find Ilsa near the cisterns when the clans stopped. He'd watched during the days to see if she'd leave the wagon, but he could not catch her alone.

On top of that, some sort of crisis involving an illness among the sheep kept Hal busy and ill-tempered, and Sora spent the days ranging.

The third such morning, he rode along the eastern edge of the caravan, getting some relief from the fact that there were no Roven between him and the Scale Mountains. The flatbread that was breakfast every morning, somehow managed to be both salty and bland at the same time. He ate it mindlessly, bracing himself for another day alone.

A horse trotted up behind him and he almost smiled.

"You missed me, didn't you?" he asked.

Sora pulled her horse up between him and the Scales. "No."

"Good." He felt something loosen inside him. "I didn't miss you either." He took a bite of flatbread.

She rode beside him calmly with her usual distant expression and he studied her out of the corner of his eye.

"Please tell me you're here to either bring me to Killien for a thought-provoking conversation," he said, "or to talk to me yourself. I'll even be happy if you're just here to tell me all the things you don't like about me."

This earned him the hint of a smile. "Killien is busy planning scouting routes with the rangers."

"You're a ranger," he pointed out.

Her leathers were the same as always, plain and well-worn. The morning was as sunny as every spring morning on the Sweep and already warm enough that her arms were bare. The band around her arm caught his eye again, the scar below it white in the morning light.

"Wait…" He took in her leathers and the assorted weapons she wore, "you are a ranger, aren't you?"

Sora shot him an exasperated look. "I don't patrol the way they do. Killien trusts me to pick my own route."

"Ahh. You mean he doesn't want to argue with you."

This time, the side of her mouth definitely lifted as she shook her head. "He knows I'll keep my eyes open and go where I need to go."

"I understand." Will nodded. "I don't like to argue with you either."

She broke into a laugh that rolled across him like one of the breezes rippling across the grass.

He stared at her a minute before realizing he was grinning. He rubbed his hand across his mouth to tone it down. Feeling oddly proud of himself, he ripped off a piece of his flatbread and offered it to her. "If Killien's busy, then you must have come here to talk to me."

She shook her head at the bread and fixed him with a calculating look. "You are usually so clever."

He waited for something more. "…thank you?"

"So why are you so fumbling around Ilsa?"

He stiffened. "Are you watching me?"

"Whatever the reason is," she continued, "stop. First of all, it's the most awkward proposition I've ever seen, and it causes me physical pain to see it."

He stared at her in disgust. "I am not propositioning anyone!"

"Second, it doesn't matter whether you're trying to impress Ilsa or get in the good graces of Lilit. Both are such bad ideas that they'll get you killed and poor Ilsa punished."

Will opened his mouth to object, appalled on so many levels he didn't know where to begin.

A cry rang out behind them and they twisted around to see a Roven ranger trotting up the column leading a young man whose hands were bound to his saddle. The prisoner's bright, wiry red hair blazed like a flame over his panicked face. He was all elbows and knees with a thin, patchy beard. He yanked and thrashed futilely against the ropes.

With a hoarse cry, the man tried to fling himself off the horse. He started to topple to the side, his arms twisted up to the saddle horn. Sora turned to ride up beside him, shoving the man back into his saddle and holding his arm. He hurled himself from side to side, sobbing.

The ranger took up a position on the other side and they trotted the man forward. He struggled against them for a few paces before his shoulders fell and he curled forward, the sound of sobs coming muffled from his chest.

Will followed Sora, riding with her back straight, her grip on the man's arm never wavering. They slowed when they reached the front of the clan and the ranger sent a child scurrying off to find the Torch.

Killien rode out of the crowd with Lukas flanking him and stopped, letting the rest of the clan pass them by.

"We've found the man who's been spying for the Sunn, Torch," the ranger announced, holding out a small roll of paper. "Arsen, son of Oshin. He was counting the herds. The writing matches the pages we found hidden in the spring shipment of wool for the Sunn."

Arsen yanked his thin arms against the hands holding him.

The ranger untied Arsen from the saddle and dragged him roughly to the ground. He tried to pull away, but Sora climbed down and held him as Killien dismounted. The Torch walked up to the prisoner until he stood only inches from him.

"I've done nothing wrong!" Arsen tried to pull back, but they held him in place.

Will stayed on Shadow, a few paces away.

"Nothing?" Killien's voice was quiet, and the man quailed. "We've intercepted two letters this winter being sent to the Sunn Clan, detailing the Morrow's stores and herds. The one in the wool shipment numbered our rangers. And our warriors."

Arsen's face turned a sickly white. Hal had arrived with a handful of rangers, spreading out in a circle around them. All of their faces were dark. Will barely breathed.

"No, Torch!" Arsen sputtered "I have a cousin in the Sunn Clan, his mother was captured when we were young. We send letters to each other. Just letters. He's a wool merchant, and he thinks that if the clans traded more—"

"You spied for the Sunn." Killien's face was a mask of fury.

"No! We just talked about the two clans, the things we could trade—"

"Why does a wool merchant need to know the number of our rangers? Of our warriors?"

Arsen said nothing, his eyes wide in terror.

"The Sunn have a dragon, and more stonesteeps than the rest of the Sweep put together. They force us to give them our crops, our wool, and our gold. They have no desire to trade with us." Killien set one finger on the man's chest and Arsen jerked back. "You betrayed the clan. You betrayed me."

The words cut through the morning like a slice of icy winter air. Will's hand smashed the flatbread into a lump.

Arsen's mouth opened and closed like a fish, his body quavering and he sank down to his knees. "I didn't...I don't..." His voice fell to a hoarse whisper. "Mercy, Torch!"

Killien stepped back and straightened. He took a long breath and let it out, his face settling into impassivity. His gaze looked through the man and his judgment cut across the Sweep, flat and empty. "Arsen son of Oshin is found to be an enemy of the Morrow Clan."

Arsen's body crumpled forward until he hung from the arms of Sora and the ranger. He began to weep, a bubbling, terrified sound and Will clenched the wad of food tighter in his hand. Desperate for the man, Will looked at Hal, but his face was stony. Every Roven stood severely silent, judgment against the man already cast.

Will opened up toward Killien, looking for any hesitation or pause. A wave of adamant resolve from Killien filled his chest. It was mirrored from the Roven around him.

The man's cries had quieted. Killien, without looking at him again, nodded to the ranger.

Another ranger stepped forward with a small knife and sliced two braids out of Arsen's beard, pulling off the silver beads and letting the hair fall to the ground.

When he pulled a silver ring off Arsen's hand, Lukas dismounted and took it. He tilted it in the sunlight, and a watery blue stone glinted. Lukas murmured something to Killien, and at the Torch's approving nod, slipped it into his pocket.

Killien looked past the man. "Take him to the Scales. Don't let his blood fall on the grasses."

Sora dropped the man's arm with grim disapproval. She mounted her horse and rode back into the clan, her back resolutely turned to Killien. Another ranger took her place and they lifted the traitor to his feet. This time he didn't resist as they pushed him away down the caravan.

Will watched them go, straining to see where they took him until they were out of sight behind other Roven. His breakfast sat in his stomach like a stone.

Hours later, when the shadow of the caravan stretched far to the east, Will caught sight of Sora riding out of the column. She didn't say anything, just fell in beside him, her face set in a darker expression than normal.

"What will happen to the man Killien sentenced?" Will asked, his voice low.

She looked straight forward not answering for so long Will began to doubt she would.

"No one who betrays the clan is allowed to live." Her words held no emotion. "The Morrow won't taint the Sweep with the blood of a traitor, though. If one is found while the clan is in Porreen, they're drowned in the sea so their spirit is pulled away with the next tide. Here, they'll have taken him to the Scales to be burned."

"Already?" His stomach sank at the idea of the terrified man. "There's no inquiry? No trial?" One of the southern dukes had been accused of treason not long after Will had become a Keeper. The investigation process had been so extensive Alaric had brought Will to the capital to help with the questioning and recording. It had taken months. In the end the duke had been found guilty of theft, but not treason, and imprisoned.

"You saw the trial."

"But…what if he was telling the truth?"

Sora turned to him, her face unreadable. "Killien didn't believe him, and Killien is the only one that matters. Did you think the Morrow Clan tamer than others?"

The question hung in the air.

Yes, he did. When had that started? Will closed his eyes, shutting out the endless view of the Roven walking next to him, spinning his ring as his thoughts swirled. It had changed somewhere among the books and the conversation and the meals. Somewhere in the midst of discussions with Killien, the Roven had lost their fierceness in his mind.

"You come here from…" Sora paused. "Wherever you come from and think the Roven are like you. You don't know what it is like to live as one. You didn't grow up with the fear of raids and battles and constant war. Don't think that because a few Roven speak to you, that they are like you. No one here is like you. No one here wants to be."

SIXTEEN

On the tenth day, from the top of a high rise, a jagged, white mountaintop rose from the horizon in the north. Within hours a handful could be seen, pristinely snowy against the sky. Will strained to see the mountains as they moved up each rise, and watched until they were out of sight as they dropped into each low place, his eyes aching for something to look at besides the grass.

The appearance of the Hoarfrost Range was the only sign that he wasn't trapped in some eternal stagnation. If they were nearing the northern edge of the Sweep, they should be at the rifts within a couple of days, and he'd made no more progress with Ilsa than to exchange quick smiles with her once through a crowd.

He'd always planned to leave the clan when they reached the rifts, but maybe he needed to convince Killien to let him stay. Maybe in the rhythm of normal life he could find more time to spend with her.

Rass found him walking beside Shadow, still stretching out the aches from sleeping on the wagon. The morning was chilly enough that Will had put on a cloak, but Rass wore the same little greyish slave shift as always, her bare feet traipsing over the grass as though it was nothing.

"Why doesn't anyone take care of you?" The words came out harsher than he'd meant them to.

Rass looked at him in surprise. "I take care of myself. And the grass helps, of course."

"Yes, the grass." He ran his hand over his mouth to block all the things that wanted to come out. "Aren't you cold?"

"No," she said carelessly. "Yesterday was so warm I can still feel it."

"I wish I could keep track of yesterday's heat." He handed her the piece of flatbread he'd been saving.

"Can't you?" She took it and squinted up at him. "Not even with your magic?"

"What?" he asked too quickly.

"That magic that you use. Like when I first met you."

His denial stuck in his throat. "What?" he managed again.

She gave him a little exasperated look. "At the festival you did something so the Roven didn't pay attention to you. The magic swirled around you like a sparkly mist."

Will's heart felt like it was being squeezed by her tiny little hands. He opened up toward her, looking for some sense of suspicion, but she was just as cheery and curious as ever. He gathered some energy from the grass reflexively, without any clear plan of what to do with it.

Her eyes widened and her gaze flickered at the air around him.

"You're doing it again," she whispered.

He stopped, staring down at her, his heart pounding against his ribs like it was the wrong size for his chest. He let the energy go, letting it seep out of him and back into the world unused.

Rass glanced around with a disappointed sigh.

"You *saw* that? With your eyes?"

She looked at him, confused. "What other way is there to see?"

There was magic that was visible. Techniques where the *vitalle* glowed as it moved. But he'd just been gathering energy. No one could see that. The Keepers talked about seeing *vitalle,* but usually it wasn't actual sight. It was a sense—like locating something with sound. Another Keeper could have sensed that he was drawing more energy into himself, but he'd never heard of anyone who could actually see it.

A dozen thoughts chased each other around Will's mind.

She could reveal him to the Morrow.

Could she manipulate the energy?

Had she told anyone?

She could *see* it!

His fear kept being shoved aside by excitement. Her light hair, her blue eyes—could she be from Queensland? She didn't look like it. With her wide eyes and her angular face, she looked foreign, even for a foreigner. Could she still be trained as a Keeper, though? She was so young to have any powers.

"Where are you from, Rass?"

She gave a little sigh and looked at him exasperatedly. "The grass."

Will glanced around. The nearest Roven drove wagons and talked to each other, their voices muffled by the creaks of the wheels.

"Do you see magic often?"

Rass shrugged. "The Morrow put it on their ugly dirt buildings. And they wear it on things like rings. They put little bits of it onto their clothes, but that's faded and weak. They don't really have any strong magic." She cocked her head and looked up at Will with her huge eyes the same bright blue as the sky. "I think you might, though."

With a smile she started humming, hopping from one foot to the next.

Will considered her for a long moment, his fingers moving to his ring, spinning it slowly. "Have you told any Roven that I have magic?"

"I don't talk to the Roven."

"Not ever?"

"They don't like me."

They walked along for a few breaths in silence. "Thank you. For not telling them."

She looked at him curiously. "Where did you learn to do magic?"

"At my home. There are other people there who can, and they taught me."

"Is there anyone there like me?

Will shook his head. "Me and a bunch of older men. But we've been looking for someone like you for a very long time."

"Are you as good at magic as you are at telling stories?"

"Not really."

"Why not?"

Will thought back to Keeper Gerone's constant prodding. "My teacher thought I had a motivation problem."

"Stories are a good thing to be good at," she assured him.

"Rass, can you do anything with magic?"

She opened her mouth to answer. Before she could say anything her brow dove down into a frown. "The mean lady is coming."

Sora rode down the caravan toward them and Rass scampered off into the grass. Will watched the little slave girl go with a strange mixture of worry and fondness. She looked stronger. Her legs and arms had lost some of their gauntness. But as she left, it felt like she pulled something away with her, leaving him feeling more vulnerable.

Will mounted Shadow as Sora came up to him.

They'd fallen into a pattern of sorts. Usually not long after the caravan had started, while the duskiness of dawn still spread across the never-ending grass, she would come by and either bring him to Killien, or ride beside him. If she hadn't arrived by the time the sun was completely above the Scales, Will knew she wouldn't come. Some days she would answer questions about the Roven, but he'd given up asking her any personal questions days ago. Those were met with biting sarcasm.

It was the days where every question was met with a silent scowl that he didn't know what to do with. Because on those days she would ride beside him for hours barely speaking, showing no interest in him, but not leaving.

He'd asked if she was on some sort of guard duty, sent by Killien to keep track of him, but she only responded with a scathing remark about not being Killien's guard dog. On those days Will pulled out a book and read, letting her stew in silence and trying not to think about her too much.

But during the days she was gone Will found himself watching for her, and this morning he felt a surprising amount of pleasure as she rode up.

"Good morning," he offered, testing the waters.

Her face was grave and she nodded absently to him. "Killien wants you."

Will motioned for her to lead the way. "Did you find anything interesting out ranging?"

A flicker of something distasteful crossed her face, but she didn't answer.

"Are you still looking for signs of frost goblins?" The urgency of the search had faded from his mind. It had been days since he'd heard Killien mention it, and while the Roven still built fires around the edges of the caravan at night, most of them seemed to be out of habit, not fear.

"No," she answered dryly. "We thought we'd just stop looking and pretend we'd never heard reports of them."

"I just...no one seems worried about them anymore."

"Anyone intelligent is."

Will looked out over the grasslands. "Have you found any?"

Sora gave a single nod.

"How many?"

"Three."

Will stared at her. "Were you alone? Are you alri—?"

"I don't want to talk about it," she interrupted his fumbling questions.

Will closed his mouth and looked around the Sweep, feeling suddenly exposed on the wide open grass. "Should I be worried?"

Sora gave a short laugh. "We should all be worried."

She didn't elaborate, and Will didn't push. He watched Lilit's wagon as they passed near it, and while he could see movement within, the interior was too shadowed to see if it was Ilsa.

When Killien came into view, Will turned to Sora. "How come you stay with the Morrow?" He pitched his voice low so only she could hear.

Sora started and looked at him as though she'd forgotten he was there. Her eyes flickered away from him and rested on the Torch, her face unreadable. "Killien pays me well."

Surprisingly, he couldn't sense any sarcasm in her answer. "That's very mercenary of you. But wouldn't your own people benefit from your skills?"

"My people have enough hunters."

"So, what?" The irritation from her terse answers rose to the surface. "You're here because you're not special enough among your own tribe?"

Sora let out a harsh laugh and turned her horse away. "That was never the problem."

He watched her ride off, wondering why he'd bothered to ask.

Turning back toward Killien, he tried to push her out of his mind. The man had been growing more irritable lately. He'd stayed distantly polite to Will, spending a few minutes questioning him about a Baylonian duke Will had written about. But he'd been short with the rangers who reported to him and snapped at Lukas for riding too close. Sini and Rett had taken to riding a little farther back.

Today, though, when he approached, the Torch was in an animated discussion with Lukas, both their faces bright as Killien clapped the slave on the back, and Lukas closed up a book. Even making eye contact with Will didn't totally dampen Lukas's spirits, and he fell away from the Torch, leaving room for Will to approach.

Killien greeted Will with an enthusiasm that was almost overwhelming. "Will! I don't feel like I've properly thanked you for all the writing you've done for me on this trip. Thank the black queen you showed up in Porreen when you did."

Will gave him a bow, his fist pressed to his chest. "It's been my pleasure. I should thank you for the books you've shared."

Killien waved off his thanks. "No, you deserve a gift. Tell me, what payment do you want? A book?" He motioned to Will's hand. "Another gold ring?"

Something glinted blue on one of Killien's fingers—the ring they'd taken from the traitor sat between Killien's other rings, and the light from the blue burning stone in it was visible even in the sunshine. He could see *vitalle* in several of his rings, actually. Maybe Killien's actually held magic.

Will shook his head and opened up to the Torch. A wide undercurrent of satisfaction and pleasure flowed into Will. Whatever Killien was happy about, it was strong.

"There must be something you'd like from the Morrow."

Yes. Will kept his eyes away from Lilit's wagon.

"There is one thing." Will paused. "Would you consider selling me one of your slaves?"

Killien raised an eyebrow. "I didn't take you for a slaveholder."

Will forced a smile. "We all have our secrets."

Killien let out a short laugh. "We do. But you haven't done nearly enough writing for me to earn a slave." He looked calculatingly at Will. "It would take three month's wages for most Roven to buy a slave, and that only gets them a mediocre one." He paused. "Although if you're talking about that tiny girl you seem so fond of, we could come up with a less expensive agreement."

Killien knew about Rass?

Will's pulse quickened.

It wasn't freeing Ilsa like he needed to do, but freeing Rass was a good first step. "Her name is Rass." He tried to keep the disgust out of his voice at the next question. "How much would she cost?"

Killien rubbed his thumb across his lips, watching Will closely. "Do you read ancient runes? I have some I need translated, and that would be worth quite a bit to me."

You've got the wrong Keeper for that. "I'm familiar with some runes, but I'm not an expert."

Killien considered this answer. "Where did you learn them?"

"When I was twelve, I moved to a place with a library." The first time he'd stepped into the library at the Keepers Stronghold, it had taken his breath away. Floor after floor of books. "The man who kept the books had some with ancient runes"—which Gerone had constantly and unsuccessfully tried to get Will interested in—"which he loved, but I was never terribly good at."

"How big was the library?"

"To my eyes, it was enormous." He glanced at Killien. "You won't like this, but the largest library I ever saw was the royal library in Queenstown."

Killien's brow darkened. "How big is it?"

"The main room is as big as the Square in Porreen."

The Torch's eyebrows rose.

"And there are a dozen smaller rooms off of it, all filled with books."

Killien was silent for a long moment. "That would be something to see."

"You should come there with me, we'll take a trip into Queensland." Will motioned to the notch in the Scales that was almost next to them. "It's only two or three days past Kollman Pass."

The Torch laughed. "Even a library that big isn't a strong enough draw."

"Is there a particular reason you hate Queensland more than other countries?" Will tried to keep his tone merely curious, while he focused on Killien's emotions. "I've never totally understood the Roven's animosity."

"Queensland drove us out of our homeland and forced us to live on the Sweep."

He chose his next words as carefully as possible. "That happened a very long time ago. When you talk about Queensland, the animosity feels…fresher."

A jab of irritation lanced across Killien's satisfaction, and he studied Will for several heartbeats.

"If that was too personal of a question," Will said, "I apologize."

"It's hardly a secret. You know that the warriors of the Morrow went with Mallon when he attacked Queensland?"

"I heard a story about it my first night in Porreen. I remember there was a giant."

"Yervant tells the story every year because their company only lost one battle during the entire war. And they were winning that one too, until a Keeper showed up."

"How many men did the Morrow lose?"

"Many." A sharp grief cut into Killien's emotions. "Among them my uncle, Andro, who had been my closest advisor, and my cousin Adaom, who was like a brother to me." Killien turned a hard gaze toward the Scales. "They were the only family I had left. And a Keeper burned them alive."

Killien's grief and vengeance flowed through Will's chest and he almost shoved them out. But the emotions were so familiar, he let them stay, mirroring his own losses, resonating in the deepest part of himself.

"Adaom was Lilit's older brother. She idolized him. It's why she hates you so much." Killien looked slightly apologetic. "And why she always will. You look too much like you're from

Queensland for her to see anything else."

They rode in silence until Will felt Killien's emotions settle. That at least explained Lilit's animosity. And why a peace offering of a story wouldn't be nearly enough. Maybe nothing would be enough. How would he ever get Ilsa away from her?

Needing something else to think about, Will asked. "Why did Mallon attack? To Queensland it seemed unprovoked. Did they do something I'm unaware of?"

Killien looked at him in surprise. "Because it was personal." At Will's blank look, he added, "Mallon was from Queensland."

SEVENTEEN

Will's mouth dropped open. "What?"

Killien's gaze turned piercing and he nodded slowly. "Mallon came to the Sweep as a child, ten years before my father was Torch. His father had debts, and to pay them, the duke sold his children to the Sweep."

Will stared at him, stunned. "Sold? They don't do that in Queensland. It's unlawful to sell slaves."

Killien let out a laugh. "And so you think it doesn't happen? Mallon was sold to the Morrow, in fact, when my grandfather was Torch. He was with us for two years and already training to be a stonesteep. Already promising to be stronger than any we'd seen." His face sobered. "Before Kachig the Bloodless took him from us."

Mallon was from Queensland?

"You thought Mallon was Roven?" Killien asked.

Will nodded. "Everyone does."

"He had black hair," the Torch pointed out.

"That does seem like a clue right now," Will admitted. "Although until I came to the Sweep, I didn't know *every* Roven had red hair. I just thought a lot of you did. I've never heard from anyone that Mallon wasn't Roven."

An idea snagged in Will's mind. "How long ago did Mallon come to the Sweep?"

"Fifty years ago."

Will's grip tightened on the reins. The fact that there were no Keepers younger than Will wasn't the only gap. Historically Keepers were born every five to ten years. Between Will and Alaric was a twelve year gap, but that length wasn't unheard of. The bigger question had always been that between Alaric and Mikal, who was seventy-one, the gap was over twenty-five years. The space between them was generally thought to have belonged to at least two Keepers who, it was assumed, had died during childhood, before their abilities were awakened. But if Mallon was born fifty-some years ago, and came from Queensland, with powers like he had—he would fit in that gap.

Mallon should have been a Keeper.

The thought struck an odd note. Keeper Mallon, puttering around the Stronghold with the other old men, browsing the library, wearing a black robe.

It was too far-fetched. What were the chances that the one child of his time who should've ended up a Keeper had been enslaved to the Roven?

Still, the Keepers hadn't known of any children born during that time with abilities.

Until now.

"Someone in Queensland knows," Killien scoffed. "The people in power know. The Queen. The Keepers."

Will clenched his teeth down on the answer that he was positive they didn't.

"They're just keeping it quiet," the Torch continued. "They wouldn't want their people to know it was one of their own trying to kill them. Better to blame the nomads, right?"

"He came with an army of Roven."

"We didn't have a choice," Killien objected. "Mallon gathered the clan Torches together and told them he was going to conquer Queensland and required our warriors. He said if we helped, he'd give us some of the land."

"Did anyone refuse?"

Killien looked at him incredulously. "You understand what he was capable of. No one refused who valued their lives or the lives of their clans. We were commanded to gain the support of our people and send all our troops."

"All of them?"

Killien nodded, his face dark. "Every man between fifteen and sixty. And to send weekly shipments of food and supplies."

Will looked away from Killien, letting his eyes run over the Scales. An uncomfortable level of sympathy for Killien vied with an illogical guilt that Mallon was from Queensland. Will shifted his cloak, pulling more of it around himself to block out the little fingers of cool morning air wriggling in through the gaps.

A half-dozen rangers appeared over a rise to the east and Killien studied them for a moment. "I'll send Lukas with the runes I'd like you to translate," he said. "When we reach the rifts, we'll discuss the little slave girl again."

Will took it as a dismissal and left, conflicting thoughts about the Roven and Killien and Mallon butting against each other in his mind. And the idea of buying Rass's freedom was bitter-sweet. Certainly he'd love to take her away from the Roven, but she was small enough he could have snuck her out. It was Ilsa he needed to get to.

When he reached the book wagon, he found Rett driving it. Will gave the slave a friendly nod and the man nodded back. There was a general sadness about him this morning.

"Looks like a big storm is coming." Will nodded toward the clouds piling up on the horizon.

"I don't like thunder." Rett kept his attention forward. Ahead of them was another wagon, loaded with baskets and sacks. And ahead of that one, another. The clan moved forward doggedly, each person and animal and wagon following the one ahead of it with no real need for thought. But Rett concentrated anyway, his hands gentle on the reins, his eyes determined and sad. Next to him sat his lumpy bag of heatstones.

Will couldn't quite figure out the man. He was older than Will by a few years, and his mind didn't seem slow as much as…distracted. As though there was too much going on and the simplest tasks required enormous concentration.

"I'm Will."

Rett glanced toward him. "I know."

"You drive the wagon well, Rett. Some of the others aren't careful about what they're doing."

Rett shook his head disapprovingly. "The Torch's books are very important."

Will agreed, and when Rett kept his focus forward, he rode around to the back of the wagon, and dismounted. Walking behind it, he moved the oilcloth out of the way and opened the red bag of his books. He pulled several out, laying them across the back of the wagon. He'd already read most of them. The only two left were genealogies, and he couldn't quite bring himself to commit the rest of the day to reading something that boring. Stuffing them all back in the bag, Will tugged at the leather straps cinching the bag shut.

The wagon creaked over the uneven ground and the bag and the boxes shifted haphazardly, making him feel slightly off balance. Will glanced up at Rett, but the man was facing forward, his shoulders slumped. He pushed the oilcloth farther to the side and opened the bag with Lukas's books, slipping out *Methods of Transference* again, even if there was nothing left to learn from it.

A rumble of thunder came from the storm clouds and Will flipped the book closed. He shoved it back into Lukas's bag and put it back where it belonged.

He was setting his own bag back in its place when the wagon wheel nearest him slammed into a hole and the entire wagon jarred to the side. Rett's bag of heatstones tumbled to the side. The wagon jolted forward again and the box in front of Will slid, its edge tipping off the back of the wagon.

Will grabbed for the box, staggering forward with the wagon hearing the thunks of dozens of heatstones falling next to Rett. Will shoved at the box, trying to push it back into place, but his own bag of books toppled down into the space where the box belonged.

Shoving his shoulder against the box, Will stretched around it with his other hand, grabbing a handful of the red bag and yanking it out of the way. He'd almost cleared it when the bag jerked to a stop, the leather strap snagged on something he couldn't see. With a curse, Will wrenched the bag toward him. The wood cracked and the bag slid clear. With a shove, he pushed the box into its place.

A rumble of thunder rolled from the dark clouds piling up to the north and Will climbed up on to the wagon to see what he'd broken. In the front of the wagon, Rett was focused on picking heatstones up and tucking them back into his bag.

A jagged piece of wood was caught in the straps of the red bag, and behind the box, one of the boards of the wagon bed had split, leaving a gap two fingers wide in the bottom of the wagon. He grabbed the broken sliver of wood and stretched around the box to put it back in place. It wouldn't be fixed, exactly, but he couldn't just leave a hole in the bottom of Killien's wagon. Just before he placed the wood in, a flash of blue shimmered from the hole.

Will glanced up at Rett, but he was looking forward. Will leaned farther over the box. There, just visible through the crack was a piece of grey oil cloth.

Why put oilcloth under the books? A bit of it stuck up through the hole and Will tried to stuff it back in. The cloth shifted and he caught a glimpse of blue leather, glimmering with silver letters.

Will's hand clutched the sliver of wood.

It was the book—the one Lukas had bought from Borto behind the wayfarers' wagons.

He pushed the cloth out of the way, the jagged edge of the wood cutting into his finger until he could read the title. *The Gleaning of Souls.*

He pulled the board farther, feeling the wood groan, and leaned over. Just at the edge of the shadow he saw the author.

Kachig the Bloodless.

In the center of the cover, where the silver medallion had been, there was only a darker blue circle of leather, rough and scarred. Will stared at the disfigured cover, confused for a moment before realizing Killien had pulled the metal off the book to keep it safe from frost goblins. Will tested the boards next to the broken one, but nothing moved. The book was well sealed in the base of the wagon.

Thunder rumbled overhead again. The round pile of clouds were surging closer, like some kind of flower that kept blooming, swell after swell of whiteness piling on top of each other. And underneath the whiteness, the Sweep was cast into dark shadows slanted with distant rain.

"The books should be covered," Rett called back to him, worried.

Will let the board fall back into place, then shoved the box of books back on top of it before covering everything with the oilcloth. His fingers itched to pull it all back apart and grab the book. Instead, he climbed down off the wagon and mounted Shadow again.

The reins stung against his hand and he looked down to see a gash in his finger from the wood. Will cast out to the Sweep. The *vitalle* of the grass was no longer little pinpoints of energy, it now covered the ground with thin strands, like humming, shimmering fur.

He found the rough edges of his cut by the tangle of his own *vitalle* crowding around the wound, beginning the long, slow process of healing, which it would work at for days. The sheer amount of energy expended in healing made anything more than small cuts nearly impossible to heal quickly. Funneling the energy from the grass into his finger, he pressed it toward the cut, bolstering the healing, drawing the deepest part of the gash back together, working his way toward the surface until new skin spread across his finger in a slash of paleness.

He rode behind the book wagon for the next several hours, reading and pondering ways to get Kachig's book out of Killien's wagon.

It wasn't Lukas who brought the runes for him to translate around midday, it was Sini.

When she appeared, Rett stood up in the still moving wagon and started to climb down. "Where are you going? I'll go with you."

"No, Rett." She pulled up alongside him, speaking gently. "We'll sit together at dinner. You need to drive the wagon and keep the books safe."

"Oh." He stopped and sat down slowly. "I forgot. Thank you."

She gave him an encouraging nod and once he was seated, rode back toward Will, carrying a roll of paper. Her face lost the serious expression it often carried around Rett and settled into something curious, but cautious as she got closer.

"Is Rett…?" Will began quietly, looking for the right words.

Sini glanced back at the big slave, her face turning pensive. "There was an accident a long time ago. They say he almost died. I don't think he remembers it, but he has trouble remembering a lot of things. He's always distracted by things inside his head."

"Do you take care of him?"

She shrugged. "He doesn't need much care, just reminders sometimes. And he's funny and kind." She brushed a bit of blond hair back behind her ear, nervously. "We like the stories you've been telling at night. Both of us knew the one you told in Porreen, about Tomkin and the dragon."

"Where did you hear it?"

"We're both from Queensland," she answered.

Will tried to ignore the complicated surge of pity and anger that thought evoked, and tried to find something to say.

But she didn't seem to need a response. "How many stories do you know?"

"I could tell you a different one every day until you turned a hundred."

She gave him a dubious look. "There aren't that many stories in the world."

"There are enough stories in the world that each of us could hear a different one every day until we turned a hundred, and we still wouldn't run out."

She considered this, biting her lip. With an almost absent expression she held the rolled papers out towards Will. He took them with thanks.

She lowered her voice and glanced around. "I'm glad you're telling stories from Queensland." With a quick smile, she turned her horse away.

Will watched her go, a convoluted tangle of emotions crowding into him. Killien might give him Rass if he could read these runes, and he'd find a way to free Ilsa, but how was he going to walk away and leave a girl like Sini here? She should be at home with her parents, growing closer to adulthood every day, complaining that they didn't give her enough freedom. Not trapped here with no hope of it. It didn't matter whether she seemed to be treated well or not, she was still a slave. The list of people he wanted to rescue from the Roven kept growing.

He unrolled the papers and his stomach sank for a completely different reason.

He'd been hoping that when Killien said "ancient runes," what he'd really meant was "old fashioned runes." A more decorated version of modern ones. But these runes were old. The deep, original-magic-workers-creating-a-language-to-hold-power old. The Keepers had plenty of books that used them. And all the Keepers could read them. To some extent.

For Will, that extent did not include being able to do more than narrow down their general meaning to a marginally more-narrow meaning.

Will's eyes trailed over the page, sliding past the precisely written, highly complex shapes.

The topmost rune was something watery. Yes. Watery.

Will tilted the paper slightly to the side.

The next was definitely something about death. Except the corner of it was odd.

The third had entirely too many pieces. He pulled it closer, trying to make out the thin lines of extra strokes drawn into the bottom.

Chicken.

It said chicken.

Will let the paper fall back against the saddle.

The translation was "dead water chicken."

That seemed unlikely.

He scrubbed his fingers through his hair, scanning the rest of the page. There were a dozen different runes. Each complex, each nonsensical.

Will closed his eyes.

If Rass's freedom depended on this, she was never going to get away from the Morrow.

<hr />

The day dragged inexorably on. Will returned, time and again to the runes, dissecting them, rearranging them, turning them on their heads. None of it was comprehensible.

The Morrow crept slowly north through the brownish green pelt of the grasslands, the sun moved slowly west through an empty, faded blue sky, and Will made no progress at all with his translations. Which began to tie his gut into a small knot of worry.

Rass appeared briefly, tugging on his foot to bring him down so she could show him the chain of flowers made from stalks and little blooms with greenish-yellow ray-like petals.

"I made it for you," she said, seriously, holding it out toward his head.

Will leaned forward and let her set it on him. When he straightened, she nodded approvingly. Her face was so much less gaunt, her arms less skeletal. She'd lost the hollow sort of look in her eyes.

He reached into his bag and pulled out a wide salt flat and handed it to her. She must have been eating almost nothing before if the little food he was able to share with her was making such a difference. She grinned and took a big bite.

"Do I look kingly?" He lifted his chin and gazed over the grass ahead of them.

She giggled. "Like the King of the Grass." And with that she ran off, stopping occasionally to yank something out of the ground.

Will watched her run, the knot of worry growing. There was no way he was leaving her here.

Ahead of him the peaks grew taller, connecting with each other until the entire northern horizon was blocked by the imposing wall of the Hoarfrost Range. He found himself staring at them more and more often, spinning his ring. His mind avoiding the impossible runes, avoiding thinking about Ilsa and Rass and Sini.

The sun wasn't remotely close to the horizon when the caravan stopped. There didn't seem to be a cistern, and Will was caught between wondering why they'd stopped and if he could come up with a good enough reason to go near Ilsa when he heard the news that Lilit's time had come. There was no reason in the world that would get him close to Ilsa tonight. Will settled down on the back of the book wagon, glad to be able to sit still during the daylight and write for Killien.

The sun had sunk low in the west when Sora rode up next to him. He hadn't seen her since that morning, and her mood had not improved. She sat down beside him on the back of the book wagon with a curt nod. He waited for a minute or two before leaning over and whispering, "Are you mad at me? Or someone else?"

A small smile cracked through her scowl.

"Good." He sat back. "It's nice when you spread your anger out among other people."

This earned him no response at all.

"Have you been doing something more riveting than walking north through grass?"

"Helping Killien." She didn't look toward him, and by the way she said the Torch's name, Will didn't have to wonder who she was angry with.

Will fiddled with the page of the book a moment, waiting for her to continue. She didn't and he let the silence go as long as he could. "Did you finish whatever he needed?"

"Yes." The word came out as almost a hiss, and Will leaned back slightly to be farther from her line of sight.

"Sometimes you're terrifying," he said.

She closed her eyes and let out a tired sort of laugh. When she opened them, her face was weary. The sun was low enough that the air had turned golden, and the copper of Sora's braid caught at the light, reflecting strands of dark red.

"Why don't you go home, Sora?" he asked. "Get out of these infernal grasses. Leave the Morrow to whatever Roven things they want to do, and go do something…anything else?"

She sank over against the wall of the wagon. "Because it's never that simple."

Will couldn't argue with that. "Well then don't go home. Go somewhere else." He paused for a moment. "Come with me when I leave."

She turned to him with an incredulous look. "And go where?"

Will shrugged. "Off the Sweep. There are a lot of interesting countries just over those mountains."

"When is it that you're leaving?" Her face was back to being unreadable.

"Once we reach the rifts, I suppose." Or he freed Ilsa. And Rass. He felt a cold doubt in his stomach at Lukas's warning that Killien already owned him. But a sudden realization struck. "Can you leave?"

"Of course I can." The scowl was back on her face.

"Does the work Killien asks you to do usually make you this mad?"

"No. This was a first."

She stopped talking and Will let the conversation end. The gnaw of doubt that had crept into his stomach was still there, and he tried to push it away.

Several minutes passed before Sora glanced over at him. "You have dead flowers on your head."

Will laughed, pulling off the crown. The dried stalks of the flower chain broke where he touched it, and one of the little blooms, which had curled in on itself into a brownish cage of withered petals, snapped off and rolled down his leg and into the grass.

"I'm King of the Grass." The whole dry chain crumbled and fell.

Her mouth quirked up in a smile. "You should get a better crown."

Will brushed his fingers through his hair, dislodging bits of dead flower. "I should get a better kingdom."

Sora didn't seem inclined to talk any more, so Will went back to flipping through the book, before the last of the daylight trickled away. When it was too dark to see the page, Will flipped the book closed and pointed out that if they didn't find Hal soon, they might not find any dinner. Sora gave a "hmm" that sounded like an agreement and mounted her horse, turning it in to the clan. Will climbed up on Shadow to follow when shouts rang out from somewhere nearby. A rider tore toward them.

It was Ilsa.

"Sora!" she cried. "Killien needs you! The baby has come, but the Flame—she's bleeding and it won't stop. She is losing her strength. The Torch begs you to come!" Her face was drawn, her eyes worried.

Sora's horse danced away from Ilsa's mare. "What does he think I can do?"

"He asks…" Ilsa hesitated, her eyes flashing toward Will for just a breath before facing Sora again, her brow creased with uneasiness. "For your blessing."

Sora's face hardened into stone. "He's a fool."

"She's dying, Sora." Ilsa voice was quiet, pleading.

Sora pressed her eyes shut.

"The Torch begs you."

With a growl torn from somewhere unbearably deep, Sora spurred her horse forward. She and Ilsa raced toward the front of the clan. Shadow, jolted into action by the others, raced after them.

EIGHTEEN

hadow galloped after Sora and Ilsa to a small tent near the front of the caravan.

What did Killien think Sora could do that a healer couldn't?

Ilsa swung off her horse and hurried into the tent. Sora sat still in her saddle gripping the reins.

Killien rushed to her. "Please!" He stood at Sora's knee like a supplicant.

"You know I can't help her," Sora hissed at the Torch.

"She's dying." Killien reached up to clench the bottom of her shirt. "It can't hurt to pray."

He wanted her to pray? Will leaned forward trying to see Sora's face, trying to understand what was happening.

A low, torn moan came from inside the tent and both Killien and Sora flinched. With a curt nod, Sora shoved his hands off her and swung down from her horse.

Fixing the Torch with a look of pure hatred, she whispered, "You and I are finished."

Without waiting for a response, she ducked into the tent.

Killien sank to his knees and dropped his head into his hands. Will sat awkward in the saddle, unable to make sense of either Killien's request or Sora's response.

Another low moan tore through the night and Killien shuddered. Will cast out toward the tent and felt three people's *vitalle* blazing like watchfires. A low, smoldering form lay at their feet.

Lilit had very little time left.

Will waited to see if Sora did anything with *vitalle* in the tent, but nothing happened. He climbed quietly off Shadow. Skirting around Killien, Will drew in some energy from the grass and wrapped it around himself like a cloak, infusing the influence spell with the idea that he was not worth noticing.

Will reached the tent door, and when none of the Roven at the nearby fire objected, he stepped inside. A lantern cast dim light on Sora and Ilsa kneeling next to Lilit's still form. Sini leaned over a basin of red water, washing blood off her arms. Tears traced tracks down her cheeks, and she dashed at them with her shoulder.

He cut off the influence spell, letting it dissolve and Sora gave him a quick, surprised glance.

"The healers gave her mutherswort," Sini whispered to Sora, "but she still bleeds from somewhere deep inside." Her voice broke. "It's too much to stop."

"The child?" Sora asked softly.

"A healthy boy."

All the fury was gone from Sora's face. With her jaw clenched, she shifted the blanket covering Lilit's legs. Beneath them, everything was soaked with blood. "Find some clean blankets," she said firmly to Ilsa, who hurried out of the tent without glancing at Will. "And fresh water," she added to Sini with a tight smile at the girl.

Sini nodded and left.

"What does Lilit need?" Will whispered.

"Strength she doesn't have." Sora gently lay the blankets back down.

Sora sank back, her hand resting on Lilit's stomach. She bowed her head and began whispering words Will couldn't understand. He cast out toward her, waiting for…something.

The words rolled out of her mouth rhythmic and heartfelt.

Killien brought her here to pray?

Will knelt down next to Lilit's head, setting a hand on her damp forehead and casting out. Her *vitalle* lay weak and thin, like tired coals of a dying fire. The little energy she had surged against the tattered edges of a tear deep inside her womb. She was weak enough that the blood flowed through it slowly.

He drew all the energy he could find from the grass beneath them. It wasn't nearly enough. If he took from the grass past the tent, it would leave a difficult to explain, enormous dead spot, and it still might not be enough. Casting out farther, he found the blazing energy of the fire and drew in as much *vitalle* as he could. It poured into him, and he felt the fire growing dim. Someone outside called for more fuel for the flames. Hopefully it would come soon, because this wouldn't be enough.

As gently as he could, he set his hands on the sides of Lilit's head and slowly funneled the energy into her, offering the *vitalle* her body needed to heal itself. Will leaned down near her ear. In a low, calm voice, he began.

"The night the nineteenth Torch of the Morrow Clan was born, the winds of the Sweep blew like a dragon, flattening the grass and driving evil omens before it."

A sound near the door caught his attention. Killien stood there, watching Will sharply, a dangerous glint in his eyes. Sora was still bowed, whispered words pouring out of her in a rhythm like a prayer. Lilit groaned quietly.

"Lilit, Flame of the Morrow," Will continued, pressing more *vitalle* into her, "had fought and bled, until her strength was almost spent."

Slowly the wound drew together. He drew in more from the fire, funneling everything into Lilit's body.

"But the Flame of the Morrow was not like the grass, she did not bend and bow before the wind."

Lilit took in a deeper breath and Killien sank down past to her feet, shrinking back from the horror.

"She reached down into the Sweep," Will continued, "down into the grasses, into where the power of her people lay."

Lilit opened her eyes and a spasm of pain flashed across her face. Sora placed both her hands on the Flame's stomach and continued whispering. Will cast out toward Sora, but she still did nothing more than pray.

"The Flame of the Morrow reached into the place where all life begins," he whispered. "Into the place where all life goes when it is worn out with living."

Lilit grimaced and shifted. The wound was almost healed, the blood barely flowing, but the fire was almost out. "She reached that place," he said, offering some of his own energy while casting out desperately to find more, "and she found the strength to fight on."

Killien stayed drawn back, his eyes locked on Lilit's face.

She was pulling energy from Will too quickly. He couldn't quite stop the bleeding. The blood kept wanting to push the tear open again. He cast out toward the grass past the tent. It would be impossible to hide a huge swath of dead grass, but he didn't see another choice.

Outside the tent the fire flared with new fuel and Will grabbed the *vitalle* from it, pouring it into Lilit.

And finally the last of the wound closed.

He waited a moment, but everything held. She was terribly weak, but the immediate danger was over. Lilit groaned and twisted and Will let his hands fall off the sides of her head.

Sini returned, bringing an armful of blankets. She lifted the filthy one off Lilit and began to clear away the soaked ones. Will sank back, his palms aching.

Sini grabbed Sora's arm. "The bleeding—" She shoved blankets out of the way and called for clean water.

Killien scrambled forward, clinging to Lilit's hand. "The bleeding stopped?"

Sora shoved herself up and stepped back, her face white. She pressed a trembling hand to her mouth, staring at Lilit. She looked at Killien, her eyes wide, shaking her head quickly. "I didn't…"

Without finishing, she spun and shoved her way into the night.

More healers rushed in, and Will slid back against the tent wall. Killien bent over his wife whose eyes were cracked open. Her *vitalle* was still more like embers than flames, but it wasn't pouring out of her any longer. Will slipped outside.

The wind whipped against him. The world had fallen into darkness and the fire burning near the tent, now blazing, lit only a small area. His feet dragged against the ground and his arms hung limp and heavy at his side. Shadow's saddle horn stung against his sore palm as he heaved himself up and headed toward his own wagon.

———◆———

The stirrings of the clan woke Will the next morning while the sky was still a faded yellow-grey. He pulled the blanket up over his face and stayed in the darkness, the rough wool warm against his face. His arms were heavy, and his eyes felt like someone had poured sand into them. He stretched his hands experimentally, but his palms were only slightly sore.

A voice called out, proclaiming the son of Torch had been born. The Roven around him let out cries of celebration, and Will shoved himself up, waiting to hear anything about Lilit. But the red-bearded man announced the caravan would move at midday, and moved on.

As the morning wore on, the ramifications of the night before grew heavier. The clan was abuzz with the news of the Torch's son, Sevien. He heard enough to know that Lilit lived, although she was weak. But did Killien know what Will had done? The Torch had focused only on Sora. What had he thought she'd done?

Questions spun tumultuously in his mind and his stomach hardened into a cold knot. Someone must have noticed what he'd done. A trio of rangers trotted toward him and Will's heart slammed into his throat. But they rode past without a word.

He scrubbed his hands through his hair. If Killien knew he'd done magic, Will would already be busy explaining himself. Which meant Killien had a new baby, and a wife who had almost died, and Will hadn't come by to show he'd even noticed.

Will pushed himself up and trudged toward the Torch. When he reached Lilit's tent, he found Killien surrounded by Roven, holding a small bundle. There was no sign of Sora or Hal or Ilsa. Will worked his way through the crowd until he reached the Torch, his heart pounding so hard in his throat he could hardly swallow.

Killien turned and Will's chest clamped down on his heart until the Torch's face broke into a grin. "Come see the future Torch!"

A scrunched face with a shock of red hair peeked out of the blankets.

"He's definitely Roven," Will said, leaning closer and trying to look calm. The baby was asleep, his brow drawn in a little scowl as though he were put out by all the activity.

"He is indeed," Killien said. "He's got a cry that will wake the dead."

"Congratulations. He looks like a fine boy." Will tried to keep his voice calm for the next question. "How is your wife?"

Killien's smile faded slightly. "She's weak. But the healers think she is out of danger. They say it is safe for her to ride in the wagons. We reach the rifts in a couple days and she'll rest better then."

Will nodded and breathed out a long breath. "Good."

"Last night in the tent, I heard you telling her that story," he said, and Will tried not to flinch. "I appreciate what you did." Killien set one hand on Will's shoulder. "Lilit doesn't remember your words, but I do. And I think they gave her some strength."

Will pressed his fist to his chest. "If I helped in any way, I am glad."

When he looked up, Killien was still studying him. With a curt nod, he said, "The little slave girl you wanted, when you leave, you may take her with you."

Will stared at the Torch. "Really?"

"But I'd still love to know what those runes say," Killien added, turning to a healer who'd just arrived.

Relief washed over Will. He could take Rass with him. And Killien had no idea what he'd done last night. He watched the Torch walk toward Lilit, wondering what he thought had happened in that tent.

There was no sign of Ilsa, so he headed back to his wagon and collapsed back down.

The day passed in an uncomfortable sort of loneliness. Will fell asleep in the wagon, which helped curb some of his exhaustion, until the caravan rolled out around midday. He caught one glimpse of Hal riding toward the herds, but no glimpses at all of Sora.

Huge storm clouds built up along the western horizon dropping the Sweep into an early shadow that night. He wrapped his cloak around himself, but the rising wind tugged at it like greedy fingers.

"This storm will be big," a little voice said behind him.

He turned to see Rass, and a blaze of affection rose in him for the girl. She looked...healthy. Still too thin, but healthier. He found a pile of flatbread and dried meat at a nearby fire and sat on the wagon, Rass's bare feet dangling down as she chattered at him.

"Rass," he said when she had quieted for a moment, "You know I'm not staying with the Morrow forever."

She looked at him and let out a little sigh, but nodded.

"When I leave..." He stopped, feeling suddenly nervous. He glanced down at her hands, stained brown with dirt. "Is there really no one here who takes care of you?"

She heaved an irritated breath. "I can take care of myself."

"I know," he assured her. "I just…" He rolled a piece of the flatbread between his fingers until it formed a snake. Taking a breath, he pushed the words out. "When I leave, would you like to come with me?"

Rass looked up at him, her eyebrows shooting up higher than he'd ever seen them. She didn't speak and something very much like terror clamped down on Will's chest. She tilted her head to the side. "Would you like me to?"

Will nodded, although the motion felt awkwardly wooden. His mouth felt dry and the next words rushed out. "I have a home, of sorts. It's a big stone tower. And you could come there with me." The idea of bringing this little, eccentric girl to the Stronghold made him grin. "The people there would love you." He leaned close to her and whispered, "They know about magic too."

She gave him a small smile, but her brow was still creased. "You'd leave the grass, though. Wouldn't you?"

Will looked out into the darkness of the Sweep. "I'd leave *this* grass, but then we'd go places with other grass. My tower is surrounded by it." He gave her a smile. "It's hard to find places with no grass."

Rass looked away, and he couldn't see her expression for an excruciating handful of heart-beats. When she turned back, though, she smiled up at him and nodded. "I think I'd like to go with you."

Will let out a long breath and wrapped his arm around her shoulders. "That makes me very happy."

She leaned against him. "You're funny, Will."

Her shoulders were definitely less boney. The idea nagged at him as he let Rass fall into her normal chatter. He'd known her less than a fortnight. And while he'd shared his food with her, he was hardly feeding her a lot. But there was no doubt she was gaining weight. Her face was filling out too, although not exactly how he'd expected. She was gaining some roundness to her cheek-bones, but the rest of her face was still thin. Her chin was still pointed and long. She looked less and less like someone from Queensland, and more like…someone more exotic. She reminded him of something he couldn't quite place.

Rass's eyes flew open wide and she scuttled behind Will.

Sora strode over, her face thunderous. Will leaned back from her fury.

"You did something," she hissed, pointing a finger in Will's face.

He batted her hand away, his heart pounding in his chest. "What are you talking about?"

"You did something to the Flame." Her voice was low, but sharp enough to cut through the Sweep itself. "Killien thinks it was *me*." The word ripped out of her throat.

Rass grabbed the back of his shirt and pressed herself up against him.

If Will had ever thought he'd seen Sora angry, he'd been wrong. Her body shook with rage, her eyes dug into him as though she could rip his heart out with a thought.

A different sort of fear jabbed into his gut. "What is Killien going to do to you?"

"Do to me?" she asked, incredulous. "Probably build me a shrine." She leaned close again and Will forced himself not to pull away. "*But I didn't do it.*"

Will stared at her at a complete loss. She was angry about getting credit for healing Lilit? He could understand a reluctance to accept it, but not this level of rage.

"Stay away from me," she said slowly, biting off every word, fixing Will with a look of pure hatred, "or, I swear by the black queen, I will tell Killien everything I know about you and you'll be dead by morning."

"Why would he build a shrine to you, but kill me?"

"Because you and I are nothing alike. Stay away from me." With a last look that threw daggers, she spun and stalked off.

He stared after her. A gust of wind tumbled around him bringing cool, stormy air and a vacant sense of waiting. Thunder growled through the clouds, and the smell of rain whipped past.

Rass peeked out around his shoulder and looked at Will with wide eyes.

"Don't wander too far away," Will told her, spinning his ring, watching the direction Sora had gone. "We may be leaving the Roven sooner than I'd thought."

NINETEEN

The storm charged closer like an attacking army, smashing into the clan with breathtaking force. Will and Rass copied the other Roven and huddled under the wagon, still pelted by raindrops shot under it like arrows. Lightning stabbed down from the clouds in a chaos of blinding flashes and howling darkness. The wind howled like a creature out of a nightmare, but it whipped the storm quickly past, driving it away to the south.

Rass ran into the grass to sleep, and Will lay watching stray clouds chase after the storm, troubled by Sora's unaccountable fury. He could understand frustration or awkwardness at getting credit for something she hadn't done, but Killien merely thought her prayers had been answered. What was so terrible about that? Of course, the question as to why Killien begged her to pray in the first place was equally unanswerable. Killien's desperation he could understand, but Sora had never given any sign of being religious.

The blackness of the Serpent Queen hung overhead, clouds scuttling across her, seeming to spread bits of her darkness across the sky. Is that who Sora had prayed to? The monster set on devouring the stars? His mind circled back on the questions, not finding any answers.

To distract himself he ran over every interaction he'd had with Ilsa. It didn't take long. The urgency to talk to her again was growing, but with Lilit needing so much attention, he doubted he'd have a chance to see her before they reached the rifts in a few days. And then, would Killien let him stay longer? At what point was the Torch going to tire of his new storyteller? All the thoughts spun in his head like a second storm.

He finally slept, but the next day turned out to be just as agonizing. Hal was busy, Killien didn't summon him, and there was no sign of Ilsa, and no sign of Sora. Although that last thing wasn't bad. Will watched Lilit's wagon, but if Ilsa was there, she was staying inside.

The caravan had just stopped for the night, and Will was sitting down to some dwarf-talk with Hal, bracing for another meal of flatbread, when a rider arrived from the north, cantering down the serpent's wake. She carried sacks of bread baked in the rift and the Roven crowded her, eagerly grabbing fresh loaves.

The ranger reported that the caravan should reach the rift the morning after next, and the news along with the bread worked a sort of magic. Will sank his teeth into the thick, spongy bread with relish, hoping he never saw flatbread again. From their spot a little away from the fire, Lukas sat with Rett. When Sini arrived Lukas handed her a small loaf with a flourish, and she squealed with happiness and sank down in between them.

Before he'd even finished eating it, another ranger raced up from the west. He galloped toward Killien, his horse staggering to a stop, its sides heaving.

"Shepherds killed, Torch, three hours hard ride west. Three Roven from the Panos Clan, and four dozen sheep."

Will felt every person near him tense. Killien's face turned stony. "Cause?"

The ranger's eyes flicked to the people around the Torch. "No sign of weapons. The meat was ripped off the sheep. The carcasses left to rot."

Murmurs of "goblins" rippled through the Roven.

Will stretched out and felt fear growing in people. A spot of coolness appeared as Sora stepped up next to Killien. Will drew back when he saw her, but she didn't even glance in his direction.

"And…" The ranger paused, his eyes wide and slightly wild. "There've been fresh signs of goblins in every ravine I've passed."

Will focused on Killien and felt a growing dread in the Torch.

"How many?"

"Dozens." The ranger twitched a nervous half-shrug. "Hundreds, maybe."

"How long ago were the shepherds killed?" Sora asked.

"Within the past day."

Sora sent a girl running to fetch a horse. "Landmarks?"

"Between the white bluffs and that rift with all the bones."

Sora fixed him with the exact same gaze she always gave to Will. "It's getting dark. Can you be more specific?"

The ranger shifted slightly. "A bit closer to the bluffs, I think. There's not much to see out there."

"Not if you don't open your eyes."

Killien looked out over the Sweep to the west, his eyes scanning the emptiness. "Word from any other rangers?"

The man shook his head. "I haven't seen anyone since I left the rift yesterday."

"Take someone with you," Killien ordered Sora.

"They'll slow me down. I'll be back by dawn."

The girl ran back with a horse, and Sora swung into the saddle. For once Will could pick out her emotions strongly enough to tell them apart from the Torch's. She was angry, which seemed to be directed at Killien, but she was also filled with a roiling fear. Feeling Sora lose her tight control was far more frightening than the ranger's report.

"Sora," Killien said, his tone dangerous. "You are not going alone."

She shot him a furious glare and galloped across the grass.

Killien's fury and sharp fear matched Will's as he watched Sora's shape shrink into the vastness of the Sweep. The Torch barked orders, sending Roven scattering.

"Hal," the Torch called, "get the wagons in tight circles tonight, the children and elderly inside. Split the animals into as many groups as you can build fires around. As much fire as you can. Form a line along the western side. Everything done before dark."

Sora's silhouette disappeared over the first ridge, outlined for just a moment against the red sky.

The dark came long before the frantic activity of the clan subsided. The wagons were drawn into wide circles around tight knots of children and elderly, protected by a ring of Roven with camp-fires. Hundreds more Roven lined the western edge of the clan, their own fires well-stocked.

North of the clan sat wagons loaded with all the metal they could find, including Will's three silver beard beads. Around the metal wagons, a wall of grass and dried dung bricks were stacked, ready to be turned into a ring of fire. The only metal left in the clan was in the weapons they'd need to fight.

The flurry of activity settled into a quiet nervousness.

And nothing happened.

Will lay on the ground at the edge of one of the circles of wagons and actually missed the hard wood of his wagon. The brooding Serpent Queen worked her way up the sky and he spun his ring, waiting, straining for any sounds of goblins in the night. The ground was uncomfortable, and no matter how he adjusted the wool blanket, cold air crept in somewhere.

The knife he'd been given felt awkward in his hand, too long, the blade weighted oddly. It was sharp though, so there was a chance his wild, unskilled hacking would turn out to be an effective fighting strategy against goblins.

He was forgetting something he should have done by now. He just couldn't figure out what.

Part of it was that he had no idea where either Rass or Ilsa was. A cold wind slid over him, sneaking down inside his blanket. Two Roven sat at a fire not far from him, and Will looked at it enviously.

He gathered in some *vitalle* from the flames. He focused on the air above it, bending it into a cloth, gathering up some heat and drawing it closer. His fingers tingled with the effort, but it reached him with a rush of warmth lasting for three or four breaths before it cooled.

Will gathered in a little more *vitalle* from the grass, an idea forming. If he created a tent of cloth from the fire to himself, then the heat would just roll along the tent continually. Slowly, starting near himself, he constructed the idea of the tent, pushing *vitalle* into it, ignoring the tingling in his hands.

He pushed the tent forward until the end of it was over the flames. The first bit of warmth rolled over Will's skin and he smiled. The warm air wrapped around him, warming his blankets and his clothes. When he was thoroughly warm, he cut off the *vitalle* and let the warm air rise into the dark sky. It didn't take long before the cold seeped back in.

He was forgetting something. The feeling nagged at him. But the harder he tried to think of what it was, the more his brain offered up the wrong answer.

You forgot to take the silver beard beads out, his brain offered for the hundredth time. He heaved a sigh. He had done that. He'd searched his bag three more times to make sure there was no metal left in it. Still the thought niggled at him. What had he forgotten?

Beard beads, his brain offered.

He pressed his face into his hands and growled. He opened his eyes and between his fingers he could just see the flicker of the nearest small fire glinting off his ring.

His wide, gold ring.

"Idiot!" he hissed, trying to work the ring off his finger. The edge of it dug into his knuckle.

He squeezed his way out of the circle between two wagons and paused at the sight of the long line of Roven warriors. Surely the goblins wouldn't attack something this large? The Morrow Clan looked prepared for an attacking army. Firelight glittered off hundreds of weapons and suddenly he felt foolish for worrying about one small ring.

Past the line of Roven, the Sweep lay still and dark. For the first time, the grassland didn't feel empty. It felt full of…nothing. Which sounded the same, but felt very, very different.

Will was jogging by the time he reached Killien at the far northern end of the clan. Hal stood by his side, huge in the dim light, a wide sword slung across his back. Farther north, separated from the clan by a hundred paces, sat the wagons holding all the metal.

Killien had a well-used, common looking sword hung at his belt. Slung across his back was another, more rustic one. It took Will a minute to recognize it as the seax Killien had been given by Flibbet the Peddler.

"Come to join the fight?" Hal asked.

Will held up his knife. "If this is the sort that needs two swords, definitely not."

"Only one sword for fighting." Killien shifted his shoulders under the scabbard on his back. "This is just for safe keeping. Svard Naj doesn't sit in the metal wagon with the common things, unprotected."

"Speaking of metal wagons…" Will held up his hand with the ring. "I forgot to take this off. But now that I see how much metal is still among the clan, does it matter? There are metal weapons everywhere."

"The weapons aren't gold," Hal pointed out. "Goblins love gold. You should get that far away from you."

"I'll get a runner to put it in my chest." Killien motioned to the wagons set fifty paces away across the grass, his voice tinged with irritation.

Will opened his mouth to explain that he couldn't get it off, when a faint horn blast cut through the silence of the night. A single fire flared larger near the sheep herds. Another horn rang out three sharp notes and other fires flamed up.

A spot of blackness raced down the nearest hill toward them. Another burst of a horn called out, this one long, and a handful of Roven rushed out in a wedge, swords drawn, facing out into the Sweep to offer protection to the rider. More fires flared, painting the rise of the Sweep in flickering orange, turning the grass to a dim, mottled red fur.

Will's stomach dropped.

Sora raced toward the clan, calling out something he couldn't hear.

The wedge opened and she galloped in, the Roven collapsing back in after her, re-forming the line.

A low growl seeped out of the ground itself.

The hillside shifted.

A wide section of the grass slid sideways, then disappeared, falling into deep blackness. It widened into a gaping, hollow maw. Another appeared beside it.

A scrambling stream of dark, ill-formed shapes vomited out of the ground. The Sweep trembled from the charge. Grating, piercing shrieks split the night.

"Heatstones!" Killien shouted and the command was echoed down the line.

Hal dropped a heatstone close to the fire. Inside it, a kernel of light like a candle flame appeared, spreading and brightening. When it was almost as bright as the fire, Hal kicked it between his fire and the next one. The stone glowed with a searing yellow light, looking almost molten. A rush of heat washed across Will, like he stood in front of an oven.

Down the line, blazing yellow spots appeared, one after another.

To the south, goblins broke through the line and reached a herd. Terrified squeals from the sheep mixed with the shrieks of the goblins. The animals panicked, crashing into each other like waves trapped in a roiling sea.

A heatstone flew in a bright arc, disappearing into the stream of goblins. Screeches rang out and the goblins scattered away from it, into the path of Roven swords and knives.

"Get that ring out of here," Killien shouted at Will, pulling two long knives out of his belt and pointing one at the seat in the front of the nearest wagon. "And then get up on something high."

The Torch turned toward the approaching goblins. Hal stationed himself by the fire, his enormous sword drawn. Will scrambled toward the metal wagons, yanking at his ring.

A long line of bonfires and heatstones edged the clan now, stretching down the Sweep like blazing teeth. Outside the line, the first row of grass hills was visible, and streaming from the wide holes came goblin after goblin. They rushed out in an endless stream a half-dozen goblins wide.

The creatures pooled along the fireline, rushing closer, their eyes reflecting back the firelight in wide, white orbs. The small, hunched goblins scrambled forward in a chaos of green, wiry legs and arms.

"More heat!" Killien called.

Whenever a fire flared up, the goblins pulled back. The stream of goblins had stopped flowing out of the hill, leaving the two holes gaping like hollow eyes.

Will wrenched at his ring, drawing in some *vitalle* from the grass to heat the gold up, hoping it would stretch. The goblins outside the fireline surged past him in a swarm of limbs and eyes and hunger. But the heatstones seemed to be working and the creatures held back a dozen paces. Roven archers shot into the horde, felling goblin after goblin. But every time, another vicious face appeared, its open mouth edged with thin, sharp teeth.

Ahead of Will, a more guttural cry rang out and the swarm raced toward the metal.

Flaming arrows shot toward the wagons, setting the ring of grasses around it into flame and Will slid to a stop, letting his hand fall from his still tight ring. Creatures raced toward fire-encircled wagons. The goblins in the front screeched and scrambled against the mob, trying to stay back, but the mass moved forward like a wave. When the first goblin touched the fire, it let out a piercing scream. Two more were shoved forward into it, then the flames were smothered below burning bodies, and goblins poured through, clawing over each other to reach the metal.

Will turned and ran back, climbing up on the wagon near Killien. The goblins swarmed against the line, screeching like birds fighting over a carcass. The Roven cut into their numbers with brutal efficiency. But they were falling too. One Roven for every twenty goblins.

There were not enough Roven.

Killien strode down the line, calling out commands. Hal stood between the nearest fire and a heatstone, his huge sword sweeping through the frost goblins like a scythe.

Will's heartbeat pounded in his ears like a drum underneath the screaming and fighting.

The goblins swarmed over the metal. The Roven retreated, re-forming a line between those wagons and the clan, hacking any goblins that chased after them. One of the Roven stumbled and a gap appeared between Will and the creatures.

A single goblin face turned toward him, eyes glinting like two flat moons. It raised its nose into the air as if catching a scent. With a hideous grin, it dropped to all fours and raced toward him, tearing into the earth.

Will's feet scrambled back against the wagon floor. He drew in *vitalle* from the ground, from the fire blazing nearby, from anything he could find, his mind scrambling for an idea of what to do with it.

Then Sora was there, stepping between the wagon and the racing goblins, two long knives in her hand. Her long braid was disheveled, her leathers glinted dark and wet.

A different level of fear wormed into him as the goblin raced closer to Sora.

Another goblin peeled away from the swarm and ran toward them. Then another.

Will cast about desperately for some way to stop them, some protection he could throw up in front of her. He opened up toward her and felt a swirl of fear wrapped in resolve and surrounded by cold, calculated waiting.

A bright glint of yellow near his foot caught his eye.

A heatstone.

He spun around. He was standing on the book wagon where Rett had spilled his heatstones. A new fear gripped him. He'd brought his gold ring to the books.

Will grabbed the stone. The goblin was halfway to Sora, more and more veered out of the main group to follow. She stood alone. At the sight of claws and teeth rushing toward her, he yanked some *vitalle* out of the grass and shoved it into the heatstone. The stone lapped it up and began to glow, the surface blossoming with heat. He threw it between Sora and the goblins.

Sora drew back from it. Will needed a way to focus the heat on the goblins—needed something like a tent of air.

No, something stronger. Thick, like the walls of an oven.

He molded the air around the heatstone into the idea of clay walls. Reaching toward the nearest fire, he drew energy in one hand, singeing his fingertips, and out his other hand until those fingers hurt as well. He wrapped the walls around the heat on three sides and over the top.

In a breath, the cool night air brushed against his skin as the heat from the stone was channeled away. From the side of the stone facing the goblins he pushed out the idea of a tunnel of clay, funneling all the heat in that direction. Thankfully, the fire near the wagon was burning strongly and he pulled more energy from it, strengthening the walls. His fingers burned from the *vitalle* pouring through them.

The heat hit the first goblin and the creature twisted back away from it, with a shriek of pain. Will pushed the heat forward and more goblins cried out in pain, drawing back. The wave of heat pushed them all the way to the metal wagons before they stopped running and sank down, their white eyes glaring towards Will.

Sora spun around and stared at him.

His fingers ached, but this wasn't enough. He needed so much more heat.

Will dropped to his knees and looked under the wagon seat. A half dozen heatstones lay shoved in the corner. Will grabbed them all, tossing them down onto the blazing one.

Sora cried out and dove away from the pile.

The heatstones exploded into searing yellow light and Will flinched back, but the clay wall held and no heat reached him. Will drew even more *vitalle* from the nearby fire, pouring it into his air-walls. The tunnel rippled with heat, rushing toward the goblins in a narrow river, flattening and searing grass in a long line before widening out into a wave of air so hot that the goblins shimmered through it.

The creatures shrieked, pulling back.

Seeing the goblins' hesitation, the Roven attacked with renewed fury, cutting at the edges of the swarm. A few Roven reached into the line of heat and spun away, crying out and cradling singed arms. Will turned his palm out instead of just his fingers, letting more and more *vitalle* flow through him to shape the walls. The energy pushed clay walls farther, wrapping the heat around the goblins until it herded them back out of the Roven lines.

Will followed the retreating goblins with his wall, pushing the heat after them. The skin on his palms blistered. He squeezed his eyes shut, shoving away the pain, and cast out again, this time searching for all the fires and all the heatstones. He visualized another long, tall wall of clay along the inside of the fire line, growing up and bending out over the tops of the fires, reflecting all the heat out at the goblins on the Sweep.

With a sharp slice of pain a blister on his palm burst, then another. Will bit back a cry and focused his mind on the wall.

The goblins paused, then with a twist like a flock of birds spinning in flight, they turned and darted toward the openings in the hills. A cry went up from the Roven and hundreds of arrows shot into the air, dropping goblin after goblin to the ground.

In moments the Sweep was empty. There was a shudder of the ground and the entrance of the goblin warren quivered and sank, turning the hillside into a mass of torn up earth.

Will cut off the flow of *vitalle*. For just a moment the clay wall held, then the air relaxed into itself and a wave of heat rolled off the heatstones next to him, burning the skin on his cheeks and sending searing pain across his burned palms. He ducked down onto the seat of the wagon, cradling his hands on his lap.

He'd never controlled that much *vitalle* before. The thought was dull and heavy. He stretched his fingers and pain lanced across his hands. Raw, red skin filled his palms, covered with blisters, some taut and shiny, some split open, dripping. His hands blurred as a wave of exhaustion rolled over him.

Celebratory shouts from the Roven echoed around him as though they came from far over the Sweep. He heard Hal bellow something incomprehensible. Will's body melted down against the wagon, his head falling back against the hard wood wall.

The earth was spinning, falling. There was nothing but the sharp pain in his hands.

Will closed his eyes.

The pain in his palms was excruciating. He closed his eyes and cast out toward his hands, feeling the energy from his own body pressing against the inside of his skin, beginning the long process of healing. Burns were much harder to heal than cuts. Instead of drawing skin back together, this required growing new skin across both palms.

Maybe he could dull the pain a little. Will cast out toward the grass below the wagon. His mind worked sluggishly, and when he reached for the *vitalle*, it dribbled through his grasp like water. His eyes slid shut and he lost focus. His arms rested heavy on his lap like two dead weights.

A crack split the night and Will's eyes snapped open. Sora stood at the side of the wagon, her knife jabbed down into the wood of the wagon seat. The brightness of the heatstones cast her face into stark light and black shadows.

Her eyes glittered with an icy coldness he hadn't seen before and her voice cut through the night like a blade. "What did you do?"

TWENTY

Sora stood by the wagon, her face livid, but he was too exhausted for it to cause more than a thin thread of fear. And he was far too tired to open up to her and deal with her anger. Will closed his eyes again and the wagon beneath him spun slowly. All he wanted to do was sleep. But Sora shifted, and the movement sounded angry.

She was always so angry.

Will had just saved her life. He, Will, the least useful Keeper in the history of Keepers, had just fought off a horde of frost goblins and saved dozens, maybe hundreds of Roven lives. He cracked one eye open and worked to focus on Sora. She stood stone-still, her glare sharp enough to cut.

If only it was Alaric standing there, not Sora. He'd appreciate what Will had done. How far had that wall reached down the line? He grinned. *Yes, Gerone,* he thought, *I had a motivation problem.*

The palms of his hands were hurting worse by the moment, but he didn't care.

"Stop grinning like an idiot," Sora hissed. "Do you realize—"

"Sora," he interrupted her, "why are you always so angry?"

"I'm angry," she hissed, "because you keep doing stupid things and I have to save your life."

He pushed himself up. "*You're* the one who got me into all this, by telling Killien about me."

She leaned over the edge of the wagon, her hands gripping the side, her voice furious. "Killien knew about you before you finished telling your foreign story at the festival. He already saw you as a threat. I came to see if you were as dangerous as he thought."

"You hid in my room and threatened me!"

"Killien had men set to take you when you left the city. I told him he should see if your stories were worth hearing.

"I was going to help you escape while the clan packed. It's not my fault you decided to play bosom friends with the Torch."

"He likes foreigners," Will objected. "He knows more about foreign people than anyone I've met in this wasteland. Everyone else jumps straight to the sword. Killien realizes not everyone outside his clan is an enemy."

"Not everyone. Just you."

A rock fell into his stomach. "I'm a storyteller."

"Stop it." Her face was taut and her shoulders tense. He opened up toward her and, for once, felt a rush of emotions. She was mad and scared and exhausted. She looked at him for a long moment, suspicion fighting with something else in her expression.

Leaning closer, she whispered, "You're a Keeper."

The word hit Will like a punch. He opened his mouth to answer her, but found nothing to say.

At his silence she shoved herself away from the wagon.

"Killien isn't opposed to magic." He shook his head, desperation growing. "He's studying it."

"He's against Queensland. And Keepers." She turned away from him and rubbed her hand across her mouth, looking uncharacteristically nervous.

To the east, the top of the Scale Mountains were visible as a dark wall beneath the stars. "What do I do?"

She looked away from the mountains. "Tonight, after first watch, I'll slip you westward into the grass. There are some small rifts that are almost impossible to find. You can hide until the Roven are gone, then you can get yourself off the Sweep."

"West?"

"Killien wouldn't imagine you'd go farther into the Sweep. He'll think you ran home."

"I want to run home. I'd run home crying if I thought it would get me there faster. What I don't want to do is go farther into the Sweep and hide in the exact places where frost goblins frequent."

She rolled her eyes. "I know. And Killien will be counting on that level of…"

"Cowardice?" Will offered, glaring at her.

"…inexperience. He won't send trackers west. He'll send me. And I'll take all the best trackers with me. When we can't find your trail, we'll blame it on your evil, deceiving magic. We just need to keep you away from him for the next few hours."

Will stared at her for a long moment. "You're very sneaky for someone who disapproves of deceiving people."

The clan spread out around him, and he had no idea where Ilsa was. Or Rass.

"I can't leave."

Sora turned a disbelieving look on him. "Why not?"

There was a loud laugh nearby and she glanced behind them and swore. A flare of anger, harsh and new blazed up. Killien's voice came from nearby and Sora raised hers at Will. "You deserve to be burned if you were stupid enough to pick up a glowing heatstone."

The Torch stepped around the end of the wagon, his eyes sharp. Two thin lines of blood slashed across a bandage near his shoulder. With a glance he took them in, his gaze coming to rest on Will's hands. Will fought the urge to hide them.

"What happened?" Killien demanded.

I saved your entire clan. Will thought. He could feel the tightly controlled fury of the Torch, and beside it, Sora's towering fury, which had risen a hundredfold as Killien approached. But she kept her glare burning into Will.

"I found some heatstones," he began. He stretched up to see over the edge of the wagon at the pile of heatstones still shining painfully bright. "I heard people calling for more heat. And the goblins were coming this way. And"—he lifted his hand to show Killien the ring, still firmly on his finger—"I couldn't get the ring off." He looked back at the heatstones. "So I heated up one stone, then threw the rest on top of it."

This was a stupid story. It explained nothing.

"And your hands?" Killien never took his eyes off Will's face.

"One of the heatstones rolled toward the wagon." The lie was so stupid he didn't need to feign embarrassment. "All the books were here…"

"So he picked it up," Sora finished for him.

"I thought it was going to reach the wagon." It felt good to snap at someone. "And I don't like the idea of blazing hot things near a pile of books."

"Enough," Killien said quietly. The fury Will could feel from him was unabated, but none of it showed up in his face.

"If the heatstones are ruined, I'll pay you for them." Will lifted his hand again. "Would this ring cover the cost? It's currently burned onto my finger, but once it heals…"

Killien let out a little huff of amusement, and Will felt the fury subside the smallest amount. "No more resting. It's time for a celebration. And for that we need stories."

Will worked a smile past his exhaustion. "Everything's better with stories."

Sora made an irritated noise, but Killien kept his attention fixed on Will. "It's a good night, Will. We're almost to the rifts. No more watching out for monsters…no more wondering what is hiding right next to us."

Will ignored the implication and heaved himself up, climbing out of the wagon and following Killien. The Torch was splattered with dark goblin blood, the sword at his hip grimy with it. Across his back, the sword from Flibbet still hung looking unused.

"Tell me, Will, are there monsters where you live? Creatures that hide close by, lulling you into the false sense that you are safe? When all along they're just waiting for the opportunity to destroy you?"

The sharp suspicion he felt from Killien cut through him and he shoved the Torch's emotions out of his chest. "No. Just people trying to live at peace with each other."

Will couldn't shake the fuzziness of exhaustion from his mind, but the conversation continued, Killien asking probing questions in his light, unconcerned voice, Will dancing along the edge of the truth in his answers. They reached a large fire surrounded by rangers. A handful of healers wrapped wounds, and children scuttled through carrying food and wineskins.

Lukas pushed his way through the crowd holding a thick roll of bandages. The slave's grey shirt was splattered with blood, but none of it looked to be his own. The blood on Killien's arm had spread and the Torch offered Lukas his arm.

"Have the healer see to your burns, storyman." Killien winced as Lukas pulled a bloody dressing off his arm.

Lukas gave the Torch a quiet apology, examining the two long, ragged gashes that ran down his arm.

Killien kept his eyes on Will. "Stay at my disposal tonight."

A slave bandaged a ranger's leg nearby, and Will sat down to wait his turn. A knot of dread sat in his stomach. He watched Sora take a seat behind the other Roven around the fire. There was no sign of Lilit or Ilsa, but he heard enough conversations to know that there'd been no injuries away from the front line of fighting.

The healer spread a thick poultice across his palms and wrapped his hands, leaving his palms pleasantly numb and Will turned his mind to which story to tell. There were several stories from Coastal Baylon that painted Queensland in a bad light, and he was tempted to use one of them, but felt reluctant even to bring his homeland up. Instead he sorted through the stories he knew that mentioned neither Queensland, nor magic, nor anyone in disguise, and most definitely not any stories where traitors were put to death.

Which left him with a surprisingly limited repertoire, and ruled out most of his favorites.

He settled on one about a shrewd merchant trapped in the garden of the indulgent Gulfind god Keelu. The fast talking merchant was funny, and hopefully no one would draw too many parallels between a trapped merchant and a trapped storyteller.

The lump of foreboding growing the longer he sat there, and when Killien finally stood to address the Roven around the fire, Will's gut was in knots.

"Our storyman," Killien announced, standing near the fire and motioning Will to join him, "is here to entertain us."

There was a general murmur of approval from around the fire, and Will stepped up next to the Torch, clasping his hands together behind his back in case they started to shake. The fire lit the closest of the faces, but the back of the group, where Sora sat, was lost in darkness.

"Our enemy in Queensland have their own magic men." Killien's voice rolled over the crowd. "They call them Keepers."

Will's blood turned icy, his entire body felt too long, and too awkward.

"The Keepers do not put their magic safely into rocks, though. They pull what they use from the world around them, then twist it to do their will."

Muttered disapproval rose around the fire.

"So they do not share their magic with the people. Here on the Sweep, our stonesteeps infuse stones with power that are available to all. They ward our houses against disaster, guard our children against illness. Give us heatstones for protection. The magic on the Sweep is used for the good of all the Roven.

"But in Queensland, the Keepers hoard all the magic to themselves. They hide away in a hidden tower, leaving only to consult with their ineffective queen."

The mutters of the group turned angry.

"You've been to Queensland, Will. Tell us a story about their Keepers." Killien's eyes were flat in the fire light. "Tell us whether they're as terrible as we've heard."

Will gave the Torch a bow, the motion stiff. A story about Keepers? That narrowed it down to hundreds of tales. None of which he was stupid enough to tell here. "In Queensland they don't have the same view of Keepers as you. The Keepers are…" He paused again. This was awkward. "The Keepers are honored there, revered even. The people there think that the Keepers protect their land and their history."

Killien's eyes glinted in the candlelight. "And what do you think of them, Will?" His voice was pitched low, but the crowd was listening so quietly that Will knew every one of them had heard.

"I think Keepers are known for preserving as many stories as they can. And in my mind, anyone who has that much respect for stories"—he nodded to Killien—"can't be all bad."

The Torch didn't move.

Will's heart was pounding alarmingly fast. He couldn't tell any of the stories he knew. They all treated Keepers like heroes, or great leaders, or brilliant strategists. They were all spoken of irritatingly well, actually. He rubbed his fingers over the bandages on his hand. Tonight, faced with the fact that the only impressive thing he'd ever done as a Keeper was about to get him killed, and would never be told to anyone, he found himself wishing for more stories about Keepers that didn't glow with adoration. Like that story from Coastal Baylon blaming one for a drought.

He bit back a grin. It was perfect.

"Queensland cannot be trusted to say anything but good about their Keepers," he began. "Whether they do so out of fear or respect, I do not know. But no group of men can be as pure, as noble, and as faultless as Keepers are supposed to be." He felt the truth of it growing in him, the need to say all these things building and gaining momentum. "They are just men. And men are not so uncontaminated.

"A person can rarely see his own people clearly. His mind is so entrenched in his own way of thinking, he can't even see where he's blind. To truly see the Keepers, let's step away from Queensland, with their prejudices and myths, and go to their neighbors, where men are not blinded by loyalty."

He told of the terrible drought that had plagued Coastal Baylon for two years after a skirmish involving a Keeper. He told of the rumors of a curse. The slow, starving deaths, the dusty, barren fields. He told of the superstitious farmers and the desperate lords needing someone to blame. How their prayers for rain were shoved away and their cries for vengeance grew. He told of the hatred that burned toward the Keeper, the oaths taken by those who vowed to bring him to Baylon and spill his blood on the ground he'd laid to waste.

"And so they went, leaving the bodies of the ones they loved behind. They climbed through barren hills into Queensland, moving toward the town where the Keeper had been.

"Their eyes had seen nothing but drought and death for so long, they didn't notice the shadows they crept through were cast by bare branches, and their footsteps were cushioned by dust and despair.

"When they found the Keeper, he lay in the corner of a cottage. His black robe, tattered and greyed with dust, was wrapped around a child. Their starved bodies clinging to each other in death."

The whisper of the fire was the only sound among the Roven.

"The vengeance and hatred they'd brought into that place breathed its last, and crumbled to dust. The Baylonese went home empty, drawing out again their brittle, neglected prayers for rain and holding them gently on their parched tongues."

The Roven before him were still. Will let the silence hang in the air, refusing to offer any more closure to the tale. He pressed his fist to his chest and bowed to the listeners, then to Killien. The Torch stared at Will with unreadable eyes. Not bothering to open up toward him, Will sat down.

Killien sat in the silence and looked at Will for a long moment. "Well," he said, "the storyman knows how to spin a tale."

It took a moment before the sounds of approval began. Exhaustion rolled over Will again as Killien called for more wine and the group around the fire dissolved into smaller conversations. Sora walked by, fixing Will with a look dripping with displeasure.

Hal moved over next to Will. "That was the most depressing story I've ever heard." He handed Will a basket of bread and cheese.

Killien came over, passing small wineskins to Will and Hal. "That was quite a tale."

Will shrugged. "You're the one who asked for something about Keepers. I had something much more upbeat planned."

"Next time let the storyman pick," Hal said, taking a huge bite of bread. "I'm so depressed I can barely eat."

"Agreed," Killien said. "Next time he can pick. For now, let's celebrate. We're still alive." He held up his wineskin toward Will. "And you put on quite a performance."

"A performance depressing enough to lower even the spirits of the victors," Hal agreed raising his wineskin.

"To the victors," Killien said with a thin smile.

Will raised his as well, and took a drink. The wine slid down his throat bitter and rough while he watched the Torch walk away.

"What'd you do to piss off Killien?" Hal asked around a mouthful of cheese.

Will took another sip of his wine to give himself a moment to come up with an answer. "Maybe he didn't like the story."

Hal grunted. "No one liked that story." He lifted his skin toward Will for a salute. "Tell something better next time. Something about dwarves."

Will laughed. Starting the story of the dwarven princess who was so ugly she'd frightened a troll, he set about passing the time until the first watch changed and he and Sora could leave.

But before he'd reached the part where the trolls showed up, his eyes grew heavy.

"Don't fall asleep on me," Hal protested, shoving Will's shoulder.

The big man slid out of focus.

"Will?" Hal's voice came from a long distance away.

Huge hands shook his shoulders, but everything spun off in strange directions and his shoulders didn't feel particularly well attached to the rest of him. The edges of the world began to turn black and Hal's words grew more insistent.

The last thing Will heard was Killien coming closer.

"Hal," the Torch said, his voice distant and cold. "Stop shaking the Keeper."

TWENTY-ONE

The walls, the floor, the very air was drenched with orange, like he lay inside a flame. Will's tongue filled his mouth, thick and dry. When he pushed himself upright, a groan scraped out of his throat.

He sat on a clay bed stuck to the clay wall, which curved up around him like a beehive. A cup and a bowl full of water sat below him on the floor. He grabbed for it and the tepid water felt like life rushing down his throat. He filled the cup three times before letting it fall from his fingers. A small window punctured the wall, showing still more orange clay. The tiny room was perfectly empty besides the cup, bowl, and bed.

He heaved himself to his feet. The world leaned to the left for a moment before pulling itself upright. Ducking through a low archway, he found another room with a wicker table and two chairs. Through the open doorway, bright sunlight raked down a cliff wall.

Will stumbled to the door.

Outside was nothing but stone and more clay. Across a thin path, no farther from the door than Will could reach, the ground dropped off sharply into a gully. Up the other side, barren cliffs rose at least three times his height. Behind him, another cliff jutted up toward a weak blue sky.

He was in a rift.

He stood at one end of it, on a path that wound past three more huts on its way to the far end where it zigzagged its way up the cliff to a pair of guards. Will cast out through the rift, but didn't find a single hint of *vitalle*. There weren't any living things closer than the guards.

He turned back, looking for the water and events of the goblin attack came back to him. He stretched his fingers and his palms ached, but not as terribly as before. They had begun to heal. A thin trickle of fear dribbled down his back. How long had he been here?

When he reached his room, a small lump at the foot of his bed caught his eye—a dead mouse. Talen knew where he was, for whatever that was worth. He sank onto the floor next to the water.

Killien knew he was a Keeper.

The thought thudded dully in his mind.

He let his head sink back against the bed. This felt…expected. As though it was the only way this could have ended.

His eyes slid shut.

A scraping noise jolted him awake. Sharp pains ran down the muscles in his back as he jerked awake.

"Hello, Will."

Will flinched at the calmness of the voice. Killien leaned against the wall relaxed, his face blank. Will opened up toward him and felt a surge of dark anger boil into his chest, dark and somehow cold.

"How do you like your accommodations?" Killien glanced around the room. "We call it the Grave."

When Will didn't answer, Killien ducked into the other room and sat at the table next to a plate of bread.

Will heaved himself up, suddenly ravenous. Three Roven guards stood at the outer door. Will sank down in the other chair, and a guard stepped behind him. None of them looked familiar. Or friendly.

"Why feed me if you're just going to kill me?"

Killien pushed the plate closer to Will. "I wouldn't have gone to the trouble of dragging you here if I was going to kill you."

Will picked up the bread, his fingers clumsy around the bandages. It crumbled a bit with staleness, but no bread in the history of the world had tasted this good.

Killien settled back in his chair. "A Keeper. Right here in my clan."

Will paused with a piece of bread halfway to his mouth.

"Sneaking and lying, right at my own table, right alongside me. For days."

"What exactly would you have had me do?" Will dropped the bread onto the plate. "Introduce myself as a Keeper? That might have dampened our friendship."

Killien's face darkened. "We never had a friendship."

The words struck deeper than Will expected, immediately followed by irritation that they had. "Would you have talked with me about books? History?" he asked, refusing to acknowledge the man's words. "Would you have told me about your father?"

"I would have killed you," Killien hissed, leaning forward. "And left your body to rot."

"Then you can hardly blame me for lying." Will picked up the piece of bread again. "If you're so keen on killing me, why am I here?"

Killien sat back, drawing in a breath, visibly trying to calm himself. "I've been reading your books."

Will stiffened.

"You've been spying on the Roven for a year now. And you learned a lot from us…" Killien nodded to a guard who brought over a book. "Now I want to learn from you."

The Gleaning of Souls glittered in silver across the blue leather.

Killien flipped open the book. Runes filled the page, similar to the ones Sini had given him. "Translate this."

Will shook his head. "I can't."

Killien grew still, his eyes dangerous.

"I'm not saying that I won't," Will clarified. "I'm saying I can't."

"Queensland and the Sweep use the same written language, and the same runes."

Will pointed at the runes. "These aren't normal."

"They're ancient."

"No. Ancient runes I can read." He paused. "Sort of. These are different. I've never seen any like this."

"I thought Keepers were brilliant scholars." Killien's voice was harsh.

"Most are. You captured the wrong one. But even if I could, I wouldn't translate something called *The Gleaning of Souls* for a power-hungry Roven Torch." Will shoved the book away. "So go ahead and kill me or whatever you have planned. Because I'm not helping you."

"You do not understand—" Killien clenched his jaw. When he spoke, his calmness sounded strained. "I could kill you. But contrary to what you think, I'm not thirsting for the blood of my enemies. I'm looking for the quickest way to peace."

Will let out a sharp laugh. "You won't find that in a book by Kachig the Bloodless."

When Killien spoke, it was quiet, spilling out onto the table like shards of ice. "I thought you might need convincing." He motioned to the door and a guard stepped aside.

Ilsa walked in.

TWENTY-TWO

A ll the air left the room and Will's body froze.

Ilsa gave the Torch a small bow and carried Will's bag over to the table, never lifting her eyes off the floor. Her hair fell in a curtain across her face. Will opened up toward her and her nervousness rushed into his chest.

She set the bag down next to the table. Her eyes flicked up to Will's face for the merest second, and he leaned toward her. She flinched away from the movement and his gut turned to ice at the spike of fear she felt. A guard took a threatening step forward.

"Thank you, Ilsa." Killien waved her away, his eyes burning into Will.

Will started to rise, but the guard shoved him back down. Ilsa kept her head down and backed up against the wall.

"You'll have to excuse Ilsa's nervousness." Killien spoke calmly, like he was discussing the weather. "Imagine her surprise when she found out she'd spoken several times with a Keeper. She's relieved she didn't anger you. She says you often seemed agitated."

Will dragged his gaze back to Killien. "How…?"

"I told you that your books made fascinating reading," Killien said.

Of course. His search for Ilsa had been written in his books starting long before he'd met the Morrow. She moved quickly back from the table and Will searched her face to see if Killien had told her, but she didn't look like someone who was worried about anything as complicated as having a new brother. She was looking at him more the way one might look at a snake that might be poisonous.

Killien set his hand on Will's bag. "They gave me so much insight into why you were on the Sweep. What you've been looking for all this time. I thought about keeping them for myself, but I've decided to let you have access to them, in case they are helpful to you while you work."

Killien stood, leaning on the table until Will had to look up to meet his gaze. "Translate those runes, Keeper, or…" He let the threat hang unfinished.

Killien walked out the door, followed by Ilsa and the guards.

Will dropped his head into his hands. It felt heavy, his arms hollow and shaky.

Killien had Ilsa. The thought stopped every other thing in his mind.

Whatever hope he'd had of freeing her from the Morrow crumbled to ash.

The gnawing fear of what Killien could do to her forced his head up. He pulled Kachig's book closer.

The silver medallion was back on the cover, a drip of hardened resin running along the edge. Four daggers split the disk into quarters. Intertwined around the blades were strings of runes connected with thin, snaking lines. Or maybe they weren't runes. There was something odd about them, something ominous. In the very center of the medallion, in a small square formed by the hilts, there was just smooth silver. Except it didn't reflect light right. It was somehow both silver and dark at the same time, and that darkness made the emptiness into something horrible.

Will leaned forward, his gaze drawn along a path of the symbols. It pulled at him gently, but persistently. None of the runes were recognizable, and the daggers themselves were part of the path. A shadowy sort of haze fell over his mind and he wrenched his eyes away and flipped the book open.

The strange runes covered the page in faded black ink. There was no way he was going to be able to read this. He scanned the page, looking for anything he recognized. Each time he found one, *age, exhaustion, coldness, death*, there was something wrong with it. As though it had been broken and put back together with too many pieces.

Something scuffed outside and Lukas limped in the door, followed by Sini. She carried a large pitcher to the table.

"I don't suppose that's saso?" Will asked.

She shook her head, with a little smile and pulled a stack of small papers and a jar of ink from her pocket.

"Prisoners don't get saso," Lukas said. "Back away from him, Sini."

"It's alright, Lukas." The girl added a short stub of a candle to the table.

"I'm not going to hurt her." Will worked to keep his voice even.

Lukas set a book on the table and Will picked it up. It was a dictionary of runes. Lukas took a step and his leg twisted awkwardly. He grabbed the chair, a grimace crossing his face.

"I might be able to help with the pain—" Will stopped at the look of undisguised hatred Lukas shot him.

"Ah, the great Keeper will fix everything." Lukas's knuckles whitened around the back of the chair. "You're fifteen years too late to help me."

Will lay the book down on the table, guilt snaking into him. "The wayfarers took my sister twenty years ago, but we thought it was an isolated event. No one knew they were still taking random children. If we knew—if the Queen knew—"

"Can you translate the runes?" Lukas interrupted.

Will fought against all the other things he wanted to say, before letting the topic of the wayfarers drop. "I'm working on it."

"I for one, don't think you'll be able to." Lukas turned and limped toward the door. "Which means Killien will kill you soon. I just hope it's before I have to walk all the way out here again. Come on, Sini." Without looking back, he left.

Sini gave Will a smile, half apologetic and half worried, and followed.

Queensland had failed these two. The Keepers had failed them. The wayfarers had been taking children all this time. He dropped his head into his hands, fury and impotence clashing against each other.

When he got home, he was taking this to the queen.

If he got home.

He forced himself to focus on the book again, and on the next page, one of the runes looked familiar. Grabbing his own bag, he unwrapped his books and flipped through one of them, search-ing through his writing for a specific page. Someone else's handwriting caught his eye. Will had recorded what he knew about the death of Killien's father, but underneath, in bold strokes, new words had been added.

Tevien, Torch of the Morrow, was betrayed by a man he trusted.

A man who lied about everything he was and everything he wanted.

A man who befriended him to sneak and spy and destroy.

Will let out a long sigh and flipped to a page with six runes he'd drawn down the side, each formed in the same sort of odd way as the ones in Kachig's book. He'd seen them months ago embroidered on a robe worn by a stonesteep in Tun. Will had walked behind him for ages mem-orizing the shapes so he could record them. Next to them were written guesses at their meaning, but they weren't good guesses.

There was a flutter at the window as Talen flew in and landed on the table, a mouse hanging from his beak.

Will ran a finger down the hawk's neck. "Good morning. How do you like our new home?" He pulled his bedroll out of his bag and took it over to the bed. "There."

Talen flew over to the blanket and picked at it with his beak.

"Have you seen Shadow?" Will sat next to the bird. "Or Rass? I haven't seen her since…" Before the goblin attacks. A little knot of worry for the little girl sat in his stomach. "Or have you seen Sora? She's sharp enough to stay safe from Killien. Right?"

Talen let out a loud squawk.

"I wonder if I'm ever going to stop wishing you could talk to me." Will slumped back against the wall. "This place is so…lifeless. I'm surprised you came back."

Talen turned and launched into the air, flapping out the door of the hut, and soaring up into the sky.

Will stared after him for a moment. "Although I suppose this place isn't as bad when you're free to fly away."

He trudged back to the table. There had to be a way to read these runes. He rubbed at his face, trying to push away his frustration and focus on the book.

Talen came back three times, bringing with him beakfuls of dead grass. The third time, Will followed him into the bedroom. Talen stood next to a neat little nest, looking at Will expectantly.

"I have no food." Will brushed the back of his fingers down the hawk's chest. "You know what would be useful? If you brought back something that had energy in it. Like living grass. Or better yet, a tree."

Talen leaned down into his nest and nudged the stalks of grass around with his beak.

Emotions resonate. They don't move.

Will considered the bird. He'd tried in the past to push emotions toward Talen, but maybe there was another way. He opened up toward the hawk and felt a nebulous pleasure that seemed to be focused more on the nest than anything else.

His finger froze against Talen's chest.

Talen felt pleased *about the nest*. Because emotions were focused on something.

Will fanned his own emotions, trying to make them strong enough for Talen to notice, willing them to resonate in the little bird.

"Or you could find Sora. Because if anyone could get me out of this, it'd be her." That was very easy to want. He let his need for her help grow until it filled his chest. "I need Sora."

Talen shifted his weight and Will held his breath. The hawk twitched his head toward the other room and launched into the air. Will, stunned that it had actually worked, watched the hawk flutter to the next room—and come back with the dead mouse. He dropped it onto Will's blanket.

"Or you could just keep bringing me mice." Will leaned back and closed his eyes, exhaustion washing over him.

Talen let out a short, self-satisfied squawk, and Will heard him rustling in his nest.

The wall and the bed spun slowly underneath him. His body felt hollow except for a gnawing fear. He considered the fear for a moment, wanting to believe it was all for Ilsa. But it wasn't. A healthy chunk of the fear was for himself. Because as sure as Talen was going to bring more mice, Will was never going to figure out these runes.

With a quick screech, Talen took off and flew out of the hut rising effortlessly out of the rift. Will had never wanted to fly so badly.

But Killien had Ilsa. Will pushed himself up.

Laying out some paper, he studied the first rune. *A page of runes is like a story,* Alaric liked to say. *Each symbol interacts with the ones next to it, altering it slightly, changing the shape of the tale.*

Except runes were nothing like stories.

He copied rune after rune, hoping to see something that made sense, but copying them was awkward. The lines were all too crowded. He flipped one rune upside down and found…something vaguely like *tree.*

This wasn't getting him anywhere. It seemed unlikely that Kachig wrote something-like-a-tree, maybe-upside-down. Or why it sat between the almost-rune for winter, and the backwards—and embellished—rune for fish.

Will paused, studying that last one. Fish or disease?

Talen flew back in the door, and winged into the bedroom.

Will shoved himself away from the table. There was no way he was going to get even a single rune translated. He walked to the door and leaned against the wall, staring up at darkening sky.

Runes are like stories.

Will let his head fall back against the hut. No, Alaric, stories were a series of events that took you someplace. Runes didn't go anywhere.

He pushed himself off the wall. The *rune* didn't move, but the *pen* did.

The room had fallen into a dark orange gloom. He set his finger against the wick of the candle and gathered a bit of *vitalle* from himself.

"*Incende.*" The candle flickered to life.

Talen had fallen asleep in the bedroom, his head turned backwards and tucked into his back, leaving him looking morbidly headless.

Will looked at the first rune. Instead of looking at the completed form, he focused on how the pen must have moved. There were two possible starting points. He picked one and drew the rune from there. A line down, more pressure at the top, lifting to gentle thinness at the bottom. A slope up to the right, a slash across. When there was no obvious next stroke, he lifted his pen, ignoring the rest of the marks.

Empty.

Clear as day, it said *empty.*

Or *hollow.* Or *void.* He couldn't quite remember the nuance between the three.

That wasn't important. At least not yet. He started on the lines left in the original rune. They began at the left, curled across and down before thinning again to a spidery line that connected to an accent mark.

Soul.

Will stared at the words, then back at the original rune. Kachig had intertwined *soul* with *empty.* The runes were stacked.

The empty soul?

No, *empty* wasn't descriptive, the rune leaned to the side—an action. *To empty.*

To empty the soul.

Will moved to the next. It split into four. *Stone, require/must, be chained, fire.*

He split the next rune, and the next, until the page was full.

When he finally put down the quill, his hand was shaking.

Absorption Stones

To empty the soul, the fire must be chained in a stone. Drawing out (or washing out?) the fire (life?) leaves _____ (possibly 'kill', but more like 'unmaking' than 'killing'.)

It went on, describing death and power and stones.

Will leaned back in his chair. This was what Killien wanted? Absorption stones.

And how could he possibly do it? There was no way he had a stonesteep with these skills hiding in the Morrow.

The candle sputtered out hours later. He stood and stretched, walking outside the lump of a hut. A swollen half-moon sat atop the cliffs, casting dim silvery shadows through parts of the rift and leaving most of it in blackness. Rising out of the east, the Serpent Queen's shadow stretched up into the sky. Her shape seemed to grow out of the darkness of the rift itself, leaving him with the eerie impressions that this rift was something she'd already devoured.

A scuff sounded just behind him. He spun, casting out. The bright *vitalle* of a person stood only paces away.

"It seems I should have snuck you away from the Morrow a little sooner," Sora said from the darkness.

TWENTY-THREE

"Sora!" he snapped, his heart slamming into his chest. "Why are you creeping around in the dark?"

"You're not supposed to have visitors," she said mildly, her voice almost agreeable. "Can we go inside?"

He blew out a long breath, trying to calm himself. "It makes me nervous when you talk nicely."

When they'd stepped inside, she pulled a cloth off a small bowl in her hands and a dim orange light filled the room.

"You have glimmer moss?" He leaned closer. A small bundle of the luminescent moss sat submerged in water. "I've never seen any outside Duncave."

"My people live in caves, Will," she said, exasperated.

Despite everything, he grinned at her. "There's your real voice."

The moss glowed dimmer than candlelight, more diffuse and gentle. She studied him with a small wrinkle in her brow. "I thought you'd be dead by now."

"So did I," he admitted, sitting down. "How'd you get past my guards?"

She raised an eyebrow. "You think I can't get past two lazy, distracted boys playing ranger in the dark?"

"Could you get me out?"

She bit her lip to hold back a smile. "I've heard you walk through the grass, Will. They could be unconscious and they'd still hear you."

He tried to smile, but he couldn't muster a real one. For a heartbeat, he considered the idea she'd been sent by Killien. But he couldn't imagine her feigning friendship like this. With more than a little surprise, he realized he trusted her.

He took a deep breath. "Killien has my sister."

She sank back in her chair and nodded. "He told me." At Will's surprised look, she added, "He doesn't suspect I knew you were a Keeper. So far all of his anger is focused exclusively on you."

"I just need to make sure he keeps it focused on me, not on Ilsa." Will sank back in the chair. "I don't *think* he's told her yet. At least Ilsa didn't seem to be trying to decide if I am her long lost brother."

Sora gave him a half-smile. "I've known Ilsa the entire time I've been here. I haven't been around her often, mostly because Lilit never warmed up to me, but we've spoken several times, and I like her. Lilit always has too, if that makes you feel any better. As far as I know, she's been well-treated." Her smile turned to a smirk. "And now I feel a little better about how horribly awkward you were around Ilsa all the time."

Will ran his hand through his hair. "I needed to talk to her without scaring her."

She raised an eyebrow. "I doubt she was scared, but she might think you're a lunatic." She sat back in her chair. "I can't figure out how to get her away from Killien, though. Any more than I can figure out how to get you away from him."

He pushed the next question out. "Does he have Rass too?"

Sora shook her head. "No one's seen the girl since the attack."

A wave of relief washed over him until he realized what she'd said and jolted forward.

"I don't think she was hurt," Sora said quickly. "There were a lot of injuries, but only twelve deaths, and all of that happened along the front line."

Twelve dead. "Did they have families?"

"Most of them." She paused. "Killien will never say it, but he knows the only reason there aren't more is because of you."

Will dropped his head down onto his fingertips, staring at the table without seeing it.

Sora shifted, and Will felt her hand on his arm. "We should have lost many more, Will. No one has ever heard of that many goblins on the Sweep." She pulled gently but persistently on his arm and he lifted his head. "The only reason the clan wasn't massacred is you."

"Twelve dead." He shook his head. "I should have done it sooner. I could have pushed the heat toward the holes in the ground as soon as they appeared, chased them back in."

She dropped her hand from his arm, leaving a cool spot in the shape of her fingers. "Why didn't you?"

He couldn't look up at her. The goblins had come so fast, like a flood.

"You didn't know you could do it, did you?"

His gaze flicked up to her, expecting her usual sharp contempt, but she was solemn.

He rubbed his hands over his face and let out a laugh. "I've never done anything remotely like that."

"Will," she said seriously, "you need to give Killien whatever it is he wants from you. I've never seen him this angry."

The blue book sat heavy and undecipherable on the table.

"I can't."

"Do something magical"—she waved one hand in the air, fluttering her fingers—"and give Killien what he wants."

Will stared at her. "I can't just *do something magical*."

"You can make a wall of heat. You can walk through a crowd and have no one notice you're there."

"Congratulations." Will glared at her. "You've named the two *magical things*"—he wiggled his fingers at her—"that I know how to do."

She sat back in her chair, looking at him in disbelief. "You can't do anything else?"

"Not anything worthwhile. Gerone, the Keeper who spent years trying to train me, says I have a motivation problem. Which maybe is true, because I just mastered the not-being-noticed thing since coming to the Sweep, and I figured out how to move the heat while the goblins"—it had been the goblins racing toward Sora. She'd looked so exposed in the face of their viciousness— "Ran toward us."

"Are most Keepers better at magic than you are?"

He gave her an annoyed look. "Yes, but it matters less than you'd think. We do a lot of reading, and writing, and research. Most of the Keepers are elderly and never leave the Stronghold. I'm the youngest. Alaric is next. He's the court Keeper. He's decently good at magic, and he could decipher these runes in his sleep."

She looked at him curiously. "Sounds irritating to have someone who's better than you at everything."

"He's not better at storytelling," Will corrected her. "And he's not irritating. He's been like a brother to me since I was ten."

She looked at him for a long moment. "If he was the court Keeper, what was your job?"

"I traveled around Queensland telling stories and learning stories and looked for new Keepers. When a child develops the ability to do magic, around the age of ten, their family brings them either to court, or to the nearest Keeper. For poorer families that can't afford to travel, it's nice if there's someone close."

"But you're the youngest."

"I was looking for new ones, not finding them. There should be at least two younger than me. The gap between us is usually less than ten years."

Sora gave him a long, probing look. "Is it true Keepers can sense people they can't see? And suck the life out of them?"

Will let out a laugh. "We're opposed to things like sucking the life out of people. But living things are full of energy—*vitalle*, and we can sense it when it's nearby."

Sora's face grew taut and she sat perfectly still.

"Grass and plants have a little *vitalle*," he continued, uncomfortable at her rapt attention. "Humans have a lot." He cast out through the rift finding only Sora, blazing bright in front of him, and the compact energy of Talen, nestled in the other room. "You, Talen, and I are the only ones in the rift."

Sora nodded slowly, her eyes losing their focus. Will waited for some sign of disbelief, or doubt. But she sat still, her eyes unseeing and her head slightly bowed.

"People are usually surprised to learn that I can do that."

Her gaze flickered up at him, more uncertain than he'd ever seen her. She was almost frightened.

Several disparate ideas he had about her clicked into place.

He leaned forward. "You can sense it too."

She flinched at his words.

Will stared at her for a long moment, then burst out laughing. "You can! Hal's right! You have creepy magic. No wonder you can—what did Killien say? Find a mountain hare in a snowstorm?" He leaned closer, grinning. "You have magic."

The edge of her lips curled into a reluctant smile.

"How much can you see?" he asked.

"It's not like seeing. It's more like a smell…or like feeling the temperature. I can tell when something is alive nearby, but not what direction it's in. I just have to move and see if it gets stronger."

"Fascinating! I've only met two people who had the ability to sense *vitalle*, but not manipulate it, and they were both in Queensland. It's unusual for people to have abilities like you."

"Can all Keepers sense things the way you do?"

Will hesitated. That was a complicated question.

"Can they sense *vitalle* as clearly as you?" she prodded, testing out the word.

"Yes. They can all sense *vitalle*."

She waited a moment, her eyebrows raised expectantly. "There's a but coming. Do they do it like I do? Without knowing really where it is?"

"No, we all send out a…wave of sorts, searching for energy, and it echoes back to us where things are."

Her brow knit together. "So what can you do that they can't?"

"I can…" He'd never told anyone this outside the Keepers.

"I don't really talk about it," he said.

She leveled a gaze at him, her face incredulous.

"And you don't talk about your creepy magic either," Will said. "Right." He rubbed his hand across his mouth. "I can feel people's emotions."

One of her eyebrows shot up. "Feel them?"

Will nodded. "Right around here." He pointed to the left side of his chest.

Sora was silent, pondering this. "Can you tell what they're thinking?"

Will shook his head. "It isn't like that. You know how if someone's angry, it can make you feel angry? Well I can feel that anger as strong as they do, but still separate from my own emotions."

"Can you read me?"

Will laughed. "I gave up trying to read you ages ago."

Her brow dove down and she looked at him, insulted.

"I've never met anyone who keeps their emotions as clamped down as you. When I try to read you, all I feel is…emptiness."

She considered him for a moment. "How many times have you tried?"

"At the beginning, a lot. You were terrifying. And finding out you had no emotions made it so much worse."

She looked satisfied by that answer. Then her eyes widened. "That's how you tell stories so well. You feel the audience. You change your story to please them."

Will shifted in his seat. "Well, it helps, of course. But all storytellers do that. They watch expressions and notice when attention starts to wander. I just have…a little more information. And I like to think that my success lies in the fact that I have some storytelling skills."

She shook her head, smiling. "I was right about you, storyman."

"In the most negative way possible."

"Let's see if I can control how much you feel. I'll try to open up." She leaned forward expectantly. It was strange to see her face so pleasant. The slight smile in her eyes was distracting and he closed his eyes before opening up toward her.

Emptiness bloomed in his chest and he shook his head. She kept her emotions too tightly controlled. As though she didn't want to feel them herself, never mind let anyone else know they existed. But then he felt a hint of…something.

"Curiosity," he said, "and a bit of worry, or fear."

She made a noise that sounded like agreement.

He focused and found the current of seething anger that he'd felt in her a few times before. It was so deep-rooted and so…foundational.

"What else?" she asked.

"You're angry," he continued, keeping his eyes shut so he didn't have to look in her face. "It's down below everything else. Like it's fundamental to everything you are."

He waited, with his eyes closed, listening and feeling for a reaction to his words.

Her silence filled the room, and there was no change in her emotions.

He was just about to crack an eye open to see if she was glowering at him when he noticed a thread of something else. Something...

"Happy."

He focused on the tiny bright feeling that was intertwined with the worry and the curiosity that floated above all the anger. It was definitely happiness.

He snapped his eyes open. "What are you happy about?"

She looked at him and laughed.

An odd thought struck him. "Are you happy to see me?"

She raised an eyebrow.

"Or are you happy to see me *captured*?"

She rolled her eyes and stood up.

"Or are you happy that you were right about me all along?"

She ignored his questions. "Killien's not a patient man, Will. Figure out a way to get him what he wants." She picked up the small cloth and draped it over the glimmer moss bowl, dropping the room into darkness. Her feet crunched softly on the hard floor as she left.

He peered into the blackness after her from the doorway. He couldn't see a thing, but he cast out toward her and felt her *vitalle* moving slowly down the path.

"What are you happy about?" he whispered after her.

Nothing but a little ripple of laughter came back to him.

TWENTY-FOUR

Morning sunlight barely dribbled over the edge of the rift, leaving it a dim honey color. Will's back felt like it had hardened overnight. Lying on the hard clay was even worse than the wagon.

He pushed himself to his feet and splashed some of yesterday's water onto his face. He tried a sip, but it tasted like clay. Outside, nothing had changed. Aside from the two guards at the top of the rift, it was empty. He sighed, sat down at the table and pulled Kachig's book towards him, his palm stinging slightly.

He cast out and felt the *vitalle* pressing against the inside of his palms, working to grow new skin. It would take more energy than he could possibly find to heal them. It had always seemed stupid that Keepers couldn't heal burned palms, when it was one injury they were almost guaranteed.

Will picked up the last page he'd translated. It was a list of gems with notes as to which held more souls, which damaged them, which tainted them.

Topaz, apparently, was what you wanted when trying to suck someone's soul into a stone.

He dropped the paper. He couldn't give this information to Killien, but before he could decide what he should do with it, footsteps sounded outside his door. He snapped his attention to the door, but it was only Sini, followed by a guard.

"I told Killien that you might work better with some saso." The girl held up a clay pitcher and a cup.

"You're amazing." Will shoved his work aside so she could set it down.

She pulled another stack of paper from a bag slung around her shoulders. "In case you need more."

He poured himself a steaming drink and the smell of dark roasted caramel filled the room.

"I told Killien I had faith in you." She picked up a page of split-up runes, holding it upside down and frowning. "You *are* figuring it out, aren't you?"

Will held the saso in front of his face for a long moment, breathing in the scent. Nothing good could come from this book. Even though Killien had no way to perform this level of magic, Will couldn't translate it for him. But he couldn't risk what Killien would do to Ilsa if he didn't.

"I thought I was on to something," Will said, taking the paper back from her and tossing it onto the others. "But it turned out to be nothing."

Sini's brow creased. "Killien will be back this afternoon. I've never seen him so angry."

"People keep saying that."

The girl hesitated, fidgeting with the papers. "That's because it's true."

She didn't continue, and Will took another drink. "I thought Lukas said prisoners don't get saso. Does this mean I'm not a prisoner anymore?"

Sini gave him a small smile. "It means that Lukas hates you."

Will sat back. "Yes. As subtle as he's been about it, I'd picked up on that. What I don't know is why."

"He doesn't hate you personally, he hates what you represent."

"The Keepers?"

She shrugged. "All of Queensland. He feels like the entire country betrayed him because it let Vahe take him." She looked down at her own hands. "It's easier than blaming his family."

The thought sank into Will, thick and bitter.

"Lukas's not as bad as you think. His hip hurts him a lot, but he still tries to be nice—to everyone but you. I was only twelve when I came to the Morrow, and he took care of me. He spent weeks letting me trail after him, introducing me to the nicest of the Morrow, helping me learn the skills that would make me useful to the Torch." She stared unseeing at the table. "He and Rett are like brothers. Lukas created a place for me here until it began to feel like home." She flickered a glance up to Will. "Not a home like my real home, maybe, but still a home."

Will set the saso down. "How long have you been here?"

"This is my third summer."

"I'm sorry…" He stopped, not knowing how to possibly say everything that needed saying.

She tapped the papers into a neater stack, not raising her eyes. "It's not as bad as I thought it'd be. The Torch treats us well. And there's always enough food. My family lived outside Queenstown, in a shed behind an inn. I used to slip into the city and steal food for us, but I had five younger brothers. There was never enough."

Queenstown. She'd been surrounded by so many people who should have protected her.

"When Vahe came to take me, we hadn't eaten in two days. My father barely put up a fight."

"Vahe?" Was he the only wayfarer who ever took children? Or was he the only one who delivered them to Killien?

She nodded, but a mischievous grin spread across her face. "He had three money bags, so, while my father tried to stop him, I tore one off and tossed it to my mother. They should have had food for a while."

Will grinned at her. "Too bad you couldn't get all three."

The guard cleared his throat loudly and Sini flinched. Will shot him a scowl which was utterly ineffective.

"Good luck, Will." The girl turned and hurried out of the hut.

Will stared at the empty doorway. Sini, Lukas, and Ilsa, all brought *here* by Vahe? Why them? And how many others had he brought?

TWENTY-FIVE

Will pulled out a new piece of paper and separated out a new page of runes, translating two more pages. "Translating" was too strong of a word. There were too many runes he wasn't sure about. The more runes he deciphered, the more chilled he felt. The human soul was nothing more than a commodity in this book. Something to be taken, stored, and used.

He couldn't give this information to Killien.

He needed to get it back to the Stronghold. The Keepers could study it, understand how Roven stonesteeps used stones for magic.

What he wanted to do was set this book on fire. He set his finger against the corner of the book and began to gather in *vitalle*. It felt deeply right to destroy something this evil.

Except he couldn't.

As evil as it was, there were things here the Keepers didn't understand. There must be more copies of this book. Destroying this one wouldn't keep the world from having the knowledge, just the Keepers. He let the energy dissipate, not entirely happy with his decision.

Still, he couldn't give this to Killien. He picked up the pages with the real translations and grabbed his own books out of his pack. He tucked his translations into empty spaces among his other writings. Thankfully his books were eclectic enough that phrases scattered about didn't seem too out of place.

When he finished he wadded the pages into balls and set them around the pitcher. It would be nice to have some warm saso. There weren't enough to surround it, so he grabbed two more blank sheets from the pages Sini had brought.

Writing on one caught his eye.

We're not random.

The letters were round and smooth. Was this from Sini?

He thought back over their conversations. He'd mentioned something being random...What was it?

His hand tightened on the paper. It had been with Lukas. Will had said no one knew that wayfarers were still taking random children.

Were Lukas and Sini not random? Had they been taken for a reason? Did that mean Ilsa had been too?

He crumpled the paper and tucked it next to the others, mulling over the idea. Gathering some *vitalle*, he set them on fire. Flames licked up the side of the pitcher, the paper turned to ash, and he still didn't know what Sini meant.

With a warm cup of saso, he set to creating useless pages for Killien, runes turned this way and that way, his best guesses at their meaning scribbled, scratched out, and rewritten.

He had fifteen pages "translated" when Killien showed up.

Killien walked in with a slight smile on his face, and for the briefest moment, he looked like the friendly, interesting man Will had talked to so often.

The three guards took up their positions around the room. Killien walked over to the table and picked up a few pages, he raised an eyebrow at Will's work and thumbed through the other pages, then looked around the room. When he saw the ring of ashes around the saso, his hands curled into fists, crushing the paper. He pressed his eyes shut, and loosened his hands, letting out a small laugh.

He set the papers down and sat in the chair across from Will. His voice was unnaturally light. "It doesn't convince me of your friendship if you start destroying the work I want to see."

Will's chair felt hard beneath him and he tried not to shift his weight. Around him the guards were attentive, but relaxed and Killien leaned back in his chair like an old friend come to visit. "Sini saw your work this morning. None of us had realized the runes were stacked."

Will's hand tightened on the quill. She'd both spied for Killien, and left Will that note? "I hadn't thought Sini was that sneaky."

"The translation should move along quickly, now. I considered taking the book and doing it myself. Lukas and Sini could help. They've spent a good deal of time learning to read runes. Sini, in particular has a knack for them. She's only been learning them for a short while, but she's picking it up quickly. Still, we wouldn't be as fast as you, Will."

The book sat heavily between them. Will almost opened up toward the Torch, but he decided he didn't want to have to face what the man was feeling.

"What do you want this book for, Killien? There isn't enough death and fighting with normal means? You need to add in more?"

"There is too much death." Killien tapped his finger on the book. "Which is why we need this. People respond to nothing but power. If the violence is going to end, it has to be crushed by something stronger."

"This—" Will stabbed a finger at the book. "—is not the answer. It speaks of dark things, Killien—things worse than killing people. Are you going to do this to Roven? Suck the life out of them and trap it in a stone? What happened to wanting to unify them?"

"I'm not going to actually *use* it." Killien's face was so intense Will pulled back. "You don't have to use such force against people, Will. What's important"—his voice dropped to a whisper—"is the *threat* of power."

For the first time since he'd been captured, Will actually looked at the man. There was no lightness, no fairness or interest in his face. The Torch's eyes were shadowed with exhaustion, his face strained. He looked driven, haggard. Angry. Like there was so much anger in him, it might rip him apart.

Something about Killien had come unhinged. Will searched the Torch's face, as though he'd find the answer to why written across it.

"The threat of power doesn't work," Will said, "unless you're willing—and able—to use it. If you had to hire someone to make heatstones for your clan, you can't have anyone skillful enough to do this."

Killien brushed off the words. "Your concern for my success is heartwarming. I'll worry about what to do with the translation, you just focus on giving it to me. You're off to an excellent start, and I think that's worth celebrating." He motioned to the guard in the doorway.

The guard moved and Ilsa walked in, carrying wine, some cups, and a plate of cheese.

Will's hands clenched. Part of him wanted to open up toward her, but too much of him was terrified of what he'd feel. He forced his hands to relax and dragged his gaze back to Killien, funneling as much hatred as he could into it. "Last time you offered me wine, it didn't go well."

Killien laughed, and it sounded slightly crazed. "There's nothing in this. I promise." He poured dark red wine into each cup and slid one close to Will. "To our…" He raised his glass and gave Will a complicated smile. "Partnership."

Will left his cup sitting on the table. "That isn't what this is."

"Relationship, then." Killien shrugged, taking a long drink of the wine. He stretched over, picked up Will's cup, and took a sip.

"See? It's just wine. Very good wine, actually. One of three bottles I bought from a Baylonian merchant last summer. Cost a fortune."

Will thought about refusing, about tossing the wine at Killien's face and hurling the bottle across the room. But the saso was cold and stale and his water had run out earlier. When he picked up the cup, Killien's smile turned almost genuine.

"I have only shared this wine with one other person. And that was the stonesteep from the Sunn clan who was kind enough to tell me the location of Kachig the Bloodless's book."

Will lifted the cup to his mouth and took a sip. It was delicious. Rich and simple and effortless.

"Best wine you've ever tasted?" Killien watched Will with a curiosity that was both eager and guarded.

Will set the cup down slowly. He stared at Killien's face, wondering how he'd missed the ruthlessness there for so long. "It's almost as good as what's served at Queen Saren's table."

The flash of ire in Killien's face was utterly satisfying.

The Torch took another drink, and when he set his cup down, his face was a mask, as cold and inhuman as the clay walls. Will's gaze flicked to Ilsa where she waited against the wall, her arms wrapped around her stomach, her eyes fixed on the floor as always.

"I think Will's done with the wine, Ilsa." Killien's eyes bored into Will.

She started slightly at his attention, then moved quickly across the room to gather his cup off the table.

"Thank you." Killien's voice was kind but his eyes never left Will's face. "Ilsa's served my wife for years, but only recently have I realized how valuable she is."

Ilsa smiled, timid and pleased. Both parts of it gouged at Will's heart. He opened up to her and her gratitude toward Killien bloomed in his chest, cutting into him like knives.

The Torch fixed Will with a smug look. "I keep finding more and more reasons to keep her near me." A streak of viciousness from Killien cut into Will.

A shiver of unease wriggled through Ilsa's pleasure and her hand tightened on the wine. A silence, taut and rigid, filled the room. Ilsa stood still, her breath shallow and quick, her apprehension growing the longer the silence stretched.

"I've done what you asked for." Will kept his eyes fixed on Killien.

"You burned what I asked for," Killien corrected him.

If Killien knew how to decode the runes, there was no point in keeping it from him any longer. Will's hands tightened into fists. "I'll write it out for you again. You'll have what you want."

"And you think you deserve a reward for doing such fine work?"

Will didn't look at Ilsa. "I'm the only one you have anything against."

Killien cocked his head to the side, he gave Will an easy smile that was stabbed in the back by the savagery in his eyes. "What exactly are you asking for?"

Will's own anger drowned out Ilsa's shrinking pleasure and Killien's cruelty.

"Leave her out of it," he whispered.

Ilsa glanced at them, her brow drawn in confusion.

"Ilsa," Killien began, leaning back in his chair, "Will has developed a bit of a…fascination with you."

Will felt a dart of fear worm its way through Ilsa's emotions and she stiffened.

"No—" he started to deny it, turning to look her full in the face.

She shrank back away from him.

"Don't speak, Will," Killien interrupted. The guard behind Ilsa shifted closer to her, unsheathing his knife.

Will dragged his gaze back to Killien, fury and impotence threatening to explode out of him.

"It's understandable," Killien said, a glint of viciousness in his eyes. "Ilsa is a lovely young woman, and you've been lonely a long time."

"That's not—"

Killien raised a hand sharply to stop him. The guard loomed grimly behind Ilsa, who held her arms close to her side. Will kept his eyes fixed on Killien's face, he pressed his fists down into the table.

"I'm sorry, Ilsa." Killien nodded to her. "I didn't mean to make you uncomfortable. Thank you for your help. You may return to your other duties."

With the tiniest glance at Killien, filled with gratitude, she bowed to the Torch and hurried from the hut.

Will turned back to Killien, furious. The sound of Ilsa's footsteps drew farther away, tearing a part of Will out with them. He slammed himself closed.

"You see, Will, you're not the only one capable of making people like you."

"If you hurt her," Will said, his voice unsteady.

"I admit I had my doubts she was your sister. Obviously you do not."

In blind fury Will cast out, found the *vitalle* of Killien and the guards, and snatched at it, not caring if it killed them. Not caring that the guards would kill him for it. Only caring that he had enough time to destroy Killien.

Nothing happened.

Drawing in the *vitalle*, was like grabbing smoke.

He stretched his hand out toward Killien. The man was a flaming beacon of energy, even the ring he'd taken from the traitor wrapped around his hand with a blaze of energy, but Will could move none of it.

Will grasped at it again. He'd never had *vitalle* be so elusive. "What did you do to me?"

The guard behind him grabbed his shoulder again, pulling him back in the chair. Each person in the room was a towering pillar of energy that Will could not touch.

"You don't think I'd walk in here and put myself at the mercy of your powers, do you?"

Killien asked. "If I were you, I'd stop trying to fight, Will. Every guard has orders concerning Ilsa if you try anything…unpleasant. At the moment she knows nothing about you beyond that you are a Keeper. She hasn't suffered anything on your account. If you cooperate, she won't have to."

Will let his hand drop to the table, a coldness spreading through him and he felt more exposed than he ever had on the Sweep. Why couldn't he touch the *vitalle*?

Killien considered Will for a moment. "How old were you when she was taken?"

Will almost didn't answer, but he couldn't see what it would matter. "Eleven." Will pushed the word out between clenched teeth.

The Torch seemed to find that answer amusing. "And did you use your magic to try to save her?"

Will clenched his bandaged hands on the table, his anger burning like searing hot coals in his chest.

"Ah." Killien nodded. "But it obviously didn't work. And even though you were only eleven, you still blame yourself."

Will stared at the man's face, pouring all his impotent rage into the look.

"Ironic," Killien said with a slight exhale of laughter.

The word caught Will off guard. "Why?" he demanded.

The Torch looked at Will with an odd expression. "Just think how different things would be today if they'd gone differently that night." Killien heaved himself out of his chair.

"But you're right about one thing. You have given me what I wanted. The beginnings of it anyway. And if you want Ilsa to stay as safe and happy as she currently is, you'll continue your translations.

"Tonight," he continued, "as a little celebration, I'm letting you out of the Grave. Not for good, of course, but for a short time. I have visitors from the Sunn Clan here. One of them is the Torch's own nephew. For the first time in ten years, the Morrow will be invited to the enclave of Torches."

Killien's face split into a broad smile. "The Sweep is being reshaped. The smaller clans are banding together and things will change, beginning with this enclave."

Knowing it was useless, Will still cast out and tried to grab at some of Killien's *vitalle*. It slipped through his grasp. Will stared at the man who'd become a stranger.

"I need the storyteller from Gulfind to impress my guests tonight, Will. Of course Ilsa will be there. I wouldn't want to deny you the pleasure of seeing her. You have a few hours to come up with a story." He walked to the door and paused. "If I were you, I'd make it something spectacular."

TWENTY-SIX

Will went to the door. As Killien and the guards topped the path and disappeared, the flat blue sky settled back down like a glass lid, clear and empty.

A smooth shape glided over the edge of the rift and toward him, Talen's white chest glinting against the sky. Will held his arm out and leaned his head away as the small bird flapped onto his shoulder. "You're getting better at landing."

A thin green shoot swung from Talen's beak, its roots still entangled in a clod of earth.

"And that's better than your usual offering of a mouse." Will let out a long sigh. "Let's take it to your nest."

Will cast out toward the bird and found the coil of energy. Even when Talen rested, he was poised to burst into flight. Gently he took hold of the *vitalle* in the little hawk. There it was, solid, malleable. Will could have drawn it out, shifted it, anything.

Whatever Killien had done to keep him from manipulating energy, had ended. Will thought back over his time with Killien. Had he ever tried to use any *vitalle* when he was that near the Torch? Maybe one of Killien's rings had the power to stop him. He'd read people's emotions. He'd used *vitalle* to heal Lilit, but Killien hadn't been as close. He'd been down near her feet, too worried and broken to come close.

Will opened up to Talen, searching for the bird's emotions. But the hawk had only a slight sense of anticipation.

"It seems like I should find some sense of loyalty. Or companionship." Will settled Talen on back of one of the chairs. "You're free to leave this charming place, and yet every day you come back."

He reached out slowly and ran the back of his finger down the front of Talen's wing. "Things don't seem to be going well. If you come back and I'm not here…" Talen's heartbeat thrummed against Will's finger. "I'm sure you'll find plenty of mice."

He sat down in the other chair. "If you get a chance, will you keep your eye out for Rass?" He tried to push the idea of the little girl at the hawk. To resonate his desire to know where she was, but he could sense no change in the little bird. "I doubt anyone's taking care of her." Talen turned his golden eyes toward Will, then with a rush of air, winged out of the door, and out of sight.

Will stared at the empty door. "I didn't think so."

He dropped his head into his hands. It really didn't feel like a night for storytelling. He needed something impressive, but easy enough he could tell in what was bound to be a stressful situation.

Sable would be a good choice. An orphan who'd joined a traveling theater company, she'd grown famous and wealthy. She'd left that life, not entirely by choice, and managed to save her people from a terrible enemy.

Yes, Sable was long enough to feel epic, intriguing enough to keep his attention even with Killien and Ilsa there. And since it was older than Queensland, there'd be no way to trace it to the current country. Yes, Sable would do nicely.

The rest of the afternoon passed in excruciating slowness while Will translated runes for Killien. Talen didn't return. Neither did Sora. Or Killien. Even Lukas's hateful glares would have relieved the boredom.

Eventually the shadows inched their way up the rift walls and the sky darkened to black, except for a reddish glow to the west. The wind tore across the Sweep, sending clouds racing past the earliest stars. To the west, the red in the sky brightened. Had they lit a bonfire? The glow stretched wider across the sky and a smudge of darkness covered the stars.

Not a bonfire. A grass fire. The smoke grew, piling up in malevolent shadows, glowing with a red-blackness. The guards still stood at the top of the rift. Will took a step toward them, wondering if they'd let him see the fire.

A small figure stepped out from the shadows next to Will. He froze, opening up and a burst of excitement exploded inside of him.

"Will!" a little voice whispered.

"Rass?"

She grabbed his hand. "Come. There's a big fire near the other rift, you can sneak out."

He almost laughed, but she sounded so serious. "The guards are still there."

"Not that way. I have a rope. Hurry!" She tugged him.

He held back. "Wait, I need my bag." He ran into the hut and grabbed it, tucking Kachig's book in it too.

He let Rass pull him around the hut and press a rope into his hands. He gave it a hard tug, and it stayed firm. Gripping it sent a thousand tiny daggers of pain into his palms, but he set his foot on the cliff wall and started to climb. With each step his feet crumbled away part of the wall. The rope was strangely textured, more like a braid of smooth vines than normal cord. Almost like—

"This is grass!" he hissed down at Rass.

"Of course it is."

It was unhealthy, that's what it was. It was unhealthy for a people to have this much of a love for grass. And this little girl was the worst. "How'd you make this?"

"I used *grass*. Hurry up."

They climbed above the height of the hut, and the guards stood clearly outlined against the reddening sky, focused by the fire. If they turned, Will and Rass would be clearly visible on the cliff.

Will pulled himself up, inch by crumbling clay inch. It took a lifetime to reach the top where the thin rope spread out into a wide net stretching up onto the Sweep. Will clawed his way over the edge and threw himself down. Wind laced with smoke and ash rolled past him and he covered his mouth with his arm.

A low line of rust-red flames spread across the ground to the west, like an army of fire demons dancing across the Sweep, the wind whipping them closer.

Will felt along the netting of grass, trying to find what the rope was anchored to. He found nothing. It merely spread out and tangled with the blades growing out of the earth. Rass climbed nimbly out over the edge.

"Rass, how did you ?"

She grabbed at Will's hand. "Hurry!"

"Wait. Where is the rift where the Morrow live?"

Rass pointed at the wall of flames. "Past the fire."

He took a few steps toward it. In the chaos, could he get to Ilsa?

Rass pulled his hand. "The fire is coming fast. We need to run!"

Will paused another moment. "I have to go back."

"After the fire!" Rass yanked at him. "You can't go that way!"

The line of flames spread unbroken to the north and south. He'd never get past it. With a growl of frustration, he nodded. Pulling two shirts out of his bag, he tied one over his nose and mouth, and the other around Rass's tiny head, then motioned her to lead the way.

The Hoarfrost Range sat to the north, close enough to touch. She ran toward a particularly jagged peak, far enough past the smoke that the snow on its peak glittered moon-white. Will ran after her, his bag bouncing against his back and his legs complaining before they had gone more than a dozen steps. The smoke whipped past them in fits, interspersed with cool night air and the fire rumbled like distant thunder.

He was utterly exhausted and the mountains seemed no closer when the wall of flame reached the nearest hillside, fingers of black and red thrashing wildly into the sky.

Rass stopped and whirled toward the flames. "It's going to catch us."

The flames flew toward them faster than they could hope to run. He spun around, but the fire was stretched out across the whole world to the west. There was no escape. Past the thick line of flames, the Sweep was black and charred. They'd be safe on the other side, but they'd be burned alive before the flames passed them.

Stepping forward, Rass closed her eyes and dropped her head down. Her hair fell over her face and she spread both her hands toward the grass between them and the approaching fire.

She was tiny and insubstantial in the face of the fire and the smoke.

"Rass!"

The flames crackled and roared like the rush of a huge waterfall, or a crashing surf. He took a step toward her and stretched out his hand, desperate to pull her away, but she flicked up her hand in a commanding gesture and he stopped.

His breath was hot and damp under the shirt, the sting of smoke burning his throat. There was no going back. The fire was already between them and the Grave. He waited a breath, then another.

A swirl of flame spun up from the grass in front of them, like a demon tearing out of the earth, showing Rass in stark relief. She clenched her hands into claws, rotated her palms up, and like a giant heaving a mountain, she hurled her hands toward the roiling sky.

The ground in front of them exploded.

TWENTY-SEVEN

Dirt and grass thundered into the air. Will spun away, throwing his hands over his head and crashing to his knees. He grabbed Rass, pulling her back, leaning over to shield her from the earth crashing down around them.

When dirt stopped pelting him, he looked up.

A swath of turned earth cut through the leading edge of the fire. Strings of grass wafted down through thick, swirling dust.

The two of them sat in a gap of darkness. Flames blazed past on either side, driven east by the wind. A wave of heat rolled by, and they were behind the fireline, kneeling in a world of blackness and soot. All around them thin trails of smoke rose like wind whipped spirits.

Rass shifted, sinking back against his chest. Her eyes were closed and her shoulders heaved with thick, heavy breaths.

He cast out across the wasteland, but there was nothing left living but roots. No plants above the ground, no animals, no people as far as he could sense. The line of fire racing eastward was a gash of bright energy.

Rass's shoulders slowly settled down into regular breathing and she pushed her dusty hair out of her face. She looked like a creature made of earth. The shirt around her face was caked with dirt, and the skin by her eyes was rough with more. Bits of grass stuck out of her hair.

Will pulled the shirt down off his face and stared at her.

"You're not just a little girl."

She pulled her own shirt down and quirked a curious smile at him. "I'm a pratorii."

Will waited for her to say more.

"I have no idea what that means."

"Pratorii. I am the grass." She tilted her head as though considering the words. "Or the grass is mine."

A memory triggered in Will's mind.

What are the elves? he'd asked Ayda during the weeks he'd spent in the Lumen Greenwood.

We are the trees. She'd spun and thrown her arms out. *The keepers of their souls.*

Will touched a lock of Rass's dirt-caked hair. It was thin and straight and stiff. Like grass. "You're an elf?"

Rass considered this for a moment. "The tree elves are our cousins. They are silvii, we are pratorii."

"So...a grass elf?"

Rass grinned up at him. "Yes."

It seemed so obvious. She didn't look like she was from Queensland. The wide eyes, the sharp chin, the cheekbones: she looked like a smaller, wilder version of a tree elf.

Will stared at her, stunned. "Why didn't you tell me?"

Her smile faltered. "I thought you knew."

"I didn't even know grass elves existed." He gestured to her little grey shift. "I thought you were just an odd little slave."

"Roven slaves don't live in the grass."

"I know, that was part of what was so odd." He frowned at the fabric she wore. "Don't tell me that's made of grass."

She plucked at the edge of it. "The veins that run down the grass blades can be woven together into anything."

Will shook his head and laughed. "It all makes perfect sense, now that you say it. Are there many grass elves here?"

She nodded. "There's a lot of grass."

"You know, I have spent a lot of time over the last few weeks imagining rescue scenarios. Never once did I include a grass elf."

Rass puffed up a bit and gave him a proud smile.

Will looked at the long line of fire, a hundred questions circling in his mind. "Does the fire hurt you?"

She let out a small laugh. "Only if we're foolish enough to be in its path. Fires are as good for the Sweep as rain and sunshine. It burns away the ghosts of the old grass and feeds the new shoots. But most fires are small, and easily avoided."

The gap of flame that had passed around them had closed, and raced eastward unimpeded.

Will cast a sidelong glance at Rass. She was an elf. The idea was both shocking and utterly fitting.

"That was well done." He pointed to the upturned earth.

Rass pushed herself up and shook her hair out, dislodging dirt clods and small bundles of grass. She set her fist on her chest and gave Will a small bow before breaking into peals of laughter. A swirl of smoke enveloped them and her laugh turned to a cough.

"We should keep going," she said.

Will hesitated. "I need to go back. I need to get someone."

Rass shook her head. "The entire clan will be on guard. If you need to go back, wait until the fire's out. You'll never get close without being caught again."

Will knew she was right, but it was still frustrating to tug the shirt back over his face and follow her north. They'd find somewhere safe to regroup, then he'd figure out how to get back for Ilsa.

With the fire racing away, the world sank into blackness. His boots kicked up ash. All of the grass was gone. Will glanced down at Rass walking silent beside him. "Are you...alright?"

She looked up at him, her brow drawn down questioningly.

He waved his hand at the wasteland around them. "The grass," he began, not knowing exactly what to ask.

"Last year's grass was dead. The fire passed quickly and the roots are fine. New grass will grow soon."

Question after question popped into his mind. "Can you talk to it?"

She considered the question for a moment. "The grass talks to me."

When she didn't continue, Will bit his lips closed to keep from laughing. "What does grass have to say?"

"It tells me about the weather and where the herds are. If the ground is wet enough. How hot the sun is. Where the Roven are."

"How much of it can you hear?"

She looked at him as though the question made no sense.

"Can you hear the grass near your feet? The grass on an entire hill?"

"All the grass is one."

Will stared at her. "*The roots of each connects with the others, so the whole world is an endless living thing,*" he quoted her from the first day they'd met.

Her eyes wrinkled in pleasure. "You remember."

"It was very story-like." He stared at this tiny girl, trooping along next to him, just as she had for days. "You can hear the entire Sweep?"

She shrugged. "The grass is one. But I can't hear anything where it's scorched. The roots never speak."

The night dragged on endlessly, each step charred and crunchy. The fire continued off to their right, but all around them, as far as they could make out, there was nothing but burnt grass and ashes.

The thought of Ilsa haunted him. Would Killien punish her because Will had left? He almost turned back three times, but he couldn't figure out what good it would do. Putting himself back at Killien's mercy would change nothing. The book by Kachig the Bloodless sat in Will's pack. It was a strong bargaining chip. Maybe he could find a way to trade it for Ilsa.

It wasn't quite midnight when they reached the end of the burned grass. They continued north through the Sweep until the ground rose into the first slopes of the Hoarfrost Range. The sun was just rising and the wind had died. Far behind them where the Sweep had burned, lines of smoke rose up like thin grey reeds out of a black swamp.

"We need a place to hide before the sun rises." Will headed uphill until the trees grew into a proper forest. The smell of evergreen filled the air, clean and fresh. It smelled like the woods at the Keeper's Stronghold, and a sharp pang of homesickness hit him. Sunlight slanted through the trunks brightening patches of the trees and tufts of bright green grass. He breathed in the air, letting the height of the forest wrap around him. For the first time in a year he felt right. If it wasn't for Ilsa, he would never step foot on the Sweep again.

Ilsa. He glanced back toward the Sweep. Killien wouldn't do anything to her, would he? Maybe Will should have done something besides run. But even as he thought it, he knew there was no way he could have even found Ilsa in the chaos, never mind convinced her to come with him.

Rass walked along next to him, looking around at the thin sprinkling of grass with a slight pucker in her brow. The forest ended and the ground sloped up to their left across a bare patch of earth, toward a rock wall. Rass scuffed her way up the slope, her shoulders slumped, but he was struck again with how healthy she looked compared to when he'd first met her. It had been less than a fortnight.

The reason was so obvious he laughed. "You're getting stronger because it's spring, aren't you?"

She nodded. "I always get thin in the winter."

"I thought it was my food."

She wrinkled her nose. "I like the bread, and the avak. But the dry meat is too hard to chew."

"You never actually lived with the Roven, did you?"

"I hadn't been near them in ages. I only came the day I met you because I do love hearing the stories from the colored wagons."

It was astonishing how many wrong ideas he'd had about her. "If you live in the grass, what do you eat?"

"Worms and grubs. But in the winter, those burrow lower than the roots of the grass, and I can't find them. There are plenty around now, though, if you're hungry."

Will tried not to let his revulsion show on his face and dampen her offer. "No thank you."

He was about to collapse with exhaustion when he saw a shadowed spot above two large boulders. He scrambled up and found a small cave. He spread out his bedroll and the two of them collapsed on the floor in a patch of warm sunlight. Using shirts for pillows, they both lay down. Will's mind searched for ways to get back close to Ilsa, but he hadn't thought of any before he sank into sleep.

He woke no less tired. He lifted his head to look outside, and the muscles in his neck cried out in protest. The woods were silent and empty in the afternoon light. He heaved himself up. The cave was high enough that he could see through the tops of the trees down to the grasslands. In the distance he could see a wide swath of blackened Sweep.

Rass came to his elbow, looking out across the Sweep, her face untroubled by the destruction. A thought struck him. "Did you start the fire?"

"No. I wouldn't have started it where it would try to kill us."

"Good point." Will thought for a moment. "Where did it start?"

"West of the rift where the Morrow live. There were people near it when it first flared up."

Will's gaze traveled over the endless black. "Who would start a fire like that?"

Something thumped in the cave behind them and Will spun around.

Two rabbits lay on the floor of the cave, and Sora climbed in after them.

"The first person most people blamed," she said, "was you."

TWENTY-EIGHT

Will stood caught between fear and relief. The smallest smile curled up the edge of Sora's mouth. "I think this is only the second time I've made you speechless. It's nice." She leaned to the side so she could see Rass. "Are you hungry?"

Rass peeked out from behind Will. "Yes."

Sora slung off her pack and pulled out some dried meat.

Rass wrinkled her nose. "I'm gonna find something for myself." She scooted past Sora, giving her as wide a berth as she could.

Sora sat down, stretching her legs out in front of her. "This is one of my favorite caves. I'm mildly impressed that you found it."

Will grabbed a piece of meat. "Are more rangers coming?"

"Not any time soon. I told them you'd run back toward Queensland as fast as your lumbering legs could carry you. We'll rest until dusk. We need to find somewhere safer to hide, but it'll be better to move after dark."

Rass scrambled back in and scurried back over next to Will, offering him one of the four squirming grubs in her palm.

Sora peered into Rass's hand. "The darkish blue ones are the best."

Rass looked at her in surprise, then smiled. "They are."

Will held up a piece of meat. "I've got plenty."

Rass considered Sora for a moment before shyly offering her the grubs. At Sora's refusal, Rass popped a thin, pink one into her mouth.

Sora watched the girl closely. "I expected you to be alone, Will."

"Rass is the one who got me out of the rift," Will said. "And saved me from the fire."

Rass swallowed the last grub. "All we needed was a rope. And a little grass ripped up so the fire would go around us."

Sora glanced between the two of them. "I saw the torn earth. I thought Will had done that." She leaned closer to the little girl, taking in her wide eyes and her angular face. "How did you—" Her eyes widened. "You're a pratorii."

Rass elbowed Will. "*She* knows what pratorii are."

"Yes. She's very wise."

Sora looked at her in wonder. "I've never met one before. I think I've caught glimpses of a couple, but was never sure. You look more human than I expected." Her gaze flicked to Will. "Why are you spending time with him?"

"Because I'm likable," Will protested.

Sora ignored him and turned back to Rass. "I've never heard of a pratorii spending time with people."

"Will isn't a normal person."

"Agreed." Sora picked up one of the rabbits and began to dress it. She glanced at Will. "Someone should take first watch."

Will nodded and started to rise, but Rass grabbed his hand. She cast a nervous glance at Sora. "I'll do it." Without waiting for an answer, she scooted out of the cave and settled into a little nook in the rocks.

"It's a good thing she's a pratorii." Sora pitched her voice low. "Because unless you have some capable wife stashed somewhere, I can't see how you're going to take care of a little girl."

"I would have done just fine. Besides, Keepers don't marry."

Sora looked up at him. "Ever?"

"Not often. We spend all our time studying and traveling. It doesn't leave much time for a family. The last time one married was sixty years ago."

"Hm," she said in a tone impossible to read. "Can you hand me some pine needles?"

A thick layer of pine needles crowded along the edge of the cave floor. He ran his fingers along the floor and scooped up a jumble of needles, their dry tips jabbing into his fingers. "We don't have wood for a fire."

She fixed him with an annoyed look. "Why would I make a fire on a clear day while the entire Morrow Clan is looking for us?" She set half of the pine needles in a pile on the floor and pulled a heatstone out of her bag. "I just need a small flame. Be useful. I know you can start this with your finger."

"Don't you have anything to start a fire with?" Will asked. "If you've misplaced your tinder, you could just give it one of your flinty looks."

"I like to save those for you. And I have several ways to start a fire. One of them is your magic finger. And since you don't have much else to contribute…"

"Fine." Will set his finger against the needles. He hesitated just a moment, at the fear that he wouldn't be able to move the *vitalle* again. But Killien wasn't here, and neither was whatever he'd done. The energy flowed easily out of Will's finger and the needles lit.

It burned for only a handful of breaths, but the heatstone began to glow with a rich, yellow light. Heat poured out of it and Will backed up.

"Why didn't you tell Killien about my magic finger the night you met me?"

"I don't know."

She rigged the rabbit up to hang over the heatstone and offered no further answer.

There was something different about her. She didn't smile, but her face was…content, her movements relaxed. She was comfortable here, in a way she'd never been on the Sweep.

He leaned against the wall, his body heavy with exhaustion. Sora's eyes were shadowed, and for the first time it occurred to him that she had been up all night as well, and probably hadn't had the luxury of sleeping all morning.

"Any chance you have anything useful in your bag?" she asked.

He dragged his pack over. "I think it's useful, but you're going to be disappointed. I have some clothes, some avak pits I'm taking back to Queensland, and I have books."

"Books. How shocking." She picked up the second rabbit, pulled out her knife and sliced into its skin.

"That is both disgusting and fascinating."

She answered him by yanking off the rabbit fur in one, quick wrench.

Outside the cave, Rass laid her head against a wide boulder next to her and hummed a catchy little tune.

"Your hawk brought me a clump of grass," Sora said.

"Of course he did. Because what people need on the Sweep is more grass. Although grass is better than dead mice."

"You didn't send him to me?"

"No. Why wou—" He sat up straight. "When did he come to you?"

"Just before I saw you in the rift."

Will's mind spun. He pointed at Rass. "Talen found her while I was there, too."

"Maybe he's in the market for a better owner."

"Or maybe," he said, "he *listened to me*.

"The first day I told him it'd be useful if he could bring me something with energy, like a tree." Will leaned forward. "And he *did*. It was barely a shoot, but the roots still had dirt in them. I'd thought it was for his nest—but he didn't take it to his nest, he brought it to *me*."

"I'm not sure a shoot counts as a tree."

"A very small tree for a very small hawk. But then I asked him for what I really needed—you." She drew back slightly.

He gave her a wide smile. "Although it turns out all I needed was Rass."

The hint of a smile appeared on her face. "I hadn't decided yet whether you were worth rescuing."

Will sank back against the wall. The sky was a bright, clear blue, without a single speck of hawk to be seen. "I can't believe Talen did what I asked."

"How'd you get him to?"

"Emotions resonate." Was it really that simple? "I think I…shared my emotions with him. My need to find you."

"You're not making sense."

"I think I am," he said slowly, sitting back and unwrapping his bundle of books. Had Talen really found Sora? And the tree? And Rass?

"What is that?" Sora pointed at the blue book.

"Killien's book. It's about fairly horrific magic by Kachig the Bloodless. And Killien is probably very angry that I have it." He opened one of his own books, starting his usual check for dampness and mites.

Sora watched him. "What could you possibly have to write down that takes up that many pages?"

"Mostly stories I've learned on the Sweep. This one's from the Temur Clan about an old woman who lives in a cave, chases the ripples of grass across the hills. And sends bats to terrorize the clan."

"What is the point of recording something like that?"

Her tone was so sharp that Will glanced up at her.

"Why write down useless, harsh things about a woman who has probably suffered her whole life as an outcast? Do you know what story might actually be worth writing down?" She leaned toward him, pointing her knife at the book. "That woman's story. She was someone's daughter. What happened to her that she ended up banished and shunned? That"—she sliced the knife viciously into the rabbit—"would be a story worth writing down."

Her face was furious and she sliced strips of rabbit meat off the creature with a frightening efficiency.

Will flipped to the next page. "It's right here."

Sora's knife stopped and she lifted her glare from the rabbit to Will's face.

"It took me three days to find her." The stench had been awful. The wind had blown past, hollow and uncaring.

Sora sat utterly still, leaning as though she might explode off the ground toward him at any moment.

"She was dead." The woman's body had been curled up in the corner of the cave. Grey hair wild and matted, gaunt cheeks, bone-thin wrists.

Sora leaned closer and Will shifted it so she could see his sketch. The cave had been scattered with clay tools and dishes. There had been goat droppings everywhere and a rickety cage along the back wall with a chicken, also dead.

"She'd had a goat, and a chicken, a small bucket, a cup, and an assortment of things made out of woven grass."

"Any bats?"

"No sign of them. The cave was covered in filth." He stared at the page unseeing. "Except for the basket her body was curled around." Her arms had held it so tightly, he'd had trouble removing it. "The rim of it was woven with withered flowers, and inside lay a set of neatly folded clothes, small enough for a young child."

Sora ran her hand over the drawing, looking at Will's notes, silent for a long time.

"But why write it down?" She spoke so quietly Will had to lean closer to hear her. "There's nothing left to do."

"I buried her." She'd been so light Will could have carried her all the way back to the Temur village. "And then I made a copy of what I'd found, describing as much of her life as I could figure out, and delivered it to the biggest gossip in the Temur clan."

Sora looked at him with raised eyebrows.

"The entire clan must have known about it in a matter of days." He paused and flipped back to the story the clan had told him about the woman, with all its meanness and fear. "I also copied this, word for word as I'd heard it, on the same sheet of paper."

A small smile curled up the edge of Sora's mouth. She nodded in approval before busying herself with the rabbit again.

"But in some ways," she said, "your story is just as bad as theirs. You wanted them to feel something about the woman. So you made your story to fit it." She looked up at him. "How you tell a story changes everything about it."

Will nodded. "There are all sorts of stories in the world. Theirs was full of fear and contempt. My story was a reminder of her humanity. Of her weakness and struggles and isolation. And ultimately of her death, neglected and shunned by them." Will stopped and flipped through the book again, phrases of fear or hope or pain jumping out from each page. "We tell stories about everything. We can't escape them. It's how we interact with each other, it's how we keep the things we value close. It's the fearful stories, the ones that strip the humanity from everyone but ourselves that cost us nothing to spread. It takes a lot of searching to find the true stories, the ones that reveal people's humanity instead of crushing them beneath the weight of hatred."

Sora was silent for a long time. "Stories are too powerful. The ones people told about that woman defined her life."

"Which is why they're important." He flipped back to the page with the sketch of the cave. "Her name was Zarvart."

"Zarvart," Sora said quietly.

Will nodded. "Names are important too."

She considered the picture for a long moment, then piled strips of rabbit onto a piece of leather. Pulling another small heatstone out of her bag, she set it next to the rest of the pine needles. She wiggled her finger in the air and looked expectantly at Will.

Leaning forward, he lit the needles. The heatstone glowed and Sora used her knife to roll it up on top of the rabbit meat. The meat sizzled as she wrapped up the leather, trapping the meat against the hot stone. She bound it with some twine, soaked the entire bundle with water, and tied it to the top of her pack.

The other rabbit cooked over the first heatstone, little drops of fat sizzling onto the stone and the hot floor of the cave next to it. Sora lay down and Will traded places with Rass at the entrance to the cave who then curled up in a corner and went straight to sleep. The next several hours passed in boredom watching nothing at all happen in the forest below.

It was late afternoon when Sora came and sat next to him. "Let me see your hands."

His bandages were grimy and shifted out of place, showing the angry red edges of his palms. Sora pulled out a small bottle from her pack and a ball of bandages.

He raised an eyebrow. "You put a lot of thought into rescuing me."

"Remembering food and medicine isn't exactly high level planning."

Will looked up at the wide blue sky. It was unaccountably comfortable here. The floor was hard, there wasn't much to eat, and if he stayed too long, Killien would find him and kill him. But somehow in the midst of all that, it felt homey.

The sky was a rich blue like home, and Queensland felt almost within reach. The Keepers' Stronghold, book after book after book, stories that made sense and had all the right feelings. A place where being comfortable wasn't restricted to one small cave, a ranger, and a grass elf.

Sora unwound a dirty bandage slowly, revealing the ugly burn on his palm.

"Do you think Killien will hurt Ilsa?" Will pushed the question out quickly before the fear behind it overpowered him.

It took her a moment to answer. "I don't."

"Are you just saying that to make me feel better? Or do you really think Killien is that decent of a man?"

"No and no. I used to think Killien was a decent man. And maybe he is, but lately he's so angry. He's done savage things when he thinks the clan is in danger. But Ilsa is the only leverage he has against you. I don't think he'd give that up. He was certain we'd find you and he needs something to control you with." She let out a long, slow breath. "It's my guess he'll do what he can to ingratiate himself to her. Because the more loyal she is to him, the more it will hurt you." Sora finished unwinding the bandage and he stretched his hand a little. She bent over his hand, inspecting the burn.

Will looked up again at the patch of right-color-blue sky outside the cave and let it call to the deepest parts of himself. The parts he'd been trying not to think about for a year. He wanted to go back home so much he almost couldn't breathe.

"I can't leave her there. You need to take me back to Killien."

TWENTY-NINE

Sora's head snapped up.

"If you take me back," Will said before she could argue, "Killien will still trust you. He probably expects you to be the one to find me anyway. Maybe you'd get a chance to help Ilsa escape."

"I'm not taking you back." She dribbled some water on his palm and rubbed at the dirty ridge of crustiness along the edge of his burn.

"There's no other way that Ilsa's ever going to get out of there."

Sora dropped his hand and looked up at him in exasperation. "If you go back, he'll kill you. Then he'll have no reason to keep her alive." She picked up the jar of salve and spread some across his palm and wrapped a new bandage around it before starting on his other hand.

She was right. He stared across the forest. There had to be a way.

Sora worked quietly, and he was struck again with how comfortable she was. He tried to pinpoint what was different. She wore the same leathers she'd been wearing ever since he met her. Her arms were bare of anything but the wide cloth band around her upper arm. The long white claw was still there, tied on by strips of thin leather, and the long puckered scar beneath it ran from her shoulder to her elbow. Her boots were worn leather, her hair hung over her shoulder in its thick braid. And every bit of it looked…at home.

"You love the mountains, don't you?"

She looked up at him sharply, as though expecting some sort of teasing. "I do."

"Why did you leave?"

Her face hardened and she picked up the salve to put on his palm. "I'm not interested in talking about my life with someone I know almost nothing about."

Will felt a flash of irritation at the return of her coldness, but his retort died on his lips. He deserved that. "You're right, you don't know much about me. What do you want to know?"

She narrowed her eyes at him.

"Alright, I'll start at the beginning. I was born outside a small town a half day's ride south of Queenstown. You already know I have a younger sister Ilsa, although I haven't seen her since she was a baby. My mother's name is Marlin. My father's name was Tell."

"Was?"

He nodded. "We lived on a small farm. I wasn't much help, I'm sure. Neither the chicken nor the cow was much trouble, but we had this goat, Tussy, who was the bane of my existence."

Will flexed his fingers slightly and saw the puckered red and white outline of his old scar, almost covered up by the new burn. "The first time I ever did magic it was because of that stupid goat."

Sora sat perfectly still, her eyes wide, searching his face. He dropped his gaze back to his hand. It had been twenty years since he'd told this story to the Keepers when he'd first joined them. But now that he started, the words pressed up inside him, and after only a short struggle, he let them out, telling her everything about Vahe and Ilsa.

"How old was she?"

Will pressed his eyes shut against the image of Ilsa's terrified face. "Two."

He felt a touch on the edge of his palm. Sora's finger brushed over it, feather light on the edge of his healthy skin, blanking out to nothing over the scar.

"All I wanted was to stop him, but after everything, he still killed my father and took my sister. And I almost killed my mother."

Sora set her hand across his palm, blocking the scar with her own long fingers.

"How old were you?"

"Eleven."

Sora said nothing, but picked up the jar of salve and began to spread it across Will's palm.

"When I was born," she said quietly, "stars flew across the sky."

The memory of his parents dissolved at her words. She focused on his hand, spreading the cool cream over the blisters, filling the air with the scent of mint and sulphur.

"A star shower?"

She nodded. "Not unusual, except this one came from the mouth of the Serpent Queen."

"Do the mountain clans think of her the same way the Roven do?"

Sora shook her head. "Among the Roven the Serpent Queen is a shadow that is devouring the heavens. But to my people she is Tanith, a serpent moving thorough the stars, giving meaning to the blackness between them. She searches out paths in the darkness and leads those lost in the night."

"I like your version better."

Sora didn't look up at him. Her face was distant as she picked up a new strip of bandage and wrapped it around his hand. "But she is not all good. She is still full of darkness, and when dark things must be done, she is the one to do it.

"The night I was born they say a hundred stars flew out from her mouth, scattering across the sky." Her hands paused for a moment. "And one gave life to a child."

"They think you came from the Serpent Queen?" Will let the idea take root and grow, seeing the effects of such a belief rippling outward, shaping all of Sora's life.

Her expression, when she looked up, had a tinge of desperation. "Everything I did," she continued in a whisper, "they said was a sign from the Serpent Queen. If I was near a sick man and he recovered, Tanith had deemed him worthy to live. If I passed a man who died soon after, I had brought the queen's judgement on him.

"For as long as I can remember, they brought people to me. Wanted me to touch the sick, bless pregnant women and hunters. And whatever happened, they claimed it was because I had doled out the will of the Serpent Queen."

"Did they blame you?" Will asked. "When things went wrong?"

"Never to my face. To speak out against me was the same as speaking out against Tanith. But they kept their distance, unless they were desperate. The other children stayed away, afraid they might anger me." She twisted the last bit of bandage in her fingers.

"It wasn't you," he said, reaching forward to set his hand on hers, stilling them. "None of it was you."

Her eyes flicked up toward him, a hollow bright green. "It didn't matter. Everyone believed it. The story shaped everything."

His hand tightened on hers. "And that's why you hate stories."

She dropped her eyes again, brushed his hand away and finished tying his bandage. Her next words were so quiet Will had to lean forward to hear her. "My mother tried to protect me from it, but the clan was relentless. I witnessed births. I sat by sick beds. The dying, in an effort to seek Tanith's mercy, confessed to me." She squeezed her eyes shut. "Terrible things. Things a child shouldn't hear."

Sora sat silent, and Will felt a deep anger growing at the thought of the small girl alone, wading through the darkest parts of people's hearts.

"The cave system we lived in was enormous. I had free range of it all. No one dared upset me, never mind hurt me. But wherever I went, I was watched. So I learned to sneak out.

"I learned to stay quiet in the woods for hours at a time so that none of the rangers or hunters would find me. I learned what sorts of things the animals did. Where they lived, what they ate.

"That's when I realized I could sense them before I saw them." She glanced up at Will. "I didn't know other people couldn't until I watched hunters walk right by some brush with a hidden deer.

"So I started to hunt."

"And they all thought you hunted so well because you were blessed."

Sora nodded. "It was nice to be outside, though. When I hunted with others, I brought them to larger herds in the mountains. There was no point in telling them the way I found things. It would have just convinced them more strongly that I was different."

"I finally understand why Killien asked you to come to Lilit."

She nodded. "He knew why I'd left the mountains. I stayed with him because he didn't believe it."

"Desperate people believe a lot of things." Will paused. "I also understand why you were so upset that he thought you healed her. I'm sorry."

She waved off the apology. "I'm a little sensitive to people thinking I did something miraculous."

"Are other people born with talents like yours in the mountain clans?"

Sora's brow knit. "The holy men and women claim to have powers. I don't know if they're real, though."

"I'm surprised they didn't try to make you a holy woman."

"They did." She ran her finger down the long claw that was tied around her arm. "Did you know the snow lynx is the enemy of the Serpent Queen? It's a creature that only hunts at night, but it is all white. It camouflages itself in white places, whereas the queen hides in the darkness. And it hunts the mountain snakes. It's supposed to be a great snow lynx that keeps Tanith up in the sky.

"I was with a hunting party. I'd chased a small hare away from the others." Sora wound up the rest of the bandage and tucked it into her pack. "I don't know why I didn't notice the lynx. But it was on me before I could do anything.

"It sliced down my arm"—she nodded to the scar that ran under her armband—"but I had just enough time to stab up into it with my hunting knife. The other rangers found the lynx lying on top of me, blood soaking the snow around us.

"For a moment I couldn't get my breath enough to call out to them."

Will let out a laugh and she looked up sharply. "I can only imagine what they thought."

A smile spread across her lips. "One of them cried out '*We are ruined! The lynx has killed the queen!*'"

"Who says things like that?"

Sora's smile widened and a short laugh escaped her lips. "I was covered in the cat's blood. It was so disgusting, and so heavy, I shoved it off with all my might."

"What did they do?"

"About fell down and worshipped me. I tried to tell them the stupid cat had leapt directly onto my knife, but no one listened. In the official story, I rose 'like a shadow of death, black against the winter snow, flinging the corpse of the lynx aside like a rag.'"

Will grinned with approval. "Dramatic."

She looked down at her hands, the smile fading off her face. "After that, things changed. They gave me the pelt as a cape. They replaced the eyes with black river stones. It sat on my shoulder and stared at anyone I talked to."

"I think I'd like to see you wear that."

Sora rolled her eyes. "I wore it once, at the ceremony where they gave it to me, then told them something that sacred should be kept in the presence of the holy woman."

"Did they give you the claw instead?"

Sora looked at her arm band. "I was terrified to step outside again. I felt too vulnerable.

"My mother went to the holy woman and claimed the claw as a trophy." Sora's lips curled up in a slight smile. "She wrapped this band around the wound, and told me it was a reminder that it wasn't Tanith who'd saved my life, it was me."

She raised her eyes to Will's face and in her eyes he could see a spark of defiance. "It was the first time I ever felt I'd done something myself. I wasn't just a tool of some great power."

Her face was set with something mutinous and despite himself, Will let out a short laugh.

"Sora, you are the most independent, competent person I've ever met. It is incomprehensible to me that anyone would think you were only a tool."

She looked at him earnestly. "They believed because of the stories they were told."

"Your people need to hear the real story of who you are. One that shows a woman who is just as human as the rest, who has been misused by the people who should have protected her, and has grown into a capable, perceptive, strong person despite it all."

Sora snorted and turned away, but Will grabbed her hand. "This is why Keepers seek out stories. Because if the truth isn't told, people are hurt."

She looked at him for along moment, before pulling her hand away. "Then I wish there'd been a Keeper in my clan."

They got a little more rest before the shadows of the mountains stretched far to the east and Sora announced it was time to leave. Will roused Rass and packed up his things while Sora cut thick pieces of rabbit for everyone to eat.

Will was packing his books when Sora came up next to him. She held a roll of leather in her hand, fiddling with the straps that tied it closed.

"Do you think Talen will find you again?"

"He's found me everywhere else."

"Then maybe you'll have a use for this." She pushed the leather towards him. "It adjusts small, so it might fit Talen…If you ever need something like this."

Will unwrapped it to find a falconry glove and a small leather hood. He slid his hand into the glove. It was darkly stained, thick leather, the fingers blocky and an extra thick layer of leather blanketing the wrist. The hood was a tiny, bulbous piece of soft leather with straps in the back and a braided tassel perched on top.

"You bought these for me?" He held up the glove, fisting his hand.

"I bought them for Talen," she corrected him. "If he stays with you long enough, I have no doubt you'll bring him to inappropriate places, like the queen's court, and the poor bird deserves to be protected from the chaos."

"Ah." He pulled the glove off and wrapped it back up with the hood. "Then Talen thanks you for such a thoughtful, and unexpected, gift."

"I like that hawk," Rass piped up.

Sora looked up at the darkening sky. "We can leave soon."

Will's body ached with exhaustion. "I can't leave Ilsa. But Killien's book…" He scrubbed his hands across his face, rubbing at the weariness. "That book should definitely get off the Sweep."

"There's no way you can get to Ilsa, Will. And even if you could…"

He sank down next to his pack. "She might not want to come with me."

Sora's face was sober. "It would be strange if she did. She doesn't know you."

He shoved the rest of his things into his bag. "I know you think I should leave. But I can't. And it's not just Ilsa. Rass is free—"

Rass raised an eyebrow at this.

"I didn't know you've always been free."

She grinned at him and rolled her eyes. "I'm going to find some grubs. Do you want any?"

"I'll be fine with the rabbit," he assured her, and the little girl slipped out of the cave.

He cinched his bag shut with a yank. "What about Sini? How can I just walk away and leave—"

He stopped. That note Sini had left him…

"Is there something unusual about Sini and Lukas? Sini said they weren't random slaves."

"Of course they're not. They're Killien's because they're training to be stonesteeps."

Will stared at her, his hand clenched on his bag.

"Maybe Lukas already is one, I don't know. Killien spends a lot of time with the two of them, but keeps their training secret."

"They can do magic?"

"Lukas does…"—Sora's face turned distasteful—"*things* for Killien. And Sini can heal people. That's why she was in Lilit's tent. She's getting better at it all the time, but Lilit was far too much for her."

The cave around him spun slowly and he set his hand against the floor. Lukas and Sini were from Queensland. And they could do magic. "Sini's fifteen…How old is Lukas?" The question came out in a whisper.

"Around twenty-five. Why?"

The truth sank into him.

They filled the gap almost perfectly. Keepers appeared every five to ten years.

Lukas was about six years younger than Will.

Sini ten years younger than that.

"Killien has the next two Keepers."

Sora's brow crinkled in doubt. "How could he?"

"Vahe found them. He must have a way…"

The fire. Vahe had thrown that fire over the crowd, and when it had reached Will, it had done…*something*. The air around him had sparkled, and right after that he'd shoved closed Tussy's gate with magic. Vahe had somehow woken his powers.

"Vahe brings Keepers to Killien."

"But Ilsa can't do any magic," Sora said. "At least I've never seen her do anything unusual."

A rock dropped in Will's gut. "She can't. It doesn't run in families like that." He could see Vahe's face in the window, reaching for him. The man's fury when Will hadn't come.

"He wasn't there for Ilsa," Will whispered. "He was there for me."

Vahe had taken Ilsa only because Will had refused. The truth felt so obvious, he couldn't believe he'd never seen it before.

All this time he'd felt guilty because he hadn't fought hard enough to save Ilsa. When in reality, his fighting had been the reason she was taken.

Will pressed his eyes shut, finally understanding Killien's comment in the rift. "Ironic," Will whispered in agreement.

He stood. "We need to find a way back into the clan."

She threw up her hands in exasperation. "We can't—"

"Will!" Rass shrieked from below.

He scrambled to the entrance.

Hal stood in the barren clearing below the cave. His huge hands held Rass's tiny form in the air at arm's length while she thrashed around, her legs flailing and her arms pinned to her side.

Sora stood next to Will perfectly still, her knife in her hand.

"You're in luck, Will," Hal said. "Bringing you back to the clan is exactly what we're going to do."

Sora's eyes narrowed and her lips tightened into their usual line. "You seem nervous."

THIRTY

"Come down. Sora first." Behind Hal a ranger stepped forward, an arrow nocked and aimed at them.

Will cast out, but the *vitalle* of the nearest trees was too far away and the ground from the cliff to the forest was just dirt.

"Anything your magic fingers can do right now?" Sora asked him under her breath.

Will shook his head. "And there's no grass nearby for Rass."

Sora waited a breath before shoving her knife back into her belt and flinging her pack onto her shoulder. Will searched for anything to do, but came up empty. Sora started down the rocks and Rass went limp at the sight. Hal lowered her until she stood on the ground, but kept this hand clamped around her little arm. When Sora reached the bottom, she dropped her pack and the ranger stepped forward, keeping his bow trained on Sora until the last moment, when he grabbed her and tied her arms roughly behind her back. He gave a sharp yank and Sora grunted in pain.

"I confess I'm a little surprised to see you here," Hal said to Sora. "When Killien said not to trust you, I doubted him."

Sora fixed him with a furious look. "You know Will doesn't deserve what the Torch has planned for him."

Hal motioned for Will to come down. "Will is a Keeper, who can suck the life out of us at any moment. Who traveled with us for weeks, and lied to us the entire time. What confuses me, Sora, is that you spent most of those weeks trying to convince us he was a liar. Then, when he proves it, you're suddenly friends with the man?"

"Of course he lied," Sora said, squeezing her eyes shut as she shifted her shoulders, pulling against the ropes.

Will climbed down while Sora's feet were bound, the truth of their situation gaining more of a stranglehold on him the farther down he went. Before he reached the ground, the ranger took Rass from Hal, gripping her shoulder with one hand and holding a long, wickedly curved knife in the other. Rass's face was set in a little mask of fury.

"Hello, Will." Hal clapped his hand on Will's shoulder and pushed him to his knees several paces away from Sora.

Will shoved against Hal's hand. "Let Rass go."

"I have no intention of hurting the girl." Hal looked at Rass with an apologetic face. "Are you thirsty?" He nodded to the ranger who, after the slightest hesitation, offered her a drink from his water skin. "She's too young to be held responsible for her terrible taste in friends."

Will cast out toward the trees again, but they were just too far away. Hal pulled a leather package from his pocket and unwrapped a long chain holding a blue stone. He slipped it over Will's head and it thunked against his chest. A crushing wave of exhaustion rolled over Will.

He cast out for any *vitalle* he could find from the trees or even Hal, but it dribbled through his grasp like water. His mind worked sluggishly. His eyes slid shut and he lost focus. His head felt like dead weight, and his body pressed heavily down into the ground.

"The compulsion stone will only work for a few hours." Hal crouched down in front of Will, studying him. "But I think the exhaustion should keep you too tired to work any magic. It's too bad we don't have a stone that could keep you from lying."

The ranger came over to Will and wound ropes around his wrists, tight and scratchy.

Will shook his head, trying to clear the fog. "The only thing I didn't tell you was that I was a Keeper." Will shifted his shoulders, trying to relieve some of the pressure in his arms.

"And that you were from Queensland, you sit on the queen's council, and you wield magic."

The ranger gave one last, sharp tug on the rope and a shooting pain sliced up Will's arm to his shoulder. With a few quick loops his feet were tied together too.

"I don't sit on the queen's council," Will muttered. "That would be my friend Alaric. He's the one who talks to the queen. And he's quite a bit better at magic than I am. Actually, he's better at translating runes too, so he's the one Killien should have captured."

"Is he nearby? I'd be happy to bring him to Killien also."

Will let his eyes slide closed. "He's too smart to come to this barbaric, ugly land."

"Ugly land?" Rass sounded sleepy too.

"Lukas made the compulsion stone you're wearing. We weren't sure it would exhaust a Keeper to the point where they couldn't perform magic, but it looks like it's a success. Which means I didn't really need to use my backup plan."

The world beneath Will spun slowly and he forced his eyes open. "If it was Lukas, I'm surprised he didn't make it something deadly."

"Lukas isn't that bad," Hal said. "Although I have noticed he doesn't like you much."

Rass swayed slightly on her feet and the ranger sheathed his knife. Will's heart lurched and he leaned toward her, but Hal held him back. Sora strained against her bonds.

"What did you do?" Will demanded.

Rass's eyes sank shut and her knees buckled. The ranger caught her and lay her down on the ground.

"Rass!" Will called, pulling against Hal's grip.

"Just an added measure of security," Hal said. "She's sleeping. Would you like a drink too? It's the same concoction Killien put in your wine the night of the attack, although a much lower dose."

Will glared at Hal, hopeless fury rising in his chest. Hal pushed Will over and he crashed onto his side, landing heavily on his shoulder. The ranger rested his knife on Rass's sleeping chest.

"I don't want to hurt her, Will, but if you give me trouble, I'll do what I need to do."

Hal opened Will's pack. "The Torch will be pleased that you still have his book." He went to a pack sitting near the trees, wrote something and tinkered with a cage. A small raven flapped out and soared out toward the Sweep. "That should let Killien know where we are." He crossed over to Rass's limp form and gave the ranger some orders. After a last check of Sora and Will's bonds, the ranger struck out down the hill. "There are rangers spread out all across the Hoarfrost looking for you. Reinforcements will arrive soon, and we'll all be on our merry way back to the rift."

Will let his head sink down on to the hard ground and watched the ranger go with a sick feeling in his stomach. Maybe it was better this way. Maybe if he could get back to Killien, he'd convince the Torch to let Ilsa go.

There was no hope in the thought.

"Let Sora and Rass go," he said to Hal. "I'm the one Killien wants. He doesn't even know Rass is here, and you can say Sora got away. He'll believe it."

"When Killien finds out that Sora helped you, he's going to want her too." He leaned back against a boulder. "Let's all just sit tight for a bit. Shouldn't take more than an hour or two for the nearest rangers to get here." He glanced at Sora. "We didn't really follow your orders, of course. We're spread all across the Hoarfrost and the Scales to catch our Keeper no matter which way he ran." He gave her a look more regretful than angry. "Killien liked you. He never likes foreigners. And yet he brought you in, trusted you, paid you better than any of the rest of us—"

"I'm better than any of the rest of you."

"—and despite your constant superior attitude, Killien still put up with you. What made you take up with this traitor?"

"I am not a traitor!" Will threw the words at Hal. He shoved his elbow against the ground, trying to push himself back up to a sitting position, but his strength gave out and he just rolled to the side, sending dust into his own face.

"Killien was generous to you, too." Hal turned on Will. "He shared meals with you. I heard him tell you his dreams of peace for the Roven."

"Oh yes," Will said, spitting out dust, "he's an amazing, benevolent leader."

Hal looked at Will as though he'd spoken in a foreign tongue. "You think that because you lied to him and he got mad, that it negates all the good he does?"

"No. I think Killien is actively searching for knowledge that only leads to tyranny and death."

"What are you talking about?" Hal asked, irritated.

"Killien has a book by Kachig the Bloodless."

Hal's eyes narrowed.

"It describes how to—how did you word it? Suck the life out of someone. And use it for your own power."

"Sounds like it should have been written by a Keeper."

Will clenched his jaw. "A Keeper would never do that.

"Ahh, you didn't deny you can."

"Yes, I can pull the energy out of you. But you don't need a compulsion stone, or to sit there threatening a sleeping girl, to keep me from doing it. Keepers believe that the energy in a person is sacred. We would never take the smallest bit from you unless you wanted us to. If we need energy for something, we pull it from a fire, or from plants. Or from ourselves." He looked at Hal, and the hardness in the man's eyes felt like knives. "You've never had anything to fear from me."

Hal's expression didn't soften.

Will shifted his arms against the tightness of the rope. "Whatever Killien wants with that book, nothing good can come of it. No matter what he's told you about wanting peace and wanting to unite the Sweep, there is only war and death in this book. And magic beyond anything Killien has the power to do. The magic in this book would require advanced stonesteeps from the Sunn Clan."

Hal's jaw clenched stubbornly. "If Killien is trying to read it, he has a good reason. Everything he does is for the good of the clan."

"So that makes it ok? Sucking life out of people is fine as long as they're not *your* people?" Will snorted. "You're lucky I don't feel the same way."

"Killien wouldn't do something like that." There was a note of finality in Hal's voice.

Weariness washed over Will again and he let his retort go.

"Who set the fires?" Sora asked.

"Our visitors from the Sunn Clan."

Sora's mouth dropped open in shock.

Will let his head sink down onto the ground. "I thought they were coming to invite Killien to some enclave."

Hal sank back against a boulder and blew out a long breath. "So did Killien. It's been ten years since he was invited. But he's been in communication with so many of the other Torches that when the Sunn wanted to visit, he thought…"

Will fought to keep his eyes open. There had to be a way out of this. He watched Sora, hoping she was working on her bonds, but he couldn't tell. "What happens at the enclave?"

"The powerful clans make demands." Hal made an irritated face. "And the smaller clans agree to them publicly. But Killien thinks that if the smaller clans can band together, they can have a voice. Together the Morrow, Panos, and Temur clans would make the third largest group on the Sweep. Both the Panos and Temur have been in talks with Killien all winter. Right now the struggle for power on the Sweep is caught between the Sunn Clan with all their stonesteeps, and the Boan with their huge army. Killien's determined to change that.

"Over the winter he managed to settle a longstanding dispute between two of the western clans over a river. It made enough of an impression across the Sweep that last night the nephew of the Sunn Torch was supposed to be coming to invite Killien to the enclave. And probably demand his support."

Sora snorted. "Killien wouldn't support the Sunn in anything."

Hal nodded slowly. "Twenty Sunn warriors hid on the Sweep and started the fire before Avi, the nephew of the Sunn Torch, had time to talk to Killien about it. So I'd say they didn't expect him to."

Sora considered this for a moment. "They attacked Killien too? With him dead, there's no good choice for another Torch in the Morrow."

"They tried. Killien hadn't trusted the little weasel, so he'd had guards in the back room. Little Avi didn't even get his knife close to Killien before they'd caught him. We killed twelve of them and captured the rest, including Avi. The man's a weasel but some say he'll be the next Torch of the Sunn. So Killien has a powerful bargaining chip."

Sora looked at Will, uneasily.

Will looked between the two of them, understanding dawning. "Killien can get stonesteeps from the Sunn, probably enough to do whatever magic he's trying to figure out."

Hal shook his head. "The Sunn have more stonesteeps than blades of grass, but most of them aren't worth the cost of feeding them."

Sora turned her head slowly, looking over the Sweep with wide eyes.

Will's mind was too sluggish to follow. "What else does the Sunn have that Killien would want?"

Neither Sora or Hal answered, but the truth hit Will like a stone in the gut. "The dragon."

"Killien was still composing the ransom letter when I left. But, yes, he's demanding use of the dragon."

"How do you use a dragon?" Will asked.

Hal pulled his hand through his beard. "The stonesteeps of the Sunn Clan control it, so whatever Killien wants it to do, they'll have to agree to it. I don't know what he has planned. But he was very pleased about the opportunity."

"He told me once," Will said, glancing up at the sky as though expecting to see an enormous creature flying across the Sweep, "that all he needed to solve the world's problems was a disposable army and a dragon." He looked back at Hal. "So he's not invited to the enclave?"

"No." Hal leaned his head back on the rock. "And even if he were, among the Sunn attackers we found three from the Panos Clan."

Will let out a long breath. "Who were supposed to be Killien's allies."

The three fell silent. Will's shoulders ached from his hands being tied behind him, his wrist chaffed from the ropes. He lowered the side of his head down to the ground again, shifting his wrists back and forth. The ropes felt as though they might be getting looser.

A very small bird soared across the sky and settled high in a nearby pine. Relief and alarm vied for control as Will glanced toward Hal to see if he'd noticed Talen's arrival, but the huge man had gone back to spinning the knife point in the ground.

Will cast out toward the hawk and felt his little coil of energy. Talen was far enough away that Will couldn't feel any emotions from the bird. What had he done before? When Talen had listened? He'd sort of pushed the idea of them, the longing for them at the bird.

Will gathered all the strength he could, firmed up the image of Talen sitting on the branch in his mind, and infused it with the feeling of contentment. He pushed the idea up toward the hawk. *Stay there.*

Talen's wings flared, and for a heart-stopping moment Will thought he would dive down. But the hawk merely shifted his feet and settled down on the branch.

Rass stirred. She stretched and opened her eyes to look around groggily. Hal set a hand on her arm.

"Are you alright?" Will asked her.

Her tiny arm looked like a stick grasped in Hal's enormous hand.

She blinked at the sunlight and peered at Will, then turned to Hal with a thunderous face. "Did you make me sleep?"

Hal laughed. "I did, little fiery girl. I see why Will likes you."

She tugged against his grip, but she couldn't even jostle his arm.

Hal sighed. "If you don't want to be put back to sleep again, stop fighting. Look at Sora and Will. We've got a nice, calm afternoon going here. No problems, no fighting, just some friends chatting on a mountainside."

Rass glared up at him. "You should let us go."

"Why's that?"

"Because Will is a mighty wizard and Sora's smarter and faster and braver than you. They're letting you sit here for now, but you can't win against them."

Hal's eyebrows rose and he let out a long, rolling laugh. The first real laugh he'd given all day. He glanced at Will. "This girl is a treasure."

Past Hal, Sora stiffened. Her gaze snapped uphill, searching.

The rangers couldn't be back so soon. Will cast out and his stomach dropped. Two people were approaching from behind him higher up the slope. And up past them waited two more.

They were out of time. He strained against the ropes at his wrists, desperation returning.

Sora's eyes, still staring up the hill, widened in surprise.

"Treasure?" a gruff voice called out from behind Will. He spoke with a rough brogue. "There's no treasure here. We've searched it before. Nothing here but rocks."

Will twisted, trying to see behind him, and caught a glimpse of the two people he'd felt. It wasn't Roven rangers.

Stumping down the side of the rockslide were two dwarves.

THIRTY-ONE

Hal's mouth dropped open at the sight of the two dwarves. Will shifted for a better view. They came down the slope with heavy steps, thick leather boots crunching against the ground. Their long beards covered their chests and tucked behind their belts. Their leather armor was darkened with age and use, and scarred blades of their battle axes sat behind their shoulders looking ruthless. Only glittering eyes were visible in their faces.

"I don't see any treasure, cousin." The darker of the two studied the group from under black, wild eyebrows.

Hal stood, pulling Rass up with him.

"Patlon," said the other dwarf, stroking his own copper beard. "We've found nothing but a bunch of humans in the midst of a disagreement."

Hal stood unmoving, his hand wrapped around Rass's thin arm, his expression caught between stunned and thrilled.

"If the giant man says they're treasure," Patlon said, "we should take them, just to be sure."

Hal's face darkened. "You're not taking anyone."

The two dwarves glanced at each other and Patlon pulled his axe over his shoulder. The shaft was a dark, glimmering purple. Sora watched the two with narrowed eyes.

"We didn't introduce ourselves," the copper-bearded dwarf said. "I'm Douglon, this is my cousin Patlon." He gestured to Will, Sora, and Rass. "I've recently started collecting needy humans, and I'd be happy to take these off your hands."

"No." Hal stepped forward, holding out the small hunting knife. "You won't."

Will heaved himself onto his back. Sharp pain shot across his shoulders and his head fell back, heavy. "I'm a Keeper from Queensland. I've been to Duncave before, visited King Horgoth's court. Even spoken to the High Dwarf himself."

The dwarves gave him their attention.

Will opened up toward them and curiosity and amusement poured into his chest. "He has a brilliant mind for strategy and is a keen negotiator." The amusement soured.

"If you keep talking about Horgoth like that," Douglon said, "I'm going to leave you with the giant."

Will glanced between the two. "I promise you, I'm a friend of the dwarves."

"Don't trust his promises of friendship," Hal said.

"Cousin," Patlon warned as Hal took a step forward.

Douglon sized up the huge man and slid his own axe out of its sheath with a glint of fiery red. "I suppose, being a Keeper," he said to Will, keeping his eyes fixed on Hal, "you are useless when it comes to using a weapon and have moral qualms about fighting with magic."

Will opened his mouth to protest, but Sora spoke first.

"It's like you already know him."

"I feel like I do." A grin flashed out from his beard. "You, on the other hand, look as though you could take care of yourself."

"Against Hal? Just cut my feet loose. I won't need my arms."

"I like her." Patlon stepped closer to Sora and pulled a small knife out of his belt.

"Stop." Hal's voice echoed off the rocks.

Patlon paused and raised an eyebrow at the enormous man.

Hal stepped forward again and Rass took the chance to wrench her arm out of his grasp and skitter out of reach. Hal grabbed for her, but she was too quick.

"Hal," Sora said, "this isn't a fight you're going to win. You couldn't take one of these dwarves, never mind both. And despite the fact their axes are"—she glanced at the two axes, the shafts shimmering with purple and red—"colorful for dwarven warriors, they seem well used."

Hal clenched his jaw.

"She likes my axe." Patlon twisted the purple shaft, catching the evening light in a deep violet glitter.

"She likes *my* axe," Douglon corrected him. "She thinks yours is stupid."

Patlon's teeth flashed from behind his beard in a grin. Rass scurried over behind Sora and Patlon tossed the knife near her. Rass grabbed it and ducked down behind Sora.

"Hal," Will said. "You don't want to be killed by dwarves. Not after you've waited so long to meet some."

"You were overpowered by a superior force." Sora rubbed her wrists. "Killien can't hold that against you." With a flick of the knife she cut the rope around her feet and came over to Will.

Hal's expression sagged and he dropped his knife by his side.

"He loves dwarves," Will explained to Douglon and Patlon. "Under most circumstances this would be the best day of his life."

"What's not to love?" Patlon asked.

Will felt the cool side of the blade against his arm, then with a quick yank, the ropes loosened and he pushed himself up with a groan. Bone-deep aches filled his shoulders, as he took the chain with the blue stone off his neck and threw it at the ground near Hal. The exhaustion that had been plaguing him blew away like smoke on a breeze.

Sora handed him the knife for his feet, and grabbing some rope, went over to Hal. She barely came up to his shoulder, but when she held out her hand, he only hesitated a moment, glancing at the dwarves before handing her the knife.

"You won't have too long to wait," Patlon told Hal. "Your ranger friends should be here before dark."

When Hal was tied up, Douglon turned uphill and gave a long whistle. Will cast out up the mountain and found the two other people.

"I met a dwarf at court once." Will watched up the hill for the others. "His name was Menwoth. He was…funny."

"Stop talking," Patlon advised.

Douglon glowered at him. "Menwoth? Slimy, fawning toad."

Despite the look on the dwarf's face, Will laughed. "He was fawning."

Douglon's face mollified a bit.

A wave rushed over Will and he snapped his gaze back up the slope.

It hadn't been a wave of anything in particular. Almost a wave of nothing, if nothing could surge like an ocean swell, and pass through you.

But it was a nothing he recognized in the foundational way he recognized home.

"Alaric!" he called.

A man stepped around one of the huge rocks.

At the sight of the black-haired man wearing the black Keeper's robe, the isolation and weight of the last year loosened.

"You were easier to find than I thought you'd be." Alaric looked pleased.

"Easy?" Patlon fixed Alaric with an incredulous look, "You've mobilized half of the dwarven outposts for the last four days!"

The sheer familiarity of Alaric was fortifying. His black hair had been cropped short, but his eyes were scanning the group exactly the way he studied every new situation. Will could almost see the questions stacking up in his mind. Seeing a face as familiar as his own broke away the last of the crust the solitary last year had built around Will.

"I have never"—Will strode up to Alaric and wrapped his arms around him, crushing Alaric to his chest—"been so happy to see anyone in my life."

Alaric laughed and patted Will on the back. "It's good to see you too."

A woman came out from behind the rock as well, walking up to Alaric.

Will stepped back, but kept his hands on Alaric's shoulders. "I'm so happy to see you."

Alaric raised an eyebrow. "You mentioned that."

Will let go of Alaric's shoulders, rubbing his hands over his face and letting out a breath. "It's been a long year."

"Long enough to grow a beard," Alaric said.

Will scratched at it. "They're popular on this side of the mountains."

"And under them," Douglon said.

"I like it," the woman said.

She smiled at Will with a hopeful sort of smile, but her green eyes watched him nervously. Blond hair hung around her face, working its way out of a braid. In contrast to the dwarves, she didn't look particularly fierce. She wore traveling clothes, simple pants and a light brown shirt, and carried no weapon besides a small knife at her belt. She stepped up to Alaric, so close that their arms almost touched. Will glanced at Alaric, waiting for an introduction.

Alaric gave him a nervous look. "Will, I'd like you to meet Evangeline—"

Will gave her a small bow as Alaric leaned against her shoulder.

"—my wife."

Will's bow stuttered to a stop. "Wife?"

Alaric's smile turned self-conscious and he nodded. He stayed pressed against Evangeline's shoulder, his expression somewhere between worry and entreaty.

Will shoved aside his surprise at the news. "Congratulations!"

Alaric's smile widened and Evangeline's shoulders relaxed.

"I'm Will. Obviously. And you married a great man. He's been like a brother to me since I was ten."

Sora stepped up next to Will. Before he could introduce her, Alaric grinned. "Did you find a wife too?"

"No!" Sora pulled away from Will her face shocked.

"Um," Will started. "It's not…"

Alaric laughed. "That's too bad. You should find one."

Sora fixed Alaric with a scowl.

"This is Sora," Will introduced her. It was nice to see her irritation focused on someone besides himself. "And despite that expression, which she wears a lot, I owe her my life. Several times over."

Sora crossed her arms, still scowling.

Will glanced up the hill. "Why were you hiding behind the rocks?"

"Because," Evangeline answered, "he is ridiculously overprotective of me."

Alaric shrugged. "With good reason."

"We need to move somewhere less exposed," Patlon said.

A glint of blue from the ground caught Will's eye, and he picked up the necklace, careful not to touch the stone. He considered putting it on Hal before deciding it would be more interesting to study it. He shoved it into his pack.

He looked up to the top of the pine where Talen still perched. He pulled a bit of rabbit from his pack and held a slice up toward the bird. Talen dove off the branch and sped down, flaring his wings at the last moment to land on Will's outstretched arm.

"We have less than an hour until the other Roven come back." Patlon pointed out.

Will nodded. "I didn't leave the Morrow on the best of terms. We should be gone by then."

"Kollman Pass is being watched," Sora said.

Alaric nodded. "We don't need the pass. There's an entrance to Duncave up the slope."

Sora's eyebrows rose and she nodded. Then she glanced at Talen. "This is a perfect example of you taking Talen somewhere inappropriate, Will." She stepped up behind him and reached into his pack. "But he'll lose track of you if we go underground." She pulled out the little hood. "Keep him calm."

Will opened up toward the hawk and pushed the idea of peace toward the creature.

Talen stilled and Sora slipped the hood over his head in one smooth motion and tied a thin strap of leather to his foot. Talen tensed, but stayed on Will's arm. With some shifting Will got the glove on and Talen settled on it while Will held the end of the strap, keeping the idea of calmness pressed into the bird.

Will felt Rass behind him, peeking around him at the new people.

"This is Rass," Will introduced her. "She's a *pratorii*, a grass elf."

"Really?" Alaric leaned to get a better view of her.

Douglon moved toward Rass and Will tensed. The dwarf, although his head only reached Will's chest, looked like a towering giant next to the tiny girl.

Sora took a step closer to the dwarf, loosening the knife in her belt.

Alaric raised his hand toward her. "It's alright."

Douglon looked at Rass like she was some sort of rare sparkling rock. He dropped down on one knee so their faces were even. "Hello."

She reached forward tentatively and touched a braid hanging from the bottom of his copper beard. "I've never met a dwarf before."

"I've never met such a tiny elf."

"Have you met tree elves?"

The dwarf stilled before nodding. "One."

Will looked up at Alaric in surprise. The other Keeper gave a small, sober nod.

"I hope I get to meet one," Rass sighed.

A heavy silence fell over the others. Something raw and broken flashed across Douglon's eyes before he closed them.

"There aren't any more," he answered.

Will's gaze snapped to Alaric's face, but he was watching the dwarf with a grave expression.

"We should go." Alaric turned up the slope.

Will and the others started after him, but Rass hung back.

"I don't want to go into the tunnels. They're too dark and quiet."

Douglon paused. "They're not quiet. The rocks talk."

Rass fixed him with a dubious look. "No they don't."

He shrugged. "I didn't used to think trees talked, but they do." He glanced over at the pine trees closest to them. "They talk so much, I wish they'd shut up."

Rass giggled. "I thought dwarves only liked rocks."

"I did, until I met that elf."

Rass looked up at him with wide eyes. "What was she like?"

Douglon's gaze traveled back to the edge of the forest. "Crazy as a bat." He turned back to Rass. "Maybe I can teach you to hear the rocks."

Rass looked doubtful.

Douglon stopped and held out his hand, "I know the tunnels are different from out here, but they have their own beauty. I'd be happy to show you. I never had the chance to show Ayda."

"Ayda?" Will asked quickly. "The elf?"

Douglon nodded, still facing Rass.

Rass studied his face for a minute, taking in his coppery beard, and his dwarfish face. His eyes were a rich, earthy color, and there was something broken in them. Whether Rass saw it or not, she set her tentative hand into his thick one.

"The rocks don't chatter like the trees. They have slow, ponderous thoughts. But there's great truth there to be heard." Douglon leaned closer to her. "It turns out, there's great truth in many different places, if you just know how to listen."

He started uphill, Rass stepping along beside him.

Will glanced at Alaric. "That's an unusual dwarf."

"Crazy as a bat." Patlon stumped up the hill after Douglon.

Will turned to Hal where he sat against a boulder, and the man fixed him with a glare. Unlike Sora's glares, which had lost much of their power from overuse, the expression on Hal's face felt like a knife in Will's gut.

"I'm glad I met you, Hal. You were the first Roven I ever thought that, if things were different, we could have been genuine friends."

Hal let out a short, humorless laugh and turned his face away, looking out over the Sweep. The setting sun cast the Sweep into a golden haze. It was past time to go. Will shifted his pack on his shoulder.

"Goodbye, Hal." He paused a moment. When Hal didn't respond, Will turned away to follow the others.

He'd only taken a step when a surge rolled over him. This time it wasn't a surge of nothing.

This was a ripple, a taste of a power so vast that Will was merely a candle flame before it, about to be snuffed out.

Sora flinched and snapped her attention to the hills, her gaze raking over the slopes around them, her face pale.

Alaric spun around and the wave of his casting out ripped past Will just as he cast his own. He searched through the trees and over the rocky slope, searching for any movement.

The casting out returned nothing for a moment.

Then, high above the Sweep, a blazing inferno of *vitalle* burst out.

Cold, sharp fear clenched around Will's chest as he spun.

Glinting blood red in the setting sun, tearing straight toward them, hurtled a dragon.

THIRTY-TWO

"**D**ragon!" Will choked out the word over the fear gripping his chest.

Still far out over the grassland, the shape was etched against the clear sky. Wide, jagged wings growing larger by the moment.

Around him, everyone spun to face the grass.

"What is it with Keepers and dragons?" Douglon shouted down to them.

"Will!" Hal's voice was taut. He yanked against the ropes tying his hands and feet.

Will ran to Hal, calling for Sora and her knife, yanking on the ropes around his ankles.

She was at his shoulder in a breath, slicing Hal's feet free.

"You'd better run, Hal." She grabbed one arm of the huge man and Will grabbed the other, hauling him to his feet.

Alaric, Evangeline, Douglon, and Patlon ran up the hill. Rass waited, her eyes flickering between Will and the dragon. Sora reached her and grabbed her hand, pulling her up after the others.

The dragon streaked toward them, growing larger and faster than Will's mind could grasp.

"Looks like you get to see Duncave, Hal. Come on."

Will ran, Talen gripping his arm. Hal's heavy steps thundered after him as they chased the others up the hill. Will caught a glimpse of the dragon and the cold fear clamped tighter in his chest.

Ridged, thin wings, spread wide across the sky, striated with tendons snaking like veins in a leaf. The sunlight shone off its scales, glinting a deep, biting red.

Voices called out and Will pushed himself faster, stumbling over loose stones. The two dwarves shouted at him, waving him up to a thin crack in the side of a huge rock.

Will's legs burned from the climb, his ankles aching from being tied up, and fear coursed through him, making his limbs clumsy.

The others reached the dwarves and Patlon slipped inside with Rass. Sora paused at the door, shouting down toward Will to hurry. Her face was terrified and a detached part of Will's brain realized he had never seen her scared before.

Without stopping or turning, Will cast out.

The massive surge of *vitalle* soaring toward them almost knocked him off his feet. The creature blocked out a huge section of the sky. With a roar that shook the earth, the dragon shot out a long spray of fire, setting trees alight and covering the ground with a churning sea of flames.

The *vitalle* released with the fire and knocked Will forward to his knees. Talen flapped his wings, panicked, but Will shot a burst of calmness at the bird. The ground trembled beneath him and the crack of rocks splitting filled the air.

"Get up!" Hal stopped in front of Will, holding one of his still-tied hands awkwardly behind him. Will grabbed it and pulled himself up, shaking his head to clear the shock of so much power. He looked up and saw Alaric bent over too, grabbing onto Evangeline for support.

Smoke poured around him, tinged red with firelight, swirling until he could barely see Hal right in front of him.

Will took a step. An overwhelming anger slithered into his chest. It wasn't human anger. It was old and savage.

He slammed himself shut, trying to close it off, but the emotions plowed into him. A desire to burn and kill and destroy. The glory of the sky, the strength of wings that ruled the wind.

And a gnawing, driving hunger to burn *someone*. A single, mindless goal.

Will dropped to his knees again, trying to shove them out, but the emotions filled him until there was nothing else—only power and strength and greed.

Talen screeched, but it sounded distant. Voices called to him, but they meant nothing. The world meant nothing.

Rough hands grabbed him, trying to pull him to his feet. Someone shouted. Will squeezed his eyes shut.

"Will." Sora's voice cut through the noise and he opened his eyes to see her face right in front of his, pale and frightened. "Will, you have to *run*."

The rush of power filled him, drowning out everything else, and Sora's face glowed red in the light from the dragon fire. Heat seared against his back.

Sora ducked down, leaning against him and pulling his head down against her shoulder. He could feel her trembling as the whole world shook. He caught a glimpse of the rocks behind them glowing like molten copper. The forest blazed with red flames, black smoke billowed around him, hiding the beast.

The dragon broke through the smoke above him and swept past. His wings stretched over the treetops and brushed the cliff, a jagged sheet of red tipped with spikes. The dragon's belly glittered dark red, reflecting countless glitters of firelight. One clawed foot tore out a huge pine and flung it down the slope.

Uphill, the others raced for shelter, and the tiny part of Will's brain that could think stared at them in horror, waiting for the flames to envelop them. But the dragon launched up into the blue sky, dwindling to a small shape and the tide of emotions receded.

"Will, please get up."

He shoved at the emotions of the dragon, but it was like pushing back the ocean.

"Will," she pleaded, pulling on his arm.

Will tried to focus on Sora's face through the chaos. For the fleetest moment he felt an emotion of his own—envy at the fact that she would never feel this.

His mind snagged on the idea of her coldness and hollowness. He grabbed her arm, squeezing his eyes shut again and instead of pushing at the swirling mass inside him, he opened himself up to her. There was none of her normal emptiness. There was only cold terror. But it was a human terror that fit inside him. Something he could understand.

He gulped in a breath. The taste of melting rock stung his throat. He opened his eyes and saw Sora.

At his look she sank down in relief. "There you are."

Talen flapped agitated on his arm and he pushed the best semblance of peace he could at the bird. The hawk quieted somewhat. Sora pulled Will to his feet and he stumbled forward. Alaric and Douglon had started down the slope toward him, but now they turned and ran back. Douglon waved them on, his face turned up to the sky. The dragon, so high he had shrunk to a small silhouette, gave one last beat of his wings and with a lazy arc, rolled over into a dive. Straight toward them.

Sora craned her head up. "That dragon is after you!"

"Me?" he demanded, his breath ragged. "Maybe it's after you!"

She spared him the shortest glare and raced forward.

They reached the entrance to the tunnel, no more than a crack, barely wide enough to fit through. Douglon stood at the entrance with his axe blocking the door, shouting at Hal.

"Let him in," Alaric yelled.

Douglon glared at the enormous man before yanking his axe out of the way and giving Hal a shove.

Evangeline stared up at the dragon, a puzzled look on her face.

"Go!" Douglon yelled.

"Evangeline," Alaric called, grabbing her hand and pulling her toward the door.

"I know that dragon…" she said, bemused.

Will glanced at Alaric, but he looked as surprised as Will at the words.

"You don't know any dra—" Alaric snapped his head upwards. His eyes widened. "You might know it, love, but it doesn't know you. Please come." He pulled at her hand, drawing her toward the rocks.

She shook her head and blinked. The two of them ran into the darkness. Sora slipped through after them and Will pushed between the rough sides of the crack, holding Talen near his chest and hearing Douglon's feet behind him. A rush of power flared outside and flames licked into the tunnel.

Douglon heaved something and the opening slammed shut, blocking out the flames and dropping them into complete darkness.

"Farther in!" Douglon cried. "Run!"

The ceiling above Will gave a low crack, and spreading his hand out to feel the walls, he ran into the darkness.

THIRTY-THREE

A low rumble shook the tunnel walls. Will's heart pounded, thrumming down even into his fingers as he ran. His eyes stretched open in the blackness, aching for some light, flickering from one formless bit of black to another.

Talen perched on his glove, still calm, but Will curled his fist closer to his body, afraid he might crash the bird into some unexpected rock. There were no unexpected rocks, though. The tunnel had the finished sort of feel that came from dwarven skill, as if any irregularity in the wall was a decision of style. The floor beneath his feet sloped gently downwards.

"Not far." Douglon's words echoed from behind. "There's an outpost just ahead."

Another resonant crack of splitting stone sent a shiver through the walls, but weaker than the last, farther behind him. Proof that they were making some progress in the black.

A dragon. Killien had sent a dragon after him.

A dim burnt-orange glow outlined Sora, and a flicker of fear shot into Will that it was dragon fire, before he realized it was only glimmer moss. Will's eyes latched onto the light and he stood straighter, seeing the vague outline of the arched tunnel.

In half a dozen steps it opened up into a wide cavern too much like a room to be called a cavern. It was domed, rising smoothly to a wide medallion carved out of the rock in the center of the ceiling. Shelves lined one wall, stocked with small crates and casks. A long table filled the middle of the room. Three maps were set out along the middle, their corners pinned by smooth black rocks. A trickling noise echoed around the room and the mosslight caught on a thin line of water sparkling down the far wall. Piles of sleeping furs were rolled against another wall.

Patlon leaned against the table watching everyone run in. Rass sat huddled next to him, looking like a little snip of grass that had gotten terribly lost. Alaric wrapped his arm around Evangeline, a bit off to the side. The naturalness of it was almost more jarring than the fact Alaric had a wife. Sora walked along the shelves, looking at the supplies. Hal stood over near the bedrolls, his hands still tied behind his back.

Douglon jogged into the room. "How often are you Keepers attacked by dragons?"

"Before this one it had been a hundred and twelve years since any Keeper saw a dragon," Alaric protested.

"This is the second one in a matter of weeks." Douglon dropped his axe on the table with a crash. "And that feels too often to me."

"But this was the same dragon as the last one."

Douglon shook his head. "It tried to kill me twice. Counts as two. You Keepers should focus a little of your study time on how to fight them. Because you're useless."

"It's a dragon!" Alaric said. "Everyone is useless against a dragon."

"Not everyone," Douglon said.

"I think you only get to count one," Evangeline said. "This dragon wasn't trying to kill you. I think it was trying to kill Will. Or maybe Sora."

"There were dragon flames shot in my direction," Douglon said, sinking down onto the end of the bench. "I'm counting two."

Alaric turned to Will. "Evangeline's right, it did seem to be after you."

"It might have been," Will answered. "I may have made Killien, the Torch of the Morrow Clan, a little angry. And he may have recently come across an opportunity to use a dragon." He explained about Killien and the attack by the Sunn Clan. "I knew he was mad." He shook his head and admitted, "I didn't realize he was send-a-dragon mad."

"Good thing the dwarves were here to save you," Douglon pointed out.

"He'll know the dragon didn't kill you," Hal said. "He'll keep sending more rangers. It's only a matter of time until he finds these tunnels."

"No one finds dwarf tunnels," Patlon said.

"Who would want to?" Rass's voice came muffled from her arms.

Douglon walked over and sat next to her. "It's not that bad." He pulled a tiny, bright red gem out of a pocket and set it on the table in front of her. "Under here there are all sorts of treasures."

Rass picked up the stone and examined it, turning it, letting it glimmer in the light of the moss.

Will settled Talen on a long wooden peg at the end of the shelves. "How'd you find me?" he asked Alaric.

"That's also thanks to us," Patlon answered.

"The dwarves had been monitoring the movements of frost goblins this spring," Alaric answered, "because they'd been more active than normal. Then about a week ago they saw the goblins attack a clan."

"The Morrow," Will agreed.

"And it seemed the frost goblins were magically forced back, chased into their warrens by something the dwarves couldn't see." Alaric dropped his gaze to Will's wrapped hand. "When their reports came back, we were in Duncave clearing up some"—he shot an annoyed look at Douglon—"misunderstandings, and the report made me worried there was some unusually strong stonesteep traveling with the Morrow. King Horgoth agreed to have the dwarves watch the clan, and imagine our surprise when they overheard two Roven rangers talking about a Keeper." Alaric paused and looked at Will expectantly.

"I was…" Will glanced at Sora who was watching him with an expressionless face. "Invited to join the Morrow on their migration north after Killien learned I was a storyteller."

"From Gulfind," Hal pointed out. "We wouldn't have invited a liar from Queensland."

"There may have been some subterfuge," Will admitted.

Alaric grinned. "You infiltrated a Roven clan?"

"Yes," Hal answered.

"That sounds more planned than it was," Will said.

"The dwarves followed the Morrow north," Alaric continued, "and saw you imprisoned in a small rift. We were working on how to get you out when the Sweep caught fire and one of the scouts saw you escape. It took us a full day to find you, but the dwarves have entrances to their tunnels all over the Hoarfrost. Once we figured out where you were, it was pretty easy to get to you." Alaric paused, then leaned closer. "What did you do? To drive off the frost goblins?"

Will felt a smile growing. "I took the heat from the fires and the heatstones." At the questioning quirk in Alaric's brow, he said, "I have to tell you about heatstones. Anyway, I took the heat and pushed it toward the goblins."

Alaric's eyebrows rose. "With a fire net? That wouldn't hold enough heat."

Will's smile turned into a grin. "With a fire *wall*."

Alaric's head tilted to the side and his eyes flickered unseeing around the room as he thought through it.

"A clay wall, like an oven."

Alaric stared at him. "That's brilliant. Show me."

Will held up his bandaged hands. "Maybe someday. Last time it hurt. A lot."

"Where's that gem you picked up?" Patlon asked Will.

Will pulled the blue necklace that Hal had put on him out of his pack. "It's a compulsion stone holding a spell that will exhaust you if you touch it."

Patlon pulled back the hand he'd been reaching.

Alaric peered at the stone. "Do the Morrow use a lot of magic?"

"No, but Killien is actively trying to change that. He has a book that talks about burning stones like this. It's based on the magic Mallon used."

"Mallon the Rivor?" Alaric exchanged glances with Douglon.

Will nodded. "The thing he seems to be studying the most from that book is how to transfer thoughts and emotions into others. They're called compulsion stones, but I don't think he's figured out how to use it."

"He definitely knows how to transfer thoughts," Sora said.

"Really? Lukas's notes said it wasn't sophisticated enough to work on humans, and he seemed to lose interest. Seems like it was meant to control beasts."

Sora nodded. "Like frost goblins."

Will tucked the blue stone back in his pack. "If Killien could control frost goblins, why didn't he drive them away from the clan?"

Sora let out a derisive snort. "He's the reason they attacked."

THIRTY-FOUR

"What are you talking about?" Hal demanded.

"On the trip north," Sora said, "Killien ordered me to bring him a goblin. Two days before the attack, I was able to capture one alive." Her mouth tightened with distaste. "He put a blue stone around the creature's neck." She stopped and stared unseeing at the bowl of glimmer moss on the table. "The goblin went mad. It was bound, but it thrashed around, trying to move toward the clan.

"It had almost torn its own hand off when Killien gave the order to kill it. When I touched it, I had this idea of a box of gold nearby, and suddenly I wanted it. I don't think I've ever wanted something as much as that."

Her hand gripped the hilt of her knife. "I pulled the stone off its neck and threw it to the ground, and the idea disappeared. But the creature didn't calm. If anything, it fought harder." She dropped her hand from the knife. "In the end, there was nothing to do but kill it."

"Killien gave a goblin the idea that there was metal nearby?" Will asked. "That's insane."

"It was more than an idea of metal," Sora said. "It was a desire for it."

Will nodded. "That makes sense. He's not trying to transfer a thought, he's transferring emotions. Lukas discovered that emotions were easy to share."

Hal shook his head violently. "That doesn't mean that Killien brought the army of frost goblins."

They had poured out of the ground like a single creature, like a hive of drones. Swarming toward the metal.

"He did. They're all connected," Will said. "Like one creature, or like a thousand spiders sharing a web. What one senses, they all sense. Killien didn't just give one goblin the desire for metal near the clan, he gave it to every goblin it was connected to."

"And they all came," Sora finished.

Hal fixed her with a look too complicated to describe, still shaking his head. "Killien caused the attack?" He sounded half angry, half appalled.

"At least now I know what Killien did that made you so mad at him." Will almost asked her why she hadn't told him, but the question felt like it presumed more secret-sharing than they'd been in the habit of. At least before today.

She nodded. "And after all of that, he has rangers trying to capture more."

"Why?" Hal demanded.

"Because he's obsessed with gaining power for the Morrow Clan," Sora said. "And he is increasingly violent about it."

Hal looked like he wanted to object, but there was something in his expression that agreed with her. "I've never seen him like this." He sank down on the bench. His next words came out slowly. "He told me nothing…about any of this."

"I'd like to see that book about Mallon's magic," Alaric mused.

"I have something better." Will pulled *The Gleaning of Souls* out of his pack and the book fell to the table with a thud. "Or maybe worse."

Alaric leaned over and drew in a breath. "Kachig the Bloodless."

"You know the name? I hadn't heard it until I came to the Sweep."

A flicker of something dark crossed Alaric's face. "The blood doctors in Napon speak highly of him."

Will glanced up at him. "You've spoken to blood doctors? In Napon?"

Alaric's eyes were dark and angry. "I don't recommend it." He sat next to Will on the bench and reached out toward the medallion on the cover. His finger paused above it. "I've seen something like this before."

"That thing is dark." Will pulled his eye away from it. "It describes how to make something called absorption stones."

Alaric nodded and opened the book. He ran his fingers over the stacked runes, tracing the lines. "They've put runes inside each other."

Will watched Alaric's finger slide over the page, heard him muttering the words. Laughter started to bubble up inside him, foreign and shocking. Like something that hadn't happened in years. It burst out and Alaric looked up in surprise.

"You're just"—Will gestured to the page—"reading it. Like it's nothing."

Alaric smiled and pointed at one complicated one. "This is fascinating. They stacked four of them here. *Fire, escape, capture, and…*" He tilted his head to the side and leaned closer. "*Broken.*"

Will leaned forward. "I thought it was *empty*."

Alaric shook his head. "This line draws it into the past, referring to a cause. The end result would be *empty* but the rune itself is talking about the brokenness that emptied it."

Sora let out a laugh too, a rippling, free sound that filled the room. "I thought you were being mopey. But you really are bad at this."

"I'm bad at everything that goes into being a Keeper."

Alaric glanced up at him in surprise, his finger set on one of the runes. "You don't believe that. Do you?"

"Name one thing I'm good at."

"People," Alaric answered, as though it was too obvious to be worth saying.

Sora sat down across the table from them, her eyes shifting between Will and Alaric, utterly amused by the conversation. Will shot her a glare before answering.

"People. That's your answer? I'm a Keeper who's fairly useless at magic and terrible at reading." He stabbed his finger at the book. "It took me over a day just to figure out those runes were stacked. And I'm not even going to let you see my attempts at translating them."

Alaric looked at Will as though he were speaking a different language.

"Could anyone but Alaric read them this quickly?" Evangeline asked.

"Probably not," Will answered. "Your husband is irritatingly good at everything. And he's freakish about runes."

Her eyebrow rose.

"No offense," he added.

Evangeline laughed. "That's my point. Alaric's obsessed with runes. He has notebooks color coded based on region of origin, but organized by meaning. And there are three extra notebooks cross referencing it all."

Alaric shrugged. "Runes are like puzzles. Like there's some enormous game going on and everyone uses the same pieces, but not always the same rules." He turned to Will earnestly. "They're like a story."

Will groaned. "No. They're not. They're nothing like a story. I want to think it's weird that you're this studious, but really, it proves that you are just better at all things Keeper."

"Except people."

"You're good at using grass," Rass piped up from where she sat, munching on a piece of hard bread Douglon had found her.

Will shot Rass an irritated look and received a cheerful grin in return.

"People?" Will demanded of Alaric. "What does that mean? The Shield sends you to court because you're the one who's good at talking crazy noblemen down from weird schemes, at giving the queen rational, useful council. That all involves people."

Alaric let out an annoyed breath and cast around the room. He jabbed a finger at Hal. "Why is he mad?"

Hal, still stood near the bedrolls, his arms still tied behind his back. The giant man's eyes were smoldering with anger, and Will could see his jaw clenched even through the bushy beard.

"He's mad," Will began, pulling out the most obvious reason, "because he just found out that the man he's been friends with his entire life endangered everyone they both love in the pursuit of power."

Hal's gaze snapped over to Will's face.

"And he's angry because he would have done anything for that man, and now he doesn't know if that's been a mistake. He's mad because all this time he thought Killien was being honest, and now doesn't know how much he's been hiding."

Hal glared at Will and turned away.

"And he's still mad at me," Will continued, quieter, "because he thought we had a friendship before all this fell apart. So that's two friendships he's afraid have never been real to anyone but him. If I were him," he finished, "I'd be mad too."

The cave was silent for a long moment.

"See?" Alaric turned back to the book. "I would have said he's mad because no one's bothered to untie him yet." He ran his finger down the page again. "You effortlessly understand people in a way I never have. In a way maybe no Keeper ever has."

Will scowled at the side of Alaric's head. "I have an advantage in reading people."

"Were you using it?"

"No."

"Then you had no advantage. The Shield has said more than once that having you be the Keeper the world meets might be the best thing that's happened to us in a hundred years." Alaric leaned closer to one of the runes, squinting at it. "Understanding people is considerably more complex than understanding runes."

Hal glared into the corner of the room. Will nodded to Sora's unspoken question, and she cut

Hal's ropes.

"I know Killien thinks I'm his enemy," Will told Hal, "but I'm not. I used to think that he and I might work together toward some kind of peace, but lately…"

Hal rubbed at his wrists and nodded. "He's changed," he admitted.

"You're not our prisoner." Will motioned toward the entrance the dragon had attacked. "I don't think the way we came in still exists, but at the next exit we find, you're free to leave."

For the first time since finding them, the anger faded off Hal's face, and he looked Will in the eye. "Thank you."

"There's an exit an hour east of here," Douglon said. "The rest of us can continue back over to the Scales. A day and a half from now you can be on your way down the other side of Kollman Pass into Queensland."

"We can take supplies from here." Patlon went over to the shelves and started rummaging. "Torgon keeps up the western storerooms and he can be counted on to keep things stocked. We'll have plenty of supplies."

"I can't leave the Sweep," Will said.

Everyone turned toward him.

"Killien has Ilsa."

There was a breath before Alaric's eyes widened. "Your Ilsa?"

Will nodded. "And there's more. When she was taken, the wayfarers were actually trying to get me."

Alaric's expression clouded. "Why?"

"Because I was going to be a Keeper. The Morrow Clan has been sending wayfarers into Queensland for over thirty years, searching for children who have the ability to do magic, and bringing them back to the Morrow to be the Torch's personal slaves. They tried to get me, but when I wouldn't go, they took Ilsa.

"And they've found others. Killien has two slaves, Lukas and Sini, who are both from Queensland and can both do magic." He turned to Hal. "And Rett too? That would explain why Killien has him."

Hal hesitated, then nodded.

"Three?" Alaric sank down onto the bench. "They found three Keepers before we did?"

"I don't care if he did it for the good of his clan," Will said to Hal. "Killien abducts children and keeps them as his own personal slaves because they have powers he wants. *Three children*, Hal."

The giant man looked down for a long moment. Then his gaze flickered up toward Will's face, troubled. When he spoke, it was almost too quiet to hear.

"There used to be four."

THIRTY-FIVE

The room fell into silence as every head turned toward Hal.

Will took a step toward him. "What do you mean, 'used to be'?"

Hal met his gaze for a breath before looking down at the floor. "It was before Killien was Torch."

Will opened up toward Hal. An old, worn out mix of sadness and anger rolled into his chest.

"Killien's father, Tevien, was the one who started trying to bring people with powers to the Morrow. He knew Mallon was from Queensland, and he turned out to be more powerful than any of our stonesteeps."

Alaric watched Hal with narrowed, searching eyes. "Mallon was from Queensland?"

Will nodded.

"Tevien learned about Keepers," Hal continued. "Thinking they would bring the Morrow power, Tevien spent a fortune on stones able to recognize people with powers, and sent them to Queensland with some wayfarers.

"The first time they brought anyone back, it was twins."

Alaric shot a questioning glance at Will. There had been three sets of twins in the history of the Keepers. The latest pair, Matton and Steffan, were nearly a hundred years old and so identical that Will had given up trying to tell them apart years ago. Since they were never away from each other, there really was no need.

"Rett was big, even for a twelve year old. His sister Raina was average sized, but it was hard to remember that because she looked so small next to her brother." Hal fixed his eyes on the floor, his voice low. "The twins were the same age as Killien and I, and we spent a lot of time with them. Raina was quick and funny and brave. And Rett was stronger than me, by a lot. The two of them were inseparable. Raina told me once that she could almost hear Rett's thoughts, that she could catch a shadow of them." He let out a small laugh. "They were constantly trying to read each other's minds. Killien was half in love with her, although he hid it well from his father."

Hal shifted his shoulders. "Tevien became obsessed with training Rett and Raina into a pair who would be more powerful than any stonesteep. He wanted them to try something from a book years beyond their training. It involved both of them putting a bit of themselves into a stone, and storing it there. Rett thought it would never work, but Raina wanted to try."

He blew out a long breath. "I think she thought that if parts of each of them were really connected, they'd finally be able to speak into each other's minds." He pressed his eyes closed for a moment, and when he opened them, they were flat. "Raina went first. The stone glowed this eerie green and when she touched it—" His voice caught.

"It happened so fast. She started screaming, and it just pulled everything out of her. She went from laughing and talking and living…to nothing.

"Rett went crazy. He tried to rip the stone out of her hands, but as soon as he touched it, it started to take him too." He squeezed his eyes shut again, twisting away from the memory.

"It was Killien who stopped it. He wrested the stone away from them both. But by the time he did, Raina was dead and Rett was…empty. He still had some abilities, but there's nothing left of *him.*" He drew in a deep breath, and blew it out. "Killien and I have never been able to figure out if he even remembers who Raina was."

"That's why Rett likes glowing green stones, isn't it?" Will asked.

Hal let out a growl. "Lukas gives him those… Something in him must remember because he watches those stones like he's waiting for something. And when the green light fades, he's heartbroken."

"Is Lukas trying to be cruel?"

Hal shook his head. "Rett begs him for them and sometimes Lukas gives in. And while they glow, he's so happy, it almost feels like the right thing to do."

"How did Killien save him?" Alaric asked. "Why didn't the stone just take him too?"

Hal closed his mouth.

"Because magic doesn't work around Killien," Will said. "Does it?"

Hal clenched his jaw, but didn't disagree.

"That's why I couldn't do anything near him." Will turned to Alaric. "He was sitting at a table with me. I could feel the *vitalle* from everyone around us, but when I tried to grab it, it just slipped through my fingers. I don't know what kind of magic he has in one of those gems he wears, but I couldn't do anything near him."

Alaric's hand felt absently for something at his chest that he didn't find. "Could you touch the *vitalle* at all?"

Will started to shake his head, then paused. "It was like smoke. I knew when I had reached it, but there was nothing to hold."

Alaric turned his eyes up to the ceiling. "Fascinating."

"What's fascinating," Hal said, his face dark, "is that after all your protesting, Will, you obviously did try to use magic against Killien."

"Once. After he'd drugged me, imprisoned me, forced me to translate an evil book, and threatened to kill my sister. After all this, you can hardly expect me to give Killien the high moral ground."

"What happened to Raina and Rett is why Killien is the way he is," Hal fired back. "Why he studies everything as extensively as he can before he does anything. Why he spends the Morrow's money on as many books as he can find."

"Like this?" Will pointed to Kachig's book. "What we need to do is free Lukas. Then Killien won't have the power to do anything."

"You can't do that to Lukas," Hal objected.

Will stared at him. "I think he'd be in favor of being freed from slavery."

"He won't leave Killien. His limp isn't from a normal injury. A few years ago he was attacked by a stonesteep. The healers fixed his leg, but the pain never went away. It's driven by some sort of magic because if Lukas is close to Killien, it stops."

Will sank back. "That explains a lot." The closeness to Killien. His foul mood anytime he was away from the Torch. How his limp seemed to change in severity. "Why doesn't Killien just give Lukas one of the gems that stops magic from working around him? Is it in one of his rings?"

Hal fixed him with a look that clearly said Will didn't know what he was talking about.

A thought struck Will. "Unless it's not in a gem. It's something about Killien himself."

Hal scowled more deeply.

Alaric's eyebrow rose. "Killien can nullify magic?"

Will shrugged. "I only tried to move *vitalle* around him once, but if it's like that all the time, I'd say yes, he can nullify magic."

Both Keepers looked at Hal questioningly. Hal's shoulders sank. "I don't know how it works," he admitted, "but no magic works near Killien. He's been like that since we were boys. So Lukas stays near Killien as often as he can. Even at night. The room he sleeps in shares a wall with Killien, and that's close enough."

Alaric's eyebrows rose more. "He can do it through walls?"

Hal nodded.

Alaric eyes were bright with curiosity. "Fascinating," he repeated.

"If Killien nullifies magic, why does he wear all the rings and have the runes on his leathers?" Will asked.

"Only a handful of people know he has the ability. He thinks it's more valuable if he keeps it a secret."

"This is all very interesting," Douglon interrupted, hefting a crate off a shelf and bringing it over to the table, "but if we're not leaving the Sweep, where are we going?"

"I need to go where Killien has Ilsa," Will said.

"He's in the rift," Hal said. "We were supposed to leave for the enclave tomorrow, but after everything that happened, I'd imagine he's waiting impatiently for us to bring you back."

"How are you going to reach her?" Sora asked.

Will scrubbed his hand through his hair. "I don't know, but I can't leave her there."

"It's gonna be tricky sneaking Queenslanders and dwarves into a Roven rift," Patlon pointed out. "We don't blend in."

That was true. It would be stupid to take this group into the Sweep. Will dropped his head into his hands. There was no way any of them were going to get anywhere near the rift, never mind Killien's own house, without the Torch finding out.

The room was silent for a few breaths while Will searched desperately for an idea. It was Hal who broke the silence.

"I can take you in."

THIRTY-SIX

Will looked up at Hal sharply. "Somehow I don't think walking into the rift with you will work out much better for us."

"We'll go in the back entrance. There's a tunnel that leads from the Sweep directly into the back of Killien's house." He ran his fingernail along a groove on the table. "Ilsa's been helping Lilit recover since the baby was born. That's where she'll be."

"Who knows about the entrance?" Sora asked.

"Killien, Lilit, Me. Lukas." Hal turned to the dwarves. "Do you have an exit closer to the rift?"

"There is one," Douglon answered. "Only a couple hours away."

"Cousin," Patlon warned. "The High Dwarf isn't fond of foreigners in the tunnels."

"I don't see Horgoth here, cousin."

"He's going to be furious."

"That's hardly new."

"Can we get into Killien's house without being seen?" Will asked.

"If we go during the night," Hal answered. "We'll have to avoid rangers, but we'll have Sora with us."

"And me," Rass said. "Rangers stomp around so much you can hear them long before you can see them."

"The hours before dawn would be the easiest," Sora said. "But what if we run into Killien before we find Ilsa?"

"Trade me for her," Hal said.

Will glanced at Sora. "Would Killien make that trade?"

"Hal's family owns half of the herds in the Morrow Clan. Killien would be stupid not to. But if we run into Killien, we won't be in a position to trade."

"Then let's not run into Killien." Will turned to Hal. "Are we going to be able to find her?"

"The tunnel comes out in a back storage room near the slave's quarters. Killien's sleeping room is one floor up. If we're quiet, we can go in, talk to Ilsa, and leave before Killien knows you're there. I'll find a different way back into the rift once it's daylight."

Sora's face was hard. "Why are you helping Will?"

Hal ran a hand through his hair. "Ilsa's served Lilit for a long time, and she seems like a good person." He glanced at Will. "And the Torch hates you with a ferocity I haven't seen before. I don't think Ilsa should be a pawn in that. You're letting me go. Killien's letting her go. It's fair."

Sora's mouth pressed into a reluctant acceptance, before she turned back to Will. "And what if Ilsa doesn't want to come?"

Will's stomach tightened at the words.

"Will you be able to leave her there?"

"I'm not taking her against her will." He pushed aside the memory of how she'd flinched away from him. "But when she hears the truth, I hope she'll come."

Sora leaned on the table and fixed him with an expression that told him how likely she thought that was. "You're following a man who's angry with you, into the home of a man who hates you, to try to convince a woman who's terrified of you, to leave everything she's ever known."

Will shook his head "You're telling the story all wrong. A Keeper is journeying through the night, using a secret tunnel shown to him by a friend, to reach the house of…an old friend, in order to save an innocent girl from slavery, and possibly death." Her expression didn't change and Will gave her a hopeful smile. "And he's taking the greatest ranger on the Sweep with him, so that counts for something."

"Changing the story doesn't change the truth."

"The truth is complex enough for more than one story."

She shook her head and stood up, walking over to where Evangeline and Patlon were discussing supplies. Will glanced at Hal who was running his thumbnail pensively along a groove on the table.

"Is my horse alright?" Will asked.

Hal nodded without glancing up. "Killien made him a workhorse in the barley fields. He'll be cared for."

Will sighed. "I liked Shadow. Although I suppose he'd probably have been eaten by a dragon by now if he was here, seeing as how he wouldn't have fit in the entrance to this tunnel."

He watched Hal run his hand along the grain of the table. "I am sorry that I lied to you about who I was."

The big man paused for a moment. "Telling us you were a Keeper would have been a death sentence."

"Does it make it any better to know that it wasn't long into knowing you that I regretted the fact that the lie existed?"

Hal grunted noncommittally and Will let silence fall between them for a moment, wondering if there was a better way to ask his next question. "Are you sure you should be helping us?"

Hal didn't answer immediately. When he did, he sounded reluctant. "I've spoken to your sister several times, and I like her. I don't think it's right, Killien using her like this."

Will thought back on the past few weeks. "I've never seen you with a slave. Do you have any?"

"My father did. I grew up with some of them. One was a girl just two years younger than me. She was…like a sister." Hal ran his fingers through his beard. "And one day my father traded her for a breeding ram." In the dim light, Hal's eyes were hard. "When my father died, I took all our slaves to Kollman Pass and sent them off the Sweep."

"You set them free?"

Hal nodded. "Never sat right with me, owning people like that."

"But you're friends with Killien, and he has plenty of slaves."

"If I kept my distance from every Roven with slaves, I'd have no friends at all," Hal answered. "Killien and I have been friends our entire lives. I love him like a brother even if we don't agree on everything."

"Won't he see this as a betrayal?"

Hal ran his hand through his beard. "Maybe. But there's a lot of what he's done lately that feels like betrayal as well. I can't believe he did that with the frost goblins, and still wants to capture more. Also, he already knows how I feel about slaves. I've tried to convince him more than once to free his."

"How did he take that idea?"

"Not well. I don't think Rett would know what to do with freedom, but Sini and Lukas deserve it. Sini is too fun and happy to be kept as a slave. And Lukas is bright, he could probably do anything he set his mind to."

Except be pleasant. "Well, thank you. I appreciate the help."

Hal gave Will a hard look. "When I met you, I thought you'd make my journey north more enjoyable. Instead you've made my life much more complicated."

"I introduced you to dwarves," Will pointed out. "And brought you into their tunnels."

A smile showed behind his beard. "True. Maybe that's the real reason I'm helping you. And I do like the stories."

"Maybe after we eat I can tell the one about a dwarf princess who was so ugly she was mistaken for a rock."

"I've never wanted to hear anything more."

Down the table, Alaric leaned close to a page in Kachig's book, squinting at a rune and muttering.

"What we need," Will said to him, "are the more elementary books on how to do magic with stones. All the books I've read expect a familiarity with a process we don't know anything about."

Alaric cleared his throat and smoothed his hand across the page. "I may have figured out a little bit of it."

"When?"

Alaric glanced at Evangeline, then began the story of how she was poisoned and how he drew out her *vitalle* into a Reservoir Stone to keep her alive.

Will stared at his old friend, stunned. "That sounds like the absorption stone that Killien's book talked about, drawing the life out of someone."

"Very much like it." Alaric told of the long, painful search for the cure, and how it led to the discovery of a wizard named Gustav who planned to awaken Mallon.

"He was the reason the dragon attacked us the first time," Douglon said.

"How did you fight it off?" Will asked.

Douglon looked away and took a bite of his bread.

"Ayda did," Alaric answered.

"Ayda the elf? I underestimated her," Will said.

"Everyone did."

Will looked back and forth between them. "I followed a wizard onto the Sweep because he claimed he was going to wake Mallon. I found him, eventually, but he was just a doddering old man. His name wasn't Gustav, though. It was Wizendor."

Alaric laughed. "That's him. His full name was Wizendorenfurderfur."

"The Wondrous," Douglon added.

They seemed perfectly serious. "That's ridiculous."

Douglon shook his head. "You can't even imagine."

"He was a master of influence spells." Alaric's distaste of the idea was obvious. "He fooled all of us."

Will shifted. "Influence spells can be useful when you're surrounded by enemies."

Alaric raised an eyebrow, but after a moment's thought, gave a nod of agreement. He explained how Ayda had been the last elf, and held the power of all the others, how she'd used it to help destroy Mallon and Gustav.

"But you said before there are no more elves." Will looked at each of their somber faces, not wanting to ask the next question. "Did destroying Mallon kill her?"

Alaric shook his head. "No, that came later."

Douglon let out a long sigh and pushed away from the table, going to rummage through another crate on the shelf.

"Douglon," Will whispered, "and Ayda?"

Alaric nodded.

"That's…" Words failed him.

"It is," Alaric agreed. "When we got back to Evangeline, she was far too weak to revive. Until Ayda…"

Evangeline looked pensively at her own hands.

"She was tired of being the only elf, tired of carrying the weight of her people. She'd done it long enough to see Mallon destroyed, and she was done."

Will sat back, taking in the whole idea. "So there really are no elves?" The idea felt so hollow. Granted he had only seen a handful of elves in his life, most of which were polite but distant emissaries at court, but elves always felt like a breath of life in the world. He'd often thought of returning to the Greenwood to find Ayda again. "Is that how you knew the dragon?" he asked Evangeline. "Whatever Ayda put in you recognized it?"

Both Alaric and Evangeline nodded.

"She put some of her memories into me," Evangeline explained. "It's like when you're doing something and you have that feeling that you've done it all before. Sometimes I see something, or Alaric says something, and I know about it. But it's like a dream. If I think about it too much, it all goes away. So Alaric's taken to slipping things into conversations to catch me off guard."

"You would not believe the things I've learned about the elves," Alaric said. "It's fascinating. And depressing."

"We should go." Douglon pulled some squash and onions out of the crate. "There's a cavern not far from here with a chimney. We can cook and get a few hours sleep before we need to head to the rift."

"I thought we'd just sleep here." Alaric glanced at the bedrolls.

"Trust me." Douglon shoved the crate back onto the shelf. "You want to get to the other one."

Patlon poured water into cup-like lanterns. As he did, each one began to glow with a faint orange light.

Sora pulled her own glimmer moss lantern out of her bag, and using a bit of Patlon's water, set hers glowing a ruddier color. Patlon peered into her lantern and grunted. "Frostweed?"

"Mixed with crushed tundra lichen."

Patlon gave her an approving nod. "You may be the most competent human I've ever met." He motioned her toward the tunnel. "You're going to like where we're headed."

Sora walked into the tunnel next to him, the sound of Patlon's voice dropping to muffled echoes. Everyone else followed.

The world shrank to the size of their group. The lanterns cast four patches of orange light. Bits of the ceiling and walls slid through them. A nagging discomfort began to plague Will that they weren't actually moving. That they were doing something like treading water. A peal of laughter echoed back from Sora, and Will craned around Hal to see her. She talked animatedly, outlined in the dim light of Patlon's lantern. It felt partly reassuring, partly irritating that she was so at ease.

"You can't listen with your ears," Douglon's voice came from behind him. "Listen with the part of you that understands the permanence of the stone. The part of you that knows that life should continue, that *you* should continue, that dying goes against what should be. The part of you that understands eternity."

Will glanced back to see Rass reach out tentatively toward the wall. "When I talk to the grass, it is always growing and dying and growing again. There is nothing lasting about it." She let her fingers trail along the rock.

"Don't think about the voice of the grasses. Think about the voice of the Sweep, lying still and strong and unmoved for a thousand years."

Rass's brow furrowed and she pressed more of her hand against the wall, dragging her whole palm along it. She shook her head.

"Give it time, wee snip," Douglon said. "The rocks speak slowly."

They walked for more than an hour. At some point, Patlon began to hum a deep, thrumming tune. The melody echoed off the walls mixing with new strands of the song. Douglon joined in, humming from the back of the group, and the echoes became more layered and rich, the pulse of the song rang through the mountain like a drum.

Eventually the darkness paled and the tunnel, which had run reasonably straight, twisted sharply to the left. Will squinted into the hazy light that filtered around another turn not far ahead. The tunnel continued in the excessively serpentine way for four more turns, each growing gradually brighter before Hal mentioned it to Patlon.

"It's giving your eyes time to adjust," the dwarf answered. "You'd have been half blinded if you just stepped into what's ahead."

Even so, when the tunnel turned the last time, Will could barely open his eyes. The air was saturated with a blue-tinged light, as though they had stepped out into the middle of the shimmering sky. After the closeness of the tunnel, the cavern gaped open taller than pine trees and wide enough that the other side was lost in hazy brightness. The faint smell of trees and earth wafted past, but everything looked like sky.

"Move in," Douglon grumbled from behind them.

Will took a stunned step forward along with everyone else, and the floor beneath him shot out fierce glints of light, flashing reflections of the glimmer moss like specks of blazing fire.

"It glitters everywhere!" Rass's little voice skipped off the walls and echoed through the chamber.

The floor itself was a pale blue, but glitters of orange from the mosslight skittered across it with every step, like infinitesimally small fairies flitting by faster than he could see. On the rough walls, the lights tripped from crevice to ridge, scattering like shattered glass.

"Welcome to Hellat Harrock'lot." Douglon's words echoed as well, deeper and richer. "The Cavern of Sea and Sky. You may be the first foreigners to set eyes on it."

"Another thing the High Dwarf is going to love," Patlon muttered.

The cavern wasn't as large as Will had first thought. His eyes adjusted and revealed the far side of the oblong cave only a hundred paces away. Four tunnels branched off, dark mouths opening in the blue-white walls. The ceiling was just the continuation of the walls, arching over them in a low hanging dome. Near the far side, the ceiling was cut by a gash letting in a trickle of light.

"We're close to the surface," Douglon said. "It's only a short climb up that shaft to an outcropping of rock on the mountainside. Judging from the light, it's close to sunset. Thanks to that little chimney, we can have a fire and a proper meal. We can get a few hours sleep before we need to leave."

In a wide, flat area there was a circle of ash on the floor and a small pile of wood stacked up against a nearby wall. Patlon lit a fire, and the flames sent millions of tiny shards of light reflecting across the cavern. Sora took out the rabbit that had been wrapped around the heatstone. The stone had stopped glowing, but the entire package was still warm. The strips of rabbit were hot and dripping with juices, and they were divided up and eaten within moments.

Will set Talen on a thin piece of firewood and ripped off small bits of rabbit, feeding them to the hawk who seemed perfectly content to sit on his perch in his hood.

Everyone gathered near the fire except Sora, who faced out into the cavern. He walked over to her, watching the floor glitter and flash below his feet, like he was treading on the stars. "Have you ever seen anything like this?"

She shook her head.

"A place like this makes me understand why you like caves."

"Everyone loves places like this. But it's the small, common caves that feel like home. The tunnels that wander through the mountains."

He thought about the passageways they'd traveled through all day, the darkness, the silence, the lifelessness. There was nothing homey about them.

"You think I'm crazy," she said.

"No, I think you're scowly," he answered, "and have an odd definition of homey."

With a small shake of her head she strode across the cavern. "Come."

He let her walk a few steps before following. "I also think you're bossy."

THIRTY-SEVEN

H e followed Sora to the nearest tunnel mouth. She paused at the opening, and with a disapproving grunt, she walked to the next.

"This one." She stepped in and turned a corner out of sight. Her voice came back in an echoey, hollow way. "Come."

Will followed her. Around the first turn, the tunnel dimmed and he found her waiting, arms crossed. The corners of the floor were lost in blackness, and shadows filled more spaces on the wall than seemed reasonable. "What are we doing in here?"

"You are going to see what tunnels are really like." She turned and disappeared around another corner, proving this was just as serpentine as the one from earlier.

"What if we get lost?"

"It'll make a great story," she answered. "Hurry up."

In two more turns the darkness crept out of the corners and seeped into the air itself. He could barely make her out in front of him. "Not to sound like a frightened child," he said, letting his hands run along the wall as he walked deeper into the darkness, "but I'd be thrilled to find out you had a bit of glimmer moss tucked away somewhere."

She turned back towards him, and he was almost certain she was laughing. She took one of his hands and started walking again, pulling him along.

"Not much farther."

One more turn and the tunnel straightened out. His eyes stretched wide, but there was nothing to see but blackness. He could feel Sora's hand in his, but there was no way to pick her out from the dark.

She walked a dozen paces more and then stopped. He tried to hold her hand loosely, fighting the urge to cling to it. The darkness was so thick it felt like a thing in itself.

"Do you hear that?" she whispered.

There was nothing at all to hear. Beyond Sora's slow, measured breathing and the unnerving sound of his own heart pounding, which he was sure she could feel through his hand, there was utter and complete silence.

"No," he whispered. "I hear nothing."

"That's what you're supposed to hear." Her words slid through the darkness, calm and pleased. "The tunnel is like a cocoon, like the walls of a fortress so thick that nothing can get through them.

Not noises, not armies, not other people's expectations, not even the Serpent Queen."

Will closed his eyes and tried to find what Sora felt. "It all feels too heavy. Like the rocks will crush us."

"You're thinking of the mountain as an enemy. It's life and shelter and warmth and endless, timeless permanence."

Her words almost made a difference. For a breath he felt the solid mass of the mountain above him like a shield. But it grew heavier until it was ready to smash down and flatten them all. His grip tightened on her hand.

"You're not seeing the mountain for what it is, Will. You're imagining what it's capable of, but you're not seeing what it is now, what it's been for thousands of years. When you walk through the forest, you don't imagine it will burst into flames at any moment, do you?"

"No," he admitted.

"This tunnel is more permanent than the trees. Think about what the rocks are, what they do. Wind and storms that terrify us don't affect them. Nothing is indestructible, but the rocks are close. They're…" She gave a short growl of irritation. "I can't explain it. Here, feel what it's like for me."

Emotion surged into his chest. Contentedness, security, belonging. Like he was a child again in the years before Ilsa had been taken, tucked under a wool blanket, lying in his bed in the dark cottage, alone but safe. The walls of the cottage surrounded him, blocking out the foxes and packs of little brush wolves that roamed the forest. All the dangers were outside the walls and inside there was nothing to fear. Just the endless night, a black backdrop waiting to be filled with imaginings.

The freedom in that moment was liberating. Freedom he hadn't noticed as a child.

The sensation drained out of his chest and he ached with hollowness in its wake. He gripped Sora's hand in the darkness of the tunnel and he understood. The tunnel walls stood solid around them, holding off the mountain, holding back the sky. The Sweep and its politics, Killien and his plans, Queensland and its responsibilities, all those things were outside the walls. And in here there was just the silence of endless years of stillness. Nothing rushed, nothing expected.

"Oh," he breathed.

"Now you see?" Her voice was quiet, low enough that he almost missed it.

"Yes."

They stood in silence for a breath and Will realized his shoulders were relaxed. He breathed in the stillness of the tunnel.

A jarring question broke through the quiet.

"How did you do that?" He wished he could see Sora's face. "Your emotions are always so tightly controlled, I can barely find them. How did you make me feel that?"

"I just did what we tried in the rift. I tried to let you feel my emotions."

"But *I* wasn't trying." He hadn't been, had he? "I have to…open up to someone. It doesn't just happen. I have to want to feel them."

"Maybe you want to know what I'm feeling more than you think you do." There was a note of amusement in her voice.

"I don't—that sounds like I'm stalking you."

Her laughter echoed off the walls, bouncing back on itself into a jumble of sound. "Do you really think that if I were trying to get away from you, you could stalk me?"

"That's not exactly what I meant."

"Shall I leave you here in the tunnel and you can try to track me?" Her fingers loosened on his hand.

"No!" He turned and brought both hands to clench hers and she laughed again. He cleared his throat. "I mean, maybe some other time. Right now, I just want to stay here and absorb all this comforting silence you just showed me."

"Of course you do." Her fingers wrapped around his hand again. "Because there's nothing better than being deep in the mountain."

The stillness of the tunnels became a palpable thing again.

"Living with your people was so bad that you won't go back? Even for this?"

She didn't answer. All he heard was the sound of their breath and the silence of the mountain.

"There was another thing my clan believed about me…"

The words trailed away, absorbed by the mountain.

"When I was twelve, Lyelle, the daughter of the holy woman, fell ill. They brought me to her and she recovered. From then on she was allowed to play with me." A wistfulness crept into her voice. "It wasn't just that Lyelle was my only friend, she was exactly the sort of girl I would have picked. She was funny and smart and brave.

"The other children never left the cave without adults." The wistfulness was gone, replaced by something Will couldn't name. "The mountains are too wild. But she wanted to sneak out with me. We went out twice with no problems, and she grew more eager to do it again.

"The third time we went…" Sora's voice stopped and her hand trembled. "By the time I sensed the wolves, it was too late. They were too close."

The horror of the idea stole his breath.

"I climbed up on some boulders." The words sounded like they were spilling out of their own will. "But Lyelle wasn't tall enough to get up. And I wasn't strong enough to pull her…" Sora's hands clenched his. She drew in a shuddering breath. "It was over so fast. I didn't…"

They stood in the darkness while she took several breaths. When she began again, a coldness had crept into her words.

"I was too young to understand why the holy woman didn't blame me."

The truth of it hit him like a fist in the gut. "She needed the people to believe everything was related to your power."

He took her silence for agreement.

"She quoted some ancient text claiming to court the friendship of the Serpent Queen was to court death. The next winter I fell sick, and in caring for me, my mother did as well.

"I wasn't even fully recovered when she died." The ache in her voice dug into Will's chest. "Terra told the clan that she'd been a good mother, but it had always been only a matter of time. Because to draw too close to the Serpent Queen brought nothing but death."

"None of this was you," Will whispered to her, pulling her hand to his chest. "None of it."

"I know." She paused. "At least most of me does. But there's a part that's still twelve, watching them take away my mother's body." She let out a long breath and her grip loosened. "So no, Will. Not even the tunnels could draw me back. Because the farther I am away from home, the easier it is to remember that I'm not twelve, I have no power, and I'm not cursed to kill everyone I love.

"Or it was. Until Lilit was dying and Killien demanded the same thing from me. I was that girl again."

She pulled gently on her hand and he let her pull it away from his chest, but didn't let go of it.

"Killien was desperate," Will said. "But still, he should have known better."

Sora didn't answer him.

"There's an easy solution to Killien, though." He felt Sora waiting. "You should curse him."

She smacked him on the shoulder with her other hand, but he heard her laugh. "If I curse anyone, it's going to be you."

Will drew in a breath of the cool tunnel air. "The stories the holy woman told about you aren't you. She doesn't have the right to choose your story. She's stolen some power over you, but if you take it back, there's nothing she can do to stop you. She's twisted and controlled the entire clan. What they need is the truth. If you tell them, if you claim your own story and stop letting her control it, you'll be free of her. And it will loosen her control over your entire clan."

When Sora didn't answer, he let the subject drop. "I see what draws you here." Will's voice echoed off the wall beside him. "But you forgot to mention the best part."

She waited in expectant silence.

"This would be a great place for storytelling. Can you hear the little echo? So dramatic. I heard a tale once in Napon about a young woman who was chased by trolls into the hill caves—"

"Will," Sora interrupted with a laugh, "let's just enjoy the silence."

"Right."

The story pushed at him, begging to be told, but he squeezed his mouth shut.

Next to him Sora shifted. "It's killing you not telling me, isn't it?"

A voice interrupted his reply, calling down the echoey tunnel to announce the soup was cooked.

"Of all the reasons to have to go back to the rest of the world," Sora said, "hot soup is one of the best." She turned and walked back the direction they'd come, and he fell in beside her, running his free hand along the wall beside him as they turned into brighter and brighter sections of tunnel.

After several turns Sora paused. He could see her clearly now, looking attentively ahead of them. He opened his mouth to start the troll story again, when she tightened her grip on his hand and motioned him to be quiet.

Voices floated down the tunnel.

Evangeline's voice bounced off the walls, jumbling with itself, "Thank you for coming with Alaric. He's relieved that you came."

"Can't expect the Keeper to get out of any troublesome situations on his own," Douglon answered. "And I didn't have anywhere else to be."

There was a long pause. And Will took a step forward, but Sora stopped him.

"Why are we stopping?" he whispered.

"Don't interrupt this." Sora's voice was firm.

"Interrupt what?"

"Do you hate me?" Evangeline's words came out in a rush and Will felt a jab of awkwardness. He leaned close to Sora. "We should not be listening to this."

"I know." She started backing down the tunnel and Will followed, but he could still hear Evangeline clearly.

"Do you hate me because I'm alive, and I'm the reason she…" She paused. "The reason Ayda isn't?"

Will's gut tightened at the question. He set his foot down as quietly as possible, backing away and barely breathed during the silence that followed.

"At first it was hard," Douglon answered. "But Ayda was exhausted. And with her people gone, she was utterly alone. In a way no one could fix." The dwarf's voice stopped and Will held his breath. "In a way I could never have fixed."

"I'm so sorry." Evangeline's words were almost lost in the tunnel.

"I'm luckier than most," Douglon answered. "When someone you love dies, you usually have nothing but memories. I have something…more." The stillness of the tunnel waited for him to continue. "Sometimes…when I listen to the trees…I can almost hear what she would say to them." His voice was soft, but the longing in it caught at Will's chest. "Almost."

"Does it make it better? Or worse?"

Douglon let out a long, jagged breath. "Both."

"I'm grateful for everything, of course, but…" She paused for a moment. When she spoke again it was determined, as though she was forcing out a confession. "Having all the knowledge from Ayda makes me somehow more equal to Alaric. He's always known so much, and I was just an innkeeper."

Douglon's answer was kind. "I don't think Alaric has ever thought of you as 'just' anything. He was ready to tear apart the world to save you. We even had to talk him out of sacrificing himself."

She murmured something to him, and there was a long, awkward pause. Will and Sora took another step backwards.

"If my cousin's finally finished cooking," Douglon said louder, "we should get there before Hal eats our portions." There was a shuffling noise. "Do you like the cavern?"

"It's amazing," Evangeline answered.

Their voices faded away.

Will let out a long breath. "I feel like I just invaded a private conversation."

"We did." Sora dropped his hand and walked forward again. "But it was that or interrupt, and she's been working up the courage to ask that for a very long time."

"How do you know?"

"We walked together earlier. What do you think we were talking about?"

Will stared at her. "You've walked for hours next to me without saying a single word."

"Maybe," she said with a smile, stepping out into the cavern, "I was waiting for you to tell me a story."

Will stopped. "Really?"

"No." She laughed. "I walked quietly with you because you let me. There's not a lot of people who will."

The cavern scattered splinters of reflected firelight across the floor.

"I thought if I talked to you," he said, "you'd leave."

"I probably would have."

"Well, that would have been a shame," he said. "Seeing as you were about the only person I was sure didn't want to kill me."

"Oh," she said, "there were plenty of times I wanted to kill you."

The soup was more delicious than a watery concoction of old vegetables had any right to be. Will told the story of the dwarf princess who was as ugly as a rock with a good deal of clarification from Douglon and Patlon. The sparkling cavern echoed with laughter and even though they'd have to wake soon, the fire burned to ashes before anyone settled for the night.

THIRTY-EIGHT

t felt like Will had barely fallen asleep before the dwarves roused everyone and they headed back into the tunnels. Will paused, taking in the cave again before stepping out of the cavern. After the glittering brilliance, the tunnel was dismal. Only the dwarves and Sora seemed to find any enjoyment in them.

An hour later, a small room opened off the side of the tunnel. Shelves lined the walls again, holding supplies, and a small table almost filled the middle of the room. Will and Sora put their packs on the table. Sora slung her bow and a thin quiver of arrows across her back.

Douglon looked at Will critically, then offered him a knife. "I'm sure you don't actually know how to fight with that, Keeper. But maybe you'll need to cut a rope or something."

Will took it and put it on his belt.

Patlon went to a wide, flat rock at the far end of the room and after a small click, it shifted and a breeze swirled in. There was a breath of freshness to the air and Rass lifted her face. "I can smell the grass."

Talen shifted his weight on Will's shoulder and Will ran a finger down the hawk's chest. "Almost out."

"The rift is a short walk southeast." Patlon set his shoulder against the rock and shoved. Slowly it swung open, revealing a slightly grayer blackness than the tunnels. The wind squeezed through the opening, humming and blustering its way in. "We'll be watching for you."

Rass hurried through the gap with Sora, and Hal followed.

Will looked through the opening with a sinking feeling in his gut. The tunnels were dark and close and lifeless. But through that door lay the exposed Sweep. He'd be shoved about by the wind, surrounded by endless nothing and endless Roven.

He turned to Alaric. "If we're not back in a few hours…"

"We'll find a way to get you out," Alaric assured him.

Will nodded and ducked out into the open night.

Huge boulders crowded around him beneath the sky. Wind swirled past him, pushing at his clothes, saturated with the scent of trees and grass. The ground rolled away in front of him, down to the vast Sweep.

A heavy moon sat low over the western horizon, washing out all but the brightest stars and spreading a stark grayness across the grass. A little east of them it turned black where the charred grass began. The wind blew in chilly, fitful gusts, twisting and pushing at the grass, whipping the Sweep into constant motion.

Talen fluttered and shifted his weight. Will pulled the hood off the hawk's head and Talen shot off his shoulder in a burst of wings.

Will cast out, but the only people he could find were Sora, Hal, and Rass. The tiny elf hurried down the hill toward the edge of the grass, her feet fairly flying across the ground. Sora stood at the end of the boulders and Will stopped next to her.

Hal stood a little away from the rocks, spinning slowly, facing up the slope, taking in the peaks behind, their snowy tops a cold white in the moonlight.

"It's that way." He pointed a little to the east. "The back entrance is not far."

Sora watched him as he headed down the slope. "Do you trust him?" Her voice came quietly through the wind.

Will pulled at the end of his beard, pushing down the fear that had been growing for the last several hours. "I think so. At least he believes he's going to help us."

The feeling of exposure the Sweep always caused wrapped around him.

"And if he changes his mind?" she asked.

"Then you'll have to use your amazing ranger skills and I'll have to use my amazing magical skills to execute a heroic escape."

The moonlight traced strands of her braid in silver and caught just the edge of a small smile. It was enough of a smile to draw out a little of his fear and let the wind snatch it away.

"Thank you for coming," he said. "Thank you actually doesn't come close to conveying how grateful I am."

"I don't trust Hal. And even though he's not much of a fighter, he could take you easily enough."

"I'd have been fine," he protested.

She shot him an incredulous look.

He wiggled his fingers at her. "Keeper."

She sized him up for a moment, then turned back toward the Sweep, the smile peeking back out. "If it was a Keeper we needed, maybe we should have brought Alaric."

Will grinned at her. He pulled his eyes away and tried to focus on the blustery motion of the Sweep ahead of them, searching for whatever Hal could be aiming for. "Maybe, but he seems a bit preoccupied with a woman."

"And you're not?"

Will snapped his attention back to her, an uncomfortably tight feeling in his chest. "I—" The moonlight etched her amusement in silver and shadows and he tried to meet her eyes, but he couldn't quite get his own to cooperate. "I'm not…" He trailed off weakly.

She laughed. "She's your sister, Will. It's alright. We'll get her out. But we should move faster."

Sora sped up, heading down after Hal. Will watched her for a moment, an awkward tangle of emotions smoldering in his chest. He blew out a long breath, hoping to push them away.

Rass waited for them at the edge of the grass. "There's no one nearby." She ran her hand across the top of the old brittle grass, then bent down and pulled a new blade of grass through her fingers. "The closest people are near the rift."

"We don't need to go that far." Hal hunched closer to the grass and set out southeast across the Sweep.

It took half an hour to reach a little pile of scrub brush and some rocks piled in the middle of the grass, only stopping once when Rass motioned them all down as a ranger passed by them to the east. They hadn't quite reached the fireline yet, but it wasn't far off. The jagged edge of the rift was easy to see here. It was wider than Will had expected, stretching away southeast from them. At the scrub brush, Hal reached under the edge of a large rock and lifted. It hinged open and thumped back with a distinctly unrocklike sound, revealing a black hole beneath.

Rass leaned forward and sniffed the air and drew back. "I'll wait here and make sure no one comes."

Hal nodded and climbed down into the hole and Sora followed.

"Be careful," Rass whispered to Will.

"You too."

"I'm in the grass. No one can hurt me." She shifted back and forth, her bare little toes digging into the soil.

"There's nothing unexpected going on nearby?"

She shook her head. "Three Roven spread out far on the other side of the rift, the one who passed us earlier is still heading south, and there's a herd of sheep with two shepherds grazing so far to the south you wouldn't be able to see them, even if the sun was up."

"You're amazing," he said, tousling the top of her head. He sat at the edge of the hole and felt along the wall until he found the rung of a ladder.

She smiled at him, then turned and tilted her head slightly. "That dragon isn't home."

Will stopped.

"He's usually down by a city that sits on a bay, with a big cliff below it."

"That's Tun," Will said. "That's the city of the Sunn Clan. They are the ones with the dragon."

"The grass goes all the way to the edges of the cliff and he lies there, looking at the ocean," Rass said. "But tonight he's much closer. Not near any cities or any people. He's just lying in the grass."

The wind shoved through scrub brush around him, shaking it against the sky. The heavy moon was almost low enough to touch the horizon, and the stars bright enough to brave the moonlight glittered clearly. Will scanned them, his mind kept offering the silhouette of wings in any dark spot. "How close?"

"It would take you more than a day to walk to him. But why didn't he go home?"

"I'm not sure, but keep track of him. We'll be back soon. I hope."

"I'd like to meet your sister," Rass whispered to him. "I hope she's happy to come."

"Me too." He grabbed a handle on the lid. It swung easily, and Will pulled the not-rock down into place. A dim orange glow illuminated the base of the ladder.

At the bottom, a rough dirt tunnel ran off to the east. Hal hunched his head down to avoid the rough ceiling and the thin roots that hung down from it. The air was damp and earthy but not as stale as Will had expected. He blew out a long breath, trying to slow his heart. Somehow being here, below the empty Sweep, was worse than being under a solid mountain. The tunnel left him feeling trapped and vulnerable at the same time.

Sora held a bowl of glimmer moss ahead of her as she peered down the tunnel.

Hal dipped his finger into another one that sat on a rough shelf. "It's wet. Someone's been in this tunnel recently."

Will cast out, but besides Sora, Hal, and the ceiling of grass above them, there was nothing living larger than a worm. "There's no one in the tunnel, and Rass says no one's nearby."

Hal frowned at the bowl before turning and heading down the tunnel. Their feet made no sound in the soft earth, and the silence and the unwavering orange light made everything feel dreamlike. And not the good kind of dream. Will had the irrational fear that this tunnel would never end, or worse—lead him to that horrible barren rift.

The tunnel ran relatively straight. When Hal held up his hand to stop, Will's fear that the tunnel wouldn't end was instantly replaced by the fear that it had, and that he was about to sneak into Killien's house. Hal motioned Will to come up with him. Will put his hand on Sora's arm as he passed her and could feel her tension. He squeezed up beside Hal and found himself looking at the back of a piece of fabric.

"Anyone there?" Hal whispered, almost noiselessly.

Will cast out past the fabric, but found no one. He shook his head and Hal pulled back the fabric and stepped through. With his heart pounding loud enough to shake the Sweep, Will followed. Sora came through with the glimmer moss and lit the small room with orange light. The wall to their left held shelves packed with books, candles and paper. Hal let the fabric fall back and Will could make out that it was a wall hanging with the image of the Serpent Queen stretching darkly across it. Most of the fabric was darkish in the dim light, but the form of the queen, which slithered over mountain peaks and coiled around the moon, was utterly black. He reached out to touch her and his fingers ran across soft, thick fabric that caught slightly at his fingertips. Pulling his hand away, he wiped it on his pants to erase the feeling.

There were other wallhangings too, overlapping on the walls. On one shelf, a pile of gems glittered dully in the dim light. Off to the side, two greenish stones glowed with a watery light, like blades of grass under a stream. In the far corner, a set of leather armor hung, silver buckles glinting in the light. Sora walked closer, holding the glimmer moss up to it, revealing intricately tooled leather with runes covering most of the surface.

"Killien's ceremonial armor," Hal whispered. "I've only seen him wear it once, the day the clan named him Torch." Hal turned toward the door and stopped so abruptly that Will almost walked into his back. He stared above the door at two empty wooden pegs.

"Killien's sword." Hal turned back to the armor, then spun slowly around the room. "Svard Naj, when we're in the rifts, it's always here. Killien never moves it. He's almost superstitious about it."

"Maybe he took it to show his new son," Sora said, irritated. "We should move."

Will looked up at the empty hooks. The seax Flibbet the Peddler had given Killien. The one the Torch had said was "too serious for a mere fight." The empty hooks looked black and slightly ominous in the mosslight.

With one last frown at the hooks, Hal pulled open the door. It squeaked and Will's heart slammed up into his throat. They all froze for a moment, but when no sounds came from the house, Hal stepped in to the hall. He led them to the right, and stopped near the end of the hall. Three doors sat closed ahead of them. Will cast out. There were two people, one behind each of the doors on the right. He told Sora and she nodded.

"Any idea which is Ilsa?"

Will shook his head.

"Stay here," she whispered. She handed the glimmer moss to Hal and walked to the first door. Easing it open, she slipped inside. She was back quickly, and with a shake of her head, moved to the other room. In moments she was out of that one as well, shaking her head again. Will sank back against the wall. He cast out again, but there was no one else on this floor. Upstairs he could just sense someone, but there was no one nearby.

Hal motioned them back to the room with the armor and they crept quietly back down the hall.

"If she's not here," he said once they'd closed the door. "She could be anywhere."

Will sank against one of the shelves. The fact that she wasn't here loomed in front of him like a blank wall.

Sora paced back and forth down the room. "You have to have some idea, Hal," she whispered.

He shook his head. "At the other end of this hall a door leads to the kitchen. Upstairs is a gathering room and Killien's sleeping quarters."

Sora froze, spun slowly around and fixed Hal with a dangerous look. "You better not be suggesting Ilsa is in Killien's quarters."

"No," Hal said quickly. "He wouldn't."

A flicker of anger pushed past the fear and Will stared at Hal. The big man turned to him and held his hands out toward Will, his face earnest. "Killien and Lilit are inseparable. And since she almost died, he barely leaves her side. He wouldn't."

Will pressed his hands against his eyes, blocking out the dim light of the moss. Sora's footsteps paced quietly, Hal let out a long, slow breath, and the fear that had been growing in Will turned icy. Where had Killien put his sister?

"I'm going upstairs." He pushed himself away from the shelves. "Killien is going to tell me where she is."

"No you're not." Sora stepped between Will and the door.

"I'm not leaving here without knowing where she is." Will stepped forward, but Sora didn't move.

"If anyone goes upstairs, it's going to be me," she said calmly.

Will stared at her incredulous. "Absolutely not. Killien will kill you."

One of Sora's eyebrows rose the smallest bit. "I wasn't asking your permission."

"And I wasn't asking yours. If my sister is here, I'm going to find her."

Sora took in an irritated breath, then froze. Her eyes flew wide and she spun toward the door, sliding the knife from her belt.

Will cast out and felt the blazing *vitalle* of someone directly on the other side of the door. He swore under his breath. Killien.

Except this person was too small. He clutched at a strand of hope. Ilsa?

The door began to swing open and the three of them backed up. Will cast out again looking for *vitalle* to draw in, but found nothing but people. He reached for the knife Douglon had given him, gripping the hilt to keep his hand from trembling.

"You'll be looking around the rift for a long time if you're expecting to find Ilsa," a woman's voice came through the opening.

The door creaked the rest of the way open and the dim orange light of the glimmer moss barely reached the face of Lilit.

THIRTY-NINE

"Hello, Hal," Lilit said lightly, looking down at the bundle in her arms. "Sevien was restless, so I thought a little walk would help him. But maybe he's a blessed child. Maybe he could sense rats in the storage room." When she looked up to consider them, her face was stony. "Sora," she acknowledged coldly, "and Will the Keeper."

The bundle she carried gave an irritated, tiny grunt and Will pulled his hand off his knife. "Where's my sister?"

Lilit stepped into the room, stopping underneath the empty sword pegs. Hal took a step back away from her, his hands held out to the side, unthreatening. Sora stood her ground, letting her knife fall to her side, but not putting it away.

"I had expected you two to return as Hal's prisoners." Lilit's eyes were cold and flat. "Not as his companions, sneaking into my house like thieves."

"We were his prisoners briefly," Sora said when Hal didn't answer. "And then he was ours."

"He wasn't our prisoner," Will said. "He was merely restrained momentarily so we could make our escape."

"And then your husband sent the dragon," Hal said, "and I would have been a charred lump on the mountainside if they hadn't saved me."

"That's very touching," Lilit said. "Which part of that compelled you to show my husband's enemies the hidden entrance that leads into our very home?"

Hal dropped his hands to his side. "Did you know it was Killien who brought the frost goblins to the clan?"

Lilit stood perfectly still, her eyes fixed on Hal suspiciously.

"It's true," Sora said.

Lilit was quiet for a long moment before she breathed out something between a laugh and a curse. "He called an army of goblins."

"Where's my sister?" Will asked again.

Lilit shifted to face him, bouncing the baby in her arms and considering him, distaste mingling with frustration on her face. "I know you were there, with Sora in the tent. The night Sevien was born. I remember your words." Her eyes closed. "*But the Flame of the Morrow was not like the grass…She reached down into the Sweep…and found the strength to fight on.*" She opened her eyes. "But it wasn't the Sweep that gave me strength that night, was it?"

He considered denying it a moment, then shook his head.

"I felt it come through your hands," she said.

"Does Killien know?" Sora asked.

Lilit shook her head. "I wasn't sure it was real." She looked down at Sevien and blew out a decisive breath. "Killien has left, taking several slaves with him, including Ilsa."

"Where?" Will asked.

Hal looked up at the empty sword pegs on the wall. "He went to the enclave." He turned back to Lilit, his face incredulous. "He took the seax, and went without being invited. They're going to kill him."

Lilit's shifted the baby and her head twitched in a nod.

"What's he going to do? How many men did he take?"

"No one, aside from the slaves. He wouldn't tell me his plans, but I think he's going to kill Torch Ohan. It was the Panos who attacked us and betrayed their word."

"He went alone?" Hal shook his head. "He's gone mad."

The baby fussed and she dropped her face down to kiss his head, bouncing him gently. When she looked up, it was at Sora. "Go after him."

Sora stepped back. "There's nothing we can do."

"They'll kill him." Lilit turned to Hal. "You have to bring him back."

"He's not going to listen to us," Hal said.

"If he kills Ohan at the enclave, they'll execute him. If he dies we have no strong choice for a Torch. The clan will be overrun. And I—" Her voice caught and her hand tightened on Sevien's blanket. "He can't die."

"He's impossible to stop once he sets his mind to something," Hal said.

"Then tie him up and drag him home." Lilit's words cut through the room. She spun toward Will, the coldness of her face cracking with desperation. "You saved my life when you had no reason to. And you have no reason to save Killien now, but stop my husband from getting himself killed and I promise you, you will have your sister and your freedom."

"Why did he take Ilsa?"

She bounced the baby for a breath before answering. "Because she's the only leverage he has against you. And he wants to make sure you don't steal her away."

Lilit clung to the baby. She was angry, but she was genuinely scared.

"How far is it to the enclave?" Will asked.

Sora blew out a frustrated breath.

"We can't get in," Hal objected. "They meet in a cave. The other clans bring legions of stonesteeps and their best warriors, all of it spread across the front of it, guarding the entrance. No foreigner could ever walk into the enclave. And even if the Morrow were invited, they wouldn't let me into the mountain unless I was with Killien."

"He left hours ago," Lilit said, ignoring Hal and walking over to a wallhanging mapping the northern half of the Sweep. She pointed at a single mountain that jutted out into the grass. "The enclave is here. It won't begin until tomorrow night. Killien will have to ride far south of the Panos and Odo rifts to avoid being seen. He'll be lucky if he reaches the mountain before the enclave begins."

"Can we get to him before that?" Will asked Sora.

She scowled at the map. "Maybe."

"You must," Lilit said.

Will nodded and Sora shot him a glare before giving Lilit a curt nod and pulling the fabric away from the tunnel opening.

"There is no way this will work," Hal grumbled, following her.

Will pressed his fist to his chest and gave Lilit a short bow. She gave him only a nod in return.

The wind shoved into the far end of the tunnel as Will climbed the ladder. Rass greeted him, peering eagerly down the hole behind Will.

"She's not there."

Her face fell as he explained.

"Can you feel them anywhere nearby?"

Rass shook her head. "This close to dawn there are more people out. Small groups of rangers and hunters are spreading out everywhere."

The wind shoved past with long gusts and fleeting moments of calm. The moon was so low it grazed the horizon, sending a thousand golden fingers dragging through the fur of the giant creature that was the Sweep.

Sora turned to him. "Was she lying to us?"

Will shook his head.

"Did you read her? Or whatever you call it?"

"I didn't need to. It's hard to fake that sort of desperation."

Sora looked unconvinced.

Hal sat on a low rock, his eyes fixed on the mountain peaks stretching to the west. "If Killien's going to the enclave, he's not going with a handful of slaves."

Sora nodded. "He's planning to call the frost goblins."

Will turned to Rass. "Can you tell if there are goblin warrens under the grass?"

"If they're not too deep." She knelt down and ran her hand along the new grass that reached a handbreadth out of the ground. "There are some, but they are small and feel…unused. There are none like the night the goblins attacked the clan."

"Makes sense," Will said. "He won't call them until he reaches the enclave."

"Which means"—Hal pushed himself to his feet—"we need to get to him before he gets there if we have any chance at stopping him. Does anyone have any idea how we're going to do that?"

"Did Patlon tell you how far west the dwarven tunnels go?" Will asked Sora.

"Not exactly, but I think a good deal farther than we are now." Sora's gaze trailed along the Hoarfrost mountains. "I had no idea the dwarves had tunneled so far from Duncave."

"Neither did I," Will said. Did they have an equal amount of tunnels stretching along the northern end of Queensland? Burrowing through the Wolfsbane range? Did their tunnels stretch down the Scales to the sea?

"We're running out of darkness," Sora pointed out.

The jagged top of the Scales cut a crisp purple line across the indigo sky, and Hal led the way back toward the dwarf tunnels. Will cast out across the Sweep, as though he'd find Ilsa and Killien walking over the next rise instead of hours away already. He found Hal and Sora, two pillars of energy moving steadily ahead of him, and the bright burst of life that was Rass, gamboling through the endless carpet of *vitalle* made by the spring grass. There were bright bits of energy from small animals scurrying across the plains and some bird soaring off to the south, but no other people.

The sky over the Scales glowed a serene blue by the time they reached the boulders at the dwarves' tunnel. Will peered at the dark lumps of rock, none of which looked like the entrance. Patlon called to them from off to the right and they wound their way to the tunnel entry. The pale sky above them was empty of any little hawk-shaped specks. Will cast out, and even though he found nothing, he lingered an extra moment before squeezing his way back into the small room.

He sank into a chair at the table while Patlon closed the entrance. The wind whistled through with a final, loud protest before it swung shut and the mountain closed around him like a shield against the vulnerability of the Sweep.

Will dropped his head into his hands. Everything was so much worse than it had been a few hours ago. The room around him was silent until Hal explained what had happened to Alaric, Evangeline, and the dwarves.

"I know the mountain you're talking about," Douglon said. "The tunnels will take us almost that far."

"Cousin." Patlon's tone was hard. "Escaping a dragon was one thing—although I'm not sure even that's enough for Horgoth to forgive us for bringing outsiders into the tunnels. We can't take a band of humans and an elf on a tour to the western end."

"You don't have to come," Douglon answered.

"Horgoth," Patlon answered, speaking slowly and clearly, "is going to kill you."

"He's wanted to kill me for years." There was a rustling of paper and Will saw the edges of a map spread out on the table and Douglon let out a short laugh. "This is one of the first times he'd actually have a reason to. Makes the relationship feel more…complete."

Patlon let out an irritated breath and dropped onto the bench.

"You with me, cousin?" Douglon asked.

"I'm always with you," Patlon grumbled.

"Excellent. The route we'll take will lead us here…"

The sound of Sora, Hal, and the dwarves discussing their route filled the room with echoing murmurs and Will stared at the table through his fingers. Killien was going to attack the enclave with an army of frost goblins. The truth of it tasted sour. He wanted to shake the man. To drag him back south on the Sweep, back to when he was rational. To break through the obsession that drove him to make the Morrow powerful. No, not obsession. Fear. The fear that if he didn't strengthen the Morrow, the Roven would destroy what he loved. And now he was going to kill hundreds of people, bringing even more violence to the Sweep.

Were all wars started from fear? He turned the idea over in his mind. Perhaps. Fear that sank so deep that it grew up in the forms of anger and greed. Anger that the fear existed, and greed for anything that would stop it.

Was he here on the Sweep because of fear? Will spun his ring slowly, pushing away the immediate refusal of the idea and forcing himself to consider it. He'd first come because he'd been afraid Queensland was in danger. But after that, what had driven him the entire time, if he really looked at it, was fear. The fear that had been planted the night Ilsa was taken, the night Vahe had stepped into his life and murdered and stole. The night when the sense of safety he'd always lived in had shattered.

Alaric leaned over the map and asked the dwarves a question. It was such a familiar sight, Alaric in his Keeper's robe, poring over some book or map. Whatever he'd asked, Douglon and Patlon both paused and considered the map before nodding. Will rubbed his hands across his face, scrubbing at the exhaustion. That was familiar too, Alaric asking the right question at the right time.

It didn't take much soul-searching to see that the last year had been fueled by another fear, more recent than Vahe. Will ran his fingers along the cuff of the greyish robe he wore. The fabric was thin and the stitches along the edge were irregular. It was simple, basic fabric with no pressure and no expectations. A small hole had formed next to the seam, and he worried at it with his finger.

The bench shifted next to him as Sora sat down. She glanced down at his hands. He tried to smile at her, but somehow the effort fell flat. He pushed his finger at the hole, widening it a bit.

"I can lend you a needle and thread," she offered, the hint of a different sort of question in her voice.

Will dropped the cuff from his fingers and ran his hands over his face again. "This isn't really worth mending, is it?"

She considered him for a long moment, her eyes dark green in the light of the glimmer moss. He spun his ring, pushing aside the edges of the bandages to get at it.

"Do you think you'll ever go home?" he asked her. "Could you ever go back and just be you? Somehow not tangled up in the expectations they have for you?"

"I don't know." She pulled his hand over toward her and began to pick at the knot on his bandage. "You shouldn't need these anymore." She picked at the knot in silence for a minute and Will watched her hands. Her nails were rimmed with dirt. Scratches and thin scars nicked her skin.

"Even with the Morrow," she said quietly, "there were expectations. They saw me partly as a ranger, but mostly as a foreigner." She worked the knot apart and started to unwrap the bandage. "But they had those expectations because it's what I gave them. If I wanted the Morrow to see me as more, I would have had to have shown them more."

She pulled the last layer of bandage off and picked up his hand, tilting his palm toward the glimmer moss. The skin was red and shiny. Sora ran her finger over the edge of where the blister had been and he flinched at the sharpness of the sensation. She raised an eyebrow.

"It's sensitive." He opened and closed his hand. There was a jolt when his fingers touched his palm, but not exactly pain.

Sora gave an approving nod and motioned for his other hand. "You're the first Keeper I've ever met, Will. I don't have any idea what a Keeper is supposed to be like. But I've seen you do some astonishing things."

"You wouldn't be impressed by pushing heat toward frost goblins, or starting candles with my finger if you'd spent time with other Keepers."

"I'm not talking about that," she said, nodding her head toward where Rass sat nestled in a corner, braiding together a wide, complicated band of grass. "It's more like what you did with Rass."

Will let out something between a laugh and a snort. "I'm never going to admit to Alaric that I knew her for weeks and thought she was just an odd little girl." He watched her fiddle with the grass, picking a new piece off the floor next to her where she had a small bundle, and weave it into the rest. "Until she exploded the ground in front of me, I had no idea she was anything else."

Sora shook her head. "You saw her as a little girl, when everyone else saw her as...nothing. No one else even noticed her."

"She came and talked to me," Will objected. "The first afternoon I was in Porreen."

"And what did you do then?"

"I talked back, Sora," he said, trying to to hide his exasperation. He shifted, wishing she'd hurry up so he could have his hand back.

Instead, she stopped and looked him in the face. "And you fed her an avak."

Will drew his hand back in surprise until her grip stopped him. "How do you know that?"

"I told you I was watching you. Your stealthy creeping around had caught my attention."

"I obviously wasn't stealthy enough."

"I hadn't noticed Rass before that." She pulled his hand closer and picked at the stubborn knot. "And I notice a lot. You set the avak on the bench and drew her out. Then you talked to her, just like she was anyone else."

"She was better than everyone else. She was the only safe person in the entire festival."

"And then somehow you convinced a *pratorii* to trust you. To walk with you, to eat food she'd never eaten." The knot came loose and Sora began unwinding the bandage. "To leave the Sweep with you."

"I didn't do anything…special to make that happen."

"I'm not saying you did. I'm saying it happened because of who you are. And it wasn't just Rass who trusted you. Hal did too." She pulled the last of the bandage off and lifted his palm to examine it. When she rubbed her finger across his palm, he almost kept it still.

Hal was over by the shelves helping Patlon sort through some supplies.

"He's never going to believe I didn't do something to trick him."

"Maybe not, but I believe you. And I believe you did nothing to trick Killien into trusting you either. Nothing more than seeing him. Seeing past the expectations that everyone else puts on him, past the expectations that he's built up around himself. And befriending what you saw."

"You don't know that." He spun his ring. It was so satisfying after not being able to reach it for so long.

"Yes I do." She let go of his hand.

He rubbed his palms together, trying to press out the weird sensitivity. She kept her eyes focused on his hands.

"Because you did it to me too."

Will's hands froze and something hitched in his throat. She started gathering up the bandages.

"So, from the little I know about Keepers," she said, "if I were in charge of choosing them, you're the sort of person I'd want to pick." She wrapped the bandages into a bundle.

He reached out and put his hand on hers to still them. Her skin and the jumbled edges of the bandage shot a painfully strong sensation across his hand.

"Come with me to Queensland."

FORTY

The words shoved their way out before Will could stop them.

Sora's eyes widened. He squeezed her hand, ignoring the sharp twinge in his palm. "Once we've found Ilsa, will you come back with me? Not forever, if you don't want to, but for a little while. I can't stay here. I'll have to take Ilsa home."

She stared at him, speechless.

"You don't have to tell me now, of course." He let go of her hands, pushing down the regret that threatened to drown him. "But if you're willing, I'd like to show it to you."

Alaric cleared his throat from behind them and Will turned to see him watching Will with a wide smile. "We should get going. The way the mountains run, if we move quickly and make tonight a short night sleep, we think we can beat Killien to the enclave." Alaric raised an eyebrow toward him and Sora. "If you two are ready."

Sora pushed herself up and walked over to her pack. Will watched her before shoving himself up from the table. Alaric stepped up and slung his arm over Will's shoulder. Evangeline asked Sora a question, and the two stood with their heads close together, looking in Sora's pack.

"I see a new future for the Keepers," Alaric said with a grin.

Will spun his ring. "That future is terrifying."

Alaric laughed. "It gets better." Then he paused. "But also it stays terrifying."

They walked for hours through the dwarven tunnels, the blackness barely ruffled by the bowls of glimmer moss they carried. Douglon led with Rass. Evangeline and Sora went behind them, talking in low voices while Will and Alaric followed behind them. Hal brought up the rear, peppering Patlon with questions about the dwarves.

"Do you think there's any chance we're going to find Ilsa?" Will asked Alaric when the featureless walk through the darkness began to feel as though it was all they'd ever done.

"I don't think finding her is going to be the problem." Alaric pulled a cord out from under his shirt with a glitter of yellow light. "The problem is going to be getting to her. The mountain where the enclave is held isn't terribly big, and the Roven are camped only on the southern side of it. Hal has been there a number of times. There's a network of tunnels near the front of the mountain. The ones that head toward the back are barred and locked to keep people from doing what we're doing, sneaking in. Patlon believes the humans tunneled all the way out the back side of the mountain, and that the locks shouldn't be a problem. The dwarves and Hal seem fairly hopeful that we can find a back entrance and get in without having to walk through an army of Roven."

"That would be nice."

Lunchtime passed, noted only by Douglon passing along a sack of hard rolls that tasted of honey and pine nuts. Sora contributed some sticks of dried meat, and they kept walking.

The day was a strange mix of tedious walking through darkness, gnawing worry about what lay ahead, and pure enjoyment of talking with Alaric. The dwarves kept up the humming song as a backdrop. Will had to stop himself from talking too fast, asking too many questions. His mind felt awake in a way it hadn't been in ages. There was something inside him that was free, reveling in the fact that there was nothing to watch out for, nothing to keep hidden. By the time Douglon called back that they were close to where they'd stop for the night, he felt more normal than he had in ages. Which considering he'd spent the day in darkness, was saying a lot.

This cave was nothing like the ones with the scattered lights. This was merely a room hollowed out of the side of the tunnel with a flat floor and more darkness. Will finished his cold meal and closed his eyes. The cave spun beneath him. It had been two days since he'd had a real night's sleep. The others murmured around him, all their voices enveloped by the silence of the cave. He leaned back against his pack. Even the stone floor wasn't enough to make him uncomfortable.

There was mention of several more hours of tunnels tomorrow, speculation on how they'd cross the open Sweep between their exit and the enclave mountain, and a debate between the dwarves about the likelihood of human tunnels actually reaching the back of the mountain. But Will couldn't get his mind to focus on any of it. Soon there was only the feeling of his body sinking down against the hard floor and the mountain wrapping around him like a cocoon.

———◆———

The next morning Will discovered Rass curled up next to him.

"I'm tired of tunnels," she groaned when he roused her.

"I'm a little tired of them myself," Will said, "but I don't think it's too much farther."

"How long until we're back near living things?" Will asked Douglon.

Douglon considered Rass with a small frown. "It's not far to the grasses now." He reached down and lifted her up. "Just a couple hours."

"I can walk," she objected. "You can't carry me for hours."

"You're just a wee snip of a thing. The only fear is that I'll drop you and not even notice."

She made a petulant little noise, but wrapped her arms around his neck and dropped her head onto his shoulder. Douglon walked back into the tunnel and began to hum. Patlon grabbed some glimmer moss and everyone followed.

The hours dragged on. To pass the time, Will told one story after another, first just to Hal and Alaric, but soon Sora and Evangeline had moved close enough to hear too. He'd told four reasonably long ones and was convinced the walk was never going to end when they spilled out into a small storage room. Patlon ordered everyone to wait, then moved to the far wall and shoved at a large rock. He disappeared through a gap while sweet, fresh, clean air rushed in and swirled through the room. Rass lifted her head from Douglon's shoulder and looked around sleepily.

In a few moments Patlon was back. "There's no one nearby. But come out slowly, it's bright."

Will filed out with the rest of them. The wind brushed across his face and the clean scents of pine and earth revived him with an almost magical power. He stepped out into a shadowed, rocky gorge with trees stretching up around them, but still, the light was painfully bright. Rass sat in a wide patch of bright green grass, squinting and beaming and running her fingers back and forth through the blades.

The grassy slope they were on angled down, interspersed with bushes and pines until it flattened out onto a wide swath of grass that lay between them and the lone mountain that held the enclave.

Mountain was too big of a word for it, really. Large hill. Oversized outcropping. Whatever it was, it sat detached from the rest of the range, surrounded by a moat of grass.

Off to the south on the far side of the enclave, smoke from dozens of campfires rose into the air. Small bands of rangers roamed across the grass between them and the mountain, and as far out into the Sweep as Will could see. The sun hadn't reached midday, and if Lilit had been right, Killien shouldn't reach the mountain for hours.

Of course, they weren't going to reach it any sooner.

The sky above them was a clear, empty blue, and Will scanned through the trees around them for Talen. Not that there was any way the little hawk could know where he was. A twinge of sadness rippled through him. He cast out into the sky, but found nothing beyond the slow, ponderous energy of the pine trees. He thought of the little bird's mind and threw an image toward it of where he stood.

The idea faded away, doing nothing. With another look across the empty sky, Will pulled his focus back to the others around him.

"You really think you can find entrances on this side of the mountain?" Alaric asked Douglon.

The dwarf nodded. "Hal says there are tunnels that come this way."

"I see three places with possible entrances," Patlon said, pointing out rocky sections of the mountainside. "What does the front of the mountain look like?"

"There's a huge cave," Hal answered. "Fifteen mounted men could easily ride abreast each other through the opening. Inside the cave is a lake that's fed from somewhere under the mountain, and it pours out of the mouth in a waterfall down to another lake down on the Sweep."

"How high is the cave?"

"A third of the way up the mountain," Hal answered.

"That makes the top entrance unlikely," Douglon said. "Unless someone just really liked digging uphill."

"I think the bottom one is too low," Sora said. "If there's water in the caves where the enclaves meet, anyone stupid enough to tunnel down would have been flooded."

"Agreed." Patlon tugged on his beard and nodded.

Sora turned to Alaric. "We're headed for that reddish cliff face about halfway up."

"You don't seem worried that there are doors blocking all the passages that lead to the back of the mountain," Hal said. "And they're locked. The Temur Clan controls the mountain. They're the only ones with keys. If there even are keys any more."

"Locked doors aren't a problem," Patlon said. "Wide open grassland is a problem."

"We'll be seen by a half-dozen scouts if we try to cross here," Sora agreed. "Most of the clans are here. And each will have their own rangers on the lookout for anything unusual."

"Good thing there's nothing unusual about this group," Patlon muttered.

A pair of Roven rangers rode slowly across the grass between them and the mountain.

Rass gave a small sigh. "We could go under the grass."

"There are no more tunnels," Douglon told her.

"No more dwarves tunnels. But"—she wrinkled her nose—"the frost goblins have tunnels all over down there."

No one answered for a moment.

"We can't go into a goblin warren," Hal said. "We'll be ripped apart."

"Only if goblins come," Sora said.

"The one thing we know," Hal answered, "is that Killien plans to call goblins to the enclave. And when that happens, I really don't want to be standing in the way."

"I can tell if they're coming," Rass said.

"From how far away?" Will asked.

She set her hand on the ground. "The closest ones are far to the west of here. There are none under the grass close by."

"How can you tell?" Hal asked.

"The roots of the grass reach down to the warrens. And when the goblins brush past them"— she shivered—"the grass knows."

"Can you tell if they're under the mountains we're on?" Douglon asked her.

Rass shook her head uncertainly. "I don't think they tunnel in the mountains. They can't get through rock, just the soft earth of the Sweep."

"I agree," Sora said. "In the mountains they travel above ground, I've seen their tracks."

"Can you lead us through the warrens?" Will asked Rass.

She wrinkled her nose and nodded, pushing herself up. "The closest one is this way."

The mouth of the warren sat at the bottom of the slope, gaping open just as the grassland flattened out. A few trees straggled out into the grass, and a small finger of bushes ran almost to where the warren started. When there were no Roven rangers in sight, the dwarves clambered down into the hole and disappeared. In a matter of breaths they were back.

"Filthy worm hole," Patlon said, brushing clods of dirt from his head.

"It's not pleasant," Douglon agreed, "but it looks stable. Rass is the only one of us that's going to be able to walk upright, though."

A hoarse screech echoed off the rocks behind them and Talen dove out of the sky. His wings faltered slightly and there were gaps in the feathers of his left wing. He landed hard on Will's arm with a weak chwirk. Feathers along his neck were disheveled and wet with blood.

Sora came over and ran her fingers gently down his neck, smoothing the feathers. Talen flinched once. Will opened up to the little hawk and felt a tangle of fear and exhaustion.

"A larger bird must have attacked him." Sora pulled out a piece of dried meat and offered it to Talen. The hawk snatched it up, his feet unsteady on Will's arm.

"You have bad timing," Will said to him. "We're about to go into another tunnel. But we'll be out soon, over on that mountain." He walked over to a nearby stump and set his arm next to it. "I'll leave you some food, and you can meet us over there."

Talen's claws tightened on Will's arm. Will rolled his forearm toward the stump, but the little hawk turned his head away from it and grabbed Will tighter. A spike of fear flashed across Will's chest.

"Ok, you can come with us, but that means the hood again."

Sora helped Will slide the leather glove on his other arm and the hawk willingly stepped onto it. Talen didn't move at all as Sora put the hood on him.

"Can we go?" Douglon asked. "Or are we going to collect any other animals that have no right to be underground?"

Will waved him on, offering Talen more meat.

"You're sure there are no goblins?" Patlon asked Rass.

She nodded and, although no one looked happy about it, the group dropped down into the hole, one at a time.

The hole was wide enough for two people to walk next to each other, but even the dwarves had to duck to avoid the ceiling of loose dirt and dangling roots. Will held Talen close to him and stretched his other hand out to run along the wall. His feet sank into the soft churned up earth on the floor and the wall crumbled off beneath his fingers while he hunched over and took a few steps into the gloom. The walls and ceiling were gashed from the scrambling mass of goblin claws that had burrowed through. The smell of the earth mingled with the fetor of rotting meat.

The tunnel ran straight ahead as far as he could see, past the stooped forms in front of him, and the dwindling light lasted long past the point when his back began to ache from bending over. Roots brushed past his head and down his back, pellets of dirt showered down on him, crumbling and rolling down his neck.

Their feet sank silently into the soft earth, so the only sound was the breathing of his companions. Something from the wall tangled wetly in his fingers and wriggled across his palm. He flicked his hand and the squirming larva gripped his finger for a breath before flinging off.

The warren dimmed to the point where the orange glow from the glimmer moss was visible, tinging the dark earth a bloody red.

Time stretched on interminably. Will's back and neck ached from hunching over and the rotten stench had settled into a sour taste in his mouth. The arm holding Talen had developed an ache that demanded he shift position. He stretched his shoulder and elbow, trying not to alarm the bird.

To pass the time he concentrated on the little hawk. It could have just been his imagination, but when he cast out toward Talen, the bird felt dimmer. Gently, Will funneled bits of *vitalle* into him. Letting it seep up from his arm through Talen's legs. Inside the hawk were three different injuries. The cut at his neck, and two slashes on his wing. Will drew in *vitalle* from the roots brushing over him as he walked and fed it into Talen, directing it toward where the little bird was healing. Slowly Talen's grip relaxed. Will offered Talen the last piece of meat, and the little hawk gobbled it up, standing straighter than before.

"We're halfway." Rass's voice trickled back, muted from the front of the group. She walked next to Patlon with her arm stretched above her head, trailing her fingers through the hair-thin roots that hung down.

Alaric fell back next to Will, holding glimmer moss up near Talen. "How did you get the hawk to come?"

"I'm not sure." Will ducked under a low-hanging clump of roots. "I sort of threw the idea of where I was out at him."

The edges of Alaric's eyes tightened in such a familiar way, Will laughed. "I know that doesn't tell you anything." Will explained the connection he'd built with Talen.

"More interesting than that, though," Will said, "is that Sora can…push her emotions at me, and I feel them when I'm not trying to."

Alaric's eyebrows rose. "Did you know that was possible?"

Will shook his head. "Gerone spent all his time developing ways to close myself off to people. We never got to the point of experimenting with anything else. And outside the Keepers, Sora's the first person I've told that I can feel them."

"The first?" Alaric said mildly. "Interesting."

"Can we stay on topic? The important part here is that she was able to do it. To show me how her childhood memories made her feel."

"Is that really the important part?" Will could hear the grin in Alaric's voice.

Will shook his head. "Evangeline has changed you."

Alaric laughed. "You have no idea." He was quiet for a moment. "Can you push your emotions into me?"

Will searched for a good emotion to share. What was the last strong emotion he'd felt? There was the conversation with Hal, but that was too complex. There was the dark tunnel with Sora, but that was even more complex.

The dragon.

Will focused on the memory of the dragon, plummeting down toward them, the flames licking the trees next to them as they ran. The rush of air from the wings, the glint of red scales. His heart quickened at the memory of being utterly defenseless in the face of such overwhelming power. He gathered that feeling and pushed it toward Alaric.

Alaric's breath caught. "I feel...scared? It's small, and distant. Like the echo of being terrified."

Will cut off the push of emotions with a surge of triumph. "The dragon."

Alaric let out a long breath. "Yes, that's what it felt like. Both times. He gets no less terrifying upon the second meeting. How have we never tried this before?"

"I don't know if I could have done it before. In Queensland I did nothing but try to close people off. It wasn't until I came here that I was nervous enough to need to read people around me. I've gotten so much better at it. I can pick out individual people in a group and filter out only their emotions. And I can feel people from much farther away."

Smaller warrens branched off to the sides, but Rass led them on without hesitation. Alaric and Will continued to test what Alaric dubbed Will's trans-emotive skills. Thankfully they soon spilled out into a slightly larger warren and there were groans and grunts as the group stretched slightly taller.

"Not far now," Rass called back over her shoulder. "This warren runs—"

She spun around. "Goblins!" she hissed.

"Where?" Patlon yanked his axe out of its sheath and turned.

"Behind us. They're pouring into the warren."

"Can we get out before they get here?"

Rass shook her head, her face terrified. "They're coming!"

"Get us out of this main warren," Will called up to her.

She nodded and ran forward, her hand dragging along the roots. She paused and pointed to the side, and everyone poured into a wide but short side tunnel.

Douglon and Patlon took up positions facing the main warren, kneeling so they could be upright, their axes out.

"This isn't going to stop them from finding us," Sora pointed out.

"We have enough metal to call an entire horde down on ourselves," Patlon agreed.

"Rass," Douglon said, "Can you collapse the warren between us and them?"

"Not without burying us too."

"So buried alive or torn apart by goblins," Patlon said. "I think I preferred the dragon."

"How many are there?" Sora asked, kneeling next to the dwarves.

Rass cowered against one of the walls. "So many."

"How far to the nearest exit?" Will asked.

"Not far. The next one to the right goes straight to the surface. But we'd still be on the grass and the Roven will see us."

"We could drop all our metal here and try for it," Patlon offered.

"Talen can fly faster than a goblin can run, right?" Will asked Sora.

"Easily."

"Then let's give them something else to chase," Will said. "What sort of metal do they like most?"

"Silver and gold," Sora answered.

"Anyone have any coins?"

Alaric offered him two, and Will, with a surge of calmness offered to Talen, pulled off the hood. The little hawk shifted and blinked into the darkness. A dislike grew in the bird, a discomfort with the closeness of the tunnel. "Tie the silver into the hood," he told Sora. "And then tie it to his leg. And let's hope it's not too heavy for him.

"A bit of coin's not going to fool them," Patlon pointed out.

"It just needs to distract them."

"What about the glimmer moss?" Evangeline asked. "Should we cover it?"

"The only thing that would make this situation worse," Douglon said, "is if it was happening in the dark."

"Agreed," Patlon said.

"Then let's at least get the light farther away from us," Alaric said. "Put the bowls out in the main warren along the edges. Then maybe we'll see them but they won't be as likely to see us. Unless that will make them suspicious."

"They're not that intelligent," Sora said. "They're driven by smell. Some odd lights won't matter to them."

"How long until the goblins reach us?" Will asked Rass as the moss was put out in the hall.

"Not long."

"Tell me when they're almost close enough to see."

She nodded and Will squeezed past the dwarves to stand hunched at the mouth of the main warren. The glimmer moss was spread along the tunnel, lighting it with the dim orange glow. Past it, the warren faded into blackness.

"There's a way out ahead," he told Talen, setting a restraining hand on the hawk's chest and putting the idea into the little bird's mind of the warren and the branch to the right, leading to wide open grass and endless sky. Talen shifted eagerly on his arm, but Will held him back.

A guttural cry cut through the darkness from behind him.

"They're here!" Rass hissed through the darkness.

Will thrust his arm forward and pushed the idea of freedom and open sky at Talen. The hawk spread his wings and flapped into the darkness of the warren.

Will ducked back in past the dwarves and sank to his knees next to Alaric. "And now we just need a wall that can block our smell."

"How can I help?" Alaric asked.

"I'm going to need a lot of energy." Will closed his eyes and cast out. Above the bright *vitalle* of the people around him, the energy of the grass dangled down in the roots. He set his hand on the ceiling and drew some in, turning to face the entrance.

Alaric wrapped one hand around Will's wrist and reached for the roots with the other. A stream of *vitalle* flowed into Will's arm.

More cries echoed down the tunnel, couched in grunts and rustles.

Concentrating on the air, he formed the idea of the wall. Not a clay wall this time, just a wall of dirt, like the rest of the tunnel. Anything to block their passage from the notice of the goblins. The energy seeped into his hand from above, singeing through the new skin on his palm and he fed it out his other hand, forming the air, shaping it, infusing it with the idea of earth. The air formed up immediately and the light of the glimmer moss shimmered as Will moved the air. The sound of the goblins faded until the warren was utterly silent.

Sora reached out and pushed her hand into it and there was a burst of pain across Will's hand as the magic was interrupted.

"Don't touch it," he gasped and she pulled her hand back.

"He's making a wall out of the air," Alaric explained to the others, his brow drawn in concentration. "It should trap any smell we have here in this tunnel."

"Should?" Douglon asked.

"Keep your axes handy." Will pushed more energy toward the wall.

"If any come through," Hal said, "kill them as quickly as you can. If they realize we're here, the rest will know too."

Sora and Douglon knelt facing the main warren with Hal and Patlon directly behind them.

Something pale flashed into view.

Will stopped and flipped through the book again, phrases of fear or hope or pain jumping out from each page.

FORTY-ONE

Grey, wiry limbs flew past the opening. Round eyes glinted like milky orbs. The group stood in silence, watching dozens and dozens of goblins rush past, scrambling past each other with sharp, jutting heads and claws that glinted in the mosslight.

The *vitalle* from the grass began to fade and Will grasped for more from above them, stretching out farther along the Sweep.

The skin around Will's wrist where Alaric touched him burned. Alaric shoved their sleeves up and pressed their forearms together, spreading out the energy until it flowed through with a bearable heat. Will funneled the new energy toward the wall.

Two goblins shoved into each other and the closest one flew into the wall of air, breaking through and slicing pain across Will's palm.

A grating screech ripped out of the creature's throat and a rotten stench filled the air. Sora grabbed the creature's neck and plunged her knife into its chest, tossing it down behind her. Douglon's axe swung down, severing the goblin's head. Blood pooled out onto the dirt in a steaming puddle of glistening black.

One of the creature's feet still stabbed into the wall and the pain across Will's hand was excruciating. Evangeline scrambled forward and grabbed the creature's arms, dragging it farther in.

The energy from Alaric faded and Will felt the wall begin to weaken.

"How many more?" he asked Rass.

She pressed back against the wall, her face terrified, her hand grabbing at the roots above her head. "So many."

Alaric grabbed the shoulder of the dead goblin and for a brief moment, Will felt a surge of *vitalle* before it faded.

"We need more energy," Alaric said.

Rass pointed to a spot on the wall of the tunnel. "There's a lot of roots behind there."

Evangeline crawled over and scraped away the dirt. Loose earth tumbled down until she was up to her elbow. With a grunt, she yanked and pulled a wide, knobby root out of the wall. Alaric stretched across the warren to grab it, and the energy poured into Will.

Another goblin tumbled through the wall with searing pain, scrambling and scratching. Patlon's axe fell almost faster than Will could see and the creature fell. Evangeline pulled it back, and the endless river of goblins flowed past.

"They're almost done," Rass said quietly. "Many of them followed Talen. The rest are heading toward the enclave."

Will's hand burned. His arm, where it touched Alaric, felt like it was pressed against hot metal. The root in Alaric's hand had withered to a thin, brittle stick and the flow of *vitalle* weakened.

The last of the goblins rushed past and the group stood still, waiting.

"Hold it as long as you can," Sora said. "Or they'll smell the metal and come back."

"They're turning down another warren," Rass said, her voice stronger. "And another past that…I think they're gone."

Alaric dropped his arm down and Will cut off the flow of *vitalle*. The air relaxed back into normal air and the glimmer moss glowed clearly through it again. The stench of rotten meat rushed in. Two of the moss bowls had been trampled.

"Let's get out of this wretched place." Douglon motioned for Rass to lead the way.

The main warren reeked of rotting meat and the sour stench of the goblins, and Will pressed the leather hawking glove to his nose while he hunched over and ran after the others. Rass turned them down a thinner warren that smelled more of earth and less of goblins. When the first hint of fresh air blew past, Will sucked it in like a drowning man.

They spilled out onto the edge of the grass near the base of the enclave mountain and streamed into the nearby trees. Rass waited at the top of the warren opening, glaring down into it.

"Are we being followed?" Will asked as he scrambled out.

She shook her head. "All the goblins near here are heading south."

Rass stood above the opening, her bare toes curling into the earth at her feet. She held out a hand, palm pointing down over the warren. Her lips pressed into a resolute line.

"I do not like these." Her fingers bent into a claw for a breath before she slowly closed them into a fist.

For twenty paces the surface of the Sweep sank down, filling the warren.

Rass kept her hand fisted, her tiny form quivering with displeasure, fixing a furious look at the sunken earth. "Let's not go in one of those again."

The group stood for a moment, looking between the tiny girl and the collapsed tunnel.

"Agreed," Will said.

"This way." Douglon led them through the trees, angling up the mountain.

Whenever there was a gap in the tree canopy, Will scanned the sky for any sign of Talen.

Sora pointed above them. "Top of that pine."

There sat Talen on a branch, gazing regally out over the Sweep. His feathers were unruffled, the hood still dangled from his leg. Will pushed his relief and happiness and gratefulness toward the little hawk and held his arm out. Talen shifted on the branch and didn't look down.

"Maybe he's mad at you," Sora said.

Will opened himself up toward the hawk.

Fierce freedom burst into him. Wind dragging its fingers over splayed feathers. Sharp heat from the sun soaking into the dark crest of his wings, seeping deep into muscles. Hunger and purpose and focus.

"There's only more tunnels ahead," Sora said to Will. "Let him stay outside. He'll find you again."

Will took another strip of dried meat out of his pack, broke it into small bits, and spread them on the top of a nearby stump. With a parting shot of gratitude toward the bird, Will followed the others up the slope.

It took only a few minutes to reach the base of the reddish colored cliffs that they were aiming for.

Douglon, Patlon and Sora spread out, looking for an entrance while the others sat with Hal. They had climbed steadily to get there and Will could see the long stretch of the Hoarfrost Range stretching to the east. The barren tops of the Scales were visible too, blocking the way off the Sweep to the east.

Will leaned a little closer to Rass. "There's a lot of new grass out there."

"I know!" Her face was so excited he thought she might burst. "Isn't it the most beautiful thing you've ever seen?"

The ground flowed over small rises and short bluffs covered with not-quite-green grass. Wind moved from one hill to the next, swirling and rippling and skittering off in different directions. The blue sky sat utterly still and vacant above it.

He cast out and instead of the tiny snips of energy he'd felt when they'd been walking north with the clan, he was met with a rising tide of life, swelling, growing, absorbing the decaying grass of last year and rising with a silent blaze of power.

"It's…" The echo of energy faded and he faced a Sweep bursting with the verdant green of spring, pushing past last year's memories.

"Yes," Rass said smugly. "Now you see it."

"When I met you," Will said, "you snuck everywhere and hid in the grass. Now you're different. Braver. Or more daring."

"There was no grass yet then." She wriggled her toes into the dirt. "I always feel weak after a long winter, and everyone else seems so strong. But now…" She flexed her hands. "There's strength everywhere."

A strange little bird trill whistled across the mountain. Douglon stood half hidden by a large rock, motioning them to come. Hunching down behind boulders as much as they could, they made their way over and found him standing at the entrance to a thin, jagged hole.

"No more tunnels." Rass crossed her arms and stood back from the entrance.

"You don't need to come," Will assured her. "You can wait for us in the grass. Hopefully, we'll be back out this way with Ilsa in…" He glanced at the others. "Not too long. But be careful. There are a lot of Roven around."

"The Sweep is awake again." She gave a little smirk. "The Roven should be careful of me." She turned and scrambled down the slope, her arms and legs twice as thick as the first time he'd seen her.

Will slid through the gap in the stones. Ahead of him a cave twisted into gloom. This definitely wasn't a dwarven tunnel. The rocks around him were rough and irregular, the passage thinned and widened erratically, piles of stones jumbled on the floor. The passage was mostly naturally made, but in the narrowest parts, rough tool marks were visible. Up at the front, Patlon stopped in the dark, muttering and shoving against a rock blocking their path. He stood frozen against the rock for several heartbeats before it tilted and rolled forward with a crushing, grinding noise.

"If you don't shut up, cousin," Douglon's voice came from behind Will. "The entire Sweep is going to know we're coming."

Patlon shoved against the rock with a growl. "I'd be alright with an honest fight about now. I'm tired of sneaking."

"You beat the rock," Douglon pointed out, as he climbed over it.

A half hour and three more shoved rocks later, the tunnel narrowed again to a point blocked by a thick wooden door. In the orange glow of the moss, the door looked like slats of black, rough wood. Iron straps held it together and it sat snuggly against the rocks around it.

"This is the back end of the enclave tunnels," Hal said, "If we can get through this, there's nothing stopping us from reaching the enclave. But it's locked from the other side."

There was no handle or hinges visible, and Douglon and Patlon brought their bowls of glimmer moss up close to the edges of the door.

"It's barely locked." Patlon knelt down next to the door and peered through the crack.

"You should break the hinges." Douglon stuck something thin through the far side.

"Messing with rusty hinges, that's a quiet idea. Why don't we just scream until they come find us. Be helpful and oil the hinges."

"If you break the latch, the hinges are still going to squeak when you open the door," Douglon pointed out,

"Are you going to be helpful?"

"Already done." Douglon tucked a little tin back into his bag. "Have you gotten through the latch yet?"

A sizzling noise and a wisp of smoke trickled out of the crack in front of Patlon. "Almost. I need—"

Douglon set the handle of a thin saw into his cousin's outstretched hand. Patlon grunted in acknowledgment and slid the blade through the edge of the door. It took barely any time before he grunted again and handed it back.

"We'd have been through by now and back with the girl if you'd just have done the hinges."

Slowly, Patlon pushed at the door and it cracked open. A low, groaning came from the hinges along with a cool, damp breeze. Patlon worked the door back and forth in little nudges until the groaning stopped.

"You didn't oil them very well," he whispered to Douglon.

"You didn't open it right."

"Let's hope the big man remembers where he's going," Patlon muttered.

"Tunnels don't change," Hal whispered back, sounding annoyed. "Even over ten years."

Hal squeezed past the dwarves, taking the lead through the tunnel. Will brought up the rear, occasionally holding his bowl of glimmer moss behind them, searching the jagged, empty tunnel.

Through the forms of the others, Will caught the gleam of the dwarves' axes in their hands. They passed caverns spilling chilled, dank air into the tunnel. Long teeth of rock hung down from the ceiling dripping water as though the mountain was melting. Rounder, lumpy stone fingers reached up out of the floor toward them.

A little farther on, Hal turned into a thin tunnel winding off to the left, and came to an abrupt stop. The glimmer moss lit a pile of rocks completely filling the tunnel.

Hal swore. "This is—This *was* the tunnel that leads to the living quarters."

"Sometimes tunnels change," Patlon pointed out.

"Is there another way?" Will asked.

Hal scratched at his beard. "Through the main cavern. The Torches' enclave meets in a smaller cave off of it, hidden enough that it will be out of view, but if the meeting has started, there could be people in the main cavern as well."

Will's heart sank a little. "Maybe we got here before it started."

Hal's answering grunt sounded doubtful, but he continued down the tunnel. Only a hundred paces farther, another cavern opened up on the left. Will followed the others in and caught the smell of mossy water. On the far side of the cavern, a tunnel wound off and the mouth of it was not completely black. Hal ordered the glimmer moss covered, and motioned for silence, then stepped into the tunnel.

Without the orange moss, the tunnel rocks were bleached to a stale grey. The tunnel was thin to the point where Will's shoulders brushed the sides occasionally, and the only noise he heard was a curse from Hal as he squeezed through a particularly tight section. The wet, green smell of moss grew stronger as the tunnel grew brighter, and a shushing noise teased at his ears.

Ahead of him, Alaric turned sharply to the right, and Will blinked into brightness. Light and the sound of rushing water poured into the tunnel from a horizontal crack in the wall. The others leaned against the wall, squinting through it. Will stepped up between Alaric and Sora, and looked out into a long, thin cavern. Straight ahead, the far side opened in a gaping maw and sunlight streamed in, landing in a blinding patch on the stone floor. The cave looked out high over the rippled surface of the Sweep, stretching away to the hazy horizon. Straight below them, down a cliff face, sat a lake. It was flat and silty brown, reflecting smudged images of the drab cavern walls. A river flowed out from it, edged with pale green moss, sliding toward the mouth of the cave until it disappeared over the edge. Just before the mouth of the cave, a thin, arching bridge crossed the river. The constant wind of the Sweep blew the edges of trees and grass outside the cave, and the smell of the grasslands mingled with the moss.

An unintelligible tangle of voices echoed loudly through the cavern against the backdrop of the waterfall, and Will leaned forward until he could see through the crack. A little to the left, a smaller cave branched off, angling sharply away from the sunlit cavern. In the gloom, dozens of torches lit rows of long tables and benches. A couple dozen Roven congregated in small knots among them, grey-shirted slaves standing along the walls or carrying pitchers. Along the far wall the tables were laden with food. At the near end, just before the tables, a wide, flat stone like a platform filled the center of the floor.

"Killien's not here," Hal said in a voice so low it was almost hard to hear over the noise of the cave. "But I do see all the other Torches."

"And Lukas," Sora said.

Lukas limped among the groups of Roven, filling cups and keeping his eyes pointed down in a more servile stance than Will had ever seen.

"There's Sini and Rett." Will nodded toward a back table where the two were busy hunched over some food.

"I don't see Ilsa," Sora said.

"Each clan has its own permanent quarters," Hal said. "The Morrow's is, of course, the smallest. I'm sure it's been ignored over the years we haven't been here. Ilsa is probably there. And if Killien isn't here with the other Torches, he probably is too."

"It'd be easier to talk to Ilsa if Killien were doing something else," Will pointed out.

"Lukas doesn't stay away from Killien for long if he can help it." Hal nodded toward Lukas who was continuing to pour drinks. "I would guess Killien will show up soon. I don't think he'll bring Ilsa to the Torches' meeting, but it might be worth staying to find out."

Will pushed back a surge of irritation at the delay, but it wouldn't do them any good to sneak into the Morrow's quarters if Ilsa was on her way to this gathering.

An older Roven man in red dyed leathers climbed up on the boulder. His hair hung down his back in long, grey braids, and his equally long beard was decorated with glints of silver and red. A severity was carved into the creases of his face and his shoulders were set resolutely. He knocked a thick wooden staff against the rock and the cavern quieted.

"Torch Vatche of the Temur," Hal said. "One of the few Torches who allies with Killien. This mountain is on his land. The powerful clans demand gifts at the opening of the enclave, beginning with the least powerful, which would be the Morrow. But with Killien not here, Vatche will have to go first."

"We are pleased to offer these gifts to our brethren." Vatche's Roven accent was harsh as he motioned for two slaves along the wall holding small chests. The first walked over to a tall, angular man wearing wine-dark leathers. His fingers glittered with rings and gems, runes were stitched or stamped into every surface of his clothes, and a large yellowish burning stone hung around his neck, swirling slowly with a viscous, murky light.

"Torch Noy, Sunn Clan," Will whispered to Alaric. "They have the most stonesteeps. And control the dragon."

"The Temur would like to thank the Sunn for their generosity in letting us hire their stonesteeps," Vatche said, his voice emotionless as the servant opened the chest, showing a pile of colored gems, the top of which shimmered with a greenish light.

"Doesn't sound very generous," Alaric whispered.

Torch Noy barely glanced at the chest before waving it away and turning back to his food.

"If the smaller clans don't offer bribes to the Sunn and the Boan," Sora said, leaning closer so Alaric and Will could hear, "the protective spells the Sunn stonesteeps place on the herds will be prone to inexplicable failures, and the Boan soldiers will *accidentally* raid their outlying settlements.

"The trick is to make both clans think they received the better bribe. One year the Boan chief thought that the Sunn clan's gift was more valuable than their own. They rode into Vatche's house, killed his servants and his two nephews."

Will scanned the main cavern, but there was still no sign of Killien. Or Ilsa. How long were they going to have to wait?

Vatche stood tall on the boulder and motioned to the other slave. The man shuffled forward and placed a slightly larger chest on the table before the enormously fat Torch of the Boan Clan. A chill dragged across Will's neck at the sight of the man. The stories of the Boan's Torch were uniformly cruel.

"Albech," Will whispered to Alaric. "Torch of the Boan. He has more warriors than the rest of the clans put together."

The slave opened up the chest and pulled out a corked glass bottle sloshing with grey liquid. Albech's eyebrow rose slightly and his hand flinched back away from the chest. With a quick nod, he flicked his hand at the servant to take it away.

"Poison." Sora let out a long breath. "The Temur dip their arrows in it. I've never seen them share it." Her eyes flicked from the Boan Torch to the Sunn. Neither man looked at the other. "Two decent gifts. At least neither wants what the other has."

With a slight bow toward the room, Vatche stepped down.

"This is taking too long," Will whispered to Hal. "Let's head to the Morrow's quarters and if Killien's there, we'll deal with it."

Hal nodded, then paused. Another Torch was approaching the boulder.

"Ohan of the Panos Clan," Hal said, his voice hard.

This Torch stalked forward like a wiry cat, his hands hung with an exaggerated ease, too still at his sides. His dark red beard was trimmed to a short point beneath his pinched face.

"The clan that betrayed Killien to the Sunn," Hal continued, "burned our grass, and tried to murder Killien in his home just days ago."

Before Ohan could reach the boulder a distant cry rang out. A shadow flickered across the sunlight on the edge of the cave and the grass along the mouth flattened to the side.

Torch Noy's head snapped toward the opening, his hand grabbing at the yellow stone at his chest. Ohan and the rest of the room turned.

A huge shape dropped into view and light scattered off garnet scales, darting through the cavern with skittering glints of blood red. The dragon flared massive wings, the membrane glowing crimson in the sunlight, dark veins and tendons stretching across them like twisted roots.

With scrambling claws, the creature sank down onto the cave floor next to the river and slithered toward the cave with the Torches, his wings curled back above him. The dragon slid forward until it reached the smaller cave and turned its emotionless face toward the Torches who had shoved back from their tables and scrambled away. Only Torch Noy stepped forward, the yellow burning stone held out before him, the other hand held up, commanding the creature to stop.

Red light rippled down the side of the dragon as he reached the boulder where Vatche had stood and stretched his head into the room. The Roven pressed against the back wall, utterly silent. Noy, his voice raising higher and higher, continued to command the dragon to leave.

With a long, ominous breath, the dragon relaxed its wings. A figure got to his feet on the wide scales between the roots of his wings, and slid down the dragon's shoulder, landing on the boulder.

"I'm glad we're still giving gifts." Killien rested a hand on the dragon's neck. "Because the Morrow have some to hand out."

FORTY-TWO

Killien stood perfectly calm, his hand resting on the wide neck of the dragon. Even on the shadowed side, with every breath the creature took, glints of red skittered along his scales. The dragon pulled back his wings, folding them along his side. Thin, jagged spikes ran from the top of his head, down his spine to the tip of his tail.

The only sound in the cavern was the muffled rush of the waterfall. The Roven were pinned against the wall of the cavern. Lukas, Sini, and Rett stood along the side wall, watching Killien closely. Lukas's face was set in a pleased expression. Torch Noy stood rigid at the first table, his hand gripping his yellow stone.

"That's Killien?" Alaric demanded in a barely audible whisper. "Your description of him didn't do him justice."

"He's less impressive when he's not riding a dragon."

Douglon shook his head. "Why is it always dragons?"

"Does anybody happen to have a kobold?" Will asked.

"Oh, Tomkin and the Dragon! I love that story!" Evangeline whispered.

"I know that one!" Sora whispered back.

"Can we focus?" Alaric interrupted.

Evangeline leaned forward. "I definitely know that dragon."

"We all know that dragon," Douglon said from behind them. "It's tried to kill us. Some of us twice."

"Anguine," Evangeline said slowly, her head tilted slightly to the side as she considered the enormous creature.

"No, Evangeline," Alaric said. "Ayda knew that dragon. Even if you think you know it, *it* doesn't know *you*."

Hal hushed them all as Killien stepped forward to speak. "The first gift is for my friend Anguine." He ran his hand down the dragon's neck. He stepped down off the boulder and walked toward Noy, pulling a short sword out of the sheath slung across his back.

The seax. Will jabbed Alaric with his elbow. "He claims that sword was given to his father by Flibbet the Peddler."

Alaric's eyes widened and he peered at the sword.

"It turns out that even though Anguine is a dragon, he and I have something in common,"

Killien said. The seax glinted a dull silver as he set the tip against Noy's chest. "Neither of us is interested in being ruled."

Noy's face was white, but his eyes blazed with fury. "You raise your sword at the enclave?" Noy hissed through clenched teeth. "You declare war on every clan here."

An unhinged laugh burst out of Killien, and Noy flinched. "A sword?" He flung his arm back at Anguine. "I brought a dragon to the enclave. Yes. It's a declaration of war." Killien reached forward and ripped the yellow stone out of Noy's hand, dragging Noy a step closer by his neck. "Your days of crushing the other clans into submission are over. You no longer have your dragon." Killien drew his sword back and slashed forward, slicing through the chain.

He turned his back on Noy and walked back toward the dragon. Noy's hand dove into a pocket and pulled out a handful of gems. Anguine's head stretched forward and a deep, low growl rumbled in his chest. Noy's gaze flickered to the dragon and he froze.

Killien tossed the stone toward Anguine. The dragon's jaws snapped shut on it, and the yellow stone sat pinned between jagged teeth for a heartbeat before Anguine bit down and the stone shattered.

A loud crack echoed through the cave and a shower of yellow sparks exploded from Anguine's mouth. The dragon spread his jaws wide and shards of yellow glittered from between his teeth. His head snaked closer to Noy. The scales on Anguine's back rose, bits of light scattering across them as he drew in a breath. Slowly he let it out and red flames flickered in his mouth with a sound like a distant wind. The fire licked along the dragon's teeth, reaching around his nostrils with clinging fingers of flame, setting the scales of his face glittering a bloody red.

When the flames stopped, the dragon's teeth shone jagged and clean.

Noy took a wooden step backwards while Anguine fixed him with a dead, reptilian gaze.

"How is Killien controlling that dragon?" Alaric whispered. "I thought you said he couldn't do magic."

"He can't."

"Could Lukas be doing it?" Sora asked.

The slave stood off to the side, gazing around the room with a satisfied smile.

"He doesn't look like he's doing much of anything," Will said.

"Look on the dragon's back," Sora said.

Nestled into the glittering red scales at the base of his neck, something flashed light blue. Like a bit of sky caught in his scales.

"That's the same stone he used to control the frost goblins," Sora whispered.

"A compulsion stone," Will whispered. "It can transfer thoughts into a creature."

"He's trying to implant thoughts into a dragon?" Hal asked. "He's completely lost his mind."

Sora studied the blue glimmer on Anguine's back. "That's what it looks like to me."

"That wouldn't work if Killien is next to it," Alaric pointed out. "He'd nullify the magic."

Will sank back away from the crack remembering Lukas's notes about compulsion stones. He spun his ring. "It could work. Killien keeps energy from being transferred near him. But Lukas discovered that if you put emotions instead of thoughts into a compulsion stone, that they'll *resonate*. Once he created a stone, the emotions would resonate into anyone the stone touched."

Alaric looked unconvinced.

"Trust me," Will said. "Emotions resonate. And he could use them to control a dragon."

"The Sunn still have stonesteeps." Noy's voice rang out shrilly. "Hundreds of them. Many of which are right outside this cave. You will never leave this enclave alive."

Killien let out a short laugh. "I also bring a gift to all the slaves in this room." There was a long moment of silence. "To you who have served these Torches, I offer you your freedom. Come to me and the Morrow will see you safely across the Scale Mountains, where you can return to the homes you were taken from."

A ripple of movement spread among the Roven and the slaves. Lukas's head snapped towards Killien, his eyes narrow.

"All you have to do is step forward. You have my word." Killien watched the huddled slaves at the back of the room patiently.

"Killien's freeing the slaves?" Will whispered to Hal.

The big man shook his head slowly, his face disapproving. "He's freeing *his enemies'* slaves, stripping the other Torches of any advantage they might have. You can tell from Lukas's expression that it's not a universal freeing."

Hal was right, Lukas's face was furious.

One elderly man stepped forward. The enormously fat Torch Albech grabbed at his arm, but the slave wrenched it away and walked toward Killien, his eyes flickering to the dragon.

"What land do you come from?" Killien asked.

"Baylon," the man answered.

Killien nodded. "We will see you returned." He faced the others again, waiting.

Slowly, other slaves stepped away from the crowd, walking over to join the old man until the only ones against the far wall were Roven.

"My final gift," Killien said, his voice as cold and sharp as the wall under Will's fingers, "is for Ohan of the Panos Clan."

Sora swore quietly next to him.

"A man I trusted," Killien continued, "a man who claimed he also wanted out from under the thumb of the Sunn and the Boan. A man who joined into an agreement with Torch Vatche and myself."

The Roven near to Ohan backed away. Vatche stepped up behind him and gave him a shove. Ohan stumbled forward. Lukas stalked over to the man and took a hold of his arm, while Vatche took the other.

Killien strode toward the man. Ohan tried to back away, but Lukas and Vatche held him in place.

"You convinced Vatche and I that you wanted an alliance. The Panos would join the Morrow and the Temur in our endeavors to break out from under the stranglehold of the larger clans."

Vatche shoved Ohan a little closer.

Killien stepped within reach of the man. "You burned my land. You sent men into my home under a sign of peace to kill me. You partnered with the Sunn, for what? To gain a little favor? To fawn at the feet of men more powerful than you?"

Ohan shrank back against Vatche, who didn't move.

"I have a question for you, Ohan." Killien stepped even closer. "And if you answer me truthfully, I will be merciful."

Ohan's entire body trembled. Killien pressed the edge of his sword against the man's neck.

"The night my father died, the night he traveled to broker peace between you and the Temur, was it a stray arrow that took his life? Or something more…cowardly?"

Ohan's jaw clenched and he stared into Killien's face, his eyes half-furious, half-terrified.

"A stray arrow." The words were rough and broken.

Killien stood very still, the blade still pressed against the man's throat.

"No, it was not." An older slave stepped forward from the knot of grey shirts who had come to Killien's side. "The arrow that killed Tevien, Torch of the Morrow, came from Ohan's own bow."

Ohan shot a blazing look at the slave and opened his mouth in rage.

"Do not speak." Killien's voice was thin. He glanced toward the slave. "Do you know this to be true?"

"I stood beside the Torch that night," the man said. "Like I have every night. He waited in ambush for your father and killed him from his hiding place. Like a coward. And the order to burn your grasses and kill you were from his very lips less than a fortnight ago."

Killien stood utterly still. A thin line of red dribbled down Ohan's throat under the sword. Killien drew in a long, trembling breath and took a step back, dropping the sword to his side.

"If you'd only told the truth, my gift to you would have been a quick death." Killien nodded to Lukas and shoved his sword back into his sheath. "You should have told the truth."

Will leaned forward, the rocky wall rough against his palms. In front of the dragon's enormous body, Killien looked small, but his posture was as vicious as the dragon's.

Lukas pulled an amber colored burning stone out of his shirt, dangling from a thick silver chain. He lifted it up over Ohan's head and Vatche yanked his hands off the man, stepping away. Lukas dropped the necklace over Ohan's head and stepped back, watching.

A strange glow formed in front of the man like wisps of fire. Tendrils of light slid out of his clothes and his neck, snaking out of his face.

"No." Alaric drew back from the rock, his breath jagged.

Evangeline drew in a sharp breath, then pressed her hands to her face, her fingers white.

"No, no, no, no," Alaric whispered, his eyes fixed on the man down in the cave.

"What is he doing?" Will asked.

Alaric pinched his mouth shut and shook his head. "That's an absorption stone—or a reservoir stone."

"It's pulling out his *vitalle*," Evangeline whispered, between her fingers, her voice pained.

Will stared at her. "Like Alaric did to you?"

Ohan screamed and Alaric flinched, turning toward Evangeline and crushing her to his chest. Ohan's screams rose, echoing through the chamber. He clawed at the necklace, trying to pull it off, but the gem stayed fixed to his chest. His screams changed to a shriek, feral and savage as he dropped to his knees.

Swirls of orange-bronze light tore out of his body and spun around the gem, sinking into it, mixing with the amber color of the stone, glowing like rusted honey.

Ohan's screams pierced into Will like daggers. Alaric clamped shaking hands over Evangeline's ears. Sora grabbed Will's arm, her face horrified.

With a final thin cry, Ohan tumbled sideways onto the ground.

His body was utterly still and the gem at his chest glowed with swirling light.

FORTY-THREE

The enclave was silent.

Lukas knelt down next to the body and dragged the stone off Ohan's head. Standing, he offered it to Killien.

Killien held up the stone, watching the orange light for a long moment. "It is a shame that the Sweep has turned into this. Clan killing clan. Roven fighting amongst ourselves when we could be banding together."

Evangeline dropped her hands and looked into the cavern, flinching when she saw the body of Ohan sprawled out on the floor. Hal's eyes were fixed on Killien, horrified.

"We should be gathering our strength to fight the real enemies." Killien's words carried throughout the cavern. "Those who live across the Scales."

"That's unsettling," Alaric muttered.

Killien stepped away from Ohan's body with a disgusted look. The slave who had betrayed him stepped forward. Grabbing Ohan's arms he dragged the body out of the smaller cave and tossed it along the wall of the main cavern.

Killien nodded to the man and climbed up next to Anguine. He hooked the swirling orange stone over a thin spike on the dragon's neck. "Nothing is ever accomplished on the Sweep without bloodshed. And today is no exception. We have never come together in peace. Every change in our land, every bit of progress comes from pouring the blood of our people into the grass.

"But let today be the last." Killien toyed with the gem for a breath before turning away from it. "Let us purge the hatred out of our clans today so that tomorrow can dawn a new age for our people."

Lukas still stood where Ohan had fallen. All semblance of servitude was gone, and he stood with arms folded across his chest, eyes fixed coldly on Killien. The Torch met his gaze for a long moment, then nodded. A vicious smile lifted Lukas's mouth and he strode away, his steps echoing as he passed through the silent cavern and into a tunnel near the mouth of the cave.

"Only a little more unpleasantness." Killien stepped away from the dragon and walked toward the back of the room where the other Roven still stood pressed against the wall. He reached the farthest table and swung his legs over the bench.

"Come join me at the tables, and let us dream of what the Sweep can be." His words echoed more with a note of command than invitation.

The other Roven shifted.

"If any of you are concerned that troops or stonesteeps from the camp below will disturb our talks, let me assure you that they will not. The Roven below have their problems and we have ours. They will fight for today, but we must sit together and fight for the whole future of the Sweep.

"Come." Killien snapped across the room.

Torch Vatche stepped forward and sat at the table across from Killien. The two warriors with him sat as well. One by one the others sat until the only Torches that stood along the wall were Noy and Albrech.

"Do you not want a say in the future of the Sweep?" Killien spoke quietly enough Will could barely hear it. "Today you lose all the power you've had. Albrech, you will lose many of your warriors. Noy, you have already lost your dragon, and your stonesteeps will soon fall. A new era is dawning."

"What have you done?" Albrech demanded. "Do you dare attack my army with your pitiful handful of warriors?"

"My warriors are safe at home with their families. It is only yours who are in danger."

A horn rang out from the Sweep. Then another. Distant shouts and clashes echoed feebly through the cavern.

"The frost goblins," Sora whispered.

The Torches shoved themselves up from the table.

"Sit." Killien's voice cracked like a whip. A threatening growl rumbled in Anguine's chest. "The way to help your clans is to sit here, at this enclave, and discuss the future of the Sweep."

With a ripple of scarlet light, Anguine raised his head until it hung high in the air over the tables. The Roven sank back down in their seats.

"Now, if you would all hand your weapons to the good people who used to be your slaves," Killien continued, "we can get this discussion underway." The slaves stepped closer, taking swords and knives. "If you wouldn't mind staying close by," Killien asked them, "you might help the conversation to stay civil."

In moments a ring of grey shirts encircled the table, knives and swords held in their hands.

"Very good. Now, let us begin. Anguine will root out any who would disturb us."

The dragon's head curved around and the enormous creature's claws scratched against the floor as it crawled back toward the sunshine.

"If we're going to find Ilsa," Hal said, his face set in hard lines, "we need to do it now."

"Agreed," Will said, stepping back from the gash in the wall.

Hal led them back out into the original tunnel.

After only a few minutes they came to a hole in the floor. Following Hal, they descended a ladder, reaching another tunnel that wound forward with a hint of brightness. A handful of doors were set on either side.

"Storage rooms," Hal whispered. "This will lead us to the main cavern. Usually the Torches clear out this area when the enclave starts, sending everyone else down to the Sweep. So it should be empty. Let's hope Killien keeps them all back in that cave, because we're going to have to walk across the cave mouth to get to the living quarters."

Will nodded for him to continue, and they walked quietly down the dim corridor. Douglan and Patlon kept their axes out. Sora held a long knife in her hand. The tunnel brightened measurably around each turn until they could see an arched doorway where it spilled out into the bright main cavern. Hal motioned them forward, and they crept toward it.

A flash of red glittered in the sunlight and Sora drew in a sharp breath. A crushing weight of emotions flooded into Will. Anger, impatience, hunger. Sora grabbed Will's arm just as the dragon's head filled the arch. With a growl the dragon drew in a breath and the group scrambled backwards.

Anguine shot out a stream of flame that filled the tunnel with a stunning burst of energy. An answering burst of *vitalle* rushed past the other direction from Alaric, and they sprinted toward the turn. Will and Hal were the last to reach it, diving around just as a wall of flickering orange flame rushed by.

"Against the wall," Alaric hissed, holding his hand toward the fire. The flames flickered along an invisible boundary that angled out from the corner, pushing the fire back from where they huddled.

The heat reached them, though. A wave of scalding heat washed over Will, and he ducked away from it.

The flames stopped and the group stood frozen. The hallway was silent, but Will could still feel the crushing hunger of the dragon. The drive to kill.

Alaric shook out his hand, wincing. "There's nothing to draw *vitalle* from in here," he whispered. "I won't be able to make another shield."

"Is there any other way out?" Will asked Hal.

"Just back to where we came from. Or down into some storage cellars."

"The dragon isn't going to stop if Killien's commanded it to root out intruders," Douglon pointed out. "I think we need to consider retreating."

"We can't leave." Will shoved against Anguine's emotions, but he couldn't push them out. They pressed down, smothering him. "Ilsa's here. And the slaves. We can't leave."

Hal's expression clearly agreed with Douglon.

Will cast out. The huge head of the dragon was pressing into the end of the tunnel.

"We need a new plan, Will," Alaric said. "We're not getting past a dragon. And Douglon's right. As long as Killien controls him, I don't think he's going to stop."

Evangeline stepped up next to them. "Maybe we can get him out from Killien's control." She bit her lip and looked at Alaric. "It's going to be alright."

Then she stepped around the corner into view of the dragon.

Alaric made a strangled noise and grabbed for her but she moved out of his reach. She held her hands away from herself, palms spread to show she held no weapon.

"Hello, Anguine." Her voice was small and thin in the tunnel.

Will felt a spark of interest flare to life in Anguine and heard the dragon draw in a breath.

"My name is Evangeline," she said, "and even though you and I have never met, I...know you."

Curiosity from the dragon bloomed in Will's chest. The hunger receded slightly and the flames didn't come.

Alaric stepped into the tunnel behind her, but Douglon grabbed his arm to hold him back. "Give her a chance," the dwarf said quietly.

"It's alright," Will whispered to Alaric. "Anguine is just curious about her."

"It is *not* alright," Alaric hissed back.

Will leaned forward to see around the corner, but Hal grabbed him and pulled him back away from the door. "You stay back. He may still want to kill you."

Will nodded and moved until he could barely see around the corner. The dragon's head filled the end of the narrow tunnel, his yellow, reptilian eyes fixed on Evangeline.

Anguine slid his head forward into the corridor, his jaw inches above the ground until his snout was within reach of her arm. She stood woodenly, but didn't back away. Alaric strained against Douglon's grip, his face white. The dragon's nostrils flared and he breathed in. From deep in his chest came a low rumble.

The elf. The words rolled through Will's mind like a wave crashing over the surf. Everyone in the group flinched.

"Yes." Evangeline let out a relieved breath. "Ayda, the elf."

You smell of her.

"I…I do?"

Alaric still leaned toward his wife, but his eyes tightened in curiosity. Anguine drew in a breath again and Evangeline was pulled a half step forward down the tunnel, her hair whipping out in front of her face.

Your life, your…being. It smells like her.

"Well, that makes sense." Evangeline nodded shakily. "You see, Ayda was a friend of my husband. And she…" The tunnel fell silent for a moment. "She sacrificed her own life to save mine. Now I know things that she knew. And I recognize you."

The dragon considered Evangeline with emotionless eyes.

What would you and your companions lurking down the hall ask of me, Evangeline Elf Scent?

"We would like—um…Elf Scent?"

It is fitting.

"Yes, but…"

Anguine stared at her, unmoving. He let out a long, slow breath and Evangeline's hair fluttered backwards.

She stepped back. "We would like to get out of the tunnel and cross the cavern behind you."

That is not something I'm willing to allow.

"I think you might."

The dragon growled and Alaric flinched. Will felt a spark of irritation wriggle through Anguine's emotions.

"I mean," Evangeline said quickly, "I don't think it's *you* who doesn't want us to cross. I—*we* think that you're being controlled."

The growl from Anguine's throat was louder this time and Alaric took a step forward. Douglon's face was stony hard as he held the man back.

"Did you know there's a stone on your back? Right between your wings? It's blue."

Anguine's eyes slid shut and the dragon was perfectly still for a long breath.

I had…forgotten that was there. His voice held a low, roiling anger. *The Torch.*

"Yes, the Torch. We think he's using it to control you. Just like he sent you before to kill someone."

The Keeper. The words were hard as granite. Will felt a spike of hatred. *I want to kill the Keeper.*

"Well, the Torch wants you to kill the Keeper. I think if you took the stone off, you might not care either way about the man." She took a tentative step forward. "If you don't mind, um, with your permission, I mean, I could climb up on your back and take it off for you."

Anguine considered her for a long time. *You know the Keeper.*

Evangeline stiffened. "I do. And it would be good for him if we took the stone off of you. But it would be good for you, too. You'll know which thoughts are yours, and which are…not."

The dragon's anger and suspicion swirled in Will's chest.

I will not be controlled. Take it off.

Anguine stretched his clawed foot toward Evangeline and she flinched back. Alaric let out a pained gasp. When the dragon didn't move again, she put one hand out slowly to touch it. The claws pressed into the floor with knife-sharp points. The tops of his scaled foot sat at Evangeline's waist. She climbed up onto it, then scrambled on her hands and knees onto his back. She kept her head low so she didn't hit the ceiling.

"It's right here," she said, peering down at Anguine's back. "It's been tied in place with leather straps around three scales." She leaned forward and tugged at something Will couldn't see. "These knots are tight."

She yanked on something and Anguine hissed and snapped his huge jaw at her.

"Sorry," she said, holding her hands up. "I think that loosened it, though."

Anguine's head drew back slightly. With a little more fidgeting, she lifted something into the air with a glint of blue. Anguine closed his eyes and shook his head as though he were shaking off water.

That is...

A deep growl vibrated the floor under Will's feet.

That is better. His words flowed smoothly into Will's mind. *You are right, I care nothing for the Keeper.*

Evangeline slid down off Anguine's side and climbed down off his foot. She slung the gem over her shoulder by the long strips of leather and stood uncertainly in front of the huge creature.

My mind clears. Thank you, Evangeline Elf Scent. He breathed in and his scales rippled waves of red light along his side. *I owe you a debt. What would you ask of me?*

"Well, aside from a different title than Elf Scent, we would still like to pass. We have business across that big cavern."

Anguine turned his reptilian head toward the others. Will felt a mild curiosity form in his chest. *You may pass.*

Evangeline nodded, then motioned to the others to come. Alaric let out a long breath. Slowly the group stepped into the tunnel and moved toward the dragon. Anguine's emotions were infinitely calmer now, a cross between boredom and vague curiosity. They were only a few steps away when he felt a flicker of recognition from the dragon.

I have met the black-robed one before.

"Yes, that is my husband," Evangeline said. "He was a friend of Ayda's. He was there the night you met her."

Will felt a low wave of anger. *I remember.*

There was a sudden spike of hatred and Will grabbed for Alaric's arm to pull him back. But Anguine continued to stare at them with an indecipherable gaze.

Will was still watching the dragon when Evangeline shifted, blocking his view. Her face twisted into a snarl and she lunged for Will, wrapping her hands around his neck and crushing his throat.

FORTY-FOUR

Alaric grabbed at Evangeline's arms, hissing words in her ear and pulling at her fingers as they dug into Will's neck.

Will's mouth stretched open, trying to draw in air. His chest burned. He shoved at Evangeline, but she leaned close to him, her face murderous, her breath hot on his face.

Black spots flashed at the edges of his vision and crept inward. Dimly, Sora's face appeared behind Evangeline with her knife raised behind Evangeline's shoulder. She sliced down and yanked the stone off Evangeline's shoulder, tossing it away.

Evangeline blinked and shoved herself back, her face filling with horror.

Will gulped in a breath of air, the coldness rushing into his lungs. He fell forward to his knees and Sora grabbed his shoulders, keeping him from toppling over. His vision cleared and he coughed, the air stinging in his throat.

Evangeline stared down at her trembling hands, backing away slowly. "What happened? Will…I'm so sorry. I don't know…"

"You were touching the stone." Sora motioned to the blue stone she'd tossed into the corner of the tunnel. "The one Killien used to convince a dragon to hunt Will."

"I hated you," Evangeline said, kneeling in front of Will, her face stricken. "I'm so sorry. I don't…I'm so sorry."

Alaric crossed the tunnel and pulled a cloth out of his pack. Carefully, keeping the fabric between his hand and the stone, he tucked the gem into the bag and tied it shut. "Doesn't seem like something that should be left lying around."

Will dropped his head forward, trying to slow his breathing.

"Are you alright?" Sora asked quietly.

He nodded, and she helped him stand.

Evangeline stepped back, her hand trembling and covering her mouth.

"It's not your fault." Will's words came out as a half-whisper. "Killien's really angry at me. That stone was strong enough to influence a dragon. Of course it would influence you, too."

"We should move," Hal whispered, pointing to the gap between Anguine's head and the tunnel wall.

Will nodded and Sora, after giving him a critical look, let go of his arm.

Alaric hesitated in front of the dragon. Anguine watched the Keeper, still calm.

"That stone." Alaric pointed to the one hanging on one of the spikes near Anguine's shoulder. "The one Killien used to pull the life out of that man, may I see it?"

I have no loyalty to that Torch, Anguine said, anger lacing the last word. *Do you intend to kill the Torch with it?*

"No." Alaric's hand went to his own necklace. "No. I'm strongly against killing people in such a manner. I want to see how much of the man has been captured, and whether there is a way to… heal the man it came from."

The dragon stared at Alaric for a long moment. *You are welcome to take the stone, but the Roven man smelled dead.* He tilted his head slightly and fixed a thin-slitted eye on Alaric. *Unless you can return people from the dead?*

"No." Alaric paused, considering the dragon. "Can you?"

No.

Alaric walked carefully between Anguine's neck and the wall of the hallway, sliding the amber stone off the long, crimson spike. He held it in his hand and closed his eyes. A flicker of darkness crossed over his face before he opened them again. "This was crudely done. There is too little *vitalle* here to do anything."

Anguine lifted his head and sniffed the air. Disgust rippled through him. *The caves fill with filth, and a battle bleeds below. Give me the sky.* The dragon's hunger returned, this time for the freedom of flight and the scent of blood.

He snaked his head around, twisting his long neck like a scarlet snake back out of the tunnel. With a dry slither, he disappeared into the main cavern.

Will cast out and felt the blazing *vitalle* of the dragon launch out of the cave and dive down toward the fighting with a swell of exultation that faded as the dragon fell away.

Sora suddenly tensed and spun looking back down the tunnel just as the scent of rotten meat slid into the tunnel. Footsteps slapped along the tunnel floor and a frost goblin scrambled around the corner.

Patlon stepped forward and crushed the creature's skull with a swing of his axe. Will cast out exactly when Alaric did and the echoes came back of three more goblins, rushing closer.

Douglon and Patlon took up positions next to each other, axes ready.

"About time we found something to fight smaller than a dragon," Patlon muttered.

"Did they follow us?" Douglon asked.

The wave of Alaric casting out ran down the tunnel again. "No. They're coming from somewhere down below."

"Storage cellars," Hal said. "They must have dug into them."

"This is our way out?" Alaric asked, pointing back the way they'd come. At Hal's nod, he turned to Will "We'll figure out where they're coming from and try to block it. You go find Ilsa."

Another goblin reached the corner and Douglon dispatched it quickly. Will cast out again. A troubling tumult of *vitalle* echoed through the rocks below them.

"Alaric," he warned.

"I feel them. Hurry." Alaric's gaze searched around the tunnel. "It'd be nice if there was something to draw energy from."

Evangeline opened several of the doors near them. "How about fires? There are things in these storage rooms that would burn."

"Fires would be perfect."

"Let's go," Hal said. Will and Sora followed him, leaving Alaric and Evangeline to their fires, and the dwarves swinging at the next trickle of frost goblins.

They hurried down the tunnel the way the dragon had gone and peered out into the sunlight of the main cavern. Far in the back, muted voices could be heard echoing from the smaller cave the Torches were in, but no one was visible. Hal motioned for them to hurry, and they followed him across. In a few steps the main opening gaped next to them, overlooking the Sweep. Cries and clashes and screams came over the ledge. Below, along the edge of the lake, hordes of frost goblins poured out of warrens, streaming into the camps of Roven.

Will hesitated for a moment. Greyish-green bodies of the frost goblins piled up, but Roven bodies lay on the ground as well. The goblins seemed disoriented as they ran out into the bright sunlight, and the Roven took advantage of their confusion, shooting and hacking into the swarm. The stonesteeps from the Sunn Clan stood near two of the warrens, shooting arcs of energy into the midst of the goblins. Wisps of black smoke rose from dark smudges on the ground.

A new warren opened as Will watched, and a stream of frost goblins spilled out, plowing into a band of warriors. A quick fear for Rass's safety surfaced, but he pushed it away. She could take care of herself.

Sora nudged his back and he started walking again. Sunlight fell warm on his arm and face. Hal hurried them across the cavern toward the hallway Lukas had disappeared down. The passage was wide and smooth, roomy enough for the three of them to walk side by side. It dimmed as they walked farther from the main cavern. They came to a turn to the left and Hal raised his hands for them to wait. He stepped around the corner and Will strained to hear anything in the silence.

In a moment, Hal came back, his face troubled.

"This is as far as I'll be able to take you." Hal held up his hand to quiet Sora's objection. "Three of the clans have left guards at their rooms. I can lead them away so you can reach Killien's rooms. The Morrow's quarters are the last ones. Get Ilsa and get out of here." He turned to Will. "After everything we just saw, after everything Killien has done, I need to go to the enclave. I don't know if he'll listen to me right now, but at a time like this, my place is next to him."

Will nodded. "Thank you for everything. And I hope you can convince Killien to..."

Hal ran his hand through his hair. "Return to sanity? So do I."

"Will you tell him we're here?" Sora asked.

Hal shook his head. "But I won't lie to him either. He'll probably figure it out on his own. You won't have much time."

Will held out his hand, and Hal grasped it around the wrist in the Roven style.

"Around this corner there's an alcove you two can hide in. I'll have to bring the guards back past here, this is the only way out."

The alcove was a natural recess in the rock only a few steps deep, but it turned to the left, and Will backed himself into the darkest part until the rough stone wall dug into his back. Sora came in and pressed her back up against him, facing out of the alcove, a knife in her hand.

Hal disappeared. The tunnel was dim, so it was almost black in the alcove. Will could just see the outline of Sora's head. She shifted her shoulders and the light glinted off her knife. Her head was right in front of him and the earthy, woody scent of her leathers filled the space.

"You smell good," he whispered and she twisted around and he could just make out her incredulous look. "You always have. I thought it that very first night when you snuck into my room. You were terrifying, but you smelled good."

The edge of a smile crept into her face. "This isn't exactly the time, Will." The dim light caught on a strand of copper in her braid as she turned away from him.

He leaned close to her ear. "If this isn't the time, do you think there will be one? Maybe later?"

He felt more than heard her laugh.

"There's not going to be a later if you keep making noise," she breathed.

"You'll know when they're coming," he pointed out. "I'm just trying to determine if it's the sentiment or the timing you're objecting to."

"I'm objecting to the volume," she whispered. "And don't even think about using your creepy magical skills to read how I'm feeling."

"There's no need for that. I'm quite good at reading people even without my amazing magical skills."

"Then you know that Hal is about to betray us to Killien?"

"No, he's not."

"The moment Killien sees him, he'll know you're here."

Will let out a long breath. "Maybe, but that's hardly the same thing as betraying us. Hal can hardly help Killien while he's creeping around tunnels with us. You have to admit that today is a significant day for the Morrow. And Killien could use some help."

"Yes, with the murders and the threats and the slaughter."

"I'm not saying I approve of it," Will said. "But Hal has a level head, and adding him to the situation can only improve it. It's not like Killien's going to listen to *me* if I ask him to stop."

"It feels wrong to do nothing."

"I agree." Will leaned his head back against the hard stone. "I just have no idea what to do. He's taken his revenge on Ohan, and he's called the frost goblins. Anything we wanted to stop has already happened."

"They're coming," she whispered.

Will cast out and felt a jumble of *vitalle* coming closer down the hallway.

"Ohan's dead." Hal's voice echoed loudly. "The Torches are discussing the future of the Sweep."

Hal passed their alcove, facing away from them down the tunnel, followed by three other Roven. Will drew in a breath and pressed himself back against the rocks, but none of them looked into the alcove. In a moment they were out of view, and a dozen heartbeats later, not even Hal could be heard.

Sora motioned him to stay still and crept out into the tunnel. In a matter of breaths, she was back. "Empty."

He followed her out and around the next turn into the long tunnel with doors lining the right hand side along what must be the face of the mountain.

"If Lukas is in there with Ilsa," Sora said, "we'll have to keep him from leaving and telling Killien."

Will nodded. Lukas's scowling presence wasn't going to make this discussion any smoother. At the end of the hall, he pushed gently on the Morrow's door and it swung open enough to let him see a sliver of a stone room, well-lit with sunlight. The shushing sound of the endless wind filled it. He pushed the door farther to reveal a small common room with a wide, open window looking out over the Sweep. Several small tables sat near the back and a fireplace was carved into the outside wall. A few closed doors filled the wall to his left.

Alone in the room, standing in front of the fire with her back to him, stood Ilsa.

FORTY-FIVE

Will's breath caught in his throat.

There was something achingly familiar about the way she stood. He was young again, standing in his home, watching his mother cook. The longing that memory evoked in him took his breath away.

Ilsa pulled a shallow pan out of the fire and the Roven smell of roasting sorren seeds cut through his memory like a rusted knife.

He stopped in the doorway, unwilling to make a sound, suddenly terrified she would turn around and see him. He spun his ring. Ilsa stood at a wooden ledge in front of the fire, mixing the seeds into something in a clay bowl. The wind outside gusted past, filling the room with its irregular shushing sound.

Giving him a little push, Sora stepped into the room and positioned herself just inside the door, scanning the room, probably wondering where Lukas was, and keeping watch down the hall. The wind filled the room with a sound more like the ocean than the Sweep.

Sora looked expectantly at Will. When he didn't say anything, she said quietly, "Ilsa?"

Ilsa glanced over her shoulder. Her eyes widened at Sora, but when she saw Will she spun around, clutching a rag to her chest.

"You!" Her face grew pale.

Will opened his mouth to say…something, but her surprised look shifted to outrage and the words stuck in his throat.

Sora waited expectantly for a moment before sighing. "Ilsa, we're not here to hurt you."

Ilsa turned accusing eyes on Will. "Haven't you done enough to the Torch?"

The strangeness of the accusation freed his voice. "To Killien?"

"He's been furious since you left, stealing some valuable book."

Will stepped forward. "Left? You mean when I escaped from the prison he was keeping me in? While threatening to kill you if I didn't cooperate?"

She paused at his words, her eyes narrowing suspiciously. "The Torch has *never* threatened me."

"When he brought you with him to the rift," he said, his anger at Killien pushing its way to the surface, "he had a warrior behind you with a knife drawn, just so I wouldn't say anything he didn't want."

She shook her head. "Those warriors were there to control you."

"By threatening you!" he shouted and Sora hissed at him to be quiet. Will rubbed his hand over his mouth and pulled it down into his beard. This was not the way this conversation was supposed to go.

"Will you please just leave?" Her face was still hard, but there was a note of pleading in her voice. She wrung the rag. "He's so angry with you." Her eyes flickered to Sora. "And with you. If he finds you two here...I don't know what he'll do."

Will took a step forward and she flinched back, pressing herself against the ledge. The fear that flashed through her eyes stabbed into him like a knife, pinning down his next words—the words he needed to say. His heart pulsed in his ears with an almost feral thrumming as he shoved the words out.

"I can't leave without you."

She dropped her hands to her side and her eyes went flat. "Leave."

"I'm your brother, Ilsa."

She leaned away from him. "He said you'd say something crazy. That if you ever talked to me, you'd try to make me come with you. But you're a liar. You spent weeks with the Morrow lying to everyone."

"I'm a Keeper, from Queensland." Will wanted to step closer but Sora put a hand on his arm. "I did lie about that, for obvious reasons. But I'm here on the Sweep because I've been looking for you. For a very long time."

Ilsa's eyes flickered toward Sora. "The Torch trusted you," she accused. "And you're here, with *him.*"

Sora nodded slowly. "Will's not what Killien says he is. He's a good man, and he really has been looking for you."

"How could you know he's telling the truth?" Ilsa's tone was scathing.

Sora paused. "I believe Will thinks you're his sister." She gave a small shrug. "And you two do resemble each other."

Ilsa let out an exasperated huff. "That means nothing."

"You were two when they took you," Will said and Ilsa's gaze snapped over to him.

"Anyone could have told you that."

"I was eleven. Do you remember anything about home?"

Her jaw tightened and she shook her head slightly, and Will felt a jab of both heartache and relief. It must have made it easier for her not to remember, but it felt like a whole new theft, a violation to have also robbed her of those memories.

"We lived in a one-room cottage with our parents on a very small farm with a goat and a dozen chickens."

Ilsa shook her head quickly, raising one hand toward him. "Stop, you could say anything, and I have no way of knowing if you're telling the truth. What I do know is that you lied to people that I respect, so I have no reason to believe you. Please," she pleaded with him, "you two are in terrible danger. Leave before the Torch returns."

Will squeezed his eyes shut as the memory of her being pulled out the window came back with perfect clarity. Vahe's furious eyes, Ilsa's terrified face, her hand clutching her doll. Will's eyes snapped open. "You had a doll."

Ilsa stiffened.

"The night they took you, you were holding a rag doll. It was...really ugly. It had no hair and the face had rubbed off. The head was squished to the side because you slept with it every night."

Ilsa's hands clenched the rag against her chest, her face pale.

"It was so ugly, but I couldn't bear to tell you that because you loved it so much. So I told you it was hideous, because I knew you wouldn't understand the word. You thought I'd named her, so you called her Hiddy."

Ilsa flinched.

"A man named Vahe took you."

At his name, Ilsa drew in a sharp breath.

"He wasn't coming for you." The pressure of it grew in his chest until he could barely speak. "He was there for me."

Her eyes snapped open, but Will couldn't meet them.

"All these years, it should have been me here, not you." The words strangled out. "If I'd have just gone with him, he would have left you alone." He forced himself to meet her eyes. "I didn't know."

Ilsa stood with her hand over her mouth, her eyes wide, her other hand clenching the rag to her stomach.

"I'm so sorry." Will almost opened up toward her, but he couldn't tell if it was hatred or hope in her eyes, and if it was the former, the feel of it might kill him.

Footsteps rang out and Sora spun toward the door.

"Will can pluck memories out of your mind," Killien's voice came from the hall. "He knows exactly what you want to hear. Don't believe anything the man says."

FORTY-SIX

A wave of relief washed across Ilsa's face, fueling the rage growing in Will. He turned to see Killien standing in the doorway, his silver seax unsheathed, his face burning with the anger that always filled him. Behind him two servants stood, their swords drawn as well.

"No, I can't," Will said, fighting to stay calm. "I've never even heard of anyone who could pluck memories from your mind."

"So it's just emotions you can read?" Killien asked.

The words caught at him, leaving him feeling exposed, like fingers pulling open his cloak and letting the chill of the cave seep in against his skin. It hadn't taken Hal long to fill Killien in. "Yes I can read people's emotions. If I try."

Ilsa's eyes were on him, wide with disbelief. When he met her gaze she stumbled back against the ledge.

"Everyone's?" Killien asked, a tight curiosity in his voice.

Will nodded, ignoring Sora's small huff. Killien didn't ask the real question. "It's not like magic that can be countered. I can just feel people's emotions all the time. Unless I work to close myself off. It's like an extra sense. I can see you, hear you, smell you, and feel what you're feeling." He glanced at Ilsa's pale face. "But I'm not doing it now."

Killien studied him, his anger seething into coldness. "A useful skill."

"Sometimes," Will answered. "But in normal life, people express their emotions clearly enough for anyone to see."

Killien shook his head. "Everyone has secrets."

"Maybe." Will shrugged. "But you'd be surprised how hard it is to suss out a secret based purely on emotions."

Killien stepped into the room, and the two slaves blocked the door. "I'm sorry I left you alone, Ilsa." Killien walked past Will and Sora without a glance. Sora kept her gaze fixed on the two armed servants. Ilsa was still backed up against the ledge, gripping the rag so tightly tendons stood out on the back of her hands. "I had a suspicion the Keeper would reappear, but I didn't think he'd follow us here.

"There is no reason you need to be subjected to whatever lies he's spun," Killien continued calmly, motioning to the nearest door. "You don't have to stay. You're welcome to wait in the other room while Will and I finish something we should have finished long ago."

She hesitated a moment, the rag still clutched in her hand. She fixed her eyes on Will as though expecting him to lunge at her, or as though she finally saw a horrible monster she'd never believed was real. Her expression lit a mixture of gut-wrenching pain and rage in him.

"Ilsa—" Will stepped forward, desperate to get that look off her face.

Killien brought his sword up and leveled it at Will's chest, the Torch's face frigid and controlled. "No more talking to her."

At the coldness in Killien's words, a flicker of something crossed Ilsa's face, but she ducked her head, and hurried into one of the side rooms before Will could figure out what it was. The door shut behind her with a grim finality.

"The sword that you said was too serious for a mere fight." Will motioned to Killien's blade. "Should I feel honored that you're using it against me?" The blade was rougher than he'd expected, more primitive. The handle was sanded wood, the blade pockmarked near the hilt. The runes carved into the blade were roughly made. *Naj.* "What does Naj mean?"

Killien ignored the question. He motioned to one of the slaves. "Bind them."

When it was done, he ordered them to stand guard at the door. "You picked a very bad time to come back, Will. I only have a short time. Hal and the slaves are holding the Torches, but I need to return."

Will searched for a hint of the man he'd thought Killien was, but found barely any resemblance. "What happened to you, Killien?" The ropes dug into Will's wrists.

The Torch paced across the small room to where Ilsa had stood. "Where's my book?"

"Far away."

"Why aren't *you* far away? You'd escaped. And then…you came back."

"I couldn't leave my sister under the control of a man like you."

Killien spun to face Will. "I have been nothing but generous to that woman. As has Lilit."

"She's lived as a slave her entire life because of you," Will flung at him. "And you're using her to control me. What happens if you suddenly latch on to the mad idea that she's a threat to the Morrow? Then anything's acceptable, right? You can suck the life out of her as a demonstration of your power, without a second thought."

"That man"—Killien slammed his hand down and shoved off the ledge, coming face to face with Will—"killed my father."

Rage burst up from somewhere old and chained, a place that had smoldered for twenty years. He leaned forward until his face almost touched Killien's.

"*You* killed mine." Will's heartbeat pounded in his head, almost drowning out every other sound. "You sent Vahe to sneak into my home like a coward."

Killien pushed him back and looked away dismissively. "And if you'd ever had the chance to kill me, you would have. Grand ideas of peace evaporate very quickly in the face of a chance to make your enemy pay."

The memory of Lilit on the floor of the stifling tent, her life bleeding out into the ground rushed into Will's mind. Her *vitalle* weak, dying like old embers.

Will thought of Killien's face, his desperation that night. "You're blind."

The Torch's face twisted in anger and he raised his sword.

"Killien." Sora sounded tired. "Stop acting like Will is something you know he's not."

Killien's sword froze and he turned toward her. He studied her for a long moment before letting out a harsh laugh. "It's all true, isn't it? You decided to help Will, and from that moment, everything he tried succeeded. He escaped me. He convinced Hal to help him." Killien raked his fingers through his hair. "He escaped a *dragon*."

The Torch shook his head and paced the room. Sora watched him, her face stony.

"I hadn't thought it was true, Sora, but you are actually blessed." He stopped in front of her, staring her in the face. "Until the night Lilit almost died, I doubted. But the cursed part is coming true too, isn't it?"

Sora's eyes hardened.

"You've come to care about Will." Killien considered Will for a long moment. "And here he is, at my mercy."

Will held his gaze. Beside him, Sora's breath quickened.

"I met hunters from your clan. They told me how you held the power of life and death. How you passed on judgment from the Serpent Queen to your people."

Will didn't need to open up towards Sora to recognize the fury growing in her.

Killien continued, his tone low and inexorable, "How being close to you was to court death… They told me about your little friend."

She flinched.

"They told me about your mother…"

Next to him, Sora's shoulders strained against her bonds as she stared at the floor.

"I didn't believe them. It took me a long time to see what you really are," Killien said, his voice dripping with disgust.

"Sora," Will said.

She kept her face down, her shoulders drawn in.

"Sora, please look at me."

She turned enough that she could just meet his eyes.

"He doesn't see you," Will said, leaning forward to hold her gaze. "There's no truth to what he's saying. He only sees what he wants."

"On the contrary, Will." Killien leaned back, satisfied. "I think I'm truly seeing her for the first time. I should thank you, Sora, for keeping yourself so distant from the people in my clan. And from me."

She closed her eyes and started to turn away.

"I see you, Sora," Will said, and she twitched to a stop.

She stood frozen. He could see her brow drawn and her lips pressed together. She stared at the ground, her face hollow.

"I see you," he repeated. "You are intelligent and strong and independent and kind." She didn't move. "And a little bossy."

She twitched at the word, a flicker of surprise crossing her face, clearing out the haunted look.

"There is no power that controls you and kills those you love. It's not the truth. It's just people grasping for power."

A spark of anger kindled in her eyes.

"You didn't go to Lilit because some distant goddess made you, you went for the same reason I did, because she was dying. You knew there was nothing you could do, but you went anyway, because of your own humanity."

Sora met his gaze. Her brow was drawn, but there was a resolve in her eyes.

"She's cursed!" Killien spat the words at them.

"Don't be stupid." Will was suddenly exhausted by everything. "And leave Sora alone. Your fight's with me."

Outrage flashed over Killien's features. "She betrayed me!" He lifted his blade to point at her. "After everything I did for you for three years, you helped Will escape. You helped him steal from me."

She stepped forward until the sword pressed against her neck. "*You* betrayed *me*. You took what I told you, the thing I hated most, and you used it against me." Her face was a mask of fury. "I told you the truth. I have no powers. I did nothing."

"Lilit was dying," Killien flung back at her. "If you have no powers, what saved my wife?"

Sora pressed against the blade, forming the next word slowly. "Will."

Killien's eyes flicked to Will, drawing the sword back slightly.

"I did nothing but pray that the Serpent Queen would take her quickly." Sora's eyes burned with hatred at him. "I told you there was *nothing* I could do. But Will stopped her bleeding. Your wife lives because of him."

Killien cast a harsh glance at Will. "Is this true?"

Will stared at him without answering.

"If it had depended on me," Sora said. "Lilit would have bled out onto the ground."

"Why?" Killien's voice was still harsh, his blade still at Sora's throat.

"Because she was dying." Will wanted to shake the man.

Killien kept his sword at Sora's neck, but his eyes shifted to Will.

"Because Sora wanted to, but couldn't. And I could." He paused, the chaos of the night coming back to him. Killien kneeling on the ground, desperate. "Also, because I believed we were friends."

Killien took a step backwards, his head shaking back and forth, his face a turmoil of anger and uncertainty.

"Lilit knows it's true," Sora said.

Killien dropped his sword to his side and he turned toward the window. A goblin screeched far below.

"You have to stop this, Killien," Will said. "Call off the goblins. Your father strove to bring peace to the Sweep. You're…"

Killien's face darkened.

Will searched again for the face he knew, but instead of finding intelligence and discernment, he saw only something raw and feral. Killien wore the same leathers. The same collection of gems glittered in rune-covered rings. But he found nothing familiar in his face.

Will felt unmoored. Like a leaf torn off the branch and tossed into the swirling winds. How could he talk to a man he didn't know at all?

"You can't convince me to be like you," Killien said.

"I'm not trying to. I'm trying to convince you to act on what you already believe."

The door to the room opened and Lukas stepped in, his customary scowl replaced by a look of satisfaction, wiping a needle-thin dagger with a cloth spattered with blackish-green stains. Sora stiffened and shifted slightly to face him.

Will's breath caught in his throat. For an instant, in Lukas's face he saw all the possibilities of what Lukas could have been. Raised by his family, brought to the Keepers, trained to use his powers. He'd have lived at the Stronghold for the last fifteen years.

A gaping void opened up inside Will. Lukas would have been another Alaric, another brother.

Lukas hesitated, taking in the room and his knuckles whitened on the handle of the knife. Will had always hated the grey slave's tunics, but the sight of it now was like a stab in the gut. Lukas should have been wearing a black Keeper's robe. Lukas stepped forward, his jarring limp a symbol of the life he must have lived. Unlike Ilsa, Lukas must remember everything. They took him when he was eleven. He knew what he'd lost.

Guilt churned in Will's stomach.

The Keepers should have known. He'd known twenty years ago wayfarers were taking children, and yet he'd done nothing. It should have been Will in Lukas's town, not Vahe. It should have been the Keepers who found him and protected him. The wrongness, the failure was so foundational and so permanent, Will shrank back.

He couldn't help feeling that he had utterly failed this man. The Keepers had utterly failed him.

"Killien," Lukas said, all traces of servitude gone from him, "it seems you're being haunted by a Keeper."

He tossed the damp rag into a corner and shoved the knife into a sheath at his belt, limping toward Killien, grimacing tightly at each step. Will's eyes were fixed on him, each step tearing something out of him. "It is done."

"Good." Killien showed no surprise at the slave's demeanor. Lukas set one hand on Killien's shoulder and blew out a short breath, pressing his eyes shut, the grimace draining off his face.

Will opened his mouth to say something, but no words came. Lukas glanced at Will with an expression of hatred.

"The bulk of the goblins should be here by now," Lukas said, stretching to see out the window.

"Call them off," Will said. "Stop the massacre, Killien."

It was Lukas who answered, "This isn't Queensland where you mindlessly follow your queen. On the Sweep power goes to the strong. Those frost goblins are crippling the powerful clans. In a few hours the balance of the Sweep will shift to the Morrow."

"In a few hours," Killien corrected him, "every clan will have a voice."

Irritation flickered across Lukas's face, but he said nothing.

"And thousands of Roven, who want nothing more than to return home to their families," Will said, taking a half step forward, "will be dead."

"Let me guess, Keeper." Lukas's mouth twisted in contempt at the word. "You're against fighting."

"No. In fact, I'd gladly join any fight on the side of the oppressed."

"We are the oppressed, Will." Killien threw the words at him. "The Sunn and the Boan demand our barley, our herds, our warriors, and all under the threat of annihilation. We are the ones fighting the oppressors."

"You were," Will said, his frustration boiling up into anger. "And you wanted to fight back with ideas that could actually change the Sweep. But now that you have power, you've become one of them. And today if I want to fight the oppressor, I have to fight you."

"Oppressor? The night the Panos attacked we caught them trying to steal my son." The raw, feral look in his eye caught at Will like claws raking into his chest.

A man poised over a child—the image loosed a deluge of anguish and fury.

In that moment he recognized what he saw in Killien's face— the same hatred Will had carried for years. It hadn't started as hatred. It had begun with the terror that someone he loved was being hurt. But that terror gnawed down deep enough that it took root, and a savage hatred grew.

It wasn't the foreignness of the hatred in Killien that was so terrible. It was how profoundly Will recognized it.

The mirrored feelings in himself clawed their way to the surface, and he wanted desperately to push them away, to close himself off to Killien. But he couldn't ignore how much he understood them. Instead of pushing it all away, he faced it.

"I know what you want," Will whispered. "I know the terror and the guilt."

Killien's face grew hard and savage.

"And I know the hatred that grows from it."

"They *must* pay."

The words rang true and familiar. Killien's eyes glittered with a new sort of ferocity, and Will stopped keeping that at a distance, stopped looking for what he wanted to find in the man. "You want to rip away everything they love."

Something vulnerable joined the viciousness in Killien's expression, opened it up. Will grasped for that opening, letting his own rawness meet Killien's.

"You want to rip it all away and make him watch it bleed out on the ground." Killien's desire to control the frost goblins blazed up in Will, and he knew that hunger. He wanted the chance to release them on Vahe, tear the man apart.

Except, of course, it couldn't end with Vahe. Will followed the hatred in himself forward to Killien and the fire faded.

"At least you want to, until you ride over the Sweep with him, and learn who he is."

Killien's jaw clenched.

"He talks of things you love. He's married to a woman and every time she is near he's useless for anything else. He has friends who respect him, a clan that needs his leadership, and a son who needs a father."

Killien's eyes stayed fixed on Will.

"But there's more than that. Somewhere along the way you realize you understand him. You recognize the things about him that you respect as things you strive for yourself. And you recognize the darkness in him too, because the same anger has lived for decades inside of you, demanding to be recognized.

"One day you realize that a Keeper from Queensland and a Roven Torch aren't foreign to each other. Then the hatred starts to cool into something different. Something more complicated. And you're left with…more than you had. A tangle of things that feels like anger and failure, but also friendship."

The Torch shifted almost imperceptibly, but Lukas's face blackened further. Sora stood perfectly still.

"It has its own form of pain. A more internal, digging pain. And it's so tempting to go back to the hatred. But the new place is more…true. And the only reason you want to go back is that it's easier just to hate. But when you can look at it honestly, you know the hatred's killing you, and killing any hope that the future could be different."

Lukas's hand clenched on Killien's shoulder. "You know nothing of hatred."

Will took in Lukas's furious face and found he had no words to answer him with. "If you don't stop, Killien, the future will not be different. The clans will strike back. Sevien will never be safe. Lilit will never be safe. The others will regain their strength and they will destroy the Morrow."

"They deserve this." Lukas's tone held an unexpected authority.

Killien spoke in a hoarse whisper. "They have so much blood on their hands."

"They do," Will agreed. "But until today, you didn't."

"Until today we didn't have the chance," Lukas said.

"The Torches are here," Will continued. "Let this be the time when a Roven could have overwhelmed with force, but instead offered peace."

Killien turned away from the window. A shadow lay on his face, but also a clarity Will hadn't seen in ages.

He took another step forward, a bit of hope kindling. "Call off the goblins, Killien."

The frenzied screech of the goblins rose and fell, slipping between the rushing sound of the wind.

"I can't."

"Yes, you can," Will said. "You obviously have a frost goblin you've used to call the others. Just change what it believes. Convince it there's a vast mountain of metal far to the north. Let it spread that idea to the rest."

The Torch shook his head. "You don't understand. I *can't*. When we give a goblin the idea of all that metal, it goes mad."

Sora let out a long, defeated breath. "You had to kill it."

Killien nodded. "The only goblin I had is dead."

FORTY-SEVEN

Sora let out a long breath that was half growl, and stalked toward Killien.

The Torch raised his sword and Will's heart lurched in his chest. Killien held the blade only a handbreadth away from her neck, his eyes fixed warily on her.

"Untie me."

Killien stared at her for a moment, his face growing incredulous. "No."

She leveled him with a look that was all too familiar to Will. "You want to stop this," she stated, and Will knew she was using a great deal of restraint to not call Killien an idiot.

Killien's eyes narrowed at her words, but the tip of his blade wavered.

Sora blew out a short, irritated breath. "It's going to be harder for me to catch another goblin if I'm tied up."

"Back away from the Torch." Lukas pointed the thin knife at Sora.

Far more than Killien's blade, Lukas's face was so dark that a dart of terror stabbed into Will and he stepped up next to her.

"You can't go catch a goblin," Will said. "There are too many of them."

Sora ignored both Lukas and Will and kept her eyes fixed on Killien. "Untie me."

Killien still didn't move, his face unreadable. "Why should I trust you?"

"I have always told you the truth," Sora said. "I didn't leave you because of Will. You and I were done the night Lilit almost died. I told you that then."

"Back away from the Torch!" Lukas repeated, his voice harsher.

Sora turned a scathing look on him. "Are *you* going to catch another goblin?"

"We don't *want* to catch one." A thin smile pulled up one side of Lukas's mouth. "Everything is going exactly as we planned."

An idea whispered into Will's mind. Lukas stood next to Killien, shoulder to shoulder, and Killien didn't object. The slave's shirt was grey, but for the first time Will realized it was a disguise.

Lukas had lived with Killien for most of his life. Killien had taught him to read, taught him how to use the skills that the Keepers should have taught him. Lukas was always well dressed, rode one of Killien's horses, stood at the Torch's side, ate next to him, lived with him. Even if he hadn't wanted to be so close to the Torch, the pain in his hip would have kept them close. Lukas was part of every one of Killien's plans.

To Lukas, Killien wasn't his owner—he was his equal.

The understanding shifted everything. Lukas's face was bleak, and Will realized this discussion wasn't just with Killien.

"Every moment you wait," Will said, keeping his eyes fixed on Lukas, "more Roven are dying. More hatred is growing and the chance for the Morrow to live in peace is growing dimmer."

"You don't understand, do you?" Lukas said. "With every moment the Morrow grow more powerful and it is our enemies who grow dimmer. We finally have the power we need."

Lukas's face was determined, almost victorious, but out of the corner of his eye, Will caught the hesitation in Killien's. Lukas stood shoulder to shoulder with Killien, and hadn't even noticed that Killien had already surrendered.

The Torch nodded to Sora and she turned around.

"What are you doing?" Lukas demanded.

With a quick slice, her ropes were cut. Sora ran across the room and grabbed her knives off the floor. Will took a step after her, pulling at his own ropes, his mind scrambling for some way to help her, but she slipped out the door. Lukas's fingers dug into Will's shoulder, pulling him back.

Will pulled toward the door. "You can't let her go alone."

"Sora always does everything alone," Killien answered with a short laugh, walking back to the window and looking down at the fighting below. "Whatever it is you two have going on, you must know her enough to know that."

Will let Lukas pull him back a step. "Nothing had better happen to her."

"What could possibly happen? She's only running into an army of goblins," Lukas said. "We should send you with her. Solve both our problems at once."

Will ignored his words. "We should be ready when she gets back. Do you need to make a new stone? Or can you reuse the last one?"

Lukas gave him an incredulous look. "We're not actually going to do it."

"Let him go," Killien said tiredly.

Lukas's hand didn't loosen.

"Let him go." Killien sounded more firm. "And get a new compulsion stone ready."

Lukas stood perfectly still. "Why?"

"Will is right." The calm in Killien's voice barely hid the anger. "If the Sweep is going to change, it has to be done differently than this. We'll call off the goblins, give the clans time to realize that they aren't the only ones with power. And then, if I haven't already ruined it, we'll find ways to build peace."

When Lukas still didn't move, Killien leveled an unbending expression. "Let him go."

Lukas shoved Will away. With a dangerous look at Lukas, Killien came over to Will and cut his ropes.

"Get the stone," the Torch commanded harshly.

Lukas wrenched the door open and turned down the hall.

Will rubbed at the skin on his wrists where the ropes had rubbed. Killien moved back to the window, his shoulders stiff.

"It's the right choice," Will said.

Killien stood unmoving, his jaw clenched. Every line in his body hummed with anger and Will felt a hint of loss that the man he'd talked to on the journey north seemed to be gone.

"What changed?" Will asked. "When did you stop looking for peaceful ways to change the

Sweep?"

Killien didn't turn around. "I got tired of doing nothing and feeling helpless. My father's plans for peace got him killed, and mine almost did the same." He scrubbed his fingers through his hair and let out a growl of frustration. "I'm so angry at all of it. So tired of the Morrow being weak."

"They certainly weren't weak today."

Killien leaned on the windowsill, looking out. "And it just made us more enemies."

"Yes, but you got their attention. Killien, you flew on a *dragon*."

Killien glanced over his shoulder at Will and a small smile flashed across his face. "You saw that?"

In spite of everything, Will let out a small laugh. "It was impressive."

Killien grinned and for a moment looked like himself. "It was…like a dream. The power in his wings, the Sweep spread out below like a rug, covering hill after hill. We flew over this mountain." He flung his hand toward the ceiling. "Over it! It was icy cold and the wind almost ripped me off. But mostly it was…so removed from everything. Somehow from up there the Sweep felt small, the clans so close to each other, they seemed like one group. The idea of a unified Sweep felt…possible."

"Maybe it is possible."

Lukas pushed the door open and came back in, carrying a light blue stone on a long chain. It was small enough to fit in Lukas's palm and shaped like an irregular, broken column.

"Put in it the idea of metal far north in the mountains," Killien ordered him. "And make the desire for it so strong they'll have no choice but to go."

Lukas shook his head quickly. "We can't do this. If we give up the power now, they'll destroy us."

"The power isn't what's important." Killien's anger flared again. "Be ready when Sora comes."

"No." Lukas's jaw was set stubbornly. "Negotiate with the other Torches once you own the Sweep. This power is all that will keep us safe."

"Lukas." The note of command rang through the room.

"Killien, this is our chance. If we stop now the Morrow go back to being worthless and helpless."

"The Morrow," Killien said coldly, "have never been worthless or helpless. This path will see us all killed. Will is right. My father knew that. I knew it before…I forgot it."

Lukas's eyes tightened at the words. "One Keeper shows up and the Torch of the Morrow rolls over like a coward?"

Will opened up a sliver toward Lukas and a churning mass of anger rushed into his chest. Frustration shoved its way through and Will clenched his jaw in an effort to push the emotions back. There was nothing servile.

Killien took a step toward Lukas, his hand on his sword hilt. When he spoke, it was deadly quiet. "You forget your place."

The sharp slice of betrayal Lukas felt cut through Will's chest, and fury laced with fear bled out of it.

"My *place*?"

"Ready the stone," Killien commanded.

The fissure in Lukas split open, pouring out a cold isolation. Betrayal clawed up from deep in the bowels of Lukas's soul, looming over him, shadowing him with black, rending isolation.

Will shoved Lukas's emotions out, slamming himself shut. "Killien," he warned.

Lukas's face hardened into a mask. "You do it." He tossed the bluestone and Killien caught it by the chain.

"This is not the time," Killien snapped. "I need your support."

"No," Lukas flung back. "You need mindless obedience."

"You owe me that!" Killien roared.

Lukas froze.

"You were *nothing*. I gave you everything. I taught you to read, to use your powers, treated you like family."

"Until the time comes when I act like I am," Lukas said coldly. "And then you prove that all I am is a slave."

Killien's hand clenched the chain. "Fix the stone."

Lukas let out a harsh breath, somewhere between a growl and a laugh. "Get your Keeper to do it."

The Torch stared daggers into Lukas for a long moment. Then he held the stone out to Will.

"I don't know if I can," Will said. With a surge of frustration, he realized Alaric probably could.

His fingers closed around the stone and a buzz of energy rushed into his hand, like he'd grabbed a bees' nest. His hand clamped around the stone and the sensation flowed up his arm. It rushed into his chest like water bursting through a dam.

Yes, Alaric was the Keeper who needed to be here. Or any other Keeper for that matter. It was time Will accepted the idea that he was an utterly mediocre person. Which made him a pathetic Keeper. The words that had always felt painful, now felt…right. They were true. These sorts of heroic things were for other people. It was nice to acknowledge that. Liberating even.

The buzzing from the stone continued, and for a single, panicked moment Will recognized the rush of emotion from that compulsion stone Hal had put around his neck days ago to exhaust him, but this was so much stronger.

But then the world flattened to dullness. The walls of the room were lifeless. The anger on Killien's face was petty and worn. Lukas's petulance was wearisome. The rush of the wind and the occasional noises from the window felt distant and unimportant. Nothing was important.

Will sank to his knees. The aquamarine was important. It was warm beneath his fingers. He wrapped his other hand around it, too, and the hum of energy surged into his fingers. His fingers glided over a facet of the stone as smooth as ice. He ran his thumb over a corner and the sharp edge scraped across his skin. A trace of light swirled inside the gem. Not filling it, just swirling in the bottom like molten stone. He tilted the stone and watched the light flow down to the other end slowly, like sluggish water.

There were voices somewhere, but he ignored them. He curled forward, trying to shadow the stone and see the light better.

A rough hand shook his shoulder and Killien's face was in front of him asking something. The Torch's face was so intense. All this intensity and scheming was so wearisome. Will ducked down, turning away from the Torch, holding the aquamarine closer to his face.

Killien tried to peel his fingers off of the stone, but when he touched it, he yanked his hand back. "What did you put in this compulsion stone?"

"Just a healthy dose of apathy," Lukas answered.

A slap on his cheek snapped Will's head to the side, and color rushed into the room along with the sound of the wind.

"Let go!" Killien's face was only inches away.

Sitting on the floor felt wrong.

Behind Killien, Lukas stood with his arms crossed, smiling. Will blinked to clear his head. Sora was coming back soon. They need to get ready for…something.

Killien shouted at him again, but what the Torch didn't understand, was that it didn't matter. The sludgy light had made it to the other end of the blue stone, and Will tipped it back the other way.

Lukas sounded terribly far away. "Let the Keeper rot."

FORTY-EIGHT

"We need to get back to the enclave." Lukas's voice was faint as he turned toward the door. "The other Torches are ripe for picking. If the fat fool Albech gives us any trouble, I have one more absorption stone. It'll be harder to fit it over Albech's fat head than it was over Ohan's." His voice took on a twang of regret. "I'd wanted to use it on Will, but I think it'd be put to better use in destroying the Boan Torch."

"Stop," Killien snapped. He clenched his fists, visibly trying to control his anger. "You're not the Torch."

Lukas froze, turning slowly to look at Killien with incredulous eyes.

Will wanted to tell them it would be easy if they just decided not to care. But it was too much work to talk. The world was dreary. Even the usually glittering gems in Killien's rings were dull.

Killien turned his back on Lukas. "Get the right stone for the goblin." He bit off the words sharply. "Now."

Lukas's body tightened and Will started to turn back to his aquamarine.

Lukas slid the thin knife out of his belt.

The movement caught at Will's mind, demanding attention. He shoved at the feelings of apathy crowding into him. Killien was still talking, chastising Will to drop the stone. Lukas continued forward, his face twisted into a silent snarl. He raised the knife.

"If you're willing to give up the power we've gained and let all of us be killed," Lukas said, his voice chilled with contempt, "you shouldn't be Torch either."

Will dragged a word up his throat. "Killien—"

The Torch looked at Will just as the knife plunged down into his back. Killien arched away from it, but Lukas drove the knife in deeper. Killien's hands clamped onto Will's arm. His eyes unfocused, and he toppled to the floor.

Will stared, his hands clenching the stone. Shock shoved against the apathy and he leaned toward Killien.

"I'm not giving up everything we've earned." Lukas pulled out the blade and wiped it on Killien's sleeve before shoving it back in its sheath. Crossing to the shelves, he picked up a small, stoppered bottle. He dumped out some dried leaves and sank down on the floor behind Killien. His face was hard, but something in his eyes tore at Will.

"Did you know," Lukas said to Killien, his words muffled and dull, "that your ability to nullify magic is carried in your blood? The night of the goblin attack, when you were cut, some of your blood landed on me. It was as though I was touching you. I felt no pain at all. Even when the blood dried it still worked almost as well as you do."

Will shoved frantically at the apathy inside him, but there was simply too much of it.

Lukas pushed the bottle against Killien's back and a thin moan escaped the Torch, the noise cutting through Will's mind. Lukas's face was drawn, but when he spoke, it was clear. "So I don't need you anymore. All I need is your blood."

Will squeezed his eyes shut and listened to the frantic part of himself. There was something about Sora, something important.

Lukas shoved a stopper into the little jar and tucked it into his pocket. "Do you know how long I've dreamed of separating your powers from you? Of bottling them up and leaving this wretched land?"

Separate. Bottle up. That was it. Sora shoved her emotions away until they didn't affect her. She kept them so tightly controlled Will couldn't even find them half the time.

He pulled himself away from the emotions for a moment, searching out their edges, feeling for the shape of them.

He pressed the apathy out his arms, shoved it back down toward the stone. Color crept into the room again.

Logically he knew he should put down the stone, but he couldn't quite cut through the deadness inside him.

Beside him, Killien lay pale, his eyes closed and his breathing shallow. Lukas leaned out the window, looking not down at the Sweep, but up into the sky. He stayed there for a moment, before turning back to the room. His gaze fell on Killien, and he clenched his jaw.

"I used to think Keepers were some sort of magical beings that knew everything. They had everything under control. They protected us." Lukas opened his hand and a faded red scar filled his palm. "Vahe triggered it. He sent that fire out over the heads of the crowd and everything inside of me…woke up.

"That's when I knew I would be a Keeper. I just wanted to run home and tell my mother, begging her to take me to Queenstown. I tried to get my brothers to come with me, but they weren't ready to leave, so I went myself."

Lukas closed his fist. "Vahe found me before I'd gone far."

He walked slowly back towards Will. "My mother wouldn't find me, not tied up in Vahe's wagon. But a Keeper…I knew a Keeper would come. I believed it until we crossed the Scales and everything disappeared except the grass." His eyes dug into Will. "For years, I waited for you to come."

A deep guilt writhed through the apathy inside Will.

"Then Sini came…And still no Keepers." His face twisted in disgust. "Sini! If anyone deserves a life of happiness, it's that girl. But they took her, too. At first, I thought you weren't coming because you were angry, because we'd begun to learn a sort of magic that the Keepers wouldn't like. But it was worse than that, wasn't it?"

Lukas's eyes searched Will's face. "You didn't even know we were gone."

Something sank into Will's gut, taking his breath away with it. He dropped his gaze to the floor.

"I believed all the lies about you," Lukas said quietly.

A complicated twist of emotions tore through the apathy and Will yanked one hand off the stone, reaching for Lukas. "If we had known—"

Lukas batted his hand away. "Now that I've met a Keeper, I know I was foolish to think they were anything but arrogant, useless men."

Will's hand dropped to the floor.

Lukas leaned over Killien and unfastened the sheath from around his chest. He slid the seax out a handbreadth and touched it with his fingertips. A grim smile crossed his face and he shoved it back into the sheath and slung it across his back. "I don't think I'll soil the seax with your blood." His gaze rested on Killien, and his jaw clenched. "This is not how I wanted things to go with Killien. I thought he could remember his anger at being controlled and make the decision to take what he needed. I had thought that together we might..." He blew out a breath and straightened. "His death is regrettable. But you, Will...I doubt I'll ever think of you again."

Will needed to move, but the part of him waking up was so small.

A voice rang in his ear. It reminded him of Sora.

Sora.

A wave of relief washed over him. She would come in and...do whatever needed to be done. Because something needed to be done, Will just couldn't pinpoint exactly what.

Lukas unsheathed his knife, his face filled with pure hatred, and Will knew it was coming. In a moment he'd be next to Killien, dying. The Torch lay still, his face grey. Will's mind recognized the wrongness of it, that he was going to be killed by a man who should have been like a brother. But there wasn't room for actually feeling it.

He dragged his gaze to the door, waiting for Sora to come and fix things.

"Why couldn't you be what you should have been?" Lukas asked in a ragged whisper.

Sora was too late. There was no one here to help. The truth flashed into his mind like a flare of light.

He was going about this all wrong. He wasn't Sora. She stuffed emotions away. He let others' emotions resonate within himself so that he could see them. Understand who they actually were. And recognize how much he was like them.

The apathy from the stone still filled him until he thought he might burst with the emptiness of it. He looked past it to his own emotions that had been shoved aside. The bright fear of the knife, the murky shame of what Lukas had been through, the hollow grief that Killien was lying so still on the floor next to him.

He latched onto the grief, and it was for so much more than Killien. It was still there for things long ago. His father. How his mother grieved for her husband and her daughter. The grief he'd carried so long for Ilsa. Even now, there was still a mourning for the years lost to knowing her.

It was his own grief and for the space of a heartbeat, focusing on it rolled the apathy back, making just enough room to open up to Lukas.

The little room left in him filled with bitterness and loss and guilt, a sharp ribbon of fear, and a fresh wound of loneliness.

And Will recognized every bit of it deep in himself.

"Lukas." He barely managed a whisper. "I see you, what you've been through. It shouldn't have happened. Any of it. But you can come back from all these things that are trying to consume you."

"You know nothing," Lukas hissed.

"I know about being alone." So much churned within Will, that he wanted nothing more than to shove it all out. But he sorted through it, gathering his own emotions bit by bit. Disappointment with himself over the sort of Keeper he was, the ever present loneliness he felt, the old, worn in anger at his father's death and Ilsa's abduction. "I know that something can happen that we don't deserve, and it can break *everything*." He gathered all the emotions and pushed them toward Lukas, letting him feel all of it.

Lukas's eyes widened, then he shrank back. "Get out of me!"

"You're not alone," Will whispered. He pulled everything back from Lukas. "It's not too late, Lukas."

"It *is* too late." Lukas's face was set in a dark look. "You don't know me."

Will felt a pang of sadness for how often he'd seen him that way. "What about Sini?"

Lukas flinched.

"She told me you're like an older brother who's always taken care of her."

For a fraction of a breath something gentle crossed Lukas's face. But then he shoved it away.

"The best thing that could happen to Sini," Lukas answered, "is that she grows up far away from me." He raised the knife and plunged the knife toward Will's chest.

Will twisted away and the knife bit deep into his shoulder.

Pain exploded in Will's arm, ripping through the apathy of the stone. Will's fingers spasmed open and the aquamarine clattered across the floor.

"Will!"

This time it really was Sora, standing in the doorway, her arms clamped around a thrashing frost goblin. Behind her Alaric and Evangeline ran into the room.

Douglon pushed past them, puffing. "Our way out is not an option any longer."

"The goblins are pouring into the cave—" Alaric stopped, taking in Killien, Lukas, and Will.

Lukas yanked the knife out. Pain shot down Will's arm and snaked across his chest. He grabbed his shoulder.

Lukas rose. The room stood still for a moment before the dwarves let out a yell and thundered across the room. Lukas fixed them with a look of pure fury, then turned and ran for the window.

"Stop him!" Sora yelled.

Douglon lunged after him and Will heaved himself up. But Lukas reached the wall, scrambled up into the window and threw himself out.

Will reached the window just as a flash of glittering red raced by. With the whip of his tail, Anguine rose into the sky, the grey form of Lukas clinging to his back.

FORTY-NINE

Douglon barreled up next to Will, scrambling toward the window and watching Lukas and Anguine fly southeast across the Sweep.

"Dragons," he grumbled.

Will sank against the wall, his shoulder throbbing. The room erupted in chaos. Ilsa yanked a door open and ran across the room, falling to her knees next to Killien crying out for someone to help. Patlon and Sora wrestled with the frost goblin, trying to get ropes around its limbs. Evangeline slammed the door to the hall closed, calling for something to barricade it with.

Alaric ran toward Will shouting question after question.

Will disregarded them all. "Help Killien, if you can."

He sank down next to the Torch and cast out towards him. Killien's body lay still. The little *vitalle* left in him sluggishly seeping out of the wound on his back. Will tried to gather some energy when Alaric knelt down next to him.

"You're in no condition. Move over."

Will nodded and sank back.

"Please help him," Ilsa whispered.

Alaric glanced up and his attention caught on her face, but he only nodded and then set his hands on Killien's shoulder and bowed his head. After a long moment he met Will's gaze and shook his head.

"He needs to live, Alaric," Will said. "He'd be an ally on the Sweep."

"The man who rode a dragon and sucked the life out of his enemy?"

Will paused. "You met him on a bad day."

Alaric's eyebrows rose. "What do his good days look like?"

"On those, he might be able to get the Roven to quit fighting. Maybe even reconcile the Sweep and Queensland."

Alaric looked skeptically down at Killien. The Torch's shoulder barely moved with shallow breaths, the ground behind him soaked with blood. Ilsa knelt behind him, tears on her face, pressing a rag to the wound.

"He's lost too much *vitalle*," Alaric said quietly.

"Give him some of mine," Will offered, holding out his hand.

Alaric waved his hand at Will's blood-soaked arm. "You don't have enough. None of us has enough—" He stopped.

"Whatever you're thinking," Will whispered, "do it."

Alaric shook his head, his face stricken.

"Alaric, please."

Alaric let out a long breath. He swung his bag off his shoulder and pulled out the swirling orange stone Killien had used to kill the Torch of the Panos.

"Is that still Ohan?"

Alaric shook his head. "Who we are isn't held in our *vitalle*. It's something more…intrinsic to us. What was Ohan is gone. This is just some of the energy that animated him. There isn't enough here to bring back Ohan, but there may be enough to save Killien."

Alaric rolled Killien onto his back and set the stone on his chest. Then, closing his eyes, he set his hands on Killien and tendrils of orange light snaked out of the stone. Ilsa gasped and pulled her hands back. Douglon stood behind her, watching Alaric with an unreadable face.

Evangeline called for help and the dwarf blinked. She stood with her back pressed to the door. "They're coming!"

Douglon ran to one of the tables along the back of the room and pushed it toward the door.

"Goblins are swarming into the caves," he said to Will. "The dragon flew off." He nodded towards the window. "Now we know why. And goblins poured into the tunnels from somewhere down below. We thought it might be time to gather you up and go. Which is when we found Sora fighting three of them, hollering about not killing one." He shoved the table against the wall and stomped back for another. "I assume this means you have some sort of plan."

Will glanced over to where Sora and Patlon had succeeded in tying up the goblin. The creature lay squirming on the floor, making a hoarse screeching sound. "We did."

Patlon went to help Douglon and Evangeline barricade the door. Will left Alaric to heal Killien and walked over to Sora. She grabbed a cloth from a nearby shelf, wrapped it around Will's shoulder.

"Do we have the stone we need to control the goblin?" she asked.

Will shook his head.

Sora pressed her eyes for a moment. With a tired sigh, she drew the knife out of her pocket and turned toward the goblin.

"Wait."

She glanced back at him. "They're pouring into the caves. This one will only draw more to us."

The goblin lay on the floor, pounding its bare, bony feet against the stone, eyes wide and feral. Its thin, wiry arms strained against the ropes, its leathery greyish-green skin scraped and raw from rubbing against it.

Will sank down next to the creature and the goblin twisted toward him. Sharp yellow teeth gnashing near his arm. Sora knelt down, pinning it with a knee to its chest.

Will opened up toward it. A howling mass of hunger and anger rushed into him. Nothing defined, nothing nuanced. It was an animal, less complex than even Talen. It was consumed with a driving hunger and…something else.

Above it he felt Sora's tightly controlled fear.

Will reached out to touch the goblin's arm. The creature hissed and squealed, but Will wrapped his hand around the loose, leathery skin.

He needed to send them back into the mountains. He'd sent Talen places by imagining a picture. But it felt more complicated than that with the goblins. Talen's mind was calm and focused.

The goblin before him was savage, and Will had no idea what the mountains looked like where the goblins were from.

Will closed his eyes against the goblin's thrashing. Almost everything was hunger. Gnawing, consuming hunger. He tasted the tang of metal on his tongue and it drove an insatiable need to possess it. Will tried to swallow the taste away and dove deeper into the hunger, searching for the anger he'd felt. Maybe he could redirect it.

He found the thread of the anger and focused on it. This wasn't one goblin's anger at being bound. This was a communal anger at…being controlled.

The goblins knew what Killien had done. They knew they were here not because they'd chosen to be, but because someone had forced them. And it was unraveling them.

Dimly he heard crashing and shouts from the door.

"Will." Sora pressed the goblin down. "Could you commune a little faster?"

"Shh."

Will focused on the anger. How could he change it? The goblin in front of him felt angry and desperate.

And hot.

Will caught the one emotion he'd missed.

The goblin didn't want to be here. The feeling was so familiar he'd passed over it as his own. The frost goblin was in a place it didn't want to be.

A loud crack came from the door and the mass of tables in front of it shifted. Long green fingers rooted through a gap in the door, scrabbling against the wood.

"Whatever you are doing," Sora hissed at him, "you are out of time."

Her words scattered the idea growing in his mind. "Stop talking!"

"Me stop talking?" Her voice was indignant. "I only talk when there's something important to—"

The door split with a long, tearing crack and a goblin wriggled through, clambering over tables. Patlon's axe swung down and the goblin collapsed on the table, but another took its place.

"I have to let go." Sora shifted her weight. "Don't let it bite you."

Will clamped his hand down on the goblin's arm just as Sora lunged off it and ran for the door. Pain ripped across the knife wound in his shoulder. The creature went mad, spinning and biting. Its teeth caught at the side of Will's pants and he shoved its head away. He grabbed the sides of the goblin's head, trying to still it enough that he could focus, but it was like trying to hold a thrashing fish—if the fish had thin pointed teeth and a great desire to eat him. Pain lanced through his shoulder and his hand loosened on the goblin's head. It twisted and bit into his arm.

A heavy weight fell onto the goblin's chest, pinning it down. It snapped its head toward the new foe, its teeth tearing across Will's arm. Hands pinned its chest down onto the floor and Will pulled back.

He looked up into Ilsa's face. She knelt on the creature, her face pale. Her terror echoed in his chest and he tried to shut her emotions out while still feeling the goblin's.

It took him a breath to find his voice. "Thank you."

Her eyes were wide with fear. "Whatever you're doing, hurry!"

Will dragged his attention back to the goblin. It wasn't the anger or the hunger he needed to work with.

He gripped the creature's arm and pulled out his own emotions. It was right there, the one he'd been living with for a year. The aching longing to go home. He thought of Queensland, trees, hills, farmland. The Stronghold, the library, the other Keepers. His mother's face that first moment when he showed up after being gone for too long.

He had found Ilsa. He could go home.

The yearning rolled through him like a wave, flattening everything else.

He let it grow until it filled him entirely, then he opened up toward the goblin and pushed the emotion toward him. Freedom to go home.

The goblin froze, its eyes wide and glazed. For a moment the longing warred with the hunger and the anger. Will pushed more of it in, letting it develop into its own sort of hunger for the familiar, the comfortable.

Will looked into Ilsa's terrified face. "Do you miss home?"

A flash of shock crossed her face and he let her longing pour into him, raw and frenzied. Will shoved her emotions toward the goblin, too.

The creature's anger dissolved, a wild freedom taking its place. In moments the craving for home was the only thing filling the creature.

It stopped straining to reach Will and stretched itself toward the window.

The door snapped and a wide gap opened. Greenish corpses were piling up inside the door, but more came every moment. Will cast out toward them feeling their hunger. But then one paused on its way through the door, a surge of homesickness filling it.

It snapped its attention to the window.

"Let it through!" Will yelled.

The dwarves and Sora paused, weapons raised. Sora stepped back and the goblin scuttled through the door, long, bony fingers grabbing the edge of a table as it scrambled over. It raced past, nails scraping on the stone floor, and clawed its way out the window.

Sora and the dwarves stepped back, leaving a clear path to the window. Goblin after goblin poured into the room, teeth and eyes glinting as they screeched and raced across the room.

Ilsa shrank back against the wall, and Will yanked at the knot holding the rope on the goblin in front of him, and threw himself over next to Ilsa. The creature thrashed itself loose and dove into the mass of goblins pouring out the window.

FIFTY

Two final goblins straggled through the room and outside. Will followed them to the window.

Down below the goblins that had been clawing their way through the Roven camp turned back on themselves like a school of fish and drained back into the gaping warrens. Hoping Rass was smart enough to stay out of the goblins' way, Will turned back to the room.

Killien groaned. Alaric had dragged him over against one of the walls, leaving a streak of blood across the floor. The last of a thin orange haze sank into the Torch's body. Killien's face had regained most of its color and he blinked slowly up at Alaric, scowling. Will came over and knelt next to him.

Killien reached a shaking hand toward Will. The moment Will touched the Torch's hand, a burning anger smoldered up in Will. He slammed himself shut, but the anger continued. He dropped Killien's hand and it faded.

A glint of blue caught his eye. The ring with the blue stones, the one Killien had taken from the traitor early in the trip north. The blue of the stone perfectly matched the aquamarine Will had just spent so long enthralled with. He reached out tentatively to touch it and the anger seeped back in.

Will twisted the ring off Killien's fingers and threw it into the corner. Killien stretched his hand, and started to take a deep breath, but cut it short with a grimace.

"What was that?" Killien looked up at Will, confused. His gaze traveled through the room and horror spread across his face. "What have I done?"

"How'd you get that ring?" Will asked.

"Lukas gave it to me," Killien said weakly. "Said it could hold magic and we should find a use for it." He shook his head, as though trying to clear cobwebs, and winced.

"It certainly held magic," Will said. "He turned the gems into compulsion stones to keep you angry. It looks like Lukas was against your plans to spread peace."

"That doesn't make sense." Killien's shook his head gingerly. "The stones wouldn't work on me—no magic works on me."

"If Lukas just used it to store emotions it would," Will answered. "He learned that emotions have their own resonance so once he created the anger in the ring, it wouldn't take any magic to transfer it to a person. The natural resonance of the emotions would do it for him. You just had to be touching it."

The Torch pressed his eyes shut. "The goblins...What have I done?" Killien breathed a long, defeated breath. He looked up at Will, stricken. "Ohan. I didn't mean to kill him...I was just going to threaten him. I..." He ran his hand over his face. "I couldn't hear anything inside of me but the anger."

The aquamarine Will had held for so long swirled with a light blue light from the floor. "I believe you."

Killien's eyes sank closed. "What have I done? I've ruined everything. I can't build peace on a murder and a goblin attack."

Will set his hand on the Torch's shoulder. "You have created a few more obstacles."

Killien opened his eyes and noticed Alaric. "Who are you?"

"This is Alaric," Will said. "Another bloodthirsty, evil Keeper."

Killien grunted. "The one I *should* have captured."

Alaric raised an eyebrow.

"Yes." Will picked up the now dark stone that had held Ohan's energy. "And the one who just saved your life. With this. Which feels...ironic."

Killien drew away from the stone. "You healed me with...Ohan?"

"It wasn't him anymore." Alaric's eyes glittered with an anger that surprised Will. "It was just the leftover energy that you didn't waste during the murder."

Killien stared at Alaric for a long moment. "So it's safe to say the healing wasn't a sign of friendship?"

"It was a sign of his friendship towards me," Will said, "not you. Alaric just saw you fly on a dragon, command an army of goblins, and kill a man in a way he's unusually sensitive to. You didn't make a great first impression."

Killien let his eyes slip closed again. "If you didn't want to save me, why did you?"

"Will seemed to think it was important. And I trust his judgment of people." Alaric pushed himself up to his feet, taking the empty stone and tucking it into his bag. "Even when I don't understand what he sees.

"And I didn't heal you, not completely. Your body won't let me. While you were weak I could pour energy into you, but the stronger you grew, the less you would let me. You're strong enough now that no magic is going to work on you. You're not going to die, but you still have a lot of healing to do."

Killien squinted up at Alaric. "Thank you."

Alaric walked across the room toward Evangeline without responding.

"You Keepers are complicated." He tilted his head and strained to look around the room. "Lukas?"

Will opened his mouth to answer, but couldn't decide what to say.

"Your man, Lukas, stabbed everyone he could, stole your sword, then flew away on your dragon," Douglon said, tossing some broken table pieces out of the way.

Killien grabbed for the strap that had held his scabbard on his back, but found nothing.

"How did he get the dragon?" Will asked. "I thought we took the compulsion stone off."

Alaric shrugged. "Maybe he had a second one?"

"So Lukas was prepared to escape on the dragon all this time?" Killien asked.

Douglon let out a snort. "People don't control dragons because they might need a quick escape. Dragons are for destruction. Who does Lukas hate?"

"Me," Killien said, his voice heavy. He pushed himself up to sit. "Obviously."

Douglon shook his head. "He already killed you. Who else?"

"Keepers," Will answered.

Douglon leveled an annoyed look at him. "So if I stay with you Keepers, I'm going to see that dragon again?" He shook his head and stumped back over towards where Sora and Patlon were clearing debris from the doorway. "I need different friends."

Killien shifted his shoulders, stretching his back. "I almost died, didn't I?"

"I thought you were dead." Will paused. "I couldn't put that compulsion stone down. I'm sorry. I wanted to, but…"

"You don't have to explain to me." Killien turned to the window. "I didn't think Lukas would…" He fell silent for a moment. "I trusted him."

"Do you…" Will paused, wondering if it were even possible now that Lukas was gone. "Do you want to know why he did it?"

Killien's attention snapped to Will. Interest warred with trepidation on his face, but he nodded hesitantly.

Will brought back the memory of Lukas's emotions and let the echo of the feelings fill him again. They came back surprisingly easy, and he opened himself up toward Killien, pushing the feelings toward him.

The sharp slice of betrayal. Fury and terror bleeding out.

The fissure split open and the cold isolation flooded him. Betrayal clawed up from the deep, shadowing him with black isolation.

Killien's breath tore out of him and he threw his hands over his face. Will closed himself off, letting the emotions fade until they were just a heart-breaking echo.

The others had cleared the broken tables away from the door. Alaric had found a stack of books and sat against the wall poring over them. Ilsa stood with her back to the wall, watching Killien and Will with a troubled expression.

"Ilsa."

Will jumped at Killien's voice, and Ilsa, after a short hesitation, came over to them.

"As far as I can tell," the Torch said to her, "Will really is your brother. What he told me matches what Vahe said."

"I know," she said quietly.

Will's heart clenched.

Her eyes flickered up to his face. "You were right about the doll. I had her until she fell apart." He opened his mouth to say something, but there was too much.

"Enjoy this," Sora said from behind him. "It's almost impossible to get Will to stop talking."

Ilsa laughed a short, nervous laugh. Her face, smiling like that, was so much like it had been when she was tiny, he couldn't breathe.

"What he'd like to say," Sora continued, "is that he's really happy to have found you. He's been looking for you for a very long time."

"Would you—" The words caught in Will's throat and he swallowed before trying again. "Would you like to come home?" At the flicker of uncertainty in her face, he added, "To Queensland."

"I believe your mother is still alive," Killien added.

Ilsa's gaze snapped to Will's face, and he nodded.

"She's always believed you'd come back."

"I think," said Ilsa, her voice wavering slightly, "I would like that."

Will wanted to smile, but something too big pushed up from his chest.

After a moment's silence, Sora stepped in front of him. "He's not always this awkward." She motioned toward the fireplace. "Let's gather some supplies while Will gathers his wits. And if you have the ability to make him speechless this often, you and I are going to spend a lot of time together."

"Speaking of going home," Douglon said, peering through the broken door, "it's probably time for us to do that. This is all very touching, but despite getting rid of goblins and a dragon, we're still not—" He stiffened and raised his axe, before muttering and pulling the door open.

Hal stepped in, stopping to take in the room and eyeing everyone warily. "The goblins are gone," he said to Killien, "but the Torches are getting restless. If you're going to talk to them it had better be soon. I don't know how long the freed slaves can keep them there, even if they are armed." He glanced around. "And you're going to lose any influence you had if you're caught with…" He gestured at the room.

Killien nodded and gingerly stood up, rolling his back muscles and grimacing slightly. Hal's face paled at the blood covering Killien's shirt, but the Torch waved it off.

"There's one more thing before we go," Will said to Killien. "Lukas should have been raised as a Keeper. Sini and Rett should have been too."

The Torch's eyes narrowed. "No."

The too-familiar frustration with Killien rose to the surface, and Will tried to keep his voice even. "What would have happened if the Panos had taken your son?"

Killien's face hardened, but there was an edge of panic in his eyes.

"Would he have been raised as a slave in their clan? Never going back to his own family? Never learning who he was or what his life should have been?"

Killien shook his head stubbornly. "You're not taking Sini and Rett. I have lost my book, my goblins, my *dragon*."

"The dragon was not my fault," Will protested.

"Really? Because it was firmly under my control."

"Oh, the stone. That part was us." Will glanced around at his companions. "You know, a few hours ago, I didn't think we had a chance at any of this."

Killien gave him a flat stare. "Yes, you've done very well."

"Sini and Rett should have the chance to go home."

"Rett won't remember what that means," Killien said, his face unreadable.

Will bit back the angry retort that came to mind and opened himself up the smallest bit to Killien. Grief blossomed in through the crack, faded and worn around the edges before he closed himself back off.

"Raina should have had the chance to go home, too," Will said.

Killien flinched at her name. "I know you think it's terrible that they're slaves, but they've been treated like family."

"Lukas thought he was family, that he was your equal. The truth that he wasn't is what finally turned him against you."

"I feel like they're family. Or something close to it." He looked up at Will. "What if they don't want to go with you?"

Will's chest tightened at the very real possibility. "Then they don't. The whole point is that they get to choose."

Killien studied him for a moment. "Hal, bring Sini and Rett here."

"You don't have time for this," Hal objected.

"Hal."

The huge man's nostrils flared in annoyance, and he walked out of the room.

"If Sini and Rett leave," Killien said, quietly enough that only Will heard, "the Morrow have lost everything."

"You still have everything that was rightfully yours," Will pointed out. "Now that Lukas isn't making you angry, maybe you can salvage the old ideas you had for peace."

"And what do I tell the Torches who just lost Roven to my goblin attack? Or the Panos Clan about Ohan. That my slave was controlling me?"

"I have no idea," Will said, "but you wanted the balance of power shaken, and you've definitely achieved that. The Morrow aren't the most powerful clan, but, in a rather belated fashion, you did choose peace over domination. And that's an idea the Sweep needs to keep hearing. You've gotten the attention of the Sweep. Now use it to say all the things you've always wanted to say."

"And if they don't listen?"

"Some of them won't. But some of them will, and it will be the start that you wanted."

Hal returned quickly with the others. Sini's eyes widened when she saw Will and Sora, and the sight of the dwarves made her step back against the towering form of Rett who set a protective hand on her shoulder. Alaric let the book sink into his lap, watching the two of them closely.

"Sini," Killien said, strained, "we've become infested with Keepers."

Sini's eyes flashed to Alaric.

"You know," the Torch started again, "if you'd stayed in Queensland…"

When he didn't continue, Will finished it for him. "You would have come to the Keepers, and we would have tested you to see what talents you have. And then, if you wanted to, you could have joined us. And Rett too." Will glanced at Killien. "Rett and Raina both would have come to us. And Lukas."

Sini's gaze darted around the room at Lukas's name. "He's gone," she said in a small voice. "Isn't he?"

At Killien's nod, she closed her eyes and let out a pained sigh. "How did he go?"

"On the dragon," Will answered.

Sini's shoulder drooped and she sagged back against Rett. "I'd hoped he wouldn't."

"You knew?" Killien asked.

"The moment you had the chance to control the dragon, he began talking about it."

Killien's jaw clenched. "Is he coming back?"

She shook her head. "He wanted to go somewhere safe, where he could learn and prepare." Her eyes flicked toward Will and Alaric. "To attack Queensland."

Will exchanged worried looks with Alaric.

"He took my sword." Killien sounded bitter.

Sini shrank back even further against Rett again. "Your seax has some kind of power. You wouldn't be able to tell, obviously, but we could feel…something in the blade. It has a…something."

"That's not very specific," Killien said.

She shrugged. "I don't know what it does. I only touched the blade once, but it made my finger tingle. Lukas doesn't know what it does either. But he thinks it's powerful."

"If it was given to you by Flibbet the Peddler," Will said, "that isn't too surprising."

He paused and spun his ring. "Sini, would you like to come back to Queensland with us?"

Sini stiffened.

"You haven't been with the Morrow long. You can come with us, back home. To your family." Sini's eyes locked onto his, a desperation rising in her making her look even younger. "Home?" Will nodded, but a flicker of distrust crossed her face.

"I know you don't trust Will yet," Sora said, stepping forward. "But I'll go with you too. I'll make sure you get back to your family."

She glanced toward Alaric, taking in the black cloak. "Will I have to join the Keepers?"

Will laughed. "No. Although you have no idea how happy we'd be if you decided to. We've been searching for you and Rett and Lukas for years, although we didn't know who you were. And if *you* joined, we'd be especially thrilled. It's been sixty years since the last female Keeper died."

"In the past," Alaric said from the floor, his fingers thrumming excitedly on a book, "female Keepers have manipulated energy in different ways than the men. I would love to know what you're capable of."

"I..." She looked around uncertainly. "I can't do the kinds of things Lukas can."

Killien looked at Will with a pointed expression. "Lukas stabbed Will in the shoulder."

Sini's gaze snapped to Will, interested.

"What does that have to do with anything?" Will demanded. "If we're comparing, he stabbed you in the back."

Sini's attention flipped toward Killien with a worried look, but he waved her away. "The Keeper healed me." A little smirk lifted the corner of his mouth. "Even if it took him a while."

"A while?" Alaric said indignantly. "You were almost dead."

Killien just laughed and motioned toward Will. Sini stepped closer, her eyes watching Will warily for a moment before she lifted her hands up near his shoulder. She set her palm on the bandage and Will tried not to wince at the jolt of pain that sliced into his arm.

"That's deep." She pulled her hand back. Her brow wrinkled as she focused on his shoulder, and traced lines in the air with her fingers. Thin trails of pinkish light hung in the air behind them, forming a rune.

Alaric scrambled to his feet and stepped closer. A strange rune that reminded Will of *sunlight* faded and she drew another one. The fingers on both hands danced through the air, leaving trail after trail of light.

A warmth started deep in his shoulder, growing hotter until Will had to try not to squirm away from it. The heat radiated down his arm as though his bone was smoldering. It burned over to his neck and he clenched his jaw. The heat moved toward the surface of his shoulder, leaving a tingling warmth behind.

With a final stretching sensation across his skin, the heat faded. Sini dropped her hands and Will pushed the bandage down off his shoulder and saw nothing but a ragged red pucker of skin. He lifted his arm and felt only stiffness and a dull ache.

Killien looked at her proudly. "You're getting better all the time."

Will raised his eyes to Sini, stunned. "How did you do that?"

Alaric stood behind the girl, staring at Will's shoulder. "There's nothing in here to pull energy from besides us. You couldn't possibly have done all that from yourself."

Sini looked up at him uncertainly. "I used the sunlight."

The room was completely shadowed.

"What sunlight?" Alaric asked.

"From out the window." She pointed outside hesitantly. "Where else would I get so much warmth?"

For a long moment, the two Keepers just stared at her. Alaric opened his mouth then closed it several times before settling on, "How did you make the runes?"

"Oh." She brushed her hair back out of her face with a nervous motion. "That energy does come from me. But it's easy." She moved her finger through the air in a long arc and left a thin pink trail behind that faded slowly away. She looked at the two Keepers curiously. "You can't make the air glow?"

Alaric blinked and reached toward the waning line.

"It looks like what the stone did," Will said, "when it sucked the life out of Ohan—and when it put that energy back into Killien."

Alaric's eyes widened. "The air glows! The energy moves through the air...and it glows. How did I not see that?" He turned toward Sini, his face so intense that she took a step back. "How does the air *glow?*"

"Alaric," Will said mildly, "you're scaring her. And the rest of us."

Alaric pressed his lips closed and backed up.

"I don't know how it glows," Sini said. "That's the first magic I ever did. Of course it wasn't a smooth line." She turned her hands over. The tips of each finger were shiny and smooth with old scars. "It was more of a...cloud."

"It came out your fingertips?" Will turned his own hands face up, showing the healing burns and the old white scars on his palm.

Alaric held out his as well, a patchwork of old faded scars filled his palms. In a tightly controlled voice he said, "*Please* come to the Stronghold. Even if you don't stay. Please come and show us what you can do. I promise you we will do everything we can to help you learn more."

"If you stay on the Sweep," Killien said, sounding desperate, "you can have your freedom. You can keep living with us as a real part of the family."

For a moment, Sini looked interested. But then she shook her head slowly. "I'd never really be free among the Roven." She considered Alaric and Will, tapping her fingers on her lips. "Lukas will come for you. I don't think yet, though. There were things he wanted to learn first, but it's always been his goal to destroy the Keepers."

"Do you know where he's gone?" Will asked.

"Probably Napon. He wants to learn from the blood doctors there."

Alaric made a disapproving noise.

Sini straightened her shoulders and a determined look settled on her face. "I'll come with you. Lukas is...I might be able to help you prepare for him. He's not as terrible as he probably seems to you right now. If I could talk to him, maybe..." She shrugged and her words trailed off.

Her gaze fell to the book in Alaric's hand. "Do you have any books at the Stronghold?"

"Eighty-two thousand three hundred and twenty. Or there about."

Killien's mouth fell open and Sini's eyes widened.

"Yes, I'll come," she said quickly. She turned to Rett and looked up into his face. "I'm going to go back home, to Queensland. Do you want to come with me? Or stay with Killien?"

Rett shook his head. "Come with Sini."

"We need to wrap this up," Patlon said. "I hear people in the hall."

"If you go out the window," Killien said, "you should be able to get around to the back of the mountain quickly. Don't linger."

"Sounds good," Douglon said, scrambling up to the window and peering out. "Everything's chaotic enough down on the Sweep that no one should pay much attention to us."

Evangeline followed him. Sini, paused before giving Killien a quick hug. Then she clambered out the window followed by Rett, Alaric, and Patlon. Sora started toward the window.

"I'm sorry," Killien said to Sora. "About the night Lilit almost died."

Sora hesitated. "I understand the desperation you must have felt. And if you hadn't called for me, you wouldn't have gotten Will, and Lilit would have died." She gave him a reluctant shrug. "So I suppose I'm glad you did."

Killien gave Will a sidelong glance. "What do you think she'd do to me if I pointed out that she'd just claimed to be the reason Lilit was saved."

Sora fixed him with a dangerous look. "I'd finish the job Lukas started on you."

Killien let out a short laugh, then grimaced and shifted his back. "If you're ever near the Morrow again, Sora, you'll always have a place."

Sora nodded in acknowledgment and went to the window. Ilsa gave the Torch a hesitant smile and followed her.

Hal gave Will a crushing pat on the back. "The fact that you introduced me to dwarves has tipped the scales. I've decided I'm glad to have met you."

"And I you."

"I have a feeling you might see Lukas before I do," Killien said to Will. "If you do, tell him…"

Will waited, but Killien shook his head.

"Maybe there's nothing to tell him." Killien held out his hand to Will, and he took it, clasping Killien around the wrist. "Thank the black queen you were here. I feel as though I should offer you some sort of reward for saving me, both from the knife and from the ring. But you might ask for more slaves, and you've already taken enough of those."

"Is that bag over there full of avak?" Will pointed to a shelf. "Because you know we don't have those in Queensland."

Killien let out a short laugh and winced. "You drive a hard bargain, but I suppose two dozen fruit will help you feed the many people leaving with you."

Will grabbed the bag and slung it over his shoulder.

"Next time you're sneaking across the Sweep," Killien said, "you should stop by the Morrow."

"I'm done with the Sweep," Will said. "It's your turn. Come to the Stronghold. We have a lot of books."

Killien opened his mouth to refuse, but Douglon interrupted from the window. "Hurry up, Keeper. Or we're leaving you behind."

Killien extended his hand, and Will grasped his wrist.

"Good luck, Will."

FIFTY-ONE

Will climbed through the window and into the warm sunlight on a slope scattered with trees. The last goblins from the battle below drained back into their warrens. Ahead of him, the others scrambled among rocks and bushes. It took endless, exposed clambering across the steep slope before they'd moved around the mountain enough that the Roven camp was out of sight. But the Roven were busy dispatching any wounded goblins and beginning a victory celebration. On the north side of the mountain, trees grew more densely, hiding the Sweep, and they hurried downhill through them. But climbing along the side of the mountain took much longer than walking through tunnels, and the sun hung low in the sky before they reached the place they'd come out of the goblin warren.

Any rangers that had been patrolling must have gone back to the camp during the fight, because the swath of grass between them and the mountain range sat perfectly empty. Douglon led, angling for the entrance to the dwarven caves. Will scanned the grass for any sign of Rass and the sky for any sign of Talen.

They were almost across the grass before Talen's little form winged out of the sky to land on Will's arm. And when they reached the last stand of thick grass before the ground rose into the mountains, Rass's face popped up out of it in time to hear Sora explain to Ilsa, Sini, and Rett that the way back to Queensland involved several days in dwarven tunnels.

Rass crossed her arms. "No more tunnels."

Will crouched in front of her. "The rest of us can't slip through the grass unseen like you can. There are too many Roven for a group as strange as ours to get home safely." He tried to keep the disappointment out of his voice and added. "If you don't want to come, I'll understand."

She frowned. "I do want to come. It's just too long away from the grass."

"It's easy enough to take some with us." Douglon studied the grass she stood on. "But that's too tall."

He climbed uphill to a little patch of short mountain grass. Taking a small shovel, he began to dig. In a few minutes he'd dug up a square of earth and grass an arm's length on each side. He rolled it up and tied it to his pack. "That should stay alive long enough to get us through the tunnels."

Rass reached her hand up and ran her fingers along the bundle, knocking loose a shower of tiny bits of dirt. "You're very smart, Douglon."

Douglon winked at her. "There are caves that get sunlight, you know. And water. Deep in Duncave there's a garden with a floor of grass. Every bit of it got in there rolled on a dwarf's back."

Unlike Rass, Sini was unabashedly excited about the idea of dwarven tunnels, and so Rett followed along perfectly happy as well. Ilsa balked only a few moments before Sora assured her she would walk with her.

Will followed behind them with Talen. A thousand questions swirled in his head to ask Ilsa, but he felt oddly nervous at the idea of asking them. Sora and Ilsa talked for a bit before Ilsa turned to him. "What's our mother like?"

In the dim glimmer moss, her face mirrored his own nervousness.

"She looks exactly like you." At her surprise, he continued, "I've been afraid for years that I might walk past you and never know it. But anyone who's met our mother would know you instantly."

She hesitated. "And our father? I heard you tell the Torch…"

Will answered before the emotions had time to make him hesitate. "He was killed the night you were taken."

Ilsa turned away for a few steps. "I think I knew that. I don't remember it, exactly, but I've never thought my father was alive." She glanced back at Will again. "Do you remember much of me?"

Will launched into every memory he could remember of her as a baby. Learning to walk, chasing the goat, dragging her ugly doll behind her wherever she went. Then he continued on with stories about their village, their mother, their father.

Ilsa turned out to have a subtle, dry wit and he found a hint of comfortableness growing. Not an ease, exactly, but the awkwardness began to smooth away. She didn't talk about herself, and he bit back the countless questions he had for her.

Ahead of them, Alaric and Sini walked together, peppering each other with questions, Douglon and Patlon hummed rhythmic, deep dwarfish tunes that echoed along the tunnel, blending back into themselves, creating their complex thrumming song. It took a couple of hours to reach the same dull cavern they'd slept in the night before. With no chimney to allow a fire, they gathered the glimmer moss together and sat around it eating a cold meal.

Douglon spread out the little square of grass, and Rass settled into it with a contented sigh.

"You're growing soft in your old age, cousin," Patlon said.

"Are you really cousins?" Rass asked.

"Patlon's father is my uncle," Douglon answered, sitting down next to her grass. "But most Dwarves call each other cousin, to remember we're all related."

"I like it," Rass said. "I've never had a cousin."

"You're too little to be a cousin," Patlon said. "You're a nibling."

Rass giggled. "Sounds like nibble."

"It's like a niece," Douglon explained. "Or a nephew."

Rass considered the idea. "Well then, thank you Uncle Douglon, for the grass." She stood and wrapped her little arms around his neck.

Douglon's eyebrows shot up, but he patted her back awkwardly. "You're welcome, wee snip."

With a contented sigh, Rass settled back down on her grass.

Ilsa, Sini, and Rett sat along one side. A thin divide of air and uncertainty formed between the three of them and the others.

Will wanted to feel celebratory, but mostly he felt exhausted. He felt a responsibility to fix the awkwardness in the group, but it was hard enough just to keep his eyes open and eat the dried meat and cheese the dwarves passed out. Will added avak to the meager meal, and everyone who hadn't tasted it before was suitably impressed with it. The fruit perked his mind up for a few minutes, but even that couldn't dull his exhaustion.

With all the humans and the small elf worn out, the dwarves carried the evening, telling tale after tale of the pranks they'd played on High Dwarf Horgoth. Douglon, it turned out, was such a close relative to Horgoth that until the High Dwarf had some children, the case could be made that Douglon was next in line for the throne—an honor he was decidedly unhappy about.

The dwarves entertained them, until one by one they fell asleep to long, slow echoes of dwarven songs.

The next day Will walked with Alaric through the darkness. Ahead of them, Sora, Ilsa, and Evangeline chatted animatedly. There was something subtle, but almost masterful, about the way Evangeline drew the other two out. Sora's laugh was as light and easy as it had been when she'd found him after the fire. And Ilsa joined in the conversation more and more as the hours passed.

Will and Alaric continued to fill in gaps for each other from the past year.

"When we reach the Stronghold," Alaric said, "I'll put Ayda's memory of the elves into the Wellstone. But I think you should be the one to write those down. The elves deserve to have the story told right."

"I can't believe they're all gone. I can't believe Ayda's gone."

They walked in silence.

"Where's her body?"

"Douglon took it to the Elder Grove in the Greenwood."

"She really *is* gone, right?" Will asked. "I mean, it sounds like Evangeline was essentially dead, and you brought her back. Could Ayda…?"

Alaric shook his head. "I've asked myself that every day. But she isn't like Evangeline. Ayda gave up everything. There's no life left in her at all. Although"—he paused, as though reluctant to continue—"she did put a lot of herself into Evangeline, and into Douglon once when he was dying. And into the Elder Grove itself. I can't find anything particularly unique about the *vitalle*, but maybe you could feel something else?"

They reached the Cavern of Sea and Sky at the end of a long day of walking. The air in the cavern glowed blue with the sunlight that trickled its way in. Glints of orange flashed across every surface from their glimmer moss. A reverent silence muted the group, both from those who'd seen it before, and those who hadn't.

Patlon and Rass made a fire, roasting some yams and onions, scattering countless glints of light across the cave. Ilsa, Sini, and Rett explored the cavern. Will took off Talen's hood, and the hawk flew in circles around the cavern.

Alaric drew Douglon and Evangeline aside and explained Will's talent. "There's a chance that he can sense what Ayda put in you better than I can."

Evangeline looked at Will sharply. "Do you think there's a chance that it's part of her? That we could somehow get her back?"

"I don't know," Will said. "That's what I'd try to find out."

He opened up to Evangeline. A rush of gratitude and unworthiness filled him, laced with guilt and something that felt like a desperate, clinging sort of…greed. Alaric squeezed her hand

and what had felt like greed settled into what it really was—a tight bundle of joy and desire and friendship and fear, all wrapped so tightly together there was no name for it except love.

Will took a breath and opened up toward Douglon. A gnawing ache flowed into him. Grief. Still new enough to be eroding everything else. Every experience of grief Will had had surged to the surface in his own emotions, resonating with Douglon's pain. The sheer weight of it threatened to overwhelm him.

There was something similar in them, but there was too much chaos to figure out what.

Sora shifted, watching them with interest. That's what he needed, Sora's calm.

"Could you help me?"

She stepped closer. "Anything."

"I need to feel what you feel." He reached out and took her hand.

A flood of emotions crashed into him. Admiration, curiosity, excitement, sympathy, and over it all, a warm, glowing blanket of eagerness, pulling him toward her, wrapping around him. His stomach twisted into a knot of nerves and he couldn't breathe.

He closed his eyes and drew in a breath. "That's very distracting."

A snag of hurt pulled her emotions back and she loosened her hand.

His eyes flew open. "No!" He tightened his grip. "It's nice—very, very nice. I like it a lot. But what I need from you is that eerie calm you have." He gave her an apologetic smile. "Just for now. There's so much here, I can't concentrate."

She laughed a self-conscious little laugh. "Oh…I'll try." She closed her eyes and he felt her emotions recede a little. She cracked one eye open. "It's harder around you than it used to be." She closed her eyes and her brow drew down in concentration. Slowly her feelings drained away until he felt a deep calmness, giving him room to sort through everything.

"Thank you."

Will started with Evangeline, pushing past the tangle of emotions. Below everything something tranquil caught his attention.

He squeezed his eyes shut. Serenity. The peace that infused forests and mountains and storm clouds. The kind that endured for eons and stretched across the heavens at night.

It did remind him of Ayda. But it wasn't the elf exactly. It was more like an echo.

He felt a twang of his own disappointment and realized he'd been hoping that he'd find something recognizably her. That somehow the elf was still alive.

What Evangeline carried wasn't just emotions, though. There was something like *vitalle* about it. He could feel it sitting like a bubble of energy inside the intangible swirl of feelings.

Will focused on Douglon, reaching past the grief. There it was, the same serenity that Evangeline had, part emotion, part *vitalle*. Instead of sitting below everything, Douglon's was completely surrounded by grief and a desperate sort of possessiveness.

Will pulled at it the way he would pull at *vitalle,* and felt it draw closer to him.

If he wanted, he realized, he could pull it out. Which was interesting, but not necessarily useful. He lingered for a moment, trying to claim a hint of the peace. But there was nothing in himself that was like it enough. The serenity of it was foreign. He could recognize it, but it didn't resonate with anything inside of him.

"It's not Ayda," he said quietly. "It's just…elfishness. I don't think there's anything of her left."

A flash of disappointment flashed through Douglon's emotions, but his face stayed impassive. "That's what I thought."

Will closed himself off from both of them, the ache of loss from Douglon still ringing in his

FIFTY-TWO

own chest. The dwarf walked over to the fire, and Evangeline and Alaric moved away together, talking somberly.

Sora, still holding Will's hand, pulled him toward a side tunnel. They turned down it, and the ethereal blue of the cavern began to darken. The tunnels felt different than they had the first time she'd brought him here. The fear of them had disappeared, replaced with the feeling of being cocooned in something safe. The disappointment of not finding Ayda couldn't quite follow him in here. It fell off somewhere in the darkening tunnel leaving just himself and Sora and the mountain.

"I'm glad you snuck into my room that first night," he said.

Sora laughed and led the way around another turn. The tunnel darkened to a deep grey. "You didn't always feel that way."

"True. You were too frightening for me to be glad." He thought back to that night. "When you said, 'I see you,' it was the most terrifying thing I'd ever heard. Because I knew you saw more than I wanted you to." The fear of her felt foreign now. "I'm not sure when it turned from terrifying to freeing."

"Somewhere on the Sweep for me." She slowed. "At first it was just frustrating that you seemed to understand me. But it kept drawing me back."

"Flibbet the Peddler has a rule that says, *It is a terrifying thing to be truly seen—but it is infinitely worse not to be.* I don't think I really understood what he meant before I met you." He laughed. "You managed to teach me both parts."

She turned toward him and he could just make out her face in the dark. She smiled, but there was a hesitation in her face. "How much past Kollman Pass is your home and Queenstown?"

"Are you in a hurry?"

She paused. "I told Sini and Ilsa that I'd see them to their homes, so I will, but then I need to leave."

"What?" He clenched her hand. "Why?"

"I need to go back home." There was an ache in her voice. "You were right. The holy woman from my clan took what was *my* story, and I've let her control it for too long. She controls who I am, who the clan is. I have to go back and stand up to her, tell them all the truth. Or they'll never be free of her...*I'll* never be free."

"I'll come with you." Her fingers felt cold. "I love telling people the truth."

She let out a little laugh and leaned against him, laying her head on his shoulder. He ran his free hand down her braid, his fingers finally tracing the plaits of copper like they'd wanted to for... how long *had* he wanted to do this?

"This isn't something an outsider can be a part of, Will. Especially one that would be chasing after me wanting to record my every word."

"Oh, this should definitely be written down." He cleared his throat. "*The Huntress and the Holy Woman: A tale of corruption and truth.*"

She breathed out another laugh and leaned into him.

He ran the end of her braid through his fingers. "When do you have to go?"

"Not yet. There's a ceremony on midsummer that I always played a main role in. She won't be able to stop me from taking that position. If I want to talk to my people, that will be the moment. But I have a couple weeks to help get Sini, Rett, and Ilsa to their homes."

"Let me come with you," he pleaded.

She shook her head against his shoulder. "You have things you need to do. Like prepare for a dragon attack."

Will wrapped his arm around her. She melted against him and he stood there absorbing the feel of her. He caught a scent of leather just like the first night she'd appeared in his room and terrified him. "Would it help if I begged? Or cried like a baby?"

"It might."

When she started to pull back, he tightened his arms, an ache in his chest. "What if I *can't* let go?"

She looked up into his face for a breath, her brow drawing down in concentration, until a rush of longing and resolve and warmth burst into him, all wrapped in a sort of grasping need and desperate hope that caught his breath.

She leaned up and pressed her lips against his, and he opened up to her, letting everything else she felt swirl in. He pushed as much of his own emotions back into her as he could, until it was impossible to tell the yearning and eagerness and hope and heartache apart. It churned around them, a tangle of things beginning and ending in the same moment.

She pulled away and it felt like she tore something out of him. "I'm not leaving until everyone gets home. And it won't be forever. If we've learned anything, it's that you're incredibly easy to track."

"You'll come find me?" He sounded desperate. "When you're done?"

She nodded and he pulled her back against him.

"You won't even have to track me. I'm very famous and important in Queensland. Just ask anyone and they'll point you in the right direction."

He could almost feel her eye roll.

Calls that food was ready echoed down the tunnel and Sora pulled away. "Food is still one of the only reasons to leave a tunnel."

They walked slowly back to the cavern. The sun must have set because the cave had dimmed to a blackness sparkling with the orange glints of firelight.

"I've talked to Douglon," Alaric said, as they drew near, "and he has an exit from the tunnels that will put us less than half a day from the Greenwood. We can get to the Elder Grove and bury Ayda." He glanced at the group. "Unless everyone's in a big hurry to get to their homes."

"We could see the Greenwood?" Sini asked excitedly.

"I haven't seen many forests," Ilsa agreed.

"I'm definitely not in a hurry." Will gave Sora a small smile. "Let's take the scenic route."

The group settled down around the fire and the split happened again. Sini, Rett, and Ilsa sat a bit apart. It wasn't as pronounced as the night before, but it was still there.

Will waited for a lull in the conversation before clearing his throat. "The night I was rescued from the rift"—he gave Rass a little bow and she beamed at him —"Killien had demanded a story from me, and I was planning to tell the story of Sable."

Alaric made an approving noise. "I haven't heard that one in years."

"If we're to have a story, we need wine." Patlon pulled a wineskin from his bag, and Douglon pulled out another. "The Roven just left these lying around. Everyone seemed too tired last night to enjoy them."

The dwarves passed the wineskins and Will pulled out the bag of avak. He took a bite of the fruit, letting the freshness wake up a little hope that the gap between them all could be closed. Passing it to Alaric, he began.

"Sable was still small enough to crawl through the broken plaster wall that led under the floor of the abandoned warehouse. And she was still small enough that finding such a place to spend the night was a necessity. Dirt, pebbles, and broken shells jabbed into her hands and bare knees as she scooted in. It was dusty and lonesome, but it was quiet and safe."

He opened up to the group and felt the normal chaotic swirl of emotions.

"Early the next morning, though, heavy footsteps broke the silence. Terrified that it was one of the dockside gangs, Sable crawled silently backwards until a glitter of fairy light caught her eye through the wood slats. Glints of red and gold and blue. She moved her head slowly, letting the colors shimmer down into the gloom where she lay."

One by one, the feelings of the people in the cave focused on the story and the first sparks of curiosity formed.

"There was laughter, but it wasn't the harsh laughter of the street packs. And there were snippets of songs, but not loud, bawdy tavern songs. She'd never heard voices like these. For it was sheer luck that a street mouse from Dockside had slept under the practice room of the Duke's Figment of Wits traveling troupe."

Sable's story continued, and the emotions of the group began to seep out from themselves and mix with those around them, creating a cloud of anticipation and amusement. It filled the cavern, each listener resonating with the emotions of the others until any divisions between them dwindled away.

The rock walls wrapped around them all, glittering with firelight. In here were no slaves, no goblins, no dragons looming on the horizon.

There was nothing but infinitesimally small glints of hope scattering across everything he could see.

THE END

SIEGE OF SHADOWS

The Keeper Chronicles Book 3

SUNFIRE

ini stopped at the cusp of the clearing, pressed back by the presence of the Elder Grove.

Behind her, the Lumen Greenwood stretched out like a sea of shadows. The trees thrummed with life. Strands of energy wove up the trunks and along the branches, spraying out into the leaves. Walking through the speckled green light of the elven forest for the last two days with her new companions, she'd thought those trees were more alive than anything she'd ever felt.

But they were nothing compared to this.

A wide, flat glade lay before them, drenched in sunlight. She stretched her arms into the light and her skin tingled. The stones in the two rings on her fingers—the small orange one for warming and the yellow for illumination—glowed dimly as they always did, leaving thin trails of light behind them as she moved. But the pricks of sunfire that danced along her fingers in pink strands of light were new.

She stared at her hands for a heartbeat before shrinking back into the shadows, rubbing her fingers. Sunlight always held sunfire, falling to the earth like a fine rain. But it had never done that before.

Everyone stopped at the edge of the trees, silent and still.

She glanced at the odd group who had rescued her and Rett from the Sweep just three days before. None of them seemed to feel the sunlight. It wasn't surprising that Evangeline and Ilsa didn't, there was no reason the human women would. Or Douglon the dwarf. But she'd thought the grass elf might and had almost expected either Keeper Will or Keeper Alaric to feel it.

Why did no one ever feel the sunlight?

Of course, the sight of the grove was enough to stop them on its own.

Enormous trees lay toppled out from the center of the wide glade. Half their roots jutted up into the air like clawed hands, the rest were still anchored in the churned earth. Deep gashes scarred the ground, and from the torn earth rose a stand of…the only word for them was trees.

Their towering trunks stood side by side in a wide ring, vicious and angry. Dark green leaves, jagged like saw blades, jutted out from between ruthless red thorns. Power thrummed out from them. The air quivered with energy. It called to Sini and unnerved her at the same time.

Even Rass's usual chatter had grown quiet. Since they'd entered the elvish forest, the grass elf had scampered among the trees, almost wild with wonder at the place. Sini had barely believed

Rass was an elf at first, but here her elfishness was obvious. Rass belonged in these woods in a way that Sini didn't, in a way none of the rest of them did.

Rass had begged Douglon to teach her to hear the trees and to Sini's surprise, the dwarf had agreed to try. Will had told Sini part of a story in half-whispers when Douglon wasn't too near about the dwarf and an elf named Ayda. She'd saved his life once by transferring so much of her own energy into him that he gained her skill of hearing the trees.

Ayda was the reason they'd come here. This story Sini had heard in its entirety. Ayda had been the last elf, and she held the power of all her people inside her. She had used it to help Alaric finally destroy Mallon.

It still felt unreal that she was free of the Roven and traveling with Keepers. She'd been almost four long years on the Sweep surrounded by people who hated them, and yet she'd never been convinced Keepers were evil. Certainly neither Will nor Alaric fit the image of a controlling, manipulative monster. In addition to the wild freedom of getting to leave the Sweep, she felt a glorious hope that maybe all the good things she'd believed about her old home really were true.

The unsettling feel of the grove made her shrink back and tuck her hands into her pockets. Her knuckle knocked against the avak pit from lunch. To distract herself, she rolled it between her fingers, focusing on the smooth surface of the pit, thinking about the way the fruit juice burst in her mouth. How it heightened all her senses.

Her fingers paused, caught by an idea. This grove reminded her of avak.

Rett stepped closer to her and she leaned into him, pressing her shoulder against his arm, reassured by his presence. In many ways, Rett was more like a child than a man in his forties, having been hurt in an accident years ago. During her slavery, though, he'd been like an older brother: always nearby, always protective, even as she grew up and he stayed forever childlike. He studied the trees with a scowl. "Don't like those."

"Welcome to the new Elder Grove." Douglon had grown quieter as they neared the grove, and now his voice was hushed. "Ayda made these trees when she found the original grove destroyed. I've seen them three times now, and they're still terrifying."

His eyes looked straight ahead, unfocused. Despite his words, his expression wasn't afraid, it was wounded. With a catch in his breath, his gaze dropped to the ground near one of the toppled trees.

A body lay among the roots, white against the forest floor.

It could be no one but Ayda.

After she had helped destroy Mallon, Ayda had sacrificed herself to save Alaric's wife Evangeline, in the process giving her, too, some of the elves' knowledge. Evangeline couldn't call upon the knowledge at will, but sometimes, unbidden, the answers to questions just came to her.

Douglon had brought Ayda back here to the elven wood in preparation for her burial. He knelt down beside her now, bowing his head.

Will, Alaric, and Evangeline stepped closer to Ayda. A thin layer of crystal, clear as glass, covered her body. Rass crept toward Ayda's feet, the little grass elf peering down at her larger tree elf cousin with a sorrowful face. Ayda's skin was pale and smooth and her hair fell over her shoulders and arms in a rich gold. She was dressed in a plain white dress with a thin chain of purple flowers wrapped around it like a belt.

Will frowned at the trees. "We can't bury Ayda here." All traces of the wariness that had shadowed the Keeper on the Sweep had fallen away a couple days ago when they had entered Queensland. He was relaxed and confident and happier than Sini had ever seen him. Or he had been until now. "She was too bright and lively to lay in the shadow of these."

Heads nodded in agreement.

Sini glanced at the vicious trees. The idea of putting anything into the ground near those brooding pillars made her shiver. The trunks were crowded close together, each so wide she couldn't have wrapped her arms halfway around them, even if she could have gotten past the thorns. But from between two trunks, something glimmered. She took a step closer and saw a narrow passage through the trees. There was definitely light inside. Bright, warm light.

Turning sideways, she slipped in, giving the red thorns as wide a berth as she could. Rett called after her, but she didn't answer. There was something treasure-like about the light, hiding inside the cocoon of the baleful trees that pulled her in.

She broke through into the center of the ring of trunks and stopped, stunned.

The glen was an oasis. Maybe fifteen paces wide, the trees that had appeared so savage outside were utterly different in here. The leaves were still a dark, rich green, but the edges were feathered and rippled gently. The red thorns were replaced with sprays of luminous scarlet petals. Sunlight poured down on thick grass and the light smell of fresh mornings filled the grove. The air shivered with sunfire.

"Sini?" Will's voice came muffled through the trees, concerned.

"It's in here!" she called back.

"What's in there?" Douglon muttered.

Sini turned slowly, her face pointed up, taking in the trees, letting the sunlight soak into her cheeks.

The others squeezed through the trees and joined her. No one spoke as they stared, awestruck, into the trees.

"I can feel them." Will's brow furrowed. "They have emotions. They're yearning for something."

Sini breathed in the air. It felt thicker, richer. She closed her eyes, trying to read the emotions of things the way Will could. She couldn't feel anything from the people around her, but the forest did feel like it was longing for something. The ache seeped into her, fanning a feeling she'd pushed away for years. Unbidden, the memory of her mother surfaced. Her little brothers, their faces always too thin. Lukas, laughing. The longing for all of them took her breath away. She blinked back tears.

"They miss Ayda," Douglon said quietly from the edge of the glen. "And the other elves. This is where she should be buried." Without waiting for any agreement, he left, and Alaric followed. They returned bearing Ayda's body. Using whatever tools they could find, everyone dug.

The earth was surprisingly soft beneath Sini's fingers, and before long they had dug a grave in the center of the ring of trees. Alaric and Douglon set Ayda's body in it. Alaric set his hand on the crystal that covered her. Orange light glowed around the Keeper's hand, and the crystal disappeared.

Sini held her breath for a moment with everyone else, as though Ayda might open her eyes, but her body was the only thing in the grove that held no life. Douglon's hands clenched a thin blanket from his pack. He climbed gently down into the grave and pressed a kiss to her forehead before covering her. Without a word, he climbed out and began to fill the grave.

Sini covered Ayda's feet, pushing the soft earth into the grave.

When they finally stood beside a mound of fresh earth, silence fell over the group.

A tremor ran through the ground.

Sini glanced around, but everyone else was looking solemnly at the new grave. Will stood on the far side with his sister Ilsa. Alaric and Evangeline stood next to Sini and Rett. Rass sat at the foot of the grave with a long, mournful face, brushing her fingers through the blades of grass. Douglon pulled his axe off his back and set the head of it on the ground, resting his hands on the end of the handle. Light skittered along a line of red flames carved into the shaft.

Next to Sini, Rett began to hum a low Roven dirge, haunting and slow.

Will cleared his throat and began speaking, with Rett's song as a backdrop. "I met Ayda before going to the Sweep. I spent three weeks with her here in the woods, wondering when she was going to introduce me to other elves. Not knowing there weren't any." He grew silent for a moment. "She was more alive than anyone I've ever met. Approachable and terrifying at the same time."

"I planned to come back through the Greenwood on my way home from the Sweep and see her again. But being here, like this—if we'd just lost her, it would be almost unbearable. But to have lost every trace of the elves as well…" He knelt down and placed his hand on the grave. "I will miss you, Ayda. The whole world will miss you."

The only sound in the grove was Rett's humming before Evangeline stepped forward. "I only knew Ayda for a few moments, but I owe her my life, and the elvish memories she left with me are priceless and precious." She sighed. "Ayda, I wish I could have known you longer. Thank you for your gifts."

Sini felt another tremble.

Not in the earth, though. In the air around them. Neither Will nor Alaric gave any indication they felt it, and Rett stood perfectly still beside her with his head bowed. Not even Rass appeared to have noticed.

Sini almost said something, but at that moment Ilsa stepped away from Will, searching the grove with a dissatisfied expression. At Will's questioning look, she said, "On the Sweep the Roven plant grass on the grave. A reminder that new life springs from the old. But…" She glanced up at the trees. "Grass feels insignificant here."

Sini reached in her pocket for the avak pit. "I have something." She held it out. "Avak are a bit magical, like this place." Alaric intercepted the pit and studied it for a moment. He made a curious noise in his throat and gave it to Ilsa. She knelt down and tucked it into the fresh dirt in the center of the grave, a handbreadth below the surface.

There was so much power in the grove, Sini half expected a shoot to burst out of the ground immediately.

Nothing happened.

Will, who'd been watching closely, nodded. "Avak belongs here."

Alaric stepped a little closer to the grave. "Ayda was nothing that I expected her to be. She started out a curiosity and ended up…a good friend. I owe her everything." He took Evangeline's hand. "I will be forever grateful to her. I only wish I could have done something different so that she was still here."

Douglon stood at the head of the grave, his head bowed. He lifted it enough to look down on Ayda's grave. "Dwarves do not bury their dead in the ground. We build a cairn of stone around them, holding them in the eternal embrace of the mountain. When you put something under the ground it is devoured by the earth itself, and I have never understood why any people would choose this."

Sini shifted her weight, shying away from the thought of the inevitable decay Ayda's body would undergo. Alaric opened his mouth as though he might protest, but Douglon spoke first.

"But even now she continues to change me. Because Ayda does not belong encased in stone.

She would have liked the idea of her body being given to the forest. She'd have been giddy at the idea of becoming part of the trees. Especially these trees."

Douglon looked up at the dark branches. "When we discovered Gustav and the dragon had torn down the old Elder Grove and stolen Mallon's body, Ayda was so angry. These trees—" he motioned around them "—were her answer. I thought what we could see from the outside was all there was. That the proof of her anger was all the world would get to keep of her. But this is what she was like, right here, the way this feels." He left his face turned up and the sunlight fell on him. It fell on everything, soaking into the trees, the mourners, and the fresh turned earth. "This is where she belongs."

They fell silent again, Rett's humming the only sound aside from the rustling of leaves.

"In the beginning," Douglon continued, "I thought she talked to the trees because…I don't know why. Because she did nonsensical things."

The dwarf's hand went beneath his beard and rubbed over a spot on his chest. "When she gave me part of herself to save me from that arrow—once I could hear the trees, too—then it all made sense. Their voices soothed that deep loneliness she carried. In the trees she could almost hear the voices of the elves she'd lost."

He looked up into the trees around them, his eyes unfocused. When he spoke again it was barely loud enough to be heard. "Because when I hear the trees, I can almost hear her again."

No one spoke, and Sini felt a shadow of the aching loss in his voice.

A pulse rippled through the air of the grove like a silent crack of thunder, and she tensed.

Rett's humming broke off, and Will and Alaric both started.

"You felt that one?" Sini asked.

Rass drew in a sharp breath and shoved her hands down into the grass, pressing her palms against the earth. She closed her eyes, her little brow knit.

Will looked at Sini sharply. "That one?"

Sini searched the glade, but everything looked calm. "There've been several. That was the strongest."

Rass scrambled forward and spread her fingers out on the ground. "This is a waking field!"

"A what?" Will asked.

"On the Sweep we have waking fields—where the new elves wake."

Evangeline's eyes widened. "Yes! The Elder Grove is where elves wake up."

Alaric's attention snapped to her. "Are you sure?"

Evangeline nodded.

"Wake?" Douglon asked sharply.

"Where they're born," Evangeline explained, her brow drawn in concentration. "The elves come here and put…something into the ground, and new elves are born." She looked at Alaric. "I'm sorry, I can't quite figure out what."

"Will burying Ayda here create new elves?" Will asked.

"I don't think so," Rass said. "On the Sweep we give the waking field part of ourselves, and care for it until the new elves become more than grass. This grove needs something from a living elf to begin with, and then elves to care for it." She peered at the trees above her. "This grove is…distant. Closed off. It's alive, but purposeless."

Sini sank down to her knees and spread her own hands into the grass. The grove pulled at her, drawing little licks of *vitalle* out of her palms before it stopped. Energy rushed past her hands, flitting back and forth beneath the surface.

"If it needs something from a living tree elf, it's going to be hungry for a long time." Alaric said. The energy below her hand felt frantic.

"I have part of a living elf," Douglon said, so quietly Sini almost missed it.

The dwarf still stood at the head of the grave, his face stony, watching Will. "Whatever she gave me when she saved my life, you said you could feel it inside me. Can you take it out?"

Will started to shake his head, but Douglon blew out an impatient breath. "It needs something from an elf. I have that."

Alaric began to object, but Evangeline touched his arm. "So do I."

Will studied both the dwarf and Evangeline with a troubled expression. A ripple rolled through the grove again, but Sini couldn't quite pinpoint whether it was in the ground or the air. The sunlight still rained down on her. But it couldn't just be the sun. Maybe the very air of the grove was alive somehow. A vibrant flower flung its petals wide on the nearest tree. Sini stood and moved over to it. The bloom wasn't just bright red. Thin lines of energy trickled across the surface. She stretched up and brushed her fingertip across it. A rivulet of crimson fire rolled down her finger like water. She pulled her hand back and the red light dissolved into the air.

"It will work, won't it?" Douglon continued, his voice low. "What we have is what Ayda had."

Will toyed with a small silver bead braided into his beard. "What is in each of you is a single thing. I can't take part of it." He hesitated. "And if I take it all, I think you'll both be back to..." He shrugged apologetically. "Normal."

Douglon's hand tightened on his axe. "We won't hear the trees any longer?"

"I'll lose the things I know about the elves?" Evangeline asked.

"Most likely."

Evangeline's gaze ran along the trees. "But you think it will help?"

Will glanced at Alaric and gave another helpless shrug. "I don't know. What you have feels like what the grove could be missing."

"Feels like?" Douglon repeated. "Could be?"

"Yes. That's how certain I am. And even if it is exactly what the forest needs, I don't know whether what you two have will be enough. There's a chance I would take it from you and still the grove wouldn't wake."

"Even if it works," Alaric broke in, "there are no elves to care for the grove."

"There are no *silvii*, no tree elves," Rass pointed out. "There are plenty of other elves."

Will looked at her sharply. "You could do...whatever needs to be done?"

"I think so, but I'd need to stay here." Rass gave him a grin. "I've never met a *silvii*."

Will knelt down next to her. "I can't stay with you."

Her little shoulders straightened. "I don't need you to—"

"I could stay," Douglon raised a hand to ward off Rass's objection. "Not because you need me to, snip. Just because I'd like to...help. However I can."

Her irritation faded. "I'd like it if you stayed, uncle."

Alaric looked at Douglon, Evangeline, and Rass. "Are you sure about this?"

"For a chance to have new elves?" Evangeline said. "We have to try."

"Why are we still wasting time talking about this?" Douglon asked.

Will motioned for Douglon and Evangeline to come closer and glanced at Alaric. "There isn't any *vitalle* here."

A shocked laugh burst out of Sini before she could stop it.

"I mean," Will clarified, "I can't take energy from the grove when I'm trying to help the grove."

Alaric nodded and Sini pressed her lips closed against another laugh. Why could no one else ever see it? "We can use the sunfire." At their blank stares, she stepped up to Will and set her hand on his forearm where she could touch his skin. "You start. I promise there'll be enough fire—*vitalle*—for anything you want to do."

The two Keepers considered her for a moment. Alaric looked as though he might question her, but Will nodded. "I believe you."

With Evangeline and Douglon standing before him, Will closed his eyes. He stretched his fingers toward Evangeline and she held still, her body stiff. Will twitched his hand and Evangeline let out a shuddering breath.

Douglon's hands were curled into fists at his side, his jaw clenched, as Will turned toward him. The dwarf fixed his gaze toward the nearest tree. Will glanced up at him once, then with an expression caught between determination and regret the Keeper made a small pulling gesture. A spasm flashed across Douglon's face.

Sini felt an ache of sympathy for them both. Will shuddered beneath her hand. He looked down and his hair hid his expression, but she could feel the tightness in his arm.

He could feel their emotions. She clenched her hand on his arm at the thought, suddenly terribly glad she couldn't. Will knelt and Sini sank to her knees.

She closed her eyes and lifted her face toward the sunlight, letting the warmth tingle across her cheeks. A trickle of energy flowed out of her hand into Will. He opened up a path for it to flow into the ground.

A wave of sunfire crashed down onto her. It poured into her like a drenching rain, flowing through her into Will.

It swelled and her hand grew hot against Will's arm. She dropped her other hand to the ground, letting the *vitalle* pour directly into it. The *vitalle* streamed down from the sky, pouring through her into the eager ground. More sunfire than she'd ever moved, more than she'd ever imagined.

The gems on her ring began to glow. This was too much for them—too much energy rushing through her hands. She tried to rein it in, but the sunfire ignored her. With two small snaps the gems in her rings split, burst from too much energy. A jab of loss shot through her as their light drained away.

The earth pulled at her, desperate. She braced for pain at the sheer amount of fire flowing through her. But there was only a buzzing tingle across her skin.

Will let out a grunt of pain and shifted his arm under her grasp, clearly feeling more than a tingle. Sini turned the energy away from him, funneling most of it into the earth.

More and more fire rushed through her, growing to a raging river. The vastness of the power threatened to overwhelm her. She tried to pull back, to cut it off, but it raced through her unchecked. She was part of the grove, part of the sky and the sunlight and the trees.

Will shoved something from himself into the earth, and the ground below her rang with a new power. The avak pit, not far from Sini's hand, shot out a burst of energy that flared through the ground. The grove drank it all in, stirring, stretching.

A wild glory sang out, blazing through the grove. The fire from her hands filled the ground, surged up the trees around them and spread out through the vast Greenwood. The forest wrapped around her, a living thing, unified, drawing her into itself. The voices of the trees rang through her mind. The earth flexed. She was exhilaratingly, terrifyingly, part of this fierce, swirling life.

"It's working." Rass's awestruck whisper came through the tumult.

Will groaned and pulled his arm away, sinking back.

The path he'd made broke off and the flow of fire disappeared so abruptly that Sini toppled forward onto both hands. The sunfire winked back into sunlight, pressing on her head with nothing more than summer warmth.

The grove was just a grove again. She was utterly cut off from it. Beneath her hands she could feel the energy, calm and purposeful, moving heedless of her presence. She had provided what it needed, and it had drawn back into itself. The memory of that vibrant life echoed hollowly inside her, leaving her alone and insignificant. The grove had no more use for her. She was shut out.

She opened her eyes to see Rass kneeling in the grass with her hands splayed into the dirt. Her face beamed with joy. "It's waking up."

Sini pressed her own hand into the ground, desperate to feel it again, but there was nothing. She turned to Will. "Where did—?" The question died on her lips.

Will and Alaric stared at her.

"How…?" Alaric started.

"She's not even burned," Will said.

"Channeling that much…" Alaric shook his head slowly. "You should be dead."

Sini's skin tingled in memory of the fire. "I've never done that much before. It was the grove. It was so hungry. And the sunlight was so…eager." She rubbed her arms to drive away the feeling.

A part of her was amazed at how much she'd channeled, but she couldn't focus on it past the emptiness left by the grove. "Couldn't you feel it?"

Will looked at the red patch on his arm where she'd held it. "The only thing I felt was an unbelievable amount of power from you." He flexed his hand. "Thank you for not sending all of it through me."

Alaric studied her like she was the most interesting person he'd ever seen. "I've never heard of a Keeper this powerful."

Sini shifted, feeling self-conscious under their attention. Her gaze caught on the dull, cracked gems in her rings. Her heart sank. Lukas had made those for her to help her channel magic.

Will leaned forward and looked at the rings. "Don't worry, we'll teach you to move energy without needing burning stones."

The thrill of the idea pushed away the loss of both the light and the gems. She'd never been able to move energy on her own.

"Whatever you did," Rass said, her eyes bright, "it was enough. The grove has what it wants."

Sini focused on the trees. The longing was gone. She placed her hand on the ground. It felt like normal earth, and paid her no heed at all. She blew out a pained breath.

Silence fell until Douglon cleared his throat, his expression ragged. "Does anyone know how long it takes for trees to give birth to elves?"

ONE

Sini stretched under the thick blankets until her feet slipped past the bottom and the early morning chill nipped at her toes. She shrank back in, curling into a ball. Stretching her mind out the window, she found the gentle power of the sunlight. Not much had managed to dribble down into the narrow valley of the Keepers' Stronghold yet, but she drew in what sunfire she could through the shutters and wrapped it around her feet, warming them. She left her eyes shut, thinking of nothing, listening to the sounds of birds and the distant stream.

It had been more than four years since she'd escaped the Sweep with Will and Alaric, and the fact that she could lie in bed as long as she wanted still felt as indulgent as it had on her first morning here.

A niggling irritation left over from the night before prodded her. Her paper on Naponese linen. She groaned. It must be almost dawn. She should have slid the paper under Keeper Mikal's door before she'd gone to sleep, but it had all been too frustrating.

A wave of something rolled through her like a ripple through water.

Her own *vitalle* lit up like a fire. A small plant by her window glowed dimly with its own energy. There was no sign of life next to her in Rett's room. The room on the other side of her was empty as it always was. She shouldn't be surprised by that after all this time, but she never could quite break the habit of checking. Couldn't quite give up the hope her younger self had held. Dim echoes of life came back from farther away in the Stronghold: Gerone below in the kitchen. The Shield puttering about his books. The twins upstairs, probably already seated at their desk.

A second wave came quickly, followed by a pause, and two more waves.

"It's so early, Rett," she mumbled into her pillow.

He'd made up the code himself. That pattern meant *come*. Seeing as he used it daily to get her attention, Sini had tried to convince him that a simpler pattern might be better, but he had grown flustered by the idea of changing it and she'd relented.

One of Rett's few skills was the ability to cast out, a process that was mostly effortless and involved flinging out a wave of curiosity, a kind of searching. To anyone sensitive to *vitalle*, the wave would light up anything living around them. Almost every other form of magic was beyond him, and after four years of valiant effort here at the Stronghold he still read only at a rudimentary level, but he could cast out.

It had been one of the first things she'd learned on the Sweep and Rett had used it daily to call her. Lukas could feel the waves as well, and had suffered it as an irritating disruption, until the day he'd wrenched his hip outside the city. It had been Rett who'd felt Lukas's call and found him.

Here at the Stronghold, all the other Keepers would have felt the waves as well, but if Rett's favorite way of calling Sini bothered any of them, they were too kind to mention it.

The waves Rett had sent were from below her and fairly weak. He must be outside. Probably wanted to show her something about that baby lamb that wasn't growing fast enough.

She sent out two of her own waves without even opening her eyes. *Where?*

Wave, pause, wave, wave, wave. *Library.*

She opened her eyes to the gloom. That was more interesting than the growth rate of a lamb.

The darkness had relented somewhat, although it would be hours before the sun was visible over the cliffs surrounding the narrow valley. Books, papers, ink, and quills were merely dark shapes on the desk near her bed. A fat candle sat on the corner waiting with a superior sort of air, but she ignored it.

Bracing against the chill, Sini pushed off her blanket and hurried to her small wardrobe. This was the third morning in a row that the air had held the crisp chill of fall. She tossed off her nightgown and pulled out the light purple tunic Will had brought back last summer. Her thick leggings were such a dark blue they looked like a black puddle in the gloom, but nothing was black in her closet except the Keeper's robe hanging off to the side. There was nothing drab, and definitely nothing grey.

Just a shadowed grey, Lukas had called the black Keeper robes. *The symbol of a slavery as real as ours.*

But her foster brother had been wrong. The robes were soft and sturdy. They symbolized something lasting and meaningful. She ran her hand over the fabric, then grabbed her wine-red cloak, instead. She pulled the wool over her head and found her boots. Unsure where her comb was in the dark, she ran her fingers through her hair. A year ago she'd cut off most of her blond locks, realizing that short hair needed less maintenance. The snipped ends tended to splay out wildly from behind her ears, but no one here was likely to care about that. She wove the pieces near her face into something as braid-like as she could manage across the crown of her head to keep any stray pieces out of her way.

Sini almost walked past the candle again on her way out, but it was so defiantly unlit that it demanded her attention. She squared her shoulders and set her fingertip next to the wick. Gently, she pushed some *vitalle* toward it. A light pink glow left her finger and clung to the wick for just a breath before dribbling down. It filled the top well of the candle and spilled over the edge the way clouds sometimes poured over the cliffs.

The wick stayed perfectly cold.

Sini hissed out an irritated breath and poured more energy into it. The pink grew brighter, but there was no path for it to follow into the wick. Enough energy to incinerate a tree slid uselessly down the candle and faded.

Rett's waves rolled through her again. *Come.*

She snapped off the flow of *vitalle* and glared at the pink mist dissolving into the air.

Irritated, she stalked out her door, into the center of the open tower.

White walls stretched up three stories to a tiled ceiling, and down two more to the dark wood floor. A ramp curled along the wall, spiraling past other arched doorways like her own. Windows dotted the far wall and the pale stones reflected the little light that trickled in, making the whole tower glow with a milky whiteness.

The tower filled her with a sense of rightness and, just as she did every morning, she breathed in the scent of freedom and safety.

At the bottom she crossed the wide floor. The library wing was a smaller building attached to the back of the Stronghold on the ground floor. She passed quickly through a short hall into the library, moving out of the white rocks of the Stronghold into warm brown stone. The hall spilled out onto an aisle running between the round walls lined with bookshelves and the wide-open center of the library. Like in the main tower, a ramp spiraled around the open center, connecting the floor she stood on to the others.

Three stories above her, a glass roof showed the pale blue of the morning sky. Four more levels lay below her. A few circles of golden light lit stretches of bookshelves, but this early the library was mostly silence and shadows. The colorfully-tiled floor at the bottom was faded to swirls of grey or black in the early light.

If the main tower smelled of safety, the library smelled of wonder. Tens of thousands of books on every subject imaginable. She wound around to her left to an open space filled with several tables. At one particularly wide one covered with a huge map of Queensland and their southern neighbors, the big form of Rett waited patiently. His distant expression cleared when he noticed Sini. A candle mounted on the wall next to him lit both his face and his feet which stretched all the way out the other side of the table. His dusty brown hair was beginning to grey, and he still wore the black Keeper's robe he'd fit into effortlessly when they'd arrived four years ago. Sini had put her smaller one on twice, but both times it had felt too much like someone else's clothes.

Rett had no such problems. Of course, Rett never overthought anything. He was…different. An accident involving magic years before Sini had met him had killed his twin sister and left his own mind damaged. He seemed aware of the fact that he was more like a child than a man, but content with it, all the same. His memories of his sister, who he'd been incredibly close to, were indistinct and confused. As far as anyone could tell, he felt only a nebulous sorrow about her, and Sini couldn't decide if that was a kindness or its own extra tragedy.

"A letter from Queenstown," he said eagerly, handing her a small piece of paper filled with script. She sat in a chair opposite him. The nearby window gave no light yet and it was too chilly outside to open the door for extra light, so he reached forward and touched the wick of a candle sitting near her. A clear green light from his finger streamed onto the wick and it instantly, effortlessly, burst into flame.

She spared an annoyed look at the cheerful flame. Despite Will's early assurances, she never had learned to do magic without some assistance. Maybe there was a reason Rett fit in a Keeper's robe better than she did.

Neither Rett nor anyone else in the Stronghold could see *vitalle* moving. In fact, they only knew of one person in history who could—Keeper Chesavia—and she'd lived almost two hundred years ago. The Keepers found Sini's abilities fascinating, and often had her watch when they manipulated energy, recording what she saw. They were endlessly fascinated by the differences in brightness and focus of the light, and the fact that each of them produced *vitalle* in a different color.

She'd give up the ability to see the energy in a heartbeat, if it meant she could actually use hers to affect inanimate objects. Living things weren't a problem. When she touched a person or an animal, the life energy in them was accessible to her. She could take *vitalle* out of them or put some in. She could even help their bodies heal, in a limited way. But inanimate things were utterly out of her reach—there was no path between herself and the object. When she'd been on the Sweep, the burning stones Lukas had made had helped her. He'd given her rings with gems that could create the path she needed. The Keepers, though, didn't approve of burning stones, and even though Alaric had used some to save Evangeline, he didn't like to talk about it.

Sini tilted the note toward the flame but hadn't even finished reading when Rett burst out with the expected question.

"Does this mean they found Lukas?"

She smiled at his unflagging hope. She'd met Rett and Lukas when she was twelve. The two men, also slaves on the Sweep, had become her foster brothers—protecting her and creating a bit of happiness amidst all the hardship. It was Rett's greatest desire that Lukas come to the Stronghold and join the Keepers like he and Sini had. Nothing would dampen that: not the four years that had passed without this happening, not the fact that every Keeper was convinced Lukas had declared himself their enemy, not the fact that he'd flown away from the Sweep on a dragon. If Rett believed the Keepers were good, there was no room in his mind to comprehend anyone thinking differently.

Sini did her best to protect Rett from the truth, but everything about Lukas was more complex than Rett could understand.

"Let me read…There was a sickness in a flock of sheep along the southern border. A wasting disease that killed fourteen ewes and caused six lambs to be born blind before it stopped." The words gave her a sour taste. "No one knows the cause or what cured it."

Rett grinned and bounced his feet, jiggling the tabletop. "That's just like on the Sweep."

Sini nodded, the similarity not striking as happy a chord inside her. It was the disease they'd seen on the Sweep, or one incredibly similar. A rival clan had used magic to poison their sheep. Lukas had been the one to find a cure.

"Lukas saved more sheep," Rett said, his voice proud. "Who else could have?"

Sini kept her eyes on the paper, trying not to let him see her disquiet. It was likely that Lukas was the only person outside the Sweep who could have healed them. Then again, a magical illness couldn't get all the way from the Sweep to southern Queensland without infecting anything before this without some help. And it was likely that Lukas was the only person outside the Sweep who could have done that as well. But why? Maybe he was perfecting the cure? She wrinkled her nose at the idea of testing it on some poor villages' sheep.

She glanced at the map. Piles of similar notes were stacked along the southern border. It had begun last year with sightings—a red dragon flying over Napon and Coastal Baylon. Seeing as Lukas had flown away from the Sweep on a red dragon, and seeing as no other dragons were known to exist, Alaric had begun sending reports to the Stronghold of disturbing events along the southern border in an attempt to figure out what Lukas was doing.

Then they'd received reports from spies embedded in Napon that Lukas had surfaced and was calling for the overthrow of Queensland, and the destruction of the Keepers. She'd managed to keep that fact from Rett's notice for quite a while, now. Lukas had always said such things on the Sweep, but Rett seemed to have forgotten.

Ever since, Sini and Rett had catalogued any odd events that Alaric sent them from the capital. There were plenty of problems they deemed natural, and unrelated to Lukas. More common sicknesses or poor crops after late spring frosts. But other events, although often small and isolated, were more difficult to explain. The ones she tracked most closely were like this one, connected to something she knew about Lukas, or something that might require magic. Animals with diseases that reminded her of ones from the Sweep, especially if they started and stopped mysteriously. Game found starved amidst lush vegetation. Small waterways that had turned bitter for a week, then cleared.

The task of determining whether these were things Lukas was capable of was complex, though. He was certainly capable of the magic needed, she just didn't know what his purpose might be. What was the point of killing off a few animals here and there? It didn't fit the Keepers' fear of a diabolical mastermind trying to destroy Queensland. The times Lukas had turned to violence in the past, he'd believed that one targeted strike of overwhelming force was better than widespread violence. These occurrences were too scattered and ineffective for him. Or maybe all of this was Lukas just practicing his skills to keep them honed.

There was an irritatingly tall pile of notes stacked on the map along the southwestern country of Gulfind. Gold merchants from the mountain country had stopped traveling to Queensland since midsummer, and no one knew why. Sini could see no connection to Lukas, but Alaric insisted these events "felt important," so she kept track of them as well.

Sini had seen two gold merchants in her life. One had come through the slums when she was small. The man must have gotten lost on his way to the vineyards. He'd hurried his wagon past with an air of panic. Sini's mother had spit at him as he passed.

Another had come through the Sweep. That was unusual enough that Sini had snuck out with Lukas to see the man meet with Killien. He'd been fatter than anyone Sini had ever seen. The two men had sat for hours, talking about Gulfind and the lands the merchant had passed through. In the end Killien had traded two good horses for a piece of gold.

"Killien doesn't care about the gold," Lukas had whispered to her. "He only wants informa-tion. Gold is like poison. Those people in Gulfind live high in the mountains. All they have is gold. They have to travel to other places to buy food or they starve, yet they love the gold too much to leave it." Her foster brother's voice had dripped with scorn, and he'd plucked his grey slave's tunic. "We're slaves because we were captured. That gold merchant chose his slavery. It's just his shackles are made of gold."

Rett interrupted her thoughts. "Lukas doesn't know where we are. The Stronghold is hidden."

Sini nodded, agreeing for the hundredth time to those words. She set this new note along the northeastern corner of Coastal Baylon where it had happened and weighed it down with a small rock.

"If he knew where we were," Rett assured her, continuing along the same line of thought he followed whenever Lukas was mentioned, "he'd come."

Sini kept her face down, the thought a dull ache. "Maybe. He doesn't know the Keepers like we do. He thinks they're…" She paused, unwilling to repeat Lukas's words. *Manipulative and impotent. Too weak to even protect those of us who should be Keepers from being taken—right out from under their noses. If I ever have the power, I will see them rooted out and destroyed.*

She'd never bought into the hatred of the Keepers that plagued the Sweep, and after four years of living with them, it seemed ridiculous that anyone could think poorly of them. But Lukas had embraced the hatred fully.

"He thinks they're bad?" Rett waved the idea away. "We'll tell him the truth."

She looked up at his eternally optimistic face and let it bolster her own hope that he was right. "We'll certainly try."

The door to the outside opened, letting in a bit of hazy dawn and a breeze that made the pinned-down notes flutter. The candle next to Sini flickered. She tried to get her finger next to it fast enough to bolster the energy before it went out, but the breeze snuffed it into a useless ribbon of smoke. The door swung shut and the map in front of her faded to darkness. She gave a low, exasperated growl.

"Help you, Sini." Rett touched the wick and it burst back into flame. He looked so pleased with himself that it dissolved a little of her irritation.

"Thank you." She glanced behind her at the approach of an older man with a perfectly combed white beard and an immaculate Keepers robe, even though he was probably returning from feeding the chickens.

Sini froze. The essay.

Keeper Mikal was one of her two tutors. While the other, Keeper Gerone, believed learning should be mostly a wild, student-led game of exploration, Mikal held more formal views—on everything. Including that essays should be at his door before dawn on the day they were due. Sini's current paper was sitting up on her desk next to that fat, obstinate candle.

He glanced at her with a slight crease in his brow and she gave him a smile that felt like a wince. "Good morning, Mikal."

"Good morning. Did you finish compiling that information on Napon?"

"I did." She bit her lip to keep from adding that it had been the most boring thing she'd ever read. "And I wrote a comparison of the two recent dynasties relating to the exports of linen." Which had been even more boring.

But the worst part had been the exercise where she was to make a small piece of linen float using only *vitalle* and record her attempts. Mikal insisted on giving her these exercises—exercises that should be simple for a Keeper—in the hopes that someday she'd be able to complete one of them. All three ways she'd tried had been utter failures. Last night's frustration rolled back into her. How was one supposed to get energy into something as dead as the air or a piece of linen?

"Modern or classic form?"

"Classic, fully annotated. And I added an appendix including a discussion of two quotes I found from Flibbet the Peddler about Naponese linen." Because even linen was interesting if Flibbet wrote about it. She'd spent hours copying his colorful, whimsical writing and doodles into her own journal. Like all the books written by the eccentric peddler, this one skipped from one topic to the next. She'd learned about bathing habits of ancient rulers (rubbing with dry dirt), the diet of the desert cactus beetles (scorpion eggs), and that Flibbet's favorite color was green.

She thought, for just a moment, that Mikal might be impressed enough to raise an eyebrow.

Instead he merely looked at her expectantly. "Did you move the linen with the *vitalle*?"

She hesitated. "No."

"Hmm." The sound might have been disapproving or a mere acknowledgement. "And where is this masterpiece?"

Sini's gaze flicked out the window. It was definitely past dawn.

"It's on my desk, quite close to the linens on my bed which I now know are Naponese in origin." She forced a bright smile in an attempt to counter his disapproving expression.

"I called Sini to come here early," Rett interrupted. "It's my fault."

Mikal's face softened slightly at the words. The fact that the man was unfailingly kind to Rett almost made up for his frustratingly strict adherence to rules. Almost.

"I'll bring it to you right after breakfast," Sini assured him.

"Or you could get it now."

"Stop plaguing the girl," a voice from above them called. Keeper Gerone walked down the ramp from a higher level of the library. His robe was permanently floured from his work in the kitchen, and starbursts of wrinkles creased the skin by his eyes. A smile peeked at her through his fluffy white beard. "You know she did the research, and you'll be impressed when you read it."

"I cannot be impressed by something I cannot see." Mikal said. "There is no reason to be wasting time on this map. It has been obvious for years that Lukas is working, not necessarily productively, on some scheme to harm Queensland and the Keepers. It is just as obvious that tracking all this isn't accomplishing anything."

Rett's shoulders sagged, and Sini bristled.

"They're doing good work," Gerone said, before she could speak. "Not everyone's as cynical as you."

Mikal shook his head. "The young generation is lazy."

"She referenced Flibbet!" Gerone threw his hands up. "That's not lazy, that's innovative."

"What it is, is late. When you are back to assigning her work, she can turn in everything tardy and crumpled for all I care."

Sini pressed her lips together. If only Gerone were back to leading her studies instead of embroiled in some strange project with the Shield involving the library roof.

Mikal turned back to Sini. "I'll wait here while you get it."

"She can get it later," Gerone said. "The Shield has a question for you about that dull paper you wrote on metalwork in Napon."

Mikal frowned. "I expect the essay at my door as soon as possible," he told Sini. Without waiting for an answer, he crossed over to Gerone and walked past him up the ramp. "Metal strengthening is a fascinating subject."

"Then why did you write about it in such boring terms?" Gerone asked. He grinned at Sini and Rett and followed Mikal, who was explaining about alloys and tension.

Rett looked after the two old men with a miserable expression. "Are we wasting time on this map?"

"No," Sini assured him. "Mikal was just…feeling grumpy. The Keepers want to know what Lukas is doing, and we're the ones who know him. It's not obvious what he's doing or why. It's important to keep up on the map."

He dropped his eyes to the table. "Did I make you forget to give Mikal your research?"

She laughed. "That paper is the most boring thing I've ever written, and Mikal should be thanking us both that his morning wasn't ruined by it." She set her hand on Rett's huge one. "Always call me when there's news. This is important."

She pushed away thoughts of Mikal and turned back to the map. This latest report was definitely about Lukas. She tapped her fingers against her lips, studying the blank space on the maps where the moors lay. Where was he headed?

"Lukas would like it here," Rett said. "We are safe here, and he always tried to keep us safe."

She nodded, not bothering to answer. Once Rett got started on this train of thought, it would be a few minutes before they could talk of anything else.

His voice dropped. "Like that time he told Killien he broke that shelf of burning stones instead of you?"

She winced at the memory of Lukas's whipped back. She'd had such poor control over the sunfire then, constantly destroying the delicate stones she and Lukas worked with.

That was one thing she was better at now. The Keepers had spent patient days teaching her ways to control the energy from the sun that none of them could even sense. What she'd never been able to do was all the things the rest of them could. Simple things like lighting candles or moving air were utterly beyond her power. She could never find a path between living things and any object that wasn't alive.

Even after all this time, if Lukas were to come here, he'd still have to do so many things for her. The thought was more bitter than she'd expected.

"If you could've healed then as well as you can now, he'd have been better by morning," Rett said.

"If I could have healed well then, Killien would have found me much more useful." She paused. Maybe he wouldn't have. "Although healing cuts isn't particularly impressive."

"I think it is," he assured her.

His face was so sincere she couldn't help smiling at him. "I'm just frustrated today about…" It was too much to explain to Rett. The irritatingly impossible exercise with the linen, the way she couldn't move *vitalle* for the simplest things. "About lighting candles," she finished.

Rett looked at her kindly. "I'll always help you, Sini."

She patted his hand. "I know you will." She turned back to the map, ready to talk about something else. The notes along the southern edge hinted at a pattern to Lukas's movements, and this latest event continued it.

Rett leaned forward. "Do you know where he is?"

Sini tapped her lips, her eyes drawn east again. The pattern didn't make any sense.

"You do know," Rett said, his voice growing more excited.

She hesitated, but he was so eager, she gave in. "It looks like he's moving toward the moors. All of the recent reports have come from the edges of it." She pointed to the wide blank area covering southeast Queensland and northern Gringonn. "But no one's going to believe me. There's nothing of value on the moors."

"I believe you," Rett said simply.

Sini smiled at him. "That's because you're very smart."

"No," he said seriously, "but you are." The big man's gaze wandered around the library. "All the Stronghold needs to be perfect is Lukas," he declared, pushing himself to his feet and stretching.

A worn, familiar ache pressed into her at his words. Lukas wouldn't want to join the Keepers at first, but if she could just talk to him…

"I agree," she said quietly.

Rett patted her on the shoulder as he passed. "Want to see how much the lamb has grown?"

"Not right now. It's time for breakfast. And I have an essay to turn in."

Rett paused by the door. Sini set her finger against her candle, letting a stream of pink *vitalle* flow out of her and into the live flame. It was so simple, once something was already using energy, to add more. The flame burned bright and high with her help, and Rett nodded approvingly before opening the door. When it shut behind him, the breeze caught the flame and it flickered dangerously. She cupped her hand around it, but one final swirl of wind snuffed it out. Sini shoved *vitalle* toward the top of the wick that was still tinted red, but the pink light dribbled away hopelessly.

She growled at the candle and everything it represented. The fat tower of wax stood like a battlement in front of every other failure. Every object she'd tried to push *vitalle* into. Every instance of trying to transfer energy into something static. There had been hundreds of tries, but every single one had been a failure.

It was so infuriating not being able to do simple things.

The map lay in semi-darkness. She could barely make out the blank space of the moors and she shoved herself out of her chair. Everything pointed to that empty rolling land, but that made no sense, and that irritated her all the more.

But the idea of the moors had nagged her for too long. She'd ask the twins about it today. A sliver of reluctance wormed into her, but she pushed it away. The twins would listen. They always took her ideas seriously. Even ridiculous ones like this.

She peered at the shadowed map. "Where are you going, Lukas?"

TWO

Her stomach reminded her of breakfast, and she cast one last annoyed look at the map before leaving it in the gloom. Crossing back through the main tower, she found the kitchen thick with the scent of warm bread. Firelight glowed out of the gaping oven in the wall. Setting three plates on a wide tray, she cut off a generous slice of bread for each, adding mounds of soft cheese and liberal helpings of avak jam.

The avak pits Will had brought back from the Sweep had thrived in the valley and the Keepers had a near constant supply of fruit and jam. Keeper Gerone, who was convinced the plant had some sort of magical power, was constantly experimenting with it.

She grabbed three cups of water and headed up the tower. Five rooms past her own, she knocked softly on a thick wooden door. At a word from inside, she opened it and stepped into a cheerfully bright room. A wide door to the balcony was swung open to let in the morning light. Nikolas and Steffan sat, as they always did, at a table just wide enough for the two of them in high-backed chairs, bent over a single thick book. One man wrote on the left page, the other on the right, filling the book with the history of the country of Gringonn. Sini couldn't imagine there wasn't already a history of the insignificant country somewhere in the enormous library, but she couldn't bring herself to point this out.

The twins were nearly identical. Their hair was long and wiry, their faces the washed-out color that skin gets when it's been facing the world for too many years. Each had a neatly trimmed beard that hung down to his chest. Their hands were gnarled, but they held their pens without any trembling.

Each man was halfway down his page, their handwriting also identical. She'd stopped trying to figure out how they did it years ago. While each wrote on their own page at the same time, the book told a single story, moving flawlessly from one page to the next. If the one on the left finished his page in the middle of a sentence, the next word would be found at the top of the right page, written hours earlier by the other man.

The first day she'd asked them how they knew what the other would write.

"I know exactly what I would write." Nikolas had shrugged. "And I trust he'll do it correctly."

Sini had stared at them speechless. "Do you ever…miscalculate?"

Nikolas had given Steffan an irritated look. "On page seventy-three he fit in an extra word. We haven't decided yet whether we should leave it at both the bottom of one page and the top of the next or sully the book by crossing one out."

"You've only mis-guessed once? How many pages have you written?"

"Today we'll finish two hundred and thirty-four."

"Can you…hear each other's thoughts?"

"No, dear. Our thoughts are all our own. But when you live with someone long enough, you can guess what they're thinking pretty well."

She'd pointed at Nikolas's hand. "You're not identical. You write with different hands." She'd felt a little bit of triumph. At least when they were writing, she'd be able to tell them apart.

"Not exactly." He had laughed. "It would be too crowded if I tried to use my right hand on this side of the page, don't you think? I'd be pushing Steffan out of the way. But we'll switch seats after lunch. Wouldn't want to exhaust one hand too much."

For the last four years, she had found them here most mornings. They'd finished the fourth volume two years ago, and had been working on the fifth, adding to it daily. She approached them and waited until they paused their writing to look up at her.

"Breakfast?" she asked with a smile.

Steffan gave her a gentle smile over the glasses perched on his nose. "Smells delicious."

Nikolas closed their book and pushed it to the side so she could hand them each a plate. She pulled a stool up to her side. "Is there anything interesting or valuable on the moors in Gringonn?"

"Valuable?" Steffan asked. "No."

"I've always thought they had a haunting sort of beauty," Nikolas said.

"As if there was more emptiness there than in most places." Steffan patted the book. "We discuss the moors in chapter three, volume 2."

Nikolas looked at her curiously. "Why do you ask?"

Sini hesitated. "Would you think I was crazy if I said Lukas was there?"

The two considered her for a moment.

"We'd be more likely to think you had a reason for saying so, and that your foster brother was the crazy one for wasting time there," Steffan said.

Nikolas nodded. "Those moors are bleak. Why do you think he's there?"

Neither man looked skeptical.

"I have no idea," she admitted. "It just feels like he's moving that way."

Steffan stroked his beard. "We'll think about it."

Nikolas coughed a wet, painful sound into a damp cloth. His elbow knocked his cup and the water spilled out toward their book.

Steffan jerked his hand forward and a stream of pale blue light shot across the table under the water, lifting and forming into a small bowl. Nikolas righted the cup and Steffan poured the water back into it from his glowing blue air-bowl.

Sini bit her lip. The twins could manipulate air so easily it seemed effortless.

Nikolas peered into his cup. "Thank you."

Steffan nodded, then turned his gaze to Sini. "Could you see the bowl shape? Or was it less distinct? I was imagining a bowl."

"It was a smooth layer of light with brighter veins running through it," she said. "Definitely bowl-shaped."

"Still blue?"

She nodded. "Yours is always blue."

"You seem troubled this morning," Nikolas said.

Sini chewed on her bread slowly. "I want to understand what Lukas is doing and where he's going." And how she could bring him here, but she didn't add that part, even to the twins.

They nodded sympathetically but said nothing, allowing her to continue if she wished.

"And I'm frustrated again by my inability to move *vitalle* in the simplest ways. Mikal gave me some exercises to move a small piece of linen, and I couldn't do it." She motioned to where Steffan had just picked up the water. "I couldn't affect the air at all."

She dropped the bread onto her plate. "I can't even light a candle. Every single Keeper has been able to light a candle. Half of them started fires as the first sign of their powers. No one has ever had a problem making a path into inanimate objects."

"I am twenty," she continued. "It's been eight years since the first time I did magic. Maybe if I had tried before I was taken to the Sweep…Or maybe I never could do the simple things everyone else can." She almost stopped there, but the twins waited quietly. Like always, their patience drew the words out. "Maybe the Roven broke something in me."

They were quiet for a moment before Steffan spoke softly. "My dear, we have never seen anything broken in you."

Anyone else would point out how much power she could find in the sunlight, or how she was perfectly able to put energy into living things, or how she could heal better than any of the other Keepers. But the twins never brushed away her words like that.

"We understand the frustration." Nikolas looked ruefully at the candle at the corner of their desk. "We've always felt inadequate around fire. Mikal can manipulate it so effortlessly."

It wasn't remotely the same thing, but the camaraderie made her feel a little better.

"It's nearly impossible not to think of our differences as limitations," Steffan said.

Nikolas chortled. "We're a hundred years old and still working on it." His laugh ended in another thick cough.

She picked up her bread and looked at him critically. "How are you feeling?"

"We have only seventeen pages left in our book." There was a deep pride in Steffan's voice.

"That's wonderful! I thought you two might just keep writing until you ran out of paper." There were certainly more than seventeen blank pages left in the book.

Steffan ran his thumb over the corner of the remaining pages. "We considered it." His voice was more somber than she'd expected.

"Well, I'm thrilled!" she said, trying to bring back his enthusiasm. "I'll read it as soon as you finish. Mikal has been assigning me the driest books ever written. It will be a joy to read something interesting."

"Ah, you should find something more fun than this to read," Steffan said, while Nikolas finished coughing with a fit that shook his thin body. "What do young people read today?"

"I have no idea what other young people read. The Shield has me researching Mallon, which is thoroughly depressing, so I try to supplement all that with happier stories before bed. I've found some fascinating ones about female Keepers. Alaric also sent me two books on anatomy so I can learn more about how the body works and maybe ways I can help it heal."

She finished her bread and stood, stepped around the table until she was next to Nikolas. "Speaking of healing…"

Clearing their lungs of the fluid that built up in them each day was simple. Their bodies were already working on it every moment of every day, they just didn't have the strength to make headway. All their bodies needed was a little help. It would take mere moments to give them relief and keep them from getting any sicker.

Instead of leaning forward in his chair as he usually did, Nikolas leaned back and looked at his twin.

Sini paused. "Do you want me to start with Steffan?"

"There's only seventeen pages left," Steffan said gently.

Sini glanced between the two of them.

Nikolas gave his brother a pointed look. "You're being too vague."

Steffan sighed. "We only have seventeen pages left before we are done with our work, my dear. So there's no need to clear our lungs anymore."

Sini's chest gave an uncomfortable lurch. "What does one have to do with the other?"

"You've been such a help to us." Nikolas turned in his chair to face her. "Without you, we certainly wouldn't have finished."

"Might not have made it past King Torroluuna," Steffan gave a wheezing laugh. "How would the world have survived without knowing about his pet squid?"

Sini didn't laugh. "Gringonn has nothing at all to do with your health." Her voice was sharper than she meant it to be. "Now which of you is going first?"

Nikolas reached out for her hand and Sini let him take it. His fingers were like leather, dry and a little cool. She had the urge to snatch her hand back.

"We owe you a tremendous debt, my dear." Steffan's face held a smile, but his honey-brown eyes were watery behind his spectacles. "All we've ever wanted was to finish the book. Before you came, we thought we wouldn't have time."

Nikolas was smiling at her too, a sad sort of smile that asked her to listen. But she didn't want to listen. Not to this.

"Seventeen pages won't take us long at all."

"All simple things too. No complicated coups or military maneuvers. Just a few weak kings and the spread of the bandit lords." Steffan set his hand on the book. "We've got plenty of time for that."

Sini pulled her hand away from Nikolas and crossed her arms. If she stopped healing them, nothing would happen immediately. Their lungs would fill slowly, and infection would certainly come, but it might be weeks, or a month before...

She shook her head. "There's a lot more to life than writing books." She'd meant to sound forceful, but her voice quavered with something that sounded much more like fear. A tightness climbed up her throat and she funneled it into a glare before it could come out as tears. "It's the simplest thing in the world to treat your lungs. Let me heal you. Maybe after you're done with these seventeen pages we could do something crazy. Like have breakfast near the window," she gestured to the side of the room. "Or if we're feeling really adventurous, maybe a picnic out in the grass."

The twins were quiet for a moment, and while they didn't look at each other, she couldn't escape the feeling that they were agreeing on something.

"A picnic would be a lovely way to celebrate finishing," Steffan said at last.

The agreement had a ring of finality to it.

"Will you let me clear your lungs?" she asked quietly.

The two men shook their heads.

"Don't worry, Sini," Nikolas said. "We're not going to disappear today."

"We do have seventeen pages left," Steffan agreed.

Sini moved back to the front of the table and sat. The old men turned back to their bread. Sini fiddled with a piece of crust on her plate. The room was stuffy and none of the breaths she took felt deep enough.

Nikolas watched her. "We've ruined breakfast, haven't we?"

"More than breakfast, I think," Steffan set his bread down and the two men waited for Sini to talk.

"If you have seventeen pages left," she said finally, biting back any tears and using her most matter-of-fact tone, "then at least let me work on your hands. There's no reason for those to be stiff." She took Steffan's gnarled hand gently in hers and traced pink runes above his knuckles. The old man let out a quiet sigh and stretched his fingers. She healed the other three hands that waited for her. She held the last one for an extra moment, but couldn't think of a single thing to say to them. She picked up her own plate, not bothering to wait for them to finish, needing to get away just to breathe. When she got to the door she looked back at the old men, who were watching her sadly.

For a moment she couldn't get the words out. Finally she whispered, "Don't write too fast."

THREE

The twins' news twisted in her gut like a knot. They couldn't do this. She clenched her hands on the railing outside their door, staring down the tower.

The Shield.

She half-ran down the ramp. Everyone listened to the Shield. He'd been the leader of the Keepers for nearly eighty years, voted into that position when the last Keeper died. Surely he could change the twins' minds.

His door was open but his room empty, which wasn't surprising. The Stronghold was bright with morning light now, and she crossed the wide floor and into the library. She leaned over the railing to see down the four stories to the swirls of color on the tiled floor far below. Books lined the round walls. Most of the levels below her lay in shadows.

"Shield?" Sini called out, her voice reverberating in the quiet library.

Someone hissed for her to be quiet, and Mikal's head appeared above her, peering disapprovingly down at her from the next level. Two floors higher than him, just under the glass roof, an old, wrinkled hand waved over the railing. Sini ignored Mikal and the reminder that she still hadn't turned in her research and ran up the ramp that spiraled between the levels. She reached the top breathless and almost crashed into a small step ladder spread across the aisle.

The Shield was perched on the top of it with a book spread open on his lap. "Good morning, my dear."

"The twins want to die," she blurted out.

He marked his place with a finger and turned to look at her fully. The Shield was the oldest of the old men in the Stronghold. Gerone figured he must be one hundred and thirty by now. He was also the only Keeper shorter than Sini. When she found him standing, which wasn't often, he barely came up to her shoulder. The top of his head was completely bald, as though years ago all his hair had climbed down and gathered into great tufts of eyebrows. There was nothing old about his gaze, though.

His customary warm smile settled into something more sorrowful.

"They only have seventeen pages left." Sini came in closer, throwing the words at the Shield.

The old man sighed. "A great accomplishment."

"No. It's just a book. And they say that this close to the end, they don't need—" The tightness in her throat cut off the last words.

He gently closed the book on his lap and tucked it back into the shelf. Climbing down from the ladder, he gestured to two nearby chairs tucked into a windowed nook. Sini grabbed the pillow off one and hugged it to her chest.

The Shield sat, scooting back into the chair and leaving his feet hanging above the floor. "For them it's not just a book."

"I know." Her voice was still too sharp. She squeezed her eyes shut and tried to calm down.

"Do you know much about their childhood in Gringonn?" At the small shake of her head, he continued. "Their parents originally lived in Greentree, but, tempted by the promise of a market for their wool, they moved their family to Gringonn and proceeded to lose every bit of money they had."

Light from the window spread across her lap, and Sini picked at a thread along the edge of the pillow. "Sounds depressing."

"That's the way with facts, isn't it? They can sound so bleak. Regardless of what happened during those years that looks so unfortunate from afar, Nikolas and Steffan developed a deep love for that land. Those twins have a way about them, don't they? I've never met a single person who didn't like them, and I've known them for almost ninety years. We're still feeling the benefits of relationships they made during the two decades they lived at court, even though most of the people they knew there died years ago. The twins were so well-loved that people's children and grandchildren are fonder of the Keepers because of them.

"In Gringonn—even as children—they befriended farmers, shepherds, milkmaids. Everyone from small local leaders to bandits. Even one up-and-coming warlord. And they found enough fascination there to fuel a lifetime of research into a country everyone else overlooks."

The Shield waited for her to say something, but she couldn't muster any enthusiasm for Gringonn this morning. The country was overlooked because it was dull. The monarchy was so weak it was constantly overrun by one of the dozens of equally-weak, squabbling warlords. But the royal family was so enormous that there was always another cousin who could step in and take back the throne. No one had enough power to actually take charge, though, and the history of the country was nothing but a muddled mess of petty coups and frail restorations.

Of course, none of this had anything to do with Gringonn. Sini took a deep breath. *Where is the real pain?* The twins would ask her. *What's sitting beneath the anger and all the swirling demands?*

"But why…" She cast about for her real question. "Why does finishing the book mean they're done with…"

There was the pain. It was childish and selfish, and tears pushed their way into her eyes. She wanted to say *breakfast*. "Everything else."

"It is everything else," the Shield answered, his words sounding as if he meant *breakfast*, "that has convinced them to stay long enough to finish."

Sini shook her head and gripped the pillow. Her chest didn't want to breathe right.

"By the summer you came to us, I thought the twins wouldn't last until the midwinter feast. You've been a miracle to them, my dear. None of the rest of us could have kept their lungs as healthy as you have. The way you interact with a body—you have a skill few Keepers have ever possessed. A skill I never thought I'd see. The twins certainly never hoped for someone like you."

Sini dashed the tear from her cheek. Then another. "And what was the point of healing their lungs for four years? To finish a book that only they care about?"

"Certainly not," he answered gently. "The book was merely a timeline."

What was that supposed to mean?

"You could continue healing their lungs for a long time, could you not?"

She nodded. The fix was so simple.

"But you must understand that every morning you heal them, and every afternoon the fluid begins to seep in again. By night they are in pain and cannot escape the truth that their bodies are worn out. Every day they go from being healthy to dying."

Sini drew back. "They never told me that."

"Because every day they decided it was worth it."

"For a book?"

The Shield raised an eyebrow. "Have you ever asked them how their day was?"

"Every morning. They tell me what they wrote the day before, or little stories about when Mikal and Gerone were young. Or funny things from their days at court."

The Shield nodded. "I suppose that is what they'd tell you. I often take my evening tea with the twins. There's a leaf Alaric brought back from Napon that has pain-deadening properties, and I like to make sure it's measured properly into their drinks."

"I could have come by in the evening and helped with the pain," she protested. "No one ever told me they needed it!"

"The tea was enough." The Shield gave her a smile. "Do you know what they tell me when I ask about their day?"

She picked at the loose thread on the pillow. "That they're miserable?"

The Shield laughed. "I've never heard either of them complain of that. They tell me about their breakfast with you."

Sini snapped her gaze up to the Shield. He looked serious.

"They talk about their hopes for the Keepers now that you have come. About how they never imagined living to a time when they could meet a Keeper who would breathe new life into this old place. Who would breathe new life into them."

Sini stared at him. "Then why stop trying now?"

"They needed a timeline, an end point when they could stop fighting against their bodies. Everyone's life has an ending. Not too many people get to choose it as they have."

"But they're still writing—they're almost done. They could take some time off. Do something else for a while." *Keep having breakfast.* "Finish it later."

"By my calculations, if they had kept writing at the speed they are capable of, they should have finished that book a year ago."

The words sank into Sini slowly. "Maybe they write slower because their hands hurt," she whispered.

The Shield shook his head. "Their hands have bothered them for twenty years." The Shield reached out his own small, knobby hand and set it on Sini's knee. "They aren't leaving in spite of you, Sini. They've stayed this long because of you." The Shield let out a snort. "They certainly didn't need another year to talk to me."

Sini's gaze traced a barely perceptible crack along the joint in the stone wall next to her. She should feel grateful, somehow, for the Shield's words. There was a truth to them. But mostly they made her feel alone and brittle, as though she was riddled with hair-thin cracks of her own.

The Shield let her sit in silence for a few minutes.

She smoothed the pillow out on her lap. "I still don't like it."

"Neither do I. But since it isn't up to you or me, we must find a way to settle with it."

The thought of the twins was too painful. She pushed it away, looking for something to distract her. The Shield had papers filled with his thin, slanting script and precisely drawn diagrams spread out along the base of the bookshelves. She picked up a stack piled next to her chair and flipped through it, breathing in the smell of paper and ink.

The library roof again.

Above them, the blue cloudless sky was visible through a starburst of glass panes that spanned the library. The eight trigonal roof sections outlined by dark wooden beams met at a diamond of glass. The overall impression was of an eight-pointed star shooting off sparks of light in every direction, frozen before they could rain down on the books below.

The little old man was obsessed with the idea that the glass roof of the library, which had covered the seven stories of books for hundreds of years, was no longer good enough. He was too well respected for anyone to point out that this strange new fixation didn't warrant as much time as he gave it. Too respected for them even to point it out to each other when he wasn't around. But it was notable that no one ever joined him in his work unless he specifically asked.

The Shield turned toward the window they sat next to, his eyes troubled under his explosive eyebrows. He was such a strange little man. Somehow, sitting there surrounded by the stone of the wall, the dark shelves of books, and the fall of the light through the roof he worried about so much, he seemed more like part of the building than a person inside it. For a moment she thought she saw something like tendrils of light swirling out from him, climbing along the stones of the window frame like a vine.

She blinked and it was gone.

"Changes are coming," he said, almost to himself.

She leaned forward. "What's coming? Can you see the future?"

"I'm not sure the future is seeable. But when you've paid attention long enough, you start to feel when changes are stirring." He turned back to her, his eyes suddenly sharper. "Can you feel it?"

She pulled back a little at the intensity of his expression. "I don't think so."

He made a disappointed noise.

Running her fingers over the papers on her lap, she pushed the next question out. "Do you know how long the twins have?"

The Shield's gaze shifted back to the sky. When he spoke, his voice was heavy. "I do not." With a heavy sigh, he scooted off the chair, grabbed a small pile of books and inspected their spines. "It's a mercy they reached this point before you left."

The page she held slipped out of her hands and she snatched it up before it could fall. Cold fingers of fear wrapped around her. "I'm leaving?"

"It feels that way." The Shield looked out the window beside them with a sorrowful expression.

She clenched the papers on her lap. The idea was appalling. "I can't leave. I have…" Rett and her studies and she didn't even know how to find Lukas yet. "Too much to learn."

"I feel the same way. Too much to learn."

Sini set the pages down on the pillow and tried to smooth out the creases she'd left along the edges. The familiar view of the valley outside caught at her heart. "Do I have to leave?"

"No one ever has to leave, my dear."

"Well then, I won't. Not for a long time."

A warm smile spread across his face. "When you first came to us, I was worried you wouldn't find a home here. That we would all be too…old."

"It's the best place I could imagine." She fought back the lump that seemed ready to shove its way up her throat again. Everything she loved was here. "I really can't imagine anything that would make me leave."

"Can you not?" He studied her for a moment. "In that case, I found four new books for you." He handed her the pile he was holding. "Alaric finished his treatise on Mallon. You can be the first to read it. He's also copied a work on Mallon that he found in Obsidian, which should be interesting.

"I ran across an early history of the Keepers shelved with the Baylonese books, the reason for which you'll see once you read it. And I found this." He handed her a thin book bound in dark green leather. His eyes sparkled. "A book of quotes by Keeper Chesavia. It was also shelved"—he scowled across the library toward the opposite shelves—"very wrongly with the Baylonese books. I have been looking for it for twenty-three years."

"Twenty-three years?" She took the book eagerly. Chesavia was a bit of an enigma among Keepers but Sini had always felt a kinship to her. Chesavia was a healer and the only other Keeper who'd had an affinity for the sunlight. Sini had read all the stories about her she could find. "What have you needed for that long?"

"A turn of phrase I couldn't quite remember."

Sini looked at him expectantly.

He sat straighter in his chair, cleared his throat, and raised one finger. "The day is shaped not by the violence of the storm, but by the fall of the light and the voice of the rain."

Sini waited, but he did nothing more than grin at her. "What does that mean?"

The Shield settled back into his chair. "Chesavia's life was one hardship chased on by another. And she speaks of them frankly. I think she was fiercer than any person I have ever heard of."

"Because she sacrificed herself to kill that water demon?"

"No, although that took great determination. She was fierce because she could always see past herself and find goodness in the world." The Shield glanced at her. "And goodness can be harder to find than a mis-shelved book in a seven-story library."

"She always struck me as," Sini hesitated, "a little meek." Chesavia had admittedly died young, but she'd never been the sort of Keeper to take charge. It had been another thing Sini had felt a kinship about.

"Indeed. But meekness can have its own form of ferocity."

Sini smiled at the idea. "What does her quote about the storm mean?"

The Shield considered this for a moment. "I'll let you read it and decide. We can discuss it once you're done."

Sini flipped through the pages, a thin hope forming. "Thank you."

A breeze blew in the window and brushed against her cheek, distracting her from the Shield's answer.

She glanced over.

There had been no breeze. The window beside them didn't even open. Sini looked outside, but the view was unchanged. Nothing but a great cliff face across the valley.

She turned back to find the Shield watching her with resigned eyes. "You do feel the change."

FOUR

The rest of the day played out like a hollow version of a normal day. An antsiness sat on her, and after trying unsuccessfully to read, she grabbed a broom and climbed the ramp to the highest room of the Stronghold—if you could call a place with no walls a room. Open stone arches surrounded her in all directions, allowing the breeze to blow through unhindered. She stood breathing it in, letting the silence sooth the edges of the raggedness inside her.

The valley of the Stronghold spread out beneath them, stretching north and south from the tower. It was widest here where the Stronghold was built, but still it wasn't wide. There was room for the orchard and a low grazing hill on one side, the horse fields on the other. The white stones from the tower gathered up the sunlight and reflected it out into the valley.

To the north the tall cliffs were etched with shadows. The open grass of the valley floor led to the neatly-rowed orchard. Behind the apple trees, pear trees, and Gerone's new thriving patch of avak bushes, the pine forest ran all the way to the end of the valley. To the south the valley lay open and rolling with low hills. A small herd of cattle and a couple dozen goats grazed. At its southern end the valley was filled again with trees. A half-dozen low buildings, stables, and workshops dotted the area around the tower.

The purpose of this room was to hold the Wellstone—a round, melon-sized gem cut with more facets than she could count. It was mostly white, but individual surfaces flashed continually with bright colors the way light flashes across new snow. Each glint of color flickered so quickly it was gone before she could focus on it, except a handful which shone with a bright, pure white.

It was small enough to pick up, but she'd never touched it. The Keepers used it to store memories. Whenever Will or Alaric came back to the Stronghold they placed into it the record of where they'd been and what they'd seen. From then on, other Keepers could access the memories. The idea of sharing so much of herself with a stone felt too exposed. The fact that someday she'd leave the Stronghold and be expected to use the Wellstone when she came back prickled at her. Yet another thing she didn't want to happen.

Threads of white light curled around the Wellstone and out into the air, then sank back into the stone. The Roven had called things like this burning stones, gems with some sort of power in them. On the Sweep the rich had hoarded them. Killien and Lukas had always worn them, trails of light dragging behind their rings or the gems that hung from chains around their necks. But Sini hadn't seen any since coming to Queensland. The Keepers were against trapping living energy into something as inanimate as a stone.

It unsettled her that a burning stone sat here, at the pinnacle of the Stronghold. It was the sort of thing that should be on the Sweep.

The burning stones on the Sweep enclosed energy like a prison. The light that swirled inside them was trapped. The trails of light they left as they moved—another one of the things only she could see—had always seemed to Sini like bits of power that had escaped.

But the light in this stone was different. The tendrils of energy that slipped out of it before sinking back in looked almost playful. The light wasn't trapped. It was more like the stone and the light were both the same thing.

She turned her back on the stone and began to sweep vigorously, cleaning dead leaves and dust from the corners of the floor. She finished the top and began working down the long ramp, funneling all her emotions into swift strokes of the broom, gathering dust and dirt into a growing pile. Finally, sore and tired, she swept the filth out the front door.

Exhausted, but less agitated, she carried her new books from the Shield outside. The sunlight fell on her like a warm mist and reflected off the white stones of the tower. She turned her face up, letting it seep into her. Taking the books to one of her favorite sunny spots, she pulled out the book of quotes by Chesavia. The leather cover was stamped with a pine tree, the edges worn smooth enough that she couldn't feel the outermost branches under her fingertips.

It was organized by topic, and she flipped through, reading quotes about light and the sun.

The sunlight falls to the ground, showering the whole world with life.

Sini nodded. It was a shame others couldn't feel the sunfire. A few pages further, her attention caught on a quote about the Stronghold.

The place I feel most at home, but am afraid I am too foreign to truly belong.

Sini's breath caught at the sentiment and she closed the book gently. This was a book for a less emotional day.

She picked up the two from Alaric. The first promised to be enlightening. *Development and Capabilities of Mallon the Rivor - compiled from the history of the elves and the Shade Seekers.* Alaric had been working on this since Sini had met him four years ago. He'd recorded everything he learned from Ayda the elf, both what she'd told him herself, and what knowledge she'd put into Evangeline when she saved her life. And Alaric had made multiple trips to the library at Obsidian, the center for the knowledge of the group of magic-workers called the Shade Seekers, a group with a loose organization and a looser moral code.

She flipped open the second book. This one promised to be even better. Written neatly in Alaric's measured hand, the title page read:

A copy of
The History and Future of the Great Lord Mallon the Undying,
Rivor of Men, Devourer of Souls, Master of the Fallen.

By Wizendœrenfürderfür the Wondrous

Reproduced and Annotated by Keeper Alaric,
Cygnus Cycle
12th *year of the reign of Queen Saren, first of her name.*

The next page held two notations, both written in Alaric's neat hand.

Author's Note:

I, Wizendœrenfürderfür the Wondrous, First Wizard among the followers of Mallon, Holder of Secrets, Caster of Spells, and Spinner of Dreams, do hereby begin this record of the ~~illustrated~~ illustrious life and triumphant acts of the Great Lord Mallon the Undying. We stand today at the cusp of domination over Queensland. Few are left who stand against us, and their powers are ~~weak~~ feeble. In the lull before this last and most terrible storm, where Lord Mallon will march across the land like ~~an army, a monster,~~ a thundercloud of wrath, and the people shall flee before him as ~~little people do~~ frightened sheep, in this tedious time of waiting while I am in danger of growing bored enough to pull out my own magnificent beard, in this time I will endeavor to record the history of our great leader so that all of posterity will know of his wondrous deeds.

Scribe's Note:

I, Alaric the Keeper, not ranked among the Keepers, as we have no ranks, Holder of Pens, Reader of Poorly Written Records, and Reproducer of Obvious Untruths, do hereby begin this replication of this ~~illustrious~~ bumbling record of the actions of Mallon, written by a doting devotee whom I knew merely as Gustav.

In this tedious time of reading this wretchedly written account, while I am in danger of growing bored enough to rewrite the entire thing from scratch and do it correctly, I will endeavor to reproduce it accurately, remaining faithful to the original form, including all spelling and grammatical errors, struck-through words, and insipid asides. I will, in addition, record all runes as written, no matter how sloppy or inaccurate. My best guess at the proper rune will be noted on the adjoining page.

This record is riddled with egregious errors in verifiable historical events. Each of these has been noted on the adjoining page, the true events recorded, and reference material listed.

I have, to the best of my ability, attempted to restrict my comments to factual errors in the text. In passages of excessive pomposity, idiocy, or blatantly poor logic, I readily admit that I have failed in this goal.

A complete record of my personal interactions with Wizendœrenfürderfür the Wondrous, more aptly named Gustav, can be found in the account of my time with him in The Final Destruction of Mallon the Rivor. *As of this writing, copies are available both in the Keepers' Stronghold and the royal library.*

Throughout the rest of the book, Gustav's writing filled the right-hand page, while Alaric's corresponding notes almost filled the left. Sini leaned forward, amused by Gustav's pompous opening, trying to follow his ridiculously convoluted sentences.

Mallon came to the Roven Sweep early in his life, sold into slavery with his entire family to pay his father's debt.

Sini flinched at the words. She had known that Mallon had come to the Sweep in that way, but reading it, the closeness to her own story pressed on her uncomfortably.

Upon reaching the Sweep, his younger brother, sold with him, fell too ill to stand on the slaver's block. When the Roven began to beat him, Mallon shot fire out of his hands, killing three Roven and gaining the attention of a nearby stonesteep. At such an immense show of power, Mallon was immediately taken to the compound of Kachig the Bloodless in Tun, where he was trained in the mystical arts by the best minds of the stonesteeps.

That's where the similarity ended. Mallon, with all his power, was trained as an apprentice, then eventually became a master among the brightest magical minds of the Sweep, while Sini's education was cobbled together from the books Killien could find and Lukas's limited knowledge. Maybe if she'd studied under Kachig the Bloodless she'd know how to light a candle.

A shiver ran down her back at the thought. Kachig would have turned her into a ruthless killer. So maybe the candle deficiency wasn't that big a problem.

There was a rather extensive, rather convoluted section describing the training Mallon had received. According to Gustav, the Rivor had instantly mastered every task set before him and bested his tutors daily. Alaric had made copious notes on the adjoining pages about the impossibility of several of Gustav's claims. Including one that asserted that Mallon had shifted the moon in the sky to prove a point.

Mallon had studied among the countries to the south of Queensland for many years before returning to the Sweep and demanding an army. By that time, he had mastered what Gustav called *liberating them from the weight of choice,* but what those in Queensland called *riving*, from the word for when a gem cutter cracks a stone so deeply it becomes worthless. Mallon could somehow leave a piece of himself in a person, controlling whatever part of their decisions he wanted, even from a great distance. The price of disobedience was terrible pain, or even death.

With these powers, no one on the Sweep dared defy him and he soon commanded a large army of Roven—perhaps the first time the clans had ever united under one banner. Gustav named it a sublime achievement, heralding an era of peace under Mallon's rule.

Sini shook her head over the book. Gustav couldn't really have believed all this.

She flipped to the next section of the book, which discussed Mallon's incursion into Queensland.

Mallon the Undying had always recognized the weakness of Queensland, her inability to protect her own subjects, and the corruption of her nobility.

Sini frowned at the sentiment. How many times had she heard Lukas complain of the same thing?

He set his mind to freeing the country of its useless leadership in an effort to turn it into a land of prosperity and safety. He was like a guiding light to the masses. A beacon of peace and tranquility.

He strove to destroy the Keepers. In his words, "They are a pestilence! A plague upon the land. A filth to be washed out! They are a disease!"

Gustav continued to list the weaknesses of Queensland, the error of her ways, the many, many ways she'd failed her people, and the uselessness of the Keepers. The wording and the tone prodded Sini uncomfortably. They were too much like the things she'd heard Lukas say. He blamed Queensland for everything that had happened to him. Blamed the local baron for not protecting him at the fair when the Wayfarers took him. Blamed the military for not guarding the borders when they weren't stopped on their way out of the country. Blamed the queen for claiming to protect the people without doing anything substantial.

But mostly Lukas blamed the Keepers for not finding him before the Roven did, and then not even knowing he was gone.

She flipped ahead to read about Mallon's attack on Queensland.

There is a small, vicious jackal on the Sweep that lives in packs. Like a brotherhood of tiny, rabid dogs. They're no taller than your knee, but they're fast and their teeth are as sharp as fangs as daggers.

They circle around a prairie deer and nip at its legs, drawing only small amounts of blood at first. But the pack follows the deer, tracking it like a pack of ferocious wolves. As fierce, but in a smaller way. And they nip, nip, nip until they wear the animal down. When it collapses, the jackals swarm in and devour it.

Mallon the Undying's army was much like a pack of persistent jackals, nipping at Queensland's borders until they weakened her.

Gustav's writing style almost made Mallon's invasion ridiculous. If she hadn't known how many had been killed, how horribly the eventual pitched battles had gone, how much Mallon had destroyed, it would have been amusing.

Alaric's notes along the side were sometimes laughable. (*For the leftmost rune, I assume Gustav meant "strengthen." What he wrote is not even a rune, but is perhaps closest to "fungus" with a diminutive tag. So instead of "strengthened Mallon" it reads "Mallon the Small Fungus"*). And sometimes depressing. (*Gustav fails to mention in his account of the "glorious" battle at Stevan's Creek, that Mallon's giant tore through a schoolhouse of children. Eighteen of them were killed, the remaining three terribly wounded.*)

There was a gap in the book when Mallon disappeared into the elven Greenwood and all the power he had over people disappeared in the span of one sunny afternoon. The notes resumed with Gustav's best guesses as to what had happened, and his hunt for Mallon's body. The book ended, very unsatisfactorily, after an entry by Gustav that he had found a dwarf who might know the location of a stone that might wake Mallon from his cursed sleep.

Alaric noted again at the end that the rest of the story could be found in his own book, *The Final Destruction of Mallon the Rivor.*

Sini closed the book feeling unsettled. It was disturbing reading Gustav's praise of a man such as Mallon.

She pushed the book away and wiped her hands on her pants. There was something repellent about it, and something churning deep in her gut that felt angry. Buried beneath Gustav's babbling she couldn't escape how much Mallon's story echoed her own. Born into poverty, enslaved on the Sweep, trained by stonesteeps.

But more than that, the resemblance to Lukas's sentiments chilled her.

Whether it was more the thoughts of Mallon and Lukas, or of the twins, a heaviness sat on her all day.

She was ensconced snugly in the library wing that evening, copying more of Flibbet the Peddler's book into her journal, trying to get the funny little man's whimsy to lift her spirits when she felt the waves roll through her. Wave, wave, pause, wave, wave. *Come.* This time Rett's call had come from the direction of the stable, so she didn't bother to cast out and ask where he was. She felt a pang of guilt. She hadn't stopped by to see the lamb Rett was so worried about all day. As she pushed herself up from the table in the library, she wished their code was more expansive. She'd have immediately sent out waves apologizing if she had more of a vocabulary to work with than *come, library, stable,* and *kitchen.*

She did find him behind the stable, eager to show her the lamb's growth, and the calmness of the evening mixed with Rett's gentleness and the soft white curls of the lamb's wool helped soothe her more than anything else had.

The next morning dawned clear and crisp again. She breakfasted with the twins, talking of her reading and the sprinkling of gold on the leaves outside. She asked them questions about Flibbet and Mallon and baby lambs. She healed their hands before leaving, pausing at the door to ask the only question she'd really had.

"How many pages left?"

Steffan gave a faint smile. "Sixteen."

She nodded past the tightness in her throat. Unable to think of anything else to say, she left.

Feeling too lonesome to go back outside, she brought her books to the library and settled at her favorite table on the top floor across from where the Shield sat again with his roof project. She could hear other Keepers occasionally too, but no one interrupted her.

The day dragged on, and she threw herself into her reading.

A scrabbling at the roof caught her attention. A miniature hawk perched on one of the beams and straightened his feathers with his beak. After a moment he peered down into the library.

"Will's back!" Sini shouted, shoving herself up from the table before realizing she was in the library. From lower floors both Mikal's and Gerone's heads peered up toward her.

The Shield studied the little hawk, troubled. "I wonder what news he has that needed to be brought by hand."

FIVE

S ini ran down the ramp through the quiet tower. It had been half a year since Will had been at the Stronghold. Twice that long since she'd seen Alaric. She stepped out through the wide front doors to find Talen winging into the sky, the sunlight edging his wings with reddish gold.

The sunlight poured down on the cliff marking the western edge of the valley. But the dark tunnel gaping open at its base was black with shadows. The sound of the horse came through before she caught a glimpse of movement. They had almost reached the end of the tunnel before she could make out Will, dressed in his black robe, riding a perfectly black horse. Will's beard was black as well, and still held the small silver beads that he'd started wearing on the Sweep. His face behind his beard was pale, and his hands gripped the reins tightly.

When he saw her, he trotted over and shook out his hands, a rueful smile on his face. "I hate that path."

Sini glanced down the tunnel as though the ghosts that guarded the path to the Wall might have slipped in behind him. Beyond a hidden door at the far end of the tunnel that only a Keeper could open, the path to the Stronghold was guarded by ghostlike apparitions that taunted people with their deepest fears. She'd only traveled the path to the Stronghold twice each year on her trips with Mikal for supplies, and that was more than enough.

The image of her own face, gaunt and accusing, floating in milky whiteness in front of a tree still haunted her dreams. And if she couldn't see the face, she could always hear the words. *You are alone.*

"What do the ghosts say to you?" she asked, still watching the dark tunnel.

"It's not what they say." Will climbed down. "I tell myself all those things every day. The problem is the way they say it. They just blurt things out. Breathing it right into your face. No buildup. No sense of story."

Sini laughed. "Well don't teach them how to. Their breathing and blurting are bad enough."

Will stepped back and studied her for a moment. "You're getting old."

She raised an eyebrow. "Don't say that too loud, they'll start expecting more from me."

"Just wait until the next Keeper is found. It shouldn't be long now, and you'll get to help train them."

"Stars help them if they're reliant on me." She paused. "We are still watching for wayfarers, right?"

"It's been three years since they were allowed into the country, and the queen has the roads watched. No one is going to abduct the next Keeper."

Sini would stop worrying about that when the new one was found, but she said nothing.

Will led his horse toward the stable. "I've heard rumors that wayfarers are being attacked in the southern countries. People have gotten the idea that they carry great piles of gold in their wagon. It's a bad time to be a wayfarer."

"I can't say I feel sorry for them," Sini said. "The Shield is trying to replicate what Vahe did to find magic users. He thinks we might be able to find new Keepers more easily. Or, he's working on that when he's not working on strengthening the library roof."

Will paused. "He's still stuck on that?"

Rett's large form appeared in the stable door, keeping Sini from having to do more than nod. He ducked his tall head under the lintel and took the reins, smiling widely and patting Will heavily on the shoulder.

Rett cared for the small herds of sheep and goats, the few horses, and the three milking cows as though they were the most precious things in the world. He had named each animal, and for the first time since he'd been injured on the Sweep he'd learned to do a bit of magic by himself. Gerone had worked with him for half a year to perfect the calming spell, *paxa,* and Rett could successfully use it on any of the animals. More than successfully, really. During a thunderstorm she'd seen him calm five sheep with one word.

"You look well," Will said.

Rett straightened. "The Shield put only me in charge of the horses, the sheep, the pigs, and all forty-two chickens. Gerone doesn't even help anymore."

"It's about time," Will said. "Anyone can see you're more skilled than the rest of us put together. Am I imagining that the stable is brighter than it used to be?"

"Rett took out part of the wall along the back," Sini said, "so the horses have an easier exit to the pasture. Fresh air actually flows through it."

"You're a genius, Rett." Will pulled his saddle off and Rett beamed as he led the horse into the stable. "I have no idea how we survived before you two came. My horse will be thrilled to be somewhere he's appreciated. You would not believe how poorly he was cared for in Barehallow."

Rett clucked disapprovingly. "How is Killien?"

Will's smile faded. "I haven't heard from him in six months. Which I find troubling."

"Sora?" Sini asked.

Will's smile disappeared entirely, and he shook his head.

It had been four years since Sora had left to go back to her people. Sini had thought she'd be back with Will before the first snow. She and Will corresponded through the dwarves, but she had yet to come to Queensland.

"Is there any chance there's still some bread left?" Will asked, his voice not quite carrying the cheerfulness it had moments before.

"There should be. The old men here eat next to nothing, you know."

Will nodded. "More for us."

"And there's avak jam."

Will's eyes lit. "Lead on!"

The kitchen was already crowded. Gerone, Mikal, and the Shield had all gathered and the room was warmer and louder than it had been in a long time.

Gerone passed Will a plate holding two pieces of bread thick with avak jam.

"There are so many reasons to miss you, Gerone." Will sat at the table and took a huge bite.

The other men settled into chairs, as well.

Sini hesitated for a moment, uncertain whether she was invited to what had turned into an impromptu council. But the Shield motioned her to a chair next to Gerone.

Will nodded. "You need to hear this too, Sin."

She sat, feeling partly excited, partly out of place. Usually when Will or Alaric appeared, they would go straight to the Shield's room to share their news, then they'd call all the Keepers to a council. There was something oddly casual about all the old men gathered here, but under everyone's calm exterior things felt unsettled. Will seemed reluctant to get the conversation started.

"I assume if you're here there is news you couldn't send by raven." Mikal prompted. "So, what's happening in the world?"

"Mostly," Will said around a bite of bread, "it's still falling apart, bit by bit. The number of small problems spread across Queensland is reaching ridiculous proportions."

"Small problems in a country as big as this is hardly unusual," Mikal said.

"This feels different." Will set the bread down. "And I'm not the only one who thinks so. Alaric is troubled by them, and Queen Saren..." He stopped and looked uncomfortably around the room. "Saren's demanding that the Keepers relocate the Stronghold to Queenstown. She's emptied the north tower for us."

Sini's mouth dropped open and there was silence at the table for a moment.

The Stronghold couldn't be relocated.

"She's not the first monarch to make such a suggestion," the Shield said.

"It's not a suggestion. Her exact words were that she 'insisted we accept her hospitality', both for our safety and because she wants us closer."

"We do not need her protection," Mikal said. "Even if someone were to figure out where this valley lies, it is inaccessible to any but ourselves. There could not be a safer place. The queen is not in a position to insist on anything. We are not under her command."

"But we do help the queen protect Queensland," Gerone pointed out, "and if she is convinced it is necessary, we should at least discuss it."

"What does Alaric think of this idea?" the Shield asked.

"He is...annoyed." Will grimaced. "Probably because Saren told him he didn't have enough information for her and she needed to be able to contact the rest of you, especially you,"—he nodded to the Shield—"more quickly than could be done by ravens."

"It does not matter what she wants," Mikal insisted. "The queen does not command the Keepers. We are outside of her land, we are outside of her authority."

Sini glanced quickly between the men. Technically Mikal was right. Queensland ended at the Marsham Cliffs, and the Stronghold lay in a valley past them. But the Keepers had always been dedicated to Queensland and its people. They served the reigning monarch any time their help was accepted.

"The problem is more practical than authority and borders," Gerone said to Will. "The twins won't be able to travel. They have almost finished their book."

Sini's gut squeezed and she looked at the table, trying not to notice the understanding that filled Will's face. When he spoke, his voice was low. "Then we cannot leave them here alone. What Saren wants is impossible."

"Some of us could go," Gerone said.

Mikal stiffened. "I'm not going back to court."

"Gerone can't go," Will said. "The rest of you would starve."

He looked questioningly at the Shield.

"I can't leave yet." The Shield's voice was firm. "The library roof isn't finished."

No one commented. The Shield looked around at their discomfort, meeting Sini's eye with a hint of amusement, but he said nothing at their silence. From outside Sini could hear the birds chirping in the sunlight that had finally reached the valley floor.

"You could come, Sini," Will said.

Sini snapped her attention to him. "What would I do there? I know less than any of you."

"After studying here for four years you know more than most people in the country do," he said. "More than most people at court, for that matter."

She shook her head. "I have too much still to learn, and I know nothing about politics or court life. There'd be no point in me going." And there was that horrible feeling there, like everyone expected her to do…something. Something amazing. Something beyond her abilities.

Will opened his mouth to argue, but the Shield raised his hand. "Will, you can return to Queenstown and help Alaric. The queen will have to make do with that. I will send her a raven with our answer."

Sini bit her lip, waiting for Will to disagree, but he didn't. Instead he traced the grain of the table with his finger, his bread forgotten.

"I gather there is more news?" the Shield prompted him.

Will glanced around the table and Sini got the sense that he was gauging the men around it. Sitting together, Sini was surprised at how old they all looked. She had lessons with Gerone in his room, surrounded by his books with his face lit with enthusiasm. Here in the bright kitchen his skin was etched with wrinkles. Mikal wasn't quite as old. Only seventy-two, which often seemed young among the other men, but judging from how stiffly he was sitting his back was bothering him again, and he rubbed his knuckles as he watched Will. His hands had been aching more often lately, even though he rarely admitted it.

The Shield was in some ways ageless. If someone ageless could be trapped in a tiny, wizened, bald little body with explosive eyebrows.

She felt Will's gaze on her and turned back to him. His face had changed some in the past four years, as well. When she'd first met him, the night he'd told the story of Tomkin and the Dragon to the Morrow Clan, he'd seemed boyish. She never would have imagined he was a Keeper.

Until he had begun that story…

Will let out a sigh. He looked tired. "There's another reason you should come, Sini. We've discovered what has happened to the gold merchants."

His gaze didn't leave Sini's face and she tried not to shift under the attention. Of all the problems Queensland was having, the gold merchants were the most boring. And the one she knew the least about. Gerone had tried to explain some of the complexities of economics to her, but it had been so boring she could barely remember it.

"Saren sent three units of the ranger company to Gulfind. They found the pass into it filled by a rockslide. It took them a week to scale the mountains around it and reach the central valley, and when they did…"

He was still talking to Sini, and something about his voice caused a little knot of dread to form in her stomach. "It was in ruins. All of the outlying land was destroyed. Burned and razed. They assume that a large part of the population has been killed. Only the city of Renndon still stood.

The mines were open and working, but they didn't see anyone doing anything else." His eyes tightened a little in what appeared to be sympathy.

Why sympathy? Sini glanced around the table, but everyone was watching him, waiting for him to continue.

"On a huge outcropping near the city was a red dragon."

A dragon? Sini dragged her gaze back to Will. "Lukas?"

Will gave a half-hearted shrug. "There wasn't anyone near the dragon, but it would be strange for the creature to suddenly decide to capture an entire country by himself.

"The valley is cut off," Will continued, finally looking around the rest of the table. "The rangers could see that the pass into Coastal Baylon was blocked, too. From their description, Saren's masons think it would take a month to clear either pass. Another well-placed rockslide could kill anyone working on it."

The Keepers began asking Will questions, but Sini didn't listen. Her stomach tightened and pushed the feeling up her throat. This couldn't be Lukas. He'd been doing annoying things along the border, certainly. Little, ineffectual attacks that bothered tiny areas of Queensland. But this? Why would he slaughter all those people? Especially people in Gulfind? Yes, he'd used the frost goblins to attack the Roven, but those were his enemy at the time. It had all been part of a larger plan to free the Morrow. He wouldn't just wipe out a whole group of people. Especially not for gold.

And it didn't make sense, anyway. Gulfind was the westernmost country along the southern coast. It was nestled against the Scale Mountains.

"Lukas can't be that far west," she interrupted, and all the old men turned toward her. "He's been moving further east for the last half a year, I'm sure of it." They all waited for her to go on. She felt stiff with tension at voicing the next thought. She couldn't prove it and it sounded so farfetched. "If he's anywhere, he's on the moors of northern Gringonn."

She waited for them to dismiss her words, but the Shield looked at her closely. "What would he want on the moors?"

"I have no idea. Neither did the twins. I just think he's been moving east."

"Has anyone else noticed that?" Mikal asked, looking around the table. No one answered.

"Not straight east," Sini said, before they could tell her it was unlikely. The chair felt unrelentingly hard under her. "There's been some back and forth, but in general he's moving east."

"His dragon sitting in the west says differently," Mikal pointed out.

Gerone was watching Sini, considering her words. "Maybe he and the dragon parted ways."

Sini felt a bit of the tension ease out of her, and she nodded.

"Then someone else is controlling the creature." Will picked up his bread again. "Dragons don't invade countries for gold, no matter what the old stories say. That's a distinctly human goal."

Sini shook her head. She knew she sounded stubborn and childish, but they didn't understand. "This isn't Lukas."

None of them answered her right away.

"No one knows him better than you, Sin." Will pushed his empty plate away. "But the number of people who can control a dragon is quite small."

"He wouldn't kill all those people." She was angry at the idea, angry at the thought the Keepers believed it, and angry at herself for how obstinate she sounded.

Will raised his eyebrow. "He killed a lot of people with frost goblins on the Sweep."

"They were enemies of the Morrow." She knew it didn't sound convincing, but this just didn't make sense. "He wouldn't kill all those people for gold."

"It is possible that he is not taking it for himself as much as keeping it from everyone else," Gerone said.

"Did they see anything that pointed to Lukas besides a dragon?" she demanded.

Will's expression said the dragon was enough. He held her angry gaze. "The only other thing they found was a…warning, maybe? There was a man hung so high on a cliff over the pass that the hunters couldn't retrieve his body to bury it."

"Someone from Gulfind? Or Queensland?" Mikal asked.

"With the condition of the body, it was impossible to tell. The only thing they could tell was that both his hands and his feet were shackled with gold."

Sini's heart caught in her throat. She could almost hear Lukas's voice. *That gold merchant chose his slavery. It's just his shackles are made of gold.*

SIX

"Shackles is what Lukas called gold." Sini glanced out the window. The Sweep felt like another lifetime. Like a different world. The colors were all different there. Everything here was more vibrant. Even the memory of Lukas's words was faded. "Worse than our slave tunics, or,"— her gaze dropped to Will's black robe—"Keeper robes." Out of the corner of her eye she saw Mikal's face tighten in disapproval, but none of the others looked surprised.

"We need you in Queenstown, Sini." The earnestness in Will's voice brought her attention back to him. "You know so much more than we do about him."

Sini looked down at the grain of the table. The old men waited patiently. They always gave her the time to think, unlike on the Sweep where she'd been expected just to obey. She glanced at the Shield. Was this the change he'd felt?

Everything in her rebelled at the thought of leaving.

"I've been telling you everything I can remember about Lukas for years." There couldn't be much they didn't know by now. "And who knows how much he's changed? I never would have expected him to do this in Gulfind."

"It isn't facts about him we need," the Shield answered. "You don't know what he's doing now, but you know him. You know his dreams and his fears and his heart in a way that maybe no one else does. If it weren't for you, we'd all assume he'd taken Gulfind out of greed. Now we know there is another reason, and it gives us a chance to understand him."

When she still didn't answer, the Shield continued, his voice kind. "It is through you that we'll be able to see his humanity. It's a dangerous thing to forget a man is a man, but it is far too easy to do with those who set themselves up as our enemies. Even this first step he's taken is hard to see as anything but savage. If we are to remember the man behind the actions—and it is of the utmost importance that we do—we'll do it through your eyes."

A fear from deep inside her worked its way up. "What if he isn't the man I remember anymore?"

"The man you knew is still there," the Shield said. "He may have taken himself deep into darkness, but it will be because he still wants what he always wanted and fears what he always feared. He's just lost track of any good paths that would bring his desires to him, and now he is trying to forge his own paths, by whatever means."

What had Lukas always wanted?

Freedom. He'd always wanted freedom. And to make those responsible for his slavery pay.

The room waited quietly for an answer she didn't have.

"Take today to think about it," the Shield said.

Sini nodded.

Gerone pushed himself up. "I'll start some soup while we catch up on everything else."

Sini stood up from the hard chair. "I'll help."

"The council chamber is a little messy." The Shield gave a self-conscious smile. At Will's raised eyebrows he added, "Drawings of the library roof."

"And piles of books and scrolls," Sini said over her shoulder, pulling the bowl of onions down from the shelf. "And a clay model of the library."

Will laughed and the Shield grinned as well. "All essential, I assure you skeptics. But we might as well talk here. Sini?"

She glanced back to find the Shield watching her with an inscrutable face.

"Whether you leave or not, it would be helpful if you shared with us everything you know about Lukas."

She paused. "That would take ages to write out."

"I wasn't talking about writing it."

It took her a moment to realize what he was saying. Her hand tightened around an onion. "The Wellstone?"

The Shield nodded. "Most likely it's the details you'd never think to share that will become meaningful as we try to understand what Lukas is doing."

"The knowledge you have could be essential," Mikal agreed.

The idea of the Wellstone felt daunting, but it was certainly better than going to court. She nodded and the Shield looked pleased.

Sini helped Gerone start the soup while Will caught them up on everything else. The vast majority of the discussion was boring. Sini tried to pay attention to the different economic ramifications of the gold trade coming to an abrupt halt. The discussion about the poor harvest was troubling, but it was just a small part of the country and a few select crops that were affected.

The Keepers circled around continually to Lukas, guessing at his involvement. Their questions to Sini skirted along the edge of accusations and she tried not to be frustrated. If even the Keepers here were tempted to see Lukas as a heartless killer, how much more would the people at court? And when Lukas was killing people in Gulfind, what were they supposed to think?

The entire conversation made her feel vaguely sick. She couldn't bring herself to believe that Lukas had killed all those people. But she couldn't quite bring herself to think he hadn't.

The valley fell into shadows and dinner time arrived, bringing even the twins down to the kitchen. Will greeted them warmly and the three of them fell into a discussion about some obscure Gringonnian tale. Sini watched the twins closely, but she couldn't see any obvious signs of discomfort. Rett came in as well, his face and hands newly washed. The twins settled themselves on either side of Sini.

Gerone had made a pastry, and the smell of the season's first apples cooking wrapped around her. The voices of the Keepers, from the quiet words of the twins to Will's rolling laughter echoed off the stone walls, brightening the kitchen until it almost glowed. Sini lost track of the words, looking from one face to the next. Never could she have imagined a place like this, where there were no servants or masters, no rich or poor. Where her own wellbeing was valued as highly as everyone else's. She could not have imagined how deeply she could love a group of men so old they'd had a hand in the histories she read.

The twins laughed with Will and a tightness formed in her throat. She couldn't leave. What if she didn't get back before…No. She couldn't leave.

Will entertained them all with stories of his latest adventures, and it was later than usual when the old men drifted back to their rooms. By the time the oven fire had burned down to coals, only Will and Sini remained.

"I need to go back to Queenstown tomorrow." Will stood. "Will you come with me?"

She shook her head. "But send me any questions you have, and I'll answer them immediately."

Will pressed his lips together but didn't argue. "Then I'm headed up to use the Wellstone. I'm sure I've forgotten to tell the Shield half the things I should have. If you want to use it, I'll show you how."

"I suppose it would help them to know Lukas better," she admitted.

"They certainly won't get any good memories of him from me."

"I forgot the Wellstone has your memories of him." She grimaced. "Those can't be good. He hated you."

Will shrugged. "I'd hate someone, too, if I thought they were supposed to protect me and they hadn't. But if you want us to know more about him than I know, it has to come from you."

Will started out of the kitchen, and Sini fell in beside him.

"Does it really take all your memories?" she asked. Someone had lit the torches along the ramp and the tower glowed with firelight.

"'Take' is misleading. You share your memories with it. Like you're telling it a story. You keep your memories, but the Wellstone does, too. And yes, it sees all of them."

"That feels…"

"Invasive?"

Sini nodded.

"It's not as bad as it sounds. No one ever goes up and rummages through people's memories. They're too busy researching things that actually matter."

"They're going to go look through mine, though."

"Your memories of Lukas, but not your entire life. No one cares what you ate for breakfast on your tenth birthday. And even if they did, it's almost impossible to find that out. It's challenging to direct the stone. I'm terrible at it. Alaric, of course, can do a decent job of finding what he's looking for.

"The memories swirl around in it like a storm. The Shield can control it. He says he can 'follow the threads', whatever that means. But sometimes I wonder…"

Sini waited, but he didn't continue. "You can't stop there."

Will grinned. "Sometimes I think he's more connected to the Stronghold than the rest of us are."

"To the building?"

"The whole valley. It's different here than the rest of the world, right? And sometimes I think he's connected to that. The man's one hundred and thirty years old, but besides the fact that he shrinks a bit each year, he never seems to age."

They passed the Shield's closed door.

"Maybe," Sini said quietly, "he'll just keep living until he gets so small we can't find him."

Will laughed. "Maybe all the previous Shields are still here too, wandering around too tiny for us to see."

They passed the council chamber and Will glanced in the door. His eyebrows shot up at the blanket of paper that covered the table and the floor. In the torchlight shining through the doorway, they could just see the clay model of the library in the center of the table. He opened his mouth as though he wanted to comment but closed it again.

"I agree," Sini said. "I've asked him what exactly the problem with the library roof is, and he says it's not strong enough. When I asked for what, he said the library wouldn't tell him."

Will let out something almost like a laugh. "See? I almost believe it could tell him. He's the same with the Wellstone, he talks to it in a way we can't."

"Is the stone alive?"

"If you ever want a really boring lecture that essentially ends up at, *We don't know*, ask the Shield that someday."

"What part of my memories does it get?" The question wasn't quite what she wanted to ask. "How I felt? What I saw?"

"What you saw and heard. But it doesn't get your emotions. It'll take our memories of dinner, but if someone else finds them in the stone, it will be like they were sitting with us. They'll hear all the words, and see the room. If they're skilled they might even smell or taste the apples, but they won't know what parts of the twins' chatter made us happy and what parts were too bittersweet to enjoy."

The ache that hadn't quite left Sini's chest flared again. Will nodded toward her. "This place won't be the same without them. I used to eat breakfast with them years ago. I always put off Gerone's lessons so I could stay longer. They are my favorite storytellers. Or storyteller? I'm not convinced they're two separate people."

"What if," Sini started, a fear suddenly occurring to her, "one of them dies before the other?"

Will looked at her out of the corner of his eye. "Do you think that's really a possibility?"

"I hope not," she said quietly.

"They've lived a good life, Sini. It's not all sad."

She walked past the twin's door in silence. "It's mostly sad."

Not far above, the ramp they were climbing passed through an opening in the ceiling and they stepped into the open room atop the tower. The valley was painted in dark blue shadows and the sky was black enough that most of the stars were visible.

The Wellstone glittered on its small table.

There was only one chair, and Will sank into it. He set his hands on the sides of the crystal, closed his eyes, and bowed his head.

Sini waited, mesmerized by the glittering lights. Slowly the stone calmed. More surfaces took on a steady grey color, flickering with bits of candlelight. Will let out a long sigh. She tried to stay quiet. The final stars came out and the breeze ran chilled fingers along her neck.

Will finally lifted his hands off the stone and shook them out. He glanced up at Sini ruefully. "Whenever I come out of this stone I'm sure I'm missing out on so much." He pushed himself up and offered her the chair. "Can you imagine how many good stories are locked in there?"

Sini forced a smile and sat. The chair was made of thick oak, the table the same. Heavy enough that they wouldn't be blown about if the wind rose. Not that it did often, this low in the valley. The Wellstone sat nestled in an intricate silver stand carved into a tree trunk with roots spreading out across the table. Her hands felt clammy and she wiped them on her tunic.

"It doesn't hurt," Will said. "Just touch it, and it will do the rest. When it finally notices you, it will look for memories it doesn't already know. Besides the unsettling experience of watching all your own memories float through your mind, it's not unpleasant."

She nodded, her eyes fixed on the stone, trying to follow the flashes of color, her mind trying to make sense of them, reluctant to sit. It was too vulnerable a thing to do.

"It's an intimidating thing to use." Will stood against a stone column between open archways, his dark Keeper's robe blending into the gathering shadows. "But the Wellstone gives us a unique chance to see the most personal stories of each other's lives from someone else's perspective. And once we've lived a story with someone, it's nearly impossible to hate or judge each other.

"Sometimes being a Keeper is difficult. Some have been put in situations where there are no good answers. Some have lied, some have hurt, some have killed. Not always for the right reasons, because no matter how long they've lived or how much they've studied, they're still human.

"But no matter what, they're still my brothers"—his smile was white in the darkness—"Or sister. So I believe that whatever of my humanity I reveal in this stone, they'll love me anyway. In fact, I think the amount of humanity we reveal to each other is one of our greatest strengths."

She did trust the Keepers. But the idea of them seeing the worst of her gave her pause.

She steeled herself. Showing Lukas's humanity was what had brought her here, and if it took revealing her own to accomplish that, so be it.

Taking one last bracing breath, she focused on the flashing Wellstone and set her hands on the cold, sharply faceted sides.

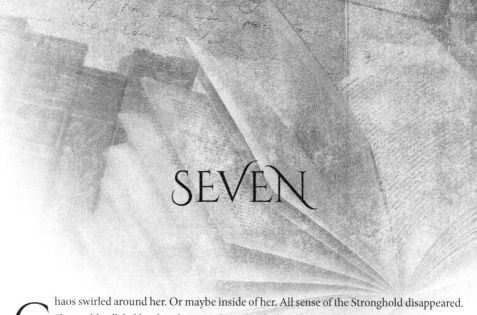

SEVEN

Chaos swirled around her. Or maybe inside of her. All sense of the Stronghold disappeared. She could still feel her hands pressed against the hard edges of the stone. But there was no breeze, no sounds of the evening.

Images blurred past her, flashing into sight then dimming, skittering away like wind over the grass. Snippets of sound caught at her ear, conversations just out of reach. The Wellstone was vast. She'd imagined something small. Something she could talk to. But this was an entire world spreading out far beyond what she could understand. There was a weightiness to it, too, an agedness. Certain sounds and images were old. That woman's face that blew past her shoulder, for instance. Although Sini didn't know how she knew.

It wasn't quite chaos. There was some sort of pattern here, some sort of purpose.

On the Sweep in the hottest parts of the summer she'd swum in the ocean and once found herself in a school of tiny silver fish, darting around her in just this way. Her movements had sent ripples of chaos through them, but as a whole, they'd moved together. The Wellstone moved together, as well, with the same chaotic fluidity.

Something caught at her. A tendril of curiosity. The maelstrom around her calmed and something focused on her. Her attention caught on a faded memory of a dirty street. Everything was cold and crumbling. Her mother's legs came closer, then her face. They stood in a hovel somewhere in the Lees, but not one she recognized. Which wasn't surprising. They'd been driven out of a new place every season.

Sini realized she'd been holding on to the memory, watching and listening to it. But all that was too long ago to worry about right now. She released it and the stone drew out more and more of her childhood in a dirty grey blur. Stealing, hiding, learning to be as quiet as she could, sneaking through alleys, away from her mother's tongue, out of range of her father's anger. The chill of it all seeped into her again. The way her bare feet always ached with cold.

The flow of memories slowed a bit with a flash of color. A wayfarer's wagon sitting in the dingy streets, Vahe's face on stage as he tossed a finger of flame through the air that lit up the world when it passed over her. A tangle of anger and regret filled her. She tried to get the Wellstone to move faster, but it seemed fascinated with the moment, focusing less on Vahe than on the magic that stirred in Sini's small body. Everything about her had tingled, like the time the innkeeper woman had given her skin a hard scrubbing. A pinkish haze seeped out of her fingertips.

The Wellstone finally moved on. A new memory filled the stone and the rest of the chaos was pushed back.

When Sini caught her mother's face, she tried to pull away from it, as well. When nothing changed, she tried to hurry it forward faster. But the Wellstone seemed to recognize this as important, and the scene moved by at a gut-wrenchingly slow pace.

Her mother looked at her with an uncharacteristically tormented expression until it fell on the smashed half loaf of bread in Sini's hands. Then the severity was back.

"That's all? We can't live on that."

"I'll go out again," Sini began, holding out the bread.

"There won't be enough," her mother snapped. The anger in her voice was deeper. It burned more than her usual impatient answers. She lowered her gaze to the bread. "There won't ever be enough."

Her mother took the bread more gently than normal, turning Sini's hands over to look at her scuffed palms. Dirt etched the lines in black. "Something must change."

Fear filled her at her mother's odd behavior. Sini opened her mouth to say she'd go over to the docks when her mother dropped her hands and turned away.

"Your father is outside." Her voice was hard again. "Go to him."

With her mother's back turned like a wall, Sini slipped outside. It was strange to hear her father's voice this early in the morning. He never woke before noon. Sini rounded the side of the shed and jerked to a stop.

He was speaking with Vahe. The wayfarer looking too bright and clean for an alley in the Lees. She stepped up as close to her father as she dared, and Vahe flashed her a smile that held more satisfaction than warmth.

"How would you like to see the world, Sini?" Vahe asked. When he held out his hand toward her thin trails of light streamed behind the rings on his fingers, just as they'd done during his show.

Sini shrank back behind her father.

"Go to the man." Her father's voice was slightly blurred from the night's drinking. He pushed her forward and held out his other hand. "The silver."

Sini froze, confused. He was trading her?

Vahe ignored him and took Sini's hand. His fingers were thin and cold and hard. She tried to pull her hand back.

"You remember the fire from yesterday? It knew you were special. You don't belong here in the filth of the Lees. Come join my family, and we will travel Queensland and the rest of the world. You'll see the beautiful parts of cities, mountains, rivers, the sea."

The sea? The sea didn't really exist. How could there be nothing but water as far as you could see? Sini stopped pulling away and Vahe's smile widened.

"We're leaving Queenstown this morning, but I wanted to find you first. Come." The word was part invitation, part command, but his hand was clamped over hers and he pulled her a step down the alley.

"The silver," snarled her father.

Vahe gave him a contemptuous look and turned away. Two leather pouches, one on his hip, and one inside his vest, caught Sini's eye. A clink from behind him told her there was a third tucked along his back.

The wayfarer was rich. He wore bright clothes. Cotton trousers dyed a greenish blue. A bright yellow shirt, even brighter than the little yellow flowers that grew in the field behind the butcher's. An orange vest like a setting sun.

Sini's father let out a cry of "Thief!" and lunged toward Vahe. The wayfarer sidestepped him smoothly and threw a punch.

Was this just a ploy to get the man's money? Sini could help with that. She tugged at the hand he gripped, and slipped her other inside Vahe's vest, working the pouch loose. Vahe didn't notice.

By the weight of the pouch, even if it only held coppers, it was a fortune. Vahe's hand locked on to Sini's hand. Her father shoved himself up, his nose and lips bloody, still bellowing. Sini's mother ran out from the shed. Sini flashed her a grin and dropped it into a nearby pile of trash where any sound it made was lost in the commotion. But instead of coming to help Sini, her mother rushed forward and jumped into the fray, beating at Vahe with a towel. Sini yanked at her hand with all her strength.

Vahe threw one more punch, sending Sini's father sprawling. Her mother rushed to his side, but Sini still couldn't free her arm. Vahe pulled her behind him as he strode down the alley.

Sini called out to her mother, reached back, but her mother met her gaze for only a moment before twisting her head away to look for the pouch.

Vahe's steps were long and Sini had to scramble to stay upright next to him. Sini stared at her mother, trying to understand why she didn't follow. She looked up one last time before Sini was pulled around the corner, and though there was something in her face Sini had never seen before, she stayed crouched by her father until the dingy boards of the inn blocked her from view.

A dart of anguish cut into Sini, an emotion the Wellstone didn't touch. It only took the images and the sounds, the feel of the cold dirt under her feet, the tightness of Vahe's hand. But it disregarded the utter confusion and panic that had filled Sini that day, and it paid no attention to the way the last expression she'd ever seen on her mother's face made her feel now that she understood it. The poverty must have been impossible, with so many mouths to feed in that broken alley. Her mother's face had been filled with guilt and desperation. But it was the relief woven through it that Sini couldn't bear.

Sini tried to catch her breath as the memories poured along faster, now. Flashes of her tiny cell in the wayfarer's wagon, forests, mountains, the sea stretching out in endless glittering light. And then another endless sea, this time of grass.

Clay buildings of Porreen rushed past until a red-haired Roven man stood before her. Killien's beard had small braids hidden in it, and his face was eager. The gems in the silver rings on his hands glowed, but none of them trailed light as they should.

"I'm Killien, and I know you feel like you've been torn from your home, but I assure you, you have been brought to the place you belong. Here you will never be hungry or cold." Beside him stood Lukas. His brown hair and short beard were styled like the Roven, but he wore a grey tunic instead of leather, and he looked at Sini with a desperation he was trying hard to mask. "Here we recognize that like Lukas, you have amazing powers, and we'll train you to use them." Killien gestured to a wall of books. "Can you read?"

Sini shook her head and Killien grinned. "Then we'll teach you."

The image shifted to a hallway as she followed Lukas.

"The room between Rett and me is empty." He was easily twenty, at least ten years older than her. He walked with a slight limp. But it was the first time since she'd been pulled from the alley that

someone looked at her with genuine kindness. "It's not as bad as it seems right now. There's always good food and clothes, even if they're grey. We'll teach you to read and you can help me with my research. We'll see what kind of magic you can do. If you're like Rett and me, Vahe woke it up but you can't do much yet. That'll change in the next few months." He glanced down at her. "I know it's a lot. When I came here there was no one to explain things. Rett is—well, you'll meet him. It was hard. But whatever you need, come find me, alright?"

"What am I supposed to do here?" Sini asked.

"Get stronger at magic and prove to Killien you're useful. If you can do that, everything will be fine."

"And if I can't?"

Lukas shot her a tight smile. "We'll make sure you do."

A different sort of pang thrummed inside Sini. Her mother's face, she wanted nothing more than to forget. But Lukas—the face Lukas had shown her that first day—that she wanted to remember. Back before the anger had festered in him. She wanted to remember the kindness and protection he'd offered, and continued to offer her, for years. To remember the excitement in his face while they were translating runes or learning some new form of magic.

The Wellstone settled on a scene in a small clay room. Lukas set a violet quartz on the table and Sini leaned gratefully into the memory. Yes. This was what the Keepers needed. Sini focused on the Wellstone. It felt open to her. She pressed a little *vitalle* into it and a slight tingling brushed along her fingertips. She urged the Wellstone to watch closely.

The stone responded. The motion slowed and the image grew more vibrant.

"I can do the mirroring, but I'll need you to put the fire into the stone." Lukas set another red glowing stone next to it.

Sini kept her hands clasped behind her. "How much fire?"

"A lot, Sin. Or I'd do it myself."

"I can find the energy, but it won't go into the stone. Let me give it to you instead."

Lukas shook his head. "I can't do both things at once. You fill it. I'll shape it. You know you can access more fire than I can." As it always did, bitterness tinted his voice when he mentioned that fact. Had she noticed it back then? She kept her mouth closed. It was useless to tell him again that there was fire in the very air around them. It filled the sunlight, it even trickled through the moonlight and starlight at night.

One time she had burned his hand terribly. After that, she'd learned to keep the flow to a gentle drip if he needed any. She'd asked him once how he knew when there was too much fire, but he spoke of broken stones and burned skin. That hadn't really been her question.

But she bit back any questions she had, lest she prompt another rant about how stonesteeps and Keepers secreted knowledge away, making it almost impossible to even find books about it.

"Maybe you could get it started," Sini began.

He gave her an impatient look, but set his finger on the quartz. A bit of fiery light trickled into it and a dim purple glow started in its core. Sini reached out for the energy that danced around the room, scattering with the sunlight. There was more even in this dim place than the stone could possibly hold. She began to draw it in, letting it seep into her arms, her face, her neck. She set a fingertip on the stone just where Lukas had, looking for remnants of the path he'd made into it. She found a thin trace of it and poured the fire into it. But the path was closing and most of the fire ran across the *surface in wisps of pink mist. She knew Lukas couldn't see them, so she poured out more and more, until her fingertip burned and the pink light flowed across the surface of the gem like a waterfall. The thinnest trickle of light flowed into the stone and it slowly produced a glow Lukas could see.*

He gave a grunt of approval and set his own finger on the quartz. The light inside shifted and changed. "More, Sini. I need a lot more."

She pulled some of the sunlight from outside. It gushed out of her fingertip so brightly she squinted. The glow of the stone increased again, but most of the pink light poured off and disappeared into the air.

Lukas made an impatient noise and she tried to push more, but the path closed completely and the light in the stone faded.

"No!" Lukas yelled, grabbing at the stone.

He leaned on the table, his hair hanging down covering his face. It was a long moment before he spoke. "You've got to work on this, Sini." He glanced up and saw her face, and his expression softened. "Go out the back so you won't run into Killien. I'll tell him…we're still working on it."

She nodded and hurried toward the door, anxious to be gone.

She was almost out of the room when he spoke, low and urgent. "We have to fix this. Before Killien finds out."

She nodded without looking back and ducked out of the door.

The familiar dull sense of inadequacy sat in her stomach. The next few years of life with the Roven flashed past. Learning to read, learning runes. Discovering she could heal small injuries, then more serious ones. She and Lukas bent over a new book, the thrill of learning new ways to use burning stones. Moment after moment of the life she'd had on the Sweep with Lukas and Rett.

She trickled more *vitalle* into the Wellstone, offering it direction through her memories. Offering it as much of Lukas as she could remember. To her surprise, the Wellstone followed her lead eagerly.

As time went by she noticed a change in Lukas she'd never seen before. He grew angrier, more impatient. Never with her, but with everything else. With her he was still enthusiastic and kind. But he grew belligerent behind Killien's back. His plans and his research became more vicious.

Vahe's face appeared again, telling a story in his wagon parked outside of Porreen. Sini's heart gave a lurch and she saw Lukas's face, twisted in hatred.

No.

She pulled at the memory. Not that one.

The Wellstone ignored her and drew more of it out. Lukas picking a small topaz out of his collection of stones.

No.

Sini yanked at it, trying to stop the Wellstone, but she was utterly helpless. In desperation she flung a different memory at it. Lukas learning about compulsion stones, studying whether they would work on a dragon.

The Wellstone paused like an animal catching a new scent. For a heartbeat both memories clamored with each other for attention. Sini gently added some energy, strengthening the thought of the compulsion stones, and the Wellstone hurried past Vahe and eagerly followed the new path.

Sini let out a breath and let the stone follow her memories to the bitter end, when Lukas flew out of the enclave on the dragon. A part of her watched what the stone learned, but another part wondered at the vast universe of knowledge spread out around her. Without her attention, the stone ran through all her memories of the Stronghold up to tonight.

A weariness started to grow in her. She lost her hold on the memories and the stone began to pull back from her. The chaos began to swirl again.

Wait!

The stone ignored her. Bits of her memories flashed past, connected to other unfamiliar ones by thin threads.

Threads. The Shield followed the threads. The Wellstone was indexing the memories. Maybe, if she helped, it would guide her to something interesting.

She started with the dragon. Letting *vitalle* continue to seep into the stone, she reminded it that Alaric already had met that dragon, and the stone lapped up the idea. A blur of color and sound settled, and Sini stood in a dark valley staring up to a sky filled with stars. Except for one spot where they were blotted out. The darkness spread until she could see a glint of red hurtling down toward them.

Ayda, alive and glittering with a sort of starlight herself, stood in the middle of a blackened swath of grass, her face turned up toward the dragon.

The creature dove toward the elf. Alaric had told her the story more than once, but to see Ayda stand there, brushing aside flames and knocking the dragon to the ground—Sini barely breathed.

The Wellstone knit bits of Sini's memory to this one. And others which must have been Will's from the enclave. The dragon became more whole somehow, more real. His scales glittered with ripples of deep red. He grew more vivid, more wild and savage.

This was the creature Lukas controlled.

It was harder this time, but she pulled up her memory of the twins at their breakfast that morning, and the stone eagerly began to connect it to a vast web of memories. She pulled her way along the threads, watching the twins grow younger, their beards darken to brown, their hands grow straighter and stronger. She followed them back until they were two boys, less than ten years old, wandering the streets of a foreign town, chattering with everyone they found.

Seeing them in Gringonn, even though the town was dingy and the landscape past it dull, shifted something in her. The country became a real place, the people around the twins became real lives with real hardships.

The sheer complexity and length of their lives sobered her. The years she'd known them were so little of what they had lived. Her claim on them felt weaker, even as they became richer, fuller people. For the first time since breakfast, she felt that the idea of only seventeen pages left was a great accomplishment. An act of love almost finished, and the chance for them to rest well-deserved.

An exhaustion began to grow in her mind. It was harder to hold the memories she wanted to see, and she let the twins drift away into the chaos. She was about to step out of the Wellstone when she remembered Chesavia.

With all the effort she could muster, she got the stone's attention and reminded it of the book of Chesavia's quotes that she'd received from the Shield. The stone shifted and a latticework of images spread out before her, stretching as far as she could see in every direction. Memories tied to other images, piled on top of each other, strung together in such a mesh of connections that she didn't know where to start. Images butted up against each other, fragments of words and songs swam past mostly unintelligible.

The word "sunlight" caught her attention. She was so tired she felt a bit like she was moving through molasses. Grabbing the memory required so much more strength than the earlier ones.

Finally, it came into focus.

The memory was of someone talking to a young woman—Chesavia?— outside the Stronghold.

"I can almost see it in the sunlight," she said, running her fingers through the air above her. A silver, moon-shaped ring glittered on her finger. "I can almost reach it. Why does no one talk about the sunlight?"

The person let out a man's laugh. "Because no one but you sees anything in it."

Sini clung to the memory. Yes! Why did no one see what was in the sunlight?

She tried to hold it, but her grip on the moment weakened and the image slipped away, sinking into the swirl of memories.

The web of images stretched away from her again. One of her memories of Lukas began to float away. He was holding Killien's sword, glancing nervously over his shoulder.

"Touch it, Sini."

The sword was crude compared to the other weapons Killien used. The hilt roughly carved wood, the blade unpolished and full of irregularities. It looked like something that would belong to some farmer, not the leader of the Morrow Clan. Except it was encased in a faint blue glow.

Her hand reached out and she set a finger on the blade. Thin tendrils of blue light poured out into her finger. She yanked back her hand. "It pushed energy into me!"

Lukas nodded eagerly. "It has some powers. And Killien doesn't even know. We should take…"

The memory drifted away, but thread after thread snaked away from it, connecting it to dozens of other memories she couldn't quite see. One silvery thread glimmered over to an image of a desolate, rolling landscape. The image closed in on a low pile of rocks set like a cairn on top of a small rise. A hand reached out to brush dirt off the largest stone, and the gloomy light caught on a silver crescent ring.

Chesavia.

Sini grabbed for the image, but it slipped through her fingers like honey.

There were runes on the rock. Sini reached after it, but the memory caught on a current swirling through the Wellstone and spun away into the chaos.

The memories of Lukas were connected to others' memories of him, as well. Sini followed the threads to one that felt new.

The room around her was stone. An enormous table filled the center, and rich tapestries hung on the wall. Alaric sat across the table with a half dozen men in grey military uniforms. Queen Saren sat at the head of the table in a tall-backed chair.

"If this man is a threat," a military man said, "then send the army. Give me three units of the rangers and we'll sniff him out."

"We don't really know where he is," Alaric said mildly. "Sini has been mapping his movements, but they seem erratic."

"Should we be worried?" the queen asked. "Is Lukas a threat?"

"Probably," Will's voice said, and Sini realized the memory was his.

Alaric glanced at Will. "He is capable of violence."

"Capable? He slaughtered Roven with frost goblins!" a man with a captain's emblem said. "He

tried to kill the man he was working for! You yourself have said he hates Queenstown and the Keepers."

"He does," Will admitted.

"Then let us take care of him before he has a chance to hurt us."

Sini lost her hold on the memory and it drifted away. She watched it disappear into the flurry of other images with a cold knot in her gut. The Wellstone pushed her out until she sat again on the top of the Stronghold, with no sounds but the quiet valley and no light beyond the sparkle of the stone.

She looked at Will, who now sat against the column. "I'm coming with you to the capital."

EIGHT

I t took ages to fall asleep. She'd organized what she needed to bring to the palace quickly enough. The map and all the accompanying notes were rolled up in leather. The few clothes she had packed up quickly, along with the two books she'd decided to bring: Chesavia's quotes and Alaric's new book on Mallon. The Shield had stopped by with a little bag of coins for her. No one had ever trusted her with money before, and it felt heavy in her palm.

On top of the busyness, her head still spun from the Wellstone. Snippets of memories flitted by. Hers, mostly, but sometimes she caught a hint of one of the others she'd seen. She hadn't thought about her mother in a long time. And Vahe…

Her chest felt raw after the emotions of the day.

The early memories of Lukas were different from the final ones. Seeing them in such quick succession, she couldn't ignore the fact that by the time Will had met him, Lukas had become bitter and angry. The earlier, happier memories were hard to hold on to.

The next morning, she woke with a gritty feeling not just in her eyes, but in her whole head. Her hand lingered on the black Keeper's robe in her closet, but it felt even more ill-suited today than usual. Maybe because going to court was intrinsically Keeperish and she felt utterly unqualified to do it. The palace had Keeper's robes, anyway. If she needed to put one on there, she could. She dressed quickly in her normal shirt and leggings, busying her mind with questions of whether she'd packed enough and what the trip would be like, doing her best to ignore the knot of nerves in her stomach.

She made it all the way to the loaf of bread in the kitchen before the thought she'd been avoiding all morning pushed its way to the surface.

Who was going to bring the twins breakfast tomorrow? She pulled plates off the shelf and set them gently on the tray. Gerone, most likely. He'd do a good job of giving them enough jam. Not a stingy serving the way Mikal would.

She cut off two thick slices of bread for the twins, and a thin one for herself, unsure if she'd be able to eat it.

Would Gerone do it every morning until she got back?

A sob rushed up her throat and her hand flew to her mouth to hold it back.

Trips to court were never quick. She'd be gone months. She pressed her eyes shut. The task of bringing the twins breakfast would end long before she returned.

Gripping the tray tightly, she headed toward their room. The ramp felt longer than it ever had, and their familiar answer to her knock almost undid her again. It must have been obvious on her face when she entered, because both twins' expressions were full of empathy.

"You've made the right choice," Nikolas said as he moved aside their book.

She couldn't bring herself to nod. "You'll write me?"

"Of course. And we expect updates from you regularly, or we'll be driven mad by curiosity."

They ate a while in silence. There should be something to talk about, now of all times, but none of their thoughts translated into words. She desperately wished that her healing was useful, that instead of just removing fluid she could actually heal the underlying sickness. Everything felt out of sorts and unfinished.

"How many pages left?" Sini asked finally.

"Fourteen." Steffan let a small smile peek out from his beard. "Yesterday was a remarkably productive day."

"Yesterday we finished almost twice as much as usual," Nikolas agreed. "Some might suggest we were looking for something to occupy our minds from more mournful thoughts."

Sini let her eyes drop to the book. "I can't wait to read it." She picked up their hands, one at a time, and traced a rune over them, drawing out the stiffness. When she finished, she gave each old man a hug. Nikolas brushed the tear off her cheek with his wrinkled finger.

"We'll miss you."

She wanted to say a million things, but she couldn't quite get any of them out. "I'll miss you too."

———— ◆ ————

She said quick goodbyes to the other Keepers on her way to the stables. When she stepped outside, the fresh air chased back her tears. There was no direct sunlight down at the floor of the valley yet, but even the weak sunfire was soothing. Will was by the stables with Rett. Her stomach tightened and she shifted her pack on her shoulder. When Rett caught sight of her, his brow wrinkled in worry.

He came out to meet her but stopped a few steps away, looking down at his hands. "Can I come with you to court, Sini?"

From behind Rett, Will shook his head regretfully.

"I don't think you'd like it there." Sini took one of Rett's huge hands. "They wouldn't let you care for the horses."

"Will you like it there?"

She hesitated. "I'm not sure."

"Then why are you going?"

"They think they've found Lukas." His gaze snapped eagerly to her face, and she pressed her lips together. If Lukas really was doing all these terrible things, how would she ever explain it to Rett?

"I'll make sure the room next to yours is clean," he said, a spark of hope in his face. "It's gotten dusty." He leaned down and engulfed her in a hug.

"Good idea." She tried to draw some of his hope into herself, but she mounted her horse without feeling any better.

The tunnel out of the Stronghold lay at the base of the immense cliff on the western wall of the valley. In the center it was tall enough she could have stood on her saddle and not reached the arched stone ceiling. It was neatly made of squared-off stones stacked smoothly against each other. If there was some kind of mortar between them, she couldn't see it.

The sunlight from the valley lit the smooth floor around them for a good distance. It ran straight under the high cliff and their horses' hoofs echoed in a tumbling chaos.

It was dim when they reached the wall at the far end, but Sini felt the subtle wave as Will cast out. The echo of a smug little rune humming with *vitalle* came back to her. Every single trip, Mikal made her try to open the door. Last spring she'd been a little afraid he wasn't going to let them back into the Stronghold until she could do it. But this rune wasn't doing anything. There was no path to it at all. Traveling with Will was going to be so much better than with Mikal.

Will reached toward it. A thin line of blue light flowed out of his hand, connecting with the rune.

"*Aperi.*" With such a small effort, the wall thinned and shifted. Green light seeped through, then the wall disappeared entirely, revealing a thick pine forest.

Talen, who had perched patiently on Will's saddle horn through the tunnel, took off into the open sky. They stopped their horses in the small grassy space between the trees and a cliff that rose immeasurably high above them. It seemed taller even than the back side of it in the Stronghold valley. The arched opening sat in a section of stone wall built directly on the cliff face.

Will raised his hand toward the opening. "Care to do the honors?"

She shot him a glare until she noticed a thin blue line snaking out from his hand to the wall. A path. She grinned, set her fingers on his hand, and funneled her own *vitalle* into the path.

"*Cluda,*" she said with an air of triumph. The stones shifted again and smoothly formed up, leaving no indication in the wall that the opening had ever existed. She considered the stones. "Do you think I'll ever be able to do that without help?"

Will turned his horse toward the forest and grinned at her over his shoulder. "Limitations are a good thing. Without them, the hero has nothing to struggle against, and the story is too dull to be worth telling."

They found the thin trace of a path leading into the forest, and Sini cast out at the nearest trees. Subtle hums emanated from the trunks along the trail. A thin black rune was barely visible against the nearest trunk, but it did nothing as they passed. Even in the calm, bright morning, she shivered at the memory of the ghostly faces those runes could create. "I suppose it's nice that the ghosts don't talk to us when we're leaving."

The first time she'd come to the Stronghold with Will and Alaric, even after being warned about the faces, the forest had been terrifying. They'd tried to get through during the day, but it was dusk when they'd finally reached this stretch of the forest and the milky faces that had leaned out of the trees toward her had spoken words that cut paralyzingly deep. *You do not belong here. You are worth nothing. You are not what they hope you are.*

In the intervening years, the taunts of the ghosts had shifted to focus more on her shortcomings and failures as a Keeper, but they always managed to throw in the original barbs for good measure.

He turned in his saddle again. "Did you know," he said with a touch of indignation, "that Alaric never saw the ghosts until the last few years?"

"What? How?"

Will shook his head. "I'd always suspected he was too saintly for them to have anything to torment him with. I guess I was right." He sobered. "Until he did all those things to save Evangeline."

Sini had read Alaric's chilling account of those days. "But that was long ago. What do they taunt him with now?"

"I don't like to ask."

In the morning light, with no ghosts, the forest was peaceful and gentle. The only sounds were the muffled clop of the horses' hoofs on the dirt path, and the scattering of forest animals. She didn't breathe freely, though, until they reached the wider road that ran toward Queenstown. She rode alongside Will while the sunlight poured down on them. The familiar sunfire seeped into Sini's skin and warmed her horse's dark neck.

It had been half a year since Sini had left the valley. She traveled with Mikal twice a year to the small market town of Brenlen a half day's ride south, but their last trip had been in the spring. It would be several weeks before Mikal would venture out again. The Keepers had standing orders from several of the merchants there for ink and paper, seeds, fabric, herbs that couldn't be grown at the Stronghold, and several different medicines sent from the court apothecary. Though the town was small and the market nothing more than a wide street swollen with local farmers and traveling merchants, even those crowds felt overwhelming after the isolation of the Stronghold.

After so long in the deep, narrow valley, passing through the cliffs felt like entering a different world. The sky stretched so low to the horizon. It always took several hours to feel comfortable with the idea that there were no walls around her. Will, of course, seemed as perfectly at ease as he always was.

Remembering something from the Wellstone, she asked, "What do you know about Killien's sword?"

Will thought for a moment. "The one Lukas stole? Almost nothing, which is a shame. If Killien really got it from Flibbet the Peddler, there must be at least one good story behind it. Probably more."

"You don't think it was really Flibbet, do you? No one's seen him in generations."

Will shrugged. "It seems impossible, but Killien certainly believes it. Why do you ask about the sword?"

Sini explained how the Wellstone had made dozens of connections to her memory of the sword.

"Wait," he interrupted her. "You saw connections between memories in the Wellstone?"

"I think so. There were webs of silvery lines. As soon as it finished drawing in my memories, it started connecting them to others. My memories of Vahe to yours. The times I saw the dragon to Alaric's encounters with it." She paused. "And I saw Ayda. She was so…" There was no way to describe the creature that had faced that dragon.

He nodded and considered her for a long moment before letting out a laugh. "I'm glad you're good with magic, Sini."

She fixed him with an annoyed stare.

He just smiled at her. "It means I don't have to be. You've really taken a lot of pressure off me."

Her hands clenched on the reins. "You realize I can do almost nothing by myself."

"You can access power the rest of us can't even find. And you're connected to it in a way we don't understand. You'll find a trick for using it yourself, or you'll decide you don't need to. Clever people always find ways around their obstacles."

"That's easy for you to say. Have you ever had any obstacles to overcome?"

"I can't read runes like you and Alaric can, I can't control *vitalle* well, and I get bored studying records that aren't well-written. I'm basically bad at all the scholarly things Keepers are supposed to do."

"But you have magic words that spill out of your mouth when you speak!"

He raised an eyebrow. "I don't think anyone's ever told me that my words were magical. At least not anyone who knew what magic actually is, so thank you."

She snorted. "It wasn't a compliment. It was a fact. When you tell stories—and sometimes just when you have something important to say—you breathe out this cloud of magic and it spreads out among everyone who's listening."

Will turned in his saddle to looked at her. "A cloud?"

"A blueish green one. It's hard to see in daylight, but at night…" The first night she'd seen him speak in the square in Porreen, she'd been mesmerized by it. "It's like sparkling mist."

Will sat back, his face stunned. "I know it happens, but I can't see it. I can…feel it there."

He considered. "I'm glad you're coming to Queenstown, Sin. Everyone there is so boring."

"I'll tell Alaric you said that."

"He already knows. Although Evangeline has helped. He's less serious all the time."

"Sora makes you more serious."

He let his gaze run ahead of them. "Maybe she did."

"She'll come back," Sini said. "She wanted to. Anyone could see that."

"Wanting something four years ago doesn't mean she wants it now."

Sini shook her head. "She'll be back. Her people needed her to free them from that awful holy woman. I assume, since she's still there, that her people still treat her like she's a holy woman herself."

"She's tried to convince them otherwise, but she does have some magical skill, the way she can feel if living things are nearby, and that's enough for her clan. In the process of getting rid of the old holy woman, she got dragged into training the new one, who's still young. I don't think she understood how hard it is to extricate yourself from a position like that." He glanced at Sini. "Which is why I've done everything I can, not to become an official part of court. Alaric's going to be stuck there forever."

Sini shuddered. "Tell me your secret so I don't accidentally become part of court. I just want to get back to the Stronghold." She glanced at Will out of the corner of her eye. "How long has it been since you heard from Sora?"

"Since early spring." Will stared ahead unseeing. "I keep toying with the idea of getting Douglon to lead me back over there. The dwarves know how to find her."

"Any news from Douglon and Rass about new elves?"

Will shook his head. "Same as always. Rass is sure the Elder Grove is awake and that new elves will come, but…"

Sini sighed. "She's been saying that for four years."

———◆———

Early that evening they reached a small inn. The innkeeper, obviously familiar with Will, beamed and bowed and doted on them, even offering Talen some strips of meat. When he discovered that Sini, despite her lack of black robe, was a Keeper as well, he offered her the best room, which turned out to be marginally larger than a closet with a lumpy bed. Will, his own Keeper's robe hanging on him quite naturally, told stories in the common room and the entire town tried to cram themselves in. The ale flowed, and Will's words spread through the room, glittering among the listeners.

Sini sat in the corner. The people were thrilled to see a Keeper, and Will thoroughly enjoyed himself, telling stories. His black robe looked different tonight. It looked…fitting. Something about it did remind her of her old slave tunic, but not in the confining way Lukas had always thought. It looked comfortable in a way she couldn't quite put her finger on.

It was late before he finished. She was on her way to her room with a short candle from the innkeeper when Will stopped her. "I forgot I have something for you." He disappeared into his room and returned with a book. "I found this on a merchant's cart in Queenstown. I showed it to the Shield, and he thought you should have it first."

The cover was faded leather, and the thin book was bent a bit. The pages inside were written in a smooth, small hand.

"This"—Will tapped the page—"is a previously unknown journal written by Keeper Chesavia."

Her breath caught. "Really?"

He nodded excitedly, handing it to her. "And you can be the very first to read it."

She stared at him, stunned. "Her journal? Why haven't you read it?"

"Two reasons." He flipped ahead in the book. Entire pages were written in runes. "First, because I'm hopeless at runes and it would take me days to decipher even a small amount of that."

She glanced at the top of the page.

8thth day, Frost Moon, 6th year of Queen Taania
I have a simmering worry…

The runes were straightforward and simple, but she didn't point that out to Will. "And the second?"

"Because I also found a book by Flibbet the Peddler which was not in runes and was utterly fascinating."

She shook her head. "How did a merchant find such treasures?"

"Some manor house in northern Marshwell flooded, and the baron had to empty a cellar they hadn't used in generations. He sold things off by the wagonload. I sent the royal librarian down to see if anything else of value was left."

"This is amazing!" Sini ran her eyes down the page. The early entries seemed to be from Chesavia's first days as a Keeper. She glanced up at Will. "I think that the Wellstone connected Killien's sword with a memory of Chesavia."

Will considered the idea. "Means nothing to me. But maybe you'll find something in there."

She nodded, her eyes scanning the page. She told him goodnight and hurried into her room to set the candle down so she could read more easily.

8thth day, Frost Moon, 6th year of Queen Taania
I have a simmering worry that I should not be here. I've begun lessons, and it is simple to find the vitalle *the other Keepers talk about. Bits of it move through the trees, the grass. Our bodies thrum with it, the animals too. It's easy to pull it out, although it stings my finger when I do. It's nothing like the sunlight.*

Her heart quickened. Yes! Nothing like the sunlight. Vitalle from living things burned on its way into Sini's body, and burned on its way out, exactly the way it did with the other Keepers.

Whenever she had to use it, it felt like something foreign, something useful but different.

The sunlight never hurt. It flowed into her naturally, like breathing, and left as smoothly.

Why can none of them find the vitalle *in the sunlight? My questions baffle them.*

Actually, none of them can see the vitalle *anywhere. They cannot see it glow around their hands or slip through the air like a stream of light. They just grope blindly for it, finding it by feel.*

I keep coming back to the sunlight. There is something there that is more…

I cannot explain it. But there is something in the sunlight.

Sini skimmed eagerly ahead, but Chesavia didn't mention the sunlight again. She talked of her lessons, of how the *vitalle* was unwieldy and impossible to focus. Every task took far more energy than it should. But whatever problem Chesavia had, at least she could create paths for the energy all on her own.

She flipped further back, landing on the pages describing Chesavia's time at court.

22nd day, River Moon, 1st year of King Lenus

King Lenus is unbearable. The man is paranoid that his advisors are against him. He's dismissed two of them this week, worthy men who had given sound advice.

Tonight, at dinner, he demanded that I declare whose side I'm on. As though there are sides. The man is petty and irritating, ranting about how his advisors have no regard for goodness or truth. Truth! From the king who twists the most common action into a new attack against himself.

The Shield bids me to do my best to stay in court, though, so I merely answered with the old quote, "I am on the side of truth and right and goodness."

I do not know how to speak in a way this man will hear. His fears control him utterly.

But I must find a way. Perhaps if I can understand his fears, we can find a way to relieve them.

I am unmoored here. There is nothing to stand on, no one to be comfortable with.

There is too little sunlight in this place.

Sini ran her fingers over the words, a knot forming in her stomach. The idea of court loomed ahead like a storm on the horizon. Why had she agreed to come?

NINE

I t took until early afternoon the next day to reach Queenstown. It turned out to be a good decision to leave behind her black robe as they traveled, as Will's drew attention from the moment they reached the highway that led into the city. Talen, with obvious disdain for the crowds, launched himself into the air.

"The falconer at the palace spoils him." Will watched him soar toward the city. "If we stay here too long, Talen gets fat and lazy."

There was a buzz of activity wherever Will went; people called greetings or nodded in a deferential sort of way. But no one paid much attention to her.

Her hands gripped the reins and she scanned the crowd continuously. She'd only seen Queenstown once since Vahe had taken her, on her way back from the Sweep with Will and Alaric. It felt odd to be back where she'd been born after being gone for eight years. Of course, she hadn't ever been in parts of it that were this nice. Still, she found herself searching for familiar things.

When she had come through with Will and Alaric, the Keepers had been pleased to introduce Sini, and Rett at court. The Queen had been thrilled to find out they existed. Especially Sini. News of a female Keeper had run through the palace like wildfire. It had been almost a hundred years since they'd seen one in Queenstown. Whatever attention the other Keepers got, she received it tenfold. Endless streams of people introduced themselves to her, offered her luxurious accommodations when she came to their duchy, declared she could take her pick of their prize breeding horses. Will had taken to escorting her everywhere in the hopes of heading off some of the chaos.

It wouldn't be long before people figured out who she was, and it all began again. She felt a little knot of dread in her stomach at it all. It wasn't just the attention, either. It was that everyone seemed to expect she'd do something amazing.

"Once we're here for a few days," Will said, leaning toward her, "the excitement settles down eventually. It's just this beginning part that's annoying."

She looked at him sharply. "Were you reading my emotions?"

He laughed. "I didn't have to. I recognize the look on your face. Alaric always has that same one. He hates the attention at the beginning, and he's not nearly as much of a novelty as you."

She caught something familiar in a woman's face in the crowd, and started. But it wasn't her mother. It was ridiculous to think her mother would be in this part of the city, anyway. The Lees sat on the far side of the palace, tucked away past the city wall. Her mother would never be all the way over here.

The complicated jumble of emotions brought on by thoughts of her family only added to her nerves. The last time she was here, she had still felt so bitter, she hadn't wanted to search for them. And her time in the city had been so short and so busy she hadn't had the chance to feel guilty about it.

Will got them to the palace as quickly as he could, and managed to usher them to the Keepers' wing with as little commotion as possible. The sitting room outside the three Keeper apartments was bright. Tall windows filled one wall, looking out over a garden. Even the comfortable chairs grouped together in friendly bunches or gathered around tables didn't help her uneasiness. Vases bursting with late summer flowers reminded her of Gerone's room but weren't enough to make it feel like home.

Three guards stood in the room, one at each apartment door, and Will paused at the sight of them. Each duchy in Queensland had its own small military force. The city guard in Queenstown was the largest of them all by tenfold. They wore grey uniforms, and the five battalions guarded not only the city, but traveled extensively around the rest of the country, as well. There were two elite companies. The ranger company ran reconnaissance missions and the queen's guard protected the palace.

"That's new." He led Sini to the room she'd stayed in last time, the second on the left.

"Let me put my bag down," he said, turning toward his own room, "and we'll go find Alaric."

Sini's palace suite did nothing to calm her. She'd forgotten how opulent everything was. And how huge. Just the entry space was as large as her whole room in the Stronghold. The hooks near the door held two Keeper's robes, one was far too long for her, but the other looked to be her size. Past the entry, the suite opened into a wide, windowed room with couches, an enormous desk, a fire crackling merrily in the fireplace, and three long bookshelves mostly full of books. Before the fire lay a thick rug made of the reddish-brown fur of a mountain bear. Sini pulled off her boots and stepped onto it. This rug was what she remembered most from the few days she'd stayed here before. This rug and the bed that lay through one of two ornately carved doors to her right. The bed had been so plush that it almost made being in the capital worth it.

The second door opened into a study with a wide desk and more bookshelves. Sini crossed to the bedroom and pulled open the wide wardrobe that stood against the wall. It was empty.

"Don't worry. They'll have it full of ridiculously elaborate dresses before dinner tonight." Evangeline stood at the door, smiling broadly. She wore a long green dress that flowed out over her extended belly.

Sini hurried over for a hug. "Is the baby coming so soon?"

Evangeline's smile turned to a grimace. "It looks like it, doesn't it? One more moon." She set Sini's palm on the side of her stomach. Sini felt three quick thumps and a roil of movement. "But the babe seems anxious to stretch."

"This is a good reason to be out of the Stronghold," Sini said. "I've been looking for one."

"Alaric is with the queen. She'll want to see you and Will immediately." She glanced back into the hallway. "Did anyone else come?" Sini shook her head and Evangeline winced. "Well, don't take the tone of this first meeting to be indicative of how it'll be all the time, then. Queen Saren was hoping that at least the Shield would come."

"No one but Saren sees the point," Will said from behind Evangeline. He hadn't changed out of his traveling clothes. "You might need your shoes back on, Sin. It's best to handle irate monarchs with good footwear."

Sini's boots looked muddy and worn in the opulence of the room.

Seeing her hesitation, Will grinned. "Presenting ourselves to the queen dirty will show her that we didn't want to waste time doing anything else before seeing her. And dispel any ideas that we'd really rather turn around and go back to the Stronghold."

Evangeline led the way through the palace, and one of the guards fell in behind them. Will raised an eyebrow, but Evangeline just shook her head and continued to the queen's personal study before excusing herself. "I'm going to disappear before Alaric sees me and I get dragged into what is bound to be a boring evening."

Will gave Sini a quick look that was half wince, half encouraging smile, before nodding for one of the guards to announce them.

Queen Saren stood at the end of a table where Alaric, a young woman with a pinched expression, and a young man dressed in the stoic grey of the city guard were seated. Dark, serious-looking wood covered the walls, loaning a somberness to the room, even with daylight streaming in the wide windows. Not even the bookshelves lining the wall made it more welcoming. She felt like a street rat from the Lees again, who had accidentally stumbled into…well, the palace.

Will bowed and Sini dropped into a curtsey, wishing she could turn around and follow Evangeline. The queen took in the two of them. After flicking her gaze behind them to the empty hall, her face hardened. "I assume the other Keepers are resting after their journey?"

Sini quailed at her tone. Saren was matronly but barely taller than Sini. Four years ago, the queen's dark hair had been streaked with grey. But the past years had taken a toll. Now almost all the brown in the thick braid hanging over her shoulder was silvered. She was only in her late forties, but her eyes looked worn and more severe than Sini remembered.

Alaric leaned back in a chair at the table. A spray of books spread out in front of him, covering the edges of an enormous map on the table. He caught Sini's eye and she felt a little relief at the warmth of his smile. His gaze, too, traveled to the empty doorway behind them, his expression resigned.

When no one answered, Queen Saren's gaze flickered impatiently to Sini. Thankfully, Will cleared his throat and answered. "The other Keepers are resting at the Stronghold. Some of them, as we suspected, are unable to make the journey here. The others remain to care for them."

"The Shield isn't wasting his day caring for sick old men," the young woman said. "He has no reason to disobey the queen's request."

Sini bristled at her words, but the queen sent the woman a quelling glance.

"I'm afraid Steffan and Nikolas's health is quickly declining," Will said.

The young woman's face didn't soften, but Alaric let out a sigh.

"I'm sorry to hear that," Saren said with genuine sympathy in her voice. "I like those two men very much."

The young woman sat stiffly at the table and Sini could feel the pressure of her gaze. The woman wore a dark red dress, expensive but understated. Her light brown hair was plaited in intricate braids held tightly in place with jeweled hair pins.

Sini ran her fingers through her own short hair, her heart sinking at how wild and disheveled she must look.

"Your highness," Alaric said to her, his voice formal, "I don't believe you've met Keeper Sini before."

The young woman gave a nod so small it was barely perceptible.

"Sini, this is Princess Madeleine. And Roan, youngest son of the Duke of Greentree."

The names shocked Sini into another curtsey. Queen Saren was widowed and childless. Madeleine was the niece of the late king, and due to some deaths in the succession, had recently been declared heir. The son of the duke of Greentree was her betrothed.

Madeleine's eyes hardened. "We thought older Keepers would be coming. Not one so inexperienced."

The words cut into Sini somewhere old and scarred, and outrage seethed through. "I believe you and I are the same age." She bit off a belated, "Your highness."

Will set a hand on Sini's arm and gestured to a chair. "Sini is the same age as yourself, your highness, and I assure you she is familiar with everything that has been going on." Will pulled gently on Sini's arm until she sat stiffly in the chair. "I have no doubt she'll be useful to us."

"Of course," Madeleine said. "She knew the dragon rider."

Dragon rider?

"Lukas?" Sini asked, surprised.

"Of course Lukas," Madeleine said, her voice dripping disdain. She turned an exasperated face toward the queen. "I hardly think someone who thinks of the murderer as a brother has a place in this council."

Indignation overcame Sini's hesitancy to speak. It had been a long time since anyone had spoken to her that way. It was the tone the Roven used with their slaves—condescending and dismissive—and an old, savage anger flared in Sini. "Yes, I know Lukas. I've been following everything happening to the south and I understand what he wants."

"He wants to destroy the Keepers," the princess said. "Or that's what you told the queen when you first came here years ago. Which he seems to have grown into a desire to cause trouble to as much of Queensland as he can manage, judging from the events along the southern border."

"Some of those things are his doing," Sini said, "some are not. I can help you determine which is which."

"Do we need help recognizing the work of a dragon?" Roan asked mildly. He was tall, but couldn't be much older than Sini and Madeleine. Clearly from Greentree, his skin was bronzed and the top of his straight hair, so dark it was almost black, was tied back from his face. The cut and grey of his clothes was the only thing out of place. Instead of the more colorful garb those from Greentree usually wore, his resembled the uniform of the city guard, but it wasn't exactly a uniform. And the plain grey of his tunic reminded her so strongly of the slaves' tunic of the Sweep, she was hard-pressed not to recoil from it. He watched Sini with an unreadable expression, mirroring none of Madeleine's contempt, but showing no warmth either.

The duchy of Greentree had been gaining power during the last generation, but now, with the son of the duke betrothed to Princess Madeleine, Greentree was about to reach a new level of influence.

"Lukas isn't using the dragon everywhere," Sini said to him, glad to speak to someone besides Madeleine. "I believe he's traveling east. Toward the moors of Gringonn. He may be there already."

He raised a skeptical eyebrow. "The moors? When we know his dragon is in the west? Can you prove this?"

Sini glanced at the queen, her earlier outrage fizzling out and leaving her feeling mostly awkward. "It's just an impression I get from studying his movements. In the past few weeks, more incidents have been reported in areas adjacent to the moors."

Madeleine didn't wait for the queen before she answered in a cool voice. "Do you expect us to act on your 'impression', Keeper Sini?" The name was said without inflection, but Sini swore she heard some contempt. "Or is it that you don't really want us to find him? I understand he was your foster brother for several years, but we are faced with a real threat from him and his dragon in the west. And you want us to turn our focus from there to a whole different part of the world?" Her grey eyes weighed Sini coldly. "Whose side are you on?"

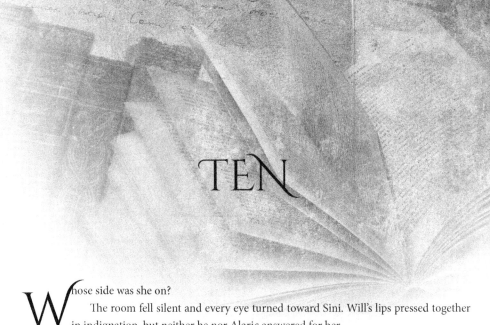

TEN

Whose side was she on?

The room fell silent and every eye turned toward Sini. Will's lips pressed together in indignation, but neither he nor Alaric answered for her.

For a moment, Sini had no answer. It wasn't a question of sides. It was a question of...what? Words from Chesavia's journal came to mind.

"I'm on the side of truth and right and goodness."

Her voice didn't sound nearly as confident as Madeleine's had, but Alaric gave a tight smile and an approving nod. Madeleine showed no sign of recognizing the quote.

The coldness in Madeleine's face made Sini continue. "Lukas isn't some evil creature filled with single-minded hatred. He's a person, like you,"—Madeleine's eyes flickered at the comparison—"and like me. If we forget that, we won't truly understand what he's doing. There's no point discussing someone if you're just going to put up a smoky shape of them and pretend you can blow them away. Surely he is more complex than that."

Madeleine sat back in her chair, apparently unmoved. The slightest hints of a smile curled her lips, not adding any warmth. "You defend him passionately."

Before Sini could gather herself enough to answer, Will cleared his throat and leaned over the map. "Sini, tell the queen what you told us about Lukas and the gold."

Sini attempted to push down her irritation and turned to Queen Saren. "Lukas thinks of gold as something that enslaves people, not something to be desired." She told her of Lukas's disdain. The queen, the Keepers, and Roan spent some time discussing the situation. Madeleine watched silently, but didn't comment.

Sini expected scorn from Roan. But he merely discussed the idea coolly. "If Lukas only wanted to keep the gold from everyone else, he would have succeeded by blocking off the valley with the rock slides. There'd be no reason to murder so many and leave a dragon there to oversee more mining."

"It's possible," Alaric agreed, "that years of living on his own has changed his feelings about money. It's easy to see it as an unnecessary evil when you don't need any of it yourself."

"But then why the dead man with the shackles of gold?" Sini asked, glad the conversation had finally turned civil.

Will nodded. "That was a message of contempt."

"Maybe it's only about control." Roan leaned forward and pulled a map toward himself. "Gold controls the merchants, and the merchants have a great deal of sway in the kingdoms of Coastal Baylon, Napon, and Queensland." He turned to Sini. "Do the gold merchants travel to the Sweep?"

She nodded. "While the clans winter in the south."

"Have you had any news from the Sweep recently?" Saren asked Will.

"I haven't heard from Killien in six months."

The queen looked at him narrowly. "Should we be worried?"

Will hesitated. "I'm not sure."

"On one level it doesn't matter whether Lukas plans to use the gold for something or just hoard it," Alaric said. "The longer he holds the gold, the more he'll destabilize the region, and we are powerless to do anything as long as the dragon is guarding it."

"Do you mean to say," Madeleine said, "that it's a Keeper—or whatever the opposite of a Keeper is—who's controlling a dragon, but the other Keepers have no way to fight him?"

"Historically," Will pointed out, "the person controlling the dragon does have the upper hand."

"I know how to make compulsion stones," Sini added. At least in theory she did. "Which is how Lukas is controlling it. But unless you know of another dragon nearby that we could use, it won't do us much good."

Alaric shot them both quelling looks. "Lukas isn't a Keeper. If he'd been raised in Queensland he probably would be. But the magic he learned on the Sweep is different than ours."

"Stronger, obviously," Madeleine continued, "since he can control a dragon and the rest of you cannot." She turned back toward the queen. "It doesn't matter that the rest of the Keepers haven't come, your majesty. I'm not sure they are quite what they used to be."

Alaric's eyebrow rose and Will stiffened in his chair and Sini's face reddened.

"One is married and starting a family." Madeleine gestured to Alaric. "Another is enamored with a foreign woman." She flicked a dismissive hand at Will. "One of them—Rett is his name, correct?— is so damaged he needs constant care."

Sini's fists clenched and she leaned forward, but Will put a hand on her shoulder.

"And then there's the best one of all—Lukas should be a Keeper, but instead he's come to hate them and has said, given the power, he'd destroy them all. And from what we've seen lately, he'd destroy Queensland with them."

Sini bit back all the things she wanted to hurl at the woman. Will said nothing either, but his hand on her shoulder was tight.

"I believe," Alaric said mildly, "you'll find the Keepers less altered than you think."

"The Keepers are quite as useful as they've ever been," the queen admonished her. "While they do seem to be going through…" She glanced around the table. "A transition of sorts, it's foolish to assume we don't need them."

Madeleine sat stiffly in her chair.

"What I need to know," the queen continued, "is the level of military threat Lukas is posing. He has a dragon. Does he also have an army?"

"The ranger company thinks not," Roan answered. "They've found no evidence of any open troop movement in Napon or Coastal Baylon, but by the time we see any, it will be too late to begin mobilization. We need to assume that Lukas is using the gold, and buying an army is the only thing I can think of that would need that much money."

Queen Saren's eyes ran over the map. "Have the garrisons at the three outposts in Marshwell and the two in Greentree tripled. How quickly can we raise a larger force?"

Sini found herself with little to add to the military conversation. She had no insight into troop movements or supply lines or the capacity of Marshwell versus Greentree for a large company.

Madeleine, raised in western Marshwell, had a great many opinions, as did Roan, who had helped his father defend the border between Queensland and Napon his entire life. Will and Alaric discussed the leadership of the different countries, calculating who would be more likely to work with Lukas. Madeleine debated them on every point. Only Sini had nothing to say.

Several servants, each better dressed than Sini, brought enough food to feed a dozen people and Sini picked at her plate of bread and fruit and roasted meat. The queen, Roan, and the Keepers turned to questioning Sini closely about Lukas, and she began to feel like she was contributing. At least when Madeleine wasn't speaking.

The princess never warmed up. She found fault with any theory Sini mentioned about Lukas, and probed any hint of sympathy, keeping Sini in an almost constant state of indignation. Neither Alaric nor Will seemed surprised by Madeleine's attitude, but Will didn't hide his annoyance quite as well as Alaric. Roan kept all his questions to the point, asking for details about Lukas in a commanding sort of tone, but leaving opinions to Madeleine. He paid special attention every time Sini spoke. She couldn't shake the feeling that she was being examined. Queen Saren, too, showed a great deal of interest in Sini's views, especially concerning Lukas.

The windows had grown dark before the queen drew the discussions to a close. "Tomorrow afternoon," she said to Alaric, "I'd like to see a proposal from you and the battalion leaders for troop deployment for different scenarios."

"We have one last matter to discuss," Saren continued. "There have been some troubling incidents near the Keepers' wing. A broken window in Will's room and some items missing. Yesterday a maid saw a man breaking into Alaric's room through the garden window while Evangeline was there alone."

Sini's gaze snapped to Alaric, his face was bleak.

"The man eluded capture," Saren said.

Will ran his fingers through his beard, frowning. "That explains the extra guards around Evangeline."

"Not just her," Saren said. "All of you. I've stationed guards in the garden outside your rooms and more at your doors. We don't know for sure that this is related to Lukas, but I don't know of anyone else threatening to harm Keepers. You will be escorted, even inside the palace, until I feel that the threat is over."

"That's not necessary," Will objected, but Saren fixed him with a stern gaze.

"The Keepers may be…in crisis, but you're the only ones we have, and you will remain safe and at my disposal. Roan is in command of the unit of the city guard assigned to protect you. And he answers directly to me."

Madeleine stood and smoothed her dress.

Roan rose and offered his arm, which she took.

"It would be better if all of the Keepers had come as her majesty commanded," Madeline said. "We cannot protect them if they are not here."

"I believe they're quite safe in the Stronghold," Alaric said.

Madeleine made a non-committal noise. After a curtsey to the queen and a cold nod to the Keepers, she left. Sini rubbed her hands across her face. The day had been the most exhausting one she'd had in years. She pushed her hands back into her hair, realizing it was still windswept from traveling. She felt a kick of defeat at her appearance compared to the queen and Madeleine.

Sini glanced over at Alaric, wondering how he stayed here and did this every day. The Keepers bowed and left as well, headed back to their own rooms. A guard detached himself from the wall and followed.

"That was a rough start for you Sini," Alaric said.

"I'm sorry," she said. "It's been a long time since someone talked to me like that, and I guess it struck a nerve. I'll try to be more…civil."

"Princess Madeleine's not quite as bad as she seems right now," Alaric said.

"Her Tightly Braided Highness is out of her depth," Will agreed, pitching his voice low. Alaric snorted and Sini grinned. "It's making her a bit combative."

Alaric led them down the hall toward their rooms. "Until last spring she was fourth in line to the throne. But when the winter gripe went through Steepdale, six members of the duke's family died. Anyone left is more distantly related than Madeleine. She discovered on her twentieth birthday that she was the heir apparent. And that she'd be wedding Roan of Greentree."

"Roan has taken quite a step up," Will continued. "His father, the duke of Greentree, a man who's always had a shrewd sense of opportunism, had brokered the betrothal between Roan and Madeleine before most of the country figured out she was the new heir apparent. Madeleine had intended to marry someone else."

Sini digested the information for a moment. All she knew about Madeleine had come from Alaric's report last spring about the succession. She had honestly not given the woman another thought until tonight. She felt a begrudging sympathy for her. Being pulled from a comfortable home and thrust into court was decidedly unpleasant. Knowing it was permanent would be worse.

"That couldn't have been easy," Sini admitted.

Will grinned at her. "She'll be queen someday. And I don't see any way it won't be you working with her."

"Me? Alaric will be here for decades more. And then you're up next, Will."

Both Keepers laughed.

"I'm certain the entire realm would vote for you to come instead of me." Will said, reaching the sitting area outside their rooms.

"He's got one foot out the palace door already," Alaric agreed. "Can't you tell?"

"There's too much arguing here, and too few stories." Will shook his head. "Too many negative emotions all wrapped up in selfishness. How soon do you think I can find an excuse to leave?"

"Not until after tomorrow, at least," Alaric said dryly. "There'll surely be a feast to welcome Sini. We'll need a good storyteller."

Will spun the silver bead braided into his beard and nodded. "Performing in the great hall is a good reason to stay. Sound carries perfectly there." He glanced out the window. The sky was almost dark. "I'm going down to The Broken Pint. Can I convince you two to come?

Alaric shook his head. "I'm going to find Evangeline."

"She can come too. It's just a quick ride down to the main square. She's more fun than you anyway."

"She's really not keen on horseback riding in her condition."

"Sini?"

"I would love—" Sini began.

"Actually, I need to talk to you, Sini," Alaric cut in.

Will raised an eyebrow. "Sounds ominous."

Alaric ignored him and faced Sini. "Gerone and I have been discussing the way you need paths to use your *vitalle*."

Her heart sank a little.

Will's eyes sharpened. "Don't depress her, Alaric. It's bad enough she had to come here."

The other Keeper shot an annoyed look at him. "I have no intention of depressing her. In fact, Sini, I think you'll be happy to hear what I have to say."

"It can wait until tomorrow," Will said. "Or until she and I get back."

Alaric glanced at the guards watching them. "I think the sooner the better."

"Have fun, Sin." Will set his hand on her shoulder, not bothering to hide his grin. "The tavern is calling. See you two in the morning."

As Will reached the hall heading back into the castle one of the guards followed. "You've picked the right Keeper to escort." Will told him. "You like the Broken Pint?"

Alaric watched him leave, and with another quick glance at the remaining guards, motioned toward Sini's door. "Let's talk somewhere quieter."

Sini led the way into her room, leaving the guards outside.

A fire burned cheerfully in the fireplace and Sini sank down into one of the chairs next to it. "Do you have any idea why I can't make my own paths?" She didn't bother to sound hopeful.

Alaric glanced into the fire. "I have some vague ideas. As soon as I have something more definitive, I'll let you know."

Sini's head dropped back against the chair and closed her eyes.

"But just because we don't understand it, doesn't mean we can't begin to work around it. Specifically…"

She cracked one eye open.

He smiled proudly. "Your trouble lighting candles."

She opened her mouth to say that the candles were hardly the real problem, when he pulled a small, silver ring out of one of the pockets of his Keeper's robe. A thin trail of auburn light trailed behind it.

Sini stared at it.

The plain silver band held a small garnet.

"This is a burning stone." Sini looked up at him. "Where did you…?"

Alaric's smile turned slightly guilty. "I made it from the information Will brought back from the Sweep. It doesn't do much, but if you give it a little *vitalle*, it'll heat something up. Light a candle, catch a slip of paper on fire. Things like that."

The ring fit snugly on her first finger. Tiny bits of energy swirled in the little stone. But the best part was it was open to her. It wanted more energy. She held the ring next to the candle wick on the table beside her and pressed a little *vitalle* into the ring. The stone lapped it up greedily and a faint copper glow seeped out from it.

Sini's heart sped up. It was nebulous and irregular, and not much like a path, but it was enough. She pushed more *vitalle* into the stone and the glow intensified to a bright copper until the energy encompassed the wick and the candle flamed to life.

Sini stared at the ring and the flame, a thrill running through her. "This is amazing!"

She blew out the candle, held her finger a little farther from the wick this time and pushed some *vitalle* into the ring again. The copper cloud formed, and the candle burst into flame.

She shoved herself out of the chair and held her hand up to a different candle on the mantle. She paused for a moment before lighting it, then put the tip of her finger near the wick instead. The coppery mist moved sluggishly up her finger, but she prodded it and in a breath it reached the tip. The wick of the candle burst into a flame so huge, Sini snatched her hand back.

Letting out a laugh that rang wildly through the room, she ran up to the side of Alaric's chair, flinging her arms around him. "I can do it! It makes a path!"

He laughed too, patting her arm. "I'm glad."

Sini sank back into her chair, tilting the ring to catch the candlelight in the little gem. "It's brilliant."

Alaric studied her. "How'd you know it was a burning stone?"

"It left a trail," she said absently, spinning the ring around her finger.

Alaric made a discontented noise. "What color?"

She grinned at him. "Sort of auburn. When I put *vitalle* into it, the light turns copper."

"I don't suppose you could teach me to see that?"

Sini shrugged. "I don't know how I do it. I've always been able to." She held up the finger with the ring. "But for this, I will put serious thought into figuring it out."

"All it does is heat things up." Alaric's voice sounded almost apologetic. "But I figured if we could get a ring to help you light a candle, then we can expand on the idea in the future. Make it more versatile."

She held her hand out, moving the ring slowly, watching the trail of auburn light.

It was a doorway flung open to the world. Everything inside her shifted toward it. The power that had been trapped blinked at the light. She blew out a long breath. There was a path between herself and everything else. The energy that had been chained inside her like some starved prisoner stirred and shifted into the light. Instead of a meek, weakened creature, a fierce being of beauty and strength stepped forward and spread wings of light.

"It's the greatest thing ever made," she whispered.

Alaric let out a relieved breath. "I wasn't sure it would work. I couldn't test it without you, but I remembered you had some like it when you first came from the Sweep."

"I broke those in the elder grove," she held up her hand to admire the garnet. "If you funnel too much *vitalle* through them they break." She smiled at him. "I've missed them ever since."

The smile he gave her back was more of a wince, and it occurred to Sini what he had done. He'd created a burning stone. Trapped living energy into an inanimate gem. Officially the Keepers didn't approve of that sort of thing. It crossed a boundary.

"Do the others know you made this?"

He gave her a half smile. "I'm pretty sure that you, Will, and I are the only Keepers with an understanding of burning stones. I knew you wouldn't be against it, and there really wasn't anyone nearby to consult with." He rubbed at his face, and she was struck again with how tired he looked. "I'm sure when I do, I'll get some disapproval. Of course, when Will realizes that stones can help move *vitalle*, he'll probably ask me for his own."

Sini considered the ring. Gerone would be concerned that she was using a burning stone. Mikal appalled. Even the Shield might not be thrilled with this solution. "Everyone is right, aren't they? The Keepers are changing."

Alaric let out a long breath and ran his hand through his hair. "It feels that way sometimes."

"Are we changing for the better?"

Alaric shook his head. "I don't know. But I hope so."

Sini blew out the candle again and lit it. She grinned at Alaric. "I don't care. This is the greatest gift anyone has ever given me."

Alaric pushed himself out of his chair. "I know what it's like to desperately want to do something you feel like you should be able to do. You have amazing powers, Sini. I think we should keep looking for ways for you to make paths by yourself, but in the meantime you shouldn't be stranded with no way to use your *vitalle*. Just in case someone really is trying to harm Keepers."

ELEVEN

A laric left and she knelt by the fire, pulling together a pile of kindling. She experimented, lighting one splinter of wood, then two at a time. She tried two pieces a fingerbreadth apart, then a handbreadth. The stone was perfect. Held inside it was just enough energy to change *vitalle* into warmth. Any energy she funneled into it came out in a copper cloud of heat looking for something to warm. If Alaric had made it well, and it seemed like he had, it would last for years.

She played with the flames until she ran out of kindling.

The silence of the room was glorious, and she scooted back until she leaned against the nearest chair, watching the fire dwindle and rubbing her thumb along the new ring.

Eventually the events of the day crowded in, and she replayed parts of the council in her mind. The palace sprawled away past the walls of her room, so different from the peaceful valley of the Stronghold. She missed the open feel of it.

The red cloak that she'd worn from the Stronghold hung next to a black Keeper's robe. Maybe if she wore that, Madeleine would treat her with more respect. She snorted. Madeleine would probably just point out that the robe didn't fit Sini well, which was too close to the truth. Wondering if Alaric would encourage her to start wearing it anyway, she grabbed her red cloak and left her room, finding the stairs to the roof above their wing. She stepped out on a wide, flat patio, railed with crenellations. A guard stationed along the wall took note of her before turning back to his watch.

The night air was crisp with the bite of fall. Most of the city stretched out to the south. Torches lit the wider street that still moved with people who hadn't made it home yet. The bulk of the palace lay south, as well, ablaze with torchlight. Torches ringed the outer walls, illuminating soldiers patrolling, and lit pathways through gardens. Other rooftops held braziers of fire and knots of people.

She cast out, feeling the energy of all the people and all the fires. She spun her ring, contemplating all the things she could do, now that she had it.

Sini wrapped her cloak tighter around her and walked to the northwest corner. Ahead of her a small wedge of the city filled the area between the palace wall and the city wall, and her gaze ran across it without stopping. The city wall snaked down into a shallow valley. Up the far side rose hills thick with vineyards and sprawling estates.

Sini let her attention sit on the specks of firelight scattered through those hills before the weight of the flatness in front of them pulled it down.

The Lees.

It was darker there than inside the city wall. The torchlight burned with more smoke and less warmth. Unlike the straight, wide streets of Queenstown, the alleys of the Lees jutted at odd angles and wound into dead ends as though they'd been crumpled by a giant fist. She found a large burnt-out house that she recognized and tried to trace the streets away from it into familiar directions. But it was too dark and the way too convoluted.

Her chest tightened. Her family was somewhere in that maze of alleys, or they had been eight years ago.

Early on, after Vahe had taken Sini from her family, she'd imagined they'd taken the money she'd stolen from the wayfarer and moved into a small house in a neighborhood where trees grew and there was enough food. It gave her comfort, as Vahe dragged her farther from home, to think she'd taken from him enough to at least give her little brothers a better life.

But the older she'd gotten, the more of her parents' wasted opportunities she remembered. The dull suspicion that Vahe's money had also been wasted curdled inside her. Her father would have drunk away the money and made his family miserable. Her brothers would have felt nothing but the absence of the little bread Sini had stolen for them each day.

After all this time, after all the vast distances she'd traveled, the Lees were still the same. It'd be foolish to think her family wasn't.

A glint of auburn from her ring caught her eye. She slid her hand across the smooth surface of the palace stones and the gem left a thin trail of light. Beneath that ring, her hand was still the same one that had stolen bread among the rough walls in the Lees and slaved away in the grass of the Sweep.

Maybe it was also foolish to think she'd changed. Maybe she didn't belong here anymore than she'd belonged anywhere else.

The door from below opened and the guard greeted someone, but she didn't bother to turn. The wind picked up, flicking the ends of her hair against her cheek. A chill ran across her neck, and she wished her hair was long enough to cover it.

Steps approached behind her and Sini turned, ready to tell the guard that she required more time alone, but she stopped when she was met with a stiff bow from Roan.

He was quite a bit taller than she was, and a few years older, in his mid-twenties. His grey clothes struck her again as not quite the uniform of a guard, but so stiff they might as well be. He greeted her with a polite "Good evening," before stepping up to the wall beside her, looking out toward the Lees, his hands clasped behind his back. "Mind if I join you?" There wasn't any question in his question.

Sini turned back toward the wall, her surprise almost chasing the irritation out of her voice. "Who am I to tell the future king no?"

"I'm not the future king," he corrected her. "Thankfully. I'm only the future lord consort. The line of succession will pass from Madeleine to our children."

"Well," Sini said, setting her elbows on the wall, and wishing the lord consort would go pester someone else, "if I'd known I was talking to someone with such meager prospects, I would have told you I do mind, seeing as I came up here for some peace."

Unlike his reserved responses in the council earlier, he smiled at her words.

"You can't find peace in as public a place as the guarded private roof above your own private wing." He leaned onto his own elbows next to her. "For true privacy I suggest locking yourself in your own room or hiding in a remote corner of the library."

He didn't say anything else, and Sini let the silence drag on for a few moments. While more relaxed than earlier, he was watchful. He closed his hands into loose fists as though he didn't trust his fingers to remain still.

She spun her ring more forcefully than before. "What is it you want, Lord Roan, the Not-Future King?" As soon as the words were out of her mouth, she knew she'd gone too far. The kindness of the old men at the Stronghold had put her out of practice in talking to people who took station and rank seriously.

But he just laughed. He felt nothing like the man from earlier. "The queen has ordered me to protect the Keepers. Alaric I'm familiar with, but I know little about you or Will."

She waited for him to say more. When he didn't, she pressed her own mouth closed. It was always like this here, being examined. She was hardly going to help him figure out what the new female Keeper was like. If he had a specific question, he could ask.

When he spoke, it was merely a statement. "I found your conclusions about Lukas from your map work to be interesting."

"Really? Because you challenged everything I said."

"I found them incomplete," he said bluntly. "I found your grouping of events misleading. You were merely using the information to track your lost foster brother, instead of figuring out what a man who is a threat is doing."

Irritation flared at the accusation, and she matched his bluntness. "So my map work was interesting, but not scholarly."

He still showed no annoyance at her tone, which was almost irritating in itself.

"You were right earlier in saying it is dangerous to simplify your enemy," he said. "We should not consider only the aspects of Lukas that show him to be our enemy." He glanced away from the city and took in her defiant look without emotion. "But I wonder if you are not doing the same thing, only seeing him as your brother." The edge of his mouth quirked up. "Surely he is more complex than that?"

The day had been too long. She wanted to keep a little lightness in her voice, but it seemed too much to ask. "Am I supposed to believe that you and I are friends and you're just here to chat with me about my poor research skills?"

Roan looked out toward the dark hills. "Friendship seems like too much to expect after a few hours' acquaintance, but I hope at some point you will think of me as a friend. And Madeleine as well."

Sini pressed her lips shut against the answer that sprang to mind.

"We all love Queensland and want the best for it. That puts us on the same side."

His voice was irritating. It bordered on smug. As though she were just expected to agree with everything he said. "Funny. It didn't feel like we were on the same side in the council."

"Feelings are deceptive," he said dismissively, and her annoyance flared stronger. "Madeleine and I want a strong Queensland. We're against anything that weakens it."

"Like Keepers?" Sini demanded.

Roan stood and faced her, folding his arms across his chest. "You have to admit that the Keepers aren't at full strength. Of the six still at the Stronghold, two are dying and one is only capable of caring for the animals."

"You know nothing about Rett," she snapped.

Roan held up his hand to stop her. "Everything I've ever heard about him says he's a good man. But you can't tell me he's an asset to Queensland like a Keeper should be."

Sini clenched her mouth shut. Her hands curled into fists and her fingernails dug into her palms.

"I'm not disparaging the man." He sounded sincere, if still pompous. "But if you take out those three Keepers we're left with the Shield, Gerone, and Mikal. We all know Mikal has no interest in coming back to court, Gerone would rather care for the Keepers at the Stronghold, and the Shield…he hasn't left that valley in forty years."

"But he is in constant communication with the queen. And if he left the Stronghold, he would lose access to the library. Which he consults often."

Roan looked unimpressed. "The Keepers here are Alaric, who's about to become a father with all the distractions that entails, and Will, who's just biding his time until he can leave court. Possibly to go to the Sweep and look for a woman."

"And don't forget me," Sini snapped. "Who's too young to be helpful."

"You are young."

She bit back the obvious response that she was only a handful of years younger than him, and no younger than Madeleine at all, since even in her own mind it sounded petulant.

"And your time on the Sweep means that you haven't trained with the Keepers as long as most young Keepers who come here. So you can understand our hesitancy."

"Because only time spent being trained among the elite of Queensland can produce a worthwhile education?"

Roan considered her calmly. "Correct me if I am inaccurate in my understanding of your history, but you had no formal education at all before joining the Keepers. Few lowborn girls attend school, and how much could you have learned from the barbarians on the Sweep?"

"Those barbarians taught me to read and write both the common tongue and runes. From the clan chief I learned politics, warfare, history, literature, and magic."

Roan raised an eyebrow. "I didn't realize you admired the Roven so much."

"I didn't say I admired them. There are many things in their culture I dislike, slavery predominant among them. But writing them off as uneducated barbarians is insulting and unwise."

She waited for a harsh answer, but he considered her words and gave a thoughtful sort of hmm. "And before the Sweep, while you lived in Queenstown, did you receive any education?"

"I didn't live in Queenstown." Sini flung her hand at the dim buildings over the wall. "I lived in the Lees."

"The Lees are right there against the wall. That's part of Queenstown as much as the hills and vineyards beyond it."

She stared at him. He was an odd mix of highborn pretentiousness and measured consideration, and it mollified the indignation that was all too ready to flare up in her today. "There's more difference between the Lees and Queenstown than there is between…say…a lord consort and a slave. It's its own small world. The city guard doesn't bother with it since it's outside the wall. There isn't enough money in the whole place to feed a tenth of the people in it. They're forgotten and ignored, left to their own devices. They care nothing for dukes or queens or lord consorts. They haven't heard of Madeleine, nor would they care about her if they had. They have no loyalty to anyone but themselves, because no one else is going to see that they eat."

Roan turned an indignant look on her. "The crown has several programs to help the Lees. Food donations, labor projects."

Sini snorted. "The crown deals with corrupt overseers who pocket the money and hire the work out to their friends. When the donations of food come, they're scooped up by the street bosses and kept for themselves."

He frowned. "There have been four schools started there, at the expense of the crown."

"I lived there for twelve years. I never went to school a single day, nor knew anyone who did. The school building nearest me had so many rooms it was used as a brothel. I did my best to never pass by it."

"We've hired three teams to update the roads, rebuild the central square, and clean out the city fountain."

Sini laughed. "I don't know what the city fountain is like now, but it was where my mother did her laundry. It didn't clean the clothes really, but it took out most of the smell."

Roan turned to look indignantly into the Lees. "Everything we've done is wasted?"

"They assume it's the government's job to waste things."

He turned toward her, his brow drawn. "What would you do to help it?"

"I…I don't know. It needs more than food or education. Or even money. Those are all part of it, but they need something more. The Lees has no faith in itself, no hope. It needs a reason to be more than it is. It's missing…heart."

Roan looked at her for a long moment, then turned back to the dimmer patch of the world that held the Lees. His face was set in an irritated frown. "Tomorrow I want to discuss this with the queen and Madeleine. Be thinking if you have any specific ideas."

Sini tapped her lips, considered his words for a moment. "Why are you driven to do this?" She gave him a wry smile. "Love of country?"

"As unimaginative as that sounds, yes. The moors of Gringonn sit along the southern border of Greentree and the poor from there come into Queensland all the time, searching for a place of safety for their families. The moors are lawless. The government of Gringonn is too weak to exert any control over the north. Small warlords have free rein there, and the power struggles between them destroy the lives of the common people. Having a strong central government keeps the common people safe. Or it should."

"Having a strong government quite close to the Lees isn't keeping it safe."

He frowned. "From what you say, the government isn't strong there."

"People here"—she flung her arm at the sprawling palace—"already know that."

"Undoubtedly. But I did not. Beginning tomorrow, help me fix it."

Sini let out a small laugh, part at the ludicrous idea, part at the commanding tone. "You're too proactive. You'll never make a good politician."

"I have no interest in being a politician. I've been put in a position where I can help the people of Queensland, and I intend to do it." He faced her stiffly, his hands closed neatly at his side as though he stood at attention. "Will you help?"

He was pompous and irritating and far too formal, but he seemed sincere. And helping the Lees was a worthwhile cause.

She curtseyed. "My undereducated mind is at your service."

He scowled. "I didn't mean—"

Sini waved it off. "But the Lees needs a way to mend its broken heart. Or everything else you do will be in vain."

She leaned back on the wall and watched the smoky torches in the Lees. A broken heart. Their food was too hard to get, their wages too low, every part of their day was a struggle.

The idea snagged in her mind. She shoved herself away from the wall. "That's what Lukas is doing. Trying to break Queensland's heart. It was Mallon's goal, to bleed the heart of the land dry so it could be easily conquered. He started at the edges and destroyed it bit by bit until everyone despaired. And now Lukas is following the same plan. He's cut off our gold and troubled Queensland along the border."

Roan turned toward her, his eyes wide. "And wants to destroy the Keepers."

"But for a different reason. That's his final goal. He believes that he's saving Queensland from the evil influence of the Keepers. Every other thing he does to hurt the country is focused on harming the Keepers."

"But it amounts to the same thing for us. It is bad for the country if the Keepers are hurt."

Sini pressed her lips closed for a moment before she trusted herself to speak. "You've just pointed out that the Keepers aren't much help."

He shook his head. "The Keepers are the soul of this land. If I'm frustrated, it's because if you fade, the kingdom fades. You hold our stories and our trust. The wisdom of the Keepers and their books stretches back to times the rest of us don't remember. We need you. You are too full of your own humanity right now, and we need you to be more.

"We need you to remind us of our history and tell us our stories matter. We need you to counsel queens and future queens—and future lord consorts." He stopped and ran his hand through his hair in the first unsure gesture Sini had seen him use. "If we're frustrated, it is because we all look to you. And we're wondering if you're strong enough to save us."

*His grey clothes struck her again as not quite the uniform of
a guard, but so stiff they might as well be.*

TWELVE

When Sini returned to her room, the maid building the fires gave her a nervous head bob. "'Scuse me, m'lady. The night promises t' be chilled," the maid said with an apologetic smile.

Sini knelt next to her and handed her another piece of wood from the stack. The maid took it with a wary expression. She was older than Sini and her deference felt awkward. "It's already chilling. I'm Sini. How are you keeping this so clean? I always manage to send clouds of ash out into the room when I set the fire."

She gave a quick grin. "I'm Dalia, and I only make clouds of ash if an overfriendly nobleman goes and gets too close when I'm working."

Sini laughed. "Have you worked in the palace long?"

"Forever. Haven't worked the Keeper's wing in years, though. We don't usually have so many Keepers. Since the intruder and the other things, they've brought some of us more experienced folk t' help."

"What other things?"

Dalia shifted. "Both Keeper Alaric and Keeper Will think someone's been in their room, goin' through their things."

"Has anything been stolen?"

"Not that they know of. The steward was furious at first, thought it was the woman who cleans their rooms, but she'd never bother their things. The reason she's here is she cleans well but leaves Alaric's work alone and don't tidy his papers." Dalia's voice lowered. "The Keeper doesn't like it when people move all his papers, and he always has lots. Spread out on the desk, the floor, sometimes stuck to the walls."

"That sounds like Alaric. If it's not the cleaning woman, then who?"

Dalia shook her head. "Didn't no one see nothing." At Sini's skeptical look she continued earnestly. "It's true. Got everybody nervous. There's no way into that garden 'cept over a guarded wall or from inside. It's nearly impossible to get through this end of the palace w'out being seen. If he'd been near the kitchens or washin' rooms, that'd be different. Those places are busy with strangers. But all the way over here, everyone knows everyone. Anyone new stands out like a pig in the throne room. We all knew Keeper Will had brought you before you'd even reached your room." She shook her head and added a last piece of wood. "It's unsettlin' that someone got to Keeper

Alaric's balcony without being seen. Then disappeared like a ghost."

Dalia struck a match, lit the fire, and stood to leave.

"It was nice to meet you Dalia." Sini held her hands out to the small flames. "Thank you for the fire."

Dalia smiled. "Always feels a bit silly lighting a fire for a Keeper when you could probably just pop one out of the air."

"I assure you," Sini laughed, "I have great respect for the skill of fire starting."

Dalia curtseyed her way out and for the first time in hours, Sini was completely alone with no noise beyond the crackling fire.

She collapsed back onto the couch. Her conversation with Roan annoyed her like a wrinkle in her sock. He'd been right about the Keepers. As much as she hated to admit it, by midwinter the twins would be gone. The remaining Keepers were few and not particularly strong. Alaric and Will had their own strengths, but they weren't what she'd always pictured Keepers to be. They weren't single-minded in their service. They were more human than that.

She thought of Will's words in the Stronghold. *The amount of humanity we reveal to each other is one of our great strengths.* Will had been talking about Keepers and the Wellstone, but it felt like more than that.

She spun her ring. The fire had grown large enough that the thin trails of amber light from the stones was almost impossible to see.

Roan had been right, but he'd been wrong too. The country didn't need the Keepers to be more than humans. It was their humanity that was essential.

That wasn't what was really bothering her, though. What was really irritating was his comments on her map work. She did not see Lukas merely as a brother. She had spent months considering all the information they had.

Sini heaved herself off the couch and took her pack into the study. This would be easy to disprove. She shoved the desk against the wall and spread out her map on the floor. Grabbing all the candles she could find, she set them around the map, seeing how quickly she could flick her finger past the wicks and still light them.

Then, putting aside fire games, she pulled out her stack of notes. Instead of placing them back in their original piles, she flipped through them again.

The night's conversations swirled in her head. Roan was right. Before, she'd been using these notes to track Lukas, to figure out where he was going so he could be found. But maybe she shouldn't be looking at where he was acting, so much as why.

It wasn't about what he was doing. It was about his goals.

Piles of notes built up slowly along the southern border of Queensland according to the type of problem instead of its location. Troubling news that affected crops or herds in one stack. Problems with water sources in another. Unusual illnesses affecting people, game, or livestock each separated out.

A disturbing pattern emerged.

Three different incidents of game dying from an unknown illness. First a few elderly sheep in the Black Hills collapsed and died. Then a sickness making the dairy goats in Marshwell collapse caused a shortage of milk. And finally the breeding sows in a small town in Greentree were almost wiped out. The report on the sows mentioned large, festering blisters on their skin before they collapsed and died. She hadn't noticed the collapsing. She'd been too focused on what sickness could have caused the blisters. But what if the sheep and goats had had blisters too, hidden under their wool and hair?

And then the water sources. Small streams all along the southern border had either dried up or turned bitter. Each incident was slightly different, sickening people or animals until the most recent one, in which the tainted water had killed a child. None of the larger rivers these spilled into had been affected, as they surely would have been if the cause was natural.

And then the wildlife. In the woods of Marshwell four deer were found dead of a wasting disease. In Greentree three moose were found dead of the same. On the border between the two, in rural hills, three dozen wild turkeys were found emaciated amidst perfectly rich food sources.

Sini knelt next to the map and laid out the last of the notes. She sank back onto her heels, the truth of it washing over her. Lukas had been systematically looking for the best way to hurt Queensland. Similar attacks had been spread so widely apart from each other, she hadn't connected them when she'd been merely tracking his location. And each of the type of attacks had continued until one sufficiently severe happened. Then nothing.

Everyone else had been right.

All this time Lukas hadn't been pestering the southern border of Queensland like a frustrated child. He'd been systematically formulating ways to harm farm animals, water supplies, crops, and wild game. It reminded her of the jackals in Gustav's book about Mallon. Lukas was nip, nip, nipping at the edges of Queensland, figuring out which nips hurt the most so he could attack and weaken her.

With a dull ache in her chest she pushed herself up and blew out the candles, taking the last one with her, leaving the notes in darkness.

Tomorrow in the council she'd have to tell them that they'd all been right. They should be ready for him to unleash his worst, as soon as he was ready.

She climbed into bed, grateful that she didn't have to explain it yet.

Once she was settled, her thoughts swirled between diseased animals and tainted water. She tried to picture Lukas's face the way she'd known him years ago. His easy smile. She could picture the way his hair had looked—light brown, hanging a bit past his shoulders. His beard, never quite coming in as thick as the Roven, still braided like them. She could picture his limp; how bad it could get if he were too far from Killien.

Had his solution to that worked? The limp, suffered when a stonesteep attacked him, had never healed. The pain from it, somehow based in magic, had lingered. For years Lukas had had to stay close to Killien to deaden the pain, since no magic worked near the Torch.

But he'd discovered that Killien's power came from his blood. And before escaping the Roven, Lukas had stabbed Killien, bottling up as much of his blood as he could and leaving the Torch to die. Alaric and Will were the only reason Killien was still alive.

Lukas had worked so closely with Killien, always scheming secret ways together to strengthen the Morrow Clan. It had been almost impossible to believe Lukas had tried to kill him.

Almost.

That had been the first day she'd had this feeling. The knot in her gut that knew Lukas was capable of the things people said he was doing. No matter how much she wanted to believe differently.

She'd forgotten that—or maybe refused to remember it. Whenever she'd thought of Lukas coming to the Stronghold, it was as she'd first met him.

But tonight she couldn't picture his younger, happier face. All she could see was him at the end: angry, and driven to destroy his enemies. Whoever he deemed them to be. He'd betrayed Killien, tried to kill him, stolen his sword, and flown away on a dragon.

When had she forgotten that was who he had become? When had she started to believe that just because she and Rett were happy and safe away from the Sweep, that Lukas would be too?

Killien's sword reminded her of the Wellstone. Why had the Wellstone connected Lukas and the sword to Chesavia?

She blew out her candle in irritation and rubbed at her face, trying to clear her mind. Trying to think of anything else.

The closeness of the Lees nagged at her. Was her family still there? Did the boys spend their early mornings trying to steal bread? What did they look like now? She tried to picture the faces of the little boys that were left in the Lees when she had been taken to the Sweep. They'd been so small. After eight years, would she even recognize them?

The last time she'd been in Queenstown, right after she'd escaped the Sweep, she couldn't bring herself to look for any of them. Will had offered to go with her, but the thought of facing the father who'd sold her, the mother who'd let her go—she'd never wanted to see them again.

And yet her mother's face in the Wellstone—it hadn't been contempt that she'd thrown at Sini when Vahe dragged her away. It had been pain and regret and terror. Her mother had been broken by too many years of hardship. And thinking of her now, Sini found her feelings had shifted from bitterness to pity. She wasn't that frightened child anymore. She wasn't frightened of the Lees, of her parents, of hunger.

Tomorrow morning, early enough that most of the Lees would be quiet, she'd go.

A large part of her protested the idea, but she paid it no heed. It was time.

———————

Sini raced through the alleys of the Lees, the ground twisting and heaving. Heavy footsteps pounded behind her. Her legs were too short and moved too slowly, as though they dragged through mud. She darted into a grimy street, her bare feet slapping the hard ground, her breath coming in gasps. Behind her the footsteps stayed close, but all she could see were leering faces leaning out of windows and doorways.

A hand shot out of the black, clamped down on her arm, and yanked her into the darkness.

Sini jolted awake, shoving herself up in bed. Her room in the Keepers wing was dim and silent.

She pressed her eyes shut and breathed deeply, trying to slow her heart. Her feet rubbed against the soft linens of the bed, not the hard, cold ground.

It had been years since she'd been plagued with dreams like that. Always chased and vulnerable.

Outside her window the world was just starting to lighten with dawn. Everything in her room had been drained of color and lay in muted greys. Too much like the dinginess of the Lees. Her trip there could wait for another day.

She reached over to the candle on the bedside table and lit it with her ring, brightening her spirits and the room.

Even this early, noises floated in from beyond her room.

She lay back down and cast out. Will still slept in the room next to her. Evangeline and Alaric further on. Guards in the sitting area outside. The floor below her was filled with people; the garden outside held several more.

As far as the wave rolled out, she found echoes of people.

It would have been handy to have been able to do that when she was little. If she could have sat in her hiding places in the Lees and cast out to discover if she was as safe as she felt.

The fear lingering from the dream sparked a new anger. She had been a child, and no one had protected her. She clenched her fists against the familiarity of the fear.

She wasn't that child any longer. Nor was she a slave. She'd spent four years at the Stronghold unlearning that fear, and she wasn't going to let it control her now.

She was perfectly capable of walking into the Lees so early in the morning that the most volatile parts were still sleeping. Mornings there had always been more peaceful than the rest of the day.

She pushed the covers off and hurried over to the wide wardrobe. Ignoring the dozen dresses that had appeared yesterday, she found her own warm pants and light blue linen shirt.

The deep green brocade cloak hanging on the side of the wardrobe would be a stupid choice to wear into the Lees, even if it was warmer than her own simple red one. Her fingers lingered on the Keeper's robe. What would the Lees do with a Keeper?

Whatever it was, it would involve more attention than she wanted. She pulled her own rustic cloak on and tugged on her boots. She glanced in the tall looking glass. Nothing about her said she'd spent the night in the queen's palace. The garnet on her ring was small enough it shouldn't be noticed. She was too clean for the Lees, but it would have to do.

Outside her door a guard stood watch over the empty sitting room. He wasn't one of the young fresh-faced men usually assigned tedious guard jobs. He was fifty at least. The grey at the temples of his short-cropped hair was spreading to the rest of his head. He didn't stand at stiff attention, as though inviting scrutiny. Instead he stood relaxed, but watchful, his arms crossed. He managed to look capably intimidating, even standing next to a table with a large vase of summer flowers. Identical sorts of guards stood at each of the other Keeper's doors.

"Good morning, soldier." She stepped up next to him and peered across the room. "Are we expecting an onslaught from the chairs?"

His expression did not change. "Good morning, Keeper. We are not concerned about the chairs, no."

"Please just call me Sini."

The guard kept his attention on the room. "That will not be possible."

Sini considered him. "Can I order you to?"

"You're free to do what you like, Keeper, but my orders to treat you with the respect due your station will override any such requests."

Sini tapped at her lips. That was annoying. "You know my name, but I don't know yours."

"Captain Liam of Ravenwick, Queen's Guard, 3rd unit."

"Captain?" Sini glanced at the other two. "The queen sent captains to guard us from the chairs?"

"These are Lieutenant Torrne and Lieutenant Branley. They are under my command."

Both lieutenants snapped off a nod to her before resuming their watchfulness.

Sini grinned at Captain Liam. "Do I require a higher level of guarding than my Keeper brothers?"

"Yes. Being the unknown entity in our mission."

Sini let out a laugh. "That makes me sound mysterious."

"You're getting less mysterious by the moment."

"I am?"

He nodded. "You woke up early, determined to go somewhere"—he glanced at her clothes before returning his attention to the room—"unofficial. Despite that determination, you diverted from your mission immediately. Which leads me to believe it is not something you are eager to do."

Sini narrowed her eyes and tried not to shift.

"Most people do not greet guards, either out of intimidation or arrogance. You have been friendly. Your uncertainty as to whether you could command me shows that you don't consider yourself in a station above us, regardless of whether you are.

"Your reluctance to either dress like a Keeper, or be named one, means that you're bound to do things I would not expect of the other Keepers. So yes, you require a higher level of guarding."

Sini crossed her own arms and studied the man. "Are you going to follow me?"

"No, Keeper. My post is here."

That was good, but the formality of it rubbed her the wrong way. Stepping around him, she snapped a small pink flower out of the vase and tucked it behind the thin brass arc pinned to the shoulder of his uniform. The pin was polished but dinged. The captain must have spent his career doing more dangerous things than watching chairs.

He spared her a tight-faced look that bordered on fatherly disapproval before turning back to the room.

"I tell you what. As long as you insist on calling me Keeper, I'll insist on calling you Daisy."

"That is not a daisy," Captain Liam pointed out.

"True. But *Pretty Pink Blossom I Don't Know the Name Of* would make for an unwieldy name." She headed across the room toward the hallway. "I hope the chairs don't give you too much trouble, Daisy."

"I believe we'll be able to handle them, Keeper."

Sini followed the only path she knew out of the palace, through the small courtyard she and Will had entered through yesterday. The sky was quickly brightening. She paused at the door. A line of city guard stood at attention receiving orders from none other than Roan. Hoping there were enough other people busy in the courtyard that he wouldn't notice her, she headed toward the gate on the far side.

Before she had reached it, he called out, "Keeper Sini."

She thought about ignoring him, but the two guards at the gate focused on her as well. Bracing herself, she turned around to face him.

Roan strode toward her, taking in her clothes with a glance. "I didn't expect you to be heading to the Lees this early."

Sini stifled an annoyed huff and thought about denying her destination. But there didn't seem to be a point. "It's as good a time as any."

"You and I are needed in the queen's council."

"Not for hours."

Roan studied her for a long moment. "Can I convince you that this is a bad idea?"

"To go to the place where I lived for twelve years?"

"A young woman going into the slums alone is asking for trouble."

"I know the Lees and their dangers better than you, Lord Consort."

His lips tightened. "Then lead on."

Sini crossed her arms. "You're not coming with me."

"It's either me or three men of my choosing."

"Three!" Sini glanced at the city guard still lingering in the courtyard. "You're worth three of them?"

"No. But it is my personal responsibility to ensure your safety. If I'm not there myself, I will make sure you are over-protected. I'm not interested in having to report to her majesty that a Keeper was killed in the Lees."

Sini glared at him in irritation. "I was under the impression that Keepers were well respected here. You're the second soldier to disregard my wishes this morning. And it's not even fully light out."

Roan gave her a satisfied smile. "Captain Liam was my personal choice to guard your room."

"I'd be safer by myself than walking with a uniformed guard."

"It's not a uniform."

"It's the most uniform-like non-uniform I've ever seen and it's going to attract unwanted attention."

He gave her a flat look. "I'm still coming with you."

Sini glared at him. "Fine." She dropped into an exaggerated curtsey. "Let's go, Lord Consort."

She stalked through the gates, shooting glares at the guards who saluted Roan as he passed.

Roan stayed several paces behind her on the avenue leading from the palace to the city wall, acting more like a real guard than she'd expected. She did her best to ignore him, which was easy amid the merchant houses with brightly painted signs lining the street. The only early morning shoppers were well-dressed servants carrying neatly-wrapped bundles, all striding down the avenue with a self-absorbed air and paying neither Sini or Roan any heed. By the time they reached the thick stone city wall at the northwestern gate, the sun had risen fully. The guards there saluted Roan and let them pass through without comment.

The broad avenue continued through more fine houses and bright shops, straight toward the vineyard hills to the north. The morning was chilly, but the early sun snuck rays in between the tall buildings and occasionally sunfire pressed against Sini's cheek with a comforting warmth. She toyed with the ring on her finger, happy to feel the weight of it.

It only took one turn down the nearest shadowed alley for the world to change. The only dignity found in these buildings was in dim echoes. Broken signs hung from rusted poles. Dark interiors squinted out through windows nailed shut with mismatched beams of wood.

The smells of the Lees hit them with almost physical force and Roan made a disgusted sound. The stench of unwashed bodies and puddles of sewage sent her heart racing. She pushed at the fear that had been dogging her since her nightmare. She was not a child. She was not running from anyone. She wasn't helpless.

The fear didn't subside, but she strode down the alley as though it had. The cobblestones beneath her feet were almost invisible under the layer of dirt and filth. The few people out watched Roan's grey uniform suspiciously. It didn't help that he walked stiffly, one hand on his sword, the other balled into a fist at his side.

Nothing looked familiar, but Sini led the way down a winding alley, heading in the direction of the central market. The alleys were so narrow that they were all deeply shadowed, and she found herself wishing she could feel the sunfire on her skin.

Roan walked behind her with his jaw clenched. "How much further?"

"I have no idea. I never got this close to the city wall when I lived here."

The street ahead of them dead-ended at a run-down shop. Sini ducked into the alley on her left.

"Do you have any idea where you're going?" Roan asked.

"Mostly." The square should be somewhere ahead of them. They just needed to find a street big enough to lead them there.

The next street was more promising. It was just too wide to be called an alley, and a block ahead it joined with the widest street she'd seen yet. The bit of building across it stood three stories high. A horseshoe was set into the stone above each window on the top floor. Sini blew out a little sigh of relief.

"That's the ironworks," she glanced at him over her shoulder. "Now I actually do know where we are."

Roan spared her an annoyed look before his eyes snapped wide at something ahead of her.

Sini spun to find a tall man in the dusty remains of a formal coat stepping into her path.

"Look at this," he said, motioning to Sini with a clay bottle that reeked of dredgewine. "What sort of treasure have we found that needs a royal guard for an escort?"

THIRTEEN

ini took a step back just as three men stepped into the alley. Roan pulled her toward the side of the alley so he could face all four. The first man crowded closer, examining Sini with a possessive, satisfied smile sliding through his wiry, unkempt beard. The hilt of a knife stuck out from his belt. He chewed a smoldering stick of gumroot. The scent of dredgeweed, a caustic spirits distilled in the Lees, burned her throat, jarring her back to all the nights her parents had reeked of it, bringing back all the fear that smell had caused.

Roan slid his sword out of its sheath with an unhurried hiss. "This treasure isn't worth the pain it would cost you."

The man with the wine raised an eyebrow. "I'm Nyle, and this is my street. No one passes through my street without paying the toll."

"I hope you're really worth three guards," Sini said to Roan.

"I'm at least better than four drunken men spineless enough to attack a woman." He held his sword low in front of him, looking more at ease than Sini had seen him yet.

In the face of a real, tangible danger, the last of the fear from her nightmare faded and was replaced by a low anger. "The Lees has too many spineless, drunken men." She took a step toward Nyle.

"Sini." Roan's voice was a cross between a warning and a command. "Don't."

"This man is the problem with the Lees, Roan." She stepped forward again and Nyle grinned at her. "There are too many people trying to intimidate and rob everyone else for…" She glanced around at the crumbling buildings. "Dungheaps like this."

Nyle's smile soured. "It's my dungheap you're in, woman. I was going to let you pass with just a fine. But I think the toll has just gone up." He mashed the end of the gumroot between his teeth and bits of brownish spittle foamed at the edges of his lips.

A spark of hatred for the disgusting root and the foul-smelling wine and the brazen, brutish attitude flared in her. This man was every problem from her childhood. Every hour spent in fear. She stepped forward until she was right in front of the man. He swayed slightly on his feet and his eyes weren't quite focused. She lifted her chin to look him in the eye, all the complicated emotions the Lees had given to her funneled into one, furious look.

"Sini." This time Roan's voice held only the snap of command.

She ignored him. "I am tired of seeing cowards like you run places like this into the ground.

You lumber around like animals destroying anything you touch." She jabbed him in the chest with her finger and dredgewine sloshed out of the bottle onto his arm.

He snarled at her and grabbed for the front of her shirt, but his motion was slow, and she swatted his hand away.

She leaned right up into his face. "It's a dangerous thing to smoke gumroot near dredgewine. Wine is flammable."

Sini slammed her elbow up into the bottom of Nyle's bottle and the wine sprayed up into his face. Rust-red liquid streamed down his beard. He roared with fury and lunged for her, just as the other men closed in on Roan. A clang rang out of Roan's sword against one of their knives.

Nyle shoved her back against the wall. Lights exploded in her vision as her head slammed into the stone. His breath was warm and rancid on her face. Dimly, she heard muffled cries from near Roan. She shook her head to clear it and grabbed a fistful of Nyle's damp beard, shoving his face back.

She poured *vitalle* into her ring. The garnet flared to life and a copper light shot out from her finger.

The wine ignited. Flames burst out from Nyle's shirt and beard.

Tongues of fire, tinted green by the alcohol, licked up the side of his face, He screamed and let go of her. She tumbled down the wall, crashing to her knees on the cobblestones. The stench of burning hair cut into her throat. Nyle's bottle smashed to the ground and he slapped at his face to put out the flames.

Nyle ran through a doorway, screaming for water. Sini's head spun. She touched the back of her head and winced at the huge lump, although her hand came away without blood. She braced herself against the alley wall, willing the world to stop spinning.

The other three men lay groaning on the ground around Roan. One had a wide gash on his forehead, one cradled his arm, and one lay unmoving.

Roan turned to her with a furious face. "Are you all right?" He pulled her to her feet and looked her over, and without waiting for an answer pointed his sword down the alley toward the iron works. "Out of this alley. Now."

She nodded and stumbled toward the street ahead.

Behind them curious faces leaned out of windows, but no one followed. She turned into the wide street running along the huge building that had once housed enough ironworkers to supply the city. The street ran due east and morning sunlight poured down into it. Merchants filled the street, selling wares along its sides. Early-morning shoppers lingered at their blankets and carts.

Sini turned her face toward the sunlight, letting it soak into her skin, funneling the sunfire toward the back of her head.

"What were you thinking?" Roan hissed under his breath. "You can't attack a drunken man twice your size."

"He attacked us," she snapped. "And I am not a defenseless child." Warm energy filled the back of her skull, and the pain lessened. Roan steered her into the shadows of a quiet nook between two tall carts.

He put his hand on her shoulders and peered into her face. "You're not hurt, are you?"

"I'm fine." She pointed to a gash on his sleeve. "You?"

He waved a dismissive hand. "One of them almost got in a lucky swing."

"I apologize for mocking you about being better than three men."

The corner of his mouth lifted. "They were hardly men."

"I'm just glad Nyle didn't bring four."

"Very funny. How's your head?"

"Healing." At his doubtful expression she set her hand against the cut on his arm. Slippery blood coated her palm. Drawing in some *vitalle* from the sun shining on the street next to them, she pressed it into his wound, helping his body knit the cut, healing muscle and skin. He stiffened under her hand. When she was done, he straightened his arm with a look of disbelief.

"Still think the Keepers aren't useful?"

"Did your head heal that quickly?"

Sini touched the back of her head gingerly. "Swelling takes longer to sort out than a cut, but it's getting better."

He rubbed his arm. "That's a useful skill."

A woman across the street stopped and stared at Roan's clothes.

"We should keep moving." Sini stepped back out into the street and he followed.

"You did well against your ruffian," Roan said.

"I did survive in this place for years without you."

He glanced at her with a smile more genuine than she'd seen from him before. "By setting beards on fire?"

Sini grinned. "No, that's a new skill."

They reached the central square and Sini paused at the nearest merchant's cart. There was more commotion here. Vendors lined the edges of the square. Shoppers, looking haggard and worn, examined their wares. A good number of children scampered through, dirty and watchful. A boy ran toward them, then skidded to a stop when he caught sight of Roan. He darted to the side and disappeared around a building.

Sini turned to look at Roan's pressed grey uniform. "You should have worn something to cover that up."

"The only cloak I own is grey regulation."

"Of course it is."

"Are you in need of a cloak, good sir?" an elderly voice spoke from behind Sini.

A short, wiry old man beamed at them. His long beard was disheveled and his hair wild. His clothes were mismatched down to two different shoes. The cart next to him had a wide bed full of colorful bundles that seemed to hold no value. Spindly sticks held a roof over it, hung with ratty blankets and unnamable bits of fabric.

The merchant pulled a long, frayed cloak off the back of his cart. The general impression of the garment was green, but it held splotches of every color from black to yellow to orange. "Two coppers."

Roan eyed it with a grimace. "No thank y—"

"Yes," Sini broke in. "A cloak is exactly what he needs." She turned to Roan. "Buy the cloak from the man."

"No. We're wasting time."

No one was going to talk to her with a royal guard hovering at her shoulder. "You can't go with me dressed like that."

"I'm not leaving your side."

"Fine." She pulled out the coins and handed them to the man.

Roan held the blotchy fabric at arm's length.

"We're not going another step until you put it on," she said.

He sniffed it before grimacing and swinging it around his shoulders. It covered a good portion of his clean greys and Sini nodded approvingly. "You look dashing."

"Let's get this over with."

"May you find whatever you seek," the old merchant said pleasantly.

"And may we find it quickly," Roan added.

With her mottled, dirty escort, Sini headed across the square. No one paid them any mind now, and she headed for the thin avenue that snaked out of the opposite corner of the square. From there it was just a few twisting blocks to the small bakery.

The buildings looked shabbier and smaller than she remembered, but the smells were still the same. Musty and dusty, with an underlying rotten scent.

Her shoulders grew tighter as more and more of the buildings and alleys became familiar. At the front corner of the abandoned hotel, the gap in the stones she'd used to shimmy through had grown wide enough for a man. The smaller children must have found a different hideout.

They turned down one last street before the crumbling old bank came into view. The gargoyle on the roof leered down past his broken nose, and she relaxed slightly. She'd been terrified of that stone face for years until one day, covered in tears of rain, he'd struck her as more sad than frightened. She'd named him Granite, because it sounded stone-like, and that afternoon she'd discovered the way up to him. It was tricky in dry weather, almost impossible in the rain. But she'd climbed up regularly and sat by him, telling him her woes. From that height she could see slivers of places beyond the edge of the Lees: the bright green hilltops of the vineyards, the point of one roof of the palace, a small wedge of the huge city wall that kept her out of anywhere respectable.

Roan scanned the area around them, watching the other people closely. Sini caught sight of the bakery and studied the old street, looking everywhere except the mouth of the alley. When they reached it, though, running alongside the tiny building that smelled of old, dry bread, she paused. The cluttered, narrow alley drew her gaze and she wiped her damp hands on her pants.

All traces of the old lean-to were gone. There was an enormous pile of trash against the bakery where her mother had knelt, watching Vahe drag Sini away. The stench was overwhelming.

Roan looked at her with an unreadable expression. "Tell me we're not going in that alley."

"No reason to." Pushing old memories away, she walked to the front of the shop. It was smaller than she remembered. The building that had once seemed so permanent and sturdy was just a ramshackle shop. Catching sight of some motion inside, Sini pushed open the door and stepped in. After glancing up and down the dingy street, Roan followed her.

Mrs. Tanning stood behind the counter, her face set in the same scowl she'd worn years ago. She watched Sini and Roan with narrow, suspicious eyes. The back corner of the shop was covered with baskets, although few of them held any bread, even this early in the morning. Sini coughed as a dusty, floury smell hit her throat. She'd expected the sort of warm bread smell she found every morning in the Stronghold kitchen, the sort she remembered coming from this bakery when she was little.

"Good morning, Mrs. Tanning." The woman's eyes widened at her name. "You may not remember me, but I lived with my family in the alley behind your shop."

Mrs. Tanning studied her before nodding. "I remember a ragged lil' thief girl."

Roan shifted in a threatening sort of way, but Sini stepped forward to ward off whatever he might say. "Yes, that was me. And I'm afraid I stole a good number of loaves from you during the time we lived there. Probably at least ten coppers' worth."

The woman pursed her lips. "I knew it."

Sini reached into her pocket and pulled out twenty coppers. She set them on the counter. "I know that doesn't make up for the difficulty I caused then, but I hope it helps now."

Mrs. Tanning's gaze flicked between Sini and the coins for a breath before she swiped them off the counter and tucked them into her apron. Her gaze softened slightly. "That's very kind of ya'. I can see ya've done well for yerself." She eyed Roan, her gaze lingering on his pants. "How'd you get a guard to marry a little street rat like you?"

Roan stiffened and Sini laughed. "Oh, he's not my husband. You wouldn't believe how high-born you need to be to marry him." She gave Roan a grin that he returned with an annoyed look. "Mrs. Tanning, I was wondering if you knew where my family has gone. I haven't seen them for…a long time."

"Got too good for us folk, they did." Mrs. Tanning sniffed. "Dunno where they stole the money from, but yer mother came to me and said she'd let a corner room above a seamstress's shop—inside the city walls."

There must have been more than coppers in that pouch Sini had snatched from Vahe the wayfarer the day he'd taken her. "Do you know where in the city? Or the name of the seamstress?"

She brushed her hands off on her dirty apron. "I don't go inside the walls."

Mrs. Tanning was no further help, and at Roan's muttered urgings, they soon left. The trip had been all but useless. The worry she'd been holding all morning—for what she wasn't quite sure—evaporated, leaving a sort of tired emptiness.

Roan examined every building critically, and at his request she took a short detour to show him one of the failed schools. The unfinished construction projects and broken cobblestone streets spoke for themselves. He grew more grim the more of the Lees he saw.

She followed busier streets out of the Lees and they reached the wide avenue leading back to the city gate with no additional excitement, at least externally. Internally, Sini's mind was tumultuous. She remembered the Lees as dirty and hard, but the reality of the poverty was jarring. It left her feeling odd. She wanted to feel relieved to be out of it, but instead she felt…wrung out.

Free of the Lees, Roan pulled the multicolored cloak off with a grimace. She caught him watching her out of the corner of her eye. "Will you continue to look for your family?" he asked.

Sini shrugged. "That they moved eight years ago to a corner room above a seamstress isn't much to work with."

"How do you know it was eight years ago?"

"Because that's when—" She almost said, "they sold me." But the words stuck in her throat. "When the Wayfarer took me."

His face darkened and he shot a black look back at the Lees.

"It's also when I stole a fat purse from Vahe's belt and left it for my parents."

He was quiet a moment. "You might not have to find them. Once word gets out that you're here, they may find you. It's not every family that lost a daughter named Sini who would be twenty."

That was true, although the juxtaposition between her current position and her family was too complicated to sort out. Sini let her mind skip among old memories, finding few worth lingering on. They passed under the city gate and neared the palace.

"I'm sorry," Roan said in a pensive voice.

She dragged her mind back to the present. "Don't be. I didn't really expect to find them. They were never the kind to stay in one place long." And it was more than that. She felt…relieved. A little twang of guilt accompanied that fact.

"I meant I was sorry I misjudged you." His expression was serious, as though he were confessing some grave wrongdoing.

He still walked next to her comfortably. Comfortable might be an exaggeration. He walked like a soldier on duty, but there was less formality about him than he'd had on the roof the night before. Something more at ease. Like a soldier whose commanding officer has stepped out of the room.

He clasped his hand behind his back. "I believe you're the first person I've met who's lived through real poverty, never mind slavery. You're certainly the first person I've met who's held such derision for an elite education."

Sini winced. "I'm sorry about that. I was tired."

"It was well-deserved. Being wealthy isn't the only way to a good education." He looked back toward the Lees. "I cannot imagine what you've been through in your life. My comments were ignorant and insensitive."

Sini raised her eyebrows. His tone was still a bit lordly, but sincere. "Thank you."

"I've been considering what you said about the Lees," he continued. "Adding to that what I saw this morning, I'm going to suggest to the queen that we form a task force to look into how resources have been used there. Can I tell her you're willing to help?"

The idea of fixing anything in the Lees felt nearly impossible, but if it could be done…

She nodded and Roan looked pleased. The idea of future children having a better life than she had felt motivational. Maybe there was something she could accomplish here in the capital.

They reached the palace gate and were waved in by the guards. As they entered the courtyard, his earlier formality reappeared, and he stopped talking.

"You were right about my map work last night," Sini said. "I'd been merely tracking Lukas, not trying to discover what he was doing. So I revisited the information." She hesitated. "It's worse than I thought."

He considered her for a moment. "That is unfortunate. You'll appraise us all at the council?"

The question held enough command in it that Sini snorted and dropped into an exaggerated curtsey. "Of course, Lord Consort."

A soldier rushed up and saluted, cutting off Roan's annoyed answer. "Sir, you and Keeper Sini are required in the queen's study immediately."

It was far too early for the council. Sini hurried alongside Roan's long strides, a knot forming in her stomach. What had Lukas done now?

When they reached the study, the queen's face was brighter than yesterday. Even Madeleine looked almost pleased.

Will greeted them with a wide smile. "An elf has been born!"

FOURTEEN

"Douglon sent a raven." Will waved a slip of paper. "There's a new elf!"

Sini took it.

Alaric,

It's finally happened!

Come to the Elder Grove.

Bring Will and Sini. And anyone else who has any semblance of power.

Douglon

Postscript: This is no time for dawdling.

"You can't all leave." Madeleine sat at one end of the table dressed in a lavender dress, her hair braided into something crown-like.

Sini sat, too aware again of her own worn clothes.

"We need to," Alaric said. "An elf has been born. This is something no one outside the elves has ever seen. And Douglon obviously needs help."

"Nothing is actually happening right now," Will pointed out. "We can be there in two days, back here in five."

"We need to go," Alaric said again.

"Of course you do," Queen Saren said tiredly. "But hurry back. It feels like we're running out of time."

"They don't all need to go," Madeleine said. "Surely Alaric can see what is happening and report back to us."

"Douglon asked for anyone with any semblance of power," Alaric said. "Whatever has happened there, he and Rass need help."

"We need help from the dwarves as well," Roan pointed out. "It's been almost a year since they gained control of Kollman Pass. If we're preparing for any sort of war, we need access to that pass to make sure there are no threats from the Sweep."

"More than that," Alaric said, "Duncave stretches far to the south. Maybe they have a way into Gulfind that we don't know about. Maybe Lukas and the dragon haven't really made the country as impenetrable as they think."

Saren nodded slowly. "Yes, it's time to talk to the High Dwarf again."

Madeleine waved her hand toward Alaric. "Your friend is a high-ranking dwarf, right?"

"Douglon?" He exchanged glances with Will. "Strictly speaking he's high ranking."

"How high?"

"Until Horgoth produces an heir, he's next in line to the throne. But he may not be of much use to us. He's spent most of his adult life trying to avoid that connection."

"Wasn't he wanted for treason at some point?" Roan asked, his voice unimpressed.

"A misunderstanding since cleared up." Alaric waved off the incident. "But he and Horgoth still aren't on the best of terms."

"Well, tell him the rest of us would like to run off and live in the Greenwood too," Madeleine said with a tight smile, "but we need his help. Have him get you access to the High Dwarf."

Will laughed. "Our friendship with him might actually hinder our access to High Dwarf Horgoth."

Saren's brow creased. "Maybe you should find a different dwarf friend. Until you do, get something useful out of Douglon. Have him at least take you as far as one of those hidden dwarf holes." She turned to Roan. "Go with them. You can see what's happening with the elves, and then have Douglon take you to Duncave. You can speak for me to Horgoth. Find out what the dwarves know and get their support."

Roan straightened, smoothing the look of surprise quickly off his face and bowing to her.

"Take a unit of guards with you," she added.

"That many people will slow us down," Alaric objected. "We'll travel much faster alone."

The queen leveled him with an unbending gaze. "No."

"I can put together a small protective guard," Roan offered.

The queen nodded reluctantly. "I want your ideas about troop deployment before you leave," she told Alaric. "I'll discuss options with the battalion generals while you're gone. Does anyone have anything else urgent?"

Sini had almost forgotten about Lukas amidst the talk of elves. "I do," she said before her reluctance to speak could grow.

Madeleine raised an eyebrow and all the eyes of the room turned toward Sini.

She cleared her throat and addressed the queen. "Roan pointed out that I'd been looking at Lukas's actions as someone searching for a lost brother, and he was right." Out of the corner of her eye she saw Madeleine smirk. "I'd been trying to track him, and I was caught up in the idea that he was moving toward the moors in Gringonn. When I went back and looked at him as someone trying to weaken Queensland, a different pattern became obvious. I believe he's refined ways to destabilize the country on several fronts."

They listened as Sini explained how she thought Lukas had perfected ways to hurt animals and water sources. Alaric jotted down notes. Will dropped his head into his hands and rubbed his forehead. The queen's face grew grim.

"If he's moved on the gold in Gulfind," Will said, "then he's probably ready to move on the rest of his plans."

A guard opened the door and offered the queen a sealed message. Her face darkened as she read it. "The Duke of Greentree"—Roan looked up at his father's name—"has just sent word that there have been multiple dragon sightings over the past weeks."

"In Greentree?" Roan demanded.

"No." The queen looked at Sini, with a raised eyebrow. "Over the moors."

Sini stared at her. "Doing what?"

The queen shrugged. "Flying. He's attempting to get more information." She dropped the paper on the table and looked over the group. "Hurry to the Elder Grove and then get the support of the dwarves." Her brow wrinkled. "And see if this new elf is in any condition to help us."

━━━━◆━━━━

In her room, Sini found two letters. One from Rett telling her all about the tiny signs of growth in his lamb, and the other from the twins asking how she was weathering her first days at the palace.

Sini packed quickly and wrote off two quick notes back to them. She told Rett about the coming trip to see the new elf, and the twins about the palace, attempting to do so without too much complaining. She was fairly sure she hadn't succeeded.

She was waiting for the others in the sitting room when Roan led in three soldiers. The first two were identically huge, identically muscular, and gave her tight, identical nods. Their skin was a deep, warm brown.

"These are the Baron brothers," Roan introduced them. Each had a belt with a sword on one side and a dagger on the other, and sleek black bows on their backs. Their military grays stretched tightly over their huge chests and arms. They looked to be in their thirties. "They have obvious attributes that will be useful if we encounter anything untoward."

"It's nice to meet you, Baron brothers," Sini said, squinting at them to see if she could detect any differences between the two. One was slightly taller than the other, and slightly more severe. "Do you have individual names?"

"Dalton and Goven," Roan answered for them. Both men nodded stonily, and Roan nodded toward the less stony of the two. "Goven is the happy one."

Sini gave them a curtsey. "Are you both barons?"

"They are not," Will said, coming up and clapping Dalton on the shoulder. "But they were bodyguards for the Baron of Whitemire a few years ago."

The name was familiar. "The one who was attacked by a mud troll?"

"His bodyguards fought off a mud troll," Will corrected her. "It's the best story to come out of Whitemire in fifty years."

Sini stared at the two huge men, her regard for them rising even more.

The third man was significantly smaller. So much so that he was barely taller than Sini. His face was thin, his hair mostly grey, and his skin looked old and weathered. Six throwing knifes were tucked into his belt. He wore nondescript, utterly un-uniformish clothes.

"This is Pest. He's good at…everything."

"Do even your friends call you Pest?" Sini asked.

Pest just gave a little smirk.

Roan shrugged. "He doesn't have any. And he's your personal shadow, Sini, anytime we're anywhere populated."

"Why me?"

"Because the queen wants the Keepers kept safe, and you like to sneak off to dangerous places. There's no way you'll sneak away from Pest."

In less than an hour the others had gathered, been introduced, and they'd ridden out of the palace gate into a blustery afternoon. The hills past the city held the slightest tinge of autumn yellow. The clouds above moved past like rounded beetles scuttling through the morning sky. Will and Alaric in their black robes and the grey uniformed escorts lent a seriousness to the group that caught the attention of the people they passed.

Pest rode next to Sini near the middle of the group, quiet but watchful. The man, for being so small, was rather intimidating. It was either all the knives or the severe sort of intensity to his gaze. Whatever it was, she found herself in danger of being too daunted by him to speak.

There really was no need to find a new gargoyle to be frightened of, so she forced herself to open a conversation. Without a better idea, she said, "Is it safe to assume you're proficient at knife throwing?"

He raised an eyebrow and nodded. Which was all the response she could fairly expect from such an inane question.

"At what range can you hit a target?"

"Depends on how big the target is." His voice was dry.

A good point. "An apple?"

He was quiet for so long she thought he might not answer.

"Twenty paces."

That seemed impressive. "Have you ever..." What did knife throwers do? Asking if he'd killed any people didn't feel like a good get-to-know-you question. He must be at least fifty, maybe older. She probably didn't want to know the number of people he'd killed. "Thrown a knife and killed a squirrel?"

His nod was curt but his face didn't show any irritation, so she continued.

"Could you hit a squirrel in the eye at twenty paces?"

"Yes."

"Really?"

He fixed her with a flat look.

"All right." She pondered her next question. "Have you ever knifed yourself?"

That earned her the edge of a smile. "Yes."

"On purpose?"

The smile grew. "Yes."

"There must be a good story behind that."

He said nothing more and they rode in silence until they'd left the buildings of Queenstown behind. At a nod from Roan, Pest galloped ahead, disappearing over the next hill.

They rode along the main western road for a few hours before turning onto a smaller track that ran southwest toward the Elder Grove. Goven led the way, humming a tune that sounded like a marching cadence. Dalton silently brought up the rear with a steely face, and Pest ranged out ahead. Roan rode next to Sini, sitting straight in his saddle, his gaze sweeping the area regularly. The guards' vigilance felt awkwardly intense, but Will kept up an unbroken stream of tales and the day disappeared quickly.

Sini toyed with the ring on her finger, catching the sun in the garnet. How close would she need to be to start a flame? She pulled a dry blade of grass out of her horse's mane and held it a handbreadth from her ringed finger. She pushed some *vitalle* into the ring and she saw the coppery glow around it, even in the bright sunlight. She tried to push the energy toward the grass, but the farthest she could get it to go was just past her fingertip. Slowly she brought the grass closer until, at barely a finger's width away, the end of it caught fire.

Sini shook it, putting out the flame. She tried several more times, but couldn't create a flame any farther away than that.

By the time the sun touched the tops of the Scale Mountains, the Lumen Greenwood was a dark blur along the bottom of the rocky range. A chilly breeze blew out of the north. Sini pulled her hands into the sleeves of her cloak and let her horse follow along with the others.

Sini found herself watching the forest, an eagerness growing in her. By midday tomorrow they should be among the trees of the elven forest.

"What's the Greenwood like?" Roan asked. He'd pulled a cloak out of his bag and it wrapped around his shoulders. It was, unsurprisingly, solid grey.

She rubbed her fingers together, remembering the energy that flowed through the trees there. "Amazing. It's more alive than other places. Walking out of it and back into the normal world was like going from a sunny day to gloom."

She stopped talking. She couldn't come up with words to explain what it was like.

Roan didn't ask anything more. She considered him for a moment. As when they'd gone to the Lees, he was more at ease here than he had been at court. While his posture was still far too straight, his hands held the reins loosely. It occurred to her that he hadn't been the future lord consort for long. Perhaps she wasn't the only one who felt out of place at court.

They crested a hill where Pest waited for them and found a cluster of buildings in the next valley cushioned in a damp, swampy smell.

Will examined the town. "Must be…Something-more."

Alaric cocked his head to the side. "An earthy name. Earthmore?"

"Loammore," Sini said. At Roan's questioning look she continued, "The smell is from the bog that stretches to the south. Most of the country's peat is dredged out of that."

"See?" Will said to Alaric. "She's as good as you are at knowing things no one else bothers to remember. You're going to lose your position as the smart Keeper."

Alaric turned to her. "All right then, why is this preferred to the peat from Marshwell?"

Sini grimaced. Gerone had assigned her that horrible book on vegetation. "Something about metal deposits." She closed her eyes. There was the issue with the smithing guild and the expensive farm tools… Her eyes flashed open. "The iron deposits have an impurity that reduces rusting."

Will laughed. "From his expression, you're right."

"At last," Alaric said, starting down the hill, "another Keeper worth talking to."

"What duchy are we in?" Roan scanned the horizon as he followed. "Doesn't Lord Taramat have an estate near here?"

"Tamarat's holding is hours north of here," Alaric answered. "Hours we'd have to backtrack tomorrow."

Roan's gaze dropped back to the little town ahead of them.

"Surely the future lord consort can stay in a common inn for a night," Sini said.

He shot her an annoyed glance that held the slightest edge of uncertainty.

"This isn't the first common inn you've stayed in, is it?" she asked.

Roan shifted. "The trip between Greentree and Queenstown takes two days, but my cousin is the Lord of Whitemire, so we always stay with him along the way."

"And you've never traveled anywhere but Greentree or Queenstown?"

"I traveled all over during my years with the city guard, but we always stayed in camps. I'm quite comfortable in camps."

"And in unrelenting grey."

He smoothed his shirt across his chest. "Grey is a respectable color."

"I'm not a fan of it."

His gaze took in her red cloak and the bit of blue shirtsleeve he could see. "I can see that."

"How long ago were you with the guard?"

"Until midsummer." He turned to look ahead again. "I had made captain of the fifth company the day before Madeleine was named heir apparent. Our betrothal was solidified by the next morning, and my time in the guard came to an abrupt halt." He had kept his voice unconcerned, but he sat more stiffly in his saddle.

"That must have been shocking."

He made a non-committal noise.

"We're supposed to be working toward friendship, I believe," Sini said. "It doesn't seem like a bad thing to admit that your life was disrupted this summer. No one joins the guard and works hard enough to be promoted to captain unless he plans to make a career of it."

Roan glanced at her. "Joining the guard was my choice. My father wasn't thrilled about the idea. He thought I should stay in Greentree and prepare to take over when he grows too old." His thumb rubbed along the reins. "Seeing as he's in perfect health and it will be decades before he'll have the chance to command death to leave him be, I convinced him that five years in the guard would be valuable experience."

"How many years were you in it?"

"Not quite three. Then a handful of the royal line died. My father took advantage of the situation before most people had figured out who the new heir even was. My betrothal to Madeleine was finalized before I reached home."

"That's…a lot to adjust to."

Roan didn't answer.

"Do you dress so close to the uniform still because it's comfortable? Or to annoy your father?"

He laughed and stretched his fingers, resuming his earlier loose grip on the reins. "Maybe this is what a lord consort wears. The country hasn't had one in one hundred twenty-three years, so no one knows for sure."

"Well," Sini said with a smile, "in something that unpresuming, at least no one will mistake you for the king."

FIFTEEN

The town of Loammore was no bigger up close than it had looked from the hills. Sini could have counted the buildings that huddled together on two hands. When Will asked a farmer whether there was an inn, he was directed to the "large building on the town square."

Sini rode next to Will into the little hamlet and took in the irregularly-shaped clearing in the center of the town. "It seems misleading to call this a square."

Will fit a little hood over Talen's head and nodded toward the inn that was barely larger than a small house. "As misleading as calling that large."

After barely fitting all the horses in the small stable, Roan set the Baron brothers to guard the front and back doors. Pest disappeared into the growing darkness.

The common room held only two smallish tables. The floor was worn and dusty, the windows dingy. The smell of weak stew replaced the boggy smell from outside. At the sound of the door opening, an older stout man with a splattered apron came out of the kitchen. His eyes widened at the sight of the large group. Will introduced himself as a Keeper, and when the man took in Alaric's black robe as well, he greeted them with stunned silence. The group waited a moment near the door, but the man seemed at a loss.

"It's a relief to find a warm fire." Will stepped up to the fireplace along the wall. "It has been a long day of riding. Some warmed wine wouldn't go amiss."

The innkeeper stammered something obliging and disappeared into the back of the inn. The back door creaked open and slammed shut in the wind. Sini stepped over to the kitchen door. The small room was empty.

Will set Talen on the back of a chair in the corner, and helped Alaric pull the two tables closer to the fire.

"He's gone to tell people there are Keepers here," Will explained. "There are so few tables we'd better arrange them before it gets crowded."

Roan stood awkwardly by the door and Sini pushed a crooked chair in his direction. "Your seat, Lord Consort."

The door opened and a handful of people hurried in. Voices called from outside and Roan tucked his chair into the corner. Sini joined him. Alaric and Will positioned themselves at the other table across the fire and Alaric pulled a book and some paper from his bag.

"This doesn't look like we're getting ready to eat," Roan pointed out. He sat stiffly in his chair, his eyes scanning the room as though watching for something dangerous.

"We'll eat before they do," Sini nodded at Will and Alaric. "They'll be stuck there for hours. No one should talk to us over here." She glanced at Roan. "Especially if you keep looking extra-lordly like that."

"I'm not looking lordly," he said to her under his breath. "This is my 'I'm trapped in a corner and just want my dinner' face."

"It's shocking how much it looks like your 'I disagree with your map work' face."

He laughed and relaxed a little.

It took a few minutes for some spiced apple cider and bread to appear. Most of the population of Loammore crammed into the small inn over the next few hours. Children ducked around the adults or perched on the thin wooden stairs that led up to a second floor.

Sini sat back and drank the cider while Will stood and introduced himself and Alaric to the room.

He asked for story requests, and after settling on an obscure legend about a sword maiden and a gang of bog gnomes, the room quieted, and he began. His words rolled across the room with the same sort of wonder they always did. Sini sat back in her chair, waiting for the moment when the story came to life. It took several minutes for the listeners to settle before it happened, but when it did his breath coalesced into a blue-green mist that spread throughout the room. No one but her seemed to notice the mist, but every hint of distraction disappeared into the wonder of the story.

Sini let herself join in. When Will drew the tale to a close, Roan sat back in his chair, looking stunned.

"Never heard Will tell a story before?" Sini asked him.

Roan kept his eyes on Will as he shook his head.

"It's like that every time," Sini said. "He tells about his time on the Sweep, and even though I was there for half of it, I'm still enthralled."

The crowd broke up into smaller groups tucked into whatever space they could find in the small inn. The innkeeper bustled about, his first timidity forgotten.

Alaric laid out paper and quills, and Will stepped up to Sini's chair. "Why don't you help Alaric?"

"I'd rather not—" she began.

"Anyone would rather read your handwriting than mine," Will said, "and these people will be thrilled to meet you."

"I have no idea what to do," she objected.

"All they need is someone to listen and write down words for them. Give yourself a chance, Sin. I think you might enjoy it."

She gave him a reluctant nod and stood.

"Wait," he said quietly, "you haven't been introduced."

"You don't need to—" she began.

But Will raised his voice. "Loammore has a great honor tonight." His voice rang out through the room and it quieted. Dozens of faces turned toward them curiously. Sini tried to step back, but Will set his hand on her back and she stopped. "It has been seventy years since the last female Keeper died." The faces in the room grew more curious, and Sini felt their attention turn toward her. "It's been over a hundred since she traveled Queensland.

"But now we have one again."

A murmur rippled across the room. And Sini leaned back a little against Will's hand. The redness of her cloak and the absolute lack of anything Keeperish about her felt awkward.

But no one seemed to mind. The faces all watched her eagerly.

"People of Loammore, I would like to introduce Keeper Sini," Will continued. "You may not have heard of her before, but I wager her life will be one of legends."

Sini's face reddened and she opened her mouth to object, but the room erupted in cheers. Will, grinning at her, motioned to the seat next to Alaric with a flourish. She dropped into it, stiffly.

Alaric leaned toward her. "Sorry, I should have done that for you. We could have accomplished it with a little less…flamboyance." He handed her some paper and a quill.

The crowd pushed forward. The first man to approach wanted Alaric to write out his genealogy. The people hung back slightly from Sini at first, until a young woman stepped up. Her face was thin, and Sini realized she must not be much older than herself. The woman clutched a baby to her chest and gave Sini a nervous smile.

"How old is your baby?" Sini asked, looking for some way to put the woman at ease.

"She was born two moons ago." The woman showed the little bundle to Sini. The baby was sleeping, her face scrunched into a look of irritation at all the movement.

"She's beautiful."

The woman gave a quick smile. "Her name is Savia. Named after th' Keeper Chesavia. Could you write 'er name down? I don't know my letters, but I'd like to have it written out."

"Of course," Sini said, smoothing out her paper. "Chesavia is one of my favorite Keepers. What is your name?"

"Pelonnia."

"And the girl's father?"

Pelonnia shook her head. "No one Savia needs t' know 'bout."

Sini nodded and turned toward the paper. "What is your daughter like?" It had always struck Sini as sweet the way parents attributed so much to their infants. Lukas had always laughed at her for the question, but it seemed that anyone who studied another person as closely as new parents studied their babies was sure to learn things.

"She's smart," Pelonnia started quietly. "And persistent." She looked down at the little face, and her own wan face was suffused with something rich. "And stronger than me." There was nothing but pride in the words.

Sini wrote out a page. Pelonnia looked uncertainly at all the words.

"The first word is your daughter's name. It says:

Savia
beloved daughter of Pelonnia,
born in the summer of the twelfth year of the reign of Queen Saren.
A girl of cleverness, fierceness, and strength
like her namesake Chesavia, renowned Keeper of old.

Below it, Sini drew out a simple rune. "This rune means *brave* and *good*, and this curl on the end says it speaks of a girl." She blew on the ink until it dried, then set it on the table before Pelonnia.

The woman ran her fingers over her daughter's name. "Thank you," she whispered, picking up the paper. She bobbed a quick curtsey and backed away from the table. Sini caught a quick, approving nod from Alaric.

An elderly woman stepped up, her back bowed so much that she stood barely taller than Sini seated in the chair.

"Good evening, grandmother," Sini greeted her.

The woman shuffled up close to the table. "My husband, Turr, died last month." Her voice was thin and wavering. "His tombstone is blank, and I'd like some words t' put t' it."

"Of course." Sini took out a clean piece of paper. "What would you like it to say?"

The old woman looked down at the blank paper for a long moment. "Dunno. None of the graves here say anything."

"How long had you been married?"

"Forty-five years." At Sini's expression the old woman smiled. "Probably sounds like a long time to live with someone to a woman as young as you."

Sini nodded. "Twelve years is the longest I've lived with anyone, and most of that I was too little to remember. Why don't you tell me a little about your husband?"

The old woman told of the years they'd been married, of his hard work in the peat bogs, of the three babies they'd had and lost. Her story was simple and halting, but the years that it covered, the life that it held brought tears to Sini's eyes.

"What was your favorite thing about him?"

"His smile," she said without hesitation, giving a toothy one of her own. "It was the first thing I fell in love with when we were young. Later in life he used it less, but when he did, it was like sunshine in the spring."

Sini reached out and gave the old woman's hand a squeeze.

"Life is shorter than ya think, lass," the old woman said. "Don't let those you love slip away if you can help it. They'll be beyond your reach soon enough."

Sini wrote on the paper then read it out loud.

"Turr of Loammore
Beloved husband
with a beloved smile,
now joined with his children.

The night continued and Sini stepped into people's lives for brief moments as they shared with her about their families or their businesses or letters to distant kin. By the time the last people trickled out of the inn, she sank back exhausted.

"That was well done," Alaric said to her, gathering up remaining papers.

The innkeeper—Sini had discovered his name was Yannek when she'd written out the words "Peat Bog Inn" for his sign—came over, clearing cups from their tables while his wife wiped off the tables with a dingy rag. "Which direction are ya headed tomorrow?"

"The Lumen Greenwood," Will answered.

The innkeeper's wife, an equally stout woman named Hattia, shot her husband an alarmed look.

"Is there a problem?" Will asked.

Hattia pressed her lips shut and focused on the table. Yannek tugged at his collar for a moment. "There's been some...strangeness in the woods lately."

Sini paused from gathering up the quills Alaric had lent her.

"What sort of strangeness?" Alaric asked.

Ignoring the scolding look from his wife, the innkeeper cleared his throat. "I don't go near the Greenwood. No reason to, of course. None of the trees are lookin' for lodgin', ya understand." He gave a weak smile.

Alaric's expression held a shadow of impatience and Yannek looked more flustered.

Feeling bad for him, Sini smiled and said, "Especially in an inn made of wood."

Yannek gave her a nervous laugh. "But folks that live out that way stop for a drink. They've all been avoiding the woods lately. No one has anything particular to complain about—"

"Which is why ya shouldn't be troublin' these good folk with yer stories," Hattia interrupted. "They're not the kind to be bothered because Tenner's bog-brained cousins think the trees chased them."

"Chased them?" Will asked.

Yannek shot an irritated look at his wife. "That's what they said. Lots of folks saying the forest is unfriendly these days. Most of the hunters won't track game much past the edges. And folk from Lorrendale, on the south side of the bogs, won't even do that."

"How long has this been going on?" Alaric asked.

Yannek shrugged. "The whole last week."

"Has anything else happened?" Will asked.

Yannek hesitated and Hattia gave him a barely perceptible head shake, accompanied by a threatening glare. Yannek waved her looks off. "In Lorrendale they say the forest took two of their children."

Hattia rolled her eyes and let out an exasperated sigh. "The folks in Lorrendale are too stupid to pick their own children out of a crowd. No one can tell ya who these children are." She turned to the Keepers. "Lorrendale is a small town. The folk there are a little...odd."

Sini bit back a smile and resisted glancing around at the tiny inn. "So you don't think it's true?"

"A couple addlebrained hunters *say* they saw two kids run into the woods three days past. Even though they called to them, the little 'uns never came back out. But they don't know which kids, and no one's missin' any children. There aren't no other towns down there for mysterious kids t' come from."

"Grown men who've hunted in the woods their whole lives aren't going in," Yannek said stubbornly.

"They're Keepers, Yannek," Hattia hissed, swatting at him with her rag. "They're not scared of trees."

Yannek shook his head and turned back to the Keepers. "If ya are headed that way, ya should be careful."

SIXTEEN

In the quiet of her very small, very sparse room, Sini set her finger next to the candle and paused. The garnet glowed with teeny bits of deep red light, only visible because her room was so dark. A shimmering, dim trail followed her hand wherever she moved it, glowing for just a breath before fading. The ring fit snugly on her first finger, and so far, that was the only finger she'd used to light anything. She curled up all her fingers but the smallest and set that near the candle. When she added a little *vitalle,* the copper glow from the ring slid smoothly across her fist, down her pinky finger and lit the candle.

She grinned at the bright little beacon of fire, blew it out, then lit it with her thumb. After playing a few more minutes with the flame, she pulled out Chesavia's journal and lay it on the table, flipping past doodles and runes, until she found a picture of the sun. Tongues of fire curled out from it, filling the entire page.

A small figure at the bottom of the page lifted its arms, embraced by the eddies of light.

Sini's breath caught.

The sunlight. Chesavia did understand the sunlight.

On the facing page was written:

Everything is light.

There is vitalle *in all living things, but sunlight is different. It is the source of all the* vitalle. *The source of everything. The light is the beginning.*

The Keepers understand this, but not in the way they should. They know that the sun gives life, but it is more than that.

Everything is light. Everything that lives glows with it. Even the dark stone is a cooled, hardened version of it. I cannot put words to it, exactly. But light is the beginning of it, and the essence of it.

On the moors the sunlight was so strong it pressed on me. When I let it in, it ran through my arms, through my body—through me. Every fiber of me, every fragment of what I am thrummed with it. It rushed through like a river of light. Warm and strong and vibrant.

She paused at the words. Part of that was thrillingly familiar. The sunfire was warm and strong and vibrant, and she'd never found anyone else who understood that. But "every fragment of what I am thrummed with it"? Sini had never felt that. Sunfire was just like a stream of sunshine that could reach past her skin and warm her, deep inside.

It was good. And pure.

For one glorious moment I wanted to join it. To let myself transform into light. To be vast and alive and free.

But there were things still to be done, and I knew I must stay.

Here—in the darkness where my skin is just skin and my flesh merely mortal, trapped in one moment and one weakened form—my soul aches at my choice.

Sini shivered at the bleakness of the thought. Was this the Chesavia who everyone lauded for her bravery and sacrifice? Instead of a sacrifice, had it been merely self-destruction?

She paused. Chesavia's death was always described as being devoured by her own fire.

That's what Keepers said when someone used too much *vitalle*. When instead of merely burning their hands, they burned too much of themselves to survive. The energy devoured them.

Sini let the book close on the table.

Chesavia hadn't been devoured by fire. She had let herself become the light.

Their path the next morning headed south through low rolling hills, sometimes forested, sometimes grassy, and the thin dirt track meandered its way along them in no particular hurry. Pest ranged up ahead, leaving everyone else hemmed in by the Barons, Goven in the lead, Dalton behind them.

Roan rode beside her in his normal grey, his dark hair as neat as it had been the first time she saw him at court. The top was pulled back into the same thin braids, and the rest hung past his shoulders, straight and orderly. There hadn't been a mirror in Sini's room, but she could imagine what the braid she'd retied hurriedly above her forehead this morning looked like. Not to mention the short ends of her hair that always splayed out with wild abandon.

Roan studied Alaric and Will. "Every Keeper I've ever met has worn the black, and I have to admit, when they're doing Keeper sorts of things like they did last night, it's fitting." He glanced at Sini's red cloak. "But I've never seen you wear one. Is it because you're young? Are you not an official Keeper yet?"

The question pricked at her. "Yes I'm 'official.'" Her voice was sharper than she meant it to be. "I've never needed to wear a robe before. The few times I've traveled since joining them, I was never doing anything particularly Keeperish. When I first came here from the Sweep, I traveled with Will, Alaric, and Evangeline to the Stronghold. Will and Alaric did a good amount of Keepering,"—Roan snorted at the word—"but I didn't. I sat with Evangeline in the corner and tried to figure out what this new life of mine was going to look like."

"Weren't you excited?" Roan asked. "Every child in Queensland dreams of being a Keeper."

"It had been a long time since I'd been in Queensland." She spun her ring, remembering how odd it had been being back among trees, and her own people. She'd expected it to feel like a homecoming, but she'd only felt out of place.

He considered her words for a moment. "I forgot you'd lived with Lukas for so long. When you lived on the Sweep, did you share his feelings about the Keepers?"

"No." It was one of the few topics they'd argued over until Sini stopped talking about

Queensland or Keepers or anything else from home. "But it wasn't just Lukas. Everyone on the Sweep hates the Keepers. As far as the Roven are concerned, they're monsters who use unnatural magic. The stonesteeps there store all the power for their magic in gems. They think the fact that Keepers just draw it through their bodies is horrible.

"I think I wanted to believe the Keepers were good, but I was scared that maybe the Roven were right." They'd crested one of many hills. It was early enough that they were only in the sunlight while they crossed the top. The warmth of it sank into her cheek. In moments they were in the cool shadows again. "So when I had the chance to join them, I needed a little time."

"That was over four years ago," Roan pointed out. "Do you still need time?"

Sini watched the horizon ahead of them. As they dipped lower into the valley, more of the world disappeared until there was nothing but their thin little road, grassy slopes, and stands of clustered trees. "No. The Keepers are more than I ever could have imagined, even as a child. They're wise and good and generous."

Roan let the obvious question hang in the air for a few moments. "Then why no robe?"

Sini plucked at the edge of her red cloak. "Maybe this is what female Keepers wear. It's been over a hundred years since the last one traveled outside the Stronghold."

Roan laughed, the first real laugh she'd heard from him. "Fair enough. You wear colors, I'll wear grey. There's no one alive to tell us that we're wrong."

Sini grinned. "The Shield is old enough on both counts. So let's not ask him."

The morning moved on uneventfully, the only real change being a brisk breeze out of the north that smelled like frost.

Sini toyed with her ring again, putting *vitalle* into it until it glowed, then trying to draw that glow back into her hand to warm it. It didn't work. It didn't do anything at all. She shifted the ring slowly, letting the garnet glitter in the sunlight. There had to be some other way to use this beyond starting fires. If not, maybe she could make another one that would let her form the air into walls or bowls like the twins were good at. Or one that would let her use *paxa* to calm her horse, the way Rett could do so easily. She sighed. It would take a good number of rings to do all the things she'd like to. Her hands would look like some Roven Torch's, with burning stones on every finger.

At the top of one hill, Pest sat on his horse looking down into the next valley, waiting.

Alaric frowned. "There shouldn't be anything out here. The nearest town is hours south of us."

Sini felt the ripple as he cast out, and the immediate flare of *vitalle* from the people and horses around her. The trees had receded from the trail, but she caught an echo of their energy as well. Over the hill, dimmed by the distance, there was an enormous pool of *vitalle*.

"What's over there?" she asked Alaric.

"Sheep," Pest called to them. "A herd blocking the way."

In the next valley the trees drew close to the road, and a huge herd of sheep moved sluggishly through the narrowest part. A handful of shepherds milled along the far side.

The herd was thinnest to the right near the trees, and Roan motioned Goven in that direction. They started slowly through, and soon the backs of the sheep spread out around the horses' legs like foamy water, slowing their progress to a crawl. The valley was shadowed, and a cutting wind rushed past. Sini pulled her cloak around her wishing the stupid animals would move out of their way.

Pest's attention snapped to the nearby trees. "Down!" He flung himself out of the saddle.

Before anyone else could react, a wet *thunk* sounded. Goven grunted in pain and slumped forward in his saddle, the tip of an arrow jutting from his back.

SEVENTEEN

"Goven!" Dalton let out a roar and dove off his horse.

Sini scrambled off hers, ducking between the sheep.

Alaric cast out, and beyond the *vitalle* of the animals Sini caught the echo of a dozen people hiding past the tree line.

Alaric dropped down next to her. Sini gripped her startled horse's reins and peered through its legs at the shadowed trees. She heard Will shout to Talen, and the little hawk burst into flight and raced away.

A knife flew into the trees from Pest's direction. A cry rang out, and a body toppled into the open.

Goven slid limply out of his saddle while his brother shoved through the herd toward the attackers. Arrows shot into the sheep around him. One knocked Dalton's arm. He plunged on, ignoring it.

"Sini!" Alaric grabbed her hand. "*Vitalle*! As much as you can give!"

Energy from the ground began to flow through her feet as he drew it to himself. She looked up at what she could see of the sky between the horses and reached for the sunfire, pulling in the lazy bits that had fallen into the valley, stretching toward full daylight higher up.

She funneled the little light she could grab into Alaric. He stretched one hand toward the sky, and a breeze ruffled her hair. Then a stronger wind shoved into her back. Sini finally reached the sunfire high above them and drew it down. It flowed into her in a stream of warmth, filling her, pouring through her hand into Alaric. It didn't cause her any discomfort, but Alaric gasped. She shifted the energy away from his arm, funneling it into the path he'd created that reached back up into the sky. The wind blew harder, pushing Sini forward. Her horse shifted, dropping his head. His tail whipped forward and snapped against Sini's neck. She hunched lower.

There was a force in the air, shoving the wind forward. A blanket of energy, or a net. The wind drove into her, and she braced herself against the ground. Another net came from behind them, pushing the wind forward. An arrow tumbled away in the gust.

"It's too bad you can't shoot the arrows back at them with the wind," Sini shouted over the wind. Alaric gave her an exasperated look. "Sorry," she said. "You're doing great."

She caught a glimpse of Dalton charging into the tree line, his sword slicing through the shadows. Another one of Pest's knives found its mark, and a body fell forward out of the trees.

The shouts and commotion scattered the sheep, clearing a wide space between Sini and the trees.

A man in a long brown robe peered out from behind a tree, watching the arrows go astray. He cried for the archers to stop, and men streamed out of the trees, knives, axes, and farm tools swinging.

Alaric cast out again. The only man left in the trees was the brown-robed leader. The Keeper stood and shook out his hands, sparing a wide-eyed look at Sini. "It's frightening how much *vitalle* you can move." Striding toward the approaching men, he grabbed a skinny stick off the ground. Strands of fiery orange vitalle wound out from his hand and wrapped around the stick.

Sini cast about for some way to help, but she had no weapon. Without Alaric, she couldn't do anything with the sunfire. She pushed energy into her ring, but how would lighting something on fire help anything? The Keepers, Pest, and Dalton met the attackers in the open space. Roan stepped in front of her, his sword drawn, facing the approaching men.

"Don't stand here like an idiot." Sini pushed him. "Go help them!"

He planted his feet and studied the approaching men. "I have orders to keep you safe."

The brown robed man raised his voice. "The Keepers are a plague! Rid our land of their filth!"

The others joined in, cries of "Plague" and "Filth" ringing through the small valley. An attacker ran toward Roan.

"I know those words!" Sini grabbed Roan's arm and peered past him. "Alaric! Those are Mallon's words!"

"I know." Alaric grunted and knocked a wild axe swing away. He slammed his thin stick into the attacker's side. Instead of breaking the stick, the man crumpled to the side in a cry of pain.

"How did you make that stick?" Will called, his own normal stick breaking against a farmer's sickle.

"Infused it with the essence of a stone," Alaric called.

"I don't really want to know," Will called, ducking back. "I just want my own!"

Alaric threw him the stick and picked up an even thinner one from the ground. Shaking out his hand, he touched a rock and closed his eyes with a grimace. Orange tongues of energy wrapped along the branch as he strengthened it. He grunted in pain and swung it at the next attacker.

Will swung the stick and knocked the sickle out of the farmer's hand. "The last few years," he grunted, "have made me wonder if Keepers shouldn't carry weapons." He grabbed the farmer's arm, and his brow drew in concentration. The man suddenly stopped fighting, his face relaxing.

"Yes," Will said, "that's better. Time to calm down a little."

The farmer blinked at the chaos around them and Will patted him on the shoulder before running past him to meet another attacker.

"Cleanse from the filth!" the leader cried.

Why were these men shouting out Mallon's words?

The brown-robed man raised his hand in the air, shouting commands, and Sini caught a glimpse of a light blue trail of light from his hand.

The trail from a compulsion stone.

She hadn't seen a compulsion stone since Lukas had created them to control the frost goblins and the dragon. And people.

"That man!" She pointed past Roan to the brown robed leader. "We need to get to him!"

Roan shook his head.

"Fine." She ducked around the back of her horse and ran toward the trees. She heard Roan swear and follow. The leader, watching his men fight, spared Sini no more than a glance. She sprinted into the trees, ducking behind a large trunk.

"Grab him!" she told Roan who rushed up next to her. "Don't kill him! I have questions."

"Why do you have to be so reckless?" Roan shot her a furious glance. "Stay here!"

He crept forward, but the man whirled and pulled his own sword out, lunging toward Roan. Sini rushed forward. "Don't kill him!"

The brown robed man swung so wildly that Roan took a step back.

"Death to Keepers and the filth who protect them!" The man raised his sword to lunge forward. His body snapped backward, and a knife appeared at his throat.

"Drop the sword." Pest held the man by the hair, his blade pressed against the man's neck. With a hiss of fury, the man obeyed.

"You have control here?" Roan demanded of Pest. At the man's nod, Roan snapped off "Keep Sini safe," and ran back toward the rest of the fighting.

"Hold him still." Sini stepped closer to the man.

The brown-robed man glared at Sini as she approached. "Get away from the Keepers while you can, woman. They are a pestilence, a plague—"

"A disease?" She grabbed his arm, careful not to touch his hand. A silver ring sat on his first finger, set with a small, uncut aquamarine that left a long trail of blue light. It was a compulsion stone. Her stomach sank at the ramifications.

His eyes widened. "You know the truth?"

"I've read Mallon's work." She took a bracing breath and grabbed the ring. Before she could pull it off, a wave of anger and hatred rolled through her.

The man curled his hand into a fist and yanked it away from her. "Don't touch that!"

"If she wants the ring"—Pest wrenched his head back further—"she gets the ring."

The man drew in a sharp breath, and a trickle of blood seeped out from under Pest's blade. Slowly the man opened his fingers and Sini, using the edge of her cloak to protect her skin, slid it off the man's finger. Through the fabric, the influence of the ring dampened to a mild anger. She dropped it to the ground.

The man blinked and drew in a deep breath. Pest peered down at the bit of silver on the ground.

"Don't touch that." Sini said to Pest. She turned to the brown-robed man. "Are you the only one with a ring?" He nodded. "Call off your men before every one of them is killed."

His eyes flickered to the men still fighting. They were untrained and wild. Only four still stood. In a strangled voice, he called for them to throw down their weapons.

As soon as the fighting stopped, Dalton rushed to where his brother had fallen.

"Watch this man," Sini told Pest. "And no one touches that ring. It's a compulsion stone, made to control your emotions. We don't need anyone else deciding they hate Keepers."

Pest gave her a nod and Sini ran out of the forest toward the twins. The sheep had scattered from the fight in fear, and most of the attackers lay on the ground, moaning. Sini cast out toward them. Her heart sank when she found two of them still and dark. The rest were injured or unconscious, but none as severely as the wounded Baron brother.

Goven lay on his side. The arrow sunk deep in his gut trembled with the man's slow, ragged breaths. His brother Dalton knelt in front of him, his own breath coming in gasps, his hands clenching Goven's sleeve. Roan stood over them, his face grim.

Sini knelt next to the wounded man and knew the truth immediately. It was too grievous a wound to heal. She'd seen too many like this with the Roven. The damage was just too much.

Dalton called his brother's name, his voice frantic.

Sini's mind rushed back to the Stronghold. What if one of the twins were succumbing faster to their illness than the other? What if right now one were watching the other die? Her heart clenched at the idea and she cast out at Goven. The damage was horrific, the amount of blood spilling out of him too much.

She pressed a fist to her mouth. She couldn't walk away. "Get the arrow out."

"No point," Goven gasped.

"Get it out," Sini snapped at Roan. "Before he loses any more blood."

Roan reached for the arrow.

"Do not touch him," Dalton warned.

"Trust her," Roan said. "She can heal." His look said this arrow was very different than a knife cut in the lees, but he snapped off the tail feathers of the arrow. Goven gave a cry of pain.

Dalton glared at Roan for a breath before grabbing Goven and holding him firmly. He gave Roan a quick nod.

"Sorry about this, Goven." Roan gave a quick pull, and the arrow slid out with a sickening wet noise.

Goven's eyes rolled back into his head and he slumped into unconsciousness. Sini set her hand on the slick warmth of the wound and reached up again for the sunfire. The sun hadn't risen enough for her to see it, but its light danced on top of the nearby trees and she drew it down into herself, pouring it into the man's body.

He was so weak his body was doing nothing at all to heal the wound. Blood seeped out his back. His gut had been pierced, and its contents spilled out, mixing with the blood. Sini pulled in more and more light, her head and chest and arms thrumming with it as she pushed it into him. Deep inside Goven, muscle and tissue drew back together.

She drew in more light, and the warmth of it grew inside her. For a moment she lost herself in the feel of it, in the current of it, the power of it. The light washed through her. And then it did more; it filled her, woke her. She breathed in, and the light spread. Her skin hummed as though it might burst with exhilaration. Everything in her grew weightless and clear and pure.

Goven shuddered beneath her hand, and her eyes flew open. She'd forgotten him. For a moment, she'd forgotten everything.

Chesavia's words echoed in her mind. *For one glorious moment I wanted to join the light.*

Appalled at herself, Sini dragged her focus back to Goven, directing more of the light into his body. The sunfire in her veins calmed and rushed into him. She found and fixed one wound after another, pushing away thoughts of the light and focusing on her work. As much of the bile and filth as she could find she worked toward the open wound at the back of his body, but there was no way to get it all.

When she finally looked up, she found Dalton pushing aside his brother's shirt and staring at the new, red scar just under his ribs. Goven's breaths came shallow, but even. Blood dripped down Dalton's arm from where he'd been grazed by an arrow himself. Gathering a little more sunfire, Sini reached over and set her hand on it. The wound was shallow and clean. After Goven's wounds, it was effortless to knit Dalton back up.

Sini sat back and cut off the stream of *vitalle* from the sunlight, letting it dispel back into the air. Her body sank down, heavy and weak. She spread out her hands and a slight golden glow faded from her fingertips. Without the sunfire streaming through her, her head drooped forward,

EIGHTEEN

and her arms fell heavily onto her lap.

Dalton caught up one of her hands.

"How—?" His hand clenched hers so tightly that she winced, and he released her. "That wound was fatal." His face was infused with a terrified sort of hope.

"It still might be." The lack of light was almost painful, like something essential had been taken from her. She rubbed her face, trying to banish the thought. "The arrow pierced his gut. I couldn't clean it all. He'll most likely get an infection. The wound on his back is still open so it can be cleaned." The dimness inside of her felt tinged with hopelessness, and she took a deep breath. "I don't know if it will be enough."

"Thank you," Dalton breathed, turning his attention back to his brother.

Her dismay at losing the light receded, and shock swelled in her at what she'd just done. She'd never healed anything remotely that severe. The sunfire—the only time she'd ever moved that much was in the Elder Grove, and she'd assumed that power was the grove's, not hers.

The commotion of the others interrupted her thoughts, and she glanced over to where Pest still held the brown-robed man. There was still a compulsion stone to deal with.

A wave of exhaustion rolled over her, and she closed her eyes.

When she opened them, Will stood several paces away, staring at her. He opened his mouth, but after staring at her dumbly for a moment, closed it again. Kneeling next to Goven, Will looked at the scar on his stomach. "I had no idea you could heal something like that."

Sini smiled weakly. "Neither did I."

Will looked between her and Goven several times, his face a cross between awestruck and troubled. She had too many questions in her own mind to wait for him to formulate one. Roan had left her side at some point to help the others tie up the remaining attackers. Despite the shaking in her legs, she stood and walked over to them.

The leader sat tied to a tree trunk. Pest was next to him, his knife still out. The other men were tied hand and foot, watched over by Alaric.

Sini stopped by each attacker. None were badly hurt. She healed two deep cuts that required only a little sunfire, then turned toward the men's leader.

"You shouldn't be with these Keepers, woman." He glared up at her, but there was less conviction in his voice than before. "They're a powerful, dangerous lot."

Will had followed her, but he cast a glance back at Goven. "You might be talking to the most powerful of us all." Sini shifted uncomfortably at the words, but Alaric studied her and nodded.

Sini ignored them both. The silver ring shone bright against the dark earth, still laying where she'd dropped it. A misty blue cloud hovered around it. Sini nudged it with her toe. The aquamarine was roughly-cut, and the light within it was turbulent but strong. It wasn't the worst cut gem she'd ever seen, but it was close. The sight of it tightened the knot in her gut. She forced the question out. "Who gave you this?"

The leader clamped his mouth shut.

"A friend, he says," Will answered.

"Let me describe this friend." She used a forked stick to pick up the ring. "He was in his mid-twenties, with light brown hair and beard, neither of which are probably braided any more. Brownish green eyes, narrow face. He had a limp, and he told you this ring did something useful."

The man's eyes flashed before he set his jaw stubbornly.

"This is troubling," Will glanced at Alaric. "Have we had any indication that Lukas was here in the west?"

Alaric shook his head.

Sini sighed. "There aren't many people who can make compulsion stones. I certainly can't." She glanced at Alaric. "Can you?"

He looked at the ring with distaste. "I've never tried."

"I hate those things," Will said.

"You would, Keeper." The man spit on the ground. "That ring protects our flocks from a wastin' disease. Give it back, or the death of all those animals, and the starvation of the people of Lorrendale will be on your heads."

"It does not protect your flocks." Sini sat in front of him and shoved the end of the stick into the ground until it held up the ring between them. "I'm Sini. What's your name?"

He glared at her. "Patrek, and I'm well respected in these parts. Folks'll be outraged when they hear you've tied me up."

"I'm sure they would be. Which is why Lukas picked you. He knew you'd be able to influence others." She nodded to the ring. "Do you feel different now that it's off?"

"Aye," he said, "but he said I would. Said it was the price of the magic. The flocks would be safe, but it would bring the evil into me. I had to fight the anger, but as long as I wore it, they'd be safe."

"That's a decent story," Will admitted.

"How long have you been wearing it?" Sini asked.

"A fortnight, plus a little."

"And where did you learn those things about the Keepers?"

"He knew it was the Keepers who'd sickened the flocks. Fifteen of our best ewes died in a week. He's the one who stopped the sickness. Said he knew Keepers were going around weakening folks who didn't live in the cities, trying to gain more power for themselves in Queenstown. Said there were lots o' towns around the land that had realized the Keepers didn't do nothin' useful, and that it was making 'em nervous." He glared at Will. "Said we were lucky. In other towns it had been the children sickened, not just the animals."

"Which other towns?" Alaric asked.

Patrek shrugged. "Towns to the south, although he said the truth about you was spreading up the western border, too. We won't just sit by and let you kill our flocks. And ye won't come near our children."

"None of what he told you was true," Sini said.

"As soon as he gave me that ring, the sheep got better."

"That's because he was the one making them sick. He's done it in the south as well."

Patrek shook his head. "I don't believe you."

She shrugged. "I've helped him make these rings before. I assure you it has nothing to do with sheep. It's just about controlling you. The words you were yelling about the Keepers? Those are quotes from Mallon."

Patrek's eyes darted from Sini to Will and Alaric.

"Lukas finds Mallon inspiring," Will said. "He's adopted Mallon's plan of attacking Queensland around the edges, over and over, until she's too weak to put up a fight. He hates Queensland, and he hates the Keepers. The more people he can get to hate us, the more divided he makes the country."

Patrek scowled at him and Sini felt a pang at the bluntness of the description.

"Have you ever heard of the Keepers being evil? From anyone but Lukas?" Alaric asked.

Patrek held his gaze for a moment before shaking his head coldly. "But when we heard there were Keepers in Loammore, we couldn't let you get this close without takin' our revenge."

"What's the best way to destroy the ring?" Will asked her.

"They're delicate. Too much *vitalle* splits the stone. Much to Lukas's chagrin, I'm good at destroying them. But since I'm not interested in touching this one, they are also destroyed by fire."

Patrek's gaze flicked from her face to the ring. "The herd has to stay healthy, or we'll all starve. Give it back to me."

Sini blew out a breath. "Lukas is long gone, right?"

The man nodded.

"He won't be back. And your sheep won't sicken." She dropped the ring onto a tuft of dry fall grass. Using her ring, she set it on fire, then piled on a few small sticks until she had a small blaze. The stone glowed blue for a few breaths until the fire grew hot enough. With a crisp snap, the stone cracked into three pieces and tumbled out of the ring.

Patrek gave a small gasp. Then he blinked and took a deep breath.

Talen soared through the edge of the trees and landed on Will's outstretched arm. Will studied the little hawk for a moment. "Talen didn't see any more people around here."

"We're going to let you go," Alaric said. "Go back to Lorrendale. When your sheep stay healthy, you'll know we were telling you the truth."

Patrek watched them suspiciously. "You're letting us go?"

"Of course," Will said. "Go tell all the other towns that you've met actual Keepers, that they aren't bloodthirsty monsters, and that Lukas lied."

"You'll find rings like this on the leaders," Sini said. "Throw them in a fire. Once the stone is broken"—she set the silver ring by Patrek's leg—"the silver is perfectly safe."

Dalton and Roan had managed to get Goven up onto his horse, and he sat slumped in the saddle. He was going to need more help with that wound over the next few days, and Sini felt a little rush of excitement at the chance to use the sunfire again.

"We're going back to Queenstown," Roan said. "Goven can't continue."

"We have to get to the Greenwood," Alaric disagreed. "If Goven and Dalton need to go back, they can. The rest of us are going on."

"Goven's better off with me," Sini said. "He'll need more help with that wound."

"We stay with Sini," Dalton said firmly.

"Then let's stop wasting time." Pest tucked the last of his knives back into his belt.

Alaric looked down at Patrek. "We can trust that you'll leave us be? At least until you can prove our words?"

The man gave a reluctant nod. "But if the sheep sicken again, we will find you."

Alaric untied the man's bonds and he hurried to his friends. Sini mounted and followed the Barons. Pest lingered behind, giving Patrek a cold look while the others left.

Sini mulled over the sunfire as they rode away. Why had it been so strong? Had she just never tried to use that much before? Possibly nothing in the Stronghold had required so much. Healing the twins was simple, and it had been a while since she'd experimented with sunfire.

In the early days after the Elder Grove, when she'd first come to the Stronghold, she'd tried to channel that much sunfire again. She'd never managed anything even half that big. A thrill went through her at the idea that they were heading back to the Grove now.

Will and Alaric had been watching her thoughtfully, exchanging quiet conversations. To them it must have looked like nothing more than healing. They were probably impressed just by that, but they had no idea what the sunlight had been like, and she didn't have the words, or the desire, to talk about it yet.

It wasn't long before Roan pulled up next to Sini, though. He'd been watching her as well, with a troubled expression.

"What's bothering you, Lord Consort?"

His expression didn't change. "How many people know you can heal like that?"

"All the Keepers. And now the Barons, Pest, and you."

"Did your family when you were young?"

She shook her head. "I didn't have any powers when I lived with them."

"Do the Roven you lived with?"

"They know I can heal. Although I can do far more now than I could when I lived with them."

He was quiet for a long time, staring ahead. "So Lukas knows?"

"Of course he does. I healed him of several bad cuts over the years."

"But never his limp?"

"That's not a natural injury." She'd probed it more than once. There was no healing going on. There was a jagged rip deep in his hip, but his body did nothing to fight it, and so she could do nothing to help. "Why do you ask?"

"What you did for Goven...Have you done that sort of thing before?"

"No. The last time I saw a wound that bad was on the Sweep, and my powers were nowhere near strong enough do anything for the man."

"Have you heard of other healers saving someone from an injury that extreme?"

"I didn't save him yet, and there have been other healers who could do it." Not many, and none as quickly as she had. She kept that part to herself. Most healers had to use normal amounts of *vitalle*, and so their work was slow and caused them pain. Chesavia was the only healer who could also feel the sunlight. But Sini had never been able to pinpoint how that old Keeper healed. Not like Sini did, not at the level of flesh and bone. Her healing involved something with the whole body.

"I can't heal everything. Closing wounds is the easiest. The flesh just needs to be brought back together, and the body heals it. Illnesses, disease, burns—those are all more complex. All I can do is help the body do what it wants, so closing a cut is easy since once it's drawn back together, there is such a little area to repair. Regrowing skin across a burn takes much longer and much more energy. Diseases and illness are spread too much throughout the body, though." She told him briefly about the twins. "It may be in their heart, but it affects the blood flow and the lungs. Everything gets weak." She sighed. "All I can heal is cuts."

Roan shook his head. "I'll tell the Barons and Pest not to mention your abilities. If the people were to find out that a Keeper could save them from death…"

"Didn't you just hear what I said? That's hardly what I can do."

"That's how they'd hear it." He turned to look at her, worry in his face. "Be careful who you tell, Sini. People will want to control something like this. It's valuable enough to be dangerous to you." He fell silent again, but the troubled expression stayed on his face for a long time.

Sini rode next to him, her own mind uneasy.

Will and Alaric fell into a long discussion about how far Lukas had reached, but Sini hung back enough that they didn't ask her opinion. A chaotic knot of emotion filled her. Lukas had been here. He'd used compulsion stones to control people and was teaching them Mallon's words. Her last hope that he wasn't really doing terrible things slipped away.

Balancing that bleakness was the memory of the sunfire. The sun had risen fully now, and whenever they rode out of the shadows and the sunfire touched her neck, she drew bits of it in. Every time she began to enjoy the feel of it though, worries over Goven, or Lukas, or Roan's warning about her powers drove the enjoyment away.

It was midmorning before, from the top of one particularly tall rise, she caught sight of the Lumen Greenwood again. Despite the chill, the land around them was drenched with light.

"Does the forest look a little…" Sini asked Roan, peering at the Greenwood. "Dark?"

Roan looked at the trees with a slight crease in his brow. "Maybe the canopy is very thick."

Sini made a noncommittal noise, and the forest disappeared from sight when they dropped into the next valley. By the time they stopped for lunch they could see the forest clearly.

Sini checked on Goven's back while Will passed out a quick meal of bread and cheese. She pulled in some sunlight, the warmth of it filling her arms as she poured *vitalle* into him, to strengthen the healing. "How does it feel?"

"Not bad," Goven answered, barely moving.

There was only so much she could do. Any more would seal the infection inside him. She ran out of things to heal long before she ran out of the desire to use the light. Alaric made a poultice out of herbs from his pack to help fight the infection and they wrapped the wound.

Sini glanced at the Greenwood. A nagging sense of unease played along her neck.

"Does it usually look like that?" she asked Will and Alaric.

"I don't remember it being that shadowed," Alaric admitted.

"It looks darker than any forest I've ever seen," Will said. "And I don't need to remind the rest of you how stories go when people walk into dark forests."

"There can't be anything terribly wrong," Sini said. "Douglon's in there, and Rass."

"Or they were two days ago," Roan pointed out. At everyone's glares, he added, "If things were going well, he wouldn't have asked for 'anyone else who has any semblance of power.'"

"He also told us not to dawdle," Will said, tucking the rest of the bread back into this saddlebag and setting off at a trot toward the dark line of trees.

The Barons took up the rear and Roan resumed his post at Sini's side.

"You're watching the forest as though you are assessing an approaching enemy," Sini said. "Are you going to protect me from the trees?"

"I certainly hope I don't have to."

Before long they could see individual trees at the edge of the forest, and despite the bright sun shining down on the tops of the leaves, past the trunks of the first trees the deep gloom was just barely too green to be black. The last time she'd left the Greenwood she'd looked behind her over and over. The air beneath the trees had glowed with a rich green that almost made her turn back and stay with Rass and Douglon. She leaned forward in her saddle, anxious to get back into it.

Pest waited for them by a large, lonely oak tree, his weathered face pointed south, considering a glint of light down the tree line. A small figure waved something shiny.

"It's Douglon," Alaric said, peering in that direction. "I think."

The person did resemble a dwarf, and Alaric turned toward him. Sini expected Douglon to come meet them, but instead he sat down against a tree.

The wind had picked up now, and the short ends of Sini's hair snapped against her cheeks. They had to skirt a steep ravine, and it took much longer than it should have to reach the dwarf. When they did, they found him sleeping against a large trunk. He was dressed for battle in a thick leather breastplate, the silver edge of mail glinting at his shoulder. Leather bracers were fastened around his forearms and the greaves on his legs were scored with scratches.

"Douglon?" Alaric called as they got closer.

The branches creaked and cracked in the wind. The leaves rustled against each other so loudly they could barely hear each other. When they reached the dwarf, Alaric called for him again, louder.

Douglon groaned and rubbed at his face, pushing himself up from the tree. At their amused expressions, he scowled. "It's so quiet here. Had to take advantage of it."

He seemed perfectly serious. And grouchy.

Everyone dismounted, greeting the dwarf. In the face of Douglon's scowl, Alaric and Will's warm welcomes cooled to pats on his shoulder.

"It's about time you got here," Douglon grumbled. "I was about to leave and let you handle things on your own." He raised an eyebrow at Sini when he saw her. "Still spending time with these boring Keepers?"

Sini shrugged, "It's better than slavery."

"Is it? Every time I'm with them I get attacked by dragons or goblins or monsters."

"Maybe it's you," Sini offered. "In the past four years, not a single dangerous thing has happened to me."

Douglon stroked his beard. His shoulders sagged. "Maybe it is me. At least I can't blame this"—he waved at the Greenwood—"on you people." He cast an irritable look at Roan and the guards. "Who are you?"

Sini motioned to Roan. "The not-future-king and our guards."

"What's going on with the forest?" Will interrupted.

Even from this close, the path next to Douglon faded into gloom so quickly it looked like they'd be stepping from midday into dusk. Sini's excitement about the forest lessened.

"C'mon." Douglon tossed his head toward the path. "Let's get in out of the wind. It's not far to a clearing. I'll explain it all there. Or I'll try." He paused. "None of you soldiers, though. You'll be no help, and flashing swords are the last thing we need."

Roan started to object, but Alaric stopped him. "They'll be no use in here. And Goven needs rest."

He frowned. "Pest, stay with Dalton and Goven. I'm going in."

Douglon crossed his arms. "No."

"I'm Queen Saren's emissary—"

"Let him come, Douglon," Alaric said tiredly. "Queen Saren sent him."

"He's your responsibility, then," Douglon grumbled.

Alaric frowned at the words. "We didn't expect you to come meet us. We could have found the Elder Grove ourselves."

Douglon glanced into the forest, his expression wary. "It'll be better if you have an escort. Not good, maybe. But better."

NINETEEN

The path into the forest was barely a game trail. Sini followed the others, walking her horse to avoid the branches hanging low across the path. They hadn't been imagining it. It was dark under the trees. Sini glanced behind her at the sliver of light she could still see from beyond the forest. Above her the leaves were locked together, blocking out almost all the sunlight. It was a gloom as deep as the last moments of dusk.

Roan walked behind her, his hand on the hilt of the sword at his waist, his eyes scanning the darkness. His hair was windblown, and he looked less sure of himself than Sini had ever seen.

The forest blocked the wind, but the branches above them swayed and creaked. Occasionally branches cracked together, and even amidst all the other noises, it made her jump. The path was so thin that twigs were constantly in her face and slapping at her arms. She pressed up tightly against her horse, spinning her ring nervously.

They reached a small clearing, and Douglon motioned everyone to come around him, rubbing his beard nervously. The sunshine landed warm on Sini's head and she squinted against the light. The trees around them looked perfectly normal. Tall trunks, bright green leaves. Sunlight danced along the top of the canopy in a blinding green. The sky above was perfectly blue. The wind could only manage to slip a few gusty fingers into this small of a clearing, so it was relatively calm aside from the creaks and groans of the forest. But back under the branches, it was dark in every direction.

Sini cast out. Even here, so close to the edge, the forest blazed with unusual energy. Each trunk was a column of fire, the leaves fingers of flames thrashing in the wind. The ground beneath her pulsed with life.

But it was different than it had been. The last time Sini had walked through these woods, she hadn't yet learned how to cast out, but it hadn't mattered. The forest had called to her, drawing her in, fanning some longing she'd never known she'd had.

Today, the trees did not call to her. The forest was drawn up like soldiers in formation standing at attention, ready for battle. "Nothing feels the same here."

Will and Alaric nodded, each watching the trees warily.

"It's not the same." The sunlight etched deep, dark circles under Douglon's eyes. His beard was disheveled, and his shoulders hung low in exhaustion. "Six days ago the first elf was...birthed, I suppose."

"The first?" Will asked quickly, running his fingers down Talen's back to keep him calm. "There have been more?"

Douglon shot him an unreadable look. "Since the last full moon, the roots in the Elder Grove began to grow knobs. They swelled larger until one cracked open and a tiny elf lay curled up inside it."

"Fascinating," Alaric said. "How big was it? Male or female?" He looked around. "Can we meet it?"

"Will you let me finish?" Douglon asked, irritably. "The elf only came up to Rass's waist. A little girl." He rubbed at his face. "She looked like Ayda. Or enough like her that for a moment I wondered…"

"If we'd somehow brought her back?" Alaric asked quietly.

Douglon didn't answer.

"I think we all hoped we could do that," Alaric said. "I gather that's not what happened?"

Douglon let out a laugh that was more resigned than funny. He slid the bracer off one arm and pulled up his sleeve. Dark red scratches raked across the muscles of his forearm. "The little elf was calm for about three breaths until she saw me, screamed, and attacked." Douglon shuddered. "She was terrifying."

"Worse than a frost goblin?" Will asked.

"That's what she was like. All of a sudden she had these pointy teeth and her hands were like claws. It was like fighting off a crazed animal. She was tearing my arms up when Rass came to help. Instead of attacking Rass too, the little elf cried and reached out for her. Must have recognized that she was an elf. The moment Rass took her the little thing calmed and smiled and was sweet again."

"That's an ungrateful way to greet the dwarf who cared for the grove for four years," Sini said.

"Yes, it was. But soon Lyara—the baby elf—started pulling something out of Rass."

"Pulling what?" Alaric asked

Douglon threw his hands out in exasperation. "Life? From the grass? I don't know. This is Rass we're talking about. Even after all this time in the forest, she's still obsessed with the grass."

"Did Lyara ever warm up to you?" Will asked.

Douglon nodded. "I have this gem thing that Ayda froze,"—he glanced at Alaric—"from the time with the dragon." He pulled a leather thong out from behind his beard with a small crystal hanging on it. It was the shape of a small tongue of fire, but it was a brilliant blue color. "Lyara pulled it out of my shirt—I was afraid she was trying to get to my neck to kill me—she just stared at it for a bit. I have no idea what she saw there, but from that moment, she was fine with me."

"Are all baby elves violent toward outsiders?" Roan asked.

"I don't know anyone who's ever met a baby elf," Alaric said.

Sini looked down at the scratched leather on Douglon's shins. "You said she was the first."

"There are two aren't there?" Will asked eagerly. "The hunters from Lorrendale didn't see children in the forest. They saw two small elves."

"Yeah, another was born," Douglon said, "just as violently as the first. Then another. And another. And a dozen more."

"A dozen?" Will asked.

"That was just the first afternoon."

"How many are there?" Alaric asked, casting a worried look into the trees.

"Forty-six."

The group stood in stunned silence.

Sini glanced at Will and Alaric. "Did you expect that many?" From their dumbfounded expressions, they did not.

"You mean to say there are almost four dozen crazed creatures who hate outsiders running around this forest?" Roan asked.

"That's why I came to escort you," Douglon said. "I'm hoping if they see me with you, they won't attack. At least not right away." He pulled a handful of frozen blue flames out of a pocket. "You might each want to take one of these and keep it visible."

Sini took one, holding it in the palm of her hand. One end was rounded and the other spread out into a trident of flames. In the sunlight it glowed like a deep blue sapphire. "These are from Ayda? From when you faced the dragon?"

Douglon nodded. "There were so many frozen flames just lying on the ground, I grabbed a couple handfuls."

"I wish I had, too," Alaric said. "I've considered going back several times to get some."

"And don't draw your sword," Douglon said to Roan. "You would not believe how hostile they get at the sight of a drawn weapon." He looked at Roan more closely. "How valuable are you?"

Roan looked uncertain at the question.

"Not too valuable," Sini answered. "Betrothed to the future queen. But he'll have no real power."

"Well then protect that pretty face of yours. The future queen might not want her trophy husband scarred." Douglon turned back to Alaric. "I called for your help because the elves are growing more agitated. At first they were fine, a little moody and unpredictable, but like normal babies. With magical abilities and retractable pointy teeth."

"Magical ability?" Alaric asked.

"They've inherited Ayda's affinity for fire. I swear they're going to burn down the Greenwood." Douglon rubbed his hand across his face again. "But they won't eat anything. Rass has tried everything she can think of, but they just won't eat."

"What has she tried?" Alaric asked.

"Leaves, grass, sap, and every acorn or nut we could find. I tried hunting a squirrel and offering some of that." Douglon shuddered. "Don't do that. The only thing they'll eat is avak—a bush grew from that pit we planted when we buried Ayda—and they stripped the plant of fruit in a matter of hours."

"What do grass elves eat as babies?" Will asked.

"Rass says the *pratorii* get life from the grass, of course. What else would she possibly answer?"

"Then do these *silvii* get life from the trees?" Sini asked.

"If they do, we can't figure out how. We've set them against trunks, put them in bundles of branches, covered them with leaves, dug holes for their feet near the roots. As far as we can tell, they can't commune with the trees at all." He tugged at the end of his beard. "And I think they're starving. They're not growing right. Their cheeks are thin." He looked at them all nervously. "You wouldn't believe how irritable they are."

"What do dwarf babies eat?" Roan asked.

"Mutton," Douglon answered as though it were the most obvious answer in the world. "We need to find a way to feed them quickly. The world isn't sturdy enough to handle them if they go out looking for food." He turned toward the thin trail leading away from the clearing. "C'mon. We need to move if we're going to reach the grove by sundown."

"We have half the day," Will said.

"It gets dark in here early."

"Why is it so dark?" Sini asked.

"The elves are doing it. As they get more agitated, the forest is growing darker." He squinted up at the bright canopy. "They're doing something to the leaves. Or the trees are imitating them, or something. We should hurry—I don't like Rass there alone."

With that, he trudged off into the woods. Exchanging wary glances with the others, Sini followed. No one spoke as they walked into the gloom. The tree trunks rose around them like tall, brooding figures. The leaves above them were such a dark green they were almost blue. Not a cheerful blue. The sort of blue reserved for shadows and caverns and foreboding places.

The wind outside didn't reach them under the canopy, but the branches swayed wildly. A sharp hiss came from somewhere above them. Sini snapped her gaze up, catching a flicker of movement among the leaves. Whatever it was disappeared into the gloom.

"Is that you, Tessian?" Douglon called out, holding his hands out in a placating manner. "It's all right boy, these are friends. They knew your mother."

"We did?" Will asked quietly.

"It's what they call Ayda. We're not entirely sure how they know about her, but they do. It took us a while to figure out who they were talking about."

"They were only born last week, but they talk?" asked Will.

Douglon nodded. A hostile chittering came from high in the trees.

"No need for that boy," the dwarf said sternly. "They're here to help."

"That didn't sound like words," Roan pointed out from close behind Sini. "Do they speak intelligibly?"

"Occasionally."

"I think we understood the gist of it," Sini said, pressing her shoulder against her horse.

The group moved forward again, and Sini caught bits of movement in the trees around them, disappearing before she got a good look. Sini cast out, feeling the huge presence of the trees. The further into the forest they walked, the more vibrant the *vitalle* was in the trunks around them. They crossed a thin stream and the air vibrated with energy. Sini didn't even need to cast out to feel the life in the forest now. Her skin tingled with it, *vitalle* thrilled along her fingertips.

Last time she was here, Evangeline had told Sini the trees were mourning. They were certainly not mourning any longer. But whatever they were doing was unsettling. The branches above them no longer thrashed in the wind. Leaves shivered and shook, but it felt more like the trees' doing than the wind's.

Sini glanced back at Roan, who was looking stone-faced into the forest, his fingers twitching toward the hilt of his sword.

"Here's the grove," Douglon called out from ahead of her, walking out into a clearing. The others followed, and Sini stepped into welcome sunlight.

The Elder Grove had changed, as well. She took only a single step into it before she stopped. The ring of huge trees Gustav and his dragon had felled still lay sprawled out from the center of the wide clearing. Their roots still pointed into the air, but moss had begun to grow over them, blending the trees into the ground.

The raw gashes the dragon had left in the ground when he tore them down had smoothed over. Grass grew everywhere, blanketing what had once looked like scarred earth with a soft rug of green.

Half of the roots of the fallen tree were still anchored in the ground, so a large portion of each tree still grew. There were bare and dry limbs, but they were surrounded by thick, living branches. The new growth from the prostrate trees had all turned upwards at the ends, reaching for the sky, giving the impression that the entire grove was reaching upward.

Inside the circle of roots, the newer trees still stood. Raised out of the earth by Ayda in her fury, they were as terrifying as they'd been the first time Sini saw them. Her memories didn't do justice to the sharpness of the red thorns or the jaggedness of the leaves. Like the rest of the Greenwood, under the vicious canopy of those trees, the trunks stood in an unnatural darkness.

But it was more than the sight that stopped her. The air thrummed with energy. It had been growing steadily stronger until the air pressed on her from all sides, tingling against her skin. Her scalp prickled with it. A soft buzzing started in her ears. Tickles of *vitalle* danced across her hands and neck and face.

"Wait here," Douglon said unnecessarily. Everyone else had stopped as well. "Let me make sure it's not too crazy inside the Vigilants."

"The Vigilants?" Alaric asked.

Douglon motioned up to the trees. "Rass named them." He glanced around. "She's named about everything…" He slipped in between two of the trunks, turning sideways and ducking his head to avoid thorns.

A part of Sini longed to go in after him, to feel the sunfire like she had long ago. To feel again how she'd felt healing Goven. But the viciousness of the trees and the frantic feel of the forest held her back.

Sini led her horse closer to the others. Alaric and Will stood looking warily around them. "Can you feel this?"

Will spared her a glance before looking back at the trees. "Feel what?"

"The *vitalle*."

"It's always more awake here," Alaric said. "I don't know how."

"No," Sini said. "Last time it was more awake. Now it's…"

Will turned a worried look toward her. "It's what?"

"Cast out," she said.

"I have been. There's at least two dozen little elves in the treetops."

Sini shook her head. "Not that, can't you feel it? In the air?"

Alaric leaned around Will, uneasy. "What are you feeling?"

The energy pressed in at her even stronger and she squeezed her eyes shut against it. "There's so much…" *Vitalle* traced flickering lines across her hands. Sini held them out, her palms up, the blue flame resting in one. She spread her fingers and arcs of pink jumped between them.

Will focused on Talen for a moment. "Why don't you scout around above the trees?" The little hawk soared up into the sky.

Sini rippled her fingers and the light flashed. "It's looking for somewhere to go. Like lightning in a storm," she explained, knowing they couldn't see the *vitalle*.

Alaric watched her with a troubled expression. "Like lightning?"

A sharp crack sounded from one of the nearby treetops. The leaves rustled. Hisses filled the air.

"We should not be here," Roan said quietly.

"I'm inclined to agree," Will said, turning slowly to watch as many trees as he could.

"The elves don't attack visitors," Alaric said in an unconvincing voice. "A sharp trill came from a nearby tree. It was echoed from another. And another.

Sini held the blue flame in her hand up higher, showing it to the creatures in the shadowed tops of all the trees nearby. Roan hurriedly did the same.

"Douglon?" Alaric called. "It's getting a little tense out here."

A flash of motion in the nearest tree caught Sini's eye and she whirled toward it.

With a shriek, a small figure no larger than a two-year-old child leapt out of the tree. Sini caught a glint of wild eyes and white claws before it crashed into Roan.

TWENTY

Roan staggered back into his horse, shoving back at the little creature clinging to his chest and screeching.

The little elf had a shock of short white hair, spiked out in all directions. Sini lunged over and grabbed at the elf's arm, trying to pry it off Roan while it strained and snapped its teeth near his neck. The little elf's arm was thin, with hard, stringy muscles, and its skin was oddly dry. The moment Sini touched it *vitalle* seeped out of her hand into it.

The elf ignored her entirely, flinging itself at Roan with everything it could muster. Its face was gaunt, its eyes wide and bulging, its cheeks sunken. Roan managed to get the creature at arm's length, but it merely turned to scratching and biting at his arms.

In a breath, a half dozen more hurtled down from the trees, landing on the others. A screeching flash of coppery skin slammed into Sini's shoulder. She grabbed its skinny torso. Tiny bony fingers clamped into her hair. Nails dug into the back of her scalp and yanked her head backwards. The little elf screamed a sound of pure hatred and slammed its head into Sini's temple. The grove spun for a moment as another hand scraped across just below her neck, sharp nails scratching her skin and clenching her shirt.

Sini squeezed her eyes shut against the spinning grove. She wrapped both hands around the elf's chest and shoved the creature out to arms' length. The elf didn't let go, and its fingers wrenched Sini's head to the side.

Sini let out a cry of pain that was lost in the shrieks of elves and the shouts of her companions. Beside her, Alaric fought with a scrambling mass of greenish elf he had driven to arms' length while another clawed at his legs. Will managed to toss one elf off. It landed on all fours, still hissing. Two more climbed up the back of his legs. Roan finally got his white elf grasped solidly in one hand and was reaching for his sword when a dozen more dropped out of the trees and rushed for them.

"No weapons!" Douglon bellowed, running out from between the Vigilants. "Do not draw that sword, boy! They'll go crazy!"

"This isn't crazy?" Sini cried, scrambling away from one near her feet.

"This is nothing!" Rass called, rushing out behind Douglon. Her hair was disheveled, and there were long red scratches crisscrossing her arms and legs. She ran to Will, pulling at an elf that clung to his legs.

Douglon pulled one off Alaric's leg. "Stand down, you stupid creatures!" he hollered at them. The horde of tiny elves paid no attention. The one in his arms slashed toward his face and Douglon gave it a thunderous look. "Derien, calm down!"

The elf Sini was holding grabbed at her wrist, and the skin where they connected burst into pain. Sini let out a yell and tried to pull away, but the elf's grip was too strong.

A wave of weakness passed over her, and Sini stumbled to her knees.

Vitalle. The elf was sucking energy out of her so fast Sini could barely breathe. This wasn't painless sunfire, the elf was sucking out her life.

She reached for the sunlight.

The energy of the grove rushed into her with a ferocity that sent her reeling. A sound like raging wind filled her ears. Her skin hummed. Energy shot from the ground into her knees. Her arms and neck and back drew sunfire in faster than she ever had before. The pain in her wrist was so excruciating, it took a moment to realize the little elf had calmed.

Its gaze was glued to Sini's wrist, its face transformed into a look of pure bliss.

It was a girl, Sini realized in a detached sort of way, with beautiful copper skin and wide green eyes flecked with gold.

Around her the sounds of struggle worked past the noise in Sini's head. "*Vitalle!*" she yelled to Alaric and Will. "They need *vitalle!*"

The copper elf loosened her grip and raised a sweet gaze to Sini's face. "Give them to me!" Sini called. "They're starving!"

Roan was the first to move, dragging the three elves that were attacking him over to Sini. A rush of pain lanced through her when he pressed the two that were on his legs against her back. It only took a heartbeat before they flung themselves off Roan and onto Sini.

The pain grew where they touched her, and where Sini touched the ground. It was the grove itself—the *vitalle* from the grass and the trees pouring into her—that burned. Gritting her teeth, she closed herself off to the energy streaming into her from the ground. It shoved against her knees, but she kept it out, letting only the sunfire pour onto her and through her.

The little copper elf chattered loudly, jumping and slapping her hands together. The chaos of elves around them turned like a school of fish and focused on her. They collapsed toward Sini, tiny hands scrambling to touch some part of her body. The pain faded as the forest's *vitalle* was cut off. The sunfire filled her and streamed out effortlessly into the elves.

Even kneeling the elves only came up to her chest, and Sini reached her hands up above them toward the sky, drawing in everything she could, feeling it rush into her arms, her face, her neck, seeping out of her into the clamoring elves.

The ones who couldn't reach her scrambled over the ones who could. Sini had a vague impression of Will and Alaric nearby, drawing *vitalle* from the ground in thin streams.

The energy flowing through her was more than she'd ever channeled. Tenfold more than when she'd healed Goven. She could feel the hands of the elves grabbing on tightly, loosening as they were fed, falling off to be replaced by more. Their screeching and scrambling were a distant tumult past the rushing river of *vitalle*.

The light filled her, swept her up in its purity and warmth, its vastness. This was life. Good and whole. No weakness, no sickness or hunger. Just light and life. Her hands glowed with a warm golden light. The skin on her fingers blurred into brightness like the edge of a candle flame, yearning to spread out, to soar into the sky. Luminous, weightless, and free.

Free.

Her skin softened, brightened, stretched toward the sunfire. It was so close. She ached to become a part of something so glorious. The golden glow on her hands grew brighter, burning along her skin with warmth and wholeness.

Dimly, she felt the number of hands on her dwindle and the pressure of the energy lessened. The light lessened as well, and Sini grabbed at it, panicked at the thought of it leaving. Her body was jostled, and she lost her hold. Exhaustion rolled over her and the light fled.

Awareness of the grove flooded into her. A crowd of tiny elves clustered around her, sitting or climbing sleepily over one another. The rushing in her ears was replaced by the sound of the elves' chatter.

The little copper elf sat in front of Sini, looking up into her face. When Sini met her gaze, the little elf smiled a wide, toothless grin and scrambled up onto Sini's lap. With a huge yawn, she snuggled into her.

Sini numbly wrapped her arms around the little creature. Her fingers on the elf's back were glowing with a golden glow. She squeezed her eyes shut against the sight. Everything was so dark and weak. Her own flesh dim and heavy. Sharp cuts stung on her arms and across the back of her neck. She breathed in deeply, letting the lifeless air fill her lungs.

The grove was so much quieter. She left her eyes closed, listening to the normal peaceful sounds of the forest. The air was empty, lighter. No *vitalle* pressed against her. She could still feel the towering energy of the elven trees, but they seemed content.

The yearning for the light squeezed her heart, and a sense of enormous loss fell over her. She understood Chesavia's words.

For one glorious moment I wanted to join it. To let myself transform into light. To be vast and alive and free…Here, in the darkness where my skin is just skin, and my flesh merely mortal, trapped in one moment and one weakened form, my soul aches at my choice.

"Sini?" Will asked quietly.

She cracked her eyes to find him kneeling next to her, his hand outstretched toward her shoulder, his face worried. She glanced at her fingers, but they were only flesh and blood. She gave him a weak smile. "I know what they were hungry for."

"Are you all right?" He touched Sini's shoulder tentatively as though he expected to be shocked.

Alaric looked at her with something akin to awe. "I've never seen anything like that. I've never read about anything like that. How did you—? Where did you get—?" He stopped and looked to Will for help.

Will let out an exhausted laugh. "Alaric, I get the feeling someday you and I are going to be remembered only as 'those two Keepers who brought the legendary Keeper Sini back to Queensland.'"

TWENTY-ONE

Legendary Keeper Sini.

The words echoed in her head hollowly. The sunfire danced on the treetops and she itched to drag her fingers through the light, to feel the warmth pour through her skin again.

"Sini," Alaric said cautiously, "why aren't you dead?"

Sini felt oddly detached from them, her mind stunned from the absence of the light.

Roan picked his way through the elves to Sini, looking down at her with a cross between shock and concern. "Are you…hurt?"

"I'm fine." She wasn't fine, not exactly.

"You should be dead," Will agreed. "Why were your hands glowing?"

His words caught her attention. "You saw that?" He and Alaric stood waiting. But she had no words to explain what had just happened. "The elves needed a lot of *vitalle*."

"We noticed," Will said.

She had glowed. A cold fear cut through her. She had glowed and her hands had blurred as though…as though they were turning into light. She swallowed down the horror that rose from the idea.

Sini shook her head and looked at the people around her. Despite her fear, she couldn't quite banish the strange longing for the light.

"They needed more *vitalle* than anyone should rightly be able to give them." Alaric turned to Will. "How many did you feed?"

"Two." Will held out his hands and showed a bright red blister spreading across each palm. "And I was terrified another would touch me." He glanced to a wide patch of dead grass that he'd pulled all the *vitalle* from. "Sorry, Rass."

"There's plenty more grass." Rass looked up at him with a weak smile from where she sat—in her own patch of dead grass—being fussed over by Douglon. "I fed four."

"You should have left the feeding to the Keepers," Douglon chided her. "You were already exhausted."

"We all should have left it to just one Keeper," Will said.

Rass patted Douglon on the cheek. "I'm all right, uncle."

Douglon gave a disapproving huff but kissed her on the top of the head before lifting two elves off her lap and settling them over by a cluster of others. He had a fresh red welt running down his cheek into his beard. Will dropped down beside Rass and she leaned against him. Sini tried to focus on the little grass elf, who looked meatier than the last time Sini had seen her. Her bare legs and arms, though scratched, looked strong. Her face was full, but dark shadows hung beneath her eyes and her shoulders slumped.

Alaric gestured to a withered tree shoot next to him. "It took a tree, but I fed three. Maybe two and a half before the last one went to Sini." He turned his palms up to show blisters matching Will's. "I believe that left thirty-nine for Sini."

"Only thirty-eight and a half," Will pointed out. "Let's not give her more credit than she deserves. Would you like to show us your hands, Keeper Sini?"

With the ends of the power just at the edge of her mind, the title almost fit, and the dry look she intended to fix him with curled into a smile. She had felt the light the way Chesavia had. One of the greatest Keepers of all time, one whose skills most Keepers struggled to understand—Sini understood her perfectly.

She unwrapped one hand from the little elf nestled against her and held it up. It still stung a little, and when she spread her fingers apart a thin arc of pink shot between them, but there were no blisters. Aside from the place on her wrist the first elf had touched, her skin wasn't even red.

"Are you part elf?" Rass asked.

The idea was so ludicrous Sini let out a laugh. "If you'd met my parents, you wouldn't ask that."

"Have you come up with any way to heal blisters?" Will gingerly stretched his fingers "O Great Keeper?"

"A wound is simply closed. A burn needs all new skin over a wide area…" Sini grimaced. "Burns are tricky."

He sighed. "That's what I thought."

An elf pulled on Will's leg and he picked up the little bluish creature. It snuggled against him and gave a sleepy yawn. "Emotional little things, aren't they?" He sat down on the ground and two others climbed onto his lap.

"Every day, all day." Douglon sat with an exhausted groan. "They're never reasonable. They're either giddy with happiness, screaming with fury, or sleeping. There's no middle ground. And here I thought grown elves were moody."

Rass threw a pinecone at him that bounced off his shoulder.

"At least now we know what they needed." Alaric sat swarmed by his own group of baby elves. They climbed onto him like a handful of sparkling jewels.

Sini shook off the last of her thoughts of the light. The elves' skin was each tinged a different color, their hair a darker version of the same. They uniformly had short hair that shot out in every direction, some in straight spikes, some in curls. There was a marked difference between the males and females. The faces of the little girls were long and lithe. The little boys were rounder, their bodies broader.

"Isn't *vitalle* what they should be getting from the trees?" Sini asked, shifting the now sleeping copper elf into a more comfortable position on her lap. "You get your energy from the grass, right Rass?"

Rass nodded. "We've been trying to get them to connect to the trees, but they don't seem to know how."

"And we can't show them how to do such an absurd thing." Douglon growled at two of the elf boys who were attempting to climb up his legs, but gently moved them onto his lap. One reached up, wrapped his fingers around a braid in Douglon's beard and gave a sharp yank. Douglon swore and swatted the hand away, then offered the elf his finger to hold instead. "Why can't you just eat mutton?" He asked the yellowish creature in his lap. The little boy smiled up at him and closed his eyes. "I don't know how to get anything from the trees either," Rass admitted. "They're not like the grass. I can feel how strong the trees are. But I can't get to them."

"We could show them," Alaric offered. "Or at least we could try."

"Unless Sini wants to stay here as a magical nursemaid for forty-six elves," Will said with a grin. Three elves were tangled together on his lap, another climbing up his back.

"That sounds exhausting." Sini glanced over the crowd of elves around them. They were all thin, their elbows and knees bony. The little copper girl in her arms had been born six days ago and hadn't really eaten? No wonder they'd been angry.

"It's brighter," Roan said, peering into the edge of the forest.

It was brighter. Sunlight filtered through under the nearest trees, landing on bright green ferns and reflecting a verdant glow onto the trunks. The leaves rustled with an utterly normal sort of sound. The whole feel of the forest had changed.

"Maybe the elves weren't making the forest angry," Sini said. "Maybe it was angry that they were hungry."

"Well, whichever it is, this is the most peace we've had in days," Rass said leaning on Will's shoulder. "I'm so glad you all came."

"We need some help of our own." Roan looked at Douglon. "Her Majesty, Queen Saren, requests that you take us to Duncave."

Douglon's eyebrow rose. "Who are you again?"

"This is Roan of Greentree," Alaric said. "He is Saren's emissary to the dwarves, and he's betrothed to the heir apparent."

Douglon grunted. "My sympathies on being so close to the throne."

"Don't worry," Sini said, "he'll just be a royal ornament." She gestured to his clothing. "A colorless, sober, level-headed ornament."

"Unless Queen Saren's court is a lot different than Horgoth's in Duncave," Douglon said, "you're not going to fit in at all."

Roan squinted at the two of them as though trying to decide whether they were serious. "Her Majesty tells me that you are of royal dwarven blood."

"I've been trying to change it out for useful blood my whole life, but so far, I haven't had much luck." He turned to Alaric. "Can you believe Horgoth still hasn't had any children?"

"These sorts of things can take time."

"Horgoth's just wasting time, like he does on everything. A council meeting that could take less time than a quick snack takes all evening. Designing a blasted throne room could be done with some snapped off commands, yet work has come to a halt over the last few years due to his indecision. I'm sure it's the same with the heirs."

"We have pressing matters to speak to the High Dwarf about," Roan broke back in. "Please escort us to the nearest entrance to Duncave. We can leave immediately."

"First,"—Douglon grinned—"you don't want me taking you to Horgoth. If you want him to listen to you, you should deny knowing me. Second, we can't leave immediately. Shall we just leave Rass with forty-six elves that may turn back into vicious monsters at any moment?"

"The elves are not my concern," Roan said stiffly. "The others can stay and help her. I am tasked with speaking to the High Dwarf, and I intend to do so."

"Without a guide into Duncave?" Douglon asked. "Good luck, ornament."

"We all need to get to Duncave." Alaric untangled a sleeping elf from his lap and set it gently on the ground. "Saren wanted to know—"

Douglon held up his hand for Alaric to stop. "I don't want to know. Every time someone tells me about a problem somewhere, I get roped into trying to fix it. I have forty-six of my own problems right here."

"That's fair," Alaric said. "I assume there is an entrance to Duncave nearby we could use?"

"No, there's not. The dwarves have never been inclined to visit the Greenwood. The nearest entrance is a hard day's ride and I'm not leaving Rass here alone."

Roan pressed his lips into a thin, disapproving line, but didn't press the issue.

The little copper elf in Sini's lap shifted and grasped Sini's arm with her hand. *Vitalle* began to flow into the elf again. Not as fast as before, but fast enough to heat up Sini's skin.

"Not so fast, little one." Sini stood up. The little elf fit snugly in Sini's arms and barely weighed anything.

"That's Avina," Douglon said, disengaging little fingers from his beard again. "The others listen to her."

"A little queen?" Sini carried her over to the nearest tree. When she pulled Avina's fingers off her wrist the elf's face darkened and she drew back her lips to show thin tips of teeth sliding out of her gums. "It's all right. You don't really want *vitalle* from me."

She set Avina's copper palm on the bark. Then, pressing her own hand to the back of it, Sini began to draw *vitalle* out of the trunk. It stung her palm but around their fingers a faint green glow appeared. Avina's eyebrows shot up and she snapped her attention to the tree. Some of the energy slid into Sini's hand, but she let most of it flow into the little elf.

Avina reached her other hand toward the trunk and Sini pulled her own hand off. A faint green light glowed from between the elf's fingers.

Avina chittered at the others, smacking the tree trunk and wriggling down from Sini's grasp. She grabbed a nearby pinkish elf by the hair and tugged at it until it woke up. The pink one snarled, but seeing Avina, settled back into a scowl. Avina grabbed the pink hand of the elf and set it against the tree, placing her own over it, the way Sini had before.

The greenish glow, very faint this time, appeared around their fingers.

"How do we know if it's working?" Will asked from behind Sini.

Sini glanced back at him. "It's working. There's a green glow."

Sini and Will stepped back as more elves roused themselves from the grass and came to the trees. The ones who had mastered feeding scampered from one tree to the next, pressing their palms into the trunks and chittering at each other.

Douglon heaved himself from the ground and stretched. "They haven't been this self-sufficient in days. Let's go eat before they all decide they need us again."

"Oh yes!" Rass jumped up. "We have a deer roasting! Douglon hunted it yesterday in the hopes that you'd be here soon."

The thought of food pulled Sini's attention away from the remaining elves, and she followed the others around the trees of the elder grove. Sini craned to see between the trunks of the Vigilants, the vicious trees guarding the center of the Elder Grove, but she couldn't see anything.

She wanted to step into that place where they'd buried Ayda—where the sunfire had been so strong. Her skin ached to feel the power of it again, but a thrill of fear went through her at the thought. If she felt the sunfire again, could she resist it? Would she want to?

She skirted the Vigilants and it struck her that the new elves were much like those trees, hostile and ferocious toward the outside, but beautiful and happy with those they'd accepted.

On the far side of the Vigilants, a thin trail wound away into the forest. The sun was moving westward, and rays slanted through the tree branches like slashes of light, glowing against the trunks and ferns on the forest floor. From the swaying of the top branches it was clear the wind was still blowing strong, but Sini could feel only the slightest breeze. It was like a whole new forest.

They walked for several minutes before Douglon turned and held up his hand for them to stop. The trees ahead of them were enormous, their trunks wider than Sini's outstretched arms.

"Ahead is the glade where the elves faced Mallon. It's…unsettling."

Beside him Rass nodded. "We buried the elves we could, but…"

Sini had heard the story from Alaric. At the height of Mallon the Rivor's power, he had put pieces of himself into people all over Queensland. The elves had tried to take all of those pieces into themselves, and intended to throw them all off at the last moment by turning themselves into trees. Sending the pieces back into Mallon would have turned him mortal, but his power had been too strong. He kept the elves from turning. They'd been trapped, not fully elves, not fully trees. All controlled by the Rivor.

Until King Andolin had convinced the elves to give up their own lives and give all their will and power to Ayda so she could escape.

Douglon motioned for them to follow, and in a few heartbeats they spilled out into a wide glade that wasn't really a glade. The tall trees of the forest ended in a huge clearing, but there were dozens and dozens of smaller trees, stunted and twisted. Sini stopped short. Not trees. Elves, trapped, half changed into trees, left in a grotesque hybrid state. The nearest tree was almost normal except for a tortured face formed into the wood, and branches that ended in clawed fingers. The one beyond it was more elf than tree. She'd toppled to her knees, her hair and arms spreading out into branches and twigs, but her body was still in the form of an elf. Her knees branched off into roots that dug into the earth. Her skin was pale and slack, but her branches held green, stunted leaves that fluttered in the breeze.

Sini set her fingers on the bark, casting out toward the tree, looking for some sense of the elven life. But all she found was a tree. Not a vibrant tree, either, just a weak, paltry thing.

There were so many of them. They grew in clumps or alone, displaying various types of bark and leaves. Some she recognized as oaks or maples, but others were foreign to her. Occasionally they looked perfectly tree-like, but more often they were a contorted amalgam of tree and elf. The ones with faces were the worst. Every expression of them was twisted in pain or fear.

Not all the elves had even begun to change into trees, though. Plenty had chosen to give up their lives while still in elf form. A mound of earth filled the center of the glade, so wide that Sini didn't want to think about how many elves must be buried there. Grass grew over the barrow, except in the center where a young sapling grew.

The breeze shifted and Sini caught the scent of roasting meat from a fire pit. At the edge of the glade rose an enormous tree, its trunk wider than four of the other huge trees. Stairs spiraled up around it and the branches themselves formed walls and arched windows.

Below it a long, squat stone cottage puffed out smoke from its chimney.

"It's been about twenty years since I was in this place for the crowning of Prince Elryn," Alaric said, "but I don't recall any cottages."

"It's unnatural to climb up into the trees all the time." Douglon led the way into the cozy little house. "Besides, they needed more substantial lodgings around here."

Inside was rustic and simple. Wood-framed chairs with seats of woven grass were quickly filled while Douglon and Rass piled food onto the table. It was a tight fit, with Sini and Rass sitting on upended crates because all the chairs were filled, but everything was delicious. Aside from the meat there was a tall pile of apples, some boiled potatoes, and baked pears. Sini sat between Douglon and Roan, serving herself a huge plate.

"We do need to get to Duncave," Alaric said, once they were all eating. He explained to Douglon about Lukas and the gold mines, and their fears that he was using the wealth to buy armies from Coastal Baylon and Napon.

"Duncave doesn't go far enough south for us to see into Gulfind," Douglon said around a mouthful of meat.

"Could you take us to the tunnels tomorrow?" Alaric asked. "I need to see if Horgoth will work with us in any way. I'm afraid if Lukas unites Baylon and Napon, the armies might be too much for us."

"Horgoth isn't going to help you. He is against the dwarves getting involved in anything outside of Duncave. Especially a war. And I can't take you anyway. I've been waiting four years for these elves to be born, and now that they're here I'm not going to leave. Is Rass supposed to take care of them all by herself?"

"This is important," Alaric pointed out, irritation bleeding into his tone.

"You know what's important? Forty-six new elves were just taught how to eat. What else are they going to need? I'm not leaving Rass here alone to figure that out." Douglon's tone was final and he turned back to his meal.

After a moment of watching the dwarf with his lips pressed together, Alaric turned back to the others. Douglon's shoulders relaxed slightly when Alaric looked away.

"Do you miss Duncave?" Sini asked him, serving herself a second helping of pears.

Roan looked over at the dwarf with an interested face. "I've heard the walls sparkle with jewels."

"Until we mine them out," Douglon pushed the last bite of meat around his plate. "But yes, sometimes I miss it. I've gone back several times over the past few years. Only for a day or two at a time. I didn't want to leave Rass here alone in case something crazy happened. I needn't have worried, though. When the elves finally did get close to being born, it was a slow process. Those knobs grew out of the tree roots over the course of a month." Douglon glanced out the window. "I do miss the quiet of Duncave sometimes, and the darkness. In the forest there's always the sound of wind or birds"—a squeal of an elf cut through the late afternoon air—"and now that. And even at night there's starlight or moonlight. If you go deep enough into the caves though…" His voice faded and he looked outside with an unfocused gaze.

Then he blinked and looked back at Sini. "But whenever I go back, they try to rope me into responsibilities. Horgoth's become unbearable. He nags at me nonstop about helping him with the crown, making me into some sort of ambassador, coming with him to council meetings." Douglon shook his head. "Don't let them snare you into all of that, Roan. And you either, Sini. You Keepers are a little too close to the throne for my liking. Look at Alaric. The man never has any fun. Once I'm in Duncave for a day or two I can't wait to leave."

"It's really that bad?" asked Sini.

Douglon laughed. "Asks the Keeper who doesn't dress like one."

Sini opened her mouth to object, but he held up his hand. "You don't need to explain to me. First you wear what they want you to, then people start expecting things from you. Before you know it, you're trapped for the rest of your life in the cold throne room while people complain to you about things that aren't your fault."

"I'd heard the throne in Duncave was amazing," Roan said.

"Who could possibly tell? The throne room walls and floors are covered in black obsidian, rough enough that it reflects no light. Something about representing the glorious darkness of the earth. But it's too dark. I like the dark—all dwarves like the dark—but that place absorbs light until you can't light it up. Part of what makes darkness so wonderful is that you can light part of it and the shadows will wrap around you and make it homey. In the throne room you can barely see who you're talking to. How Horgoth can spend so much time in there, I'll never understand."

Sini glanced between Roan and Douglon. "It seems unusual to find people close to the throne who don't actually want it."

"It's the weight of all that responsibility," Roan said with a grimace.

"The throne changes a person," Douglon agreed. "My uncle, Horgoth's father, became High Dwarf when I was twenty. Before that he was fun, energetic, happy. But the weight of the crown crushed him. He had no time for Horgoth or me or anyone else. It destroyed his family and his health. He died young, leaving the throne to Horgoth when he was young." Douglon stared at his plate, unseeing. "He hasn't been the same since, either."

"Don't you miss other dwarves?" Sini asked.

Rass let out a peal of laughter at the other end of the table where she was seated between Alaric and Will. A fondness softened Douglon's face.

"It's not really a question of missing them, or of wanting to go. Sometimes life changes you, and the people you used to know aren't as comfortable of a fit as they used to be. And people you thought you'd never want to be near turn out to feel like family."

The same grief Sini had seen in Douglon's face four years ago was back. It wasn't as ragged as it had been. It had mellowed, but not lessened. Maybe it had worn itself in.

She looked away from it and focused on her pears. There was a sweet syrup on them that pooled on the side of her plate, and she pushed the last of the fruit into it. Down the table she heard Will and Alaric laugh. There was something grounding about them. Their faces were familiar. She'd never have thought the strange group of Keepers could feel like family. She'd been too close to Lukas to even consider it. But there they sat, more like family than anything she'd ever known.

She took the last bite of pear.

What did that make Lukas?

TWENTY-TWO

y nightfall it was obvious the elves had figured out how to feed themselves. Chirps and gig-
gles and shrieks filled the evening. Sini watched with Rass and Douglon out of one of the
cottage windows as the elves scampered up trees and skipped along the ground.

Two of the little elves tumbled into the cottage. One climbed up Sini's leg. She picked the silver
elf up and it snuggled up on her shoulder.

"They like you," Rass said. "They know you're the one who fed them."

Sini smiled at the foreign little creature in her arms. He was humanlike enough that his
strange-colored skin and chirpy squirrel-like-ness were mesmerizing.

"I'll be fine for a day or two, uncle," Rass told Douglon. "Will and Alaric need your help."

"I'm not leaving you alone," he said stubbornly.

It took more arguing to convince either Alaric or Douglon that this was a good idea, but eventually they did admit that, with Lukas's activities in Queensland, being in the Greenwood with the
elves—as long as they stayed well-fed—was probably safer than being out on the road.

Sini almost asked if she could sleep up in the elven house in the tree, but it felt too important,
and she didn't feel elvish enough. So, laying in Douglon's cabin on a thin mattress of grass Rass
had made, her mind went back to the sunfire.

Nighttime always felt empty. Occasionally under a full moon she could feel a little sunfire, but
usually the night air was just empty. Tonight it was hollow and bleak. The thought of the energy
she'd channeled settled into a cold lump. The more she thought about it, the more certain she was
that had she brought in much more, it would have killed her. And she'd have blissfully let it.

The truth of it felt like a betrayal. The sunfire had always been reassuring and safe. But now…

For the first time in her life, she feared that dawn was coming.

The next morning Sini was grateful for the shadows of the forest, and that gratitude left an ache
in her chest.

The elves were like whole new creatures. They were sleepy and relaxed, scampering to the
trees and drawing energy from them.

"An entire forest of nursemaids," Douglon grunted. He tousled the hair of the nearest elf, who was curled up against a tree trunk. "This is a good development."

He still didn't seem perfectly comfortable leaving Rass, but after the dwarf had given a stern talking to the elves—and after they paid him little heed, rolling around on the ground, hanging from branches, or reaching up to tug on the end of his beard—Douglon was satisfied enough to leave.

Will wrote a message to the queen explaining about the elves and fixed it to Talen's leg. "Go be pampered by the falconer at court." He ran his hand down Talen's chest. "You wouldn't like the tunnels of Duncave anyway. Don't get too fat while I'm gone." He raised his arm and the little hawk burst into the air. Above the treetops the morning sunlight laced his wings with gold. Sini flinched at the brightness.

Douglon led them out of the woods, and Sini felt a slight nervousness that they would have to pass through the Elder Grove again, with all its power. But he took them by a different path and when they found Pest and the Barons the sun was still hidden behind a tall hill, leaving the edge of the forest in shadows.

Dalton and Pest were awake, but Goven still slept. His face was pale, but better than yesterday. Sini knelt next to him and set her hand on his shoulder gently. She cast out and felt his *vitalle* pressed up against the edges of the wound. His body was strengthening and healing itself. A pocket of darkness marked the beginnings of an infection.

He needed help, and Sini braced herself before reaching tentatively toward the sunfire. Her hand on Goven's back trembled, but she fed the *vitalle* into him. In the dimness, the sunfire was easy to control. She did the little she could for him and cut off the light as soon as she could.

Despite Douglon's complaints about time being wasted, Sini and Dalton cleaned the wound as best they could. Dalton thanked her over and over.

"He's not out of danger yet," she told him. "There's infection."

"Take him back to Queenstown," Roan told Dalton. "He needs rest and medicine." He glanced at Douglon. "But we'll need your horse."

Douglon watched Sini with a raised eyebrow. "That's a handy skill you've got there, lass. Never thought I'd meet a useful Keeper."

Sini smiled weakly at him, and caught Roan frowning at the dwarf. She mounted her horse and Dalton came up beside her. "My brother and I are forever in your debt."

Goven stirred in an uneasy sleep.

"Don't say that until he recovers."

Dalton shook his head and looked at her sincerely. "He'd be gone already if it weren't for you. You've given him a chance. No matter how this ends, if you are ever in need of anything, anything at all, I am at your service."

Sini nodded and shifted in her saddle at his intensity. "I hope you reach Queenstown in safety."

"As long as he's not with Keepers, he should be fine," Douglon grumbled. "I'm leaving. If no one follows, I'm going back to Rass."

Dalton returned to his brother and Sini nudged her horse to follow the others. Roan pulled his horse up beside her. "I've known the Barons for three years and that's the longest speech I've ever heard Dalton give."

Behind them the huge man hovered over his brother like a nursemaid. "I may only have prolonged the inevitable," Sini said.

"I think Dalton would still be thankful to have a little more time."

The trip north was hurried, with Douglon keeping up a brisk trot. The day clouded over early and Sini felt relieved to not have the sunfire pouring down on her. The entrance to Duncave was a long day's ride, and Douglon wasted no time. They skirted the edge of the Greenwood, keeping to open land as much as they could, ducking through bits of forest when they had to. The Scale Mountains drew closer, and the deep gash in them that was Kollman Pass fell behind them by midday.

Sini hadn't been able to shake her complicated emotions about the sunfire. In the afternoon she found Pest riding nearby. Grey stubble covered his chin, and his hair was disheveled, but his gaze was still intense enough that it bordered on alarming. To distract herself she rode up next to him.

"Have you ever..." she began and at the smile on the edge of his mouth, she continued, "thrown a knife and killed a dwarf?" She asked quietly enough that Douglon wouldn't hear.

"Yesterday was the first time I'd ever met one."

"An elf?"

"Same."

She thought for a moment. "A goblin?"

"Still haven't met one of those."

"You'd want to throw a knife at one if you had."

"Maybe we'll get the chance."

"I dearly hope not. Have you ever won a knife throwing contest?"

He considered the question. "Isn't that what every fight is?"

"I suppose." Goven came back into her mind, and the men killed the day before, mostly by Pest's knives. The memory felt heavy, mixing with all the Roven she'd seen die on the Sweep in their endless, pointless skirmish. The futility of it all weighed on her.

"Have you ever cried after killing someone?"

He paused. "Yes." He didn't look at her. "Have you ever cried after using your magic on someone?"

The thought of Lukas and the small topaz rushed into her mind. Helping him pour *vitalle* into it, sewing it into the lining of the money bag that would be given to Vahe the wayfarer in payment for a new delivery of slaves. "Yes."

She snuck a look at Pest. His face was flinty. "Would you do it again?"

His expression didn't change. "Yes. Would you?"

She thought of Vahe in his wagon, trundling away with the leeching gem at his belt. How he had never returned. "Maybe."

They did not stop for dinner, and night was falling quickly when Douglon paused. He held two strips of cloth from his bag out toward Pest and Roan. "You two will be blindfolded 'til we're in. We don't need random humans finding our doors and pestering us."

"Absolutely not," Roan said.

Pest gave the dwarf a flat stare.

"Then you can all wander around the hillside knocking on rocks trying to find the entrance yourself." Douglon said. "I'll go back to Rass."

"Just put them on," Alaric said. "It's reasonable for him to keep these entrances secret."

Roan glared at Douglon, but held out his hand for a blindfold. It took a direct order from Roan before Pest did the same.

Once the blindfolds were set, he led them to a rocky outcropping that looked like every other one they'd passed for the last several hours.

He swung down from his horse, pulled his axe off his back, and pounded the butt of it against a boulder. Nothing happened, and Douglon pounded again.

"Ragnoor, I know you're in there, you lazy oaf. Open the door now, or I'll report you to Horgoth for neglecting your duties."

"Douglon?" a muffled voice asked. "Sorry, my lord. I didn't know t'was you." The boulder shifted and a dark split appeared.

Douglon stared into the darkness. "My lord? What's gotten into you? Open the door far enough for us to get in. Hurry up."

"Yes, my lord." The rock shoved over until a wide doorway gaped open.

"Bring in the horses," Douglon muttered to everyone. "Ragnoor will care for them while you're in Duncave."

"Horses? No, no horses. It'll smell in here for a fortnight."

Douglon ignored him and led his horse in. The others followed. Roan and Pest removed their blindfolds to navigate a short, winding tunnel. It opened into a clean cavern filled with the gentle orange glow of mosslight, the subterranean moss that glowed orange when wet. A younger dwarf, his golden yellow beard hanging only to the middle of his chest, directed them to a stable-like adjoining cavern.

He kept casting nervous glances at Douglon.

"What's gotten into you, lad?" Douglon demanded. "You're acting like a frightened sheep."

"I just didn't expect you here, m'lord."

Douglon turned to face him. "If you call me m'lord one more time, I'll knock your teeth out."

Ragnoor pressed his mouth closed and nodded quickly.

"These people need to get to Horgoth," Douglon continued. "They'll be sleeping here tonight, and the moment they say they're ready tomorrow, you'll take them to see my addleheaded cousin. Not that he's bright enough to actually help them with what they need."

"But I can't—"

"Ragnoor," Douglon growled. "I'm not asking. If Horgoth gives you trouble blame me. Tell him I threatened to kill you if you didn't do it. I am going to kill you right now if you don't wipe that stupid expression off your face. You'd think you'd never had anyone come to the door before."

"But you must go to the High Dwarf," Ragnoor stuttered. "He's ordered it."

"Horgoth is used to me ignoring his orders. Find out what he wants. Tell me next time I stop by." Douglon turned to Alaric, "I'm starting back tonight. Good luck with Horgoth. You'll need it." He stumped toward the exit.

Ragnoor bit his lip, then blurted out, "High Dwarf Horgoth is dying."

Douglon froze and turned back slowly, his face thunderous. "What do you mean dying?"

Ragnoor glanced at the others. "He broke a leg in a fall a fortnight ago, and th' leg's sickened. He wouldn't let the surgeon cut it off, an' now…he's dying. With no heir of his a'comin', he's commanded everyone to be on the lookout for you, m'lo—" he cut himself off. "Says you must come back to Duncave at once."

Douglon stared at the dwarf, his face livid. "He is not going to die. He will *not* do that to me." He spun toward Sini. "You, come with me. You will heal that sorry excuse for a dwarf before we have a nightmare on our hands. Get the horses."

Ragnoor huffed. "You can't take horses into—"

"Get us some food." Douglon snapped at him "We have hours of riding before we reach those miserable royal quarters."

Douglon's expression sent Ragnoor rushing to nearby shelves.

Douglon snapped at everyone to get their horses. And Alaric nodded. "Let's hurry. The world isn't ready for Douglon to become High Dwarf."

"I am not becoming High Dwarf!" Douglon yelled from the stable.

* * *

Douglon led them at as fast of a trot as the tunnel would allow. Even with mosslight lanterns hanging around their horses' necks, the way forward was barely visible. The tunnels were smooth dwarven passages though, and the horses moved quickly, the echo of their hoofbeats on the stone floor almost deafening.

Sini rode behind Douglon, who kept up a constant stream of muttered curses and threats directed at the High Dwarf, the surgeon, and anyone else he could think of.

Her eyes strained into the darkness, growing gritty with exhaustion. Alaric called for Douglon to slow, and the dwarf snapped back that they were welcome to fall behind if they thought they could navigate the tunnels on their own.

It must have been long past midnight when the first hanging lantern came into view and they trotted out into a wider, taller tunnel. Several dwarfs stared in shock at the six horses running into the light.

Douglon hurried on, careening around corners, scattering groups of dwarves, until he raced into a huge open cavern. Dozens of tunnels of all sizes opened out of it, and the ceiling stretched higher than Sini could see. Hundreds of lit windows around the walls looked like shopfronts on a city square. Small stone buildings were clumped together, encroaching into the cave from all sides and creating winding narrow alleys.

Douglon rode diagonally across the huge cave, the hoofbeats echoing more quietly and more chaotically off the distant walls. Dwarves scrambled out of his way. He galloped down a wide, straight avenue between larger stone houses until he reached a bright tunnel burrowing into the wall of the cavern. He swung out of his saddle and called for Sini to hurry.

She climbed down on aching legs, unsteady after the long ride. She leaned against her horse until Douglon shouted for her.

The tunnel was bright with a mosslight much more yellow that what they'd been using. Sini squinted into it and followed Douglon's angry voice. The floor and walls of the tunnel were smooth, showing a perfect reflection of the hallway. Sini's short hair was wild and disheveled, her face tired. Douglon stormed ahead.

Huge wooden doors lined the tunnel. Guards at one near the end bowed at the sight of Douglon before pushing open the door. Douglon glowered at them and entered. "That one is with me." He gestured back at her. "And a pack of other humans. Let them all in."

The dwarf guards at the door were big for dwarves, but no taller than Sini. They watched her with stern, disapproving glares, but let her pass. The chamber beyond was enormous and opulent. Columns of black rock rose along the wall, interspersed with huge, richly-colored tapestries. The stone floor was inlaid with a pattern of stars in grey and white. A carved stone bath large enough for ten dwarves sat along the far wall, and jutting out into the middle of the room was a four-poster bed, each post a stone column wider than Sini's body, carved with fantastic creatures and inset with gems. Along the wall across from the bed a real fireplace, wide enough for a bonfire, held actual flames—the first Sini had seen since they entered the tunnels. Guards and servants hovered along the walls.

A putrid stench filled the room. In the middle of the huge bed, under a pile of covers, was a dwarf with a grey face and a withered expression.

"Horgoth!" Douglon bellowed, striding across the room. "What in the depths of the deepest pit have you done?"

The High Dwarf cracked an eye open and let out a groan. "Douglon, you good-for-nothing excuse for a dwarf. Where have you been? I've needed you for ages, but you're never here. You're always off with humans. And elves." His breath caught in his throat with a jagged noise and he grimaced in pain.

"It smells like a rubbish heap went rancid in here," Douglon said. "Someone get new linens."

A servant hurried from the room.

Horgoth reached out and clutched Douglon's arm. "They tried to take my leg, cousin." He laughed a gurgling, horrible noise. "But I wouldn't let them. No surgeon's gonna hack me into bits."

Douglon lifted the edge of the cover and threw his hand over his nose. Sini caught a glimpse of the High Dwarf's leg. The skin was purplish, eaten away in huge red, oozing chunks. The foot was almost black, and the wave of foul stench that rolled out made her gag.

Douglon dropped the blanket and Horgoth let out a hiss of pain. His breathing was ragged and shallow.

"You fool," Douglon said. "Why didn't you let them take it? If I'd been here, I'd have held you down and chopped it off myself."

"I'd have had you executed, you ungrateful clod," Horgoth yelled, a wild edge to his voice.

"Executing me would've been better than you dying without an heir!"

"You always did hate me." Horgoth closed his eyes and turned his face away. "The idiot surgeon says it's bad, but I threw him in the dungeon. Tried to kill me, he did. Until I'm back on my feet, you will stay here and be useful."

"You fool," Douglon said more quietly. "It'll take a miracle to get you back on even one foot. Lucky for you, I brought a miracle worker."

Horgoth squinted at Sini. "Is that a human? Get her out of here!"

The guards stepped forward, but at a glare from Douglon, paused. "This is Sini. She's a Keeper and a healer. And she's going to heal you. If you complain about her again, or say anything unkind, I will muzzle you until she's done."

Horgoth glared at Douglon but said nothing more.

Douglon motioned Sini closer. "What do you need?"

Sini kept her hand over her face to ward off the smell. There was no sunlight here. Nothing living at all except the dwarves and the other humans who were standing by the door. There wasn't nearly enough energy here to heal him. "How big of a fire can you build?"

"In that ridiculous thing? As big as you need. Stupid extravagance. Took six years to carve the chimney all the way up to—"

"Then build a fire," Sini cut him off. "As big as you can." She cast out toward the High Dwarf. The *vitalle* in his body moved sluggishly. His entire leg and whole sections of his gut were dark and lifeless. Maybe even the fire wouldn't be enough.

Douglon shouted commands and the fire was stoked. Sini went to the other side of the bed, pulled some energy from the fire and began to feed it into Horgoth's body. Unlike sunfire, the *vitalle* from the fire was thin. It burned as it flowed into her hand, and burned as it went out into the

High Dwarf. She couldn't find the edges of the dying flesh at first, and she searched around, lost, before she realized there was nothing to find. His body wasn't fighting. Stagnant energy hovered near his chest and his head. The rest of his body was wasting away.

She funneled more *vitalle* into his chest, burning through her palm, pushing at the edges of the living parts, spreading it into the damaged flesh. His body didn't grab at the energy the way it should, and the excess *vitalle* just faded away.

The fire blazed higher and Sini drew in more energy from the flames, grimacing against the pain in her hands and wishing for the painless power of the sunfire. She picked a spot near Horgoth's gut to funnel it into. The energy along the edges of the dark spot flared a bit and attacked the dying flesh but made no progress. She grabbed more energy, testing different places, pushing against the coolness at the base of his lungs, at the top of his leg, deep into his gut.

Horgoth thrashed his head, his breathing ragged.

Nothing worked. There was no wound to heal here. Or if there was, the flesh around it was so weak it wasn't trying. His leg was dead and dark. The death had crept up through his blood, spreading everywhere else. Anything that should have been healing was decaying instead.

She pulled her hand off him and glanced up at Douglon. "There's nothing I can do."

Douglon's face hardened. "Heal him."

"This isn't healing," she said quietly. "His body isn't just damaged. Huge parts of it are dead. His leg, his gut." Douglon shook his head, but she continued. "I can't bring them back to life."

Horgoth's eyes were closed, and he made no indication he'd heard. Douglon sank to his knees next to the bed and dropped his head into his hands.

He made no sound for a long moment. "How long?" he asked in a muffled voice.

Sini cast out again. "I don't know." Leaning against the bedpost, she set her hand on Horgoth's good foot over the blankets and funneled in *vitalle* again.

Alaric crossed the room to the bed and Sini felt the ripple as he cast out toward the High Dwarf. "It's no use, Sini. He needed help a week ago. It's too late."

Douglon heaved a sigh and looked toward the soldier. "Go find Patlon."

"He's not here, m'lord."

"Do not call me that, Haldar."

The guard shifted, but gave a reluctant nod. "Patlon left to find you at the Elder Grove several hours ago."

Douglon closed his eyes. When he opened them, they were resigned. "Well, track him down. And find all these humans rooms with beds long enough for their ridiculous legs."

———•———

The dwarven beds were surprisingly comfortable. Being only slightly taller than dwarf height, no one had any trouble finding Sini a bed near the royal apartments, and she collapsed into the thick wool mattress the moment she was left alone.

A distant commotion woke her. Her room was lit with the same mosslight as before, and it was impossible to tell how long she'd slept. From the fogginess in her head, it wasn't long.

Pest leaned against the wall outside her door.

Sini cast a dramatically suspicious look down the hallway and whispered, "Am I in danger from the dwarves?"

A dwarf came down the hall, giving both humans a disapproving look. Pest met it with his own flat stare.

Sini sighed, "Maybe I am. The dwarves aren't terribly welcoming, are they?" The commotion she'd heard came from a different direction than Horgoth's bedchamber.

"The throne room," Pest said. "The other Keepers are there."

"I suppose we should join them." She spun her ring and peered down the tunnel they stood in. It was quiet, but it emptied out into a busier one not too far away.

"Would you like the quick route, or the quiet route?" Pest asked.

"Quiet," she answered immediately.

He nodded approvingly. "Follow me." Turning the opposite direction, he led her into a maze of tunnels.

"How do you know where you're going?" she asked after the fourth turn. "Have you been to Duncave before?"

"No. Roan took first watch at your door, and I explored." He shot her a grin.

"Do you enjoy skulking in dark hallways?"

"Very much."

Sini laughed. "It's nice to know you have pleasures beyond knifing."

"If we're lucky, we'll get to do both at the same time."

"Yes," she answered, "that sounds lovely."

After far more turns than she could possibly have retraced, they turned into a wide hall. At the end of it, heavy wooden doors braced with iron bands were flung open to an enormous cavern. At least the impression of the room was enormous. The far walls and ceiling were lost in darkness. To the left, a huge stone mantle stood with a real fire burning in it. But the fire was set far back in the gaping opening and only cast light directly out onto a long, low table. The floor was black stone, and the brightness of the flames somehow sank into it instead of brightening it. Dozens of mosslight lanterns were lit, but the room remained locked in shadows.

Will, Alaric, and Roan stood at the end of the table next to Douglon. Sini joined them and Pest positioned himself in the shadows alongside the fireplace, disappearing completely aside from the glints from his knife handles.

"...the absolute worst thing that could happen to either me or the dwarves." Douglon was saying. He glanced at the tall chair at the end of the table, then sank into one of the smaller ones along the side. "I have to abdicate."

Will and Alaric exchanged glances. "Who's next in line?" Alaric asked.

"My imbecile cousin Tolroth. He hates everyone who isn't a dwarf." He glanced at Alaric. "He stopped speaking to me after I traveled with you. And when I decided to stay with Rass he tried to have me banished for consorting with and abetting a dangerous enemy."

"He's clearly never met Rass," Will said.

"The dwarves need to wake up and realize they're a part of the world. If Tolroth has the crown they'll just hide deeper in these caves and never even pop their heads out." Douglon leaned on the table and dropped his head into his hands. "But I can't stay here. I can't abandon Rass."

"Aside from his isolationist ideals," Alaric asked, "Would Tolroth make a good high dwarf?"

"No," Douglon answered emphatically, looking up. "He's selfish and childish and spoiled. He picks fights with anyone he thinks has insulted him. He has never once seen any situation from any point of view besides his own."

"Then you can't abdicate to him," Will said.

"Why do you think I haven't already? He's the one dwarf in Duncave worse for this position than me!"

"I don't think you'd make a bad high dwarf," Sini said, sitting down across from him. "Over the last four years the Keepers have made me read about a lot of rulers." Douglon looked unimpressed. "A lot. Like every ruler of Queensland, every ruler of Coastal Baylon or Napon that we know of, the three elvish rulers we know. I studied everything we have about High Dwarves Bellrott the Grim,"—Douglon's eyebrow rose—"Frita Mossflinger, and Lugg Hammerston the Younger." There had been at least one more dwarf she'd read about, but she couldn't quite remember her name. Besides, Will always said groups of three sounded more dramatic. "You have everything a good ruler should. You're levelheaded. You've traveled widely and learned to understand people different than yourself. You're loyal."

"We all know you'll delegate tasks and not take on too much yourself," Will pointed out.

Douglon glared at him.

"And you've lost someone," Alaric added, "which changes a person." He studied Douglon for a moment. "You could be the best thing that's happened to Duncave in a long time."

The dwarf shook his head slowly. "It'll destroy everything I love. I know it will."

"You're not your uncle," Alaric said. "Just because he couldn't handle the throne doesn't mean you can't."

"And Rass? What happens to her?"

No one answered.

"The dwarves need a leader now, Douglon," Will said. "It's you, or you put Tolroth on the throne. No one will blame you for stepping away from something you've never wanted. If you're abdicating, then Queensland will get no help from the dwarves and we'll be on our way, and you can go back to the Greenwood."

Douglon sank back in his chair. Footsteps rang out near the door and the dwarf sighed. "I can't let Tolroth take the throne. I love my people more than that." He looked up at Alaric. "For now, at least until this crisis is done, I'll take the crown." He glared at them all as though it were their fault. "But I can't promise I'll do it forever."

"You might want to keep that feeling to yourself," Will said quietly as a handful of dwarves entered the room. "That's not the sort of sentiment that breeds loyalty."

"They probably already know," Douglon said miserably.

One of the dwarves called out a greeting to Sini and she recognized Douglon's cousin, Patlon, who'd helped rescue her from the Sweep.

"You got here quickly." She stood to greet him. "Unless I slept longer than it feels like."

"It's a little after dawn," Patlon answered. "I traveled a different way than you, but reached Ragnoor not long after you had, and followed you back here." He frowned. "You got taller, lass. You were shorter than me a few years ago."

She was barely taller than him now, but she grinned. "This is the only place on earth I'm tall. It feels odd."

"I heard the elves are all wee little things now," Patlon said.

"True. I suppose I'm tall there too." The dwarf looked exactly the same as he had four years ago. His beard, so dark it was almost black, hung over his broad chest. He wore leather armor nicked and worn from years of use. Sini leaned forward and gave him a hug. He stiffened before patting her back awkwardly. She released him with a grin. "You look well."

Patlon shrugged. "I was better before I was turned into Douglon's advisor."

The rest of the dwarves started laying their axes along the wall near the door.

"Don't bother with that," Douglon waved at the weapons. "I'm not Horgoth. I'm not paranoid you're all trying to kill me. In fact, I'd take it as a kindness if one of you would axe me before I have to sit on that wretched throne." He flicked his hand toward the darkness of the room.

Far across the cavern a vague grey shape rose from the floor like some huge, rough pillar of silver that thinned up to the right, reaching toward the unseen ceiling. Sini peered through the darkness at it, but she couldn't make much out except the occasional glitter from the torchlight.

"Everybody sit, and let's get this over with," Douglon said.

"How's Horgoth?" Sini asked Will quietly, sitting down in the chair next to him.

"Alive, barely. Douglon retrieved the surgeon from the dungeon. He says it'll be any time now."

"Stop dawdling in the shadows," Douglon snipped at the newcomers. "We have things to do. Most of you know Keeper Alaric from his earlier visits. Listen to him." Douglon dropped into a tall-backed chair at the end of the table and waved impatiently for Alaric to speak.

Alaric stood and told the dwarves about Lukas and the current threats to Queensland.

"As you can see," Alaric concluded, "there are problems all along our southern border, the gold trade with Gulfind looks to be permanently cut off, and the towns along our western border are being controlled by Lukas and primed for revolt." He paused. "No one's sure how much time we have, but it's clear we have a good deal of trouble coming."

"Oh," said a voice from the door, "you have a lot more trouble than you know."

TWENTY-THREE

ini turned with everyone else to see a man hobbling into the room, leaning heavily on a cane. The firelight glinted red off his beard.

"Killien!" Will jumped up and strode across the floor to him.

Sini's stomach tightened and she almost stood before she caught herself, a mixture of happiness and nerves swirling inside her. Killien limped forward a step and she fought the compulsion to help him. The man wasn't her master any longer and she was under no obligation to him. Clenching her hand on her lap, she stayed seated. The act felt defiant.

Killien's face was so familiar it made her chest burn with emotions she could not name. But he wasn't exactly the same. His normally neat beard, which had always been accented with a few thin braids, was wild.

He embraced Will with enthusiasm and a grunt of pain before coming over to the table. Killien caught sight of her and his smile faltered. "Hello, Sini," he said cautiously.

His face was thin, and sharp lines of worry were creased into his brows. But more than that, there was a haunted, defeated look in his eyes.

Her rebellious feelings evaporated. There was nothing to rebel against here. This man had no say over her. She was free of him, and free of everything about that life. Despite a pang of pity at his appearance, she couldn't help smiling at the thought. "Hello, Killien."

Before he could answer, Douglon broke in. "You can catch up later. Who let you into Duncave, Killien?"

"I did," Patlon said. "He's been recovering here for the better part of a week. And you need to hear what he has to say."

Will sat back down next to Sini. Killien on his far side.

"Killien?" Roan asked, looking coldly across the table. "The Torch of the Morrow clan?"

"Sorry." Will said. "This is Killien, Torch of the Morrow. He and I have been in correspondence since my time on the Sweep. Yes, he is a Roven, but he is trusted by the Keepers."

Killien cleared his throat. "It's not only in Queensland that Lukas has been busy. Over the summer he reappeared on the Sweep. He's united the clans and gathered an army."

Sini stared at him. The Sweep? Lukas had been as far east as the moors of Gringonn, and as far west as the Sweep? Was there anywhere he hadn't been?

"Are you sure it was Lukas?" Will asked. "I can't imagine him walking onto the Sweep and telling everyone who he was."

"He didn't," Killien answered. "He flew over it on his dragon and landed next to the Sunn Torch. He seems to have developed a taste for the dramatic. Lukas managed to convince the Sunn Torch—or intimidate him—into supporting his cause."

"Conquering Queensland?"

"What else could unite the clans?" Killien asked. "Lukas also claims he has forces ready to attack Queensland from both Coastal Baylon and Napon."

Sini's stomach sank.

"Already?" Alaric asked.

"We've seen no sign of any troops," Roan agreed.

Killien shrugged. "Lukas was convincing enough that the whole Sweep has mobilized."

"Even the Morrow?" Will asked. "Surely your own clan won't follow Lukas."

Killien shifted. "The Morrow are no longer my clan. Somehow our correspondence was discovered, Will. Someone strategically shared parts of it to make it sound like I was a spy for Queensland. A few of my distant cousins incited a riot among my people. I barely escaped with my life."

"Is Lilit all right?" Sini asked. "And Sevien?"

"My wife and son are fine. We managed to escape to the mountain clans."

"To Sora?" Will asked sharply.

Killien nodded. "The Morrow have a new Torch, an upstart nephew of mine who must have been bought off by Lukas. He's groveled before all our enemies, letting them bleed him dry of money and herds, then offered every warrior in our clan to Lukas's great cause."

"Killien arrived here five days ago," Patlon said. "With Horgoth…unavailable, I took the liberty of sending some scouts south and they confirm that more and more Roven forces are funneling into a valley that leads to Gulfind. If they continue to come, a good-sized army will have gathered in the next fortnight."

"But Gulfind is blocked off," Roan said. "Our rangers say rockslides block every way into the country, even from the Sweep. There's no way an army could get through."

Will frowned. "Why would Lukas lead them into a dead end?"

"Maybe there's a way through we don't know about," Alaric said.

Patlon grunted. "I'll send more scouts today. We'll pinpoint where the army is and see where it's headed."

Alaric sat back. "If Lukas really has troops from Napon, Coastal Baylon, Gringonn, and the Sweep, Queensland will be overrun."

Sini's stomach fell at the words and the room was silent for a moment.

"You have the support of the dwarves," Douglon stated.

A murmur of dissent rippled down the table. Douglon fixed them all with a glare. "When Mallon came, we hid in our holes and let the humans and elves fight. This time we will not burrow in the dark like cowards. The dwarves will stick their noses out those holes and join the rest of the world.

"I've met this newest threat, Lukas. Skinny human. Limps. Likes to kill people. We're not going to sit by and let him."

"He can't get to us," one of the dwarves protested. "He's no concern of ours."

"He has a dragon," Alaric pointed out.

"Even a dragon can't reach us in here."

"He doesn't have to reach us," Douglon said. "All he has to do is raze our planting valleys and massacre our herds. And then what will we eat? Rocks? It's time that the dwarves stopped pretending they aren't part of this world."

"Horgoth still lives," another dwarf objected. "Our orders come from him."

Douglon leveled him with a flinty gaze. "As soon as he regains consciousness, he can countermand everything I'm saying. Until then, unless you can produce someone else to stand in his place—and I would kiss you if you could—I'll be making the decisions."

Sini glanced down the table. Though there were a good number of scowls, no one objected.

Douglon pointed at Roan. "You speak for Queen Saren?"

Roan straightened and nodded.

"Good. Let's set up daily runners between Duncave and Queenstown. There is a ridiculously small town halfway there called something stupid like Tall Mountain." He looked at the humans expectantly.

"High Peak?" Sini offered. That town was so small it only showed on the most detailed maps of the area.

Alaric nodded. "High Peak is about halfway."

"High Peak, Tall Mountain, same thing. Stupid names. Why not just call it Wet Water, or Green Tree?

Sini let out a snort. At Douglon's irritated look she pointed at Roan. "His father is the Duke of Greentree."

Douglon sighed. "Humans." He turned his attention back to Roan. "If you will supply human messengers from Queenstown to High Peak, the dwarves will send one of our own from here to the town. I've stayed there often enough that they're used to dwarves."

Douglon turned back to Patlon. "Use the Moorwen boys as runners. They're so proud of winning the tunnel sprints every year, let them put those legs to more use than chasing the Rochkellun girls."

Patlon raised an eyebrow. "That sounded almost kingly."

Douglon gave him a dangerous look then turned to face a female dwarf wearing an ornate leather breastplate. "Torgon, how many troops do we have ready?"

"Fifteen hundred," she said. "A thousand more could be ready within a month."

"Make it two thousand more. You have two weeks."

Torgon's eyes narrowed slightly, but she nodded.

Patlon leaned closer to Douglon. "You would sound more official if you were sitting on the throne."

Douglon's brow dropped and he turned toward his cousin. "I'd rather have my beard chopped off. But as soon as you're in charge, feel free to use it."

"Me?"

A wolfish grin peeked through Douglon's beard. "I'm putting you in charge in my place. You, Torgon, and—is Nurthrum around?"

"What do you mean in your place?" Patlon demanded.

Douglon ignored him and waited for an answer.

"Northrum's here," Torgon said. "But he's been retired since returning from the Queen's court a year ago."

"Well, rouse the greybeard out of retirement. He's more hale than the rest of us put together. And smarter. He also knows the humans well enough to not make blockheaded mistakes.

"The three of you will be in charge. Get the troops ready to fight. There's a storm brewing, and we'll feel it even here under the mountains. The humans need more fighters, and the elves are…" Douglon blew out a long breath. "The elves aren't much use at the moment."

The room fidgeted, the dwarves casting looks between one another.

"I know what you all think of me," Douglon said. "Trust me when I say that I am the person here who most fervently wishes I was not"—he grimaced—"the next High Dwarf. But you who stay locked up in these tunnels don't see the world for what it is. It's time we stepped out and made ourselves useful. At the very least there's a dragon coming. I can tell you from experience that the Keepers—the best the humans have to offer—are useless against one. Any hope the elves had of beating it died four years ago." Douglon's voice didn't waver, but Sini thought something in him did. "We do not deserve the sacrifice the elves made for the world. Or the sacrifice the humans made trying to protect it. But we bloody well will try to earn some of that now. It's time the world remembered what the axe blades of the dwarves can do."

The room stirred with nods and a low rumble of agreement.

"Ah, not to distract from that rousing speech, cousin," Patlon said, "but what exactly are you going to be doing while we ready the dwarves?"

"I'm going with the Keepers."

The rest of the room sat in silence for a moment before a roar of dissent rang out.

Patlon raised his hand for silence. "That's not how being High Dwarf works, cousin."

Douglon stared at his cousin for a long moment before turning back to the room. "Who here thinks I would run things better than Nurthrum, Patlon, and Torgon working together?"

No one spoke.

"You can't leave," Patlon said flatly.

Douglon leveled a gaze at him. "I am breaths away from being High Dwarf. Who's going to stop me?"

Patlon shifted and glanced at the others. "Your conscience?"

"My conscience is what's driving all this. You are more than capable of taking care of things yourselves." Douglon stroked his fingers through his long copper beard. When he spoke again, his voice was resigned. "None of you are any more pleased than I am that I'm about to be High Dwarf. Let it be known there's a standing reward of a dozen diamonds from the royal vault for anyone who can discover another contender for the throne. I'll double it if they have a few brains to knock together in their thick skull and have a long, healthy line of children. Until one is found, we all have things to do.

"I'll stay for a few days until…to see what happens with Horgoth. But those runners better get to Queenstown with news of this entire mess before I do."

The dwarves stood and headed out of the throne room with a low hum of conversation. Some of them left immediately, some of them congregated into knots. Alaric, Douglon, and Patlon stayed at the end of a table, talking over a map. Will and Killien fell to talking quietly beside Sini.

She leaned her elbows on the table and dropped her head into her hands.

Lukas had gone back to the Sweep and sought an alliance with the people he'd despised. Her eyes felt gritty from the little sleep she'd gotten. How could he have come to align himself with everything she would stand against? The last hope that she knew him crumbled away. Whoever Lukas had become, it wasn't someone she recognized.

"You've seen Sora?" Will interrupted her thoughts. She glanced over to find the Keeper looking hesitantly at Killien.

Killien nodded. "You'd better go find her soon. She'll kill both of us for not telling her you're here."

Will started. "She's here?"

Killien laughed. "Of course she's here. Do you think I could find Duncave on my own? She's been pining for you non-stop. It's made her even less fun than usual."

"I have not been pining over anyone," Sora said from behind them.

Will spun around.

Sini turned to see the ranger. "Sora!" Like Killien, Sora looked tired, and one of her hands was bandaged.

Despite Sora's words, a smile creased her face and after a heartbeat of stunned silence, Will shoved himself up from the table and wrapped his arms around her.

She returned the hug and buried her face in Will's shoulder.

"I thought you'd…" Will said, still holding her tightly. "I was afraid…I didn't…"

Sora pulled a little away from him so she could see his face, and touched the braids in his beard. "I remember a more eloquent man."

Will laughed and stepped back. He took her bandaged hand gently. "Are you all right?"

"She's fine," Killien interrupted. "I'm the one with the terrible leg wound."

"You twisted your ankle," Sora said, not taking her eyes off Will. "The only terrible thing is your constant whining about it."

Killien grinned at them. "I still don't really understand you two."

"I do," Sini said, standing up.

Sora took her hand back from Will and gave Sini a hug. "I heard a female human was here trying to heal Horgoth," Sora said. "I was hoping it was you."

Sini set her hand on Sora's bandage and cast out. There was a deep cut along the back of her hand. Sini pulled some energy from the fire and funneled it into the wound, drawing it together. The *vitalle* tingled along her fingers, but it didn't take much.

Sora stretched her hand and raised an eyebrow. "You've gotten better."

"It's too bad Horgoth's problem isn't a cut," Sini said quietly.

"So," Will interrupted, taking Sora's hand back. "You were pining for me?"

Sora raised an eyebrow. "No."

It was such a familiar expression and tone that Sini grinned. "Will's been pining for you."

"And moping and fretting," Alaric added. "It's nice to see you Sora."

She gave him a nod.

"They have no idea what they're talking about," Will said. "How long are you here? Why are you here?"

"I'm finished with my clan," she answered. "It took a lot longer than I thought. When the old holy woman died, there was no one to take her place. Her replacement was only fourteen, and I just ended up drawn into doing…everything."

"That's what happens," Douglon grumbled. "It's dangerous to even look at the throne. There are forces waiting to drag you into it."

Will ignored him. "But how did you and Killien get here?"

"I found them," Patlon said. "It had been so long since either Sora or Killien had sent any messages that when Horgoth broke his leg a fortnight ago, it seemed like a good reason to make myself scarce." He sighed. "I thought I'd just be avoiding some work, I didn't realize I'd be missing his last days."

"I was chased out of the Morrow," Killien said, "And they followed me to Sora's clan. We hid my wife and son there, and Sora and I drew away the Roven who were after me."

Patlon grinned. "When I found them, they were surrounded by rangers. Got a good scuffle out of it and brought them into Duncave."

Douglon called Patlon and Alaric's attention back to his map. Will and Sora drew away slightly from the others.

Still at the table, Killien cleared his throat. "It looks like your time with the Keepers has treated you well, Sini." The smile he gave her was a little unsure.

"It has," she answered, sitting back down.

He turned his attention back to his hands, clasped on the table. "You don't dress in the black robe?"

"Somewhere along the line I developed an aversion to grey"—Killien winced—"that spills over into black." Unwilling for the topic of her slavery to sour the conversation, she attempted a smile. "I'm working on it."

Killien didn't smile back. He ran his fingers along the grain of the table. "This past year has taught me a lot, Sini. For the first time in my life, I have no power at all." He ran a short, broken fingernail along the wood. "I really thought when I was Torch that I was a good leader. That I cared for and protected the people whose lives were in my hands. But I only cared for them in as much as they served my purpose. I don't think I really saw them."

He twitched as though he would look at her, but his gaze got no further than the table in front of her. "It seemed to me that if I treated you well, especially knowing where you came from, that it would be enough to cover the fact that I'd taken your whole life." He risked a look at her face. "I know it wasn't enough."

She looked at the man who had once controlled every aspect of her life. The one who had taken her from her family and raised her among the Roven. The one who'd kept her from becoming a Keeper for years. She wanted to feel angry with him, but there was something too broken in him for her anger to settle on.

"I don't know if I can forgive the Torch who forced me into slavery," she said honestly. Killien dropped his gaze and nodded. "But I'm just now realizing that I'm no longer the girl who was a slave. And if you are no longer a Torch, perhaps we can begin there while our pasts sort themselves out."

Killien looked up at her hopefully.

She motioned to his ankle. "I'd help you if magic worked on you."

He moved his ankle gingerly, "Sora's right, it's just a sprain."

She paused before her next question. "Did you see Lukas on the Sweep?"

Killien shook his head. "He didn't come to the Morrow. At least not while I was there. I heard he'd visited the Sunn and the Boan. I honestly don't know what I would have done if he'd come to us."

"If he was on his dragon, probably nothing," Sini pointed out.

Killien groaned. "I still can't believe Lukas has that creature. And that he's controlled it for four years. The more I learn about him, the more I think I didn't really…know him."

Sini shook her head. "I feel like I've misjudged him at every turn. Maybe neither of us actually knew him."

A heavy, bitter regret settled on her at the thought, and the darkness of the throne room felt suddenly oppressive. In effort to shift the mood, she said, "Tell me of Sevien. He must be so big."

Killien launched into a long, glowing account of his son and Sini listened, letting her more leaden thoughts fall to the wayside.

A dwarf ran into the throne room, bowing to Douglon. "The High Dwarf's condition worsens, my lord. The surgeon bids you come quickly."

Douglon's shoulders slumped. He turned back to Alaric and waved a hand at the map. "We've discussed as much as we can now, anyway. Make yourselves comfortable. I'll make sure everyone treats you better than they want to treat humans. We'll leave after Horgoth…"

Without finishing, he followed the messenger out of the throne room.

Will and Sora had disappeared, and Killien joined Roan and Alaric at the map. Pest rejoined Sini from the side of the fireplace and offered to take her back to her room.

Grateful for the chance to escape to somewhere quiet, she agreed. "The quickest way this time, please."

TWENTY-FOUR

Horgoth did not die quickly. Though the surgeon gave omens of death nearly every hour, the High Dwarf lingered. The surgeon gave him herbs to dull the pain, and he stayed blissfully unaware of his surroundings and how slowly the infection was killing him.

Douglon swung back and forth between despondency and agitation. To avoid a constant stream of dwarven nobility seeking him out, he took the humans on a tour deep into Duncave. Patlon, despite his disapproval of Douglon's responsibility-shirking, came along as well. The first evening they visited a mining cave where dozens of dwarves were tinking on walls with tiny hammers. Casks full of glittering blue gems lined the walls. Pest, who'd been shadowing Sini, apparently decided the cave was safe enough for him to lurk near the casks.

Still tired from the long ride the night before, Sini sank down onto a rough bench along one wall.

"What have you done to warrant so much watching?" Sora asked, sitting beside her and watching Pest. "This is the first I've seen you without one of your two bodyguards."

"I wish I knew. They've been commanded to guard me."

"Just you?"

"So it would seem."

Sora studied Pest and Roan for a moment. "Ordered by who?"

"The queen, I assume."

Sora gave a noncommittal grunt. "I'm not sure I trust Pest."

Sini watched the man lingering by the gems. "Why not? Aside from the fact that I'm pretty sure he's stealing from the dwarves right now."

"He skulks."

Sini laughed. "You skulk, and I know many people who trust you, including one Keeper who's quite in love with you."

A grin slipped out of the edge of Sora's mouth. "Will's too nice. He trusts everybody. And I don't skulk, I track."

"There's a difference?"

The ranger nodded and leaned against the wall, stretching out her legs, seemingly perfectly at ease. But her gaze shifted to Roan.

"Do you trust Roan?" Sini asked.

She shrugged. "I wonder if your soldier there took it upon himself to decide you needed guarding."

"He's not my soldier," Sini objected "and why would he?"

"Because he admires you."

Sini felt a slight flush at her words. "He does not!"

"He definitely does. I just can't decide if he's inappropriate about it. He's a formal sort of fellow."

Sini laughed. "Yes. He does nothing inappropriate. Ever. He takes his position and his engagement to the future queen seriously. If he feels anything toward me that is even positive, this tedious guarding began long before that."

Howls of laughter came from across the cavern where Will was regaling three dwarves with some story. Sini could see a light mist of blue green air around him as he filled his words with enthusiasm. Sora's face softened.

She glanced back at Sini. "Just be careful with yourself."

"Not all of us fall in love with someone we're not supposed to."

Sora's smile turned self-conscious. "It's easier than you think."

With no change in Horgoth's condition, the next afternoon Douglon led them to an enormous cavern that was so bright he handed out thin blindfolds before they reached it. Sunlight snuck in through small holes in the roof and an assortment of metal disks reflected the light down into the garden. Through the gauzy blindfold Sini could see bright green plants growing in endless rows. Dwarves were sprinkled throughout the room, tending them.

"This is our greenhouse," Douglon explained. "We grow wheat out on the mountainsides, but in here it never gets too hot or too cold, so we have fruit trees and spices. The sunlight comes down chutes from the surface. Every fall we burn the old crops and let the soil lie. Every spring we shovel new dirt down the chutes."

Until she stepped into the frail sunlight, Sini hadn't realized how deeply she'd missed the sunfire. It rested gently on her skin, greeting her like an old friend. She worked the blindfold off and blinked into the brightness. Tentatively she drew some sunfire in. She braced herself for the longing for more to return, but she felt nothing beyond a comforting warmth.

"You have sheep herds too, right?" Roan asked. "Is there a cave somewhere housing them?"

Douglon laughed. "They eat too much. We keep them in valleys too isolated for humans to reach."

Sini breathed in the sunfire and felt something inside her loosen. The light was still the same as it had always been. When Douglon led them back into the dark caves, she followed reluctantly.

Duncave was intriguing, but the shadow of Horgoth's health hung over them whenever they were in the main city. There was a tavern not far from their rooms, and Sini found herself there more often than not with whoever else was unoccupied.

Pest could navigate the caves well and when he was on guard duty, she had him lead her back to the sun cave just so she could sit in the sunlight and read. Slowly, bit by bit, she found comfort again in the light, and the fear that had eaten at her since feeding the elves faded.

On the third day Alaric and Douglon were tied up in council meetings. Roan and Sini went to lunch at a tavern not far from their rooms where their group ate most of their meals. They found themselves alone until Douglon stumped in and sat down heavily on the bench beside Roan.

A dwarf brought Douglon a large tankard of ale. He took a deep drink and dropped his head into his hands. "What am I going to tell Rass? She can't come here with me. There's no grass. She'll grow weak within a couple days in the tunnels."

Sini searched for something comforting to say.

"In my study of history, I have noticed," Roan continued, "when a king chooses his advisors wisely and lets them do their jobs with little interference, the country prospers."

Douglon looked up at Roan. "You're saying I'm superfluous?"

Roan laughed. "I'm saying that a government runs a country, not merely a king. Or a high dwarf." Roan paused. "Three generations ago, our king Tunnred had a wife with fragile health. They had built their home in one of the southernmost valleys of Greentree to take advantage of the warmth. When he became king, she couldn't follow him to the chilly winters of Queenstown, and as he was unwilling to be absent from her constantly, he spent one month out of three in Greentree."

Douglon's bushy eyebrow rose. "And did Queensland prosper?"

"We enjoyed a prolonged season of peace and growth because Tunnred had good people running the country."

A grin split Douglon's beard. "One out of three months, huh? Might need to make it one out of two, but that has possibilities." He considered Roan. "Is Queen Saren going to keep you as ambassador once you're tethered to the future queen?"

"I hope so." Roan looked around the tavern. "Trips to Duncave would be vastly preferable to staying at court all the time. But my decisions seem to be made by higher powers."

"You'd think once you became the higher power you'd actually have freedom." Douglon peered into his tankard. "But what you lose is the choice of how to spend your day, and who to spend it with."

Roan let out a long sigh. "I've noticed."

Douglon glanced at Sini. "Keep your head down, and hope the next Keeper they discover is so spectacular everyone forgets who you are."

"After listening to you two moan," Sini said, "I certainly will do my best."

Douglon was summoned to something official sounding, and Roan escorted Sini back to her room before joining him.

"Are you really as upset about your position as you sound?" she asked him.

Roan blew out a long breath. "I was handling it all better before this trip. I'd almost forgotten how much I loved traveling, having concrete goals and destinations. Seeing new places." He rubbed the back of his neck and gave Sini a troubled glance. "It's going to be hard to go back to court."

A bell rang out, echoing down the hallway, signifying the beginning of a council, and Roan smiled a little. "The councils here are far more interesting. The dwarves mostly shout over each other and occasionally bang their axe handles on the floor. And Douglon cuts off anyone who gets too pompous. You want to come?"

"Not at all."

He laughed. "Then I'll send Pest when I find him."

In her own quiet room she lay down, letting her mind shift over the last few days. She thought of Horgoth's failing body, how odd it was to see Killien, how happy Will and Sora seemed. But her mind kept shifting back to Lukas. How had he gathered such an army?

Annoyed with the worry of it all, she pulled Chesavia's journal out of her pack to distract herself. She had barely read any of it.

She lay in bed, her eyes skimming over pages of writing and sketches of people or scenes, only paying the barest attention to any of it.

Until her attention caught on a word.

Naj.

Sini blinked.

Naj? Svard Naj was the sword Lukas had stolen from Killien.

She sat up.

The Wellstone had been right to connect Chesavia to the sword.

She flipped quickly back to the beginning of the entry.

4th day, Wolf Moon, 8th year of King Lenus

I found Naj!
I've tracked his Monnton tribe across the moors.

Below the words was a sketch of low hills covered with coarse, stunted plants. The barren place where Chesavia had stood in the Wellstone was the moors of Gringonn. There was a connection between Lukas and the moors.

Sini turned the page so quickly she tore a small rip in the edge.

I've never seen such a desolate place. The hills go on forever in a blue-green nothing. The plants are scrubby and short, they scuff at my legs as I walk, making each step a battle. There are no paths to follow, so I kick more plants out of my way and aim toward the smoke on the horizon.

The vastness of it is daunting. But it is better than court.

I wonder, now that I have found Chief Naj, will I find his sword?

Naj was a man? Killien had assumed it was the name of the sword.

6th day, Wolf Moon, 8th year of King Lenus
I've met him.

It took some work to keep the guards from killing me, and I feel bad about the one who wouldn't listen. He'll recover quickly, I'm sure.

Naj is…not what I expected. He is almost civilized. When I was finally taken to him, he was suspicious, but treated me well. I am now a personal guest in his tasarr. The tasari of the others in the tribe are small, drab, serviceable tents, but his is extravagant. It has six rooms. The ground has been cleared of scrub bushes and covered with thick animal hides. The incessant wind is blocked by the thick walls woven out of bright colors. It is almost comfortable.

Naj himself was raised in a wealthy shipping family along the coast. When I asked him how a merchant becomes a warlord on the moors, he merely answered, "Life does not let us choose our paths." I wish he had answered me honestly, instead.

He is smarter than I expected, and more educated. Yet he is entrenched in only this insignificant bit of the world, consumed by the goals of his small tribe.

9th day, Wolf Moon, 8th year of King Lenus
I have seen the swords!
Yes. <u>*Swords.*</u> *There are two of them, not one.*
To look at them, you'd never know they were valuable. They're so rough they'd look at home in a farmer's cottage.
But they are what I've been looking for, there is no doubt. When they are together, they glow—one blue, one smoky black. Naj couldn't see it, of course. But the power in the swords is unmistakable, even to him.
He found them in a shipwreck and claims they are blessed. Anyone who carries them into battle cannot be defeated.
I fear it is much worse than that.

Beneath the entry was a sketch of two swords, identical except for the runes. Svard Naj was unmistakably the sword that Lukas had stolen from Killien.

11th day, Wolf Moon, 8th year of King Lenus
Naj and I are quite comfortable now. So much so that I worry he's entertained thoughts of making me his twelfth wife. I doubt he'd force the matter, but it may be time to finish here. He's given me a silver ring shaped like a crescent moon. It's lovely.
He let me touch the swords.
I claimed an interest in the runes hammered into them. The hammering is as rough as the rest of the blades. The blue blade says Svard Naj, or sword of Naj, the shadowy one says Swift Death. The Monnton are experts at metalwork. Their other weaponry has intricate words and runes and pictures on them. Naj says these are rough because the metal was almost impossible to mark.
Now I know how the Monnton have gained so much power so quickly. The swords are much more than blessed. Or maybe much less. 'Blessed' is the wrong word.
Touching the handle of either sword does nothing. But the blades…
The blue one is filled with an energy that seeped into my hand when I touched it. It burned enough that I was reluctant to hold it longer, and I have little sense of what else the energy would have done. It did not feel wholesome.
The blade with the dark glow…that should be destroyed. I merely brushed my finger along it, and it drew vitalle *out as quickly as the blue blade had offered it. My finger grew cold to the second knuckle and hours later it still aches.*
Naj does not notice the effect of either. Perhaps it isn't noticeable to someone who can't move vitalle. *In battle, he says the blue blade does more*

damage than he can explain, and the black kills more quickly, although he says its power only comes rarely. It will kill a first opponent almost instantly, filling Naj with an exultant power, but then it is like a normal sword for a long spell, before it will kill quickly again.

My best guess is that the black blade draws out life, but only of one person before it needs to...rest. Swift Death indeed. I would guess it transfers that energy to the wielder and the blue blade, empowering both to fight.

These weapons trouble me. They were not made to be wielded by an ordinary person. In Naj's hands they wreak destruction in this small part of the world. But I dread how terrible they would be were they wielded by someone who understood them, who could use the power in them.

The idea unsettles me greatly.

Sini bit her lip. Unsettling was an understatement.

13th day, Wolf Moon, 8th year of King Lenus
I write in haste before I lose the light. The Monnton have mobilized for a battle. Another warlord was spotted to the south. Naj had become possessive of me, and I worried he would not let me go, so I left during the commotion, leaving him only a note. It felt cowardly, but I believe it might have been my last chance. While the man is almost civilized, he does have a feral streak. I think I will not risk a fire tonight.

I am still unsettled over the swords. The black more than the blue.

It is my consolation that there are almost no people here on the moors. It is probable that Naj's tribe will fall, like every other small war tribe here, and the swords will be lost. They are so plain compared to the rest of Naj's belongings that no looter would bother to pick them up.

At least that is my hope.

Chesavia's journal entries after that went back to her life at court, new entries coming only every few months to say that King Lenus was still difficult. Sini skipped ahead, looking for anything else.

She had almost given up when she caught sight of the word 'Naj' again. The entry was a full ten years later.

27th day, Blood Moon, 1st year of King Rushua
I am troubled.
I have just returned from the moors. I found the grave of Naj. He was killed by an arrow, his tribe wiped out or enslaved. There is nothing left of the Monnton.
Naj was buried under a stone cairn.
I left his grave alone until the sun was high in the sky. I had no desire to see those swords without access to sunlight. Under the stones, the rough twin blades lay crossed on his chest. None of his more valuable looking weapons were there. His enemy, who had fulfilled the tradition of burying their foe,

had probably thought leaving these swords was an insult.

But they were the reason I found him. Even beneath the earth it was easy to find their vitalle.

His grave saddened me more than I expected. He could have been more than a warlord. If only he hadn't been so focused on blood, he could have built something better here.

But perhaps that was not possible, as long as he had the swords.

I have heard the stories of his ruthlessness over the last ten years. They hold little resemblance to the man I met. Was it the swords that drove him to brutality? Or was he on that path on his own?

I do not think the swords should remain together and the Shield agrees. I will take the blue sword away, and bury the black one deep beneath the earth. Not under a cairn though. I will leave its grave unmarked.

The black sword lay on top, and while moving them, I touched both blades at once. The surge of energy between the two knocked me to my knees. A terrible coldness gripped my chest and my hands locked on the blades.

Without the sunfire I never could have pulled my hands off. I believe I would have been dead in a matter of breaths.

I wrapped the black blade in a blanket before moving it to a new place. It is buried deep, the location unmarked. The blue blade I wrapped in the thickest fabric I could find and then again inside my bedroll.

I encountered the Shield in Greentree and have passed off the blade to him. I can't say I'm sorry to be free of it.

Sini reread the entry, an ache forming in her own chest to match Chesavia's words. This was the reason Lukas was on the moors. This dreadful sword.

Sini breathed in the sunfire and felt something inside her loosen.

TWENTY-FIVE

S ini opened her door, finding Pest leaning against the wall outside. "I need to talk to Alaric and Will. And even Killien."

He pushed himself off the wall and led her to the tavern. The Keepers, Sora, and Killien sat around a table in tall-backed chairs, eating a rich smelling stew that made Sini's mouth water. She dropped into an empty chair, surprised to find it dinnertime already. She eyed the soup, and explained what she'd read.

"This is about my sword?" Killien asked. "The one I got from Flibbet the Peddler? How old is that journal?"

"Chesavia died almost 200 years ago," Alaric answered.

"I think Lukas knows about the black sword," Sini said, ignoring Killien's shock. "I think he really has been on the moors, that the dragon sightings are real, and that he's looking for the twin sword to the one he has."

"How could he know about them?" Alaric asked. "Unless he found a copy of Chesavia's journal before we did, which seems unlikely."

"Lukas has spent time in Coastal Baylon," Will said. "Tales of the warlords of the moors are popular there. If Naj was a well-known chief on the moors, there's a good chance his story is known by the Baylonese." He spun one of the beads in his beard. "I'm inclined to believe Sini is right. There's too strong a connection for this to be coincidence. I wonder how Naj's sword got from the Shield to Flibbet the Peddler."

A dwarf woman set down a bowl of soup with a thick chunk of bread in front of Sini, and Sini gratefully began to eat.

"If this is talking about my sword," Killien interrupted them, "and it really was the same Flibbet the Peddler who's been around for hundreds of years who gave it to my father, then why did he tell my father the sword was intended to "help mend the torn?" A sword isn't particularly good at mending anything, but this one sounds particularly ill-suited."

Alaric shook his head. "I don't know. Douglon agrees that it's time we head back to Queenstown. We can leave tomorrow. Maybe there's something there in the library."

"I'll send word to the Stronghold," Will said. "Knowing this about Chesavia gives the Shield a good place to start researching this sword. Maybe the Wellstone can tell him something."

Alaric nodded. "Douglon and I have decided we are going back to the Elder Grove to see

Rass and check on the elves. I think the rest of you should go straight to Queenstown. I'll have the dwarves send ravens ahead to the queen and to the Stronghold, telling them what we've learned."

Sini mopped up the end of her soup with her bread before following the others.

She'd packed and was walking back to the tavern with Pest when the bells began. If their somber tone didn't convey their meaning, the reactions of the dwarves around her did.

Horgoth was dead.

Douglon arrived not long after. "The horses are supplied and ready."

"Don't you have to stay for some sort of crowning ceremony?" Sini asked him.

"That'll take months to plan," Douglon muttered. "I've made sure everything is set for me to leave. I'm going before anyone tries to stop me. Killing a dwarf would be a poor beginning to my illustrious reign."

One of Douglon's cousins offered to take Killien to an exit from Duncave near where his family hid. Sora, on the other hand, agreed to go with Will to Queensland, which made him happier than Sini had ever seen him. Alaric and Douglon immediately headed south, toward the Elder Grove, while Patlon led the rest of them as far as the nearest exit to the east. With Patlon on foot, they led the horses until they came out from behind a boulder on a bright mountainside.

Sini tensed as the full strength of the sunfire fell on her cheeks, but it was gentle and warm. The air was chilly after the warmth of the caves. She drew a little sunfire in to warm her hands but balked at bringing enough in to warm the rest of her.

There were still several hours of light and they hurried toward Queenstown.

They reached a small town with an inn long after dark. Sini was relieved to find that the common room was empty, and they went straight up to their sleeping quarters. Despite the fact that the mattress was straw, Sini fell asleep almost immediately.

Early the next morning, she woke to voices outside her window and a sharp tap on her door. The sky was still dark, and she groaned and shifted on the lumpy bed.

"Sini," Roan's voice came quietly from the hall. "We need to leave."

One of the voices outside called out something angry. She sat up and looked out the window over her bed, reaching her ring toward the candle wick. A dozen people were gathered in front of the inn, holding lanterns. Sini caught a flash of something metal and her hand paused.

Roan knocked again. "Quickly, Sini!"

Sini dressed in the dark and grabbed her bag. The others were converging in the tight hall. The innkeeper wrung his hands at the end of the hall, apologizing.

"There are townspeople outside who aren't pleased that there's a Keeper in town," Roan said. "We are leaving out the back. Pest and I moved the horses when the first unhappy guest appeared. He has them in the trees out back. We should go before it gets any brighter."

"Yes," the innkeeper agreed. "Follow me. I'm so sorry. I don't know what's gotten into folks. They're saying terrible things 'bout Keepers out there."

"Wait." Sini ducked back into her room. She slipped to her window looking through the crowd for anything with trails of *vitalle*. Sora appeared silently at her shoulder. As far as Sini could see, there were no lights beyond the lanterns, but she heard the word Keeper being tossed about in a decidedly unfriendly way.

"Do you see anything...unusual?" Sini asked Sora. The ranger shook her head.

Sini went back to the hallway. "I don't see any sign of a compulsion stone, but I can't see the whole group well. And it could be under someone's clothes."

Will shook his head. "They might not need one any more. Once rumors begin like these, they have a life of their own."

"You led me to believe that you were something of a hero here," Sora said to Will, her voice lighter than Sini felt. "But this is exactly how they'd treat you on the Sweep."

"Let's hope it's not that bad yet." Will shrugged out of his Keeper's Robe. "But I should probably tuck this away for a bit."

Roan nodded and motioned for the others to follow. They passed down the stairs and through the common room, heading back into the kitchen. The crowd was louder, and someone pounded on the front door. The sound made Sini jump.

"Give us enough time to get into the trees," Will told the inn keeper, "and then let them in. We don't want them harming your inn." He handed the man a handful of coins. "I'm sorry if we caused you any trouble, and I hope no one is hurt through all this."

The inn keeper clasped Will's hand and hurried them through the kitchen and out into the chilly night. Sini ran to the nearby trees. The first hints of dawn were lightening the sky and Sini could feel the first tickles of sunfire.

"Should we try to talk to them?" Sini asked Will as they mounted their horses.

"Probably," answered Will, "but there are a lot of them, armed, and I'm not interested in having another battle where I have to fight people we're supposed to protect. There are better ways to fight rumors than with weapons." He glanced back at the inn. "The inn keeper met us and can attest to the fact that we weren't monsters."

They rode quickly away from the town, heading southeast. The roads they followed toward the capital were small and little used. The sun rose into a clear sky, and the sunfire on Sini's cheeks was a welcome warmth. Without Will's Keeper robe or the Baron's military uniforms, they didn't garner much attention.

Pest had disappeared up the road to scout and Roan rode beside Sini. Ahead of them Will and Sora rode together, and Sini thought she'd never seen Will so happy. Or Sora, for that matter. Roan watched the two of them with a narrow expression.

"Stop frowning," she told him. "It's good that they've found each other."

Roan gave a noncommittal grunt.

"I like Sora, and if you make any effort to get to know her, you will too. She's exactly the sort of person a guard would rely on. She's competent and resourceful and independent. Will's been lonely for years now. I don't see how this is bad, unless you're against the fact that she's foreign."

"It's not that she's foreign." He frowned. "Not completely. It's the fact that she distracts him from more important things."

"Some people would say that love is the most important thing. And being loved makes people better. Maybe even helps them to do all the other things well."

"Who says that?"

"Poets, probably," she said offhand. "You put no stock at all in love, Lord Consort?"

"There's never been any chance I would marry for love," Roan said matter-of-factly. "I never expected to marry the heir to the throne, but I've always known my marriage, like the rest of my life, would serve Greentree more than myself."

"There's never been any girl you've loved?"

He rubbed his thumb over the saddle horn thoughtfully. "I know you don't put much stock in the nobility's formal education, but I've been kept busy with it for… ever. Even before I joined the guard, I never had time for chasing girls." He brushed off the top of the horn with a flick. "And I can't think of anything my father would have liked less."

"They would have distracted you from more important things?"

He let out a long, annoyed sound and closed his eyes. "I'm turning into my father."

"If you want to counter that," Sini offered, trying not to laugh at him, "you can begin by being happy for Will."

Roan snorted and she was struck again with how relaxed he was on the road. She'd caught him staring into the distance ahead several times this morning with a tight expression, as though he were waiting for Queenstown to pop over a hill and capture him. Suddenly she felt a pang of pity.

She was reluctant to say the next thing, but she forced herself to before analyzing why. "It's not unreasonable to think you and Madeleine may end up happy."

His hand tightened on his reins. "It's possible. I admire her, which feels like a better start than many I'd imagined." He glanced at Sini. "I know you're not fond of her."

Sini tried to keep a grimace off her face. "You and Will and Alaric all admire her. If I had never met her, your opinions would have been enough. So I suppose I should realize that the problem is my attitude, not her."

He looked earnestly at Sini. "Give her time to grow used to her new role. Once she is more comfortable and knows you better, she will feel less threatened."

Sini stared at him. "Threatened? By me? I've only met her twice and both times I was dressed in traveling clothes. I didn't even have my hair combed."

"It has nothing to do with your hair." He looked at her thoughtfully. "Although, your lack of concern for the formality of court may be part of what is throwing her off. Someday, assuming we all survive Lukas and his dragon, I imagine you and she will work closely together." A smile quirked his mouth. "Knowing you both even a little, I rue anyone who tries to stand against you."

Sini sighed. "I don't know which is worse. You thinking I'm too young and stupid to do anything, or you thinking I'm more impressive than I am." She spun her ring. When had what Roan thought begun to matter at all?

Roan laughed. "Just preparing you for palace life, where you're bound to be disappointing half the court's expectations at any given moment."

Grey clouds moved in from the west, and before they'd gone far, the sun was covered and a thin, chill drizzle began. Sini pulled up the hood to her cloak and hunched forward in the saddle, her hands cold on the reins. Pest took a break from scouting ahead, and Roan spurred his horse forward out of sight.

Pest fell in beside Sini, seemingly unbothered by the rain but as quiet as ever. The chill and wet bogged down Sini's thoughts until they swirled slowly inside her head, finding no good places to settle.

Lukas had raised a Roven army, and two more from Coastal Baylon and Napon. He was looking for a sword that could give him horrible powers, and he'd killed hundreds, maybe thousands, of people in Gulfind for their gold. The people of southern Queensland were worn out and disheartened by all the things Lukas had done to them. The people in the west were nursing a growing hatred for Keepers.

Sini watched Will's back ahead of her. There were no towns between them and the capital, and he'd donned his Keeper's robe to ward off the rain. It was comforting to see him in it. For the first time, Sini felt a pang of regret that she had shunned wearing one for so long. It wasn't a grey slave's tunic. It didn't constrain. It was a symbol of what Will aligned himself with. And Alaric. And the Keepers at the Stronghold. Every Keeper throughout history.

The people in the towns around here were wrong about the Keepers, and Sini wished she had a robe of her own to wear in a silent declaration—not that the Keepers owned her, but that she stood with them.

When they reached the palace, it would be time to throw off the lingering trappings of her old life and declare where she stood in her new one. It seemed to have taken an inordinately long time to reach that decision, but it finally felt right.

Sini glanced at Pest. Tiny drops of water beaded on his grey hair. "Did you always dream of being a knife thrower?" She tried to keep her tone light but wasn't sure she succeeded.

Pest considered the question. "I always dreamed of surviving." He cast a quick sidelong glance at her. "I grew up in the shadow of the ironworks."

Sini straightened. "In the Lees?"

He nodded. "Next time you decide to venture in there, take me, not Roan."

TWENTY-SIX

"You grew up in the Lees? How did you…? When did…?" Sini pulled her cold hands into her sleeves and searched for the question she really wanted. "No one from the Lees joins the city guard."

"I'm not exactly in the city guard."

"But the queen trusts you with something like this." Sini waved at the group around them. "And Roan obviously has a great deal of faith in you. How did you get where you are?"

Pest was quiet for a long time. The rain continued to cast flecks of chilliness onto her cheeks, no matter how far forward she pulled her hood. She couldn't see Pest's face well, and regretted turning the conversation so personal.

"My younger sister and I were raised by our uncle near the ironworks," he said finally. "If you can call what he did raising. My sister only ate what I could steal. When I was seventeen, I stole from the wrong man." He smiled wryly. "He was a captain in the queen's guard, and he tracked me home. Seeing where we lived, he offered me an alternative to being arrested. I could clean the barracks for a year at a small wage. I figured I could find some good things to steal from there, so I accepted. He was smarter than that, though, and I wasn't allowed even a moment's privacy. I had no intention of keeping at the job, but it was the first time I had earned regular money, and the first time my sister had eaten regular meals. And so, to my great surprise, I continued cleaning. It wasn't long before I also helped with training exercises." He shrugged. "Somewhere along the line I joined the guard."

"What about your sister?" Sini asked. "Has she found a better place than the Lees?"

Pest nodded. "Not somewhere I'm pleased with, but this current job pays well, and soon I will get her somewhere better."

"Good." Sini shifted in her saddle. "I don't know if I have any power to do…anything, at court. But if you need…anything…" She laughed at the vagueness of it all. "Just ask and I'll do my best."

Pest's attention fixed on Roan riding quickly down the road toward them. He tensed in his saddle until Roan waved.

"Queenstown," Roan called. "No more than an hour ahead."

They reached the palace without incident, their party receiving barely any notice at all in the busy streets of the capital. While Will stopped to talk with a steward about a room for Sora, Sini hurried to her own room, desperate to find some warm clothes. Captain Liam once again guarded her door.

"Nice to see you, Daisy," she greeted him.

"And you, Keeper."

She found the maid Dalia pouring hot water into a huge basin by the fire. "A hot bath for you, Keeper." She bobbed off a quick curtsey. "If you're interested. I thought you must be shiverin' from this weather."

"I am very interested." Sini pulled off her wet boots. "And please just call me Sini."

"The steward wouldn't let me keep my job if I did." Dalia helped Sini off with her wet cloak and began gathering the rest of the damp, dirty traveling clothes.

The heat stung Sini's skin, but she sank down until her entire body was surrounded by the warmth. Dalia stoked the fire and Sini let the heat sink all the way into her bones.

"Have there been any more signs of the intruder?" Sini asked.

"It's been perfectly quiet. All the extra guards must have scared the fellow off."

"Good." Sini rested her head back on the side of the tub. Her eyelids drooped and she let her hands float weightless in the water.

A sharp knock at the door jolted her eyes open. Dalia cracked the door and returned with the message that Sini was expected in the queen's council. Taking the maid's offered towel, Sini reluctantly climbed out of the tub. Dalia rummaged in the wardrobe and held up two dresses, one a silvery grey, the other green.

"Green," Sini said without hesitation.

With Dalia's help she dressed quickly, and then accepted the maid's offer to fix her hair. Dalia plaited three thin braids over the top of Sini's head like a band, holding her hair out of her face, and wound green ribbon between the plaits. The effect was much neater, and much more elegant than anything Sini ever managed. The woman looking back at her from the looking glass still didn't look refined enough for court, but her dress was tasteful, and her blonde hair curled out in an almost organized fashion around her head.

Sini straightened her shoulders. She went to her wardrobe and pulled out one of three black Keeper's robes. The fabric felt heavy in her hands. Dalia held it open for her. Before she could change her mind, Sini slipped her arms inside and let the maid settle it on her shoulders.

"Your light hair looks striking against the black," Dalia said with an encouraging smile.

Closed, the robe was too dark, but Sini left the front open and with the green dress beneath it, it felt…right.

Dalia gave an approving nod. "It suits you."

Sini smiled at her through the mirror. "More than I ever expected it to."

One of the handful of guards in the sitting area escorted Sini to the queen's council. Raised voices came through the door as the guard opened it, and Sini straightened her shoulders before stepping into the room.

This wasn't the queen's study. This was the formal council chamber, and while the table was large enough to seat twice as many people, the dozen that sat around the far end still felt like an enormous crowd.

The queen raised her hand to stop an impassioned speech by an older man. "Keeper Sini, please take a seat. We're discussing the extent of Lukas's armies."

She caught Roan staring at her, his normal court formality slipping enough to show surprise. Whether at her black robe or the fact that she wasn't disheveled for once, she didn't want to know. Sini gave him a tight smile, but she received nothing but a frown from him before he smoothed his reserved expression back on. Sini felt a flare of irritation and tried to hide it in a curtsey to the queen, then another in the general direction of Roan and Madeleine. The future queen dismissed Sini without even a nod, but Will caught her eye and gave her a wide smile. Will leaned over an enormous map next to four men in military uniforms. The man who'd been speaking when Sini entered fixed her with a stern look.

"May I introduce my father," Roan said, his voice tight. "Duke Heath of Greentree."

Sini curtseyed again, but the man's face didn't soften. She sat down in the nearest empty seat.

"If what your deposed Roven Torch friend says can be trusted," the Duke of Greentree said, continuing the conversation from before she'd arrived, "and Lukas has armies along the southern border, especially if they're being reinforced with men from the Sweep, we need to mobilize our own troops quickly. Since delaying until we know the truth could prove perilous, I will send a message south to Greentree and Marshwell immediately."

"If he has as many armies as he claims," a man with a general's insignia on his sleeve said, "we need to mobilize the city guard south."

Everyone began talking at once.

"We don't need the city guard," the Duke of Greentree insisted. "Marshwell and Greentree have kept the southern border safe for hundreds of years. Even when we were under attack by Baylon, we've never needed support. We don't need it now."

"That is foolish," Queen Saren said. "We have never faced a combined army from Baylon and Napon, never mind one swelled by the Roven. We are sending the guard. What we need to determine is how many of them to send."

"If you take the city guard," the duke said, "you empty Queenstown of its defenses."

"I agree," Will said. "Douglon promises fifteen hundred dwarves within days, two thousand more within a fortnight."

The queen nodded. "That will help."

The general made a derisive noise. "We won't know if it will help until we see what they send. If they send anything. Queenstown is days away from the border. There is no way an attacking force could get past us to reach the capital. We should send the city guard. We can call them back if they're needed."

"I don't think it wise to take the guard away from the city," Roan said.

"If you must send some," his father agreed, "perhaps the first and second battalion could be sent, and the rest left here to protect the queen."

"And the Keepers," Saren said firmly. She turned to Will. "I want the Keepers brought here immediately."

Duke Heath nodded. "It is ridiculous that the Keepers do not live here. I have always thought so. Why do we bother with two different libraries? Here they could be cared for by the finest staff and have more time for studies."

"The palace isn't really conducive to quiet study," Will said. "And we believe that it is easier to see things clearly from a distance, rather than embroiled in court life."

The Duke waved away his words. "If they are loyal to Queensland and to her Majesty, they can have no objection to being a part of us. They cannot be protected well anywhere else."

"With all respect," Will said, "being in a hidden valley which none but ourselves can access is safer than anywhere else in the country."

"You will write to the Shield today," the queen said, "and tell him I require his presence here immediately."

Will let out a short sigh. "I will convey your message, but I don't expect him to acquiesce."

"How dare he?" Madeleine flung an outraged glare at Will. "How dare he ignore a direct command from his queen?"

"He does not do so lightly, I assure you," Will said. "If he stays at the Stronghold, it is because he believes it essential that he do so."

"Or he wants to hide in his tower and let the rest of the world burn," Madeleine leaned forward. "And where is Alaric? Is he hiding away as well?"

"I believe Alaric will be here tomorrow," Will said evenly. "If he is not delayed."

Sini felt a little twinge of nervousness. Hopefully Alaric wouldn't travel back to Queenstown in his Keeper's robe.

"Sini," the queen said, and Sini snapped her attention back to the conversation. "Do you have any additional information about this sword that Lukas is supposedly searching for?"

"No." Sini had found nothing else about the sword in Chesavia's journal. "And I don't know whether he's found it."

"We've looked into the dragon sightings," Duke Heath said. "It's been three weeks since the last report of a sighting over the moors."

Fear pricked the back of her neck. Maybe Lukas had found the black blade.

"The dragon has obviously turned its attention somewhere else," Duke Heath continued. "Along with his rider."

"The dragon rider has been busy with armies and gold," the general agreed. "He's most likely given up his search...if that was what he was doing."

Sini hesitated. "I don't think he would give up."

"He has more to worry about than ancient swords," Madeleine said.

Sini glanced at Will. "The way Keeper Chesavia hid the sword, I think it represents a serious threat."

Will nodded. "I don't think we should ignore the fact that Lukas may already have it."

"And what should we do about that?" Madeleine asked. "Besides find fault in the Keepers of old for not hiding such a thing well enough?"

Sini looked at Roan for some support, but his face was stony. "Lukas would put more faith in a powerful magical object than in armies." She tapped her fingers against her lip. "It's worrisome that he's stopped looking."

"Only a fool would think a single sword more important than an army," Madeleine said firmly. "As a man who's never been in charge of anything, he's likely realizing how much work it is. His little treasure hunt will take a back seat to the realities of leadership."

Sini pressed her lips closed.

Roan finally looked up at her, but she found no warmth in his eyes. "We'll send to Greentree for more information," Roan said, his voice stiff. "Perhaps the fanatics were too busy watching the dragon to report it over the last few weeks."

A surge of gratefulness rolled through Sini, but Roan looked away before she could even nod her thanks.

Within a few minutes, the queen dismissed them all. Will headed off to find Sora, and Roan announced he would escort Sini back to her room.

"You must think the sword is a problem," she whispered as soon as they'd left the room. "You saw how concerned Alaric was about it. I'm not overstating this."

"It doesn't matter what I think," Roan answered stiffly.

"Right." Her irritation flared. "You're just there to support Madeleine. I forgot."

Roan glanced at her. "I am there to support her. I have little to no knowledge about the sword. Why would I speak?"

"Because I thought—" Sini clenched her mouth closed. Because she'd thought they'd started to develop something resembling a friendship. She searched for a better topic, or one that would at least make him as annoyed as she was. "When did your father arrive?"

"The day after we left," Roan said, no hint of emotion in his voice, though his expression was darker.

"He's..." she couldn't figure out a polite way to end the thought.

"Used to getting his way."

"He must be proud that you were sent as Saren's emissary to the dwarves."

He cleared his throat. "Now that you're wearing the black robe," he said, changing the subject with an annoyingly stern tone in his voice, "you need to be more careful. Guards will escort you around the palace. Please do not leave it." His voice held considerably more command than request. "After the unrest we found on the road, I can't imagine things will stay peaceful in the city for long."

Sini let out an annoyed huff. "Don't worry. I won't drag you into the Lees again."

He didn't let her words ruffle him. "I hope you're done going to the Lees altogether."

"Pest informed me he grew up there. I've already assured him I will take him if I venture back into that part of town, not you."

Roan paused, choosing his words carefully before continuing. "You shouldn't go there with Pest either. He and his sister were raised in the Lees by an uncle with an ugly reputation. The man...disappeared under suspicious circumstances."

Sini turned in surprise. "Pest killed him?"

"No one can prove it. But the uncle was...unkind to Pest's sister." Roan clasped his hands behind his back as they walked. "Regardless, Pest's services were for while we traveled. Now that you're in the city, you will be protected by the city guard."

"That's too bad," Sini answered. "He and I were just starting to become friends."

"Pest has no friends," Roan said firmly.

Sini felt another jab of irritation. "Maybe he just doesn't like you."

"He doesn't like anyone. He doesn't talk to anyone."

"He talks to me."

They had reached the sitting area outside Sini's room and Roan turned to face her, scowling. "I know. But I don't know why."

Sini crossed her arms. "Maybe I'm more fun to talk to than uptight city guards."

"I hope that's what it is," he said coldly.

Sini glared at him. "I thought you of all people would understand that if I find someone here I like to talk to—preferably someone who's not stiff and formal and attached to a woman who hates me—I'm going to talk to him."

His jaw twitched and he fixed her with a stern look. "Be careful, Sini."

She wanted to slap the stuffiness off his face. "Daisy?" she said without turning.

"Yes, Keeper Sini?" Captain Liam's voice was not amused.

"In your professional opinion, does the younger son of the Duke of Greentree, even if he is betrothed to the future queen, have the rank to command a Keeper?"

Roan's gaze flickered past her to the man. There was a moment's silence.

"No, Keeper," the captain said at last. "I do not believe he does."

"Neither do I." She didn't wait for Roan's response before turning and stalking into her room. Captain Liam gave her a flat look. She ignored it, letting the door close behind her with a satisfying thud.

TWENTY-SEVEN

Roan did not improve over the next few days. In fact, nothing improved over the next few days. The weather stayed chilly and damp and the only topic anyone spoke of was war.

Alaric arrived at the palace the next morning with word that Douglon would follow shortly, but that the dwarven messenger system was in place. The dwarves had fifteen hundred troops stationed at the border between Duncave and Queensland, and were working on getting the other two thousand ready well within a fortnight.

Sini joined Alaric in Will's room as soon as he returned.

"Now that the elves know how to eat," Alaric said, dropping heavily into a wide chair near the fire, "they're growing so fast you can almost see it. Elves live so long I figured their childhood would last for decades. But most of them are as tall as my waist already, and they speak fluently."

"Are they happier?" Sini asked.

Alaric nodded. "Thanks to Douglon, half the time they talk like dwarves. When they're angry they'll yell at the 'blasted trees'." He let out a tired laugh and shook his head. "The homes they've begun to build themselves are mostly on the ground instead of up in the trees. They've taken to making stone-walled houses centered around a single, large tree trunk. Then they convince the tree to bend its branches down to the top of the wall as a roof. So there are all these half-stone, half-tree houses."

"They sound cozy and ingenious." Will sat with his feet propped up on a stool, stretching toward the fire.

"But not elvish." Alaric dropped his head back and closed his eyes.

"You didn't really think we'd manage to bring back elves exactly as they were before, did you?" Will asked.

"No. I just wish I knew what we did bring back." Alaric sighed. "Actually, I wish everything would just calm down for a little while." At their silence he gave them a small smile. "The apothecary says Evangeline's time is coming sooner than we expected. He expects it to be less than a fortnight."

Their hearty congratulations were interrupted by a messenger calling them to the queen's council.

The meeting took place in the full council chamber again, this time with at least two dozen generals, dukes, and nobility. Each duchy had its own troops in addition to the massive city guard, and there were endless discussions about which to mobilize. Sini quickly realized that she had absolutely nothing to add to the discussions of troop movements and supply routes.

When it was over, she begged Alaric to get her out of future meetings. He agreed, if she promised to spend the time researching Lukas's swords and continue the studies on Mallon she'd been working on at the Stronghold. She gladly spent the next few days in the library as everyone else planned for war. She tried, as much as she could, not to think about the fact that Lukas was behind all of this. It felt almost like they were talking about some stranger who happened to have the same name as her foster brother. She couldn't reconcile her memories of him with this.

A suspicion began to grow in her after rereading Chesavia's journal. What if these swords were doing something to Lukas? Chesavia's entries blamed the sword for Naj's continued violence. If Lukas had just found the black sword a few weeks ago when people had seen the dragon on the moors, that was just before he'd slaughtered all those people at the gold mines in Gulfind. That event was certainly an escalation of anything Lukas had done before.

She found Will and Sora and mentioned the idea.

"It's possible," Will admitted, "but be careful that you aren't making excuses for him. On the Sweep we saw him attack the Roven with a swarm of frost goblins. So we know he's willing to use mass violence when it suits him."

Sini just nodded, caught between frustration and disappointment. Will was the most sympathetic ear she was likely to find. She filed the idea away in her own mind and didn't bring it up again.

On the second afternoon she received a letter from Rett. She opened it to find his halting handwriting filling almost all of the small paper. There were almost no spelling mistakes, so one of the other Keepers must have helped him. The idea of Rett laboring in the library, his big body bent over the small paper with Gerone or Mikal or the Shield patiently spelling words made her smile. This must have taken him ages.

The lamb is walking strong like the others! Still little, but growing. Gerone made apple sugar bread. I wanted to save you a piece, but I ate it. I miss you Sini.

She let out a little groan at Gerone's apple sugar bread. She should write to him for the recipe so they could make it here at the palace. That bread might be the best part of fall.

The war plans went on slowly. The dwarves reported that Killien's information about the Roven army was correct. They were gathering in a valley in the Scale Mountains along the edges of Gulfind. But, as Saren's rangers had found earlier, the pass into Gulfind ahead of them was blocked by a landslide. Currently the numbers of Roven swelling in that valley were threatening the fragile truce between clans who had been lifelong enemies.

A part of the council took this as a sign that Lukas's entire invasion would be inept. The rest were alarmed that they were missing something important.

She'd sent a message by raven to the twins, asking if they knew anything about the warlord Naj, and if the Shield had discovered anything new in the Wellstone about the sword Lukas was searching for.

Whenever she was bored, which was often, she experimented with her ring. Lighting small sticks and tossing them into her fireplace, lighting blank or useless pages from her notes, just because she could. She began a list of other burning stones she would like. Maybe one that could interact with the air so she could shape it the way the twins could. And one that would connect her in a way that she could use *paxa* to calm animals. When all this was over, she'd need to sit down with Alaric and see which were possible. Maybe she could have a whole handful of rings.

Roan continued to be insufferably stiff and ill-humored until Sini was glad he was seldom out of the council room.

As the days went on, she spent more and more time reading books by Flibbet the Peddler. At first it was in the hopes of finding something about the swords, and how the odd little peddler had come to possess the blue one that eventually made its way to Killien.

But she kept seeking out more of his books because they were just plain fun. Flibbet wrote in multi-colored ink, with doodles lining each page. He told heroic tales as well as stories of small people in small villages. He recorded jokes and insightful quotes with wild, whimsical disorganization. She found nothing of any value, but the time was spent so much more pleasantly in his writing than all her other studies, that she kept coming back to him.

Flibbet was an enigma. The first records of him were over two hundred years old. For a time he had interacted with the Keepers regularly, bringing them his strange books and providing useful information from his travels. But he must have died a hundred years ago, at least. The idea that Killien's father had gotten Svard Naj from Flibbet was impossible. Maybe one of Flibbet's descendants had inherited the odd collection of things the peddler had collected. The idea piqued her interest. It would be interesting to meet Flibbet's grandchild. Maybe they had more of his wonderful books.

On the third afternoon spent in long, lonely study, a raven returned with a tiny scroll written in the twins' hand, containing no more information about Naj and his swords than she already knew. The Shield had been searching the Wellstone but had found nothing significant.

The post script on the letter caught at her chest.

All is well here, if a little lonely in your absence. Rett is mournful but has taken to breakfasting with us, and we do our best to cheer him. He says he will be well when "his Sini" returns. We hear great things of you, dear one, which brings us no surprise, but a great deal of pride.

Because you would ask: five pages left.

We are in no great discomfort and speak of you often.

If you find court to be lonesome, remember that once even we were strangers to you, and you are undoubtedly surrounded by future friends.

She dropped the scroll onto the messy library table, glancing around the small room she'd commandeered. She was surrounded by nothing but books.

Which, all things considered, might be better than the friends she would find here.

She closed her eyes. Five pages left. They'd finish in a week at the most. And there was no way she'd be back at the Stronghold for…maybe months.

She dropped her head into her hands and let the tears that were filling her eyes fall.

That evening, Douglon showed up at court with the little copper elf, Avina. Every single person in the palace was in a tizzy over the elfling, and Avina hated all of them. After she tried to bite the Duchess of Marshwell, Douglon kept her isolated. The queen had given them a room that opened into a private garden that held two large oaks, and Avina was content climbing their branches.

"Rass wanted to come with me," Douglon explained to them, "but the elves got nervous at the idea. She wasn't thrilled with staying but she agreed if I promised to keep her apprised of the situation. A dwarven messenger is supposed to meet her at the edge of the Greenwood every third day."

Will raised an eyebrow. "Do you think they really will?"

"They'd better," Douglon grumbled. "Last I looked it was treason to disobey a direct order from the High Dwarf."

Will grinned at Sini. "He's drunk with power."

Avina was overjoyed to see Sini, who became her primary caretaker whenever Douglon had to attend councils. She was taller than Sini's waist now, with coppery red hair that hung past her shoulders and darker copper skin. She prattled incessantly about trees and leaves and sunlight and grass and missing Rass and how she was sure the other elves were terribly lonesome without her. After so many days of isolation, Sini was perfectly happy to listen.

The next morning, Sini had to endure a breakfast attended by the queen, Madeleine, Roan's father, and a taciturn Roan himself. The Duke of Greentree was his usual overbearing self, lecturing Sini on how the Keepers should have already responded to Queen Saren's orders to come to Queenstown. Madeleine chimed in her support whenever there was a break. Saren didn't contribute to the conversation; instead she flipped through a thick stack of papers with a worried crease in her brow.

Sini, not given a moment to speak, looked to Roan for some support, but aside from one faintly apologetic look, he stared fixedly at his plate and said nothing.

She excused herself as quickly as possible and stormed back to her room, unsure of whether she was more furious at the Duke or his spineless son.

It was yet another gloomy day and her room was all shadows and chills. She threw herself down in front of the fire and flung a piece of wood onto it, sending up a huge cloud of embers.

"Have you ever…" a voice said from behind her and she spun to see Pest at her balcony door. "Thought of what you would say to your mother if you found her?"

"Pest!" Sini pressed her hand to her pounding chest. "You scared me to death! Why are you in my room? And why didn't you use the normal door?"

"Sorry to startle you." He came over to hold his hands out near the fire. "I came with a proposal for you, but Roan did not approve of it and told his guards not to let me near your room." The little man, who was dressed in a grey guards' uniform that matched his grey hair, grinned. "I thought I'd find my own way in and ask you anyway."

"Good," Sini snapped, sitting back down. "Because Roan has absolutely no say over me."

Pest laughed. "But he does have some over me. I was informed that I was not to speak to you, and my deployment was moved up to this afternoon when the second battalion heads south."

"He's shipping you off to war?"

"Everyone's being shipped off to war. Before I left, though, I thought you deserved to hear what I had to say." He nodded to the door leading to her balcony. "I apologize for letting in a bit of the cold when I let myself in."

Sini waved away his apology. "Roan's been insufferable. He'll be furious about this."

"I know." Pest gave her a wicked grin. "But I thought you should know, I've found your mother."

She stiffened, and a ripple of disquiet rolled through her gut. "In the Lees?"

"No, near the market square."

The square. Sini couldn't imagine her mother in such a clean neighborhood.

"Would you like to see her?"

Sini watched the flames crawl around the edges of the logs. "I don't know."

He waited for her to say more, then nodded. "I'll write you directions so you can find her whenever you are ready." He started for her desk.

Her breath caught in her throat. "Wait. I…would like to see her…I think."

He considered her for a moment, as though trying to decide if she meant it. "Roan will disapprove of you leaving the palace."

"Well Roan can tighten up his stiff little uniform and deal with it."

Pest laughed and jerked his head toward the balcony. After only a moment's hesitation, she pulled on the thickest Keeper's robe in her wardrobe and followed him outside. He helped her over the ledge and down the short drop into the garden. They rounded the edge of the Keeper's wing and passed two guards who did nothing more than nod at Pest. A quick jaunt through an enormous kitchen found them weaving through a courtyard full of carts delivering vegetables.

Sini's trepidation grew as they walked. Did she want to see her family? What would she say to them? What would they want from her? "How did you find them?"

"Not a lot of people leave the Lees. Those who do find their new neighbors to be distrustful. It makes it hard to become a part of their new neighborhood, but it also makes them easy to find."

The rain had stopped, but the air was chilly, and the cobblestones held enough puddles that her feet were soon soaked through. Pest turned up his collar and hunched into his own thick cloak. She drew the Keeper's robe tighter around herself.

She glanced down at the dark fabric. "Should I be wearing this? Have you seen any unrest in the city toward Keepers?"

He shook his head. "Not yet. And there are enough black robes in the city that no one will notice yours."

"Not yet? You think it will come, though?"

"If the Keepers can't stave it off, yes. Those sorts of rumors get a life of their own."

Sini pulled the robe tighter and hurried after him. Pest turned down a wide avenue with neat cobblestones and well-kept shops. The way was crowded with people shopping or hurrying home. The noise and the activity and the bright merchandise in the shop windows distracted her until Pest turned into a smaller street that wound among more modest shops. Her gaze scanned each sign, looking for a seamstress shop. Pest finally drew up at a corner and pointed across the street.

A solid, plain grey building stood shoulder to shoulder with the shops around it. The sign with a painted needle and thread was nailed above a dark, thin door. The building was two stories tall, the windows on the top floor dingier than the ones at ground level.

"A woman lives there with two boys. She came from the Lees eight years ago, and the shop across the street"—he motioned toward an equally plain shop with an equally rough sign depicting scissors and what must be a piece of fabric—"tries to steal her business by telling everyone that she sold her daughter into slavery so she could buy this shop."

Sini's stomach clenched. "Have you seen her?"

Pest shook his head.

"And my father…?"

"There's no man living there."

A light brightened the window for a moment, then faded, and Sini shrank back, wrapping the black robe tighter, trying to block out the chill of the afternoon. She felt suddenly conspicuous to be dressed as a Keeper.

She stood awkwardly, wanting to go in, but reluctant to start. The street was so foreign. This wasn't the Lees, where she'd felt ready to see her mother. Here there were no old memories, no way to gauge how much she'd changed against the backdrop of her childhood. All she could picture was the way her mother had let Vahe take her. Was that the face she was about to see?

"Have you ever forgiven someone who's done something terrible to you?" she asked Pest quietly.

"No." He answered flatly. "But I'm certain you're a better person than me." When she didn't answer, he continued, "There's a difference between forgiving your mother and meeting her again. Perhaps you can go not for her, but for your brothers."

The boys' small, always-wary faces came to her mind. The thought of them being left without her for so long wrung her heart. "Yes, maybe I can meet her for their sakes."

Pest nodded. "I would do anything for my sister."

Roan's suspicions about Pest's uncle came to mind, and the hardness in Pest's face did nothing to belie the idea that he might have killed the man.

"Will you..." she almost asked if Pest would come with her, just to have a person she knew alongside her. But the fear of what her mother might be like made her reluctant to have any witnesses. "Will you wait for me here?"

Pest looked unhappy at the idea, but nodded.

She took a deep breath and stepped forward.

"Sini." He set his hand on her arm to stop her. His face was conflicted, and he opened his mouth twice before actually speaking. "Sometimes, people from our past are...worse than we remember them."

Her stomach clenched in apprehension at the words.

"Sometimes they're someone you should stand against." He dropped his hand. "Not someone you should try to save."

At the earnestness in his voice, she nodded, although the idea of wanting to save her mother felt off.

"Just remember who you are." He turned his gaze back to the shop front. "And you'll be fine."

She wasn't sure what sort of response that deserved, but she managed a "Thank you." Before she lost her courage, she crossed the street.

The door to the shop squeaked open and she stepped into a small, dim room. A wide hall led to the back where warm firelight glowed out of a doorway. Sini took a deep breath and smoothed the Keeper's robe. She toyed with her ring as she walked down the hallway, rubbing her fingertips over the tiny garnet, wondering what it should feel like to remember who she was.

"Hello?" she called.

A response she couldn't quite make out answered, and with a last bracing breath, she stepped into the doorway.

Instead of her mother, a man stood near the small fireplace.

His hair was shorter than she'd ever seen it, his face clean-shaven.

"Hello little sister," Lukas said with a wide smile.

TWENTY-EIGHT

ukas stood next to the mantle like a lord deigning to step into squalor. In sharp contrast to the serviceable, plain room around him, he wore a cloak of dark, red fabric rich enough to rival anyone at court. He turned toward her and a dozen trails of light followed him. From rings, necklaces, glitters of gems sewn into his cloak. There was even a mist of green light trailing from his shoes.

Her immediate reaction to all the burning stones was one of disgust. He trailed *vitalle* like a Roven Torch. Her hand tightened on her own ring, the idea of making more of them suddenly repellant.

He watched her speechlessness, amused, waiting for her to find her voice.

"Lukas?" She took a step forward. Her mind scrambling to make sense of this. "How are you here? In my mother's shop—"

The room around them was mostly empty. Heavy dust covered the surface of the long table and the meager bits of fabric crumpled on the floor next to it. The clarity of the truth hit her with a surprising amount of dismay.

"This isn't my mother's shop."

Lukas let out a laugh. "Of course not. How do you track down a woman from the Lees who's too stupid to save her family, even when she's handed a fortune?"

Sini pulled back at the harshness of the words, her mind scrambling to catch up to the situation.

Lukas stood right in front of her. Lukas! A part of her wanted to rush forward and hug him, but she couldn't reconcile this man with her foster brother. He looked so wealthy, and his voice was…different.

"Put your mother out of your mind, Sini. She's not worth a thought. She sold you." He took a step closer, his voice taking on a fanatical edge. He flung his hand toward a tiny window. "She's what's wrong with this world, Sini. She cares for nothing but herself. She's probably sold both your brothers by now,"—Sini flinched—"and with any luck, killed the sorry excuse for a man who was your father."

Sini opened her mouth, wanting to defend her parents, but her brain offered no clear thoughts. Lukas crossed the final two steps and set his hands on Sini's shoulders, looking into her face with a wild intensity.

"But you and I can fix the world, Sini."

He was so changed, so gaunt and pale. His motions were twitchy, his eyes sunken in, his skin thin. His gaze dropped to her shoulders and he snatched his hands off her Keeper's robe as though it might bite him. His expression darkened. "Pest said you didn't wear the black."

Pest.

Her emotions caught up to the situation with a sharp jab of betrayal. That lying, sneaking traitor.

"What else did Pest tell you?" she demanded.

Lukas laughed again, and it was not the laugh she remembered. "Don't blame him. His sister is currently a guest at one of the homes I keep here."

The complexity of that answer snagged on one, shocking fact. "You have *homes* in Queenstown?"

"Only a few. Until my armies move through, it's not safe to have more. Pest has been helping me in exchange for a level of care his sister has never received. She has trouble walking, you see. Some injury from her childhood. I believe that man would do anything for her. Aside from his weakness for his sister, though, he's been an ideal mercenary." His face sobered and he studied Sini. "Until the point where he was reluctant to bring you to me." His smile was calculating. "I forgot how winsome you can be. Even to a man as rough as Pest."

Lukas stepped forward and Sini shrank away from him. His smile faltered for a moment before he walked past her and closed the door. "More surprising, I didn't think it possible that Pest could earn your trust." His tone was almost friendly. As though they hadn't been parted for four years. As though he wasn't threatening an entire country.

"Hired?" Sini backed up until against the table, her emotions finally settled into something concrete. Anger. "By threatening his sister?"

Lukas frowned. "I didn't threaten her, I took excellent care of her. Yes, I hired Pest and he took the work willingly."

A truth struck her. "Pest was the intruder at the palace. That's how he could move through without anyone noticing."

"He did a fine job of getting me information. The best of which was that you had arrived. That's why I was shocked when I told Pest to bring you here and he refused. The only thing that would convince him was the chance to take his sister from the good care she's receiving and leave Queenstown, which is hardly in her best interest." He frowned, focusing on Sini. "Take off that ridiculous black robe and let's talk."

The command raised a flare of indignation. "No."

His smile evaporated. "I've waited too long and worked too hard to let them keep you—" He clenched his jaw and made a visible effort to stay calm. "Let's start this over, Sini. I came here to get you, and it has not been easy."

"To get me?"

"I tried to come back for you on the Sweep," he stepped closer, "after Will and his cohorts ran me out. I couldn't leave you or Rett with the Roven. When I found you two gone, I assumed that the Keepers had taken you against your will. That somehow they'd discovered how much power you had and wanted it for themselves." His expression hardened. "Imagine my surprise when I heard rumors of a new female Keeper."

"The Keepers are not what you think."

Lukas's jaw clenched. "Still, everything I heard was that you weren't really one of them.

That you didn't wear the black." He plucked at the sleeve of her robe. "That they kept you captive in the Stronghold and never let you out."

"They didn't—"

"Stop!" he yelled over her. He scrubbed his hands over his face. "It doesn't matter," he continued in a tightly controlled voice. "Whatever they have over you, you can throw it off now. I'm taking you and Rett. We leave tonight."

Sini stared at him, stunned.

"Sini, I have worked very hard, for a very long time to get you free. I have a castle." He laughed again and the unhinged sound felt like a stab into her chest. "A castle! I have a room for you so big you'll get lost in it! I have gold. More gold than entire countries. You can have anything you want. Finer dresses than this"—he motioned to her green dress—"a cloak in any color, in any fabric you want. You want a crown? I'll make you a crown. You can have books and pets and jewelry. Anything you want." He motioned to his own clothing and toward an ornate pack that lay against the side of the mantle. "Just as I have anything I want."

A scabbard holding two identical swords leaned against the pack. Sini's stomach dropped. One sword let out a thin cloud of blue light, the other a smoky black cloud. "You found it," she whispered.

His gaze snapped to her face. "You know what those are?"

"Just that they exist." She started to ask what they did, but Lukas interrupted her with a laugh.

"Of course you know about them." He lunged forward and hugged her. His thin arms around her shoulders felt skeletal. From the burning stones on his hands and chest and robe, bits of *vitalle* seeped into and out of her in a chaos of impressions.

He pulled back and gripped her shoulders.

"What are you going to do with swords?" she asked. "Carry them into battle like some warlord?"

He snorted. "Do I look like the kind of man who strides into battle? These aren't weapons for a common war. Killien was right about that. They're swords for a purpose. A blade to surgically cut out infection, not an instrument to hack up a whole body." He grinned at her. "Oh, how I've missed you, Sin. I have had so many puzzles and runes to decipher, and no brilliant sister to help." He grinned, and for just a moment she saw the old smile. "You don't know how happy it makes me that we're together again. Name anything you want and it's yours."

The smile gave her a little hope. "I want you to stop."

He looked at her without comprehension.

"Stop hurting people and crops and animals."

"You always were too sensitive, Sin. Those things were the smallest things I could use. I could have hurt so many more, but I did only what was necessary."

"How many people did you kill in Gulfind?" Sini asked him. "Hundreds?"

"That was not my fault," he answered sharply. "I asked for a fair amount of gold. I offered to take it and leave them in peace. But they refused! They loved their gold too much to part with even a few cartloads!"

Sini stared at him. "And so you killed them?"

"Their greed killed them," Lukas spat at her. "The world is not simple and easy. Sometimes you have to do unpleasant things. Do you think I wanted to kill them?"

"I don't know," she whispered.

"It had been years. I had to do something big. Something big enough to get their attention."

"Whose?"

He cocked his head to the side, surprised at her question. "The Keepers. I had to create enough problems to draw out the Keepers. To draw out you."

She stared at him. "You hurt all those innocent people, just to get the Keepers out of the Stronghold? Lukas, all you had to do was come to Queenstown and ask for them. They would have met you. You could have seen once and for all what they were like."

"The Keepers"—his voice curled around the word with disdain—"would have killed me on sight."

"No, they wouldn't." His face hardened as she said the words, and she knew he wouldn't listen.

"I understand that you feel a loyalty to them. I expected it. After all, we both felt a loyalty to Killien, didn't we? And he kept us in slavery."

"Please stop," Sini said, trying to get him to listen. "I know you've read Mallon. I know you've been imitating him, eating away at the edges of Queensland to weaken her. But how could you model your actions after such an evil man?"

Lukas let out a little huff of disbelief. "You've bought into so many of their lies. Mallon wasn't evil. He was just brave enough to try to break the current system and give the people something better. Like Mallon, if I succeed, this war will be the last. I'll create a lasting peace and remove any of the leaders who lie to the people. We'll have real peace, Sini. And we'll have no masters or Keepers or owners." There was a fanatical fire in his eyes.

"You don't have to do any of this," she pleaded. "Come back with me to the palace. Come meet the Keepers. They're—"

"You have the power to stop all this," Lukas interrupted her. "No other innocents have to be hurt."

She backed up a step. "I'm not doing any of it."

"Everything I've done is to draw the Keepers out so I could reach them. But if I have you with me, I don't have to. Tell me where the Stronghold is, and I'll go straight to them. I'll leave everyone else alone."

She stared at him incredulously. "No."

"Sini, you can stop protecting them. I've been looking for you for ages, and now you're safe. Safer than you've ever been in your life." The look she recognized came back into his face. "You're free."

"Lukas,"—she took a step toward him—"I'm already free. I've been free since the moment I stepped away from Killien."

He turned away and paced over to the fire. "I know Will and Alaric are at the palace, but I need to know where the others are."

Sini shook her head. "I'm not telling you where the Stronghold is."

"I could force it out of you," he said offhandedly.

"You wouldn't," she raised her chin. "You promised me long ago that you would never use magic against me. That I was safe with you, and I have always believed that. I still believe that."

"I've never wanted to hurt you. But you know I can get anyone to do anything I want."

Sini's stomach tightened, whether with anger or fear, she wasn't sure. "With one of your compulsion stones?"

Despite her tone, his face brightened. "I've improved them so much. The original versions were like a huge hammer, pounding into someone." He started pacing again, this time with a nervous energy. "The ones I make now, they're like a chisel. I can select an exact thought or emotion, I can direct it toward a goal."

"Yes." A coldness sank into her at his excitement. "I ran into one of your rings along the western edge of Queensland."

"Wasn't it fantastic? You're acting like it's bad, but every time I used one it only took a few sheep dying before the people began to listen. I didn't really harm those people. I just gave them the truth of who the Keepers are."

"The truth? By lying to them about who sickened the sheep?"

He shrugged. "A small deception to teach a greater truth. The Keepers do not keep them safe. And they should stop expecting them to."

"Those men attacked us! One of my companions almost died. Several of the attackers did."

"And you, I heard, performed a near-miraculous healing. Don't you see, Sini? Both you and I have learned so much. Let's throw off the people who taught us by trying to control us, and step into the life we deserve. Between you and me and the dragon, we'll be unstoppable."

He grinned at Sini and pulled out a necklace from under his shirt.

It glinted red and blue, and Sini took a step closer. It was a dragon scale, blood red and shimmering in the fire light, and set in the center of it was a bright blue aquamarine. The stone left a long, glittering trail of blue light as it moved. "Sini, I've learned so much. I've been dying to talk to you about it. I don't even need to touch Anguine any longer to control him. I just need to be nearby."

"Anguine?"

"The dragon."

"You can control him? Fully?"

"Not with words, but with emotions. And I've discovered how to make it go both ways. I can feel what he's feeling, get a vague impression of what he sees." An excitement glittered in his eyes. "He doesn't see like we do. He sees…more. The warmer something is, the brighter it is. Cold things are muted, but he can see a deer in the woods at night as though it were glowing!"

"That's…terrifying."

Lukas laughed. "It is. But I control him. I put desires in Anguine's mind for specific things and he acts on them, as long as I'm asking him to do dragon-like, predatory things."

"Doesn't Anguine know he could overpower you? Why does he submit?"

"Because I have something he wants more than anything else." Lukas gestured to the outside. "Like Pest. Everyone can be controlled if you know what to offer."

"You can offer Anguine something he can't get on his own?"

"Oh, yes." Lukas smiled enigmatically. "He'll obey you, too. I'll see to it. He's amazing. So much power and fire. To ride on his back with the whole world spread out beneath you…" He shook his head. "You're going to love it."

He let out a long breath. "We have a long way to go, but I want to send word to my troops. I'd rather be rid of all those groveling fools, anyway." His face was relieved. "Now that you're here, we can stop the invasion and I don't have to use any of the weapons I made. No killing animals or tainting water supplies. Just tell me where the Stronghold is. Everything else can go away."

She searched his face for something familiar, something to give her hope.

The shock of seeing him had faded, and for the first time—maybe ever—she could truly see him. His face was not the one she'd trusted when she'd first been made a slave. His eyes were not the ones that had seen her and understood her. The way he stood breathed arrogance and hatred and hardness. He was his own person, utterly separate from what she had thought of him. Utterly unconcerned with who she wanted him to be. The image of him she'd clung to blew away like smoke. Whoever that had been, it was not Lukas.

She glanced back at the swords. The black one had definitely changed him. He couldn't hear anything but his own violent plans.

The truth of it wrung something in her heart. "I'm not going to tell you."

"Things are already in motion, Sini," he said, a hint of exasperation in his voice, "Tell me where they are and I can stop it all."

"No." Something deep inside her cracked as she accepted the truth. "I wish things were different. I wish you were different. Or maybe I wish you were the same person I used to know. Or I was the person I used to be. Whatever has happened to us, we are not who we once were."

He fixed her with a stern look. "That'll all go back to normal once you're out of here. You've been my sister for years—that's not something that disappears. Even when you join my enemy and betray the goals we once had."

"Join your enemy?" A flicker of anger cut into her sorrow. "I have defended you at every turn. I have spent months studying your movements to see where you are, to prove that you weren't the threat everyone thought you were."

"I told you they hated me."

"You are the threat!" She flung the words at him. "You're everything they said of you and more!" The small fracture inside her widened. Tears pricked her eyes and she blinked them away furiously. "I believed—I actually believed—that you were still the man I knew. I know you're angry at what happened to us. But your anger has twisted everything. You're not seeing anything clearly."

Lukas's gaze turned cold. "You're not a child any more, Sini. Stop being naive. Tell me where the Stronghold is so I can make arrangements and you and I can leave."

"No."

The muffled sound of voices outside came through the small window.

Lukas looked up sharply. "Did you tell anyone where you were going?"

Sini looked at him. It ached to admit it, but he was too changed, too damaged to even hear her.

"Goodbye, Lukas."

He spun around. "You're not leaving."

"Think about what you're doing. Please think about the lives you're ruining." She turned her back on him and reached for the door.

"You are not leaving."

Her legs froze, her feet locked into the floor. Fear swirled in her gut as she tried to yank them free. She heard his footsteps come up behind her.

"I don't want to do this to you, Sini." His voice sounded strangled.

"You promised me you'd never use magic on me." She twisted to look him in the eye, wrenching at her legs. They didn't budge. A wave of anger rolled over her. "You promised me."

Lukas's face was tortured, but he clenched his hand into fists. "You are leaving me no choice," he snarled. "Tell me where the Stronghold is."

"No." Sini cast out toward the tiny window, looking for *vitalle,* trying to draw in any sunfire she could find. But the window was too grimy, the world outside too clouded. The bit of sunlight that leaked through was barely enough to feel. She drew *vitalle* from the fire and poured it into her legs, searching for some way to break the hold, but her legs were being held by something she couldn't find.

Someone outside shouted something that might have been her name.

"Here!" she shouted.

Lukas clamped a hand over her mouth, his fingers pressing into her cheeks. His eyes burned with a savage fury, and he pulled a thin silver circle out of somewhere in his robe. It was large enough to be a crown, and trails of blue light bled from a handful of small gems set in it.

He breathed heavily, his face in front of hers. "Why are you making me do this?" His voice was hoarse with anger. "Tell me what I need to know."

Outside there was no more noise, and when she didn't try to scream again, he loosened his grip on her mouth.

Sini tried to pull her legs away from the floor, fury and anguish warring in her. "You promised," she whispered.

Lukas pressed his eyes shut and waved his hand. Sini's arms froze as well.

"Lukas!" she pleaded. "Stop!"

Without meeting her gaze, he gave the circle a tug and it opened. He wrapped it around her neck, and it clicked together behind her. The cold metal lay around her neck like a collar.

He stepped back and Sini felt a wave of peace push away everything else. The fury in her faded to the background and a new feeling grew. She wanted to make Lukas happy, wanted to see the smile she remembered from long ago. It would be so easy.

She scrabbled to keep hold of her anger. She shoved again against whatever held her legs, but everything faded away but Lukas. If she made him happy, it would make her happy. There was nothing else worth being bothered with. Her shoulders relaxed and at another wave of Lukas's hand, her arms were freed.

She felt tears roll down her cheek, but she couldn't fathom why. Lukas had tears of his own, and it broke her heart to see them. She couldn't stay quiet, not when she could help her brother.

"The valley lies behind the Marsham Cliffs." She brought her hand up to wipe the wetness off his face as she told him how to find it. And he did smile. Not with the happiness she'd hoped for, but it was a start.

"Thank you, Sini," he said quietly.

Some part of her mind cried out an alarm. The Keepers were there. Rett was there. "Lukas—"

Another yell came from outside.

She paused. That voice sounded familiar.

"It's time to go." Lukas's voice grew stronger. "I can't carry you, I have my own things to carry. So I'm going to release your legs and we'll head out the back. We'll be home before you know it. You'll stay calm?"

"Yes."

Her legs stumbled forward, free. Lukas grabbed her arm to steady her. He gave her a probing look. "Ready?"

She nodded again and he smiled at her. Her heart soared at the expression and she grinned back at him.

Promised! The word rang in her mind like a feral beast, pounding against the tranquility that filled her. It held so much agony that she paused.

"Let's get Rett out of the palace," he said, leading her toward the door. "I'm sure you can convince him to come with us."

"But Rett…"

"Sini!" The muffled voice from outside *was* familiar.

"Roan?" she whispered.

Lukas slung the belt with the swords over his shoulder and picked up his pack. He set a hand on her elbow and guided her toward the door. "It's no one, Sini. A ghost from your past. Not important any longer."

She nodded, but she cocked her head to listen again. A woman's voice called out her name. The angry voice in her mind wanted her to listen. She pushed back against his hand. "Wait, that's Sora."

Lukas stiffened. "She tracked Pest?"

There was a tingling at Sini's neck. *Vitalle* seeping in along the cold line of silver. She raised her hand to feel the band. She tried to look at it, but it was snug up against her throat, and all she saw was the trail of blue light.

Compulsion stones.

The anger in her flared again, and before the foreign serenity could drown it out, Sini grabbed for the sunlight from the window. It was too little. She pulled energy from the fire. The collar was already open to her, pouring in a need to help Lukas. She used those paths to pour in whatever *vitalle* she could find. These stones were so much stronger than the ring the man in the woods had worn. These must be well-cut, unflawed gems and they drew in the *vitalle* gladly.

But there was still a limit. There was always a limit to what the stone could hold. She poured in the energy from her own body. She drew it from Lukas where he still touched her arm. He yanked his hand away.

"Stop it!" He reached for her again, his face furious, but stopped before touching her. She grabbed his arm and the skin on her palm burned as she pulled *vitalle* from him and shoved it into the stones.

One stone cracked. Four more continued to lap up the energy.

Lukas wrenched his arm away with a cry.

Voices outside the window grew louder. Someone pounded on the front door of the shop.

The front door shouldn't be locked. The thought wormed its way through Sini's mind. Had Pest locked her in?

She shoved more energy into the collar and another gem split. Its *vitalle* dribbled out harmlessly.

Lukas stared at her, his face furious. A huge part of her wanted to stop, to fix things. To fix him.

But the wild voice inside her was too strong.

It was her voice. Not a Keeper's voice, not the voice of Lukas's sister, or a slave, or a poor girl from the Lees. This was her own voice and it combined all those things to become something more. Something stronger.

And she listened.

Every place the collar touched her neck, she forced energy into it.

A third stone split and Lukas snarled. From the front door of the shop came a sharp crack and Lukas let out a growl.

His face twisted in fury and he set a red ring against Sini's temple. She was drawing in so much energy, that a flood of *vitalle* poured into her head.

"Sleep." Lukas's voice broke at the end of the word.

Everything went dark.

TWENTY-NINE

"Sini!"

The voice came from far away, clawing at her. She floated in the deepest, emptiest sleep and all she wanted was to be left alone.

"Sini!" It was more urgent this time, and someone shook her. A man. His voice sounded familiar.

The hard floor pressed against her back. Her eyelids felt thick and heavy and so happy to be closed.

Lukas. His name shot through her mind. What if it was Lukas trying to rouse her? Something tingled gently around her neck. For him she'd open her eyes.

"Lukas?" she whispered. A face came into focus above her. "Will?"

Relief washed over his face. "She's awake," he called over his shoulder. He peered back into her face. "Sin, are you all right? Why are you here?"

The memory of the past few minutes flooded in like someone had shoved back the curtains. She let out a groan and tried to sit up. "Lukas was here. Pest brought me to him." Will's arm slid under her shoulder and he helped her to sit. "Lukas left when you were at the door. Out the back."

"What was he wearing?"

A revulsion came over her at answering. She couldn't betray her brother like that. He needed to be safe.

But that was the collar talking, and Sini grabbed it, trying to yank it off. The metal stayed latched and dug into the back of her neck. "A red cloak," she said through clenched teeth. "It was really…" Her mind searched for the word, battling to want to keep talking. "Fancy."

What else? She thought of the deep red stone he'd pressed to her temple, and a surge of fury rose. She grabbed Will's arm. "He wore burning stones. Lots of them. If you get close and cast out, you'll feel them." She squeezed her eyes shut. "So many of them."

Roan knelt on Sini's other side.

"You have her?" Will demanded.

Sini shook her head, trying to banish the sleepiness, and the room tilted.

Roan set his hand on her back, holding her steady. "Go."

Sora stood at the door, her arms crossed, her face livid. "I take it back," she said, her voice hard. "You do need protecting." Will rose and motioned for Sora to follow him before Sini remembered the other important thing.

"Will!" Sini called out. "He has both swords."

Will's face darkened and he nodded. He and Sora disappeared toward the back of the shop.

"Are you hurt?" Roan's face was worried and furious. "What do you need?"

Sini tugged at the collar around her neck. "The sunlight."

"There is no sunlight, Sini. It's raining."

"Get me outside." She tried to stand, and he helped her. "There's always sunlight."

Her legs didn't want to hold her weight. Roan half supported, half carried her out of the room. They stepped past the front door, hung broken on its hinges, into the chilly rain. The clouds were thick, but to their left the sky was slightly brighter. Sini sank down on a bench along the front of the building. Ignoring the urge to just close her eyes and go back to sleep, she reached up toward the sunfire, drawing in the bits of it that fought their way through the clouds. She shoved it into the collar and the final two stones cracked.

The last of the compulsion to please Lukas scattered. The sleepiness did not, and she leaned her head back against the wall and closed her eyes. She cast out inside her own body, looking for some way to fight it. But there was nothing specific. Just an overwhelming urge to lay down on the bench and go to sleep, despite the cold drizzle.

"Are you…"

She cracked one eye open. Roan stood in front of her, his face drawn in worry.

"I'm fine."

"You don't look fine," he said bluntly. Then he bit his lip and knelt down in front of her. He studied her, his face still a mix of anger and concern. "Did he hurt you?"

The question sent an ache deep in to her chest. Lukas had promised. He had promised and she had believed him. She pressed her eyes shut at the memory of her legs fixed to the floor. She dug her fingers under the collar at her neck and yanked at it, but it did nothing more than cut into the back of her neck.

A sob tore out of her, and she covered her face.

He had promised.

"Can I help you take that off your neck?" Roan asked gently.

A brand-new surge of fury rolled through her. She wanted to rip it off and fling it into the gutter. She nodded quickly and leaned forward. Roan's fingers ran along the back of the collar.

"There's nothing here. No break, no latch…I was going to wait here for Will and Sora, but let's get you back to the palace. The blacksmith will have to cut it off." He ducked back into the shop and found paper for a note. *Took S. back home.* He propped it up in the window and pulled the door closed as well as he could. Sini considered the note for a moment. If only she was going home.

The Stronghold.

Her stomach dropped.

She'd told Lukas how to find the Stronghold. The guilt tasted sour in her mouth. "I need to get to Alaric. As fast as we can."

"The palace is our goal. Can you stand?"

Roan helped her up, and with a hand on her elbow to keep her steady, started them down the street.

The sleepiness was beginning to fade in the face of the rain, but Sini's tongue felt thick and dry, and everything inside her ached at the fact that she'd told Lukas how to find the Stronghold.

"I'm thirsty," she whispered.

"We'll be passing through the market soon. I'll find you something."

He looked more like a real guard with his uniform wet and his shoes muddy. "How did you find me?"

He gave her a slightly guilty look. "The guards at the gate were to notify me if you left the palace."

She raised an eyebrow. "You're watching me?"

"No, I am doing my job and making sure you are safe."

"Are you watching the other Keepers? Will leaves the palace all the time with Sora."

Roan shifted. "We keep tabs on Will as well, for his safety. Today, it was reported to me that Pest had taken you into the city. Since he was supposed to be on his way to Marshwell, that needed investigating. Will was with me at the time, and said he'd had some lingering doubts about Pest's intentions toward you."

"His intentions?"

"Something about Pest's emotions being more guilty around you than was necessary." Roan looked at her pointedly. "How does Will know that?"

"That's a question for Will to answer." She frowned. "He said nothing to me about Pest."

"Apparently he said nothing to anyone. He told me that complicated emotions were common enough that if he investigated every time it happened, he'd never get anything else done." Roan waited, as though she would explain that to him. She kept her eyes forward and tried to not think about how thirsty she was. "Regardless," Roan continued, "the news troubled him, and he sent his hawk to follow Pest." This earned Sini another pointed look. "How exactly is Talen trained to help him follow someone?"

Sini's legs felt heavy. "Another question for Will."

With a disapproving look he continued. "Between Talen and Sora, we were able to track you to that shop. While Talen seemed to believe Pest had moved on, Sora was sure there were people inside the shop. Care to tell me how she knew that?"

She felt a flicker of irritation. "Will you stop asking me questions about other people and just finish the story?"

"You know the rest. When we found the door locked, Will and Sora were both convinced you were inside, so we forced our way in. We found you alone, lying on the floor." His grip tightened on her arm. "For a moment I thought you were dead."

The street gradually grew busier and the drizzle ended. They turned a corner into the wide square that held the bustling city market. Sini stumbled on an uneven cobblestone and her legs almost gave out. Roan helped her to a bench set against a statue, surrounded by merchants. The commotion set Sini's head spinning and she reached up for more sunfire. The warmth of it helped a little and her mind perked up.

"How long is the tiredness going to last?" Roan asked.

"I wish I knew." She tried to swallow. "Is there anything to drink?"

Roan stepped out past the edge of the merchant carts. "Nothing close. And I'm not leaving you here. There are enough guards in the market that one should pass shortly. You can rest until we see one."

Sini nodded. The dryness in her mouth was growing unbearable. She leaned back and closed her eyes, trying not to think about her thick tongue. The merchant from the cart next to her called out to folks passing by. Sini glanced over at him, surprised to find him familiar. He caught her eye and gave her a wide smile.

He turned to face his new captive audience. "Scarves, jewelry, perfumes, trinkets!"

"You're the merchant from the Lees," Sini said.

The man grinned. "The young lady and her guard friend."

The man's merchandise was all pushed well inside the roof of his little cart lest the rain begin again. Roan plucked at a silk scarf hanging down inside the cart. Made from thin, bright green silk, it fluttered gently. "Your fortunes have improved." He ran a skeptical gaze across the finery in the cart. "Earned all this from selling musty cloaks in the Lees, did you?"

"My cart never holds all my wares," the wiry old man assured him. "Different people need different things. Sometimes the same people need different things on different days." He glanced at Sini. "For instance, you again look like a young woman who's in need of…something."

"Do you have anything that will change someone back into the person you used to know?"

The man stroked his beard, which was much tamer than the last time they'd seen him. "That would be expensive. But I have found that most other people haven't changed more than I have myself."

She considered his words. "What if they've grown cold and let hatred taint their mind?"

"More's the pity." His old face grew somber. "Those things usually have roots in some great pain. The most hateful among us are often worthy of a great deal of pity." He shot her a smile. "Is there something more concrete you're after today?"

"Water would be lovely."

"No water." He pulled out a drawer at the back of his cart and rummaged through it, pulling out a glass bottle. "But I do have fine old yellow wine from Greentree."

"I don't feel up to wine at the moment."

"Yellow wine is medicinal." Roan peered at the bottle. "And rare. Neither of us are carrying nearly enough money for that."

The old man waved away his words. "We can always trade." He dismissed Roan with a quick glance, then turned to Sini. "That garnet ring on your finger?"

She closed her hand into a fist. "No."

"Perhaps the silver circlet around your neck?"

Sini let out a tired breath. "If you can get it off, it's yours. We can't seem to manage it."

"I've seen quite a few clasps in my time." He shuffled over and Sini turned so he could see the back of her neck. "Ah, yes." His fingers tickled along the collar for a moment before she heard a click. "Naponese. There's a hidden spring. Takes only a slight pressure, but it has to be in just the right place." The silver band hinged open and he took it off her neck. Sini rubbed the skin under it, expecting to feel some sort of freedom. All she felt was the chill air against her newly bare skin.

"Did it used to hold gems?" the merchant asked, examining the silver.

Roan frowned at the man. "They've been lost."

"No matter, the silver is lovely, and the clasp is in excellent shape." He clicked the collar closed and tucked it into his drawer. "Your wine, my lady." He popped the cork out with a flourish and handed it to her.

The glass was smooth and elegant, the neck wrapped in a band of purple ribbon dotted with glass beads and dangling a round yellow tag. She took a sip and the light-yellow liquid flowed through her mouth like a burst of life in the desert. She took another drink and felt a warmth start in her chest and spread outward. The flavor was light and lemony with a hint of something spicier, and the combination perked up her mind.

"That is delicious." Sini blinked and sat up straighter.

"Can you walk again?" Roan asked. "We should get back to the palace."

At her nod, he helped her up and offered his arm. She leaned on it as they started through the square.

"What is this?" Sini held up the yellow tag. It wasn't a perfect circle, more like a rounded flower petal, or a seashell. The underside was light, almost a pearly gold, and perfectly smooth. The top was rougher, dimpled with hundreds of tiny impressions. The bright yellow glittered in the dim sunlight. Ripples of something lighter, like frosted cream, shimmered across the surface when she tilted it. "It's beautiful."

"Dragon scale." Roan stretched to see over the crowd with an irritated expression. His hand on her back exerted enough pressure to keep her moving. "Where's the guard?"

"A dragon scale?"

He spared her a glance. "Not a real one. The story is that yellow wine was first made in caverns that had once held dragons and the floor was littered with dragon scales. So they decorate the bottles with them. Today they're made of glass. Or painted silver, if the bottle is expensive enough."

She took another drink of the wine and her mind cleared a bit more. "This doesn't look like glass or silver." Her mind might be waking, but her feet still felt like they were tied to stones.

"C'mon, Sini. Put your arm over my shoulders. Where is the useless excuse for a city guard?"

She complied and Roan half urged, half carried her forward. In the next street they found a guard, and Roan commandeered his horse. He helped Sini up and, ordering the guard to come with them, they moved quickly toward the palace.

By the time they reached it, Roan had collected three more guards. Sini felt a bit like a prisoner surrounded by the serious young men. The yellow wine had worked wonders, though. Her head was clear, and she felt mostly-normal by the time they reached the queen's study, where, although there was no queen, Madeleine and Roan's father sat at the table and Alaric leaned over a map of Greentree.

"Lukas knows where the Stronghold is," Sini blurted out.

Alaric straightened. Madeleine frowned at Sini's wet hair and muddy pants and Sini fought off a moment's irritation that once again she had shown up before this woman looking like a gutter rat. Madeleine's frown deepened when she took in Roan's condition.

"What is she talking about?" the duke demanded of Roan.

The irritation flared into anger at the idea that she couldn't answer for herself. She forced herself not to snap at the man. "Pest lured me away from the palace," she said, speaking to Alaric.

The Keeper's brow dropped at the word "lured."

"He offered to show me where my mother was living. But it wasn't my mother he took me to, it was Lukas."

Alaric stared at her "Here? In the city?"

"He has houses here."

"Houses? Plural?" Alaric sat down hard in his chair. "And he knows where the Stronghold is?"

Sini tried not to notice the appalled expressions on Madeleine and Duke Heath's faces. "I didn't want to tell him." The word wrung out of her. "He…forced me to."

Roan tensed at the words.

"Forced you?" Madeleine's voice dripped with scorn.

Understanding dawned in Alaric's face. "A compulsion stone."

Sini sank into a chair and rubbed the skin on her neck.

"He put some sort of necklace on her," Roan said, "with blue stones."

Alaric moved around the table to sit next to her. "It's not your fault, Sini."

"Then whose fault is it?" demanded Madeleine.

Guilt washed over Sini again and she closed her eyes.

"Sini?" Alaric set his hand on her shoulder and waited until she met his gaze. "It's not your fault. When Lukas used a compulsion stone on Will, it took him ages to fight it off."

"I wanted to fight it, but there was no sunlight. There was a small fire, but I couldn't get enough energy to do anything."

Alaric squeezed her shoulder. "Now you know what the rest of us feel like all the time."

"If the Keepers had been here at the palace like the queen has commanded more than once," Madeleine said, "this would not matter."

Alaric's jaw clenched, but he nodded. "They should certainly be brought here now." He grabbed a piece of paper from the table and wrote a hasty note.

"Send this by raven to the Stronghold immediately," Alaric commanded a guard standing by the door. "Find the queen and Douglon," Alaric ordered another. "And notify me the moment Keeper Will returns to the palace; we have to go get the others. Roan, prepare a carriage to leave immediately. The Shield and Mikal will need to sit, the twins will need to lie down. Rett and Gerone should be able to ride. Bring at least a dozen guards."

Roan nodded and started for the door.

Madeleine and the Duke both watched him obey with narrowed eyes.

"You're not going," Madeleine declared to Roan.

He paused. "I am. Excuse me."

Before he could leave, his father stood. "Your place is here, with Madeleine."

Roan stiffened. "The queen has given me orders to see to the protection of the Keepers. And I intend to do just that."

Before either Madeleine or the Duke could protest, he strode out of the room. Roan's father sat back down, his face furious.

Sini hesitated before speaking. When she did, she addressed it to Alaric. "There's more." Sini told him how Lukas had troops already in motion. "He made it sound like an attack is imminent."

"Did he say where?" Alaric asked.

Sini shook her head.

"The first and second battalions of the guard are already moving south." Alaric leaned over the map. "I think we should send the third and fourth as well. The fifth can stay in the city."

"All of the Greentree and Marshwell troops stand ready," the duke snapped. "The first and second battalions of the city guard are more than enough."

"No one doubts the strength of your troops, sir. But we cannot afford to underestimate Lukas. As it seems we have done too many times." Alaric turned to Madeleine. "Please tell the queen that I strongly suggest she send more troops.

"Sini," Alaric said, offering her his hand to help her stand, "we should be ready to leave for the Stronghold when Will returns."

Madeleine rose, her face incredulous. "You are not all leaving."

"Yes. As soon as we can. If Lukas is threatening the Stronghold, we need to go. With luck we'll get there before Lukas and bring the other Keepers back safely."

"The queen must be consulted before you all go do something so perilous." Madeleine declared, crossing her arm. "What happens now is her decision."

Alaric's hand tightened on Sini's before he dropped it and turned to the future queen. In a perfectly polite voice he said, "Not this time. Tell the queen the Stronghold is in grave danger. We will return with the others as quickly as possible."

"Keeper Alaric is right," Duke Greentree said. "They must leave immediately."

Madeleine fixed Alaric with a black look, sparing a sliver of one for the duke.

Alaric bowed to both of them, seemingly undaunted by either the approval or the censure. Sini did as well, and the room spun slightly at the motion. Alaric offered Sini his arm, and she took it gratefully. Beneath her fingers his arm was tight with tension.

"You can't leave now," she said quietly when they'd reached the hall. "Not with Evangeline so ready to give birth."

He squeezed his eyes shut. "They think it won't be for at least a week."

"How can they know?"

He shook his head. "I can't stay here if the others are in danger. Start from the beginning of today, Sini. Tell me everything."

THIRTY

L ess than an hour later, Sini leaned against her horse, her head resting on the saddle. A frosty wind blew through the courtyard. Around her, grooms finished readying horses and stocking the carriage with blankets and pillows. More than a dozen mounted guards surrounded them, waiting to leave.

"Talen will be able to find us with the Stronghold's response," Will assured Alaric, fastening a note to the little hawk's leg.

"Even while we're traveling?"

"I have no doubt." Will rubbed his hand down Talen's chest. "Go see the Shield, little one," he said quietly, then raised his hand, and the hawk soared away to the east.

Sini mounted and pulled her Keeper's robe tightly around her. Sora sat nearby on her horse, her hunting leathers covered by a thick wool cloak. Her gaze followed Talen as though she wanted to soar away with him.

"We'll move with haste," Roan announced. "The carriage will follow with as much speed as possible." The soldiers began to form up into a line.

"You know we're not going to get out of this without running into that dragon," Douglon grumbled, leading his horse up between Sini and Sora. "I can't decide which is worse. Facing that dragon—again—or going home to face that wretched throne."

"Stay with us and face the dragon," Sora told him. "It might give you a chance to use that big red axe you carry everywhere."

"I want to see a dragon," Avina said, clinging to the horse's neck while Douglon climbed into the saddle.

"If I could trust you to behave," Douglon told her, a disapproving look on his face, "I would get you as far from the dragon as I could. But since you're set on biting noblewomen, I can't leave you behind."

"She touched my hair," Avina said, as though that explained everything.

"That's because your hair looks like veins of copper." He tousled her head and she swatted at his hand. "Everyone wants to touch it."

"If you want me to stay," the elfling said, "why are we going?"

"Because Alaric is my friend," he answered patiently. "And friends don't let friends ride toward dragons alone."

With an order from Roan, the guards nearest the gate began to move out.

"I gave up carrying my axe in the Elder Grove," Douglon said to Sora, his face pensive. "It sat against the wall in my cottage for over a year."

She glanced at him. "Did you miss it?"

Douglon grinned. "I did."

"They're going to make you give it up when you're on the throne."

He scowled. "I'll be High Dwarf, I'll carry my axe anywhere I choose."

"That's not the way the crown works." Sora prodded her horse forward. "I'd be looking for an exit strategy. Quickly."

Douglon's shoulders sank and he followed her, muttering into his beard.

Sini fell in behind them. The sleepiness Lukas had caused was gone, but she felt numb and vaguely ill. Thick wool pants and a heavy sweater helped her Keeper's robe ward off the cold, but the dull truth of Lukas's betrayal sat deep inside her like a cold stone.

She spun her ring and ran through the conversation with him over and over. His unhinged laughter, his face as he clicked the collar around her neck. She had trusted him. The thought made her furious and sick. And then the guilt returned. She shouldn't have let him put that collar on her. She should have been able to fight it off. Destroying compulsion stones wasn't hard.

Past the gate the guards formed up around them and Sini gladly placed herself between two silent and stern grey uniforms. The group, large enough to attract attention, trotted at a quick pace out of the city. Her thoughts swirled in the same circles and she hunched down under her robe.

Lukas's assumptions that she'd been duped by the Keepers stung. Not because of the Keepers, but because she had been so naive when it came to him. And Pest. She felt a sharp jab of anger at the weasel. How could she have trusted him so easily when both Roan and Sora had warned her? Of course Pest had never mentioned anything to Roan about Sini's mother. He had merely snuck into Sini's room and lied. And she'd fallen for every word.

Roan was livid about Pest. To Roan's credit, he never pointed out to Sini that he'd warned her, only apologized endlessly and set such a high reward for Pest's capture that all of Queenstown was searching for the man. Roan also sent runners to every military outpost in the country with Pest's description and orders to arrest him on sight.

A trail of wide streets led out of the city and across the long bridge spanning the river. Rolling hills dotted with farm houses spread out ahead of them. Scattered stands of trees were brushed with the golds and reds of early fall. Even that scene couldn't raise her spirits. When they reached the open ground on the far side, the guards spread out and set a ground-eating pace. They rode hard until they reached a stream crossing, and Sini gratefully dismounted. Her horse drank and grazed while she stretched. Her thoughts still swirled around Lukas. She should have been able to resist him. The Keepers were in terrible danger because she hadn't been strong enough.

When Will came up beside her, she forced herself not to cringe. "I don't want to talk."

"I'm not expecting you to," Will answered easily. "I only want you to listen and know that no one blames you. Compulsion stones are no simple thing. Lukas handed one to me, and I sat on the floor staring into it while he stabbed Killien and tried to kill me."

"But you didn't know what it was," she pointed out. "I knew it from the moment it touched my skin, and I still couldn't fight it."

"I knew," Will said quietly. "A part of me knew the entire time. I knew all I had to do was drop it and I'd be fine. Afterward, I kept asking myself why I didn't just put the stone down. But I couldn't. I didn't want to. And everyone knows you couldn't refuse Lukas, either. So there's no point torturing yourself. Lukas violated your trust and stole from you."

The truth of the statement cut deeply but lessened her guilt a little. "I should have played along with him earlier," she said dully. "If I'd cooperated before he put that collar on me, I could have lied about where the Stronghold was and escaped later. I just…"

She'd never imagined he'd use a compulsion stone on her. That was her real mistake.

"What I don't understand," Will said, "is why he left you there. I would have thought he'd make you go with him once you were wearing the collar."

"He tried. I was going to go, but then I heard you all calling me, and his hold faltered enough that I could break a few of the stones."

"A few of them?"

"There were five."

Will stared at her, open-mouthed. "You fought off five stones?" He ran his hand through his hair. "Never mind. I'm done trying to console you. You're not even human. Next time Lukas needs to put you in a cave created completely out of compulsion stones and maybe he'll get somewhere."

"He did get somewhere!" Sini snapped. "He found out the location of the Stronghold."

"He has a dragon, Sin," Will said. "He can fly. It was only a matter of time before he found it."

"How long do you think before Lukas can reach Anguine and fly to the Stronghold?" she asked.

"No one's reported seeing a dragon in Queensland. So the closest he could be is the northern edges of Coastal Baylon or Napon. Lukas will have a two-day trip to get to him. It'll be tight, but we should be able to get the old men out of the Stronghold before then."

The wave of guilt rolled over her again. "And what will happen to the Stronghold itself?"

Will didn't answer.

"I'm sorry," she said, spinning her ring. "I should have listened. You have all been telling me for years how awful he was, and I couldn't see it."

"You had faith in his humanity," Will said. "That is a good thing."

She thought of how tortured Lukas had looked at the end.

"It seemed like he didn't want to be what he is now," she almost whispered. "But he's become it anyway."

"He didn't want to hurt Killien either," Will said. "But he did. He left him to die. Lukas is too driven by fear and hatred to listen to what he really wants."

She felt the stirring of something new, a pity for Lukas. "He was…frantic. Haunted." She looked at Will. "He can communicate with Anguine the way you can with Talen."

Will raised an eyebrow.

"Lukas said he can feel Anguine's emotions and almost see through his eyes. It's not clear, like our vision, but he gets impressions. Apparently the dragon can see heat. Living things are bright."

"Talen sees in different colors than we do. Things are more colorful. There are more blues and purples than we see."

"Lukas can give Anguine commands too, desires for things."

Will nodded. "That's how I convinced Talen to go to the Stronghold."

Sini shook her head. "Can you believe that after all this, the Shield was right? The library roof isn't strong enough to stand against a dragon. No part of the library is strong enough." Her stomach sank. "All the books will be lost."

Will glanced up into the sky. "I have spent a decent amount of time wondering what that old man sensed. Dragon attack never entered my mind."

An unsettling thought struck Sini. "You can call Talen, can't you? When he's far away?"

"To some extent. If he's within a few minutes flight I can." He squinted at the sky. "I honestly am not sure exactly how it happens. But if he were traveling with us, flying nearby, I could call to him with a desire to come back, and he would."

"But it doesn't work far away?"

"I don't know, honestly. I've never tried."

Sini looked toward the southern horizon. "If Lukas can call Anguine like that, we have less time than we thought."

A thought occurred to her and she did a quick count of the days that had passed. "I think tomorrow is the day the twins thought they'd finish their book. A few days ago I was wishing I could be there for it. But not like this."

Will sighed. "Maybe we'll get to see them pen the last words."

Once the horses had rested, they pushed ahead again. The afternoon remained cold and a mist rose, leaving them walking through a greyish world with no horizons. Though the soldiers kept up a quick pace, it was hard to shake the impression that they were making no progress at all. She kept wishing she could see the sky, wondering if even now a dragon was flying over unseen. Regularly, she reached up for the thin sunfire slipping through the fog, pulling the energy down and warming herself with it.

The fog persisted and the only sign that the day was progressing was a gradual darkening of the world to blackness. They rode long into the dark, trying to make as much progress as possible. When they finally stopped, the soldiers set up a camp in a copse of trees a little off the road. The cluster of tents was set up with a speed and precision Sini had never seen, and she gratefully climbed into the tent designated for her and Sora.

She felt like she'd barely closed her eyes when the sounds of the camp roused her. Sora was already gone, and Sini lay for a moment, deeply envious of herself just a few weeks ago. It had been so recent that she'd been able to lie warm and lazy in her bed at the Stronghold, her biggest worry how to account for Lukas's odd behavior.

Lukas.

She shoved herself out of her blankets and into the cold air before the guilt could even settle. She'd slept in her clothes and just added her warmest cloak before ducking out of the small tent.

The sun was just rising, and the morning was stunningly beautiful.

The trees above her glowed, their golden leaves drenched in sunlight. Between them a brilliant blue flung itself gloriously across the sky. The edges of the grass were touched with frost. Wherever the sun touched it, the ground glittered like gemstones. Sini stepped out of the trees and turned her face toward the sun. She closed her eyes and sunfire pressed against her skin. She breathed it in, letting it seep into her muscles. She blew out a long breath and opened her eyes to see it cloud up into a puff of whiteness.

She heard footsteps and turned to find Roan approaching. A soldier called to him and he answered with an easy nod. Their camp was a flurry of activity as the soldiers pulled it down as efficiently as they'd set it up the night before.

He stopped next to her and looked at her critically. "Are you recovered from yesterday?"

"I'm getting there." She glanced at the soldiers who were efficiently pulling down the tents. "Are you recovered from the days we had to be at court?"

He laughed and ran his hand through his hair. "Yes. Being on the road cures me almost instantly."

"How are you going to survive a life at court?"

He blew out a long, frosty breath. "Madeleine and I have discussed how well-suited I am for the job of ambassador. Not permanently stationed anywhere, of course, but we both agree that the kingdom is large enough that having an emissary of the crown travel regularly is a good thing."

"That's a good idea. The Keepers believe the same thing. Thus Will's near-constant travel."

"I doubt my travel will be as enjoyable as his, but it will be better than court."

"Will you get to begin soon? After Duncave and now this, it seems like Madeleine and the queen are in favor of you traveling."

"I will be officially named emissary in a fortnight." His gaze grew distant.

"You don't seem excited."

He cleared his throat. "It becomes official on our wedding day."

Sini stared at him. "You're marrying Madeleine in a fortnight?"

"That is the reason my father came to Queenstown. He felt it was better for the kingdom in a time of crisis, to have the heir's marriage solidified."

"And he has the power to decide this?"

"He has the influence and the skill to convince those who do. The queen, who is more worried about Lukas than she appears, was easily swayed."

"How does Madeleine feel about it?"

Roan grimaced. "Livid, last I saw."

Sini paused. "And is your father angry that you came with us?"

"I imagine so. He thinks I should stay there as an advisor." He shrugged. "Let him be mad. He can play advisor while I'm gone. It's what he really wants anyway."

The chill morning air pushed on her again, and Sini drew in more sunfire, letting it flow down into her hands and feet.

Voices called out in the camp that everything was readied to leave. She started to turn back when he touched her arm. His face was pained. "I know at court I'm..." He stopped.

"Insufferable?" she offered with a smile.

He almost smiled. "I was going to say formal. I don't mean to be. But everything there weighs on me so heavily. When my father is there, he criticizes everything from my wardrobe to my posture to my words to my silences." He rubbed his hand across his mouth. "You are the only person there who I consider a friend." He looked at her earnestly, and there was a hint of fear in his eyes. "Be patient with me?"

She reached out and grabbed his hand. His fingers were cold, and she funneled some of the sunfire into him. His eyes widened and he started to pull back, but she tightened her grip. "You'll be cold the rest of the morning. Take the heat while you can get it." He looked at her for a moment before offering her his other hand. She wrapped her hands around his fingers and in moments they were warm against her palms. She let go.

She pushed aside the idea of him marrying Madeleine. It felt too lonely to dwell on. "There's nothing to be patient with, Roan. We all have to adjust." She started walking back to the horses and he followed, his face unhappy. Trying to shake the gloomy mood, she said, "But more support for my opinions when we're in a council would go a long way toward mending your horrible insufferableness."

The edge of his mouth quirked up. "If your map work improved, I'd be more likely to support it." His smile faded. "After all this is done, do you think you'll even be at court much?"

Sini sighed. "I'm fairly certain it will be impossible for me to get out of it."

THIRTY-ONE

They left the campground at a hurried pace. They were making good time and should reach the Stronghold by the afternoon. Roan rode at the front of the column, and Sini felt glad to have some distance from him. His marriage to Madeleine felt…irritating, and she didn't want to examine that feeling too closely.

It felt like ages before they rested the horses at a small lake. Her back ached from all the trotting and she made her way to where Will and Alaric were talking. "When we were attacked on the way to the elves," she said to Alaric, "How did you strengthen the sticks you fought with?"

Alaric considered her for a moment. "Inanimate things have an essence that is different than the *vitalle* that fills living things. It infuses the object with its own sense of being. Take your ring." He motioned to the silver band on her finger with the garnet. "If you cast out toward the silver, you'll find it filled with tiny drops of…silver-ness."

She cast out toward it, but saw only the bright *vitalle* of her hand and the flare of energy around the garnet. "I see nothing." She glanced at Will.

"Don't look at me," he said. "If you can't see it, there's no hope for me."

"It takes practice." Alaric picked up a piece of grass and reached over to touch Sini's ring with one finger. She cast out toward the ring again and felt something shift inside it. Very slowly, a faint stream of something dark trickled out of it and into Alaric's finger. He moved his finger to the grass, and she saw the something slide into it. Creeping forward the tiniest bit at a time, a thin line of *vitalle* wrapped around it. When it was done, Alaric shook out his hand and gave the grass to Sini. It felt like a cold, hard needle in her hand.

"That won't last," Alaric said. "The silver essence won't bind to the grass, not without a lot of coaxing, but it will remain hard until maybe midday."

"How did you find the essence of the silver? I've never read anything about doing that."

"The Keepers aren't fond of the idea," he admitted. "But I was convinced at one time that Evangeline's cure lay in understanding how the Shade Seekers manipulated inanimate things, so I was motivated to learn." His face grew pensive. "It helped save Evangeline's life. The older Keepers don't agree with me, but I think it's just another way to think about energy." He motioned to her ring. "They won't be excited about that either, but I think burning stones can be useful tools."

Sini tried to bend the grass, but it stayed rigid. "Could we use this to strengthen the Stronghold?

It's already made of stone, but I doubt that will be enough. What would make it stronger than a dragon?"

Alaric laughed. "Another dragon?"

"Please don't let there be another dragon," Will groaned.

Sini sat up straight in her saddle. "What about a dragon scale?" She searched through the pockets of her Keeper's robe and pulled out the thin yellow scale.

The yellow glittered so brightly in the sunlight that Alaric drew back. "You have a dragon scale?"

"I don't know that it's real." She tilted it and a ripple of frosty cream-colored light raced across the surface.

He took it and held it up in the sunlight. "Where did you get this?"

"It came on a bottle of yellow wine from a merchant in the city square. Roan said they are traditionally decorated with dragon scales, but today they're made of thin painted metal."

Alaric closed his eyes and Sini felt something like a gentle casting out. His eyes flew open. "This is real!"

Will took it and examined it. "Breathtaking."

"Where was this merchant?" Alaric asked.

"In the market square in Queenstown. And Roan and I also met him in the Lees one morning."

Will tried to bend the scale but it refused. "It's stronger than it looks." He handed it back to Sini.

"Maybe strong enough to protect against another dragon," Alaric agreed. Roan called out that it was time to continue. "Keep that safe," Alaric said. "And available."

She held it in her palm and the light danced across the yellow in shimmers of glittering wintery white. A real dragon scale. She tucked it back into her deepest pocket and with one last stretch, mounted her horse.

By midmorning they could see the Marsham Cliffs rising like a wall on the eastern horizon. The road wandered toward it over hills and around stands of trees. But the real barrier to the Stronghold wasn't the cliffs. At the base of the rock face, the blue-green shadow of a pine forest stretched as far to the north and south as they could see. Sini gripped the reins tighter when she caught sight of it. They were close enough to it by lunch that they ate the rations the guards handed out without stopping.

Talen soared out of the sky not long after they'd eaten, flaring his wings to land on Will's saddle horn with a note that the Keepers would be ready to leave when they arrived.

When they reached the edge of the trees Alaric called for a stop.

"This is as far as the guards go," he announced.

Roan began to protest, but Alaric stopped him. "The path through the woods to the Stronghold is already protected and I'm not bringing a dozen strangers to a hidden valley."

"They don't want to go in anyway," Will said.

Sini looked into the woods. "They really don't."

"The forest won't let you through," Alaric continued, speaking to the soldiers. "Without the escort of a Keeper, you'd likely wander in it until you died."

The soldiers exchanged tight glances.

"We may need help carrying the other Keepers out, though, so Roan, Douglon, and Sora can come," Alaric said. "And we'll need the stretchers in case the twins are too weak to ride."

Roan took the stretchers on his own horse, and Alaric led the rest of them farther up the edge of the forest, out of view of the soldiers. They rode on, Alaric looking intently into the trees over two more hills before he stopped next to a thin game trail.

The path didn't look familiar. Sini knew there were a half dozen small paths that led into the woods, and if they were followed correctly, to the Stronghold. But she'd never been on this one.

"I'll go first," Alaric said.

"How do you know we won't lead people back here in the future?" Douglon asked him.

Alaric spared him a short glance. "You won't want to. The forest does not want you to get through. There are things that will attempt to scare you into leaving the path."

Douglon shifted to peer into the forest. "I'm not afraid of trees." In his lap, Avina peered at the woods curiously. He glanced down at her. "Very often."

"It's not the trees. You'll hear wolves. They cannot hurt you if you stay on the path." He squared his shoulders and looked into the trees. "And there are ghosts."

Sini shivered at the memory of the white faces.

"They can read your deepest fears," Alaric continued. "Just remember, no matter what you hear, none of it will hurt you as long as you stay with us on the path."

"And if we leave the path?" Roan asked.

"Don't do that," Will said grimly.

Alaric glanced at Douglon. "You might want to cover Avina's ears. I don't think a crazed elf will help this go any smoother."

Douglon nodded and shifted her until she faced him, tucking her in tight to his chest. He set his huge hands over the sides of her face. "Just keep looking at me, little one." She nodded, her eyes wide, and he pressed his hands over her ears.

Alaric nudged his horse forward and entered the wood. Douglon came next, followed by Roan. Will motioned for Sini to go before Sora. Will brought up the rear.

The forest was almost like any other. Sunlight streamed down from above in long rays of light. A thick layer of dead pine needles covered the ground, muting their horses' steps. The air held the clean smell of pine and the damp smell of moss. Birds chittered and small unseen animals rustled through the undergrowth. But there was something watchful. Something biding its time.

Roan rode ahead of Sini with his hand on the pommel of his sword. Douglon twitched toward each new sound.

"Worse than the Greenwood," he muttered.

"Keep a tight rein on your horses," Alaric called back. "Nothing will hurt us on the path."

Roan shot a concerned look over his shoulder at Sini.

"We should hear the wolves soon," she said.

The first howl rang out to their right, and the entire group twisted to face that way. More sounded from the left and Sini's horse flicked his ears.

"Keep moving," Will called.

They hurried their horses forward, flinching at the howls ringing out around them until around a sharp corner in the path, the baying stopped and the forest fell quiet. No birds sang and no little animals scurried along the branches or the forest floor.

"I think I liked the howls better," Roan muttered.

"You'll like them better than the ghosts," Sini said. "They try to convince you that your worst fears are true."

"That doesn't sound too bad."

"It is."

They rode through the unnaturally quiet forest for several long minutes before Sini caught a glimpse of Alaric flinching at something. Douglon swore a moment later and curled himself over Avina. The reaction trickled down the line as each person passed a large pine standing on the left edge of the path.

Roan looked around warily until his eyes snapped to the trunk. He drew in a sharp breath and pulled away.

Sini braced herself.

As her horse drew even with the tree, a milky white face slid out of the bark. "You are alone," it whispered.

Even knowing it was coming, the words struck deeper than she'd expected. The face was an old man, gaunt and thin. Stringy bits of hair hung from the sides of his head. His eyes were empty black holes.

"I am not," Sini whispered back, gripping her reins tightly. "I have seven friends here. Which is a lot for me."

"They won't hurt you," Will said, his voice tight. "Just keep riding."

When Sini reached the next tree a child's face leaned toward her. "Your powers are uselesssss." The hiss followed after her, creeping along the back of her neck.

A ray of sunlight slanted through the trees ahead of her and she rode through it, drawing in the sunfire, letting the power of it fill her.

The next face emerged slowly from the tree, lifting his chin and staring at her with black eyes. Lukas.

She gripped the reins tighter.

He looked as he had on the Sweep, his hair long, his beard braided. Sini drew in a gasp and waited, but he said nothing, merely watched her with disdain. She turned to watch him disappear behind her.

"I'm glad to be free of you," his voice snapped her attention back forward and she shrank back from his cold, accusing eyes. "I shouldered your weight for too long."

"We just kept you around for your power," he whispered from ahead of her. She snapped her head around and saw his face glaring at her with disgust from the next trunk. Every tree ahead of her on the path held a milky, thin image of his face.

"They don't want you," one said.

She flinched lower in her saddle.

"You offer them nothing," said the next.

"You've done nothing but hurt them."

Sini's heart pounded and she shut her eyes, letting her horse follow Roan's down the path on its own. Alaric's voice startled her into looking up. His face, pale and severe, floated at the next trunk. "You betrayed us." His voice cut into her. "You're so naive."

Her breath caught in her throat and she flinched away as Will's face appeared ahead of her. Instead of angry, he looked tired, defeated. "I should have left you on the Sweep."

She shrank away from the words, from the truth of it. Rett's familiar, gentle face slid out of the next trunk and she pressed her hand to her mouth. Not Rett too.

"Tired of helping you, Sini." His voice dripped with disgust.

She pressed her eyes shut. *That's not Rett. It's not really him.* Her heart pounded and a sob rose up her throat anyway.

"We wish," the Shield's thin, old voice began, and her eyes were drawn to his face against her will, "that you'd never been found."

She ducked her head down so she wouldn't have to see them.

"You don't belong," Rett's voice said.

"You've never belonged," agreed Lukas.

The truth of it crashed into her.

Ahead, the real Alaric let out a strangled yell and spurred his horse into a gallop to reach the edge of the trees. Douglon and Roan followed, and Sini pounded after them, flying out past the last tree, the voices of the ghosts fading into the forest. She let her horse run across the swath of grass to stop by the others along the base of a huge cliff.

The words still pounded in her head. ...*never belonged*...

Above them the Marsham Cliffs jutted up into the sky. Sunlight poured down on them and Sini drank it in, letting the sunfire infuse her, driving back the fear that gutted her. Sora and Will spilled out of the forest behind her, hunched over their horses' necks.

"What—" Douglon's voice came through rough, "—was that?" The dwarf's face was pale behind his beard and Sini caught the glimmer of wetness on his cheeks. Avina clung to him sobbing and he had his arms wrapped around her so tightly it was a miracle she could breathe. "I thought this place housed kindly old men. Why is it guarded by those demons?"

"Those wards were placed here centuries ago," Alaric said, his voice unsteady. "We're not sure why this particular form of protection was chosen, but it's generally effective. Even we Keepers don't really want to come through these woods."

Most of the others stared at the ground. Sora curled forward in her saddle, her arms wrapped around herself. Will rode up next to her, and even though his own face was haunted, he set his hand on her shoulder.

"Deep breaths," he told everyone, his voice quiet. "The ghosts play on your emotions. None of those words are things you haven't told yourself. They strike deeply because they are familiar." His voice strengthened as he spoke. In the bright sunlight Sini could just see the mist of blue-green light forming from his words. It reached her and she felt a breath of peace. "But every one of you is feeling the same thing."

Sini glanced at him, realizing that not only could he feel his own fear, he could also feel everyone else's.

"The ghosts used different words," he continued, "but it causes the same result in each of us. They want you to feel hopeless and alone.

"The forest fed your fear so that you would run away, because it knows your fears can overcome almost everything else. But love can overpower things too, as can the truth that we are not hopeless or alone. Breathe deeply. Look at each other."

Sini did take a full breath. The air in the clearing was fresh and calm. Roan's face was drawn, his shoulders curled in.

"Look at each other." Will rode slowly between them all and stopped near Alaric who sat stiffly on his horse, his breath coming quickly. Will managed a small smile, his voice steadier. "Those emotions aren't the full truth about you, but it's easier to recognize that about someone else. These friends around you—you'd banish their fears if you could. You'd convince them that the truth of who they are is so much vaster."

Alaric rubbed at his face and looked around the group.

"As clearly as you know that about them"—Will caught Sini's eye—"remember the same about yourselves. If you can't hear your own voice telling you that your fears do not define you, then believe the words your friends would speak."

Sini straightened in her saddle, taking another breath, and the others stirred around her.

"Trust me," Will said, his smile coming easier now. "You are all much more than a single emotion."

Roan pushed his shoulders down and sat up taller. He met her gaze and offered her an exhausted smile.

"Now," Will said, "we need to get the Keepers out. Don't worry," he added, "the forest is perfectly happy to let us leave. There'll be no ghosts on the way out."

He climbed off his horse and walked toward the cliff. The short section of wall that covered the entrance to the Stronghold sat flush against the rock face. Alaric dismounted as well and stretched, and Sini and the others followed suit.

Roan walked up close to Sini's shoulder. "How many times have you ridden through there?" he asked quietly.

"Too many."

He gave her a sidelong glance. "Does it ever get easier?"

She pressed her eyes shut. "No."

He considered her for a moment, opening his mouth twice before he actually spoke. "You're a good Keeper, Sini. Alaric and Will already trust you. And I, for one, am glad you are one. If that matters."

The words sank into her like sunfire, and she leaned into them. "And you," she told him, "will be an excellent lord consort. Madeleine is lucky to be marrying you, and court will be a better place for having you in it."

He smiled, a little wearily, but thanked her.

Alaric cast out toward the wall, and Sini felt the quiet hum of the rune that controlled the entrance.

"It's so peaceful." Will looked up into the clear blue sky. "At least we know we arrived before the dragon."

Avina let out a long hiss at his words, her little face turned upwards.

Sora's head snapped up toward the sky, as well. Her hand gripped the knife at her belt.

Sini cast out, flinging the wave into the sky. Will and Alaric's waves washed over her in the same heartbeat.

For a breath the casting out returned nothing.

The horses flinched, their ears flicking back and forth.

And then an inferno of *vitalle* blazed out above the forest. Sini shrank back against her horse, her eyes fixed on the clear blue sky.

Dark red flashed between the tree tops.

Anguine soared into view, blocking half the sky. His wings were spread wide—a jagged membrane stretched between thin ridges, letting through dark red sunlight. Tendons splayed through them like black veins.

He soared over the cliff toward the valley of the Stronghold, black shadows rippling across the red scales of his belly like dark, grasping fingers.

THIRTY-TWO

S ini's blood chilled in her veins. Her horse jerked away. Roan's reared up, hooves flying dangerously close to her head.

Alaric sprinted to the wall and slammed his hand onto the stones. "*Aperi!*"

The wall shifted. Alaric and Will raced in before the dark entry to the tunnel was clearly visible. Sini tore into the shadows after them. The running steps of the others followed.

The tunnel was longer than it had ever been, the bright arch at the other end so small she could see only a patch of light beyond it. The air was cool and silent except for the sounds of their pounding feet—until a crash thundered from the valley, shaking the floor and knocking dust loose from the ceiling. A cloud billowed across the end of the tunnel and Sini's heart clawed up into her throat.

The Shield. The twins. Gerone. Mikal. She gasped in a breath. Rett.

Tiny rocks pelted her from the ceiling and she pushed herself faster. Alaric reached the end first and stopped short at the exit. Beyond him the valley was hazy with dust. Sini ran up beside him, expecting the entire tower to be a pile of rubble.

The main tower of the Stronghold still stood, glowing white in the bright midday sunlight.

Tucked up beside it, the shorter brown library wing was unharmed, as well. The other low buildings dotting the valley near the tower looked fine, except where dust settled around the barn, now crushed under an enormous boulder that must have been flung down from the cliffs.

Sini searched frantically for the dragon. She caught a glimpse of red arcing high above the cliffs. In the yard behind the stable, the closest building, Rett stood amid a herd of sheep and stared stunned at the ruined barn.

"Rett!" Sini called.

Will took a step toward the man. "Get the animals into the tunnel!"

Rett stood frozen for just a breath until the tiny lamb in his arms bleated in terror. He set his hand on its head. "*Paxa*, little one." The lamb relaxed. He held his hands out over the animals. "*Paxa.*"

Sini felt a twinge of astonishment. He'd calmed the entire flock. Still talking softly to the animals, he herded them out the gap in the fence toward the tunnel.

"We need to get the Keepers out of the tower." Alaric leaned out of the end of the tunnel, searching the sky for the dragon.

Motion at the top edge of the far cliff caught Sini's eye. The red dragon hovered, beating his wings and tearing off a huge boulder with his claws. A shower of smaller rocks cascaded into the valley below. Between the mouth of the tunnel and the tower lay a long stretch of open grass.

"You'll need a distraction," Douglon said, hefting his axe. Avina crowded close to him, her arms wrapped around his leg. The dwarf leaned down to look at her. "That is the dragon that tore up the Elder Grove."

The little elf's face darkened, and she drew back her lips. Sharp teeth slid out of her gums and she hissed.

"Let's go say hello." Douglon lifted her with one hand and Avina swung herself up onto his shoulders, glaring over his head at Anguine who now flew toward the tower, gripping the huge rock in his claws.

Douglon let out a long, deep battle cry and ran out into the grass. Avina held out one hand. She curled it into a claw and a ball of fire burst into life in her palm. With a screech, she hurled it at the dragon. The fireball fell to the ground before it reached him, but Anguine's attention snapped to her.

"Come down and fight, ya' coward," Douglon boomed.

While the dragon was distracted, Will sprinted out of the tunnel toward the tower. Sini followed, with Alaric on her heels.

Avina flung another fireball. Anguine rushed closer but the ball of flames still fell short. The dragon dismissed her and shifted his attention back to the tower, diving toward it. One of Sora's arrows ricocheted off the scales beneath Anguine's eye.

The dragon closed on the tower before the Keepers had run halfway. Mikal and Gerone stumbled out the front doors, spinning to look into the sky.

"Run!" Sini shouted at them.

The old men caught sight of the dragon and broke into a run. They'd only taken a few steps when Anguine hurled the boulder at the base of the tower and shot out a stream of flames. Mikal and Gerone stumbled and fell as rocks exploded from the tower. The wooden front doors burst into flame and huge chunks of rock showered down on the old men.

Sini's heart leapt into her throat. The two men were buried in stone. She raced up to them as Anguine sped off down the valley.

From the front edge of the pile, she caught sight of a hand. She dove to her stomach and looked into a small cave under the rocks. The underside of the stones shimmered slightly. Gerone's wide, shocked eyes blinked out at her. Grabbing his hand, she pulled. Will grasped Gerone's other hand and they drew him out while Alaric pulled out Mikal. Once the Keepers were free, the pile of rocks shifted and collapsed, sending a cloud of dust into Sini's face, stinging her eyes and catching in her throat.

Gerone gripped Will's arm tightly. "How...?"

"The twins," Will said, nodding up toward the top of the tower.

Sini's eyes raked the Stronghold until she saw them—Nikolas and Steffan, standing together on their balcony, unprotected and vulnerable, peering down at them. Their skin was bone-white and one of them leaned heavily on the railing.

Sini grabbed Will's arm. "We need to get them down!" But there was no more entrance to the tower. The doors, what could be seen of them past the pile of rubble, were alight from dragon fire. There was no way in.

"Strangers!" Hissed Mikal, pointing at Douglon, Avina, Sora, and Roan. "You brought strangers into the valley?"

"People!" Gerone interrupted him. "Just in time! They look like they can fight!"

Sini started to explain, but the Shield rushed out of a small door at the side of the library wing. "Alaric! Sini!" he called, his voice steely. "I have need of you."

Alaric ran toward him without hesitation.

Sini sprinted after him. "But the twins!"

"The Shield needs us," he called back to her, angling for where the tiny old man stood, peering at the library.

Over her shoulder she saw Anguine soar up to the top of the cliffs at the far end of the valley, breaking loose another huge stone while the sunlight flashed scarlet on his scales. The sun was high in the sky and sunfire poured down. She drew it in, the warmth of it driving off the chill of the air. It filled her chest and her arms and drove her legs faster.

She cast out and could feel the *vitalle* of the dragon like an inferno hurling into the valley behind her. She cast a glance over her shoulder. He raced up the valley toward them, skimming over the grass, sending out a stream of flame that blasted into the side of the white tower. Chunks of charred rock toppled off the far wall, and the dragon streaked past before launching back into the sky. Two arrows in quick succession from Sora skipped off his scales.

Sini ran past Alaric, reaching the Shield first at the brown stone wall of the library. He turned toward her, his normally serene face frightened. "I can't save the books." He grabbed her sleeve, his fear churning a rush of her own in her stomach. "I need something strong!"

"The scale!" Alaric yelled running up to them.

The dragon scale. Sini dug it out of her pocket and handed it to the Shield. He stared at it for a moment before comprehension dawned. "You can get its essence?" he demanded of Alaric.

The tall Keeper nodded and took the scale. The Shield ran his hand over his bald head, his face regaining some of its composure. "Clearly we need to strengthen more than the roof." He turned to Alaric. "How much can you give me? Enough for the tower, too?"

Alaric's face was bleak. "Only enough for the library, and even that might be a stretch."

The Shield spared a stricken look for the tall white tower of the Stronghold before facing the library.

"*Vitalle*, Sini," he said gravely. "As much as you can find."

Alaric knelt down and placed the scale on his palm. Sini drew in the sunfire that poured down on her. She looked up at Steffan and Nikolas, leaning on their railing, surveying the valley.

"They can't stay there," she said.

"The twins know what they're doing," the Shield said without looking. Alaric held out the scale and the Shield touched it. His eyes widened, and he set his other hand on the library wall. "That *vitalle*, Sini! Now!"

She felt a rush of energy pour out of the tiny man. A huge stream of bright white light shot out of his palm toward the library wall. The *vitalle* flowing into him was more than she'd ever felt near Alaric or Will. A hundredfold as much. It seeped out of the ground through his feet, but it also streaked toward him from the white stones of the Stronghold itself. She was blinded for a moment by the light flooding from all directions into the tiny man.

"Sini!" he called, in a strangled voice.

She brought her hand next to his and let the sunfire stream out of her, pouring her own pink river of *vitalle* into the path of light he'd created. The magic he'd started lapped greedily at the extra energy. She closed her eyes and turned her face toward the sun, drinking in the heat and the power.

Her body began to thrum with it. The sunfire warmed her, filled her, called her to itself.

She opened her eyes to see Alaric drawing bits of yellow from the dragon scale, sliding them into the stream of light like seeds bobbing in a river. The Shield's arm shook, funneling the energy and the essence of the scale up into the wall. A web of light crawled upward and around the brown stone of the library, covering the walls and sliding up onto the roof. Where the library connected to the white tower, the web disappeared into the building.

The sunfire filled Sini with light. Her mind stretched out in it, reaching across the valley, out into the boundless sky. The tips of her fingers began to glow, not with the pink light, but with a radiant gold. The edges of her fingers tingled and blurred. Her thoughts of the Shield and Alaric and the library faded. She breathed in the goodness of the light. The wholeness of it. It pressed against her skin not with pain, but with a longing for freedom.

A crash above her snapped her vision back to the valley. The dragon's red tail flicked overhead, catching the edge of the tower below the twin's window. A white chunk of rock, larger than her whole body, ripped out of the tower and plummeted down toward the library roof. When it hit, the library shook and the ground beneath Sini's feet shuddered. But the rock splintered and cascaded over the edge of the roof, leaving the arched ceiling undamaged.

The Shield sank to his knees next to Alaric, cutting off the *vitalle* to the building. "That should hold," the Shield managed.

With nowhere else to go, the sunfire filled her, infusing her with warmth and light and hope.

"Sini." The Shield's quiet voice tugged at her. She clenched her fists and with a tremendous effort closed herself off to the sunfire, letting it drain out of her, leaving her empty and dark. She fell to her knees next to him. His face was white and his eyes unfocused.

"Are you hurt?" she asked, turning his hand so she could see his palm. A blister, red and split, leaked clear fluid.

He shifted their hands until her own palms were facing up. They were perfectly smooth and healthy. "Well done, my girl. Well done."

Before she could answer, he slumped forward. A sharp crack sounded, this time directly above her. Another huge white stone slid out of place and plummeted toward them. An earsplitting crash sounded just above her, and Alaric clenched his arms around them. Above them the rock burst into pieces and bounced off a thin, wavy layer of air. Rubble shot in all directions and when it cleared she saw, high above her, the twins stretching their hands toward her. The air smoothed itself out and the final bits of white rock pelted down on them. The twins peered down long enough to see her, Alaric, and the Shield stir, then turned back to the sky.

The dragon roared out a burst of fire to her left and she spun to see him send the roof of the stable up in flames. She looked for Rett but saw no sign of him or the sheep. Hopefully they were tucked away in the tunnel by now.

Around her the valley was ablaze. The workshop was a smoldering pile of ash, the barn was not only crushed, but burning. The stables were in flames. Huge swaths of grass were charred down to the earth. The forest on the south end of the valley poured out huge plumes of smoke. Roan, Sora, Douglon, and Avina were huddled together against a tall stone wall that ran along the stables. The dragon shot up past the face of one of the cliffs and Sini spun to face the tower. Huge chunks of stone had been knocked loose.

Only the library was unharmed.

A dozen paces from the door of the Stronghold, Will, Gerone, and Mikal pulled balls of water out of the well and hurled them at the burning front doors, quenching most of the fire.

The dragon flew up over the cliff and disappeared from sight. The Shield moaned and Alaric knelt to look at him. The old man's head drooped, and his eyes rolled back into his head.

"Is he…?" Sini asked.

"Just exhausted," Alaric answered, his face uncertain. "I think." He picked the tiny old man up and ran with him toward the safety of the tunnel.

Sini sprinted to the well, arriving at the same time as Douglon and Avina. The dwarf's sleeve was charred and his face was furious. "Singed my beard!" He pointed at shriveled, blackened ends of his copper-red beard.

"Dragon gone?" Asked Avina, peering into the sky.

"It won't be that easy," muttered Douglon.

Sora and Roan joined them. Sora limped slightly and Roan had a gash on his arm.

"What do we do now?" Sini asked as Alaric and Rett joined them.

"Never fight a dragon in the air," Mikal quoted the famous poem "Dragonsbane", by Flibbet the Peddler.

"We ground him," Gerone agreed. "And keep him down."

Sini stared at them, almost more shocked at their agreement than at their idea. "How are we supposed to do that?"

"Gerone and I will knock him down," Mikal said, still looking up, waiting for the dragon to reappear. "Will, maybe you can control the beast the way you control that hawk."

"He doesn't control the hawk," Gerone argued. "He befriended it."

"That's worked before with this dragon too," Mikal pointed out.

"He's not going to stay still long enough for me to do either," Will said. "Besides, it's not just the dragon. There are two distinct entities in that creature. I can feel the dragon's emotions and Lukas's as well."

"He must be nearby," Sini agreed, "or he wouldn't have enough control." She scanned the top of the valley. A lone figure stood on the top of the eastern cliff. She pointed up at him and everyone turned. "Lukas is using compulsion stones to control Anguine." There was plenty of sunfire raining down. "I can break them and free Anguine if I can touch him." She glanced at the others. "We might be able to convince the dragon to leave us alone." She swallowed the bitterness of the next thought. "We'll never convince Lukas to."

"Anguine has cooperated in exchange for his freedom in the past," Alaric agreed.

"How many times do we need to free one dragon?" Douglon grumbled. "And why is it that no matter who is controlling it, they always want it to attack you Keepers?"

"If we can get the dragon grounded," Sora said, ignoring the dwarf, "we could pin his wings." Everyone stared at her blankly. "In my home caves there are ice bats. They're enormous. But you can hold them if you grab the thin membrane of their wings. If they pull too much, the membrane will tear, so they stay still until you release them."

"And you think the dragon's wings are thin?" Douglon asked.

"Not that thin, but if he were grounded we could roll some heavy rocks onto the thin parts between the thin bones. Enough rocks would pin him." She looked around at the rest of them. "Right?"

"That's the craziest plan I've ever heard." Douglon grinned. "I like it. Let's pin the monster and destroy it!"

"I doubt the destroying part is feasible," Will said, "but Anguine has been reasoned with before—"

Sora twisted to look north. The red silhouette of the dragon soared into view, far to the north, high above the cliffs.

"And I don't have a better idea," Will finished.

"This is ludicrous," Roan said, but he hefted up a large white rock.

"Someone's going to explain to me at some point who all of you are," Mikal said, scowling at the newcomers, "but for now, if you lure him to this open space, flying low, a strong enough wind should ground him. At least for a short time."

Gerone nodded. "You get him here, we'll bring him down."

Sini looked up at the top of the cliffs, a cold fear growing in her. There was only one person that Lukas might pay attention to. "Lukas can see through the dragon's eyes. If he sees me, I might be able to get him to fly closer down…and I don't think he'd kill me." The words sounded unconvincing, even to herself.

"Lukas wouldn't," Will agreed, "but Anguine might."

"Then let's hope Lukas has good control over the dragon," Sini answered. She pulled her black robe off and handed it to Will. "I need to look…familiar."

"This is a terrible idea," Mikal said.

"It is," Will agreed, "but she's right. She's the only one who can get Lukas's attention." He squeezed Sini's shoulder with a look more worried than reassuring. He turned to the older Keepers. "Bring it down near that wall, and we'll use those rocks to pin it. We'll need help with the bigger ones."

"We should be able to roll some of them with *vitalle*," Alaric said.

"Then let's find some big rocks." Will sighed. "Those of us who can't move rocks with *vitalle* can use brute strength."

Everyone but Mikal and Gerone ran back to the broken rock wall along the far end of the yard and began to pull rocks loose.

Anguine began a long, slow dive into the valley and Sini walked over to the grass in the middle of the yard, her heart pounding in her chest. Taking a deep breath, she yelled, "Lukas!"

The air shimmered slightly. Sini glanced up and saw the twins stretching their hands out toward her. She swallowed. Would their shield deflect dragon fire?

"Lukas!" she yelled again, spreading her arms wide.

Anguine shifted his flight slightly and hurtled toward her, his belly brushing over the tops of trees, his claws ripping off branches. The sunlight glittered along his neck and sides, sending shimmers of lighter red and black chasing each other across his body.

When he reached the edge of the grass, Gerone pulled a wavy ball of water out of the well and floated it almost to the wall where the others waited. Mikal waited until the dragon was almost on top of the water before blasting it with a huge stream of fire from the stable.

The fire hit the water and a geyser of steam shot out from it, exploding into the air and catching the dragon under the back of its wings. Anguine's body flipped forward, his tail whipping over his body. He tumbled all the way over, crashing to the ground on his belly and slamming his wide, scaled head into the ground.

The dragon lay stunned, his wings spread crookedly along the ground. The spindly bones that ran down them like stretched-out fingers almost poked through the web of tissue and scales spread between them.

His snout was as tall as Sini's waist. Her heartbeat thrashed in her ears and she stood frozen before the huge shape, every muscle clenched.

The others ran forward, piling rocks on the thin membrane. Large stones rolled forward, directed by the Keepers, and smaller ones were dropped in piles by the others.

Sini forced herself to step toward Anguine's head. Sunlight glinted off his scales in a mesmerizing display of reds and orange and black. Every movement of her head sent splinters of light shooting across the surface of his snout. Each scale perfectly nestled into the ones around it.

Anguine stirred.

Douglon and Roan each dropped a final large stone onto the outermost sections of his wings, pinning them to the ground.

Anguine shook his head and his eyes focused on Sini. She drew in a breath that quivered her entire body, watching to see any sign of recognition from the dragon. A low growl began deep in the red scaled chest.

"Hello, Anguine." Sini's voice was small and tremulous. "And hello, Lukas."

The dragon shifted. The front of his wing lifted off the ground, sending ripples of light across it. But the rocks sat heavily on the thin skin of his wings and the movement jerked to a stop. He twisted his head around, snapping his jaw in fury. The rocks on his other wing cut the motion short.

He snapped his head around and sent a jet of fire at the people behind him. They dove behind the small wall. Anguine's head swung back around and Sini dropped to her knees, ducking as the fire poured out over her head.

Anguine stopped to draw in a breath and Sini faced him. "Lukas!" She stood on shaking legs and held her hands out toward the dragon, wishing they'd stop trembling. "Lukas, stop!"

Anguine's eyes flashed with recognition just as the next burst of flames came. His head whipped away from her and fire charred the grass beside her. The heat hit her like a wall, and she threw her arms up before a shimmery barrier spread between her and the fire, blocking it off. The coolness was like a spray of water on her singed cheeks.

The fire stopped and Anguine drew in a breath, fixing Sini with a glare of absolute hatred. *He bids you remove yourself if you would live.*

"I can free you," Sini said, her voice still sounding too thin. "I can destroy the stones Lukas uses to control you. If you promise to leave."

Anguine's eyes slitted with anger. Douglon inched forward, peering at the place where the dragon's wing met his body. The dwarf held his axe out. Avina, who still sat on his shoulder, formed a little fireball and held it to the blade. When the blade glowed red, Douglon placed the tip of it against the scales at the base of Anguine's wing. There was a small hiss and Anguine's whole body jolted.

"Looks like you've got a weak spot here," Douglon called, pulling out the axe.

Sora's head appeared over the dragon's back on the other side. She pulled out her sword and it chinked across the scales until Anguine flinched again. "Can't be too far inside here before we'd reach something essential," Sora said over Anguine's back.

Douglon grinned at her. "Can't be far at all."

"You want to be free," Sini said drawing the dragon's attention back to herself. "And we want to free you."

"Do we really?" Douglon grumbled.

"We would like," Will said, stepping up next to Sini and sending a quelling look at the dwarf, "to never see you again. Ever."

"That we agree on," the dwarf said. From his shoulder, Avina hissed.

"Sini," Will warned her quietly. "I can feel Lukas fighting for control, trying to get Anguine to stop listening."

Anguine stretched his neck forward until his snout was within Sini's reach. His eyes were amber in the center with flecks of gold, darkening out to a deep red on the edges. His pupils, tall and thin like a snake's, tightened into slashes of hatred. His body trembled.

"Promise me you'll leave," Sini said, her voice strengthening, "Leave Queensland forever, and I'll free you from Lukas."

It is more than the stones, Anguine's voice was laced with rage. *He holds what is mine.*

"When you're free," Will said, "you can take it back."

Anguine rumbled a long, threatening sound and Sini forced herself not to take a step back. *Yes. Even his sword that wields death could not stop me.*

Sword that wields death? Sini's stomach sank. The black sword. "What does it—?"

She was cut off by Anguine thrashing his head wildly to the side. Will grabbed her arm and pulled her back.

"Lukas is gaining control." Will's eyes were wide. "He's making Anguine angrier."

The dragon snapped his head forward and stretched until his muzzle was within Sini's reach, his body quivering. Cautiously she set her hand on the red scales of his nose. "I can help you."

Scalding hot breath shot out of his nostrils, singeing her arm. Measured footsteps came up from her left and Rett came into view.

Sini's heart stuttered. "Stay back, Rett!"

"Dragon not hurt Sini," the big man said, his voice soothing. He reached out and set his hand on Anguine's neck just behind his jaw. "*Paxa,*" Rett crooned softly. The dragon shuddered. "*Paxa,*" Rett ran his hand over the red scales. A trail of green light flowed out of him and seeped into Anguine. The dragon's head settled onto the ground. Alaric set his hand on the scales along Anguine's tail and the dragon's entire body relaxed.

The dragon's eyes were still fixed on Sini and his breath still came in hot, quick bursts. His scales were warm beneath her hand, but he was still.

"That helped," she said, trying to keep her voice calm. She cast out, looking for the compulsion stone Lukas must be using to control him. But the *vitalle* from the dragon was overwhelming. He burned with energy, every bit of him infused with power waiting to be unleashed. It took forever to notice the spattering of bright spots along the back of Anguine's neck, sparkling like a trail of stars.

She craned her neck to see around Anguine's head and caught the glimmer of light blue gems set deep into his scales. Compulsion stones. Dozens of them.

She faced Anguine's terrifying, unblinking eye. "I can destroy the compulsion stones. Promise me you'll leave."

Anguine's eyes bored into her and she fought not to step back.

"That made Lukas nervous," Will said quietly.

Sunfire warmed the top of Sini's head. The heat from the still-smoldering grass and nearby barn was hot and dry and destructive. But the sunfire rested on her like a gentle hand. She could feel it on her shoulders. She turned her face up toward the light and let the wholesomeness of it sink into her skin, healing the sting leftover from the dragon's heat, driving back her fear. The light seeped into her and she pressed it out into Anguine. It ran along his neck, searching for the pinpricks of *vitalle* burrowed deep in his scales.

Each stone trickled energy into the dragon like a dripping icicle. Sini pushed the *vitalle* from the sun back through those paths and into the stones. One compulsion stone cracked, its energy spilling out uselessly down the scales of Anguine's neck. Another split and darkened. Then a third.

Anguine drew in a sharp breath.

"I can destroy them all," Sini said softly.

You do not have the power, Anguine's voice came through strangled.

"That was Lukas," Will said. "He's scared."

The dragon tossed his head, and his voice boomed out, wild and commanding. *Destroy them all!*

Will flinched. "That was not Lukas."

FREE ME! Anguine's voice roared into her mind with enough force that she stumbled back into Will. Anguine's head began to thrash, his wings strained against the stones. *Unchain me and I will take what is mine!*

"His wing is ripping!" Roan called from the far edge of one wing.

The dragon showed no sign of noticing. He flung his body to the side, whipping his tail at the people standing along his wings.

Sini flung more *vitalle* into him and another handful of compulsion stones shattered.

Anguine let out a savage snarl. *Do it,* he choked out. *Do it and I will not harm—* His words were cut off in a roar of pain. He lifted his head and shot a stream of fire high into the air.

"Sini!" Will yelled, "Get away from him! He'll tear himself apart! Lukas is driving him mad!"

She dove around Anguine's face to the side of his neck as his head thrashed to the side, spewing fire. Will, too, lunged out of the way and Sini caught a glimpse of a shimmer following him. She glanced up at the twins and saw them, on their knees now, reaching down toward the group. How could they still have the strength for shields?

Sini slammed herself against the heat of the dragon's neck, splaying her hands across his scales. She poured *vitalle* into him, streaming it toward the compulsion stones. The nearest blue gems split so fast they burst out of the scales, leaving blackened pockmarks.

Her *vitalle* rippled along his neck, breaking stone after stone. The sunfire thrummed in her again, a blanket of warmth instead of the dragon's vicious heat. Bright. Blazing with freedom. Compulsion stones snapped one after the other until all that remained were three larger stones set on the back of Anguine's head.

The dragon thrashed to the side, gushing fire. He turned trying to snap at Sini, his teeth biting the air beside her, the flames rushing past, deflected by a thin, wavering shield. She pressed herself against his neck, funneling more and more sunfire through his glittering red scales.

There was a horrible rending sound and the end of his wing came free, blood streaming from a deep rip. She closed her eyes, feeling the sunfire light her muscles, her bones.

Her fingers glowed and the edges blurred as bits of light floated off them. She shook her head to clear it. "Keep him grounded!" she yelled.

Anguine's whole body shifted and he turned his head, trying to reach Sini along his own neck. Sora gave a yell from the other side and Sini caught a flash of her sword before the ranger stabbed it into the chink behind Anguine's right wing. The dragon whipped his head away from Sini, spraying fire as Sora dove over his tail.

Avina leapt off Douglon's shoulders and raced over the dragon's wide back, her bare feet flitting over the bright scales, flinging fireball after fireball at his face. The dragon yanked and his left wing came completely free. He spun, snapping at the tiny elf on his back.

Sini clung to Anguine's neck, pouring more energy into the stones.

Douglon shouted, raising his axe and driving it home into the gap behind the left wing. Anguine let out a roar and twisted, dragging his other wing out from under the rocks.

"I have wanted to do that for so long!" Douglon yelled, swinging again with his axe. This time he caught the scales and his axe skittered harmlessly off Anguine's side.

Sora, Rett, and Roan backed away from the dragon's whipping tail. Avina leapt off the dragon's back to Douglon and clung to him as he ran for cover. Will ran to the four of them, pushing them back toward the nearest wall. Anguine twisted, spraying fire, and Sini was slammed by the front of his wing. She grabbed it and funneled in more sunfire, pushing it through the long path up to the remaining compulsion stones in Anguine's neck. Over the tattered wing she saw Will throw protection for the others. His own shield didn't shimmer the way the twins' did, but the flames deflected against an unseen barrier and everyone scrambled over the short wall.

Anguine hurled himself off the ground and Sini lost the connection to him. Her body thrummed with sunfire, but she had no path to the dragon. Anguine's wings flung streams of blood as they flapped, and he hurtled forward a few feet off the ground before crashing back down.

She ran after him, funneling energy into her ring and trying to shoot fire at the dragon, just to give herself a path. There were still compulsion stones left—but he was too far away.

"Alaric!" she cried, "give me a path!"

The Keeper ran to her and stretched his hand toward Anguine as the dragon pitched himself into the air again. "Doing what?"

"Anything!"

"*Paxa!*" A shot of orange light shot out of Alaric's hand and into the dragon. Sini hoped for an instant that it would calm the dragon, but the creature was too enraged.

Sini put her hand next to Alaric's and threw her own *vitalle* into the flow, driving the energy toward the dragon's head. One more compulsion stone burst with a flash of light. The light filled her, still. Sini squinted at the dragon, trying desperately to keep her mind focused. She felt light enough to float into the air. The muscles in her arms filled with so much power she could have thrown the dragon into the air. Alaric's hand was normal flesh, but hers glowed a bright gold.

"Lukas is still fighting for control!" Will yelled.

The dragon shoved himself up again and his wings caught the air. His wing dipped to the side and a spray of blood flung out from its tip. He flapped once and rose high enough that Alaric's light struggled to reach him.

Anguine continued rising unsteadily into the air, flying away from them. He let out a ground-shaking roar, and veered sharply to the right, almost falling into the still burning barn. Regaining his balance, he pushed himself higher in the air.

Alaric cut off the now-useless flow of *vitalle*.

With no more path, the sunfire filled Sini and her desperation to reach the dragon faded.

Warmth, light, peace, hope.

The chaos and smoke of the valley faded. The roars of the dragon were lost in the hum of light that infused every fiber of her body. The last thoughts of the dragon faded away and she breathed in the light.

Someone called her name. It might have been Alaric, but even his voice was too dark to pay attention to. Hands shook her shoulders, but all of that was darkness and chaos and she wanted no more of it. If only she could rest in the light. Embraced by it, a part of it.

Her fingers stung like candle wicks burning away in a flame.

There was nothing but the light.

A crash thundered through the valley, knocking Sini to her knees.

From far away she heard Alaric cry out.

Rubble pelted her face, snapping her attention back to the world around her.

She was holding her hands up towards the sun. Her arms glowed golden almost to her elbows, shining like miniature suns.

A horrible grinding noise dragged her attention to the Stronghold tower. Anguine's glittering body thrashed against it, his left side smashing through white stones. His legs scrambling for purchase. He thundered out a stream of fire at the rocks above him until they glowed red and began to soften. With a roar he shoved himself out of the tower and flung out his wings. Free, he flapped heavily upwards toward the top of the cliffs, his twisted wings shuddering in the air.

The remaining compulsion stones glittered blue on his neck among the ripple of red scales, and Sini watched them go with a sense of dread. Had she destroyed enough stones? Was the dragon free?

Anguine clawed at the top of the cliffs, dragging himself over the edge near Lukas. The dragon let out a bellow of fury laced with pain. He opened his mouth at Lukas to douse him in flame, and terror clamped down on Sini's heart. But Lukas thrust out a hand and Anguine twisted his face upward, spraying fire into the sky. The dragon let out a roar of anger, but stretched himself low so Lukas could scramble on.

With another thundering cry the dragon shoved himself into the sky and with jagged, faltering thrusts of his wings, flew south.

Sini stared after them, numb, terrified they'd turn back.

Behind her came the sound of a deep, rending crack.

She spun back around as the main tower of the Stronghold, in a slow, ponderous movement, tilted. A wide crack formed between it and the library.

The breath rushed out of her lungs. She stretched her glowing hand out toward the twins kneeling next to each other on their high balcony as though the sunlight could catch them.

With a sound like a mountain crumbling, the tower leaned.

The twins clung together, burying their faces in each other's shoulders.

The tall white tower pitched to the side. Sini screamed as the stones slipped apart, crashing to the earth one after another with a deafening roar.

A cloud of dirt and debris enveloped her in darkness.

His eyes were amber in the center with flecks of gold, darkening out to a deep red on the edges. His pupils, tall and thin like a snakes', tightened into slashes of hatred.

THIRTY-THREE

The collapse of the tower shook the valley and Sini fell to her knees. The ground trembled as though the earth might split apart. A cloud of dust shot out from the tower and pelted her with tiny fragments of rock. She twisted away and buried her face in her arms until the ground stilled.

Her arms still glowed almost all the way to her elbows, pulsing with her heartbeat. Her fingers shone bright enough they were hard to look at.

Multiple Keepers cast out at once and the waves rolled in through her from all sides. Sini pressed herself smaller, not casting out, wishing she couldn't feel what they were going to discover. Bright points of *vitalle* glowed around her where the others sat or crouched in the wake of the collapse. But the tower itself was completely dark. Not one wave found any life amid the rubble.

Roan called her from somewhere nearby. She curled up tighter, leaning forward over her knees, her eyes pressed closed. Her arms felt too warm, and she couldn't block the memory of the twins clinging to each other. She felt like a tiny pebble sinking in a vast ocean.

"Sini!" Roan called again, closer this time. He dropped to the ground in front of her. "Sini?" His voice rose with fear. "Are you hurt?"

She kept her face down, but shook her head. He shifted to sit beside her.

Roan's arm wrapped around her and she drew in a gasping breath. She felt the hard ground beneath her and the dust in her mouth. The sunfire worked its way through the hazy air and rested gently on the back of her neck. Her next breath caught and came out as a whimper and Roan's arm tightened around her shoulders. She leaned into him and wept.

———————◆◆———————

It was Gerone who finally roused her.

"Rett is injured," the old man said gently. "He needs your help. As do that dwarf and the human woman, and Mikal."

She lifted her head and blinked into the brightness. Her eyes stung with dust. She sat with her back to the tower, facing toward the forest at the southern end of the valley. Smoke poured out of it in more places than she could count.

Numbly she turned and Roan loosened his arm around her shoulder.

It was almost too much to take in. The valley was in ruins. Every building was crushed or burning. Trees were knocked down, stone walls tumbled into the grass.

And the tower—only the first floor still stood, its walls cut off jaggedly. The rest was a trail of white stones flung across the valley floor.

The brown stone library was the only thing undisturbed. The three stories of it that stood above ground were unharmed. The portion of the white wall where the Stronghold had connected to it was still intact. The whole library was covered with a layer of dust, and chunks of rock had rolled down the arched roof to gather at the edges. But it was intact.

Slowly she noticed the others. Alaric and Will stood together near the fallen tower. Douglon, his head and arms bloody, held Avina by the rock wall they'd hidden behind. Sora sat next to him, her arm bloody, pressing something to Rett's head. It came away bright red.

The sight cut through her shock and she tried to push herself up, but her limbs felt weak and she sank back down.

"Do you need help?" Roan asked.

She shook her head. "Just give me a moment." The sun was still high in the sky over the valley. It felt wrong that it had barely moved from when they'd run into the valley. She hesitated, thinking of how brightly her arms had glowed, but she wouldn't need a lot of sunfire for this. Turning her face toward the sunfire, she let it warm her, strengthening her arms and legs, letting the goodness of it ease the ache in her chest.

Bracing herself on Roan, she stood and moved over to Rett. He lay on the ground with his eyes closed, his face pale. A gash ran across his forehead, and he had several cuts on his arms. Sini knelt down next to him and put her hand on his cheek, funneling sunfire into him. The wound started to close and Rett opened his eyes.

His face split into a wide smile at the sight of her. "Happy you're back, Sini," he said, letting his eyes slip closed again.

"Rett threw himself in front of the dragon's tail," Sora said, "keeping us from the worst of the blow."

Beyond Rett's cuts he had a burn on one arm and his ribs were badly bruised, but nothing was broken. Sini focused on the others, healing gashes, reducing swelling where they'd been hit with rocks. The burns were harder to help, but they kept her mind focused on the simple task of moving the warm sunfire.

When she was done, she finally turned to face the tower. A pang of guilt washed over her at the destruction. How could she have let Lukas find out where this valley was? The white tower strewn across the ground felt like a dream she couldn't quite understand.

The loneliness of the library standing amid the rubble pierced her.

Drawn by the rightness of the library amidst the wrongness of the rest of the ruins, she left Will and Alaric and fled the destruction through the same little door the Shield had run out when they arrived. The dry, papery smell of the books almost undid her. It smelled like home, like family and peace, like an afternoon of studying. The serenity of the library might have been on the other side of the world from all the destruction outside.

At ground level, there were two stories above her. She walked to the open center of the library and looked at the glass roof. It wasn't even cracked. Dust and bits of rock coated it, blocking out the sunlight, leaving the library dull and gloomy. On the top floor she caught the glow of a candle. Her mind shut out thoughts of everything outside, as though none of it had happened. She walked along the railing, brushing her ring across every candle she found, leaving a path of golden light behind her. When she reached the top of the ramp, she found the Shield slumped in a chair at his table overflowing with notes about the library roof.

She sat down next to him, looking him over to see if he was hurt.

"I'm fine, my dear. Alaric tucked me into the tunnel where I managed to stay unconscious for most of the dangerous parts of the afternoon."

On top of all his notes sat a pile of 4 books, bound in matching dark leather. A fifth sat open before him. The Shield pushed it toward her.

It was the twins' writing. The page was half-filled and ended with their signatures and yesterday's date. She sat forward to see it better. "Their book? They finished?"

"Just yesterday. They wanted to be done before we needed to leave." He held his hands gingerly and Sini caught sight of blisters on his palms.

"I can help those…a little," she offered.

He shook his head. "They'll heal in time." He nodded toward the book. "You should read the dedication."

Sini turned to the front.

To Sini, whom we love not for all the deeply appreciated healing, or your astounding power, but for the joy you brought us by deigning to breakfast every day with two old men. For brightening each day with your light. You were the granddaughter we never knew we needed, and we miss your presence more than you'll ever know.

Her throat tightened at the words. She felt like tears should fall, but everything still felt too unreal. She read the words again, trying to make them sink in. "I'm glad they finished," she said finally.

"So were they."

She closed the book. "We could have come up through here to reach them." She gestured around the library. "Even after the front doors of the tower were destroyed, we should have come through here."

"The twins had plenty of time to get down." The Shield sank back in his chair. "They chose to stay up there and protect the rest of us. I think,"—he smiled the slightest bit—"they were enjoying themselves. It's been a very long time since they were needed like that."

She ran her fingers over the words of the dedication. "I wish…" She closed the book and set the fifth and final volume of their book on Gringonn on top of the others. What did she wish? "I wish the tower had lasted a little longer."

"They would still be gone," he said gently. "They were already weak, and they didn't have the strength in them to do half of those shields without causing themselves irreparable damage. Even if the tower still stood, we'd have lost the twins today. They saved Gerone, Mikal and Will. They protected you and me and Alaric. And that's just what I saw from the beginning. Without them there might not be a single Keeper alive right now. The dwarf and the humans would probably be dead as well."

"There's a baby elf out there too."

The Shield's bushy eyebrows rose. "Is there really?"

"Will did see the whole thing," Sini said thoughtfully, "so the twins are bound to be immortalized in a story."

The Shield smiled a tired smile. "As will we all, I'm sure. I hope he emphasizes my work on the library and minimizes the fact that I missed the rest of the fight."

"How did you know this?" She waved at the drawings strewn over the table. "How'd you know the roof would need help?"

"She told me." At Sini's blank look he added, "The Stronghold."

She waited to see if he was making some sort of joke. "The Stronghold really talks to you?"

"Not often. But sometimes."

"How…" The number of ways she could finish that question was almost paralyzing. "How did the Stronghold know the roof would need help?"

"That is an excellent question. I have no idea what the answer is."

She stared at him. "The Stronghold has never talked to me."

He laughed. "When I was voted Shield, two things changed. First, the moment I stepped into the Stronghold she greeted me. Not with words, exactly. But she was welcoming all the same. Second, the Wellstone began to…pay attention to me. You saw how independent it is. But when I became Shield it knew. It…put itself under my control. Not completely, and often not in the most helpful ways, but I'd barely been able to direct it before."

Sini sat up. "The Wellstone! Is it gone?"

"It's fine," he assured her. "It was flung out past the end of the rubble when the tower fell. It has rolled up against a tree."

Her mouth dropped open. "Does the Wellstone talk to you too?"

He let out a little, raspy laugh and shook his head. "I saw it fall."

She laughed, for the first time in what felt like days. It loosened something inside her.

"I was by the tunnel, so I had a good view. I'm not certain it's against a tree, but it did roll into that stand of oaks past the workshop—or where the workshop used to be."

They both sobered.

"When I used the Wellstone," she said, "I saw connections between different memories."

He raised a bushy eyebrow. "Did you? Not many do."

"How does it…" She cast about for the question she wanted to ask. "Is it intelligent?"

The Shield rubbed his hand over his head. "I don't think so. It organizes the memories, and that feels intelligent, but…it also might just be magic. The stones are created in the Greenwood and I don't think anyone, maybe not even the elves, know how." He sighed. "When I tried to find out anything about those swords through Chesavia, though, I didn't have much luck. There are so many memories of her and about her. It was a bit like searching through the forest for a specific twig. Maybe if you try, you'll have better luck."

A little nag of worry nipped at Sini. "Did you see all the memories I put in there?"

"Most of them." He smiled gently. "I see why you trusted Lukas. He took good care of you once."

She shook her head. "I should have listened to all of you."

"Not necessarily. Believing the best about someone is usually a good idea."

"Not in this case."

"I think it was." He peered at her. "Even now, do you think he's truly lost?"

The anger at everything he did swelled in her, but she remembered how tortured he sounded as he used his magic on her. "I don't know. I don't think he necessarily wants to be doing it all, but he continues to choose it."

"A common enough trait." He smiled weakly. "Thankfully most people who share it don't have access to a dragon."

She sank back in the chair. Lukas still had the dragon. Everything she'd tried to do had been useless. The valley was in ruins, the twins were gone, and Lukas still had his dragon. She wanted to be angry at him, furious for all the destruction he'd caused. But the truth of what had happened pushed up inside her until she thought she might be sick. She let her head fall back on the chair, closing her eyes. "I failed," she said quietly. "He still has the dragon."

"A wounded dragon," the Shield pointed out.

The sense of defeat filled her until she could feel nothing else. "None of this is over."

"No," The Shield's voice was low. "Not yet." He was quiet a moment. "But we saved the books."

Sini cracked open her eyes to see the little bald man looking warmly at the bookshelves. He had always seemed like the perfect Keeper. He knew everything about everything, had read books from all over the world, always managed to have the right sort of advice. But today…

"You used the essence of the dragon scale to strengthen the library."

At the hint of accusation in her voice the edge of his mouth quirked up.

"I thought Keepers didn't approve of using the essence of inanimate things," she continued. "Alaric said it took a lot of practice. He strengthened a blade of grass for me and it took several minutes. But you…" She thought of him standing there, webs of light stretching out from him, covering the library. "You were amazing."

He straightened and beamed at her. "Thank you."

"That was more of a question than a compliment."

He grinned. "It has less to do with being amazing and more to do with being very old."

She narrowed her eyes at him. "How did you learn to do it?

He lifted his eyes to the glass of the dust covered roof. "That is a long story. One for after all this is done, perhaps. But for now, you are right, none of this is over and Lukas still has a dragon."

She considered pushing him for the story, but he was right. There were more pressing things to discuss. "I think the sword is more of a problem than the dragon. Chesavia noted in her journal that the black sword seemed to exert a power over the warlord Naj. If Lukas found it when we had those reports of dragon sightings over the moors, that was right before the massacre in Gulfind at the gold mines."

The Shield considered the words. "There was definitely an escalation of his violence there."

She nodded and looked around the library. Even though everything looked perfectly familiar, something felt off.

"It keeps changing," the Shield said quietly.

"What does?"

"The way this place feels."

She looked at him sharply.

"The first time I left the Stronghold, when I returned, it felt…wrong. It took me days to feel comfortable again, and even then, it was different. I never have been quite as at ease here as I was in my earliest days."

Sini sank back in her chair, her shoulders slumping forward. "I don't want it to change."

"Sometimes change is good. For instance, it shouldn't be long until a new Keeper is discovered. And though every time I'm nervous that this next Keeper might not really fit with us, I have found each new one to be a joy. Each new Keeper changes this valley a little bit."

"Except some, who destroy it."

"It is not your fault that Lukas came. And in some ways, he is connected to this valley too. Had he stayed in Queensland he would have been brought here almost a decade before you were.

Somehow it still feels a bit like he belongs, doesn't it?"

She thought of him standing atop the cliff, directing the dragon. Of his face as he clicked the collar around her neck. "Not anymore."

"Well then, I hope it brings you some peace to know that even though I have never felt quite as comfortable here as I did in the beginning, I love this place more every year."

"Even now that it's ruined?"

"It's hardly ruined. The books are safe. The Wellstone is safe, and we lost no Keepers today that we haven't already been preparing to lose." He patted Sini's hand. "Towers can be rebuilt, my dear."

The idea felt nearly impossible, but the Shield's face was so hopeful she didn't say anything. "I think I'll go look for the Wellstone," Sini said, pushing herself up from the table. "I'll bring it back here to the library. It feels wrong just to let it lie outside somewhere. Besides, we all have plenty of new memories to add."

"I'll come with you," he said, hopping down out of his chair. "I just needed to come in here and assure myself that the dragon scale really strengthened the building enough. I needed to know it was all unharmed."

They stepped out into the bright afternoon and Sini let the sunfire warm her. The others rummaged at the sides of the crumbled tower, not accomplishing much of anything. The Shield walked along the white stones, stopping at a place that looked just like the rest of it. "Their bodies are under here. Almost on the ground, about ten paces in."

The group looked at the Shield with varying levels of disbelief until Alaric nodded and began shifting rocks. "They deserve a proper burial."

Douglon, leaning on his axe, watched them for a moment before dropping the weapon to the ground and stomping over. "You're doing it all wrong." He waved them out of the way. "Back up, back up. If they're low down, we tunnel in. Two of us shifting stones at a time. Roan, with me. The rest of you, find good, thick branches."

Sini left them and walked alongside the fallen tower. The rubble was as tall as she was, taller in spots, the white stones shining brightly in the sunlight. It felt like she was walking beside the fallen body of some ancient hero. She felt oddly numb next to the destruction. The sunfire that reflected off the stones warmed her just like the standing tower used to do. She touched the edge of a huge block of stone next to her, expecting…something. It was just cool stone.

The top of the tower had flung out farther than the rest, the blocks of rock rolling out into a large grouping of oak trees. Sini cast out when she got near and a bright beacon of *vitalle* glowed from further within the trees, far past the ends of the tunnel. She found the Wellstone glittering in a nook between two gnarled roots. In the shadow of the tree the flash of white light from its facets cast bright spots on the trunk. Sini almost picked it up with the intention of bringing it back to the Shield, when she paused. As soon as she touched it, it would draw in the memories she'd made since the last time she'd touched it. Could that have been barely more than a fortnight ago?

She'd planned to do it somewhere quiet in the library.

Despite the chaos of the day, the valley had settled back into normal sounds of birds and the occasional rustle of trees. The sunfire fell exactly as it always did, in thin streaks where it could sneak through gaps in the branches, in wide diffuse clouds of green light where it had to go through the leaves. From where she stood the only sign of destruction she could see were two white stones that had tumbled into the trees.

She sank down onto the root. This is what she'd been longing for since she left the valley. This peace. But like the library, it wasn't quite right any more. The anger she'd been expecting since the tower fell started to form deep in her stomach. Lukas had torn apart the Stronghold. The best place she'd ever found, and he had destroyed it. It grew to a fury inside her. How dare he come and destroy her home out of ignorance and viciousness? Her hands clenched into fists. She should have stopped him when she had the chance. In that little sewing shop, she should have…

The flickers of light on the hundreds of facets of the Wellstone caught her eye. Her anger chased away any reservations about using it. Let it take her memories, let everyone see how often she failed and how she'd let Lukas control her.

As long as it helped her fight back. Chesavia had known about the black sword. There had to be information in the stone that could help. With a deep breath, she picked it up and settled it onto her lap.

She stood in the chaos again. Images and sounds swirled around with wild abandon. She stepped out into it, willing it to slow. The Wellstone paid her no heed. She caught a glimpse of Alaric, looking much younger, and the Shield, with a little bit of hair actually growing out of his head. Even though the Wellstone surrounded her, she could still feel her hands set on each side of it. She willed a little *vitalle* into it and the chaos shifted like a flock of birds. A brush of curiosity swept past her and paused. Her own memories began to roll out of her. She let them flow as quickly as the stone would take them. Queenstown, talking on the roof with Roan, the Lees, traveling to the Greenwood.

The stone slowed as she hovered over Goven, watching him heal. Then it rushed ahead again. When Sini stepped into the Lumen Greenwood, the stone slowed drastically, drawing out every sight and sound. It focused on the darkness of the trees, taking in every detail of the Greenwood. Every detail of the new elves.

With the scenes moving so slowly, Sini noticed threads of light stretching out from each, winding into the surrounding storm of memories. They left the Greenwood and the flow sped again, moving past Duncave and Queenstown. She saw Lukas again, then the dragon. The stone took an inordinate amount of interest in the battle with the dragon. Every glimpse Sini got of the twins' faces, she studied. It was obvious they had begun exhausted and weakened themselves with every shield they cast. Without having to focus on the dragon, she caught the moment when Anguine's tail had smashed into Rett, and all the other injuries she'd missed while they were happening.

The twins weakened, leaning against each other, casting shield after shield, far more than she'd noticed at the time.

When the tower finally fell, she saw their faces and knew the Shield was right. They knelt together almost as white as the tower. One lay limply against the other, his face already slack. As it toppled, neither of them moved.

The Wellstone backed away from her a little, the memories in it beginning to swirl again as though it had forgotten she was there. She grabbed at her own memories, which were winding away into the chaos.

Everything shifted. Spread out around her was her life. Glimpses of the Lees, the Sweep, the Stronghold. New memories slid in between others, her latest journey connecting images of Douglon, the elves, Sora, or Killien to earlier memories of them put in the Wellstone by Will and Alaric.

Sini remembered her hands on the Wellstone, and funneled a little *vitalle* in through them, directing the stone to show her Lukas.

The first memory that drifted close was Lukas handing her the small topaz stone. "We'll need a lot of energy, Sini. Just funnel it in slowly."

She shoved that one away, but not before she saw her own hands sewing the glowing stone into the lining of Vahe the Wayfarer's money bag.

Her most recent conversation with Lukas drew near and she grabbed for it, focusing on his swords. Several threads stretched away from the image. One led to her own memory from the Sweep as she and Lukas examined the blue sword.

The second led to the image she'd found before: Chesavia on the moors, her hand, with the crescent ring, brushing dirt off the stone cairn where Naj was buried. Sini held onto the memory she'd already read about in Chesavia's journal and let it play.

The afternoon was bright. Chesavia held her palm up toward the sunlight and stretched her other hand toward the grave. A violet-tinted stream of light poured out from her fingers toward the cairn, bits of the energy splitting out from the main stream and shooting uselessly into the air. The amount of light was incredible before the topmost stones shifted to the side, then the ones beneath it. In a few breaths, they had revealed Naj's body. His face was severe, his hair and beard unkempt. His skin was pale with death, but he could not have been dead long.

Two swords lay crossed on his chest. He gripped the hilts with each hand. One blade let off tendrils of blue light; on top of it, the other was wrapped by fingers of darkness. Chesavia reached out to move the blades. Her hands touched them both at once and her fingers clenched. She yanked back from them, but her fingers wouldn't release.

The blue blade was sending arcs of blue into Chesavia, while the black one…

Chesavia's fingertips on it blurred slightly, the edges becoming unfocused.

She turned her face up toward the sun and Sini could almost feel the sunfire streaming into her. With a cry, Chesavia threw herself back and her hands flew free of the swords.

A strand of light led away from that memory and Sini followed it.

She caught sight of Naj in more than one nearby image. He was slightly wild-looking, with two thick, unruly braids catching the auburn hair that hung down his back. She was surrounded by Chesavia's memories of the war chief. He sat in a tent, or rode a horse on the moors, his face attentive and intelligent. There was a private dinner, his face split in a smile.

Sini let all those images flow by, following the thread from the swords.

Chesavia's hand gripped the top of a low rock, hiding on the edge of a battle. The moors stretched out into the distance under a grey, formless sky. Men cried out and swords clashed. But one man strode through the center of the chaos, slicing through the fight holding two swords.

It was Naj, utterly changed.

The sword in his right hand was black like a sliver of the night. Chesavia shifted to the other side of the rock and Naj plunged the black sword into a man on the edge of the fight. The man's body convulsed and fell.

Naj drew in a deep breath and the blue sword flashed brighter. Chesavia's hand clenched on the rock. The warlord's face was gaunt, sunken. His eyes flashed with a dark viciousness. He swung the blue blade and it cut through the man as though he were mist. The black sword hung at his side, seemingly worthless after its one kill.

But still, no one could stop Naj, and the battle was short and swift. Chesavia sank down behind the rock and buried her face in her hands.

Sini let go of the brutal image and moved on, following the trail of Chesavia's memories.

She let Chesavia's life move past her quickly until she caught a glimpse of a wide lake against the backdrop of snowy mountains. From far across the water, a creature rose, formed out of black water. It was vaguely human-sized, but its arms and legs were too long, its torso too thin. Its eyes were nothing but holes, glowing a dark, deep blue.

Chesavia stood on the shore. Sini realized she must be watching through the eyes of Bernn, the Keeper who'd traveled with Chesavia on her final trip.

Of course Chesavia couldn't have given this memory to the Wellstone herself.

Above her the sky was clear and blue. Sunlight glittered on the lake and off the edges of the water demon. The creature clutched a large, wriggling fish in its hands and thin streams of yellowish light flowed out of the fish and into the demon.

"They say it's killed four already," Bernn said, "and grown stronger each time. They hit it with a lit ball of pitch, but the monster devoured it and grew."

"It is drawing in the energy of the things around it," Chesavia answered. "The fire was more food."

"Then how do we destroy it? If you pour sunlight into it, it will just go stronger."

"Everything has its limits."

"Do you?" His voice reflected his growing fear. "Does your sunlight?"

She looked up into the sky. "There is no end to the sunlight. Everything is light."

"That thing doesn't look like light."

The creature moved closer.

"It is. It's just hiding in a different form. Get the people back into the trees. It won't reach the shore."

The creature slid closer over the surface and Chesavia stepped up until her feet were in the edge of the water. She held her hands out toward the demon and Sini saw…nothing. Bernn, unable to see the stream of *vitalle* almost certainly flowing out of Chesavia's hands already, backed up until he stood in the trees with several others. Chesavia was a small figure at the edge of the lake. The energy must have reached the demon because it flung its arms out in surprise, then took a faltering step forward, reaching hungrily toward Chesavia. With each step, the creature grew.

Sini knew how this story ended, and she watched with dread as Chesavia stood on the water's edge, holding her arms out toward the monster. Bernn gasped when her fingertips began to glow with a golden sheen, then her hands. The demon drew closer, it loomed twice as tall as a man now, its chest swollen. A watery maw opened, nothing more than an empty hole surrounded by shifting water. The creature made a deafening wordless sound. The tree next to Bernn trembled at the noise.

The water demon reached forward with dozens of fingerlike rivulets.

Even from this distance Sini could see Chesavia's breath coming in gasps. This is where the well-known story said Chesavia was fighting against the pain of the *vitalle*. But Sini saw the way Chesavia turned her face toward the sun. She wasn't in any pain. Her struggle was against the desire to let the sunfire consume her.

The monster was within a dozen paces of the shore. Chesavia's arms stretched forward, the glow reaching past her elbows. Her arms were like molten gold, her fingers too bright to look at. Bernn stepped forward, reaching helplessly toward Chesavia. Deep inside the creature something glowed like sunlight through the water.

"Stop." Chesavia voice was ragged. Her hands clenched into fists and the golden glow dimmed.

The creature froze, caught off guard by the absence of the light.

"You,"—Chesavia's voice was a wrenching mix of determination and sorrow—"can come no closer to those people."

Sini's stomach dropped at the words.

Chesavia flung her hands open again and lunged forward into the water, grasping the creature's arms.

The water demon twisted back and the light inside it grew brighter. With a roar from its shapeless mouth, it swelled to an enormous size. Chesavia's head tilted back, her gaze drifting up toward the sky and she sighed with utter contentment.

The glow spread up her arms, across her chest, filling her body. The water demon lit like a torch and exploded into glistening shards of light.

Bernn shielded his eyes with his arm, and when he looked again, the lake was perfectly empty. Sini caught a glimpse of the water glittering with a million golden flecks of light before it faded.

Sini dropped her hold on the memory and the images in the Wellstone surged past her. She pulled herself out of the chaos of images, growing aware again of the valley around her.

A claw of cold worry gripped her chest.

Sitting in the shadows of the oak, Sini's arms warmed with the memory of sunfire flowing through them. But the thought of how far the glow had moved up her own arms chilled her.

The thought of what might have happened felt like ice, and she tried to push it from her mind. She thought about the other memories from the Wellstone.

She knew what the black sword did. Like the water demon, it pulled energy into itself. When Naj had wielded it, any enemy he touched with it was sucked dry of *vitalle*. That energy fed the blue sword, and seemed to flow into Naj himself, changing him, feeding a darkness in him.

Chesavia's journal entry about the swords came back to her. *They were not made to be wielded by an ordinary person. In Naj's hands they wreak destruction in this small part of the world. But I dread how terrible they would be were they wielded by someone who understood them, who could use the power in them.*

How much more would the sword do in the hands of someone like Lukas? Could he focus the blades? Draw life out of anyone nearby, even without touching them? Could he draw all that power into himself and make himself more powerful the more he killed?

Sini rubbed the ring on her finger.

Everything has a limit.

Every magical item she'd ever seen did. She'd certainly broken enough of them on the Sweep. Everything has a limit.

Except the sunfire.

The facets of the Wellstone flashed at Sini with colors and bursts of white.

Lukas needed to be stopped. The fact sat like a dull piece of rubble surrounded by the destruction of what she'd wanted for so long. Maybe it had been naive to believe Lukas could come here and be free of all the dark things that drove him. Maybe it had been love that had driven her to think the best of him. Either way, she finally saw who he was. Whether he wanted to be vicious and destructive or not didn't matter. What mattered was that he was headed south to join his armies. He'd spread destruction all the way through Queensland unless someone stopped him.

His dragon wasn't strong enough for battle now. It might not even still be under Lukas's control.

But he still had the swords.

And now Sini knew how to destroy them—and that she was the only one who could.

THIRTY-FOUR

ini found the Keepers sitting near the fallen tower, resting while Douglon and Roan took a
shift trying to reach the twins' bodies.

"I know what the swords do," she said, setting the Wellstone down next to the Shield.
"And I know how to stop them."

She sat down between Rett and Gerone. Rett moved over until his arm was against hers, and
he smiled warmly at her. She leaned against him, letting his sturdiness prop her up, and explained
everything from Chesavia's memories.

"Lukas will be able to do much more with the swords than Naj ever could, I'm sure of it. If we
are going to stop Lukas, we'll need to destroy at least the black blade."

"Do you think you can pour enough energy into the sword to destroy it?" Alaric said.

"Assuming it's daytime, yes." She paused. "I saw Chesavia's battle with the water demon. She
didn't die from moving too much *vitalle*. I've discovered something new about the sunfire."

All the Keepers looked at her with interest.

Haltingly, searching for words to try to describe the longing, she explained the hint she had
of the sun's power while she was healing Goven. How in the Elder Grove she'd funneled so much
that she'd known if she just kept going, she would become the light herself.

The Shield nodded slowly. "I've always wondered about the way Chesavia's arms glowed."

Sini rubbed her own hands, remembering how they'd glowed against Anguine's scales. "There's
something that happens when I have enough light. It seems there's no real difference between the
light and me. That I'm just a cruder stage of it, frozen in solid form. I can feel how everything is
connected. How everything comes from the light, and how we're all destined to go back to it."

She stopped. The words sounded strange once they'd been said. She wasn't explaining it right
at all.

"Everything is light," Will said. "That's what Chesavia said before she died."

Sini nodded. "She knew that she was using too much, that she wouldn't be able to resist it.
It didn't kill her—I mean it did, but it didn't destroy her body the way we've always thought. She
became light."

The men were quiet for a long moment.

"It still killed her," Mikal pointed out, his face set in a worried expression, focused more on
Sini than the story.

Rett made a worried sound.

"But not as hopelessly as we'd thought," Gerone pointed out. Despite his words, he looked at Sini with an equally worried face.

"This is good to know," the Shield said, his own face more thoughtful than worried. "Excellent work, Sini."

Sini looked away from Gerone and Mikal, knowing they'd disagree with her next idea. She addressed the Shield and Alaric instead. "I think I should go south with the soldiers."

"Absolutely not," Mikal said.

"No," Gerone agreed.

"If the black sword works like I think it does, then I'm the only one who could get enough *vitalle* into it to destroy it. It kills one person at a time. I don't think it's made to draw in huge amounts at once."

"You can't know that," Mikal objected. "You know nothing about this sword."

"True, but I know a lot about other things made to hold magic. On the Sweep I dealt with plenty of burning stones. And there were metal objects too: shields, knives, even a hammer. Making an object hold energy is difficult. It doesn't want anything to do with life. Making it give off energy is easier, because it follows the nature of the object to push out the *vitalle*.

"But to make an object draw energy in..." She glanced at Alaric. He'd made such a stone to save Evangeline. "That is challenging and has many limitations."

Alaric's face was dark at the memory, but he nodded. "The absorption process was very structured."

Gerone and Mikal seemed to be the only two who were really troubled by the idea of harnessing *vitalle* in inanimate objects. The Shield watched closely, without any sort of judgement. Alaric had spent the last several years trying to convince them there was nothing intrinsically bad in the storage of energy, but he'd only had moderate luck.

"That sword draws in the energy of the people it touches. But we all know it doesn't require taking much energy from a person before they die. The sword will only draw in so much at a time. Chesavia said the sword rarely killed—it needs breaks before it could draw in energy again. I think it's not made to take in more energy than one person can provide. If I can get near it, I can pour much more into it than it would get from one person, and I can destroy it."

"Assuming it's sunny," Mikal said.

She glanced at him. "It doesn't have to be sunny. There is always sunfire, even on the cloudiest days. It just needs to be daytime. And I was under the impression soldiers planned their battles for daylight hours."

The other Keepers were quiet.

"We don't know Lukas will still attack," Gerone said. "The dragon was gravely injured. I'm not sure it will even have the strength to fly him out of Queensland to his armies."

"He will, and it will be soon," the Shield said quietly, "before Queensland can consolidate her troops in the south. Or he's a fool."

"Sini should not go with the army," Rett said decidedly.

"No, she shouldn't. This is a terrible idea." Mikal said. "Set every archer we have to shoot Lukas from a distance and our problem will be solved. That's how Naj died."

"Lukas isn't stupid enough to leave that angle open," Sini said.

"I agree," Will said.

The Shield's expression had turned sorrowful. "When I sensed change in your future, Sini, this isn't what I was expecting." He considered her for a moment. "The Shield from Chesavia's days wrote, after her death, that she'd had so much power he'd never expected her to live into old age. That she willingly offered too much of herself too often. I would like a different path for you, Sini."

"I can't sit by, safe in Queenstown, while Lukas kills people. Not if I'm the only one who can stop him."

"We don't know that's true," Mikal insisted.

She turned to him. "I know it's true."

Mikal's eyes narrowed, but Gerone next to him laughed and patted the other old man on the shoulder. "It's too late. She's found herself now. You're not going to sway her. Stop arguing about everything.

"I'm not—" Mikal began irritably.

"We'll get the Shield, Gerone, and Mikal settled at the palace," Will interrupted. "And then we'll head south."

Alaric nodded and the Shield sighed but didn't object.

Sini opened her mouth to thank Will, but shouts from the rubble interrupted her.

"We've found the twins!" Douglon called out, and Sini flinched.

Rett, Will, and Alaric rose to help, but she stayed seated. A finger of guilt dragged across her chest. She should go help, but she didn't even want to look.

Gerone put his hand on her shoulder. "Just rest for a bit, my dear. The others are more than able to take care of this. Tell us of your adventures while we wait."

"Yes, the last fortnight has changed you," Mikal said.

Sini's shoulders sank.

Gerone shot Mikal a frown and patted her back. "Obviously in good ways."

"Of course that's obvious," Mikal said. "Anyone who knows Sini knows she's strong enough to use these sorts of things for the better. Why do you always feel the need to explain these things?"

Gerone let out a huff somewhere between amusement and exasperation. "Tell us everything that's happened, my dear."

"And start at the beginning," Mikal said. "No jumping around and confusing us."

———◆———

They stayed in the valley that night. The twins' bodies were buried next to each other in the glade at the north end of the valley next to the dozens of other Keepers' tombstones. The leaves around the clearing glowed with golden light in the gathering evening.

Sini's emotions were thin. There was grief, certainly, but not with the strength she'd expected. Mostly she just felt an empty sort of ache.

The library was warm and dry, and the entire group slept on the floor on the lowest level. Gerone and Mikal created a wind with enough force to clean the dust off the library roof, and the stars glimmered brightly through the glass.

Early the next morning, when the first hint of brightness lightened the sky, Sini took some day-old bread out of her pack and walked out to the twins' grave. The morning was chilly, and she looked at the fresh earth for a long moment before she squeezed in to sit between the tombstones.

"Good morning." Her words were hesitant at first. She closed her eyes, imagining their room in the tower. "I brought breakfast." She broke it into thirds and placed a piece on each grave. "It's old, but I can't imagine that bothers you anymore. And I can stomach it if it means one last breakfast together." She leaned her head against one of the tombstones. "I don't know what you two found to like about court. The place is awful, and even the people you do like get stiff and awkward there."

She let the details of the last few weeks pour out. Not just where she'd gone and what she'd seen, but the people. Madeleine's arrogance, the Duke of Greentree's oppressive presence, Pest's betrayal, the Baron twins, the baby elves, the dwarves. The more she talked the lonelier it all sounded.

"Roan is...sometimes he feels like a friend. But as soon as he's at court, he's this annoying, distant, nothing. It's like he just shuts off." She chewed the last bite of dry bread. "It's irritating."

Neither the gravestones nor the graves nor the trees around the glade gave any answer, but she heard what the twins would say anyway.

"I know he's not happy there either," she answered, "but Alaric's busy and Will has Sora and..." She sighed. "I guess I just miss having someone I could rely on to be...available." The stones were cold where she leaned against them. "I thought I'd been healing you two over the past four years, but it just now occurs to me how much you healed me simply by listening. Before you, I don't think I knew I had a voice that wanted to speak." Her throat tightened. "I wish you were coming to court. I can't find my voice there. Alaric can talk and they hear him. Even Will manages to make himself heard. But I can't...I couldn't even get Lukas to listen to me. He just talked through me." She stopped. "Maybe he doesn't know me any more than I know him."

Two waves rolled through her from the direction of the Stronghold, or what remained of it. A pause, then two more waves.

Come.

She blew out a long breath and brushed the crumbs off her hands before she stood. "Rett's calling." She faced their graves. "Thank you for the shields yesterday. It's the only way any of us stayed strong enough to survive." The sun was hours from being high enough to shine directly in the valley, but the leaves around the glade caught the indirect morning light and shimmered with gold. This place was peaceful and beautiful. The edges of the hollow ache that had grown inside her since she'd watched the tower fall softened. "Thank you for...everything."

* * *

The entire group left the Stronghold an hour past dawn, in what all the Keepers agreed was the first time the valley had ever been emptied. Rett had salvaged four saddles from the corner of the ruined stable and collected horses from where they'd bolted. Mikal, Gerone, and the Shield could ride to where the guards waited at the edge of the forest. Hopefully the carriage from Queenstown had caught up by now. Mikal had objected that someone should stay in the valley and begin the long process of reconstruction, but the Shield had shaken his head and shut the library door.

Sini ate some cheese Gerone passed out without tasting it as they filed into the tunnel and left the Stronghold. After yesterday, the peacefulness felt unreal. The forest let them leave without any sounds other than birds chirping. The runes on the trees stayed dormant, the only faces in the trees belonged to squirrels.

In response to Douglon's grumbling about how horrible the ghosts had been, Mikal launched into a history lesson on the formation of the Stronghold. "These ghosts are a holdover from the time when the common folk believed in supernatural forces and would have been terrified by the mere sight of the apparitions."

"Superstition has nothing to do with it," Gerone disagreed. "The Keepers were smart enough to know that if you control the emotions, you control the man. And nothing makes someone want to run away more than fear. These ghosts are a perfectly painless defense along the path. And have always been effective."

"Hardly painless," Douglon muttered as the two old men continued to debate.

Alaric led them out of the forest into the bright, clear morning. They turned south toward where they'd left the guards. They hadn't gone far when a soldier galloped toward them.

"Armies of Coastal Baylon and Napon approach the southern border!" he shouted.

Sini's heart clenched. So soon?

"There have been skirmishes, and the queen expects a full attack within days. As many of us as can go are ordered south immediately."

They followed him back to the other guards at a gallop. The entire escort stood ready to leave. The Shield, Mikal, and Gerone were quickly settled into the carriage and sent back to Queenstown with half the guard. There was some discussion about Rett joining them, but the man adamantly refused to go back to the palace if Sini was heading south.

Douglon toyed with the idea of heading west as well, seeing if he could find the dwarves and hurry them along. But he'd lose two days getting to Duncave, and if they had done as he'd commanded, they would have started marching south already. Assuming messengers were going between Queenstown and Duncave, the dwarves should already be heading south.

He'd hesitated to bring Avina near the battle, but she hissed at him so viciously at the thought of going back to the Elder Grove he dropped the idea.

"The last report we have says the battle will happen in southern Marshwell," the captain of the six remaining guards reported to Alaric, "across the river from Rillborne Hold."

"Good," Alaric said. "That's where we expected it. At least our troops are headed in the right direction."

"It'll take a full two days to ride there, if we push," the captain said. "We should ride to Brenlen instead and hire a boat."

Alaric nodded. "The Tellryn River will take us within a few hours' ride of the hold. If we continue through the night we can be there by tomorrow morning."

The captain nodded, then paused, a worried look on his face. "I have heard reports that the queen intends to go south herself."

Alaric's face darkened. "Then we need to hurry all the more."

Sini had traveled to Brenlen twice a year with Mikal, but in their wagon the trip took half a day. At the pace the soldiers set, they reached Brenlen barely past midmorning. A wide lumber barge was headed south, and there was just enough room for their horses, a quickly-purchased bundle of hay, and the rest of the group. As long as no one was particularly interested in sleeping anywhere comfortable.

The boat was wide and low, the center of its deck filled with stacked pine logs that still smelled of sap. A low railing ran along the front, back, and port side, while the starboard was left open for rolling the logs on and off.

Sora and Roan set up a little camp along the back end of the barge with the guards. Avina scampered along the railing, while Douglon followed after her, calling for her to be careful, reminding her she couldn't swim and that he wasn't interested in jumping in after her. Will, Alaric, and Rett stood at the front, facing downstream in their black robes. Sini considered joining them but climbed over the lumber to the empty side of the boat and leaned on the railing instead. The sunfire reflected off the water in bursts of warmth, but it couldn't brighten the somberness of her mood.

Once the barge started moving, Roan came up beside her. He didn't speak for a few moments. Finally he brushed a pine needle off the rail. "Lukas is different than I imagined him."

She glanced at him.

He smiled self-consciously. "Somehow with all this talk of what a threat he is, I'd pictured some hulking brute of a man. Some huge warrior with long hair." He grinned. "He's skinny."

A smile spread across Sini's face, and the motion felt unexpected and rusty. "He's skinny and has a bad limp from an old injury that won't heal. It's not his muscles everyone's been nervous about all this time."

"He must have been…" Roan paused. "Was he different when you first met him? He must have been, for you to love him as much as you do."

"It feels like he was." The garnet in Sini's ring caught the sunlight and she shifted it slightly to watch the stone glitter. "I think I always knew he was capable of hating people, but he protected me for years on the Sweep. He taught me the magic he knew, he taught me to read…he taught me how to survive among the Roven. And he shielded me from the worst of it all. When I couldn't get my magic to work right, he claimed he'd caused the problems and took the punishments." She risked a glance at Roan. His face was darker than she'd expected, and she realized it was at the idea of the punishments, not Lukas. "No one in my life had ever protected me from anything, and it saved me during those first years."

Rett stood with Will at the front of the boat, gripping the rail. She felt a slight guilt that she hadn't even talked much to Rett since yesterday. But Will's voice floated back infused with enthusiasm, and he gestured to something in the water. She caught sight of a wide smile on Rett's face and thanked Will silently for helping.

"Lukas and Rett were my family, and they were both kind to me. But if I'm honest, I knew Lukas had the ability to do all these things. Even on the Sweep he never cared if he hurt those he considered enemies." She paused.

"Maybe the real difference between him and me is that he had no one to protect him when he was brought to the Sweep. Lukas could never let down his guard, never be safe." The idea rang true. "No one ever protected him," she said slowly.

"If someone had been there to take care of him, someone more aware than Rett, maybe Lukas would have ended up different. Maybe he wouldn't feel the need to fight everything. By the time Will met him, he was perfectly willing to hurt his enemies. But somehow I convinced myself that his attacks on the Roven and on Killien and Will were…I don't know what. An anomaly. A moment of weakness brought on by his constant attempts to keep us safe, and the fear that he was losing everything."

She watched the water ripple along the side of the boat. "I think I believed he wasn't a threat to other people just because he wasn't a threat to me."

Roan was quiet for a moment. "It's hard to think poorly of your family." He shifted. "When you get the chance to think better of them, it's…nice."

Sini glanced at him.

"Ever since my father arranged my marriage to Madeleine, I've been trying to figure out why." Sini laughed. "Having his son become lord consort isn't enough?"

"That's such a long-term goal for him. Most of his plans result in more immediate gratification. And they almost always come at the expense of someone else. As far as I can tell, this arrangement hurt no one."

"One immediate result is how influential he is in court now."

"But his importance is secondary to mine." He frowned and stared into the water, unseeing. "He doesn't like being second to anyone." He shot a self-conscious glance at Sini. "Despite the fact that I keep wondering why he did it, I can't help being just a little proud that he's orchestrated something that's not utterly self-serving and damaging to others."

He stood silent for a few minutes. "I'm sorry about your friends, the men in the tower. Will told me you were close to them."

Her chest tightened but she told him of their book and the breakfasts they'd had and how safe their room had always felt.

"You make me wish there'd been twins living in a tower at my home."

She gave him a small smile. "Every home should have a pair." She glanced up the river. "It feels strange to have all the Keepers leaving the Stronghold."

"Being at court puts them near people who would use them. I'm not sure how I feel about them being around people like my father."

"Do you really think he could control Keepers? The Shield isn't going to be duped by someone at court a quarter of his age."

"He'll try to control them. He'll use anyone he thinks will gain Greentree any power."

Sini glanced at Roan. He was so comfortable outside the palace. "Even you?"

Before the question was out, she regretted it. Of course even Roan. Especially Roan. Why else would the betrothal to Madeleine exist?

"So far, I haven't used my influence to do anything I regret. I'm not going to change that for him."

The thought of the burning stone she and Lukas had hidden in Vahe's money bag came back to her again. The truth of what she'd done sat heavy in her stomach. "Good. Don't."

Roan glanced at her with a small smile. "That sounded grim. I can't imagine you've ever used your powers for anything nefarious."

She ran her finger over her ring, but didn't answer. At her silence, Roan shifted. "I'm sorry, that was insensitive. If I'd been through what you have in life, I'd…I'm sorry," he finished lamely.

"I was taken to the Sweep by a wayfarer named Vahe," she said, still focused on her ring. "He took me from my parents and sold me to Killien."

She felt the pressure of Roan's gaze. "How old were you?" he asked quietly.

"Twelve. Vahe left me caged in a small, windowless room at the back of his wagon for the entire trip. He fed me scraps."

Roan's hand tightened on the rail and she shook away the memory, continuing without looking at his face. "When I reached the Sweep and met Lukas, I discovered that Vahe had brought him as well, and Rett. And Vahe just kept returning, bringing Killien slaves, all mistreated, some so sick or wounded they never recovered."

She ran her thumb over the garnet in her ring, feeling the bit of *vitalle* swirling in it. "And so the third spring I was there, Lukas and I stole a small topaz from Killien's collection and Lukas turned it into a burning stone that would slowly draw energy from anyone near it. It took a huge amount of energy to complete and he never could have done it without me, but I helped him willingly. And then I sewed it into the lining of the money bag that Killien would pay him with and handed it to Vahe myself."

Roan stood silently next to her.

"His face was so smug, and so cruel…I gave it to him happily." Vahe had tied the pouch to his belt, as she'd known he would. "He left that morning, and never returned."

"Did it kill him?"

Sini shrugged. "I don't know. If he carried it long enough it would have weakened him gradually. It may have killed him. It may have just weakened him to the point where some other sickness killed him. I don't know. All we know is that he never returned."

"Are you still happy you gave it to him?"

She felt the familiar pang of guilt. "I don't know."

Roan's hands were tight on the railing. "I'm happy you did."

They stood in silence for a few moments, listening to the splatting and sloshing of the water on the side of the boat. Sini turned her face up to the sunfire and let it trickle into her, warming her against the chill of the air and chasing away the dark thoughts.

"If you go to face Lukas," Roan asked, "will you have to use your powers in a way you might regret again?"

"I don't know. I think I can destroy his black sword. And I won't regret doing that."

"But if you're pouring energy into the sword, and Lukas is holding the sword, what will that do to him?"

"That depends on how fast the blade transfers the energy out. If it's slow, like I think it should be, I'll destroy the sword before it can send the power to Lukas."

"And if not? Will you just strengthen him?"

She nodded, fear worming its way into her. "Either that or I'll kill him."

The trip south was expected to take until morning, and while they were making far faster progress than they could have on horseback, their forced idleness left everyone restless. Sini was sitting by herself again, letting the motion of the boat and the sounds of the river lull her when she felt the wave of Rett's casting roll through her twice, a pause, then twice more.

He sat in the front corner of the edge of the barge looking sadly into the river. She crossed to him and sat, her shoulder leaning against his. For a few moments neither of them spoke.

"Don't like the twins falling," Rett said finally.

Sini reached over and took one of his hands, leaning her head on his shoulder. "Neither do I."

He paused again before continuing quietly, "The twins were sick."

"Yes," she whispered.

His next words came out troubled. "Too sick for Sini?"

She pressed her eyes shut against the tears. "Yes, Rett."

"The Shield says sometimes people can't be healed."

All she could manage was a nod.

He patted her hand, then turned it to see the garnet on her ring. "A burning stone?"

Taking a deep breath, she blinked away the tears. "Yes. Alaric made it for me." She picked up a sliver of tree bark from next to her on the deck and lit it on fire with her ring.

Rett drew in a sharp breath, his whole body brightening with excitement. "You can light it!"

His enthusiasm brought a smile to her face. "Yes." She tossed the burning bark into the river.

Rett scooped up more from beside him and offered her another piece. She lit it and he let out a whoop that echoed across the water. She sat with him, lighting small pieces of wood on fire and catching up on things like the growth of Rett's lamb, until one of the horses got restless and Rett went to calm it.

Sini was perfectly happy to sit alone after that. The sunlight shining off the water was mesmerizing, and she rested against one especially large log and watched the light play. Fall colors dusted everything. The grass along the river was yellowing. The leaves shone gold and red as they fluttered down to bob on the water.

She worked the ring off her finger and studied the light swirling in the small garnet. Despite Rett's enthusiasm, she wasn't as excited about it as she'd first been. It was glorious, of course, to be able to start fires. But warring thoughts swirled in her own mind, matching the light: the distastefulness of Lukas and his dozens of burning stones, the relief every time the garnet created a path for her, the tight-lipped disapproval both Mikal and Gerone had shown when they saw it. It was nice to have, but compared to the sunlight, the *vitalle* in the gem was such a feeble little thing. It felt frustratingly like a weak crutch.

She sighed and put it back on, still undecided about whether she liked it or not.

Her mind strayed back to the valley and the dragon. The sunfire had been so bright, so consuming. The warmth of it called to her again, tickling at her skin. The sunlight from above was smooth and calm, the flashes reflected off the water weaker, but playful.

She rubbed her hands together. They had glowed gold. The thought tightened around her chest. The ends of her fingers looked whole, but there had been bits of her floating off, she was sure of it. The fear of how close she'd gotten again took her breath away. If the dragon had stayed any longer, if she'd been able to hold on to him long enough to destroy those last compulsion stones, what would have happened?

Even here, not doing anything, she could feel the draw. Part of her wanted to draw the sunfire in, another part cringed at what she would become if she did.

The daylight finally dwindled, and the night fell. In contrast with her fear of the coming day, the night settled with an eerie peace. She'd watched the skies to the south as though she might see a dragon flying in the distance. But Lukas was probably far ahead of them.

Unless Anguine was too wounded to fly that far. His wings had been tattered, and Douglon and Sora had cut deeply into the gap in the scales behind them. Maybe the dragon hadn't made it far. Maybe Lukas was stranded somewhere in the desert that lay at the top of the Marsham Cliffs. The tall rock faces stood like an insurmountable wall to the east, stretching as far as she could see to the north and south. No one traversed the cliffs. There was nothing above them but endless desert. If Lukas was up there, he'd have to walk south almost to the Southern Sea to get back down the cliffs. If he survived that long.

An idea nagged at her about the dragon. *I have something he wants more than anything else,* Lukas had said. *Everyone can be controlled if you know what to offer.*

And Anguine had said something similar. He wanted freedom from Lukas for a reason. *Unchain me and I will take what is mine!* he had roared.

Lukas had something Anguine wanted.

What did a dragon want?

The question nagged at her. The boat was quiet, and whether or not anyone slept any easier than she did, it was a question that could wait until morning. Maybe Alaric or Will would have an idea.

The further south the barge went, the more she realized her plan to stop Lukas was absurd. If she could get close to him, there was a good chance she could destroy the sword. But how was she going to reach him in the middle of a battle? If he was even with the armies?

She must have fallen asleep at some point on the hard deck of the boat. It wasn't long past a cloudy, dim dawn when the loggers docked along a bend in the river, and pointed the way toward Rillbourne Hold.

They let the horses graze for a few minutes and Sini shared her questions with Will and Alaric about what Lukas might have that Anguine wanted. Neither had any better guesses than she did. Before they had time to discuss it further, it was time to set out. They took the wide grassy hills at a canter. The entire sky was clouded, but a troubling brownish haze smudged the western sky, as well.

The cloud cover was a little unnerving. Sini reached up through it and found plenty of sunfire, but without the strong sunlight hitting her back, it didn't warm her the way she wanted it to. And the want she felt for the sunfire unnerved her more.

The darkness in the western sky grew more pronounced as the morning went on. They soon joined a well-traveled road running southwest. It dipped through hills and valleys until it crested one large hill and the world opened up before them.

Rillbourne Hold, a low, stocky walled keep, presided on a hill overlooking the great river that flowed south out of Queensland. The river was wide and spanned by a single bridge directly beneath the hold. But it wasn't the flurry of activity at the bridge that arrested their attention.

Across the water lay a wide plain surrounded by the barren foothills of the Scale Mountains on the west and south, and the dark slopes of the Black Hills on the north.

Two armies marched forward along the southern edge. The force farther away carried the dark green flags of Napon, and the light blue of Coastal Baylon fluttered above the near one. Rank after rank of enemy soldiers formed up onto the plain, pouring out from the mountains onto the southern edge of Queensland.

THIRTY-FIVE

Will sent Talen ahead to scout as the rest of them galloped toward a crowd of tents pitched outside the walls of the hold. The attacking armies marched inexorably across the field and over the river as Sini, feeling utterly helpless, raced with the others to the command tents. The entire flatland was easily visible from that vantage point. The area swarmed with generals and battalion commanders. Riders hurried from the command tents, down the wide road that ran to the river and across the bridge to where the troops waited on the field.

While Rillbourne Hold was part of Greentree, the plain where the battle would commence lay across the river in the duchy of Marshwell. The southern side of the plain connected with one of the few valleys that allowed access between Queensland and the countries to the south. Historically, almost every battle between Queensland and her neighbors began here. But despite the countries never being friendly, few armies had bothered to invade because the plain was surrounded on three sides by steep, rocky hills, and on the fourth by the wide and fast-moving Great River. There were only two ways to march further into Queensland: cross the bridge into the duchy of Greentree to gain an unimpeded way north into the heart of the country, or stay in Marshwell and pass through the narrow gap between the river and the edge of the Black Hills.

Queensland's forces blocked both of these options. The forces of Marshwell stood with their yellow shields along the shrinking slopes where the Black Hills approached the river. Two battalions of the city guard stood in the gap between the end of the hills and the river, and Greentree's forces, their verdant tunics showing beneath mail shirts, defended the land at the end of the bridge.

Sini stood at the edge of the command tents with her heart pounding in her throat. The near edge of the river was down a sharp embankment and several hundred paces across a cultivated field. The bridge was easily three hundred paces across, but the soldiers lined up across it with their backs to her, facing the approaching enemy, seemed alarmingly close and so utterly human. She felt a grasping need to protect them, offer some sort of help. The sunfire drizzled through the clouds and she drew in a bit of it, looking for any way to help.

The idea both thrilled and terrified her. She had to help, but the sunfire…She let go what she held, feeling a shiver of fear at how the warmth soothed her. The fact that she couldn't think of any way to help was both maddening and a relief.

Commanders from the city guard, Greentree, and Marshwell were all crowded into the command tent, bickering over a map. A general in the grey of the city guard shouted over them, but no one paid any heed.

Alaric frowned at the chaos for a moment before stepping up to the table. "Who's in command?" he demanded.

Sharp looks shot at him from around the table until the general straightened. "I am, Keeper Alaric."

At his name the others quieted. They glanced at Will and Sini, both in their black robes. No one else spoke.

"Then why is there so much arguing?" Alaric asked. "The enemy is at the doorstep and you're bickering over details." He addressed the general. "Is the queen expected to arrive, General Viso?"

"We received word this morning that the queen fell ill," he answered, "and will be delayed by several days."

"Better ill in Queenstown than here." Alaric turned to the map. "With any luck we'll be done before she arrives. Describe to me the troops we have available. City guard first."

"Only two of the battalions have reached the field," General Viso answered. "If we had all five, our numbers would be slightly higher than the enemy, but as it stands, battalions one and two man the gap."

"Marshwell guards the hillsides to the west of the gap so they cannot flank us," a man with the yellow tunic of Marshwell under his mail shirt said. "But we'd be better used in the gap. We know the terrain."

"Greentree has been pushed along the river," Greentree's commander added. "The river is running too fast for them to cross. We're wasted there."

Arguments again broke out across the map, until Alaric held up his hand for silence. "We all serve the queen and we will work together as one body, or the enemy will roll over us as though we were children." He pointed at the map. "Tell me about the hills near the gap. Can the enemy get through them?"

The commander from Marshwell began to describe the land.

Sini stepped back from the table, looking across the river at the enemy. Naponese and Baylonian troops were forming into tight, organized files. Queensland's troops were scattered and clumped.

Next to her, Roan scowled and muttered something. A soldier dressed in the deep green of Greentree passed by. "Where's my father?" Roan demanded.

The man gave Roan a quick bow. "In the hold, my lord."

"Doing what?" Roan spun to examine Greentree's troops lining the far side of the bridge. "Who's in command on the field?"

"Captain Long, sir."

"Where's General Rutter?"

"In the hold as well, sir." The soldier fidgeted under Roan's furious gaze. "I think, sir."

Roan spun and glared at the hold above them on the slope.

Alaric sent runners sprinting down to Queensland's troops. From across the river Sini heard echoes of orders being called out, and the disorder of the different armies began to smooth into one line of defense.

Sora stepped up beside Alaric. "Where can I go?"

"You can't go down there," Will objected.

She shot him an annoyed look. "You need all the fighters you can get." She turned back to Alaric. "Which unit?"

Alaric looked between her and Will, at a loss.

"You can join Greentree," Roan said. "Second unit has two women in it already. I'll take you down." Roan sent a runner to the hold for a tunic in Greentree's colors. "We don't need them thinking you're the enemy."

Will glared at them both, but Talen darted in through the open tent wall and landed on Will's shoulder. "Talen saw one battalion of city guard coming from the north," Will told them, focusing on the hawk. "We should be able to see them soon. He didn't see any others."

The soldiers glanced at each other uncertainly. But Alaric nodded. "We'll use them in the gap."

"We have reports that bridges farther up the river have been damaged," General Viso said. "I think the final two battalions are stranded north near the Steepdale bridge. Whether they have to find a way to cross the river or follow it along the eastern bank, it could be days before they arrive." The general tapped the map at Gulfind. "The Roven army is still unaccounted for. We haven't had any reports on them in over a week." Douglon stood with Avina on an outcropping a little to the north, watching the distant hills. "Duncave was advised of the impending attack two days ago," General Viso continued. "It would take that long for them to have come this far south, though. I don't think we should expect them until tomorrow at the earliest."

"Douglon assures us they'll be here," Alaric said.

If the general was unconvinced, he didn't say so.

Will glanced at Sini. "Talen didn't see any sign of Lukas."

"Has anyone reported seeing a dragon?" Alaric asked the general.

"Thankfully no," the general answered. "We have rangers in the hills to the south, but they've seen nothing. We've been expecting Lukas and the beast, but we haven't seen any sign of either." He motioned to the mouth of the valley the enemy troops had emerged from. "It's possible he's in that valley, but I don't know why he'd keep the dragon out of the fight."

"His dragon can't fly particularly well right now." Will grinned. "I don't think he's up for a battle." He ran a finger down Talen's chest. "Why don't you see what's in that valley? But stay high above the ground." Talen burst off his arm and shot high in the air, angling toward the valley.

The general watched him soar away. "I don't suppose you could teach someone else to do… whatever you're doing with that bird?" Will shook his head and the general turned his attention back to the field, folding his arms across his chest. "That's good news about the dragon. I think our lines should hold. Especially after the third battalion arrives—"

Horns rang out from the enemy lines, and a low rumble rolled across the plain as the attacking armies marched forward. Sini's heart pounded at the noise. Queensland's forces were still reorganizing, but the field was wide and it seemed to take ages for the army to cross. They came unrelentingly forward as Queensland's forces hurried into place along the line.

The armies finally joined with the grinding of metal striking metal. Sini stood with her fists clenched at her stomach, watching as soldiers from both sides fell. Cries of the battle and cries of pain echoed across the river. The soldiers moved like a flock of birds, like leaves floating on the water. Pushing forward, sliding back, drifting toward one side.

The invading armies edged forward, focusing their attack on the gap.

Slowly the city guard was pushed back.

A distant horn blast rang out from the north. The third battalion streamed into view over a hill near the river in three long lines. Matching horn calls sounded from the battalions already embroiled in the fight, and the general gave an approving grunt.

A ripple went through the invading forces at the arrival of the new troops and they reformed into lines. A trail of Queensland's wounded began to file from the battlefield across the bridge to a field hospital that had been set up below the command tents, and Sini took a bracing breath. Here was something she could do. Cold fear gripped her at the idea, but at that moment a soldier let out a cry of pain as he was lowered to the ground. His side was red with blood and his face pale.

She forced herself to turn to Alaric. "I can help in the hospital."

He glanced toward the growing line of wounded and nodded. "Don't go any further than that. If we find Lukas, we'll need you."

"I'll take you," Roan said. "I'm going to the battlefield. If my father isn't going to bother to even be out of the hold, someone needs to keep track of Greentree's troops."

Sora had donned a tunic with Greentree's colors and the three of them started down the hill. The thought of Roan and Sora going into battle made Sini's gut clench even harder than it had been before.

When they reached the hospital Roan bid her to be careful, and he and Sora headed toward the river. The fighting was still far from the edge of the bridge, but she watched them go with a knot in her stomach.

When she stepped between the first two injured men, everything but her sympathy disappeared. One soldier's leg was covered in blood, the other had a deep gash in his head that ran all the way to his cheek. Sini sank down next to a woman cleaning the injured leg with water. As soon as the wound was clean, Sini set her hand on his leg. She cast out, finding the edges of the deep cut. Reaching up for the sunfire that streamed through the clouds, she began to knit the wound back together, repairing the worst of the damage. Not wasting time to close up the now more superficial cut, she turned to the man with the head wound. The nurse beside her was staring at the leg Sini had just healed, and Sini gave her a small smile. "You clean the wounds, and I'll heal them." The woman's mouth dropped open, but she nodded quickly.

The cut on the man's face had spread apart and she could see the white of bone once the nurse cleaned it. Sini grit her teeth against the brutality of it and set both hands on his head, funneling sunfire into him, healing the deepest parts, covering the bone, knitting the flesh back together. The sunfire began to warm her, running through her arms like liquid heat.

She ignored it, moving to the next soldier. This one's gut was pierced and the nurse, after hovering over him for a moment, shook her head and moved on. Sini cast out, but the man's body was lifeless.

More and more injuries came back from the field and Sini moved down the line with the nurse. Soldier after soldier. Wound after wound. At first she searched each new face to make sure it wasn't a friend, but soon they began to blur together. Her hands turned red and slick with blood; the front of her robe grew damp with it.

Her back ached from bending over the wounded. Her legs were tired, her hands cold and wet. The sunfire didn't hurt, and it didn't wear her out to use it, but she began to slow anyway.

Word of what she was doing spread through the field hospital. She caught whispers of her name. "A Keeper...Keeper Sini...the woman Keeper..."

The other healers began to prioritize for her, cleaning and preparing the worst wounds for her to work on. They passed by still bodies and her heart broke each time. The sunfire poured through her. She could feel the draw of it, the glorious goodness of the light—the wholeness of it in such opposition to the violence and death that lay before her.

Kneeling next to one man, fatigue and hopelessness rolled over her. For every man she helped, two more came. She closed her eyes and felt the warmth fill her. She could go with the sunfire, leave these horrors.

But the smell of the blood and the filth of the hospital brought her back. She forced herself to focus on the wounds. The moans of the men tore at her and she shoved away the call of the light. It could heal these men, and she was not going to let it stop her.

The light kept up its sweet, glorious call, but the face of the next soldier drew her on.

There was too much suffering here, too much she could do. She felt the echo of Chesavia's words.

...there were things still to be done, and I knew I must stay.

And so she worked. The power to resist the sunfire was obvious at last. The needs before her trumped any relief she could seek for herself. The sunfire was a tool. It flowed through her, healing the worst of the wounds if she got to them in time. The goodness of the light, even in its vastness, settled into something familiar, something she'd known her whole life. The call was still there, but she was able to see it and turn away. She called upon more sunfire than she ever had, and, in the midst of the death and blood, felt a new strength growing, a new confidence.

The sun began to drop toward the west and despite her increasing weariness, a sense of urgency grew. Once night fell she'd have nothing to offer these men. The moonlight would never be strong enough.

The only good thing about the night coming was that the fighting would stop. She cast glances into the field, wondering if Queensland could hold their ground. She looked for signs of Sora or Roan, but there was no way to pick them out from the chaos. As time went on, another worry nagged her. There had still been no sign of Lukas, and she began to fear he wouldn't appear during daylight. She glanced up at the sun. Without sunfire, she'd never be able to destroy the sword.

A different sort of horn echoed across the flatland. Sini's attention snapped to the field. That hadn't come from the enemy forces. It had been further away. The field seemed to hold its breath for a heartbeat. Then the horn sounded again, from across to the west at the mouth of the Scale Mountains.

Horses poured out of one of the thin valleys. Hundreds and hundreds of mounted Roven warriors poured onto the field and galloped toward the westernmost troops of Marshwell. The troops from Napon and Baylon attacked with renewed fury. Queensland's troops scrambled to face them, funneling more troops west to help stop the Roven without depleting the defenses at the bridge and across the gap.

Roan ran up from the bridge. "Come with me to the hold!" he called.

"Not while there's light!"

He came up to her and lowered his voice. "If those troops break through the line they'll be across the bridge in moments."

She glanced across the water. "If they get close to breaking through the line," she agreed, "I'll come to the fort."

"Sini, please."

"Not while there's light," she repeated firmly. "Where's Sora?"

He glanced at Greentree's lines across the river. "With the second unit. But something's wrong." His voice was even lower. "Greentree's army has five units. Only three of them are on the field."

She glanced up at him. "Where are the rest?"

"I have no idea. I assume my father is saving them for something, but we need them now. Since he seems to be hiding in the hold, I'm going to find him. Please come somewhere safer."

"When the sun sets. But not before."

He clenched his jaw but nodded. "Be careful."

Sini stood and looked out across the field. The Roven warriors cut across the field like wild men, their long swords glinting in the cloudy afternoon, their calls making her flinch. For a moment she searched the flags of the Roven for the Morrow's colors, paralyzed at the idea that she might know some of them.

A groan next to her brought her back to herself. She swallowed down a terrible dread. Lukas had everything he'd claimed. Armies from Coastal Baylon, Napon, and the Sweep. His soldiers outnumbered their own now.

She glanced involuntary into the sky. At least Anguine was too wounded to fight. The last thing this battle needed was a healthy dragon.

There was still no sign of Lukas on the field, or anyone who seemed to be directing all three armies. She began to think maybe Anguine hadn't even been strong enough to get Lukas back here.

The man next to her called her name softly and she knelt down next to him, setting her hand next to a wound that slashed across his ribs. Her hand felt heavy. She'd been with the wounded for hours. She cast glances over her shoulder at the battlefield. There was too much chaos to tell who was winning. The troops near the bridge held strong, so she continued her work, funneling the sunfire down into the bodies before her, healing wound after wound.

The sun sank lower and Queensland's line near the gap started to falter. Sini's anxiety swelled as the day grew old. The sunlight would fade soon, the wounded kept coming, and the grey of the city guard was pushed back slowly, inevitably.

The first Naponese warrior cut through the line and her hand flew to her mouth. Three more surged through and the city guard was cut in two. Horns sounded, calling for reinforcements that were too tied down to come.

Sini stood at the edge of the line of wounded, her hands pressed to her chest, staring across the river as Queensland's line broke in two.

Suddenly a rumbling sounded on the hillside bordering the gap. From behind a rocky outcropping a stocky figure in dark metal armor appeared, bellowing and running down the slope toward the invaders.

The Naponese soldiers stopped at the sight of the dwarf. Another one rounded the boulder, and another. Dozens of dwarves came into view, streaming down the hillside hoisting axes and crying out in deep voices. They cut into the Naponese forces and pushed them back, plugging up the hole in the line of the guard and shoving the invaders back onto the field where they'd begun.

Sini threw up her arms and cheered. Above her on the slope she heard Douglon bellow something in dwarvish as he raced down the hill toward the bridge. Avina stood on the outcropping where she and Douglon had been keeping watch, like a blazing copper torch, leaping and shouting in victory.

The sun was lower. Sini could see a bright spot behind the clouds, but she had much less than an hour before the sun would be gone. She looked around her at the rows of the wounded and her heart sank. She needed more time. Pushing back panic that more wounded would come who she wouldn't be able to help, she knelt down and got back to work.

Until she heard the first shouts.

They weren't war cries or cries of pain. These were pure fear.

She spun around. A ripple ran through the troops and they turned to face the mountains along the southern border.

Against the grey clouds, two dragons spread their wings and shrieked before plummeting toward the bridge.

THIRTY-SIX

Dragons!

Two of them—and neither was red.

They glittered with color in the grey afternoon light. One dark green, one sapphire blue. Sini's chest tightened in fear, but something about them was off, as though they were farther away than they looked.

They drew closer, letting out spine-scraping shrieks. They weren't far away, they were small—a third of the size of Anguine.

The truth hit her like a punch in the gut. Young dragons.

Lukas had young dragons.

The green one soared past, banking and spreading it's wings like a glittering emerald bat. She caught flashes of light blue dotting its neck.

Compulsion stones.

That's what Anguine wanted. He served Lukas because Lukas controlled two immature dragons.

The blue dragon dove toward the bridge and Sini braced to see flames shoot out over Greentree's troops. Instead it darted down over the men, who threw themselves to the ground. The creature might be smaller than Anguine, but it was still twice as long as a man, its wingspan stretching from one rail to the other of the bridge. It might not be a full-grown dragon, but it was still terrifying. Green claws reached into the crowd and snatched up a soldier. The talons pierced his armor, digging into his flesh as he was lifted over the army and flung screaming into the river.

Arrows shot out from the troops, bouncing harmlessly off glittering scales.

The green dragon plummeted again into the men and dwarves filling the gap, and Sini shrank back. It slashed at them, dragged them into the air and flung them down, breaking their bodies on the earth.

A dwarven axe hurled at the creature deflected off its wing. The dragon reeled to the side, but recovered quickly and dove back into the fray.

The enemy soldiers took advantage of the chaos and pushed forward again. The line near the bridge wavered as it faced both the surge of enemies and the dragon. The Roven kept eating away at the western flank, pushing ever closer to the river.

Sini stood frozen, watching the soldiers of Queensland attempt to hold their lines.

The blue dragon wheeled up into the air and she caught a ripple of lighter blue along its neck. More compulsion stones.

The implications hit her. Lukas could control what the dragons did as long as he was close. Lukas was here.

She spun, searching the edges of the battlefield, scanning the flatland behind the approaching army. Where was he? She swallowed down a knot of dread. He had every army he'd claimed. He had more dragons. She clenched her jaw. All that was left for him to use was the black sword.

Two soldiers ran up the hill, carrying another whose shoulder had been torn open by the dragon's claws, and Sini pulled her attention away from the field. There wasn't much sunlight left.

The men put down their wounded friend and she grabbed one of them with her blood covered hand. "Get to the command tent now! Tell Keeper Will that Lukas is nearby."

The man's attention caught on her black robe and he snapped off a nod before running up the hill.

Sini knelt down next to the soldier with the torn shoulder and closed her eyes, blocking out the chaos and focusing the light. The cut was deep and clean. She shuddered at how sharp the dragon's claws must be.

From the battlefield the shrieks of the dragons mingled with the cries of men and her heart sank. The dragons had turned the tide. The sun was near the tops of the mountains, but Queensland's troops wouldn't hold until darkness forced the invaders to pull back.

Avina screeched something, still standing on an outcropping of rock. The elf stared across the river, past the fighting dwarves to the hillside above the gap. Her little hands fisted at her side and she raised her voice in a long, high call.

It echoed back, slightly different.

Even from where she knelt, Sini could see Avina grin. Her teeth lengthened into long spikes. Flinging herself off the rock, she raced down the hill. She sprang onto the rail of the bridge, her feet barely touching the wood as she sprinted into the chaos.

New calls rang out from the hillside. High and bright, filled with a fierce fury.

Glints of color moved in the treetops on the hillside. A flash of silver tore out of the edges of the trees and sprinted down the slope. Sini jumped to her feet.

An elf!

Another dove out of the trees, this one glimmering purple. With screeches and cries, elves poured out of the trees like a wave of jewels spilling down into the battle.

Avina's copper head appeared above the soldiers. Sini took a step closer. Douglon held the little elf up as the green dragon pelted toward them again. It was almost upon them when Douglon hurled Avina up into the air. She screamed, and Sini could have sworn her fingers stretched into long claws.

The elf clenched onto the dragon's neck, swinging herself onto it and shimmying up toward its head. The dragon thrashed and flew over the water, heading toward the hospital. Avina held up one hand and a ball of flame appeared between her clawed fingers. With a cry she slammed the fireball into the dragon's face.

The green dragon twisted away from the flames and careened toward the water, its wing beats turning into frantic attempts to escape upriver.

The battle had paused as everyone—human and dwarf—stared at the elfling and the dragon.

With a shout, the other elves started hurling fireballs into the enemy line, and the sounds of battle resumed.

Sini thought the dragon might flee north, but as it flew past the edge of the battle a tremor rolled through it. With a furious cry it banked into a wide arc, heading toward the hill where Sini stood, bringing it back around toward the fighting.

The compulsion stones—Lukas was forcing it to stay and fight. The dragon flew closer, bright green ripples scattering across its body, glittering unnaturally bright against the leaden sky. Avina straddled its neck, her legs gripping the scales tightly, her clawed hand forming a new fireball.

"Avina!" Sini cried, waving her hands to get the copper elf's attention. Avina glanced at Sini, her teeth bared. "Hit the stones! The blue compulsion stones in its neck!"

Avina glanced down. With a vicious grin she scooted back and slammed the fireball down onto the dragon's neck. The creature shuddered, and a trail of blue light from the broken stones curled up into the flames.

The copper elf thrust her fists into the air in victory just as the dragon let out a wild, liberated roar and veered back over the river. The move dislodged Avina and her little body tumbled to the side. She caught the front of its wing and clung to it until the dragon spun to the side and then fell, plummeting into the river along the far bank.

The green dragon raced down the river to the south, away from the fighting.

Sini began running toward the copper elf flailing in the river, but she was too far away.

With a strangled cry, Douglon burst out of the crowd of soldiers along the river, threw his axe down and dove into the river after her, but she was floating downstream too fast, bobbing under the water.

Then, Sini saw long tendrils of grass stretch out into the water near the bridge, wriggling like snakes across the surface. Rass stood on the shore, her hands buried in the greenery at the water's edge. Avina's little hands grabbed the grass and she clung to it until Douglon reached her. More and more grass dammed the edge of the river and the dwarf pulled them both to the shore while Avina clung to him.

On the battlefield, the other elves called to each other like birds and skipped over soldiers' heads and shoulders as though they were racing through the treetops. The blue dragon, who still bombed the soldiers on the bridge, flew close. With a mighty leap a yellow elf shot into the air. The dragon twisted, catching the elf in its teeth, crushing his body.

The elves on the ground raced forward, flinging themselves at the sapphire dragon, screaming and clawing over the people in their way. A bronze elf leapt onto the dragon's wing, pulling himself up. Another, light purple, jumped into the air and grabbed the tail. Two green elflings sprang onto the dragon's wings before the bronze one slammed a fireball against the compulsion stones in its neck. Blue light streaked out from them and the dragon thrashed his head to the side.

The green elves yanked at the wings and the dragon careened to the side. The purple elf opened her mouth wide and her teeth slid out long and sharp enough to be fangs. She bit down on the thin end of the dragon's tail. The blue dragon screeched in pain and plummeted down to smash into the river bank. A dozen elves piled on top, slamming fireballs onto it, gouging at it with tooth and claw.

The blue dragon flailed, biting viciously at the elves and another elf body was tossed, lifeless, from his jaws before the green dragon dove down, scraping through the crowd of elves with its claws. The elves scattered and the blue dragon launched itself into the air.

The two dragons, free of the compulsion stones and free of the elves wheeled away and tore south through the sky.

A cheer went up from Queensland's troops at the sight and they surged ahead with renewed vigor. The invading armies fell back, bit by bit, further from the bridge and the gap leading north. Dwarves and city guard fought side by side, pressing back the enemy. The elves darted between the legs of the other soldiers slinging fireballs at the invading forces. Several dozen of the Roven peeled off from the rest and began to gallop back toward the Scale Mountains.

Sini watched as the Roven forces splintered into individual clans and broke apart. The forces of Marshwell along the western edge cheered and the forces of Napon and Baylon sounded a full retreat.

The captains of Queensland's troops called for their men to stand, cutting off any pursuit of the enemy. Sini heard shouted directions to dig in at their position, preparing for whatever would come tomorrow. She went numbly to a basin of water tinged red. Her hands were slick with blood almost to her elbow, and she cleaned them as well as she could. Everything inside her settled to a numbness. When her hands looked reasonably clean she left the hospital and sank to her knees, looking toward the battlefield. There would be more wounded coming, but the sunlight was all but gone.

The humans, dwarves, and spattering of gemlike elves intermingled on the field. Sini watched them interact, tentative at first, then with more enthusiasm. A wave of exhaustion rolled over her and she let herself just sit. The night darkened and the first campfire was lit. A dwarven song rolled across the water and Sini stood, explaining to the nearest nurse that she'd be back in the morning when the sun rose to help with the healing again.

The events of the day left her feeling dull. The enemy had been held back, but there had been so many deaths, so many horrible wounds.

And she hadn't even caught a glimpse of Lukas or the black sword.

She dropped her head into her hands. Where was Lukas? When she finally looked up, more fires had been lit. It was too lonely here by the wounded when she had no way to help them. She felt tired and powerless. She couldn't bear to go back to the command tent and hear them talk about the dangers tomorrow would bring. Instead, she pushed herself up and started down the slope, hoping she'd be able to find Douglon and Avina in all the commotion. No one she'd known had come to the hospital, but she needed to know they were alright.

She struck out down the dark hill toward the bustle of the bridge. Shadows spread around her, joining together into the blackness of night. The lack of sunfire left her feeling exposed, like she'd walked into the cold without a cloak.

A hand on her arm from behind startled her, and she spun around.

Only paces away stood a hooded guard, his face in shadows. Sini drew back a step.

"Have you ever done something you regretted?" He reached up and pulled back his hood. The evening light fell on Pest's face. "Even before you'd finished doing it?"

THIRTY-SEVEN

Sini stumbled back away from him, a chill fear gripping her. "Get away from me!"

She grabbed for sunfire before she could remember there was none. At the emptiness of the sky she lifted her hand, pouring *vitalle* into her ring.

Except nothing happened. Her hand was empty.

Her fear turned ice cold. Where was her ring?

The nearest soldiers were down by the bridge and she drew in a sharp breath to cry for help.

"Wait!" he begged. He grabbed the neck of his own shirt and pulled it down.

Sini's breath caught. Trails of faint blue light from three compulsion stones set in a silver collar shimmered in the night.

"Help me," he pleaded. "He's made me…" He gritted his teeth. "I can't resist him."

"How long…?" She stopped. Pest carried his full set of knives and she took another step back. "What is he making you do?"

Pest pressed his eyes shut, his face tortured. "It's already done." He looked at her with desperation. "Destroy it before he makes me do anything else."

"What did you do?"

He grabbed at the collar and yanked at it. "I know you can destroy these stones. Get this off me and I'll tell you everything I know."

She took a tentative step forward. The stones were well-made. This was something Lukas had spent time on. She felt a shiver of revulsion at the collar, remembering how helpless she'd felt, controlled by hers. "I can't destroy them, not without the sunlight. But I may be able to get it off you. Turn around."

He did and she pulled the back of his shirt away from the silver band. Bracing herself for whatever the stones would do, she slipped her fingers around it. A wave of contentedness filled her. Like when she'd worn her own collar, she was filled with a longing to make Lukas happy. She gritted her teeth against it and forced herself to feel along the inside of the collar. The little merchant had said there was a spring. She squeezed along the band until she heard a faint click and the collar cracked apart. She pulled the two sides apart and Pest yanked it off his neck and threw it to the ground.

He rubbed at his neck and glared at the thin strip of silver. The three compulsion stones still gave off trails of blue light.

"How long have you been wearing that?" Sini asked him, staring at the collar. She felt a sliver of hope about the man. "Is this why you lied to me and took me to him?"

Pest was silent, but when she looked up at his face, she knew his answer.

He had betrayed her without being controlled. "Then why?"

Spreading his hands out away from himself in as unthreatening a gesture as he could manage, his face turned pleading. "I didn't understand who Lukas was at first. All I knew is that he offered my sister a safe place to live. Finding out some information about the Keepers seemed like a small price to pay for that. When we returned from Duncave and he found out I knew you..." He shrugged and the action looked almost helpless. "I didn't want to take you to him. He had my sister."

She stepped away from him. "You could have told us. We could have helped you."

He dropped his gaze. "I don't expect forgiveness."

"Good," she snapped, "Because I have none to give. Lukas tore information from me and destroyed the Keeper's Stronghold."

He flinched at her words. "You need to know the rest of it." He stepped closer and she tensed. "You cannot trust the Duke of Greentree. He's been working with Lukas for...I don't know how long. Longer than I have been."

"That's ridiculous."

"If I had to guess," Pest continued, "Their relationship started last summer when all those heirs to the throne mysteriously died of a wasting disease, and Lady Madeleine found herself as the heir apparent."

Sini stiffened. They had died of a wasting disease—just like the animals along the southern border. "Lukas killed them?"

Pest shrugged. "I don't know, but the Duke of Greentree knew before anyone else in the kingdom who would be the next heir. He went from no interest in Lady Madeleine to solidifying a betrothal between her and his son before the rest of the country even realized that the six heirs between her and the throne had actually died."

Sini's mind reeled at the idea. Roan had said his father had jumped on the opportunity so quickly that Roan hadn't even understood the reasoning at first. "Is that why the duke has been trying to keep the queen from sending more troops south? To keep our army weak for Lukas?"

Pest shrugged. "I don't know what Lukas and the duke planned."

He stood before her less confident than she'd ever seen him. His shoulders were bowed, and his face twisted in unhappiness. "What did Lukas make you do?" she whispered, afraid of what his answer might be.

Pest's hands clenched into fists and he shrank in on himself. "The queen is dead."

Sini's jaw dropped open.

"He had me poison her food." His voice was strangled. "She grew ill yesterday and by this morning..."

"You killed her?" Sini's mind tried to grasp the idea.

"I didn't want to!" He reached for her, his face desperate. "I tried not to! The collar—"

"You're here," she interrupted. "You must have left Queensland yesterday, maybe they cured her since you left."

He shook his head slowly. "He made me stay long enough to make sure that even if they'd figured out it was poison, it would be too late to do anything."

Sini turned toward the battlefield, staring at the flickering fires along Queensland's lines.

Across the field fires burned among the enemy troops as well. The queen was dead?

"So Madeleine is queen," Sini said, "and the Duke of Greentree has a great deal of influence over both her and Roan." She straightened. "We need to tell Will and Alaric." She picked up the collar with a stick, keeping it far from herself. "And we need to find a fire to destroy this in."

"Thank you," Pest said quietly, backing away.

She looked sharply up at him. "Come with me and tell them what you know."

He dropped a hand to a knife hilt and shook his head. "They'd kill me on sight."

"Maybe." She glared at him. "But after all the harm you've done, come do something good."

He paused and for a moment she thought he might agree. "I'm sorry," he whispered. Before she could answer he broke into a sprint, running south along the river.

"Coward!" she called after him, but she'd already lost him to the darkness. She turned and ran uphill toward the bright torches around the command tent. She threw the collar into the first fire she reached, letting the stones crack and the blue light flutter away in with the flames. Then she ran into the command tent. Alaric and Will were both there, surrounded by military men, many of whom wore Greentree's colors. Not sure who she could trust, she pulled them outside the tent door before whispering everything Pest had told her.

"The queen is dead?" Alaric asked, stunned.

"So Pest says," she answered. "And I don't know who we can trust from Greentree." A new fear gripped her. "Has anyone seen Roan? Do you think…he's not working with his father, is he?"

Will shook his head. "I can't imagine he is. I've never sensed anything traitorous about him. His father though…" He ran his hands through his hair. "The duke has always felt duplicitous, but scheming people always do." He glanced at Alaric apologetically. "I didn't suspect anything like this."

"None of us did," Alaric answered. "Can you read the men we're working with here? See if anyone's feeling guilty?"

Will nodded and ducked back into the tent. Sini glanced after him into the lit interior. "Where's Rett?"

"The battle was upsetting him, so we sent him to the stables inside the hold."

"Good. Have you seen Roan?"

"Not for hours," he answered. "I thought he was across the river."

"Not since right after the Roven arrived." A terrifying thought struck her. She grabbed Alaric's arm. "He said he was going to confront his father in the hold."

"The duke was in the command tent on and off today, but I haven't seen him since—" He looked toward the battlefield, frowning. "Since before the dragons came."

"Did any more of Greentree's troops report? Roan said several of their units weren't on the field."

"Not that I saw." He stared over the river with a dark look before turning back to her. "Don't tell anyone what you know. Not until we figure out who can be trusted."

She nodded. "I'm going to go look for Roan."

"Not by yourself." Alaric glanced up at the hold. "Rett is up near the stables. At least bring him with you. He might even know where Roan is. And be careful."

He ducked back into the tent and Sini hurried up the hill toward the hold. Traffic streamed in and out of the gate as people brought supplies and water to the troops. She jogged into the courtyard and headed for the main doors. The hold was squat and solid-looking, made from a reddish-brown rock. It wrapped around three sides of the courtyard. Her heart sank at the sheer size of it. The building was low except for one tower that rose high enough to look over the wall toward the river. The stables were a bustle of light and activity to her left and she headed for them. Maybe Rett had seen Roan.

A wave rolled through her, then another. A pause, then two more.

Rett? Sini's gaze snapped up the tower. Those waves had come from above her. What was Rett doing in the hold?

She changed course and hurried in the front doors, stepping into a long hall severely void of decorations. People bustled through doors along the walls and up and down a long stairway at the far end.

Come.

The second call sent her running for the stairs. He was above her. From the weakness of the wave, he must be near the top of the tower. A knot of fear formed inside her. Why was Rett in the tower?

She took the stairs two at a time. Smaller stairs headed up from the second floor.

Come.

The waves were getting stronger. Sini cast out herself. There was no code for her to answer with, but at least he would know she was coming. The tower was mostly empty. She caught the echo of *vitalle* one more story up, and she sprinted up the last flight of stairs into an ornate hall-way. Lit torches showed tapestries on the walls and a floor lined with plush rugs. These must be the apartments the duke was using. The thought was a cold knife to her gut. Why was Rett with the duke?

She cast out again and felt *vitalle* in a room near the end of the hall on the left. There wasn't much, though. Only one person. Was he here alone? She ran down the hall, her footsteps muffled in the thick carpet. The door to the room was open and she peered around the doorway into a dark room.

A low fire burned along the wall to the left, but the rest of the room lay in darkness.

In front of the fire, crumpled face down on the floor, was a body, too limp and too awkwardly positioned to be conscious.

"Rett!" She ran across the floor and knelt by him, knowing immediately that something wasn't right. This body was far too small for Rett. This close to the firelight she could see that the clothes were grey. She rolled him over and froze.

Not Rett. She looked into Roan's pale, slack face.

Her heart caught in her throat and she cast out into his body. There was such a tiny bit of *vitalle* that she let out a little sob. The skin on his face was a dusty grey, his hair black against it. She could find no wound. Sluggish energy flowed through his torso and his head, but his arms and legs were almost an extension of the darkness in the rest of the room. She set her hand on his cheek and felt nothing but coldness.

She needed sunlight.

Stretching one hand toward the fire, she pulled *vitalle* in and funneled it out her other hand into Roan's body. The fire dimmed slightly, and her fingers stung. The *vitalle* flowed into him like a dribble of light in an ocean of darkness.

Sini's breath came in little shallow hisses. The fire would never be enough to help him. A tickle of fear ran across her neck. Roan was barely alive, so who had she felt—?

"Leave him be, Sini," a voice said softly from behind her. "He's past even your skills. At least at night."

THIRTY-EIGHT

Sini whirled.

Lukas stood behind her, burning stones on his hands and around his neck oozing trails of light and the drawn sword in his hand sheathed in tendrils of darkness.

Sini's hand clenched Roan's shirt at the sight of Lukas.

It took her several heartbeats to make the connection. Rett hadn't called her here, Lukas had. She felt an instant's relief that Rett was safe before a wave of fury filled her and she wanted to fling herself at Lukas, cursing him for the battle and the Stronghold and the twins.

But his face stopped her anger cold. He smiled at her almost warmly, with a hint of smugness at her surprise.

"I hoped you'd hear my call." He leaned easily against an ornate desk with a window open wide to the starry night sky behind him. His smile was familiar, but his face had changed, even over the last few days. The differences were small—a harshness in his eyes, a cruel twist to the edge of his mouth—but they changed it profoundly.

A chill loneliness seeped into her, pushing back the anger. Everything she'd wanted to say to him died on her lips. She gripped Roan's shirt and stared at the dark sword in Lukas's hand.

"What did you do to Roan?"

"The lord consort was unable to see reason," Lukas said. "I warned him not to attack. A common sword is no match for this."

The chaos of what she was feeling shrank into a heavy knot in her stomach. The shape of the sword in Lukas's hand was identical to Svard Naj. The wooden hilt looked as though it had been hastily carved, merely to be functional. The blade, what she could see of the silver behind the swirl of shadows, was rough and slightly irregular. Runes along the blade caught the light. *Swift Death.*

"It is a shame," Lukas admitted, "that the Duke of Greentree had to sacrifice his son for the good of the realm, but it will play well with the people. And it will be easy enough to find Madeleine another suitably accommodating husband. Had I known Roan was so stubborn and naive, I would never have told the duke to use him. I hear he has a younger cousin who is not as short-sighted."

"How are you so selfish?" She demanded, turning back to Roan, trying to swallow the dread rising in her. He was so weak. She pulled more *vitalle* from the fire, pushing it into his body. It wouldn't be enough, but she did it anyway. He just needed to survive until dawn.

"Come away from him," Lukas said quietly. "There's nothing for you here any longer. You can't save him, he's all but gone already. None of this is your fault, and if you want to blame me for it, I understand. But I love you, and someday I hope you'll see that I'm doing all this for your own good."

The words and the familiarity of his voice caught at her. That voice had given her sanity on the Sweep. But his words—had his words always been this twisted? Everything inside her felt too chaotic, too afraid. Roan's body was so cold.

"We'll go soon," Lukas continued. "I'm not leaving you to this place after I worked so hard to free you from all of this."

Sini shoved herself to her feet, the anger back in force. "By starting a war?" she flung at him. "By destroying the Stronghold? By killing people I love?"

"I know you don't understand. No one wants to hear that the Keepers aren't the saviors we thought they were. But these aren't the Keepers of the old days, Sini. They've lost all the things that make them great. They can't fight enemy hordes or water demons. They couldn't contribute to this small battle."

He gave a derisive snort. "They didn't even know that the Duke of Greentree was working for me all this time. They don't offer the protection they claim to, and it's time Queensland was free of their lies. After a short time, no one will even miss the Keepers. Even you'll get over them, the way everyone gets past childhood heroes."

There was a scuffling at the window and the darkness shifted. A glitter slipped into the room and a trail of light blue light slithered down behind the desk. A black reptilian face came into the firelight next to Lukas. He set his hand on the inky black dragon's head.

Sini took a step back. A third young dragon.

"This is Umbra." The creature fixed Sini with white, emotionless eyes. "Isn't she beautiful?" The rings on his hand left thin lines of light as he stroked her head. His jaw tightened. "Anguine is useless. He barely had the strength to fly and is nearly free of my compulsion stones." For a breath he glared at Sini. "And now Umbra's brothers have been taken—" He took a calming breath. "But that may be for the best. It was exhausting trying to keep control of four dragons. Now we can raise Umbra to be everything we need."

He stood surrounded by so much darkness.

"Everything around you is black," Sini whispered.

Lukas snorted. "Don't be dramatic, Sin."

The swirls of shadow around the black sword had lessened. Fingers of it still drifted up Lukas's arm.

"What's that blade putting into you?" She could feel the pull of it, tugging gently at the edges of her *vitalle*. Hungry and waiting.

"Strength." Lukas shifted so she could see the blue blade sheathed across his back. "Mostly it pours energy into the other blade, but some of it comes into me. I never tire when I hold it. It's amazing."

She cast out and felt the energy of the sword not only wrapping around Lukas's arm, but delving deep inside him. It wormed into his chest, snaked up his neck and into his mind before flowing out through his back into the blue sword, Naj.

It moved an incredible amount of energy. The *vitalle* from the fire and the little bits of the candles would be nothing to it. She stepped closer. Without the sunlight, how was she going to have enough *vitalle* to destroy the blade?

"How much energy can it take in?" She let a begrudging interest into her voice.

"Close enough to an entire healthy person"—he nodded to Roan—"that they're essentially dead when it's done. It takes it from them in a breath, but the energy moves slowly through me. There's no pain at all. When it happens…" He closed his eyes and drew in a long, luxuriant breath. "It won't take anything more until it's moved everything into the blue sword. That blade is so strong it can slice through armor with no effort at all. Until this one is ready, if anyone else were to threaten us, Naj could deal with them. Of course, it's been long enough since Roan attacked me that this blade is almost ready again."

Sini kept her eyes fixed on the shadows wrapped around the blade. "It's black."

"What?"

"The light around Naj is blue, but this blade has nothing but shadows."

"Really?" he asked eagerly. "Have you ever seen anything else like it?"

She shook her head. "It's so violent."

"That's the point, Sini. They're both so violent you only need to use them once or twice, then the threat of them is enough."

The pull of the black sword grew stronger. Fingers of darkness began to reach out of it toward her and made her skin crawl. "That blade is a terrible thing."

"Only in the wrong hands." Lukas's fingers wrapped around the hilt. All the burning stones in his rings oozed little clouds of energy. Bits of the blackness merged with them, wrapping around the other swirls of color, tainting them darker.

She raised her eyes to his face. "Yours are the wrong hands."

"But I've accomplished so much," he objected. "Tomorrow we will sign a peace treaty with Queensland."

"Who will sign it?" Sini demanded. "You killed the queen!"

He looked puzzled for a moment before grinning. "I didn't expect you to know that yet. You always surprise me. Saren was an impediment to peace. Madeleine will sign the treaty tomorrow. It will give her access to the gold merchants just as before and will ensure that no one bothers us."

Sini fixed her attention on his sword. She needed the sunlight to destroy it. Maybe if she agreed to go with him, she could destroy it at first light and then escape. Roan lay on the floor, though. She'd never get back in time to heal him. Of course, even if she was here, dawn might be too late.

Shouts echoed from outside and Lukas cocked his head to the side, listening with a pleased air. "There is the final step. We can leave. The Duke of Greentree has proved invaluable."

Sini swallowed down a new fear. "What is he doing?"

Lukas sighed. "Why do you ask questions you don't want to know the answers to?"

"Tell me."

He paused for a moment. "The duke kept several of his units in old barracks behind the hold. They're now spreading the news that Queen Saren was assassinated by a city guard who was a personal friend of the Keepers. A whole unit is being tasked with…bringing the Keepers here to face justice for the crime."

She stepped toward him, furious, and Umbra let out a low hiss.

"Careful, little sister. Umbra is viciously protective of me. I'll teach her to protect you too, in time. But for now, you should stay back."

More shouts came in the window and Sini flinched.

"There's nothing you can do for them," he said gently. "Not against trained soldiers. At night."

The truth of his words stung, and she turned her attention back to his sword. Maybe she couldn't help anyone outside, but she could do something about that monstrosity.

He followed her gaze and held the sword. "Do you have any idea how much power this gives me? I don't need to touch someone to draw life out of them. Roan didn't even get close, and I gain more control all the time. Together with you, Sini, I could…" He laughed wildly. "Can you imagine? Is there anything that could stop us?"

Lukas stepped toward her. "Do you know how many times I've wished I had your powers? And your mind?" He grinned. "I have missed you!"

Coldness gripped her, freezing her anger into something sharp. His words rang like a hollow, twisted form of the dedication in the twins' book. …*Sini, whom we love not for all the healing…or your astounding power, but for the joy you brought us.*

Sini searched Lukas's face for something she couldn't find. "Did you ever want *me*?"

"Those things *are* you." His voice was tinged with exasperation. "Without your powers, your life would be utterly different. You'd still be a street rat in the Lees. Vahe would never have noticed you. Killien would never have trained you. The Keepers would never have taken you to the Stronghold. Everything that has ever happened to you has been because you have amazing powers. Without them, you wouldn't be you."

The words snapped something inside her; some power his words had held broke. She wanted to shake him. "Your view is so small and twisted, you can't even see anyone. You can't even see me." She stepped closer to him. "I keep hoping you'll open your eyes."

The black sword pulled at her again. The shadows wrapping it were thin now, brushing gently over Lukas's hand.

Everything has a limit.

Drawing *vitalle* from the dying fire, Sini funneled it into the sword. The shadows grew and climbed up Lukas's arm.

His eyes widened and he looked at the sword. "What are you doing?"

She pulled more *vitalle* from the fire. The flames sputtered and Lukas twitched. "Stop it."

The blade was like a vast, hungry emptiness. The little bits of light dripped into an ocean of black. The sword must have a limit, but it was far more energy than she could find.

She needed sunlight.

The more she put into it, the more the strands of darkness thickened, wrapping up to Lukas's shoulder.

"It's changing you." Sini watched the darkness sink into Lukas's body. Chesavia had been right. Maybe the war chief Naj would have been a better man without these swords. She cut off the flow of *vitalle* into the blade. "You don't have to be like this. You're doing all of this because of the sword."

He snorted. "I've been planning this for years. I didn't even know the sword existed before I heard a story about it in Napon last summer, and I only found it weeks ago. It's doing nothing beyond helping me to achieve things I've worked towards for a long time."

"But before you found it," Sini said, "you only did what was necessary. You sickened a few animals, you caused trouble along the border, planted the idea of unrest and that the Keepers weren't trustworthy. But after the sword…" She looked up into Lukas's face. "That's when you went to Gulfind, isn't it?"

Lukas's eyes narrowed. "I only did what was needed there, too."

She almost didn't ask, but Lukas needed to understand, and maybe she did too. "How many people did you kill?"

Lukas's hand tightened on the sword. "It was Anguine, he was too…enthusiastic."

"You controlled the dragon," she pushed. "You caused it. That was the first time you did anything like that."

Lukas looked down at the sword, shaking his head dismissively. "It had to be done. I didn't intend to, but there was no other choice…" An edge of uncertainty crept into his voice.

"What happened?"

Lukas blinked down at the sword, his brow drawn as though searching for the answer. "When I arrived, I had a meeting with the leaders of their merchant guild. They refused to just give me the gold I required, as I had expected, but when I called Anguine to threaten them… they attacked me," he said sharply. He paused. "Or they were about to." His voice lost its certainty. "I didn't intend to kill anyone. But it started and Anguine came…"

"Put the sword down, Lukas," she said gently.

He shifted away from her. "I have no desire to put it down," he snapped. "It's what I've always needed. Have you ever—" He chewed on his lip. "Have you ever found something so strong that you wanted to be part of it?"

She stretched her fingers, the memory of the sunfire thrumming through them. "That sword is death and destruction."

He shook his head. "It is power. It is safety from any who would harm us. Forever."

"Put it down," she pleaded. "When dawn comes, I can destroy it."

Lukas took a step away from her. "When dawn comes, we'll be long gone." He started toward the door, but Sini stepped in front of him.

"No. That sword needs to be destroyed."

Lukas fixed her with an irritated look. "I know you don't approve of my methods, but after tonight, we'll have nothing but peace." The blade in his hand still swirled with tendrils of darkness.

"That sword wasn't made for peace."

Sini studied it. If the sword took in less than the *vitalle* of a healthy person before stopping, then its limit must be near that. All she needed was more *vitalle* than a healthy person.

She could light a fire—her stomach dropped. Her ring was gone. A surge of fury rushed through her at how little power she had. After all the sunfire she'd controlled today, without her ring she couldn't even start a fire.

She cast out through the room. There was Lukas, the now weak fire, Roan's dim body…and the dragon.

It was the dimness of Roan's body that made her decision. He needed as much help as she'd be able to give him tonight if he was to survive until dawn when she could really help him. She straightened. It would require actually touching the dragon. She stifled a grimace.

First she'd gather everything else she could find. The burning stones Lukas wore glowed like tiny fireballs. The energy twirled out of them, creating a path she could easily access. Knowing Lukas wouldn't be able to see the light, she began drawing the energy out of them. Streams of colored light flowed out of every burning stone on Lukas's body into her hand.

"On the Sweep," she said quietly, "you always protected me."

"You're my sister," he said simply.

"No, I was a stranger, and you still protected me. But I never protected you."

"You were only a child. You shouldn't have been protecting anyone."

"But I'm not a child now. And it's long past time someone protected you." She straightened. "That sword is damaging you. Put it down."

He looked at her in disbelief. "You already lost me my dragon. If I put down this sword, I might as well have nothing."

"You'll have yourself back." She paused. "And you'll have me."

"You've always been too naive," he snapped.

The words stabbed into her, but she forced herself to keep trying, "Aren't you tired of being controlled?"

He held the blade out. "No one controls me. This sword is my freedom."

The sound of fighting grew out the window and Sini pushed away worry for the others. The dark blade was flat for a handbreadth where it came out of the hilt before the cutting edge grew sharp.

She took a bracing breath. There were too many people here that would need her help come dawn. This needed to end now.

Sini shifted slightly towards Lukas. Umbra's eyes narrowed and she let out another hiss.

Good.

Sini pushed back the panic rising in her. This was going to hurt.

"I hope someday," she told Lukas, "you'll understand I'm doing this because I love you."

Sparing one breath filled with longing for the sunlight, Sini thrust her hand forward and clutched the flat portion of the blade.

The metal was ice cold against her skin and her fingers clenched around the sword of their own accord. She was grateful for a heartbeat that her hand fit between the hilt and the sharpened edge of the blade—then the *vitalle* rushed out of her hand.

"Sini!" Lukas twisted the sword away, but not before Umbra shot forward and sank her teeth into Sini's forearm. Pain exploded in her arm as the teeth cut into her flesh. She clamped her eyes shut and fought to concentrate through the pain, slowing the flow of her own *vitalle* and funneling the dragon's into the sword.

She'd expected to see pink light rushing out of her fingers with the *vitalle*, but her hand only darkened.

"Let go!" Lukas yanked the sword away from her. "It will kill you!"

She couldn't have let go even if she'd wanted to. Her hand clamped down on the blade as though her fingers had turned to steel. Umbra shook her head, trying to free her teeth and sending daggers of pain into Sini's arm, but her jaw was locked shut.

This wasn't the painless energy of the sunfire. This was common *vitalle* and the energy burned her skin.

Darkness crept up Sini's arm, her flesh somehow losing light.

Light.

Everything is light.

Not everything will become light the way Chesavia had. Everything is light.

The *vitalle* in her body was light, that was easy to see. But the flesh of her hand—was it just light in a different form?

The sword wasn't just taking *vitalle*, it was somehow taking light.

She could feel the sword now, could sense how empty it was, how much it would take to overfill it enough to break it. Between herself and the dragon, she might have enough.

Except energy was pouring out of the sword into Lukas. The shadows swarmed up his arm.

"Too much of it is going into you." Her voice sounded more strained than she'd expected. "I can destroy it if you let go."

"No," Lukas pulled again, turning his face away. He was growing stronger, and Sini could feel her own body weakening. Already her legs shook with the effort of standing.

"Look at me," she begged him, bracing herself on his arm so she didn't fall.

Slowly he turned back to her, his face twisted with anger.

"Come back to me, Lukas. Let go of the sword."

"So you can destroy it?" He glared at her with so much raw hatred that she flinched back. "You will not destroy me!" he snarled.

Reaching over his shoulder, he wrenched the other sword from its sheath in a wide arc of blue light that cast an icy gleam over the twisted hatred in his face.

She tried to pull back, but her body moved sluggishly, and the dragon thrashed on her arm.

A strangled cry sounded from behind her and a huge form crashed into them. Rett threw his arms around Sini just as the blue blade sliced down, cutting deep into his side. He let out a bellow of pain.

A flood of energy surged from the blue blade into Rett, sending a wave of destruction through his body. The *vitalle* she'd been pouring into the black blade rushed out to replace it, leaving the shadow blade nearly empty again.

Rett's weight dragged them all down and Sini stared helplessly into his face as he crumpled away from her. Umbra's teeth tore out of Sini's arm and the dragon shrank back into a corner.

Rett's face was deathly pale, his expression faintly confused. Lukas threw the blue sword down and reached toward him in horror.

"I'm sorry," the words bubbled out of Lukas like a desperate child. "Rett! I'm sorry. I'd never—" He pressed his hand to Rett's ravaged side helplessly. "What have I done?" He turned to Sini. "Heal him!"

Sini stared into Rett's face. "I can't," she whispered.

Lukas fixed her with a furious look. "Heal him!"

"There's no sunlight!" The words tore out of her like a sob. "There's no sunlight!"

Understanding dawned in Lukas's face and he sank down, staring in horror at the black sword. "Destroy it…destroy it, Sini!"

So much of the energy she gave the sword was pouring into Lukas. "Let go," she whispered. His hand twitched on the blade but didn't release. "I can't." He looked at her wildly. "I can't!'

Sini tried again to pull her own hand off, desperate to help Rett, but everything felt cold below her elbow.

"Need more energy," she gasped. "Need sunlight."

"There's no sunlight," Lukas's voice was rough with fear. "Take energy from me." He grabbed Sini's other hand with his free one and she tried to pull energy out of him. But everything was rushing into him. Nothing would come out.

Her chest started to feel dark and cold.

The bands of darkness from the black sword wove into Lukas's body, piercing into his chest, sliding out his back and wrapping up around his neck. Fingers slid down his arms, around his stomach. Darkness shrouded his legs. Sini cast out and there was no division at all between the blade and the man.

She clamped down on the light leaving her hand, fighting against the raging pain in her arm. She was weak enough that the flow had lessened, and she could almost cut it off. "The darkness of the sword is everywhere inside you," she told Lukas.

Lukas leaned heavily against her shoulder, his head fallen forward. "I can feel it. It's cold. Destroy it, Sini."

A chill fear gripped her. "It's part of you now. If I destroy it," she whispered, "it will kill you."

Lukas raised his eyes to meet hers. Shadows seeped out of his skin. His eyes were pained and panicked. Rett let out a ragged moan and Lukas clenched his jaw. A new resolve filled his face. "It's fitting."

"I'm not going to kill you, Lukas. I only wanted to free you."

Lukas shook his head, staring at the floor with distant eyes. "You are the only person I've never hated." Lukas's eyes turned back to Rett, who lay unmoving. "Even Rett…" he whispered. "Sometimes I hated him for being hurt, for not being strong enough to…" He shook his head. "When you came to the Sweep, you saved me. You gave me someone to fight for."

The light flowing out of her now was slow enough that she barely needed to stop it. The truth struck her. The blade still had room and she didn't have enough energy left to fill it. Her fear of hurting Lukas faded. He wasn't the one this would kill.

"I can't destroy the sword," she said. "I'm sorry. I don't have enough left. Destroy this thing or bury it or drop it in the bottom of the sea." She looked into his face. "Promise me you'll let it go."

Lukas gripped her free hand. "Find more energy. Find a way to take mine." He grabbed the blue sword off the floor. "Take this!"

She pulled away from it. "You'll die."

"And if you don't, you'll die. So find another way. Find a way to use this blue sword to help us both. Killien said this sword was meant to 'help mend the torn'. Mend this!"

Reluctantly, Sini reached toward the blade wreathed with bright blue ropes of light. The metal felt hot against her skin, but she couldn't grab the energy. It was as though it were held away from her by an invisible wall. It seared her skin with heat, but she couldn't reach the power there.

She dropped her hand to her lap.

"Sini," Lukas whispered. "Find more."

She rested her head against his shoulder. Her body felt so heavy. An ache as sharp as another blade pierced—a longing for the sunfire. Not even to help, just so she could feel the warmth and the goodness of it. Everything in her was so dark and empty and dead. "Just tell me you'll destroy it once I'm gone."

"You need to live," he said, "to heal Rett."

Sini looked at the still form of Rett collapsed on the floor. A pool of blood spread out beneath him. "I can't, there is no way. But I'm glad the choice has been taken away," she closed her eyes. "I could never have chosen between you and Rett."

The shadows were thick around Lukas, but he strengthened. "I can." He turned toward the dark corner of the room. "Umbra."

Sini's heart fell. "Don't," she pleaded.

"She has more than enough, doesn't she?"

"Lukas, it'll kill you." It was hard to focus on him. Everything felt heavy and dim.

He gave her a weak smile, barely visible through the shadows. "You were right. I've been selfish."

He closed his eyes and Umbra twitched and hissed.

"This once, let me not be selfish."

Sini tried to pull her hand away, but Lukas held the sword still as Umbra moved forward and set her nose on Sini's arm.

The dragon's energy shot through her with searing pain, pouring into the sword.

Umbra growled but her nose pressed harder, pushing into Sini's bloody arm.

Lukas cried out and threw his head back. Shadows poured out of him, wrapping around his neck, surging into his open mouth until he was a pool of darkness in the room. The edges of his fingers smudged into darkness on the hilt.

A tiny brittle noise came from the sword, then a loud crack. A burst of light exploded out of it. The dark shadows ruptured into tiny shards of blackness and were engulfed in the light.

Sini's hand went limp and slid off the blade and the dragon twisted away. The sword, now a dull silver, clattered to the floor.

Lukas, toppled to the side, his skin unshadowed, his eyes wide and empty.

THIRTY-NINE

ini grabbed Lukas's hand, but it was still. She cast out into him but there was no *vitalle*. Scales scuffed over the stone floor and Umbra launched herself out the window into the darkness where battle sounds still rang out, but she was too numb to worry about either of those things.

Her body felt cold and sluggish and she cradled her bitten arm against her stomach. She turned to Rett, sliding over to him. She cast out and found life still pulsing weakly. The wound in his side reached so far into him that she knew it was hopeless. Even with sunfire this would be hopeless. When she lifted up his hand, he groaned. Her heart clamped down at his pain and she froze. It was better that he was unaware.

The room was dark except for moonlight coming in the window. Sini reached out toward it, looking for the weak sunfire she could find in it, but there was such a little bit it wouldn't accomplish anything. Underneath Rett, the rug was dark and wet.

But he cracked an eye open. "You safe, Sini?" His voice was less than a whisper.

"Yes, Rett." She squeezed his hand. "I'm safe. Thanks to you."

He closed his eye. "Hurts."

Sini cast out again, frantic to do something. Her own arm throbbed, but it must be nothing compared to what he felt.

Lukas was cold, Rett was dimmer even than he'd been a heartbeat ago, and Roan was still crumpled on the floor over near the fire with so little *vitalle* she could barely find him. Even the fire in the hearth was nothing but coals.

"I can't do anything," she whispered to Rett, her hand hovering over him, afraid to touch him and cause him pain. "I can't—There's no sunlight. I need energy—I lost my ring, Rett. I can't even start—" Her throat tightened around the words. None of that mattered. Fire would not be enough. Even sunlight wouldn't be enough.

He squeezed her hand, the pressure almost too small to feel. "The Shield says sometimes people can't be healed."

"I don't want that to be true," she whispered.

"Find a candle. Help Sini with the fire."

She didn't even think of arguing. Her body felt leaden, but she crossed to the desk and brought him back a candle. He tried to lift his hand, but it fell back to the floor. She held the candle, shaking, with the hand on her injured arm, and lifted his hand with the other. The green light from his finger was so weak it was barely visible, but the candle slowly flamed to life. She set it near his head.

It was almost worse, having light. She kept her eyes focused on his face so she wouldn't have to see the rest of him.

"Where is Lukas?"

She swallowed. "He's gone, Rett. He sacrificed himself to destroy that sword."

Rett was silent for so long that she cast out again. "See," he whispered finally. "Lukas wasn't bad. He always kept us safe."

Sini dropped her head down onto Rett's shoulder and pressed her face into him. His body rose with a shallow breath. "Don't go," she whispered.

"Doesn't hurt anymore," he said so quietly she almost didn't hear him.

She felt him take one shuddering breath, and he stilled.

Dreading the result, she cast out. Rett's body was empty.

She gripped his huge hand, but his fingers were slack. He didn't grip her back, or wrap his huge arm around her shoulder, or tell her everything would be alright.

He smelled of hay from the stables and the bright metallic tang of blood. His motionless chest was still warm and stable beneath her head, like some foundation stone that she'd rested on for years.

"I'm sorry," she whispered. "I'm so sorry."

She cast out again and again, as though she could conjure life inside him from pure will.

He was nothing but darkness.

Something behind her caught her attention. It wasn't alive, exactly, but there was a... something.

She turned to find the blue sword half covered by Lukas. Tendrils of blue light snaked around it. Sini fixed it with a glare of fury. Her body was still sluggish, and it took her breath away when she shifted her hurt arm, but she scooted over and picked it up by the hilt, sliding it out from under Lukas. She pushed herself to her feet, leaving the candle be for a moment, and headed for the fireplace. She'd build a fire, as big as she could, and throw this sword in.

The sight of Roan stopped her.

Roan wasn't wounded. He had nothing that needed healing. What he needed was energy, light. She looked at the blue sword. It hadn't let her take the energy before, but maybe that was because she was holding the black sword too.

She brushed her finger quickly over the flat of the blade and a rush of energy poured into her finger so fast it burned her. Yanking her hand back, she knelt next to Roan. The energy moved too fast for her to just touch it to Roan, but maybe she could control it.

She focused on her finger, focused on letting in only a little *vitalle* from the sword, and touched it again.

It pressed on her like a huge wave, but only a small amount flowed into her finger. Warm instead of hot. She set the blade on the floor next to her and laid one hand on Roan's back. Shaking her head to clear the exhaustion that threatened to overwhelm her, she braced herself and touched the sword blade.

Keeping the flow gentle, she let energy come in from the sword, and pressed it into Roan.

It was almost like healing. There were brighter parts of him, and she funneled the energy there, in his chest and his head. She bolstered the life that was there already, and let it spread itself through the rest of his body.

The tip of her finger against the sword began to burn and she pressed more fingers to it, spreading out the energy. They burned as well, but there was too much to be given to Roan for her to pay attention to it.

Little by little, Roan's body filled with energy. It was like slowly filling a dark hole with light. The blue stone was draining quickly, though, and Roan needed more.

Her exhaustion weighed on her like a sodden blanket. When the sword was empty Sini shoved herself up and built a fire, lighting the kindling with the candle Rett had left her. The flames were small at first, and she nearly fell asleep waiting for them to grow, but once it was burning she started again, drawing energy out of it slowly and funneling it into Roan.

The fire had burned low before he groaned. A wave of relief rolled over her and she cast out. His body was weak, but *vitalle* flowed through all of it.

Her vision was blurry with weariness. She lay her head on his chest and let sleep take her.

• • • —

Everything was quiet, but there was a brightness past her eyelids. Sunfire brushed against her skin, weak and indirect. Her chest held a deep, hollow ache, and her arm throbbed.

Sini opened her eyes slowly. She lay in a stone room. The shutters were thrown open and late afternoon light slanted onto the floor. Her arm was wrapped in a clean bandage and her bloody black Keepers robe was gone.

Roan leaned back in the chair next to her bed, his eyes closed.

She was still so tired. She stretched out toward the sunfire and drew it in. Tingling warmth filled her fingers, flowing up her arms and wrapping around the wounds from the dragon's teeth. The light seeped into her chest, bolstering her, strengthening her.

She took a deep breath and Roan stirred. When he saw her eyes open, he leaned forward and grabbed her good hand, a wide smile filling his face. "Hi."

Her own smile felt tired. "Hi." The significance of the sunlight hit her, and she sat up. "It's late!" Pain shot through her arm and she groaned.

He winced at her pain. "Nearly dinner time. Everyone will be glad to know you're awake."

"What happened?" She listened for a moment but while there were noises outside, she heard no battle sounds. "Was there more fighting?"

"The Roven had left by dawn. Will's hawk saw them skirmishing with each other as they rode back through the mountains toward the Sweep."

"How did they get through?"

"A scout arrived late last night with the news that the pass had been cleared. He theorized the dragon had done it. Since he arrived too late to warn anyone that the Roven were coming, no one really cared about the details."

"What about the armies from Napon and Baylon?"

"Seeing the Roven gone and realizing the dragons weren't coming back must have been enough. They started a full retreat out of Queensland by midmorning."

The memory of what Lukas had planned came back to her. "And your father—? Are Will and Alaric alright?"

"They're fine. My father's troops were…reluctant to carry out their orders, and while there was a nice long skirmish, they merely captured Will and Alaric and didn't harm them at all. I was able to convince our men that my father was the problem, not the Keepers, and it didn't take them long to put him under arrest." Roan studied their hands. "He's being taken back to Queenstown to stand trial for treason."

"I'm sorry." Sini squeezed his hand. "Is anyone else hurt? Sora? Douglon? Avina?"

"Sora and Douglon have minor wounds, but nothing serious."

"How did the dwarves get here in time? And how did the elves get here at all?"

"The dwarves were already headed south when news came of the skirmishes, so they picked up their pace. And apparently the dwarves had been talking to Rass. When she heard what was going on, she roused all the crazy elflings and they hurried down to join the fun."

She let out a tired laugh. Besides looking tired, he looked perfectly healthy. "How long have you been awake?"

"I woke up in the middle of the night on the floor in the study," he raised an eyebrow, "with your head on my chest."

She let out a small laugh. "I was…really tired."

"I gathered that when I couldn't wake you up." He sobered. "When I saw Rett and Lukas, I went for help."

Something clamped down on her chest at their names. "Both of them died saving me."

He squeezed her hand but didn't answer.

She tried to shift her pillows, and Roan helped her so she could lean back on them. It occurred to her that instead of his normal drab grey, he was wearing a real guard's uniform. She set her arm down gently across her stomach and fixed her attention to him. "Your father is being charged! Are you…?" She fumbled the question. "Do they blame you? Are you…accused of anything?"

"No." He blew out a long breath. "Sadly, everyone could see I was just a pawn. Lukas needed a husband for Madeleine so she would be a strong heir. And my father offered me."

Sini could think of nothing to say.

"No one else in Greentree seemed to have any knowledge of it, either. My older brother has been named duke. He was worried we'd be stripped of the title. We weren't, but it will be ages before Greentree is trusted again." He ran his free hand through his hair. "The betrothal is off, obviously."

Sini's attention caught on the last words and her hand tightened on his. "Are you…" The question felt awkward. "Disappointed?"

He gave her an incredulous look. "What possible reason could I have for being disappointed?"

She had no answer to that. "What will you do now?" She realized she was gripping his hand. She loosened her hold, but he held hers firmly.

"Madeleine—" He shifted. "I mean, the queen is allowing me to rejoin the guard. I have two years left in my original contract and she's decided that I can continue as though there was no interruption. As long as I 'continue my exemplary service' and have no communication with my father."

A tumultuous series of emotions greeted this news. "Where will you be stationed?"

"For now, the battalion is in northeast Marshwell."

Marshwell sounded far away from either Queenstown or the Stronghold. She stopped at the thought. It would be a long time before anyone lived at the Stronghold again. "When do you leave?"

"I petitioned to stay until after Will and Sora's wedding and Madel—the queen agreed."

Sini started. "Wedding?"

"Oh." He grimaced. "I probably should have let Will tell you that. They're planning it for as soon as we get back to Queenstown. I'll join my battalion once it's over."

She was surprised at how much her stomach sank at the news. "That's so…soon."

"True." He ran his hand through his hair, looking uncertain. "The mail system between the troops and the capital is quite good. Would you mind if I wrote to you?"

She smiled. "I'd be honored, lord cons—" She clapped her hand to her mouth. "I can't call you that anymore!"

He laughed. "Thankfully."

"But what will I call you now? The Not Future Lord Consort is too unwieldy."

"I suppose Roan is out of the question?"

She nodded and considered him for a moment. The captain's pin on his collar was a bright bronze. "I'll have to settle for captain. I've never written to a captain before."

"I'll be the only captain in the guard getting personal letters from a Keeper."

"Unless I meet another interesting captain," she pointed out. "Then I may decide just to write to him."

"I'll have to work hard to get a promotion so I can order him to stop writing you."

She grinned. "Two years of wearing unrelenting grey is going to be nice for you."

"Not two straight years," he pointed out. "Captains get a fortnight off twice a year. If you're in the capital, I'll be able to find you easily."

"Don't say such a horrible thing! I hope I'll be back at the Stronghold long before two years is up."

"Well I know how to find that now too."

She smiled. "You'll have to come through the ghosts."

He made a pained face, but his hand tightened on hers. "It'd be worth it."

FORTY

There was no rush to get back to Queenstown and the trip was put off until Sini and Roan were both fully recovered. Sora, too, had been injured, receiving a cut on the leg during the fighting, but was recovering quickly.

Both Lukas and Rett's bodies were cremated and their ashes brought north to be buried in the Stronghold. Sini had thought that Will or Alaric might object to the idea of Lukas in the Stronghold, but all Alaric said was, "I only wish we'd been able to bring him there years ago."

"Speaking of Lukas," Will said. "I think you should have this, Sini." He handed her the dull sword that had once been so horribly dark. The runes *Swift Death* looked more worn than threatening.

She took it, cringing. "Why?"

"Does it have any light?"

"No." She held it at arms' length. "It never did though. It only had shadows."

Will ran his fingers through his beard. "It has emotions."

Both Sini and Alaric stared at him.

"Something like…" Will focused on the sword. "Regret? But it's tinged with hope."

Sini tightened her grip on the hilt. "Lukas's emotions?"

Will shrugged. "I don't know. But from what you told me, it fits. And you and Rett were the only ones who ever felt anything like hope for Lukas. So I think you should have this."

"What happened to Svard Naj?"

"The Shield has it," Alaric said. "There are discussions going on as to whether it should be kept somewhere safe or destroyed."

"Flibbet the Peddler told Killien that sword was meant to mend the torn." She pressed her eyes shut against the image of Rett's broken body. "That's not what it did."

"I don't know," Will said slowly, "It did terrible things, but in the end, it healed Roan. And maybe it somehow healed Lukas too."

"At a terrible price," she said.

"Yes." He considered the dull sword in Sini's hand. "Maybe the words applied to both swords together."

She fixed him with an incredulous look. "How? This one is even worse."

"Is it? I can feel the hope in it." Will touched the flat of the blade with his finger tip. "And if a piece of cold metal can hold onto hope, maybe the rest of us can too."

———————◆◆———————

By the next day, when Sini was feeling good enough to walk and she'd been able to heal her arm from the worst of the injuries, the field hospital had been disbanded. The worst of the wounded had been moved into the hold where they could receive better care, and those who could travel had headed home. Sini and Roan searched the area for her ring, but the ground was stained red. Even if the ring had fallen off there, a bloodied ring with a red garnet would have been nearly impossible to find. She cast out, hoping to find a trace of the gem's *vitalle*, but found nothing.

Her finger felt empty without the ring, and she couldn't decide if that was good or bad.

The day was gloriously sunny, and she drew in a little sunfire as she walked with Roan along the river. The day of the battle had proven both the power and the limitations of the sunfire. How tempting it could be, and how she could control it.

She felt a wave of frustration. If only she'd had light that night. There was no doubt she could have destroyed the sword with it, and then Lukas would still be alive and Rett would not have been hurt.

But everything that had happened was too complicated to throw such a simplistic wish at. If Rett hadn't been hurt, Lukas might not have realized who he'd become. Maybe he'd have escaped. Maybe he'd have brought back the dragons, continued the war. Maybe he'd still be the twisted shadow of himself that he'd thrown off in the end.

She sighed, her mind tangled in the thoughts.

"Have you seen Douglon?" Roan asked.

"No, why?"

A smile pulled up the side of his mouth. "Patlon brought him very good news. Something about a perfectly scandalous dalliance between Patlon's great-grandmother and Douglon's great-grandfather. The implications of it being that the line of succession *should* have been in Patlon's family for the last two generations."

Sini laughed. "Douglon must be overjoyed."

"He relinquished the position of High Dwarf to Patlon as soon as he could find two dwarves of high enough rank to witness the transfer. As of late this morning, Douglon is a free dwarf."

"I'm glad. It was sad to think of him being separated from Rass."

Roan nodded. "The two of them feature heroically in the story of the battle Will's already composing."

"Of course they do."

Roan glanced at her and a little smile crossed his face. "People are calling you a hero too, you know."

Sini frowned, then groaned. "I told Will what happened with Lukas."

"I know. Everybody knows. Last night, while the last battalion of the city guard was still here, Will went down to their camp and told the whole story. You're getting quite a reputation."

"That explains some of the looks I've gotten today."

"I went down myself to hear it," he grinned. "You were very heroic."

She sighed. "Who knew living through heroic moments was so painful?"

His smile softened. "Probably all the other heroes."

When they finally reached Queenstown three days later, it was in time for one more surprise. They'd arrived, Sini had enjoyed a long, warm bath, and they'd prepared for a formal dinner with the new queen when someone knocked on her door.

She opened it to find Alaric, beaming at her, gingerly carrying a small bundle. "Sini, I'd like you to meet my daughter, Lillan."

A very small, very scrunched face was nestled in the blanket, fast asleep. Sini reached out to touch her cheek. "She's beautiful!"

"She's the most beautiful baby ever born," Alaric said seriously. "She was born this morning.

"Lillan is a beautiful name."

"It's elvish for spring. It means new beginnings and growth and freshness. Douglon is already calling her Lilly."

"Hello, Lillan," Sini said softly. "We need more freshness and new beginnings."

Everyone gathered for Will and Sora's wedding on a sunny afternoon in the private garden outside Douglon's room at the palace in Queenstown. Will had suggested a formal state affair in the great hall, but Sora had informed him that if that was his plan he could find a different bride.

The leaves of the two oak trees in the garden were a glorious gold near the trunk, darkening to brilliant red at the ends. In the sunlight they looked like enormous lanterns draped in scarlet silks.

Avina, who'd come back to Queenstown with Douglon and Rass, sang happily among the branches in a haunting, birdlike song. Two elves had been killed in the fighting, and another had died the next day from his wounds. The other elves had taken the bodies back to the Elder Grove. The deaths had shaken them and they'd grown more somber.

Douglon listened to Rass chatter. Gerone, Mikal, and the Shield sat with Alaric, seriously discussing Lillan, who was fast asleep in Alaric's arms. Sora hadn't arrived yet and Will paced nervously along the far wall. He wore his Keeper's robe as all the Keepers did, but somehow managed to look more formal than usual.

The absence of the twins and Rett was like a cold hole in the courtyard. The three of them would have been overjoyed to see this day. Sini sat alone on a bench near the back wall, letting her black robe soak in the sunshine. The emptiness inside her from the loss of the twins and Rett and Lukas refused to warm.

Roan walked out into the courtyard and Sini raised an eyebrow. Instead of his normal greys, he wore the charcoal dress uniform of the city guard. He saw her and smiled, coming to sit next to her.

"You look nice, captain," she said. "Maybe military greys aren't that bad."

He glanced at her. "You look like the rest of the Keepers." His gaze lingered on her hair. Dalia had fixed it again, stringing thin ribbons dotted with tiny pink gems into a series of braids. The overall effect had been almost too crownlike for Sini's taste, but Roan gave her an approving nod. "Although I do think you're the prettiest of the bunch."

She glanced at the group of men sitting in the courtyard. "Thank you for that high praise."

He grinned.

There was a small commotion near the door and Queen Madeleine entered, her dress more understated than Sini was used to seeing and only the front of her hair arranged up in braids. The rest hung down her back. She received bows from everyone, stopping next to Alaric to admire the baby, before coming back to where Sini and Roan sat. They stood and Sini curtseyed, bracing for some unpleasantness, while Roan gave the queen a formal bow.

Madeleine considered them with an unreadable expression before turning to Sini. "I've heard the story of what you endured, and I'm sorry for your loss."

Caught off guard, Sini barely managed a "thank you."

The queen smiled faintly. "I admit I misjudged the former Duke of Greentree," she flickered a glance at Roan, "and I know we disagreed on Lukas's intentions, but I hope it brings you some peace that you were right about him in the end."

"I was terribly mistaken about him almost the whole time," Sini said. "I couldn't believe he'd lost himself that much. But in the end, I think he found himself again."

"I'm also sorry," Madeleine continued, "that the Stronghold has suffered such damage, but I am glad, Sini, that you will be at court a while longer. I think," she bit her lip, "that together, you and I could accomplish many things."

Sini found herself speechless again, and curtseyed.

Madeleine took a seat next to the older Keepers and Sini stared after the queen. At that moment Evangeline came into the courtyard and announced that Sora was ready.

The Shield, beaming, took his place at the front of the courtyard with Will next to him. Sini and Roan joined the others in the chairs. Even Avina came out of the tree and sat next to Douglon.

Sora stepped into the courtyard in the first dress Sini had ever seen her wear. It was long and green and suited her perfectly. Will stared at her with his mouth partway open until Alaric cleared his throat and Will blinked. He walked over to her and offered his arm to lead her up to the Shield.

The ceremony was short and simple. The words the Shield spoke had the feel of age, of being handed down through generations. They spoke of being a Keeper and Sini realized that despite the fact that most Keepers didn't marry, there was an obvious precedence for it.

Even Mikal's face softened at the obvious tradition encompassed by the words.

Will kissed Sora, and Rass burst into cheers.

Servants brought out tables of food and two musicians appeared, setting up in a far corner of the garden.

"Congratulations," Sini told Sora, after waiting her turn to talk to the bride. "You look happy."

"I am happy," Sora answered, watching Will talk animatedly with Roan. "Your personal guard looks handsome today, and less entangled than he used to be."

Sini let out a half laugh. "He's entangled with the city guard for another two years, but at least I'm not risking some court scandal by admitting that he does look handsome."

A familiar face appeared at the door to the courtyard. Captain Liam stepped in, motioning for people behind him to follow.

"Daisy!" Sini hurried forward to greet him. "I've missed you by my door."

"I've heard the story of your battle with Lukas," the captain said with a smile, "and I'm willing to admit that maybe you didn't need a guard after all." Before she could answer, he turned. "Someone you know came to the Keepers' wing looking for you today." From behind him the huge form of Dalton appeared.

Sini clasped his hand. "How is Goven?"

"Healing more every day," Dalton said, "thanks to you."

"I'm so glad." Behind him a family waited, looking awkwardly into the courtyard.

"He's recovering at the army hospital along the western edge of Queenstown," Dalton continued, "and last night this family arrived asking to see a Keeper." He motioned them forward.

A skinny, red-haired, freckled girl of about twelve slowly stepped toward Sini and opened her hands, showing wide blisters on her palms.

"A new Keeper!" Sini reached out and gently took her hands. "I'm Sini."

"I'm Kate," the girl said shyly.

Alaric knelt down next to her, looking at her hands closely. "What happened?"

"My little brother was walking too close to the river," she said. "He fell in and…" she hesitated. "I used the water to push him back out."

Alaric showed her his own hands, scarred from old burns. "I bet it hurt."

Kate nodded nervously.

Sini smiled at her. "I'm so happy to meet you. I'm Sini, and I've been worried you wouldn't find your way here."

Kate looked up at Sini in awe. "I heard a story about you and a black sword."

Sini paused, not sure what to say to that.

"Excellent," Will said, coming up beside her. "That one's spreading quickly."

The party devolved into a dozen happy conversations. Kate and her family met the Keepers, Rass and Avina retreated up the tree with a plate of fruit to sit in the branches and watch the others.

Sini and Roan were talking with the Shield, discussing plans to rebuild the Stronghold when a back gate into the courtyard opened. A small, rickety cart full of colorful trinkets rolled in. The short, wiry old man pushing it nodded his thanks to two guards who held the gate long enough for him to get through.

"It's our merchant!" Sini said to Roan. The same little man with the long beard who they'd met in the Lees, and again who'd sold her the yellow wine after she'd seen Lukas.

Roan looked at the man narrowly.

"Let's go thank him for the dragon scale," Sini said, heading toward him.

"Let's go ask him how he got into the palace," Roan muttered.

"Ah!" the merchant said as they approached. "My friends! I told them I knew the two of you, and they agreed I could come give you gifts on your wedding day!"

Sini drew to a sharp stop. "It's not our wedding day!"

"Not yet!" Roan agreed.

She turned to look at him with raised eyebrows. "Yet?"

"I mean," he said, not meeting her eyes, "it's not our wedding, it's theirs." He pointed toward Will and Sora.

"Ah," the merchant said, amused. "My mistake." He peered at Will and Sora for a moment. "They look rather content with each other, and seeing as I came to give you gifts, I'm still going to give them." He gave Roan a sly glance. "For whenever the happy day occurs. Now, what do you need?"

Roan looked at him blankly.

"He'll need to be writing letters regularly in the near future," Sini said.

The merchant flashed him a smile and handed him a flat wooden box. It was plain, but well-made. The top hinged open and inside was a stack of paper and three writing sticks.

"A letter writing kit, small and light enough for even a traveling soldier to carry," the merchant explained. He turned to Sini, but she shook her head.

"I have plenty of paper and pens. I don't think I need anything."

"Ah," he said, raising one finger in the air and taking on a pedantic air. "A person at ease with themselves needs for nothing."

"A quote from Flibbet the Peddler!" Sini looked at the man with a new respect.

"That man was a genius," the merchant said. He studied Sini for a moment. "But I already have your gift picked out. And perhaps it is not much of a gift, because unless I am mistaken, it already belongs to you." He reached into a small dish on his cart and pulled out her garnet ring.

Sini's mouth dropped open and she took it. Little bits of *vitalle* swirled in the gemstone. She slipped it on her finger. "How did you find this?"

"After battles, soldiers always have things to sell. Although usually they're more along the lines of weapons than jewelry. I decided if it was important enough to you that you wouldn't trade it for yellow wine when you looked desperate for a drink, that maybe it was something you would like back."

She pushed a little *vitalle* toward the ring and the garnet flared brighter. "Thank you." She gripped his hand. "I thought this was lost."

He cocked his head to the side. "Maybe it's something you needed that you didn't even think of."

"No." The ring didn't look quite the same on her finger. It still fit, but she'd grown used to her hand without it over the past few days, and she realized that even if she wore it, it wasn't part of her. It was like a quill or a book. Something useful. "I don't need it. It's just a tool given to me by a friend." Remembering why she'd first come over, she added, "The dragon scale you gave us turned into a handy tool as well."

"Excellent, excellent," he nodded, blinking at them kindly.

Will called for everyone's attention. The sun was low over the hills to the west. "In Sora's clan," he said, standing next to a brazier that had just been lit, "they have a tradition at weddings to burn away old fears and begin anew. Everyone participates, and I have plenty of paper. So come up, toss your old fears into the flames and begin anew."

Sini and Roan gave their thanks to the little merchant and walked up to the fire. Little slips of paper were set next to it on a table, and Sini picked one up. There were a handful of beautiful long feather quills, as well, and she rolled one between her fingers as she thought.

Roan scribbled down his answer quickly and she leaned over to read it, but he folded it up, then with a flourish dropped it into the fire. Flames licked at the paper immediately.

Sini turned back to her own. What old fear was it time to give up?

The last weeks had been full of so many different fears, she couldn't choose just one.

The night before, in the book of quotes by Chesavia, she'd again come across the words the Shield had quoted to her so long ago in the library.

The day is shaped not by the violence of the storm, but by the fall of the light and the voice of the rain.

The people in the courtyard milled around her in a comfortable buzz of conversation. Whether they were Keepers or friends or dwarves or elves, they felt like family. There were gaps still, places where Rett should be, and Lukas. But the ones who were here felt like home.

The storm had been violent and the losses from it were still raw, but the voices around her and the play of the sunlight over it all changed things.

It was obvious what old fear to write.

I do not belong.

She folded the paper, then folded it again until it was a thick, hard little rectangle. Then she held her hand out, set the paper against her garnet, and set it on fire.

EPILOGUE

The Shield waited until the young people had stepped away from the little old merchant before he stood. His back had ached more than usual since the long ride here to the palace, and he gladly took a seat next to the old man on a bench near his cart.

"Hello, old friend," the Shield said quietly, watching people drop their fears into the fire. "Would you like an avak?"

The merchant's face lit up. "I would!" He took a big bite and chewed it with relish. "What happened to your hair?"

The Shield smiled. "I ran out of a use for it long ago."

"And your height?"

"That's what happens when people get old. They shrink."

"I wouldn't know." the merchant answered. "This is a nice group you've got here."

"I'm rather proud of them. I don't suppose you'd like to be introduced?"

"No. This is a day for them, not for old men."

The Shield sat in silence for a few minutes, enjoying the bright taste of the avak. "A few of the Keepers think these fruits have magical powers."

"Maybe they do. I've always found them surprisingly refreshing." The merchant took another bite. "Although I think any magic they may have is the little, everyday magic. Like the smell of a rainstorm. Or the way a bright flower lifts a heavy heart."

The Shield grunted and finished his fruit. "I thought you were done interfering."

"Well, I was already involved in this whole thing from long ago. I thought I might as well see it out. Retirement can be a bit dull, honestly. Although I get more writing done than I used to."

The Shield's fluffy eyebrows twitched up in interest. "I don't suppose you brought any with you?"

"Now you want a gift too?"

"I'm always looking for books."

"Only because you take such good care of them,"—the merchant leaned over and pulled a set of three slim books out of the back of his cart—"and because I know you'll do anything to protect your library." He handed them to the Shield.

The tiny bald man grinned broadly. "This has been a very good day."

"It has. Well—" The merchant stood. "—good luck with all the changes you have going on." He waved his hands at the others. "Things look to be headed in a nice direction."

"They do indeed."

The merchant lifted the handles of his cart and started to push it toward the gate again.

"Do you think we'll meet again?" the Shield asked.

"Who can tell the future?"

The guards outside the gate pulled it open and the old man pushed his rickety cart out of the courtyard. The gates closed behind him and the Shield opened the cover of one of the books on his lap.

Retirement: Friend or Foe?
by Flibbet the Peddler.

The Shield ran his fingers over the colorful, swirly letters. "Goodbye, old friend."

THE END

From the Author

Thank you for reading *The Keeper Chronicles!*

Did you enjoy them? They were more fun to write than I could have ever imagined.

<u>Did you know a review is worth more to an author than a way to actually fight off a dragon would be to the Keepers?</u>

If you enjoyed The Keeper Chronicles and have the time to leave a review, I would be unbelievably grateful if you did so on Amazon.

WAYS TO READ MORE:

1) Want a short story? **The Black Horn, a story set in the Keeper's world, is free** when you sign up to my mailing list. I promise only fun emails about bookish things, and you can unsubscribe at any time.

To get your free copy of *The Black Horn,* go to jaandrews.com.

2) This wraps up the **first set of stories** in the world of the Keepers. I'm currently working on a new trilogy, set in the same world, about the first queen of Queensland, and the first Keepers.

Dragon's Reach (**The Keeper Origins Book 1**) is already out, and can be found on Amazon.

3) After that, well, I also have about a hundred ideas for stories based on the characters in this series. Everyone from Douglon to Ayda to Avina to Sora deserve their own tales. Flibbet the Peddler has so many interesting things about him, he's pestering me for his own series. How are things going with the Roven? What will Sini look like in ten years? What were the twins like when they were younger?

What I really need is Hermione Granger's time turner. If anyone finds one of those for me, I pledge to get all these things written. Until then, I'll just work as fast as I can.

To be kept informed of when new books are published, you can sign up for my newsletter: jaandrews.com.

Thank you,
Janice

Tomkin and the Dragon

A bookish, unheroic hero, a maiden who's not remotely interested in being rescued, and a dragon who'd just like to eat them both.

"When they request a story from you,
tell *Tomkin and the Dragon*. I love that one."
~ Evangeline

If you'd like to read the story of Tomkin and the Dragon that was mentioned in the Keeper Chronicles, it is published under the title ***A Keeper's Tale: The Story of Tomkin and the Dragon*** and you can find it for sale on Amazon.

Dragon's Reach
(The Keeper Origins Book 1)

The truth is neither plain, nor simple

"[Will] set to writing out a story with the most powerful woman he could think of. Sable's story was epic enough in proportions to need a whole book, but certain episodes of her life were excellent tales themselves."

~ Pursuit of Shadows

You can find **Dragon's Reach** on Amazon.

Experience The Keeper Chronicles anew! Now in audiobook format, narrated by Time Gerard Reynolds!

Acknowledgments

To my readers, thank you so much for your support. It means more than you could ever know and is a huge reason why the beginnings of Alaric's story actually became a full trilogy.

Thank you to Cheryl Schuetze for your unending patience with my questions, rants, insecurities, and updates through phone calls, emails, texts, and any other form of communication I could think of to bother you with.

To Karyne Norton, thank you so much for your invaluable advice. It is true that this book should read "by JA Andrews wiz Karyne Norton."

To Karen Kubin, thank you for the amazing edits and advice.

To my favorite group of authors who are always there with knowledge and snarkiness, I adore you all, whether you're living, passed on, or have gone over to the dark side.

Thanks to my three kids for your patience while I worked like crazy to get this one done. Thanks for being willing to hold all your questions about life and quotes from books you were reading until my writing time was over. And thanks for always being willing to put off the home-school school day until I had time.

But most of all, thank you to my husband for your unfailing support and enthusiasm. Thank you for willingly playing xbox at night so I can write more and for discussing plot questions and character development. I'm so excited for the future and all the new things. Love you to the top of the sky.

About the Author

JA Andrews is a writer, wife, mother, and unemployed rocket scientist. She doesn't regret the rocket science degree, but finds it generally inapplicable in daily life. Except for the rare occurrence of her being able to definitively state, "That's not rocket science." She does, however, love the stars.

She spends an inordinate amount of time at home, with her family, who she adores, and lives in the Rocky Mountains of Montana, where she can see more stars than she ever imagined.

For more information:
www.jaandrews.com
jaandrews@jaandrews.com

.